# The Watcher's Guide

**Christopher Golden** *and* **Nancy Holder**

*with* **Keith R.A. DeCandido**

POCKET BOOKS
New York   London   Toronto   Sydney   Singapore

*Special thanks to the people at Pocket Books, Twentieth Century Fox, and* Buffy the Vampire Slayer *who made this book possible:*

Gina Centrello, Donna O'Neill, Lisa Feuer, Julie Blattberg, Gina DiMarco, Nancy Pines, Patricia MacDonald, Twisne Fan, Jennifer Sebree, Debbie Olshan, Caroline Kallas, Todd McIntosh, and Lili Schwartz.

The sale of this book without a cover is unauthorized. If you purchased this book without a cover, you should be aware that it was reported to the publisher as "unsold and destroyed." Neither the author nor the publisher has received payment for the sale of this "stripped book."

An *Original* Publication of POCKET BOOKS

Edited by: Lisa A. Clancy
Design by: Lili Schwartz

POCKET BOOKS, a division of Simon & Schuster Inc.
1230 Avenue of the Americas, New York, NY 10020-1586

TM and copyright © 1998 by Twentieth Century Fox Film Corporation. All rights reserved.

All rights reserved, including the right to reproduce this book or portions thereof in any form whatsoever.
For information, address Pocket Books, 1230 Avenue of the Americas, NewYork, NY 10020-1586.

ISBN: 0-671-02433-7

First Pocket Books trade paperback printing November 1998

20 19 18 17

POCKET and colophon are registered trademarks of Simon & Schuster Inc.

Printed in the U.S.A.

*In memory of my father, J. Laurence Golden Jr., who used to wake me up in the middle of the night to watch* Kolchak: The Night Stalker. *this one's for you, Dad. You would've loved it.*
—CG

*In memory of my grandmother, Lucile M. Jones, and my father, Kenneth Paul Jones, who both hoped I would write someday. And for the mensch and the friend and the writer he is, thank you, Chris Golden. You made it happen.*
—NH

*For Laura Anne Gilman. She knows why.*
—KRAD

A book of this magnitude requires the infinite patience and the invaluable assistance—not to mention the simple moral support—of a great many people. For all of that, the authors would like to thank the following:

Joss Whedon and the entire cast and crew of *Buffy*, with a very special thanks to Caroline Kallas (your name should be on the cover, Coywoman!), Todd McIntosh and Jeff Pruitt; our editor, Lisa Clancy, and her tireless assistant, Elizabeth Shiflett; and our agents, Howard Morhaim and Lori Perkins.

Christopher would like to thank: Lucy Russo, Colleen Viscarra, Stefan & Carole Nathanson, Jeff & Gail Galin (for their forbearance), Ruth and Rachel Satrape, and Tom Sniegoski, for his help in juggling. And thanks to Nicholas and Daniel, for their love and laughter, with hope that they grow to be as brave and noble as Xander and as clever and gentle as Oz.

Nancy would like to thank: Lindsay Sagnette, Leslie Jones, all the Simpsons and the Holders, the Baby-sitter Battalion (Ida Khabazian, April Koljonen, Andi Craft, and Bekah "Bah" Simpson), Maryelizabeth Hart, Stinne Lighthart, Karen Hackett, Linda Wilcox, Susan Klug, Barbara Nierman, Brenda Van De Ven, Susie Johnson, Margie Morel, and all my other friends who so politely ignored me.

Keith would like to thank: Helga Borck, Peg Carr, Cathy (a.k.a. BuffyChic4), Amiee Collier, GraceAnne Andreassi DeCandido, Livia DeCandido, Robert L. DeCandido, Edward DeVere, John S. Drew, Laura Anne Gilman (a.k.a. Meerkat), Orenthal V. Hawkins, Alan "Anime Nut" Hufana, the Inner Circle of *Buffy* Geeks (you know who you are), Kate (a.k.a. hrprobe), Andrea K. Lipinski, Peter Liverakos, Dave Logsdon, Sonja Marie, Pam McLaughlin, John Nestoriak, Carolyn Oldham, John Edward Peters, RayneFire, Leslie Remencus, Scott Robinson, Rainier Robles, Lisa Rose, Wendy Tillis, Jack Welsh, Jennifer Whildin, Sarah Winsor, and generally everyone on Buffy-L@planetx.com.

And most of all, we'd like to thank our respective, long-suffering spouses: Connie Golden (you were right, sweetie, but it looks phenomenal! —CG); Wayne Holder (*Dai suki*—NH); and Marina Frants (hey, look, dear, it's finally a *book!*—KRAD)

# CONTENTS

| | |
|---|---|
| v | **Foreword** |
| 1 | **The Mythology of Buffy** |
| 11 | **Rules of the Game** (or The Slayer Handbook According to Buffy Summers) |
| 13 | **Sunnydale Guidebook** |
| 19 | **Character Guide** |
| 51 | **Episode Guide** |
| 53 | First Season |
| 81 | Second Season |
| 123 | **Monster Guide** |
| 163 | **Bloodlust** |
| 195 | **Behind the Scenes** |
| 197 | Cast |
| 240 | Joss Whedon |
| 243 | Crew |
| 295 | **Music** |

# FOREWORD

*Buffy the Vampire Slayer* wasn't always the hip success it now is. Before the show aired, there was often a certain amount of derision involved in conversations about it. A cheerleader named *Buffy*, who slew vampires. It sounded a little goofy, truth be told.

But the first time you saw it, you just knew.

Joss Whedon has proven to Hollywood that it isn't impossible to mix action, comedy, drama, and horror and still have a compelling hour-long show...in fact, one of the most compelling hours on television. Critics fall all over themselves naming it one of the best shows on the air.

Here is a series unlike anything else on TV. Things *change.* Characters feel pain. Yes, this is a world of horror and fantasy, but the ongoing subplots don't feel like storylines. They feel like people's lives. It's a world of angst and the terror of simply being a teenager that anyone can relate to. Joss Whedon is often, mostly in fits of hyperbole, called a genius. And while it might not have taken genius to come up with the basic plot of *Buffy*—high school girl chosen to save the world from vampires—it certainly took genius, or something like it, to make of that idea a series that speaks to viewers of all ages on a universal level. Nobody knows what it's like to be a Slayer, because there's no such thing. (No such thing as vampires, either.)

But we all can relate to what Buffy and her friends are going through.

As the series progresses and the characters move through high school, graduate, and go out into the world, we can be certain of one thing. There will be a great deal of change. And, as always, change will bring some joy, and a great deal of pain.

We wouldn't miss it for the world, and we know you'll be right there with us.

You hold in your hands a very special book: the official companion and guide to the hit television series *Buffy the Vampire Slayer*. It contains nearly forty exclusive interviews with principal cast members and major guest stars, the executive producers, the production crew, and the creator of *Buffy* himself—Joss Whedon.

Illustrated with photographs from the set, as well as from the personal archives of *Buffy* professionals such as makeup artist Todd McIntosh and stunt coordinator Jeff Pruitt, the *Watcher's Guide* offers a behind-the-scenes look at what it takes to transform Joss Whedon's unique vision into a series that continues to intrigue and delight devoted fans...and capture new ones each week.

Everything you need to know about the series and its mythology, as well as everything you'd like to know about how the show is put together and the people who bring it to you week after week—it's all in here.

On the following pages, you'll find out things about this series you can't get anywhere else!

It was a true pleasure putting this book together for all of you. We hope that you enjoy it as much as we did.

*Christopher Golden & Nancy Holder*
*with Keith R.A. DeCandido*

# THE MYTHOLOGY OF BUFFY

# Who and What is a Slayer?

Don't you get the feeling that the Watcher Rupert Giles knows an awful lot more than he's telling "The Harvest," part two of the two-hour premiere of *Buffy the Vampire Slayer,* opens with Giles beginning to explain to Willow Rosenberg and Xander Harris just what it is they have gotten themselves involved in by discovering Buffy Summers's secret identity as the Slayer.

"This world is older than any of you know, and contrary to popular mythology, it did not begin as a paradise. For untold eons, demons walked the Earth, made it their home, their Hell. In time, they lost their purchase on this reality, and the way was made for mortal animals. For Man. What remains of the Old Ones are vestiges: certain magicks, certain creatures. . . .

"The books tell that the last demon to leave this reality fed off a human, mixed their blood. He was a human form possessed—infected—by the demon's soul. He bit another and another . . . and so they walk the Earth, feeding. Killing some, mixing their blood with others to make more of their kind. Waiting for the animals to die out and the Old Ones to return."

Not a pretty picture, is it? Fortunately, the forces of good reacted almost instantly. As Giles says later in that very same episode, "As long as there have been vampires, there has been the Slayer." More precisely, "a" Slayer, for each time a Slayer dies, a new one is ready and waiting to take her place, with a Watcher prepared to instruct and guide the new Slayer in her role as the scourge of Darkness.

How all this happens is still quite a mystery. Since the Slayer herself is slightly more than human—stronger, faster, more resilient—it is probably safe to assume that, even as the forces of Darkness created the vampires, there are forces of good that have created the Slayer legacy as counterpoint to the evils of the world.

*Giles:* "Into each generation, a Slayer is born. One girl, in all the world, a Chosen One. One born with the . . ."
*Buffy:* ". . . the strength and skill to hunt the vampires, to stop the spread of evil, blah blah. I've heard it, okay?"
—*"Welcome to the Hellmouth"*

Indeed, there are many questions unanswered. Who was the first Watcher? How does a Watcher know that it is his time and the time for his Slayer? Is there some ruling council among Watchers? This is fertile territory, fascinating questions whose fascinating answers still exist only in the mind of Joss Whedon. For the moment, let's take a look at what we do know.

## Slayer

The current Slayer is Buffy Summers, a seventeen-year-old junior at Sunnydale High

School. After her parents' divorce, Buffy believed that her and her mother's move to Sunnydale was their own choice, but obviously larger forces were at work. After all, upon her arrival, Buffy discovered that Sunnydale was once also called "Boca del Infierno" or "the Hellmouth."

*Giles:* "Dig a bit into the history of this place and you'll find there's been a steady stream of fairly odd occurrences. I believe this area is a center of mystical energy. Things gravitate toward it that you might not find elsewhere."
*Buffy:* "Like death."
*Giles:* "Like werewolves. Zombies. Succubi. Incubi. Everything you ever dreaded was under your bed and told yourself couldn't be by the light of day. They're all *real*."
*Buffy:* "What, did you send away for the *Time-Life* series?"
*Giles:* "Uh, yes."
*Buffy:* "Did you get the free phone?"
*Giles:* "The calendar."
—*"Welcome to the Hellmouth"*

> Later, Giles did indeed get "the calendar." The erstwhile Watcher's only love interest on the series thus far has been technopagan Gypsy computer teacher Jenny Calendar.

"A Slayer hunts vampires; Buffy is the Slayer; don't tell anyone. I think that's all the vampire information you need."
*Giles,* in *"The Harvest"*

Information about other Watchers and Slayers has been revealed sparingly over the course of the first two seasons. The very first episode began with a short trailer that discussed some of them, including Lucy Hanover, in Virginia, 1866. But other references have been even more vague. We do know, interestingly enough, that the vampire Spike has killed two Slayers in his time, and his lover, Drusilla, has also killed at least one—namely, Kendra.

**"Virginia, 1866: The disappearance of local Civil War widows shocked an already devastated community. These events ended when Lucy Hanover arrived in town. Chicago, May**

**1927: Forty-one bodies were found near Union Station. Shortly after the arrival of this young woman, the mysterious murders stopped. Now, in 1997, it's starting all over again."**
*Voice-over narration at the beginning of "Welcome to the Hellmouth"*

"I knew a Slayer in the '30s. Korean chick. Very hot. We're talking muscle tone. Man, we had some times."
*Sid,* the demon-hunting dummy, in *"The Puppet Show"*

"So this is the Slayer. You're prettier than the last one."
*The Master,* to Buffy, in *"Nightmares"*

"You know what I find works real good with Slayers? Killing them. . . . Oh, yeah, I did a couple Slayers in my time. I don't like to brag. Oh, who am I kidding; I *love* to brag. There was this one Slayer, during the Boxer Rebellion . . ."
*Spike,* in *"School Hard"*

Yes, time is unkind to Slayers. They don't tend to live very long. Take Kendra, for example.

When Buffy drowned, only to be revived by Xander, she was, technically, albeit temporarily, dead. Thus, Kendra was "activated" as the Slayer, and her Watcher, Mr. Zabuto—whom Giles notes is "very well respected" among Watchers—sent her to Sunnydale because of the great evil rising there.

*Willow:* "Is that even possible? I mean, two Slayers at the same time?"
*Giles:* "Not to my knowledge. The new Slayer is only called after the previous Slayer has died. . . . Good Lord, you *were* dead, Buffy."
*Buffy:* "I was only gone for a minute."
*Giles:* "Clearly it doesn't matter how long you were gone. You were physically dead, thus causing the activation of the next Slayer."
*Kendra:* "She . . . died?"
*Buffy:* Just a *little*."
—*"What's My Line? Part 2"*

In the end, Kendra didn't live very long.

But why? What is it that keeps Buffy going? That keeps her alive? Her training, certainly. Her determination. But even in the face of prophecies about her death, what seems to keep Buffy alive more than anything else is this: she's unpredictable. The very thing about her that frustrates Giles to no end—her lack of attention to tradition—may be what makes her so very hard to kill.

For starters, Buffy uses her street smarts as much as she does the profound perception of a Slayer.

*Giles:* "Can you tell me if there's a vampire in this building?"
*Buffy:* "Maybe?"
*Giles:* "You should know! Even through this mass and this din you should be able to sense them. Try. Reach out with your mind. You have to hone your senses, focus until the energy washes over you, till you can feel every particle of—"
*Buffy:* "There's one."
*Giles:* "What? Where?"
*Buffy:* "Down there. Talking to that girl."
*Giles:* "But you don't know . . ."
*Buffy:* "Oh, please. Look at his jacket. He's got the sleeves rolled up. And the shirt . . . deal with that outfit for a moment."

*Giles:* "It's dated?"
*Buffy:* "It's carbon-dated! Trust me: only someone who's been living underground for ten years would think that was the look."
—*"Welcome to the Hellmouth"*

*Kendra:* "My parents—they sent me to my Watcher when I was very young."
*Buffy:* "How young?"
*Kendra:* "I don't remember them actually. . . . I've seen pictures. But that's how seriously the calling is taken by my people. My mother and father gave me to my Watcher because they believed they were doing the right thing for me—and for the world. [Then, off Buffy's look] Please. I don't feel sorry for myself. Why should you?"
*Buffy:* "It just sounds very lonely."
*Kendra:* "Emotions are weakness, Buffy. You shouldn't entertain them."
*Buffy:* "Kendra, my emotions give me power. They're total assets."
—*"What's My Line? Part 2"*

Yes, even in the nastiest of situations, Buffy's ability to improvise has saved her time and again.

"There was this time I was pinned down by this guy that played left tackle for varsity. . . . Well, at least he used to before he was a vampire. Anyway, he's got one of those really thick necks and all I've got is a little Exacto knife. . . ."
—*Buffy, in "The Harvest"*

*Buffy* (looking at some crossbow bolts): "Huh, check out these babies; good-bye, stakes, hello, flying fatality. What can I shoot?"
*Giles:* "Nothing. The crossbow comes later. You must become proficient with the basic tools of combat. And let's begin with the quarterstaff. Which, incidentally, requires countless hours of rigorous training. I speak from experience."
*Buffy:* "Giles, twentieth century. I'm not gonna be fighting Friar Tuck."
*Giles:* "You never know with whom—or what—you may be fighting. And these traditions have been handed down through the ages. Now you show me good, steady progress with

the quarterstaff and in due time we'll discuss the crossbow."
Buffy demolishes him with the quarterstaff.
*Giles* (on the floor, breathing hard): "Good. Let's move on to the crossbow."
— *"Angel"*

Of course, given Buffy's penchant for doing things her way, she has clashed time and again with both Giles, as her Watcher, and particularly with Kendra, whose training was far more traditional ... and restrictive in a way that Buffy would never stand for.

*Buffy:* "Then why the hell did you attack me?"
*Kendra:* "I thought you were a vampire."
*Buffy:* "Ooh, a swing and a miss for the rookie."
— *"What's My Line? Part 2"*

*Kendra:* "Here. In case the curse does not succeed ... This is my lucky stake. I have killed many vampires with it. I call it Mr. Pointy."
*Buffy:* "You named your stake."
*Kendra* (embarrassed): "Yes."
*Buffy:* "Remind me to get you a stuffed animal."
— *"Becoming, Part 1"*

*Giles:* "Kendra. There are a few people—civilians if you like—who know Buffy's identity. Willow is one of them. And they also spend time together. Socially."
*Kendra:* "And you allow this, sir?"
*Giles:* "Well ..."
*Kendra:* "But the Slayer must work in secret. For security ..."
*Giles:* "Of course. With Buffy, however, it's ... some flexibility is required."
— *"What's My Line? Part 2"*

*Kendra:* "We can return to your Watcher for orders."
*Buffy:* "I don't take orders. I do things my way."
*Kendra:* "No wonder you died."
— *"What's My Line? Part 2"*

*Giles:* "You see, Spike has also called out the Order of Taraka to keep Buffy out of the way."
*Kendra:* "The assassins? I read of them in the writings of Dramius."
*Giles:* "Really? Which volume?"
*Kendra:* "I believe it was six, sir."
*Buffy* (to Kendra): "How do you know all this?"
*Kendra:* "From my studies."
*Buffy:* "So, obviously you have a lot of free time."
*Kendra:* "I study because it is required. The Slayer handbook insists on it."
*Willow:* "There's a Slayer handbook?"
*Buffy:* "Handbook? What handbook? How come I don't have a handbook?"
*Willow:* "Is there a T-shirt, too? 'Cause that would be cool."
*Giles:* "After meeting you, Buffy, I was quite sure the handbook would be of no use in your case."
— *"What's My Line? Part 2"*

*Kendra:* "Buffy's a student here?"
*Giles:* "Yes."
*Kendra:* "Right. Of course. And I imagine she's a cheerleader as well."
*Giles:* "Actually, she had to give up cheerleading. It's quite an amusing story, really ..."
— *"What's My Line? Part 2"*

Buffy's most persistent crisis, however, has little to do with vampires or Demons. Instead, it is the struggle to create some kind of life for herself, some sort of "normal" teenage existence, and still do her duty as the Slayer. Surely she cannot be the first Slayer to have struggled with these issues, but before she was approached by the late Watcher Merrick, at Hemery High, where she spent her freshman year in Los Angeles, she was living the life of a typical, popular, fifteen-year-old girl: boys, clothes, cheerleading, and dreaming about the future, those were her primary topics of conversation. All of that has changed.

*Kendra:* "Did anyone explain to you what 'secret identity' means?"
*Buffy:* "Nope. Must be in the handbook. Right after the chapter on personality removal."
— *"What's My Line? Part 2"*

*Buffy:* "I'm guessing dating isn't big with your Watcher, either."
*Kendra:* "I am not permitted to speak with boys."
*Buffy:* "Unless you're pummeling them."
— *"What's My Line? Part 2"*

*Buffy:* "Have I ever let you down?"
*Giles:* "Do you want me to answer that, or shall I just glare?"
— *"The Dark Age"*

*Buffy:* "I told one lie, I had one drink."
*Giles:* "Yes. And you nearly got devoured by a giant demon-snake. I think the words 'let that be a lesson' are a tad redundant at this juncture."
— *"Reptile Boy"*

**FROM THE ORIGINAL TELEPLAY "WHAT'S MY LINE? PART 2"**

*Kendra:* "I'm not allowed to watch television. My Watcher says it promotes intellectual laziness."
*Buffy:* "And he says it like it's a bad thing?"
— *"What's My Line? Part 2"*

"Do you think any of the other Slayers ever had to go to high school?"
*Buffy,* in *"School Hard"*

> In "The Harvest," we see that Buffy keeps Slayer supplies in a false bottom of a trunk in her closet. Later, in "School Hard," we see that she also keeps such supplies in a drawer in her dresser, including stakes, a cross, a bottle with "Holy Water" inscribed on it, and spiked brass knuckles.

*Angel:* "I thought we had...you know."
*Buffy:* "A date? So did I. But who am I kidding? Dates are things normal girls have. Girls who have time to think about nail polish and facials. You know what I think about? Ambush tactics. Beheading. Not exactly the stuff dreams are made of."
— *"Halloween"*

*Giles:* "Buffy, maintaining a normal social life when you're a Slayer is problematic at best."
*Buffy:* "This is the '90s! The 1990s, in point of fact, and I can do both. Clark Kent has a job. I just wanna go on a date."
— *"Never Kill a Boy on the First Date"*

*Giles:* "Buffy, you think I don't know what it's like to be sixteen?"
*Buffy:* "No. I think you don't know what it's like to be sixteen, *and* a girl, *and* a Slayer."
*Giles:* "Fair enough. Well, I don't. . . ."
*Buffy:* "Or what it's like to stake vampires while you're having fuzzy feelings toward one."

*Giles:* "Ohh...ahh..."
*Buffy:* "Digging on the undead doesn't exactly do wonders for your social life."
— *"Reptile Boy"*

Given the life she leads, Buffy is often cynical about being the Slayer. She frequently talks about what life might be like if she didn't have that burden.

*Willow:* "You're not even a teensy-weensy bit curious about what kind of career you could have had? I mean, if you weren't already the Slayer and all."
*Buffy:* "Do the words 'sealed' and 'fate' ring any bells for you, Will? Why go there?"
— *"What's My Line? Part 1"*

*Buffy:* "I wonder if it would be so bad, being replaced."
*Willow:* "You mean, like, letting Kendra take over?"
*Buffy:* "Maybe. Maybe after this thing with Spike and the assassins is over, I could say, 'Kendra, you slay, I'm going to Disneyland.'"
*Willow:* "But not forever, right?"
*Buffy:* "No, Disneyland would get boring after a few months. But I could do...other stuff. Career-day stuff. Maybe I could even have, like, a normal life."
— *"What's My Line? Part 2"*

*Giles:* "I'll research all the possibilities, ghosts included. Xander, if you're not doing anything, would you like to help me?"
*Xander:* "What, there's homework now? When did that happen?"
*Buffy:* "It's all part of the glamorous world of vampire slaying."
— *"Out of Mind, Out of Sight"*

*Joyce:* "A little responsibility, Buffy, that's all I ask. Honestly, don't you ever think about anything besides boys and clothes?"
*Buffy:* "Saving the world from vampires."
*Joyce:* "I swear, sometimes I don't know what goes on in your head."
— *"Bad Eggs"*

**FROM THE ORIGINAL TELEPLAY "WHAT'S MY LINE? PART 1"**

*Buffy:* "This career business has me contemplating the el weirdo that I am. Let's face it—instead of a job I have a calling. Okay? No chess club or football games for me. I spend my free time in graveyards and dark alleys."
*Angel:* "Is that what you want? Football games?"
*Buffy:* "Maybe. Maybe not. But you know what? I'm never going to get the chance to find out. I'm stuck in this deal."
— *"What's My Line? Part 1"*

Despite her many complaints, however, Buffy is dedicated to her sacred duty. Never was there a Slayer who had to bear so much horror. That may well be because she refuses to turn her heart off, to her friends and family, and to Angel, the vampire she loves. Still, in the end, Buffy is a Slayer, through and through.

"If the apocalypse comes—beep me."
*Buffy, in "Never Kill a Boy on the First Date"*

"...and you never let her do anything, except work and patrol and—I know she's the Chosen One, but you're killing her with the pressure. I mean she's sixteen going on forty!"
*Willow, to Giles, in "Reptile Boy"*

"Who needs a social life when they've got their very own Hellmouth?"
*Buffy, in "Reptile Boy"*

*Kendra:* "You talk about slaying like it's a job. It's not. It's who you are."
*Buffy:* "You get that from the handbook?"
*Kendra:* "From you."
*Buffy:* "I guess it's something I really can't fight. I'm a freak."
*Kendra:* "But not the only freak."
*Buffy:* "Not anymore."
— *"What's My Line? Part 2"*

*Buffy:* "You know, I'm the Chosen One. It's my job to fight guys like that. What's your excuse?"
*Angel:* "Somebody has to."
— *"Angel"*

"Grown-ups don't believe you, right? Well, I do. We both know there are real monsters. But there are also real heroes, that fight monsters. And that's me."
*Buffy*, in "Killed by Death"

*Angel:* "That's everything, huh? No weapons, no friends. No hope. Take all that away and what's left?"
*Buffy:* "Me." —"Becoming, Part 2"

*Giles:* "He seems like a nice lad."
*Buffy:* "Yeah, but he wants to be Dangerman. You, Xander, Willow, you guys know the score. You're careful. Two days in my world and Owen really would get himself killed. Or I'd get him killed."
—"Never Kill a Boy on the First Date"

*Willow:* "Come on, Buffy. One night of rest isn't going to kill you."
*Buffy:* "No. But it might kill somebody else."
—"Killed by Death"

*Buffy:* "Open your eyes, Mom. What do you think has been going on for the last two years? The fights, the weird occurrences—how many times have you washed blood out of my clothes? You still haven't figured it out?"
*Joyce:* "Well, it stops now."
*Buffy:* "It doesn't stop! Do you think I chose to be like this? Do you know how lonely it is? How dangerous? I would love to be upstairs watching TV or gossiping about boys, or God, even studying. But I have to save the world. Again." —"Becoming, Part 2"

"Mom, I'm a Slayer, not a postal worker. The cops just can't handle demons. I have to do it."
*Buffy*, in "Becoming, Part 2"

No matter how she might fight it, in the end, Buffy will accept her destiny. Even if that destiny is her death. That is a kind of courage that is rare in the human race, and it is even rarer for one so young to be mature enough to understand the nature of sacrifice.

*Merrick:* "There isn't much time. You must come with me. Your destiny awaits."
*Buffy:* "I don't have a destiny. I'm destiny-free. Really."
*Merrick:* "Yes, you have. You are the Chosen One. You alone can stop them."
*Buffy:* "Who?"
*Merrick:* "The vampires." —"Becoming, Part 1"

> Some of Giles's books include *The Black Chronicles*, *The Tiberius Manifesto*, the *Writings of Dramius*, *Legends of Vishnu*, and *The Pergamum Codex*.

*Giles:* "Some prophecies are a bit dodgy. They're mutable. Buffy herself has thwarted them time and again. But this is *The Pergamum Codex*. There is nothing in it that does not come to pass."
*Angel:* "Then you're reading it wrong."
*Giles:* "I wish to God I were. But it's very plain. Tomorrow night, Buffy will face the Master. And she will die."
*Buffy:* "So that's it, huh? My time is up. I remember the drill. 'One Slayer dies, the next is called.' I wonder who she is. [Then, to Giles] Will you train her? Or will they send someone else?"
*Giles:* "Buffy, I . . ."
*Buffy:* "Does it say how he's gonna kill me? [small voice] Do you think it'll hurt? [Angel reaches out to comfort her.] Don't touch me! [beat] Were you guys even gonna tell me?"
*Giles:* "I was hoping I wouldn't have to. That there was some way around it."
*Buffy:* "Oh, I've got a way around it. I quit."
*Angel:* "It's not that simple."
*Buffy:* "I'm making it that simple! I quit! I resign! I'm fired! You can find someone else to stop the Master from taking over."
*Giles:* "I'm not sure that anyone else can. The signs all indicate—"
*Buffy:* "The signs? Read me the signs! Tell me my fortune! You're *so* useful, sitting here with all your books. You're really a lot of help!"
*Giles:* "I don't suppose I am."
*Angel:* "I know this is hard . . ."
*Buffy:* "What do *you* know about this? You're never gonna die."

**Angel:** "You think I want anything to happen to you? Do you think I could stand it? We just have to figure out a way—"
**Buffy:** "I already did. I quit, remember? Pay attention."
**Giles:** "Buffy, if the Master rises . . ."
**Buffy:** "I don't care! I don't care. Giles, I'm sixteen years old. I don't want to die."
—*"Prophecy Girl"*

"Bottom line is, even if you see 'em coming, you're not ready for the big moments. No one asks for their life to change, not really. But it does. So, what, are we helpless? Puppets? No. The big moments are gonna come, can't help that. It's what you do afterward that counts. That's when you find out who you are."
*Whistler, in voice-over, as Buffy discovers Kendra's corpse, in "Becoming, Part 1"*

"She's gonna have it tough, that Slayer. She's just a kid. And the world is full of big bad things."
*Whistler, in "Becoming, Part 1"*

## Watcher

As we have previously noted, one of Buffy's strengths is that she does not work alone. All Slayers have had a Watcher, but it is certain that few are as dedicated, as loyal, and as passionate as Rupert Giles. His perseverance in the face of Buffy's inner struggle, and his position at her side in many of her physical battles, mark him as a tremendously courageous man.

**Giles:** "I was ten years old when my father told me I was destined to be a Watcher. He was one, and his mother before him, and I was to be next."
**Buffy:** "Were you thrilled beyond all measure?"
**Giles:** "No. I had very definite plans about my future. I was going to be a fighter pilot. Or possibly a grocer. My father gave me a very tiresome speech about responsibility and sacrifice."
—*"Never Kill a Boy on the First Date"*

"Buffy, I have volumes of lore, of prophecies and of predictions. But I *don't* have an instruction manual. We feel our way as we go along. And I must say, as a Slayer you're doing pretty well."
*Giles, in "Never Kill a Boy on the First Date"*

"It's who you are? The Watcher? Sniveling tweed-clad guardian of the Slayer and her kin?"
*Ethan Rayne, to Giles, in "Halloween"*

**Buffy:** "Maybe you should consider a career as a Watcher."
**Willow:** "Oh, no. I don't think I could take the stress."
**Xander:** "And the dental plan is *crap*."
**Willow:** "I don't know how Giles does it."
**Buffy:** "I don't think he has a choice."
—*"The Dark Age"*

**Willow:** "How is it you *always* know this stuff? You always know what's going on. I *never* know what's going on."
**Giles:** "Well, you weren't here from midnight to six researching it."
—*"Angel"*

*Giles:* "I've studied all the extant volumes, of course. But the most salient books of Slayer prophecy have been lost. *The Tiberius Manifesto, The Pergamum Codex*—"
*Angel:* "The Codex..."
*Giles:* "It is reputed to contain the most complete prophecies about the Slayer's role in the end years. Unfortunately, the book was lost in the fifteenth century."
*Angel:* "Not lost. Misplaced. I can get it."
*Giles:* "That would be most helpful. My own volumes seem to be rather useless of late.... There's an invisible girl terrorizing the school."
*Angel:* "That's not really my area of expertise."
—*"Out of Mind, Out of Sight"*

*Buffy:* "There's something supernatural at work. Get your books. Look stuff up!"
*Willow:* "What are you going to do?"
*Giles:* "Get my books. Look stuff up."
—*"The Pack"*

**Now, for those of you who believe you have the courage and the fortitude—and particularly the lack of any real social life—which will make you perfectly suited for the position of Slayer, we have provided here a step-by-step program to train you for the job in the event you are the Chosen One.**

# Rules of the Game
## or The Slayer Handbook According to Buffy Summers

### Rule One:

**Walk tough. Talk tough. Be tough.**

"I don't think we've been properly introduced. I'm Buffy and you're...history."
*Buffy*, in *"Never Kill a Boy on the First Date"*

"I've lost friends tonight, and I may lose more. If you have information worth hearing then I am grateful for it. If you want to make jokes then I will pull out your rib cage and wear it as a hat."
*Buffy*, to Spike, in *"Becoming, Part 2"*

### Rule Two:

**Provide whatever assistance you can, but know your strengths and weaknesses.**

*Buffy:* "You have to admit, I kinda lack in the book area. You guys are the brains. I'd only be here for moral support."
*Xander:* "That's not true, Buffy. You totally contribute. You go for snacks."
—*"What's My Line? Part 1"*

*Xander:* "So. Okay. Get started, Buffy. Dissect it or something."
*Buffy:* "Dissect it? Why me?"
*Xander:* "Because you're the Slayer."
*Buffy:* "And I slayed! My work here is done."
—*"Bad Eggs"*

### Rule Three:

**Be properly respectful about your calling and its traditions.**

"Sacred duty, yadda yadda yadda."
*Buffy*, in *"Surprise"*

### Rule Four:

**Keep your cool. Don't let little things like homicidal boyfriends distract you.**

"I know how hard this is for you. But as the Slayer, you do *not* have the luxury of being a slave to your passions. You mustn't let Angel get to you, regardless of how provocative his behavior may become."
*Giles*, in *"Passion"*

"It should simply be *plunge* and move on, *plunge* and . . . "
*Giles*, in *"Never Kill a Boy on the First Date"*

### Rule Five:

**Don't be fooled by a lull in Slayage. Stake all you want, they'll make more.**

"When you live atop a mystical convergence, it's only a matter of time before a fresh hell breaks loose. Now is the time that you should train more strictly, you should hunt and patrol more keenly, you should hone your skills day and night."
*Giles*, in *"Reptile Boy"*

"Just because the paranormal has been more normal and less . . . para lately, is no excuse for tardiness or letting your guard down."
*Giles*, to Buffy, in *"Reptile Boy"*

### Rule Six:

**Seek a proper balance in your life.**

"Buffy, when I said you could slay vampires and have a social life, I didn't mean at the same time!"
*Giles*, in *"Never Kill a Boy on the First Date"*

### Rule Seven:

**Be vigilant in regard to personal morale.**

"A cranky Slayer is a careless Slayer."
*Buffy,* in *"Never Kill a Boy on the First Date"*

### Rule Eight:

**Personal appearance is important in making a good first impression.**

*Xander:* "Is she gonna be okay?" [re: an electrocuted Buffy]
*Giles:* "She was only grounded for a moment. [then, to Buffy] Still, if you'd been anyone but the Slayer...."
*Buffy:* "Tell me the truth. How's my hair?"
*Xander:* "It's great. It's your best hair ever."
*Giles:* "Oh, yes."  —*"I, Robot, You Jane"*

### Rule Nine:

**When faced with the unknown, go with your instincts.**

*Xander:* "You don't know how to kill this thing."
*Buffy:* "I thought I might try violence."
*Xander:* "Solid call."  —*"Killed by Death"*

### Rule Ten:

**Wherever you can, inspire faith in your allies and loathing in your enemies.**

"Not to state the obvious, but this looks like a job for Buffy."
*Xander,* in *"Never Kill a Boy on the First Date"*

"He was young, and he was careful. And still the Slayer takes him, as she's taken so many of my family. It wears thin."
*The Master,* in *"Angel"*

### Rule Eleven:

**Be patient.**

"Ninety percent of the vampire-slaying game is waiting."
*Giles,* in *"Never Kill a Boy on the First Date"*

### Rule Twelve:

**Safeguard your identity as the Slayer at all times.**

"If your identity as the Slayer is revealed, it could put you and those around you in grave danger."
*Giles,* in *"Never Kill a Boy on the First Date"*

*Spike:* "What, your mum doesn't know?"
*Joyce:* "Know what?"
*Buffy:* "That, uh, that I'm in a rock band.... Yes, a rock band with Spike here."
*Spike:* "Right, she plays the ... triangle."
*Buffy:* "Drums."
*Spike:* "Drums, yeah, she's hell on the old skins, you know."
*Joyce:* "And what do you do?"
*Spike:* "Well, I sing."  —*"Becoming, Part 2"*

"Buffy, you aren't by any chance giving away your secret identity just to impress cute boys, are you?"
*Giles,* in *"Lie to Me"*

**Follow these words of wisdom, and one day perhaps your Watcher will arrive, and you, too, may be called to save the world from Darkness.**

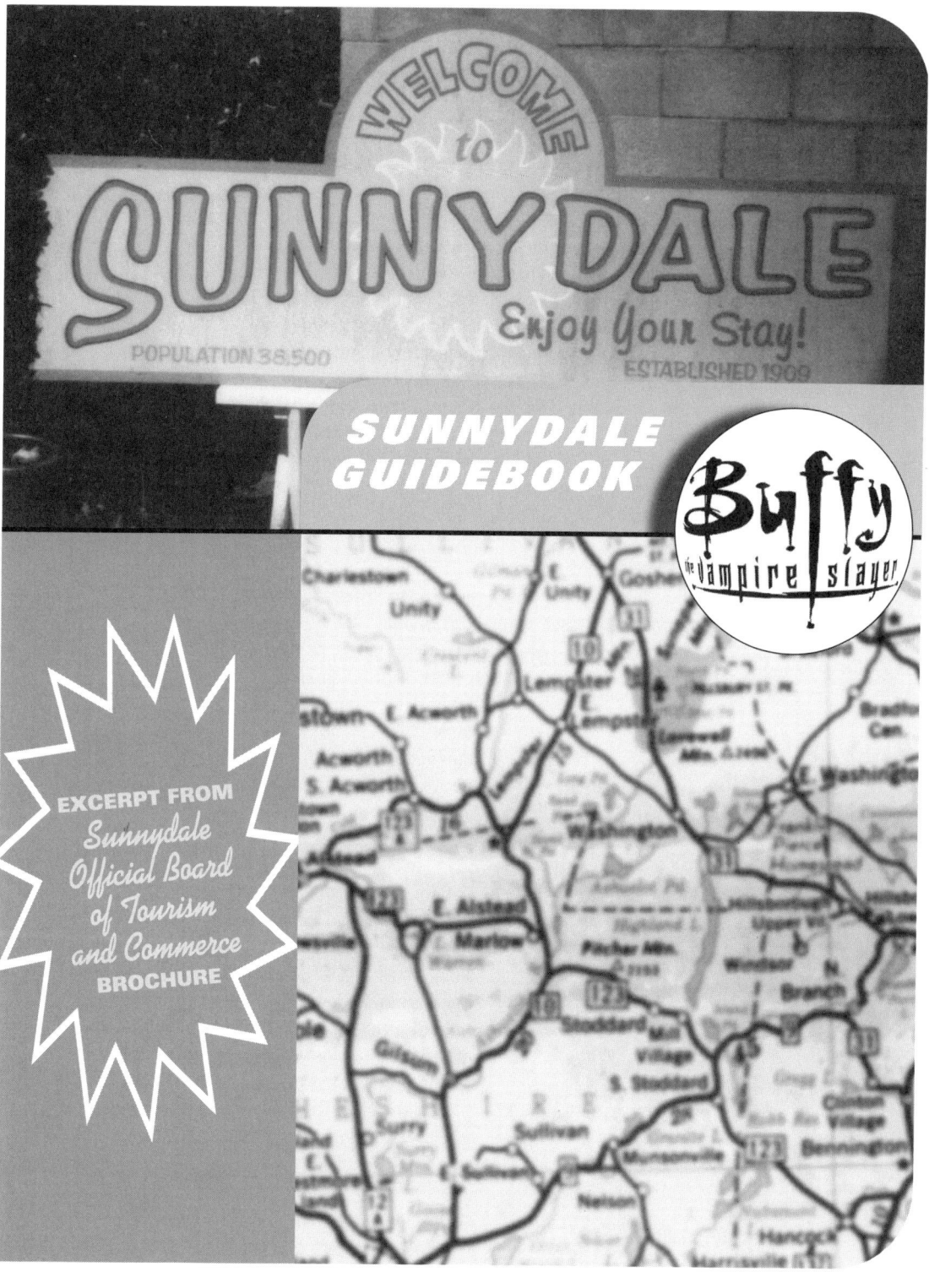

# SUNNYDALE GUIDEBOOK

EXCERPT FROM *Sunnydale Official Board of Tourism and Commerce* BROCHURE

# Welcome to beautiful Sunnydale!

> "It's two hours on the freeway past Neiman Marcus."
> RE: SUNNYDALE, **BUFFY** IN "WELCOME TO THE HELLMOUTH"

The Sunnydale Chamber of Commerce welcomes you to lovely Sunnydale, home to many scenic attractions, including a pristine strip of Southern California beach, a world-class museum, and the fully accredited Crestwood College, a magnet for liberal-arts majors from all corners of the globe. Browse for curios at our art gallery, have a cappuccino at our young people's "hangout," the Bronze...and get to know the friendly locals, who are always glad to show you around their town. Colonized by the Spanish centuries ago and given the quaint and colorful name Boca del Infierno, Sunnydale is a community steeped in history. Nowadays, all kinds of interesting folks make their homes in Sunnydale...and once you've been here for a little while, you'll see why!

**Sunnydale...come for an hour...stay for a lifetime!**

The Historical Society has prepared this Tour of Sunnydale. Many of the attractions are clustered in our central downtown section, while the beach, docks, skating rink, and other places of interest make diverting excursions by car or bus (a map to our **bus depot** and **airport** is located on the back of this brochure).

Sunnydale is a town on the grow . . . and our young people are our lifeblood. The lovely Spanish-style campus of the **Sunnydale High School** features an attractive **Quad**, where the annual May Queen is announced, and an Olympic-sized **swimming pool**, complete with an exquisite **underground grotto**. Sunnydale High is home to the fierce Razorbacks. In 1977, our cheerleading squad won the tri-county championship, and this year we took state semifinals in boys' swimming. Everyone turns out to view the exhibits at our annual science fair, and it's standing room only at the spectacular talent show in our large, professionally equipped **auditorium**. Come have a snack and "hang out" with the class of '99 in our student-decorated **lounge**! Our **cafeteria** recently won "Best Burritos" for the third year in a row. We have a fully computerized **library**, and we're also members of the "Let's Get Together" foreign-exchange-student program.

There are 43 churches in Sunnydale...but some claim there are 44! Ghost stories about a **sunken church** across from the school persist,

> THE LIBRARY
> According to Willow, in the pilot, it's "where the books live."
>
> "Ew, libraries. All those books. What's up with that?"
> MITCH, IN "OUT OF MIND, OUT OF SIGHT"

> "Ooh, Sunnydale bus depot. Classy. What better way to introduce someone to our country than with the stench of urine."
> XANDER, IN "INCA MUMMY GIRL"

> XANDER: "Buffy, this is not about looking at a bunch of animals. This is about not being in class."
> BUFFY: "You know, you're right! Suddenly the animals look shiny and new."
> —ON A FIELD TRIP TO THE ZOO, IN "THE PACK"

> WILLOW: "Everything seems normal. Not a snake, not a wasp."
> CORDELIA: "Yep. School can open again tomorrow."
> XANDER: "Explain to me again how that's a good thing."
> CORDELIA: "I'm drawing a blank—"
> —"I ONLY HAVE EYES FOR YOU"

despite the fact that no such structure has ever been located. Museum archeologists have explored the vast warren of tunnels beneath the town itself, but to no avail. Still, the legend of the Master's Lair never dies . . . will you be the one to unlock its secrets?

Continue on a few blocks directly from the campus, and you'll come across another very nice example of Spanish architecture. These multi-storied buildings have been turned into condos. **Rupert Giles,** the school librarian, lives here.

Doubling-back to the campus, take a short walk toward the edge of town. **The Bronze** is the local hangout for high school students and older young adults. The place has an appealingly dive-y earthiness; no waiting in line for the bouncer to decide if you're cool or not! Just pay the cover and get your hand stamped if you're old enough to drink.

The Bronze is dark, crowded, noisy…and fun! Live bands play almost every night of the week, and the club also hosts the annual May Queen dance, a spooky celebration of Halloween, the World Culture fiesta, and other exciting community get-togethers. The coffee bar serves a delicious array of croissants and pastries.

Approximately ten blocks to the northeast of the Bronze are a number of abandoned warehouses, where, until recently, an attractive brick **factory** occupied most of a city block. Discussions with the city fathers were under way to transform the factory into a spaghetti restaurant or possibly a wax museum, when, unfortunately, a fire burned the factory to the ground.

Also located in this part of town are two very "colorful" establishments, the rough-and-tumble **Fish Tank** and **Willi's Alibi Room.** (No one under twenty-one admitted.)

In addition, you'll need to know "the password" to enter the private **Sunset Club**. And the word is . . . "Lestat"! This Goth club, it is said, once played host to some "real vampires" . . . but you be the judge as you walk among its denizens clad in black lace and blood-red velvet! (Hours vary.) Admission by invitation only.

A ten-block walk east will lead you to the main gate of the **Sunnydale Armory**. Currently under the command of Colonel Newsome, the Armory is home to the 33rd (the legendary "Skull & Crossbones" unit). The Armory offers a tour of its Weapons Museum on Saturdays from 1–3 P.M. A number of interesting armaments have been recovered during excavations in and around Sunnydale (including our new and exciting high-rise towers!). These fascinating objects of battles gone by are showcased alongside examples of the military's most up-to-date weapons systems. (Civilians, please check in at the Visitors' Gate.)

> THE BRONZE
> "The perfect breeding ground for vampire activity."

> "An affluent Southern California school."
> JOSS WHEDON'S DESCRIPTION OF SUNNYDALE HIGH IN THE SCRIPT FOR "WELCOME TO THE HELLMOUTH"

> OZ: "Hey, did everybody just see that guy turn into dust?"
> WILLOW: "Uh, sort of."
> XANDER: "Yep. Vampires are real; lot of 'em live in Sunnydale. Willow'll fill you in."
> WILLOW: "I know it's hard to accept at first…."
> OZ: "No, actually, it explains a lot…."
> —"SURPRISE"
>
> BUFFY: "There's this amazing place you can go and sit down in the dark—and there are these moving pictures. And the pictures tell a story."
> GILES: "Ha ha. Very droll. I'll have you know I have many relaxing hobbies."
> BUFFY: "Such as?"
> GILES: "Well, I enjoy cross-referencing."
> BUFFY: "Do you stuff your own shirts or do you send them out?"
> —"HALLOWEEN"

# Sunnydale Guidebook

Rounding the perimeter of the Armory and headling back west, you'll come to the **Sunnydale Hospital**. Our E.R. is a busy, bustling trauma center, and our on-site physicians are ready to service your every need, be it a gang-related incident, a run-in with a backed-up sewer line, or an inconvenient tumble down the stairs. Our viral-containment unit is world-class. All our blood products are irradiated, and we have a twenty-four-hour pharmacy.

Continue past the **police station** and the city administration building, and you will come to our lovely **Sunnydale Mall**. Recently refurbished, it boasts a multiplex cinema offering first-run movies, as well as many shops and a lavish food court. Be sure to check out the cool video-game parlor on the upper level!

Leaving the mall and continuing past the community parking lot, our business district offers more fascinating shopping. Not for the faint-hearted, the **Dragon's Cove Magic Shop** carries voodoo dolls, love potions, and Ouija boards. It also sells an attractive line of crystal globe paperweights called "Orbs of Thesulah." Pick up a few for your New Age friends! Nearby, a number of shops specialize in theatrical-costume rentals and Halloween gear. Flash those vampire teeth and say, "Blood!" The oldest costume shop is **Party Town**, and last year, **Ethan's** was a big hit. (Currently closed.)

> XANDER: "Hel-lo! Excuse me, but have you ever heard of knocking?"
> STUDENT: "We're supposed to get some books on Stalin. For a report."
> XANDER: "Does this look like a Barnes & Noble?"
> GILES: "Xander! This is the school library."
> —"PASSION"

After an hour or so of browsing, continue down the lane that leads into one of our loveliest residential areas. Wide boulevards and Deodora pines grace the yards of several Arts and Crafts homes on **Revello Drive**, as well as typical Southern California ranch and Mediterranean styles on the attractive cross streets.

If you continue on, you'll come to **Weatherly Park**, a meeting place for young people and senior citizens alike. This large park is suitable for biking, hiking, and picnicking. Skateboarding is prohibited. (A note of caution: it's probably best to stick to the trails and paved walkways. The occasional unlicensed dog may run loose.) The gates are locked at 10 P.M.

A few blocks farther north, you'll come to the local **playground**, where children can let off steam on the jungle gym and the swings. There are picnic tables, too.

Continue on for approximately another mile, and you'll come upon one of the largest and most beautiful buildings in Sunnydale: the **Sunnydale Natural History Museum**.

> "Uuhhggh. Parts."
> **BUFFY** AT THE SUNNYDALE FUNERAL HOME, "NEVER KILL A BOY ON THE FIRST DATE"
>
> WILLOW: "Oh, I'm good with medical stuff. Xander and I used to play doctor all the time."
> XANDER: "*No*, she's being literal. She used to have these medical volumes and diagnose me with stuff. I didn't have the heart to tell her she was playing it wrong."
> —"KILLED BY DEATH"
>
> GILES: "A transport vehicle is delivering a supply of blood to the hospital."
> BUFFY: "Aha. Vampire meals-on-wheels."
> GILES: "Well, hopefully not. We should meet in front of the hospital at 8:30 sharp. I'll bring the weapons."
> XANDER: "I'll bring the party mix."
> —"THE DARK AGE"

Boasting several impressive collections of anthropological artifacts as well as scientific specimens, the museum also plays host to several touring exhibitions each year. Recently, the Inca Princess exhibit drew record crowds. Be sure to visit the Douglas Perren Memorial Room, where a large collection of curios from in and around Sunnydale is on display.

> "Typical museum trick. Promise human sacrifice, deliver old pots and pans."
> **XANDER**, IN "INCA MUMMY GIRL"

Beyond the museum are a number of lovely homes. Rumor has it that members of the popular local band Dingoes Ate My Baby live in this area. Watch out for groupies!

The next stop on any tour of Sunnydale would have to be the **Sunnydale Zoo**. Home to many rare and exotic species, the zoo is a favorite field-trip destination for all ages and grades. Open year-round. (Sorry, the Hyena House is under repair and will be closed until further notice.)

Our youth like to stop to admire the view at "the point," which actually affords a nice view of our town. Make sure that emergency brake is on! Another well-known congregating spot is the humorously named "Makeout Park," near the zoo. Teen Angel, where are you?

Next stop...surf city! Hang ten at the **Sunnydale Beach**. Take I-17 west (municipal bus #13, "Beach" stop.) There's plenty of free parking in the lot. Bonfires are permitted; however, alcoholic beverages and glass containers are not permitted. (*Note:* There have been several unverified shark sightings, but the Sunnydale Water Safety Commission advises that there is, at present, no cause for alarm.) **Our waters are safe**.

And speaking of sharks, if it's fishing you're after, be sure to visit the **Sunnydale Docks**! Home to a healthy shipping industry, the docks house deep-sea fishing boats that are available for charter, from half-day excursions to long, lost weekends lazing in the sun, waiting for that good, strong tug....Call 555-FISH for details.

Take I-17 in the opposite direction, go past the Sunnydale exit, and take the Kallas off-ramp, for a cool spin at the **Sunnydale Ice Rink**. (Bus #66, "Ice Rink" stop.) Go for the gold—and be sure to warm up with some nice hot chocolate and a sugary *churros* at the concession stand. Closed Tuesdays.

Head back into town to spend a few quiet moments in the "Graveyard in the Woods," **Sunnydale Cemetery**. The Mausoleum is also on the grounds. In this hallowed ground, the town's deceased are buried. Prominent Sunnydalians laid to rest here are: Sunnydale principal Robert Flutie, all-state football star Daryl Epps, and many, many others. The historic **Sunnydale Funeral Home** is located nearby. A full-service funeral home providing burial services and with a fully licensed, on-site crematorium, its motto for over four generations has been: "We'll take care of the rest."

> **XANDER:** "We saw the zebras mating! Thank you, very exciting..."
> **WILLOW:** "It looked like the Heimlich. With stripes."
> —"THE PACK"
>
> **CORDELIA:** "The Bronze. It's the only club worth going to around here. They let anybody in, but it's still the scene. It's in the bad part of town."
> **BUFFY:** "Where's that?"
> **CORDELIA:** "About half a block from the good part of town. We don't have a whole lot of town."
> —"WELCOME TO THE HELLMOUTH"
>
> **GILES:** "We'll deal with that when we've ruled out evil curses."
> **BUFFY:** "Someday I'm going to live in a town where evil curses are just generally ruled out without even saying."
> —"INCA MUMMY GIRL"

Abutting the cemetery's south wall stand the Sunnydale woods, a bucolic wonderland of deciduous evergreens, and just beyond the woods, the abandoned but still splendid **Delta Zeta Kappa fraternity house**. Once chartered by **Crestwood College**, on whose campus the house stands, the fraternity chose to disband last year after a scandal involving questionable initiation rituals. The college itself remains in excellent academic standing. Last year, the drama department mounted an excellent production of *The Sound of Music*.

About two miles past the north wall of the college stands **Sunnydale Technology Park**, home to a small but prosperous cluster of high-tech companies, including Lorrin Software. The park was also home to CRD, now unfortunately in Chapter 11 bankruptcy proceedings. The structure recently sustained some damage due to an electrical problem and has been condemned.

> WILLOW: "Now there's a killer? We don't know there's a—"
> GILES: "No. But this being Sunnydale and all..."
> —"REPTILE BOY"

A quick turn down the street and you're at the **Mini-Golf**! Providing wholesome family entertainment, Sunnydale's miniature golf course is a great place to catch up with old friends...or get better acquainted with new ones!

On the outskirts of town stands a **mansion**, which is reputed to be the home of a retired silent-film star who deeded it to the town upon her death. The Historical Society recently leased it to a reclusive gentleman named "Mr. A." Movers report that the mansion is filled with beautiful Art Deco statuary and fixtures. Perhaps one day Mr. A will open his doors for a *grande soiree*, as has been suggested by some "in the know."

We hope that this brochure has added to your enjoyment of our beautiful town. Who knows? Maybe once you've spent some time in Sunnydale, you'll find you just can't leave!

---

> "Not a lot happens in a one-Starbuck's town like Sunnydale."
> XANDER, IN "WELCOME TO THE HELLMOUTH"
>
> BUFFY: "And on your right, once again—the beautiful campus. I think you've now seen everything there is to see in Sunnydale."
> FORD: "Well, it's really..."
> BUFFY: "Feel free to say 'dull.'"
> FORD: "Okay. Dull's good. Or maybe not so dull.... Is that more vampires?"
> —"LIE TO ME"
>
> GILES: "There are forty-three churches in Sunnydale? That seems a little excessive."
> WILLOW: "It's the extra evil vibe from the Hellmouth. Makes some people pray harder."
> —"WHAT'S MY LINE? PART 2"

> GAGE: "So that . . . was the thing that killed Cameron?"
> BUFFY: "No, that was something else."
> GAGE: "Something else?"
> BUFFY: "Unfortunately, there are a lot of 'something elses' in this town."
> —"GO FISH"

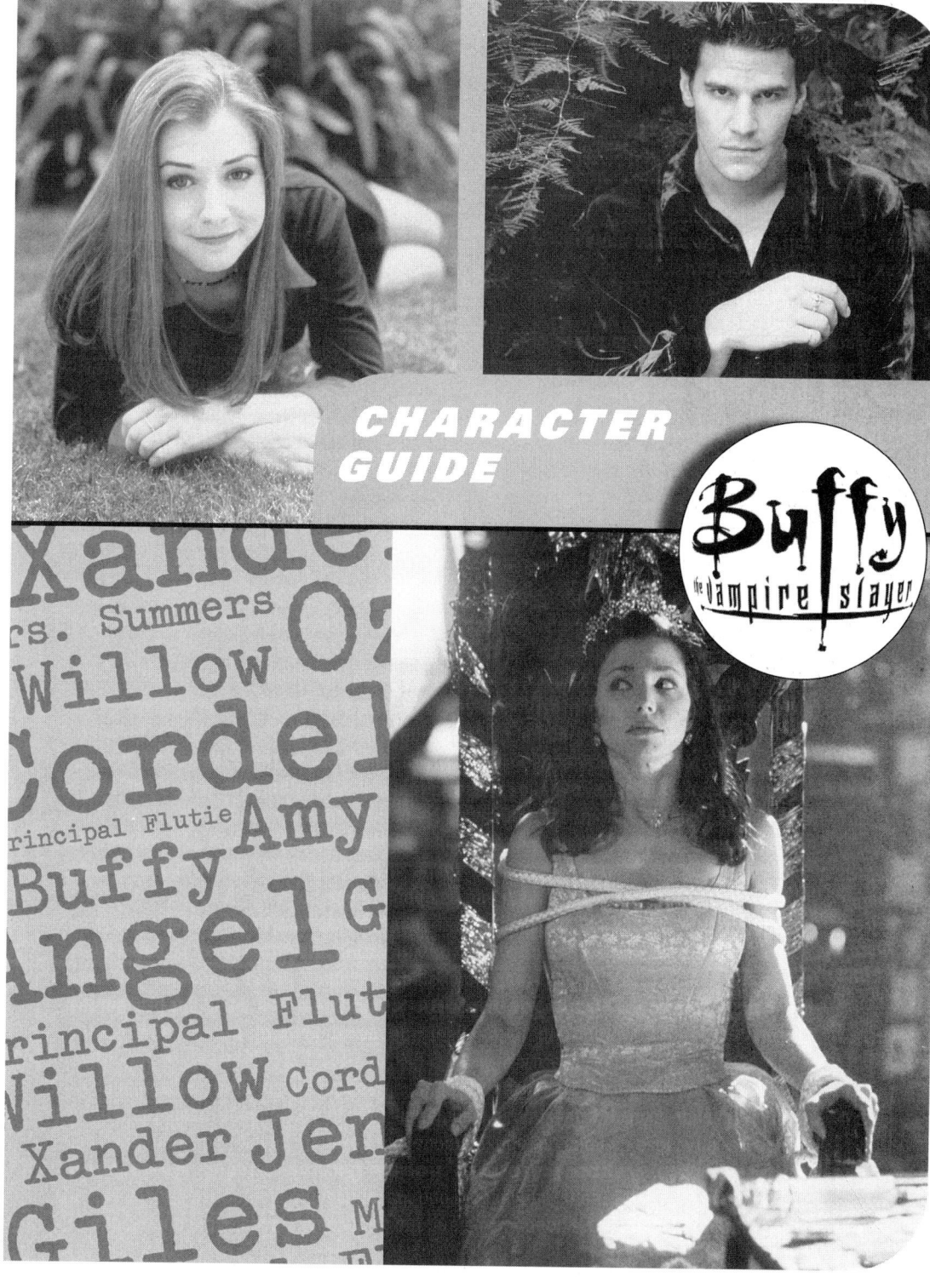

# CHARACTER GUIDE

**Buffy the Vampire Slayer**

## Buffy Summers

Buffy Anne Summers was born in 1981 ("Nightmares," "Surprise," "Innocence") to the now-divorced Hank and Joyce Summers. As a child, she would pretend to be the superhero Power Girl, which would turn out to be a prophetic choice of alter ego. She was very close to her cousin Celia until Celia died in a hospital, leading Buffy to hate hospitals ("Killed by Death").

Buffy started attending Hemery High School, in Los Angeles, in the fall of 1995. She was elected the equivalent of the May Queen in 1996 ("Out of Mind, Out of Sight"), and it was also then that she learned from a Watcher named Merrick that she was the Chosen One, the Slayer of vampires ("Welcome to the Hellmouth," "Becoming, Part 1"). During her initial foray into Slayerhood, Merrick was killed and she burned down the school gymnasium ("Welcome to the Hellmouth"). Her parents—who had been having marital difficulties for some time ("Becoming, Part 1")—finalized their divorce that same year ("Nightmares").

Her mother gained custody of Buffy in the divorce, and the pair moved to a house at 1630 Revello Drive ("Angel") in Sunnydale, California, and Buffy enrolled as a sophomore at Sunnydale High School ("Welcome to the Hellmouth"). Reluctantly at first, she again took up her duties as the Slayer, with Rupert Giles as her new Watcher ("The Harvest").

In addition to her increased strength, agility, and stamina thanks to being the Slayer, Buffy is also a skilled ice skater—she went through a "Dorothy Hamill phase" as a child, down to the haircut ("What's My Line? Part 1"). She also sometimes has prophetic dreams ("Welcome to the Hellmouth," "Prophecy Girl," "Surprise," "Innocence"). Giles seemed to think that she should be able to sense vampires ("Welcome to the Hellmouth"), an ability Buffy has been developing over the last two years.

Buffy's success with relationships has been limited. Her fifth-grade crush on Billy "Ford" Fordham went unrequited, though the two had been very close friends through to high school ("Lie to Me"). She briefly dated a boy named Tyler, but dumped him in fairly short order ("Becoming, Part 1"). She became vaguely involved with two Sunnydale High boys, Owen Thurman ("Never Kill a Boy on the First Date") and Cameron Walker ("Go Fish"), but the former was more interested in Buffy's wild lifestyle than in Buffy

> "I think I speak for everyone here when I say, 'Huh?'"
> —to Giles, in "Out of Mind, Out of Sight"

> "Everyone has them in L.A. Pepper spray is so passé."
> —about her stake, in "Welcome to the Hellmouth"

> "Giles, CARE. I'm putting my life on the line, battling the undead! Look, I broke a nail, okay? I'm wearing a press-on. The least you could do is exhibit some casual interest. You could go 'Hmmm.'"
> —"Prophecy Girl"

herself, and Cameron turned out to be as dull as dishwater (and a gill monster, to boot). A college boy named Tom Warner came on to her, but he was interested only in sacrificing her to the Demon his fraternity worshiped ("Reptile Boy"). She turned down two other propositions ("Halloween," "I Only Have Eyes for You"), as well as Xander's numerous advances ("The Witch," "Prophecy Girl"). Her only successful relationship—with Angel—ended very badly ("Angel," etc.). Buffy and Angel, a vampire with a soul, fell in love and actually managed to sustain a relationship.

Unfortunately, the curse that gave Angel his soul was predicated on his suffering forever for his past evil deeds; having sex with Buffy led to him to revert to his former vampiric self, Angelus ("Surprise," "Innocence"), which put something of a damper on the relationship.

Buffy's style of Slayerhood has proven to be unique. She has a support system beyond her Watcher (Xander, Willow, Cordelia, and Oz, plus Angel, until he reverted, and Jenny Calendar, until she was murdered), the peculiarity of which was commented on by Spike ("School Hard"), and her training has focused almost exclusively on the physical elements of Slayerdom, Giles having foregone the intellectual side ("What's My Line? Part 2"; until that episode, Buffy had no idea there even was a Slayer's handbook). However, she has done a superlative job, having killed the Master, one of the oldest and most powerful vampires ("Prophecy Girl"), and prevented Hell from spilling over onto Earth ("Becoming, Part 2").

Buffy is played by Sarah Michelle Gellar. Her eight-year-old self was played by Mimi Paley in "Killed by Death," and she was also played by an anonymous rat for parts of "Bewitched, Bothered, and Bewildered."

> "Well, it's the weirdest thing. He's got two little holes in his neck and all his blood's been drained. Isn't that bizarre? Aren't you just going 'Ooooh'?"
> —"Welcome to the Hellmouth"

> FROM THE ORIGINAL TELEPLAY "INCA MUMMY GIRL":
> Giles: "You're twisting my words."
> Buffy: "No, I'm just using them for good."
> —"Inca Mummy Girl"

> "Loser."
> —to the bones of the Master, in "Prophecy Girl"

> "Cordelia, your mouth is open. Sound is coming from it. This is never good."
> —"When She Was Bad"

> "You won't tell anyone that I'm the Slayer, and I won't tell anyone that you're a moron."
> —"When She Was Bad"

---

"When he wakes up, tell him...I don't know. Think of something cool; tell him I said it."
—after knocking Giles out to save his life, in "Prophecy Girl"

"I wish people wouldn't leave open graves lying around like this."
—"Some Assembly Required"

"I may be dead, but I'm still pretty. Which is more than I can say for you."
—to the Master, in "Prophecy Girl"

# Quotable Buffy

"She's the gnat in my ear. The gristle in my teeth. She's the bloody thorn in my bloody side!"
— **Spike, on Buffy, in "What's My Line? Part 1"**

**Buffy:** "I wasn't gonna use violence. I don't always use violence, do I?"
**Xander:** "The important thing is, *you* believe that." —**"Inca Mummy Girl"**

"Now, we can do this the hard way, or . . . well, actually, there's just the hard way."
—**"Welcome to the Hellmouth"**

"I've had it. Spike is going down. You can attack me, you can send assassins after me . . . that's fine. But nobody messes with my boyfriend."
—**"What's My Line? Part 2"**

"When this is over, I'm thinking pineapple pizza and teen-video movie fest—possibly something from the Ringwald oeuvre."
—**"What's My Line? Part 2"**

**Buffy:** "I kill vampires. That's my job."
**Giles:** "True, although you don't usually beat them into quite such a bloody pulp beforehand." —**"Ted"**

**Xander:** "Can you say 'overreaction'?"
**Buffy:** "Can you say 'sucking chest wound?'" —**"Ted"**

**Willow:** "Don't forget, you're supposed to be a meek little girlie-girl like the rest of us."
**Buffy:** "Spoil my fun." —**"Phases"**

**Ted:** "Buffy, your mother and I are taking one step at a time, and if things go the way I hope, someday soon I may just ask her to tie the knot. How would you feel about that? It's okay to have feelings, Buffy, and it's okay to express them."
**Buffy:** "I'd feel like killing myself." —**"Ted"**

**Willow:** "I'm sure it wasn't your fault. He started it!"
**Buffy:** "Yeah, that defense only works in six-year-old court, Will." —**"Ted"**

**Giles:** "Let's not jump to any conclusions."
**Buffy:** "I didn't jump. I took a tiny step, and there conclusions were." —**"Phases"**

**Cain:** "You know, sis, if that thing out there harms anyone, it's going to be on your pretty little head. I hope you can live with that."
**Buffy:** "I live with that every day." —**"Phases"**

"The Master. I went by his grave last night and they have a vacancy." —**"When She Was Bad"**

"Destructo-Girl, that's me." —**"Teacher's Pet"**

**Buffy:** "So what's the scuttlebutt? Anybody besides Larry fit our werewolf profile?"
**Willow:** "There is one name that keeps getting spit out. Aggressive behavior, run-ins with the 'authorities,' about a screenful of violent incidents."
**Buffy:** "Okay, most of those weren't my fault. Somebody else started this. I was just standing up for myself."
**Willow:** "They say it's a good idea to count to ten and say you're sorry."
—**"Phases"**

"I am trying to save you! You are playing in some serious traffic here, do you understand that? You're gonna *die*. And the only hope you have of surviving is to get out of this pit right now and, my God, could you *have* a dorkier outfit?"
—to "Diego" and the True Believers, in "Lie to Me"

"I'd suggest a box of Oreos dunked in apple juice...but maybe she's over that phase."
**Ford's first line, in "Lie to Me"**

"We need to find the rest of the swim team and lock them up before they get in touch with their inner halibut." —**"Go Fish"**

**Coach Marin:** "You've got quite an imagination, missy."
**Buffy:** "Right now I'm imagining you in jail....You're wearing a big orange suit and—oh, look! The guards are beating you!" —**"Go Fish"**

"Can you vague that up for me?"
—**"Welcome to the Hellmouth"**

"People, listen to me. This is not the mother ship, okay? This is ugly death come to play."
—**"Lie to Me"**

**Joyce:** "Are you going out tonight, honey?"
**Buffy:** "Yeah, Mom, I'm going to a club."
**Joyce:** "Will there be boys there?"
**Buffy:** "No, Mom, it's a nun club."
—**"Welcome to the Hellmouth"**

**FROM THE ORIGINAL TELEPLAY:**
"I'm not a big secret-sharer. I like my secrets. They're secret." —**"Inca Mummy Girl"**

# Angel

An Irish gentleman born in the early 1700s, Angelus was a ne'er-do-well who was more interested in drinking than in doing an honest day's work. On one such drunken binge, he encountered a vampire named Darla, who turned him into a vampire ("Angel," "Becoming, Part 1"). Although he had never left his home of Galway as a human, as a vampire he traveled extensively. In England in 1860, he murdered the family of a woman named Drusilla, driving her mad before finally turning her into a vampire ("Lie to Me," "Becoming, Part 1"). In Romania in 1898, he killed the favorite daughter of a Romany tribe and was thereafter cursed by the tribe's elders: they restored his soul to him, forcing him to live in anguish over the acts he had committed as a vampire ("Angel," "Becoming, Part 1").

From that point on, Angel suffered. He drifted, eventually winding up as a homeless person in a New York City alleyway in the 1990s. It was there that the demon Whistler found him and encouraged him to make something of himself ("Becoming, Part 1"). He traveled to California and

decided he would help the Slayer. Initially, his help came in the form of cryptic advice ("Welcome to the Hellmouth," "The Harvest," "Teacher's Pet," "Never Kill a Boy on the First Date"), but his and Buffy's growing feelings for each other led to him becoming closer both to her and to her circle of friends. He also revealed to her that he is a vampire and how he came to regain his soul ("Angel"). Angel became a valued ally to Buffy, Giles, and the Slayerettes, and his vampiric strength and abilities proved especially useful against the demon Eyghon ("The Dark Age"), the minions of the demon Machida ("Reptile Boy"), and against the various vampires that have infested Sunnydale ("Angel," "School Hard," "Lie to Me," etc.).

> "Angel's our friend. Except I don't like him."
> —Xander, in "What's My Line? Part 2"

> "Don't worry, I'm not here to eat."
> —"Out of Mind, Out of Sight"

Despite the lunacy of it (though Giles called it "poetic" in "Out of Mind, Out of Sight"), Angel and Buffy fell hopelessly in love with each other, eventually consummating the relationship on Buffy's seventeenth birthday ("Surprise"). Unfortunately, the Romany curse was predicated on Angel remaining tortured. By experiencing joy, the curse was lifted and he reverted to his old self ("Innocence"). He remained un-souled until Willow recast the spell—but, right after that Buffy was forced to impale him and send him to Hell to prevent the world from being destroyed ("Becoming, Part 2").

Angel is played by David Boreanaz.

> "Aren't you a 'throw himself to the lions' sort of chap these days?"
> —Spike, in "What's My Line? Part 2"

> "If I can go a little while without being shot or stabbed, I'll be okay."
> —"Angel"

## Quotable Angel

**Willy:** "I'm living right, Angel."
**Angel:** "Sure you are, Willy. And I'm taking up sunbathing."
—"What's My Line? Part 1"

**Buffy:** "It's Angel. He's Drusilla's sire."
**Xander:** "Man, that guy got some major neck in his day!"
—"What's My Line? Part 2"

**Angel:** "I want to learn from you."
**Whistler:** "Okay."
**Angel:** "But I don't want to dress like you."
—"Becoming, Part 1"

**Angel:** "The [Romany elders] conjured the perfect punishment for me."
**Buffy:** "What, they were all out of boils and blinding torment?"
**Angel:** "When you become a vampire, the demon takes your body. But it doesn't get your soul. That's gone. No conscience, no remorse…it's an easy way to live. You have no idea what it's like to have done the things I've done, and to care. I haven't fed on a living human being since that day."
—"Angel"

**Spike:** "No more of this 'I've got a soul' crap?"
**Angel:** "What can I say? I was going through a phase." —"**Innocence**"

"I can walk like a man, but I'm not one. I wanted to kill you tonight."
—to Buffy, in "**Angel**"

**Buffy:** "I invited you into my home. And then you attacked my family."
**Angel:** "Why not? I killed mine. I killed their friends and their friends' children. For a hundred years, I offered an ugly death to everyone I met. And I did it with a song in my heart."
—"**Angel**"

**Buffy:** "...I know what you are."
**Angel:** "I'm just an animal, right?"
**Buffy:** "You're not an animal. Animals I like."
—"**Angel**"

**Angel:** "What?"
**Xander:** "You were checking out my neck! I saw that."
**Angel:** "No, I wasn't."
**Xander:** "Just keep your distance, pal."
**Angel:** "I wasn't looking at your neck."
**Xander:** "I told you to eat before we left."
—"**Prophecy Girl**"

# Xander Harris

Alexander LaVelle Harris has lived in Sunnydale, California, all his life. His best friend growing up was Willow Rosenberg—they used to play literal "doctor," with Willow using actual medical texts ("Killed by Death"), Willow was at Xander's sixth birthday party when he was menaced by a clown ("Nightmares"), and each used to regularly sleep over at the other's house ("Bewitched, Bothered, and Bewildered")—and they remain best friends to this day. He was also best friends with Jesse, until he was turned into a vampire and Xander inadvertently staked him ("The Harvest"). Xander learned of Buffy's secret by overhearing her and Giles speaking in the library about it ("Welcome to the Hellmouth"), and, along with Willow, he insisted on helping Buffy in her subsequent adventures ("The Witch").

Little is known about the Harris family. Xander's father supposedly once considered selling his son to some Armenians ("Inca Mummy Girl"), and apparently neither parent can cook—Xander once invited Willow over for dinner by saying, "Mom's making her famous phone call to the Chinese place," prompting Willow to ask if they even had a stove in their house ("Out of Mind, Out of Sight").

Although not unintelligent by any means, despite referring to himself as the "king of cretins" ("The Witch"), Xander has never excelled academically ("Bewitched, Bothered, and Bewildered," "Go Fish," etc.), relying on Willow to tutor him in many subjects, especially math ("Welcome to the Hellmouth," "The Pack," "Becoming, Part 2").

Xander's love life has not been the most successful. Remaining cheerfully oblivious to how Willow feels about him (except for one moment in "When She Was Bad" and "Innocence"), he instead pursued a variety of women who were no good for him, ranging from a sexy substitute teacher who turned out to be a praying mantis out for his head ("Teacher's Pet"), to an exchange student who turned out to be a mummy that needed to drain the life out of people ("Inca Mummy Girl"), to Buffy, for whom he has carried a torch from the moment he saw her and crashed his skateboard ("Welcome to the Hellmouth") but who has not shown any interest (except for one moment in "Phases" and under a spell in "Bewitched, Bothered, and Bewildered"). Although he had often declared himself treasurer of the We Hate Cordelia Chase Fan Club ("Innocence"), Xander and Cordelia found themselves necking when they were trapped in Buffy's basement ("What's My Line? Part 2"), and the pair of them have become, against all odds, an item. After Cordelia broke up with him, Xander conscripted Amy Madison to cast a love spell on her, which backfired rather spectacularly, causing every woman in Sunnydale *except* Cordelia to fall for him and nearly starting a riot. The desperate gesture, however, was enough to make Cordelia give the relationship another chance ("Bewitched, Bothered, and Bewildered").

He continues to pine for Buffy, which irks both Cordelia and Willow and caused a great deal of friction between him and Angel before Angel's soul was taken ("Surprise")—and led to a not-entirely-unjustified "I told you so" ("Passion") and a lack of desire to see the vampire re-souled ("Becoming").

Xander's primary contribution to the Slayerettes is not really physical—Buffy, Giles, and Angel are all better suited to the hand-to-hand stuff—nor intellectual—Willow and Giles are more inclined in that direction—though he has done both (he's slain a vampire or two in his time, e.g., "Phases," and it was he who came up with a way to stop the Judge in "Innocence" and the maggot assassin in "What's My Line? Part 2"). His most important qualities are his loyalty to Buffy and the others and his willingness to do whatever is necessary to help out (overcoming his inner demons in "Nightmares," going undercover on the swim team in "Go Fish," challenging the vampires in their lair in "The Harvest," "Prophecy Girl," "When She Was Bad," "Innocence," and "Becoming, Part 2," rescuing Cordelia from a fire-filled room in "Some Assembly Required," etc.), though sometimes that gets in the way of his better judgment (e.g., shadowing Buffy and Cordelia to the frat party in "Reptile Boy").

Xander is played by Nicholas Brendon.

### XANDERISMS

"The dead rose! We should've at least had an assembly." —**"The Harvest"**

"I don't like vampires. I'm gonna take a stand and say they're not good." —**"The Harvest"**

"I laugh in the face of danger. Then I hide until it goes away." —**"Witch"**

"It's funny how the earth never opens up and swallows you when you want it to." —**"Teacher's Pet"**

"We could grind our enemies into talcum powder with a sledge hammer, but, gosh, we did that last night." —**"When She Was Bad"**

"For I am Xander, king of the cretins. May all lesser cretins bow before me." —**"Witch"**

"You're certainly a font of nothing." —to Jesse in **"Welcome to the Hellmouth"**

# Quotable Xander

"Okay, this is where I have a problem, see, because we're talking about vampires. We're having a talk with *vampires* in it."
—**"The Harvest"**

"Rodney Munson. God's gift to the Bell Curve. What he lacks in smarts, he makes up for in lack of smarts." —**"Inca Mummy Girl"**

"Can I just say one thing? HEEELLLLPPP!"
—**"Teacher's Pet"**

**Ampata:** "You are strange."
**Xander:** "Girls always tell me that. Right before they run away."
—**"Inca Mummy Girl"**

**Ford:** "I'd love to go [to the Bronze], but if you guys had plans—would I be imposing?"
**Xander:** "Only in the literal sense."
—**"Lie to Me"**

"Cavalry's here; cavalry's a frightened guy with a rock, but it's here."
—**"Becoming, Part 2"**

**Buffy:** "Xander, how do you feel about rifling through Giles's personal files, see if you can shed some light?"
**Xander:** "I feel pretty good about it. Does that make me a sociopath?"
—**"The Dark Age"**

"Wow. Wow, I think I'm having a thought. I am. I'm having a thought. And now I'm having a plan. [The lights go out.] And now I'm having a wiggins." —**"Innocence"**

"I'm seventeen. Looking at *linoleum* makes me wanna have sex." —**"Innocence"**

**Mr. Whitmore:** "How many of us have lost countless productive hours plagued by unwanted sexual thoughts and feelings? [Xander's hand shoots up.] That was a rhetorical question, Mr. Harris. Not a poll." —**"Bad Eggs"**

"Man, Buffy. My whole life just flashed before my eyes. I've got to get me a life."
—**"Killed by Death"**

"Ready to get down, you funky party weasel?"
—to Giles, in **"Surprise"**

"Buffy! I feel a pre-birthday spanking coming on—" —**"Surprise"**

**Giles:** "I suppose there is a sort of Machiavellian ingenuity to your transgression."
**Xander:** "I resent that! Or possibly, thank you..."
**Giles:** "Bit of both would suit." —**"Bad Eggs"**

**Giles:** "The She-Mantis assumes the form of a beautiful woman and lures innocent virgins back to her nest."
**Buffy:** "Well, Xander's not a...I mean, he's probably . . ."
**Willow:** "Going to die!" —**"Teacher's Pet"**

"Principal Snyder! Great career fair, sir. Really. In fact, I'm so inspired by your leadership—I'm thinking principal school. I want to walk in your shoes. Not your actual shoes, of course. Because you're a tiny person. Not tiny in the small sense, of course . . . Okay. Done now." —**"What's My Line? Part 1"**

"Whatever comes out of your mouth is a meaningless waste of breath. An airborne toxic event."
—**Principal Snyder to Xander, in "What's My Line? Part 1"**

**Jenny:** "Cordelia is going to meet us."
**Xander:** "Ooh, gang, did you hear that? A bonus day of class, plus Cordelia! Mix in a little bit of rectal surgery and it's my *best day ever!*"
—**"The Dark Age"**

**Buffy:** "Winning equals trophies equals prestige for the school. You see how they're treated. It's been like that forever."
**Xander:** "Sure, discus throwers got the best seats at all the crucifixions."
—**"Go Fish"**

"That's it. This has gotta stop. It's time for me to act like a man. And hide."
—**"Bewitched, Bothered, and Bewildered"**

**Giles:** "I can't believe you'd be fool enough to do something like this."
**Xander:** "Oh, no. I'm twice the fool it takes to do something like this."
—**"Bewitched, Bothered, and Bewildered"**

"On behalf of my gender: Hey!"
—**"Phases"**

"I can translate American Salivating Boy-talk. He said 'you're beautiful.'"
**Buffy, translating Xander's reaction to Ampata, in "Inca Mummy Girl"**

"This is just too much. I mean, yesterday my life is like, 'uh-oh, pop quiz.' Today it's 'rain of toads.'"
—**"The Harvest"**

"That's creepy on a level I hardly knew existed."
—**"Ted"**

**Buffy:** "Willow, grow up. Not everything is about kissing."
**Xander:** "Yeah. Some stuff is about groping."
—**"When She Was Bad"**

## Willow Rosenberg

Willow Rosenberg was born and raised in Sunnydale, the daugher of Ira Rosenberg and his wife in a very Jewish household ("Bad Eggs," "Passion"). A fairly reserved and shy person, she is best friends with Xander and had established a reputation as the person to go to for tutoring help ("Welcome to the Hellmouth"). Willow can be charmingly naive at times—when she was a child, her idea of playing "doctor" was to actually read medical texts and test them out on Xander ("Killed by Death").

Willow's computer skills are both prodigious and legendary. During Sunnydale High's Career Week, she was one of only two students (the other being Oz) selected to be interviewed by an unnamed but very prestigious computer-software company ("What's My Line?"), and she was chosen to substitute for computer-science teacher Jenny Calendar after she was murdered ("Passion"). When an adequate replacement couldn't be found, Principal Snyder asked her to fill in for the remainder of the term, an impressive request to make of a junior ("Go Fish"). Acquiring the latest software tends to make her incoherent ("Ted"), and she has continually upgraded her own equipment, having gone from a desktop

("I Robot, You Jane") to a laptop ("Lie to Me"). She was also involved in Jenny's project to scan several texts into the school computers ("I Robot, You Jane").

Willow and Buffy became friends soon after they met. Unfortunately, Buffy's encouragement for her to seize the moment led to her flirting with a boy at the Bronze who turned out to be a vampire ("Welcome to the Hellmouth"). Buffy rescued her; Willow later helped locate the Master's lair by hacking into the city records ("The Harvest"). Like Xander, Willow insisted on helping Buffy out on subsequent adventures ("The Witch"), and her computer skills in particular have come in handy, especially given Giles's technophobia. (at one point she comments, "I'm probably the only girl in school who has the coroner's office bookmarked as a favorite place" ("Some Assembly Required").

Willow has long carried a torch for Xander. They "dated" when they were five years old, but she broke it off when he stole her Barbie doll ("Welcome to the Hellmouth"). In adolescence, she has waited for Xander to notice her but, aside from a fleeting moment shortly before the start of junior year ("When She Was Bad"), he has remained only a friend to her and nothing else, preferring to lust after praying mantises ("Teacher's Pet"), mummies ("Inca Mummy Girl"), Buffy ("Welcome to the Hellmouth," etc.), and Cordelia ("What's My Line? Part 2," etc.). Throughout all this, Willow has remained a true friend even as her heart has broken, encouraging Xander to invite Ampata to a dance ("Inca Mummy Girl").

She carried on an on-line correspondence with a boy named Malcolm, who turned out to be the demon Moloch, which was a pity, as she seemed to have had more success with him than any other boy up to that point ("I Robot, You Jane"). She met up with Oz at the Career Fair, shortly after which he saved her life ("What's My Line? Part 2"), and they eventually started dating ("Surprise"). The later revelation that Oz is a werewolf did not deter their relationship ("Phases"), and when Willow awakened from a coma, Oz was whom she first asked for ("Becoming, Part 2").

After Jenny's death, Willow started going through the techno-pagan's programs, Web sites, and books on the occult, and when she and Buffy discovered the translated spell to restore Angel's soul to him, it was Willow who cast it, despite the risks ("Becoming"). It has yet to be determined whether or not she will continue to dabble in magic.

Willow is played by Alyson Hannigan.

> "Once again, I'm banished to the demon section of the card catalog."
> —"The Puppet Show"

> "So he is a good vampire. I mean, on a scale of one to ten, ten being someone who's killing and maiming every night and one being someone who's . . . not."
> —"Angel"

# Quotable Willow

**Willow:** "About the spiders. Did you talk to Giles about . . ."
**Xander:** "Oh. The spiders. Willow's been kinda . . . what's the word I'm looking for . . . insane about what happened yesterday."
**Willow:** "I don't like spiders, okay? Their furry bodies, their sticky webs—what do they need all those legs for anyway? I'll tell you: for crawling across your face in the middle of the night. *Ew*." —**"Nightmares"**

"I'm not okay. I knew those guys. I go to that room every day. And when I walked in there . . . it wasn't our world anymore. They made it theirs. And they had fun."
**—to Buffy, about vampires slaughtering students right there in school, in "Prophecy Girl"**

"Uh, Angel, if I say something you don't really wanna hear, do you promise not to bite me?"
—**"Lie to Me"**

**Willow:** "I know—we could go to the Bronze, sneak in our own tea bags, and ask for hot water."
**Xander:** "Hop off the outlaw train, Will, before you land us all in jail."
—**"Reptile Boy"**

**Willow:** "I don't get wild. Wild on me equals 'spaz.'" —**"Halloween"**

"I swear, men can be such jerks sometimes . . . dead or alive." —**"Passion"**

". . . and you, I mean, you're gonna live forever, you don't have time for a cup of coffee?"
**—to Angel, in "Reptile Boy"**

**Xander:** "Angel was in your bedroom?"
**Willow:** "Ours is a forbidden love."
—**"Lie to Me "**

**Xander:** "You gotta take care of the egg; it's a baby, gotta keep it safe and teach it Christian values."
**Willow:** "My egg is Jewish." —**"Bad Eggs"**

**Willow:** "Our friends are in trouble. Now we have to put our heads together and get them out of it. And if you two aren't with me a hundred and ten percent, *then get the hell out of my library!*"
**Cordelia:** "We're sorry."
**Xander:** "We'll be good." —**"The Dark Age"**

**Buffy:** "I'll fight [Angel]. If I have to, I'll kill him. But if I lose or I don't find him in time . . . Willow might be our only hope."
**Willow:** "I don't want to be our only hope. I crumble under pressure. Let's have another hope."
—**"Becoming, Part 1"**

**Angel:** "I guess I need help. And you're the first person I thought of."
**Willow:** "Help? You mean like on homework? No, 'cause you're old and you already know stuff."
**Angel:** "I want you to track someone down. On the Net."
**Willow:** "Oh! Great. I'm so the Net girl."
—**"Lie to Me"**

**Xander:** "Sheila's definitely intense. That guy with her? That's the guy she *can* bring home to mother."
**Willow:** "She was already smoking in fifth grade. Once I was lookout for her."
**Xander:** "You're bad to the bone."
**Willow:** "I'm a rebel." —**"School Hard"**

**Willow:** "I'll give Xander a call. What's his number? Oh, yeah: '1-800-I'm-Dating-A-Skanky-Ho.'"
**Buffy:** "Me-ow!"
**Willow:** "Really? Thanks! I've never gotten a 'me-ow' before." —**Phases**

"Even I was bored. And I'm a science nerd."
—**about a particularly dull biology class, in "Prophecy Girl"**

"Oh, Will, you're supposed to use your powers for good!" **Buffy, in "Ted"**

"Don't warn the tadpoles!"
—**upon awakening from a dream in "What's My Line? Part 1"**

# Rupert Giles

Rupert Giles comes from a family of Watchers—both his father and grandmother also served in that capacity—and he was told at age ten that he too would become one, which disappointed him since he had plans to be either a fighter pilot or a grocer ("Never Kill a Boy on the First Date"). He attended Oxford University, where one of his friends, Carlyle Ferris, fought a She-Mantis and lost both the battle and his sanity ("Teacher's Pet"). Giles eventually rejected the family destiny and dropped out of Oxford, choosing instead to dabble in the occult—he and five friends summoned a demon called Eyghon to the Earth. Only two of that group—Giles and Ethan Rayne—still survive, the others having been killed by the demon ("The Dark Age"). Although he is no longer the practitioner he was in his youth, his skills in spellmaking have proven useful on more than one occasion ("The Witch," "I Robot, You Jane," "Bewitched, Bothered, and Bewildered").

He was the curator at a museum in England, possibly the British Museum, prior to being assigned by the Watchers to Buffy ("Welcome to the Hellmouth"). He also plays the guitar ("The Dark Age") though one suspects it's been a while since he picked the thing up, can read five languages "on a good day" ("Nightmares"), has some skill in fencing ("Reptile Boy") and in shooting a tranquilizer gun ("Phases," "Go Fish"), and lists cross-referencing among his favorite hobbies ("Halloween").

Giles is presently the school librarian for Sunnydale High ("Welcome to the Hellmouth"). It is presumed that he has either a master's degree in library science or the British equivalent in order to qualify for his current position. It is also presumed that Principal Flutie gave him broad discretion in choosing the contents of the library, since it includes several ancient texts that would be out of place in an ordinary school library ("I Robot, You Jane")—these are extremely useful when he needs information to help Buffy fight a particular demon or counter the latest plot from the Master, Spike, Drusilla, or Angel.

Aside from Jenny Calendar ("I Robot, You Jane," etc.) and Dr. Gregory ("Teacher's Pet"; after Gregory was murdered, Giles professed that he liked him), his relationship with his fellow faculty members has not been extensively chronicled. He did date Jenny for some time, though Jenny's possession by Eyghon put a hitch in things ("The Dark Age"), and the truth about her Romany background and that she was sent to Sunnydale to keep an eye on Angel put in an even bigger hitch ("Surprise," "Innocence"). They had made steps toward a reconciliation right before Angel murdered her ("Passion").

Although not a Slayer, Giles has proven quite physically resilient. He has suffered several attacks on his person ("Never Kill a Boy on the First Date," "The Pack," "Prophecy Girl," "The Dark Age," "Bad Eggs," "Passion," and "Becoming"), Jenny once shot him with a crossbow bolt at frighteningly short range ("Ted"), and he was able to resist giving Angel information under torture ("Becoming, Part 2"; he did eventually give in to Drusilla's hypnotic manipulations).

As a general rule, Giles is the picture of the stiff-upper-lip Brit: restrained, stuffy, always wears tweed, somewhat befuddled, what little humor that escapes is dry as toast. However, he also has a ferocity that tends to show through when his emotions are engaged, whether negative—as seen in his rather brutal treatment of Ethan ("Halloween," "The Dark Age") and his attack on Angel ("Passion")—or positive his tremendous protectiveness of and devotion to Buffy ("The Witch," "Nightmares," and "Bewitched, Bothered, and Bewildered," in particular). His time in the company of the Slayerettes, and dating the rather freewheeling Jenny, has loosened him up somewhat. His witticisms are coming more frequently, and he seems more relaxed around Buffy and the gang. He appears, however, to be suffering some residual mental trauma from Jenny's brutal murder ("I Only Have Eyes for You"), the full extent of which has yet to be explored.

Giles is played by Anthony Stewart Head.

> "So, you like to party with the students? Isn't that kind of skanky?"
> —Buffy, to Giles, in "Welcome to the Hellmouth"

> "I don't believe it [a crossbow bolt] went in too deep. The advantages of layers of tweed. Better than Kevlar."
> —to Jenny, in "Ted"

> "Rupert, you have to read something that was published after 1066."
> —Jenny, to Giles, in "School Hard"

> "Giles? Who counts tardiness as, like, the eighth deadly sin?"
> —Buffy, in "The Dark Age"

> "Since Angel lost his soul, he seems to have regained his sense of whimsy."
> —Giles, in "Passion"

> "He's like SuperLibrarian. Everyone forgets, Willow, that knowledge is the ultimate weapon."
> —Xander, in "Never Kill a Boy on the First Date"

> "The vid library. I know it's not books, but it's still dark and musty; you'll be right at home."
> —Buffy, to Giles, in "Teacher's Pet"

**Giles:** "I've been indexing the Watcher Diaries covering the last couple of centuries. You'd be amazed at how numbingly pompous and long-winded some of these Watchers were."
**Buffy:** "Color me stunned."
—**"What's My Line?, Part 1"**

**Cordelia:** "What?"
**Giles:** "I'm sorry . . . your hair."
**Cordelia:** "There's something wrong with my hair? Oh, my God." [She exits]
**Giles:** "Xander was right. It worked liked a charm." —**"The Puppet Show"**

**Willow:** "...that they had...they had...you know . . . . Uh, you *do* know, right?"
**Giles:** "Oh, yes. Sorry."
**Willow:** "Oh, good. Because I just realized, you being a librarian and all, maybe you didn't know."
—**re: sex, in "Passion"**

**Giles:** "Two more of the Brethren were here. They came after me, but I was more than a match for them."
**Buffy:** "Meaning?"
**Giles:** "I hid."
—**"Never Kill a Boy on the First Date"**

**Ethan:** "How does Ripper inspire such goodness?"
**Buffy:** "Because he's Giles."
—**"The Dark Age"**

**Xander:** "I knew this would happen. Nobody can be wound as straight and narrow as Giles without a dark side erupting. My uncle Rory was the stodgiest taxidermist you ever met—by day—by night, it was booze, whores, and fur flying . . . . Were there any whores?"
**Buffy:** "He was alone."
**Xander:** "Give it time." —**"The Dark Age"**

**Buffy:** "It's not noise. It's music."
**Giles:** "I know music. Music has notes. This is noise."
**Buffy:** "I'm aerobicizing. I must have the beat."
**Giles:** "Wonderful. You work on your muscle tone while my brains dribble out my ears." —**"The Dark Age"**

"One of these days, you have to get a grown-up car."
—**Buffy, disparaging Giles' mode of transportation, in "Inca Mummy Girl"**

**Xander:** "Giles lived for school. He's still bitter there were only twelve grades."
**Buffy:** "He probably sat in math class thinking, There should be more math! This could be mathier."
**Willow:** "Come on. You don't think he ever got restless as a kid?"
**Buffy:** "Are you kidding? His diapers were tweed." —**"The Dark Age"**

**Buffy:** "I was a little sloppy on the roundhouse. You want me to try it again?"
**Giles:** "No, that's fine. You run along to class and I'll wait for the feeling to return to my arms." —**"The Pack"**

"The Bay City Rollers, now *that's* music."
—**Giles, "The Dark Age"**

## Giles: Hero Librarian

It should come as no surprise that *Buffy the Vampire Slayer* in general and the character of Rupert Giles in particular have been embraced by the library community. After all, one of the three male leads is the school librarian and the library is the Slayerettes' central meeting place.

The show is a hot topic of conversation on Stumpers Talk, an e-mail list created to discuss reference questions and other minutiae. The "listserv" was founded by and is primarily populated by librarians, many of whom have waxed enthusiastic about that rarest of rarities, a librarian hero on television. "I think this is the first time in years, if not decades, that a librarian is a major character in a television show," says Pam McLaughlin of the Warren-Newport Public Library. "Not only that, but what a librarian!" (The Fox series *Party Girl*—based on a feature film—also had a librarian as its lead character, but the show was canceled after only a few episodes.) Library consultant GraceAnne Andreassi DeCandido used Giles as a shining example of a pop-culture librarian icon in a speech that she gave to both Oxford University librarians (Giles's alma mater) and the California Library Association (to which Giles likely belongs).

> **Buffy:** "See, this is a school, and we have students and they check out books and then they learn things."
> **Giles:** "I was beginning to suspect that was just a myth."
> —**"Never Kill a Boy on the First Date"**

Recognizing this enthusiasm, the American Library Association has made *Buffy* the focus of its latest "READ" promotional poster. The poster includes the entire *Buffy* cast and the caption "Slay Ignorance at the Library." It can be ordered from ALA Graphics at 1-800-545-2433 (press 7 to order a poster) or at their Web site: http://www.ala.org/market/graphics/index.html.

In a world where the general public is mostly unaware that librarianship is a profession that requires a master's degree, a show such as *Buffy* that presents the librarian and the library as focal points of the Slayer's ongoing battle against evil is deeply heartening. So is the fact that the librarian isn't a middle-aged woman who says "Shhh!" a lot. Most episodes of *Buffy* hinge on hours of research by Giles (aided and abetted by Willow, Xander, and Cordelia), and the show rarely soft-pedals the difficulty of that research.

Not every librarian thinks Giles is the ideal, however. For one thing, he is rarely seen actually doing what school librarians do. As Priscilla E. Emrich, library director of the Murphy Memorial Library, points out, "The one time that I saw someone come in the library other than Buffy and her friends, Rupert ran them off."

> **Xander:** "Hel-lo! Excuse me, but have you ever heard of knocking?"
> **Student:** "We're supposed to get some books on Stalin. For a report."
> **Xander:** "Does this look like a Barnes & Noble?"
> **Giles:** "Xander! This is the school library."
> **Xander:** "Since when?"
> —**"Passion"**

More to the point, Giles is a technophobe, which makes him something of an oddity. As Carolyn Oldham, director of library resources at American InterContinental University, says, "Most librarians these days are expected to be technology literate." Will Caine of OCLC adds, "It's anachronistic that Giles—since he's not dumb and not working at an underfunded school in the slums—is not a computer user. Librarians today are big-time computer users; everything's on-line, on CD-ROM, on the Web, etc., and it has been that way for a decade or so. In many schools, the librarian would be the primary computer user." Libraries have been on the cutting edge of information technology, and librarians have been among the top professionals making use of the Internet in recent years.

> **Giles:** "Ms. Calendar, I'm sure that your computer-science class is fascinating, but I happen to believe that one can function in modern society without being a slave to the idiot box."
> **Jenny:** "That's TV. The idiot box is the TV. This is a good box."
> **Giles:** "Well, I still prefer a good book."  —"I Robot, You Jane"

Still, the library and the librarian's critical role on the show is important to librarians. That importance is best summed up by library/pro-literacy advocate and cartoonist Edward DeVere (who was instrumental in getting the *Buffy* READ poster to happen): "The *Buffy the Vampire Slayer* series sets a precedent as far as presenting a first-time-ever hero who is a librarian. If ever there was a ready-made message just waiting for representation on a poster, it was this series being used to promote the idea that books, reading, libraries, and their many available avenues of research are a vitally important tool in combating the forces of Darkness—a metaphor for ignorance if ever I saw one."

## Cordelia Chase

The prototype of the most popular girl on campus, Cordelia Chase is attractive, snobby, completely self-centered, fashion-conscious (and makes sure no one else is copying her outfits, "Angel," "Bewitched, Bothered, and Bewildered") head cheerleader (as of "Some Assembly Required," having gotten on the squad in "The Witch"), the object of desire of much of the school's male population, was elected May Queen in her sophomore year ("Out of Mind, Out of Sight"), and is often surrounded by a group of admirers who hang on her every word.

Cordelia was born and raised in Sunnydale. Her mother has Epstein-Barr syndrome ("The Harvest"). Her parents gave her a car ("Prophecy Girl") after she passed driver's ed (some time after "The Witch"). Her dating calendar tends to be full and varied. She used to be very fond of Daryl Epps before his tragic death ("Some Assembly Required"), she took Mitch Fargo to the May Queen dance ("Out of Mind, Out of Sight"), and she dated Devon, the lead singer of Dingoes Ate My Baby ("Inca Mummy Girl"), though she eventually dumped him because he wasn't paying sufficient attention to her ("Halloween"). She has also made plays for both Owen Thurman ("Never Kill a Boy on the First Date") and Angel ("Some Assembly Required," "Reptile Boy," "Halloween"), both of whom preferred Buffy to Cordelia, to the latter's disgust. She also attempted to get into a relationship with Richard Anderson, from the local college, but he was interested only in sacrificing her to the demon he worshiped ("Reptile Boy"). Cordelia and Xander found themselves wildly kissing after arguing while trapped in Buffy's basement by a Tarakan assassin ("What's My Line? Part 2") and, against all odds, have actually managed to build a relationship despite having gone through most of their lives despising each other (dating back to when they were small children, according to Willow in "Out of Mind, Out of Sight").

> "People who think their problems are so huge craze me. Like the time I sort of ran over this girl with my bike, and it was the most traumatizing event of my life, and she's trying to make it all about *her* leg! Like my pain meant nothing!"
> —in Out of Mind, Out of Sight"

Cordelia initially made friends with Buffy, thinking that, being from Los Angeles, she had to be cool, but when Buffy *a)* mistakenly attacked her with a stake while searching for a vampire in the back area of the Bronze and *b)* started hanging around with "losers" like Willow and Xander, Cordelia shunned the Slayerettes as the lamest of the lame ("Welcome to the Hellmouth," "The Harvest," etc.). This changed when Cordy was threatened by an invisible attacker, and she went to Buffy for help, figuring, based on all the violence that surrounds Buffy, that she was in a gang or something ("Out of Mind, Out of Sight"). Cordy had the truth about vampires in Sunnydale shoved in her face when the Master was freed from his imprisonment, and she was there when Buffy slew him ("Prophecy Girl"). She found herself hanging around with the Slayerettes more and more as time went on, becoming "official" when she was awakened early in the morning to drive Xander to Buffy's house after she'd gone missing ("What's My Line? Part 1").

When her relationship with Xander went public ("Innocence"), she became alienated from her roving band of followers, and she initially broke up with him to appease them. However, realizing that her "friends" were just sheep who hung around her because they wanted her cool to rub off on them, she decided she'd date anyone she wanted, "no matter how lame he is" ("Bewitched, Bothered, and Bewildered").

> "Hello? Can we deal with my pain, please?"
> —to the Scooby Gang, in "Some Assembly Required"

> "This exchange-student thing has been a horrible nightmare. They don't even speak American!"
> —in "Inca Mummy Girl"

Cordelia once summed up her own character perfectly: "Tact is just not saying true stuff. I'll pass" ("Killed by Death"; Giles later described her as "Homerically insensitive"). She expresses her opinion and isn't interested if she hurts anyone's feelings. This might be the reason she has found herself gravitating to the Slayerettes, who have also been completely open in their feelings for her (usually by insulting her, but still...).

Cordelia is played by Charisma Carpenter.

# Quotable Cordelia

"Being this popular is not just my right, but my responsibility, and I want you to know I take it very seriously."
—in her May Queen speech, from "Out of Mind, Out of Sight"

"What an ordeal. And you know what the worst part is? It stays with you forever. No matter what they tell you, none of that rust and blood and grime comes out. You can dry-clean till judgment day; you're living with those stains."
—after Buffy has saved her from becoming a human sacrifice, in "When She Was Bad"

**Eric:** "Cordelia is so fine. You know, she'd be just perfect for us."
**Chris:** "Don't be an idiot. She's alive."
—"Some Assembly Required"

"I think you splashed on just a little too much 'Obsession for Dorks.'"
—to Xander, in "Phases"

**Xander:** "Wendell, what is wrong with you? Don't you know that she [Cordelia] is the center of the universe…the rest of us merely revolve around her."
**Cordelia:** "Why don't you revolve yourselves out of my light?"
**Xander** (to Buffy and Willow): "Wendell was in Cordelia's light."
**Wendell:** "I'm so ashamed."
**Willow:** "Why is she so Evita-like?"
**Buffy:** "It's the hair."
**Willow:** "Weighs heavy on the cerebral cortex."
—"Nightmares"

"Gym is canceled due to the extreme dead guy in the locker."
—"Welcome to the Hellmouth"

**Giles:** "Do you know, I don't recall ever seeing you here (the library) before."
**Cordelia:** "Oh, no. I have a life."
—"Out of Mind, Out of Sight"

**Cordelia:** "You're really campaigning for bitch of the year, aren't you?"
**Buffy:** "As defending champion, you nervous?"
**Cordelia:** "I can hold my own."
—"When She Was Bad"

"I am, of course, having my dress specially made. Off-the-rack gives me hives."
—in "Out of Mind, Out of Sight"

"God, what is your childhood trauma?"
—to Buffy, in "Welcome to the Hellmouth"

"'I aspire to help my fellow man.' Check. I mean, as long as he's not, like, smelly or dirty or something gross."
—"What's My Line? Part 1"

**Cordelia:** "She (Buffy) is like this Superman. Shouldn't there be different rules for her?"
**Willow:** "Sure, in a fascist society."
**Cordelia:** "Right! Why can't we have one of those?"
—"Ted"

"Darn, I have cheerleader practice tonight. Boy, I wish I knew you were gonna be digging up dead people sooner; I would have canceled."
—"Some Assembly Required"

**Giles:** "She (Buffy) has taken a human life. The guilt... is pretty hard to bear. It won't go away soon."

**Cordelia:** "I guess you should know since you helped raise that Demon that killed that guy that time."

**Giles:** "Yes, do let's bring that up as often as possible." —**"Ted"**

"Feels like home. If it's the '50s and you're a psycho." —**in "Ted"**

"Is murder *always* a crime?"
   **Xander, waxing homicidal about Cordelia, in "What's My Line? Part 1"**

"She's a wonderland tour."
   —**Oz, on Cordelia, in "Inca Mummy Girl"**

"Did I ever tell you about when Buffy attacked me? With a spear when I came out of the ladies' room at the Bronze. I still relive the trauma every time I see a pencil. I can only use felt-tip now."
   — **in "Out of Mind, Out of Sight"**

"Boy, that Cordelia is a regular breath of vile air." **Xander, in "Angel"**

"Cordelia, I don't want to hurt you...some of the time...."
   **Xander, stating the obvious, in "Bad Eggs"**

"And almost sixty-five percent of that was actual compliment. [to Cordy] Is that a personal best?"
   —**Xander, in "Becoming, Part 1"**

**Cordelia:** "I hope you guys weren't planning on going to this Sadie Hawkins dance tonight—because I'm totally organizing a boycott. Do you realize that the girls are supposed to ask the guys—and pay and everything? I mean, whose genius idea was that?"

**Xander:** "Obviously some hairy-legged feminist."

**Cordelia:** "Really. We have to nip this in the bud or things could get way scary."
   —**"I Only Have Eyes for You"**

**Cordelia:** "And do what? Besides be afraid and die?"

**Xander:** "Nobody's asking you to go, Cordy. If the vampires need grooming tips, we'll give you a call."
   —**"Innocence"**

**Giles:** "The more I study the Judge, the less I like him. His touch can literally burn the humanity out of you. A true creature of evil can survive the process. No human ever has."

**Xander:** "So what's the problem? We send Cordy to fight this guy and we go for pizza." —**"Surprise"**

"I just don't see why everyone is always ragging on Marie Antoinette. I can so relate to her. She worked really hard to look that good. People don't appreciate that kind of effort."
   —**participating in history class, in "Lie to Me"**

**Cordelia** (re: Giles): "No, he was perfectly normal yesterday when I saw him talking to the police."
**Buffy:** "And you waited until now to tell us because . . . ?"
**Cordelia:** "I didn't think it was important."
**Xander:** "We understand. It wasn't about you." —**"The Dark Age"**

**Xander:** "...Cordy, you should go with Giles."
**Giles** (petulant): "But why do I have— [stops himself] Good thinking. I could use a research assistant."
**Cordelia:** "Let's go, tact guy."
—**"Killed by Death"**

**Cordelia:** "Nobody told me I was supposed to bring a gift. I was out of the loop on gifts."
**Giles:** "Well, it's common among . . . people."
—**"Killed by Death"**

"Well, let me know when you want to move up to the big leagues."
—**to Owen re: Buffy, in "Never Kill a Boy on the First Date"**

"Doesn't Owen realize he's hitting a major backspace by hanging out with that loser?"
—**re: Buffy and Owen, "Never Kill a Boy on the First Date"**

"Buffy, love your hair. It just *screams* street urchin."
—**in "Halloween"**

"Half the school is out with this flu. It's a serious deal, Buffy. We're all worried about how gross you look."
—**in "Killed by Death"**

"Excuse me, I have to call everyone I ever met right now."
—**reveling in Buffy's bizarreness, in "Welcome to the Hellmouth"**

# Oz

"I'm shot. Wow. It's . . . odd. And painful."
—**"What's My Line? Part 2"**

"I was on the phone all night, listening to Willow cry about you. I don't know exactly what happened, but I was left with the very strong urge to hit you."
—**to Xander, in "Bewitched, Bothered, and Bewildered"**

Many details about Oz are still unknown. He is a senior at Sunnydale High School ("Surprise"), and the guitarist for the rock band Dingoes Ate My Baby, which plays regular gigs in the area, including at least two special-occasion concerts at the Bronze, a costume dance in honor of the arrival of foreign-exchange students ("Inca Mummy Girl"), and the Valentine's Day dance ("Bewitched, Bothered, and Bewildered"), which indicates that the band is well regarded by the Bronze's management.

Oz is apparently quite brilliant—he was one of only two Sunnydale High students recruited by a large, unnamed computer-software company during Career Week ("What's My Line? Part 1")—but shows very little ambition, beyond mastering the E-flat, diminished ninth chord on the guitar which he refers to as "a man's chord—you could lose a finger," ("What's My Line? Part 2"). He tends to not pay attention in class ("Innocence"), though he does test very well.

Midway through his senior year, Oz was bitten by his cousin Jordy, who, it turns out, is a werewolf. The bite transmitted the lycanthropy to Oz, and he now changes into a werewolf on the night of the full moon as well as the nights before and after. His initial foray into werewolfdom nearly caused a panic—not to mention almost getting him killed by a hunter after his pelt—but he now knows to lock himself up three nights a month ("Phases").

Oz tends to take things in stride. He was very nonchalant at the revelation that *a)* his cousin is a werewolf and *b)* so now is he ("Phases"), and he was equally blasé when he discovered that there are vampires in Sunnydale and Buffy is the Slayer ("Surprise"). He has joined the inner circle of Slayerettes, so far providing transportation in his van ("Innocence," "Becoming, Part 2") and tracking down Buffy when she was turned into a rat ("Bewitched, Bothered, and Bewildered").

Oz found himself attracted to Willow from the moment he saw her in an Eskimo outfit ("Inca Mummy Girl"), and more so when he saw her in her rather revealing Halloween outfit ("Halloween"), though they didn't actually speak until they found themselves together in the recruitment area for the software company ("What's My Line? Part 1"). Oz saved Willow's life from one of the Tarakan assassins ("What's My Line? Part 2"), and they started dating a short while later ("Surprise"). His lycanthropy has not noticeably interfered with their relationship, though Oz was willing to break it off if she wanted (she didn't, "Phases").

Oz is played by Seth Green.

## Quotable Oz

**Willow:** "Do you guys have a…gig tonight?"
**Oz:** "Practice. The band's kind of moving toward this new sound where we suck. So, practice."
—**"Surprise"**

**Xander:** "Vampires are real; lot of 'em live in Sunnydale. Willow'll fill you in."
**Willow:** "I know it's hard to accept at first.…"
**Oz:** "No, actually, it explains a lot.…"
—**"Surprise"**

**Devon:** "What does a girl have to do to impress you?"
**Oz:** "Well, it involves a feather boa and the theme from *A Summer Place*. I can't discuss it here."
**Devon:** "You're too picky, man. You know how many girls you could have? You're lead guitar, Oz, that's currency!"
**Oz:** "I'm not picky. You're just impressed by any pretty girl that can walk and talk."
**Devon:** "She doesn't have to talk.…"
—**"Inca Mummy Girl"**

# Jenny Calendar

Born Janna, of a very old Romanian Gypsy tribe, she took on the name Jennifer Calendar when she was sent to Sunnydale, California, to keep an eye on the vampire Angelus, who had been cursed by her tribe eighty years before ("Angel," "Surprise," "Innocence"). Presumably, Janna was sent after the demon Whistler brought Angel from New York to Sunnydale ("Becoming, Part 1"). Jenny was hired as a computer-science teacher at Sunnydale High School. It was there that she met Rupert Giles and worked with him when she initiated a project to scan several of the school library's works into the computer system; when the demon Moloch was scanned into the Internet via this project, Jenny helped Giles exorcise the demon ("I Robot, You Jane"). Jenny also saw the signs of the Master's eventual freedom from imprisonment and offered to help Giles and Buffy stop him ("Prophecy Girl"). A very modern woman, Jenny dressed in similar fashions to her students, spoke in slang, and had an excellent rapport with her students.

Despite their differing philosophies—Giles is very much a technophobe—Jenny and Giles were attracted to each other, and, after months of flirting, started dating in the fall of 1997 ("Some Assembly Required"). Their relationship stalled when Jenny was possessed by Eyghon, a demon that Giles had helped conjure up twenty years before ("The Dark Age"), though Jenny eventually was able to forgive him ("Ted"). Less easy to forgive was the revelation that Jenny was, for all intents and purposes, a spy for the Romany elders ("Innocence").

She was the one who explained to Buffy and Giles the specifics of the curse on Angel—that if he achieved even a moment of happiness, the curse would end ("Surprise," "Innocence"). Wanting to make up for deceiving her friends, and having no desire to see Angel continue to be evil (among other things, he murdered Jenny's uncle Enyos, "Innocence"), Jenny tried to find a way to retrieve the spell that had cursed Angel the first time ("Becoming, Part 1"); using a computer program she wrote, she translated it, but was murdered by Angel before she had a chance to use it ("Passion"). Angel destroyed the hard copy and hard drive, but Jenny had backed the file up to a disk that was eventually found by Willow and Buffy ("Becoming, Part 1"). Willow was able to cast the spell, with the help of Oz and Cordelia ("Becoming, Part 2"), thus fulfilling what was, in essence, Jenny's dying wish.

Jenny was played by Robia LaMorte.

> "Wrong and wrong, snobby. You think the realm of the mystical is limited to ancient texts and relics? That bad old science made the magic go away? The divine exists in cyberspace same as out here."
> —to Giles, in "I Robot, You Jane"

## Joyce Summers

Joyce Summers met Hank Summers, her future husband, at her high school prom. She didn't have a date and so went alone. She was miserable for the first hour, then met Hank. He *did* have a date, but they still met and clicked, and later married ("Prophecy Girl"). By the time their daughter, Buffy, reached high school, their fighting had escalated ("Becoming, Part 1"), and they were divorced in her first year ("Nightmares"). The pair seem to be getting along well since the divorce ("When She Was Bad").

Joyce works at an art gallery, where her duties include acquiring and selling pieces, a job which requires long hours and keeps her away from home sometimes ("What's My Line?"). She has tried to connect with her daughter, but—despite their occasional bonding over movies and ice cream ("Ted," "Bewitched, Bothered, and Bewildered")—finds understanding of her daughter elusive. She appreciates that her daughter can take care of herself ("School Hard"), but has grown frustrated with Buffy's inability to do what she is told for no obvious reason ("Bad Eggs") and for not confiding in her about anything, such as the fact that she was dating Angel ("Passion"). Despite having seen some evidence of the bizarre activity in Sunnydale ("Angel," "School Hard," "Bad Eggs"), she remained oblivious to her daughter's secrets right up until circumstances compelled Buffy to spell it out for her ("Becoming, Part 2"). The ultimate consequences of Joyce learning that her daughter is the Chosen One have yet to be established.

Joyce is played by Kristine Sutherland.

> "That much quality time with my mom would probably lead to some quality matricide."
> —**Buffy, to Amy, in "Witch"**

> "Seeing my mother frenching a guy is definitely a ticket to therapyland."
> —**Buffy, in "Ted"**

---

**Buffy:** "But . . . don't you understand? This is so important!"
**Joyce:** "It's an outfit. An outfit you may never buy."
**Buffy:** "But . . . I looked good in it!"
**Joyce:** "You looked like a streetwalker."
**Buffy:** "But a *thin* streetwalker! That's probably not gonna be the winning argument, is it?"
**Joyce:** "You're just too young to wear that."
**Buffy:** "I'm gonna be too young to wear that till I'm too old to wear that."
**Joyce:** "That's the plan."
—**"Bad Eggs"**

**Willow:** "I just hate to think of you solo on Valentine's Day."
**Buffy:** "I'll be fine. Mom and I are gonna have a pig-out and vidfest. It's a time-honored tradition among the loveless."
—**"Bewitched, Bothered, and Bewildered"**

Quotable Mrs. Summers

## Quotable Mrs. Summers

**Buffy:** "Did I ask for backseat mommying?"
**Joyce:** "What's the matter, did your egg keep you up all night?"
**Buffy:** "You're killing me."
**Joyce:** "Wait till it starts dating."
—**"Bad Eggs"**

**Buffy:** "I made a mistake."
**Joyce:** "Don't just say that to shut me up, because I think you really did."
**Buffy:** "I know that. Mom, my life is so... I can't tell you everything."
**Joyce:** "How about *anything*? Buffy, you can shut me out of your life, I'm pretty much used to that, but don't expect me to stop caring about you, 'cause it's never gonna happen. I love you more than anything in the world."
—**"Passion"**

**Joyce:** "So, what did you do on your birthday? Did you have fun?"
**Buffy:** "I got older." —**"Innocence"**

**Joyce:** "Was he the first?"
**Buffy:** "...Yes. He was the first. I mean, the only."
**Joyce:** "He's older than you."
**Buffy:** "I know."
**Joyce:** "*Too* old, Buffy. And he's obviously not very stable. I really wish... I thought you would show more judgment."
**Buffy:** "Mom, I—he wasn't like this before."
**Joyce:** "Are you in love with him?"
**Buffy:** "I was."
**Joyce:** "Were you careful?"
**Buffy:** "Mom—"
**Joyce:** "Don't 'Mom' me, Buffy—you don't get out of this. You had sex with a boy you didn't even see fit to tell me you were dating." —**"Passion"**

**Joyce:** "So does seventeen feel any different than sixteen?"
**Buffy:** "Funny you should ask that—You know, I actually woke up feeling more mature, responsible, and level-headed."
**Joyce:** "Really? That's uncanny."
**Buffy:** "I now possess the qualities one looks for in a licensed driver." —**"Surprise"**

"Try not to get kicked out."
—to Buffy, in **"Welcome to the Hellmouth"**

# Principal Bob Flutie
# Principal Snyder

Sunnydale High School has gone through two principals in the past two years. The first was Bob Flutie. Flutie was a more "touchy-feely" type of principal, concerned with how the students felt and with relating to them as people, not just faceless students under his care. He assured Buffy that she would be starting at Sunnydale High School with a "clean slate" (though he did put the fact that she burned down the Hemery High gym on her permanent record) and that she would be given every opportunity to start over ("Welcome to the Hellmouth"). When the dead body of Dr. Gregory was found in the cafeteria, Flutie insisted that everyone who saw the body attend a session with a counselor ("Teacher's Pet"). In an attempt to foster school spirit, Flutie purchased a pig to serve as a mascot for the Sunnydale High Razorbacks (it is unclear which team the pig was meant to be a mascot for, since all the school sports teams are named "the Razorbacks"—perhaps it was an all-purpose pig); that pig, however, was devoured by five students possessed by the spirit of a hyena. Four of those five students—notorious troublemakers even before they were possessed—were summoned to Flutie's office, wherein they proceeded to eat *him* alive ("The Pack"). The official story was that wild dogs ate him.

Flutie was apparently married—he wore a wedding ring ("The Pack")—and tried to be friendly with his students—he wanted them to call him "Bob," though none of them did ("Welcome to the Hellmouth").

His replacement, Principal Snyder, is somewhat more authoritarian and less interested in the needs of his students. Indeed, he decried Flutie's attitude as the kind of "woolly-headed liberal thinking that leads to getting eaten" ("The Puppet Show"). He hates children—which led Giles to question his choice of vocation ("When She Was Bad")—but was apparently given this position by the Sunnydale City Council because he could "handle this job" ("I Only Have Eyes for You"). He is also fully aware that Sunnydale sits on the Hellmouth and has twice been seen coming up with cover stories for the strange events in the town ("School Hard," "I Only Have Eyes for You").

The one characteristic he shares with Flutie is a desire to foster school spirit. To that end, he has encouraged such events as a school talent show ("Puppet") and done what he could to boost the position of the swim team when it started winning ("Go Fish").

He seems to have it in for Buffy in particular, having singled her out for discipline on more than one occasion ("School Hard," "Halloween," "What's My Line? Part 1," "I Only Have Eyes for You"). Not until he expelled her when she was on the run after mistakenly being accused of Kendra's murder is it made clear that he knows who Buffy really is—and either doesn't care or wants to see her fail ("Becoming, Part 2"). The full consequences of Snyder's actions and the full story behind what he and the city council and the mayor of Sunnydale know have yet to be explored.

Flutie was played by Ken Lerner; Snyder is played by Armin Shimerman.

## Amy Madison

The only daughter of Catherine Madison, Sunnydale High's most decorated cheerleader and Homecoming Queen, Amy was raised by Catherine alone after her father, the Homecoming King, ran off with a woman identified only as "Ms. Trailer Trash" when Amy was twelve. Catherine insisted that Amy follow in her mother's footsteps and trained Amy to become a cheerleader, though Amy herself had no interest in it. Frustrated with that disinterest and her daughter's increased weight, Catherine took to witchcraft. By the time cheerleading tryouts for the 1996–97 school year took place, Catherine had switched bodies with her daughter, then—when she proved unable to make her unfamiliar new body do what she wanted, leaving her only as third alternate on the squad—she cast spells on other cheerleaders to clear a space for herself. Amy was left to stay at home in her mother's body and do her homework for her. Catherine's actions were discovered by Buffy and Giles, and all the spells were reversed, putting Amy back in her own body. Catherine's attempt to banish Buffy to a nether realm was reversed in a mirror to a banishment of Catherine herself. Amy then went to live with her father and stepmother ("The Witch"), which she found "cool."

Although never interested in following in her mother's footsteps as far as cheerleading went, she was apparently intrigued by the occult. By the following school year, she had mastered several spells, including one to make a teacher believe she had handed in homework when she hadn't and another to transform a person into a rat. Her attempt at a love potion did not work as intended, however, and instead of making Cordelia love Xander, it made every woman in Sunnydale *except* Cordelia love Xander—including Amy herself. With Giles's help, that spell was reversed ("Bewitched, Bothered, and Bewildered"). It is unknown whether Amy will continue her pursuit of witchcraft.

Amy is played by Elizabeth Anne Allen.

# Kendra

Very little is known about Kendra. Her accent suggests a background on a British, or formerly British, Caribbean island, but her homeland is never identified by name. However, her people are aware of vampires, as Kendra's parents knew that she was destined to become a Slayer and sent her to be trained with her Watcher, Sam Zabuto, at a very early age ("What's My Line? Part 2").

Kendra's training has been much more traditional than Buffy's—she was given the Slayer handbook to read, which Buffy had never even heard of ("What's My Line? Part 2")—and she works in less overt ways than Buffy, including hitching a ride from her home to Sunnydale in a cargo hold rather than traveling openly in an airline seat ("What's My Line? Part 1"). Her life has been very cloistered, with no friends or family (and she doesn't hug), and her manner of living is quite Spartan—she seems to own only one shirt ("What's My Line? Part 2"). Her one concession to whimsy was to name her favorite stake "Mr. Pointy" ("Becoming, Part 1").

Kendra became active as a Slayer after Buffy died fighting the Master ("Prophecy Girl"). When Spike found the du Lac manuscript and the key to deciphering it, signaling that he would be trying to revive Drusilla, Zabuto sent Kendra to Sunnydale ("What's My Line?"). She appears to have all the same abilities as Buffy—and a similar fighting style—though, like Buffy, she has not mastered the ability to sense vampires ("Welcome to the Hellmouth"), since she mistook Buffy for a vampire based on her kissing Angel ("What's My Line? Part 1"). After

> "Get a load of the She-Giles."
> —Buffy, to Willow, in "What's My Line?, Part 2"

> "A Slayer? I knew this 'I'm the only one, I'm the only one' thing was just an attention-getter."
> —Xander, in "What's My Line? Part 2"

> "It's all right. Kendra killed the bad lamp."
> —Buffy, in "What's My Line? Part 2"

helping Buffy stop Spike and Drusilla, Kendra returned home, coming back to Sunnydale, when Angel stole the sarcophagus of Acathla, to provide Buffy with a sword that would aid in defeating the Demon. She was killed by Drusilla while trying to protect the Slayerettes ("Becoming, Part 1").

Kendra was played by Bianca Lawson.

## Quotable Villains

### Spike

"You have your way with him [Giles], you'll never get to destroy the world. And I don't fancy spending next month trying to get librarian out of the carpet." —**to Angel about Giles, in "Becoming, Part 2"**

**Willy:** "What're you gonna do with him [Angel] anyway?"
**Spike:** "I'm thinking—maybe dinner and a movie. I don't want to rush into anything. I've been hurt, y'know."
—**"What's My Line? Part 2"**

"Do I have anyone on watch here? It's called security, people. Are you all asleep? Or did we finally find a restaurant that delivers?"
—**on Ford's arrival at the Factory in "Lie to Me"**

"It's paradise! Big windows and lovely gardens. They'll be perfect for when we want the sunlight to *kill us*."
—**on their new mansion, in "I Only Have Eyes for You"**

**Spike:** "A Slayer with family and friends. That sure as hell wasn't in the brochure."
**Drusilla:** "You'll kill her. And then we'll have a nice party." —**"School Hard"**

**Buffy:** "It's your lucky day, Spike."
**Kendra:** "Two Slayers."
**Buffy:** "No waiting."
—**"What's My Line? Part 2"**

"I'll only kill you this once."
—**to Willy, in "What's My Line? Part 2"**

### Drusilla

"My mummy used to sing me to sleep at night. 'Run and catch, the lamb is caught in the blackberry patch.... What will your mummy sing when they find your body?"
—**to a small boy, in "Lie to Me"**

**Spike:** "Are we feeling better then?"
**Drusilla:** "I'm naming all the stars."
**Spike:** "Can't see the stars, love. That's the ceiling. Also, it's day."
**Drusilla:** "I can see them. But I've named them all the same name, and there's terrible confusion. I fear there may be a duel."
—**"Innocence"**

"I met an old man. I didn't like him. He got stuck in my teeth." —**"Becoming, Part 1"**

## The Master

"My ascension is at hand. Pray that when it comes, I'm in a better mood."
—in "The Harvest"

"You've got something in your eye."
—to a vampire henchman he's just blinded with a talon, in "The Harvest"

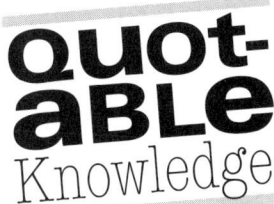

"I defined something? Accurately? Check me out. [He slams a book on the table shut.] Guess I'm done with the book learning!"
Xander, in "I Only Have Eyes for You"

**Xander** (to Giles): "After classes, I'll come back and help you research."
**Cordelia:** "Yeah, you might find something useful—if it's in an 'I Can Read' book." —"Innocence"

"You remember: you fail math, you flunk out of school, you end up being the guy at the pizza place that sweeps the floor and says 'Hey, kids, where's the cool parties this weekend?'"
Willow, to Xander, in "The Pack"

**Cordelia:** "This is not right. School on a Saturday? That throws off my internal clock."
**Xander:** "When are we going to use computers in real life, anyway?"
**Jenny:** "Let's see, there's home, schoolwork, games—"
**Xander:** "Computers are on the way out. I think paper is about to make a big comeback."
**Willow:** "And the abacus." —"The Dark Age"

"Well, evil just compounds evil, doesn't it? First I'm sentenced to a computer tutorial on Saturday, now I have to read some computer book. There are books about computers? Isn't that the point of computers, to *replace* books?"
**Cordelia, in "The Dark Age"**

**Jenny:** "I'm reviewing some computer basics for a couple of students who have fallen behind. Willow's helping for extra credit."
**Xander:** "Hah! Those poor schlubs. Having to give up their Saturday—"
**Jenny:** "Nine A.M. okay with you, Xander?"
—"The Dark Age"

"Buffy, this is not about looking at a bunch of animals. This is about *not being in class.*"
—Xander, on a field trip to the zoo, in "The Pack"

**Joyce:** "She talks about you all the time. . . . It's important to have teachers who make an impression."
**Giles:** "She makes quite an impression herself."
**Joyce:** "I know she's having trouble with history. Is it too difficult for her, or is she not applying herself?"
**Giles:** "She lives very much in the now, and history, of course, is very much about 'the then. . . .'" —"Angel"

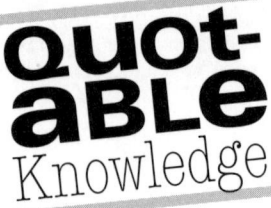

# Quotable Knowledge

**Buffy:** "Mom, this is Mr. Giles."
**Joyce:** "The librarian from your school? What's he doing here?"
**Giles:** "I just came to pay my respects, wish you a speedy recovery."
**Joyce:** "Boy, the teachers really *do* care in this town...."
—**in Joyce's hospital room, in "Angel"**

**Willow:** "This means I can't help you study for tomorrow's finals."
**Buffy:** "I'll wing it. Of course, if we go to Hell by then, I won't have to take them. [sudden fear] Or maybe I'll be taking them forever...."
—**"Becoming, Part 1"**

"I mean, in the real world, when am I ever gonna need to use chemistry, math, history, or the English language?"
—**Buffy, in "Becoming, Part 1"**

**Willow:** "I'm gonna get you through this semester if I have to sweat blood."
**Xander:** "Do you think you're likely to? 'Cause I'd like to be elsewhere."
**Willow:** "It was only metaphor blood."
**Oz:** "I think you'd sweat cute blood."
—**"Becoming, Part 1"**

**Buffy:** "We'd better get back. I haven't even *started* studying for finals."
**Xander:** "Oh, yeah, finals. Why didn't you let me die?"
—**"Becoming, Part 1"**

"Sorry. I pretty much repress anything math related."
—**Buffy, in "I Only Have Eyes for You"**

"Oh. Yeah.... I remember now. Weren't there chalkboards and pencils and desks and stuff?"
**Buffy, on her late, great Algebra II class, in "I Only Have Eyes for You"**

**Cordelia:** "School can open again tomorrow."
**Xander:** "Explain to me again how that's a good thing."
—**"I Only Have Eyes for You"**

"Ha! This time I am ready for you. No F for Xander today. No, this baby's my ticket to a sweet D-minus."
**Xander, on his homework, in "Bewitched, Bothered, and Bewildered"**

**Jenny:** "You here again? You kids really dig on the library, don't you?"
**Buffy:** "We're literary."
**Xander:** "To read English is makes our speaking English good."
—**"I Robot, You Jane"**

**Giles:** "Does this look familiar to either of you?"
**Buffy:** "Yeah, sure. It looks like a book."
**Xander:** "I knew that one."
—**"I Robot, You Jane"**

**Jenny:** "Honestly, what is it about [computers] that bothers you so much?"
**Giles:** "The smell."
**Jenny:** "Computers don't smell, Rupert."
**Giles.** "I know. Smell is the most powerful memory trigger there is. A certain flower or a whiff of smoke can bring up experiences long forgotten. Books smell—musty and rich. The knowledge gained from a computer has no texture, no context. It's there and then it's gone. If it's to last, then the getting of knowledge should be tangible. It should be smelly."
—**"I Robot, You Jane"**

"You start a school, you get desks, some blackboards, and some mean kids."
—**Xander, in "The Pack"**

**Giles:** "So, apparently, Angel has decided to step up his harassment of you."

**Cordelia:** "By sneaking into her room at night and leaving stuff? Why not just slash her throat or strangle her in her sleep or cut out her heart? ... What? I'm trying to help."

**Giles:** "It's a classic battle strategy to throw one's opponent off his game. He's trying to provoke you. To taunt you... goad you into a misstep of some sort."

**Xander:** "The 'nyah nyah nyah nyah' approach to battle."

**Giles:** "Yes, Xander, once again you've managed to boil a complex thought down to its simplest form." —**"Passion"**

**Willow:** "Buffy. How come you weren't in class?"

**Buffy:** "Vampire issues. Did Mr. Whitmore notice that I was tardy?"

**Xander:** "I think the word you're searching for is 'absent.'"

**Buffy:** "Oh. Right."

**Willow:** "And, yes, he noticed. So he wanted me to give you this." [Hands her the egg.]

**Buffy:** "As punishments go, this is fairly abstract." —**"Bad Eggs"**

**Buffy:** "Homework."

**Willow:** "It's my way of saying, 'Get well soon.'"

**Buffy:** "You know, chocolate says that even better."

**Willow:** "I did all of your assignments. All you have to do is sign your name."

**Buffy** (awestruck): "Chocolate means nothing to me." —**"Killed by Death"**

"A couple more days and we'll get to do the two things every American teen should have the chance to do. Die young ... and stay pretty."
   **Ford, to the True Believers, in "Lie to Me"**

**Buffy** "'Cause I'm *not* well. I feel all oogy."

**Xander:** "Increased oogy-ness. That's a danger signal." —**"Killed by Death"**

# EPISODE GUIDE

## Buffy the Vampire Slayer

**Angel:** "They're children, making up bedtime stories of friendly vampires to comfort themselves in the dark."

**Willow:** "Is that so bad? I mean the dark can get pretty dark. Sometimes you need a story."

—"LIE TO ME"

Here it is, your handy-dandy guide to each and every episode from the first two seasons of *Buffy the Vampire Slayer*, including writer and director credits, complete cast list, and a plot summary, plus pop-ups, sidebars, and the following subsections:

### Quote of the week:

"Could you vague that up for me?"

### Love, Slayer style:

The relationships on *Buffy* are complex and critical to the overall plots (Angel/Buffy, Giles/Jenny, Xander/Cordelia). This section shows the major relationship turning points for each episode.

### BUFFY'S BAG OF TRICKS:

A catalog of Buffy's weapons in each episode.

### POP-CULTURE IQ:

The characters in *Buffy* are almost preternaturally aware of pop culture—it's part of their hip factor. We'll note some references from the show here, and explain them to the uninitiated.

### CONTINUITY:

A hallmark of *Buffy* is the show's sense of its own internal history and chronology. This section will detail bits of continuity, character-establishing moments, references to past episodes, and foreshadowing of future ones.

### From the Original Teleplay:

Exclusive text from the original script that was cut solely to accommodate the required length of an episode for broadcast.

# FIRST SEASON

| EPISODE NUMBER | EPISODE NAME | ORIGINAL AIRDATE |
|---:|---|---:|
| 1 | Welcome to the Hellmouth | 10-Mar |
| 2 | The Harvest | 10-Mar |
| 3 | The Witch | 17-Mar |
| 4 | Teacher's Pet | 25-Mar |
| 5 | Never Kill a Boy on the First Date | 31-Mar |
| 6 | The Pack | 7-Apr |
| 7 | Angel | 14-Apr |
| 8 | I Robot, You Jane | 28-Apr |
| 9 | The Puppet Show | 5-May |
| 10 | Nightmares | 12-May |
| 11 | Out of Mind, Out of Sight | 19-May |
| 12 | Prophecy Girl | 2-Jun |

### ★ STARRING ★

Sarah Michelle Gellar.................Buffy Summers

Nicholas Brendon....................Xander Harris

Alyson Hannigan ...................Willow Rosenberg

Charisma Carpenter...................Cordelia Chase

Anthony Stewart Head ..................Rupert Giles

# Welcome to the Hellmouth/ The Harvest

**WRITTEN BY** Joss Whedon; **DIRECTED BY** Charles Martin Smith (Part 1) and John T. Kertchmer (Part 2). **GUEST STARS:** Mark Metcalf as the Master, Brian Thompson as Luke, David Boreanaz as Angel, Ken Lerner as Principal Flutie, Kristine Sutherland as Joyce Summers, Julie Benz as Darla; with Mercedes McNab as Harmony.

Buffy Summers and her mother, Joyce, have moved from Los Angeles to the suburb of Sunnydale, California, and Joyce drives Buffy to her first day at the prosaically named Sunnydale High School. Her first day at the new school, Buffy meets a new world of people who will have a profound effect on her life. Principal Bob Flutie says that he believes in clean slates and won't hold the fact that she burned down her previous school's gymnasium against her. Cordelia, popular girl on campus, gives Buffy a test for her "coolness factor" and extends the hand of friendship—until Buffy starts to hang out with Willow, a horribly shy computer nerd, and her friends Xander and Jesse. Giles, the school librarian, not only knows that Buffy is the Slayer but has been assigned to be her Watcher.

Later that night, Buffy meets the mysterious Angel, who informs her that Sunnydale is located on the Hellmouth, a focal point of demonic activity of all sorts that attracts vampires like moths to a flame, and that she needs to be ready for the Harvest. Buffy ignores both Giles and Angel, hoping to return to some semblance of a normal life after her experience with vampires in L.A.

In the catacombs underneath the town, the vampiric Luke awakens the Master so he will be ready for the Harvest. The Master, a very old, very powerful vampire, has been trapped underneath Sunnydale for sixty years, ever since his attempt to open the Hellmouth was foiled by an untimely earthquake. The time is right for the Harvest, which will give him the power to break free.

Luke sends vampires out for food, and Jesse is captured, although Buffy saves Willow and Xander—and also realizes that she must fulfill her duties as Slayer, or people will die. She goes to rescue Jesse, with some unwanted help from Xander, only to find that Jesse has been turned into a vampire. They escape and then must stop Luke, who serves as the Master's vessel and is attacking the Bronze. With assistance from Giles, Willow, and Xander, Buffy kills Luke and several other vampires (Xander winds up inadvertently staking his old friend Jesse), though Darla survives.

> The high school used for external and some internal scenes in the series is Torrance High, the same school used when the *Beverly Hills, 90210* kids were still in high school.

> According to Joss Whedon's script, the Master's real name is Heinrich Joseph Nest.

> Brian Thompson, who plays Luke, also later appeared in both "Surprise" and "Innocence" as the Judge.

### Quote of the week:

**Cordelia:** "It's in the bad side of town."
**Buffy:** "Where's that?"
**Cordelia:** "It's about half a block from the good side of town. We don't have a whole lot of town here."

### Love, Slayer Style:

Xander's first sight of Buffy causes him to crash into a railing while skateboarding, and he gamely attempts to flirt with her. Angel and Buffy meet and are immediately at odds, thanks to his being overwhelmingly cryptic.

## POP-CULTURE IQ:

**"Don't go all *Wild Bunch* on me."**
Buffy's warning to Giles, Willow, and Xander when they storm the Bronze, referring to the famous ending of that film

### BUFFY'S BAG OF TRICKS:

Buffy carries a stake and uses several random items (tree branches, pool cues, and the like) as substitute stakes. She beheads one vampire with a drum cymbal. At the climax, she unpacks her supplies from a trunk with a false bottom, which include several stakes, vials of holy water, garlic, and crosses.

### CONTINUITY:

Viewers of the movie *Buffy the Vampire Slayer* might be confused at the repeated references to Buffy burning the gym down, since that didn't happen in the movie. The solution is simple: Joss Whedon has spun this series off of his *original* movie script for *Buffy*, which did indeed have Buffy performing a touch of necessary arson on the gym. Two previous Slayers—Lucy Hanover in 1866 Virginia and an unidentified woman in 1927 Chicago—are mentioned in an opening montage, thereby extending the Slayer lore, although neither reference is to be found as such in Whedon's screenplay, nor in any other episode.

Buffy has the first of many prophetic dreams ("Prophecy Girl," "Surprise," "Innocence"). Joyce's parting words to Buffy as she drops her off are to extract a promise not to get kicked out of this school, a promise she will wind up breaking a year and a half later ("Becoming, Part 2"). Angel acts as if he's never seen Buffy before, which belies the flashback in "Becoming, Part 1." The Master's first attempt to open the Hellmouth was in 1937; his next will be in "Prophecy Girl."

## From the original teleplay:

The following exchange was cut from the "Welcome to the Hellmouth" script because of length:

**Mr. Flutie:** "Oh! Buffy! Uh, what do you want?"
**Buffy:** "Um, is there a guy in there that's dead?"
**Mr. Flutie:** "Where did you hear that? Okay. Yes. But he's not a student! Not currently."
**Buffy:** "Do you know how he died?"
**Mr. Flutie:** "What?"
**Buffy:** "I mean—how could this have happened?"
**Mr. Flutie:** "Well, that's for the police to determine when they get here. But this structure is safe, we have inspectors, and I think there's no grounds for a lawsuit."
**Buffy:** "Was there a lot of blood? Was there *any* blood?"
**Mr. Flutie:** "I would think you wouldn't want to involve yourself in this kind of thing."
**Buffy:** "I don't. Could I just take a peek?"
**Mr. Flutie:** "Unless you already are involved . . ."
**Buffy:** "Never mind."
**Mr. Flutie:** "Buffy, I understand this is confusing. You're probably feeling a lot right now. You should share those feelings. With someone else."

# Witch

**WRITTEN BY** Dana Reston; **DIRECTED BY** Stephen Cragg.
**GUEST STARS:** Kristine Sutherland as Joyce Summers, Elizabeth Anne Allen as Amy Madison, and Robin Riker as Catherine Madison; with Amanda Wilmshurst, Nicole Prescott, Jim Doughan, and William Monaghan.

Cheerleading tryouts at Sunnydale High prove to be more exciting than expected, when Amber Grove, the most talented of the girls who try out, catches fire. Meanwhile, Amy Madison is under fierce pressure from her mother, Catherine, the former cheerleading champion of Sunnydale High, to live up to her own reputation from years before. Unfortunately, Amy is the third alternate, which means she only gets on the squad if something happens to three people on the team. Sure enough, something happens to three people on the team—Cordelia is struck blind, Lishanne's mouth is sealed over, and then Buffy is turned into a gibbering idiot, as the result of a Bloodstone Vengeance spell.

Giles and a weakened Buffy go to the Madison house to discover that it isn't Amy who's casting the spells at all—it's her mother, Catherine, who has switched bodies with Amy in order to relive her glory days. Fortunately, Giles is able to reverse all the spells, even as Buffy battles Catherine, whose final spell is repelled and ironically traps the witch herself inside the cheerleading trophy she won when she attended Sunnydale High.

### Quote of the week:

"I laugh in the face of danger—then I hide until it goes away."

Xander, summing up his approach to life

### Love, Slayer style:

Xander gives Buffy a charm bracelet that reads, "Yours, always," then queries Willow as to whether he should ask Buffy out, to Willow's obvious-to-anyone-but-Xander chagrin.

### POP-CULTURE IQ:

"So Amber has this power to make herself be on fire. Like the Human Torch, only it hurts."

Xander, speculating on Amber's combustion, referring to the Marvel Comics superhero

"She's our Sabrina."

Buffy, describing Amy, referring to the Archie comics and TV show character Sabrina the Teenage Witch

**Buffy:** "Mom, I accepted that you've had sex. I'm not ready to know that you had Farrah hair."
**Joyce:** "This is Gidget hair. Don't they teach you anything in history?"
—Dishing about the hairstyles of sex symbols from the '60s and '70s.

### CONTINUITY:

Willow coins the term "Slayerettes," and Joyce's occupation as the owner of an art gallery is first discussed. Cordelia is taking driver's ed, having failed twice before—sometime between this episode and "Prophecy Girl," she passes her driver's test. Giles's affinity for the occult is first revealed ("The Dark Age," "I Robot, You Jane," "Bewitched, Bothered, and Bewildered"), though he claims that the spell he casts here is his first casting, a statement proven false in later episodes ("Halloween," "The Dark Age").

### From the original teleplay:

There are a lot of lines in the original script that don't show up in the finished episode. Xander, at one point, says, "Hey, we've fought vampires. Anything else'll be a walk in the park." Giles observes, "If I had the power of the black mass, I'd set my sights a little higher than making the pep squad." And then there's this exchange:

**Xander:** "Wow, you've got a killer streak I've never seen before. Hope I never cross you."
**Willow:** "I do, too. Then I'd have to carve you up into little pieces."

Finally, when Giles is searching for a test to figure out if Amy is a witch, he comes upon something in a book . . . "Yes, the ducking stool! We throw her in the pond. If she floats, she's a witch; if she drowns, she's innocent...[then, off their looks]...some of my texts are a bit outdated."

> When Buffy wakes up in bed, early in "Witch," she's wearing a T-shirt with a black cat on the front, a symbol sometimes synonymous with witchcraft.

## Teacher's Pet

**WRITTEN BY** David Greenwalt; **DIRECTED BY** Bruce Seth Green. **GUEST STARS:** David Boreanaz as Angel, Ken Lerner as Principal Flutie, Musetta Vander as Natalie French, Jackson Price as Blayne Mall, Jean Speegle Howard as Claw; with William Monaghan as Dr. Gregory, and Jack Knight, Michael Ross, and Karim Oliver.

Buffy receives an encouraging pep talk from her biology teacher, Dr. Gregory, who, sadly, turns up the next day without his head. His substitute is a sultry, sexy woman named Natalie French, who talks at length about praying mantises and has all the boys' hormones in overdrive. Buffy at first suspects Claw, a vampire whose hand has been replaced by sharp implements, as the culprit for the biology teacher's murder, but is surprised when she sees that very vampire whimper and flee at the sight of Ms. French.

Giles seeks advice from his friend Dr. Carlyle Ferris, who is an expert in entomology and mythology, and who is also quite mad since hunting a She-Mantis at Oxford. Meanwhile, Ms. French, apparently the same creature that Carlyle hunted, has taken both Xander and Blayne prisoner, with the intent of mating with them then killing them. Buffy manages to kill the creature before the boys are decapitated.

### Quote of the week:

"You were right all along, about everything....Well, no, you weren't right about your mother coming back as a Pekingese."

Giles's half of the conversation with Carlyle

### BUFFY'S BAG OF TRICKS:

She uses a machete on the She-Mantis, after driving it bonkers with an audiotape of bat sonar.

## POP-CULTURE IQ:

**"We're talking full-on *Exorcist* twist."**
Buffy, describing Ms. French's head twisting all the way around, referring to the most famous scene from *The Exorcist*

**"Oh, this is fun. We're on Monster Island."**
Xander, complaining about the Hellmouth, in reference to the Pacific island where Godzilla and friends reside in Japanese monster movies

### *Love, Slayer style:*

Xander continues to moon for Buffy and is not thrilled when Angel gives her his leather jacket. However, the minute Xander lays eyes on Ms. French, he only has eyes for her—as does every other male in the school. Xander refuses to believe Buffy's warning that Ms. French is a praying mantis, preferring to delude himself into thinking that she's jealous.

### CONTINUITY:

Xander's falling for a She-Mantis becomes a running joke throughout the series ("Inca Mummy Girl," "What's My Line? Part 2," etc.).

### From the Original teleplay:

The following scene was cut from the "Teacher's Pet" script because of length.

**Buffy:** "Dr. Gregory didn't chew me out or anything. He was really cool. But Flutie showed him my permanent record. Apparently, I fall somewhere between Charles Manson and a really bad person."

**Willow:** "And you can't tell Dr. Gregory what really happened at your old school?"

**Buffy:** "I was fighting vampires? I'm thinking he might not believe me."

**Willow:** "Yeah, he probably gets that excuse all the time."

**Cordelia** (just arriving): "Here lies a problem. What used to be my table occupied by pitiful losers. Of course, we'll have to burn it."

**Buffy:** "Sad, you have so many memories here. You and Lawrence, you and Mark, you and John. You spent the better part of your 'J' through 'M' here."

---

Xander fantasizes about being a guitar god, impressing Buffy with his amazing musical talents. Of course, we later learn that Giles did actually play guitar in a rock band in his youth, and Oz is lead guitarist of Dingoes Ate My Baby. So, clearly, guitar is the hot instrument of the moment.

## X-MAN'S MUNCHIES!!!

Xander Harris, Buffy's self-proclaimed knight in shining armor, is like all other great heroes in that he has one tragic flaw: snack food. A Hostess cake or a chocolate bar waved in front of his face during battle would be all an opponent would need to cause a fatal distraction. Check out these examples of the X-Man's obsession….

"Ho-Ho's are a vital part of my cognitive process."
—*What's My Line? Part 1"*

"Someone else's loss is my chocolaty goodness." — *"Nightmares"*

**Giles:** "A full moon tends to bring out our darkest qualities."
**Xander:** "Yet, ironically, also led to the invention of the moon pie."     —**"PHASES"**

"It's a delicious, spongy, golden cake, stuffed with a delightful, white creamy substance of goodness. And here's how you eat it . . . . Good, huh? And the exciting part is, they have no ingredients that a human can pronounce. So it doesn't leave you with that heavy food feeling in your stomach."
—re: Twinkies, in "Inca Mummy Girl"

"Okay. On sleazing extra candy. Tears are key. Tears'll usually get you a double-bagger. You can also try the old 'you missed me' routine—but it's risky. Only go there for chocolate. Understood?"
—trick-or-treat advice, from "Halloween"

Yep. Keep an eye on that Harris boy. His sweet tooth is going to turn out to be his Achilles' heel for sure.

## Never Kill a Boy on the First Date

**WRITTEN BY** Rob Des Hotel and Dean Batali; **DIRECTED BY** David Semel. **GUEST STARS:** Mark Metcalf as the Master, David Boreanaz as Angel, Christopher Wiehl as Owen Thurman, Andrew J. Ferchland as the Anointed One, Geoff Meed as Andrew Vorba; with Paul Felix Montez and Robert Mont.

The Master wishes to raise the Anointed One, who will be his primary weapon against the Slayer. Meanwhile, Buffy kills a member of the Order of Aurelius, the presence of which alerts Giles to the Master's plan. While Giles tries to decipher the prophecies relating to the rising of the Anointed One, Buffy attempts to have a social life with Owen Thurman, a

> Cemetery sequences in season one were shot at Rosedale cemetery in Los Angeles.

> All the books in the stacks of the library are real books.

quiet student who likes Emily Dickinson. Their date, however, is cut short by the need to save Giles from a vampire attack at a funeral home—where he went in Buffy's place to see if the Anointed One would rise, so Buffy could have her date—made more complicated by Owen following Buffy. They believe that the vampire they find and kill is the Anointed One. Unfortunately, Owen turns out to be a danger junkie, and Buffy has to refuse to date him again in order to keep him safe.

### Quote of the week:

**Giles:** "All right, I'll just drop in my time machine, go back to the twelfth century, and ask the vampires to postpone their ancient prophecy for a few days while you take in dinner and a show."
**Buffy:** "Okay, at this point, you're abusing sarcasm."
—Discussing the inconvenience of the prophecy of the Anointed One coming to pass on the night Buffy has a date

### Love, Slayer style:

Buffy has a crush on Owen, which does not make Xander (or Cordelia, or Angel) happy. Xander does what he can to sabotage the relationship (and also continue his own fawning after Buffy, including sneaking a peek at her changing clothes), but Buffy eventually breaks it off herself.

### POP-CULTURE IQ:

**"Here endeth the lesson."**
The Master, parroting dialogue from both Sean Connery and Kevin Costner in *The Untouchables*

**"Clark Kent had a job."**
Buffy, referring to her desire to have a life, citing the DC Comics character Superman's secret identity

### CONTINUITY:

> "Dusting" a vampire using computer graphics costs the producers $5,000 a pop

The Master creates the Anointed One, a small boy who remains a factor in the series until the second season events of "School Hard." Buffy and the gang think they've taken care of the Anointed One, and don't learn the truth until "Prophecy Girl." Giles says he has no instruction manual, which belies information learned in "What's My Line? Part 2" about the Slayer handbook.

# CONSPIRACY THEORY

Throughout the second season, the creators of *Buffy* have been developing a subplot one tiny bit of dialogue at a time. It's a conspiracy fit for Oliver Stone, and it's happening right here in Sunnydale! The mayor. The chief of police. Principal Snyder. They know Buffy's the Slayer. They don't like her—particularly Snyder. Whatever their super-secret agenda is, it's probably sinister, and it is definitely something they'd like to keep Buffy from finding out!

Here are some of the moments that have led us to formulate this conspiracy theory.

**Police Chief:** "I'll need to say something to the media."
**Snyder:** "So?"
**Police Chief:** "So . . . usual story? Gang-related, PCP?"
**Snyder:** "What did you have in mind? The truth?"
**Police Chief:** "Right. Gang-related. PCP." —**"SCHOOL HARD"**

**Police Chief:** "Schoolboy prank?"
**Snyder:** "Never sell."
**Police Chief:** "Backed-up sewer lines?"
**Snyder:** "Better...I can probably make that one fly. But this is getting out of hand. People will talk."
**Police Chief:** "You'll take care of it."
**Snyder:** "I'm doing everything I can. But you people have to realize—[as people pass]—backed-up sewer line, this happened in San Diego just last week—[the people are gone]—that we are on a Hellmouth. Sooner or later, people are going to figure that out."
**Police Chief:** "The city council was told you could handle this job. If you feel you can't . . . perhaps you'd like to take that up . . . with the mayor."
**Snyder:** "I'll handle it. I will." —**"I ONLY HAVE EYES FOR YOU"**

"Just give me a reason to kick you out, Summers. Just give me a reason."
Principal Snyder, in *"Becoming, Part 1"*

**Snyder:** "In case you didn't notice, the police in Sunnydale are deeply stupid. It doesn't matter, anyway. Whatever they find, you've proved too much of a liability for this school....These are moments you want to savor. You wish time would stop so you can live them over and over again. You're expelled."
**Buffy:** "You never ever got a single date when you were in high school, did you?"
**Snyder:** "Your point being?" [Buffy leaves; he speed-dials on a cell phone.] "It's Snyder. Tell the mayor I have good news." —**"BECOMING, PART 2"**

## The Pack

**WRITTEN BY** Matt Kiene and Joe Reinkemeyer; **DIRECTED BY** Bruce Seth Green. **GUEST STARS:** Ken Lerner as Principal Flutie, Eion Bailey as Rhonda, Michael McRaine as Kyle, Brian Gross as Tor, Jennifer Sky as Heidi, Jeff Maynard as Lance, and James Stephens as the zookeeper; with Gregory White, Jeffrey Steven Smith, David Brisbin, Barbara Whinnery, Justin Jon Ross, and Patrese Borem.

> The zoo segments in this shot were filmed at the Santa Ana Zoo.

Among the attendees at a school field trip to the zoo are Buffy and the gang, as well as the four biggest troublemakers in the school—Kyle, Rhonda, Tor, and Heidi—and Lance, the nerdy object of their scorn. The quartet leads Lance into the closed hyena exhibit. Xander goes after them to keep them out of trouble—and all save Lance find themselves imbued with the predatory spirit of the hyena. Xander starts to hang around with the quartet, acting very un-Xander-like—including verbally abusing Willow. The five of them devour Herbert, the school's new pig mascot, and later, when Principal Flutie brings Kyle, Rhonda, Tor, and Heidi to his office to accuse them of attacking the pig, they eat the principal alive as well.

Giles digs up references to "Primals," animal worshipers who can draw the spirits of animals into themselves. The keeper of the Hyena House—to whom Giles and Buffy turn for help—is, in fact, one such Primal, and he attempts to draw the power into himself and out of the students. He succeeds, but then Buffy tosses him to the actual hyenas.

### Quote of the week:

*"It's devastating—he's turned into a sixteen-year-old boy. Of course, you'll have to kill him."*

Giles, initially skeptical after Buffy describes Xander's odd behavior

### Love, Slayer style:

> One line that was cut: Xander says, "Welcome to the jungle."

Buffy and Willow discuss their respective attraction for Angel and Xander in the Bronze. (Willow on Xander: "He makes my head go tingly.") This makes it all the more devastating for Willow when Xander publicly humiliates her in front of the rest of the Pack. The possessed Xander is also much more aggressive in his pursuit of Buffy. (Buffy hits him with a desk for his troubles.)

### POP-CULTURE IQ:

*"I cannot believe that you of all people are trying to Scully me."*

Buffy, to Giles, when he refuses to accept that something's wrong with Xander, referring to Dana Scully's skepticism on *The X-Files*

*"Oh, great, it's the winged monkeys."*

Buffy, talking about the Pack, in a reference to *The Wizard of Oz*

**CONTINUITY:**
Xander will find his experiences as a hyena useful when Buffy and her friends are trying to find a werewolf ("Phases"). Buffy is still wearing the leather jacket Angel gave her in "Teacher's Pet."

**WRITTEN BY** David Greenwalt; **DIRECTED BY** Scott Brazil. **GUEST STARS:** Mark Metcalf as the Master, David Boreanaz as Angel, Kristine Sutherland as Joyce Summers, Julie Benz as Darla; with Andrew J. Ferchland as the Anointed One; with Charles Wesley.

After hovering on the periphery for several episodes, Angel's secret is finally revealed: he's a vampire. This realization does not come until he and Buffy admit their feelings for each other and share their first kiss. At first this leads Buffy to think that Angel's past actions are part of a plot to set her up for a fall, especially after she finds her mother in Angel's arms with bite marks on her neck. (In light of Angel's actions in the latter half of the second season, this is an even more reasonable assumption.)

Soon enough, Buffy learns the whole truth. Angel was "sired" (vampire language for turning a human into a vampire) by Darla 240 years before. Eighty years ago, he tortured and killed a Romany woman, and her clan put a curse on him: they restored his soul. He became a vampire with a conscience, a unique creature among the undead. Darla's attempts to bring him back to the Master's fold fail, and she winds up on the wrong end of a stake wielded by Angel.

**Quote of the week:**
"Angel's a vampire. You're a Slayer.
I think it's obvious what you have to do."
Xander, laying it out for Buffy after
Angel's vampirism is revealed

> It takes an hour and a half to apply Angel's vamp face to David. One of his favorite parts of being a vampire is the weird yellow contact lenses.

### *Love, Slayer style:*

The Angel/Buffy relationship goes into full bloom here, starting with his spending the night in her bedroom (though he is, as she says, a perfect gentleman), continuing to their first kiss, and ending with another kiss that, thanks to Buffy's crucifix necklace, leaves a burning impression on Angel's chest. Their continued insistence that "This can't ever be anything" rings hollow even as they say it, more so in light of where the relationship does actually go.

Meanwhile, a hint of the future with Cordelia and Xander comes in an early scene on the dance floor ("Boy, that Cordelia's a breath of vile air"), and Willow continues to moon for Xander to Buffy, though Buffy's continued urges for Willow to actually say something are met with vehement refusal ("No, no, no, no. No speaking up. That way leads to madness and sweaty palms").

### BUFFY'S BAG OF TRICKS:

Giles trains Buffy in both quarterstaffs and crossbow. She uses the latter on Darla (piercing her in the stomach rather than the heart), and tries and fails to use it on Angel (the impression being that her shot went wild on purpose).

### *CONTINUITY:*

> Angel's duster is from Hugo Boss and cost $1,000.

The Master has begun training the Anointed One ("Never Kill a Boy on the First Date"). Buffy invites Angel into her home for the first time ("Passion"). Angel describes Darla making him and his cursing at the hands of the Romany, both later dramatized in "Becoming, Part 1."

## I Robot, You Jane

**WRITTEN BY** Ashley Gable and Tom Swyden; **DIRECTED BY** Stephen Posey. **GUEST STARS:** Robia LaMorte as Jenny Calendar; with Chad Lindberg, and Jamison Ryan.

> The lead monk in the ancient-Italy sequence is "Thelonius," obviously a reference to jazz great Thelonius Monk.

In fifteenth-century Italy, a monk is able to imprison the demon Moloch, the Corruptor, in a book as the actual text of the tome. Since the demon can be freed only if the words are read aloud, the monk seals the book in a box, where it remains for over 500 years—until it is opened in Sunnydale High School's library as one of Giles's new acquisitions. The book is scanned into the computer as part of a project developed by the school's computer-science teacher,

Jenny Calendar—a freewheeling, hip-dressing, slang-speaking young woman who seems to be the diametric opposite of Rupert Giles. Scanning the book, however, releases the demon into cyberspace, and Moloch soon begins his work. As "Malcolm," he begins an on-line relationship with Willow, subverts Fritz and Dave, the school's biggest computer geeks, and uses a now-defunct electronics company to build himself a robot body.

> Alyson Hannigan is hooked into the Net, but says she's not the "Net girl" that Willow is.

With the unexpected assistance of Jenny—revealed to be a technopagan who is familiar with Moloch and other such creatures—Giles manages to bind the Corruptor into the robot body, giving Buffy the opportunity to kill the demon by blowing up the robot with a handy wiring box.

## Quote of the week:

"I know our ways are strange to you, but soon you will join us in the twentieth century— with three whole years to spare!"

Jenny, in one of her many book vs. computer arguments with Giles.

## Love, Slayer style:

Jenny and Giles go from open hostility to grudging respect over the course of the episode, and Jenny makes something of a pass at Giles at the very end, sowing the seeds of their future relationship (if not its tragic end). Xander also shows fierce jealousy when Willow starts cyberdating "Malcolm."

## POP-CULTURE IQ:

"I can just tell something's wrong. My spider-sense is tingling."

Buffy, when she, Giles, and Xander are discussing the odd behavior of both Willow and Dave, referring to the Marvel Comics character Spider-Man's ability to sense danger

## CONTINUITY:

Buffy and Xander attempt to cheer Willow by pointing out that, yes, Willow's boyfriend turned out to be a demon, but Buffy has the hots for a vampire ("Angel") and the teacher Xander had a crush on was a praying mantis ("Teacher's Pet"). Jenny's assisting Giles will lead to her being brought into the "inner circle" of Slayerettes ("Prophecy Girl").

> The episode features the first appearance of Ms. Calendar. Though her first name is never used in this episode, it was originally to be "Nicki" and was later changed to avoid any confusion on set with actor Nicholas Brendon, whose friends call him Nicky.

## THE REHABILITATION OF CORDY

At first, Cordelia Chase seemed like the stereotypical shallow, popular, vapid, bitchy…well, you get the idea. It was very easy to picture her in the role of Buffy's school-bound nemesis. And that would have been the easy way to go. But, interestingly, though Cordelia remains somewhat shallow, bitchy, and still very popular, over time, she's turned out to have a heart and soul after all.

Witness, then, the rehabilitation of Cordelia.

At first, Ms. Chase was best known for her cruel, humorless barbs. In one scene in the premiere episode, Cordelia gets off several nasty lines. Spotting Buffy hanging out with Willow and Xander, she says, "I don't want to interrupt your downward mobility…." and moments later, sneers at Xander, "Don't you have an elsewhere to be?" Not exactly the winner of the How to Make Friends and Influence People contest. Actually, Cordelia's enormous lack of charm is the subject of quite a bit of humor among our heroes for the first season.

But then, something begins to change. Slowly at first. In "Out of Mind, Out of Sight," Cordelia first approaches Buffy for her help, realizing that there's more to the Slayer than meets the eye. Then, discussing the hapless "invisible girl," we get our first glimpse at the human side of the wicked witch of Sunnydale High, with this exchange.

**Cordelia:** "It's awful to feel that lonely."
**Buffy:** "Oh, so you've read something about the feeling?"
**Cordelia:** "Hey, you think I'm never lonesome 'cause I'm so cute and popular? I can be surrounded by people and be completely alone. It's not like any of them really know me. I don't even know if they like me half the time. People just want to be in the popular zone. Sometimes when I talk, everyone's so busy agreeing with me, they don't hear a word I say."
**Buffy:** "If you feel so alone, why do you work so hard at being popular?"
**Cordelia:** "Well, it beats being alone all by yourself."   —**"OUT OF MIND, OUT OF SIGHT"**

At the end of the first season, in the episode "Prophecy Girl," Cordelia takes her biggest step toward her rehabilitation, when she saves Willow and Ms. Calendar from an army of vampires. Then, in the first episode of season two, "When She Was Bad," the amazing Ms. Chase actually steps in when she sees how badly Buffy is screwing up her relationships with her friends. "Whatever's causing the Joan Collins 'tude, deal with it, embrace the pain, spank your inner moppet, whatever," Cordy tells Buffy. "But get over it, 'cause pretty soon you won't even have the loser friends you've got now."

Okay, so maybe she could have come up with a nicer approach, but this *is* Cordelia we're talking about here!

Already involved with the Slayerettes because, well, she knows Buffy is the Slayer and there are monsters and vampires and demons and…hey, she lives in Sunnydale too…Cordelia also begins to think Xander's not quite such a nerd after all. In fact, at the end of "Some Assembly Required," she thanks him for saving her life. Xander immediately rebuffs her, but observant viewers knew something was brewing in that exchange.

Despite her frequent collaboration in their efforts to save the world, it was difficult for Buffy and friends to accept Cordelia. But in the first part of "What's My Line?" she officially becomes one of them, with this exchange:

**Cordelia:** "I can't even believe you. You drag me out of bed for a ride? What am I, mass transportation?"
**Xander:** "That's what a lot of the guys say. But it's just locker-room talk. I never pay it any mind."
**Cordelia:** "Great, so now I'm your taxi and your punching bag."
**Xander:** "I like to think of you more as my witless foil—but have it your way.... Come on, Cordelia. You wanna be a member of the Scooby Gang, you gotta be willing to be inconvenienced now and then."
**Cordelia:** "Oh, right. 'Cause I lie awake at night hoping you tweekos will be my best friends. And that my first husband will be a balding, demented homeless man." —**"WHAT'S MY LINE? PART 1"**

And, of course, it's all cemented when, later in that same episode, Cordelia and Xander—under the duress of being attacked by a bug man—make out for the first time.
Cordelia Chase. Purposefully tactless. Materialistic. Sarcastic. Patronizing. Arrogant. And coming around.

## The Puppet Show

**WRITTEN BY** Rob Des Hotel and Dean Batali; **DIRECTED BY** Ellen Pressman. **GUEST STARS:** Kristine Sutherland as Joyce Summers, Richard Werner as Morgan, Burke Roberts as Marc, and Armin Shimerman as Principal Snyder; with Chasen Hampton, Natasha Pearce, and Krissy Carlson.

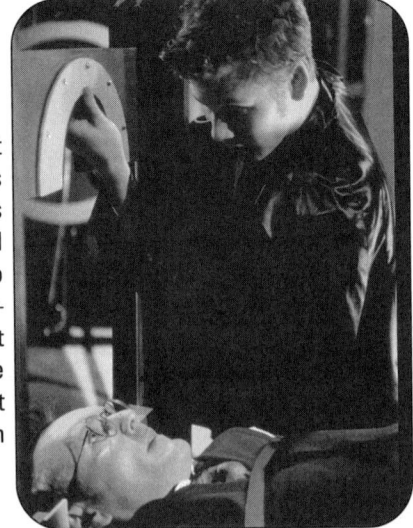

Giles faces a true horror—running the annual Talent Show—at the instruction of Principal Snyder, Flutie's somewhat militant replacement. Snyder also instructs Buffy, Xander, and Willow to be in the Talent Show, and generally makes a nuisance of himself. To add insult to injury, one of the Talent Show entrants is found dead—with her heart cut out. At first the Slayerettes think it might be your basic serial killer, but Giles finds a text on the Brotherhood of Seven, a clan of demons who must obtain the heart and brain of a human youth every seven years to keep up their own guise as youthful humans.

Suspicion falls upon Morgan, the class genius, who seems to be talking to the wooden dummy he uses for his performance and who is also suffering from headaches—right up until Morgan is found dead with his brain removed, and Buffy realizes that Sid, his dummy, is alive. Could he be the demon?

Sid turns out to be a demon hunter who has been imprisoned in a dummy's body. Once he and Buffy realize neither is the demon, they pair up to find the demon, which proves necessary once they realize that Morgan suffered from brain cancer, and so his cranium would be useless. And the magician really wants to demonstrate his magic trick involving a guillotine to Giles....

Willow's running off in terror at the end of the episode, midway through the drama piece that she, Buffy, and Xander are performing, was not part of the script. Though it seems prophetic, considering that in the next episode, "Nightmares," Willow's primary fear has to do with stage fright.

## Quote of the week:

**"That's the kind of woolly-headed liberal thinking that leads to getting eaten."**
Principal Snyder, on the shortcomings of his predecessor

## Love, Slayer style:

More foreshadowing of Xander and Cordelia's future, as Cordelia cries, "All I can think is, it could've been me!" prompting Xander's reply of, "We can dream."

## POP-CULTURE IQ:

Xander has Sid-the-dummy crying "Red Rum!" a reference to a line from *The Shining*—it's "murder" spelled backward.

As Xander is trying to convince Buffy and Willow that Sid is just a piece of wood, he operates the dummy's mouth and cries "Redrum! Redrum!" The reference to Stanley Kubrick's *The Shining* was added by actor Nicholas Brendon and was not in the original script.

**"Does anyone else feel like we've been Keyser Soze'd?"**
Xander, in reference to the manipulative villain in the film *The Usual Suspects*

## CONTINUITY:

The wild-dogs-ate-Principal-Flutie story from "The Pack" seems to be holding up. Sid mentions that the Slayer in the 1930s was a Korean woman, with whom he had some "good times."

**From the origial teleplay:**

The following two exchanges were cut from the script to "The Puppet Show" because of length:

**Buffy:** "And I don't think we'll be featuring Xander's special gift . . ."
**Xander:** "Okay, some people are jealous that they can't burp the alphabet."
**Buffy:** " . . . so we're back to drama. We'll just do it quickly. Get in, get out. Nobody gets hurt."

**Buffy:** "Pretty good. I never heard 'Flight of the Bumblebee' on the tuba before."
**Lisa:** "Most people aren't up to it."

> Sid is just one in a long line of terrifying puppets and talking dolls in film and television, from "Talking Tina" in a classic episode of *The Twilight Zone* to the horrifying dummy in William Goldman's *Magic*.

## DEEP THOUGHTS: A GUIDE TO SLAYER PHILOSOPHY

**Buffy:** "You know, it's just, like, nothing's simple. I'm constantly trying to work it out, who to hate or love . . . who to trust. . . . It's like the more I know, the more confused I get."
**Giles:** "I believe that's called 'growing up.'"
**Buffy**: "I'd like to stop now then, okay?"  —"LIE TO ME"

**Giles**: "To forgive is an act of compassion, Buffy. It's not done because people deserve it. It's done because they *need* it."
**Buffy:** "No. James destroyed the person he loved the most in a moment of blind passion. And that's not something you forgive. No matter why he did what he did. No matter if he knows now that it was *wrong* and *stupid* and *selfish*. He's just going to have to live with it."  —"I ONLY HAVE EYES FOR YOU"

"There's moments in your life that make you. That set the course of who you're gonna be. Sometimes they're little, subtle moments. Sometimes...they're not."

Whistler, in "Becoming, Part 2"

**Buffy:** "Does it ever get easy?"
**Giles:** "You mean life?"
**Buffy:** "Yeah. Does it get easy?"
**Giles:** "What do you want me to say?"
**Buffy:** "Lie to me."

**Giles:** "Yes. It's terribly simple. The good guys are always stalwart and true. The bad guys are easily distinguished by their pointy horns or black hats, and we always defeat them and save the day. No one ever dies . . . and everyone lives happily ever after."
**Buffy:** "Liar."
—**"LIE TO ME"**

**Buffy:** "And don't lie to me. I'm tired of it."
**Angel:** "Some lies are necessary."
**Buffy:** "For what?"
**Angel:** "Sometimes the truth is worse. You live long enough, you find that out."
—**"LIE TO ME"**

**Buffy:** "Life is short."
**Willow:** "Life is short."
**Buffy:** "Not original, I'll grant you. But it's true, y'know? Why waste time being shy, worry about some guy and if he's gonna laugh at you? Seize the moment. 'Cause tomorrow, you might be dead."
—**"WELCOME TO THE HELLMOUTH"**

**"It was wrong to meddle with the forces of Darkness, and I see that now."** Xander, in "Witch"

**"We saved the world. I say we party. I mean, I got all pretty."**
Buffy, at the climax of "Prophecy Girl"

**"I think anyone who cuts dead girls into little pieces does not get the benefit of any doubt."**
Buffy, in "Some Assembly Required"

**"Love makes you do the wacky."**
Willow, in "Some Assembly Required"

**"'I aspire to help my fellow man.' Check. I mean, as long as he's not, like, smelly or dirty or something gross."**
Cordelia, filling out a questionnaire, in "What's My Line? Part 1"

**"Sorry, I'm an old-fashioned girl. I was raised to believe the men dig up the corpses and the women have the babies."**
Buffy, in "Some Assembly Required"

**Buffy:** "Vampires are creeps."
**Giles:** "Yes, that's why one slays them."
—**"TED"**

**"Loneliness is about the scariest thing there is."**
Angel, in "Ted"

# Nightmares

**STORY BY** Joss Whedon, **TELEPLAY BY** David Greenwalt; **DIRECTED BY** Bruce Seth Green. **GUEST STARS:** Mark Metcalf as the Master, Kristine Sutherland as Joyce Summers, Jeremy Foley as Billy Palmer, Andrew J. Ferchland as the Anointed One, Dean Butler as Hank Summers; with Justin Urich.

Everyone's nightmares start coming true in Sunnydale, with the only common element being the occasional appearance of a young boy. One student's recurring dream of spiders attacking him in class actually happens; Xander walks into a class wearing only his underwear; Willow is forced to sing onstage; Giles gets lost in the stacks and forgets how to read; Cordelia has *really awful* hair and loses her fashion sense; and then Buffy is told by her father she was the reason her parents divorced.

Things get worse when the Master is freed—a nightmare Buffy has in the teaser made reality—Buffy is killed (Giles's nightmare) and comes back to life as a vampire (Buffy's). The chaos is finally traced to a young boy in a coma who was beaten by his Kiddie League coach, and whose constant reliving of that nightmare has been made real by the power of the Hellmouth—unless Buffy can make him confront his fear.

### Quote of the week:

"So you're the Slayer. You're prettier than the last one."

The Master's first comment upon finally meeting his nemesis

### CONTINUITY:

The Master's instruction of the Anointed One ("Never Kill a Boy on the First Date," "Angel") continues. Buffy's nightmare of the Master attacking and killing her serves as a teaser of sorts for their confrontation in "Prophecy Girl."

### From the original teleplay:

Material cut from the script because of length includes the following gem from Xander:

"Okay, despite the rat-like chill that just crawled up my spine, I'm going to say this very calmly: Helllppp...."

Also cut was the following exchange:
**Giles:** "Are you all right? You look a bit peaked."
**Buffy:** "Hospital lighting. It does nothing for my fabulous complexion."
**Giles:** "Are you ... sleeping all right?"
**Buffy:** "I'll sleep better when we find this guy. Nothing like kicking the crap out of a bad guy to perk up my day."

> This is the episode where Xander officially grows up and turns from nerd into hero. Not by saving anyone's life, exactly, but by facing his own childhood fears and punching out a clown he's had nightmares about for a decade.

## THE SOMEWHAT BRIGHTER SIDE

Living on the Hellmouth, there's rarely a bright side to look on, still our stalwart heroes do their best to be optimistic about things.

**Buffy:** "We averted the apocalypse. You gotta give us points for that." —**"THE HARVEST"**

"That is the thrill of living on the Hellmouth—
one has a veritable cornucopia of fiends, devils, and ghouls to engage . . .
[off their looks] Pardon me for finding the glass half full."

Giles, in "Witch"

"If it weren't for you, people would be lined up five deep waiting to get themselves buried. Willow would be Robbie the Robot's love slave, I wouldn't even have a head, and Theresa's a vampire!"

Xander, as Theresa is reborn, in "Phases"

"I'd give anything to be able to turn invisible—but I wouldn't use my power to beat people up. I'd use my power to protect the girls' locker room."

Xander, in "Out of Mind, Out of Sight"

**Cordelia:** "It's about time our school excelled at something."
**Willow:** "You're forgetting our high mortality rate."
**Xander:** "We're number one!" —**"GO FISH"**

**Xander:** "Hellmouth. Center of mystical convergence, supernatural monsters. Been there."
**Buffy:** "A little blasé there, aren't you?"
**Xander:** "I'm not worried. If there's something bad out there, we'll find, you'll slay, we'll party."
—**"NIGHTMARES"**

"We're still the undead's favorite party town."

Xander, on Sunnydale, in "When She Was Bad"

**Giles:** "Grave robbing. Well, that's new. Interesting."
**Buffy:** "I know you meant to say 'gross and disturbing.'"
**Giles:** "Yes, of course. Terrible thing. Must put a stop to it...dammit."
—**"SOME ASSEMBLY REQUIRED"**

**Willow:** "By the way, are we hoping to find a body or no body?"
**Xander:** "Call me an optimist, but *I'm* hoping to find a fortune in gold doubloons."
**Buffy:** "Well, 'body' would mean flesh-eating demon. 'No body' points more toward the 'army of zombies' thing. Take your pick." —**"SOME ASSEMBLY REQUIRED"**

"I must admit, I'm intrigued. A werewolf. It's one of the classics.
I'm sure my books and I are in for a fascinating afternoon."

Giles, in "Phases"

# Out of Mind, Out of Sight

**STORY BY** Joss Whedon, **TELEPLAY BY** Ashley Gable and Tom Swyden; **DIRECTED BY** Reza Badiyi. **GUEST STARS:** David Boreanaz as Angel, Armin Shimerman as Principal Snyder, Clea DuVall as Marcie Ross, Mercedes McNab as Harmony, Ryan Bittle as Mitch, Denise Dowse as Ms. Miller, Mark Phelan as Agent Doyle, Skip Stellrecht as Agent Manetti; with Julie Fulton.

Cordelia is campaigning to be crowned Sunnydale High's May Queen. Mitch, her prospective date for the occasion, is clubbed in the locker room with a baseball bat—a bat seemingly acting of its own accord! Later, Cordelia's friend Harmony seems to fall down the stairs, but Harmony insists she was pushed. Everything points to an invisible person, and Buffy finds evidence of someone living in the ductwork: a girl named Marcie Ross whom nobody remembers, yet who has a Sunnydale High yearbook signed by most of the class, including Xander and Willow (*everyone* signed, "Have a nice summer").

Having been treated as if she were invisible for so long—especially by Cordelia and her "Cordettes"—she has become literally invisible, and is now wreaking havoc on Cordelia's life. Buffy manages to stop her—though not before Marcie attempts to kill Giles, Xander, and Willow and almost mutilates Cordelia—at which point some federal agents take her away to a special school with some other invisible students to "rehabilitate" her.

The Giles/Buffy exchange about listening (Giles: "You may have to work on listening to people." Buffy: "Very funny." Giles: "I thought so") was not in the original script, and was added in postproduction as a transition voice-over.

### Quote of the week:

"Being this popular is not just my right, it's my responsibility."

Cordelia, upon accepting the honor of May Queen, summarizing her approach to life

### Love, Slayer style:

Angel and Giles meet for the first time, and they discuss Angel's feelings for Buffy. ("A vampire in love with the Slayer.

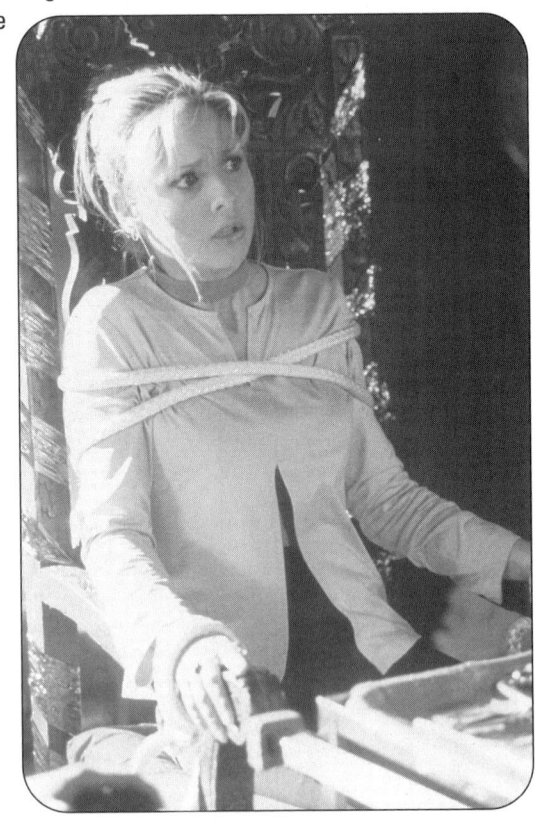

74

When Marcie arrives at her new school, the teacher has her open to Chapter 11. That chapter's title is "Assassination and Infiltration." The first case study: "Case Example D: Radical Cult Leader as Intended Victim."

That's rather poetic," says Giles, a line used regularly in the "Previously on *Buffy the Vampire Slayer*" montages.)

## POP-CULTURE IQ:

**"Monsters don't usually send messages. It's pretty much 'Crush! Kill! Destroy!'"**

Buffy, referring to a famous line uttered by the robot in the television series *Lost in Space*

## CONTINUITY:

The seeds of Cordelia's eventual induction into the Slayerettes are sown here, as she comes to Buffy and the others for help when she egotistically yet correctly realizes that the attacks are directed at her. Giles mentions *The Pergamum Codex* to Angel, which has various prophecies regarding the Master and the Slayer, which Angel obtains for him—said prophecies prove vital in "Prophecy Girl."

## A MATTER OF PRINCIPAL

The philosophies of Principals Flutie and Snyder are very clearly at odds.
Here, for your edification, the words of wisdom
from these two titans of education.

**"We all need help with our feelings, otherwise we bottle them up,
and before you know it, powerful laxatives are involved.
I really believe if we all reach out to one another, we can beat this thing.
I'm always here if you need a hug—but not a real hug, because there's
no touching in this school. We're sensitive to wrong touching."**
Principal Flutie, to Buffy, in "Teacher's Pet"

**"My predecessor, Mr. Flutie, may have gone in for all that touchy-feely,
relating nonsense. But he was eaten. You're in my world now.
Sunnydale has touched and felt for the last time."**
Principal Snyder, in "The Puppet Show"

**"Kids today need discipline. That's an unpopular word these days.
'Discipline.' I know Principal Flutie would have said kids need
'understanding.' Kids are 'human beings.' That's the kind of woolly-headed
liberal thinking that leads to being eaten."**
Principal Snyder, in "The Puppet Show"

**"A clean slate, Buffy. That's what you get here. What's past is past."**
Principal Flutie, in "Welcome to the Hellmouth"

**"Kids. I don't like 'em."**
Principal Snyder, in "The Puppet Show"

**"All the kids here are free to call me 'Bob.'"**
Principal Flutie, in "Welcome to the Hellmouth"

**Principal Snyder:** "I mean, it's incredible. One day the campus is completely bare, empty . . . the next, there are children everywhere. Like locusts. Crawling around, mindlessly bent on feeding and mating, destroying everything in sight in their relentless, pointless desire to exist."
**Giles:** "I do enjoy these pep talks. Have you ever considered, given your abhorrence of children, that school principal is perhaps not your true vocation?"
**Principal Snyder:** "Someone's gotta keep an eye on 'em. They're just a bunch of hormonal time bombs. Why, every time a pretty girl walks by, every boy turns into a jibbering fool." —**"WHEN SHE WAS BAD"**

"There are things I will not tolerate. Students loitering on campus after school. Horrible murders with hearts being removed. And also smoking."
Principal Snyder, in "The Puppet Show"

"Buffy, don't worry. Any other school, they might say 'watch your step' or 'we'll be watching you,' but that's just not the way here. We want to service your needs and help you to respect our needs."
Principal Flutie, in "Welcome to the Hellmouth"

**Principal Snyder:** "There are some things I can just smell. It's like a sixth sense."
**Giles:** "No, actually, that would be one of the five."
**Principal Snyder:** "The Summers girl? I smell trouble. I smell expulsion. And just the faintest aroma of jail."
**Giles:** "Well, before you throw away the key, you might consider giving her the benefit of the doubt. She may surprise you."
**Principal Snyder:** "You really have faith in those kids, don't you?"
**Giles:** "Yes, I do."
**Principal Snyder:** "Weird."
—"WHEN SHE WAS BAD"

"That's the Buffy Summers I want in my school. The sensible girl, with her feet on the ground."
Principal Flutie, just before Buffy leaps the fence in "The Harvest"

"A lot of principals tell students, think of your principal as your 'pal.' I say, think of me as your judge, jury and executioner."
Principal Snyder, in "School Hard"

**Principal Snyder:** "This is my school. What I say goes. And I say this isn't happening."
**Joyce:** "Well, then I guess the danger's over."
**Parent:** "I'm not waiting for them to break down the doors. I'm getting out."
**Joyce:** "Don't be an idiot."
**Principal Snyder:** "I'm beginning to see a certain mother-daughter resemblance."
—"SCHOOL HARD"

# Prophecy Girl

**WRITTEN AND DIRECTED BY** Joss Whedon. **GUEST STARS:** Mark Metcalf as the Master, David Boreanaz as Angel, Kristine Sutherland as Joyce Summers, Robia LaMorte as Jenny Calendar, Andrew J. Ferchland as the Anointed One.

On the eve of the prom, Giles translates a rather devastating prophecy in *The Pergamum Codex*: "The Master shall rise and the Slayer shall die." Several portents—noticed by Giles, Jenny Calendar, and Buffy—point to the Master finally freeing himself from his imprisonment. Giles tries to keep the prophecy from Buffy, but she overhears him discussing it with Angel. Though at first she rejects both the prophecy and her continuing as the Slayer ("Giles, I'm sixteen years old—I don't want to die"), the news of two students' deaths at the hands of vampires on schoolgrounds makes her realize her duty, and she goes after the Master. Angel and Xander go after her, arriving in time to find Buffy drowned and the Master free. Use of CPR revives Buffy, and she, Angel, and Xander return to Sunnydale High to find that the Hellmouth is opening—right under the library—despite the best efforts of Giles, Jenny, Willow, and Cordelia. Buffy confronts the Master once again, and this time he is the one who dies. "We saved the world," says Buffy at the end of it all. "I say we party."

### Quote of the week:

"*By the way, I like your dress.*"

This is said by Willow, the Master, and Angel to Buffy at various times; Buffy's mother bought her the dress to wear to the prom

### Love, Slayer style:

Xander finally comes out and expresses his feelings for Buffy in the form of a labored attempt to ask her to go to the prom with him. Buffy turns the offer down, not feeling that way about Xander, prompting a snide comment about how one has to be undead to get her attention. ("I don't handle rejection well. Funny, considering all the practice I've had.") Later on, Xander recruits Angel to follow Buffy in going after the Master ("You're in love with her," Angel says, to which Xander replies frankly, "Aren't you?").

Xander practices his pickup line to Buffy on

The moment Willow discovers the corpses of Kevin and his friends in the audio/visual room is a major turning point for the character. From that point on, Willow becomes more proactive about her involvement with the Slayer. In that moment, she grows up.

> Both Willow and the Master compliment Buffy on her dress, but the final exchange (Angel: "I really like your . . ." Buffy: "Yeah, yeah. It was a big hit with everyone.") was added during production and was not in the original script.

Willow, which is some comfort for her, though not enough for her to accept his post-Buffy's-rejection offer of the two of them going to the prom.

## POP-CULTURE IQ:

> "Calm may work for Locutus of Borg here, but I'm freaked and I intend to stay that way."

Xander, upset by Giles's maddening reserve, referring to the emotionless cyborg characters on *Star Trek*.

## CONTINUITY:

The Master's imprisonment finally comes to an end, with the help of the Anointed One, and he makes his second attempt to open the Hellmouth ("Welcome to the Hellmouth"). For the second time, but not the last, Buffy has a prophetic dream ("Welcome to the Hellmouth," "Surprise," "Innocence"). Buffy and the Slayerettes finally realize that the vampire they killed in "Never Kill a Boy on the First Date" *wasn't* the Anointed One. Jenny reminds Giles of her help in destroying Moloch ("I Robot, You Jane") when she tries to pry some solid information out of him. Since "Witch," Cordelia has passed driver's ed and obtained a car. Unlike other vampires, the Master's bones remain intact upon his death, which proves important in "When She Was Bad."

> The massive demon coming up out of the Hellmouth at the end of "Prophecy Girl" had to be frightening, but the budget didn't allow for computer-generated images. The masterminds at Optic Nerve ended up making tentacle "costumes." Each of the tentacles has a human being inside, manipulating it from within.

## From the original teleplay:

The following scene, right after Buffy has turned down Xander's request that she go to the prom with him, was cut from this episode's script because of length:

Xander bails, wandering off under the archway. Buffy sits by herself on the bench, bummed.

Which is when the hail of pebbles starts.

The first few get Buffy's attention, tiny hard pellets hitting the ground around her. She stands as more start coming down.

People—including Buffy—all run for cover as the real shower starts. Buffy stands under the archway, watching the hail come down.

ANGLE: XANDER

Walking away, not near Buffy. He hears:

**Student** (O.S.): "Check it out! It's raining stones!"
Xander looks back over his shoulder.
**Xander:** "Figures."

# SECOND SEASON

| EPISODE NUMBER | EPISODE NAME | ORIGINAL AIRDATE |
|---|---|---|
| 1 | When She Was Bad | 15-Sep |
| 2 | Some Assembly Required | 22-Sep |
| 3 | School Hard | 29-Sepr |
| 4 | Inca Mummy Girl | 6-Oct |
| 5 | Reptile Boy | 13-Oct |
| 6 | Halloween | 27-Oct |
| 7 | Lie to Me | 3-Nov |
| 8 | The Dark Age | 10-Nov |
| 9 | What's My Line? Part 1 | 17-Nov |
| 10 | What's My Line? Part 2 | 24-Nov |
| 11 | Ted | 8-Dec |
| 12 | Bad Eggs | 12-Jan |
| 13 | Surprise | 19-Jan |
| 14 | Innocence | 20-Jan |
| 15 | Phases | 27-Jan |
| 16 | Bewitched, Bothered, and Bewildered | 10-Feb |
| 17 | Passion | 24-Feb |
| 18 | Killed by Death | 3-Mar |
| 19 | I Only Have Eyes for You | 28-Apr |
| 20 | Go Fish | 5-May |
| 21 | Becoming, Part 1 (Season Finale) | 12-May |
| 22 | Becoming, Part 2 (Season Finale) | 19-May |

## ★ STARRING ★

Sarah Michelle Gellar . . . . . . . . . . . . . . . . .Buffy Summers

Nicholas Brendon . . . . . . . . . . . . . . . . . . . . .Xander Harris

Alyson Hannigan . . . . . . . . . . . . . . . . . .Willow Rosenberg

Charisma Carpenter . . . . . . . . . . . . . . . . .Cordelia Chase

David Boreanaz . . . . . . . . . . . . . . . . . . . . . . . . . . . . . .Angel

Anthony Stewart Head . . . . . . . . . . . . . . . . . .Rupert Giles

# When She Was Bad

**WRITTEN AND DIRECTED** by Joss Whedon. **GUEST STARS:** Kristine Sutherland as Joyce Summers, Robia LaMorte as Jenny Calendar, Andrew J. Ferchland as the Anointed One, Dean Butler as Hank Summers, Brent Jennings as Absalom, and Armin Shimerman as Principal Snyder; with Tamara Braun.

Buffy returns from spending summer vacation with her father. Willow and Xander are relieved at first, as the summer has been exceedingly dull, though Buffy returns just in time to save the pair from a vampire—the first such they've seen since the Master was killed. The relief turns to concern, however, as Buffy is withdrawn, snappish, a little too eager to continue her training, and more rude to Cordelia than even she deserves. She also has a nightmare about Giles attacking her while Willow and Xander calmly look on.

When the Master's buried bones go missing, everyone is concerned. Giles learns of a revivification rite that requires those "closest" to the Master when he died. It turns out to be a bad translation from Sumerian to Latin, and by the time he realizes it means "nearest," he and Willow are taken, along with Cordelia and Jenny, all of whom were next to the Master when he was impaled. Buffy, Xander, and Angel must stop the Anointed One and his new deputy, Absalom, from completing the ceremony.

### Quote of the week:

**Snyder:** "There are some things I can just smell. It's like a sixth sense."
**Giles:** "Actually, that would be one of the five."

### Love, Slayer style:

The romantic entanglements kick into high gear in this episode. Xander and Willow come within microns of actually kissing each other in the teaser after Xander licks ice cream off Willow's nose—interrupted by the vampire attack and Buffy's return to Sunnydale. Willow's attempt to re-create that mood later in the Bronze fails miserably, as Xander has returned to full panting-after-Buffy mode.

Giles and Jenny return from their summer vacation and immediately begin flirting, with an oblivious Principal Snyder carrying on about how teenagers are driven by their hormones.

> David Boreanaz became a regular cast member beginning with this episode

Buffy, still reeling from her experiences with the Master and refusing to outwardly deal with it, plays mind games with all her friends. She is cold to Angel. ("Could you contemplate getting over yourself for a second? There is no us.") She dances a hormone-tingling slow dance with Xander at the Bronze, which manages to make Willow, Angel, and even Xander himself squirm, prompting Cordelia, of all people, to tell her to get over it ("Spank your inner moppet, whatever"). It isn't until the climax, when she cathartically smashes the Master's bones with a sledge hammer, that she seems to come out of it.

### BUFFY'S BAG OF TRICKS:

She makes excellent use of a torch to simultaneously stake one vampire and burn Absalom to a crisp.

### POP-CULTURE IQ:

Xander and Willow's movie quote contest includes T*erminator, Planet of the Apes, Star Wars,* and *Witness:*

"I mock you with my ice cream cone, Amish Guy...."

### CONTINUITY:

The entire episode picks up from "Prophecy Girl" showing that it *wasn't* as simple as, "We saved the world; I say we party." Buffy's slow dance with Xander will continue to have consequences ("Some Assembly Required")

### From the original teleplay:

The following exchange between Buffy's parents was cut from the script for "When She Was Bad" because of length:

**Hank:** "Oh, I'm spoiling her. Did I forget to mention that?"
**Joyce:** "What you forgot is that I'm gonna have to deal with another year of 'Daddy would let me buy that.'"

---

**WRITTEN BY** Ty King; **DIRECTED BY** Bruce Seth Green. **GUEST STARS:** Robia LaMorte as Jenny Calendar, Angelo Spizzirri as Chris Epps, Michael Bacall as Eric, Ingo Neuhaus as Daryl Epps, Melanie MacQueen as Mrs. Epps; with Amanda Wilmhurst.

## Some Assembly Required

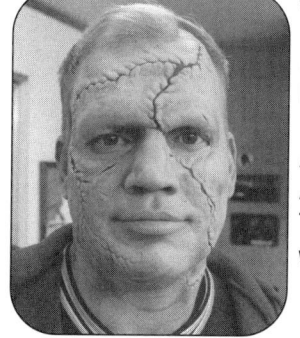

After Buffy slays a newly minted vampire in the graveyard, she and Angel find that a body has been dug up and removed from its grave. The body belonged to a student from another school—a girl who was killed in a car crash with two fellow cheerleaders. The gang digs up one of the other graves to find that body missing as well. Meanwhile, Angel, while looking for Buffy, sees Cordelia in the parking lot, and they both stumble across body parts that turn out to belong to the three dead girls—but not enough parts for three *whole* girls. And all three heads are present.

> Cordelia's science-fair project, "The Tomato: Fruit or Vegetable?" is completed by Willow in three words. "It's a fruit."

It turns out that Chris Epps—the Science Club's prize student—and his friend Eric are trying to pull a Victor Frankenstein and create life from lifelessness. A disgusted Buffy tries to stop them and soon learns that the Frankenstein analogy is closer to the mark than she thought: Chris had already brought his football-jock brother Daryl back from the dead, albeit in a hideous form, and has now promised to give him a companion. But they need a freshly killed head to complete the body, and so they're going after Cordelia....

### Quote of the week:

**"I'm an old-fashioned gal. I was raised to believe that men dig up the corpses and women have the babies."**

Buffy, on why she and Willow don't help Xander and Giles dig up a grave

### Love, Slayer style:

Angel and Buffy argue in the teaser, with Buffy accusing Angel of being jealous of Xander—which Angel finally admits at the episode's end. Giles is found working on a pickup line for Jenny in the library, prompting both ribbing and advice from Xander and

Buffy ("She's a technopagan, right? Ask her to bless your laptop"). His attempts to use it later are hesitant and befuddled, prompting Jenny to ask him out instead, to the football game.

The first real seeds of the Cordelia/Xander pairing are sown here, as Xander saves Cordelia from a fire while Buffy is fighting with Daryl. At the end, Xander discusses with Willow how everyone is "paired off" (Buffy with Angel, Giles with Jenny) except them. Interrupted by Cordelia trying to thank him for his bravery, he blows her off, then turns to Willow to ask what they were talking about. "Why we can't get dates," Willow replies dryly.

### POP-CULTURE IQ:

**"Sorry to interrupt, Willow, but it's the Bat-signal."**

Buffy, summoning Willow to the library for Slayer research, referring to the signal used by Commissioner Gordon in DC's *Batman* comics to summon the dark knight

> The episode sees the destruction of the "old science building," the only structure remaining of the original school after the earthquake of 1937.

> **"If you don't mind a little Gene and Roger . . ."**
> Buffy, about to offer Giles criticism, referring to film critics Siskel and Ebert

## CONTINUITY:

Buffy's slow dance with Xander ("When She Was Bad") continues to have ramifications, mostly with a jealous Angel, but also in ribbing from her friends.

# School Hard

**STORY BY** Joss Whedon and David Greenwalt, **TELEPLAY BY** David Greenwalt; **DIRECTED BY** John T. Kretchmer. **GUEST STARS:** Kristine Sutherland as Joyce Summers, Robia LaMorte as Jenny Calendar, Andrew J. Ferchland as the Anointed One, James Marsters as Spike, Alexandra Johnes as Sheila, Gregory Scott Cummins as Big Ugly, Andrew Palmer as Lean Boy, Juliet Landau as Drusilla, and Armin Shimerman as Principal Snyder; with Brian Reddy and Keith Mackechnie.

There are a couple of new vampires in town: Spike and Drusilla. The former is a rebellious sort who goes his own way rather than stick with the traditional vampire rituals; the latter is the love of his life, who is completely insane and very weak. They show up in time for the Festival of St. Vigeous, when vampires' powers are at their height. Before that, though, is a much greater horror for Buffy: Parent-Teacher Night, and she's scared to death of what her teachers (not to mention the misanthropic Principal Snyder) will say to her mother. However, Spike—a.k.a. William the Bloody—decides to jump the gun and attack the school on Parent-Teacher Night, two days prior to St. Vigeous.

Buffy manages to drive them all off, with some help from Angel, Xander, and, at the end, her mother, who clubs Spike with a fire ax. Spike runs off, and is then soundly criticized by the Anointed One and his cronies. Spike replies by throwing the Anointed One in a cage and exposing the boy to sunlight, then going to watch TV with Dru.

### Quote of the week:

"If every vampire who said he was at the Crucifixion was actually there, it would've been like Woodstock."

Spike, debunking the claims of his peers

> Spike's car, in the original script, was intended to be a Cadillac. In reality, it is a Desoto Sportsman, California license-plate number HIA 873.

### Love, Slayer style:

Spike and Dru are the first vampires who are shown to be in love with each other, and Spike is obviously completely devoted to Drusilla.

### CONTINUITY:

Angel reveals that he knows Spike, and Spike refers to Angel as his sire in front of Xander (though Xander doesn't know what that means). Spike makes reference to Prague, which we later learn is where Drusilla was believed killed ("Lie to Me"). The reign of "the Annoying One," as Spike calls him, comes to a sudden end ("Never Kill a Boy on the First Date," etc.). The first hint that Principal Snyder and other authorities in Sunnydale know, at the very least, that *some* kind of weird stuff happens in this town are provided—Snyder and Bob the Sheriff discuss what to tell the media, and decide to say it was gangs on PCP, since telling the truth is considered ludicrous ("I Only Have Eyes for You," "Becoming, Part 2").

### From the original teleplay::

There are several lines cut from the "School Hard" script for length, including Spike insulting Big Ugly ("Would it kill ya, a little mouthwash every couple hundred years?") and Xander talking about planning a good party ("The important thing in punch is the ratio of vodka to schnapps....That was obviously far too sophisticated a joke for this crowd"). Also cut was a humorous exchange between Buffy and Giles (Buffy: "I don't suppose this is something about happy squirrels?" Giles: "Vampires." Buffy: "That was my next guess").

## Inca Mummy Girl

**WRITTEN BY** Matt Kiene and Joe Reinkemeyer; **DIRECTED BY** Ellen Pressman. **GUEST STARS:** Kristine Sutherland as Joyce Summers, Ara Celi as Ampata, Seth Green as Oz, Jason Hall as Devon, Danny Strong as Jonathan; with Samuel Jacobs, Kristen Winnicki, Joey Crawford, Bernard White, Gil Birmingham, and Henrik Rosvall.

Sunnydale's exchange program brings students from all over the world to the school, and Joyce Summers is among the parents who volunteered to house the foreign kids. Buffy is not relishing the thought of sharing her house—nor is Xander when he learns that Ampata Gutierrez from South America is a boy. After a field trip to a local

museum, a young student tries to steal the seal on an Incan princess's mummified remains, and breaks it. This awakens the mummy, allowing her to drain the life, first from her would-be grave robber, then from Ampata, who is waiting for the late Buffy to pick him up at the bus station. Assuming the identity of Ampata, the princess learns about the modern world—and she and Xander fall for each other, to Willow's chagrin. As Xander and "Ampata" share a slow dance at the Bronze, Buffy and Giles realize that the exchange student is an imposter, and that they must find her and put the seal back together.

## Quote of the week:

"Oh, I know this one! 'Slaying entails certain sacrifices, blah blah bliddy blah, I'm so stuffy, give me a scone.'"

Buffy, anticipating one of Giles's lectures

## Love, Slayer style:

Xander finds someone who loves him, only to learn that she must periodically drain the life out of people in order to survive. Willow spends most of the episode moping (not aided by her overhearing a conversation between Xander and Buffy, where the former makes it clear that he sees Willow as his best friend and no more than that), but still suggests to Xander that he invite "Ampata" to the dance. Cordelia is dating Devon, the lead singer of Dingoes Ate My Baby, in this episode.

## POP-CULTURE IQ:

"I am from the country of Leone. It's in Italy, pretending to be Montana."

Xander, explaining why he's dressed like Clint Eastwood in an old Sergio Leone-directed spaghetti western, for the World Culture Dance

## CONTINUITY:

Oz and his band make their first appearance, and Oz notices Willow for the first time at the dance—though, as with "Halloween," his initial attempts to strike up a conversation don't quite work. Xander briefly wonders if "Ampata" is a praying mantis ("Teacher's Pet"). Some disturbing parallels are drawn between the Inca princess's life and that of the Slayer. At the end, Buffy tries to comfort Xander with how she felt when she heard the prophecy that she would die—when Xander points out that she made the sacrifice anyhow, Buffy reminds him that she had a friend (Xander) to bring her back ("Prophecy Girl").

> The Natural History Museum, where the students go on a field trip in this episode, is in real life located at 900 Exposition Boulevard, near the University of Southern California, in Los Angeles.

87

**From the original teleplay:**

The following exchange was cut from this episode's script for length:

**Ampata:** "He [Xander] has a way of making the milk come out of my nose."
**Buffy:** "And that's good?"

> Ara Celi, who plays Ampata, and Nicholas Brendon each wolfed down eight to ten Twinkies for one scene.

## SHOPPING WITH BUFFY

> "I am, of course, having my dress specially made. Off-the-rack gives me hives."
> Cordelia, in "Out of Mind, Out of Sight"

Costume designer Cynthia Bergstrom puts just as much time and effort into Buffy's wardrobe as Buffy would herself. She buys the show's "contemporary clothes" (as opposed to historical costumes) in stores in Los Angeles. Some designers send her things directly, such as Cynthia Rowley and Vivienne Tam.

Here's a list of where she shops in Los Angeles for some of our heroes:

### BUFFY
Fred Siegel • Barney's • American Rag on La Brea • Cynthia Rowley

### WILLOW
Contempo Casuals • Rampage • Macy's • Chenille sweaters from Wuiff Design • Fred Siegel • Barney's

### CORDELIA
Neiman Marcus • Bloomingdale's • Barney's • Tommy Hilfiger on Rodeo Drive

### ANGEL
Cashmere wool duster from Hugo Boss • Traffic in the Beverly Center • Barney's • Macy's

**WRITTEN AND DIRECTED** by David Greenwalt. **GUEST STARS:** Greg Vaughn as Richard Anderson, Todd Babcock as Tom Warner, Jordana Spiro as Callie Megan Anderson, Robin Atkin Downes as Machida, Danny Strong as Jonathan; with Coby Bell, Christopher Dahlberg, and Jason Posey.

In a period of relative inactivity for the Slayer, Buffy is feeling especially put upon by the demands of her duties. She also feels that her relationship with Angel is going nowhere fast. So when an older boy named Tom presents an opportunity to go to a fraternity party at the local college to Cordelia, she decides to take it.

Unfortunately, the frat worships a demon known as Machida and once a year has to sacrifice three teenage girls to it. Cordelia and Buffy turn out to be the second and third (along with a girl who has gone missing from another school). They are drugged and chained to a wall—leaving it up to Giles, Willow, Angel, and Xander to learn the truth and rescue them.

### Quote of the week:

"This isn't some fairy tale: When I kiss you, you don't wake up from a deep sleep and live happily ever after."

Angel to Buffy in the graveyard. Her reply:

"When you kiss me, I want to die."

### Love, Slayer style:

Buffy has been dreaming about Angel, and they argue in the graveyard over whether they can have a relationship. Cordelia also puts several moves on Angel, all the while trying to make an impression on college-boy Richard (she seems to have thrown over Devon, though she's sort of back with him in "Halloween"). Xander, meanwhile, is a teeming mass of jealousy regarding both Angel and Tom, and sneaks off to keep an eye on Buffy at the party.

> The frat party is the first, and thus far only, time we have seen Buffy and Cordelia drink alcohol. (Xander was the first of the group to drink alcohol, in "Teacher's Pet.")

### POP-CULTURE IQ:

"You could go on to live among rich and powerful men— in the Bizarro World."

Cordelia, dissing Xander, referring to the world in DC's *Superman* comics where everything is the reverse of what it is in our world

> "I, for one, am giddy and up. There's a kind of hush all over Sunnydale."

"A Kind of Hush" was originally a Herman's Hermits song, although the Carpenters did cover it.

> Sarah Michelle Gellar, Alyson Hannigan, and Charisma Carpenter all wear the same shoe size.

### CONTINUITY:

Angel and Buffy at the end agree to go out for coffee, a date-like event which they attempt to follow through on in "Halloween."

# Halloween

**WRITTEN BY** Carl Ellsworth; **DIRECTED BY** Bruce Seth Green. **GUEST STARS:** Seth Green as Oz, James Marsters as Spike, Robin Sachs as Ethan Rayne, Juliet Landau as Drusilla, Armin Shimerman as Principal Snyder, Larry Bagby III as Larry; with Abigail Gershman.

It's Halloween at the Hellmouth—a slow time for vampires, but not for mischievous mystics. Ethan's Costume Shop is the newest store in town, and many buy their costumes from there—including Buffy, who wants to dress up like the noble women Angel would have known two centuries earlier, based on drawings she and Willow see in a purloined Watcher diary.

However, the shop owner, Ethan Rayne, has other things in mind. Invoking the Roman god Janus, he casts a spell that turns everyone who purchased a costume at his store into the persona their costume represents. Xander becomes an army grunt (with real machine gun), Willow becomes a ghost (the generic nature of her costume meaning she, at least, keeps her personality, but is physically completely insubstantial), Buffy becomes an actual eighteenth-century maiden, and several little kids become demons. Spike sees the resulting chaos—and the fact that the Slayer is now useless in that particular role—and decides to party.

Cordelia's lack of transformation reveals that only people who got their costumes at Ethan's were changed (Cordy obtained her cat costume elsewhere). A trip there finds Giles confronted with old friend Ethan—and the ostensibly stuffy and befuddled librarian proceeds to literally beat the method of reversing the spell out of the costumer, just in time to save Buffy from the business end of Spike's teeth.

### Quote of the week:

> "This is...neat!"

Spike, on the chaos that results from Ethan's spell

> Originally, Buffy's house was shot on location, but the production later re-created its interiors on a soundstage.

### Love, Slayer style:

Angel and Buffy's semi-date (planned in "Reptile Boy") is ruined by Buffy's lateness thanks to actual vampire slaying. Cordelia takes this opportunity to make a move on Angel, also later telling Oz that she's no longer interested in Devon. However, by the end, Angel and Buffy are actually necking in her bedroom, establishing the pair of them as a true couple at last.

In the denouement, Xander and Cordelia have a brief moment of bonding over Angel and Buffy, as Xander tells Cordy that there's no chance of getting between the two of them, as he knows from bitter personal experience.

As part of her distracting of Giles to allow Willow to swipe an old Watcher Diary, Buffy blurts out, "Ms. Calendar said that you were a babe!" This notion intrigues Giles, to say the least. ("A babe. I could live with that.")

> Alyson Hannigan had makeup wiz Todd McIntosh do her up as a vampire for a Halloween party in 1997.

### POP-CULTURE IQ:

**"She couldn't have dressed up like Xena?"**
Willow's plaintive cry after Buffy's shrinking-violet behavior goes into overdrive, referring to the tough title character of the TV series *Xena: Warrior Princess*

### BUFFY'S BAG OF TRICKS:

She uses a pumpkin-patch sign to stake a vampire, a bit of ingenuity noted by Spike, who had the fight videotaped by one of his cronies.

### CONTINUITY:

The first hints of Giles's dark past are dropped here, to be picked up on in "The Dark Age." Cordelia is told that Angel is a vampire, but she doesn't believe it. (It is never revealed when Cordy learns the truth, though her lack of reaction when the vampiric demon inside Angel defeats Eyghon in "The Dark Age" indicates she found out some time prior to that.) Oz and Willow continue to fly by each other, first bumping into each other while Willow's in her ghost suit, then Oz passing her in the street later on, again wondering who that girl is.

> According to set decorator David Koneff, "We would have found out a lot more about Oz if you had seen the inside of the van. It was just like a little sugar shack, a love shack, with black light and a mirror ball, black-light posters on the ceilings and a bean-bag chair, and the whole van was carpeted and wild."

# Lie to Me

**WRITTEN AND DIRECTED BY** Joss Whedon. **GUEST STARS:** Robia LaMorte as Jenny Calendar, James Marsters as Spike, Jason Behr as Billy Fordham, Jarrad Paul as "Diego," and Juliet Landau as Drusilla; with Julie Lee and Will Rothhaar.

After observing Angel talking to a strange, attractive woman, Buffy starts moping—right until the arrival of Billy Fordham, "Ford" to his friends. Buffy's former crush and best friend for many years back at her old high school, Ford says he's transferred to Sunnydale High. In due course, Ford reveals that he knows that Buffy is the Slayer. A suspicious Angel has Willow check up on him, and they discover that he hasn't actually transferred and that he's part of a club that worships vampires and wishes to become like them. Ford's plan is to give Spike the Slayer in exchange for becoming a vampire—a preferred alternative to dying of a brain tumor, which is his expected fate. Buffy, however, manages to turn the tables on him and prevent the club members from being massacred by Spike and Dru.

The entire episode continues to turn on the theme of lies, and the title becomes particularly valid in the poignant conversation at the episode's end between Buffy and Giles, as she asks him to lie to her, to tell her that everything will be all right.

### Quote of the week:

"Things used to be pretty simple. A hundred years, just hanging out, feeling guilty. I really honed my brooding skills. Then *she* comes along."

Angel, describing to Willow how Buffy has changed his life

### Love, Slayer style:

Buffy is jealous when she sees Angel with Drusilla and latches onto Ford as soon as he arrives, even hanging around with him to the exclusion of Angel at the Bronze. Later, though, she finally comes out and admits that she loves Angel.

Jenny and Giles go on their second date, which Jenny keeps a surprise; it turns out to be a monster truck rally.

### POP-CULTURE IQ:

"It was terrible. I moped over you [Ford] for months. Sitting in my room listening to that Divinyls song, 'I Touch Myself.' [suddenly sheepish] Of course, I had no idea what it was about."

Buffy, getting herself into hot water

### CONTINUITY:

Spike has one of his vampires steal the du Lac manuscript from the library (later used in "What's My Line?"). Buffy learns of Drusilla's existence; Giles had believed her killed in Prague ("School Hard"). Willow points out to Angel that he's acted jealous in the past ("Some Assembly Required"). Willow has also upgraded from a desktop to a laptop since "I Robot, You Jane" ("Passion"). Angel details how he tortured Drusilla and made her insane before he finally changed her into a vampire ("Becoming, Part 1").

### From the original teleplay:

The following line of Angel's was cut from this episode for length:

> "Yeah, I eat too. Not for nutritional value—
> it just kind of passes the time."

---

## DISSING THE BRITS

In the world of *Buffy*, there are many references to England and things English. Which makes sense: Joss Whedon lived in England, attending Winchester "public" boarding school for boys. Set designer Caroline Quinn is British, as is the show's producer, Gareth Davies. Anthony Stewart Head is English (although James Marsters and Juliet Landau, who play Spike and Dru, are not). Here are few bits from the scripts, which deal with lampooning the "matter of Britain"—all in good fun, of course.

> **"You could have just gone, 'Shhh.'
> Are all you Brits such drama queens?"**
> Xander, to Giles, in "Surprise"

> **"You know, raiding an Englishman's fridge is like dating a nun.
> You're never gonna get the good stuff."**
> Whistler, to Buffy, in "Becoming, Part 2"

In "Teacher's Pet," the following exchange took place:

**Giles** (gazing at the sky with loathing): "God, every day here is the same."
**Buffy:** "Bright, sunny, beautiful. How ever can we escape this torment?"

But the script provided for another version, if the typically sunny Southern California skies were overcast on the day the scene was to be shot.

**Giles** (gazing at the sky): "Reminds me of home."
**Buffy:** "Dark, dank, dreary. You must be so happy."

Here's another bit of dialogue from the original script that pokes fun at the Brits:
**Buffy:** "Do they know about 'fun' in England?"
**Giles:** "Yes, but it's considered very poor taste to have any." —"LIE TO ME"

And some bits that stayed in the episodes:

> "Oh, I know this one. 'Slaying entails certain sacrifices, blah blah blah-bity blah, I'm so stuffy give me a scone.'"
>
> Buffy, to Giles, in "Inca Mummy Girl"

> "You also might want to avoid words like 'amenable' and 'indecorous.' Speak English, not whatever they speak in…"
>
> Buffy, also to the long-suffering Giles, who replies, "England?" in "Some Assembly Required"

## The Dark Age

**WRITTEN BY** Dean Batali and Rob Des Hotel; **DIRECTED BY** Bruce Seth Green. **GUEST STARS:** Robia LaMorte as Jenny Calendar, Robin Sachs as Ethan Rayne, Stuart McLean as Philip Henry; with Wendy Way, Michael Earl Reid, Carlease Burke, Tony Sears, Chris O'Hara, and John Bellucci.

*Anthony Stewart Head visited an American high school library to prepare for his role as Rupert Giles.*

A British gentleman comes to Sunnydale looking for Rupert Giles, but is killed by a dessicated creature he calls Dierdre. After the murder, the creature dissolves into blue goo. Giles later identifies the body as Philip Henry, and denies knowing what the tattoo on Philip's right arm is—though Giles has the same tattoo in the same spot on his left arm. Later, Philip awakens and leaves the morgue, obviously possessed by whatever had taken over Dierdre.

Buffy knows something is wrong when Giles misses a planned meeting, instead choosing to remain home and drink a lot. When Buffy finds Ethan Rayne lurking in the stacks, he informs her that it involves something called the Mouth of Eyghon. Giles tries to

keep Buffy out of it, but when the demon moves from Philip to Jenny, Giles realizes he needs Buffy's help. He explains that he and five friends summoned Eyghon; the demon then killed one of them. Now the demon's back. It is Willow who comes up with a solution—get the demon to move from Jenny to Angel, who already has a demon inhabiting his body, and one that is much older and stronger.

### Quote of the week:

"Do you want me to answer that, or shall I just glare?"

Giles's dry response to Buffy's asking if she's ever let him down

### Love, Slayer style:

Giles and Jenny share their first kiss after she returns a book he lent her and the planning of a weekend excursion. Said plans are derailed by the return of Eyghon, and Eyghon's possession of Jenny puts something of a damper on their passion. At the end, Jenny makes it clear that she needs some distance from Giles.

### POP-CULTURE IQ:

"I'm not running around, wind in my hair, 'the hills are alive with the sound of music' fine, but I'm coping."

Jenny, after her possession by Eyghon, referring to the famous film

"I'm in a little restaurant [...in Florence, Italy], having ziti, and there're no more tables so they have to seat this guy with me, and it's John Cusack."

Willow, in "Anywhere But Here"

### CONTINUITY:

The hints of Giles's past dropped in "Halloween" are expanded on here.

## What's My Line? PART 1

**WRITTEN BY** Howard Gordon and Marti Noxon; **DIRECTED BY** David Solomon. **GUEST STARS:** Seth Green as Oz, James Marsters as Spike, Eric Saiet as Dalton, Kelly Connell as Mr. Pfister, Bianca Lawson as Kendra, Saverio Guerra as Willy, Juliet Landau as Drusilla, and Armin Shimerman as Principal Snyder; with Michael Rothhaar and P.B. Hutton.

The hold of the plane in which Kendra arrives was constructed on the set and later turned upside down and redesigned as a sewer tunnel.

It's Career Week at Sunnydale High School, which just drives home to Buffy that she can't possibly have a normal life. She proceeds to mope for some time, leading Angel to invite her to a skating rink. It cheers her up—right until she is attacked by a huge biker-dude type who is wearing a ring that identifies him as part of the Order of Taraka, a group of supernatural assassins. Three have been sent after Buffy by Spike, who doesn't want any distractions from curing Drusilla. The method for doing so is in the du Lac manuscript that had been stolen from the Sunnydale High library, which Spike eventually translates. Angel's attempt to find out what is going on is interrupted by a woman who attacks him and locks him in a cage until sunup. The same woman then attacks Buffy, who has taken refuge from the assassins in Angel's empty apartment, and identifies herself as "Kendra, the Vampire Slayer."

> The ice rink where Angel and Buffy skate in this episode is, in real life, a place called Iceland, which is located at 8041 Jackson Street, in Paramount, California, about twenty-five miles from the actual set of the show.

### Quote of the week:

"It's a statisstical impossibility for a sixteen-year-old to unplug a telephone."
—Xander

### Love, Slayer style:

Angel is waiting in Buffy's bedroom when she returns from slaying, saying he's worried; she tells him, "You're the one freaky thing in my freaky world that still makes sense to me." They also neck at the skating rink (observed by Kendra, leading to the new Slayer attacking the old one at the episode's climax).

### POP-CULTURE IQ:

"You wanna be a member of the Scooby Gang, you gotta be willing to be inconvenienced now and then."

Xander, to Cordelia, referring to the crime-busting kids who hung around with that famous cartoon Great Dane, Scooby-Doo

### CONTINUITY:

The truth of the du Lac manuscript stolen from Giles in "Lie to Me" is revealed. Oz and Willow finally meet ("Inca Mummy Girl," "Halloween"), as both are chosen as recruiting fodder for a computer-software megacorporation in Seattle (never identified by name) during Career Week. Willow's fear of frogs is first mentioned ("Killed by Death").

**What's My Line? PART 2**

**WRITTEN BY** Marti Noxon; **DIRECTED BY** David Semel.
**GUEST STARS:** Seth Green as Oz, James Marsters as Spike, Saverio Guerra as Willy, Bianca Lawson as Kendra, Kelly Connell as Mr. Pfister, and Juliet Landau as Drusilla; with Danny Strong.

Kendra and Buffy call a truce and realize that the former truly is a Slayer. When one Slayer dies, another is activated, and Buffy did die, however briefly. To Buffy's chagrin, Kendra seems more dedicated, more studious, and seems to get along better with Giles—but she also has had no life to speak of, and is long on duty but short on passion.

Meanwhile, Angel has been rescued from his cage by the slimy bartender, Willy, who hands him over to Spike. The two other Tarakan assassins attack, one going after Xander and Cordelia at Buffy's house, the other shooting at Buffy in school.

As the Slayerettes figure out for themselves, the ritual to restore Drusilla to full health requires the presence of her sire—Angel. Brutal questioning of Willy by the two Slayers reveals the location of the church where the ceremony will be performed, and they attack. Buffy manages to end the ceremony before Angel is drained of all life, then literally drops a church organ on Spike's head while the church burns around them. With the bad guys defeated and Angel saved, Kendra heads back home. But Drusilla has survived the church burning and rescued Spike—and she's stronger than ever....

### Quote of the week:

"'Cause I've had it. Spike is going down. You can attack me, you can send assassins after me, that's fine. But *nobody* messes with my boyfriend."

Buffy, getting her dander up

### Love, Slayer style:

While trapped in Buffy's basement by one of the assassins, Xander and Cordelia get into a knockdown, drag-out argument that culminates in a kiss, followed by a heartfelt, "We *so* need to get out of here." An attempt to redistance themselves at the climax fails miserably, and they wind up in each other's arms again, following yet another nasty argument, thus setting the tone for their relationship.

Oz and Willow make the first steps toward their eventual relationship, as Oz saves Willow's life from one of the assassins, then proceeds to flirt with her while discussing animal crackers.

Buffy tells Kendra to watch the movie on her flight home unless it's a "movie with a dog in it and Chevy Chase." This is a reference to *Funny Farm*, a 1988 movie starring Chase that Gellar had a small, uncredited role in.

### POP-CULTURE IQ:

**"Back off, Pink Ranger!"**

Buffy, admonishing Kendra to not go off half-cocked, referring to one of the title characters in *Mighty Morphin Power Rangers*

> "It's a little more complicated than that, John Wayne."
>
> Buffy, once again admonishing Kendra, referring to the legendary movie hero

### CONTINUITY:

Kendra's activation as the Slayer apparently happened after Buffy died in "Prophecy Girl." Drusilla tortures Angel prior to the ceremony, reminding him of what he did to her ("Lie to Me," "Becoming, Part 1"). When Xander reveals that he and Cordelia encountered an assassin that is literally made of maggots, Buffy asks, "You and bug people, Xander—what's up with that?" ("Teacher's Pet"). Spike and Drusilla have their roles reversed at the end of the episode, as Spike is badly injured and Drusilla is at full strength.

> The "Pink Ranger" line has additional significance beyond being a standard Buffy pop-culture reference: Sarah Michelle Gellar's stunt double, Sophia Crawford, used to play the Pink Ranger on *Mighty Morphin Power Rangers*.

### From the original teleplay:

The following exchange was cut from the opening of this episode's script for length:

**Kendra:** "Your English is very odd, you know."
**Buffy:** "Yeah—it's something about being woken by an ax. Makes me talk all crazy."

> Willow wears a backpack that has a little lion poking its head out from under a rainbow.

## MOST OF THE RIGHT MOVES

Xander, the man, the myth, the dance machine. Xander does a lot of dancing, but where has it gotten him?
Aerobicizing at the Bronze:
**Cordelia:** "Ouch! Please keep your extreme oafishness off my $200 shoes."
**Xander:** "Sorry, I was just—"
**Cordelia:** "Getting off the floor before Annie Vega's boyfriend squashes you like a bug?"
—**"Angel"**

Then there was this scene from "Reptile Boy," which was expanded during filming. Although the shooting script called for a dark-haired wig, Xander actually wore a blond one. And he wore the bra over his bare chest:

A hideous wig of long, dark curls parked on [Xander's] head; an extremely large bra strapped over his shirt; a painful smile plastered on his face. Some of the guys swat him with paddles.
**Linebacker:** "Come on, dance, pretty boy! Come on, shake it! Don't break it!"
**Xander:** "Okay, big fun. Who's next?"
**Tackle:** "You are, doll face. Keep on dancing."
—**"Reptile Boy"**

**Xander:** "Aw, you just need cheering up. And I know just the thing [a few wild moves]. Crazed dance party at the Bronze!"
**Buffy:** "I don't know."
**Xander:** [restrained moves] "Very calm dance party at the Bronze." [no moves] "Moping at the Bronze."
—**"Lie to Me"**

**Xander:** "Having issues much?"
**Buffy:** "I am not!"
Xander points, with a mock-childish dance.
**Xander:** "You're having parental issues, you're having parental issues."
**Willow:** "Xander..."
**Xander:** "Freud would have said the exact same thing. Except he might not have done that little dance."
—**"Ted"**

**Willow:** [nailing crosses around her French doors], "I'm going to have a hard time explaining this to my dad."
**Buffy:** "You really think this'll bother him?"
**Willow:** "Ira Rosenberg's only daughter nailing crucifixes to her bedroom wall? I have to go to Xander's house just to watch *A Charlie Brown Christmas* every year."
**Buffy:** "Yeah, I see your point."
**Willow:** "Although it is worthwhile just to see Xander do the Snoopy dance." —**"Passion"**

# Ted

**WRITTEN BY** David Greenwalt and Joss Whedon; **DIRECTED BY** Bruce Seth Green. **SPECIAL GUEST STAR:** John Ritter as Ted Buchanan. **GUEST STARS:** Kristine Sutherland as Joyce Summers, Robia LaMorte as Jenny Calendar; with Ken Thorley, James G. MacDonald, and Jeff Langton.

Buffy comes home to find her mother kissing a strange man. He is introduced as Ted, and he and Joyce have been seeing each other for some time. Buffy is leery of this new man in her mother's life. Xander and Willow disagree—sure, he talks like a '50s sitcom character, but he's a magnificent cook, and her mother seems happy. But Buffy is not convinced, especially after he threatens her during a miniature golf game when the pair of them are out of sight of the others.

When Buffy returns from a night of slaying, she finds Ted in her bedroom, having gone through her diary. She is justifiably angry at the invasion of her privacy, but her attempts to complain result in his striking her. That gives her the excuse she needs to wallop him—so much so that he falls down the stairs, dead. The police question her, and let her go for the time being.

Buffy is devastated at this abuse of her powers as the Slayer. But then, while Xander, Willow, and Cordelia dig deeper into Ted's life—finding drugs in his cookies, marriages dating to 1957, and odd things in his closet—Ted himself turns up alive at the Summers' house. He turns out to be a robot, and what's in his closet are his four previous wives....

## Quote of the week:

"Buffy, I believe the subtext here is rapidly becoming text."
Giles, trying to find out what is irking Buffy

## Love, Slayer style:

Giles makes an attempt to reconcile with Jenny, which she initially rebuffs. Later, when Giles is doing Buffy's rounds in her place following Ted's apparent death, Jenny attempts a reconciliation and proves that love means never having to say, "I'm sorry I shot you with a crossbow bolt." Cordelia and Xander's tryst continues in secret (Xander later says pointedly, "I sometimes like things that are not good for me"), and Angel and Buffy indulge in smoochies while she helps him recover from his injuries.

> In the final fight scene between Buffy and Ted, both Sarah Michelle Gellar and special guest star John Ritter were sick. Sarah had the flu, and John had food poisoning from the night before.

> John Ritter had once worked with Joss Whedon's father, Tom, also a writer, and John's son had appeared in a play written by Joss's brother, Zack.

## POP-CULTURE IQ:

In the teaser, Xander and Willow argue about the Captain &Tenille. At the episode's end, the Summers women want to rent a movie that has no horror and no romance, prompting Buffy to say, "I guess we're *Thelma & Louise*-ing it again."

## CONTINUITY:

> At the end of the Captain & Tennille conversation in the teaser, there was one last line that didn't make it into the episode. Willow says, "I'm just saying that if Tennille were in charge, she would have had the little captain hat."

Cordelia mentions Giles's summoning of Eyghon after Giles talks about how hard it must be to be responsible for another's death ("Do let's bring that up as often as possible," Giles says tartly in response), and Eyghon's possession of Jenny continues to haunt both her and her relationship with Giles ("The Dark Age"). Angel is still recovering from Drusilla's revival ceremony ("What's My Line? Part 2").

**WRITTEN BY** Marti Noxon; **DIRECTED BY** David Greenwalt. **GUEST STARS:** Kristine Sutherland as Joyce Summers, Jeremy Ratchford as Lyle Gorch, James Parks as Tector Gorch, Danny Strong as Jonathan; with Rick Zieff, Eric Whitmore, and Brie McCaddin.

## Bad Eggs

The Gorch brothers—who were a couple of lunatic hellraisers in the Wild West *before* they were turned into vampires—have arrived in Sunnydale. Buffy is busy helping Giles research them, and so misses health class, wherein the students are broken into pairs and given the responsibility of eggs to care for as if they were children. Buffy, having been absent, gets to be a single mother to "Eggbert."

However, these are not ordinary eggs, but the offspring of a bezoar that lives under the school and has now come to life. The offspring bond to human hosts, and several students and adults—including Willow, Cordelia, Giles, and Joyce—become drones for the bezoar. Only Buffy—who slays the offspring before it can bond with her—and Xander—who hard-boiled his "child"—escape unharmed. Of course, Buffy's attempts to stop the bezoar are hindered by the Gorch brothers deciding to attack.

> The shopping sequences were shot at the Sherman Oaks Galleria.

### Quote of the week:

"They're such a—oh, I don't want to say burden, but, uh...Actually, I kind of do want to say burden."
— Joyce Summers, on children and parenting

### Love, Slayer style:

Xander and Cordelia continue their tryst, complete with constant arguing, both in private and in public, the latter particularly in health class. (Xander: "This would work a lot better for me if you didn't talk." Cordy: "Well, it would work a lot better for me with the lights off.")

Angel and Buffy can't keep their hands off each other when they're supposed to be patrolling. When discussing possibilities of the future, Buffy says, "Angel, when I look into the future, all I see is you—all I want is you," which is fairly tragic in retrospect.

### BUFFY'S BAG OF TRICKS:

She uses one of the pickaxs the drones are using to slay the monster.

## Surprise

**WRITTEN BY** Marti Noxon; **DIRECTED BY** Michael Lange. **GUEST STARS:** Seth Green as Oz, Kristine Sutherland as Joyce Summers, Robia LaMorte as Jenny Calendar, Brian Thompson as the Judge, Eric Saiet as Dalton, Mercedes McNab as Harmony; special guest stars Vincent Schiavelli as Uncle Enyos, James Marsters as Spike, Juliet Landau as Drusilla.

On the morning before her seventeenth birthday, Buffy has a dream that Drusilla is still alive and that she will kill Angel. This worries Buffy and the Slayerettes, but does not deter the latter from planning a surprise party for Buffy at the Bronze the following night. Meanwhile, a wheelchair-bound Spike and a restored Drusilla are planning to reconstruct the Judge, a creature whose purpose is to literally burn the humanity out of humankind, leaving only the evil to survive.

Though it cannot be killed "by any weapon forged," it was once dismembered, the parts spread to the four corners of the Earth—but now being brought to Sunnydale. Buffy intercepts the delivery of an arm, and Jenny and Angel agree that Angel should take it somewhere far away—a journey that would take months.

Buffy is reluctant to part with Angel, but as they kiss and say good-bye at the docks, vampires attack and retake the arm. Angel and Buffy brave the Factory to try and stop them, but the Judge is already assembled, and the pair barely escape with their lives. They return to Angel's apartment and find refuge in each others' arms, making love for the first time. But afterward, Angel feels strange....

### Quote of the week:

**"My boyfriend had a bicentennial."**
—Buffy to Willow, re: Angel

### Love, Slayer style:

Angel finally comes out and says he loves Buffy, though his feelings have been obvious since "Teacher's Pet." Before his planned departure, he gives Buffy a claddagh ring, which is as close to a wedding as these two are ever likely to get. After their abortive attack on Spike, Drusilla, and the Judge, they finally give in to their passion—with, as shown in "Innocence," devastating consequences. Buffy convinces Willow to take a shot at dating Oz. The pair agree to go on a date in an adorable and hilarious scene. Xander makes an attempt to convince Cordelia to make their relationship public, but Cordy will hear none of it. And Spike and Drusilla are as devoted to each other as ever—indeed, the Judge smells the "stink of humanity" on them thanks to their affection for each other.

### CONTINUITY:

> The tent-like building where all the Buffy sets are constructed is called "the El Niño building."

Jenny Calendar is revealed to be Janna of the same Romany tribe that cursed Angel eighty years previous ("Angel," "Becoming, Part 1"), and she is warned by her uncle that Angel is becoming too happy. Buffy once again has prophetic dreams ("Welcome to the Hellmouth," "Prophecy Girl," "Innocence"). Oz finds out the truth about vampires and joins the ever-expanding Slayerettes.

### From the original teleplay:

The following scene was cut from this episode's script for length:

**Jenny:** "I guess it makes sense. I mean, all of Buffy's senses are heightened. Why should her intuition be different?"

**Giles:** "Precisely. It's not unheard-of for the Slayer to start having prophetic dreams and visions as she approaches adulthood."

**Jenny:** "Adulthood? Buffy's seventeen tomorrow, Giles. Don't rush her."

**Giles:** "I'm not the one rushing her. While I'm loathe to say it, the fact is, the Slayer rarely lives into her mid-twenties. It follows that she'd exhibit signs of maturity early on. Her whole life cycle is accelerated."

**Jenny:** "Still, you should be careful about treating her like a grown-up. Like—this thing with Angel. Have you even talked to her about it?"

**Giles:** "I . . . I suppose I try not to pry."

**Jenny:** "Maybe you should, a little. The way she talks, it's clear she has intense feelings for him."

**Giles:** "Well, yes. They're friends. . . ."

**Jenny:** "They're more than friends, and you know it."

**Giles:** "I'm not her father, Jenny."

**Jenny:** "She looks up to you. She'll never actually say that, but she does. And I just think, at her age, it's easy to get in over your head. She could make some bad choices here. Trust me on this one."

**Giles:** "I'll keep an eye to it. Right now, I'm worried enough trying to think of the right birthday present."

> Spike's duster cost more than Angel's, a whopping $1,600. It was heavily "distressed" by the costume department.

> The docks sequence was filmed in San Pedro. The water was not as cold as anticipated, because of a warm, El Niño current.

## Innocence

**WRITTEN AND DIRECTED BY** Joss Whedon. **GUEST STARS:** Seth Green as Oz, Kristine Sutherland as Joyce Summers, Robia LaMorte as Jenny Calendar, Brian Thompson as the Judge; special guest stars Vincent Schiavelli as Uncle Enyos, James Marsters as Spike, Juliet Landau as Drusilla; with James Lurie, Carla Madden, Parry Shen, and Ryan Francis.

Angel's soul is again lost, and he has reverted to the same old vampire he was prior to the Romany curse. Spike and Drusilla are thrilled to find their sire back in the saddle, and invite him to join them in destroying the world with the Judge. Buffy, meanwhile, knows only that Angel has disappeared, and the Slayerettes are no closer to finding out anything useful about how to stop the Judge.

When Buffy finally finds Angel, he is standoffish and dismissive of her feelings. Then he attacks Willow at the school, though Xander and Buffy manage to drive him off. Jenny, under pressure from Buffy, reveals that she knew about the curse, that it was removed, and that she had been sent to Sunnydale to keep an eye on Angel. She takes Buffy to her uncle, but Angel has gotten there first and killed him. Xander, meanwhile,

comes up with a plan: to use a missile launcher, a weapon that is made, not forged, against the Judge. It works, but Buffy finds it impossible to kill Angel when she confronts him.

### Quote of the week:

"My God! You people are all— Well, I'm upset, and I can't think of a mean word right now, but that's what you are, and we're going to the Factory!"

Willow, insisting, along with Xander, that they go after Angel and Buffy, who have not checked in since their attack on the Factory

### Love, Slayer style:

Angel and Buffy obviously are on the outs; indeed, Angel is disgusted with the way he acted around the Slayer, and is determined to hurt her in much the same way he hurt Drusilla before he turned her into a vampire. His initial foray is a textbook example of the Insensitive Male After Sex, culminating with, "I'll call you." He also starts his campaign to come between Spike and Drusilla ("Bewitched, Bothered, and Bewildered," etc.).

Xander and Cordelia are caught kissing by a devastated Willow. ("It's against all laws of God and man!") Xander's attempt to explain that it doesn't mean anything fall on deaf ears, as Willow realizes that, "You'd rather be with someone you hate than be with me." Later, Willow asks Oz if he wants to make out with her, which he politely declines, knowing that she's only doing it to get back at Xander; the maturity of this response charms Willow.

The Giles and Jenny coupling comes to a screeching halt with the revelation of Jenny's true reason for being in Sunnydale.

> Often the scripts will contain some wry humor even in the stage directions. In the script for this episode, Joss Whedon wrote, "A couple of soldiers pass. Xander suavely nods to them. They nod back and pass without comment, because they are extras."

### CONTINUITY:

Buffy continues to have prophetic dreams ("Welcome to the Hellmouth," "Prophecy Girl," "Surprise"). Xander's memories of his transformation into a soldier remain intact ("Halloween") and allow him and Cordelia to successfully break into an armory and make off with the missile launcher, and also allow Xander to instruct Buffy in its use.

### From the original teleplay:

The following exchange was cut from this episode's script for length:

**Gypsy Man:** "You! Evil one!"
**Angel:** "Evil one? Oh, man, now I've got hurt feelings."
**Gypsy Man:** "What do you want?"

**Angel:** "A whole lot. Got a lot of lost time to make up for. Say, I guess that's kind of your fault, isn't it? You Gypsy types, you go and curse people, you really don't care who gets hurt. Of course, you did give me an escape clause, so I gotta thank you for that."

**Gypsy Man:** "You are an abomination. The day you stop suffering for your crimes, you are no longer worthy of a human soul."

**Angel:** "Well, that pesky little critter's all gone. So we can get down to business....Don't worry, it won't hurt a bit...after the first hour."

> The multiplex/mall set was in a closed Robinsons/May department store on South Grand Avenue in Los Angeles. A moat was built around the set to catch the water from the overhead sprinklers.

> Another Whedon stage direction, regarding Xander and Cordelia kissing: "They haben der big smootchen."

## WILD KINGDOM

**Angel:** "I'm just an animal, right?"
**Buffy:** "You're not an animal. Animals I like."
—"ANGEL"

Animals are important to the denizens of Sunnydale, on and off the set. David Boreanaz has a dog named Bertha Blue, who has "one ear that goes up and one ear that goes down." Sometimes he brings her to his trailer, but she's run away a number of times. Still, they've always found each other again.

Nicholas Brendon rescued his dog from the streets, where a kid was feeding him bubble gum. David B. says, "Nick's a dog freak." In their spare time, David and Nicholas hang out together and sometimes take their dogs to the dog park together.

Alyson Hannigan keeps Alex, a Jack Russell terrier, in her trailer. When she walks him around the lot, she says to producer Gareth Davies, "This is a mythical dog," as animals are not officially allowed. At home, with her roommate, she has another dog, Zippy, and five cats: Dr. Seuss, Jupiter, Tear Drop, Rain, and Lucky.

Costume designer Cynthia Bergstrom has a beautiful Keeshond named Sammy, who spends the occasional day in the wardrobe department.

And Buffy—Sarah Michelle Gellar—also has pets, including a white Maltese named Thor.

As for the animals in *Buffy*, let's have a moment of silence for Sunnydale High's late (crunchy) mascot, Herbert the Pig. And for a dog named Spritzer, whose demise at the hands (and teeth) of demon Jenny Calendar was cut from "The Dark Age." And, finally, for Willow's fish, which Angel kills in "Passion."

> And fish are not all that Angel kills:
>
> **Giles** [reading aloud]: "Ah, here's another. Valentine's Day, yes, Angel nails a puppy to—"
> **Buffy:** "Skip it."
> **Giles:** "But—"
> **Buffy:** "I don't want to know. I don't have a puppy. We can skip it."
> —**"BEWITCHED, BOTHERED, AND BEWILDERED"**
>
> **Willow:** "Thanks for having me over, Buffy. Especially on a school night and all."
> **Buffy:** "Hey, no problem. Sorry about your fish."
> **Willow:** "It's okay, we hadn't really had time to bond yet. I just got them for Hanukkah. Although, for the first time, I'm glad my parents didn't let me have a puppy."
> —**"PASSION"**
>
> On the lighter side and in happier times, Angel seemed to enjoy spending quality time with Buffy's stuffed-animal porker, Mr. Gordo.
>
> And then there's that werewolf deal with the lead guitarist of Dingoes Ate My Baby:
>
> > "You're talking obedience school, paper training. Oz would be burying all their stuff in the backyard. And that kind of breed can turn on its owner."
> > Xander, in "PHASES"

# Phases

**WRITTEN BY** Rob Des Hotel and Dean Batali; **DIRECTED BY** Bruce Seth Green. **GUEST STARS:** Seth Green as Oz, Camila Griggs as the gym teacher, Jack Conley as Cain, Larry Bagby III as Larry, Megahn Perry as Theresa, and Keith Campbell as the werewolf.

Xander and Cordelia are making out in Cordy's car when they are interrupted by the vicious attack of a werewolf. Giles is intrigued by the idea of a werewolf in Sunnydale—"one of the classics"—but intrigue turns to concern as he and Buffy encounter a hunter named Cain who wants to kill the werewolf for its pelt, and then a Sunnydale High student named Theresa is found dead. As the Slayerettes try to figure out who the werewolf might be—Xander's theory that it's Larry, one of the school jocks, turns out to be very erroneous—Willow tries to determine why Oz is acting so weird.

When she goes to his house to confront him, she finds him transforming into a werewolf. Buffy, Giles, and Willow manage to bring the werewolf down and keep Cain from killing their friend.

> The pines outside Buffy's window are deodara pines.

## Quote of the week:

"That's great, Larry, you've really mastered the single entendre."
Oz, after Larry makes a crudely sexual remark about Buffy and Willow

### Love, Slayer style:

Oz and Willow have started dating (the episode begins with them discussing the movie they went to the previous night), but Willow is frustrated that he hasn't made a further move. ("But I want smoochies!") At the end, after Oz's lycanthropy is revealed, they decide to keep the relationship going, and they have their first kiss which Willow initiates.

Buffy is still smarting from Angel's reversion to type. When she learns that Theresa's death was caused not by the werewolf, but by Angel—confirmed when Theresa rises as a vampire and tells her that Angel says hi—Buffy finds comfort in Xander's arms briefly before leaving, causing the latter to mutter, "Oh, no, my life's not *too* complicated." Meanwhile, Xander and Cordelia's relationship continues apace, thus prompting a catty comment from Willow: "What's his number? Oh yeah: 1-800-I'm-dating-a-skanky-ho.'" Despite this, Willow and Cordy find themselves bonding in the Bronze over the inadequacies of the men in their lives.

Giles appears to be having trouble dealing with Jenny's apparent betrayal, as his behavior is slightly off throughout the ordeal—he even laughs at one of Xander's jokes.

### BUFFY'S BAG OF TRICKS:

Not wanting to kill the werewolf, Buffy tries using a chain on it when they first clash at the Bronze. Later on, Giles employs a tranquilizer gun, which Willow actually wields in the end. Xander uses an easel in the funeral home to stake Theresa.

### CONTINUITY:

Oz first discovers that he is a werewolf in this episode. Oz also notices the moving eyes of the cheerleader trophy ("The Witch"). Xander cites his temporary infusion with the spirit of a hyena as evidence that he understands where the werewolf is coming from ("The Pack"; by doing so, he also inadvertently reveals that he does, in fact, remember that entire experience, despite his claims at the end of that episode).

Seth Green and Alyson Hannigan, whose characters officially become boyfriend and girlfriend in this episode, also appeared as boyfriend and girlfriend in the film *My Stepmother Is an Alien*.

Oz seems to have a particular affection for New York City. In his first appearance, he wore a New York Rangers T-shirt. In this episode, his shirt says, "New York City Yoga."

### From the original teleplay:

The following exchange, during a self-defense class, appeared in the original script but not in the episode because of length:

**Xander** (to Cordelia): "Be gentle with me."
**Cordelia** (to Willow): "You first. I wouldn't want to be accused of taking your place in line."
**Willow:** "Oh, I think you pushed your way to the front long before this."
**Cordelia:** "Hey, I can't help it if I get the spotlight just because some people blend into the background."
**Willow:** "Well, maybe some people could see better if you weren't standing on the auction block, shaking your wares."
**Cordelia:** "Sorry, we haven't all perfected that phony 'girl next door' bit."
**Willow:** "You could be the girl next door, too. If Xander lived next to a brothel!"

**WRITTEN BY** Marti Noxon; **DIRECTED BY** James A. Conter.
**GUEST STARS:** Seth Green as Oz, Kristine Sutherland as Joyce Summers, Robia LaMorte as Jenny Calendar, Elizabeth Anne Allen as Amy Madison, Mercedes McNab as Harmony, James Marsters as Spike, Juliet Landau as Drusilla; with Jennie Chester, Lorna Scott, Kristen Winnicki, and Tamara Braun.

## Bewitched, Bothered, and Bewildered

It's Valentine's Day, and all is not well. Giles is concerned for Buffy, given Angel's past history of tormenting people on this particular holiday, and Cordelia has noticed a downsurge in her own popularity since her relationship with Xander went public. As Angel leaves a box of roses for Buffy with a note saying, "Soon," Cordy breaks up with Xander just after he gives her a gorgeous silver locket as a Valentine's Day present. Now the laughingstock of the entire school, a heartbroken Xander turns to Amy—who has decided to take on her mother's calling of witchcraft—for a love spell that would make Cordelia love him and allow *him* to dump *her*, giving her a taste of the humiliation he's enduring. The spell backfires and instead makes every woman in Sunnydale *except* Cordelia fall for Xander. This leads to fierce jealousy and mob rage (Amy at one point transforms Buffy into a rat), as the entire female population of Sunnydale—including Drusilla and Joyce Summers—tries to kill both Xander (for not loving them) and Cordelia (for daring to break his heart). With Giles's help, Amy reverses the spell, and things revert to something resembling normal.

The script called for Buffy to be changed into a rat for a good portion of the episode to free up Sarah Michelle Gellar to spend a week in New York hosting *Saturday Night Live*.

### Quote of the week:

**Buffy:** "Slaying is a tad more perilous than dating."
**Xander:** "Obviously, you're not dating Cordelia."

### Love, Slayer style:

Xander buys an expensive gift for Cordelia, which he gives to her just before she breaks up with him. Xander—who had asked Buffy to pick his clothes for the evening (she picks a wardrobe that looks like it comes straight from Angel's closet)—is devastated, to say the least, especially given that the breakup is on Valentine's Day. ("Were you running low on dramatic irony?") After learning the extent to which she broke Xander's heart, not to mention the realization that dumping Xander to satisfy her shallow friends was simply not worth it, Cordelia gets back together with him. ("I'll date who I want to date—no matter how lame he is.")

Oz and Willow's relationship continues apace (Willow gets to enthuse, "My boyfriend's in the band!" at one point), and when Willow's love-spelled heart is broken by Xander not returning her affections, she spends all night crying on the phone to Oz.

On the vampire side of things, the love triangle among the bad guys thickens: Spike gets Drusilla a piece of jewelry, but Angel gives her a heart—ripped from the chest of a "quaint little shop girl"—which she seems to like better, to Spike's annoyance.

### POP-CULTURE IQ:

In the script, when Oz is searching for the Buffy rat, he's singing Michael Jackson's ode to rats, "Ben."

> Oz's guitar is inscribed with the words "Sweet J."

### CONTINUITY:

Jenny makes two attempts to reconcile with Giles following the events of "Innocence," but the first is cut off by circumstances, and the second by Jenny falling victim to the love spell.

## Passion

**WRITTEN BY** Ty King; **DIRECTED BY** Michael E. Gershman.
**GUEST STARS:** Kristine Sutherland as Joyce Summers, Robia LaMorte as Jenny Calendar, James Marsters as Spike, Juliet Landau as Drusilla; with Richard Assad.

Buffy wakes up to find a charcoal drawing of herself sleeping left on her bed by Angel, and Willow finds her fish dead in an envelope in her bedroom. At their behest, Giles searches for a spell that will uninvite the vampire from the Summers and Rosenberg residences. The spell comes from Jenny, meant as a reconciliation gesture. Angel, meanwhile, plays the stalking ex-boyfriend role on Joyce, complete with mention of the

> Director Michael Gershmann is also the series' director of photography. The first two seasons of *Buffy* were shot on super 16mm film stock.

fact that they made love, which leads to a rather difficult conversation between Joyce and her daughter.

Meanwhile, Jenny is working to try and translate the spell that would return Angel's soul to him. Late one night, she finally does so, saving the file to a disk and printing it out. However, Angel has learned of this project, thanks to a prophetic vision from Drusilla, and destroys Jenny's computer and the printout, and brutally kills Jenny. He then places the body in Giles's bedroom, setting the place up with champagne and flowers, making it all the more devastating when he finds the corpse. The move backfires rather spectacularly, as Giles firebombs the Factory and manages to do some serious damage to Angel before the vampire gets the upper hand. Luckily, Buffy shows up and proceeds to pound Angel, though she is forced to cut it short in order to save Giles from the fire.

### Quote of the week:

"You're supposed to kill her, not leave gag gifts in her friends' beds."
Spike, criticizing Angel's methods

### Love, Slayer style:

Jenny has a few heartfelt conversations with Giles ("I know you feel betrayed." "Yes, well, that's one of the unpleasant side effects of betrayal"), even admitting she loves him. Despite Buffy's anger at Jenny, the Slayer does encourage Jenny to try to reconcile with Giles because he misses her, even if he won't admit it. Her death puts Giles in full "Ripper" mode.

The Angel-Drusilla-Spike triangle gets worse. Dru gets Spike a puppy that she names Sunshine, which makes Spike feel like he needs to be fed like a child, and Angel's jokes about Spike's wheelchair-bound condition grow crueler.

### POP-CULTURE IQ:

"If Giles wants to go after the fiend that killed his girlfriend, I say, 'Faster, pussycat, kill, kill!'"
Xander, on Giles's course of action following Jenny's murder, referring to the title of a Russ Meyer movie

### CONTINUITY:

The Slayerettes cast a spell that uninvites Angel from the Summers house ("Angel"), the Rosenberg house ("Lie to Me"), and Cordelia's car ("Some Assembly Required"). When Buffy warns her mother about Angel possibly coming around, Joyce remembers him as, "the college boy who's tutoring you in history" ("Angel"). Using a computer program, Jenny manages to re-create the spell that originally cursed Angel ("Angel," "Surprise," "Innocence"), but the only copy is on a disk that falls under her desk, where it remains until "Becoming, Part 1." At the end of the episode, Willow becomes the substitute computer-science teacher, a post she winds up retaining for the balance of the school year

("I Only Have Eyes for You," "Go Fish," "Becoming, Part 1"). The Factory, which has been vampire headquarters all season ("When She Was Bad," etc.), is destroyed by Giles, which will lead Angel, Spike, and Drusilla to take up residence in the mansion ("I Only Have Eyes for You").

### From the original teleplay:

During the sequence just after Jenny is killed, we hear Angel in voice-over while we watch through the window of Buffy's home as the phone rings and she and Willow learn of Jenny's death. What follows is the dialogue the viewer can't hear:

**Willow:** "So was it horrible?" (referring to "The Talk" between Buffy and her mom)
**Buffy:** "It wasn't too horrible." [phone rings] "Hello?"
**Giles** (on the phone): "Buffy?"
**Buffy:** "Giles! Hey, we finished the spe—"
**Giles** (on phone): "Jenny... Ms. Calendar...she's been killed."
**Buffy:** "What...?"
**Giles** (on phone): "It was Angel."
Buffy drops the phone.
**Willow:** "Buffy?" [She picks up the phone] "Giles?"
**Giles** (on phone): "Willow. Angel's killed Jenny."
**Willow:** "What? No...oh...no..."
**Joyce:** "Willow! My God, Buffy! What's wrong? Has something happened?"

## IN MY ROOM

Besides a desk drawer filled with stakes and holy water and a trunk with a false bottom loaded with communion wafers, yet more stakes, garlic, and holy water, what does today's Slayer keep in her bedroom?

With a framed picture of Xander and Willow by her bedside, Buffy's room looks very much like that belonging to any other seventeen-year-old girl. Here are some of the objects in the Chosen One's private abode:

- dolls and stuffed animals, including: a big Harlequin witch doll, a cow doll, a pink pig, a blue teddy bear, a black and white panda, and a green creature in a dress
- an umbrella with Chinese characters on it and a small dressing screen with a similar design
- a snow globe
- a straw hat and scarves hanging on the wall
- a black-light lamp

- two lamps with upside-down shades
- a purple and black pyramid candle
- celestial matters: a sun-and-moon art object with a face and a green-and-yellow moon box on the second shelf of her bookcase
- a wicker chair and a wicker shelf
- butterflies

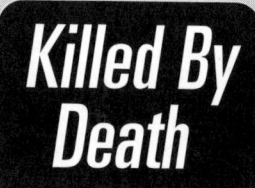

## Killed By Death

**WRITTEN BY** Rob Des Hotel and Dean Batali; **DIRECTED BY** Deran Sarafian. **GUEST STARS:** Kristine Sutherland as Joyce Summers, Richard Herd as Dr. Backer, Willie Garson as Don, Andrew Ducote as Ryan, Juanita Jennings as Dr. Wilkinson; with Denise Johnson as Celia, Mimi Paley as little Buffy, Robert Munic as the E.R. intern, and James Jude Courtney as Der Kindestod.

Buffy is out patrolling, despite suffering from a flu bug. After a run-in with Angel, she collapses and is brought to the hospital. After she is stabilized and admitted, she has a dream about a strange-looking creature and a young boy—except the young boy is really in the kids' ward with a similar flu, and he has also seen the creature. The boy, Ryan, says that the creature is Death, informs her that children have died because of him, and then gives Buffy a drawing of the creature, which only kids can see. Initial research points to a more mundane source of the kids' deaths: Dr. Backer, who has used unorthodox cures in the past. However, Buffy discovers the slashed corpse of Dr. Backer, killed by an invisible creature that attacks Buffy.

Eventually, Giles and Cordelia discover that it's Der Kindestod—German for *child death*, a monster that can be seen only by children and also feeds on them. Buffy realizes that she can see it only when she's feverish and convinces Willow to give her a small dose of the fever to make her sick enough to see it. The question is, will she be too sick to fight it? Of course, the answer is no. She's the Slayer, after all.

> Cordelia brings Xander Krispy Kreme donuts, considered by many to be elite among donuts. There is also only one Krispy Kreme in the Los Angeles area, so there's an implication that Cordelia went quite a ways to get Xander his breakfast.

### Quote of the week:

**"Tact is just not saying true stuff. I'll pass."**
Cordelia, summarizing her character in ten words or less

### Love, Slayer style:

Angel and Buffy's tête-à-têtes continue, first with his attack on a weakened Buffy in the graveyard, then in an attempt to visit her at the hospital, stopped by Xander, of all people. Xander spends most of the episode playing Buffy's White Knight, to Angel's amusement ("You still love her," he sneers. "It must eat you up that I got there first") and Cordelia's annoyance. Indeed, Xander and Cordelia snipe throughout the episode, with Cordy making a sweet peace gesture by bringing Xander—loyally standing guard at the hospital against Angel's returning—donuts and coffee.

> The script originally called for Willow's distraction to involve bats. This was changed to make use of Willow's frog fear, established in "What's My Line? Part 1."

## POP-CULTURE IQ:

*"If he asks you to play chess, don't even do it. Guy's like a whiz."*

Xander, on Death, referring to the portrayal of Death in the Ingmar Bergman film *The Seventh Seal*, as well as *Bill and Ted's Bogus Journey* when the heroes meet Death.

It's also established that Buffy used to pretend she was the DC Comics superhero Power Girl as a kid—a character who is also blond, tough, and super-strong

## CONTINUITY:

It's established that Buffy encountered Der Kindestod as an eight-year-old, when she saw her cousin Celia die in a hospital—that trauma would keep her hating hospitals ever since.

Joyce expresses her sympathy to Giles on the death of Jenny Calendar, and Giles later expresses concern that, in the wake of that murder ("Passion"), Buffy is making up the "death" creature to give her something to fight. Willow makes use of her fear of frogs ("What's My Line? Part 1") to distract hospital security. Xander tells Angel, "You're going to die and I'm going to be there," a semi-foreshadow of "Becoming, Part 2."

## I Only Have Eyes for You

**WRITTEN BY** Marti Noxon; **DIRECTED BY** James Whitmore Jr. **GUEST STARS:** Chris Gorham as James, John Hawkes as the janitor, Meredith Salinger as Grace Newman, James Marsters as Spike, Juliet Landau as Drusilla, and Armin Shimerman as Principal Snyder.

On the night before the Sadie Hawkins Dance, Buffy is heading toward the library, only to encounter a boy about to kill a girl with a gun. As soon as Buffy knocks the gun from his hand, though, both of them regain their senses—the pair have no idea why they were fighting—and the gun disappears. Later, in Principal Snyder's office,

something knocks the 1955 yearbook off the principal's shelf in front of Buffy, and then, while bored to tears in history class, she gets a vision from the '50s of a Sunnydale High student named James and a teacher named Miss Newman, who seemed to have a relationship.

Strangeness continues as Xander is attacked by a dessicated arm in his locker, snakes start appearing in the school, and a janitor and a teacher play out the exact same scene as the two students did earlier—but without Buffy to interfere, the scene results in the janitor shooting the woman. Willow discovers the story of James and Miss Newman, who had an illicit affair in 1955, and on the night of the Sadie Hawkins Dance, he killed her and then shot himself in the head. The Slayerettes figure it's a poltergeist: James's spirit trying to resolve the conflict. An attempt at an exorcism fails, and finally the spirits confront each other yet again—this time with James inhabiting Buffy and Miss Newman inhabiting Angel.

*All the actors' shoes have rubber soles to cut down on noise that might be picked up while shooting.*

### Quote of the week:

**"Don't walk away from me, bitch!"**

Said by James, the boy at the beginning, the janitor, and Buffy, and written on the blackboard at the poltergeist's urging by Mr. Miller

### Love, Slayer style:

*Writer and story editor Marti Noxon loves ghost stories. She said of this episode, "I know my mom will cry when she sees it."*

Willow gives Giles a stone that she found in Jenny's desk. "She told me it's rose quartz—that it has healing powers. I thought she'd want you to have it." Later, Giles convinces himself that the poltergeist is Jenny, even though there's no evidence to support it.

Buffy's unresolved issues over Angel color her judgment throughout the episode, both preventing her from accepting an invitation to the dance and in dealing with James's spirit, for whom she has no forgiveness.

### POP-CULTURE IQ:

*Costume designer Cynthia Bergstrom is haunted by Jenny Calendar. She finds herself shopping for Robia LaMorte's character, though she's no longer on the series.*

**"Yeah, but if I see a floating pipe and a smoking jacket, he's dropped."**

Xander, in an oblique reference to *The Invisible Man*

**"Are you crazy? I saw that movie. Even the priests died!"**

Cordelia, upon Willow mentioning an exorcism, referring to the movie *The Exorcist*

## CONTINUITY:

Buffy has a dream with visions, but unlike her prophetic dreams ("Welcome to the Hellmouth," "Prophecy Girl," "Surprise," "Innocence"), this shows the past, is very specific in its imagery, and is provided by the ghost of James. Willow is still teaching Jenny Calendar's computer classes ("Passion," "Go Fish," "Becoming, Part 1"). Angel, Drusilla, and Spike move into the mansion following the destruction of the Factory ("Passion"), and Spike secretly gets up out of his wheelchair at the very end ("Becoming"). More hints that Snyder and the town authorities know more about the local weirdness are dropped ("School Hard," "Becoming, Part 2").

> Although the show has dealt with many a disturbing subject, this is the first one that has prompted a public-service announcement. Following the end of the final act, Sarah Michelle Gellar did a voice-over on the dangers of teen suicide and giving information on the American Association of Suicide Prevention.

**WRITTEN BY** David Fury and Elin Hampton; **DIRECTED BY** David Semel. **GUEST STARS:** Conchata Ferrell as Nurse Ruth Greenliegh, Wentworth Miller as Gage Petronzi, Charles Cyphers as Coach Carl Marin, Jake Patellis as Dodd McAlvy, Jeremy Garrett as Cameron Walker, and Armin Shimerman as Principal Snyder; with Danny Strong as Jonathon.

The Sunnydale High swim team has become the darling of the school, thanks to its actually winning several meets, putting it one up on the school's other teams. This extends to Principal Snyder's encouraging Willow to give a swimmer with an F a better grade and refusing to see Buffy's side of the story when she attacks another swimmer who tries to grope her. To make matters worse, the two best swimmers have apparently been killed by something that skinned them alive. Suspicion initially falls on Jonathon, a boy who was tormented by the team, but all he did was pee in the pool.

When Gage, the third-best swimmer, is attacked by Angel—who proceeds to spit out Gage's blood as if it were battery acid—they

> Though we knew there were docks nearby, this is the first time we find out that Sunnydale is actually a coastal town with a beach.

suspect steroid enhancement. When Gage transforms into a gill monster, leaving his skin behind, the slayerettes realize that none of them died, and it was more than steroids. Xander goes undercover, joining the swim team to get to the bottom of things. In the end, the newly mutated fish-men eat their coach and swim out to sea.

> Sunnydale High students have interesting reading tastes. Some of the magazines the school receives for its library are *Vegetarian Times, Women's Sports and Fitness, Upscale, National Geographic, PC World, Slam, Skin Diver, Sports Illustrated, ArtNews, Smithsonian, Bon Appetit,* and *Horseman.*

### Quote of the week:

**"That is wrong. Big, fat, spanking wrong. It's a slap in the face to every one of us that studied hard and worked long hours to earn our D's."**

Xander, expressing outrage over Snyder's encouraging Willow to raise Gage's grade from an F to a D

### Love, Slayer style:

Buffy finally gives in and decides to go on a date—with Cameron, who turns out to be stultifyingly dull and a pervert (and, later, a gill monster). Cordelia sees Xander wearing a Speedo and thinks that dating him isn't such an awful idea after all.

### BUFFY'S BAG OF TRICKS:

She uses a lacrosse stick on two of the gill monsters.

### POP-CULTURE IQ:

**Giles:** "He was eviscerated. Nothing left but skin and cartilage."
**Xander:** "In other words...'This was no boating accident!'"
—Referring to a famous line from the film *Jaws*

**"Swim team. Hardly what I call a team. The Yankees. Abbott and Costello. The A. Those were teams."**

Xander, bitter over the attention the swim team is receiving, referring to baseball, the classic comedy duo, and the '80s action series *A-Team,* starring Mr. T

### CONTINUITY:

Willow is made a permanent substitute computer teacher through to the end of the term ("Passion," etc.).

> The long shots of the Bronze, which imply that it is on a block of warehouses, actually show the building that houses the sets where the series is filmed.

### ANGEL'S RETREAT

Angel's dimly lit apartment is rather sparse for someone who's 242 years old. Apparently, he enjoys a Spartan lifestyle. He has a striking chair upholstered in a blue feather design, a table with an antique ashtray and cigarette lighter, a statue in a glass case, and the many sketches he has drawn of Buffy and her loved ones. Also, a desk that looks as though he uses it, which begs the question, does Angel pay his own utility bills?

## Becoming PART 1

**WRITTEN AND DIRECTED BY** Joss Whedon. **GUEST STARS:** Seth Green as Oz, Kristine Sutherland as Joyce Summers, Max Perlich as Whistler, Bianca Lawson as Kendra, Julie Benz as Darla, James Marsters as Spike, Juliet Landau as Drusilla, and Armin Shimerman as Principal Snyder; with Richard Riehle as Merrick, Jack McGee, and Nina Girvitz.

The construction of a new housing project has unearthed the sarcophagus of Acathla, a demon that was turned to stone by a knight. Angel makes off with the sarcophagus and wishes to use the demon to bring about Hell on Earth, destroying everything. Meanwhile, Buffy and Willow discover the backup disk that Jenny Calendar had made with the translation of the spell to restore Angel's soul. Though Xander thinks re-cursing Angel is a mistake and Giles thinks Willow isn't ready to channel that kind of magic, Willow prepares to cast the spell.

Kendra reappears with the sword blessed by the knight who imprisoned Acathla, and a warning from her Watcher that something awful is about to happen. Angel's first attempt to make that something awful happen fails, and so he lures Buffy away from the library so Drusilla can lead a raiding party to kidnap Giles. That raid leaves Willow comatose with a nasty head injury, Xander with a broken wrist, Giles kidnapped, and Kendra slaughtered. Buffy returns to the library just in time for Kendra's dying breath—and the arrival of the cops, accusing her of the murder.

### Quote of the week:

"It's a big rock. I can't wait to tell my friends. They don't have a rock this big."

Spike, less than impressed with Acathla's sarcophagus

### Love, Slayer style:

In one of the episode's many flashbacks, Angel gets his first look at Buffy when Merrick first tells her she is the Chosen One, and it's obviously love at first sight.

### BUFFY'S BAG OF TRICKS:

She is given a sword by Kendra to stop the demon, and Kendra also gives Buffy her favorite stake, which she has named "Mr. Pointy."

### POP-CULTURE IQ:

Buffy mispronounces Acathla as "Alfalfa" (likely referring to the *Little Rascals* character) and "Al Franken" (referring to the comedian/writer/actor).

### CONTINUITY:

This episode is festooned with flashbacks that detail important events in the lives of the characters: Darla turning Angel into a vampire ("Angel"), Angel torturing Drusilla ("Lie to Me"), Angel being cursed by the Romany people ("Angel," "Surprise," "Innocence"), and Buffy's first learning that she is the Slayer ("Welcome to the Hellmouth"). The disk with the spell to restore Angel is rediscovered ("Passion"), though Willow's attempt to cast it is interrupted; her next chance comes in "Becoming, Part 2." Angel's diversion of Buffy to get at the Slayerettes mirrors the similar stunt executed by the Anointed One and Absalom in "When She Was Bad," of which Angel reminds Buffy.

### From the original teleplay:

The following line was cut from the script for length:

**Whistler:** "There are three kinds of people that no one understands: geniuses, madmen, and guys that mumble."

---

The stuntwoman who was set on fire for the vampiric "immolation-o-gram" is named Cindy Folkerson. She has been set on fire more times than any other stuntwoman in Hollywood.

# Becoming PART 2

**WRITTEN AND DIRECTED BY** Joss Whedon. **GUEST STARS:** Seth Green as Oz, Kristine Sutherland as Joyce Summers, Robia LaMorte as Jenny Calendar, Max Perlich as Whistler, James Marsters as Spike, Juliet Landau as Drusilla, and Armin Shimerman as Principal Snyder.

> Joss Whedon's stage directions this time around included, "Yes, it's sunrise. Sue me." Sunrises and sunsets are almost impossible to film because they are so brief and difficult to schedule, much less capture on film.

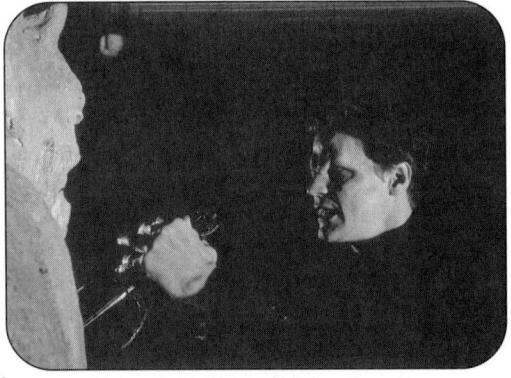

Buffy runs from the cops before they can mistakenly arrest her for Kendra's murder. She later goes to the hospital to learn that Xander's arm is broken but fine and Willow's still in a coma. Whistler shows up and tells Buffy she has to know how to use the sword, but his importuning falls on frustrated ears. Spike then approaches Buffy with a proposal: a temporary alliance against Angel in exchange for Spike and Drusilla's being allowed to leave Sunnydale. Reluctantly, Buffy agrees. Meanwhile, Willow awakens from her coma and insists on trying to cast the spell again, and Angel is physically torturing Giles for information on how to awaken Acathla, which the librarian is handily resisting. However, Giles breaks when Drusilla creates the illusion of Jenny Calendar in his mind. Angel learns that his blood must be used to open the portal to Hell—and, as Buffy learns from Whistler, only Angel's blood can subsequently close it. She goes to the mansion, determined to free Giles and kill Angel, and unaware—through Xander's omission—that Willow is attempting the ritual again. With Spike's help, she does fairly well, but Angel manages to open the portal anyhow. When the curse takes effect and Angel's soul is restored, Buffy realizes that she has to impale the man she loves and send him to Hell in order to close the gate. She does so, and then departs from Sunnydale on a bus, leaving only a note for her mother.

> Exterior shots of the mansion are filmed in a residential neighborhood on a hill. The crew had to get special permission to drive a 6,000-pound crane on the street, and all filming had to be wrapped by 10 A.M. This is called the "taillights at ten" rule.

### Quote of the week:

"I want to torture you. I used to love it, and it's been a long time. I mean, the last time I tortured someone, they didn't even *have* chain saws."

— Angel, describing Giles's immediate future

### Love, Slayer style:

Xander admits he loves Willow just before she awakens from her coma—so, naturally, the first thing she does upon awakening is call for Oz. Drusilla is able to use Giles's grief over Jenny Calendar's death to her and

> The Factory set was torn down to make room for the mansion set on a *Buffy* soundstage.

Angel's benefit. The re-souled Angel and Buffy exchange a passionate kiss and declare their love for each other right before she is forced to stab him.

## BUFFY'S BAG OF TRICKS:

She uses the sword Kendra brought for her.

## CONTINUITY:

The police talk to Joyce regarding Buffy's possible involvement in Kendra's death, referring to her history of violence. After a vampire attacks Joyce, Buffy is forced to finally tell her mother that she is the Slayer—a concept Joyce has understandable problems facing. When Joyce asks Spike if they know each other, Spike reminds her that she hit him with an ax ("School Hard"). Spike's speech on how much he likes the world and doesn't want to destroy it ("Billions of people walking around like Happy Meals with legs") belies his actions with the Judge in "Surprise" and "Innocence." Buffy is expelled by Snyder, making Buffy two-for-two regarding high schools ("Welcome to the Hellmouth"). More hints regarding the apparent conspiracy among the authorities in Sunnydale are dropped via a phone call Snyder makes to the mayor ("School Hard," "I Only Have Eyes for You"). Spike and Dru leave Sunnydale the way they came in: driving in a fast car ("School Hard"). Again Angel is cursed with a soul ("Angel," "Surprise," "Innocence," "Becoming, Part 1"), but Buffy has to send him to Hell regardless.

> To put himself in an "agonizing" frame of mind, Tony Head chopped chili peppers into small bits and popped them into his mouth before every take of Giles's torture scene.

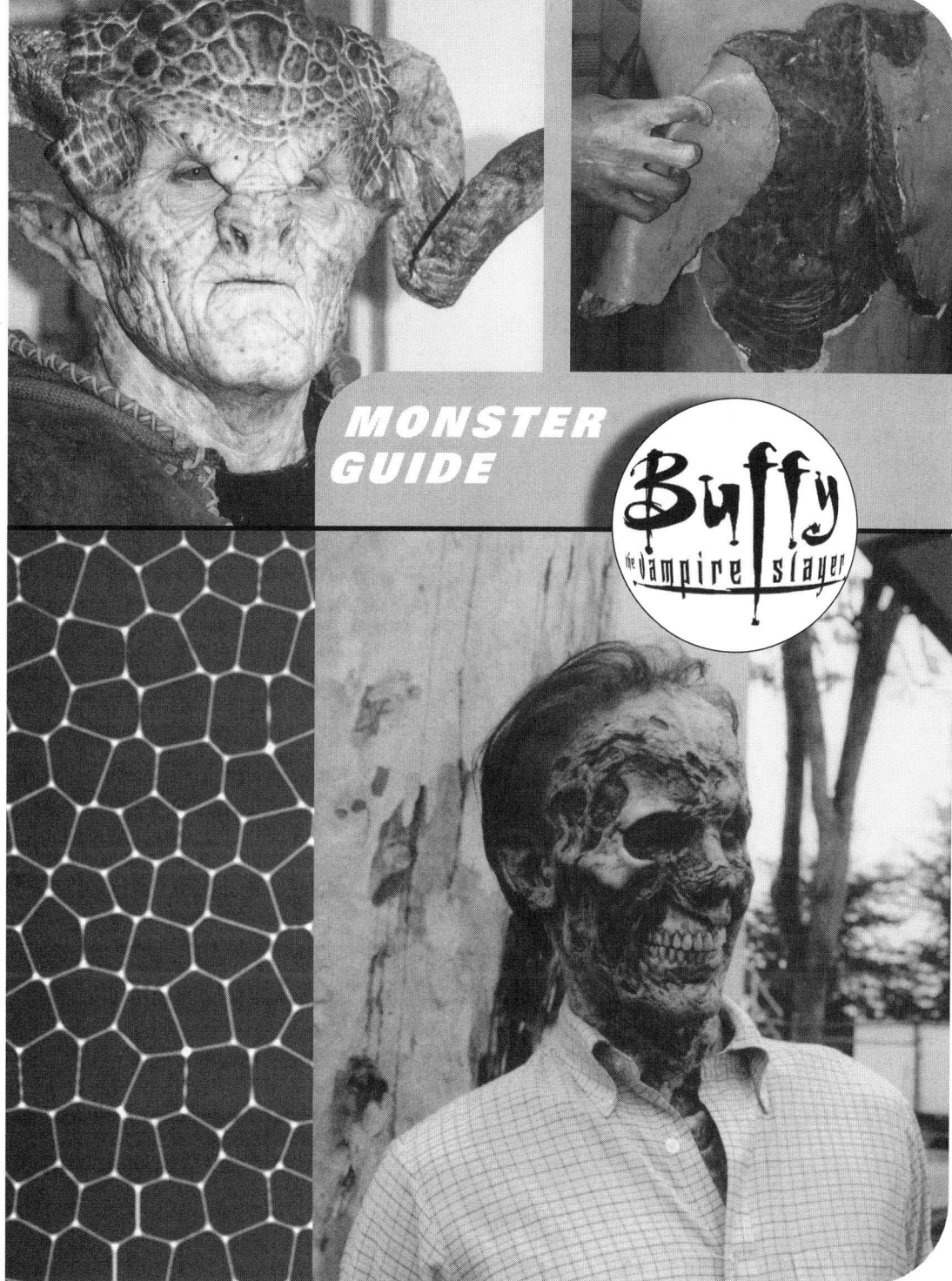

# MONSTER GUIDE

### Buffy the Vampire Slayer

# VAMPIRES

The legend of the vampire has existed, in one form or another, as long as there have been legends. From China to Ireland—in nearly every region of the world—there is some version of the vampire legend. There are those who believe that biblical references to a "screech owl" are actually comments about vampirism, since the word in Latin, *strix*, also means "vampire." The myths existed in ancient Babylon, and references have been found in ancient Assyrian and Chaldean tablets. Which, in a way, is disturbing. It makes absolutely no sense that similar ancient legends should exist in such diverse lands, unless there is some truth to those legends, some inspiration for them. Food for thought, at least.

From the horrifying tales of the Malaysian *penannglan*, to stories of the *nachzehrer* of Germany, belief in vampires seems to have always existed. It would be simple enough if we could distance ourselves from that mythology by placing it in a historical context. But, oddly enough, despite—or perhaps partially because of—the vibrant pop-culture existence of vampire mythology, belief in vampires actually thrives even to this day. There are groups of people around the world who still believe in, and in some cases believe themselves to be, vampires. A small "cult" of alleged vampires were responsible for several murders in the southeast United States in 1996. However, most modern "vampires" seem to be nonviolent and confine their blood-drinking to within their own circles. Thus far, none of them have exhibited any of the traditional powers or abilities of vampires, and there is no record of any modern vampire having died and come back to life.

Perhaps more so than any other supernatural legend, vampires owe much of their popularity, and certainly their endurance, to literature and the media. Though a number of writers had taken a crack at the vampire story before him, Bram Stoker certainly wrote the definitive vampire story in 1897—*Dracula*. For many decades thereafter, Stoker's work set the "rules" in place for vampire tales. Though the myriad legends from around the world each had their own wildly variant concepts about how vampires were created, what they actually did, what their weaknesses were, etc., there were now hard and fast rules.

Vampires could not be seen in mirrors. They cast no shadows. They could not cross running water, and direct sunlight could destroy them. They commanded the low creatures, bats and rats and wolves, and could transform themselves into those creatures. They slept on beds of their native earth. They had a powerful hypnotic gaze and could transform another person into a vampire by draining the blood from a living human, who would then, after death, rise from the grave. They feared the crucifix and garlic, and holy water could burn them. A stake through the heart and decapitation were the appropriate combination to kill a vampire once and for all.

Despite film and television creators and writers having worked their own twists on this basic formula for decades, the average consumer of Western pop culture still likely accepts Stoker's formula as an unassailable truth. Films such as *The Hunger* and *Near Dark*, among many others, have challenged those perceptions. Novelists such as Kim Newman, Dan Simmons, and particularly Anne Rice have radically altered those rules in creating their own vampire mythologies.

> "To make you a vampire, they have to suck your blood and then you have to suck their blood; it's like a whole big sucking thing. Mostly they're just gonna kill you, just take all your blood."
> **Buffy, in "Welcome to the Hellmouth"**

When it came time time for Joss Whedon to invent the mythology for *Buffy the Vampire Slayer*, he chose what suited him. The greatest diversion from Stoker's formula is that Whedon went back to an interpretation of ancient vampire mythology that few but scholars remember: some legends say that vampires are not humans at all, but demons who have taken up residence inside human corpses. From there, Whedon has built his own monsters. Built a better vampire, one might say, particularly since these vampires are not quite as all-powerful as their legendary and fictional forefathers.

> "Well, I've got a newsflash, braintrust. That's not how it works. You die. And a demon sets up shop in your old house. And it walks and talks and remembers your life, but it's not you."
> **Buffy, to Ford, in "Lie to Me"**

Vampires, in the world of *Buffy*, cannot fly. They cannot turn to mist. They cannot shape-shift at all. Though they cast no reflections in mirrors, they do cast shadows. In addition, they can be videotaped. While they do not actually need to breathe—at least not in the sense that humans do, with the intake of oxygen—their lungs do perform a function that simulates breathing. One possibility is that this process fouls whatever oxygen they do take in. It seems likely that the false act of "breathing" is somehow a comfort to them—and perhaps makes them feel less like the walking dead.

Whedon's vampires have a capacity for hypnosis, but some are much more skilled in its uses than others. Drusilla, for one, uses her hypnosis in Becoming, Parts 1 and 2 to great effect in the final episode of the second season, mesmerizing Giles into giving up valuable information and distracting Kendra long enough to cut her throat.

> "Xander, listen to me. Jesse is dead. You have to remember that if you see him. You're not looking at your friend. You're looking at the thing that killed him."
> **Giles, to Xander, in "The Harvest"**

> "A vampire isn't a person at all. It may have the movements, the memories, even the personality, of the person it takes over, but it is a demon at the core. There's no halfway."
> **Giles, in "Angel"**

Like Stoker's vampires, Whedon's cannot enter a private home without an invitation, but once they have been invited, they can return at any time. The traditional vampire cannot enter houses of worship or tread on hallowed ground, and they fear religious symbols, particularly the Christian cross.

> "We are defined by the things we fear. This symbol, these two planks of wood, it confounds me. Suffuses me with mortal dread. But fear is in the mind. Like pain, it can be controlled. If I can face my fear, it cannot master me."
> **The Master, about the crucifix, in "Nightmares"**

Whedon's creations have no problem entering a church, but touching actual consecrated earth causes them great suffering, and they do fear the cross. One thing Whedon's vampires share with Stoker's that many other creative imaginations have ignored over the years is the exposure to sunlight. In most recently created vampire mythologies, the sunlight will actually destroy a vampire. But for both Whedon and Stoker, in order for the sun to kill a vampire, it must be direct light. A heavily overcast day or some other kind of covering is sufficient to keep the creature alive for a period of time.

"I can't fly. There's no sure way to guard against the daylight."

**Angel, on airline flight, in "Surprise"**

In addition, vampires have frequently been portrayed as having almost instant healing abilities, save for the stake through the heart. Whedon's vampires can recover from just about anything, but it takes a lot longer to get there. Hence Darla's comment in "Angel" that "Bullets can't kill vampires. They can hurt them like hell...."

As to the origins of the vampires themselves, Whedon, through the character of the Watcher, Rupert Giles, has a very specific idea of their origins:

> "This world is older than any of you know, and contrary to popular mythology, it did not begin as a paradise. For untold eons, demons walked the Earth, made it their home, their Hell. In time, they lost their purchase on this reality, and the way was made for mortal animals. For Man. What remains of the Old Ones are vestiges: certain magicks, certain creatures....

> "The books tell that the last demon to leave this reality fed off a human, mixed their blood. He was a human form possessed—infected—by the demon's soul. He bit another and another...and so they walk the Earth, feeding. Killing some, mixing their blood with others to make more of their kind. Waiting for the animals to die out and the Old Ones to return."

Toward the goal of returning their ancient ancestors to the Earth, the demons who reside within the vampires have created their own "families" and societies, tribes or clans of vampires who work and live together to further their chaotic impulses. As Buffy points out in "Lie to Me," however, "vampires are kind of picky about who they change." Frequently, a clan will include a group of vampires and their "sire," the vampire who turned them into vampires in the first place. The best-known vampire clan thus far in the *Buffy* mythology is the Order of Aurelius, which was led by the Master for centuries and whose Brethren, or adherents, have included Angel and Darla and, by implication, very likely Spike and Drusilla as well.

Indeed, Joss Whedon seems to have purposefully moved away from the vampire fictions of recent years, finding a middle ground between ancient legends, Bram Stoker's "rules," and his own unique twist on the subject. Witness, for example, the following exchange from "School Hard":

ANGEL: "I taught you to always guard your perimeter. You should have someone out there."
SPIKE: "I did. I'm surrounded by idiots. What's new with you?"

ANGEL: "Everything."
SPIKE: "Come up against this Slayer yet?"
ANGEL: "She's cute. Not too bright, though. Gave the puppy-dog, I'm-all-tortured act. Keeps her off my back when I feed."
SPIKE: "People still fall for that Anne Rice routine? What a world."

Without question, the vampires in *Buffy* are unique characters, and viewers are eagerly awaiting every new bit of information provided as the show moves forward.

## ANGELUS

Without a doubt, Angelus is the most important vampire in the world of *Buffy*. He is both Buffy's great love and her worst enemy, the source of her greatest happiness and her deepest despair. Here in the Monster Guide, we will discuss the dark side of Angel, referring to him as Angelus.

As we learn in the first part of the second-season finale, in 1753, in Galway, Ireland, Angel was a drunken young scoundrel intent upon filching some of his father's silver to buy himself a night of love at the local brothel. He is distracted in his purpose by the appearance of Darla, to whom he boasts:

"My lady, you will find that, with the exception of an honest day's work, there is no challenge I am not prepared to face."

Darla, amused, takes him at his word and not only invites him into her vampiric embrace, but sires him into eternal life as a vampire.

There is an interesting parallel between Angel's initiation into his new world and Buffy's, when, as a shallow fifteen-year-old, she meets her first Watcher, Merrick. They share this exchange:

BUFFY: "You're not from Macy's, are you? 'Cause I meant to pay for that lipstick."
MERRICK: "There isn't much time. You must come with me. Your destiny awaits."
BUFFY: "I don't have a destiny. I'm destiny-free. Really." —"Becoming, Part 1"

But while Buffy becomes the heroic Slayer, the Irish lad Angel becomes Angelus, "the one with the angelic face," the scourge of Europe. The Master calls him "the most vicious creature I ever met."

One of his many evil deeds revealed thus far in the series was his insidious manipulation of Drusilla, a young English girl who is plagued by visions. The year is 1860. Her mother has told her that her clairvoyance is the work of the Devil, and the sadistic Angelus, posing as a priest in the confessional, takes full advantage of her confusion:

DRUSILLA: "My mum says I'm cursed. My seeing things is an affront to the Lord. That only He's supposed to see anything before it happens. But I don't mean to, Father, I swear. I try to be pure in His sight and do my penance. I don't want to be a thing of evil."
ANGEL: "Hush, child. The Lord has a plan for all creatures. Even a devil child like you."
DRUSILLA [mortified]: "A devil . . ."
ANGEL: "Yes, you're a spawn of Satan, all the Hail Marys in the world aren't going to help. The

Lord will use you and then smite you down. He's like that."

DRUSILLA: "What can I do?"

ANGEL: "Fulfill His plan for you, child. Be evil. Perform evil works. Attack the less fortunate. You can start small: laugh at a cripple. You'll feel better. Just give in . . ."

DRUSILLA: "No . . . I want to be good. . . . I want to be pure. . . ."

ANGEL: "We all do, at first. World doesn't work that way."

DRUSILLA: "Father, I beg you...help me."

ANGEL: "Very well. Uh, ten Our Fathers and an Act of Contrition. Does that sound good?"

DRUSILLA: "Yes, Father, thank you."

ANGEL: "The pleasure was mine." [She starts to go.] "Oh, and my child?"

DRUSILLA: "Yes?"

ANGEL: "God is watching you."

—"Becoming, Part 1"

Angelus drives poor Drusilla mad, exploiting her troubled mental state and killing everybody she loves. In desperation, she flees to a convent, and on the day she takes the veil, he turns her into a vampire.

He had also earlier killed his own family, and for over a century thereafter offers an ugly death to everyone he meets. "And I did it," he later tells Buffy, "with a song in my heart."

Eventually, Angelus leaves England—apparently in the company of his sire, Darla, with whom he is at least occasionally romantically involved—and they wreak havoc throughout Europe. In Budapest, they pluck human beings "like fruit off the vine." He delights in torturing both animals and people, as when he tells the captive Giles.

"I want to torture you. I used to love it, and it's been a long time. I mean, the last time I tortured someone they didn't even have chain saws."

—"Becoming, Part 2"

Angelus would probably have continued his career as "a vicious, violent animal"—to quote Giles—except that one fatal night, Darla brings him a Gypsy girl to feed on. Upon discovering her dead body, her clan, the Romany, decides to take its revenge against Angelus by returning his soul to him. As Angel explains to Buffy:

"When you become a vampire, the demon takes your body. But it doesn't get your soul. That's gone. No conscience, no remorse . . . it's an easy way to live. You have no idea what it's like to have done the things I've done, and to care."

—"Angel"

From that time until now, the Romany send clan members to spy on him, ensuring that their vengeance curse— "a living, breathing thing"—makes Angel's life a Hell on Earth.

But what Angel did not know that if he was ever completely happy, even for one second, his soul would once more be lost and he would revert to his evil state. After his night of passion with Buffy, in "Surprise," the curse is "lifted"—and Angelus howls into the night with pain as his soul leaves his body.

His first act as the newly restored Angelus is to feed upon a living human being—something he has not done in a century—and then he seeks out Drusilla and Spike to reassert his dominance over them. Engrossed as the couple are in their new toy, the Judge, it takes them a moment to realize what has happened when he strides boldly into their lair:

**THE JUDGE** [urged by Spike to burn all the goodness out of Angel]**:** "This one cannot be burned. He is clean."
**SPIKE:** "Clean? You mean he's—"
**THE JUDGE:** "There's no humanity in him."
**DRUSILLA:** "Angel?"
**ANGEL:** "Yeah, baby, I'm back." —*"Innocence"*

Angelus immediately sets about to establish himself as the head of "the family" that consists of Drusilla, Spike, and himself. He taunts the weakened, wheelchair-bound Spike, calling him "roller-boy" and "Sit 'n' Spin." He leers at Drusilla and implies at every possible turn that he is sleeping with her, instilling in Spike no end of jealous fury.

Angelus's next order of business is to destroy anything and everything that had made him feel like a human being when he was the brooding, guilt-ridden Angel—most especially, the young girl who had given him the first true happiness he had known in over a hundred years—Buffy. First he attempts to murder her friends, beginning with Willow. He is thwarted only when Jenny Calendar, knowing what has happened to him, distracts him with a cross long enough for Buffy to attack him and save her friend ("Innocence").

Hating the Slayer for making him feel love, yet fearing her—she's the strongest Slayer he and Spike have ever crossed—he wages a relentless campaign of mind games against her—sneaking into her bedroom and leaving sketches of her asleep; killing Willow's aquarium fish; threatening to harm Joyce Summers, then revealing to her that he has slept with her daughter—with the same unrelenting cruelty that he once used on the hapless Drusilla.

**DRUSILLA:** "You don't want to kill her, do you? You just want to hurt her. Just like you hurt me."
**ANGEL:** "Nobody knows me like you do, Dru."
**SPIKE:** "She'd better not get in our way."
**ANGEL:** "Don't worry about it."
**SPIKE:** "I do."
**ANGEL:** "Spike, my boy. You really don't get it, do you? You've tried to kill her, and you couldn't. Look at you. You're a wreck.... Force won't get it done. You gotta work from the inside. To kill this girl...you have to love her."
—*"Innocence"*

But his plot backfires; the sheer magnitude of evidence that this is not some version of Angel on a bad day but a different creature entirely, eventually allows Buffy to accept that fact, and to resolve to destroy him.

Around this time, Angelus realizes that Jenny Calendar, the Gypsy woman sent to spy on him, is trying to curse him once again—to restore his soul. In one of the most chilling sequences in the entire first two seasons, he comes upon her in the school, smashes the Orb of Thesulah that was to house his soul until it could be returned to him, and destroys what he believes to be every copy of the incantation itself. Then he hunts Jenny down and, with no passion, no hatred, just simple satisfaction, breaks her neck.

Soon after, Angelus announces that he's done with his personal vendetta against the Slayer. He has decided that rather than bothering with her, he will send every non-demon creature on Earth into Hell by bringing the demon Acathla back to life. With this decision, he has finally divested himself of everything that once made him human—including his passion, whether it be clothed as love or hatred, for the Slayer.

Now Angelus, the one with the angelic face, is a complete monster.

## THE MASTER

"This is what we know. Some sixty years ago, a very old, very powerful vampire came to this shore, and not just to feed."

That's the gospel according to Giles, from "The Harvest," the second half of the two-hour premiere of *Buffy the Vampire Slayer*. For the entire twelve episodes of the first season, the Master, leader of the Order of Aurelius, was Buffy's primary enemy, the most evil creature in a town filled with them. Though the Master's real name and history are never revealed on screen, the true master of Buffy, the show's creator, Joss Whedon, wrote in his script of the pilot that the Master's real name was Heinrich Joseph Nest. Whedon called him "the most powerful of vampires," and marked his age at roughly 600 years.

The Master was originally drawn to Sunnydale because it is situated directly over the Hellmouth, which Giles describes as "a sort of portal between this reality and the next." The next, obviously, meaning Hell. Based upon the basic mythology of the series, we know that this Hell is the dimension wherein the race of demons that walked the Earth before mankind currently reside. The worst and oldest of these demons are called the Old Ones, a term reminiscent of the Cthulhu mythos created by horror forefather H.P. Lovecraft.

As a worshiper of the Old Ones, the Master hoped to open the Hellmouth and allow the demons to walk the Earth once more. At the time of his arrival in Sunnydale, the evil one might well have succeeded with his plan if not for a horrible stroke of luck; bad luck for the Master, the good kind for the rest of the world. In 1937, an earthquake rocked Sunnydale, swallowing "about half the town," including an old church which, ironically, became the Master's lair. For it was in this shattered, now buried building that the Hellmouth began to open, only to be blocked by the earthquake and, it seems, by the Master. According to Giles, "Opening dimensional portals is tricky business. Odds are he got himself stuck. Like a cork in a bottle."

Thus, the Master remained stuck in an odd limbo between Earth and Hell from 1937 until 1997. He tried several times over the course of the first season to free himself. In fact, he was actually, very briefly, free during the episode "Nightmares," thanks to the reality-warping powers of a comatose boy named Billy Palmer. Fortunately for Sunnydale, when Billy awoke from his coma, the Master was returned to his limbo captivity.

Finally, however, in the last episode of season one, "Prophecy Girl," the Master did manage to get free. A prophecy in *The Pergamum Codex*—which Giles pointed out had never been wrong—predicted that the Slayer would face the Master and the Slayer would die. At first, Buffy did not want to face him, but in the end, she descended into his underground lair. Little did she know, but that was exactly what the prophecy had meant. By entering the Master's lair, Buffy exposed herself to his attack. It was the power the Master received from tasting her blood in traditional vampiric fashion that allowed him to break free. After he had bitten her, the Master dropped Buffy in a pool of water, where she drowned and died. However, Xander was able to perform CPR and bring her back.

The Master had achieved his dream. The Hellmouth was open and the tentacled Old Ones were emerging when Buffy caught up with him. Their battle ended when the Master was impaled on shattered furniture in the school library and died. Over the intervening summer, Giles, Willow, and Xander buried the Master's bones in consecrated ground. In the second season opener, "When She Was Bad," the Master's remaining followers attempted to revive him, but Buffy stopped them, and then used a sledge hammer to pound the Master's bones to dust.

At this point, we can only assume that he is gone forever. But you never know.

## SPIKE

Also known as "William the Bloody," Spike first appears in "School Hard," when he drives his car into the Welcome to Sunnydale sign on the outskirts of town. His first words as he reaches the Hellmouth, "home sweet home," are apparently a reference only to the idea that the Hellmouth is, de facto, home to all vampires, rather than any implication that he has ever been to Sunnydale before.

As the episode continues, the Anointed One holds court, and his followers argue over who will take the place of the Master, who will actually lead. A pair of vampires, referred to in the script only as "Big Ugly" and "Lean Boy," are arguing when Spike enters the Factory, wherein the Anointed One has set up shop.

**BIG UGLY:** "This weekend, the Night of St. Vigeous, our power shall be at its peak! When I kill her [the Slayer], it'll be the greatest event since the crucifixion. And I should know, I was there."

**SPIKE:** "You were there? Oh, please. If every vampire who said he was at the crucifixion was actually there, it would have been like Woodstock."

**BIG UGLY:** "I ought to rip your throat out."

**SPIKE:** "I was actually at Woodstock. That was a weird gig. Fed off a flower person, and I spent the next six hours watching my hands move. . . . So, who do you kill for fun around here?"

—"School Hard"

Spike goes on to brag that he has killed two Slayers in his life, one during the Boxer Rebellion. Then he brings Drusilla into the room. The two are obviously a couple, though Drusilla seems less than sane. She is a sickly vampire who also has prescient visions, and Spike's entire world seems to be about caring for her. That and his thirst for power. To prove himself, he vows to kill the Slayer.

Shortly, we see Spike and Big Ugly visit the Bronze. According to Spike's plan, Big Ugly draws Buffy out and into combat. Despite his bragging, he is easily dispatched by the Slayer as Spike watches, taking her measure. Later, Buffy and crew are discussing the arrival of Spike, and Angel reveals that he is familiar with the vampire. "Once he starts something, he doesn't stop until everything in his path is dead," Angel explains. Later,

Giles finds references to Spike in the Watcher diaries.

"Our new friend, Spike. 'Known as William the Bloody, earned his nickname by torturing his victims with railroad spikes....' Ah, but here's some good news: he's barely 200, not even as old as Angel."

**Giles, in "School Hard"**

On Parent-Teacher Night, Spike and his hordes are defeated, and Spike himself is hit with an ax by Joyce Summers. He withdraws to consider an alternate plan. However, the Anointed One is less than pleased. Spike solves this problem quite simply: he kills the Anointed One. "From now on," he tells the other vampires, "we're gonna have a little less ritual and a little more fun around here."

The next time Spike appears is in "Halloween," when it is revealed that he has been videotaping Buffy fighting other vampires to watch her technique. Later that night, he makes his second attempt on Buffy's life, but once again, he is overpowered and forced to flee.

In "Lie to Me," Spike has yet another shot at the Slayer, but this time Buffy fends him off by threatening the weakened Drusilla's life. In the same episode, Spike begins to show the jealousy he feels over Drusilla's former involvement with Angel, a topic that later takes on a new significance. In the two-parter "What's My Line?" Spike finally manages to return Drusilla to health, only to become an invalid himself. After he is wheelchairbound, Spike becomes quieter, almost morose. Even when he and Drusilla put the Judge together in "Surprise," Spike seems merely to be playing along because of his love for Dru. However, when Buffy and Angel make love at the end of that episode, causing Angel to lose his soul and revert to the demonic Angelus once more, the fire begins to burn in Spike again. For when Angel comes to stay with Spike and Drusilla, Spike's jealousy grows and grows. Of course, Angel's constant taunting doesn't help matters.

In fact, Angel's taunting, and Spike's anger continue to feed on each other, and Spike presses him time and again to kill Buffy and be done with it. However, at the end of "I Only Have Eyes for You," we begin to realize that Spike is not as docile as he has seemed. William the Bloody is up to something, for certain. In the last moments of that episode, when nobody else is around, Spike stands up out of his wheelchair, unaided, obviously strong again.

In the two-part season finale, "Becoming," his deceit takes on an entirely new meaning. Spike has decided that Angel's plan to destroy the world isn't exactly good for the vampire race. He's also realized that the only thing that really matters is that he gets Drusilla back. In order for that to happen, he allies himself with the Slayer, an unthinkable act for a vampire. He vows to Buffy that he will betray the others if she lets Drusilla live, that the two of them will leave Sunnydale and Buffy will never see them again.

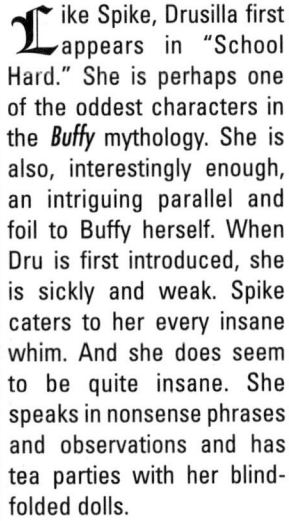

"We like to talk big, vampires do. 'I'm gonna destroy the world'—just tough-guy talk, strutting around with your friends over a pint of blood. Truth is, I like this world. You got dog racing, Manchester United, and you got people. Billions of people walking around like Happy Meals with legs. It's all right here. But then someone comes along with a vision. A real passion for destruction. Angel could pull it off. Good-bye, Picadilly, farewell Leicester bloody Square, you see what I'm saying?"
**Spike, in "Becoming, Part 2"**

Though events do not unfold as planned, Spike and Dru do manage to escape in that second season finale, driving off in the same car in which they first arrived, its windows blacked out against the sun. Though Spike vowed that Buffy would never see him and Dru again, the fact that in the final battle he abandoned her to Angel—decidedly not part of their bargain—chances are Buffy may have a very serious bone to pick with him if they ever do hook up again.

## DRUSILLA

Like Spike, Drusilla first appears in "School Hard." She is perhaps one of the oddest characters in the *Buffy* mythology. She is also, interestingly enough, an intriguing parallel and foil to Buffy herself. When Dru is first introduced, she is sickly and weak. Spike caters to her every insane whim. And she does seem to be quite insane. She speaks in nonsense phrases and observations and has tea parties with her blindfolded dolls.

"Do you like daisies? I plant them, but they always die. Everything I put in the ground withers and dies. Spike, I'm cold."
**Drusilla, to the Anointed One, in "School Hard"**

"Miss Edith speaks out of turn. She's a bad example and will have no cakes today."
**Drusilla, about her favorite doll, in "School Hard"**

"You know what I miss? Leeches."
**Drusilla, in "Halloween"**

Drusilla also has prescient visions, seen through the kaleidoscope of her madness, and yet Spike never fails to interpret them. The Slayer has prescient dreams, and that is one trait they share.

The other thing, of course, is their feelings for Angel.

In Drusilla's first appearance, we learn a bit about her past. She notes that she misses Prague, and Spike has to remind her that she was nearly killed by an "idiot mob" in Prague. Though she spends much of her time swooning and having visions, Drusilla does manage a late-night outing, during which she runs into Angel. It is here, in "Lie to Me," that we first get an inkling of their past. Later in that episode, Buffy grills Angel about Dru's identity.

**Angel:** "I did a lot of unconscionable things when I became a vampire. Drusilla was the worst. She was . . . an obsession of mine. She was pure and sweet and chaste."
**Buffy:** "You made her a vampire."
**Angel:** "First I made her insane. Killed everyone she loved, visited every torture on her I could devise. She eventually fled to a convent, and the day she took her Holy Orders, I turned her into a demon."  —**"Lie to Me"**

In the two-parter "What's My Line?" it is Angel's blood—as Dru's sire—and a ritual conducted by Spike that returns Drusilla to health. "Say 'Uncle,'" she says as she tortures Angel. "Oh, that's right, you killed my uncle." Ironically, at the end of that same episode, Spike is badly injured and is left confined to a wheelchair for a time, allowing Drusilla to take center stage.

"You've been a very bad daddy."
**Drusilla, to Angel, her sire, in "What's My Line? Part 2"**

**Drusilla:** "My mummy ate lemons. Raw. She said she loved the way they made her mouth tingle. Little Anne, her favorite was custard . . . brandied pears . . ."
**Angel:** "Dru . . ."
**Drusilla:** "Ssshhhh. And pomegranates. They used to make her face and fingers all red. Remember little fingers? Little hands? Do you?"
**Angel:** "If I could, I . . ."

**Drusilla:** "Bite your tongue! They used to eat. Cake. And eggs. And honey. Until you came and ripped their throats out."
—**"What's My Line? Part 2"**

In "Innocence," when Angel appears once more, now without a soul, Drusilla is thrilled. Spike, on the other hand, is less than pleased. Drusilla seems either ignorant of the tension or pleased with it, for she completely ignores Spike's jealousy and discomfort. It seems evident that Angel and Drusilla have become involved once again, although this is never confirmed, only implied. The tension continues to rise throughout subsequent episodes.

Perhaps Dru's most amusing appearance is when, affected by the love spell Amy Madison cast for Xander, she offers Xander eternal life in "Bewitched, Bothered, and Bewildered." In "Passion," she adopts a puppy whose owner has had a small accident—courtesy of her own fangs.

We get another look into Drusilla's past in a flashback sequence in the first half of the second season finale, "Becoming." It is an encounter in London in the year 1860, and apparently the first meeting between Dru and Angel. Angel begins to toy with Dru's mind, the beginning of the horrors he would later inflict upon her.

"I met an old man. I didn't like him. He got stuck in my teeth. And then the moon started whispering to me. All sorts of dreadful things."
**Drusilla, in "Becoming, Part 1"**

It isn't until the end of "Becoming, Part 1" that we see Drusilla at her most evil, however. In that scene, she first hypnotizes Kendra, the *other* vampire Slayer. Then she cuts Kendra's throat. In part two, she also uses her hypnosis to convince Giles that she is Jenny Calendar to get him to reveal the last bit of information Angel needs to wake the demon Acathla and destroy the world.

During the final battle, however, Drusilla is overwhelmed by Spike, who has struck up an alliance with the Slayer, and she is forcibly removed from the battle. Spike and Dru then leave Sunnydale, presumably forever. But there is certainly a sense of unfinished business there.

## DARLA

Other than the Master and, of course, Angel, Darla is the most important figure in the vampire mythology from season one. A member of the Brethren of Aurelius, she is the first vampire we see in the series—when she kills a teenage boy in the opening teaser of "Welcome to the Hellmouth." In the same episode, she also becomes the first vampire to actually fight the Slayer in the series (Buffy is first attacked by Thomas, but she "dusts" him without any actual combat).

Darla is an interesting character because, while the Master habitually tortures or kills those who disobey him, Darla is able to be almost flippant, and, in fact, to disobey him without any obvious repercussions. Tasting Jesse's blood before handing him over to the Master in "The Harvest" is a good example of her disobedience. And yet, when Luke is killed in that very same episode, Darla takes Luke's place as the Master's primary acolyte.

The next time Darla appears is in "Angel." The Master has sent a trio of vampire warriors to kill Buffy, but "the Three" fail, and Darla gleefully kills them for the Master in punishment. In the same episode, a great deal is revealed during Darla's visit to Angel in his apartment. It is made quite clear that the two were involved for quite some time. In fact, the implication is that they were linked romantically, at least off and on, for the entire time that passed between Angelus becoming a vampire and the Gypsy curse that restored his soul. Darla brags that it was she who brought that very girl to Angel in the first place, and there is some suggestion that this took place in or near Budapest, about the time of an earthquake there.

It is also revealed that Darla was Angel's sire, that she was the one who turned him into a vampire in the first place.

Darla formulates a plan, hoping to bring Angel "back to the fold." If she can force him to kill Buffy, he will surely be evil again, she believes. To that end, she bites and bleeds Buffy's mother, Joyce, becoming the only vampire to bite any of Buffy's circle of family and friends (not including Buffy herself, of course). Darla then tries to frame Angel for this attack. In the long run, it does not work, and in the end of that episode, it is Angel who ends up killing Darla.

The Master mourns Darla's passing. "She was my favorite," he says. "For 400 years."

## THE ANOINTED ONE

There will be a time of crisis, of worlds hanging in the balance. And in this time shall come the Anointed, the Master's great warrior. The Slayer will not know him, will not stop him. And he will lead her to Hell.

"As it is written, so shall it be . . .
Five will die, and from their ashes the Anointed One shall rise. The Brethren of Aurelius shall greet him and usher him to his immortal destiny. . .
"As it is written, so shall it be."

**The Master, reading from the writings of Aurelius in "Never Kill a Boy on the First Date"**

The Anointed One in mortal life was a sweet-looking little boy named Collin, whose last words as a human were, "I went on an airplane." When born into eternal life, he was to be the Master's greatest weapon against the Slayer.

He first appears in "Never Kill a Boy on the First Date," and he retains his angelic appearance, aside from a gravelly, echoing voice and soulless black eyes. Dropping stones into a pool of blood, holding hands with the Master and later with Buffy herself, he appears very much a small boy, save for his focused determination to rid the Master of the Slayer and his heartless assessment of various changes in the Master's situation. For instance, when Angel stakes Darla, the Master rages and sobs. Darla had been his favorite for 400 years, and Angel, the ultimate betrayer, was to have sat at the Master's right hand "come the day."

But, in "Angel," Collin calmly tells the grief-stricken Master in a flat, strong voice: "Forget her...she was weak. We don't need her. *I'll* bring you the Slayer."

Although he never physically attacks Buffy, it is he who leads her to the Master's lair in "Prophecy Girl." He also orchestrates the attempted resurrection of the Master (in "When She Was Bad"). After that fails, he serves as the leader of the Master's vampire family...until Spike and Drusilla arrive on the scene. Spike kills the "big noise" in "School Hard," by trapping him in a cage and exposing him to direct sunlight.

The coming of the Anointed One was prophesied in the twelfth century by one Aurelius, the founder of the Order of Aurelius. Aurelius foretold that the Brethren of his Order would come to the Master, to bring him the Anointed One. "Five shall die, and from their ashes shall rise" this very special vampire.

Giles's research indicates that the Anointed One will rise on the evening of the 1,000th day after the advent of Septus . . . that very night, in fact! The Master sends the Brethren out to fulfill the prophecy, which they accomplish by killing the passengers as well as the driver on an airport bus—five in all, including Andrew Borba, a lunatic who was sought by the police for questioning in a double murder. Giles, Buffy, and the Slayerettes all assume that Borba is the Anointed One when he rises from his slab in the Sunnydale Funeral Home as a full-fledged, very crazy vamp. After they dispatch Borba, Buffy and company assume all is well—unaware that little Collin is holding court beside the triumphant Master.

However, in "Prophecy Girl," Ms. Calendar tells Giles of "some crazy monk from Cortona" who has e-mailed her about some Anointed One. Giles later asks her if she managed to get in touch with him.

JENNY: "As far as I can tell, no one can. He's disappeared. He did send out one last global, though. Short one."
GILES: "What did it say?"
JENNY: "Isaiah 11:6. Which I dutifully looked up."
GILES: " 'The wolf shall live with the lamb, the leopard shall lie down with the kid, the calf and the lion and the fatling together, and a little child shall lead them.' "   —**"Prophecy Girl"**

When the Anointed One sees Buffy coming on the night she is prophesied to die, he begins to feign crying, a lost little boy. Buffy says, "It's all right. I know who you are."

She takes his hand, and he leads her to her destiny.

## LUKE

The second vampire revealed to the audience is Luke. He is one of the Brethren of Aurelius, the Master's chief acolyte as the series begins, and is obviously quite powerful. In fact, his strength and prowess as a warrior is indicated by a conversation he has with the Master in "The Harvest":

THE MASTER: "A Slayer...have you any proof?"
LUKE: "Only that she fought me and yet lives."
THE MASTER: "Very nearly proof enough. I can't remember the last time that happened."
LUKE: "1843. Madrid. And the bastard caught me sleeping."

It is also a measure of Buffy's strength that she is the first opponent to survive a battle with Luke in more than a century and a half. Still, to be clear, none of Luke's opponents during that time were Slayers, since he later confesses that he had always "wanted to kill a Slayer."

In "The Harvest," the second hour of the premiere, it is explained that once every hundred years, the Master may gain power through a ritual or event called the Harvest. Luke is chosen as the Master's "Vessel." A symbol is painted on his forehead in blood, and a ritual is conducted, after which, according to the Master, "Every soul he takes will feed me. Their souls will grant me the strength to free myself."

Luke and the rest of the Master's minions attack the Bronze, and the Harvest begins. Unfortunately for the Master, and even more so for Luke, Buffy shows up to save the day. It isn't long before Luke is first outwitted, and then slain by the Chosen One, Buffy Summers.

## DALTON

Unlike any other vampire we see in the first two seasons, Dalton seems quiet and bookish, almost like a demonic Willow. When we first see him, in "What's My Line? Part 1," Dalton is attempting to translate an ancient manuscript that Spike hopes will help cure Drusilla. Interestingly, despite his reserve, Dalton is willing to question Spike's judgment several times in this episode.

DALTON: "I'm not sure . . . it could be . . . *Deprimere ille bubula linter.*"

SPIKE: "'Debase the beef . . . canoe.' [beat] Why does that strike me as not right?"
—"What's My Line? Part 1"

In that same episode, he is sent off to retrieve the cross of du Lac, which will allow him to translate the ritual for Spike. However, we don't see Dalton again until "Surprise," wherein he is helping Drusilla and the now wheelchair-bound Spike collect the pieces of the Judge. Drusilla nearly kills him at one point, but Spike stops her, suggesting instead that he rectify his error.

"Dru, sweet. You might give him a chance to find your lost treasure. He's a wanker, but he's the only one we've got with half a brain. If he fails, you can eat his eyes out of the sockets for all I care."
Spike, on Dalton, in "Surprise"

An interesting character, despite his few appearances, Dalton meets an untimely end as the Judge's first meal, in "Surprise."

## THOMAS

Thomas is a relatively young, and not very bright, vampire who appears only in the very first episode of the series. He is also the first vampire Buffy actually spots in Sunnydale, ruffling Giles's feathers because she does so with her own teenage instincts rather than the instincts of the Slayer. Thomas dresses in '80s fashions, which is what tips her off in the first place, suggesting that vampires get stuck in the fashions of the time in which they "died." In the same scene, Thomas flirts with Willow and ends up convincing her to go get ice cream with him. Outside, he manages to lead her into the cemetery and to a large crypt that is an entrance to the Master's underground lair. Shortly thereafter, Thomas thinks he can sneak up on Buffy and instead becomes the first vampire killed by the Slayer in the series.

## CLAW

Claw, a.k.a. "Fork-Guy," was once a member of the Brethren of Aurelius, the Master's followers. Apparently, he "displeased the Master and cut off his [own] hand for penance." Claw then seems to have replaced the severed hand with a kind of metal claw or, to Buffy, a big "fork." Prior to the events in "Teacher's Pet," Claw apparently battled Angel, wounding him, but both of them survived the encounter. Angel tells Buffy, "Don't give him a moment's mercy; he'll rip your throat out."

In "Teacher's Pet," Claw is stalking people in Weatherly Park and fights Buffy early on, only to flee. Buffy follows and watches him stalk substitute biology teacher Miss French, who turns out to be the She-Mantis. Claw is afraid of her. Later, Buffy actually uses Claw's fear of the She-Mantis to track the creature and then "dusts" Claw without any obvious difficulty. Not as tough as we were led to believe.

## THE THREE

In the opening sequence of "Angel," the Master reports to Darla that Zachary, a strong and careful member of the Master's vampire family, has been slain by Buffy. Supremely irritated, the Master decides to step up his war against the Slayer and summons the Three—much to Darla's delight.

The Three are a trio of imposing warriors, muscular, battle-scarred vampires who dress in leather and body armor. Without breaking stride, they clear Sunnydale's streets of terrified gangbangers in their search for the Slayer. Once they find her, they launch a brutal attack, and it's pretty clear that Buffy will lose this one—until Angel arrives on the scene. Still, despite the fact that he was once the most vicious vampire on earth, Angel and Buffy barely escape with their lives, and Angel is severely wounded.

Later, Giles tells Buffy, "You're really hurting the Master; he wouldn't send the Three for just anyone. We must step up our training with weapons."

Meanwhile, the Three, having failed in their mission, offer up their lives as penance. The Master dallies with them for a moment, allowing them to believe that he is going to spare them, while Darla circles behind them and, with great glee, stakes each one and they explode into dust.

## LYLE AND TECTOR GORCH

These vampiric cowboy brothers appear in "Bad Eggs," arriving in Sunnydale for no apparent reason other than that the evil energy of the Hellmouth has drawn them there. Lyle tangles with Buffy first and decides that he and Tector should go after the Slayer when the moment is propitious. Originally from Abeline, Texas, they massacred an entire Mexican village in 1886...and that was *before* they became vampires. Not the sharpest tools in the shed, they finally attack Buffy while she is trying to deal with the Bezoar threat. The Bezoar kills Tector, and Lyle finally realizes that where this Slayer is involved, his wisest course is to head for the hills.

Lyle Gorch is still at large.

## ABSALOM

Appearing in the second season opener, "When She Was Bad," Absalom is the mouthpiece for the Anointed One. Though the Anointed One is technically the leader of what remains of the Brethren of Aurelius, Absalom seems to be their spokesman and the chief organizer of the effort to resurrect the Master.

**ABSALOM:** "Your day is done, girl. I'll grind you into a sticky paste. And I'll hear you beg before I smash in your face."

**BUFFY:** "So, are you gonna kill me? Or are you just making small talk?"  —**"When She Was Bad"**

Of course, at the end of the episode, Buffy shoves a torch into Absalom's face, and he goes up in a blast of flame, cinder, and ash.

## ST. VIGEOUS

St. Vigeous is a sort of patron saint of vampires. In ancient times, he led a vampiric crusade that swept through Edessa, Harran, and points east, destroying everything in its path.

The Feast of St. Vigeous is a time when the power of the vampire is at its peak. According to Giles, "For three nights, the Unholy Ones scourge themselves into a fury, culminating in a savage attack on the Night of St. Vigeous." In an expurgated bit of dialogue, Jenny Calendar refers to it as "a Holy Night of Attack."

# DEMONS

Even more so than with vampires, entire volumes can and have been written on the subject of demons. The concept is a broad one, but rises out of a mixture of religious world views, as well as popular and cultural myths, folklore, and superstitions. The idea of a lord of an underworld is found in many hierarchies of gods and goddesses: the Romans had Pluto, the Greeks Hades, and the Norsemen had Hel, to name a few. In addition, a vast array of mischievous spirits, faeries, wood sprites, poltergeists, and so on populate the religious and mythological landscape.

In the Judeo-Christian system, Satan (or Lucifer) has his subordinate demons, whose purpose is to harry humanity with aggravation and temptation. In the Old Testament, Satan was an angel whose occupation was to test humanity's loyalty to God. Only later do we have the tale of Satan's rebellion against God and the casting out of Satan and the angels who had sided with him. After which, of course, they became known as demons.

Later in the history of the Christian church, around the twelfth and thirteenth centuries, there was a general consensus that demons were actually all the old gods and goddesses, not only the lords of the underworld, all of whom had animal incarnations of some kind. At baptism, Christian souls were commanded to renounce "Thor and Odin and Saxnot and all evil beings that are like them." But the older notion that demons were fallen angels serving Lucifer is the belief that proved more resilient and became the more traditional definition of demons in Christian teachings.

As noted in the vampire section, however, in the mythology of *Buffy the Vampire Slayer*, the traditional story of creation is considered a myth. The demons in this series are based not on Judeo-Christian and Western tradition, but are more influenced by Eastern traditions, and to some extent by the works of prominent horror forefather H.P. Lovecraft, whose own mythology seems to have been based largely on ancient Sumerian demonology. Lovecraft's fiction included references to a race of "Old Ones" or "Ancient Ones," who existed on Earth before humanity and who were constantly trying to regain control of our world. Various acolytes and half-demons (for instance, the human twin in *The Dunwich Horror*) labored to open the gates and let the Old Ones through.

Also, as previously discussed, the vampires in *Buffy* are corpses inhabited by demons, and thus it follows that in the *Buffy* mythology demons are more often described by their function than by the form they have currently taken:

Ms. CALENDAR: "I knew this would happen sooner or later. It's probably a mischief demon, you know, like Kelkor or—"
GILES: "It's Moloch."
Ms. CALENDAR: "The Corruptor."
—**"I Robot, You Jane"**

And from "Killed by Death":

CORDELIA: "*Ew. What does this do?*"
GILES: "It, um, extracts vital internal organs so that it can regenerate its own mutating cells."
CORDELIA: "Wow. What does this one do?"
GILES: "It elongates its mouth to engulf the head of its casualty between its teeth."
CORDELIA: "Ouch. What does this one do?"
GILES: "It asks endless questions of those with whom it's supposed to be working but they're not getting anything done!"
CORDELIA: "Boy, there's a demon for everything."

This stated function is generally some kind of static goal, from a mindless reflex to lash out and destroy to a more sophisticated need to dominate and control. This is a limitation of demons, as opposed to the more fluid and multidimensional "living of a life" that humans engage in. As Spike says to Angel in "School Hard":

ANGEL: "Things change."
SPIKE: "Not us! Not demons."

As demon-inhabited corpses, vampires are evil, and they remain evil, despite the assertion of the Judge, who says of Drusilla and Spike that they stink of humanity, sharing affection and jealousy (in "Surprise.") In a sense then, what makes them human is their *capacity* for feeling emotion; what makes them demons is their inability to change; their emotions don't grow or lead to good as human emotions can. They are what they are, and they remain that way. And if evil is the inability to choose good, or feel love, for instance, then perhaps that explains the fury Angelus exhibits when he contemplates how completely he was changed when his soul was restored.

However, there are also good—or perhaps a better word is "neutral"—demons in the *Buffy* universe. Whistler is one such demon, and even he describes himself in terms of his function:

ANGEL: "You're not a vampire."
WHISTLER: "A demon, technically. But I'm not a bad guy—not all demons are dedicated to the destruction of all life. Someone has to maintain balance, you know. Good and evil

can't exist without each other, blah blah blah. I'm not like a good fairy or anything. I'm just trying to make it all balance—do I come off as defensive?"

—"Becoming, Part I"

The introduction of a character like Whistler suggests that in Whedon's universe, at least, there seems to be a continuum running between the opposite poles of human and demon; in other words, some demons are more human than others, and some humans behave like demons. Or, to put it another way, what makes us human is our capacity to change, to feel emotions, to choose good over evil. As Buffy herself says to Ford, the terminally ill young man who wants to become a vampire so he won't "die":

"You have a choice. You don't have a *good* choice. What's behind door number three is pretty much a dead fish, but you have a choice. You're opting for mass murderer here and nothing you say to me is gonna make that okay."

**Buffy, in "Lie to Me"**

Having chosen such a versatile approach to the demon, Joss Whedon has provided vast opportunities for more stories about demons, what makes them different from and similar to humans, and the choices they make or fail to make in the ongoing battle between good and evil.

## ACATHLA

Acathla, the demon, came forth to swallow the world. It was killed by a virtuous knight who pierced the demon's heart before it could draw breath to perform the act. Acathla turned to stone, as demons sometimes do, and was buried where neither man nor demon would be wont to look. Unless, of course, they're putting up low-rent housing." —Angel in, "Becoming, Part 1"

The entombed demon Acathla has been unearthed during the construction of low-income housing outside Sunnydale. He is stolen by Angel, Drusilla, and their henchmen and taken to their mansion. The lid of his coffin is opened, and the vampires react to the sight of the grimacing demon, a stone sword sticking out of his chest:

DRUSILLA: "Ooh, he fills my head.... I can't hear anything else...."

Angel approaches Acathla slowly, reverently.

SPIKE: "Let me guess. Someone pulls out the sword—"

DRUSILLA: "Someone worthy—"

SPIKE: "... the demon wakes up and wackiness ensues—"

DRUSILLA: "He will swallow the world."

ANGEL: "And every creature living on this planet will go to Hell. My friends, we're about to make history...end." —"Becoming, Part 1"

As explained by Giles, "The demon universe exists in a dimension separate from our own. With one breath, Acathla will create a vortex, a kind of whirlpool that will pull everything on Earth into that dimension, where any non-demon life will suffer horrible, eternal torment."

As is true of demons in the world of **Buffy the Vampire Slayer**, then, Acathla exists to serve a purpose. He is almost like a machine, with an on-off switch that, when pressed, will finally cleanse the Earth of humanity once and for all. His threat lies not in what he is, but in what he can do. And in the second-season finale, that threat is very real. In fact, only by sacrificing Angel does Buffy finally defeat Acathla.

## EYGHON, THE SLEEPWALKER

In his twenties, Giles rebelled against his inevitable destiny to become a Watcher, and together with Ethan Rayne, he organized a circle that dabbled in the occult for their own amusement. "And then," Giles explains, "Ethan and I discovered something a little bigger."

This was Giles's "Dark Age" when he and Ethan learned how to summon the ancient Etruscan demon Eyghon. They would put someone into a deep sleep and the others would summon the demon to inhabit the sleeper's body. According to Giles, the possession induced "an incredible high." However, Eyghon asserted control over one of the sleepers—Randall—and they could not send it back.

Each member of the circle—including Giles—bears a tattoo called the Mark of Eyghon, and this mark acts like a homing beacon to the demon as it searches out the people who tried to kill it, possessing each and destroying each in turn. As Willow tells her friends, reading from one of Giles's books, in "The Dark Age":

> "Eyghon, the Sleepwalker, can only exist in this reality by possessing an unconscious host. Temporary possession imbues the host with a euphoric feeling of power....Unless the proper rituals are observed, the possession is permanent, and Eyghon will be born from within the host....Once called, Eyghon can also take possession of the dead, but its demonic energy soon disintegrates the host and it must jump to the nearest dead or unconscious person to continue living."

In the opening of the episode, Eyghon is wearing the decaying corpse of Deirdre as it shambles after Philip Henry, intent upon killing him. "She" easily snaps his neck, and then she liquefies into a pool of ooze. This is Eyghon, as it rolls down an incline and washes over the dead hand of Philip, into whom it now enters.

Using Philip's corpse to pursue its next victims—two of them are in Sunnydale, namely Ethan Rayne and Giles—Eyghon jumps next into an unconscious person—Jenny Calendar, whom it attacked as Philip. During her possession, Jenny becomes more and more grotesque, until she resembles the demon in its natural state—an ugly, horned creature. Filled with Eyghon's rage and aggression, she beats Giles in anticipation of killing him, until Buffy arrives on the scene. Then the demon jumps through a window to escape.

Eventually, the demon is tricked into jumping from Jenny into Angel—it believes that Angel is trying to kill it by choking Jenny—a chilling foreshadowing of what is to come. Once inside Angel, it wrestles with the demon already in residence there...and loses. As Angel explains:

BUFFY: "You [Willow] knew that if the demon was in danger, it would jump into the nearest dead guy."
Willow nods, even smiles.
ANGEL: "I put it in danger."
WILLOW: "And it jumped."
ANGEL: "But I've had a demon inside me for a couple hundred years just waiting for a good fight."
BUFFY: "Winner and still champion."

Eyghon, the demon within, serves as a metaphor for the dark secrets and longings that we wish to hide from others. Buffy and her friends have always seen Giles as a steadfast, stuffy Brit with most, if not all, of the answers to every question they ask. Now, however, he has been revealed as less than perfect:

GILES: "I never wanted you to see that part of me."
BUFFY: "I'm not gonna lie. It was scary. I'm used to you being, you know, the Grown-Up. And then I find out that you're a person."
GILES: "Most grown-ups are."
BUFFY: "Who would've thought?"
GILES: "Some of them are even very short-sighted, foolish people."
BUFFY: "So after all this time, it turns out we do have something in common. Which, apart from being a little weird...is kind of okay."

It's telling that now that Buffy has seen this side of Giles, she, too, bears the Mark of Eyghon. But with the resilience of youth, she complains about the expense of having it removed—she was saving up for some "very important shoes."

# THE JUDGE

The Judge is a hideous blue demon (in fact, nicknamed "Big Blue" by Spike) that was brought forth to rid the Earth of the plague of humanity. "He would separate the righteous from the wicked...and burn the righteous down," Angel tells the others. In his last visit to Earth, it proved impossible to kill him, but an army finally managed to dismember him. The pieces of his body were scattered to the far corners of the Earth, each piece buried separately. In a scene expurgated from the episode for length, Xander quips: "Do you think they left his heart in San Francisco?" Oz replies, "I had that thought, too."

In "Surprise," the Judge's living arm nearly chokes Buffy to death when she opens the box containing it at her surprise birthday party—a gift originally meant for Drusilla, from Spike. Unsure if this is the only piece of the Judge in town, Angel is elected to take it far, far away, possibly Nepal, possibly somewhere even more remote.

Unfortunately, Spike's henchvamps steal back the box, and at the climax of Drusilla's party, the last piece of the Judge is put in place—his head. Energy surges around him. He's enormous, dressed in armor, with a horned head and solid black eyes.

His "righteousness radar" activated, his first impulse is to burn Drusilla and Spike who "stink of humanity." In their place, he is given the nebbishy Dalton, who is burned to a cinder because of his love for books. However, it's clear that the Judge needs to recuperate from his long ordeal—for now, he must touch his victims in order to burn them. But with each life he takes, his strength will increase. In time, he promises Spike, he will not need direct contact. In an expurgated sequence from "Innocence," the second half of the two-parter, he explains to Spike: "I fought an army. They hacked me to pieces. For 600 years, my living head lay in a box buried in the ground. I've learned to be patient."

It is because he isn't fully recovered that he briefly touches the Slayer and yet she lives.

It is the Judge who reveals to Spike and Drusilla that Angel has become Angelus once more, stating that "this one is clean." There is nothing human inside to burn.

Round-the-clock research yields no answer on how to destroy the Judge, until Willow's offhand comment, "Where's an army when you need one?" prompts Xander to come up with a plan to steal a rocket launcher. Since the Judge is a demon, an unchangeable being, modern warfare has caught up with him: an old-fashioned army may have had to physically hack him to pieces, but the Slayer, with one well-aimed shot with a rocket launcher, takes him out in a rain of blue fragments. The pieces are collected and kept separated...the implication being that the Judge will never be put back together again.

# MOLOCH, THE CORRUPTOR

"There's a demon in the Internet."
   **Giles to Jenny, in "I Robot, You Jane"**

In these, the latter years of the century, there has been much concern over the awesome potential for harm afforded by misuse of the Internet. Story after story appears on TV news shows and in the papers about pedophiles luring young children into tragic situations and shady characters of every stripe preying on the shy, the lonely, and the trusting by involving them in long on-line conversations that grow increasingly more familiar and intimate.

Add to this the strong public fear over the wealth of data available about individuals—credit-card numbers, medical histories, and supposedly private e-mail messages—and you have the ingredients for the rich subtext of "I Robot, You Jane."

In the Middle Ages, it was books and reading that were generally regarded with suspicion, an occupation better left to monks hidden away in shadowed monasteries. So it follows that it was believed, as Giles states (in a section expurgated from the script):

> "There are certain books that are not meant to be read. Ever. They have things trapped within them....In the Dark Ages, demons' souls were sometimes trapped in certain volumes. The demon would remain in the volume, harmless, unless the book was read aloud."

In medieval Italy, the horned demon Moloch, the Corruptor, held sway over a group of devoted disciples, to whom he promised love, wealth, and power. Despite his leathery, distorted features and clawlike hands, he was eerily elegant in his velvet clothes, moving among his followers like a Borgia prince. His standard way of thanking them for their devoted service was to summarily break their necks.

Finally, he was bound by a group of monks, sucked into a large book, and shelved.

Since the essence of a demon is an entity, not necessarily a form, Moloch has dwelled for centuries within the infernal volume. When the book arrives in a shipment for Giles, he is too distracted to take much note of its distinctive cover, directing instead that it be placed on "Willow's pile." To his intense unease, his library has been invaded by Jenny Calendar, the beautiful computer-science teacher, and she is presiding over the wholesale scanning of the library's holdings into the "idiot box," i.e., the school computer system.

While Giles sequesters himself "in the Middle Ages" section of the library, Willow innocently opens the book and scans the strange characters within into the computer's memory. Intent upon her work, she doesn't see the single question that appears across the computer screen, signaling that Moloch has been freed: "Where am I?"

"A very deadly and seductive demon," Moloch's specialty is preying upon "impressionable minds." As soon as he realizes that he's been released into the Internet, he begins a campaign to enlist a new army of followers. Sensing that the computer-literate Willow is also lonely, he presents himself as a boy named Malcolm Black and begins to send her a series of friendly e-mail letters, ostensibly from his hometown of Elmwood, eighty miles away. Willow, who has never had a real boyfriend, is flattered by his attention and begins an on-line romance with him that gives Buffy pause and makes Xander jealous.

Moloch also connects with Dave and Fritz, two Sunnydale High computer nerds. Dave is shy and quiet, while Fritz is more aggressive and intense about his opinions: "The printed page is obsolete," he says. "Information isn't bound up anymore, it's an entity. The only reality is virtual. If you're not jacked in, you're not alive."

Moloch soon manages to hold Dave and Fritz in his thrall, and they join with other computer experts at a shut-down computer facility to create a robot body for the incorporeal Moloch. A body of his own is the thing the demon craves: "To be able to walk...to touch...to kill."

He also wishes to give Willow the world, or so he says:

MOLOCH: "You created me. I brought these humans together to build me a body, but you gave me life. Took me out of the book that held me. I want to repay you."

WILLOW: "By lying to me. By pretending to be a person. [weakly] Pretending . . . you loved me."

MOLOCH: "I do."

In a mirroring of the unquantifiable capacity of the Internet, once Moloch inhabits the robot body his minions have created for him, he is capable of being bound. Working with Ms. Calendar and her Internet circle of fellow technopagans, Giles traps Moloch in his robot body and Buffy electrocutes him. The question remains: if he had remained within the Internet, could he have ever been destroyed?

## WHISTLER

As previously mentioned in the general overview on demons, Whistler describes himself as "technically" a demon whose function is to maintain the balance of good and evil. He is young and very badly dressed, "like a low-ranked mafioso." He tells Angel, whom he approaches in Manhattan in 1996, that his real name is hard to pronounce "unless you're a dolphin."

In "Becoming, Part 1," Whistler offers the half-sane vampire a choice: "You could become an even more useless rodent than you are right now, or you could become . . . someone. A person. Someone to be counted." Whistler then brings Angel to the spot where he sees Buffy for the first time, as she discovers she is the Slayer and must learn to fight the forces of evil. He is giving Angel a purpose—to help the frightened young girl—and he is giving Buffy an ally, for he says of her: "She's gonna have it tough, that Slayer. She's just a kid. And the world is full of big bad things."

Angel replies that he wants to help her. Whistler's impressed, but reminds Angel that this will not be an easy road. Angel asserts that he wants to learn from Whistler.

But he doesn't want to dress like him.

The demon next appears to Buffy, in "Becoming, Part 2." She guesses who he is—"an immortal demon sent down to even the score between good and evil"—but she's not impressed:

BUFFY: "Why don't you try getting off your immortal ass and fighting evil once in a while? 'Cause I'm tired of doing this by myself."
WHISTLER: "In the end, you're always by yourself. You're all you got. That's the point."
BUFFY: "Spare me."

Whistler's function, then, is not to actively even the score between good and evil, but to inspire others to do so. He can also give information, telling Buffy that using the sword blessed by the knight who slew Acathla isn't enough to thwart Angel's plan to send every non-demon being on Earth to Hell. As with all demons, he has limitations, and he cannot change.

But he can make bad jokes: "You know, raiding an Englishman's fridge is like dating a nun. You're never gonna get the good stuff."

## MACHIDA

Also known as "Wormy," "the One We Serve," and "Reptile Boy," Machida appeared in the episode of the same name. Machida is an enormous demon snake-monster which inhabited the dungeon-like basement of the Delta Zeta Kappa fraternity house on the Crestwood College campus. Accompanied by subsonic rumbling as he shoots from a pit in the basement floor, Machida's "terrible countenance" is terrible indeed as he towers high above his worshipers and their victims. In the words of "Reptile Boy" writer-director, David Greenwalt:

> "Machida is half man, half snake. He has a muscular body (from the waist up) and the enlarged and frightening head of a man with the fangs and horrible eyes of a snake. His skin has the diamond pattern of a snake—thus the diamond carvings on his "people." From the waist down, he is all snake—and a big 'un, too, his snake body trails behind him into the depths of the pit: God knows how long this guy is."

Once a year, the frat brothers of the DZK "psycho cult" lure unsuspecting high school girls to wild parties, drug them, and offer them as sacrificial offerings to the "enhungered" Machida. In return, Machida showers the fraternity members with riches and power. This has gone on for over a century, until Buffy slices Machida in two and she and the Scooby Gang—plus Angel—bring the DZKs to justice.

Originally, Machida was supposed to survive Buffy's attack, but according to Greenwalt, there was not enough time in the production schedule to shoot the sequence, and so Machida met his untimely end. This is the section of the shooting script that was cut to make this adjustment.

(from scene 86):
Tom comes to near the altar. And, unbeknownst to any of our heroes, the snake body begins slowly moving. Until it joins up with the torso. A squooshy sound of flesh and protoplasm meeting and the two halves rejoin!

(cont'd)

CORDELIA (to Tom): "And you, you're going to jail for about 15,000 years. Oh, God, it's over . . . it's really . . ."

That's when Machida, rejoined, suddenly pops up again. Angel takes a threatening step forward next to Buffy, growls. Machida towers over Tom:

MACHIDA: "For a hundred years I have given your forebears wealth and power. And this is how you repay me? From this day forth, you are alone in the world."

Machida slides back down. Cordelia is afraid to breathe. With good reason. Machida pops back up, grabs Tom.

MACHIDA: "Li'l somethin' for the road."

Machida disappears into the pit with Tom. We hear Tom's screams, a quick couple of chomps and then silence.

## THE KINDESTOD

At first glance, the monster in "Killed by Death" appears to be a hallucinatory projection of the Slayer herself, as she thrashes feverishly in a hospital bed, suffering from both the flu and severe injuries sustained in a battle with Angelus. But that's not it at all.

At the age of eight, Buffy was the lone witness to the bizarre and violent death of her little cousin Celia, who was in a hospital at the time. Now, at seventeen, Buffy is still terrified of hospitals and begs her mother not to make her stay despite her condition.

Adding to the air of menace is the fact that Angelus attempts to "visit" her. Xander blocks his entry and serves as sentry during Buffy's hospital stay.

Buffy's fever dream of a bizarre figure dressed "like a nineteenth-century undertaker" but with a pasty white face, beaky nose, and a mouth full of very ugly, sharp teeth propels her to investigate the hospital. In the children's ward, two doctors quarrel over the proper course of treatment for the children afflicted with the same virus Buffy has. As she observes them, a small boy and girl approach her, and the boy solemnly explains to her that the monster was with Tina, and he will come back for the rest of them.

The monster, he continues, is Death.

In the morning, Tina's sheeted body is wheeled out of the children's ward, and Buffy tries to explain to Giles and the others what Ryan told her. With her usual tact, Cordelia says what everyone else seems to be thinking:

"So this isn't about that you're afraid of hospitals 'cause your friend died and you wanna conjure up a monster that you can fight so you save everybody and not feel helpless?"

And despite the obvious truth that Don, the creepy security guard, shares with Cordelia—sometimes children die—Xander offers to help Buffy investigate Tina's death.

For a time, the doctor with whom Buffy's own doctor quarreled over treatment for the children—Dr. Backer—is suspected of being the culprit. But Buffy is eyewitness to his murder by an invisible assailant, who slashes his body and drags him down the hall. She is thrown against the wall by the unnamed, unknown force.

Ryan has given Buffy a picture of the monster, and she in turn hands the childish scrawl over to Giles to serve as a mug shot. At last he takes her seriously and heads to the library to do research. It is Cordelia, serving as his assistant, who pinpoints the monster:

CORDELIA: "It's called 'Der Kindestod.'. . . The name means 'child death.' This book says that he feeds off children by sucking the life out of them. *Blech*. Anyway, afterward, it looks like they died because they were sick."
BUFFY: "So it *did* kill Tina?"
CORDELIA: "Yeah. That's my take. 'Cause it would be looking at the children's ward as basically an 'all-you-can-eat' kind of thing, you know."
BUFFY: "Backer was curing the kids—and taking away the Kindestod's food."
CORDELIA: "Hence the slice-age."

Buffy puzzles over why she could at one time vaguely make out the figure of the Kindestod but since then he has been invisible. She finally realizes that she was sick—near Death—when she saw him. Ingesting a live virus, she faces him at last, to discover that he is a fearsome opponent. His method of killing the children is gruesome—worth every one of Cordelia's *"ews"* as she reads about him to Buffy: "His eyes bulge and protrude out of their sockets. Then they extend downward and push into the forehead of his victim." It's no wonder that Buffy's cousin Celia thrashed and screamed as she died.

Buffy is weak from the fever from the virus, and for one terrifying instant she finds herself on the receiving end of the Kindestod's terrible method of killing...until she manages with her last bit of strength to grab his head and break his neck.

It really doesn't look like we'll be seeing Der Kindestod again.

# THE BROTHERHOOD OF SEVEN

The "seven" in their name reflects both the number of demons, as well as the length of the cycle of their evil. The Brotherhood of Seven originally were seven demons who had the capacity to take the form of young human beings.

"Every seven years, these demons need human organs—a heart and a brain—to maintain their humanity. Otherwise, they revert back to their original form, which is slightly less appealing."
**Giles, in "The Puppet Show"**

In "The Puppet Show," there is a series of murders relating to the Sunnydale High Talent Show. Due to the missing organs, Giles surmises that one or more of the Brotherhood of Seven is responsible. He is, of course, correct. However, at first, Buffy, Giles, and company believe the demon is a student named Morgan, a budding ventriloquist. Later, they come to believe that one of the Seven inhabits his dummy, named Sid, and for good reason.

"On rare occasions, inanimate objects of human quality, such as dolls and mannequins, already mystically possessed of consciousness, having acted upon their desire to be human by harvesting organs."
**Giles, in "The Puppet Show"**

To everyone's surprise, it becomes evident that, although Sid is indeed mystically alive, he is not the demon. In fact, Sid was a demon hunter, cursed to live the rest of his life in the form of that dummy by the Brotherhood of Seven. By the time this story takes place, Sid has already dispatched six of the seven. When the last has been killed, his curse will be lifted. In the end, the seventh demon turns out to be a student magician named Marc. When Sid finally does kill that demon, his soul passes on to the next world at last, and the Brotherhood of Seven is destroyed forever.

# WITCHES AND SORCERERS

The subject of witchcraft has become, particularly over the past two decades or so, a controversial one. For although the presence of a tribal shaman, magic user, "witch," or the equivalent, was a pivotal position in many ancient cultures, the rise of "New Age" groups, societies, communes, and "alternative religions" has brought new awareness and attention to old practices. Consequently, witches are once again in the news. Of course, much of what is popularly referred to as "New Age" is not new, but instead is an outgrowth of shifts in political, social, and cultural thinking. The feminist and civil rights movements, changes in health care, and educational programs are but a few of the influences leading to a revival of interest in "the old ways." Modern paganism is one example of a type of "new" religion which prides itself on its relationship with ancient Druidic styles of worship. Some members prefer to be known as "witches" or devotees of the goddess Wicca. Sadly, they must battle the pop-culture impressions of witchcraft, which have their foundations in Christian theology, dating to the beginning of the twelfth century.

Over the subsequent six centuries, Christian doctrine would be completely altered, and Europe itself would be changed forever. The idea that Satan had gathered his forces and was systematically attempting to corrupt Earth and subjugate humanity had really not developed until this time. Nor had there been a literate population across the continent, joined by religion and communication for the first time, that would have been able to mount the horrors of what would come to be called the Inquisition.

The Inquisition consisted mainly of Christian "investigators" and "judges," whose mission was to weed witches out of society. Sadly, we have no space for a detailed examination of this era and phenomenon here. Suffice it to say that the majority of those killed—and the numbers were horrifying—were not witches at all (and, of course, we point out that witches themselves were hardly the Satanic agents the Inquisition portrayed them as, but rather members of oppressed religious sects). If you were accused as a witch, you would be tortured until you either died or confessed. And, if you confessed, you would likely be burned to death. Therefore, accusation alone was a death sentence. Of course, this quickly became a political tool. Want to get rid of an enemy? Accuse them of witchcraft!

The madness of the Inquisition spread to America in 1692, in Salem (now Danvers) Massachusetts, where many women in the town were hanged as witches. Amazingly, there were people burned as witches in Europe as late as the 1780s. Popular culture—particularly in the form of film and television—kept alive the Inquisition's image of the witch for most of the twentieth century. Only now have we begun to separate the myth from the reality.

The relationship between modern witches and actual magic, or spellcasting, is something we will not address here. In fact, even attempting to define magic beyond the popular-culture image of it is not what we're after. In that, we are little different from the creators of *Buffy the Vampire Slayer*. Witches, in *Buffy* parlance, seem to be powerful female magic users. Little else of their nature is explained. However, a line is clearly drawn between witchcraft and paganism, because Jenny Calendar is specifically referred to as a pagan, but the two witches (mother and daughter) discussed in the series so far are never portrayed with any kind of religious belief. At one point, Giles actually asks Jenny if she is a witch, and she replies: "I don't have that kind of power," suggesting that the "source" of power—or the use of that power—is a distinguishing factor. Also, both Giles and Willow use magic at one point or another, and are not classified as witches. So what else is necessary to make one, in the world of this series, a witch? We'll just have to watch and see.

We get very little solid information on witches in the two episodes in which the craft is used. However, Giles does discuss a test that reveals Amy/Catherine as the culprit in "Witch." The test requires some of the witch's hair, mercury, nitric acid, and...eye of newt. "Heat ingredients and apply to witch. If a spell has been cast in the previous forty-eight hours, witch's skin will turn blue." Simple as that. The beauty of it, of course, is that it works. At least on television.

GILES: "Witchcraft. Blinding your enemy to disable and disorient them is a classic."
XANDER: "First vampires, now witches. No wonder you can still afford a house in Sunnydale."
—"Witch"

"Intent has to be pure with love spells."
**Amy, in "Bewitched, Bothered, and Bewildered"**

"People under the influence of love spells are deadly, Xander. They lose all capacity to reason."
**Giles, in "Bewitched, Bothered, and Bewildered"**

One particular spell cast by Catherine as Amy is the Bloodstone Vengeance Spell, which, according to Giles, "hits the body hard, like drinking a quart of alcohol, then eradicates the immune system." In fact, it is with this spell that Catherine nearly kills Buffy.

We also learn in that episode that a witch's spells can be reversed with the use of the witch's "spell book," which seems to be some kind of journal of the witch's activities—or by cutting off the witch's head. To cast spells, the witch needs "a sacred space with a pentagram, a large pot . . ."

Also, the presence of a black cat guarding the witch's spell book in "Witch" would indicate at least a passing acknowledgement of the concept of "familiars" in the *Buffy* mythology. Familiars are animals with whom the witches can communicate.

## CATHERINE MADISON

In the episode aptly titled "Witch," the Slayer faces her first witch. Technically, this is the first use of magic on the series as well. Catherine Madison was the homecoming queen and cheerleading star of Sunnydale High when she was a teen. But when her own daughter didn't show an interest in such things, Catherine did something horrible. She used her witchcraft to actually switch bodies with her daughter, Amy.

No matter how hard Catherine worked to get Amy's body into shape, the change of bodies was too much for her, and she could not perfect the moves necessary to become a cheerleader. Instead, she made only the "alternate" list. To make the squad, Catherine used magic to eliminate the competition. She caused Amber Grove to spontaneously combust, made Lishanne's mouth disappear, and nearly killed Cordelia Chase by blinding her.

In the end, Giles managed to return Catherine to her own body, after which an enraged Catherine tried to use her witchcraft to destroy first her daughter and then Buffy. Buffy was able to put a mirror between herself and Catherine, reflecting the magic back at the witch. Ironically, to this day, Catherine remains trapped in a trophy case in the high school's front hall, inside the small cheerleading trophy she had won for the school when she was a teen cheer queen.

## AMY MADISON

Though Amy is not evil, she is, indeed, a witch. After being trapped for some time in her mother's body, one would have thought Amy would have learned not to toy with magic. Instead, it becomes obvious in "Bewitched, Bothered, and Bewildered" that Amy has been studying witchcraft. She casts a spell on one of her teachers to make the woman believe she has handed in homework that she never did. Amy is also coerced by Xander into casting a love spell on Cordelia, but the spell backfires with hysterical and discomforting consequences.

## ETHAN RAYNE

Ethan Rayne is a sinister friend from Giles's youth in London. As leaders of a circle that dabbled in the occult, they were responsible for the death of one of their associates who was possessed by the demon Eyghon. Ethan stands for everything Giles has repudiated, and it seems that he has come back into Giles's life only to cause him misery.

Ethan first appeared in "Halloween" as the proprietor of a shop filled with costumes, which he cursed by praying to the two-faced god Janus. His second appearance comes in "The Dark Age." He and Giles are being stalked by Eyghon. Giles suffers from paralyzing remorse over having summoned the demon in the first place and orders Buffy as her Watcher—his highest mantle of authority—to stay out of it. Ethan tattoos Buffy with the Mark of Eyghon and destroys his own tattoo with acid so that the demon will come after her instead.

Ethan has a dry wit, which may be one of the reasons he and Giles became friends:

**BUFFY:** "I know you, you ran that costume shop."
**ETHAN:** "I'm pleased you remember."
**BUFFY:** "You sold me that dress for Halloween and nearly got us all killed."
**ETHAN:** "But you looked great."

But he's also an immoral dilettante, explaining why Giles has repudiated that friendship:

**ETHAN:** "What? No hug? Aren't you pleased to see your old mate, Rupert?"
**GILES:** "I'm surprised I didn't guess it was you. This Halloween stunt stinks of Ethan Rayne."
**ETHAN** (proud): "Yes, it does, doesn't it? Don't want to blow my own horn, but—it's genius. The very embodiment of 'be careful what you wish for.'"
**GILES:** "It's sick. Brutal. And it harms the innocent."
**ETHAN** (wry): "Oh, and we all know that *you* are the champion of innocence and all things pure and good, Rupert….This is quite a little act you've got going here, old man."
**GILES:** "It's no act. It's who I am."

In both "Halloween" and "The Dark Age," Ethan Rayne disappears into the night. We can only wonder when he'll turn up next. . . .

# WEREWOLVES, SHAPE-SHIFTERS, AND PRIMALS

The origins of werewolf and shape-shifter myths are intertwined heavily with those of vampire legends. Vampires could, according to some legends, change their shapes, including transforming themselves into wolves. However, the best-known pieces of the mythology of lycanthropy, or werewolfism, are predicated on the fact that the werewolf or shape-shifter is a living human being somehow cursed or gifted with the ability to alter his or her form.

Like vampires, werewolf legends are found throughout history. Unlike vampires, however, stories about lycanthropy abound in the works of the most respected ancient historians. Herodotus, Pliny, Petronius, Virgil, and even, in his *Metamorphoses,* Ovid, discuss the transformation of men into werewolves, though in the majority of these cases the change is either permanent or it is an annual rather than a monthly event.

Indeed, werewolf stories or stories of similar shape-shifting, are to be found throughout ancient history and mythology, and into the nineteenth century. Norse mythology and Scandinavian folklore are rife with references to wolf-men, apparently in conjunction with the legend of the berserkers (literally, "bear-shirts," warriors cloaked in the skins of bears). Although in this case, rather than bear skins these wolf-men would wear wolf skins, and many had the power to make an actual change. Of course, this is but one example of a phenomenon found in folklore from around the world.

There are countless examples throughout history of man-beast creatures, and man-into-beast transformations, of which the traditional werewolf is only one. The *azeman* of South America is a human woman by day and a savage beast by night. There are legends of were-hyenas and were-lions in Africa, were-jaguars and were-boars in South America and kindly were-seals, or selkies, on the coastal islands of Scotland. Navajo legends discuss "skinwalkers," men who would wear the skins of wolves and thereby literally transform themselves into faster, more savage wolves. And these are merely a few examples.

"I must admit, I'm intrigued. A werewolf. It's one of the classics. I'm sure my books and I are in for a fascinating afternoon."   **Giles, in "Phases"**

In the mythology of *Buffy the Vampire Slayer,* there seems to be no end to the variations upon the lycanthropic or shape-shifting theme. Each time the subject has been touched upon, it has been in a manner entirely different from the others, and completely in keeping with the program. Boys transformed by science into giant sea creatures. An ancient half-human, half-insect shape-shifter. Demonic hyenas able to possess the souls and minds of human beings. And werewolves, of course.

GILES: "A werewolf is such a potent, extreme representation of our inborn, animalistic traits that it emerges for three consecutive nights—the full moon and the two nights surrounding it."
WILLOW: "Quite the party animal."
GILES: "Quite. It acts on pure instinct, no conscience, predatory and aggressive." —**"Phases"**

Interestingly, the werewolf concept presented in the series is much closer to its traditional representation than the vampires and demons in the series are. A werewolf, in Buffy's world, is a human being who had the misfortune to have been bitten by a werewolf and survived. This person will, from that day forth, transform into a wolf for the three nights of the full moon, every month. A werewolf can be killed only with weapons made of silver—most commonly a silver bullet.

One major departure for the series, however, is that the presentation of the werewolf is a sympathetic one. The werewolf is the victim of a curse and is not responsible for his or her actions while in the wolf state. Which makes things wonderfully complicated, of course.

## OZ

Oz is a werewolf. Apparently, he was bitten on the finger by his toddler cousin, Jordy, only to discover later on that Jordy was a werewolf. Jordy's parents, Uncle Ken and Aunt Maureen, may or may not be werewolves as well. This subject has yet to be addressed. However, Oz did seem strangely stoic about the revelation that he had become a *loup garous*.

"Is Jordy a werewolf? Uh-huh…and how long has that been going on? Uh-huh…no reason. Thanks. Love to Uncle Ken."
**Oz, in "Phases"**

For the three nights of the full moon each month, Oz chains himself up to stop his wolf-self from hunting the nighttime streets of Sunnydale. The chains were supplied by Buffy's Watcher, Rupert Giles. The Slayer and all her friends are aware that Oz is a werewolf. Even his girlfriend, Willow Rosenberg, is sympathetic.

"Well, I like you. You're nice, and you're funny and you don't smoke, and okay, werewolf, but that's not all the time. I mean, three days out of the month *I'm* not much fun to be around, either."
**Willow, in "Phases"**

As a werewolf, Oz has yet to take a human life. In wolf-form, he is huge and quite powerful. His only known natural enemy is the werewolf hunter, Gib Cain, who was forced to leave town without the werewolf pelt he wanted so badly. Cain hunts werewolves to skin them and sell their pelts in Sri Lanka. Chances are, we may see Gib Cain again, particularly with Oz taking a more prominent role in the series' third season.

## THE PACK

In high school, as in any jungle, there always seem to be those mean kids who run together and pick on other, more timid classmates. They practice a kind of brinksmanship, rarely crossing the line into overt cruelty (for which they could be punished), but still satisfying some inner need to dominate.

Joss Whedon has commented that his high school years were difficult and that much of ***Buffy the Vampire Slayer*** springs, at its core, from those memories and experiences. They certainly resonate with the show's audience, which might explain why the viewership is so varied. All of us can remember a time in school when we felt put on the spot, laughed at, or misunderstood.

Four of the five "monsters" of "The Pack," begin the show as just this sort of bullying group. Kyle, Tor, Rhonda, and Heidi spend the field trip to the zoo picking on shy, bookish Lance, an easy and tempting target. They intimidate him into joining them on a forbidden tour of the Hyena House and half-threaten to throw him to the quarantined animals.

Xander arrives on the scene to help Lance. He and Kyle are practically on the verge of blows when the hyenas' eyes flash yellow…and the eyes of each member of the pack glow in turn. As do Xander's. Now he is possessed by the spirit of the hyenas.

Xander begins to change, subtly at first—he seems more aggressive, a little rude, and he starts sniffing his friends. The four other hyena-people seem to respect him in some way, perhaps even to include them in their sphere of influence.

The changes grow more pronounced, until Buffy appeals to Giles, certain that something is wrong. He responds by tut-tutting her concerns:

GILES: "Xander's taken to teasing the less fortunate?"
BUFFY: "Uh-huh."
GILES: "There's been a noticeable change in both clothing and demeanor?"
BUFFY: "Yes."
GILES: "And otherwise all his spare time is spent lounging about with imbeciles?"
BUFFY: "It's bad?"
GILES: "It's devastating. He's turned into a sixteen-year-old boy! Of course, you'll have to kill him."

It's not until Xander and the other members of his pack devour the school mascot that Giles does his research, and he recalls the story of a sect of animal worshipers called Primals. Their goal is to become possessed by the spirits of the most predatory animals—hyenas, for example:

"The Masai of the Serengeti have spoken of animal possession for generations. I should have remembered that.…They believe that humanity, consciousness, the soul—is a dilution of spirit. To them, the animal state is holy. They were able, through trans-possession, to pull the spirit of certain animals into themselves."

As the possession continues, the victim, or host, takes on the characteristics of the animal that is possessing him or her, until they are little more than a savage beast. The hyena-people devour the principal, and Xander attacks Buffy. The stakes upped, Giles visits the zookeeper in charge of the hyenas and discovers that he knows of the legend of the Primals. He explains that the transference requires a predatory act and the presence of a totemic symbol. One of which, Giles notices, is drawn on the floor of the hyena house.

In his own case—for the zookeeper is revealed as a Primal believer—the predatory act is Buffy's attack on him as he threatens to cut Willow's throat. The hyena-people burst into the Hyena House, intent upon devouring Buffy in a scene reminiscent of William Golding's *The Lord of the Flies*, a novel about British schoolboys who "revert" to savagery when they are marooned on an island.

The zookeeper chants sacred words, and the spirits inside the hyena-people leap into him all at once, completely obliterating his humanity. As Xander and Buffy fight to protect Willow from him, he falls to his death inside the hyena enclosure, devoured by the very animals he wished so desperately to commune with.

ZOOKEEPER: "A Masai tribesman once told me that hyenas can understand human speech. They follow humans by day, learning their names. At night, when the campfire dies, they call out to a person. And once that person is separated . . . the pack devours him."

## SHE-MANTIS

Though she took on the identity of an aging substitute teacher named Natalie French when she came to Sunnydale, the true name of the She-Mantis is not revealed during her single appearance, in "Teacher's Pet." The creature is either a "perception-distorter" or possessed of the power to alter its physical mass between a human form and its true form, that of a giant praying mantis which has a taste for young male virgins. In "Teacher's Pet," it first dispatches biology teacher Dr. Gregory, so that the school will have need of a substitute. Then it sets its sights on and abducts a pair of young male students, Blayne Mall and Xander Harris. The She-Mantis is a terrifying creature, fierce enough that it frightens even vampires.

Like her tiny cousins, the She-Mantis is a cannibal who eats her mate's head during the act of mating. She "lays her eggs and then finds a mate to fertilize them." She can turn her head 180 degrees, even in human form.

> "No, no, I'm not saying she craned her neck. We are talking full-on *Exorcist* twist."
>
> **Buffy, in "Teacher's Pet"**

Giles has a former associate, Dr. Ferris Carlyle, who, according to the Watcher, "spent years transcribing a lost, pre-Germanic language," wherein he first read of the She-Mantis's existence. When several teenage boys were murdered, Carlyle went hunting for the creature.

> "This type of creature, the Kleptes-Virgo or virgin-thief, appears in many cultures: the Greek Sirens, the Celtic sea-maidens who tore the living flesh from the bones of…"
>
> **Giles, in "Teacher's Pet"**

Dr. Carlyle was committed to an insane asylum after his run-in with the creature. When Giles contacted him, Carlyle recommended that Buffy cleave all its body parts with a sharp blade. Which is, of course, what she did in the end. It is Buffy, however, who pointed out that they would be able to use the recorded sounds of bat sonar to distract the creature so that she could get close enough to kill it.

## Fish-Men

In "Go Fish," it at first appears as though the swim team is being attacked and devoured by huge fish monsters. However, over the course of the episode, it is revealed that the members of the team are actually evolving into these enormous fish-men. Dodd McAlvy, Gage Petronzi, Cameron Walker (with whom Buffy goes on a date early in this episode), and another swimmer, named Sean, lose their humanity, thanks to a type of steroid experimentation by Coach Marin and Nurse Greenleigh. On an interesting note, Buffy begins to suspect something is wrong with the swimmers when Gage is attacked by Angel, only to have Angel spit out the swimmer's blood.

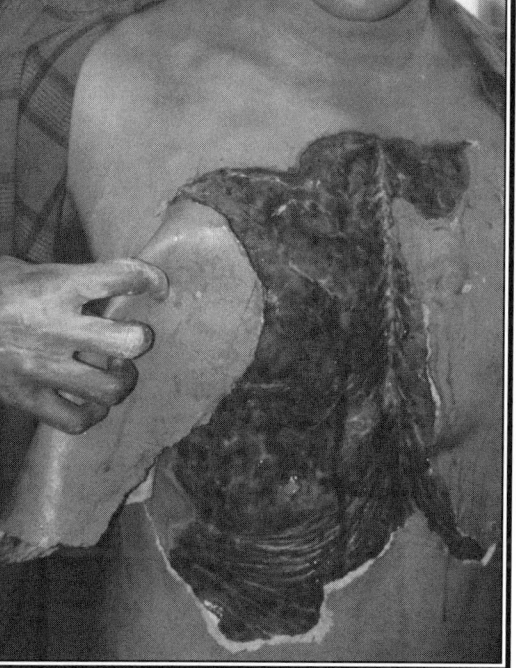

> **Buffy:** "It's all here in their school medical records."
>
> **Willow:** "All symptomatic of steroid abuse."
>
> **Xander:** "But is steroid abuse usually linked with 'Hey, I'm a fish'?"
>
> **—"Go Fish"**

When Xander goes "undercover" and joins the swim team, he discovers that the "steroids" are being given to the swimmers as part of their steam bath. They're breathing them in. When Nurse Greenliegh tries to talk Coach Marin into abandoning the treatments, the coach feeds her to the fish-men. All that matters to the coach is that they win. When Buffy presses him, he reveals the source of these mutations.

> "After the fall of the Soviet Union, documents came to light detailing experiments with fish DNA on their Olympic swimmers. Tarpon, mako shark—but they never cracked it."
>
> **Coach Marin, in "Go Fish"**

Though the "team" has already eaten, Coach Marin ends up dropping Buffy down into the grotto where the fish-men are waiting. They aren't hungry, but the coach apparently has decided they can use Buffy to satisfy other needs. "This is just what my rep needs," she quips. "That I did it with the entire swim team." In the end, Coach Marin ends up down in the grotto, where the fish-men tear him apart. Finally, they are seen swimming out into the Pacific, and it is implied that this is home to them now and they won't be back.

# GHOSTS

The words "ghost" and "guest" spring from the same source, the Germanic "Geist." In northern England, the words are still pronounced identically. In most early belief systems, ghosts were the spirits of dead ancestors invited to tribal events, ceremonies, and feasts, such as Samhain (Halloween). In Europe, the heads or skulls of the dead were preserved and decorated, and the spirits of the deceased were considered to be present when these objects were displayed. They were also consulted as oracles after being given an offering.

As Christianity established itself as a religious and political force, these customs were discouraged because the church's doctrine of the resurrection of the body insisted that a buried body be kept as whole as possible. Thus, the hanging of the heads of executed traitors on pikes or gates represented a direct threat against any kind of life in the hereafter. Yet the custom of preserving heads continued well after the establishment of the Christian church: in the days of Henry VIII of England, the daughter of Sir Thomas More retrieved the head of her executed father and rather than burying it, is reputed to have kept it with her until she died.

This concern is no doubt the source of many ghost stories in which the phantoms carry their heads under their arms—"The Headless Horseman," by Washington Irving, comes to mind.

Other beliefs attached to ghosts are that they are the restless spirits of people who died violently or committed suicide, were buried in unconsecrated ground, or had been possessed by evil spirits. They haunt the places where they dwelled as living beings or where they met their untimely ends.

In an expurgated sequence in "Out of Mind, Out of Sight," Giles talks about having seen a ghost: ". . . in Dartmoor. A murdered countess, very beautiful. She used to float along the foothills, moaning the most piteous..."

In a sequence left in the episode, he explains that he has never touched nor been touched by a ghost, and they make the deduction that what they're dealing with is not a ghost:

GILES: "From what I've read, having a ghost pass through you is a singular experience. It's a cold, amorphous feeling, makes your hair stand on end."

BUFFY: "Okay, this is my problem. I touched the thing. It didn't go through me, it bumped into me. And it wasn't cold."

XANDER: "So this means, what— That we're talking about an invisible person?"

Though different cultures have adopted different "takes" on ghost lore—for example, Japanese ghosts are said to have no feet and are drawn to water—there seems to be universal agreement that they are the spirits of someone, or something, who has died.

## JAMES STANLEY AND GRACE NEWMAN

In Western belief, a variant of the standard ghost is the poltergeist, or "noisy ghost." In the episode "I Only Have Eyes for You"—thus far the only episode that deals with ghosts—Giles deduces that the malevolent force at work within the school is a poltergeist. It seems that in 1955, a Sunnydale High student named James Stanley was in love with a teacher named Grace Newman. Though she loved him in return, she knew their affair must end and tried to tell him so on the night of the Sadie Hawkins Dance. In a blind panic at the thought of losing her, he shot and killed her. Then, filled with remorse, he turned the gun on himself.

Now, in present day, as the dance draws near (and, one assumes, the Hellmouth charges the situation with its energy), individuals who pass through the same part of the school where James and Grace fought and died become possessed by their spirits and reenact the tragedy. Buffy breaks up a fight between two quarreling students (who are reciting, we later learn, the last conversation James and Grace had before he shot her) and is sent to the principal's office for her trouble. While there, a yearbook from 1955 falls from the shelves, apparently moved by a ghostly hand.

In history class, she dreams of James and Grace during their tragic romance, and when she drowses awake, discovers that her teacher, Mr. Miller, is scrawling, DON'T WALK AWAY FROM ME, BITCH, on the blackboard, apparently without realizing it.

Concerned, Buffy talks to Xander, who replies: "I'm not trying to poo-poo your wiggins, but a domestic dispute and a little case of chalkboard Tourette's? Sounds like 'Hellmouth Lite' to me—"

His tune changes when a blue decaying arm bursts from his locker and tries to drag him inside. They hurry to Giles:

GILES: "Fascinating. It sounds like paranormal phenomena."
WILLOW: "A ghost? Cool!"
XANDER: "Oh, no, not cool. This was no wimpy chain-rattler. This was more like—'I'm dead as hell and I'm not gonna take it anymore.'"
GILES: "Exactly. Despite the Xander-speak, that's an accurate definition of a poltergeist."
XANDER: "I defined something? Accurately? Check me out. Guess I'm done with the book learning!"
BUFFY: "So we've got some bad boo on our hands?"
GILES: "Well . . . A poltergeist is extremely disruptive—and what you described certainly fits the bill."
WILLOW: "But why is it here? Does it just want to scare people?"
GILES: "It doesn't know exactly what it wants. That's the problem. Many times the spirit is plagued by all manner of worldly troubles. But, being dead, it has no way to make its peace. So it lashes out. Growing ever more confused, ever more angry."
BUFFY: "So—it's like a regular teenager. Only dead."
WILLOW: "What can we do? Is there any way to stop it?"
GILES: "The only tried-and-true way is to figure out what unresolved issues keep the spirit here—and resolve them."
BUFFY: "Great. So now we're Dr. Laura for the deceased."
GILES: "Only if we can find out who this spirit is. Or...was."

Giles, in a radical departure from his usually cautious approach to the presence of any kind of supernatural phenomenon, jumps to the conclusion that this troubled spirit is Jenny Calendar. Even after the school janitor shoots and kills Miss Frank, a teacher, Giles clings to this belief...a false hope at best, a poignant testament to his love for Jenny. Meanwhile, Buffy and company do the research that Giles usually does and discover the story of James and Grace. They conclude that the violent spirit is the ghost of James, in terrible need of forgiveness.

What is particularly interesting about this interpretation of a poltergeist is that not only can it wreak havoc, but it can possess individuals and move them to repeat the act which doomed it in the first place. And while the suffering spirit of James enters Buffy, who herself is burdened with guilt over the change in Angel—a change she feels entirely responsible for—the gentle ghost of Grace, who wishes to forgive James, manages to infiltrate the demonic Angel, completely obliterating—at least temporarily—his savage and brutal nature.

# REANIMATED CORPSES

Legends and myths abound the world over about people coming back from the dead. The vampire myth itself is very much about life after death, or "undeath," as it is often called. So are ghost stories. But reanimated corpses are slightly different. These are people whom, for one reason or another, rise up from death in their own bodies, with their own minds (for the most part), usually for some sinister purpose or another. Once upon a time, our popular culture was able to make the distinction between a zombie—a human being raised from the dead, usually by magic or voodoo, and bound to obey the person responsible for their revival—and a ghoul, a person raised by some malevolent purpose and driven by the urge to eat human flesh. After George A. Romero's *Night of the Living Dead,* in 1968, however, the two became almost inextricably joined. Zombies and ghouls were, essentially, one and the same.

There are, of course, other theories about ways to reanimate a corpse. Primary among them is through scientific means. Mary Shelley's legendary novel *Frankenstein* introduced that enduring piece of mythology to the world. The mad scientist playing god, the corpse brought back to life, and the tragedy that ensues, have been portrayed by writers and filmmakers time and again, inspired by Shelley.

But how do these things translate into the world of *Buffy the Vampire Slayer?*

## ZOMBIES

Zombies do exist in Buffy's world, although technically, we have yet to actually see one. However, there are several discussions about them in "Some Assembly Required." The specific mythology of zombies in the series has few established facts, but Giles does tell Xander that "zombies don't eat the flesh of the living." That, of course, leaves the door open for ghouls down the road, although ghouls were usually thought to frequent gravesites and eat the flesh of the newly dead.

It also implies that zombies, according to the series, do eat the flesh of dead humans.

In addition, in the same episode, when Giles discovers that someone has been robbing graves, he suggests that it might be a voodoo practitioner. When Xander asks him if he means somebody might be "making a zombie," Giles replies, "...or zombies. For most traditional purposes, a voodoo priest would need more than one."

Thus far, this is all the information we have on zombies in Buffy's world.

## DARYL EPPS

"Some Assembly Required" is clearly, in part at least, an homage to Mary Shelley's *Frankenstein.* In this instance, however, the mad scientists in question happen to be two high school boys, Chris Epps and his friend Eric. Their monster is Chris's older brother, Daryl, who died in a fall, "rock climbing or something," according to Willow. But Chris wasn't content to let his brother stay dead. With Eric, he sewed his brother back together and, through some unrevealed scientific process, brought Daryl back from the dead.

Daryl remained in his family's basement, while his mother grieved endlessly upstairs. He needed a companion, and he asked Chris and Eric to make him a woman who was like him so he wouldn't be alone. When their plans were ruined by Buffy's interference, Daryl died a final death because he refused to leave the partially constructed companion to burn in the old science building where the experiments were taking place. Daryl Epps is one monster we can reasonably expect to never see again. Except, perhaps, as a ghost. On this series, you never know.

## AMPATA GUTIERREZ, A.K.A INCA MUMMY GIRL

Five hundred years ago, the Incan people chose a beautiful teenage girl to become their princess..." so that they could sacrifice her to the gods. Mummified and imprisoned in a tomb in a state of living death, the mummy was bound in that state by a ceramic seal clasped between her withered hands.

When Rodney, a Sunnydale High student, tries to steal the seal, the mummy rises from her sarcophagus, kills Rodney, and leaves his freeze-dried corpse in her place. In the process, the protective seal is broken.

Ampata is actually the name of the South American exchange student who is slated to stay with Buffy and her mother. By the time Buffy is to pick him up at the bus station, the mummy has sucked the life out of him, renewing her own once more. She introduces herself to Buffy as Ampata.

Ampata's hunger not only for the life force of others but for the experience of life itself, makes her one of the most sympathetic monsters to appear in the first two seasons:

"She was sixteen. Like us. She was offered as a sacrifice and went to her death. Who knows what she gave up to fulfill her duty to others. What chance at love?"
**Ampata, to Buffy, in "Inca Mummy Girl"**

She is a tragic figure, given no choice in her fate. She is even described as the Chosen One by the Peruvian man who hunts her, seeking to stop her from taking the lives of others and return her to her hellish existence inside her cramped, dark tomb.

She also is the first girl other than Buffy to attract Xander, who cannot believe his good fortune that the beautiful, exotic girl seems to return his affection ("You're not a praying mantis, by any chance, are you?"). She grows to love him, and though desperate, struggles not to take his life away from him. She tries to deflect her need onto others—Jonathan and even Willow:

XANDER: "If you're going to kiss anybody, it should be me."
AMPATA: "Xander, we can be together. Just let me have this one."
XANDER: "That's never gonna happen."
AMPATA: "I must do this *now*, or it is the end. For me and for us."  —**"Inca Mummy Girl"**

And it is not until she is almost completely decayed that she approaches Xander with her fatal kiss.

After the mummy is destroyed, Buffy underscores the tragedy of "Ampata's" life, while Xander emphasizes Buffy's heroism when confronted by a similar destiny:

BUFFY: "She was gypped. She was just a girl, and she had her life taken from her. I remember when I heard the prophecy that I was going to die. I wasn't exactly obsessed with doing the right thing."
XANDER: "But you did. You gave up your life."

# OTHER MONSTERS

## INVISIBLE PEOPLE

Though it's reasonable to assume that in the *Buffy the Vampire Slayer* mythology there are many different ways for someone to become invisible, we're going to concentrate on the one documented brand of invisibility.

"Greek myths talk about cloaks of invisibility, but they're usually just for the gods....Research boy comes through with the knowledge."
**Xander, in "Out of Mind, Out of Sight"**

In "Out of Mind, Out of Sight," there is a series of attacks on unsuspecting students by an invisible person. At first, Giles considers several possibilities, including ghosts and telekinesis, but it's soon obvious that they are dealing with a living human capable of invisibility.

Soon, Buffy discovers the identity of the "invisible girl." Marcie Ross was a student at Sunnydale High—a student nobody spoke to, or remembered. Even Xander and Willow, kind to a fault, seem to have been oblivious to her existence. This leads Giles to the astonishing revelation that Marcie is not invisible because of any supernatural event, but rather because of a scientific one. In a line cut from the script, Giles explains that "reality is shaped, even created, by our perception of it." The answer lies in quantum mechanics, according to Giles, who realizes that Marcie was perceived as invisible, and so she became invisible.

Marcie is understandably angered, and perhaps even slightly insane, due to her condition. She attempts to get her revenge, and, in the end, plans to carve up Cordelia's face as an example to everyone and a lesson to Cordelia. Of course, Buffy manages to save the day, but in the end, Marcie is spirited away by FBI agents Doyle and Manetti. "This isn't the first time this has happened, is it?" Buffy asks. "This has happened at other schools." Of course, Doyle and Manetti don't bother answering the question. Marcie is taken to an FBI compound and into a classroom filled with invisible people who are learning about "assassination and infiltration" in their textbooks. Obviously, Marcie and a lot of others like her are still out there.

## The Order of Taraka

The Order of Taraka first appears in the two parter, "What's My Line?" Spike, desperate to cure Drusilla and fearing Buffy's interference, decides that extraordinary measures are required. As such, he calls in the Order, to the surprise of his followers.

DALTON: "The Order of Taraka? I mean, isn't that overkill?"
SPIKE: "No. I think it's just enough kill."
—"What's My Line? Part 1"

At this point, the only hint as to the nature of the Order is a single reference, when one of the vampires, Dalton, refers to them as "the bounty hunters." But they are far, far more than bounty hunters. They are, in fact, a "society of deadly assassins dating back to King Solomon," or so Giles informs us.

"Their credo is to sow discord and kill the unwary....They're a breed apart....Unlike vampires, they have no earthly desires except to collect their bounty. They find their target and eliminate it. You can kill as many of them as you like. It won't make any difference—where there is one, there will be another. And another. They won't stop coming until the job is done. Each one of them works alone. His own way. Some of them are human. Some are not. We won't know who they are...until they strike."
Giles, in "What's My Line? Part 1"

Members of the Order of Taraka also wear a particular ring that identifies them as assassins of the Order. They are, according to Kendra, also discussed in detail in volume six of the *Writings of Dramius*. In this two-part episode, we are exposed to three of the Order's assassins. First is a woman known only as Patrice, who disguises herself as a police officer and attempts to shoot Buffy during Career Week at school. Patrice ends up living longer than the others, though she seems in many ways less frightening. The first to attack Buffy, and also the first to die, is Octarus, whom the original script described as "a GIANT. Seven feet tall in boots and a hard 400 pounds. A thick milky cataract covers one eye. His other eye is set deep in the fleshy mask of assorted scars and carbuncles he calls a face." Fortunately, the Octarus that reached the final version of the episode was just as horrifying. Unfortunately, he doesn't last very long.

The most disturbing assassin from the Order of Taraka, at least that we have seen thus far, is Mr. Pfister. Probably a demon of some kind, Pfister is a being who looks human but is actually composed entirely of maggots and other bugs. In an unfortunately expurgated moment from the second half of this two-parter, Xander says it best: "You know, just when you think you've seen it all, along comes a worm guy."

BUFFY: "You and bug people, Xander. What's up with that?"
XANDER: "No, this dude was different than praying-mantis lady. He was a man *of* bugs, not a man who *was* a bug."
—"What's My Line? Part 2"

In the end, while Octarus and Patrice are defeated in straight combat by Buffy and Kendra, respectively, Mr. Pfister takes a bit more ingenuity. He can be killed only when he is in his disassembled state. Thus, Xander and Cordelia taunt him, then hide behind a door so that he must break up into his true self, the horde of bugs. When they crawl under the door, they find themselves trapped in a pool of white paint that Xander and Cordelia have spread there . . . and they stomp him to death.

> "Hey, larva boy! That's right. I'm talking to you, the big cootie!"
> **Xander, in "What's My Line? Part 2"**

After the finale, we don't hear anymore about the Order until the next episode, "Ted," where Buffy tells Willow and Xander that "Angel's sources" say the contract is off. However, since the Order of Taraka is made up of all kinds of creatures—human, demon, vampire and otherwise—chances are, we may well end up seeing them again.

## BEZOAR

From "Bad Eggs" little Bezoar grow....

A Bezoar is a prehistoric parasite. The mother hibernates underground, laying eggs that look identical to chicken eggs. While still in the egg, the Bezoar sends out long tendrils that spread over the intended host's face, preparing its prey for subjugation. The Bezoar hatchling is an ugly creature that looks like a chicken breast riding on crab legs, reminiscent of the early stages of the Alien in the *Alien* film series.

Buffy, the gang, and the other students in their Teen Health class accidentally (?) receive Bezoar eggs to "parent" in a section on sex ed. As the eggs hatch, the offspring attach themselves to the unsuspecting students, taking control of their minds and bodies through "neural clamping." Cordelia and Willow, as well as their health teacher, Mr. Whitmore, Giles, and Buffy's mother are all taken over. Xander is spared because he boiled his egg to lessen the chances that it would break while he was parenting it, and Buffy catches her Bezoar hatchling as it breaks out of its shell and kills it.

The mother Bezoar is "a slimy expanse of black that moves and breathes below the cave" that lies beyond the school's boiler room, opening one sole eye to observe her surroundings. Her hatchlings are directing their human hosts to break open the floor under which she lies and free her. The hosts are directed to kill any humans who have not been subjugated, which they attempt without hesitation. With a whiplike tentacle, the mother Bezoar lassos the vampiric cowboy Tector Gorch and pulls him down into the pit, apparently consuming him. Tector's brother, Lyle, tries to feed Buffy to the monster, but the Slayer destroys the creature and then emerges from the Bezoar's pit covered in the blue goo that is the Bezoar's blood.

## THE UGLY MAN

The Ugly Man is a fascinating monster, in that he exists only as a construct of the imagination of young Billy Palmer. After a Kiddie League baseball game in which he missed a critical play, twelve-year old Billy was attacked and brutally beaten. Billy was comatose after the attack, and his attacker remained unknown to the authorities. Only after Billy had regained consciousness did Buffy, Giles, and the others realize that it had been Billy's baseball coach who had attacked the boy.

While comatose, Billy suffered horrible nightmares, and somehow his mind interacted with the Hellmouth to reach out to others in the town and bring their own nightmares to life. While all of this was occurring, however, Billy's own nightmare, "the Ugly Man," was also running free in the town. The Ugly Man was Billy's nightmare version of the man who'd beaten him. As an interesting aside, it seemed that Billy was also astrally projecting an image of himself into the real world, an image which only the Slayer could see. Giles postulates that it is this projection that has caused Billy's nightmares to "leak" into reality.

The first actual appearance of the Ugly Man is at the end of the first act of "Nightmares." A student named Laura ducks into the school boiler room for a cigarette and is attacked and savagely beaten by the Ugly Man, who says only "lucky nineteen." This turns out to be a reference to Billy's jersey number on the baseball team—it was what the coach called him, at least before he missed an important catch. The Ugly Man also has a thick club arm, and is, hence the name, hideous to look at. For most of the rest of the episode, he hunts Billy and Buffy, and in the end Buffy not only defeats him, but helps Billy "unmask" him. Billy wakes, and all returns to normal. A short time later, his coach, the real-life inspiration for the psychically created

Ugly Man, enters the room. When he realizes his crime has been discovered, he attempts to flee, but Xander and Giles stop him.

## TED BUCHANAN

Ted Buchanan would have been enough of a monster if he'd been human. In the episode simply titled "Ted," Buffy comes home to find her mother "Frenching a guy" in their kitchen. This turns out to be Joyce's new boyfriend. To everyone else, Ted seems to be the perfect father figure. He's a great cook, obviously has great values, and gets along well with everyone. But…

BUFFY: "So far, all I see is someone who apparently has a good job, seems nice and polite, and my mother really likes him.…"
XANDER: "What kind of a monster is he?!?!"
—"Ted"

Needless to say, Buffy's friends don't take her concerns very seriously, even though Ted, in a private moment, actually threatens to slap Buffy. Later, he reads her diary, and when they argue over it, he does finally hit her. She fights back, and as the Slayer, overpowers him. Ted ends up falling down the stairs and apparently dying.

Later, however, Buffy's suspicions are proven correct: Ted comes back to life, psychotically obsessed with Joyce. We quickly discover that Ted was never what he seemed, particularly after Xander, Willow, and Cordelia visit his address and find his four previous wives or, rather, their preserved corpses.

"Feels like home. If it's the '50s and you're a psycho."
**Cordelia, on visiting Ted's abode, in "Ted"**

As it turns out, "Ted" isn't Ted Buchanan at all, but a robot that the brilliant but mad Buchanan built when he was dying. To put it in terms Xander could understand:

"'I'm Ted the sickly loser; I'm dying and my wife dumps me. I build a better Ted. He brings her back. She dies in his little love bunker, and so he keeps bringing her back over and over.' That's creepy on a level I hardly knew existed."
**Xander, in "Ted"**

In the end, Buffy destroys Ted. Later, she tells Joyce that she is certain he's on the "scrap heap." But anyone who's seen *The Terminator* will tell you that you can't keep a good robot down. After all, there's no telling how many "Teds" the original built.

# SPELLS, CHANTS, AND INCANTATIONS

"The sleeper will awaken. The sleeper will awaken. And the world will bleed."
**Luke, chanting in "Welcome to the Hellmouth"**

"And like a plague of boils, the race of Man covered the Earth. But on the third day of the newest light will come the Harvest, when the blood of men will flow as wine, when the Master will walk among them once more, the world will belong to the Old Ones, and Hell itself will come to town. Amen."
**Luke, quoting from "the sacred text" in "Welcome to the Hellmouth"**

**MASTER:** "My blood runs with yours. My soul is your province."
**LUKE:** "My body is your instrument."
**—preparing the Vessel, in "The Harvest"**

"The center is dark. *Centrum est obscurus*. The darkness breathes. *Tenebrae respiratis*. The listener hears. Hear me. Unlock the gate, let the darkness shine. Cover us with holy fear. Show me. Corsheth and Gilail, the gate is closed. Receive the dark, release the unworthy.... Take of mine energy and be sated! Be sated, release the unworthy!"
**Giles, casting the spell to switch Amy and Catherine back to their own bodies, in "Witch"**

"I shall look upon my enemy. I shall look upon her and the dark place will have her soul. Corsheth! Take her!"
**Catherine, trying to zap Buffy into oblivion, in "Witch"**

"For the Old Ones, for his pain, for the dark."
**The Brethren of Aurelius, chanting for the Master's resurrection in "When She Was Bad"**

"St. Vigeous, you who murdered so many, we beseech you, cleanse us of our weaknesses: mercy, compassion, and pity."
**Lean Boy's prayer to St. Vigeous, in "School Hard"**

"Diana, goddess of love and the hunt, I pray to thee. Let my cries bind the heart of Xander's beloved. May she neither rest nor sleep until she submits to his will only. Diana! Bring about this love and bless it!"
**Amy's love spell in "Bewitched, Bothered, and Bewildered"**

"Goddess Hecate, work thy will. Before thee let the unclean thing crawl!"
**Amy, turning Buffy into a rat, in "Bewitched, Bothered, and Bewildered"**

"Diana! Hecate! I hereby license thee to depart! Goddess of creatures great and small, I conjure thee to withdraw!"
**Amy, turning the rat back into Buffy, in "Bewitched, Bothered, and Bewildered"**

"Eligor, I name thee. Bringer of war, poisoners, pariahs, grand obscenity! Eligor, wretched master of decay, bring your black medicine. Come restore your impious, murderous child. From the blood of the sire she is risen! From the blood of the sire shall she rise again.... Right, then. Now we let them come to a simmering boil, then remove to a low flame."
**Spike, intoning the du Lac ritual, which will restore Dru to health, in "What's My Line? Part 2"**

"Diana, goddess of love, be gone! Hear no more your siren's song!"
> **Giles, breaking the love spell, in "Bewitched, Bothered, and Bewildered"**

"And there will be a time of crisis, of worlds hanging in the balance. And in this time shall come the Anointed, the Master's great warrior. And the Slayer will not know him, will not stop him. And he will lead her into Hell. As it is written, so shall it be. Five will die, and from their ashes the Anointed shall rise. The Brethren of Aurelius shall greet him and usher him to his immortal destiny. As it is written, so shall it be."
> **The Master, reading from the writings of Aurelius, in "Never Kill A Boy on the First Date"**

"By the power of the Circle of Kayless, I command you, demon. Come!"
> **Thelonius Monk, binding Moloch into the book, in "I Robot, You Jane"**

"By the power of the divine...by the essence of the word, I command you. By the power of the Circle of Kayless, I command you! Demon, COME!"
> **Giles, speaking and Jenny typing, getting Moloch "off-line," in "I Robot, You Jane"**

YOUNG MAN: "I pledge my life and my death...."
RICHARD: "To the Delta Zeta Kappas and to Machida, whom we serve."
YOUNG MAN: "To the Delta Zeta Kappas and to Machida, whom we serve."
RICHARD: "On my oath, before my assembled brethren."
YOUNG MAN: "On my oath, before my assembled brethren."
Richard: "I promise to keep our secret from this day until my death."
YOUNG MAN: "I promise to keep our secret from this day until my death."
RICHARD: "In blood I was baptized, in blood I shall reign, in His Name!"
YOUNG MAN: "In blood I was baptized, in blood I shall reign, in His Name!"
RICHARD: "You are now one of us."
YOUNG MAN: "In His Name!"
> **—initiation ceremony into the DZK fraternity house, in "Reptile Boy"**

TOM: "Machida...We who serve you, we who receive all that you bestow, call upon you in this holy hour."
OTHERS: "Machida."
TOM: "We have no wealth, no possession, except that which you give us. We have no power, no place in the world, except that which you give us."
OTHERS: "Except that which you give us."
TOM: "It has been a year since our last offerings . . . a year in which our bounty overflowed....We come before you with fresh offerings . . . we hope you find them worthy. Accept our offering, dark lord, and bless us with your power, Machida! Come forth and let your terrible countenance look upon servants and their humble offerings! We call you, Machida!"
OTHERS: "In his name! Machida!"
TOM: "For he shall rise from the depths and we shall tremble before him. He who is the souce of all we inherit and all we possess. MACHIDA!"
OTHERS: "Machida!"
TOM: "And if he is pleased with our offerings, then our fortunes shall increase."
OTHERS: "Machida, let our fortunes increase."
TOM: "And on the tenth day of the tenth month, he shall be enhungered and we shall feed him. Feed, dark lord."
> **—ritual for feeding Machida, in "Reptile Boy"**

"The word that denies thee, thou inhabit. The peace that ignores thee, thou corrupt. Chaos, I remain, as ever, your faithful, degenerate son. [Then, in Latin] Janus, hear my plea. Take this as your own. Come forth and show us your truth. The mask is made flesh. The heart is curdled by your holy presence. Janus, this night is *yours*."
> **Ethan Rayne, incantation to enchant the wearers of his costumes, in "Halloween"**

"...*his verbes, consesus rescissus est.* [By these words, consent repealed.]"
> **Willow, repealing Angel's invitation to enter Buffy's home, in "Passion"**

"I shall confront and expel all evil...out of marrow and bone—out of house and home—never to come here again."
> **Willow, Cordelia, Xander, and Buffy performing a ritual of exorcism, in "I Only Have Eyes for You" (Cordy adds "totally")**

In Rumanian: *Nici mort nici al flinçtei*
  *Te invoc, spirit al trecerii*
  *Reda trupului ce separa omul de animal*
  *Cu ajutorul acestui magic glob de cristal.*

"Not dead, nor not of the living. Spirits of the interregnum, I call. Restore to the corporal vessel that which separates us from beast. Use this orb as your guide."
> **Gypsy woman, chanting the Spell of Restoration of the Soul, in "Becoming, Part 1"**

"I will drink...the blood will wash in me, over me, and I will be cleansed. I will be worthy to free Acathla. [to Spike and Dru]: Bear witness as I ascend. As I become."
> **Angel, reciting the ritual to awaken Acathla, in "Becoming, Part 1"**

"*Quod perditum est, in venietur.*" [What was lost, shall be found.]
> **Giles, reciting the Spell of Restoration of the Soul in Latin, in "Becoming, Part 1"**

"Not dead, nor not of the living. Spirits of the interregnum, I call. Let him know the pain of humanity, gods—reach your wizened hands to me, give me the soul of—" [she's interrupted]
> **Willow, reciting the Spell of Restoration after Giles, in "Becoming, Part 1"**

"Gods bind him, cast his heart from the demon...realm...return his...I call on...I...*Te implor Doamne, nu ignora accasta rugaminte! Lasa orbita sa fie vasul care-i va transporta sufletul la el!* [I call on you, gods, do not ignore this supplication! Let the orb be the vessel to carry his soul to him!] *Este scris, aceasta putere este dreptul poporului meu de a conduce...* [It is written, this power is my people's right to wield...] *Asa sa fie! Acum!* [Let it be so! Now!]"
> **Willow, attempting the Spell of Restoration one more time, in "Becoming, Part 2"**

**BLOODLUST**

*Buffy the Vampire Slayer*

*Love may make the world go round, but in Sunnydale, it can kill you. Do the wacky with the wrong vampire, demon, robot, or bug woman and you may be the next to die. Maybe it's the Hellmouth and maybe it's hormones, but Sunnydale is one smoldering berg when it comes to 'der big smootchen.' Thrill, therefore, as the fireworks go off—and the smoke alarms—for these...*

# Sunnydale Love Connections

## Buffy and Angel

For ne'er was there a tale of more woe . . .

The course of true love has never run less smoothly than for the Slayer and the tormented Angel. Introducing himself as "a friend" (though not necessarily *her* friend) in the premiere episode, "Welcome to the Hellmouth," Angel's earliest meetings with Buffy generally consisted of warning her about impending danger...neither of them dreaming that he would ultimately pose the greatest threat of all the evil forces she has ever faced.

In the second episode, "The Harvest," he takes a risk by telling her his name. After all, her Watcher may eventually make the connection between Angel and Angelus. But apparently his courage has limits...or could it simply be that he understands that the Slayer has a sacred duty, while he does not?

**Buffy**: "If this Harvest thing is such a suckfest, why don't **you** stop it?"
**Angel:** "Because I'm afraid."
**Angel:** "They'll be expecting you."
**Buffy:** "I've got a friend down there—or, a potential friend. [joking] Do you know what it's like to have a friend?"
He doesn't answer.
**Buffy** (gently): "That wasn't supposed to be a stumper."

In "Teacher's Pet," the fourth episode of the first season, it is established that Angel has made it a practice to come to Buffy when he has heard of possible dangers in her midst:

**Buffy:** "Well, look who's here."
**Angel:** "Hi."
**Buffy:** "I'd say it's nice to see you but we both know that's a big fib."
**Angel:** "I won't stay long."
**Buffy:** "No, you'll just give me a cryptic warning about some exciting new catastrophe and then disappear into the night, right?"
**Angel:** "You're cold."
**Buffy:** "You can take it."
**Angel:** "I mean you look cold."
Angel takes off his leather jacket.

Nevertheless, this mysterious man—"dark, gorgeous, in an annoying sort of way" (as she decribes him to Giles)—continues to intrigue her. A solitary figure, he seems haunted and lonely. Perhaps she is drawn to him because of aloneness...something she shares, for although she has good friends in Willow and Xander, she alone in all her generation is the Slayer.

Yet Angel has revealed to her a shared sense of purpose—"to kill them, kill 'em all—" which bonds them to each other almost before Buffy realizes what is happening. This man, this guardian Angel, has become important to her, though she knows very little about him. And though she tries to be "a real girl," having real crushes on boys and going out on dates, the importance of all they share overshadows everything else:

**Angel:** "Buffy. I was hoping I'd find you here."
**Buffy** (a little flustered): "You were hoping—?"
**Angel:** "There's severe stuff happening tonight. You need to be out there."
**Buffy:** "Oh, no. Not you too."
**Angel:** "You already know?"
**Buffy:** "Prophecy, Anointed One, yada yada yada."
**Angel:** "So you know. Fine. I just thought I'd warn you."
**Buffy:** "Warn me?" [indicating Owen] See that guy over at the bar? He came here to *be* with me."
**Angel:** "You're here on a date?"
**Buffy:** "Yeah. Why is that such a shock to everyone?"

—**"NEVER KILL A BOY ON THE FIRST DATE"**

The next episode Angel appears in is the one that bears his name, promising revelations. Buffy has not been successful in her bid to be a regular girl:

**Willow:** "It's a lot of fun [the Bronze fumigation party]. What's it like where you are?"
**Buffy:** "I'm sorry. I was just...thinking about...things."
**Willow:** "So we're talking about a guy."
**Buffy:** "Not exactly. For us to have a conversation about a guy, there would have to be a guy for us to have a conversation about. Was that a sentence?"
**Willow:** "You lack a guy."
**Buffy:** "I do. Which is fine with me, most of the time, but . . . "
**Willow:** "What about Angel?"

**Buffy:** "Angel. I can just see him in a relationship. 'Hi, honey, you're in grave danger. I'll see you next month.'"
**Willow:** "He's not around much, it's true."
**Buffy:** "When he's around, I think it's like the lights dim everywhere else. You know how that happens with some guys?" —AT THE BRONZE, IN "ANGEL"

Later, when he joins in her battle against the Three and they escape together into her house, the tension builds. He takes off his shirt; they stand close as she tends to his wound; still, attracted though she is, the Slayer tries to stay in control of the situation:

**Buffy:** "I was lucky you came along. How did you happen to come along?"
**Angel:** "I live nearby. I was just out walking."
**Buffy:** "So you weren't following me? I just had this feeling you were...."
**Angel:** "Why would I do that?"
**Buffy:** "You tell me, you're the Mystery Guy who appears out of nowhere—I'm not saying I'm not happy about it tonight—but if you *are* hanging around, I'd like to know why."

Meanwhile, Joyce Summers has told Buffy to go to bed, and Angel can't leave because "the Fang Gang" may be loitering nearby. And so together they climb the stairs to her bedroom, as the tension rises.... "So, uh-oh, two of us, one bed—that doesn't work—" And the next evening, when she returns from her life in the daylight, he confesses: "I did a lot of thinking today. I can't really be around you...because when I am...all I can think about is how badly I want to kiss you—"

Unable to conquer his passions, he does kiss her, fiercely, until, bloodlust upon him, he pulls back and reveals his true face:

He is her enemy.

He is a vampire.

"I can't believe this is happening....One minute we're kissing, the next minute [to Giles]...can a vampire ever be a good person? Couldn't it happen?"

**Buffy, in "Angel"**

Still, Buffy wavers in her duty as the Slayer: "He's never done anything to hurt me." And she and Willow talk about him pretty much as they would talk about any boy they were interested in:

**Willow:** "Okay, here's something I gotta know: when Angel kissed you, I mean before he turned into....How was it?"
**Buffy:** "Unbelievable." —"ANGEL"

**Willow:** "And it is kind of novel how he'll stay young and handsome forever—although you'll still get wrinkly and die—and ooh, what about the children—I'll be quiet now."
—"ANGEL"

Then, in what for her is the ultimate betrayal, Buffy is horrified to find Angel bent over her mother, his fangs lowered near the bleeding puncture wounds in her neck. Still, Buffy does not stake him. She throws him through the window and calls 911. But later, at the hospital, she realizes that the time has come to destroy Angel.

Showdown, as terrible truths are revealed:

**Buffy:** "Why? Why didn't you just attack me when you had the chance? Was it a joke? To make me feel for you and then.... I've killed a lot of vampires. I've never hated one before."
**Angel:** "Feels good, doesn't it? Feels simple."
**Buffy:** "I invited you into my home. And then you attacked my family."
**Angel:** "Why not? I killed mine."

This is a pivotal moment, because it shows the depth of Angel's remorse. Rather than correct her false conclusion—his sire, Darla, attacked Buffy's mother, in order to both frame him and get him to feed on a living human, thus returning to the vampire fold—he tells her more horrible things about himself: "I killed their friends and their friends' children. For a hundred years, I offered an ugly death to everyone I met. And I did it with a song in my heart."

When he does admit that he didn't attack her mother, he makes another confession: "I wanted to. I can walk like a man, but I'm not one. I wanted to kill you tonight."

Buffy sets down her weapon—a crossbow—walks to him, and offers him her neck, saying, "Go ahead." When he only looks at her, they reach an understanding: it's not as easy as it looks. Their relationship is deeper and more complex than that.

When they meet again, agreeing that they must part, they tenderly kiss...the Slayer's cross-shaped brand searing the heart of Angel.

Angel vanishes for three episodes, and when he returns, in "Out of Mind, Out of Sight," he is avoiding Buffy:

**Giles:** "Is that why you're here? To see her?"
**Angel** (shakes his head): "I can't. It's . . . it's too hard for me to be around her."
**Giles:** "A vampire in love with the Slayer. It's rather poetic, in a maudlin sort of way."

In the first season's finale, "Prophecy Girl," the joy Buffy feels upon seeing Angel is wrenching...once she knows that he's discussing the fact that she will die in less than twenty-four hours. "You think I want anything to happen to you? You think I could stand it?" he asks her.

And though Angel loves her, it is Xander who forces him to go down into the tunnels with him to rescue Buffy. And it is Xander who brings Buffy back to life with CPR. But it is Angel who finally, publicly attacks his own kind as the Hellmouth opens. And Angel who is finally accepted as Buffy's companion...at least for this evening...as they set off for the prom.

In the second-season opener, "When She Was Bad," Buffy is having a hard time dealing with her own fate at the hands of the Master...as well as her destiny as a Slayer. She is cold and cruel to all her friends, including Angel:

**Buffy:** "Is that it? Is that everything? 'Cause you woke me up from a really nice dream."
**Angel:** "Sorry. I'll go."
He heads for the window. Stands facing it as Buffy hunkers down in bed, facing away from him.
**Angel** (quietly): "I missed you."
She can't reply, but the hardness in her face melts away. After a couple of beats, she turns, her true emotions about to spill out.
**Buffy:** "I missed—"
But he's gone. She stares at the window, unhappy.  —**"WHEN SHE WAS BAD"**

> "Uh, could you contemplate getting over yourself? There's no 'us.' I'm sorry if I was supposed to spend the summer mooning over you, but I didn't. I moved on. To the living."
> **Buffy, to Angel, in "When She Was Bad"**

**Angel:** "Why are you riding me?"
**Buffy:** "Because I don't trust you. You're a vampire. Or is that an offensive term? Should I say 'undead American'?"
**Angel:** "You have to trust someone. You can't do this alone."
**Buffy:** "I trust me."
**Angel:** "You're not as strong as you think."
**Buffy:** "You think you could take me."
**Angel:** "What?"
**Buffy:** "Come on, you must have wondered . . . a vampire, the Slayer, I know you've thought about it. If it came down to a fight . . . could you take me? Why don't we find out?"
**Angel:** "I'm not gonna fight you."
**Buffy:** "No? Big strong vampire like yourself?"
**Angel:** "Buffy..."
**Buffy:** "Come on. Kick my ass."  —**"WHEN SHE WAS BAD"**

When Buffy finally grinds the Master's bones into dust, she collapses into Angel's arms, sobbing out her fear, her frustration, and her victory to the one she loves best.

In the next episode, "Some Assembly Required," they move on, becoming more of a twosome. Which includes quarreling:

**Buffy:** "Are you jealous?"
**Angel:** "Of Xander? Please, he's just a kid."
**Buffy:** "Is it 'cause I danced with him?"
**Angel:** "'Danced with' is a pretty loose term. 'Mated with' might be a little closer...."
**Buffy:** "Don't you think you're being a little unfair? One little dance, which I only did to make you crazy, by the way; behold my success!"
**Angel:** "I am not jealous!"
**Buffy:** "Oh, you're not jealous. What, vampires don't get jealous?"
**Angel:** "See? Whenever we fight, you always bring up the vampire thing."
**Buffy:** "I didn't come here to fight."  —**"SOME ASSEMBLY REQUIRED"**

By the end of the episode, Angel can laugh at himself a little and make an admission:

**Buffy:** "Love makes you do the wacky."
**Angel:** "What?"
**Buffy:** "Crazy stuff."
**Angel:** "Oh. Crazy like a 241-year-old being jealous of a high school junior?"
**Buffy:** "Are you fessing up?"
**Angel:** "I thought about it. Maybe he bothers me a little."
**Buffy:** "I don't love Xander."
**Angel:** "But he's in your life. He gets to be there when I can't. Take your classes, eat your meals, hear your jokes and complaints. He gets to see you in the sunlight."
**Buffy:** "I don't look that good in direct light."
**Angel:** "It'll be morning soon."
**Buffy:** "I should probably go.... I could walk you home." —**"SOME ASSEMBLY REQUIRED"**

And they have their miscommunications, the same as any other new couple:

**Angel:** "You said you weren't sure if you were going."
**Buffy:** "I was being cool. C'mon, you've been dating for what, 200 years, you don't know what a girl means when she says maybe she'll show? Work with me here." —**"SCHOOL HARD"**

Things go from bad to worse in "Reptile Boy":

**Buffy:** "I was just thinking, wouldn't it be funny to see each other sometime when it wasn't a blood thing? Not funny ha ha."
**Angel:** "What are you saying, you want to have a date?"
**Buffy:** "No—"
**Angel:** "You don't want to have a date?"
**Buffy:** "Who said 'date'? I never said 'date.'"
**Angel:** "Right. You just want to have coffee or something."
**Buffy:** "Coffee?"
**Angel:** "I knew this would happen."
**Buffy:** "Really? And what do you think is happening?"
**Angel:** "You're sixteen years old, I'm 241."
**Buffy:** "I've done the math."
**Angel:** "You don't know what you're doing, you don't know what you want."
**Buffy:** "Oh, I think I do: I want out of this conversation."
**Angel:** "Listen. If we date, you and I both know one thing's going to lead to another."
**Buffy:** "One thing's already led to another. It's a little late to be reading me the warning label."
**Angel:** "I'm just trying to protect you. This could get out of control."
**Buffy:** "Isn't that the way it's supposed to be?"

**Angel:** "This isn't some fairy tale; when I kiss you, you don't wake up from a deep sleep and live happily ever after."
**Buffy:** "No. When you kiss me, I want to die." —"REPTILE BOY"

In "Halloween," Buffy hopes to please Angel by dressing as a noblewoman after seeing a sketch of one in a Watcher's Diary about him. After their misadventures, they debrief:

**Angel:** "I don't get it, Buffy. Why did you think I'd like you better dressed that way?"
**Buffy:** "I—I just wanted to be a real girl, for once. The kind of fancy girl you liked when you were my age—what?"
**Angel:** "I hated the girls back then. Especially the noblewomen."
**Buffy:** "You did?"
**Angel:** "They were just incredibly dull. Simpering morons, the lot of them. I always wished I could meet someone...exciting. Interesting." —"HALLOWEEN"

But the lightness of this interlude is shattering in "Lie to Me," when Buffy must learn more bitter truths about Angel. As she had to accept that he had been sired by Darla in "Angel," she now must learn that the beautiful girl she has seen him with is not only a vampire and Spike's "paramour," but someone Angel hideously wronged:

**Angel:** "I did a lot of unconscionable things when I became a vampire. Drusilla was the worst. She was...an obsession of mine. She was pure and sweet and chaste."
**Buffy:** "You made her a vampire."
**Angel:** "First I made her insane. Killed everybody she loved, visited every mental torture on her I could devise. She eventually fled to a convent, and on the day she took her Holy Orders, I turned her into a demon." —"LIE TO ME"

Buffy absorbs this shock as well, and their love continues to grow. In "What's My Line? Part I," as it hits home to Buffy that no matter what the results of the school Career Fair, her destiny is unalterable, she assures Angel of her love:

**Buffy:** "Angel, it's not you. You're the one freaky thing in my freaky world that makes sense to me. I just get messed up sometimes. I wish we could be regular kids."
**Angel:** "I'll never be a kid."
**Buffy:** "Okay, then. A regular kid and her cradle-robbing, creature-of-the-night boyfriend." —"WHAT'S MY LINE? PART 1"

Later, after Angel takes Buffy skating in an effort to recapture her lost girlhood dreams, they do battle with an assassin from the Order of Taraka. Angel is still wearing his vamp face when she tends to his wounds, even as he's urging her to flee:

**Angel:** "I—you shouldn't have to touch me when I'm like this."
**Buffy:** "Like—what?"
**Angel:** "You know. When I'm . . . "
**Buffy:** "Oh. I didn't even notice." —"WHAT'S MY LINE? PART 1"

In "Bad Eggs," Buffy prophetically speaks the line that foreshadows their doom: "Please. Like Angel and I are just helpless slaves to passion. Grow up."

But their passion is growing as their relationship matures past the dating stage and into serious love. And while Angel, as the older and more mature of the two of them, begins to look at their future and worry, Buffy struggles to hold onto her dream with the hopefulness of any seventeen-year-old:

**Buffy:** "Like, I'm really planning to have kids anytime soon. Maybe someday, when I'm done having a life. But I think a kid would be a little too much to deal with."
**Angel:** "I wouldn't know. [then, carefully] I don't . . . Well, you know, I can't."
This sinks in.
**Buffy:** "Oh. [regrouping] "Well, it's totally okay. I figured there are all kinds of things vampires can't do, like, you know, work for the telephone company, volunteer for the Red Cross. Have little vampires."
**Angel** (skeptical): "So you don't think about the future?"
**Buffy:** "No."
**Angel:** "Never?"
**Buffy:** "No."
**Angel:** "How can you say that? You really don't care what happens a year from now? Five years from now?"
**Buffy** (with difficulty): "Angel. When I try to look into the future, all I can see is you—"
—"BAD EGGS"

Now their relationship has reached the apex of its growth: they have faced many dangers together; Buffy has discovered and accepted the terrible truths that lie behind her beloved's face. She loves him completely...and she is pondering her next step...to love him utterly. She has accepted that death stares her in the face each night—her death, but perhaps Angel's death—as she has a terrible dream, only to be reassured by his loving presence when she runs to him:

**Buffy:** "...I like seeing you first thing in the morning—"
**Angel:** "It's bedtime for me."
**Buffy:** "Then I like seeing you at bedtime...I mean...you know what I mean. That I like seeing you. And the part at the end of the night where we say good-bye, it's getting harder."
**Angel:** "Yeah, it is."
—"SURPRISE"

It's a more reflective, thoughtful Buffy who discusses her feelings with Willow:

**Buffy:** "Want isn't always the right thing...to do. To act on want can be wrong."
**Willow:** "True."
**Buffy:** "But, to not act on want. What if I never feel this way again?"
**Willow:** "Carpe diem. You told me that once."
**Buffy:** "Fish of the day?"
**Willow:** "Not carp. Carpe. It means seize the day."
**Buffy:** "Right." [a long beat] "I think we're going to . . . seize it. Once you get to a certain point, then seizing is sort of inevitable."
—"SURPRISE"

Buffy has had many things taken from her: she comes from a broken home; she has been essentially exiled from Los Angeles. Nightly, while other girls are gossiping on the phone and trying out new nail polish colors, she is keeping those same girls safe until another sunrise. As the Slayer, she cannot look forward to a normal future. Loving Angel, she cannot hope for a white picket fence and a yard full of kids.

So when it appears to her that Angel might be taken from her in "Surprise," and he is given back to her one more time, it makes sense that Buffy would do everything in her power to claim him. To claim her love for him, and for life.

Buffy gives herself to Angel. They make love.

And their world shatters.

For in that one moment of true happiness, Angel loses his soul and Buffy's nightmare begins.

**Angel:** "Lighten up. It was a good time. Doesn't mean we have to make a big deal."
**Buffy:** "It is a big deal! It's—it's—"
**Angel:** "Fireworks. Bells ringing. A dulcet choir of pretty little birdies. Come on, Buffy, it's not like I haven't been there before."
**Buffy:** "Why are you saying these things to me?"
**Angel:** "I should have known you wouldn't be able to handle it."
**Buffy:** "Angel...I love you."
**Angel:** "Love ya too. I'll call ya." —"INNOCENCE"

**Buffy:** "Angel...there must be some part of you inside that remembers who you are...."
**Angel:** "Dream on, schoolgirl. Your boyfriend is dead. You're all gonna join him."
**Buffy:** "Leave Willow alone and deal with me."
**Angel:** "But she's so cute and helpless. It's really a turn-on." —"INNOCENCE"

As she realizes that the beautiful gift she gave to him—her complete and unconditional love, forsaking all others, cleaving to him, has made him into a monster.

He hounds her, terrifies her with threats toward her mother and her loved ones, delighting in her fear as he sits beside her bed, stroking her hair as she sleeps, leaving portraits and roses in his wake....

Yet with each morning, her resolve strengthens: this is not the man she loved. This is the final, terrible truth: her love killed that man.

**Angel:** "You know what the worst part was? Pretending that I loved you. If I'd known how easily you'd give it up, I wouldn't even have bothered."
**Buffy:** "That doesn't work anymore. You're not Angel."
**Angel:** "You'd like to think that, wouldn't you? Doesn't matter. The important thing is, you made me the man I am today." —"INNOCENCE"

He begins to taunt her, as in "Phases," when he "sends his love" by turning a schoolmate into a vampire. Or as Valentine's Day nears:

**Giles:** "There's a disturbing trend. Around Valentine's Day, he's prone to rather brutal displays of...what he would think of as affection, I suppose."
**Buffy:** "Like what?"
**Giles:** "No—no need to go into detail." —"BEWITCHED, BOTHERED, AND BEWILDERED"

**Giles:** "He's doing this deliberately, Buffy. He's trying to make it harder for you."
**Buffy:** "He's only making it easier. I know what I have to do."
**Giles:** "What?"
**Buffy:** "Kill him." —"INNOCENCE"

With the murder of Jenny Calendar—the person the Watcher held most dear, the Slayer is compelled to act against the murderer . . . he demon who has taken the place of her beloved: "Because I know now that there's nothing that's ever going to change him back to the Angel I fell in love with."

And yet, there is an odd resonance to the discord of his actions:

**Buffy:** "It's so weird....Every time something like that happens, my first instinct is to run and tell Angel. I can't believe it's the same person. He's the complete opposite of what he was."
**Willow:** "Well...sort of, except...."
**Buffy:** "Except what?"
**Willow:** "You're still the only thing he thinks about." —"PASSION"

Angel proves this to her, in "Killed by Death," when he tries to "visit" her and Xander staves him off. Then, in "I Only Have Eyes for You," Buffy cannot forgive herself for sleeping with Angel and tearing his soul away from him. She is awash in misery, and yet, as the ghost of someone who desperately needs to be forgiven fills her spirit and Angel and his demon are possessed by the one who was wronged and who needs to forgive, there is a moment—brief and gossamer—where grace descends.

Finally, in the climactic season finale, Angel is saved...only to be damned. When, as the demon, he decides to send the entire world to Hell, he believes that he has lost his passion for Buffy. And she, having loved him through the first shock of his vampirism, through the sins he committed as a demon, to the realization that she must sacrifice him just as he has regained his soul, becomes the ultimate tragic hero. Their last words:

**Angel:** "What's happening, Buffy?"
**Buffy:** "Sh....It doesn't matter."
She pulls away to look at him. Kisses him passionately.
**Buffy:** "I love you."
**Angel:** "I love you . . ."
**Buffy:** "Close your eyes."

And then the Slayer sends Angel, a redeemed soul and her one true love, straight to Hell. For never was there a tale of more woe...

# Three Strikes...

**BUFFY AND FORD:** Buffy "loved" Billy Fordham in the fifth grade, but he was a manly sixth-grader who had no time for younger women. When "Ford" arrives in Sunnydale, he tells Buffy that his father has been transferred and that he'll be attending Sunnydale High.

He's lying. Terminally ill, he doesn't even bother with registering in school. Instead, he meets as soon as possible with Spike and offers him a deal: if Spike will agree to turn Ford into a vampire, Ford will lure the Slayer to the Sunset Club, a private Goth hangout, and Spike can come to collect her.

Buffy is devastated when she discovers Ford's betrayal, moved though she is by his revelation that he is dying. When he rises as a ravening, mindless vampire, she stakes him without reaction; the Ford she knew and loved had already died.

**BUFFY AND OWEN THURMAN:** Buffy did not choose to be the Slayer. By some whim of fate yet unknown to us, the universe did the choosing, and Buffy must deal with the consequences. But having a crush and getting asked out on a date, as any normal sixteen-year-old would love to do, are "problematic at best" (to quote Giles) for Buffy. When shy, handsome Owen finally asks her out, Buffy is delighted...until he becomes involved in a vampire battle at the Sunnydale Funeral Home and she discovers that he has a yen for danger. Realizing that her world is too dangerous for Owen, she breaks up with him...unable to tell him the real reason why, nor to say that she still cares for him just as much.

**BUFFY AND CAMERON WALKER:** Initially, Buffy is interested in Cameron, a member of the Sunnydale swim team. He waxes poetic about the ocean and he's good-looking...and he seems equally interested in her. However, the bloom is off the rose by the end of the first date: he's boring and self-absorbed. When he won't take no for an answer, she breaks his nose...and gets blamed for leading him on. And, of course, any hope Cameron might have had with Buffy is dashed when he becomes a giant fish-guy...

And one more:

**TOM WARNER:** Tom is the fraternity brother of Cordelia's love interest, Richard Anderson. The fraternity, Delta Zeta Kappa, worships Machida, a giant demon-snake, and Tom is their leader. He lures Buffy to a fraternity party for the express purpose of feeding her to Machida as a sacrifice. Naturally, this relationship was doomed from the start.

# Love Is Strange.
# Very, Very Strange.

Xander has likewise had his share of bizarre romances. If, as Willow says, "Love makes you do the wacky," it can also make you date the wacky. *Par example*—as they say in France—with regard to:

**XANDER AND MISS NATALIE FRENCH:** Miss French murders the science teacher, Dr. Gregory, and takes his place as a substitute teacher. Sexy and mesmerizing, she is actually a huge praying mantis intent upon mating with young male humans in order to fertilize her eggs. Her first two targets are Blayne Mall—who has been bragging about his many conquests to Xander—and Xander himself, who has been bragging back. Of course, once the She-Mantis is dispatched and the two are rescued, it comes out that the She-Mantis only selected young male *virgin* humans as her potential mates....

**XANDER AND AMPATA:** Ampata is actually the name of a male South American foreign-exchange student who is to live with Buffy and her mother for two weeks. However, the millennia-old mummy of a sixteen-year-old Inca princess has been freed from her sleep and literally sucks the life out of Ampata when she kisses him. He becomes a shriveled corpse. As the female foreign-exchange student Ampata, the mummy falls in love with Xander. At first she finds she cannot kill him, even to perpetuate her own life, and in desperation attacks Willow. When Xander stands between Willow and Ampata, it appears that in her hunger for life, she may actually take his. But with Buffy's intervention, the once-beautiful Inca princess decays and falls to pieces before his very eyes.

**BEHOLD THE WEIRDNESS: XANDER AND CORDELIA:** What's up with that? Astute *Buffy* viewers of season one may have sensed that beneath the caustic remarks and rapid-fire banter, Cordelia and Xander were racking up passion points. But for the rest of us, it was quite a shock when, facing death from Mr. Pfister, the Tarakan bug-man assassin in "What's My Line? Part 2," they clung to each other in an embrace that can only be described as it is in the shooting script:

A beat. They FALL INTO A KISS. A kiss of steel-melting, ground-shaking intensity. It just goes on and on and on....

Finally, they break. LEAP apart as if they've been electrocuted....

Naturally, Cordelia wants to keep this strange lust connection a secret, and perhaps she is right: for when Willow finds out, she is devastated:

**Willow:** "I knew it! I knew it! Well, not 'knew it' in the sense of having the slightest idea, but I knew there was something I didn't know. You two were fighting way too much. It's not natural."
**Xander:** "I know, it's weird...."
**Willow:** "Weird? It's against all the laws of God and man! It's *Cordelia!* Remember? The 'We Hate Cordelia Club,' of which you are the treasurer?"
**Xander:** "I was gonna tell you...."
**Willow:** "Gee, what stopped you? Could it be *shame?*"
**Xander:** "All right! Let's overreact, shall we?"
**Willow:** "But I'm—"
**Xander:** "We were kissing. It doesn't mean that much."
**Willow** (softly): "No. It just means you'd rather be with someone you hate...than be with me."

—**"INNOCENCE"**

If the course of true love never ran smooth, the course of unadulterated passion has practically no chance for pothole-free driving, as Xander and Cordelia quickly discover.

**Xander:** "You know, it's really better for me if you don't talk."
**Cordelia:** "Well, it's really better for *me* with the lights off."
**Xander:** "Are you saying you can't *look* at me when we . . . whatever we do?"
**Cordelia:** "It's not that I can't. It's more that I . . . don't want to."
**Xander:** "That's great. That's just dandy. We're repulsed by each other. We hide from our friends—"
**Cordelia:** "I should hope. Please."
**Xander:** "All and all. This thing is not what I'd call a self-esteem booster." —**"BAD EGGS"**

They struggle to define what it is they have; if it's only lust, why are they jealous of other people?

**Cordelia:** "Excuse me. We did not come here to talk about Willow. We came here to do things I can never tell my father about because he still thinks I'm a good girl."
**Xander:** "I just don't trust Oz with her. He's a senior, he's attractive. Okay, maybe not to me, but . . . oh, and he's in a band. We all know what element that kind attracts."
**Cordelia:** "I've dated lots of guys in bands."
**Xander:** "Thank you!"
**Cordelia:** "Do you even want to be here?"
**Xander:** "I'm not running away."
**Cordelia:** "Because when you're not babbling about poor, defenseless Willow, you're raving about the all-powerful Buffy."
**Xander:** "I do not babble. I occassionally run-on. And every now and then I yammer..."
**Cordelia:** "Xander, look around. We're in my daddy's car. Just the two of us. There's a beautiful, big, full moon out tonight. It doesn't get more romantic than this....So shut up!"
—**"PHASES"**

But are they even dating?

**Xander:** "So, you're going. And I'm going. Should we—maybe—go?"
**Cordelia:** "Why?"
**Xander:** "I don't know. This thing. With us? Despite our better judgment—it keeps happening. Maybe we should just admit that we're dating."
**Cordelia:** "Groping in a broom closet isn't dating. You don't call it a date until the guy spends money."
**Xander:** "Fine. I'll spend—then we'll grope. Whatever. I just think it's just some kind of whacked that we feel we have to hide from all our friends."
**Cordelia:** "Well, of course you want to tell everybody. You have nothing to be ashamed of. I, on the other hand, have everything to be ashamed of."
**Xander:** "Know what? 'Nuff said. Forget it. Must have been my multiple-personality guy talking. I call him Idiot Jed, Glutton for Punishment." —**"SURPRISE"**

And then, the payoff . . . finally:

**Cordelia:** "Me? I'm not the one who embraced the black arts just to get girls to like me. Well, congratulations, it worked."

**Xander:** "It would have worked fine! Except your hide's so thick not even magic can penetrate it!"
**Cordelia:** "You mean, the spell was for me?"   —**"BEWITCHED, BOTHERED, AND BEWILDERED"**

As Cordelia realizes how much Xander cares about her, she courageously takes a stand that could bring her down socially until the end of time:

**Cordelia** (to Harmony): "I'll date whoever the hell I want to date, no matter how lame he is! [she walks away] Oh, God...oh, God."
**Xander:** "It's gonna be okay. Just keep walking."
**Cordelia:** "Oh, God, what have I done? They're never gonna speak to me again."
**Xander:** "Oh, sure they are. If it helps, when we're around them, you and I can fight a lot."
**Cordelia:** "You promise?"
**Xander:** "You can pretty much count on it."   —**"BEWITCHED, BOTHERED, AND BEWILDERED"**

## XANDER AND THE ENTIRE FEMALE POPULATION OF SUNNYDALE

"Dammit, Xander, what is going on? Who died and made you Elvis?"
**Cordelia, on Xander's sudden irresistibility to all but her, in "Bewitched, Bothered, and Bewildered"**

In "Bewitched, Bothered, and Bewildered"—an episode rewritten to give Sarah Michelle Gellar more days off for her appearance on *Saturday Night Live*—Xander blackmails Amy Madison, the witchly daughter of Catherine Madison, into casting a love spell on Cordelia. As mentioned above, Queen C is crumbling under peer pressure: the Cordettes are snubbing her because she is dating the lamest of the lame...Xander. In an attempt to regain her hard-won popularity, Cordelia dumps him, although it is clear to us, the viewing audience, that she still cares about him.

Xander retaliates. But the spell goes awry: instead of enchanting Cordelia, the spell works on every *other* female in Sunnydale . . . including Jenny Calendar, Buffy, Joyce...and, in a lucky misadventure that saves Xander's life . . . Drusilla!

As Angel grabs him and prepares to kill him, Drusilla steps in and saves Xander's life:

**Drusilla:** "If you so much as harmed one hair on this boy's precious head—"
Angel can't believe his ears.
**Angel:** "You've got to be kidding? Him?"
**Drusilla:** "No, now. Just because I finally found a real man...."
Angel shakes his head, uncomprehending.
**Angel:** "A real man? I guess I really *did* drive you crazy."
   —**"BEWITCHED, BOTHERED, AND BEWILDERED"**

**Drusilla:** "Your face is a poem. I can read it."
**Xander:** "Really? It doesn't say 'spare me,' by any chance?"
**Drusilla:** "Ssshhhh. How do you feel about eternal life?"
**Xander:** "We couldn't just start with a coffee? A movie, maybe?"
   —**"BEWITCHED, BOTHERED, AND BEWILDERED"**

Xander discovers that it's not wonderful to be the object of mass obsession, as the women of Sunnydale literally attack him in a mob of possessive, love-crazed Xander groupies. Armed with axes, knives, and sheer *need*, they trap him and Cordelia in Buffy's basement.

When things go back to as normal as they get, Cordelia takes her place in the sun once more...on Xander's arm.

**XANDER AND...KENDRA?** One can only speculate about Kendra's flustered reaction around Xander. It's true that she hasn't had a lot of contact with boys her own age, but in "What's My Line? Part 2," she's clearly unsettled by him:

**Xander:** "Welcome. So you're a Slayer, huh? I like that in a woman."
Kendra can only look at her shoes. Totally flustered.
**Kendra:** "I—I hope.... I thank you. I mean, sir... I will be of service."
**Xander:** "Good. Great. It's good to be a giver."
Xander looks to Buffy—what's with her? Buffy shrugs.

When Xander and Kendra meet again, there's no time for such exchanges. But one wonders what might have been, if only Kendra had had more time....

**LOVE IS CRUEL: XANDER AND BUFFY** From the first moment he sees her, Xander is attracted to Buffy. Oblivious to the fact that he's wounding Willow, who has carried a torch for him ever since they were five and he stole her Barbie, he discusses his feelings about the new girl with his best buddy on an almost constant basis. It takes the entire first season for him to ask Buffy out, with less-than-sterling results:

**Xander:** "You know, Buffy, Spring Fling is a time for students to gather and...oh, God. Buffy, I want you to go to the dance with me. You and me. On a date."
**Buffy:** "I don't know what to say...."
**Xander:** "Well, you're not laughing, so that's a good start. Buffy, I like you. A lot. And I know we're friends, and we've had experiences, we've fought some bloodsucking fiends, and that's all been a good time, but...I want more. I wanna dance with you."

**Buffy:** "Xander...you're one of my best friends. You and Willow..."
**Xander:** "Hey, Willow's not looking to date you. Or, if she is, she's playing it pretty close to the chest."
**Buffy:** "I don't want to spoil the friendship that we have."
**Xander:** "I don't want to spoil it, either. But that's not the point, is it? You either feel a thing or you don't."
**Buffy:** "I don't...Xander, I'm sorry. I just don't think of you that way."
**Xander:** "Well try, I'll wait."
**Buffy:** "Xander..."
**Xander:** "No, forget it. I'm not him. I guess a guy's gotta be undead to make time with you."
—**"PROPHECY GIRL"**

The "him" that Xander is referring to is Angel, of course. It really hurts Xander that Buffy prefers "Dead Boy," and Xander stands alone in his continuing mistrust of the "good" vampire, even when other people chalk up his concern to jealousy.

"Hey, it's *me*. If Angel's doing something wrong, I need to know.
'Cause it gives me a happy."
**Xander, in "Lie to Me"**

As previously mentioned, it is Xander, not Angel, who insists that the two of them go down into the tunnels to rescue Buffy in "Prophecy Girl." And Xander often acts as the leader of the group when mobilization is required, assigning tasks for himself and the others. Despite the fact that when Angel's not in the picture Buffy goes out or hangs with other boys—Owen, Ford, Tom, Cameron—and that when she is desperately angry and unhappy, she flirts with Xander only to provoke reactions in others ("When She Was Bad"), Xander's yen for Buffy never diminishes:

"Buffy. My Lady of Buffdom. The duchess of Buffonia. I am in awe.
I completely renounce spandex."
**Xander, upon seeing Buffy in her costume, in "Halloween"**

Still, Xander, Buffy, and Willow continue to be a special threesome, spending idle hours together, watching Indian TV, sharing their lives. Not even Xander's strange new relationship with Cordelia can lessen his love for Buffy. Cordelia repeatedly accuses him of being obsessed with the Slayer, pouting that while he would die for his beloved Buffy, he would never die for *her* ("Innocence"). And on occasion, Willow still tests the wind, even though she eventually moves on to Oz:

**Willow:** "When Buffy was a vampire, you weren't still, like, attracted to her, were you?"
**Xander:** "Willow, how can you... I mean, that's really bent, she was grotesque."
**Willow:** "Still dug her, huh?"
**Xander:** "I'm sick. I need help."
**Willow:** "Don't I know it." —**"NIGHTMARES"**

Angel, reborn as Angelus, taunts him:

**Angel:** "Buffy's white knight. You still love her. It must just kill you that I got there first."
**Xander:** "You're gonna die. And I'm gonna be there." —**"KILLED BY DEATH"**

There are moments when it seems that Xander's faithfulness will be rewarded, as in "Phases," when Buffy destroys the vampire Theresa, created and sent by Angel as a token of his own "affections":

> "Oh, no, my life's not too complicated."
> **Xander, after a too-long embrace with Buffy, in "Phases"**

Now, after the second-season finale, Buffy has sent Angel to Hell and left town. Will Xander ever see her again? Will she ever return his loyal and lasting love? At this point, we can only speculate.

# And the Torch Is Passed, Sputtering at First

**WILLOW AND MOLOCH:** In her sweet, wry, and unsure way, Willow has yearned after Xander nearly all her life. Encouraged numerous times by Buffy to make the first move, Willow demurs. "No speaking up. That way leads to madness and sweaty palms" ("Angel").

Xander makes it very clear that Buffy is the girl he wants, and so Willow tries to move on. In "I Robot, You Jane," she meets "Malcolm Black" on the Internet, and they begin a romance via e-mail that deeply concerns Buffy, much to Willow's disappointment:

**Willow:** "You're having an expression."
**Buffy:** "I'm not. But if I was, it would be saying...this just isn't like you."
**Willow:** "Not like me to have a boyfriend?"
**Buffy:** "He's...boyfriendly?"
**Willow:** "I don't understand why you don't want me to have this. I mean, boys don't chase me around all the time—I thought you'd be happy for me."
**Buffy:** "I just want you to be sure. To meet him face-to-face. In daylight in a crowded place—with some friends. You know, before you get all obsessive."
**Willow:** "Malcolm and I really care about each other. Big deal if I blow off a couple classes."
**Buffy:** "I thought you said you overslept."
**Willow** (Turning away): "Malcolm said you wouldn't understand."
**Buffy:** "Malcolm was right."
—**"I ROBOT, YOU JANE"**

Unfortunately, this being Sunnydale and all, it turns out that Malcolm is not what he seems. Rather, he's a demon Willow inadvertently freed into the Internet when she scanned the book he was bound in into the school library computer system. Now housed in a terrifying robot body, Moloch, the Corruptor, used to tempting humans into his service with promises of love and riches, has Willow kidnapped and brought to him:

**Willow:** "I don't understand. What do you want from me?"
**Moloch:** "I want to give you the world."
**Willow:** "Why?"

**Moloch:** "You created me. I brought these humans together to build me a body, but you gave me life. Took me out of the book that held me. I want to repay you."
**Willow:** "By lying to me. By pretending to be a person. [weakly] Pretending...you loved me."
**Moloch:** "I do."

But of course he doesn't, and when Willow tries to "break up" with him, he prepares to kill her. And in the last scene of the episode, the immortal wisdom of the three friends—Buffy, Xander, and Willow—is laid bare:

**Willow:** "The one boy that's really liked me, and he's a demon robot. What does that say about me?"
**Buffy:** "It doesn't say anything about you."
**Willow:** "I mean, I thought I was really falling—"
**Buffy:** "Hey. Did you forget? The one boy I've had the hots for here turned out to be a vampire."
**Xander:** "Right! And the teacher I had a crush on: giant praying mantis."
**Willow** (brightening): "That's true...."
**Xander:** "Yeah. It's life on the Hellmouth."
**Buffy** (cheerfully): "Let's face it. None of us are ever going to have a normal, happy relationship."
**Xander** (laughing): "We're doomed!"
**Willow:** "Yeah!"

They all laugh together. Then it kind of sputters out, and they all sit there, incredibly depressed.

# Burning Bright

**WILLOW AND OZ** In "When She Was Bad," the second-season opener, just as it seems that Xander may indeed finally notice Willow—kissing the ice cream off her nose—Buffy shows. And the moment is lost. Forever—for Willow tries vainly to recapture it and must admit defeat.

But on the horizon for this brave little boat sails a conquistador: Oz, the equally wry, very laid-back lead guitarist of Dingoes Ate My Baby. For two episodes—"Inca Mummy Girl" and "Halloween"—Oz admires Willow from afar with but a single question: "Who is that girl?!" Then in "What's My Line? Part 1," they discover they are the two students singled out by a hush-hush computer organization, and he utters his first word to her: "Canapé?"

In "What's My Line? Part 2," they discuss their feelings about being candidates for the computer company, then move on to Oz's real ambition: to play the manly chord of E-flat, diminished ninth.

Then the spark is definitely ignited:

**Oz:** "Oh, hey, animal cracker?"
**Willow:** "No, thank you. How's your arm?"
**Oz:** "Suddenly painless."

**Willow:** "You can still play guitar okay?"
**Oz:** "Not well, but not worse."
**Willow:** "You know, I never really thanked you."
**Oz:** "Please don't. I don't do thanks. I get all red and I have to bail. It's not pretty."
**Willow:** "Well then forget—that thing. Especially the part where I kind of owe you my life."
Oz pulls a cracker from the box, hoping to change the subject.
**Oz:** "Look. Monkey. And he has a little hat. And little pants."
**Willow:** "Yeah. I see."
**Oz:** "The monkey is the only cookie animal that gets to wear clothes, you know that.... You have the sweetest smile I've ever seen.... So I'm wondering, do the other cookie animals feel sort of ripped? Like, is the hippo going, 'hey man, where are my pants? I have my hippo dignity.' And you know the monkey's just, 'I mock you with my monkey pants,' then there's a big coup at the zoo...."
**Willow:** "The monkey's French?"
**Oz:** "All monkeys are French. You didn't know that?" —**"WHAT'S MY LINE, PART 2"**

Then Willow musters up the courage to invite Oz to Buffy's surprise birthday party in "Surprise"—and he is immediately initiated into the Scooby Gang when he sees a vampire explode into dust. He joins in the heist of the rocket launcher without so much as batting an eye: "So, do you guys steal weapons from the army a lot?" he asks. And he makes it very clear where he stands:

**Oz:** "Sometimes when I'm sitting in class, I'm not thinking about class, 'cause you know that could never happen, I think about kissing you and then it's like everything stops. It's like, freeze frame. Willow kissage...but I'm not gonna kiss you."
**Willow:** "What? But...freeze frame..."
**Oz:** "Well, to the casual observer, it would appear like you want to make your friend Xander jealous. Or even the score or something. That's on the empty side. See, in my fantasy, when I'm kissing you...you're kissing me. It's okay, I can wait." —**"INNOCENCE"**

So Willow has clearly connected with a wonderful guy. But—this being Sunnydale and all—the course of true love never runs smooth for anyone. In "Phases," Willow discovers that Oz has a secret:

**Willow:** "What am I supposed to think? First you buy me popcorn, then you put the tag in my shirt, and then you're all glad I didn't get bit. But I guess none of that means anything, because instead of looking up names with me, here you are all alone in your house doing nothing by yourself."
**Oz:** "Willow, we will talk about this tomorrow, I promise."
**Willow:** "No, darn it, we will talk about this now! Buffy told me that sometimes what the girl makes has to be the first move, and now that I'm saying this, I'm starting to think that the written version sounded pretty good, but you know what I mean!"
**Oz:** "I know. It's me. I'm going through some ... changes." —**"PHASES"**

Oz is a werewolf. A bit shocking at first, but in the end, sort of okay:

**Oz:** "You mean ... you'd still ..."
**Willow:** "Well, I like you. You're nice, and you're funny and you don't smoke, and okay,

werewolf, but that's not all the time. I mean, three days out of the month I'm not much fun to be around, either."
**Oz:** "You are quite the human."
**Willow:** "So I'd still if you'd still."
**Oz:** "I'd still. I'd very still." —**"PHASES"**

And at last, Willow has not only a boyfriend, but a very cool boyfriend:

"My boyfriend's in the band!"
**Willow, in "Bewitched, Bothered, and Bewildered"**

Clearly, there is more...much more...to Oz than meets the eye. At the end of the second season, we can only imagine the adventures he and Willow will share.

**WILLOW AND XANDER:** Willow and Xander have been best friends for years . . . and through those years, Willow has come to love Xander in a more-than-best-friends kind of way. Xander, of course, has no clue. In a section cut from "Angel," he sums up the situation perfectly, without the slightest idea that with every word, he's wounding Willow:

**Xander:** "Love sucks. Ever since I was in grammar school, it's the same old dance...you dig someone, they dig someone else. And then that someone else digs someone else."
**Willow:** "That's the dance."
**Xander:** "I mean, I'm right for her. I'm the guy. I know it. She's so stupid! She's not stupid. But . . . it's too much. We're such good buds, I'm *this* close to her, and she doesn't have a clue how I feel. And wouldn't care if she did. It's killing me."
He exits into class. She stands alone a moment.
**Willow:** "Gee, what's that like?" —**"ANGEL"** (expurgated)

Willow struggles with her feelings, trying to replace Xander in her heart with someone else. But it's difficult at best when your one prospect turned out to be a demon, and no one else is beating down your door.

**Willow:** "Well, you know, I have a choice. I can spend my life waiting for Xander to go out with every other girl in the world before he notices me, or I can just get on with my life."
**Buffy:** "Good for you."
**Willow:** "Well, I didn't choose yet...." —**"INCA MUMMY GIRL"**

Finally, Oz arrives on the scene. And maybe that's the wake-up call Xander finally needed . . . or maybe he realizes his love for her far exceeds the boyfriend/girlfriend thing:

> "Come on, Will... [he takes a moment, continues.] Look, you don't have a choice here. You gotta wake up. I need you, Will. How am I gonna pass trig? Who am I gonna call every night to talk about what we did all day. You're my best friend, you've always ... [He leans in close.] "I love you."
> 
> **Xander, in "Becoming, Part 2"**

And Willow wakes up, speaking Oz's name.
What will happen here?
Only time will tell.

# The Many, Many Loves of Cordelia Chase

**CORDELIA AND THE ENTIRE Y-CARRYING POPULATION OF SUNNYDALE HIGH:** Cordelia has always prided herself on her fine taste in men. She knows what she wants: the best. She knows what she deserves: the best. Anything less would be...less. As she explains to the Cordettes in "Welcome to the Hellmouth":

> "Senior boys are the only way to go. They're just a better class of person. The boys in our grade? Forget about it. They're children. Like Jesse— did you see him last night? The way he follows me around? He's like a little puppy dog: you just want to put him to sleep. Senior boys have mystery, they have...what's the word I'm searching for? 'Cars.'"

But being Cordelia's boyfriend can be bad luck of the worst kind: in the first two seasons, Cordelia racks up more dead or severely injured boyfriends than a black widow spider:

**CORDELIA AND DARYL EPPS:** Former all-state champion football star Daryl appeared in "Some Assembly Required." He was severely injured in a rock-climbing accident and presumed dead. But his science-fair-winning younger brother, Chris, stitches him back together a la Frankenstein and his monster, and now Daryl dwells, quite alone, in their basement. As with the original *Frankenstein*, Daryl prevails upon Chris to build him a mate. And Cordelia will be the crowning achievement . . . the head.

**CORDELIA AND MITCH FARGO:** Mitch is Cordelia's "hunk du jour" in "Out of Mind, Out of Sight." He is to reign beside Cordelia as May King, preferably in a lot of pancake makeup after Marcie Ross, the insane, invisible girl, takes a baseball bat to him.

**CORDELIA AND KEVIN:** Kevin was to have escorted Cordelia to the prom, but vampires attack and kill him in the school's AV room...also nixing his ability to help Cordelia with the sound system at the Bronze.

**CORDELIA AND RICHARD ANDERSON:** Richard is a fraternity brother of the Delta Zeta Kappas, a cult that sacrifices beautiful young high school girls to their demon lord, the giant snake-man, Machida. Initially, Richard goes after Cordelia; then, needing more girls, the cult leader, Tom, invites Buffy to their party.

> "The Zeta Kappas have to have a certain balance at their party—Richard explained it all to me but I was so busy REALLY LISTENING to him that I didn't hear much—anyway, the deal is they need you to go. And if you don't go... [her eyes moisten] I can't! I'm talking about Richard Anderson, okay? As in Anderson Farms, Anderson Aeronautics... [she can no longer hold back the tears] and Anderson Cosmetics!"
> —Cordelia, in "Reptile Boy"

In the end, Buffy kills Machida and she and Cordelia are rescued by the Scooby Gang, pretty much putting the kibosh on this romance.

**CORDELIA AND JONATHAN:** Jonathan has appeared in four episodes thus far: "Reptile Boy," "Inca Mummy Girl," "Bad Eggs," and "Go Fish." In "Inca Mummy Girl," the Incan princess/mummy Ampata nearly sucks the life out of him in a stolen kiss. In "Reptile Boy," Cordelia favors him with her presence (although he scarcely deserves it, having forgotten the extra foam on her cappuccino). He is neurally clamped by a Bezoar hatchling in "Bad Eggs." He escapes becoming a gill-man in "Go Fish," but so far, Jonathan has more lives than Catherine Madison's black cat.

**CORDELIA AND DEVON:** Devon is the lead singer for Dingoes Ate My Baby. He first appears in "Inca Mummy Girl," when Oz first notices Willow. By "Halloween," Cordelia is dating him—and it appears that he's been standing her up. Still, she hovers at the edge of the stage—even though she informs him not to expect her there.

**CORDELIA AND ANGEL:**

> "Hel-lo! Salty goodness. Pick up the phone. Call 9-1-1. That boy's going to need some serious oxygen after I'm through with him."
> **Cordelia, spotting Angel, in "Never Kill a Boy on the First Date"**

> "Oh. He's a vampire. Of course. But the cuddly kind. Like a Care Bear with fangs.... You know what I think? You're trying to scare me off because you're afraid of the competition. Look, Buffy, you may be hot stuff when it comes to demonology or whatever, but when it comes to dating, *I'm* the Slayer."
> **Cordelia is told that Angel's a vampire, in "Halloween"**

Just like any other girl who has eyes would attest to the fact that Angel is a honey, Cordelia attempts several times to attract/distract him from Buffy. She never gets anywhere, despite the fact that Buffy's own insecurities lead her to assume that Cordelia could pose a serious threat, and Cordelia takes advantage of that when it suits her:

**Buffy:** "I'd say it's about time for you to mind your own business."
**Cordelia:** "It's long past. Nighty-night.... I'll just go see if Angel feels like dancing."
—**"WHEN SHE WAS BAD"**

Incredibly, Angel never starts dating her, despite the fact that she showers on a regular basis and spends as much time on her hair as Marie Antoinette.

**CORDELIA AND OWEN:** Owen Thurman also prefers Buffy, even though, technically, Cordelia asks him out first:

**Cordelia:** "Owen, a bunch of us are loitering at the Bronze tonight. You there?"
**Owen:** "Who's all going?"
**Cordelia:** "Well, I'm going to be there."
**Owen:** "Oh. Who else?"
**Cordelia** (genuinely confused): "You mean besides me?"
**Owen:** "Buffy, what about you?"
**Buffy:** (caught off guard): "What?"
**Cordelia:** "No, no, no. She doesn't—like—fun."
**Owen** (to Buffy): "How about we meet there at eight?"
Cordelia glares at Buffy.
**Buffy:** "Yeah. Eight. There." —**"NEVER KILL A BOY ON THE FIRST DATE"**

**CORDELIA AND XANDER:** And then, there is "the weirdness of them," as she discovers her one true passion:

**Cordelia:** "I can't believe that I'm stuck spending what are probably my last moments on Earth with you!"
**Xander:** "I hope these are my last moments! Three more seconds of you and I'm gonna..."
**Cordelia:** "You're gonna what? Coward!"
**Xander:** "Moron!"
**Cordelia:** "I hate you!"
**Xander:** "I hate you!"
(Then big smootchies, and then...)
**Xander:** "We so need to get out of here!" —**"WHAT'S MY LINE? PART 2"**

In an expurgated section from "Surprise," Cordelia tries on new clothes as Xander's girlfriend:

**Cordelia** (too casual, to Harmony): "Hello. I'm having, like, a totally random thought. [then] Xander Harris. Is it just me, or does his shirt almost match his pants?"
Harmony looks. Shrugs.
**Harmony:** "Almost. Why do I care?"
**Cordelia:** "Well. If you look at him a certain way—is he vaguely...cute?"
THEIR POV
As XANDER does some spazzy dance for Willow's amusement.
RESUME
**Harmony:** "Oh, yeah. I'm hot for spaz boy. Are you tripping, Cordelia?"
A beat. Cordelia laughs a little too loud.
**Cordelia:** "You thought I was serious? Please. I was just testing you. Ha. [Sighs.] I'm hot for spaz boy. Good one." —**"SURPRISE"**

# Angel's Demon Lovers

**ANGEL AND DARLA:** In her human form, Darla is a beautiful young blonde who can pass herself off as a high school student. She sired Angel in Galway in 1753:

**Angel:** "God, but you're a pretty thing. Where are you from?"
**Darla:** "Around. Everywhere."
**Angel:** "Never been anywhere, myself. Always wanted to see the world, but..."
**Darla:** "I could show you."
**Angel:** "Could you, then?"
**Darla:** "Things you've never seen. Never even heard of."
**Angel:** "Sounds exciting."
**Darla:** "It is. And frightening."
**Angel:** "I'm not afraid. Show me. Show me your world."
**Darla:** "Close your eyes."

—"BECOMING, PART 1"

Angel is involved with Darla at least periodically for the next century. But when his soul is restored, he forsakes all other vampires—including Darla—and lives alone. Darla flourishes as the reigning favorite of the Master, presiding with joy over the executions of those who fail her demon lord. When it comes to light that Angel is keeping company with the Slayer, Darla concocts a plan to pit Buffy and Angel against each other. Either Buffy will kill him, or Angel will kill Buffy . . . and hopefully, return to the vampire fold.

Unfortunately for Darla, her plan backfires. After she taunts Buffy with her past relationship with Angel—"There was a time when we shared everything"—Angel kills Darla. Her last word—his name—is uttered with shock and astonishment, as if, to the last, she cannot believe she has lost her hold over him.

**ANGEL AND DRUSILLA:**

**Angel:** "I did a lot of unconscionable things when I became a vampire. Drusilla was the worst. She was...an obsession of mine."

**Angel, in "Lie to Me"**

Angel sires Drusilla in London in or around 1860. In the full glory of his demonic existence, he torments her in the confessional as she speaks tremulously of having visions. Her mother has told her this is the work of the Devil, and she turns to the Church for absolution. But Angel gives her no release, only more pain, as he tells her she is the spawn of the Devil.

Angel kills all her family and drives her completely insane. When she is left with nothing and no one—not even her own identity—he enfolds her in the vampire's kiss.

When his soul is restored, his agony over seeing Drusilla again in "Lie to Me" is palpable. If vengeance is a living thing, as Jenny Calendar's Gypsy uncle posits, so is remorse. And it is a hungry living thing, demanding constant feeding....

**Angel:** "Drusilla, leave here. I'm offering you that chance. Take Spike and get out."
**Drusilla:** "Or you'll hurt me? [ looks down.] No. No, you can't. Not anymore."
**Angel:** "If you don't leave...it'll go badly. For all of us."
**Drusilla:** "My dear boy's gone all away, hasn't he? To her."

**Angel:** "Who?"
**Drusilla:** "The girl . . . the Slayer. Your heart stinks of her. Poor little thing. She has no idea what's in store."
**Angel:** "This can't go on, Drusilla. It's gotta end."
**Drusilla:** "Oh, no, my pet . . . [She leans in for what looks to Buffy like a kiss, whispers in Angel's ear.] This is just the beginning."

## DRUSILLA AND SPIKE:

**The Judge:** "You two stink of humanity. You share affection and jealousy."
**Spike:** "Yeah, what of it?" —**"SURPRISE"**

Drusilla and Spike are an adoring couple when they burst upon the Sunnydale scene. Drusilla is incredibly weak and wraithlike, having barely survived an angry mob in Prague. She and Spike set up shop in Sunnydale, joining the Anointed One's court while they plan their strategy. Which is: to get rid of the Slayer and restore Drusilla to health in "Sunnyhell."

Spike clearly worships Drusilla. When she enters the Factory for the first time ("School Hard") to greet the Anointed One and his court, Spike loses his vampire face and turns to her with the adoring eyes of a young human man.

They discover that Angel is in town ("School Hard"), and the audience learns that Angel sired Drusilla, who, in turn, sired Spike—which makes Angel Spike's grand-sire. Now the jig is up: the vampire couple knows that Angel has somehow become good, that he is the Slayer's lapdog...and their enemy.

On occasion, Drusilla uses her madness to manipulate Spike:

**Spike:** "You, uh, meet anyone? Anyone interesting? Like Angel?"
**Dru:** "Angel."
**Spike:** "It's a little off, you two so friendly, him being the enemy and all that." —**"LIE TO ME"**

When he flares up on learning that she has indeed seen Angel, impatiently pointing out to her that the bird she is coaxing to sing for her is dead because she forgot to feed it, Drusilla begins to keen. Spike is immediately contrite, dropping entirely the subject of her clandestine meeting with Angel.

> "I'm sorry, baby. I'm a bad, rude man."
> **Spike, to Drusilla, in "Lie to Me"**

Spike's world revolves around Drusilla and getting her well again. But even in that effort, foreshadowing of things to come darken his finest hour as he allows Drusilla to torture Angel before performing the ritual that will cure her and kill Angel:

**Spike:** "I've never been much for the pre-show."
**Angel:** "Too bad. That's what Drusilla likes best as I recall."
**Spike:** "What's that supposed to mean?"
**Angel:** "Ask her. She knows what I mean."
**Spike:** "Well?"
**Drusilla:** "Ssshhh. Bad dog."

**Angel:** "You should let me talk to him, Dru. Sounds like your boy could use some pointers. She likes to be teased...."
**Spike:** "Keep your hole shut!"
**Angel:** "Just take care of her, Spike. The way she touched me just now.... I can tell when she's not satisfied."
**Spike:** "I said, shut up!"
**Angel:** "Or maybe you two just don't have the fire that we did." —**"WHAT'S MY LINE? PART 2"**

When Angel finds true happiness in the arms of Buffy, he loses his soul, and in that moment, Drusilla cries out in "orgasmic pain." Then:

**Spike:** "Are we feeling better, then?"
**Drusilla:** "I'm naming all the stars."
**Spike:** "Can't see the stars, love. That's the ceiling. Also, it's day."
**Drusilla:** "I can see them. But I've named them all the same name, and there's terrible confusion. I fear there may be a duel." —**"INNOCENCE"**

She is so very right....

### ANGEL AND DRUSILLA AND SPIKE

When Angel changes, he goes immediately to the Factory to reunite with Spike and Drusilla, who are delighted.

**Angel:** "It's really true."
**Drusilla:** "You've come home."
**Spike:** "No more of this 'I've got a soul' crap?"
**Angel:** "What can I say? I was going through a phase."
**Spike:** "This is great! This is so great."
**Drusilla:** "Everything in my head is singing. We're family again. We'll feed, and we'll play...."
**Spike:** "I gotta tell you, it made me sick to my stomach, seeing you being the Slayer's lapdog—"
**Drusilla:** "How did this happen?"
**Angel:** "You wouldn't believe me if I told you."
**Spike:** "Who cares? What matters is, now he's back. Now it's four against one, which are the kind of odds I like to play." —**"Innocence"**

But soon the invalid Spike's pleasure turns to acute discomfort and jealousy as Angel taunts him with suggestions that he has taken Spike's place in Drusilla's arms:

**Angel:** "Well, maybe next time I'll bring you with me, Spike. Might be handy to have you along if I ever need a really good parking spot."
**Spike:** "Have you forgotten that you're a bloody guest in my bloody home?!"

**Angel:** "And as a guest, if there's anything I can do for you.... Any... responsibility I can assume while you spin your wheels [purposeful leer toward Dru], anything I'm not *already* doing, that is...."
—**"PASSION"**

Spike attempts to give as good as he gets, but Angel is an old hand at cruelty in the matters of the heart:

**Spike** (re: Angel): "All hat—no cattle."
**Angel:** "I don't know about that."
**Drusilla:** "Oh, Angel's got cattle all right. *Mooooo*."
**Angel:** "Yeah. I think this whole Buffy thing has run its course. I'm ready to focus my energy elsewhere."
**Spike:** "Really?"
**Angel:** "Oh, yeah. What with you being special-needs boy, I figure I should stick close to home. You and Dru can always use another pair of hands...."
—**"I ONLY HAVE EYES FOR YOU"**

**Spike** [to Dru]: "I won't have you feeding me like a child, Dru!"
**Angel:** "Why not? She already bathes you, carries you around, and changes you like a child."
—**"PASSION"**

**Angel:** "I know Dru gives you pity access, but you have to admit, it's so much easier when I do things for her."
**Spike:** "You'd do well to worry less about Dru and more about that Slayer you've been tramping around with."
**Angel:** "Dear Buffy. I'm still trying to decide the best way to send my regards."
**Spike:** "Why don't you rip her lungs out. That might make an impression."
**Angel:** "It lacks poetry."
**Spike:** "It doesn't have to. What rhymes with 'lungs'?"
—**"BEWITCHED, BOTHERED, AND BEWILDERED"**

When Angel decides to send the non-demon beings in this world to Hell, Spike frets:

**Spike:** "Darling, if this works, everything changes. Think about it. In this world, we can be kings. In the next . . ."
**Drusilla:** "My Spikey's getting cold feet. Don't you worry about the next world. You'll always have me."
**Spike:** "Will I?"
—**"BECOMING, PART 1"**

And it is really because of his fear of losing Drusilla, and not so much of bidding a final farewell to Piccadilly, that Spike betrays Angel by forming an alliance with Buffy.

"I want Dru back. I want it like it was before he came back. [Disgusted] The way she acts around him . . . "
**Spike, to Buffy, in "Becoming, Part 2"**

In the end, Spike betrays Angel and Buffy both, thinking only of saving himself...and getting Drusilla as far away from Angel as possible.

# The Sorrow and the Pity: Jenny and Giles

**GILES AND JENNY:** Jenny Calendar, the beautiful technopagan and Sunnydale computer-science instructor, makes her first appearance in "I Robot, You Jane." Although she is lovely, at first Giles seems more put off by her invasion of his library with her book scanners than interested in the woman herself.

**Giles:** "I'm just going to stay and clean up. I'll be back in the Middle Ages."
**Jenny:** "Did you ever leave?" —**"I ROBOT, YOU JANE"**

Once he learns that she's a "technopagan" who not only knows what he's talking about when he tries to tell her there's a demon in the Internet, but helps him cast the demon out of the Net, he's smitten...and intrigued.

**Jenny:** "Well, you really are an old-fashioned boy, aren't you?"
**Giles:** "Well, it's true I don't dangle a corkscrew from my ear."
**Jenny:** "That's not where I dangle it." —**"I ROBOT, YOU JANE"**

He determines to ask her out . . . but finds himself tongue-tied and shy. Buffy and company are more than happy to offer him advice:

**Buffy:** "You also might want to avoid words like 'amenable' and 'indecorous.' Speak English, not whatever they speak in…"
**Giles:** "England?"
**Buffy:** "Yeah. Just say, 'Hey, I got a thing, you maybe have a thing, maybe we could have a thing?'"
**Giles:** "Well, thank you so much."
**Buffy:** "I'm not finished. Then you say, 'How do you feel about Mexican?'"
**Giles:** "Mexicans."
**Buffy:** "Mexican! Food. You take her for food. For which you then pay."
**Giles:** "Right."
**Xander:** "So this 'chair' woman? We are talking Ms. Calendar, right?"
**Giles:** "What makes you think that?"
**Xander:** "Simple deduction: Ms. Calendar is reasonably dollsome, especially for someone in your age bracket; she already knows you're a school librarian, so you don't have to worry about how to break that embarrassing news to her...."

**Buffy:** "And she's the only woman we've ever actually seen speak to you. Add it all up, it spells 'duh.'"
**Xander:** "Now, is it time for us to talk about the facts of life?"
**Giles:** "I am suddenly deciding that this is none of your business."
—**"SOME ASSEMBLY REQUIRED"**

The sweetness of their budding romance is underscored by her more matter-of-fact approach. He wants to lead, but it's really best if he just gets out of her way.

**Giles:** "I just think it's rather odd that a nation that prides itself on its virility should feel compelled to strap on forty pounds of protective gear just in order to play rugby."
**Jenny:** "Is this your normal strategy for a first date: dissing my country's national pastime?"
**Giles:** "Did you just say…'date'?"
**Jenny:** "You noticed that, huh?"
—**"SOME ASSEMBLY REQUIRED"**

"Nothing's safe in this world, Rupert. Don't you know that by now?"
—**Jenny, in "The Dark Age"**

Their romance continues. And then bitterness overshadows the sweetness: Giles's past is brought to light, and Jenny is possessed by the demon Eyghon. Giles is overcome with guilt, which makes Jenny's dishonesty all the more difficult to excuse, once it's revealed that she has been sent by the same Gypsy clan that cursed Angel over a century ago. Because she did not speak up, Angelus has returned, Buffy is bereft, and there's a good chance the Judge will cleanse the Earth of mankind.

She attempts to apologize, but to no avail.

**Jenny:** "Rupert, I know you feel betrayed."
**Giles:** "Yes, that's one of the unpleasant side effects of betrayal."
**Jenny:** "I was raised by the people Angel hurt the most. My duty to them was the first thing I was ever taught. I didn't come here to hurt anyone. I lied to you because I thought it was the right thing to do. I didn't know what would happen. I didn't know I was going to fall in love with you."
—**"PASSION"**

But no one can hold anger toward the kind and well-meaning Jenny of the Kalderash people for very long, not even Buffy:

**Buffy:** "Look, I know you're feeling bad about what happened and I want to say…good. Keep it up."
**Jenny:** "Don't worry. I will."
**Buffy:** "Wait. I, uh … He misses you. He doesn't say anything to me, but I know he does. I don't want him to be lonely. I don't want anyone to."
—**"PASSION"**

And when she thinks that she can restore Angel's soul—an act of redemption not only for Angel, but for her, she plans to share the wonderful news with Giles first. These are the last words between Giles and Jenny:

**Jenny:** "I spoke to Buffy today."
**Giles:** "Yes."
**Jenny:** "She said you missed me."
**Giles:** "She is a meddlesome girl." [But the truth of it is on his face.]
**Jenny:** "Rupert, I don't want to say anything if I'm wrong, but I may have some news.... I have to finish up—can I see you later?"
**Giles:** "Yes. You could stop by the house."
**Jenny:** "Okay."
**Giles:** "Good."

—"PASSION"

# Other Lovers:

**LOVE IS FOREVER: JAMES AND GRACE:** In 1955, James Stanley was a Sunnydale High student who fell in love with Grace Newman, a teacher. Realizing that their love was wrong, Grace attempted to break off their affair on the night of the Sadie Hawkins Dance. In desperation, he shot and killed her, and their ghosts have haunted the school ever since, doomed to repeat their tragedy.

**James** (in many guises, possessing many people, including Buffy): "Come back here! We're not finished. [He grabs her arm. Stops her.] You don't care anymore? Is that it?"
**Grace** (also in many guises, possessing many people, including Angel): It doesn't matter. It doesn't matter what I feel."
**James:** "Then tell me you don't love me. [She's silent. He burns. Shakes her—hard.] Say it!" [She starts to cry.]
**Grace:** "Will that help? Is that what you have to hear? [lying] I don't. I don't. Now let me go!" [James is devastated—disbelieving.]
**James:** "No.... A person doesn't just wake up one day and stop loving somebody. [Now he raises his gun.] Love is forever."

—"I ONLY HAVE EYES FOR YOU"

When James possesses Buffy and Grace possesses Angel, they play out this scene and the ensuing one, where Grace finally appears to James and forgives him. Released from his unending cycle of guilt, James is finally freed, and the school is cleansed of his self-hatred. Buffy is not quite as lucky; she still blames herself for Angel's loss of his soul. But at some deep level, she has experienced, perhaps, a lifting of some of the burden she carries.

The poignant subtext of this episode is that Giles so wants the spirit haunting the school to be Jenny that he virtually ignores any detail that undermines his assertion. He misses her terribly.

He is haunted by her.

**DADDY DEAREST: JOYCE AND TED:** Joyce Summers has a difficult life at best. The single mother of a daughter she doesn't understand at all, forced to move from Los Angeles to some tiny, strange town called Sunnydale...it's frightening and lonely. Still, Joyce is more than a match for the task, giving voice to the notion that the fruit never falls far from the tree. After all, she is the mother of a Slayer.

When she falls in love with Ted Buchanan, it seems like a dream come true. He's kind, thoughtful...and he cooks! In fact, he makes pizzas and cookies people can barely stop scarfing.

Yet there is discord between Buffy and Ted, which hurts and disappoints Joyce.

**Buffy:** "I mean so far all I see is someone who apparently has a good job, seems nice and polite, my mother really likes him. . . ."
**Xander:** "What kind of monster *is* he?!"
—**"TED"**

A robot monster, it turns out, who tries to reinvent the perfect wife and family he never had in life. Before this is known, Buffy is hauled up on a murder charge when she sends him hurtling down the stairs, quite by accident...severely testing the limits of her mother's love for her. And yet, Joyce comes through when Ted comes back as if from the dead:

"Oh, my God, Buffy.... Ted, I swear she never meant to hurt you; you have to believe me."
**Joyce, to Ted, in "Ted"**

Though she loves this man, she loves her daughter more.

# INTRODUCTION

Joss Whedon says of the world of *Buffy the Vampire Slayer:* "At the core, it's an emotionally safe place to be." The main characters care deeply about one another (yes, even Cordelia), and when the chips are down, they can count on one another. They share a common vision, and they serve a common purpose. They are loyal and true, and yes, they would die for one another.

What all that is, is love.

The entertainment industry as a whole is not about sharing vision, purpose, or love. It's not a safe place to be. Despite the proliferation of TV channels, networks, a new appreciation for independent film, and quirky, risk-taking films in general, as well as the current new trend of putting short QuickTime movies on the Net as "job applications" for new directors, it is still incredibly easy to be pushed off whatever mountain you have managed to scale. Shows are canceled after three episodes, or they're never picked up in the first place. Beautiful movies that took years to make it to the screen fail because they are released at the same time as a cynical, commercial blockbuster.

(Frankly, book publishing is not a safe place to be, either, but that's neither here nor there.)

Yet, there exists within the arts a place where the heart and soul are safe: in the knowledge that you had your chance to do your best on a project you care deeply about.

Welcome to the Hellmouth.

An emotionally safe place to be?

No way.

Because on the lot, and in the interviews, and through the day-to-day encounters we had with the cast and crew, we came to understand the dedication everyone connected with *Buffy* brings to their craft.

They talked about having to spar with their agents over accepting positions at *Buffy* ("the vampire what? Are you nuts?"). They shared with us the painful truth that when the twenty-minute presentation of *Buffy* was shown to "the suits" around town, no one wanted it. *It was passed over. It was not picked up.* And then, finally, twelve episodes were ordered so that *Buffy* could serve as a mid-season replacement series. Hardly a sign of enthusiasm or confidence.

It was the critics who found *Buffy* first, and then the fans. And it was a huge, diverse audience of fans: horror devotees, teenagers, Boomers—anyone who watched the show and realized this wasn't just about icky things that go bump in the night. This was a show about the heart...by people who were pouring their hearts and souls into it.

A shared vision.

# SARAH MICHELLE GELLAR

Wandering around the set, conducting on-site interviews, and in later phone interviews, we hear the same things about Sarah over and over again. She's a true professional. She was a child prodigy. Her natural ability as an actress is astonishing. She tends to mother cast and crew alike, taking an interest, solving a problem.

She works too hard.

That's something that is echoed time and again. Indeed, between her last day of work on *Buffy's* second season and the first day of work on the third, she'll have something like three days off. In the meantime, she'll be filming two movies, a *Dangerous Liaisons* update called *Cruel Inventions*, and a romantic fantasy called (for the moment) *Vanilla Fog*. When does she sleep?

Does she need to sleep?

Apparently not, because, despite the concerns of her coworkers, this is a pace Sarah seems to have been on since birth. Or, at the very least, since she began making television commercials at the age of four. From that moment on, she was the kind of girl, the kind of actor, who got noticed.

Marcia Shulman, casting director for the first two seasons of *Buffy*, remembers Sarah from her days as a child actor in New York City. In fact, she cast Sarah and Seth Green in a commercial together when the two were barely old enough for kindergarten. She stood out from the crowd. Even more so when, at the age of four, she was sued by McDonald's for a Burger King ad in which she, just a little girl, had teased the other company about its allegedly less substantial burgers.

Marcia is also the one who reveals that the producers had a very good idea of what they wanted in the actress who would play the title role—until Sarah came along. When they knew she was what they had been looking for all along, they revised their ideas about the character slightly to accommodate the actress they had found. As has been said, Sarah was there to audition for the role of Cordelia. To her incredible good fortune, Joss Whedon and the other producers saw her in another role.

Julie Benz, who played Darla, remembers screen-testing along with Sarah for the role of Kendall Hart in *All My Children*. They were in the same small audition group. She knew Sarah was going to get the part, she says. Just knew.

Sarah, by the way, is apparently meticulous about keeping a record of her career. The ad she did with Seth Green? When Marcia reminded her of it, she knew right where to find a copy. Same with her *All My Children* screen test. And the blooper reel for *Buffy the Vampire Slayer*? Last seen in Ms. Gellar's hands, perhaps never to surface again.

Sarah grew up in Manhattan, where she attended the Professional Children's School. She has appeared in countless commercials. Her TV credits include the series *Swan's Crossing* and the miniseries *A Woman Named Jackie*, in which she played a teenage Jacqueline Kennedy. As the world knows by now, Sarah won an Emmy for her stint on *All My Children*. Her film credits include *Funny Farm*, *Scream 2*, and *I Know What You Did Last Summer*. And all of that was before she kicked it into total overdrive.

Driven doesn't even begin to describe her.

While we're on the set, Sarah jokes with producer Gareth Davies and story editor Marti Noxon, and frightens away a crew member who offers to relieve her of her not-quite-finished yogurt before grinning wickedly. Before she has to run back over to hit James Marsters again, she quickly tells a story about her recent trip to the Blockbuster Movie Awards. There are workmen doing some renovations on her house. On that day, they were completely redoing her driveway. In her gown and heels, Sarah couldn't figure out how to get out to her limo without ruining her outfit. Fortunately, the blue-collar heroes offered to carry her out to the waiting car. She's surprised at how nice these guys were...as if this chore were actually a hardship in some way.

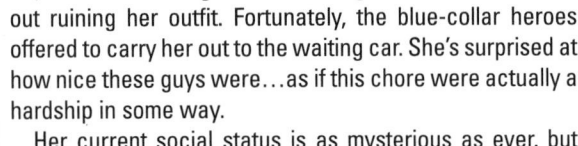

Her current social status is as mysterious as ever, but then, a woman with this kind of schedule likely doesn't have much time for romance. Or much else, for that matter.

Indeed, Sarah must be very pleased. It wasn't all that long ago, September 1994, that she was modeling back-to-school fashions on *Regis and Kathie Lee*. Things have changed considerably since then. Sarah bought her first house and her first car, among other things, including her much-talked-about tattoo.

Her own life reflects Buffy's dilemma quite dramatically, though Sarah's mission is one she herself chose, rather than being the Chosen One. Due to her work habits, it seems that Sarah has never really had time to kick back and just be "a kid." In fact, she sometimes has to ask Joss Whedon what some of the slang in the scripts means.

When she has a few moments when she isn't being filmed or photographed or interviewed, Sarah does spend time with other members of the cast, particularly Alyson Hannigan. In fact, Sarah credits the addition of Alyson to the cast (another actress was originally cast as Willow) as the final ingredient needed to make the rapport among the main characters truly click. When Sarah does hang out with the cast, a typical get-together might be like the night Sarah, Alyson, and Charisma Carpenter went to the Hard Rock Café and then to the movies to see *Scream*.

Where would Sarah find the time? What she does find the time for is her dog, a white Maltese named Thor, after the Norse god of thunder. Also John Cusack movies. And, sometimes, vanilla wafers.

How busy is she? Well, let's just say she made no secret of the day she drove to work in knee-high boots and a slip—but forgot to wear her dress. It's a story she's told several times, and the busier she gets, the more likely it becomes that it might happen again! But maybe next time she won't be in a convertible.

Ever since the series premiered, Sarah's star has been skyrocketing. She hosted *Saturday Night Live*, appeared on the covers of *Entertainment Weekly, Rolling Stone, Seventeen, YM, Cinefantastique*, and just about every other magazine out there. Her "Got Milk?" ad ran everywhere from mainstream publications to the backs of Marvel comic books. *Entertainment Weekly* called her star turn in *Buffy* one of the great performances of 1997.

Sarah, and the show in which she stars, are big enough that when asked by *EW* to define the level of pop-culture excitement over the release of *Scream 2*, director Wes Craven said, "The idea that Buffy the Vampire Slayer has a relatively minor role shows you how big this thing is."

As Buffy, Sarah is far more afraid of emotional wounds than physical ones. But in her two horror films, the tables were turned, and she became a more traditional "scream queen." What is Sarah herself afraid of? Not much, but she has admitted a terror of an intruder in her home, as well as a fear of cemeteries and the idea of being buried alive. And, as far as being a scream queen is concerned, as Sarah told *YM* magazine, "Some of the best work for girls my age is in this genre."

## NICHOLAS BRENDON

Nicholas Brendon isn't Xander. Right off the bat, that's clear. He's quick-witted, a bit mischievous, yes. But where Xander is open and spur-of-the-moment, Nicholas seems more guarded and contemplative.

We meet outside his trailer. These "Star Wagons" are split into two compartments, and Nicholas shares his with Alyson Hannigan. While we talk, he sits in a rocking chair he brings out of the trailer (though he first offers it to us: a gentleman). Alyson comes out walking her little dog. Charisma comes and wants to talk about plans for them to hang out after shooting is completed for the day.

We talk about auditioning in general first, and the way he has of delivering his lines so they sound natural, rather than like "acting."

"If I have to go in and read for something, [I try to] use an unusual but natural beat. Take a breath where I shouldn't be taking it. It also helps you slow down; in real life people think about what they are saying."

It is perhaps impossible to turn auditioning into a formula—otherwise a casting director could choose anyone for a part. But something of Nicholas's philosophy and strategy must work. For an actor with a relatively short resumé, he snagged the role of Xander more quickly than anyone could have expected.

"I met with [casting director] Marcia Shulman," he recalls. "She brought me back that day. I met Joss and Gail and did my thing and got a phone call about an hour later saying I was going to Fox to test. I went to Fox and was very nervous and tested. They allowed me to go to Warner Brothers the following Monday. There were two of us, and then Tuesday I found out that I got the role."

Four days. That's fast.

And acting was not Nicholas's first career choice. Born and raised in Granada Hills, California, he attended College of the Canyon, where he played baseball. That was his dream: the majors. A dream that ended when he broke his arm in a manner which would impede his baseball performance.

It wasn't long before Nicholas was working in TV commercials. Unsatisfied with the way things were going, he switched to the other side of the camera, becoming a production assistant on the series *Dave's World*. After acing an audition for a guest spot on that series, his luck started to change. Nicholas also appeared in a recurring role on the daytime soap *The Young and the Restless*, as the lead in a pilot called *Secret Lives*, in a guest spot on *Married...With Children*, and as a homicidal corn worshiper in *Children of the Corn 3: Urban Harvest*.

Then came *Buffy*.

"My twin brother, Kelly, dyed his hair blond because he was sick of people coming up to him [for autographs]," he says in wonder.

Hmm. Nicholas has a twin brother. While that thought will send many a female fan's mind whirling, it also makes one wonder how long it can be before the "evil doppelganger" episode of *Buffy*.

"You never know," Nicholas says. "The show's been sold into syndication already. They're going to need to do about a hundred episodes. So you never know what's going to happen down the road. And you've *got* to have a doppelganger episode. But we've got to find a doppelganger for each individual."

The differences between Nicholas and Xander aren't limited to just personality, either. There are some, well, physical differences as well.

"I had my belly button pierced for three or four years," he says. "I took that out because of the show. I had to have my shirt off a few times and Joss said, 'Xander wouldn't have a belly-button ring.'"

**Do you have any scars, tattoos or other distinguishing marks?**
**NICHOLAS:** "The scar on my elbow from my baseball injury. And as my girlfriend just said, there are scars all over my heart because she's broken it so often."

**Are you expecting Speedo backlash over your performance in "Go Fish"?**
**NICHOLAS:** "I'm not looking for backlash. I'm looking for forward lash."

**Do you have any skills or talents you haven't showcased as Xander yet?**
**NICHOLAS:** "I *discover* new talents. Like dancing. Whatever comes up, I'll do it. I've done a lot of pratfalls and stuff like that."

**What were you afraid of as a child?**
**NICHOLAS:** "I'm afraid of that question. I don't talk about my childhood that much."

**Which isn't all that unusual for actors.**
**NICHOLAS:** "That way you know there's a reason we're acting."

**Which member of the Scooby Gang are you?**
**NICHOLAS:** "I'm both Scooby and Shaggy. Maybe a little bit of Fred in there as well."

**You have a great love for old movies. Your favorite actor is Jack Lemmon, your favori film is *Some Like It Hot*. What else do you like, and where does that love come from?**
**NICHOLAS:** "Cary Grant. Looking at his whole body of work. Most of those actors were vaudeville-trained. Cary Grant was one of those and was great at physical comedy but had leading-man looks. If anyone ever said of me that 'he's like a poor man's, '90s, Cary Grant' I would be very, very happy about that. Jimmy Stewart, of course. Ernest Borgnine in *Marty* is one of the best performances I've ever seen. Hollywood was so different. Some ways better, some ways worse. But not being born in that era, you fantasize. Everything seems so epic."

**During season two, Alyson pantsed you on the set. You still haven't gotten her back.**
**NICHOLAS:** "I can't do it. Instead, I'll take that anger out on some guy driving the car. Road rage. Someone's goin' down."

**Do you have a favorite moment, on or off camera, from your tenure on the series?**
**NICHOLAS:** "Probably the day I did my Speedo stuff. The crew was so supportive. I was so terrified of it. When we finally did my scene it was four minutes of sheer hell. Walking in, doing my dialogue, then diving into the pool. Then, coming up from the water, I heard this weird smattering, and then I emerged and the whole crew was applauding. It was really nice. Everyone was very supportive."

**Even David [Boreanaz]?**
**NICHOLAS:** "Heh. Dave wasn't there. Yeah, he's a wiseguy."

**You've kissed or been in some intimate situation with each of the female cast members. Is this the best job you've ever had?**
**NICHOLAS:** "It's not bad. I'm sure I can get paid to do worse things."

**Everyone on the set seems to think that *Buffy*'s success, and the team that came together to make it happen, was almost destiny. Do you share that feeling?**
**NICHOLAS:** "It's one of those things where everything worked. When you're creating a successful show, it's ninety percent luck. Joss has the talent, but when it comes to casting, it's all luck. It was my first pilot season, and I kind of won the lottery."

## ALYSON HANNIGAN

She isn't Willow. That's patently obvious. The veteran actress, who has been working since the age of four, is confident and outgoing, funny and mature. But then again, there's that smile, those expressive eyes, the warmth and sincerity. And then you have it. This is what Willow might be like when she grows up.

Born in Washington, D.C., Alyson spent years working in commercials in Atlanta before moving to Los Angeles at the age of eleven. She has appeared in several TV series as a guest star, including *Picket Fences, Roseanne,* and *Touched by an Angel,* and was a regular on the short-lived *Free Spirit*. Her feature films include *Dead Man on Campus* and *My Stepmother Is an Alien,* in which she first performed opposite Seth Green, who played her boyfriend in that film, just as he does in *Buffy*.

On the question of how much she's like Willow, Alyson, of course, has her own opinions. So does her boyfriend. When asked, he replied that Willow was "one of her personalities."

"I love that," Alyson says happily.

Though, unlike Willow, Alyson has not achieved computer nerd-dom just yet.

"I have a computer, and I'm signed onto the net," she says. "I'm not nearly as literate as Willow but definitely can make my way around the computer and programs and everything. I have a Packard Bell. It is kinda slow now; in fact, it discourages me from going on the Net, because my modem is not very fast. I think I need to upgrade my computer."

Like many of the actors on the series, Alyson loves animals. She has, in her words, "an army of pets," including two dogs, and, together with her roommate, a total of five cats in the house. Her dog Alex, who is a Jack Russell terrier, is on the set with her, though officially pets aren't allowed. Alyson insists that Alex is a figment of the imagination of anyone who might see him running about. The other dog is named Zippy, and the cats are Dr. Seuss, Jupiter, Tear Drop, Rain, and Lucky.

One has to wonder, given Willow's naivete, if playing such an innocent character has made Alyson want to act, well...naughty.

"No," she says dismissively. "You know, we sort of dabbled in the different wardrobe with the *Halloween* episode. Perhaps if the character were completely different...but to be Willow in that outfit, I was self-conscious. But if I were playing a different character that was just evil, then I could be more comfortable with the wardrobe. But, no, I don't ever want to be evil. I love Willow as she is."

The way she is. Interestingly enough, Alyson figured out "the way she is" by instinct, and the way she read her lines in her audition has defined the character ever since. We like to call it "the Willow cadence."

"I was sitting in the parking lot in my car waiting for the audition," she recalls. "I was reading the lines, and it was just sort of depressing. She was saying, 'Oh, boys don't like me, and this and that, and I can't really speak around guys.' I just didn't want to feel sorry for her. How are [viewers] going to like her if they're saying, 'Oh, look at her feeling sorry for herself'?

"There was a scene between Buffy and Willow, and in the beginning of the scene Willow says, 'Xander and I went out when we were four or five, and then we broke up.' Buffy says, 'Why?' 'Because he stole my Barbie.' It changed once we got to [shoot] the actual scene, but in the [original version] Buffy says, 'Did you ever get your Barbie back?' And Willow's line was: 'Most of it.' And so I thought, you know what, I'm gonna make that a really happy thing. I was so proud that I got most of my Barbie back. And then that clued in how I was going to play the rest of the scene. It defines the character. That was the one line that triggered it. Then I went back and said, 'Okay, now how can I play the whole scene like that?' And it really helped me. And Joss said later, 'Oh, yeah, *most* of it!' It was a funny line, and he didn't even know there was a joke there. I made the right choice."

**Do you have any scars, tattoos, or other distinguishing marks?**
**ALYSON:** "I have all of the above. I have a bunch of scars. Let's start with the one on my nose from a dog ripping it open when I was two. He was kissing me, and then his tooth got caught in my nose, and he was trying to get it out, and he just ripped my nose apart. And then I have a scar in my eyebrow, from— I was in the bathroom with my friend when we were little kids. We were about to take a bath, and for some reason, I don't understand why, my foot went into the waste basket, and I tripped, and my head fell onto the track from the sliding door. I also have a scar on my chin that I got when I was a little baby. I was running around with a glass bottle, and I fell.

"Then I have a scar under my chin from— The story my mom knows is I just fell on the chain-link fence, but the real story is that I was playing Marco Polo with my friend, and my mom said, 'Go get the mail.' I said, 'I can't, I'm playing Marco Polo.' I was the one with my eyes closed, I guess that's Marco. So I decided, 'Okay, fine, I've got to go get the mail, but I still want to play the game. I'll do both.' So, I decided I'd walk to the mailbox from the backyard swimming pool with my eyes closed. I was doing quite a good job, I thought, until I was in the carport, and I was walking through, and we had just gotten the chain-link fence removed from the front yard, and the people just put it into the carport. I guess I forgot about that, so I tripped over it, and my chin landed on the top part of it. I was probably about seven. You know, that's just my face. I guess I wasn't a very graceful child.

"As for tattoos, I have tribal dolphins on my ankle, and I have a Japanese *kanji* on the lower part of my back."

**Tribal dolphins?**
**ALYSON:** "They're black, and they are in more of the tribal form. It's not like Flipper or something."

**And what does the *kanji* say?**
**ALYSON:** "It's the *kanji* for luck and happiness."

**Do you have any skills or talents you haven't been able to use on the show that you'd like to showcase?**
**ALYSON:** [laughter] "No. I don't think so. I can't think of anything right now."

**You worked with Seth on *My Stepmother Is an Alien*. Do you have any other connections with any other cast members or crew members from previous jobs?**
**ALYSON:** "I worked with Seth on a couple of things actually. The other was *Free Spirit*, this sitcom that I did."

**Were you interested in horror and fantasy growing up?**
**ALYSON:** "Yeah. I mean, I was a chicken. I still pretty much am, you know. I'm the screamer in the theater, but it was always fun to get spooked."

**What were you afraid of as a child?**
**ALYSON:** "Tests that I hadn't studied for? I was sort of afraid of my spelling teacher. She was mean. Obviously, you go through the phases of, 'Okay, there are monsters moving under my bed,' so I was obviously afraid of anything that could be under there. That's why I kept all of my toys under my bed. You know, my mom thought I was just messy. No, no, it was protection."

## CHARISMA CARPENTER

Just out of makeup, Charisma Carpenter is wearing a long overcoat that covers whatever Cynthia Bergstrom has dressed her in for this episode. She has only a few minutes before she'll be called to the set, so while we sit at a picnic table, Charisma enjoys a light lunch. The picnic table is located on a patch of lawn in the middle of the parking lot. A patch of lawn which also sports portions of a cemetery set.

The first thing that comes to mind upon meeting Charisma is, of course, "How much is this girl like Cordelia?" The immediate answer is "not at all." It is evident that Charisma Carpenter is intelligent, focused, and thoughtful, three things her television counterpart has never been accused of being.

Charisma was born and raised in Las Vegas, Nevada, where she lived until she was fifteen, at which point her family moved to Mexico. Charisma's interest in the performing arts was evident from childhood. At the age of five, she began to study classical ballet. She continued to dance through high school, during which she commuted between Mexico and San Diego to take classes at the School of the Creative and Performing Arts.

After her high school graduation, and a jaunt through Europe, Charisma entered junior college in San Diego and worked the usual jobs in restaurants and video stores, and was also an aerobics instructor. In 1991, she spent a brief period as a cheerleader for the San Diego Chargers—experience that would come in handy later as cheer-queen Cordelia.

Eventually, the actress moved to Los Angeles.

"I was working in a restaurant, saving my money to go back to college," she recalls. "I wanted to be an English teacher. When I was working in this restaurant, a lot of people would ask, 'Are you an actress? Are you a model? Why don't you consider that?' Finally, one person specifically said, 'I know somebody. I want you to meet them.'"

Then she met a commercial agent who recommended several acting schools. After visiting the most reputable on the list and auditing classes, she wound up at the well-known Playhouse West, where she studied for eighteen months.

"That was when I discovered how much I enjoyed acting and what an outlet it was—and that I could actually make a living at it," Charisma notes. "It gave me a lot of confidence. That school made me feel like 'This is possible; if I worked hard, I could really do this.' This is what I want. I love doing this."

Still, despite her blossoming career, Charisma hasn't forgotten her interest in teaching.

"I'm sure I would be a good teacher, and maybe down the road, that [could] happen," she says. "I mean, I love children, and I love the aspect of giving and loving and nurturing in an educational environment. It would be great. But it's not me right now."

While attending Playhouse West, Charisma began to do commercials. She appeared in more than twenty before her first real break came in the form of a guest shot on *Baywatch*. Shortly thereafter, Charisma auditioned for Aaron Spelling, who cast her in the role of Ashley in his short-lived NBC series *Malibu Shores*.

It was while she was working for Spelling that Charisma first found out about *Buffy the Vampire Slayer*.

"Working with Aaron Spelling was a great experience," Charisma says fondly. "But I was working on his show, and the vibe was that it wasn't 'going.' Thankfully, my agent sent me out on the *Buffy the Vampire Slayer* audition."

Charisma first auditioned for the role of Buffy.

"I was wearing overalls and these bright orange flip-flops and a jacket, and I was just kind of hanging, you know, because I felt that Buffy could really just be herself," she remembers, a wry smile playing at the edges of her mouth. "She could wear the flip-flops, and she could be low-key and still be very—it wasn't about looking as cute as I could to get the part. It was about just being cool, just being fun with your identity. And that's how I felt. The other girls in the room were really dressed up, and they were wearing very high school trendy clothes with knee-high stockings and short skirts."

To Charisma's surprise, however, the producers asked her to audition for the role of Cordelia as well. To say the least, the actress was unprepared. She had, after all, come to read for *Buffy*.

"I was thinking, *I'm never going to get this part because of the way they're seeing me.* Sometimes you

have to show people. Cordelia is definitely a character to dress for. You have to kind of give it to them and let them work on that. It was an interesting experience, because I had about fifteen minutes to go outside and prepare for Cordelia when I had spent all this time on Buffy."

Obviously, it went well. The producers soon had Charisma scheduled for a screen test for Cordelia. All did not go as smoothly as one might imagine, however.

"I was super, super late for the screen test, because I was working all the way down on the beach for *Malibu Shores,* and I had to go to Burbank, which was on the opposite end of the city. I was late, and there was traffic, and it was raining," she remembers. "My agent called me right when I was at the exit, paged me, 911, and I went 'Oh, gosh, I better answer this.' So I pulled over, even though I was tremendously late. I said, 'What? I'm on the exit right now.' She tells me, 'They're going to leave, you'd better hurry up.'"

Most actors would have been in a panic by that time. Not Charisma.

"I said, 'You tell them that they'd better order a pizza or something, because I did not drive an hour and a half in all this traffic to not go in there and at least audition.' Obviously, I was panicked."

Fortunately, when she finally arrived, the audition went well. The producers were "laughing, really responsive," Charisma recalls. She left with a rush of confidence. "After it was over and they had all left, I called my agent and said, 'I got this part.' She said, 'No, don't say that, you don't know.' But I knew I had the part, I could tell."

She was, of course, absolutely correct. During the first season, the character of Cordelia seemed little more than Buffy's snobby nemesis. But in the season finale, the character learned the truth about Sunnydale. From that point on, Charisma knew that her character was going to be much more involved with the Slayer's posse. Ironically, she admits that this news caused her some anxiety.

"I wasn't sure how I felt about it, because I didn't want to lose my edge. I didn't want her to be nice; I didn't want her to change because that's who she is," she says thoughtfully, although she notes that Cordelia's somewhat rough edges can make for difficult experiences with fans.

"Sometimes it's hard when they don't expect you to be anything but snobby. They don't necessarily want to approach you. Fan letters often ask, 'When are you going to be nice to Buffy?' Fans don't know how to take me, they don't know that I'm nice, they don't know that I'm normal, and Cordelia is just a character. People get confused. It's a TV show. I provide conflict, and that's what good drama needs."

Perhaps because of that element of conflict, Charisma didn't want her character to change too much. In fact, when discussing a moment of kindness Cordelia exhibits toward Xander in the second-season finale, Carpenter asserts in no uncertain terms that: "We don't want too many of those nice moments." In fact, she has often urged the producers to "make her meaner."

"It would be boring if she was too one-dimensional. It's a challenge for me to find that balance. That's why I enjoy playing her so much. She's got to be somewhat tolerable or why would they hang out with her? But I [try] not to lose her edge, her honesty."

Which brings us round to that first question: does Charisma Carpenter share anything with Cordelia Chase beyond her initials? Before our interview, she would have said absolutely not. Now, though, she's not so sure.

"Now that we're talking about it, in this context, I am kind of like her. That's the first time I ever realized it; that's how I am," she admits. "Sometimes I'll say things, but it's just the truth, you know? You kind of have to learn the balance, so you don't offend people. Sometimes I do get in that situation where I have said something outspokenly, and based on [somebody's] reaction, later wondered, *Ooh, how did that come across?* I have a good heart, I'm a good person, honest."

But what about in high school? Was she Cordelia in high school, or was she more like one of the other characters on the show?

"Well, I wasn't Willowish, I wasn't terribly academic," she says quickly. "I wasn't in the clique, either; I wasn't Cordy. I was kind of a loner, and nobody really is a loner in this cast."

Conversation eventually turns to the future, of course. But Joss Whedon, the series' creator, plays things very close to the vest. So close that cast members rarely know what will happen to their characters next season, or in some cases, even next month. Charisma will say only that she's "curious," and who can blame her?

**Do you have a favorite moment, either off camera or on, since you've been on the show?**
**CHARISMA:** "I have a lot of favorite moments, most with Xander. A lot of Cordy's conflict, and a lot of who she is, comes out around Xander. Because she is in love with him in spite of herself, or in spite of him. I have my best moments with Nicky (Nicholas Brendon)."

**Are you more of a preparatory or an instinctual actor?**
**CHARISMA:** "A little bit [preparatory]. But I leave room for whatever's going to happen instinctually. I read the scripts, and if I find something that I don't like, it's up to me to deliver it in a way that makes me happy and is true to [the character]. Fortunately, I have been working as Cordelia for two years, so I'm getting to know her really well, and that's a benefit of television."

**Do you have any tattoos or distinguishing marks?**
**CHARISMA:** "Just a beauty mark on the hip."

**Scars?**
**CHARISMA:** "I do have a scar, actually, a really nasty scar on my stomach. Do you want to see?"

**Ow, that looks like it hurt. How did you get it?**
**CHARISMA:** "I was five years old, and I had snuck into the backyard when I wasn't supposed to. The pool was being built. I guess the construction workers had left the gate open. So me and my adventurous friend were in the backyard. We ran around to the deep end, where he bumped me, so I fell forward, and I impaled myself on a rebar (one of those metal bars that stick up out of the cement in any new construction). It almost punctured my stomach. I don't know how I came to. I don't remember lifting myself off or any of that, but I must have, because nobody else did it. The next thing I remember is going into my downstairs bathroom and taking the toilet paper in both hands, just getting gobs and gobs of toilet paper and putting it on my tummy and going upstairs.

"My mom was getting ready in the bathroom and I came in and said, 'Mommy, I have a boo-boo.' She said 'Okay, let me kiss it better,' and she turned. I took [the toilet paper] off, and she started to freak out. That day my dad was at work, and the car was in the shop. So my mom was carrying me in her arms, pounding on the neighbor's doors to take me to the hospital. I got stitches, and that was a painful part. That was a drama.

"I almost died."

**What were you afraid of as a child?**
**CHARISMA:** "My brother. And that's not a joke."

**Do you have any talents or skills that you haven't used on the show that you'd like to?**
**CHARISMA:** "I dance. I love ballet. I sang [on the show], and that's not a gift. That is specifically why they had me sing, I think. 'Do you sing?' 'No.' 'Well great!' I did classical ballet all my life, growing up."

## DAVID BOREANAZ

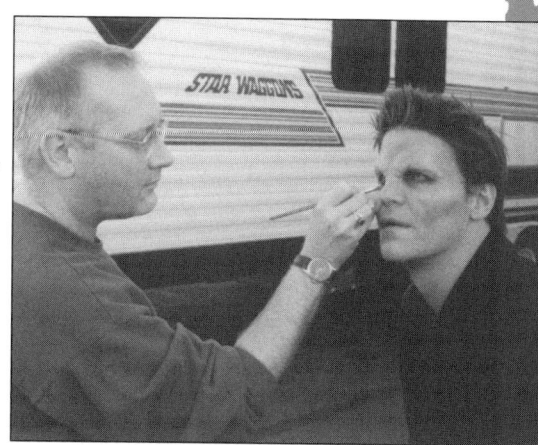

He's as arresting in person as he is on camera. Very kind, very gracious. He ushered us over to some overstuffed chairs and couches on part of the mansion set, but just as soon as we settled in, the grips started moving things around. So he suggested we move. As soon as we got settled into our new chairs, someone started vacuuming. David seemed apologetic, but we assured him everything was fine there.

David Boreanaz was born in Buffalo, New York, grew up in Philadelphia, and graduated from Ithaca College in New York before moving to Los Angeles to try his luck at acting. His luck, it must be noted, at first didn't seem to be all that good. He parked cars, painted houses, and handed out towels at a sports club. He did some local theater and managed to get a guest spot on a single episode of *Married...With Children*. But his big break is a story right out of 1940s Hollywood.

Casting director Marcia Schulman had seen just about every young actor in L.A. for the role of Angel. One day, she received a phone call from a friend, a manager, who had just signed a new client—a guy he had seen out the window of his home. David had been walking his dog when the man approached him. In no time, he was off to audition for the role of Angel. The moment he walked in, Marcia Shulman, who had already seen so many actors for the role, wrote in the margins of the casting sheet, "He's the guy."

He was the guy.

As an actor, he is intense and focused. Off the set, however, he has earned a bit of a reputation as a wiseguy. Both sides are in evidence during our visit.

Both sides, angel and devil. Or, if you prefer, Angel and Angelus. Which brings us round to the question of David's preference: which of his character's personae has he most enjoyed portraying?

"There are pluses and minuses to each," he points out. "With Angel's good side, I wasn't really exploring as much, as far as his being as outgoing as I wanted to be. But I know when I go back to being good, then I'll have learned from that. I think they both balance each other out pretty well....Yeah, I've done some bad things."

Bad things, perhaps, but that's Angel. David's intensity tells you he's capable of that, but mention his dog, Bertha Blue, and he turns into a softie, sad that he must leave her at home.

"It's terrible. Terrible," he says. "Sometimes I bring my dog on the set. It is hard: she's in the trailer and you don't want to bring her out and you are afraid that she might run away. But it is good to come home and see her all happy. [To know that] she is okay.

"I've had her about four years. She has her own house. She has one ear that goes up and one ear that goes down. She has been lost many times, but she has always found her way home or I've found her. She's got a collar on and tags; so she'll come up somewhere eventually. I just don't stress. I home in on her."

Not exactly brooding, is he? And yet, other than the subject of Bertha Blue, David does seem to have some of that Angelic demeanor to him. Let's face it, Angel is cool. But as for David—observations about the present aside, we want to know about the past. As a child, was the man who went from walking his dog to talking about his own television series, well, *cool?*

"Ahhh, was I cool?" he repeats, a bit mystified by the question. "I liked the Fonz. Arthur Fonzarelli [from *Happy Days*]. I thought he was cool. But I don't know. I felt good about myself, I guess that is being cool."

Moments before the interview, we had been watching David shoot several takes of a very intense scene. It can't be easy to prepare as an actor, particularly emotionally, for each new scene.

"It's tough," David admits. "You have to find a focus. You do your homework and you come to the set prepared and you [just] have to go out the door and see what happens. That is the most exciting thing. You've got everything down and you have it in your body and you let things happen. That is when it really starts to get fun. You get those magical moments where something goes wrong but it turns out good. That is the best thing about it."

Hmm. So, homework, then. What is an actor's homework, exactly? To David, the answer is: whatever it takes.

"Everything an actor goes through for a specific scene—whatever it calls for," he says. "And, no, I don't practice in front of a mirror. There are some secrets you have to keep; there is a fine line. And those are the things that you cherish. You go home, memorize your lines, get that over with, then you add to your character. You bring certain things to the rehearsal, and they either work or not. The director might like them, or he might not like them. Then when you are finished, you drive home and you think how you could improve. When I've finished a scene, there is always something more that I want to do. Even if it was great, that's fine, but there is always something more. You want to push yourself, to find a different level. It is tiring."

David admits that he is being recognized more and more frequently, but he is resolved to whatever may come.

"It goes with the territory. You kind of embrace it," he says. "More and more people are coming up to me to say they are enjoying the show or the character. It is pretty wild. It is nice to be recognized. You are doing work and you are on a good show."

As for the break between seasons two and three, David had no real plans.

"I'm just going to go on vacation and take some time to relax. When I come back from vacation, I'll see what happens. I'm a real patient person. I let things kind of happen. I'm young and I have my whole life in front of me. I want to enjoy this time. I really don't want to overindulge myself in work or push things, because you can really wear yourself out. And I don't want to do that. I want to kick back, have a margarita," he says with a smile.

"Also, I don't want to be overly exposed. I don't want to push anything. I don't want to be in a film or a project that I'm not passionate about and have it flop. Then where are you five years from now?"

On the subject of the future, the conversation turns to ways in which David would like to explore his character, if he could choose.

"I'd like Angel to be able to go to Las Vegas on road trips, spend the night with my vampire friends," he says. "You don't want to take your work home and think about the show, but you do inevitably because you are part of it and it is part of you. There is a lot to him that I would like to explore. He's got a good side, and he's got a bad side. How you keep that balanced is pretty interesting. Sure, he can mope around and be sad and brooding. Or he can try to make a difference, somehow, in somebody's life. You know what I am saying? Sure, you make your amends and go on with it."

**How do you feel about being a sex symbol?**
**DAVID:** "Oh, geez, I didn't know I was. Am I a sex symbol? I'd have to thank my mom and dad; they made me. That was pretty easy. Those are the two that started it. I was conceived in Toronto, too, did you know that? Yeah, my parents conceived me in Toronto."

**It must be difficult for an actor to start a new series, for the cast to work together without knowing one another and yet still try to be an effective ensemble.**
**DAVID:** "Well, you're thrown together. In my case, I've been blessed that things have been very, very good. I haven't had any problems with people I'm working with. My fellow actors have all been very giving. There are tense moments, but that is because of the time and because of the hours. You can catch somebody at a very vulnerable spot sometimes and they won't find that amusing and/or they just want to get the day over with. And you've got to respect that. So, I think it's all been pretty good. I can count on the cast. You don't really try to create that, I think it just happens."

**What was your schedule today?**
**DAVID:** "I got up at five. I had a six A.M. call."

**Were you interested in the horror genre at all when you were growing up?**
**DAVID:** "I remember being terrified by *Frankenstein* when I was a kid. The old *Frankenstein*. Boris Karloff. When he came and visited the little girl playing by the lake. Terrible, I couldn't watch it. That and I like Godzilla movies."

**Do you want to direct?**
**DAVID:** "Yeah, definitely. I love people. I studied film in college, so I understand it. I love moving the camera. I just need to understand a little bit more about the technical side of the camera."

**Do you have a favorite moment, either on or off camera, from your work on the series?**
**DAVID:** "There were a couple actually. When I had the scene in the Factory—just after I had changed—and I was striking the match off the brick table. That was a really cool moment. That whole scene seemed to really gel.

"Also, I work with Sarah a lot and there is good chemistry between the two of us. We are able to grasp each other's insights pretty easily. That's really pleasant. There have been a lot of moments with her that I would walk away and say, 'Wow, that was really great.' And there are moments where you say 'Wow, that was really bad,' but it comes out great. You can't really judge yourself. You've just got to do it. You learn from your mistakes; you grow from them."

## ANTHONY STEWART HEAD

Anthony Stewart Head is at present the resident "grown-up" among the cast regulars. He portrays Rupert Giles, Buffy's Watcher, and the librarian at Sunnydale High School.

Born in Camdentown, England, he has enjoyed a long and successful career with roots in musical theater, following completion of his training at the London Academy of Music and

Dramatic Arts. His first break came playing Jesus in *Godspell* in the West End. He has also appeared in British theaters in *The Rocky Horror Show* as Frank N. Furter, *Julius Caesar*, *The Heiress*, *Chess*, Peter Shaffer's *Yonadab*, and *Rope*.

In America, he attracted attention as regular cast member Oliver Sampson on *VR5*. He has guest-starred on *Highlander*, *NYPD Blue*, and many BBC productions (including his first TV role, in *Enemy at the Door*.) He also appeared with Jim Belushi in the Showtime movie *Royce*, and in feature films, including *A Prayer for the Dying* and *Lady Chatterley's Lover*.

His long-lasting fame as the romantic and intriguing "coffee guy" on the long-running Taster's Choice coffee commercials is gradually being supplanted by his new image as the sexy librarian on *Buffy*. When he asked to visit an American high school library in order to research his role, the librarian he interviewed was thrilled at the prospect that a librarian would be featured so prominently in the show—and played by a handsome man, at that.

"She said it was really good to have a spokesman for librarians because somebody could finally tell the true story of the hard time that librarians have. For instance, she said, did I know that there were more libraries in state prisons than there were in schools? I promised that I would try to get that in a script somewhere."

Of his role as a heroic librarian, Tony adds, "I don't think Giles is a very good librarian, actually. No one ever comes into his library. The library's all over the place, and I think that's part of his charm."

He was surprised by the strong reaction to Giles as a sex symbol.

"I have played a number of types before now," Tony says, "but usually on TV I have played dark, the character himself quite sexy. Nice sort of thing. I have to thank Jeri Baker [of the *Buffy* hair department], because when I first sat down in her chair and we talked about what we were going to do, I suggested parting my hair on the side and flattening it down for a really, really geeky look.

"She said, 'No, please, don't do that. You're a good-looking man, and I promise you there are going to be women out there who would rather see you looking attractive.' So I said, 'All right, fair enough.' So I am thankful to her, because otherwise Giles wouldn't have had any fans at all."

Fans he does have, including his loyal GASPers on the net and members of the American Library Association. He is quite appreciative of their attention. They have sent him many gifts, including a T-shirt laden with "Buffyisms."

In addition to soliciting his input on his character's appearance, Tony has been consulted by the *Buffy* production staff about how to decorate his haunts: the library, his office, and his apartment. He and production designer Carey Meyer share a love of Art Deco, which shows in Giles's furnishings. Tony suggested having a bedroom loft. A support beam in the apartment reminded him of one of the tenets of Feng Shui, and he decided that Giles would probably be a devotee of the Chinese spiritual philosophy.

So Tony was quite charmed to discover that someone had added some hanging crystal prisms used in Feng Shui to his apartment set. In addition, he decided that Giles had at one time been an archeologist, and so there are photographs and memorabilia about digs in his school office. He based this part of his characterization on a friend from his youth, "who is or was" a librarian and an archeologist, and was fascinated by the occult.

"It always used to worry me," Tony confides. "I have always hated those Ouija boards and things. I've always thought they were dangerous."

His suggestions for his transportation—Giles drives a barely functional Citröen DS—were not heeded, however, as he explains, with a grin:

"I was severely pitching for a motorcycle and sidecar. With Sarah on the back of a 1950s, 1960s BSA. An English bike. You used to be able to get a double sidecar. Willow and Xander would ride there. I think I got the image from *The Aristocats*.

"But Joss says there are times for humor and times for seriousness, and rolling up like that in a moment of great urgency wouldn't work."

Tony comes from a theatrical family. His mother is an actress, probably best known for her role of Madame Maigret in the BBC television series, *Maigret*. His father, a documentary-film producer, founded the British production company Verity Films. And his brother sang the role of Judas in the original recording of *Jesus Christ Superstar*.

He's working on a script of a musical he's written with a collaborator, as well as talking to a stateside producer interested in reworking a project into an animated feature. He misses singing, "because it is a great means of self-expression, a completely different buzz" from acting. The only singing he does at the moment is at charity functions and the like. As he removes his makeup, he chuckles at the memory of a recent benefit casino night, where he sang one of his favorite songs, by the Police: "Every breath you take, every move you move, I'll be watching you," without making the connection to the fact that Giles is a Watcher, prior to selecting the song. The audience loved it.

However, he's very pleased with the acting opportunity that *Buffy* presents him: "It is a wonderful thing being able to do the story arc of a character. It is extraordinary. I thought I was pretty lucky in *VR5* to have the story arc that I had then, but this is even better."

**Do you have a favorite moment, either off camera or on, since you've been on the show?**
**TONY:** "There was a moment in 'The Dark Age.' Certainly as an English actor, real emotion is consummate to be discovered and looked for—not having to create an emotion, just finding an emotion there. I have always had great technique, but it is something to really break down and cry. There was a scene with Buffy, and my line was that I didn't know how to stop the demon without killing Jenny. I just wept. Ever since then I have not had any problem with emotions at all.

"It was a huge breakthrough, a lovely moment. Although they used a slightly less emotional take, it was still there."

**Do you know why they used a less intense take?**
**TONY:** "Joss's feeling is that you shouldn't push the emotion. The tear welling up is enough. The tear rolling down the cheek is too much. You have done the work for the audience, and the audience can move on. As another example, in 'Passion,' after I have assaulted Angel, I come out sobbing. It was dry sobbing. It was basically a man who is just spent of his emotion, at the end of his rope. They turned the sound down a little and muted it.

"A number of people on the set who saw the scene actually had to walk away because they said it was really embarrassing watching it. A grown man sobbing. The found the moment almost too powerful. You don't want to take the audience out of the story. You want to keep them with you. You don't want to turn them off.

"Joss walks a very fine line, but I have to say, I take my hat off to his instinct. He is a very sharp cookie."

### Do you have any scars, tattoos, or distinguishing marks?

**TONY:** "When I was seven I fell off a coal bunker and broke my nose. This was in the 1960s; in England, it's cold, so you had coal. At least, some households did. We were playing in the garden and I jumped up on this thing, which is about five feet tall. I put my foot through the lid, went straight off the end, and landed on concrete. And so I have an interesting-shaped nose.

"Another time, I was playing a villain, running away from somebody. The scene was being filmed in three sections, and in each [my pursuers] were supposed to get closer. Like an idiot, I said to the director, "Why don't I turn around to look and see where they are?" Which obviously slows me down.

"The director thought it was a good idea. I completely lost my balance and found my legs running away from me, and just piled into the concrete. I tucked and rolled, as I had learned to do in drama school. So I dislocated my shoulder. I could have an operation, but I don't have the time to have my arm in a sling for two to three months."

### Do you really wear glasses?

**TONY:** "I have astigmatism. I wear them for driving and for the theater and the movies. But in fact, I believe very strongly that you can tell when glasses are fake on TV and in the movies, and so it was important to me for them to be integral. I have prescription lenses and I wear them most of the time unless they reflect the lights during a shot, and then I will wear a flat, nonreflective pair. I try to avoid that as much as I can. I've been wearing my prescription lenses a lot."

### Has it affected your vision?

**TONY:** "A little. I went bowling last night and bowled a few frames very badly. I thought maybe I should put my glasses on. Suddenly I could see everything. Not that it actually improved my game very much, but I could see.

"Actually, I have to pretend that Giles wears bifocals. My prescription is for shortsightedness, while Giles wears glasses to read. I saw somebody take his glasses off to read in a movie the other day, and I think that would have been quite cool, a nice bit of business. Real stuff that brings your life outside of the scene into the scene is what I find interesting; the reality outside the theater. The choices you make against the scene that make the scene live.

"There was a scene I did with Alyson and just off the top of my head, I thought I should be eating an apple, perhaps one a student left me. I was munching away and she gave me something of Ms. Calendar's, and so I suddenly forgot the apple and just put it down. It means the scene is about people and life and it is not just about what is written on the page."

### So are you a method actor?

**TONY:** "I don't know what 'method' really is, but I just know there are things that you can do to help yourself. I tried something today [for a torture scene]. I wanted to cause myself some discomfort while I was being tortured. I asked Jeri [for advice] because she used to be a nurse. She came up with the idea of chili peppers.

"I got the hottest peppers I could. My fear then was that I was going to be kissing these girls and set their lips alight. I must admit that I was buzzing.

"I was able to use the discomfort and went into a bit of a shudder, which wasn't difficult, and I felt a bit sweaty. It made me feel right.

"But there are times when the director says, 'I want you over there. Find something to do.' Something I was pleased with the other day, was that they stuck me behind my desk because it looked good in the shot and I thought, 'What the hell am I going to do down here?' Everyone else was [on the other side of the library] and Buffy was coming in to say something big. I think it was in 'Passion,' when she comes to say that Angel has been in her room.

"I decided to stamp the school address in the library books. Then, because Buffy has said something earth-shattering, I wandered into the scene with the stamp in my hand. It was just a little thing, but those are the kinds of things that bring life into scenes. I don't look for props for their own sake."

**How did it feel to do the scene when Giles discovers Jenny Calendar's body?**
**TONY:** "Joss is a genius. I thought it might be better if we didn't see Jenny killed when Angel chases her. That we might leave it over the commercial break . . . did he or didn't he? Then you would see someone entering my apartment and think it was Jenny, and then you would get the big revelation: 'Oh, my God, she *is* dead.'

"But Joss knew the audience's discomfort would be that much increased knowing. It was really clever writing."

Tony smiles for a moment when we discuss Marcia Shulman's delight in casting him for Giles on her first day. He says, "When I went to audition, it felt very good. I remember going to the Fox [screen] test and seeing Joss there, and I knew that I was going to know him....[It's like] when you see somebody and you just know that you are going to know them for a long time and they are going to be a friend. I just knew it."

# KRISTINE SUTHERLAND

Kristine Sutherland is the immensely talented actress who plays Joyce Summers (Buffy's mom), a role that has provided her with both heartbreakingly familiar moments of maternal tribulation, and some exceedingly odd ones as well. She's been bitten by a vampire, stricken by a love spell that caused her to lust for a seventeen-year-old, and romanced by the robot doppelganger of a long-dead mad scientist.

Without question, Kristine sounds like she's having the time of her life.

The actress, who has appeared in such films as *Honey, I Shrunk the Kids* and *Legal Eagles*, was born and lived most of her adult life in New York before moving to Los Angeles. She is married to *Mad About You* scene-stealer John Pankow, and the couple have one daughter, seven-year-old Eleanore. Kristine, who admits to feeling protective of her younger cast mates, is using her experience as the fictional mother of a teenage girl as preparation for the time when her own daughter comes of age.

"I look forward to someday being the kind of mother to an adolescent that allows that [process of growing up] to sort of happen in a good way. I really enjoy playing Buffy's mother, because it is kind of like a dress rehearsal. I get to explore these feelings and situations that someday will be mine because I have a daughter and I will go through that," Kristine reveals.

"Everyone says it is going to be awful, and I am sure it will have its moments, but I just think adolescence is such an interesting time," she says. "It was such a struggle for me, that in many ways I think I identify—personally, heavily—with adolescents. Some adults remember, and some don't."

Kristine is quick to note that series creator Joss Whedon "definitely remembers."

Interestingly, she feels protective not only of her real-life costars, but of their fictional counterparts as well.

"As a mother, I can't help but be concerned about Buffy not having a father figure and not having a father around. My parents were divorced, so I have some sense of what it is like to grow up in a divorced household. The dynamic, at least from my experience, was very different, because for me, when my parents got divorced, it was such an admission of failure on their part somehow, that they lost a tremendous amount of authority in the household. They both had their own emotional problems, which I suppose contributed to that, but as an adolescent you take that and you wedge it wide open: 'What would you know? You screwed up in such a big way, and *you* are going to tell me what to do?'

"That makes it difficult for a single parent to wield authority over an adolescent. Actually, I have gotten a number of letters from parents in their early thirties who write to me about their empathy with Joyce as a single mother and the struggles involved."

Gradually, the conversation turns back to her young cast mates, and Kristine notes that playing Buffy's mom, as well as working so closely with Sarah Michelle Gellar, has made her feel "very protective" of the young star.

"I worry about her working too hard," Kristine says. "You know, it's like, 'You should get an assistant; you shouldn't be doing that by yourself; you are working much too hard.'"

As for her character, Kristine thinks Joyce Summers is coming along very nicely, thank you.

"I think everybody was sort of finding their way, and there were other things to establish the first season," she notes. "I have been really, really thrilled with the writing and some of the stuff we have had to do this year. It has been really nice. I think one of my favorite scenes was the one at the end of her birthday, that two-part story ["Surprise" and "Innocence."]. When [Joyce and Buffy are sitting] on the couch. I thought Joss did something so wonderful in that scene with Joyce being her mother and *knowing* that something is going on that is very hard for her. Just being there and not asking what it is. Knowing that. You just have to be there and hope for the best for them. You can't say, 'Oh; let me be your best friend and tell me everything that is going on.' That's not your place; you're a mother."

Though she's biased, of course, Kristine is a very enthusiastic fan of the show.

"I get very caught up in the story," she says happily. "I remember so much of what it was like to be an adolescent, and it just rings so true in so many ways." And as for the second-season finale, she reports having been "stunned" by it.

"I read it in my car," she says incredulously. "I couldn't wait to read it and I had picked it up, but then I had to go to this morning voice-over thing. Well, the first free moment I had, I am sitting in my car, baking without air-conditioning, parked somewhere in Hollywood. I just had to find out what happens and I just sat there and read it. I was in shock. I mean when she gets on the bus and leaves. I was just sobbing in the car."

It should come as no surprise, at this point, that Sutherland loves her job. The beauty of it is that, as with many of the cast and crew members interviewed for this book, her participation in the series seemed to fall into place almost as though it were fate.

"I was actually kind of hiding," she recalls. "I had left New York and I had come back to L.A. and my daughter was out of school. I hadn't really told anybody I had left New York, and I hadn't really told anybody in L.A. I had gotten back. I was in limbo somewhere and thought they'd never find me. I was just sort of taking it easy and being with my daughter. It was August and nobody was around, and suddenly the phone rang and it was my agent. I thought *Damn it, how did they find me?* He said, 'Oh, Kristine, I'm so glad to find you, I have been calling everywhere looking for you because I have got this audition and I just think you are really right for this part.' He sent me the [script pages] and I just sort of toddled off to the audition. I walked in the room and it just immediately felt good. I had really loved the material. It was a very short scene, but I really enjoyed working on it and enjoyed auditioning with it. It was one of those weird things where you leave the room and go, 'Wow, I might actually get that job!'"

That feeling of destiny is strong on the *Buffy* set.

"I feel so privileged to be a part of that," Kristine says. "I really believe in the show. I think it has a great message for kids. I don't know if all parents would necessarily think so, because it is wrapped in the garb of kidspeak and trendy clothes. It is amazing how many parents who are older don't get it. It is so great because Buffy struggles. It is not all easy. She really has to struggle with things—her loyalty to her friends, issues of popularity. There are really wonderful messages in those stories."

By way of example, Sutherland points out "When She Was Bad," the second-season opener.

"How many times, when you are a kid, and even as an adult, do you have a day when you are just not proud of your behavior at the end of the day? Where you just don't feel like you acted as responsibly to your friends or your peers as you should have? At the end of the day, you review it and you think, *I really screwed up today. That wasn't cool what I did.* That had a lot of resonance for me as an adult, because all those issues that we grapple with as teenagers still resonate for the rest of your life. You never really completely grow up."

**Were you a fan of horror or fantasy growing up?**
**KRISTINE:** "I loved fantasy and science fiction, but I could never stomach horror. In fact, when I rented the movie *Buffy the Vampire Slayer*, I had to have my husband sit and watch it with me. I know it is funny and everything, but I am so terrified of horror films. I am waiting for Sarah to do a film that isn't a horror film so I can go see it. I don't know if I could even watch the show if I wasn't in it. I'm terrible. I get scared watching the show even when I'm in the episode and have seen most of it being shot."

**What were you afraid of as a child?**
**KRISTINE:** "Demons, strangely enough. I used to lie on my bed, and I used to think the whole room was just filled with evil spirits. I would break into an absolute sweat and be so terrified I couldn't talk, I couldn't move. I was convinced that there were demons under the bed. Demons and skeletons under the bed and—I think because I would be home with my mother and I didn't have a man in the house—I was always terrified that somebody was going to climb in the window. Intruders were going to come in and kill my whole family. To this day, I hate living on the ground floor. I am a New Yorker. I like to live on the eleventh floor, behind the doorman and ten locks."

**Do you have a favorite moment, on or off the screen, from your work on the series?**
**KRISTINE:** "It has been really fun for me this year, because last season almost all my work was just with Sarah, and I felt I didn't know the rest of the cast that well. So this year has been really fun, getting to know everybody else and feeling much more a part of the group. But my favorite day this year was Halloween. I was working Halloween day—which was a slight bummer because I didn't get to go trick-or-treating with my daughter—but what better place to be on Halloween than on the set of *Buffy the Vampire Slayer* with vampires running around? A lot of us came in costume, which was really fun. We were shooting the episode "Ted" that week. I came in a whole '50's garb as Ted's first wife. Sarah was Dorothy from *The Wizard of Oz,* and [her dog] Thor was Toto."

**Did you have any professional history with any of the cast or crew prior to this series?**
**KRISTINE:** "No, but I auditioned the day that David auditioned as well. I remember walking into the room. There were couches over in the corner. There were about five guys there—I figured out later that they were auditioning for Angel—and David was one of them. I saw these five guys, and he just leapt out at me. What a striking-looking guy. So it was so interesting when he showed up for Angel. I just happened to be there when they were auditioning, and I knew he had it."

**Do you have any talents or skills you haven't been able to use on the show as yet that you would like to showcase? Just as a for-instance, by the way, Armin plays trumpet.**
**KRISTINE:** "Well maybe we could do a duet. I play the piano. Actually, that was a big thing between me and my mother when I was a kid. I just hated taking piano lessons so much, and I thought it was just a curse that she put on me, just to torture me, of course. I had taken lessons since I was maybe seven, and I finally managed to quit when I was about fourteen. I picked it up again and started taking piano lessons again about a year and a half ago. Actually, just about the time that we started doing the first season of Buffy...and I love it. I love playing the piano. [Those lessons] actually turned out to be a marvelous gift."

**Do you have any scars, tattoos, or other distinguishing marks?**
**KRISTINE:** "Well, I do, but they are not that interesting. I'm riddled with scars. Fortunately, they are all small. But there are only two that are really interesting at all. I have a scar on my face, which you can't really see. You have to look very closely for it. My brother attempted to tear my eye out during one of our sibling battles. I have another scar high up on my forehead, which my hair covers, from me trying to do my brother in at a very early age. Sticking him in a wagon and going down a really, really steep hill...running off the road, over the bridge and into the creek."

**The same brother?**
**KRISTINE:** "Yeah."

**Was this payback for trying to rip your eye out?**
**KRISTINE:** "No, I think trying to rip my eye out was the payback."

**Angel is a big-time sex symbol, but a lot of women we've spoken to seem to like Oz as well.**
**KRISTINE:** "You know what it was? It was the scene in the van where she asks him to kiss her and he says, 'I don't want to kiss you until you want to kiss me.' That is the kind of man that every woman is looking for."

**Your series and your husband's (*Mad About You*) air opposite each other. Any competition there?**
**KRISTINE:** "We only have one TV. Sarah offered to take up a collection for a second one, but it's okay, we already ordered one."

**What about you and John working together sometime?**
**KRISTINE:** "We try to keep our lives and our careers separate, that works best for us. When we first came out here and he was doing *Mad About You*, they all said, 'Great we will get a part on it for Kristine.' I just didn't want to do that. It works great for some people, some people work together all the time, but we have always had different agents, different jobs, everything."

**Does Joyce think that Giles is sexy?**
**KRISTINE:** "Yeah, I think she does."

# ARMIN SHIMERMAN

Once upon a time, Armin Shimerman planned to be a lawyer. To the relief of millions of fans, he scrapped that idea in favor of what some would call a similarly provocative profession. These days, he's one of the most in-demand character actors in Hollywood. But when he started, Armin had no real interest in television.

"I studied for and apprenticed in classical theater," he notes. "If you had asked me twenty years ago if I would be on TV, I would have answered with a big fat '*no!*' No, I was set on being a stage actor. Which I became. For many years, I appeared in regional theater and Broadway in classical plays. But I was seduced by the dark side of the force and moved to Hollywood. Even today, I always think of myself primarily as a classical actor on hiatus. In fact, should the TV work end for me, I will most assuredly go back to my first love. That is what I am trained to do. That is what makes me most happy. However, it may be that my classical training, that sort of larger-than-life approach to material, is what gets me parts in the fantasy programs I frequent.

"A classical approach to a fantasy show is required. You need an actor who is not going to just mumble and worry about an itch on the left side of his arm. You need somebody who is going to deal with larger issues—life and death issues—in both a serious way and sometimes in a comedic way."

Armin knows whereof he speaks. The actor has been a regular on several successful television series, including a number of popular fantasy and science fiction series. He spent two and a half years playing Pascal in *Beauty and the Beast* before moving onto a period series called *Brooklyn Bridge* (obviously not a fantasy series), in which he starred with *Happy Days* alum Marion Ross. He has played at least half a dozen different roles on the *Star Trek* franchise, most notably fan-favorite Quark, and has also appeared on *Alien Nation* and *Stargate SG-1*. Armin also regularly appears as a judge in both of David E. Kelley's lawyer series, *Ally McBeal* and *The Practice*.

The man gets around.

His path to *Buffy*, however, was not as direct as some might think. Originally, Armin had auditioned for the role of Principal Flutie, the first-season administrator who died in "The Pack."

"Ken Lerner got the part, but I suppose that months later, when they decided to kill off Principal Flutie, they remembered me from that audition. I am assuming that is how that happened. It could very well be that they knew me from *Star Trek* and requested me from my work there, but I am assuming it was from that audition I had for Principal Flutie."

Though he grew up on the other coast, Armin's hometown of Lakewood, New Jersey, is probably not very different from the fictional Sunnydale. "I had a very nice childhood, in a wonderful small town," he recalls. "It was an incredibly good childhood, except for the fact that I came from a very poor family. But when I look back and I hear about other people's growing-up process, mine was [idyllic] in comparison."

On the subject of the obvious conspiracy being conducted by Snyder, the mayor, and the police chief, Armin is in the dark, just like the rest of us.

"I have asked Joss once or twice," Armin admits. "He won't share. I don't know if Joss has decided where he is going or not, but it does *look* like it is definitely going somewhere and, of course, I appreciate that. It is great fun for me to play a role so different from Quark."

Other than the obvious differences in character, of course, Armin is also talking about the fact that, much to his relief, his *Buffy* character is (apparently) human. No full head mask or makeup! That's one aspect of the series that thrills him. In fact, when asked if he laughs silently as actors walk by in full makeup, he says, with obvious glee, "I laugh out loud! I just smile at them, and they probably don't understand why this guy is grinning at them. I look at all the vampires and say, 'Drink a lot of water,' because it is so much pleasure not to have to be in it. I am very pleased. I think one job with makeup is sufficient.

"I am sure for the rest of the cast and the crew, this is their job, they do it every day. It's hard work, but for me it is a vacation. I get to be with very nice people doing very creative things and playing a character that is normal. So going to work [on *Buffy*] is really a vacation for me. It is delightful, and it is different, and it is creative."

Juggling his schedule isn't easy, but Armin chalks it up to the cooperative efforts of *Buffy* producer Gareth Davies and *Deep Space Nine*'s unit production manager, Steve Oster.

"There was one day recently where Steve was able to get me out of *Star Trek* at about 11:00 and gave me two hours so I could drive to Malibu to be there at 1:00 for *Buffy*. It was a good day. It is a good day when an actor gets to do two jobs in one day," Armin says happily.

At least until the end of season three, when the cast will presumably graduate from high school, the series is immersed in high school culture. A large part of that, since his first appearance in "The Puppet Show," has been the foreboding presence of Shimerman as Principal Snyder. Surprisingly, Armin admits that there are certain traits he shares with the youth-hating Snyder.

"Principal Snyder bristles much more so than I, of course, but I am not particularly easy around children. I have a lack of communicative skills with people that age and younger. So that is what I draw upon. Some of the principals that I remember growing up were major authoritarian figures who had a disdainful aura about them.... And I draw upon that as well."

In fact, Armin believes that, to a point, Snyder is more threatening to the teen characters on the series than the vampires.

"He really holds power over their future," he explains. "If they get expelled from the school, then they'll really be screwed over. They can attack a vampire, but they can't attack a school record. To our younger viewers, that's a real threat."

**What were you afraid of as a child?**
**ARMIN:** "I was afraid of snakes, which I just had to recently deal with in *Buffy*—not as close as Charisma did, but close enough. I was afraid of chickens, because I grew up on a chicken farm and they constantly pecked at me, and that was pretty unnerving. And certainly, as far as the show is concerned, I was certainly afraid of not being liked. That is probably what endears the show to me the most. Here are teenagers who are desperately dealing with the angst of growing up amidst a group of people that they are not a part of."

**Do you have any scars, tattoos, or other distinguishing marks?**

**ARMIN:** "*Ah-h-h*, that is an interesting question. I never have been asked that. I have no tattoos. I adore scars, by the way. I love scars on people. I find them fascinating. I, indeed, do have a scar. Little noticed but there it is. It is over my right eye. It was acquired when I was six years old. I was hanging onto my dog, Brownie, and I was sitting on a trash can. My father was a painter, and there were several open paint cans below. The dog pulled me and I landed on the edge of one of these paint cans, which required about seven stitches. I have always been fascinated by scars. I find them very erotic."

**Do you have any talents or skills you haven't been able to use on either *Star Trek* or *Buffy* that you want to showcase?**

**ARMIN:** "Yeah, I want to play trumpet. I do play trumpet a little, not very much anymore and not very well, but it would be kind of a hoot to play trumpet somewhere. Any other skills? I juggle, but I can't picture Principal Snyder juggling."

**Do you have a favorite moment, on or off screen, from your tenure on *Buffy*?**

**ARMIN:** "It happened the very first day. I knew that I wanted my new character to be something totally different from Quark and I wanted it to be serious and comic at the same time. I was blessed from the very start. It is the scene where Tony and I are walking down an aisle of the school auditorium. As it went on, I remember thinking, *This is exactly the character; this is exactly right; right off the bat this is working exactly right*. I was elated. When I did *Deep Space Nine*, it took six full episodes before I realized, *Ah, this is who Quark is!* But when I walked down that aisle with Tony in that first scene and talked with the four of them on my first day, I thought, *This is it*. It was a great feeling of achievement. Sometimes I try to re-create that specialness. Sadly, my acting moments aren't always as good as that first encounter. But that first meeting was just something magical for me; when I worked with those people for the first time and slipped flawlessly into character the first time. It was perfect."

## ROBIA LaMORTE

The actress who plays Jenny Calendar has done a great many different things in her career, from dancing to touring with Prince, from music videos to major TV ad campaigns, from *Beverly Hills, 90210* to Sunnydale. Without question, it's only the beginning.

Robia was born in Queens, New York, but moved around a great deal growing up.

"I had kind of a gypsy childhood," she recalls. "I traveled all around the country. My mom is not a freaky gypsy, but she's kind of a nomadic type. I grew up everywhere. I lived in Aspen, Colorado. I lived in Maryland. I lived in a bunch of the [Florida] Keys, and then I lived in Connecticut right before I moved out here with my dad when I was fourteen."

Robia pursued her first love, dancing, vigorously upon her arrival in California. She had studied "back east," and then spent six months at the Los Angeles County High School for the Arts. She took the GED and left high school early to follow up on a scholarship offered to her by the Dupre Dance Academy. But by the age of sixteen, Robia was already making her first music video, Debbie Gibson's "Shake Your Love."

She has also appeared in videos by artists as diverse as Yanni and Donny Osmond ("nothing tacky or gross," Robia says), been in fashion shows around the world, and toured with various bands, including the Pet Shop Boys and, most notably, Prince.

Indeed, for many months, Robia traveled the world as "Pearl" in Prince's *Diamonds and Pearls* world tour. She appeared as Pearl in all the music videos tied to that album, and is also on the disc's holographic cover.

"That was the pinnacle of my dance career," Robia says. "I started out auditioning for one video. He was looking for a set of twins and they couldn't find any twins they liked. The dance circle is pretty small, and I knew a girl, Laurie. We thought the twins part would be not really featured, so we didn't even want to be the twins. They told us to dress alike, and we said, 'No, no, no.' We wound up getting hired for the twins, and we started rehearsing with him. We had great chemistry, and he loved us, and he got the idea, because the album was *Diamonds and Pearls*, that one would be Diamond and one Pearl. It turned into five, six, seven videos.

"We went on tour with him all around Europe, and that's when he wasn't speaking at all, so we did all the press for the album," Robia recalls. "I did *The Joan Rivers Show*, Howard Stern, *Hard Copy, Current Affair, Inside Edition*. We went all over the place signing albums. It was a pretty awesome thing. For a year and a half, that was basically my life. Flying back and forth to Minneapolis and shooting videos, flying around to the other side of the world and hosting parties and doing fabulous things.

"That was really the perfect time for me to make the transition. After I had done that, there was really nowhere else to go with dancing, and I was training as an actress. I thought, *Okay, this is the time.*"

Robia quit dancing and quickly landed a several-episode guest shot on *Beverly Hills, 90210*.

"People still recognize me off the street, and this must have been four or five years ago," she says of her stint on the popular series.

Robia played Jill Fleming, a New York girl who was spending the summer in L.A. and was romantically involved with Ian Ziering's character, Steve Sanders.

"I think they were going to develop my story line, but then that's right where Brandon started to get involved with a teacher. That was that."

Robia has worked in a number of television commercials for companies such as Oil of Olay, GE, The Gap, and Budweiser. Most memorable, perhaps, is her Mitsubishi commercial. She is sitting in her car, using an audiotape to learn Italian, when a darkly handsome man pulls up beside her in an identical vehicle. Hearing her speak Italian, he believes she is Italian and speaks to her in that language.

Not long thereafter, Robia found herself working on *Buffy*. Already familiar with the fame game from her work with Prince and the *90210* gang, she realizes that *Buffy* has raised the bar a little higher. For one, she's likely to be attending conventions until she's ninety. For another, well, the fans are everywhere....

"A few months back, I was at 7-Eleven," she recalls. "It was ten at night. I pop out of my car. This homeless guy is sitting at 7-Eleven panhandling for money. He looks at me and says, 'Hey, you're a friend of Buffy's, aren't you?' I look at him, and I smile, and I say, 'Yeah.' And I'm starting to walk in the 7-Eleven and he says, 'Can we spare a little change, Ms. Calendar?' I've seen him a few times now, and I'm like, 'Hey, how are you?' And he says, 'I'm starstruck; I can't talk to you.' He never misses the show."

Though it seems like karma now, Robia came to the series through the usual audition process. But she knew right off that this was something different.

"Sometimes you get scripts, and you just know," she says. "The words just fit in your mouth a different way when you know you're supposed to speak them. And I kind of knew I was going to get it. I came in and auditioned, and they liked me, and I came back and met with everybody, and Tony [Head] came in to read with me. I think it was me and one other girl, so they wanted to see the chemistry. But I didn't know who he was. I thought he was a producer, so he was talking with me, and I was joking with him, and we walked into the room, and I was chewing gum, and I gave it to him, and said, 'Here, hold this.' I didn't even know. I was just playing around with him. They hired me, I think, the next day."

**Do you have any scars, tattoos, or other distinguishing marks?**
**ROBIA:** "No, I'm clean. [Pauses, then points to an attractive birthmark on her neck.] This is my only distinguishing mark. [Producers] either love it, or they hate it. Half the time when I do jobs, they cover it, and half the time they think it's great." [The *Buffy* producers didn't have it covered, by the way.]

**What were you afraid of as a child?**
**ROBIA:** [long pause] "A few things. Bugs. I grew up in Florida, and there were always bugs, and I don't like bugs. And, um, not really the dark, but what could happen in the dark. What might be there. Also, I've always been scared of sharks. I love to swim, though. I've never not gone in the water, but I have this crazy fear of sharks, even to the point where I dream I see a wave coming up, and I'll see the outline of the shark in the wave, and it's coming toward me. I have that dream all the time. So, one thing I would do when I was little, and this is crazy, I would just play with my mind. I would go into the swimming pool, and I would close my eyes, and I would swim around under there, and just see it all dark and oceany, and I could get myself so scared that there were sharks in there that I'd have to jump out of the pool. You know? I would freak myself out."

**Do you have a favorite moment, on or off screen, from your time on the show?**
**ROBIA:** "The moment I loved, loved, loved, is in the very first episode I did. As soon as I saw it on tape, I said, 'Praise God that I get to say this kind of line, because you don't get the chance to do it very often.' It's when Giles is returning her earring. I loved it on the page; I loved the way it came off. 'No, that's not where I dangle it.' Yeah, that's a classic."

**Do you have any professional history with anyone else on the series?**
**ROBIA:** "No, but you want to hear something crazy? You want to go all the way back. Last year, I was in my grandmother's house, and I was going through some jewelry. You know how grandparents always have all this crazy stuff in their drawers. There was a *TV Guide* in there. I opened up the *TV Guide*, and I'm thinking, it's from my *90210*. I open it up, and it is. There's my *90210*, with my name circled. I go to the front of the *TV Guide*, and there's a big picture of Sarah Michelle Gellar from an article on her about *All My Children*, and I thought, *Whoa, who would have thought five years later?*"

**Unlike many of the other characters, you didn't get much chance to kick butt. Are you disappointed?**
**ROBIA:** "I have not gotten to kick as much butt as I would have liked, but I did get to do a little bit of stuff in my demon episode. I jump out the window, and I throw Giles. I got to slam his head into the table and throw him and do some stuff like that. That was a fun episode."

**Is LaMorte your real name?**
**ROBIA:** "Yes. 'The Death.'"

# SETH GREEN

Like his cast mates Sarah Michelle Gellar and Alyson Hannigan—both of whom he had worked with prior to his stint on *Buffy*—Seth Green has pretty much grown up on camera.

Born in Philadephia, he began in New York City, making television commercials as a toddler. One of those commercials also featured a four-year-old girl named Sarah Michelle Gellar, a fact the actors didn't realize until Marcia Shulman—*Buffy*'s casting director and the woman who cast that commercial so long ago—reminded both of them.

Seth has gone on to appear in such television series and miniseries as *The X-Files*, *The Wonder Years*, *Beverly Hills 90210*, *Evening Shade*, and *Seaquest*. He had starring roles in *Stephen King's It* and *Byrds of Paradise*. Seth has also appeared in a number of feature films, including *Hotel New Hampshire*, *Radio Days*, *Pump Up the Volume*, *Austin Powers*, and *My Stepmother Is an Alien*, in which he played the boyfriend of a young girl played by…you guessed it: Alyson Hannigan. Even as this is being written, he has several films on the way, including *Can't Hardly Wait*, starring Jennifer Love Hewitt, *Stonebrook*, a con caper, and *Idle Hands*, a thriller.

In this interview, he's all over the place. He's driven, but he also seems like he's having a very good time. And who can blame him? On top of the movies he has coming up, he's just been offered a gig as a regular on *Buffy*, one of the hottest shows on television.

"In a way, I was kind of welcomed from the very start. I had someone that I have known a long time, who was already ingratiated into the fold. Alyson and I have stayed friends for the last ten years or so. I wasn't an outsider from the start. I was just kind of included. When things went on, I was invited. When everybody left the set to go to the service table, they asked me."

Interestingly, Seth is content to remain a background player on the series, though he'll be a regular cast member in season three.

"If you're there all the time and you're in the forefront, then it is so over, so fast. I would rather be a supporting player for the rest of my life. I would be very content with that," he says.

In fact, though most young actors (and older actors, come to think of it) seem to have a longing for the director's chair, Seth has no interest in directing. Instead, he'd like to produce and act in feature films and is working toward those ends with some close friends.

"Directors have to have a vision, and they have to have stamina, and I have neither," Seth says amiably. "I just want to take things from their very earliest points and I want to put the people into them and make them something special."

The conversation turns to Hollywood and politics, and Seth decides fairly abruptly that it's a tangent he doesn't want to go off on. Instead, we talk about fun stuff. Like Oz's van.

"It was carpeted, there were bean-bag chairs, there was a bench. It had black-light posters, there were shrunken heads, there was a disco ball, a dart board, a fridge. There was just all this stuff. They went all out. They so defined the van. It was really funny. They did a great job finding cool stuff."

Oddly enough, there is apparently an Internet group devoted solely to Oz's van. Seth has spent some time on the official *Buffy* posting board, and enjoys it, but he doesn't let the attention go to his head.

"It's just nice because the people who like the show, the fans of the show, are very, very supportive, and it is such little effort to show them that you appreciate it," he says of his chatting on the board. "So long as it doesn't take focus away from the work. Because if you get too wrapped up in your own ego, you stop working as hard. So as long as I avoid that, then, yeah, it is nice to know that people are into it.

"Somebody gave me a piece of advice a couple of years ago that I wasn't quite in the place to receive then. But it has resonated in my head ever since. That advice was to treat every audition like it's the Super Bowl and treat every day of your job like it is your first audition. Never lose the same commitment and intensity. If you just always try to do your best work every day, and never become complacent and never become satisfied, then you will always be successful."

Seth is looking forward to his promotion to "series regular" status.

"I'm very excited about it, and it's nice to know that I have a steady job. I look forward to developing the character. Also I think it makes everybody a little bit more comfortable knowing that we don't have to worry about making a deal show by show. We know that they can do longer character arcs and plan ahead. I also told them that I would just as soon sit in a scene without saying anything than say something that is uncharacteristic or some fluffy dialogue."

Not that he's expecting any fluffy dialogue. Not with the writers on this show.

"Between Joss and Marti and Rob and Dean and everybody else that has contributed, they have really helped me to find this character, and I want to make sure that we all keep sight of that. There is a tendency to forget where each character came from or all the things you are setting up. You have a scene and you want a character in that scene. You just want to give them something to say so that you don't forget that they are there. But at the same time, I feel that Oz is defined by a few specific moments.

"One of them is that scene [in *Innocence*] where we are stealing the weapons from the armory and I am sitting in the van with Alyson. I haven't said anything, this whole episode I haven't said a word. And then she says, 'Do you want to make out?' And I remember this so specifically: I say, 'Well, to the casual observer, it would appear that you are trying to make your friend Xander jealous, or even the score, or something like that, and to me that is on the empty side.' Right away, you get the impression that Oz knows what is going on. He pays attention, not only to what people are doing to him but to what people are doing to each other.

"He just takes things as they come and recognizes them for what they are. So, while I would love to explore the more emotional side of him, I think it is going to necessitate a huge and very powerful catalyst to even break through that. It's the werewolf thing. The way that his family has reacted to the whole thing, too, because no one else seemed too upset about their kid being a werewolf. He has been conditioned in one way or another, and while there is a little bit of an emotional reaction, it is pretty internal. It is so much more cerebral than that. He's like, 'Well, all right, how am I going to deal with that?'"

Of course, Oz wasn't always intended to be a werewolf. In fact, when Seth first came onto the show, it was with a three-episode commitment.

"Then they saw that Aly and I got along really well, and I saw the wheels spinning in Joss's head and he was like, 'I can work with this.' He came to me really early on and said...well actually Alison said it to me first....She said, 'If they asked you to be a regular, would you do it?' I was like, 'Hell, yeah...absolutely. Absolutely.' Then I talked to Joss and I said I just wanted to know what he was thinking, because that was integral in my decision whether this was the show that I was going to commit to.

"He said, 'Well, there is talk of making him into a werewolf, but we don't know exactly how we would handle that.' I said, 'Okay, let's keep our minds open and see where it goes.' He told me a couple of weeks later to read episode fifteen. 'That is what I am going for. If you like that, we will go into negotiations.' Fifteen was "Phases," the werewolf episode, and I loved it. It was perfect."

Soon, we discover a little-known piece of trivia. Seth is connected to the series through Alyson and Sarah and Marcia Schulman. But he's also connected to it in a more direct way. He's the only member of the series cast who was in the movie.

Yes, really.

"I was cut out of the film, but I'm on the back of the video box," he says. (Go on, check it.) "I was awful in it, and I really hope the footage never surfaces, because in retrospect I realize how bad I was in it. At the time, I was very excited. You see me really early on as sort of a geeky guy that Sasha kind of makes fun of in passing, like knocks books out of my hands or something like that....And then he is walking through the woods toward the merry-go-round.

"The way it goes in the movie now, Sasha says, 'I'm going to turn around, and when I do, you are not going to be there.' When he does, it is Paul Reubens on the merry-go-round. There are five minutes cut out of that, where he turns around and I'm standing there and I have the face of a vampire, and I call him by name, and he says, 'What are you doing here?' and he comes over and I just start laughing, and he picks me up. He lifts me up threateningly, gripping my collar, and he lets me go and I stay floating in the air. I start laughing like crazy, and I grab him and I bite him.

"It was terrible. For some reason, I told them I had a thirty-two-inch waist, so the harness they gave me was five sizes too big. I just look like I'm wearing a diaper....It was impressive," Seth concludes with a dry chuckle.

**Were you interested in horror and fantasy growing up?**

**SETH:** "Absolutely. There was a time when I was very into vampire mythology and things like that. Then it got a little spoiled for me. It is difficult for it not to be spoiled when there are all these people running around with dyed black hair and Marilyn Manson T-shirts talking about how they suck blood. Quite frankly, when you have something that you take relatively seriously, just made so laughable by a few ignorant people, it is difficult to still hold it with the same amount of respect. That is why I am glad there is a show like *Buffy*, where even though the show is a little tongue-in-cheek sometimes, they take their monsters seriously and it is scary. It is not a joke. Like *Buffy* the movie was just on TV a couple of times, and I always get that kind of sadness when I see it."

**Oz is the lead guitarist for Dingoes Ate My Baby. Do you play guitar?**

**SETH:** "I can fake it, can't I?"

**That's not what I asked.**

**SETH:** "No, I sure can't. I can strum. I know where notes are on the guitar, but I really don't have any dexterity when it comes to it. But our music coordinators on the show [help], and my friends who do play guitar. I get the tapes well in advance and I sit and practice and practice and practice, and it is all for naught because you really never see me playing guitar on the show."

**Do you have any scars, tattoos, or other distinguishing marks?**

**SETH:** "I have two scars on my head in the same place. I was five years old and my sister and

I were running around our living room. I just dove headfirst into the corner of our coffee table and split my head right open. And then, this is the best part, about two years later I was playing super-jock football with my dad and I go to run out of my room, and I hit my head on the protruding corner of the wall, right in the same place. Split my head right open again."

**There you have it. The question is sort of another version of something Cordelia says in one episode: 'What is your childhood trauma?'**
**SETH:** "My childhood trauma was when I realized I was going to Hell very early on in my life because I saw an old lady fall when she was trying to get off the bus and I laughed. It was bad, man. It was a very slight fall, and we helped her up, mind you. We raced to help her up, but at that moment I realized I had laughed at an old woman falling off a bus. I was going straight to Hell. As a result of that, I have lived my life with the theory that I'm already going, so I might as well live it up."

**What were you afraid of as a child?**
**SETH:** "I don't know...stupid stuff. When I was four years old, there was this episode of *Starsky and Hutch* on TV and they opened up a closet and there was a decaying body inside, and that scared me. But I never had an ongoing fear....Then, over the course of my life, I have seen so many horror films I am conditioned to not jump at the big scare, and as a result, I don't jump. Creepy is so much better than the big scare."

**What other actors do you admire?**
**SETH:** "Breckin Meyer, who I think is one of the best young actors around. Definitely one of the most underused talents around. He is up and coming, just a huge sex symbol. And if there were a man that I was going to be in love with, it would be Breckin Meyer."

**Is he standing right there next to you?**
**SETH:** "Kinda."

**So you have to say that?**
**SETH:** "Well, Breckin and our friend Ryan and I intend to produce stuff, and we're trying to work toward that. If I could sound any more arrogant and pretentious."

**Do you have a favorite moment from your tenure on the series?**
**SETH:** "There was a day when we were making "Innocence." They had built that whole mall in this warehouse in downtown Los Angeles, and we had a kind of mini-revolt, and Aly and Charisma and Nick and Tony and I all went to the mall across the street and we ate lunch there. It was so bad, we were told there was a Chinese place and they wouldn't serve us. They were like, 'We're only doing lunch orders now.' We said, 'Yeah, we want lunch.' 'No, no bulk orders for delivery,' and they wouldn't give us food. So we wound up eating at McDonald's or something, and then we started scouring the mall for board games, and we wound up buying TVopoly, which is like TV monopoly. It was just like a long time between setups. Juliet and David and Sarah were all on set; they were working. We didn't have anything to do, so we just sat in Charisma's trailer playing board games. It was so much fun."

# JAMES MARSTERS

It's just after dusk. James Marsters comes over to say that he has a short break while the lighting setup is changed. We go and sit on the steps in front of the trailer he shares with Juliet Landau, and he lights a cigarette. In full Spike costume, the smoking is eerily appropriate. But other than that, James is about as unlike Spike as you could imagine. He's a genuinely nice, enthusiastic man with undying affection for the theater, for his craft, and for *Star Trek*. He jokes freely, comfortably chuckles at his own humor, and—it seems—at the very idea that he's being interviewed.

James is originally from Modesto, California. He has appeared in several films and as a guest star on several TV series, including *Northern Exposure*. James studied at Juilliard and came to Los Angeles in 1997 after spending more than ten years on the regional-theater circuit. The decision was based on a conversation about pragmatism that he had with an idol.

"I was talking to Michael Winters, who I think is the best actor in America. Primarily stage. He's been my idol since I was ten years old," James says. "I was lucky enough to do table readings of *The Cider House Rules* in Seattle with him, which Tom Hulce was directing.

"I was driving Michael home and he was saying that his car was on the fritz and he didn't have enough money to fix it and he was damn tired of being poor. Michael is fifty years old. He told me that everyone told him if he pursued stage acting he'd end up poor, and he never believed them. For the first time in my life, there was something about Michael that I didn't want for myself.

"He went down to L.A. and got a recurring role in *The Single Guy*. He's got a TV movie coming out, and he's doing quite well. He's a marvelous actor. So I decided to come down here and try to make enough money to stow away so that I wasn't poor. I came down here willing to be the new ALF if I needed to, to do about anything. I didn't want to be one of those stage actors who came down here and who whined about not doing Shakespeare.

"The irony of it is, I think I'm working on a show with better scriptwriting than many of the original plays that I worked on in theater. I'm very lucky. It doesn't hurt to be known first as 'cool sexy killer guy.' You can't overstate enough how lucky it is to be cast in a project with good writing and good producing and good actors. Quite frankly, the other good thing about this is that I've been learning film acting. There's a lot about stage acting that you take years to learn which is of absolutely no use at all [on film]."

Interestingly, when James auditioned for the role of Spike he had dark wavy hair, not unlike David Boreanaz, who plays Angel. In order to cast him, the producers had to look at his performance alone and imagine what he might be like as Spike. Obviously, his audition went well.

"Juliet and I hit it off really well, and I thought I auditioned really well," he remembers. "But I have to say that the people around here realize that the look of a character is really malleable. They really want to cast off of who fits the part internally. They trust that they'll be able to make the visuals of the character work the way they want them to work. I think the casting office is more in tune with acting than with 'type.'"

Particularly since Spike is British, and James couldn't be more American. The accent didn't intimidate him, though.

"I've done lots of plays with different accents," he explains. "When I got the call for the audition I was doing a production of *The Tempest* with Shakespeare Festival L.A. There was a gentleman from North London playing Caliban, so I asked him if he could go over some lines with me. Tony Head's been very helpful as well. He doesn't want his friends in England being embarrassed."

One thing James did have to adjust to early on (though it wasn't as much of an issue in the latter half of his run on the series) was the vampire prosthetic.

"I have to say that the advances they've made in both the foams they've used to create the appliances and the adhesives they use to glue it onto you are so much improved in the last ten years that it's actually comfortable," he says. "The foam is so pliable that it moves with your face. You can almost forget that it's there."

That doesn't mean, however, that an actor can use his or her free range of facial expression with the prosthetic on.

"I learned very quickly to let the mask have its own expression and not try to add too much to it. It's damn scary, and [you should] act with your eyes. At first I was practicing what expressions would be good through the mask. And that's called bad acting [smile]. Pre-planning what you're going to do is just not good. The mask makes me scary and Joss's words make me funny, and that's all there really has to be."

**Do you spend time with any of the other cast members off the set?**

**JAMES:** "Yes, very much. We get along really well. In fact, David and Nick and Todd McIntosh and Seth Green and I all went over to Todd's for dinner. He's a great cook. We had a marvelous time. Todd wanted us to get on-line, and we were all like, 'What are we going to say?' By the time we actually got in there, they couldn't put us out.

"Last Halloween, Alyson and I got made up as vampires and went out. She's hot as a vampire.

"I have to say, the people who do the hiring around here really understand how important it is that people work well together. A lot of people would sacrifice that for other things, but I think it makes it a nice place to work."

**Do you have a favorite moment, on or off screen, from your tenure on the series?**

**JAMES:** "By far, my favorite moment was in the first episode I did when I put my vampire henchman's head through the glass of the fire extinguisher. I love playing Spike because I get into fights and no one has to go to the police station, and no one has to go to the hospital."

**And unless it's against Buffy, you get to win!**

**JAMES:** "Yes. Which is very nice. But I have to say the stunt guy was just incredible with that. He put his head through inch-thick candy glass three times, and I was the one who looked like the tough guy. He really sold it. My favorite parts are always the violent parts."

**Any idea what's to come for Spike and Drusilla?**

**JAMES:** "He realized that Dru is drawn to Angel like an alcoholic is drawn to booze. And for their relationship and her health, he needed to get her the hell out of Sunnydale. There's a lot of jealousy, but there's also a lot of understanding. He's her sire. It makes it easier for Spike to forgive her for going with him, since it's a sickness more than an attraction."

**Were you interested in horror growing up?**

**JAMES:** "Very much. I grew up on *Creature Feature*. I think fantasy and horror have the ability to use metaphor to a much better extent than shows that are more tied to realism. You often find issues that are taboo in any other realm except for horror and science fiction. It's kind of like the jester in the old medieval courts. He could say whatever he wanted, as long as it was a joke. I think it's quite important, actually. Most television, movies, and stage are in the death grips of naturalism. I'm quite happy not to be doing it. Robert Heinlein said 'In good science fiction, you ask your audience to suspend their disbelief once. The rest should follow from there.'"

**Do you have any scars, tattoos, or other distinguishing marks?**
**JAMES:** "I have a scar on my left leg that I got in fifth grade playing a game called Hot Box or Pickle. I was sliding downhill and caught my leg just below my knee on a sprinkler head. It ripped my flesh to the bone two-thirds of the way around my leg. My leg slid down my bone like a sock. The only thing holding it was about an inch and a half of flesh on the back. They had to take a skin graft from my left thigh, and put it there because my skin wasn't growing back. I was off my feet for almost a year. So all the hair on my lower left knee grows sideways, because they took the skin and rotated."

**Do you have any talents or skills you haven't used on the series?**
**JAMES:** "Yeah, I play guitar and sing. I paint. I write."

**What do you do with your spare time?**
**JAMES:** "I have a little house near the beach. I like to spend time down there. I have a girlfriend I've been with for about eight months. Actually, I don't enjoy time off."

**What were you afraid of as a child?**
**JAMES:** "Not getting everything done. I did a lot of stupid things in my youth, because I didn't have enough fear. But I'm better now. I'm recovered. With my leg, I found out that it's possible for the worst thing in the world to happen to you and you still live. And I also found out that if you're in a position where you can get away with whining and you don't, you score big brownie points with everyone."

## JULIET LANDAU

As Drusilla, Juliet Landau portrays a slightly insane, slighty clairvoyant, British vampire torn by her attraction to two other vampires. Needless to say, it's an odd role. Which, for an actor, is a little bit like gold.

Juliet is a second-generation star, the daughter of the inimitable Martin Landau and Barbara Bain, neither of whom were strangers to television themselves. In an era when many actors and producers are just beginning to accept the idea that actors can work successfully on both large and small screens, it should be remembered that Juliet's parents were among those who paved the way.

In a very short time, however, this young actress has made a name for herself. Aside from her role on *Buffy the Vampire Slayer*, she is perhaps best known for her role in the quirky Tim Burton film *Ed Wood*. Juliet has also appeared in *The Grifters, Pump Up the Volume,* and *Neon City,* among others.

We're fortunate enough to catch up with her for a few minutes on one of her final days of shooting. While the crew is changing the lighting for the next scene, we sneak away to an abandoned set, with Juliet in full Drusilla makeup and costume. A true professional, she

seems at first distracted—loath to break from character. But after only a moment or two, Juliet relaxes and it's obvious she is warm and open, quite unlike the Hollywood stereotype.

She is a unique actress, an observation borne out by the fact that, unlike nearly everyone else in this cast—and nearly everyone else in Hollywood making less than ten million a picture—Juliet did not actually audition for her role in the series.

"Joss had seen my work in *Ed Wood*. He called my agent, and they sent over a reel, and I came in for a meeting with Joss and David Greenwalt, Gail Berman (both executive producers), and [casting director] Marcia Shulman. It was an incredibly creative meeting. It was great. All I had read was a couple of pages in the script about Spike and Drusilla, and the character description. And I got a real strong sense from what was written about what I felt about the character. Joss apparently had these characters running around in his brain for years. So it was this amazingly creative meeting, and then I left, and within half an hour they called my agent and said that they wanted me to do it."

Apparently, as part of that meeting, on the spur of the moment, Juliet began to go into what we would now call her "Drusilla mode," with fluttering hands and distant stares. The producers loved it. So did Juliet. When Drusilla first appears, in a weakened state, she is reminiscent of classical opera heroines, dying of consumption or some other debilitating disease. But the idea that she would start this way and become strong really appealed to the actress.

"There are so many colors to this character: going from weak to strong; being a villain. There's also this sweet sort of love story in a way between Spike and Drusilla. It's a little kinky and strange, but it's also sweet. You just have these different dynamics. She's evil, but there was a side to her when she was ill that was sort of fragile. Ethereal. Joss described us as Sid and Nancy as vampires. And the look of Drusilla is fun, this sort of cross between Victorian period heroine and Kate Moss."

Interestingly enough, Juliet does not think of Drusilla as evil.

"I'll say that to Joss, and he just says, 'Yeah, and I can tell that you think so, and it shows.' She's so creepy, but she doesn't think of herself that way. 'And so I eat a few people, it's no big deal.'"

Indeed, from Drusilla's perspective, it's perfectly reasonable to kill people and suck their blood.

Juliet makes a point of discussing how fortunate she and the rest of the cast are to be working on this series, where characters do develop and change over time.

"It evolves," she says appreciatively. "Angel goes from being the good guy to where he's come to be with Spike and Drusilla. Then there's my character's whole journey, and the fact that the second I become healthy, I have to take care of Spike while *he's* in a wheelchair."

Conversation turns to the subject of Juliet's British accent. American by birth, she did spend four years in London as a child. It paid off.

"There was an Englishman who was the double for the Judge (in "Surprise" and "Innocence"). That day I guess I had been speaking mostly in dialect. He came up to me afterward and asked where I was from. I said, 'Actually, I'm from here,' and then he said 'Oh, my God, I can't believe you fooled me.' And I thought, that was really good."

**Do you have a favorite moment, on or off screen, from your time on *Buffy*?**

**JULIET:** "After they hired me, they paired me with their two final choices for Spike. James [Marsters] came in and immediately we just bounced off each other. There was a moment during his audition—it was our very first scene of our first episode, and [Spike and Dru] are talking to the Anointed One. James came up to me as if we were going to kiss, and then we didn't and we turned [away from each other]. And we ended up doing it in that scene, and it was kind of fun that it came from that initial meeting. Then they actually used it in the promo—'Evil has a few new faces.' They used that actual thing."

**Were you interested in horror as a child?**
**JULIET:** "No, actually, not really. But it's funny, because the show doesn't feel like horror to me. The dark forces are used to show the high school experience to the absolute extreme. High school is a horror movie, which we all can relate to. It's got this humor and this dark edge, and it bounces between being scary and funny and tragic."

**Drusilla is the most powerful female villain we've seen on television in a long time. How come Buffy has never beaten the crap out of you?**
**JULIET:** "Actually, what's been interesting with Buffy and me is that [my character has] these visions and sees things, and her character has these dreams and premonitions. It's been sort of mind-to-mind [combat], women battling with their minds. It's been interesting."

## JULIE BENZ

Things are really taking off for Julie Benz. Not only did the actress have a role in the smash comedy *As Good As It Gets*, which had her in nearly every commercial for the film, but she's recently gotten married, and has a new film, *Jawbreakers*, with Rebecca Gayheart, Rose McGowan, and Pam Grier, on the way.

Julie has also appeared in *Inventing the Abbotts*, *Black Sheep*, and *Two Evil Eyes*, as well as making guest appearances on such series as *Diagnosis Murder*, *Step by Step*, *Married...With Children*, *Sliders*, and *Fame L.A.* She also had a recurring role on *All My Children*.

For the woman who played Darla, the vampire who sired Angel into the "nightlife," it's been a very good year. Still, no matter how busy she's been, she was more than happy to return to the series for the two-part second-season finale.

"I was very excited, especially when I found it was set in 1760 Ireland," she says. "I had never done a period piece before, so I was very happy to return to the show. They sent away to London for my costume."

Julie was a bit surprised when she found out that Darla would be back. After all, the powerful blond vampire girl was...well, dead.

"I *was* really surprised, even though when I died, they kept saying, 'Oh, we will bring you back somehow. We want to have you come back at some point.' They can't ruin the reality of how vampires die. I was cooked," she says. "When you are cooked, you are dead. You have to stick to that reality because they have killed about a hundred vampires that way. So I was really surprised when they actually did bring me back, and in the way that they did."

As things go forward and Angel's past is delved into, there will likely be many opportunities for Darla to appear. If that comes up, no matter how high her star rises, Julie will be there.

"Our characters have an interesting past," she notes. "It would be so interesting to flash back to different time periods when we were together. It is very fun and creative as an actor to have that. I love the show."

Interestingly enough, Julie originally read for Buffy, and it wasn't the first time she tried out for a role that eventually went to Sarah Michelle Gellar. But we'll get to that.

"Like every actress in Hollywood, I had originally gone in and read for the role of Buffy," Julie says. "Sarah is just so wonderful as Buffy. When they were doing the pilot, they came to me and asked if I would play the vampire, and I was like, 'Sure, sure, okay.' It was interesting. I had never played a vampire before. I didn't have to audition for it, which makes me glad because I don't know if I would have gotten it.

"So I did the pilot for them, and then they wrote me into a couple of episodes, which was really nice. I honestly thought that I would just be in the pilot and that would be it. I would never see those people again."

Unlike some of the other actors who have appeared on the series, Julie is rarely recognized in public from her *Buffy* work. She suspects it is because most of Darla's scenes involve her being in full-vamp mode. Although, interestingly enough, people do sometimes recognize her by her voice alone.

Though she's always enjoyed horror films, Julie admits that even the bad ones frighten her. It was a nice opportunity to turn the tables by working on this series.

"In the first or second episode, we were sitting in this really creepy cemetery late at night. I had on full vampire makeup and it was pretty scary. It freaked me out. I mean, here I was supposed to be scaring everybody else."

### What were you scared of as a child?

**JULIE:** "The dark. I was terrified of the dark, and I was also terrified that there were people under the stairs. In the dark, I would creep up the stairs, and I always thought somebody was under there ready to grab my legs. I was always afraid that someone was in my closet, so my closet was always a mess as a kid. I would never hang up clothes and stuff to make sure that nobody was there. And the closet door had to be open. Because if it was closed, somebody was in there."

### Do you have a favorite moment, on or off camera, from your work on *Buffy*?

**JULIE:** "David and I had a lot of fun working together. In the episode where I get killed, he stabs me in the back with the stake. I turn, and I look at him and I realize it is Angel. We had the giggles. We could not stop laughing, and it was so hard to do that scene. I would turn and look in his eyes and I would just bust up laughing and so would he. I mean, here we were in the whole vampire faces and we had the giggles. The whole thing seemed absurd. And then in that moment, I am supposed to fall out of frame onto a mattress but I missed the mattress and hit the floor. We felt like kids. 'Oh, no, we can't stop laughing.' And the more you try to stop laughing, the more you laugh."

### Do you have any scars, tattoos, or other distinguishing marks?

**JULIE:** "Well, I have two tiny little scars on my chin, two little ones. I was an ice skater growing up. When I was a kid, I accidentally tripped over my own skate and split my chin open on the ice. I was in first grade when it happened, and I had to go get two stitches, and I thought it was the ugliest thing in the world. Then I got the stitches out, and two weeks later I did the exact same thing and reopened the exact same part of my face. I had to get two stitches again."

**Did you have any professional history with any of the cast and crew prior to working on *Buffy*?**
**JULIE:** "Actually, Sarah and I both tested for the role of Kendall Hart in *All My Children*. It was a long time ago, but we tested together. She went first. I actually remember what order we were in. She went first, and I was fourth; there were six of us there. When I went to work on the pilot, I told her we had tested together. [I reminded her that] I had short hair then, then she remembered me. Then she went back and watched the audition tape....I was really embarrassed to find that out because it was a long time ago. She was very sweet. I remember watching her test and knowing right away she was going to get it. She is really amazing: her work ethic, being as young as she is and working as hard as she does. It is really an admirable thing. I admire her."

**What's your latest film, *Jawbreakers*, about?**
**JULIE:** "It's about three high school students. We kidnap our best friend on her birthday and we accidently kill her. It's a very dark comedy, like in the vein of *Heathers*."

**If you have the opportunity to play Darla again...**
**JULIE:** "Darla is one of my favorite characters ever. It is so much fun playing a vampire, because you can do so many different things and you have a freedom there to play. I love it even though the sight of blood makes me faint. I love Darla, and the great thing is that they don't use blood on the show. Even fake blood makes me want to faint."

# BIANCA LAWSON

She was there to die.

Bianca had come to the set just to die. The actress, who played Kendra the Vampire Slayer for four episodes of the second season, had returned to film her last scene. Her death scene.

The scene, shot on the library set, was directed by co-producer David Solomon. Makeup master Todd McIntosh was there, overseeing every moment, as Juliet Landau, playing Drusilla, slashes Bianca's throat. Bianca holds in her hand a small sponge filled with stage blood. When she is "slashed," she slaps the sponge to her throat, and blood drips down her neck.

Bianca has appeared in many television series as a guest, including *Sister Sister, In the House, Saved by the Bell: The New Class,* and *Parenthood* (coincidentally, a series Joss Whedon wrote for). Bianca began her acting career at the age of nine in a Barbie commercial, and she's been working ever since. She had a small role in the John Travolta film *Primary Colors*.

When Bianca was cast for Kendra, the scripts for the two-part "What's My Line?" were still being written. The night they called to tell her she had the part, they asked her what accents she could do. Eventually, they went with Jamaican.

"I have a friend who is a dialect coach, and I ran through it with him. But some people had ideas of what they wanted that were a little bit different. Do I want to be upper class? Do I want to be, like, smart but upper class? Sounds very British. So it was like the lower class, with a heavier patois."

Once they had determined what her accent would be, it was up to Bianca to get it down right. She worked hard with her dialect coach and, in fact, the producers weren't certain exactly what her accent would be until she showed up to start shooting. Obviously, they were pleased enough to bring her back for two more episodes. Her hard work paid off.

As far as the impact *Buffy* has had on her, Bianca was very pleasantly surprised.

"It was only one two-parter," she says with wonder. "I wasn't even in the previews for it. I was surprised that so many people saw it, so many different kinds of people. All these adults in the mall, married women, mothers; they're like "Oh, my God, you were so good, I saw you last night.""

**Do you have a favorite moment, on or off camera, from your work on the series?**
**BIANCA:** "I have a lot of fun doing the fight scenes. That was when I knew I really enjoyed being here. In the past, I have done a little bit of kickboxing and a little bit of boxing, but it was never anything I did consistently. It's been so much fun."

## ARA CELI

One of the first things you notice about Ara Celi is her laugh: a beautifully lilting and infectious sound that instantly dispels the glamour of Hollywood. This is a laugh, it is easy to believe, that springs not from managers and agents and image-makers, but from the heart of a real person. The pleasant, inclusive laughter one hears among friends.

No surprise, then, that Ara, the exotic-looking young actress who portrayed the "Inca Mummy Girl" in the episode of the same name, is quickly making plenty of friends in Hollywood.

In fact, the *Buffy* role came as the result of a conversation between casting director Marcia Shulman and ultra-hot, maverick director Robert Rodriguez. Rodriguez was considering Ara as the title character in *The Hangman's Daughter*, the *From Dusk 'Til Dawn* prequel (a role she eventually won), and recommended that Shulman see her. On her third audition, she met with the series' producers and later that day learned she had the tragic role of a sixteen-year-old girl who died for her peoples' beliefs, cursed for eternity. In fact, of all the monsters on *Buffy*, the "Inca Mummy Girl" is perhaps the most sympathetic. Certainly according to Ara's fans.

"Everybody says, 'We didn't hate you. Usually we hate the bad guys on that show. Even though you were the villainess, we liked you, and we didn't want to see you die. We wanted to see you and Xander get together.' It's funny."

And clearly, fans were not the only ones who didn't want to see Ara go.

"It worked out well. I mean, everybody really liked the show. People kept saying, 'I wish there was some way, why do we have to kill you off? Why do we have to kill you off?' Really, the cast was great to me—everybody was great. They were trying to figure out a way they didn't have to kill me so that they could bring me back on."

The actress is a former Miss Texas, originally from El Paso. In addition to *The Hangman's Daughter*, Ara also has the lead in a film scheduled for release in late '98 titled *Looking for Lola*. Her career is taking off quickly, but she promises that no matter how successful she might be, she would never turn down a chance to reprise her role as Ampata. Her experience on that episode was overwhelmingly positive, thanks in large part to Nicholas Brendon, with whom she shared most of her scenes.

But it wasn't until after the episode aired that Ara realized that her feelings about the show were echoed by millions of fans.

"I'll tell you when it hit me," she says. "The day after the first time that episode aired, I went to the movies. My friends and I were walking up to the movie theater and a crowd of about ten or twelve guys said, 'Oh, my gosh, it's her.' And we were looking around, thinking, Who are they talking about? And they said, 'You were great on *Buffy* last night.' And my friend, Ally, said, 'Dude, they're talking about you.'

"I did not believe it. I promise you. The guys were like, 'You were awesome.' I just said, 'Thanks,' and I waved, and I could not believe it. And then I was at the Super Bowl in San Diego, and there was this huge party in the Gas Lamp District. They close off the street. There were 130,000 people. I cannot tell you how many people rushed me asking for my autograph. 'That's Ampata, that's Ampata!' and yes, that is when it became pretty relevant. I mean, one episode! So, yeah, I think it's great. I don't know. People pray for stuff like this. You do one thing, and everybody knows you."

**Do you like Twinkies?**

**ARA:** [laughter] "That is such a classic question. As I child, I used to love, love Twinkies. They were my favorite snack. I mean I loved Twinkies. Well, I'll tell you what, shoving eight to ten in my mouth at one time, ooh...but I do still like Twinkies!"

**Is that how many you ended up having to eat?**

**ARA:** "Yeah, we did about ten, myself and Nicholas. And after every take, we turned yellow. We both turned yellow in the face. It was wild. We laughed a lot."

**Do you have a favorite moment, either off camera or on, from your adventures on *Buffy*?**

**ARA:** "My favorite moment was the part where Xander and I were dancing. It was just like a fairy tale come true, because we're like standing around, and we're lost in each other's eyes at the dance. I just love that moment, because it was really magical. I forgot about everything. I forgot about the cameras. I forgot about acting. I was really, really in that moment, and just staring into his eyes. It was unbelievable."

**And he didn't even call the next day.**

**ARA:** "Actually, he was great. We did exchange numbers as friends. He's really, really a nice guy. He's wonderful."

**Were you ever a horror fan?**

**ARA:** "You know what, I'd never even seen the show before I was booked on it. What I did know was, when I read the character, about this Inca princess, I liked it, I liked her. I liked the way she was naive, and I liked the fact that she never really had the chance to fall in love, and I thought that was kind of fun."

**Very sad, though.**

**ARA:** "Yes, it was sad, but she got kind of lucky. At least she got a little taste of it."

**What were you afraid of as a child?**
**ARA:** "As a child, I was afraid of the dark. I was afraid of being alone. I didn't like to be anywhere, even in my front yard, alone."

**Do you have any scars, tattoos, or other distinguishing marks?**
**ARA:** "Oh, I have a great scar."

**See, this is the weirdest thing. It must be actors, I don't know.**
**ARA:** "It must be. I don't have any tattoos, but I do have a scar over my top lip. It's clearly visible. It looks like a little Frankenstein scar. When I was very small, I wanted to get out of my crib, and my mom wouldn't get me out, so I decided to jump. I leapt out of my crib and hit the floor, and I had to get stitches. I think I got seven or eight stitches across my lip. The funny thing about this scar, which is so beautiful, is that when I was a little baby, my mother said to my grandmother, 'I can't believe she did this, she ruined her face.' My grandmother said, 'Oh, it doesn't matter, it's not like she is going to be an actress or a beauty queen or anything.' And then I was Miss Texas. And of course, I act, so my grandmother constantly tells me that story. Over and over again. But I love my scar. When I first moved out here to Hollywood, this man lived with me who's a casting agent, and he said, 'You know, if you just had that scar removed off of your face, your face would be flawless.' And I said, 'I like it, it gives me character, I'll never remove it.' And he said, 'You're going to do fine in this business with that attitude.' I like it. I don't think I'll ever get rid of it."

**You know all the female viewers are going to want to know if Nicholas is a good kisser.**
**ARA:** "Yeah, actually I've been asked that quite a bit. And yes, he was a wonderful kisser."

**You kind of have to say that.**
**ARA:** "Yeah, I know. No, he was really great."

## JOHN RITTER

One of the best-loved sitcom stars ever, for his roles on *Three's Company* and *Hearts Afire*, John Ritter also starred in such films as *Skin Deep*, *Problem Child*, *Hero At Large*, and *Sling Blade*. In the episode "Ted," he plays Buffy's mother's new boyfriend, a man who isn't what he appears to be. It afforded him an opportunity to play against his image, and it gave *Buffy* one of the best ratings it had received up to that point, not to mention an opportunity for the show to explore the series' mother/daughter relationship in more detail.

As for John, he had a great time. Even better because he was already a fan of the show.

"It was so much fun," he says. "And it was interesting because my agent said, 'Do you want to do *Buffy the Vampire Slayer*?' I had really liked the movie, but when the TV show came on, I liked the TV show so much better because there was a quality to it that I hadn't seen on TV before. It was stylized and so funny and so hip. They were creating teenage jargon that I hadn't heard before. Very sarcastic and intelligent dialogue, as opposed to that kind of *Beavis and Butt-Head* thing.

"And there was a real sexiness to it, and it was scary and action-packed. The fights were thrilling and creative. Not just exchanging punches but using the environment around the combatants. I took a couple of years of karate—I'm so old it was when Bruce Lee was alive. These guys have come up with so many creative things. The way the vampires explode, and the makeup....I would say, they can't possibly do this every week. I sat down with my three kids to watch the first episode, and we were hooked.

"So when my agent called and said, 'They want you for *Buffy the Vampire Slayer*,' I said, 'Absolutely. I'd love to see the script.' Well, when I called my agent and said, 'What happened to that script?' they said, 'Oh, the *Sabrina, the Teenage Witch*?' I said, 'Wait a minute, I thought it was *Buffy*.' Then I got the script. Usually you have a suggestion, but I just thought it was really well written and well worked out. It was a really fun turn."

Doing the show also scored big points for John with his children.

"My kids visited me as much as they could," he says with a chuckle. "I've always said, 'I'm going to do this and this. Do you want to come down to the set? Do you want to come to the theater?' 'No, that's okay, Dad.' Then it was, 'I'm doing *Buffy*.' 'All right, we'll be there at lunch, and then when we get out of school.' That was the one thing that really impressed them."

But John's appearance on the series impressed a lot of people besides his kids.

"Garth Ancier from Warner Brothers said, 'John, it was the highest-rated *Buffy* we ever had.' So many people have come up to me and said, 'Do that thing with your head.'"

"Aside from the adventure and everything else, it's a girl and her friends going through all the teenage angst that normal kids go through, except there are vampires and monsters and creepy things. It's such a metaphor," John observes. "Some of the worst times you can have—at least it feels that way—are when you're a teenager. The greatest upsets, the highest highs, [then] you can't get out of bed. You're so sad because of a heartbreak or something.

"'Ted' fed on the fear of being somewhat abandoned by your mother for a stepdad or a step-parent. It turned out that I was *reaaaally* bad. Everybody else really liked Ted, as long as they kept eating the cookies and brownies with drugs in them."

And, as Ted, John was very effective, very disturbing, even for *Buffy*'s creator.

"Joss's one note to me every day was, 'John, that was just a little too creepy.' He said, 'Be as normal as possible. You've got to really take the audience by surprise.' I was just looking, staring with too much subtext. He asked me to lighten it up a little bit," John says, amused.

The other thing that made this a unique experience for John was working with the series' talented young actors.

"I'm really knocked out by that cast," he says. "They're really good. There's a technique to acting for camera. A lot of people treat every line like it was handed out by your professor in college and you've got to say every word clearly or Homer, who wrote the *Iliad* and the *Odyssey*, will come out of his grave and tear you apart. There's a way of throwing away dialogue, like people do in real life. There's a kind of nonchalance, or planned casualness, that is really appealing sometimes. This kid Nicholas Brendon and Alyson Hannigan just really knocked me out. They're all so good.

"Sarah is such a professional. She's just adorable, but you assume someone that young can do one or two things, but she can do it all. She's been around since she was a zygote. I think she started acting as a fetus. She was really fun to act with. At the dinner table, which was done the first day, I think that's where I went, 'This little girl is a major talent.' You see a whole lot of subtext in her eyes. She's always thinking. The camera is the one invention by man that can record thought as it's taking place. Actors who know that are off to a great start.

"Then she went off and did *Scream 2* and *I Know What You Did Last Summer* and then she comes right back to the TV series with nary a break in between. I think that's smart of her. When I did *Three's Company* and it started to be a hit the first year, I got very busy during my hiatuses because I knew that I didn't want to just sit on my laurels. That introduced me to different casts and crews, and the idea that I could do things other than sitcoms. I thought that was really smart, when I was young enough to do three things at once."

Unfortunately, though he persevered, it wasn't all good times on the set for John.

"It turned out that Sarah and I both got the stomach flu on the last day," he remembers. "We were both saying 'excuse me' and visiting our respective toilets in our trailers. I was in really bad shape. Then we had to do the fight scene. The most convincing thing I did that day was be dead, 'cause that's how I felt. But the thing is, I've been around and I know there are some days you feel good and some days you feel bad. If you're freezing cold, you can't show the audience. I have a way of shutting down."

Conversation comes round, almost inevitably, to some of the films John has done, including the average-joe turned superhero flick, *Hero At Large*.

"That was the first major film that I did," he says. "I think that was released in late '79 or early '80. That was one of the things I did during hiatus from *Three's Company*. The author was this guy, A.J. Carruthers, this sweet guy, a real optimist. He wanted it to be a Capra film. The film was so sweet."

Though many readers might not remember that film, John went on to make the *Problem Child* films, as well as a film that combined drama and comedy called *Skin Deep*.

"That was a dream of mine—to work with Blake Edwards. I just love him. He and I became really great friends after *Skin Deep*. I don't remember how we got through some of those days. I've never worked with a director who encourages you to break up, and might do something in the middle of a scene to make you laugh. Like tell another actor to give you a false line to see how you'll respond. Many, many times I've ruined takes with my laughing out loud or his laughing out loud. To me that was so helpful, because I felt there was an underlying sadness to that film."

**We hear that you're a hell of a ball player. You saved the cast and crew of *Buffy* in their game against *Seventh Heaven*.**

**JOHN:** "Where's a stake when you need one? No, it was really a fun thing. I love playing."

**What were you afraid of as a child?**

**JOHN:** "Unrequited love."

**That's an adult fear, too.**

**JOHN:** "I was very mature for my age. Early on I realized that's my problem. Unrequited love, and in a totally unrelated matter, quicksand. Actually, that's sort of a metaphor for unrequited love, but let's not get into my psyche."

**Do you have a favorite moment from your *Buffy* adventure?**

**JOHN:** "I think it was throwing the baseball around with Nick Brendon. I knew I could really dig being a part of this company. Also, I have three really, really nice and loving kids, and I just remember taking them around the set. The whole place is just Buffyland. I would take them to wardrobe and makeup and props, and I remember showing off the set and the cast to my children. It was just really family-friendly, even though it's about vampires. They're trying to make an hour show under Herculean challenges, and they make it. And they still have time to be friendly. I think that reflects Joss and the deep respect everybody has for what he's trying to do, and that incredible, extraordinary crew they have over there."

**Did you have any previous professional experience with any of the cast or crew?**
**JOHN:** "No, but I had worked with Tom Whedon, Joss's father, years ago. And my son Jason had done a one act play by Zack, Joss's brother."

**Would you like to do it again?**
**JOHN:** "I really had a wonderful week with those folks. We were talking about how I could get back. Willow, being a computer genius, said, 'Well, I just kept a little bit of him.' She could accidentally build one or something."

## ROBIN SACHS

Born in London, England, Robin Sachs is, to all appearances, everything his character, Ethan Rayne, is not. Good natured. Courteous. Decidedly not a wizard. His background is in London theater, but he has appeared in many films and TV series in Britain and America. His TV work includes guest stints on *Diagnosis Murder, Nowhere Man, Nash Bridges, Walker Texas Ranger, Brideshead Revisited, Babylon 5,* and *Murder, She Wrote.*

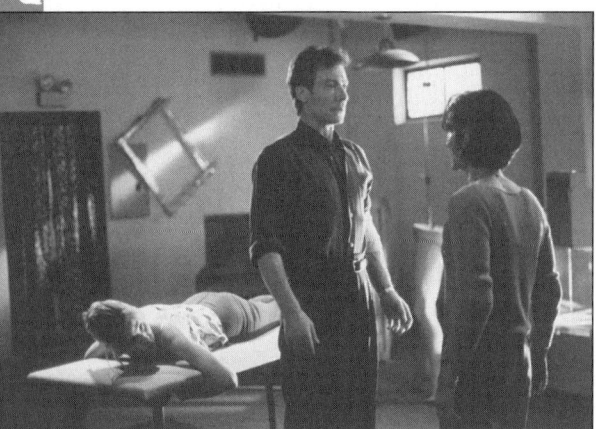

As for his work on *Buffy*, Robin was already familiar with the series when his agent put him up for the part of Ethan Rayne. "I had seen it before, and I thought it was a very good show, well written, well produced, well directed," he recalls. "I liked it."

Though he has no special affinity for horror, Robin has always been intrigued by it, "so long as it is well done. I have always loved watching TV, and I have loved going to the movies, and all parts of the visual media appeal to me in any form. I used to watch Boris Karloff when I was a kid, and wonderful horror movies that seemed horrifying at the time, they are nothing compared to what we do now."

The subject of Hammer Studios, the classic British horror production company, comes up, and Robin notes that he was in a Hammer film called *Vampire Circus,* now a cult classic.

As it is for Armin Shimerman, working on *Buffy* is a pleasure to Robin, who has frequented *Babylon 5.* At the moment, he has just completed an episode of the series in which he recurs "occasionally as people wearing latex heads." The actor has also done a number of voice-over projects.

And what about the character's future? While it seems likely we will eventually encounter Ethan Rayne again, Robin has his own version of the character worked out all too well.

"I have the feeling his mother didn't like him too much and left him in the broom closet when she went shopping," he says. "It certainly has something to do with childhood."

**Did you have any professional history with any of the cast or crew before working on the series?**
**ROBIN:** "I knew Tony Head briefly back in England."

**Assuming Ethan will return, which, as we said, we all hope, do you have any particular talents or skills that you would like to see them work into the character?**

**ROBIN:** "I have a lot of talents and skills outside of acting that I would love to see worked into characters, but you know, I am delighted to work with whatever they have. I am a black belt in karate. I have boxed; I play tennis; I ride horses. I would love to ride horses on screen. I haven't done that since I was in England. I suppose the likelihood of my playing a cowboy is pretty minimal. It would be great. I would love Ethan to come back as a cowboy."

**Do you have any scars, tattoos, or other distinguishing marks?**

**ROBIN:** "I have scars all over myself. I ripped my arm open on a metal railing when I was eight. I have scars in my eyebrows from playground fights. I have a recent scar, two scars that happened just before I started filming *Buffy*. I was putting in a new air conditioner on an old window and there was no one around to help. I was taking the old one out by myself, and as I took the old one out, of course, the window fell apart and I went through it with the air conditioner. So I ripped open my shoulder and my neck, just on my Adam's apple.

"I bled a lot. It doesn't usually bother me too much, but after I sort of mopped up and put the air conditioner in, I went to look in the mirror and one of my shoulders was okay, but it needed stitches. The one on my neck was very clean, right across the Adam's apple. Every time I bent my head back, it looked like a little mouth. I was filming in two days, so I decided to go to the hospital, and they stitched it up with clear stitches, which didn't show on film. I have this British thing about not going to doctors or hospitals too often. I am glad. Actually, my wife persuaded me to go.

**Giles and Ethan have this horrible dark past of something really, really stupid that they did when they were younger. What have you done that has come back to haunt you, if anything?**

**ROBIN:** "Me, personally? Oh, God. Nothing major. Nothing huge. When I was in my early twenties, I had a set of head-shot photos done. I was extremely buff at the time, or so I was told, and so the photographer said, 'Well, why not do some bare top shots, just in case they come in useful for later?' And I did them, and I sent them to my agent to pick out and he obviously kept one because it got circulated."

# JOSS WHEDON

We were fortunate enough to be on the set while Joss was directing the two-part second-season finale. Though he was on an insanely tight schedule, as always, he used several of his breaks to sit down and chat with us about his creation. Strangely, the greatest testament to what Joss has created did not come from the modest writer/director/producer, but from the rest of the cast and crew.

And they all know the vision that he brought to the show. This isn't really about vampires and demons, though Joss loves those things. It's about personal demons. It's about high school. As David Greenwalt said, "If Joss Whedon had had one happy day in high school, none of us would be here."

Indeed, that has been the magic of the show from the beginning. People can relate to Buffy and company not because they face the forces of Darkness, but because they are also facing the horrors that we all face growing up. In fact, the monsters are frequently metaphors for things teens have to face as they mature.

It's one of the hottest series on television. It almost single-handedly put the WB Network on the map. And yet *Buffy the Vampire Slayer* made an unlikely journey from Joss's original script to a movie that never became more than a cult hit, to a television series that is both hugely popular with mass audiences and a critical darling. The movie varied greatly from his original story. The series, though, is right on target, because Joss is at the controls.

But to do that, he had to take a detour from his burgeoning career as one of the hottest feature-film writers in Hollywood.

Joss is a third-generation television writer. His grandfather wrote for such programs as *The Donna Reed Show* and *Leave It to Beaver*, and his father, Tom Whedon, for *The Dick Cavett Show*, *Alice*, and *Benson*, among others. Before moving on to major success, writing such features as *Alien: Resurrection*, and *Toy Story*—for which he was nominated for an Oscar—Joss wrote for the hugely popular sitcom *Roseanne* and for *Parenthood*, a series adapted from the eponymous film.

He grew up in Manhattan and attended high school at Winchester, an all-boys school in England, before returning to the States to attend Wesleyan College, in Connecticut. After a year writing "a sickening number of spec scripts," Joss was hired by the producers of *Roseanne*. As he has said, he literally went from "working at a video store on a Friday to working on *Roseanne* on Monday."

Still, after all the things he has achieved, Joss says that *Buffy* "is the most personal work I've ever done. Which is funny. The opportunity to mythologize my crappy high school experience makes it extremely personal, but also sort of exorcises it. It isn't just reliving it, it's sort of reinventing it, so it moves me more than anything I've ever done. The opportunity to keep developing the characters and finding out what's going to happen to them and how they're going to grow apart or together is…the more it goes on, the more personal it gets."

With all that soul-searching, one would think that Joss would begin to change his feelings about his high school years. Joss disagrees. He also notes that, contrary to popular opinion, "my high school years were not all terrible. There was that Thursday...." He laughs.

"No, I did have a couple of friends, and I had a lot of good times, but all the bad high school stuff definitely went down. This lets me come to peace with that. But really, I'm at enough of a distance, and it's not like 'That girl, and I'll get her....' There's nobody I harbor any particular malice toward from high school.

"I think that's part of why I like doing the show so much. I'm able to look at high school and say, 'There's the dumb jock who was mean to me. Well, what's his perspective? He's going through something, too. There's the teacher who flunked me.' I suppose in that sense, it is sort of revelatory. It's nice because I can go to the pain, but at the same time, I have a much more pleasant view of it, because I am seeing it from a bit of a distance."

That pain, in fact, has become almost more important to the series than the horror or the humor of the characters.

"When we realized how much we could really live these characters' lives, we found that we could go to that dark place," Joss says. "I made a joke that, 'The key to the show is to make Buffy suffer.' Sarah said, 'Why do you do this to me? Another crying scene? Do you know what I go through here?' and I said, 'America needs to see you suffer, because you do it really well.'"

Joss laughs, but he isn't really joking.

"We're doing these sort of mythic-hero journeys in our minds," he says. "A lot of times, the story doesn't make sense until we figure out who's suffering and why. Including the bad guy. If the bad guy's not hurting, not relating to her, then it's just a cardboard guy to knock down. And the same thing goes for the audience. If they're not feeling it, if her relationship to what's going on isn't personal, and if ours isn't, then it's just guys with horns running around and some good jokes, but it's not going to resonate."

It's amazing, given how personal a project this is, that Joss ever got to do it at all. The film was not what he had originally envisioned, and he thought he'd had his chance. Then Gail Berman and Fran Kuzui came to him to ask if he wanted to do the TV series.

"I had never thought of doing it myself, but I was like, 'Oh, wow, that's sort of neat!' And I thought about it, and the more I thought about it, the more I realized how many stories there were to tell and how excited I was," he recalls. "I was pretty much out of TV completely at that point, and my agent asked me, 'Now, come on, really, what do you want to do?' I said, 'I'm already writing scenes for this in my head,' and he said, 'Fine, I'll make the deal.' I did not expect it to take over my life like this. I did not expect it to move me as much as it did."

And, though he loves horror and always has, it isn't really the horror that moves him.

"I love invoking all those [old horror] movies, but at the same time, the core of this series, emotionally, is a very safe place. These are people who care about one another and when their world is upset, *you* care about it. Whatever horror is out there is not as black and terrible as what is already within and between us. A lot of my friends never watch horror, and they get scared and don't like that part. But they respond to the show."

With the wonderful cast on the series, one can't help but think of the adage that writers are frustrated actors. Joss goes one step further.

"I'm a frustrated writer, I'm a frustrated actor. I'm frustrated at everything I don't do. But that is why I love this so much, I get to do everything, including some set dressing and some costume work. That is the fun thing about producing television, you're doing all of that," he says.

Still, horror has and will always have a special place in Joss's heart. His knowledge of films, comic books, and movies is encyclopedic, and his influences are many and varied.

"I have a lot of influences," Joss says. "So many, in fact, that I can't even think of them all. I've sort of hodge-podged together my favorite bits of everything. I take what I need for the series. For example, vampires look like vampires part of the time, because I want to see demons so you don't have a high school girl just stabbing people. At the same time, I want her to see people that [the viewer] doesn't know if they're vampires or not. They turn to dust because it's cool, but also so we don't have to have twenty minutes of body-cleaning-up at the end of every show.

"I read *Tomb of Dracula,* and I'm a huge *Blade* fan and a fan of [comics artist] Gene Colan. I always loved Morbius, and I loved anything that smacked of the undead and tortured souls. I just rock on that stuff. The old horror comics.

"The movies? Well, *Lost Boys* is in there, obviously. Their vampires change, they get ugly-face when they feed. And *Near Dark,* because it's just so important. The Langella *Dracula,* which I actually saw onstage. *Night of the Comet* is an underrated flick. The remake of *The Blob,* too. I really loved that movie. I actually have a picture of Shawnee Smith with an M-16 on my desk. She was a big inspiration."

**Do you have a favorite moment, on or off the screen, from the series?**

**JOSS:** "At the end of 'I Robot, You Jane,' when they're all sitting there realizing how pathetic their love lives are, that was my favorite ending. That was very nice. For me, there have been a bunch of things. I think one of them was definitely when I shot 'Innocence.' Things came together for me. That's when everything just completely fell into place. And I thought we had created something that is more than the sum of its parts. And I'd always been proud of its parts, but that was the first time the thing really just completely talked back to me.

"That was really neat, and then, everyone was like, 'You must be so happy you did well?' And I would say, 'Oh, yeah, but I was so happy before.' I didn't even notice the ratings because I was already on such a high.

"There was a moment when we were shooting that scene in 'Innocence' with the rocket launcher: the guys are flying, a big explosion, and I was quite literally jumping up and down. I was so happy. And the next day, we shot the last scene with Buffy and her mom, and I was watching the two shots of Kristine and Sarah, and I thought, *Yesterday, I had the rocket launcher, and this is better.* They were so good in that, and it looked so beautiful, and it felt so right, and that to me was just ... we had everything. We had the kitchen sink on this show, but it's still the small stuff that holds it together."

**Has the cast ever inspired the evolution of their characters?**

**JOSS:** "Oh, absolutely. They certainly inform the way the characters behave and the way they talk. They can't help but bring some of themselves to it. Although I'm still pretty strict about what they have to do. But the more we write the characters, the more Willow becomes like Aly...all of them. As I get to know them more as people. They bring so much more depth to it. They all become the heroes to their own stories because I know them as people."

**Are the vampires in the *Buffy* mythology organized as clans?**

**JOSS:** "I don't really think of them as clans. I think of them more like people. There are religions, there are religious leaders, different sects. What do they say in C.S. Lewis books, 'We all worship the same god, we just call it different names'? Well, they all worship evil, they just call it different names. It's not so much clans where different vampires have different appearances or powers. What you have are certain charismatic figures who find themselves surrounded by stuntmen."

**Is there a Council of Watchers?**

**JOSS:** "There is an actual little Watcher Bureaucracy based in England that Giles works for. But they're very loose and pretty incredibly inefficient. Since nobody ever seems to know what anybody else is doing. But so much of finding the Slayer and training her and figuring out who's going to be next is magic and luck. And nowadays, people are just not that dedicated. Giles tried to get out of it. It's a little bit muddy. Things get balled up at the head office."

**Are you prepping Willow to be a Watcher?**

**JOSS:** "No, I'm not. I've never thought of Willow as a Watcher. I've got something else in store for Willow."

**What were you afraid of as a child?**

**JOSS:** "I'm going to have to go with standard-issue dark and monsters, and pretty much my older brother. I was sort of terrified of my father, too, but he turned out to be a really nice guy, so I got over that. And *Horror Hotel*. That stuff was scary. Witches in cowls, hooded figures walking through graveyards chanting...every time I get scared."

**Do you have any scars, tattoos, or other distinguishing marks?**

**JOSS:** "I have a scar on my wrist. I always like to pretend I tried to commit suicide, but I really didn't. It was a rusty nail."

**We saw you wolfing Hershey's Kisses on the set. Are you a chocolate fiend?**

**JOSS:** "I wouldn't call myself a chocolate 'fiend.' I'm a friend to chocolate. Occasionally, I eat a lot of chocolate, but I'm not one of those scary people who eat it all the time."

**Everyone involved with this show seems to think of it as some kind of destiny. Does that spook you?**

**JOSS:** "It's only spooky when I think, *Jeez, I'm going to work on other shows where this doesn't happen.* It does feel like Manifest Destiny. It's such luck and chance that everybody from our D.P. to David Greenwalt to the entire cast just happened upon this project. And if they hadn't...I break into a cold sweat thinking about what I would do without any of them. Let alone Sarah. It does have a kind of inevitability to it. It seems like it just flowed into being."

# DAVID GREENWALT

If you saw him walking around the set, you'd swear he was one of the actors. Actually, though, David Greenwalt is the series' co-executive producer, and has written more than his share of episodes. He works hand in hand with Joss Whedon each day and may well be the only member of the staff besides Whedon who truly knows where Buffy's destiny lies.

David is a Hollywood veteran who has worked as a screenwriter, a producer, and a director for more than twenty years. Series that have been positively influenced by his work include *The Wonder Years, The Commish, Shannon's Deal, Doogie Howser M.D.,* and *Profit,* which he co-created.

We met with David in his office, and he was kind enough to give us all the time we needed. We started off talking about Angel, whom David said "was tortured, and then he's good when he comes back, and then eventually he will probably go his own way."

Accordingly, there will be some very serious reservations among the other characters about Angel's return. At first, David says, "Buffy will keep him secret for a while."

As far as the quality of the series itself, David modestly deflects any praise to *Buffy*'s creator. He's one of several people who refer to Joss Whedon as a "genius."

"This stuff just pours out of him," David says. "He is very, very emotionally connected to all of these characters. He has an excellent idea of who they are, and he has a pretty good idea of where they are all going at any given time in the universe. The world [of *Buffy*] has become more complex, which is all part of his master plan. These are adolescents becoming young adults. It's a lot about the veils dropping from your eyes and realizing these essential facts of life, which is what happens. Next year they'll graduate from high school, and some of them will go to college, and some of them will go away, and they'll go on with their lives.

"Now some things, like Jenny being a Gypsy, we're seeing develop sort of after the fact. We're saying, 'Wouldn't it be cool if she had an agenda?' because everybody has some kind of agenda. Then there are other elements, like Angel turning bad. Most shows like to just choose the same person every week, doing the same thing. There's a certain comfort level in that. But Joss takes a lot of risks. He gives the audience what it wants, but he also gives the audience what it needs: a deep emotional connection to the characters and the knowledge that anything can happen in the show. Regular characters can die, people you love and trust can turn completely evil, and there's a good metaphor for that, too. That whole arc of Buffy and Angel finally consummating that relationship and then him turning so vile, it's the metaphor for 'he doesn't call the next day.' So it's the metaphor for your worst fears realized. That's also a metaphor for going a little too far, too fast, too young, biting off something bigger than you can chew."

David, who obviously has passed some of his snack-food frame of reference on to Xander, started out in the entertainment industry as Jeff Bridges's stand-in. From there, he became a screenwriter and co-authored three films: *Class, American Dreamer,* and *Secret Admirer*. The latter film was his directorial debut, and he later directed several television movies for Disney. From there, he continued to "dabble" in television.

"I really liked it," David says. "I felt there was a slightly better class of professional. As a person who has directed features, I'm not a snob against TV at all. Show me a guy who can make a great show in eight days, I'll show you a guy who could make a great show in 180 days. People work harder and longer, and, by and large, better in television than they do in movies.

"We make twenty-two hours of television a year. In terms of film on a screen, that's at least the equivalent of eleven movies. That's a lot of stuff. Plus, we do other things, plan other shows. For me, it's a throwback to the old studio system in the '30s or '40s, where someone would have belonged to a studio and would have been making five movies a year. Maybe the geniuses can, but I don't feel I could learn anything making a movie every four years. Now making three every week, I think I can learn something, so it's wonderful, it's stimulating."

David ended up writing and directing several episodes of *The Wonder Years* and *Shannon's Deal* before going to work on *The Commish* for Stephen J. Cannell. After two years on that series, he teamed up with a friend, and together they created a series called *Profit*. *Profit* is rare in the history of television because, though every major critic in America praised it vociferously, "nobody watched it," as David says.

Still, the series, which was unique because it had "a villain as its centerpiece," got David Greenwalt noticed in the television industry. In fact, that series helped land David a deal with Fox which would have him working on *The X-Files*, right after he helped them out with this little experiment they were doing, a new series called *Buffy the Vampire Slayer*. He never expected to fall in love.

"I remember saying to my wife, 'Anybody want to know what the best pilot of the year is? The best-written pilot is *Buffy*.' Joss had worked on *Roseanne*, he worked on *Parenthood*, his work in movies is pretty well known, but you know, he just really got this thing on its feet. He's totally devoted to it. It's always hard in a TV series, to come up with a hundred episodes. But with this show, it's worth telling a hundred stories. There is so much richness in these characters, that while it is hard, like on any show, we just feel as if we have more stories every day to do."

Needless to say, giving up *The X-Files* was quite a decision. But it's obvious David doesn't regret it at all. Still, though he's more Buffy's godfather than father, David is quite satisfied with his role on the series and his life.

"I feel incredibly satisfied," he says, and then smiles. "On the series, we say 'into every generation one is born.' That's this guy [Joss Whedon]. Mark my words, Steven Spielberg, watch out. This guy is only thirty-three years-old. By the time he's fifty, he will be as rich, and as successful, as Steven Spielberg. I have no doubt of it.

"Joss understands stories. Breaking stories with him is like playing tennis with a pro. You go play with a pro, the pro hits the ball back really hard, and really sure every time, so you're forced to be better and better in your game. I've been working long and hard to learn story and structure and emotion and humor and heart and dialogue and all these elements that we play with here. I'm playing with one of the very, very best in the business. And while he certainly runs this show, he's also very willing to let you go and do your own thing, too. He's very open to suggestion, and he's a big team player and very big on acknowledging other people's contributions to it. I can't sit here and lie and say I'm fifty percent of the show: it's just not true. But I'm the number two guy, so I'm very happy."

As for how he explains *Buffy*'s popularity, David attributes a lot of it to the show's willingness to delve deeper into the shadows than most.

"A lot of the time, television is considered a clean, safe world, as opposed to movies. There's sort of a tradition—I don't think a good tradition—of safe, easy stories, easy on the psyche," he explains. "Joss just keeps going deeper. For example, 'Lie to Me' is very disturbing. It's about the idea that there is no innocence, there is no good in the world. The bad guys and good guys aren't clearly delineated. Some of the episodes [Joss has written] I find very disturbing. You can have more depth, but you don't have to distance your audience to do it. I think that's quite an art in its own."

As for the future of the series, David says that *Buffy* is just getting warmed up.

"I actually think that this year is going to be our big year. I think we're very hot within the industry. Certainly we're ahead on the WB, which is somewhat of a fledgling network. *Buffy* is in the consciousness now. The show is mentioned on radio programs, it's mentioned on *Jeopardy!*, it's in the lexicon already. We've only been on the air a year, really. So twelve months in the national consciousness. I think season three is the year that we will come into our own. I think we'll become more mainstream. I'm sure that Sarah will get an Emmy nomination eventually, and the show will get more and more recognition. You know there are some people who are never going to come to a show called *Buffy the Vampire Slayer*. But I think there are enough people who are going to be hearing from their friends and other people that 'Oh, you should see this.'"

**Of all the hats you wear on this show, which is your favorite?**

**DAVID:** "Always the writer. Writing the story is the very hardest thing to do, but, in a sense, the most satisfying. A lot of people who want to be writers make a similar mistake: writing is not putting words on paper. Writing is understanding the way the character is, what the arc of the story is, where you want to be at the end of the story. Laying it out. That is the hard work. The writing is also challenging, but kind of fun. So that's my very favorite thing. The next thing is directing and editing."

**Do you have a favorite moment from your tenure with the series?**
**DAVID:** "Probably when I directed 'Reptile Boy,' where Buffy is dancing with the frat boy who turned out to be evil. It was a nice moment with Tom, and I had all these fancy ideas on how to shoot this thing. Sarah came in and said, 'This is really hard to choreograph, just let us dance, just shoot it, and just let us dance and move, and watch what happens.' Sure enough, it just happened, and it was great: just watching two people relate and dance, and I didn't do anything so terribly fancy, showing off with the camera. You have these moments on the set…if you're lucky maybe you get one a day, or one every few days, where you go, 'This feels true, this feels honest, this feels really funny, it just feels right.' There's that kind of quiet that comes, that sort of hush that says this is the moment, this is the little pearl for the necklace."

**Were you a big fan of genre films and fiction growing up?**
**DAVID:** "Nothing like Joss. I'm a Billy Wilder, John Ford, Preston Sturges, romantic-comedy guy. My movies were romantic comedies, and most of the TV I've done had sort of a comedic bent to it. I've learned dramatic structure form over the years, and there were horrific elements, but it's not my natural bent. Through working with Joss, I've discovered that it's really cool because…we say that people have demons, but in our world *they really have demons*. It's just making it bigger."

## FRAN RUBEL KUZUI

Only Joss Whedon has a longer history with our favorite Slayer than Fran Kuzui. She was, as they say, there at the beginning and ushered the film version into being by helping rewrite and then directing the original feature film. Fran is married to producer Kaz Kuzui and together they own Kuzui Enterprises, one of the largest independent motion-picture distribution companies in Japan. How she got there, however, is classic Hollywood.

"I wanted to make films from the time I was about twelve years old," she recalls. "I was the president of my drama club in high school, and I directed all of the plays. My high school drama teacher was my mentor and really encouraged me. When I went away to college, I started taking film courses my freshman year and always knew that that's what I would do.

"In my senior year at New York University, I wrote a treatment for a TV show as part of an assignment for one of my professors. It was my final project for my last year of school. He had just been appointed head of PBS Public Affairs. He hired me on the basis of the treatment that I had written for class. I went directly from graduation to a job at the PBS station in New York, and within three weeks I was an associate producer in the public-affairs department, and I was producing documentaries."

After working in television for a time, Fran went on to produce educational films for Encyclopedia Britannica. Then came the next major turning point in her career, when she met renowned film director Milos Forman.

"I told him that I was really inspired to make movies," Fran recalls. "He had just come to live in the United States from Czechoslovakia, and his wife was a script supervisor there. He said to me, 'Why don't you become a script girl, and I'll teach you how to do it?' So I became his personal assistant, and I worked for him for two years. In the course of that time, he introduced me to his script supervisor and taught me how to be a script supervisor and helped me get into the union. I went from being an associate producer at a TV station to running errands for somebody, and I think that's sort of the dues you pay in the entertainment business."

Fran went on to write and direct the 1988 film *Tokyo Pop*, which received much acclaim at Cannes Film Festival upon its release. Her latest project as producer is *Orgazmo*, a film by *South Park* creators Trey Parker and Matt Stone.

Her involvement with *Buffy* came about almost entirely through instinct.

"After *Tokyo Pop* was shown at the Cannes Film Festival, and as soon as I came home from there, my agent sent me a script I loved, which eventually turned out to be *Cool Runnings*. I fell madly in love with this script and spent the next two-plus years trying to get the film financed as an independent film. The options on the script expired without my knowing it because I was not the person who had optioned it. I was just the director. I wasn't the producer. Without my knowing it, somebody else optioned the rights, and I lost the opportunity to direct *Cool Runnings*.

"I was really, really down in the dumps. I ran into Howard Rosenman at a birthday party, and he said, 'Oh, I have a script that you're going to fall in love with. Why don't you come to my office next week?' So the next week, I went to his office, and he threw the [movie] script down on his desk, and I opened it up, and it said *Buffy the Vampire Slayer*, and I said, 'I'll do it. Anything called *Buffy the Vampire Slayer* has to be a wonderful script. I'm in.' So I called Joss, and I got together with him, and I told him how much I loved the script.

"After we optioned it, Joss and I sat down and discussed ways that it could be re-focused. I suggested, since I was an enormous fan of John Woo, that we add martial arts. My idea, since I like to do comedy, was to make this more comedic than scary. What I do is pop art. Or what I'm interested in is pop art. So I saw the original script more from a pop sensibility or a pulp sensibility than as a genre piece. So I suggested that every time she saw a vampire she should do martial arts before she puts the stake through its heart, kind of like John Woo's *The Killer*.

"John is a friend of mine. I thought, *Well, in* The Killer *there's all this violence, but it's not very violent because it's treated as ballet.* And it's done so tongue-in-cheek, more like comic-book violence than Jean-Claude Van Damme violence. I think that's the biggest change that Joss and I made in this script.

"As we rewrote it, there were several times I said to Joss, 'Oh, that's such a silly thing for her to say, could we take that out?' And Joss said, 'But I said that myself when I was in high school,' and we started to laugh at how funny you are when you are in high school. High school is not only a scary place, but a funny place. For me, what I wanted to do in the movie was balance the scary and the funny. I think, at that point, Joss's vision was more toward the scary, but he was incredibly supportive of what I wanted to do and refocused the script more along the lines of my vision and how I wanted to make the movie.

"You know, *Buffy* has been blessed from the very, very beginning, because it took Joss several months to do the rewrite and give it to me, and I just loved it," Fran recalls.

After sending the script to Fox, Fran and Kaz took off for a vacation in Hawaii. Things in Hollywood don't usually happen very quickly. But the morning after they arrived in Hawaii, they received a call from Fox saying that Joe Roth wanted to give *Buffy* the green light and wanted them in L.A. as soon as possible. Fortunately, when Roth learned of their vacation, he gave them a week in the sun before they needed to come in for a meeting.

"The whole process from our optioning it, having it rewritten, and then green-lighted, took about six months," Fran notes. "In the movie business, that's like lightning."

As for its middling reception at the box office, Fran chalks it up to a lack of focus in the marketing of its release.

"I know the film has an enormous number of fans, but I think it was never clearly marketed to one audience. I think the film found an audience. I don't think the marketing found an audience. Gail Berman, who loved *Buffy*, came to me and said, 'Someday I'm going to turn this into a TV show.' I was still smarting from the experience of the theatrical release of the film and said, 'Well, I don't really think this is *Buffy*'s moment.' But several years later, I just had the sense that it was time for *Buffy*.

"For me, from the very beginning, *Buffy* was always about 'girl power.' I started seeing so much around me that was beginning to emerge that was similar to that. I called Gail, and said, 'Hey, remember you wanted to do this TV series? Let's go.' And the next thing we knew, everybody in town was fighting over who got to make it. It's always been pretty blessed."

When it's pointed out that her career path is a perfect example of that 'girl power' that she saw as a trend, Fran pauses a moment.

"The real challenge for me is to have made a movie that was perceived as not successful and to pick myself up and not quit," she says. "To turn the creative focus of *Buffy* [the show] over to Joss Whedon and to say, 'Well, okay, I will enable Joss to express himself through the TV show,' is where the guts come in. That's what *Buffy*'s about: dealing with the consequences of what you do, and moving on and not folding to the vampires is the really important part. Having the grace to say to Joss, 'This is yours now.' The grace to say to Joss, 'I know you had an original vision. Let's go back to that, and let's make this TV show along the lines of what you want to do.' That's the guts, and that's the girl power."

Fran also wants to make it clear that she believes "girl power" is almost more important for boys than girls.

"For me, *Buffy* was always about creating a role model for girls, but unless you show boys what that is, they're not going to step aside and let girls be that," she says proudly. "You can educate your daughters to be Slayers, but you have to educate your sons to be Xanders."

**Do you have a favorite moment from your involvement with the series?**

**FRAN:** "I'm very fond of the praying-mantis episode. Also, the entire [atmosphere] of the set. Since I'm not there all the time, there are people who don't know who I am. One day, I was on the set and asked one of the Teamsters for directions, and he said, 'Hi, what do you do?' and I said, 'Believe it or not, I'm the executive producer,' and he looked at me, and he said 'Thank you, thank you. This is one of the nicest experiences of my life. Thank you for making this.'"

## GAIL BERMAN

Now that she's added running a new company to her duties as executive producer on *Buffy*, Gail Berman has had to move her office. But don't worry, she hasn't gone far. Only a few hundred feet from her old office is the new one, the home of Regency Television. When we sit down to interview her, everyone is still moving in and there's a very sort of temporary look to everything. She's a remarkable woman, sharp and in control. She had all her calls held, with the single exception of her daughter, and the warmth and pride in Gail's voice as she spoke to her were wonderful to hear.

Gail got her start shortly after graduating from the University of Maryland. She produced *Joseph and the Amazing Technicolor Dreamcoat* at the Ford Theater in Washington, D.C. "Then nine months after it closed in Washington, it opened off Broadway, and two months later it went to Broadway. So I was the youngest female Broadway producer. My first project was one of those *wunderkind* things. Then I was a Broadway producer, having never been a production assistant. I did that for ten years."

Among Gail's theater production credits were *Hurly Burly, The Nerd, Blood Knot*, as well as "all the road companies of *Joseph* at the time." She was on the Board of Trustees of the League of American Theaters and Producers, "and I was younger by thirty years than my next colleague," she says.

In 1989, Gail decided it was time for a change.

"It was a very dramatic move at that time. I had no idea what I was going to do next." She took a job at the then-fledgling Comedy Channel (now Comedy Central), her first "real" job since graduating college. "It was an extraordinary thing to have happen, because when you are starting something new, you have to learn it all. This was an operation where the day-to-day business was taking place where the production was taking place. It was really a great experience, and I learned a tremendous amount about television." During her time there, she served as the supervising producer for a new show from Minnesota called *Mystery Science Theater 3000*, among others.

After her husband's career took him to California, Gail resigned and went to work for Sandollar in L.A. "I wasn't sure what I wanted to do, but I figured it was a good way to start my career in Los Angeles. That's been my career in Los Angeles, one place. I started as the vice president and I became the CEO of the company, and then in June, I left to just do *Buffy*." In addition to her duties as one of *Buffy*'s executive producers, Gail is the president of the television studio Regency Television—a joint venture with Fox.

Gail was instrumental in getting *Buffy* to the small screen.

"When I came to Sandollar, I read a script called *Buffy the Vampire Slayer*. I thought it was a great script, I thought it was really amazing, and they were making a movie of it. Before the movie was going to be released, I went to Sandy Gallin and I said, 'I think this would make a great television series. I think we should sell it as a television series before the movie comes out.' Sandy [Gallin, president of Sandollar] said, 'Great idea, let's see if we could do that.' I called the various parties. Nobody was interested in pursuing it as a television series at that time.

"I was very disappointed and went home with my tail between my legs. I couldn't go ahead with it, so I put it on the shelf and thought, *someday*. A couple of years later, Fran Kuzui called me and said, 'You know, someone has come to see me about *Buffy*'—talking to her about it sort of theoretically, and she said that they might be interested in doing it. I said, 'Fran, nobody else is going to do this but us.' We started to work on it together. I didn't know Joss, I had only read the original script. We were contractually obligated to offer this to Joss. Everybody said he was a big movies guy now, and he'll never want to do this, including his agent, who said that to me on the phone. Then his agent called me back and said that, in fact, this was the only thing that Joss *was* interested in doing. So for me, that was fantastic. I met him, we hit it off very well, we had a very similar vision, and we went to go about selling it eventually."

Gail is quick to point out that it's Joss Whedon's show, top to bottom. "It was my idea to do this as a series, but it's his creation. Every single thing you see, every line you hear, it's him.

Obviously, there are episodes I like better than others, but I never am disappointed in the vision. The vision is unbelievable to me."

She is very grateful for the show's success, especially since it didn't seem as if it had much of a chance at first. "We were like the bottom of the barrel. We're on the WB mid-season, thirteen episodes, a show called *Buffy the Vampire Slayer,* based on a movie that was considered less than successful. You can't have any more strikes against you."

Indeed, the title was a source of contention. "The network did not want to keep this title at all. They had a lot of different ideas, none of which we were interested in. It was a very big battle to the finish. Now, of course, it seems fine, because everybody calls it that, but at the time their research told them that the title was a killer. 'Definitely don't call it *Buffy!*'"

Gail's ability to cut and run when she's had enough of something is in direct contrast to the heroine of *Buffy,* who is stuck with her destiny no matter what. When this comparison is mentioned to Gail, she says, "I just know when it's time to move on." As to Buffy Summers's inability to move on even if she is "spent," she says that is "one of the things that makes her pretty extraordinary, I think. It's something that I think Suzanne Daniels from the network pointed out in an early episode that she wasn't pleased with. She felt that it was very important that Buffy not be reluctant. She is a heroine, she accepts her responsibilities, she accepts her fate. That doesn't mean that every day she loves it, but it means she totally accepts. I think about that often when we think about the show. She is mature enough to understand her destiny."

**There are a lot of strong girl-driven shows right now. Do you think this is something that is going to last, or do you think this is just a fad?**

**GAIL:** "I'm not prescient in these matters. The only thing I can tell you is, a lot of women out there respond to this kind of material. I think women are looking for role models, or strong characters, that they can identify with in some way. I don't think that that is a trend; I think it has taken all this time to catch up with what's going on with women. Now, sooner or later, people are going to say, 'Hey, there are too many shows like this on television,' and you'll see there will be an emphasis on male shows. That will happen just simply because that's the nature of television. You sort of have to be above the curve to anticipate new trends, but I think, in the end, what we've learned here is that women are not going back to the same place they were before this all started. So this trend has moved women forward."

**Who is your favorite character?**

**GAIL:** "Willow. Young people respond so much to Willow, because so many people see themselves as her. Young girls who are scientifically oriented, or they're into math, and they're always on the sidelines. What I love so much about Willow is that she maintains that, she keeps that. It's not that all of a sudden Willow became a glamour girl for having known Buffy—she is the same Willow, but all of her strengths come out thanks to this friend of hers. Her loyalty, her brilliance, her cuteness, her everything comes out because she has been empowered by her friend. I love Willow's character, I love what's going on with her and Xander, and Oz—it feels real to me. I love the fact that she is Jewish—I can't recall ever having a Jewish character on television that isn't portrayed in some stereotypical way. For me that is very helpful to say to my daughter: Willow's Jewish."

**Has there been a moment where you felt really satisfied with something, a moment where you can kind of sit back and say, "This is really cool"?**

**GAIL:** "Well it's a much earlier moment than anybody else will remember. There was a moment at the end of the presentation [reel] where Buffy throws a stake at a poster of *Nosferatu*, and the music starts—it's not music that we ever used again, just for the presentation, and she's so satisfied with herself and she is sort of welcomed into the group. I thought to myself, *This is the best show*, and I just knew it in my heart at that moment. It was a very private moment, it's not a moment that I really shared with anybody else. It's the eeriest thing with this show, because people ask me, 'Well, when did you know?' and I can't explain it other than saying that I just have always known. It's never been something where I thought, *Well, it's not going to happen that way*. It's happening where I always knew it in my heart. It's like when people used to say to me, 'How did you know that *Joseph* was going to go to Broadway?' I just knew it. Remember the show wasn't picked up. *Buffy* was not ordered. We almost didn't make it then, and yet I thought, *We're going to get picked up*. I don't know why. Knowing Joss, believing in him, just seeing his vision, being around that kind of creativity, just watching that is an awesome thing."

## SANDY GALLIN

Ask executive producer Sandy Gallin how he got where he is today, and his answer is typically direct and self-effacing: "I eat breakfast, lunch, and dinner."

A personal manager, Gallin has represented superstars as Barbra Streisand, Michael Jackson, Mariah Carey, Dolly Parton, Cher, Whoopi Goldberg, Luther Vandross, Lisa Stansfield, Renee Zellweger, and Nicole Kidman. As a film producer, he has brought to life such features as *Fly Away Home*, *Father of the Bride*, *Sabrina*, and the original film version of *Buffy the Vampire Slayer*. On the television side, Sandy has produced dozens of specials and series, including the original, long-running *Donny and Marie Show* and the Margaret Cho sitcom, *All-American Girl*, as well as the Academy Award-winning AIDS documentary, *Common Threads: Stories From the Quilt*.

Sandy's place in entertainment history is assured by his extraordinary accomplishments, but his place in the history of America itself is marked by the single most important booking he made in his early career as an agent for General Artists Group (which would later become ICM): it was Sandy Gallin who booked a little-known British band called the Beatles for their legendary appearance on *The Ed Sullivan Show*, after which he was promoted to senior vice president at the tender age of twenty-seven.

"I started in the mailroom. I became the head of the television department. I moved to California, running their music and television department, which is now ICM, and I became a personal manager. I brought the Beatles to the United States. And in 1985, I formed Sandollar Productions with a very good friend and client, Dolly Parton."

Sandollar was the main force behind getting the original *Buffy* film onto movie screens. The film, released in 1992, was written by Joss Whedon and directed by Fran Rubel Kuzui. It starred Kristy Swanson, Luke Perry, Donald Sutherland, Rutger Hauer, and Paul Reubens.

"The movie was sort of a cult success," Gallin recalls. "Not a big commercial success, but I had asked Gail Berman, who was then running Sandollar Television, to please go through all of our inventory and see what we could turn into a television series. Gail came up with *Buffy the Vampire Slayer*. We partnered with Fran Kuzui and made a deal with Joss Whedon to create, write, produce, and direct the series. In all the years I've been involved with any project, television or motion picture, this is the first time that when the creative head of the show took over as producer and director, there actually were no problems. Joss did such a brilliant job. When we made his deal, that was a difficult thing. He's a very hot screenwriter. But he was passionate and wanted to do this and is totally and completely responsible for its success in my opinion, in every way."

Though it was all very hush-hush at the time of this interview, Gallin confirms that there is a *Buffy* spinoff in the works, featuring Angel as the lead character.

When asked, as the interview draws to a close, when he knew that *Buffy* was going to be as big a hit as it has become, Gallin's answer was immediate: "When I was told that it redefined the advertising prices for the WB."

## GARETH DAVIES

We met Gareth Davies in his second-floor office in the *Buffy* production wing. Most of his office wall space is taken up with production stills, air-date schedules, and the other paraphernalia of being a producer. His desk faces a rogue's gallery of guest stars, with large red dots on the ones who have been killed. He speaks with a British accent and is very gracious, very relaxed, despite the fact that it's around 9:30 P.M. There's a location shoot of the mansion going on, and the residential area in which the mansion is located has requested a "taillights at ten" curfew. This means that the shoot must be finished, wrapped, and on the way out of the area by 10 P.M. People with radio phones periodically walk by the open door of his office to report on the shoot's progress at making the curfew. If they don't make it, there will be a hefty fine. (*Note:* They *do* make it.)

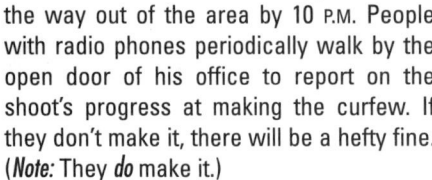

Gareth is impressed with how suddenly *Buffy* has gone from obscure WB show to hot pop-culture phenomenon. "I've done a lot of shows but never had a show that got as hot so quickly as this one. I went with Sarah to the premiere of *Scream 2*, and I was shocked at the reaction to her as opposed to the others." As a result, the production office is a trifle skittish. "You might notice," he says, "there are no names up on the outside of the studio or anything like that, and we have just left the owner's name up on the building. We don't want to draw attention to ourselves."

Gareth started out his career as an actor, but got out of it because, "I was not a very brilliant actor and didn't want to be anything less. And in England there is a huge pool of actors and, unless you're really good, you can make a sparse living, but that's about all." He went to work on the production side, first for the BBC, then for ATV. "I was sent to do a documentary all around South America, which is when I got the bug to travel. As I sat in first class going over the Andes, drinking champagne, I thought, 'Do I really want to go back to London?' I went back anyway—I was broke by the time I got to Rio—and when I arrived, a new show was being scheduled called *Broadway Goes Latin*. I asked what it was and was told, 'Oh, you don't want to do it, it's a co-production with the Americans.' Okay, but what is it? Turns out, they took the one Latin American orchestra in Europe, along with some dancers and musicians in the Caribbean and brought them to London with an American choreographer and basically orchestrated all the Broadway hits, but with Latin rhythms. I said, 'I'll do it.'

"The first show was a disaster. The American producer called me the next morning and said, 'We need to talk. Meet me tomorrow at seven.' So we went for coffee and I told him the problem was that he was an American, nobody wanted to work with him, and he stocked the deadwood for the entire network. So he said, 'Well, how do I get rid of it?' I said, 'Here, I'll give you a list of names. You go into the production office and say, "These are the guys I want."' And I gave him the names of all the young turks, and we put together a helluva show. We did nine months worth of shows. Six months later, he came back to England and said, 'You know, I want you to come to the States.' He brought me to the States with his company. His name was Milton Leer, and he had a production company called International Video Productions in Miami, and did a lot of work in Puerto Rico. With him I went to Yugoslavia, Spain, Puerto Rico, all over. A lot of work in Miami. But eventually, we were going nowhere. We did an unfortunate movie in Yugoslavia, where I realized that I had to get away. So I left him after three years and came to Los Angeles, not knowing anyone, but I thought, *I'll give this a whirl*. I got very lucky, and since then it's been one job after another, once I got the start."

His credits, once he arrived in California, included *The Best of Families*, a 1976 PBS miniseries with Sigourney Weaver, William Hurt, and Jill Eikenberry ("We nearly got Meryl Streep except her agent wouldn't let her get tied up to PBS for nine months"), which got very little notice thanks to coming out at roughly the same time as *I, Claudius*; *Andersonville* ("We got a lot of enemies for that"); and a number of television shows, among them *Flamingo Road, Remington Steele*, and *Shannon's Deal*.

It took Gareth some time to get into *Buffy*. "When I first saw the presentation, I thought, *Hmmm, it's okay*. It grew on me as we went along. The more I got into it, the more I saw how clever it is."

In addition to the high praise that everyone has for Joss Whedon, Gareth also singles out the set designers. "The art department is amazing."

### What are the difficulties in producing a show like Buffy?

**GARETH:** "The amount of stunts we do, the amount of fighting, because that means stunt doubles all over the place, and it takes forever. When we first start to do the climactic scene of the show, we can board it normally, which means six or seven pages a day. Then we would find two pages we couldn't get finished in the day, because there are stunt shots all over the place. On one show, we had a situation where the director had seven vampires just beating up on everybody. So about ten pages of dialogue went to a fight there, and he went on and on about this. Eventually, I got called on the set to plead with the director, to tell him it's okay and put him out of his agony. This poor guy was sitting in the chair going, 'Oh, I'm dead.' I explained to him that it was fine. We know it's going to be tough. I would hate to be a director that had to shoot that stuff! The other problem is the prosthetic makeup. When we do it, it's a couple of hours each. When we have a fight with sometimes six vampires, we've got more makeup guys down there than almost any other department. Then the other thing from the financial point of view is that those people could be in at six o'clock in the morning and not get used until eleven o'clock. Then, at the end there's all the taking off, so their work span is terrific. That's a very expensive episode."

**How did you get involved in *Buffy*?**

**GARETH:** "I got a call from my agent, who said, 'Would you be interested in doing *Buffy the Vampire Slayer*?' I said, 'You have to be joking!' He told me to go out and see the movie. So I saw it and said basically the same thing. He said, 'Look, take a meeting.' So I did. I hadn't seen the presentation, and I didn't think we got on very well, and I walked away. Then one day I called my agent because there was something else that I wanted to do, and he said, 'Wait a minute, let's not dismiss *Buffy*.' I told him it wasn't going to work and that they didn't particularly like me anyway. So I came over and met Charlie Goldstein, the senior vice president of production. I had met him years ago and liked him a lot. Ultimately they offered me the job and I came on.

"Since then it's sort of been a love affair in that it's been great. Joss makes my job easier, because I don't always have to say no, but I can go to him and say, 'Look, Joss, this is the situation. This or that, which do you want?' Nine times out of ten he'll be very rational. Sometimes, of course, he is irrational about something he's really in love with and really wants. But he's great. And the whole group is just terrific."

## DAVID SOLOMON

Co-executive producer David Solomon is in charge of postproduction, which basically includes all the things that occur to the film after it is shot: the editing of the episode, the sound effects and special effects, mixing the show's sound, and so on. He also directs all the second unit (generally, sequences where the main actors are not used) and the inserts (someone's hand opening a book, for example). In addition, to his great delight, he directed "What's My Line? Part 1."

During our visit, we watch David direct Drusilla as she slashes Kendra's throat. This is a "pickup," where bits and pieces of an episode are shot after the episode is wrapped. Although he is under pressure to get the shot finished quickly, the set is relaxed, even jovial, as Juliet Landau and Bianca Lawson go through their paces. There is a great deal of care and discussion over how much blood there should be—*Buffy* strives to be "tasteful" in that regard—and he and Todd McIntosh try various methods such as attaching a tiny tube to Bianca's throat and giving her a "blood"-soaked sponge to press against it when Juliet slashes her. It is very important that the actors maintain their "eye lines"—their line of sight—so that this shot blends seamlessly with the previously shot footage. Some directors find this difficult to achieve, but thanks to David's editing background, it's second nature to him.

Though he works at pretty much the same pace throughout the season, the beginning of a season is less hectic for him than the final weeks. However, since *Buffy* uses Avid, a very sophisticated, high-end Macintosh editing software program, he is able to move fast. In addition, Avid allows Joss to oversee every aspect of each show. "And he does," David assures us. Additionally, the more special effects in an episode, the more work there is for him in postproduction. He works closely with Digital Domain in this regard.

However, the amount of work per episode seems to "even out," he observes. "It seems that the fewer visual effects there are, the more second unit there is to be shot." He mentions "Go Fish" as an example: no visual effects, lots of second unit.

David also oversees blue-screen effects, where the actors have to act before a large blue screen, freezing and reacting to various visual elements that will be put in later. David tells us that the fifty-year-old method is very demanding for the actors.

"But we have an unbelievable group of actors," he says. "I don't know how they do it. They all work a minimum of fourteen hours every day…and there's no such thing as five minutes late."

Armed with a degree in biology from UCLA—"I use it every day," he jokes—David's first job in the entertainment industry was cutting sound effects for Hanna-Barbera cartoons. He worked in animation for a while, but like *Buffy* director of photography Michael Gershman, decided he wanted to move to live action. He was an assistant editor on a Billy Wilder feature called *Buddy Buddy*, starring Jack Lemmon and Walter Matthau.

"I had the best time in the world," he recalls fondly.

He went on to do a lot of editing on various features and TV series including *Hill Street Blues* ("those leather jackets were such a pain, drowning out the sound") and the pilot for *Miami Vice*. He went on to edit, line-produce, and direct more than thirty TV movies and pilots for Viacom. He also directed *Matlock* and the Shadoe Stevens series, *Loose Cannons*, among other TV shows.

It was in his capacity as an editor that he met Joss. An executive at Twentieth Century Fox put them together, and David edited the twenty-minute presentation that Joss and Kuzui/Sandollar showed around town in hopes that *Buffy* would be picked up.

He enjoyed editing the *Buffy* presentation and was delighted to work on the show when it was bought. By the third episode ("Witch") he says, "the show really took on a life of its own for me. Buffy is a great character, but I didn't know how great the show would be until we started rolling. The second season took off with much more complete and sophisticated shows, deeper and better ones, really, and even the humor is funnier."

We talk about "What's My Line? Part 1," the episode that he directed. He was thrilled to get the chance, as he had "drifted from directing to producing and stayed there." He was very pleased to be able to cast Kelly Connell, one of his favorite actors, as Mr. Pfister, the Tarakan assassin also known as Bug Man.

"There was a stand-in bug wrangler for the arm sequence," David recalls, but Connell assured him he wouldn't mind putting up with "a bug or two." Everyone else stayed well away of the critters. "They were disgusting."

"I was lucky," David continues. "I had a lot of interesting characters" to work with, including Spike and Drusilla.

"What's My Line? Part 1" is the episode for which Kendra's cargo bay was built. The cargo bay provided the inspiration for the sewer system beneath Sunnydale and its attendant grimy appearance for the vampires' world.

"It almost didn't get built," David recalls. "It was very expensive for use in a small scene." However, he points out that it would have cost three times as much to rent one, and it would have been even more expensive than that to go to an airport to film a real cargo bay. "So Carey has used it over and over."

**Did you have any professional associations with anyone on Buffy prior to working here?**
**DAVID:** "It's interesting that you should ask that. When I was editing *Hill Street Blues*, Gareth Davies was down the hall working on *Remington Steele*. I saw him every day for years, just to nod to in the hall."

**Do you have any scars, tattoos, or distinguishing marks?**
**DAVID:** "When I was twenty, I dumped a motorcycle on the island of Corfu. I have a big scar on my knee filled with gravel. You can see it." It is the same knee he injured as a boy growing up in Tarzana, California.

**Do you have a special moment working on Buffy?**
**DAVID:** "When I found out I would be directing an episode, I thought it wouldn't be for a while, but the scheduled director [for "What's My Line? Part 1"] dropped out. David Greenwalt called me in to the office to tell me. I'm sure I was very professional, said something like, 'Well, thank you very much for this opportunity,' but inside I was bouncing off the walls and shouting, 'Omigod! Omigod!'

"Directing is the best kind of exhaustion there is. It's a fully concentrated day."

**Since your work on *Buffy* requires you to work with intense scrutiny on a myriad of details, does it take away the "magic" of watching the finished shows for you?**
**DAVID:** "I watch *Buffy* at home if possible, and I watch just like everyone else. I rarely take a tape home. I watch it while it's being aired, with the commercials and everything. I really enjoy it."

## MARTI NOXON

It's hard to imagine Marti Noxon as a Hollywood power broker, though that seems to be where her career is quickly taking her. She straddles an interesting line. One moment, she's all professional, intensely scrutinizing the events taking place on the set of *Buffy the Vampire Slayer*, and absorbing everything she feels she can learn from. The next, she's all social butterfly and fan girl. Everybody on the set seems happy to be here. But Marti seems as if she still can't quite believe her good fortune.

It isn't luck, however. Not at all. Marti rose to the position of story editor in *Buffy*'s second season, with a promotion to co-producer for the third. She is heavily involved in all the story conferences and has written five second-season episodes, co-writing a sixth with Howard Gordon. Among her credits are the pivotal two-part episode "What's My Line?" and the turning-point episode "Surprise."

Marti goes out of her way to be friendly to people. She is very, very "up." And she has good reason to be. She worked for seven years to break into Holllywood as a writer, and now she's not only here, she's on a series famous for its scripts.

"I was working as a secretary until last year," Marti recalls. "But I had been writing that whole time. I had had little successes here and there, and a lot of encouragement, but nothing had clicked. I finally got a better agent last year."

Amazingly enough, Marti almost passed on the chance to work on *Buffy*.

"They [the new agents] sent my material to Joss, but I had actually already gotten an offer from another show, so I turned Joss down. The other show was on a network, and I was intimidated [by the *Buffy* gig]. I just thought that these guys were so smart and so good, and it was my first job ever. I think I was afraid the bar would be too high."

In addition, it was only logical to assume that a small show on a fledgling network would be a risk.

"There were very few people saying this show was going to be a hit. There were even people at my agency who were discouraging me from taking this job. But then I called someone who knows Joss—my sister-in-law's brother went to school with him—and he said to me, 'If you don't work with Joss Whedon, you're crazy.' That's when I changed my mind, and I backed out of the other deal and came over here."

In her first year, Marti would still get the occasional odd look. "When I first started, people were like, '*Buffy*?' They would give you a kind of, 'Oh, that's nice,' and then discount you like you couldn't get a better job."

What Marti likes most about the show is the character progression, though she admits that it makes it that much harder for aspiring screenwriters. "I have a number of friends who are writing specs, and it's really tough for them, because things change so dramatically. 'Xander and Cordelia are together now? What's that all about?' That's one of the things about Joss, one of the reasons I think this show is so good, because he does things with characters. He is willing to take them places, where most average TV writers would stop. 'This is a franchise, you don't want to alienate your viewers.' And guess what? They *want* to see these radical things happen. We all crave that motion, that sense that things are happening, and they're just going to keep moving forward. It's very exciting.

"Next year's senior year, and there are all the paces we get to put them through that come with that, and all the questions about, 'Who am I going to be, and what am I going to be doing?' They all get to change; no one is going to remain static.

"When Joss pitched me the end of the second season, I went, 'What, you can't!'" Marti says. "My first reaction was, 'You can't do that to our audience.' Then I thought, 'Of *course* you can do that.' You've got to give them what you think they don't want, because if you fulfill [their expectations], it's the old *Moonlighting* thing: get those two people together and it loses its energy."

The story editor has nothing but fulsome praise for her boss.

"Thank God I get to work with a Mozart—maybe *I'll* get a little Mozart, you know? Maybe just a touch, just a pinky of Mozart, from being around him."

She knew that this was the right place for her shortly after she turned in her first couple of scripts.

"I was riddled with anxiety, and I got a call from both David Greenwalt and Joss on my home machine. The first thing they said was, 'You know, we're really sorry to have to tell you this...'—I think this is my second script, and they called me from the set, and they were saying—'God, you really just haven't worked out at all.' Then they both started cracking up. Then they said, 'You did a really good job, and this is just great stuff, we're real excited.' I felt like, if they can tease me, then I must be okay. They must want me to stay."

**We heard that you had a special guest for the *Buffy/Seventh Heaven* softball game.**
**MARTI:** "John Ritter came out and played! He was just a guest star [on 'Ted'] that week, and he came out and played for our team. He was just the greatest. He turned out to be a great hitter, too; he was amazing. He really helped our team. Of course, *Seventh Heaven* won. God was on their side."

**Could you describe your day-to-day work and responsibilities?**
**MARTI:** "The cool thing is it changes all the time. It depends on what I'm doing. We get together and break story, no matter whose script it is—it's usually David and Joss, and then sometimes David, Joss, and me and the guys. We all sit around in a room and eat and talk about everything under the sun except for what we are supposed to be talking about. We spiral down to having really no other anecdotes, no other shockingly bad jokes to tell, right until you are really desperate enough to actually talk about the story. Then we will talk for seven or eight days. Once we have locked on the story idea, if it's my script, they send me off to take the story beats and then write out an outline. If I have ideas or pitches for jokes or things that will happen in that scene, I'll put it all in the outline, then hand it back. They'll give me notes on that, and then I go away and write a first-draft script. That usually takes between five and seven days. I usually try to write an act a day, then I try to spend a couple days and just let it sit, then I read it over. Then comes the agonizing day when you turn it in and you wait for someone to put their head in your office and say something nice to you. Those are sort of vomitory days, seasickness days."

**Do you have a favorite moment, either off screen or on?**
**MARTI:** "Recently I got asked to teach a day of school for aspiring writers, high school–age writers, through the Museum of Television and Radio. That made me almost cry, because I got to pass on my passion and my love for this thing to other people, and I have a credential now to do that, so that was kind of an amazing thing.

"The other time I remember is when we were first breaking story, everybody was working through lunch, and someone said, 'We've got to get lunch.' I stood up and started to go to the phone because I knew I had to start making calls about where we were going to have lunch. Somebody said, 'Marti, you know one of the guys who works with us, he'll get the lunch; you don't have to do that anymore.' And I was like, 'Wait a minute, I don't get the lunch?'

"It's all those little things, but in terms of the actual show, there are so many moments when I know that probably half the people watching the show just felt something, either laughed or maybe cried, if we're lucky. To me, that's the big win, if you get someone there, and that to me is so overwhelming I can't even take it in."

**Are you interested in horror at all?**
**MARTI:** "Yeah, I've written three spec features that are about ghosts. I love ghost stories. For me it's always been the metaphysical types of horror, like *The Haunting*, *The Exorcist*, and *The Silence of the Lambs*. It's always been about that sort of transcendence, about trying to communicate with the dead or reconcile your past—all those kinds

of things. Those are the themes that I kept working on, and for some reason horror always fit. I think about reconciling your high school experience. We all had those nightmares in high school."

**Do you have an affinity for any character in particular?**
**MARTI:** "Willow is probably closest to who I really was. I was an egghead, and I didn't date until college. I was totally antisocial, and I was very, very shy. I couldn't talk to boys. So I was much more Willow, although Willow is way cooler than I was. You know, there's no one as geeky as me on this show. There's nobody as awkward and introverted, and creepy as I was. I scared my friends. I was just a big drama nerd—I was too gregarious, too silly, then I would withdraw, and then I was too quiet. A couple of other girls and I were the biggest nerds in the universe. We were pizza-faced and just completely couldn't talk. There was a hall that wasn't actually a classroom, like an in-between place, called Room 6—it didn't lead anywhere, it was just a dead end. We would stay in Room 6 because no one ever walked through there. That's where we would hide so we wouldn't have to talk to people.

"It wasn't the hardest time of my life, because I had a support system. I had what Buffy has. I had my Xander and my Willow and we had each other and we got through it. Man, thank God those weren't my glory days. I hope my glory days are still ahead."

## ROB DES HOTEL AND DEAN BATALI

We met Rob Des Hotel and Dean Batali in their large, shared office. Rob's desk faces the door; Dean's is perpendicular to it. They talked about naming various characters after relatives—"Spritzer," the dog whose role was ultimately cut from "The Dark Age," is the name of one of their family pets.

From their rapport, it was clear they were a team, and comfortable working as such. Both were articulate, bright, and funny. Rob and Dean come originally from the sitcom world. They started out as writers' assistants on various shows, meeting on *Bob*. They were writers on *Hope and Gloria, Bob,* and other shows. They wrote spec scripts together—*The Simpsons* and *Duck Man*, but it was their scripts for a Nickelodeon show called *The Adventures of Pete and Pete* that attracted Joss Whedon's attention.

Rob tells us, "[Joss] was reading everything at the time. He was reading one-hour dramas, half-hour sitcoms. *Pete and Pete* was a one-camera comedy drama that actually, in retrospect, is the closest thing to this show at the time because it had some edge to it—but obviously, no vampires. *Pete and Pete* had a lot of the same character issues."

They pitch Joss a number of ideas, and Joss will pick one or more from the batch. They go off and develop those. The secret to consistent excellence comes from sitting with him and David Greenwalt "for hours and hours and try to break the story out," in other words, separating it into "beats" and acts. Then the team goes back into its office, to its white board, where the two "try to piece stuff together," then go back to Joss. This process usually lasts a week or two.

Their "beat sheet" usually consists of one line or so for each scene. After Joss approves that, they do an outline of around ten pages.

Rob adds, "For the most part, it's a lot of planning. It's one of the great things about this show is that it's planned in the story stage. We've been on plenty of shows where you're doing rewrites every day all day because you didn't have the story broken in the first place. You just sort of had an idea, and then find, to no one's surprise, that the script doesn't work at all, so then you have to go back and do what you should have done in the beginning. So I think Joss is really really good at planning ahead, knowing where he wants to go."

As an example of their creative process, Rob and Dean discuss their favorite episodes. Rob's was "Phases," and Dean's was "The Puppet Show." Rob tells us, "Werewolf was what Joss gave us for the story. He said, 'Okay, Oz is a werewolf.' It was his basic idea, and then we went to him and said, 'Here are some ideas....How about if there's a bounty hunt going on here?'"

Dean says, "Last season's episodes—especially the early ones—were really big on teen situations. 'The Invisible Girl' was about people who had a lack of popularity, for

example. And even 'Puppet Show' was at one time more about being the geek of the school and being around all the other geeks at the school. We felt that in 'Puppet Show,' the angle that everybody freaks out worked. But once we got deeper and deeper into the script, that just kind of stood out. In rewrite, the basis became a subtle kinship between Buffy and the puppet."

Rob gives us another example of the way in which stories are devised: "Joss said, 'Giles did something bad in his past, so pitch ideas about that.' It felt like we pitched at least a hundred ideas. About things that he could have done or things that could have happened, and we had all sorts of 'could be this, could be that,' different things, different ways things are happening."

Once the idea is approved, the team does a first draft. They get notes back. Then they rework the material into a second draft, and then "usually the third and sometimes the fourth. From first to fourth, that can change a lot."

As with "Killed by Death," the "hospital episode," as they shorthand it: "The first draft actually took place at a day-care center, so that tells you the transition that can happen. Story ideas will change, things can move around, the monster can be different. The only person who really changes [things] is Joss, mostly, although David does a little bit here and there. We've done a rewrite of a script or two for other people, but normally it just goes from the writer to Joss. And even if we do a rewrite, Joss still takes it after that."

So moving from pitch to completed final draft of the team's script is probably an eight-week process.

"Getting the story down is, of course, always harder than the actual writing of the script."

They also point out that they can—and have—sped the process up. They've had to turn scripts around in five or six days. They wrote the second draft of "The Puppet Show" in thirty-six hours straight.

Pitching stories to Joss can sometimes amount to a discovery process of Joss's long-term vision of the show: "He has story arcs and stories that he wants to tell through this season and next season and next season. Occasionally, you do come up with a happy accident. Jenny Calendar [being a Gypsy and then getting killed]—that just sort of fell in place perfectly at the perfect time in the perfect way. And really, you know, sometimes you have an element in your story, and you're not sure what it is that's not making it work and it presents itself.

"So, like we were saying, [when we] pitch to him, probably thirty to forty percent of them, something's already being done like that in a future episode, or he's got an arc plan that negates it. So sometimes we do find ourselves pitching stand-alone type things—one episode, a contained episode, like "Puppet Show" or the hospital show that we just did. Often he'll give us stories where he says, 'Okay, here's a story where by now this is happening, and I want this kind of development happening.'"

But they add, "It's really rare that any one episode can just be plunked down anywhere in the season and still work. Even 'Killed by Death' had part of the Angel–Buffy story. You can't throw it anywhere."

"Killed by Death" was originally scheduled to be one of the first thirteen episodes, but there were production problems in that they would have to shoot on a hospital location for at least half the time, so they postponed it. By then, so many developments had occurred in the show that the script had to be reworked. In its original incarnation, Buffy and Angel were fighting side by side, and Angel was the one who brought Buffy to the hospital.

In fact, it was almost the "great lost *Buffy* episode." Rob and Dean explain that it had some conceptual problems in the beginning as they tried to get a bead on what the *Buffy* story of it was. "And the monster was just way too difficult to comprehend.

"In the second or third draft, there was an old lady sharing Buffy's room, and instead of the cousin who had died, it was Buffy's grandmother who had died. So that changed things."

### How do you break down the work when you work together?

**DEAN:** "I do most of it." (They laugh.)

**ROB:** "We are a weird drama team. We write like comedy. We do everything face-to-face, word for word. We do it all together."

**DEAN:** "One of us sits at the computer. Occasionally, once we have an entire script, we'll take it away and work on our own, and then come in with pitches written on the script and say, "We could do this here, or this here" and go back and forth and decide what we like the best. It's usually Rob's stuff we like the best. That's weird because then we look back over the script, and in all honesty, it's hard to tell who came up with what. We might remember a line or something."

**ROB:** "And hope we have something that flows."

### Would you say it is the strengths you brought into your work as sitcom writers that have given you your longevity on *Buffy*?

**ROB:** "Yeah. The staff from last year, of which I guess we remain, was a real combination. There were two or three teams and a single person. We were a comedy team, and the single person was a comedy team. The other two...were hourlong teams, so it was a real mixture. Then Dana Reston came on. She did the witch episode. And then Kiene and Reinkemeyer were hourlong writers. They'd come from *Space* and *Law and Order*. And then Gable and Swyden, who were hourlong writers. They were brand-new, but they got this off their hourlong scripts."

### From studying the shooting scripts, we have seen that actors almost always deliver their lines exactly as written. Do the actors request many dialogue changes prior to this final draft?

**DEAN:** "Well, Joss is the final arbiter on that, ninety-nine percent of the time. Nicholas wanted to say 'red rum' in the 'Puppet' episode. Sarah had a good note for us a few months ago, in "Phases." She thought there was a word in there that Buffy wouldn't know, and that she was being too pushy in her advice to Willow. [We] thought she had a good point, so we toned down the advice and rephrased it. But usually that's a thing that Joss deals with."

**When you come up with your pitches, do you keep budgetary considerations in mind?**
**ROB:** "Well, our best example of that was right in the beginning where we knew what the budget was, but we had no clue as to what that would buy or what we could do. In our first episode, 'Never Kill a Boy on the First Date,' there was going to be a [vampire] uprising. Giles had this prophecy that he was reading to Buffy, and it was something like, 'Seven will die, and five will rise.'

"As production went on, Joss would poke his head in about once a week and say, 'Okay, five are going to die, and how many are going to rise?' By the time production came around, it was 'Five will die, and one will rise.'

"We had this fight choreographed with Buffy, Xander, Willow, Giles, and Owen—her date—and five vampires. It included urns crashing down, flipping over caskets, falling into caskets, and none of us had any idea if this was possible or not, and that was actually why we had to do a third and fourth draft of that particular script, because we had done two drafts, and we were done. But Joss came in a few weeks later and said, 'We can't do this anymore, we're going over budget, and we really have to tone down a lot.'

"So we rewrote a big thing like a duel from the movie, *Duel*, with the two vampires who take the van off the road. And then it became the airport minivan with both vampires standing in the middle of the road. We still had them crash into the light post. It was cool."

**Do these budget considerations frustrate you?**
**ROB:** "It's almost not fair in horror to have a huge budget because it's so easy then to manipulate the audience the way you want to. With our little budget, we have to rely more on classic, old-fashioned scares. More eeriness and suspense rather than huge special effects.

"We catch ourselves occasionally going, 'That'll be too expensive.' We try not to, but then [the producers] will go, 'No, we can't do that, it's too expensive. That sounds like a lot of outside stuff' [location shooting]."

**So, any tidbits for next season?**
**DEAN:** "Nothing you'll hear from us. We don't even tell our wives. We don't tell our friends. Oh, there is a chance that Xander is an alien....'"

# MICHAEL GERSHMAN

In the egalitarian dress of production professionals, Michael Gershman wears the standard jeans and casual shirt. A quiet, affable man, he is perhaps the antithesis of the stereotypical director of photography, very soft-spoken, although extremely enthusiastic about his work.

Michael began his career as an animation cameraman in the late '60s, shooting *Peanuts, George of the Jungle, Tom Slick,* and Captain Crunch cereal and other animated commercials. But as he sat all day in a semidarkened room, his colleagues were on the streets of Hollywood shooting movies, and he decided live action was where the real action was.

While continuing to shoot animation, he began working for Pylar Camera Systems, which specializes in aerial cinematography. They trained him on the job and then began throwing jobs his way, until he dropped the animation work and concentrated on the aerial jobs. He worked in aerial cinematography for about five years, but became increasingly nervous about flying so much. As he had before, he started transitioning into another line of work: episodic television and movies of the week. One of his first projects was *Columbo*.

He worked on *Days of Heaven*, a feature that was shot in Canada and went on to win an Academy Award. He worked with famed cinematographers, such as Haskell Wexler and Vilmos Zsigmod, on such films as *The Deerhunter, The Rose,* and *Heaven's Gate*, moving from assistant cameraman to camera operator.

Then, in the mid 1980s, Michael's life took a big turn: he became a single parent as a result of a divorce. He eliminated travel and concentrated on working in Los Angeles, which led him back into television. He worked on the pilot of a show called *Shannon's Deal* as camera operator and moved up to director of photography when the show was picked up. Through that project, he became DP on *Middle Ages,* and that was where he met Gareth Davies, *Buffy's* producer. They worked together on a number of other shows before Gareth persuaded him to come to *Buffy*.

Recalling his initial reluctance, he tells us, "I thought, *Buffy the Vampire Slayer,* 16 mm. [the format the first two seasons have been shot in]...no.' Gareth called me a number of times and said, 'You just have to meet with them.' I just kept saying, 'Well, I don't really want to get involved with that.'

"Finally, I said, 'Okay. Within ten minutes of meeting Joss, I wanted to work with him. So here I am."

**So this actually...is a sort of shift content-wise. A little different from the other stuff you have done.**

**MICHAEL:** "It is different because of the subject matter. I have tried to bring a look to most of the shows I have done. I have always tried to make them interesting. This [show] gives me the ability to be much more interesting than anything else around. There are no rules. In a normal situation, you would not put a light on someone from below and bring it up. But I can light from below; I can light from above; I can use camera moves, and I pretty much have carte blanche.

"Joss told me what he likes and what he doesn't like...and I think that the material that we are dealing with is so good and so well-written, I feel an obligation to keep the show looking on par with the information we are delivering. I am just trying to make it interesting all the time."

**What about the challenge of shooting in 16 mm? Does this affect the look of *Buffy*?**

**MICHAEL:** "To me, it is much harder to make it look interesting. It tends to flatten everything out....The *Buffy* look is just to stimulate the audience's interest and to keep it original. To light it with depth in the frame and put texture in the frame. I use colors and I use pools of light to set up contrast, so that I will have light, dark, light, dark, light, dark. To set up areas of contrast for perspective. Then I will use various colors, warm colors, or cool colors, to help shape and mold the actors a little bit."

**What about the Bronze set?**

**MICHAEL:** "It is really one of the easiest sets to shoot. Because I have so much lighting in place, I can leave it very dark. I try to keep the show dark. . . . I let things go into darkness, where another show may not.

"I like to keep it simple. I like to work with as few units as I can. . . . I like camera movement. We use Steadicam. We use all the tools. At night we use helium weather balloons, white balloons that I fly and bounce light off of to light the sets. I just use any tool that I think will do the job. There is not a set pattern. If I need something, they [the producers of *Buffy*] have been very good. I explain to them what I think I will need to do in the scene and why, and they say okay when at all possible."

**When we were watching you work today, we thought it looked very much like a tag-team kind of operation between director and DP. Is it difficult for you with the TV system of rotating directors, given that you are the constant and they are the variable?**

**MICHAEL:** "It is difficult, inasmuch as it is physically demanding. It is difficult in the area...that some of our directors who come in don't communicate as well as others. When I work with Joss, he can start a sentence and I can finish it or vice versa, because our minds go the same way about where to put the camera and what we are trying to get. And, of all the directors, he is my favorite director. So we have fun.

"It is very much a collaborative effort when it comes to the camera. [Joss] knows what he wants, and he says, 'What if we put the camera over here; yeah, move it over here instead, that is exactly what I want.' It's great when you can work with somebody like that."

**"Passion" was your directorial debut. How was that experience?**

**MICHAEL:** "I had a great script [by Ty King], and I was able to do things. I know the sets, I know the actors. The actors were incredibly helpful to me. All of our producers were helpful to me. They left me alone and just let me do my thing. I think we got a great show out of it."

**Do you light actors in different ways?**

**MICHAEL:** "All of our actors on the show photograph so well. They are young. They have character. The camera loves them. If I were working with actors who were twenty years older than this, it would be more difficult, but you can't light these people badly. Sarah takes any kind of light you can throw at her. She takes it and she looks beautiful. The same with Aly and Charisma. And the guys. You can do anything you want and they look good.

"Again, it is really about keeping it interesting and keeping up with the material, the written word. That is where it all comes from, it comes from Joss. These are Joss's visions that I am trying to interpret. The show is about him. That is where it stems from. Sarah brings it all to life, Sarah and the other actors. These kids have such great personalities. They are kids. They are fresh. Sarah, at twenty, being the youngest member of the cast, has as much or more experience than any of the rest. Other than possibly Tony.... But she nails it time and time again. She is right on. She finds the light, she finds the camera angle, she clears herself if another actor blocks her. She is special.

"I love the show. Everybody on the show works so hard to make it into the show that it is. It's not like any other series that I have ever worked on....

"Everybody loves it, even when we complain, even when we get tired . . . and we're saying, 'We have been here too many hours, let us go home, and we are hungry'...the bottom line is that we all still love it."

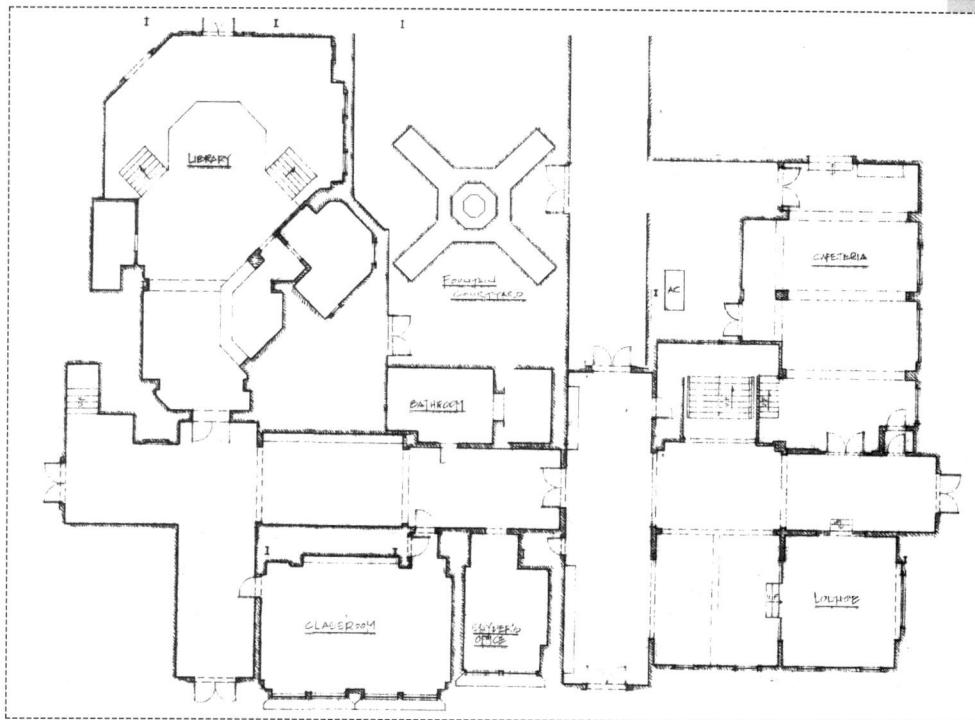

## CAREY MEYER

Carey Meyer became the production designer for *Buffy* at the beginning of the second season after working as the first-season art director. That means he heads the art department, designing all the sets and overseeing their construction and decoration. The title came into being because the art director of *Gone with the Wind* had such a huge impact on the set work, and became such an involved person in the production as well, that the producers felt they needed to give the person a more meaningful credit.

When he begins designing for a new episode, Carey gets the script from Joss and the writers, taking careful note of the list of new sets and locations that he and his team "have to sort of make real."

A soft-spoken man, he sits behind his desk in an office filled with sketches, blueprints, a drafting table, color wheels, and assorted design paraphernalia. A number of sketches dot the wall behind him, including one of the new mansion set.

Armed with a degree in architecture, he studied production design at the American Film Institute in Los Angeles. Then he realized that "nobody wants to hire production designers just because they have a degree," and set out to get some practical experience. He worked as a swing man (a grip) on a few productions, then became a production assistant. Around that time, he had a chance to design a "really, really low-budget" independent film. He got together with a friend who was fresh out of architectural school and they created a team for the film—"very unorthodox, but we put a lot of fun into it."

After that, he started getting more design work, in commercials, music videos and a few more small independent films. He was also art-directing for other designers on various low-budget shows. One of those designers hired him to art-direct a show called *VR Five*—a show on which Tony Head was a regular cast member. All this took approximately six years to achieve after graduating from the AFI.

He worked on TV series, including *Nash Bridges*, and then Steve Hardy, the first-season production designer for *Buffy*, asked him to be the first-season art director. Carey was delighted. "Steve was somebody I had been wanting to work with for a really, really long time. We sort of crossed paths several times, but just hadn't had the opportunity to hook up."

So Carey came to *Buffy*. He "just got really into the show, had a great time, and really, really loved working for Steve." They worked together on a feature titled *Denial* with Adam Rifkin during the first-season hiatus.

Hardy decided to concentrate on feature work, so *Buffy* producer Gareth Davies called Carey and asked him to move up to production designer. It was a big opportunity for Carey, and he decided to cement his position by pitching the idea for the Factory, Spike and Dru's lair, which Buffy burns to the ground during the second season.

Carey reminisces that he wanted to prove to Joss that he could design the show, so the Factory set was very important to him. Though he looked at many pictures of factories from different time periods, what eventually inspired him most was an English library from the Craftsman period. Since much of the vampire look of the show is industrial, he enjoyed creating a set that retained that flavor, yet was layered with something more.

"There's this bizarre kind of amalgamation of different styles and things. As long as it has a feel that is cool.…You know, things happen by chance," he says. "It's not like something that you set out with the rule books saying that 'this is going to be this.' It just evolves."

As an example, Carey tells us the genesis of the underground motif for the vampires:

It began with the lair of the Master, the underground church where he was imprisoned. To get to the lair from aboveground, Steve Hardy introduced sewer pipes. Over time, it became established that there was an extensive sewer system beneath the town. As a result, the underground world of the vampires became "industrial, low-ground, cement, dirt, rust, and grime and that kind of stuff."

Carey recalls that when Kendra was scripted to emerge from the cargo bay of a 747, "We had a bunch of curved walls and things from the set, and I said, 'We could make a really great sewer tunnel out of this stuff, and so all of a sudden, we started shooting all this sewer, this great sewer.…'"

The sewers got used in more and more creative ways. Floors broke away beneath characters to drop them into the sewers; characters chased vampires down into the sewers; or someone popped up from beneath a manhole or a grate. The underground grotto in "Go Fish" is another extension of the underground sewer theme. As is the cavern of the Zeta Delta Kappas in "Reptile Boy."

Over time, the *Buffy* team also realized that the sewer system worked almost like a "transporter" à la *Star Trek*, allowing them to move from one place to another in a confined area.

"It allows us to get somebody in and out of the set in an interesting fashion and having [a connection] from one set to another . . . getting somebody to go somewhere [while trying] to keep the time line going in real time."

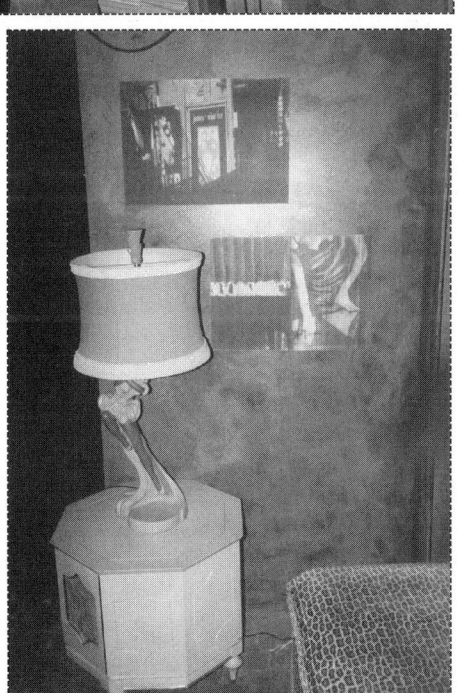

It was also very important to the *Buffy* production company because it cut back on the need to go on location and do big night exteriors. It's more technically difficult and expensive to go on location, especially night location. Carey tells us that a typical day shooting on location lasts for fourteen or fifteen hours, while shooting the equivalent amount of footage on a stage takes twelve or thirteen.

"When we're here on the lot," he continues, "we don't have to do a whole night out. We can have a slightly later call and do the work inside on the stage, and move out to our little graveyard and do half a night, then do the same thing the next night. So it's enabled us to keep all the night work in the show, but also not have to go out for a whole night. If you go out, you're going to go out at six o'clock sundown and be out until morning.

"Gareth [the producer] really got excited about building sets this year and bringing the show to the stage as much as possible.... We've been able to just go hog-wild and build tons of stuff."

### How much stuff?

**CAREY:** "On every other show I've done, we've built one or two permanent sets and then built like one and a half, maybe two, sets per episode. With twenty-two episodes, you figure you can have maybe twenty-five or thirty sets. But this show, I've easily done three sets an episode, so on top of eight permanent sets that we have on stage, we've built between sixty and eighty sets this year, easily. And Caroline Quinn (the set designer) has drawn every one of them."

### Where do you build all these sets?

**CAREY:** "Everything is built essentially in the El Niño building or on the stage. The El Niño building is a temporary structure that we built outside to cover up material and have a dry workspace during the rain, because we didn't have enough space inside to build, and sometimes there will be shooting on both stages. We're constantly creating scenery, and we do everything right here. We don't build anything away from here and then bring it here."

### How big are the stages?

**CAREY:** "Stage I is 26,000 feet. Stage II is 19,000 feet. And the third stage [will be] 14,000 square feet, wedged between the two."

### Did you have any professional connections with anyone prior to working on *Buffy*?

**CAREY:** "I knew some of the costume people from working on *VR5*. Cynthia Bergstrom, the costume designer. And I worked for my decorator, David Konoff, as a swing man on my second job in Los Angeles. It was on *Eve of Destruction*. David and I have worked together ever since I moved to Los Angeles; we've known each other for eleven years."

### Tell us about the new mansion set.

**CAREY:** "When we first started conceiving of the mansion and the secret garden, Joss was driving out of the lot one day and stopped his car, and said, 'By the way, we're working on burning the Factory down.'

"It was a really fun set and I really loved it, and I hated to see it go, but you know Joss. I think Joss likes chaos. Which is good. I like it that way. I don't get very precious about [the sets]...you build them for the camera, you film them, and you rip them down.

"And now we were looking at trying to create a new permanent site. I had to think of a way to utilize the same structural stuff and the same space to create the mansion. So I conceived a floor plan that would mesh with the space of the Factory before I even thought about what the mansion would be like. The geography of the set.

"From there, I found a very Gothic mansion, arches and fireplaces and things like that. But what really attracted me was the coloring of the photograph. It was a photo shoot, so there was a very pretty lady in a large dress, standing in the middle of this decrepit place, which had been in an earthquake or something. The vampires have a sort of different look than Sunnydale, which is very pastel and bright in daytime, aboveground. Our underground spaces for the vampires are industrial and dirty. So I really liked the photograph.

"Joss hated it because it was very Gothic. He wanted to stay away from Gothic because that's very Anne Rice. He said, 'Maybe it could be [Art] Deco or something.' I can do Deco, but I wanted to keep it very cement. If you notice, the set looks like cement."

**Do you have a special moment where it all just clicked for you?**
**CAREY:** "I feel like that seventy-five percent of the time. I really love putting these sets together, bringing everything to a point of completion. We are able to generate sixty or eighty different spaces, making everything look different...without cramming everything into every nook and cranny. It's something you can be proud of."

## MARCIA SHULMAN

A native New Yorker, Marcia loves all things Italiano: the food, the culture, and the language, which she now speaks because she goes every year to Tuscany, where she hopes to eventually retire.

When asked about her professional life and how she came to *Buffy*, she chuckles at the memory. "I was so naive," she says, that when she graduated from college, she went to an employment agency and informed them that she would take their typing tests and all the rest, "but that I really wanted to work in show business."

The agency placed her in a secretarial position at Children's Television Workshop. She was promoted very quickly to the title of talent coordinator, "which had nothing to do with talent. It was more like a production manager kind of function."

A freelance producer had an office next door, and he noticed that not only did Marcia have a photographic memory, but she was obsessed with keeping track of actors and roles: "I always had to know, as long as I can remember, [maybe I was] three years old.... I used to watch credits, look at *TV Guide*, and match the names to the actors. I call myself the Rain Man of casting." The producer informed her that she was a casting director.

As a result of working for CTW, she knew every child actor in New York, and in her capacity there had negotiated contracts. The producer suggested she open her own casting agency, which she did. Her first project was *A Christmas Story*. From then on she did many after-school specials, and then went out to the West Coast to do television. She was on her way back to New York in January 1996 when Gail Berman, her best friend, asked her to talk to Joss about *Buffy*.

She remembers the meeting with fondness: "I think part of it was because I wanted to go home, [so I] threw caution to the wind [with her casting suggestions]. If he didn't like them, I could go home.

"So I said to Joss, 'I read your script and I know casting directors come in with lists and ideas, but I have a problem: Everyone I thought of while I read your script is dead.' And I started naming these really obscure character actors from movies of the '30s and '40s.

I mentioned the name Franklin Pangborn to him. [Pangborn] used to play the butler in Fred Astaire movies."

Marcia chuckles. "Joss said, 'I can't believe it. You're the only person who has ever mentioned that to me. In the *Buffy* movie I made a reference to Franklin Pangborn and they cut it.' It was just such a funny meeting. We have always had that connection. . . . It is really easy to cast for Joss because there is so much trust there. He knows what he wants."

When we asked her about the process of casting for *Buffy*, Marcia explained that she has three different ways of casting: Sometimes when she reads a script, she immediately thinks, "I know who this is." She gets a tape of that actor to show Joss, who knows everybody himself, and he has never disagreed with her suggestion. Sometimes she will jot down a short list of four or five names and ask them to come in and read for the part.

The third process is perhaps what most people think of when they think of casting. Marcia uses it primarily for smaller speaking roles: She breaks down the part, then looks through the voluminous numbers of submissions (she points to an enormous file cabinet brimming with agent submissions), and then she sits down on the floor and looks through all of them. Then she does a pre-read of those actors who make that cut, and then she presents Joss, David Greenwalt, or Gail Berman with a handful of possibilities.

In some ways, she tells us, it is more difficult to cast the smaller roles. Generally, the actors have less experience, and are hungry for a chance to show their stuff. So they "try to do more, but they only have one line to do and then it becomes over the top. It is really hard for somebody to come in and throw it away."

She gives the example of the shoot today, when they were filming the "Buffy gets arrested" scene. When she was casting for the cops' roles, "there were people who came in and they were like, 'FREEZE!' It was like the *Airplane* version. We said, 'This is a cop, he does this every day, these are kids.' Less is more."

She adds, "The thing about *Buffy* is that it is very real. The acting is very real. You can't comment on the show [in your acting]. When I first started casting for the pilot, people would come in and do *Dracula* kind of readings. But now that it has been on the air, people see it, and they get it."

Casting about seven parts per episode, she says that the process takes "as long as you have. It's like water seeking its own level. It's like production: if you have five days to shoot something, it will take five days. If you have eight days, it will take eight....There have been many times in my career where a director I am working for will say, 'It's fine. I got it', and I will just continue to cast, secretly. I have to keep looking. Thank God I have this job."

She adds, "The other very interesting thing about this project as opposed to a lot of stuff is that there are really fun, great, fantastic characters to create. We sort of live in a world of typecasting, and on this show, which is what I love about the show so much, actors get a chance to act and create. These are characters. It is like why you want to be an actor. It is playing. You really don't get a chance to do that on other television shows."

**What about the famous "David Boreanaz was walking his dog" story?**

**MARCIA:** "[Angel] was supposed to be in just the first episode. Sort of like a vision. . . . The character was supposed to start working the next day. I said to Joss, 'Just give me one more day. I don't feel like he is there yet.'

"[The person who became David's manager] was looking out the window as David was walking his dog. He's a friend of mine, and he called me and he said, 'I am telling you, I just saw Angel. I can send him.' David walked in and I ran down the hall [to Joss.]"

*She flips through her casting book.* "9-9-96. I wrote, 'He is the guy.'"

**How did you know Sarah Michelle Gellar was Buffy?**

**MARCIA:** "We didn't know she was Buffy. I knew Sarah from New York, when she was a kid, as I knew Seth Green from when they were eight years old. At the time we were all trying to find our way to make the show something, its own thing apart from the film. Sometimes it's sort of hard to get a new vision going. So we didn't think of Sarah as Buffy because we thought she [Sarah] was too smart and too grounded and not enough of a misfit in a sense, because Buffy was this outsider. How could Sarah be an outsider? She's so lovely.

"So we brought her in as Cordelia, and she was fantastic as Cordelia. We still kept looking for Buffy. Then when we went to the network, they [knew] that Sarah was a star [from her previous work], and that she could be a Buffy, and that we could do that Buffy. It was a different Buffy. It was a great Buffy."

**Then how did you cast a new Cordelia?**

**MARCIA:** "I had met Charisma before, and I brought her in and she just nailed it. She was hysterically funny. . . . She was just great and beautiful and she brought so much to it."

**What about Willow?**

**MARCIA:** "Willow was really hard. Because when you think about it, the kind of character Willow is—a sort of shy, insecure person—is the exact opposite of what somebody has to be as an actress. So it was like working against who came in and had the nerve to audition.

"When Alyson came in, we all got her immediately. I had pre-read her first and then brought her to everyone else and we felt good. She just brings so much vulnerability. She makes me cry all the time and she is also funny. She is an 'everygirl.' I think Willow is the kind of character that there is someone like her in high school...or most of the girls in high school are like her."

**What about casting Nicholas Brendon as Xander?**

**MARCIA:** "Nicky also came in [via the pre-reading process]. I read him and then I brought him to the guys and every time he came for callback, he brought more and more to it. When we went to the network for everybody to see him, he improvised a line, which was, 'Let's go get some schwarma.' And now we have used it in the show. I think that gave him the part. We all just died and so the part was his."

**Tell us about Tony Head as Giles.**

**MARCIA:** "I had brought him in the first day and we all just completely fell in love with him. I was so happy because when you start working for somebody new, you always want the first day of casting to be good. Because you want [your boss] to say, 'Good,' so you can stay for the second day. When everybody responded to Tony the first day, I said to Gail, 'I'm so happy Joss is happy today.' Tony was a no-brainer. Like David [as Angel]."

**And the newest regular, Seth Green.**
**MARCIA:** [smiling] "Seth and I...we get each other. When I knew Sarah Michelle Gellar and Seth [in New York], you brought them in on everything. They were really star kids. And now they are star adults, and no surprise."

**What about some guest stars?**
**MARCIA:** "James Marsters came in on the pre-read process. But I am always partial to theatrical training on a résumé [which James had]. In New York, it's not even a question. Out here it is very different. With Juliet Landau, I knew her. I got a tape of her and I went in to Joss. Same with Armin Shimerman. Merrick is Richard Riehle, a really wonderful actor I know from New York."

**Did you have professional associations with anyone prior to the show?**
**MARCIA:** "When I met Joss, I didn't think it was appropriate to say anything, but when he hired me, I said, 'I have a question for you: is your father Tom Whedon?' When I was just out of college, and working on *Sesame Street*, Tom was a writer on *The Electric Company*. And Gail and I have been best friends for seventeen years, and we get to work together. That is so great for me. That never happens. You know, you get to work with one of your best girlfriends every day, and we have this sharing and this mutual respect. It is an incredible thing."

**Do you have any tattoos, scars, or other distinguishing marks?**
**MARCIA:** "Since I started working on this show, I have broken both my ankles. . . . I kept saying, they're going to talk about me like, you know, 'that casting director, the one with the limp.'"

**Do you have a special moment?**
**MARCIA:** "Well the David moment, because it was so hard to find [Angel] and he walked in the day before we were shooting, but there are so many moments. This is a really special group.

"Joss has such a complete vision and you sort of come not to expect in your career that [working on a show] is going to be such a cohesive thing. It is crazy to produce this number of shows on this schedule. That goes with the territory. I am always amazed that a group of people can carry out a vision that it is somehow communicated through the writing, and through who Joss is as a person. It is a very unique situation. It is why I want to do *Buffy*."

## CYNTHIA BERGSTROM

From the chaos of the set, we enter the relative calm of the costume-design department. At first glance, it seems like either a particularly odd flea market or the private closet of a particularly eclectic dresser. Either way, it's fascinating. Off to the left is the office of the series' costume designer, Cynthia Bergstrom. A former model, Cynthia is tall and beautiful...and an impeccable dresser.

The office is unlike any other we see on our visit. Candles burn brightly within. When she wants a glass of water, Cynthia pours from a crystal decanter. Her dog, Sammy, who has an injured paw, makes himself at home. It's a very soothing retreat for a woman whose job is often the opposite. But you don't hear Cynthia complaining. She loves it. Clothing and fashion have always been her passion.

"I've been doing costumes for about ten years, but I've always been involved in fashion;

when I was a little girl, I was a runway model and I did some print work. I used to sit with the encyclopedias as a kid and look at the history of clothing. Look at period clothing and historical pieces and patterns to see how the clothes were constructed. I'd watch old movies.

"One of things that really sort of, I think, tied Joss and me together was the fact that we both grew up watching *Creature Feature*. I watched all those bad horror movies, and I loved them. I especially loved the Dracula movies—the vampire movies—because I just was so mystified by everything. I loved the fantasy of it. So that kind of solidified our relationship right there. We had bonded through Bela Lugosi and Christopher Lee."

Cynthia attended Brooks College in Long Beach, California, where she majored in fashion design and merchandising. She entered the working world as a wholesale rep for ESPRIT.

"I handled thirteen western states, and then I went to another company, and I was really longing for something else. I just felt there was something else. Then I remembered watching movies and watching television as a little girl and wondering who put the clothes on these people. I just woke up one day and I said, 'I want to be a costume designer.' It must have been one of those things that was meant to be because a friend called me a week later and said he was doing a film and he needed my help. One thing led to another, and ever since then, I have been designing."

That initial film was a low-budget horror piece called *Zombie High*, with Virginia Madsen. Though it was never what she set out to do, it seems Cynthia's early love of horror films set a course for her. From that first picture, she worked on several other horror films, all the way up to the smash hit *Scream*, which is what drew the attention of *Buffy*'s producers.

"As I recall, Joss really liked the way the kids looked, because they were so believable; they were so real," she says. "So they tracked me down. I'm not one hundred percent sure on that story, but that is what I've gathered from Joss and the producers."

Interestingly, though she worked on so many horror films, Cynthia confesses to a distaste for most of the current crop.

"I like the older ones," she says. "I don't like the new horror films. I don't like slash gore. I like stories. Like in this show [*Buffy*]. There is nothing like it out there. It is fantasy, yet it is real at the same time. A lot of the story lines are so metaphoric for what really goes on in life."

Cynthia buys much of the show's "contemporary" wardrobe (as opposed to historical costumes) in stores in Los Angeles. Some designers send her things directly, such as Cynthia Rowlie and Vivian Tam. In L.A., she often shops Fred Siegel, Barney's, American Rag, Contempo Casuals, Rampage, Macy's, Neiman Marcus, Traffic (in the Beverly Center), Bloomingdale's, and the Tommy Hilfiger store on Rodeo Drive.

"I really go just about everywhere," she says.

On historical or "period" costumes, there is a great deal of research involved. Cynthia enjoys the challenge.

"I look at costume books," she explains. "I'll pick a painter that I particularly like that was of that time and look at his treatments of color. I have some books here and I have tons of books at home. Sometimes I'll call the research houses and I'll have them pull things for me, but I am typically a pretty hands-on designer, so I like to do my own research. I always figure there is something that I'm going to see that nobody else is going to see. I go to museums and I study paintings; knowing your periods is part of being a costume designer. Knowing the construction of a garment; being able to look at something and being able to say, 'This is the sixteenth century; this is the seventeenth century.' It is important to know those things. I do continually study, and also movies are a great way to study periods, you know. You can always turn on AMC and catch those period films."

It isn't just the look of the clothes that's important, however. A Hollywood costume designer has to worry about other things, including how the clothes **sound**. It sounds like a joke, perhaps, but it isn't. Cynthia puts rubber soles on the bottoms of all the actors' shoes so they don't make noise that could be distracting if picked up by the sound equipment during shooting.

"I've taken fabrics and washed them in softener," she adds. "Especially rayon, because it can get kind of noisy. Heat will soften the fabric as well."

The clothing also has to be treated to fireproof it.

"Everything has to be of natural fibers: wool, cotton…rayon is actually a natural fiber. But I can't use any synthetics because they'll burn. We have a certified fire-proofer that does it. It's dipped and sprayed. A lot of things are taken into consideration when the clothes go on these people. Buffy has multiple costumes. She is either getting dunked in water or she is fighting, whatever might be happening, she needs a change."

Cynthia needs to have a philosophy about each character she dresses. To understand exactly how that is developed, it would help to know how she analyzes them. Jenny Calendar for instance.

"Though she was a computer instructor, she was a very beautiful woman," Cynthia explains of Jenny. "She was a combination of old-world guile and the kids she was teaching. A combination of her past as well as today's technology. I knew that she was a Gypsy and that she was sent to watch over Angel and that her family had cast a spell on him. With all that in mind, I gave her colors and silhouettes and textures and patterns that were somewhat of that Romanian Gypsy influence. If you notice, her colors have sort of a vibrant, earthy tone, and I used really tiny little paisley, and everything was new yet old. Her jewelry was always some sort of reproduction of a vintage piece. She was the easiest one to find things for, because I was so specific about what I wanted for her. It was really hard to stop looking for clothes for her when I was out in the stores. Cindy [Rosenthal, one of Cynthia's costumers] and I would go around shopping, and she'd say 'You know, Jenny isn't on the show anymore.'

"Then there's Angel," she continues. "Angel's shirts have to be spectacularly different and European. But lot of times you don't get all of the detail on TV that is really there in his wardrobe. I've taken that into consideration and—especially now that he is bad—I've really toned down a lot of detailing on his shirts. The clothes on him should be sexy, whether he is good or bad. I experimented with lighter colors in the beginning, when he was still good; it just didn't work, it wasn't really his thing so I stuck with the darker colors."

Drusilla has also changed, Cynthia notes. As Angel went from good to bad, Dru went from weak to strong.

"We first saw her in her ivory gown that to me was a timeless image of a woman," she recalls. "She was killed in 1860, and this dress is about the late 1800s, from the romantic period. She started out as a very sort of insane, willowy, soft, sickly, consumptive woman. I was really taking off from the women that you sometimes saw in the Dracula movies from the '60s. I sort of saw her like that, but not quite so, you know, girly. I toned down the dress, and I just gave her an empire waist. Then, as she grew weaker, I put her in bad clothing, and I had that nightgown she walked out of the Factory in [in the second part of "What's My Line?"]. Then when she does her ritual, she's in a black dress. I wanted something that looked very medieval, but yet still had a sense of the future. It needed to look powerful yet soft at the same time, that is why I chose velvet."

Then there's Drusilla's paramour:

"Spike is just a bad-ass character," Cynthia says. "He's just great. He's really funny, and he's quirky, and he's got this white-blond hair and this English accent. He just needs to be a bat; to just sweep in like a bat. His coat cost $1,600, and we literally beat the heck out of it. We took down the shine and sandpapered and really distressed it. And his clothes are also just a bit distressed."

Cynthia loves the writing on the show, particularly when it offers her a challenge.

"When I am able to do something different, when I see an opportunity to build something, that's exciting," she says. "In 'Inca Mummy Girl,' there was a dance where we had people coming dressed as their nationality, and that was so fun. Then, of course, the 'Halloween' episode; it wasn't just dressing people in Halloween costumes, it was doing Buffy in her dress and Cordelia in her cat suit, and I just went to Joss and asked, 'Can I do something a little fun?' It is such a wonderful opportunity, because I know they trust me. I am given a lot of creative freedom. It's a great feeling."

It's impossible not to ask if Cynthia envies the wardrobe she buys for the characters. What does she like?

"I like all of it. Fridays I'm in jeans and T-shirts. But I have a tendency to dress a little conservatively. Some of the miniskirts that I put the girls in, I'll try them on. It is so fun. Little black miniskirts and knee-high boots, which I did end up buying a pair of for myself. It is so much fun to dress like that. I couldn't wear that to work, of course. In my personal life, I'll go a little bit more out on the edge, but at work I have to keep things rather serious."

## JEFF PRUITT

It's impossible to look at Jeff Pruitt and believe a word of his résumé. He seems far too young to have risen so high in his chosen field. Now stunt coordinator for *Buffy*, Jeff has held that position on more than fifteen feature films and five television series, including *Mighty Morphin Power Rangers* and *The New Adventures of Robin Hood*. Previously, he had performed stunts in dozens of films and TV series.

Jeff is the only American stunt coordinator to have belonged to an Asian stunt team. He has specialized in Hong Kong–style stunts for more than ten years. He has more than twenty years experience in martial-arts combat, and, surprisingly, Jeff himself directed and edited more than half of each episode for the second season of *Power Rangers*.

During our visit to the set, Jeff was omnipresent. Setting up stunts, or "gags," he was informative and inclusive at all times. We interviewed him at a picnic table on the grass by the cemetery set on the lot. He was friendly and forthcoming and broke the news that he was engaged to Sophia Crawford, the stunt double for Sarah Michelle Gellar. Sophia is also one of only four women in America who do both stunts and martial-arts fight sequences. The two seem quite evenly matched. When they see each other on the lot, their faces light up.

He's at the top of his game. But one must wonder, what leads a person to get into this very dangerous game to begin with?

"In the '60s I watched *The Green Hornet, Our Man Flint; Wild Wild West* was a big show. All of these shows and the 007 films—they all got me interested in stunts. I knew that's what I wanted to do, and that is where I headed—especially with the martial-arts action. *The Green Hornet* was the first time I had ever seen someone leaping and kicking and I knew this is what I wanted to do.

"From the time I was a kid, I trained in martial arts and I did motocross racing and I raced cars and things like that. As things progressed, I started working on films and also worked as a production assistant and as a cameraman and things like that, until I was able to break through. This is a tough business. Finally, when I made it to Hollywood in the late '80s, it took me a couple of years to get in the door here, even though I had some credits. I started coordinating some shows here in about '89, and that's all I've been doing."

Though his time is at a premium, Jeff knows the value of his fans. He spends time on the official *Buffy* Web site talking to them. "I have a whole closet full of sweatshirts and T-shirts made by the fans," he says happily. "They know all about me and Sophia and our show."

"I normally block everything out with my story boards and choreograph the fight with Sophia. Then Sarah and I will watch it. We shoot closeups of her doing the stunts, and then we edit it together."

Now that Jeff's brought her up, of course, we want to know everything about his love, Sophia Crawford.

"Sophia trained in Hong Kong," Jeff says. "She came here and starred in a film series. When I did *Power Rangers*, I hired her to be the Pink Ranger, so she did all the stunts for the Pink Ranger. We worked together for four years before *Buffy* ever started."

They didn't come as a package deal, however. Sophia was on the series from the beginning. After the first season, a new stunt coordinator was hired, but he didn't work out after the first episode. "I wanted to come in and meet Joss, but he was nervous because of us being a couple. He'd seen my work, and he liked my work but he thought *Well, we've had problems with people who are couples and then have a fight and then they don't want to work together.* For the girl who does all the fighting for Buffy and the guy who designs all the fights...for them not to be able to get along would be terrible. But, he gave me a chance, and I started working, then he saw that we worked together well."

In the early days, though, Jeff and Sophia spent a lot of time just checking each other out.

"For two years, she would wear the Pink Ranger helmet and she would be looking at me. But I couldn't see that she was looking at me and I would try to work on my story boards, but I was really looking at her. We kept doing this for so long. Finally, during the Power Ranger movie, we started dating and we never stopped. And we are going to get married now."

Jeff reveals their impending nuptials casually. You'd never know there was a moment of anxiety that spurred on his proposal. It was after a stunt that, Jeff says, "scared me so much that I decided that I had better marry her now.

"It was during the episode 'Phases.' Sophia had to walk onto a net, and the effects guys had rigged the net with 300 pounds of counterweight. I told them that I weigh 150 pounds and normally when we do stunts like this, I just jump down and jerk her straight up. They felt that they needed extra weight. They said they had tested it with some dummy weights before and it was okay. So we did it and she shot up....We had the camera up at about thirty feet in the air. She went past the camera and came out at the top of the net. Then as she

was falling, she grabbed hold of the outside of the net and snapped to a halt before she hit the ground, and it snapped her neck back. She was okay. She got up and she did it again. We took all the weight out and we did it the right way. After that, that same night, I asked her to marry me.

"We do so many hard stunts, and we're not blasé. Sometimes Sophia and I will fight each other, I have her really kick me, really hit me, because we come from that background of more Hong Kong–style fighting. They're not really used to seeing that, so it freaks them out a little bit, but it's our job; it seems like normal, everyday stuff to us. It was just that one time it did bother me, because I wasn't in control of it. As long as we're in control, it's okay. Equipment failure I don't like."

## *BUFFY THE VAMPIRE SLAYER*
Stunt Coordinator: Jeff Pruitt

PAGE 13.

BUFFY & KENDRA EXCHANGE HAND TECHNIQUES AND BLOCKS BUFFY'S PUNCH...

KENDRA TURNS AND THROWS BUFFY OVER ONTO THE COFFEE TABLE – SMASHING IT TO PIECES.

AS KENDRA REACHES DOWN, BUFFY KICKS UP BOTH FEET TO KENDRA'S FACE – KNOCKING HER BACK.

Even though he's the coordinator, Jeff doesn't miss out on the action. Anytime he gets the itch, he jumps right in.

"Sometimes I put myself in just for the heck of it. I still like getting out there. As a matter of fact, in the episode "Lie to Me," you see Buffy whaling on this guy with a trash-can lid. That's me. That was one of those days when I told her to just go ahead and hit me as hard as you can. So every shot she was hitting me and the crew was just freaking out. Certain stunt guys I know will do that."

Though at times, fights are described in the series' scripts, and Jeff doesn't necessarily follow those directions.

"I find out what the feeling is before, during, and after the fight. Unless there is something specific, some specific prop or someplace a character has to be...then I know that's where they have to end up. But what happens during the whole thing is pretty much up to me. I guess Joss has come to trust me pretty much on that.

"This final fight that we are going to do [for season two] involves some very specific attitude between Buffy and Angel and how they feel about each other. So that was not as fancy as some of our other fights but more emotional. Each fight has a different flavor to it."

In the case of Buffy, because Sophia has exactly the same body type as Sarah and the ability to do fights and stunts, she does all the doubling for Buffy. For other characters, however, Jeff chooses from a range of stunt people whose services he calls upon depending on what the particular fight calls for.

Of his favorite moments on the set, Jeff says there is one that doesn't have anything to do with stunts or fighting. That would be working with John Ritter.

"'Ted' is not a great fighting episode," he says. "But I enjoyed John Ritter. Now there was a nice guy to work with. He was so sick that day, and he brought me my pads back all separated neatly and put in little plastic bags and gave them back to me. No one had ever done that before. They usually just rip them off and fling them. I have never met a guy like him before, he is so great. He's super."

Despite the fact that there isn't much fighting in "Ted," Jeff remembers that episode for another reason. After shooting a fight from several angles, one particular shot was included that was from the wrong angle.

"There is a miss," Jeff says incredulously. "There is an actual miss. There is a high angle of John Ritter's stunt double just before he goes upstairs, and it is a big miss. I made a big deal about that, because it makes me look bad. But those things happen."

One of the things that Jeff enjoys most about working on *Buffy* is that it is a story-driven show.

"I've walked into a room full of executives as they are rewriting a script," he recalls. "These are guys whose experience in movies is watching movies when they were in law school. That was their experience in making films. But there they are, saying, 'And then the old master trains them….' and I'm saying, 'We've seen all of that before a million times.' So many shows have been like that. But now, with *Buffy*, the writers are actually in charge of the show. God, it's great. It is original, it is witty, it is different, and it is cool."

## TODD MCINTOSH AND JERI BAKER

Todd McIntosh is more than merely the makeup supervisor for *Buffy the Vampire Slayer*. He is friend, father-confessor, and sometimes even chef to many of the people who work on the series with him. Chef? Well, don't tell Hanna Mourad, who is the on-set chef for the series, but Todd has been known to whip up a meal now and again. One particular night, he cooked for David Boreanaz, Nicholas Brendon, and James Marsters, who all then went online on the official *Buffy* web site's posting board. Marsters called the meal "amazing," and everyone enjoyed chatting on the posting board. That's something else Todd does a lot of—taking care of the fans. Everyone talks about the series' star, Sarah Michelle Gellar, as being nurturing. It's a sure bet that Todd gives her a run for her money.

He's also one of the best makeup men in the business.

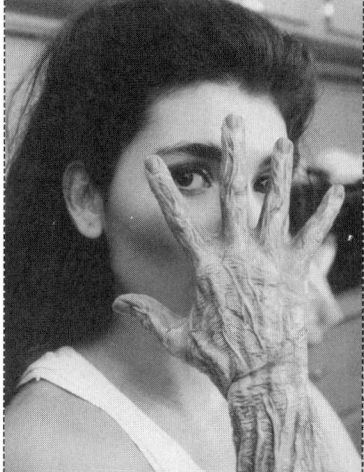

After the morning's makeup session is through, Todd and hair department head Jeri Baker invite us into the trailer where the makeup and hair crew work. The room is festooned with photographs of actors and stuntmen in very nasty-looking monster makeup and, of course, in the glamour makeup that the cast wears while filming.

As makeup supervisor, Todd is also the department head, and liaison to Optic Nerve, the special makeup effects house that creates the prosthetics for the show.

"The design phase of everything that we do goes on between Joss and whoever upstairs needs to do the budget and John Vulich at Optic Nerve," Todd explains. "They design, then they send me the drawings. I look at the drawings, give my input, then when it comes to actually doing the makeup, they drop the appliances on my doorstep. I pick them up and take them to work. I put the makeup on that day, and the coloring and finishing of the makeup is my end of the deal. So it's a complete symbiotic group among Jeri Baker, John Vulich, the actor, myself, and, of course, Joss, who comes in to see what I've done with the coloring and okay it."

The department includes Todd, his second-in-command, John Maldonado, Jeri Baker, Dugg Kirkpatrick and Francine Shermaine. When necessary (for instance, when there is a larger-than-usual number of vampires in an episode), Todd and Jeri both use union makeup and hair artists for additional coverage.

As for how long the actors have to sit in the makeup chair, the answer differs, of course, depending on exactly what needs to be done that day.

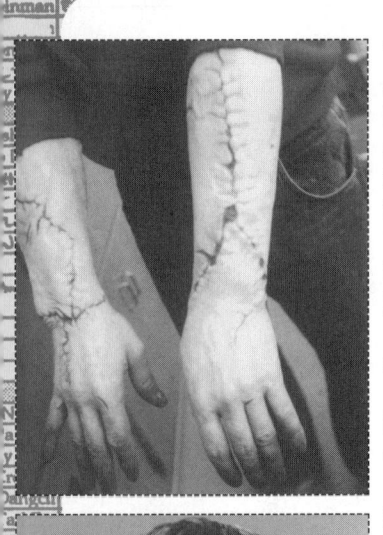

"Beauty makeup on our show takes no more than half an hour," Todd says. "The monsters, if you're doing regular vampires, take about one to two hours. If I do it, I can get it down to forty-five minutes, but if new people who have never done the show do it, they all get two hours to put one on. The removal time is about half an hour to forty-five minutes, whether it has been put on to last all day or put on for five minutes."

He notes that when an actor, in this instance, David Boreanaz, has to morph into vamp face only briefly, they are able to put the vampire prosthetic on with a water-soluble glue.

"It's not very stable and won't stay on for long, but we can peel it off without damaging the skin too much," Todd explains.

The conversation turns to the subject of stunt doubles, and the difficulty involved in making them look like the stars they're doubling for on film.

"Unlike feature films again, where you can take the time to make a prosthetic so that the stunt double looks like the actor, we don't have that luxury," Todd explains. "Buffy's stunt double is Sophia Crawford. Sophia is a magnificent martial-arts person. There are times when we will be watching the show and it's her, but it's so perfect, and Sarah and Sophia have found a way to look like each other. Sarah watches Sophia, and Sophia watches Sarah, and the two of them have merged into twins, in their expressions, turns and movements. You really have a magnificent combination of actors and stunt people, hair and makeup people."

Obviously, McIntosh and Baker are true professionals, individuals working a fine craft that is often overlooked. But how does one prepare for a career doing makeup or hair in film and television? Good question, but one without a simple answer. Or, perhaps, many different answers. For instance, one would be hard put to find two individuals who came at the industry from more divergent origins.

Todd McIntosh knew what he wanted to do from childhood.

"I was about seven years old, watching *Dark Shadows* on TV, and I was so totally fascinated with what I was seeing," he recalls. "*Star Trek* was on at the same time. I started to do what makeup I could, to make myself into a vampire or whatever, with my mother's eyeliner pencil that was lying around. I used to Scotch tape my ears into a point like Mr. Spock, and that moved me into theater makeup.

"I was in the theater by the time I was twelve, doing makeup. I was at a TV studio at seventeen, being paid to do makeup, and in my early twenties I was chairman of the local union in Vancouver, doing makeup full-time. I moved here when I was in my thirties. So I'm over twenty years in the business now. But it all started with *Dark Shadows*, and that, to me, was a perfect makeup show. Again, you had beauty makeup—you had Angelique, you had all the pretty young girls—your regular characters and your monsters. It was the closest possible thing that I could ever hope for as a model for this show.

"For me, *Buffy* is like coming full circle. I'm doing a vampire show, which I've always been fascinated by, doing beauty and horror, and it's a chance to really shine in all of those fields. There have to be at least 800 makeup artists in the Hollywood local. Out of that 800, there are really not very many who do beauty makeup and special makeup in equal quantities, with equal dedication. For those of us who do that, and like to shine that way, this is the place. This is the best gig in town."

Jeri Baker's background couldn't be more different from Todd's. She didn't start out with any intention of working in Hollywood. In fact, she was in medicine.

"I was a surgical nurse for thirteen years," she explains. "I developed an allergy to one of the chemicals we used. Allergies are all the same. If you don't find out what the allergy is, you keep on getting exposed to it until your body builds up so much resistance to it that it is dangerous. By the time they figured out what was wrong with me, I was too toxic, and they told me I wasn't going to survive. For two years, the therapist was trying to keep me alive and when they finally did, they decided I had to have a new career, so they came in and retrained me.

"Hairdressing was the only thing that they felt was cheap enough to put me through. So I went through hairdressing school, but I had problems with some of the chemicals. Then a makeup artist in Burbank named Laurie Stein helped me do a project, and he liked my work, and we started talking and he asked me what my background was, and when I told him he was quite interested. He felt my nursing background and art talent would be great assets. So I did all the training films for the medical corps for the Navy and makeup simulation and then one thing led to another....When you're breaking into the industry you have to do both hair and makeup and climb the ladder. So that's what I did.

"I was on a television series that turned union, and I had to make a decision," she recalls.

The union required that members be one thing or the other. Jeri was leaning toward makeup, but was already working with one of the best-known makeup artists in the business. In order to stay with the show, and make a decent salary, she chose to do the hair on the series. She hasn't regretted it for a moment.

"In nursing, you're problem-solving, and in this you're doing the same sort of thing. You have to figure things out, some things I didn't know, or weren't possible, but I made do and it worked. For instance, one of my first experiences was with a wig that the director hated. He didn't know what he was going to do since the whole story hinged on the actor—who had very short hair—having long hair. I took the wig and took the actor with me and opened up the wig and started to find all these little bands inside. I cut them out and placed each one of them at the hairline, all the way around, so it looked more like hair. It became what today would be called hair extensions, but in 1990 hair

extensions for Caucasians weren't that big. It wasn't something you were taught in school, just something you had to figure out.

"That's the fun part about the job. A lot of our work is pulled out of our imagination and has to be done quickly. Sometimes it's the best work we do, because it's done with a whole lot of energy. Without a doubt, it's a craft; it's a skill, but then after you learn a skill, you have to be able to take it further than that."

Jeri has her own take on vampires as well, one that ties in rather nicely with the bloodsuckers on *Buffy*.

"Vampires are the ultimate seduction. This a creature that can seduce on any level. It can seduce a dog, a child, an adult, an elderly person, on their level. There has to be a certain amount of physical attraction for anyone to start a seduction. If you make everything ugly, there is no seduction. You have to make it so that you're pulled into it. Like, I want to be there but 'ooh that's bad.' That gives the woman the feeling of 'Wow, the big bad boy.' That's what Angel came out of. It had to be beautiful. There had to be something about them that you would rather be with them than be safe."

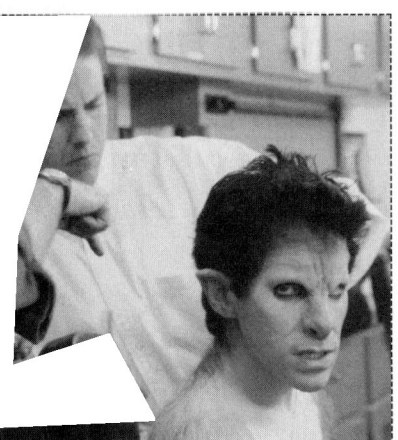

One aspect of doing makeup for television and motion pictures that people rarely consider is the lighting. How a set is lit is something that makeup artists must consider very carefully.

"The makeup that you use for film and television is already color-balanced for the lighting and for the circumstance. So I don't need to change the makeup for each scene when they change the lighting. But, if I walk through a scene and everything is amber and I didn't expect it to be, then all my colors have to be changed. I may have to take makeup out there [onto the set] and do the final touches in that lighting.

"The first season, we had a character called the Master who required a lot of subtle highlight, shadow, and coloring because he was so white. Every time I did it, he went out onto the set and the thing was lit for candlelight [amber] and everything was gone, and he just looked like a big, blobby head. So I finally had them light this end station [in the makeup trailer] with gels that matched the set. I would come in here, turn out all the lights, close the doors and paint the appliances under that light so it would look normal. I finally got this system down, painted the appliances, put them on him, took them up to the set and they hit him with a white spotlight! I don't know, you do the best you can. That's all you can do.

"The lighting alters all the colors. Sometimes you've got a problem area on a prosthetic; if the light is coming from one direction, the edge is huge. If it's coming from another direction, it's gone. So we often coordinate with Michael Gershman, the director of photography. I tell him what my problems are, and he does what he needs to do to adjust it. If he sees something that he thinks I can help him with, I go in and do that. We work very hand-in-hand, and Michael is really good that way. He's one of the few I have found who is very open to communication both ways. A lot of DPs are just, 'That makeup doesn't look any good. Change it,' when really the problem is the light. There's no back-and-forth communication. But we work very well on this show."

Despite that teamwork, however, Todd and Jeri agree that some mistakes just can't be helped.

"Sometimes you can't do anything about it. We knew it was a mistake, we knew going in it was a problem, but couldn't get it changed," Todd says.

"People are walking in and out of lights," Jeri notes. "At one point, they may look absolutely fabulous, and the next thing they walk into the light and it's turning them a whole other hair color, and you just look at it and people are saying, 'Look how it keeps changing back and forth!' The light sources make the effect."

Because synthetic hair will change color differently, and because it almost never looks quite right, Jeri tries to use real hair whenever possible. Even better when a desired 'look' can be achieved with an actor's own hair.

"Ninety percent of the time, we try to work with what we have, because of the lighting problems," she notes. "Nothing looks more wonderful than someone's natural hair. If I have to do a piece, I like to try to match the person's hair or try to use the hair piece in the back of the head, with the front of their own, and try to make a great color blend. Wigs are wigs. You can spend $5,000 on a wig, but it doesn't necessarily mean the audience is going to buy it. That's when you really have to talk to everyone involved and try to come up with a solution that works best. The worst thing that can happen to a hairdresser is that you get this gorgeous hairstyle going and then somebody comes along and dumps a hat on it, or they put the actor up against a dark background when they're brunette and the hair just kind of fades off into the background. We spend so much time trying to make something happen, and then all of a sudden it's gone in the light."

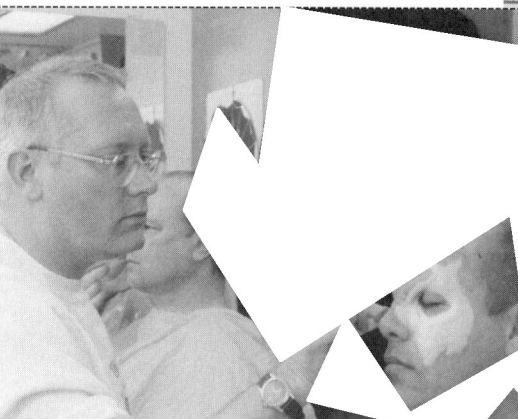

Talk in the trailer turns to the looks of individual characters, and then Jeri drops a bombshell. She whips out a head shot of James Marsters before he was cast as Spike. The dashingly handsome brunette actor looks more like a soap opera star than a punk bloodsucker.

"He was so flamboyant that he needed to be either one way or the other, either have black hair or white hair," Jeri says. "But since Drusilla has dark hair, I thought he should go to white hair. It needed to be a statement one way or the other. So they were afraid, and asked that I just make him blond, so I sent him out to a friend of mine, asking that he be made white. I took a chance. His hair was very curly and very close to his head, but when he came back after having his hair bleached, the texture of the hair had changed. So when I cut it, I came up with this beautiful wave pattern because the bleach allowed the hair to mellow out. He walked into wardrobe, put his outfit back on and walked in front of Gail and Joss, and they all just went crazy. 'That's what we wanted all the time!' When everybody's ideas come together, it's the best.

"That's what I really love about Joss and Gail and David, is that they have allowed us and trusted me with changing some things that they were kind of not sure would be the way to go, but they trusted me. They've let me do some really cool things. I don't think Spike would be Spike without it. We had a character called the Master, and his original design came up with hair. Todd showed me the pictures of it, and I said no, I didn't want that. So he said, you go fight for it.

"I went to the producers and told them that he had to be bald. So they said, 'You're a hairdresser, why are you going to take someone's hair off?' 'Well, this is a character that's been dead for a long time and has no human characteristics and no heart for anyone. Hair is a very human characteristic. If you take hair away from them, all of a sudden they lose their human connection. Just like that. That's the way I think we should go with it.' They agreed to give it a shot and the Master was amazingly cold and cruel and heartless, and you felt nothing for him in any sense as a human being. As a hairdresser, it's hard to give up the idea of hair, but Todd is a magnificent artist, and we talked about it, and he agreed with me that it was a good fight, and he fought for it."

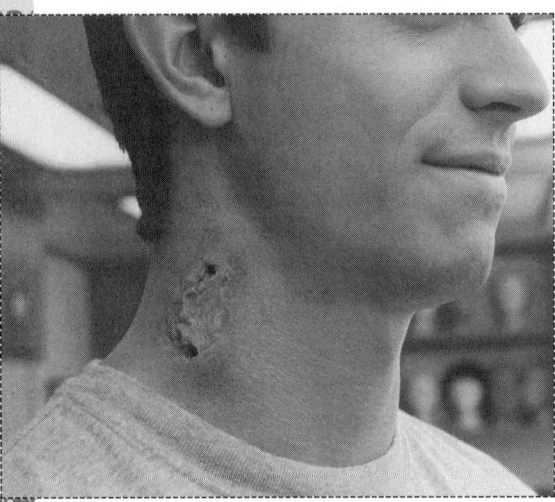

Back to Todd and monsters. It's interesting to note that the maestro waxes poetic about beauty makeup and about monster makeup. One wonders if he has a preference.

"*Buffy* is the perfect show for me, because I like both in equal amounts," he explains. "I started out wanting to do special makeup, but I was raised in Vancouver, and at that time there was nothing up there. Now they have *Outer Limits,* but at that time I couldn't get a job. There was nothing. So I taught beauty makeup and ended up doing beauty makeup in film and television more than effects. While it wasn't my first love, I grew to enjoy it very much, and this is an example of the kind of show that is a perfect meld between the two. I enjoy that more than anything else about it. There's not one makeup I like more or one person I like working on more. People keep asking me what's the most difficult makeup, what's the most elaborate—it's the whole show. It's being able to have two stations set up at a time and jump from a beauty makeup to a prosthetic makeover, all within the same morning. That's what makes this exciting, for me anyway."

Todd is also quick to note that one isn't necessarily more elegant than the other. Though it might be hard to imagine for those who have seen too many low-budget horror films.

"The trouble is that people seem to think that if you throw a lot of blood on something, everybody goes, 'Ooh, isn't that wonderful?'" he notes. "But if you take the blood away and take a good photograph of the work, it's often really crude, you can see the edges sticking out, where they've used a false strip and it's not even glued down properly."

"I'm never going to do shows with a lot of gore. I have done them. I did *Hideaway,* for example, but most of the gore effects were cut out at the end to get the ratings down. But that's not where true artistry lies. [Watch] a movie that Dick Smith has done, such as *Marathon Man.* When the old man gets his throat cut in the street? I have gone over that frame by frame on laser disk, and it is so beautifully done, so artistically done, I can't even see the edges. There are very few zombie-type films that would stand up to that kind of scrutiny. So that level of artistry is what I'm striving for. I want each thing, whether it's a vampire that we paint or Sarah's beauty makeup, to be as good as it can be, as polished as it can be, within the realm of TV."

Soon, the talk begins to turn toward fans and how the television audience perceives what it has seen on the small screen.

"A lot of people want to know 'How do I get my hair to look like so-and-so's?'" Jeri observes. "They go to their hairdresser with a picture and say, 'I want to look like that.' Now, first of all, styling hair in the television industry does not necessarily have anything to do with a haircut. It's styling, and the audience has to realize that this is a style that is maintained all day long. They don't walk out of the trailer and never get touched again, like normal people in the regular world. They have somebody chasing behind them, making sure that every hair is in place. So to take a photograph of an actor and expect to look like that, they can cut your hair the same way, but if you don't do the styling, all you're stuck with is a haircut you don't know what to do with.

"I think the most important thing is that everybody needs to seek their own look, what makes them beautiful. It has nothing to do with what the actress looks like and nothing to do with wanting to be like them. You have to be yourself. I'm hoping that's what has evolved on *Buffy*. She kinda looks like herself. She doesn't try to create a hairstyle that takes hours to do. Fifteen minutes. Sometimes you have to work with the hair that you have. She is sixteen years old. I don't want her hair to look like she came out of a salon. I'm hoping that we're creating things that people can do, they're not difficult to do. It's a matter of really liking your face and being able to stand in front of the mirror and move [your hair] around until you balance your face."

Todd is very pleased that Jeri brought up the fact that hair and makeup are constantly touched-up during a day's shooting.

"People who don't really know our business seem to think that we come in in the morning, put the makeup on, and we go home. It is the weirdest thing. What do they think we do all day?" he asks, mystified. "We are there every minute of the day during filming, making sure that everything is still on. Lipstick has to look fresh for fifteen hours, and that's our job, to wipe their noses and make sure there are no problems. Every five minutes, you are going in and primping."

On a side note, our experiences on the set bear this out. Todd and Jeri seem to be there before almost anyone else arrives, and they're on set until "cut" is called for the last time that night.

The conversation continues on the subject of the Hollywood image versus reality, and it's clear that both parties wish people knew a bit more about Hollywood. Perhaps people wouldn't be quite so uptight about their appearance.

"They went through a period in movies where they would take the classic Greek face, with a set of actual measurements that the Greeks used in their sculptures. They measured the distance between the eyes, lined up the nostrils with a certain part of the features, and came up with a mathematical formula. That's what it was all about, looking at an actress's face and seeing how far off it is from 'perfection,' and then adjusting the face through the illusion of makeup to make it perfect. That's insane in the same way that all of the current controversy about what a woman's perfect figure is and weight is. It's insane to try to fit everybody into a common mold. What we do in the movies is all illusion. It's all about creating something that isn't real.

"When you've got Marlene Dietrich up on that screen, that's not what she looked like when she went shopping at Ralph's. She had this mask that was built for her, the makeup illusion, which included lighting and film stock, and everybody worked together. In the old days, for example, when an actress stepped out of makeup, she went straight onto the set and got her closeups. Then they would pull back and do the master. Because it was fresh and she looked perfect."

In case anyone was wondering, by the way, the men wear makeup, too.

"Xander [for instance] doesn't wear a ton of makeup. He wears a foundation. We do have a problem when his beard shows. It's a little heavy, so to make him look younger we do a beard correction. It's not a huge amount of makeup."

And on the subject of the actors in the makeup trailer, Jeri really enjoys watching them. Sarah, for instance, "comes into character" in the chair.

"I start putting in her hair pieces, and before I know it, she's moving like this, like that. It's really fun," she says.

Working on *Buffy* is a delight for both of them, and Todd is always amused to hear from other makeup artists.

"I got a little bit of a last laugh," he says. "On the first season, before we hit the air, I could not get a makeup artist to come and help me on the show. '*Buffy the Vampire Slayer*, I don't think so.' This season, they're calling us, two or so a week."

## JOHN VULICH

As the driving force behind Optic Nerve Studios, the company that supplies *Buffy the Vampire Slayer*'s demons and other nasties, John Vulich is living his childhood dream.

"I'm the classic kid who had the *Famous Monsters* magazines kind of stuck behind my textbook in class. I've always had an interest in filmmaking. I was always making 8 mm horror films, and, inevitably, I ended up doing my own effects for them. I was just a kid in Fresno, and I learned how to do effects as a by-product of being interested in being a filmmaker."

Vulich's interest in filmmaking consumed him. So much, in fact, that he dropped out of high school his senior year to work on an installment of the *Friday the 13th* movie series.

"At a certain point, I realized that I needed to go and get a job, and really all I knew how to do was make monsters and make films. It seemed more practical to try doing something like makeup effects rather than trying to jump into directing right off the bat. It seemed more accessible to me, I think."

Because of his interest in horror and monsters, John made contacts with makeup wizards like Tom Savini. Savini promised that the next time he worked in L.A., he would hire Vulich, and he "stuck to his word."

Vulich and his team at Optic Nerve came to *Buffy* via an existing relationship with the series' makeup maestro, Todd McIntosh.

"We had originally worked with Todd on a series called *Great Scott*, which was really kind of a neat Walter Mitty kind of show," Vulich notes. "That was a clever show, but it never really found an audience. There was another [similar] show called *Pete and Pete*, which is on Nickelodeon and is one of my secret favorite shows."

Unbeknownst to Vulich, two of *Buffy*'s staff writers, Dean Vitale and Rob Des Hotel, actually wrote for *Pete and Pete*. Another bit of kismet among a cast and crew who seem to have been literally made for one another.

But, back to *Great Scott*, where Vulich hooked up with Todd McIntosh. That relationship led to Optic Nerve working on a pair of Mel Brooks films, including *Robin Hood: Men in Tights*. Optic Nerve went on to become the special makeup and prosthetics provider for *Babylon 5*. When McIntosh began to work on the "presentation reel" for *Buffy*—essentially a *Reader's Digest* version of the pilot to show to network execs—another special makeup and prosthetics firm was being used by the producers. Fortunately for Optic Nerve, the other firm turned out to be too expensive; McIntosh recommended them, and Optic Nerve was in!

"It was a very good opportunity," Vulich notes. "At that point, we had done three or four years of *Babylon 5,* and I feel I learned a lot of the ins and outs of getting it done on that kind of [severely deadline-oriented] schedule."

Indeed, *Babylon 5* required Optic Nerve to create special makeup effects in extraordinary volume and with incredible speed. In comparing their job on *B5* to any of the *Star Trek* spinoffs, Vulich believes that the amount of work his team does for *B5* is "certainly comparable, if not more work—or more elaborate work—than on *Star Trek.*

"So much of what we do, other than trying to learn, is trying to work faster and [find] ways to cut corners without really affecting the quality," he notes, before confirming that Optic Nerve will also be working on the "sequel series" to *Babylon 5,* currently titled *The Crusade.*

For all three shows, the amount of work Optic Nerve has done continues to pay off in other, very cost-conscious ways.

"We have a decent backlog of a lot of, like, backs of the heads, ears, necks—all kinds of different things—that we tend to recycle from project to project. We kind of pull a 'Mr. Potato Head.' We'll have four or five sets of demon horns, two or three sets of demon ears. Out of respect to the original people that we had built it for, we won't necessarily reuse the same face twice. But we might use the back of the head, something that's not as recognizable."

*Buffy* has been a challenge for a number of reasons; among them, of course, are the eight-day shooting schedule (each episode is shot in eight days) and the tight budget. But what's the biggest challenge the Optic Nerve team has had to face on the show?

"I would say maybe the Hellmouth, in the first season's finale," Vulich replies. "We only had a week and a half to do this really large, elaborate creature. If we were to have done it for a feature, it could easily have cost half [*Buffy*'s per-] episode budget."

Obviously, Vulich had to come up with some other options for the enormous, tentacled demon that seemed to be the embodiment of the Hellmouth itself—or perhaps just the first of the Old Ones to cross over. And he had to come up with it quickly—the producers needed a resolution in about four days. Vulich's first instinct was to go with CGI, a prospect he quickly abandoned."

"Our next idea was that maybe we could do it in miniature. But the creature had to interact so much with people, and a miniature copy of the set seemed prohibitive. We can't spend $500,000 to do this, and we only had a week and a half to do it."

Vulich's answer was the last thing anyone might have expected in an era so filled with technology.

"The Hellmouth beast is really three guys inside these tentacles, who are holding these mechanical poles, and the [tentacles] are actually almost like suits. We used a different technique to make the [tentacles]. The standard technique is to sculpt something in clay, mold it, and then pour rubber into the molds that you make, and that's how you end up with the piece. That is a simplified version."

The technique Optic Nerve went with required them to use sheets of a certain type of foam, cut and glued to form the desired shapes.

"It's a type of technique they use a lot for walk-around suits that you see at amusement parks," Vulich explains. "It cuts out the sculpting and the molding process, so that saved us about a week, a week and a half right there. It's not quite as refined a look, but you try to make up for it in a paint job. We knew it was going to be gooped up and all that, and that would help. Some elements were sculpted, like the teeth and the mouth and the eyes. We did sculpt those.

"I also made some suggestions to the producers as to how to shoot it. They were very gracious about listening to my ideas—which oftentimes doesn't happen—but they actually took me seriously. I suggested [they use] a couple of cameras and shoot some very tight closeups, so you almost don't know what you're looking at. You're just looking at masses of flesh, and one of my big beliefs with creatures is that oftentimes context is almost everything. If you were to see the alien in the movie *Alien*, in full-frame, walking through a shopping mall, it would [look] kind of stupid."

Vulich was happy, however, with the end result of this challenge when it finally aired in "Prophecy Girl."

"I thought it all came together very nicely. It was a lot better than I thought it would be," Vulich admits. "We were basically using the same stuff they would have used in *Lost in Space* back in the '60s, so we had to try to pull every trick we could to make it look that much better."

Vulich is also proud of the "suit" for the demon Machida, from "Reptile Boy." Once again, the look was achieved with a mixture of techniques. The upper body was sculpted, and the lower, tail portion, made use of the same foam construction used for the Hellmouth tentacles.

"We were very pleased with that," Vulich notes. "We hid the actor's body in there, in a kind of slip he fit into, which bound his legs together. It was made of different plastic sections that were glued together with foam wrapped around it, kind of interlocking. It was almost a forced perspective, in a way. The tail is actually a lot smaller toward the back than it is in the front, something we did hoping to make it look longer than it really was. Again, it's using whatever illusions or tricks you can, you know, to make these things look more dynamic."

In both cases, Vulich observes that the final product works on film in large part because of the environment. In the case of "Reptile Boy," he notes that Machida lived in a "really neat basement, and was kind of coming out of this pit."

An observation that leads to a discussion of the show in general, and his feeling—as a long time horror enthusiast—about why the show works as well as it does. For instance, he says of "Reptile Boy" that "there is certainly some kind of Freudian symbolism going on, the idea of a snake coming out of a hole in the frat." He also notes the date-rape subtext of Cordelia and Buffy's abduction by frat brothers.

"It's kind of indicative of the show in general, to basically take teenage angst and turn it into some kind of metaphor through a monster. I think that is really the brilliance in the show. For any kind of fantasy, horror, or sci-fi to really touch anybody, it has to be a metaphor for some real, true emotion; otherwise, why would anybody care about it if it is pure fantasy? You have to somehow relate to it in a way that actually touches you. A lot of the episodes are about taking real teenage angst and then doing the nightmare version of that."

From there, the conversation quickly turns to the creative process and the balancing of the intent to entertain with the urge to share one's philosophy through that entertainment. And it is a balance Vulich believes all artists reach for on some level, conscious or otherwise.

"Intuitively or through trial and error, creativity is just editing. You generate a lot of ideas, and you pick the good ones or the ones you like. You can't even necessarily explain why it feels right. If you try to rationalize it intelligently, at a certain point you just like it. I'm sure there is a reason, but it's probably so deeply buried, and there are so many layers of your consciousness, there's no point in even trying to go after it, and probably not even healthy to try to do that," he reasons.

Back to the series in question, however. We've heard from Vulich about the things he's proud of having pulled off. It's tempting, then, to wonder what he was unhappy with. The answer: the werewolf.

"[The producers] weren't pleased with the way it turned out, but I maintain that a lot of it is the context. It was shot in people's living rooms and stuff, and I think it makes it that much tougher to make the monster—it's a lot easier if you're in the basement, because the basement is half the mood, you know?

"We looked at a lot of videos, and there wasn't anything we really liked, except for *The Howling*. I think a lot of what made the werewolves in that film work was the way it was shot and the context it was all within—they are all silhouetted and backlit. Actually, oddly enough, sometimes a lot of tighter shots are better. If they are quick, close shots, they are disorienting enough. To me, that always seems to be the answer when you're shooting something that you're not quite sure about."

Of later episodes, the entire team at Optic Nerve was quite happy about the fish-boys from "Go Fish." That "team" will, at any given time include about fifteen people. Among them, Vulich's right-hand man, studio supervisor Mark Garbarino; John Wheaton, who does a lot of the designs with Vulich; and a number of others, including Andrew Sands, a novelist and screenwriter who is part of the studio's office staff. One key player Vulich wants to be sure to mention is Mike Pack, who makes all the fangs for the series' vampire characters.

The basic vampire prosthetic was something that Optic Nerve and Joss Whedon differed on originally. While Whedon wanted something distinct and dramatic, Vulich and his staff were thinking of something more subtle. Subtlety had worked well for them in the past, on the remake of *Night of the Living Dead*.

"If it's bloodier or more rotted or more angry or has an evil-looking forehead, to me, that's not necessarily what makes it scary. To me, what makes things scary is if they're believable. The fact that it's a wrinkled, shriveled puppet doesn't necessarily make it believable. That's why we tried [in that film] to think of them as characters instead of monsters. That was our whole aesthetic on that, and I think that to a certain degree, we were successful. We try to look for little holes, things that other people would miss, and that's why we did oversize ears [on the zombies]. We also took contact lenses and made people's eyes look bigger, because in real life certain parts of your features don't shrink.

"Cartilage doesn't shrink, so when you see emaciated people, their ears look huge because the rest of them is shrinking but ear cartilage doesn't. There are all these little things we tried to do to make them look more natural. When we started doing that with *Buffy*, we were trying to go in that direction, and it just wasn't really the tone that they were looking for. They encouraged us to be a little bit more heavy-handed in it."

Obviously, the process of putting an episode of the series together is complex and rigorous for all involved. It requires, more than anything, vast amounts of cooperation. As soon as Optic Nerve receives a script for an episode of the series, Vulich and his staff do a breakdown of the scenes and what they need to supply for that episode. Then they begin to create designs for a meeting with the series' producers. Usually, they bring no more than three designs for any one creature, to limit the choices to the best they have to offer. Once again, aesthetics come into play.

"Our primary concern is to figure out what serves the story. We try to be really aware of the fact that we're providing elements that are part of the story-telling process. We are not just making the cool monster, but we're making a story-telling device. What does this design need to be? Is it scary? Is it something that you start thinking of as scary but later on is benevolent? The design needs to reflect that. Not that we want it to be obvious, but we want a kind of resonance to it. With 'Reptile Boy,' there is a certain kind of phallic aspect to the story. That should be reflected in the design, so instead of making him green, we went for lighter flesh tones.

"Secondly, we try to find what's been done before," Vulich says. "We'll scour magazines, books, and videos. We usually have a day or two to do this. We'll try to find out what everyone else has done before, bring in photos, and figure out if there's anything anyone else has missed. Or how we can avoid some clichés."

Once Vulich's designs are approved, it becomes a question of budget.

"I will try to make whatever suggestions I can to try to make it as cost-effective as possible," he admits. "The show is very limited financially, and that's a really major concern. Part of what makes me valuable in what I do is actually saving people money. In the case of the fish-guys [for "Go Fish,"], we had to build three of them. We used some existing body casts that we had, and pretty much told them what size person to get to fit into it."

Once again, cooperation appears to be the key. And that doesn't seem to have been any problem. Vulich and Whedon share a love of horror, and of films in general, that makes their communication very simple and direct. Any reference Vulich can think of, Whedon is likely to be familiar with. That communication has served both John Vulich and the producers of *Buffy*.

"I think we're very much simpatico with Joss's vision," Vulich notes. "Once we initially got the tone down, from the first few episodes, I think we really got a good feel for what he was looking for."

## DIGITAL MAGIC

**"It's really cool when you can say part of your job is blowing up vampires."**
—Stephen Brand, 3D and visual effects supervisor, Digital Magic

And how do they blow up those vampires?

Loni Peristere of Digital Magic, the computer-graphics company that creates *Buffy*'s "CG" effects, told us that it was an exciting challenge to create the show's signature effect...and to do all the other things they've been asked to do. But Digital Magic was up to it: founded in 1990, it has worked on shows such as *Star Trek Voyager, Teen Angel, Early Edition, You Wish, Dawson's Creek, Rodgers and Hammerstein's Cinderella*, and *Dr. Quinn, Medicine Woman*, as well as the feature films *Mortal Kombat: Annihilation* and *Species II*. A dedicated team working in a 30,000-foot facility in Santa Monica, they searched for the perfect image to represent what happens to a vampire when Buffy stakes it: all the moisture is sucked out of its body, which then turns to dust and explodes.

To their delight, the teeth fall out last.

Loni explained that to create this effect, a "dust man" double of the live character is created, then positioned frame by frame to match the live action actor. As Loni continued:

"Stephen [Brand's] integrated dust elements are designed around the scene. They possess as many realistic qualities as the scene provides, as well as the dramatic impact suggested by the actors. They can be languid and touching, as Angel's turn in Buffy's nightmare sequence in "Surprise," or pointed and quick, as Xander's killer lunge in "Bewitched, Bothered, and Bewildered." Each shot is layered with detail. The skin turns, the teeth fall, and the body crumbles."

In addition to the vampire "dustings"—each episode averages a minimum of two—Digital Magic provides two to four more effects per show. They provided the sequence where Drusilla's and Angel's blood mingles in "What's My Line? Part 2." They've risen demons and mummies from their sleep, and opened the mouth of Hell in the second-season finale, "Becoming, Part 2."

They also transformed a certain Dingoes Ate My Baby guitarist from his creature self back to Oz. Again, as Loni vividly describes it:

"Lying on the floor of a very realistic wood setting is an actor dressed in an impressively frightening six-foot werewolf costume (created by makeup and prosthetics specialists Optic Nerve). Later on, he will be replaced by two increasingly less-hairy actors, before the real actor takes his place on the set." (Indeed, Todd McIntosh told us how they painstakingly inserted the hairs onto Seth Green's body one by one.)

"It will then be up to our special-effects team to blend these four different stages into a seamless transformation from werewolf back to man."

Working on a relatively tight budget, and required to produce completed effects on a schedule unheard-of in the world of feature film, Digital Magic usually receives the scripts for *Buffy* two weeks before they must provide two to eight graphic sequences for the episode in question. Co-producer David Solomon adds that since *Buffy* isn't a show heavy on special effects, the few they do use in an episode need to look "fantastic."

Back to that dusting thing. It seems that in an effort to find just the right look, Digital Magic filmed exploding bags of flour and smashed plaster models. They researched their vampire lore, watching cinematic vamp death scenes from the old masters, including Bela Lugosi. They decided they wanted to find an "organic" look, rather than go for the super-slick hi-tech superclarity that often betrays a shot composed of computer graphics. They refer to this organic look as "CGI gore."

Live actors are combined into the computer-graphic elements much more often than one might expect. Loni told us that when shooting the demon-possessing-Angel sequence in "The Dark Age," David Boreanaz had to repeat his "wild involuntary convulsions" in three different makeups. Alyson Hannigan had to let the floor fall out from under her for the vortex scene in "I Only Have Eyes for You," and in that same episode, Charisma Carpenter "marched through stage after stage of extra makeup and applications" for the snakebite infection sequence.

And he excitedly remembers the first successful test shot for that all-important dusting: "...and the 4 A.M. realization that what we had on screen was right, that yes, indeed, a vampire turns to dust just like that, and Joss, Sarah, David, Alyson, Nick, Tony, Charisma, and all the show's creators believed it just as we did. This first experience set the precedent for the year, and we've all continued to work together as such."

### The Digital Magic Visual Effects Team includes:

**JEFF BEAULIEU,** executive producer

**STEPHEN BRAND:** 3D and visual effects supervisor

**LONI PERISTERE:** visual effects producer-supervisor

**BILL LAE:** Henry compositor (an editing and special effects "suite in a box")

**KIKI CHANSAMONE:** flame compositor

**DAN SANTONI:** CGI animator

**CASEY DAME:** CGI animator

**MICHAEL SCHNEIDER:** Telecine colorist (converts film to digital video format)

FUMIGATION PARTY
Find a cockroach, get a free drink

DRIVING DRUNK?
TWISTED

# MUSIC

> **Buffy:** "It's not noise. It's music."
> **Giles:** "I know music. Music has notes. This is noise."
> **Buffy:** "I'm aerobicizing. I must have the beat."
> **Giles:** "Wonderful. You work on muscle tone while my brain dribbles out my ears." —**"THE DARK AGE"**

The post-production department has a policy of listening to every demo sent to them. They are particularly delighted when they find songs from up-and-coming groups to help them get exposure.

The band that really plays for Dingoes Ate My Baby is called Four Star Mary. If you listen closely, you can hear Giles humming very softly in the segue from the scene with Buffy in front of the burning Factory to their standing beside Jenny's grave. (And did you spot the uncredited appearance of Sean Lennon in one of the Bronze's headliners?)

Here are the songs and the bands who played in the first two seasons of *Buffy*:

## SEASON ONE song list

| Artist | Song Title | Episode # |
|---|---|---|
| Sprung Monkey<br>Surfdog—1995's "Swirl" | *Saturated, Believe, Swirl, Things Are Changing, Right My Wrong* | 4V01 |
| Mindtribe<br>Independently recorded; not yet available | *Losing Ground* | 4V01 |
| Dashboard Prophets<br>No Name Recordings—1996's "Burning Out the Inside" | *Wearing Me Down, Ballad for Dead Friends* | 4V02 |
| Superfine<br>(a.k.a.: Abbey Normal)<br>Fish of Death Records; available on label's website | *Already Met You, Stoner Love* | 4V04 |
| Three Day Wheely<br>Capitol—1996's "Rubber Halo" | *Rotten Apples* | 4V05 |
| Velvet Chain<br>Overall—1997's "Warm" | *Strong, Treaon* | 4V05 |
| Rubber<br>Independently recorded; not yet available | *Junkie Girl* | 4V05 |
| Kim Richey<br>Mercury Nashville—1995's "Kim Richey" | *Let the Sun Fall Down* | 4V05 |
| Sprung Monkey<br>Surfdog—1995's "Swirl" | *Reluctant Man* | 4V06 |

| Artist | Song Title | Episode # |
|---|---|---|
| Dashboard Prophets<br>No Name Recordings—1996's "Burning Out the Inside" | *All You Want* | 4V06 |
| Far<br>Epic/ Immortal—1996's "Tin Cans with Strings to You" | *Job's Eyes* | 4V06 |
| Sophie Zelmani<br>Epic/ Immortal—1996's "Sophie Zelmani" | *I'll Remember You* | 4V07 |
| Patsy Cline<br>MCA—1961's "Patsy Cline Showcase" | *I Fall to Pieces* | 4V12 |
| Jonatha Brooke<br>Blue Thumb and Refuge/MCA | *Inconsolable* | 4V12 |

## SEASON TWO song list

| Artist | Song Title | Episode # |
|---|---|---|
| Cibo Matto<br>Warner Brothers—1997's "Super Relax" | *Sugar Water, Spoon* | 5V01 |
| Alison Krauss and Union Station<br>Rounder—1997's "So Long, So Wrong" | *It Doesn't Matter* | 5V01 |
| Nickel<br>Independently recorded; available on band's website | *Stupid Things, 1000 Nights* | 5V03 |
| Four Star Mary<br>Independently recorded; available on band's website and at Aaron Records in Hollywood, CA | *Fate, Shadows* | 5V04 |
| Act of Faith<br>Expansion—1997's "Release Yourself" | *Bring Me On* | 5V05 |
| Louie Says<br>RCA—1997's "Cold to the Touch" | *She* | 5V05 |
| Epperley<br>Triple x—1996's "Epperley" | *Shy* | 5V06 |
| Treble Charger<br>RCA—1997's "Maybe It's Me" | *How She Died* | 5V06 |
| Willoughby<br>Fuzz Harris Records—1996's "Be Better Soon" | *Lois on the Brink* | 5V07 |

| | | |
|---|---|---|
| Creaming Jesus<br>  Import—"Dead Time" | *Reptile* | 5V07 |
| Shawn Clement and<br>Sean Murray<br>  Independently recorded; e-mail requests to smurray@cinenet.net or clemistry@aol.com | *Blood of a Stranger* | 5V07 |
| Rasputina<br>  Sony—1996's "Thanks for the Ether" | *Transylvanian Concubine* | 5V13 |
| Shawn Clement and<br>Sean Murray with vocals by Care Howe<br>  Independently recorded; e-mail requests to smurray@cinenet.net or clemistry@aol.com | *Anything* | 5V13 |
| Lotion<br>  Warner Brothers—1996's "Nobody's Fool" | *Blind for Now* | 5V15 |
| Four Star Mary<br>  Independently recorded; available on band's website and at Aaron Records in Hollywood, CA | *Pain* | 5V16 |
| Naked<br>  Red Ant—1997's "Naked" | *Drift Away* | 5V16 |
| Average White Band<br>  Atlantic—1974's "AWB" | *Got the Love* | 5V16 |
| Morcheeba<br>  WEA/Sire/Discovery2—1996's "Who Can You Trust?" | *Never an Easy Way* | 5V17 |
| Puccini | *La Bohème: Acte 10<br>Soave Fanciulla* | 5V17 |
| The Flamingos<br>  Collectables—1959's "Flamingo Serenade" | *I Only Have Eyes for You* | 5V19 |
| Splendid<br>  Independently recorded; CD in spring 1999 | *Charge* | 5V19 |
| Naked<br>  Red Ant—1997's "Naked" | *Mann's Chinese* | 5V20 |
| Nero's Rome<br>  Lazy Bones—1995's "Togetherly" | *If You'd Listen* | 5V20 |
| Sarah McLachlan<br>  Arista—1997's "Surfacing" | *Full of Grace* | 5V22 |

Ypsilanti District Library

# Lecture Notes in Physics

Edited by J. Ehlers, München, K. Hepp, Zürich,
H. A. Weidenmüller, Heidelberg, and J. Zittartz, Köln
Managing Editor: W. Beiglböck, Heidelberg

## 41

## Progress in Numerical Fluid Dynamics

Lecture Series Held at the von Karman Institute
for Fluid Dynamics
1640 Rhode-St.-Genèse, Belgium
February 11–15, 1974

Revised and Updated Version

Edited by H. J. Wirz

Springer-Verlag
Berlin · Heidelberg · New York 1975

## PREFACE

This Lecture Series "Progress in Numerical Fluid Dynamics" being organized at the von Karman Institute for Fluid Dynamics and partly supported by the Consultant Exchange Programme of AGARD (Advisory Group for Aerospace Research and Development) reviews recent developments in the area of computational fluid dynamics.

More than 130 participants from almost all European countries and from even further afield attended and contributed during the discussions to the success of the Lecture Series.

The present material, being revised and updated, comprises two- and three-dimensional transonic and supersonic flows, the numerical treatment of the incompressible and compressible Navier-Stokes equations, two- and three-dimensional boundary layer flows, including unsteady layers, the foundation of the finite element method with applications to fluid dynamics, the treatment of problems of numerical stability in the presence of boundary conditions and methods to improve numerical solution using analogue subroutines.

Expressing my thanks to my colleagues, who did not hesitate to update and rewrite their contributions, to Mrs N. Toubeau who carefully assembled the material, I finally wish to address my appreciation to the Springer-Verlag and in particular to Prof. Dr. W. Beiglböck, Editor of the "Lecture Notes in Physics", for arranging this publication.

Hans Jochen Wirz<br>
Lecture Series Director

Rhode Saint Genèse,
   June 29, 1975

## TABLE OF CONTENTS

| | page |
|---|---|
| BAILEY, F.R.: On the computation of two- and three-dimensional steady transsonic flows by relaxation methods . . . . | 1 |
| CHENG, Sin-I: A critical review of numerical solution of Navier-Stokes equations . . . . . . . . . . . . . | 78 |
| FRAEIJS de VEUBEKE, B.: Variational principles in fluid mechanics and finite element applications . . . . . | 226 |
| KRAUSE, E.: Recent developments of finite-difference approximations for boundary layer equations . . . . . . . . | 260 |
| KUTLER, Paul: Computation of three-dimensional, inviscid supersonic flows . . . . . . . . . . . . . . . . . | 287 |
| MUELLER, Thomas J.: Numerical and physical experiments in viscous separated flows . . . . . . . . . . . . . | 375 |
| SMOLDEREN, J.: Stability of explicit time dependent treatment of hyperbolic boundary problems . . . . . . . . . | 410 |
| VANSTEENKISTE, G.C.: Improving of the numerical solutions by using analogue subroutines . . . . . . . . . . . . | 419 |
| WIRZ, H.J.: Computation of unsteady boundary layers . . . . . | 442 |

ON THE COMPUTATION OF TWO- AND THREE-DIMENSIONAL STEADY

TRANSONIC FLOWS BY RELAXATION METHODS

by

F. R. Bailey

Ames Research Center

NASA, Moffett Field, Calif., U.S.A., 94035

## TABLE OF CONTENTS

|  | Page |
|---|---|
| TITLE PAGE | 1 |
| TABLE OF CONTENTS | 2 |
| LIST OF ILLUSTRATIONS | 3 |
| 1. INTRODUCTION | 5 |
| 2. RELAXATION METHOD APPLIED TO THE SMALL DISTURBANCE EQUATION | 8 |
|     2.1 Introduction | 8 |
|     2.2 Transonic Small Disturbance Theory | 8 |
|     2.3 Finite Difference Method | 14 |
|     2.4 Results | 24 |
| 3. EXACT ISENTROPIC PROCEDURE IN TWO DIMENSIONS | 29 |
|     3.1 Introduction | 29 |
|     3.2 Steger and Lomax Procedure | 31 |
|     3.3 Garabedian and Korn Procedure | 32 |
|     3.4 Jameson Procedures | 34 |
|     3.5 Jameson's Rotated Difference Scheme for Supersonic Regions | 38 |
|     3.6 Results | 41 |
| 4. AXISYMMETRIC FLOW | 44 |
| 5. COMPARISONS WITH EXPERIMENT | 45 |
|     5.1 Introduction | 45 |
|     5.2 Viscous Effects | 45 |
|     5.3 Wind Tunnel Wall Effects | 51 |
| 6. SMALL DISTURBANCE PROCEDURE IN THREE DIMENSIONS | 55 |
|     6.1 Introduction | 55 |
|     6.2 Basic Formulation | 55 |
|     6.3 Relaxation Procedure | 58 |
|     6.4 Nonrectangular Planforms | 59 |
|     6.5 Results | 61 |
|     6.6 Swept Shock Waves | 65 |
| 7. JAMESON'S EXACT ISENTROPIC PROCEDURE FOR YAWED WINGS | 68 |
|     7.1 Introduction | 68 |
|     7.2 Transformed Equation | 69 |
|     7.3 Numerical Method | 70 |
|     7.4 Results | 71 |
| 8. CONCLUDING REMARKS | 71 |
| REFERENCES | 74 |

## LIST OF ILLUSTRATIONS

Sketches                                                                                      Page

A . . . . . . . . . . . . . . . . . . . . . . . . . . . . . . . . . . .   5
B . . . . . . . . . . . . . . . . . . . . . . . . . . . . . . . . . . .   8
C . . . . . . . . . . . . . . . . . . . . . . . . . . . . . . . . . . .  11
D . . . . . . . . . . . . . . . . . . . . . . . . . . . . . . . . . . .  15
E . . . . . . . . . . . . . . . . . . . . . . . . . . . . . . . . . . .  21
F . . . . . . . . . . . . . . . . . . . . . . . . . . . . . . . . . . .  31
G . . . . . . . . . . . . . . . . . . . . . . . . . . . . . . . . . . .  36
H . . . . . . . . . . . . . . . . . . . . . . . . . . . . . . . . . . .  38
I . . . . . . . . . . . . . . . . . . . . . . . . . . . . . . . . . . .  56

Figures

1. Comparison of FCR and NCR solutions for 6 percent parabolic arc airfoil at $M_\infty = 0.872$ (K = 1.8). . . . . . . . . . . . .   25

2. Comparison of FCR and NCR solutions for 6 percent parabolic arc airfoil at $M_\infty = 0.909$ (K = 1.25) . . . . . . . . . . .   26

3. Comparison of computational methods for 6 percent parabolic arc airfoil with detached bow wave at $M_\infty = 1.15$. . . . . . .   27

4. Hodograph plots for detached bow wave . . . . . . . . . . . .   28

5. Comparison of hodograph and relaxation solutions for NLR quasi-elliptical airfoil; $\delta = 12.12$ percent, $\alpha = 1.32°$, $M_\infty = 0.7557$ . . . . . . . . . . . . . . . . . . . . . . .   42

6. Comparison of hodograph and relaxation solutions for Garabedian-Korn airfoil . . . . . . . . . . . . . . . . . . . .   42

7. Comparison of conservative time-dependent and nonconservative relaxation solutions of exact isentropic equation for the NACA 64A410 airfoil at $M_\infty = 0.735$ and $\alpha = 1°$ . . . . . .   43

8. Comparison Jameson relaxation solution with data for Boerstoel airfoil; $M_\infty = 0.834$ . . . . . . . . . . . . . .   46

9. Comparison of small disturbance solutions with data for NACA 0012 airfoil at $\alpha = 0°$ . . . . . . . . . . . . . . . . . .   46

10. Shock-wave pressure jump on airfoils in transonic flow. . . .   48

11. Comparison of Jameson relaxation solution with data for Garabedian-Korn airfoil . . . . . . . . . . . . . . . . . . . .   49

12. Comparison of FCR solutions with data for Garabedian-Korn airfoil; $\alpha = 1.38°$, $M_\infty = 0.768$. . . . . . . . . . . .   50

13. Effect of wall conditions on body surface $C_p$ for parabolic arc of revolution with sting ($M_\infty = 0.99$ and $f = 10$) . . .   52

14. Variation of surface pressure drag coefficient (based on body length) with Mach number for a parabolic arc of revolution with sting (f = 10) . . . . . . . . . . . . . . . . . . . . . .   53

## LIST OF ILLUSTRATIONS (Continued)

| Figures | | Page |
|---|---|---|
| 15. | Lift and pitching moment curves for NACA 0012 airfoil in perforated wind tunnel and free air, $M = 0.80$ . . . . . . . . . | 54 |
| 16. | Comparison of FCR solutions with data, NACA 0012; $\alpha = 0°$, $M = 0.8$ . . . . . . . . . . . . . . . . . . . . . . . . . . . . | 54 |
| 17. | $C_p$ distribution on C-141 swept panel model, $M_\infty = 0.752$, $\alpha = 2°$. . . . . . . . . . . . . . . . . . . . . . . . . . . . . | 62 |
| 18. | $C_p$ distribution on C-141 swept panel model, $M_\infty = 0.853$, $\alpha = 2°$. . . . . . . . . . . . . . . . . . . . . . . . . . . . . | 62 |
| 19. | Calculated upper surface isobars for simulated C-141 wing at $M_\infty = 0.825$ . . . . . . . . . . . . . . . . . . . . . . . . | 64 |
| 20. | Wind tunnel, flight and computed upper surface $C_p$ distribution for C-141 wing at $y/b \approx 0.4$ and $M_\infty = 0.825$ . . . | 64 |
| 21. | $C_p$ distribution on cylinder-wing combination at $M_\infty = 0.908$ . | 65 |
| 22. | Values of $(u_1 + u_2)$ from Eq. (6.22) and Eq. (6.19) for $M_\infty = 0.85$ . . . . . . . . . . . . . . . . . . . . . . . . . | 67 |
| 23. | Yawed wing results for $M_\infty = 0.866$, $\alpha = 3°$, $\theta = 30°$ . . . . . | 72 |

ON THE COMPUTATION OF TWO- AND THREE-DIMENSIONAL STEADY
TRANSONIC FLOWS BY RELAXATION METHODS

by

F. R. Bailey
Ames Research Center
NASA, Moffett Field, Calif., U.S.A., 94035

## 1. INTRODUCTION

Transonic flows are characterized by the presence of adjacent regions of subsonic and supersonic flow that are usually accompanied by weak shock waves. For example, sketch A illustrates schematically the development of the transonic flow pattern over a lifting airfoil for increasing free-stream Mach number. The flow pattern progresses from a predominantly subsonic flow with embedded supersonic regions to a predominantly supersonic flow with embedded subsonic regions.

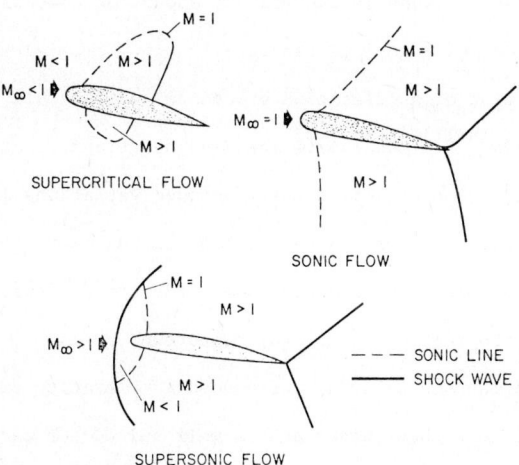

Sketch A

Mathematically, the description of steady transonic flows requires the solution of "mixed" equations that are elliptic in subsonic regions and hyperbolic in supersonic regions. The problem is essentially nonlinear, and solutions usually contain discontinuities representing shock waves. The only well-known analytical method for treating transonic flows solves the two-dimensional equations in the hodograph plane, where they are linear. This approach has proven useful for generating shock-free airfoil shapes[1,2] but is not well suited for solving flow fields with embedded shock waves. In the past several years, however, finite difference methods have been developed to treat steady transonic flows with shock waves. These methods follow two distinct approaches — unsteady and relaxation.

In the unsteady methods, the steady flow solution is obtained as a large time asymptotic solution to a real or pseudo time-dependent formulation. The approach is based on the extensive development of finite difference methods for initial value problems[3] and was first introduced by Magnus and Yoshihara[4,5]. For an overview of the unsteady methods, the interested reader is referred to the reviews given in references 6-8.

In the relaxation approach, the steady transonic flow equations are solved by an iteration algorithm in a manner similar to the standard procedure for solving elliptic boundary value problems. The main advantage of the current relaxation methods over the unsteady methods is the smaller amount of computational effort required — about an order of magnitude less.

The first application of a relaxation procedure to transonic flows was by Emmons in the late 1940s[9-11] who solved the density-stream function formulation of the inviscid steady equations of motion that included variations in entropy. Shock waves were explicitly fitted according to the Rankine-Hugoniot jump relations. Unfortunately, the method appears to require a decision process that is too complicated to be well suited for programming on digital computers.

More recently, Murman and Cole[12] introduced a relaxation procedure that automatically accounts for weak shock waves and is well suited for machine computation. The scheme was originally applied to the transonic small disturbance equation with a perturbation potential serving as the single dependent variable. The method has been extended by others[13-15] to include the exact isentropic formulation, in which it is assumed that any shock waves present are sufficiently weak that vorticity can be neglected. The unique feature of the method is that separate difference operators are used in elliptic (subsonic) and hyperbolic (supersonic) regions. In elliptic regions, central difference operators are used to account for the domain of dependence of subsonic flow equations. In hyperbolic regions, upwind difference operators are used to account for the absence of upstream influence in supersonic flow equations. Because of the absence of an entropy inequality, the isentropic flow equation contains discontinuous solutions that are not unique, and both expansion and compression jumps can exist. However, the use of upwind difference operators introduces directionality into the numerical method and creates a positive dissipative truncation error term which acts, in a sense, as a source of entropy production. Thus, expansion jumps are eliminated and uniqueness is restored. The compression jumps evolve naturally in the method and are considered as approximations to the true Rankine-Hugoniot shock jumps.

The present paper discusses recent developments in applying the Murman and Cole scheme to steady, inviscid transonic flow problems in two and three dimensions. Considerable emphasis is placed on two-dimensional methods since they form the basis for three-dimensional algorithms. The basic details of the scheme are described in terms of the original small disturbance formulation of Murman and Cole. In particular, Murman's recent introduction of fully conservative difference operators[16] to obtain the correct shock jumps is discussed. The extension to treat the exact isentropic equation is then covered with special attention given to Jameson's new rotated difference scheme[17] for supersonic flow regions. Following is a brief discussion of axisymmetric methods. Consideration of two-dimensional procedures is concluded by a discussion on comparisons with experiment, emphasizing the effects of viscosity and wind-tunnel walls. Finally, the paper concludes with discussions of the treatment of the three-dimensional small disturbance equation for swept wings and the exact isentropic equation for yawed wings.

## 2. RELAXATION METHOD APPLIED TO THE SMALL DISTURBANCE EQUATION

### 2.1 Introduction

We begin the discussion of the transonic relaxation method by considering its application to steady, transonic small disturbance theory for lifting airfoils. The theory is derived under the assumptions that the flow is inviscid, that airfoil slopes are everywhere small so that flow quantities are small perturbations about their free-stream values, and that the free-stream Mach number is near unity. Consequently, the airfoil must be thin and angles of attack small. In practical situations, these assumptions are not always strictly met, particularly at blunt noses, at large angles of attack, and if extensive flow separation is present. Nonetheless, many cases of engineering interest may be adequately described by the theory. Small disturbance theory is a considerable simplification of the exact inviscid theory in both the boundary conditions and governing equations. The resulting governing equation still retains the essential nonlinear, mixed elliptic-hyperbolic character, and its solution contains discontinuous jumps that approximate shock waves.

In the following, we discuss in some detail the transonic small distrubance formulation of Cole[18,19] and the application of the Murman and Cole scheme to lifting airfoils.

### 2.2 Transonic Small Disturbance Theory

#### 2.2.1 Introduction

The transonic small disturbance equations can be formally derived by an asymptotic expansion procedure[18,19] applied to the inviscid equations of fluid flow in which the airfoil thickness ratio $\delta$ (see sketch B), tends to 0 while the

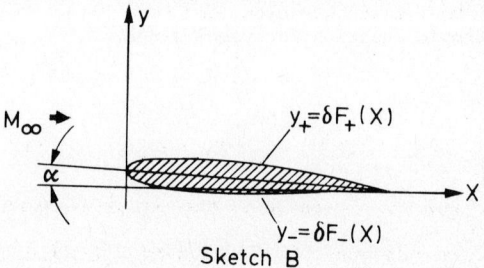
Sketch B

free-stream Mach number, $M_\infty$, approaches 1. Thus, the flow is represented as small disturbances on a uniform stream. The large lateral extent of transonic disturbances is taken into account by use of the scaled coordinate $\tilde{y} = \delta^{1/3} y$. The limit process is $\delta \to 0$, $M_\infty \to 1$ while $K, x, \tilde{y}$ remain fixed where

$$K = (1 - M_\infty^2)/\delta^{2/3}$$

is the transonic similarity parameter. It should be noted that the definitions of $K$ and $\tilde{y}$ are not unique and may be multiplied by functions like $g(M_\infty^2) = O(1)$ where $g(1) = 1$. In the above, we have followed the scaling of Cole[19], although the more usual scaling is given in reference 20. For a more detailed summary of the theory, the reader is referred to Cole[19].

## 2.2.2 Transonic Equations

The asymptotic expansions of the form

$$q_x/u_\infty = 1 + \delta^{2/3} u + \delta^{4/3} u_2 + \delta^2 u_3 + \ldots$$

for the x-component of velocity,

$$q_y/u_\infty = \delta v + \delta^{5/3} v_2 + \ldots$$

for the y-component of velocity,

$$p/p_\infty = 1 + \delta^{2/3} p + \delta^{4/3} p_2 + \delta^2 p_3 + \ldots$$

for the pressure, and

$$\rho/\rho_\infty = 1 + \delta^{2/3} \sigma + \delta^{4/3} \sigma_2 + \delta^2 \sigma_3 + \ldots$$

for the density, are substituted into the inviscid equations for conservation of mass, momentum, energy, and entropy (but allowing for a jump in entropy across shock waves). Taking into account the shock relations, various integrals are found, of which two give the first-order transonic equations

$$\left\{ K u - [(\gamma + 1)/2] u^2 \right\}_x + v_{\tilde{y}} = 0 \tag{2.1a}$$

$$v_x - u_{\tilde{y}} = 0 \tag{2.1b}$$

Eq. (2.1a) is a transonic version of the continuity equation, and Eq. (2.1b) shows that the flow is irrotational to first order (it turns out to be irrotational to second order also). Thus, a perturbation velocity potential can be introduced by

$$\left.\begin{aligned}\phi_x &\equiv u \\ \phi_{\tilde{y}} &\equiv v\end{aligned}\right\} \quad (2.2)$$

which yields the governing equation in divergence form as

$$\{K\phi_x - [(\gamma + 1)/2]\phi_x^2\}_x + \phi_{\tilde{y}\tilde{y}} = 0 \quad (2.3a)$$

or alternatively, in nondivergence form, as

$$[K - (\gamma + 1)\phi_x]\phi_{xx} + \phi_{\tilde{y}\tilde{y}} = 0 \quad (2.3b)$$

The essential nonlinearity of the governing equation allows the local formation of either an elliptic equation, representing subsonic flow $[\phi_x < (K/\gamma + 1)]$, or a hyperbolic equation, representing supersonic flow $[\phi_x > (K/\gamma + 1)]$.

### 2.2.3 Shock Jump and Drag

The shock jump relations, which are of great importance in transonic calculations, are contained in the governing equation in the sense that the weak solution[21] to Eq. (2.1a) and (2.1b) yields a consistent approximation to the usual Rankine-Hugoniot relations — that is, the surface integral forms of Eq. (2.1) integrated across a jump in (u,v) yield

$$\langle Ku - [(\gamma + 1)/2]u^2 \rangle (d\tilde{y})_s - \langle v \rangle (dx)_s = 0 \quad (2.4a)$$

$$\langle v \rangle (d\tilde{y})_s + \langle u \rangle (dx)_s = 0 \quad (2.4b)$$

where

$\langle \ \rangle$ is the jump

and

$( \ )_s$ is a shock surface element.

Eqs. (2.4a) and (2.4b) can be recast into the shock polar representation

$$[K - (\gamma + 1)\bar{u}]\langle u \rangle^2 + \langle v \rangle^2 = 0 \quad (2.5)$$

where

$\bar{u} = (1/2)(u_1 + u_2)$

is the average across the shock. The shock angle relative to the positive y-axis is given by

$$\theta_s = dx/d\tilde{y} = -(\langle v \rangle / \langle u \rangle) \tag{2.6}$$

and the continuity of tangential velocity across the shock yields

$$\langle \phi \rangle = 0 \tag{2.7}$$

The shock jumps given by Eqs. (2.4a) and (2.4b) will give good approximations to the Rankine-Hugoniot jumps for the ranges $0.8 \lesssim M_\infty \lesssim 1.3$ and $M_1 \lesssim 1.3$.

The consistent approximation to the Rankine-Hugoniot shock jumps contained in the transonic small disturbance theory has an important bearing on the calculation of drag, which in a two-dimensional inviscid flow about a closed body can only be due to shock waves. The drag on the airfoil is given by the x-momentum integral

$$D = \oint_C \{(\rho q_x) q_y \, dx - [p + (\rho q_x) q_x] dy\} \tag{2.8}$$

where C is a contour enclosing the airfoil. Inserting the small disturbance expansions and taking into account jumps across shock waves yields, to the lowest order (for closed bodies),

$$\frac{D}{\gamma p_\infty} = \delta^{5/3} \left\{ \oint_C \left[ uv \, dx + \left( \frac{\gamma + 1}{3} u^3 + \frac{v^2}{2} - K \frac{u^2}{2} \right) d\tilde{y} \right] - \frac{\gamma + 1}{12} \int_S \langle u \rangle^3 \, d\tilde{y} \right\} \tag{2.9}$$

The last integral in Eq. (2.9) is over that part of the shock surface S enclosed in C (see sketch C).

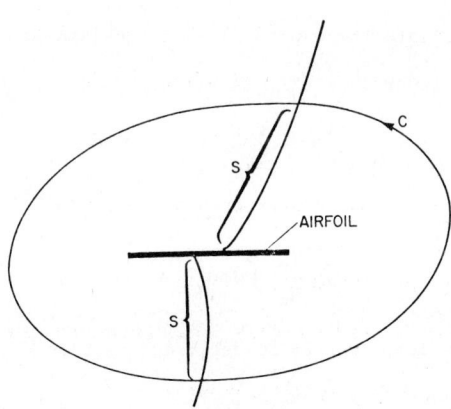

Sketch C

If the contour C is collapsed to the wing surface, $\tilde{y} = 0$, Eq. (2.9) becomes

$$\frac{D}{\gamma p_\infty} = \delta^{5/3} \int_0^1 [(uv)_- - (uv)_+] dx \tag{2.10}$$

which is the usual expression for pressure drag where $v$ is the local body slope.

If the contour C is extended to infinity, the only contribution comes from the shock surface and is the wave drag

$$\frac{D}{\gamma p_\infty} = -\delta^{5/3} \frac{\gamma+1}{12} \int_S \langle u \rangle^3 \, d\tilde{y} \tag{2.11}$$

Thus, the drag on the airfoil is due to the presence of shock waves and although the drag is a third-order quantity, it may be computed from the solution of the first-order transonic equations. Furthermore, the drag may be computed by (i) integrating surface pressures (assuming leading-edge singularities are integrable), (ii) integrating shock jumps, or (iii) integrating along an intermediate contour, Eq. (2.9).

It is important to note that momentum conservation is satisfied to the first two orders, and in particular the first-order solution has the correct first-order momentum conservation. The drag, however, has been shown to arise from nonconservation of third-order x-momentum across the shock wave. It can also be shown to be equal to that which is due to the entropy jump across weak shock waves. Substituting the transonic expansions into the expression for the jump of entropy across weak shocks yields to lowest order

$$\frac{\Delta s}{R} = -\frac{\gamma+1}{12} \gamma \delta^2 \langle u \rangle^3 \tag{2.12}$$

Substituting Eq. (2.12) into the Oswatitsch drag relation[22]

$$D = \frac{T_\infty}{q_\infty} \int (\rho q_x)_n \Delta s \, dy \tag{2.13}$$

gives Eq. (2.11). Therefore, drag to lowest order is also due to the jump of entropy across the shocks.

## 2.2.4 Boundary Conditions

The formulation of the problem is completed by specifying the boundary conditions. The condition that the flow be tangent to the airfoil is linearized by the assumption $\delta \to 0$ and applied on the mean surface $\tilde{y} = 0$ in the form

$$\phi_{\tilde{y}}(x, +0) = F_+'(x) - \frac{\alpha}{\delta} \tag{2.14a}$$

$$\phi_{\tilde{y}}(x, -0) = F_-'(x) - \frac{\alpha}{\delta} \tag{2.14b}$$

For lifting airfoils, the Kutta condition is satisfied by requiring that $\phi_x$ (pressure) be continuous across the line $\tilde{y} = 0$, $x \geq 1$ and $\phi_{\tilde{y}}$ (flow angle) be continuous across $\tilde{y} = 0$, $x > 1$. The disturbance potential remains single-valued by introducing a cut in the $x, \tilde{y}$ plane ($\tilde{y} = 0$, say) at which $\phi$ jumps by an amount equal to the circulation $\Gamma$ defined by

$$\Gamma = -\oint d\phi \tag{2.15}$$

with the integration taken around the airfoil.

The far field boundary conditions require that the perturbation velocities vanish at infinity with the disturbance potential given by

$$\phi = \frac{\Gamma}{2\pi} \theta \tag{2.16}$$

where $\theta$ is the angle between the position vector and the positive x-axis.

## 2.2.5 Some Singularities

Before discussing the small disturbance numerical procedure, it is instructive to look at the singular behavior expected to occur in small disturbance solutions at the airfoil edges. From solutions for wedges, it can be expected that the pressure has a log singularity near sharp edges of a nonlifting symmetric airfoil. This singular behavior is sufficiently weak that it provides no difficulties to the numerical method. In addition, Nonweiler[23] (also see Cole[19]) has shown that, for moderately blunt leading edges, Eq. (2.3) possesses a solution with an integrable singularity. For a nose shape given by $y = x^n$, the pressure approaches infinity in an integrable manner for $n > 0.4$ (slightly blunter than a parabola, $n = 0.5$) to

$n = 1$ (wedge). No drag contribution (other than wave drag) is obtained by small disturbance solutions within this range of bluntness. It appears from numerical calculations that this criterion also holds for the numerical method. The addition of lift (either by angle of attack or camber) compounds the singular behavior at the nose. For example, the linearized boundary condition, because it does not allow the stagnation point to move off the geometric leading edge, causes a loss of expansion around the nose.

There exists still another important singularity, which occurs downstream of a supersonic to subsonic shock wave on a convex curved surface. In an inviscid flow, the shock must be normal to the surface so that the flow remains attached. The curvature of the surface induces an increasing pressure away from the surface in both the supersonic and subsonic regions near the shock. However, the jump conditions imposed by the normal shock cannot accommodate the downstream normal pressure gradient and, consequently, the shock must become oblique immediately off the surface. Their analysis predicts that the shock wave compression will be followed by a rapid expansion. Unfortunately, the scale is unknown, thereby preventing precise modeling of the post-shock expansion. It should be noted that this singularity is a consequence of the inviscid flow assumption and occurs in more exact treatments as well as in small disturbance theory.

## 2.3 Finite Difference Method

### 2.3.1 Introduction

The mixed differencing relaxation scheme for solving transonic boundary value problems was introduced by Murman and Cole[12] in their treatment of the small disturbance formulation for nonlifting airfoils. Soon afterwards, their scheme was extended to the lifting case by Krupp[25,26]. Most calculations are obtained by using unequally spaced grids, but in the following, we confine our discussion to evenly spaced grids and refer the reader to the cited references for more details.

The important type-dependent feature of the method is that, in subsonic regions, central difference operators are used to account for the domain of dependence of elliptic equations; in supersonic regions, backward or upwind difference operators are used to account for the absence of upstream influence in hyperbolic equations.

### 2.3.2 Difference Equations

Consider the finite-difference grid shown in sketch D, with $\Delta x$ and $\Delta \tilde{y}$ assumed constant and velocities defined as

$$\left. \begin{array}{l} u_{i+1/2,j} \equiv (\phi_x)_{i+1/2,j} \equiv \dfrac{\phi_{i+1,j} - \phi_{i,j}}{\Delta x}, \\[1em] v_{i,j+1/2} \equiv (\phi_{\tilde{y}})_{i,j+1/2} \equiv \dfrac{\phi_{i,j+1} - \phi_{i,j}}{\Delta \tilde{y}}, \text{ etc.} \end{array} \right\} \quad (2.17)$$

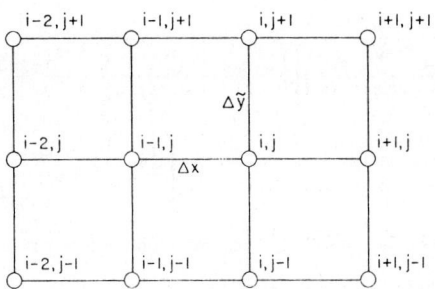

Sketch D

A central difference formula at point $i,j$ approximating the governing equation, Eq. (2.3), may be written in conservation form as

$$\frac{\{K\phi_x - [(\gamma + 1)/2]\phi_x^2\}_{i+1/2,j} - \{K\phi_x - [(\gamma + 1)/2]\phi_x^2\}_{i-1/2,j}}{\Delta x}$$
$$+ \frac{(\phi_{\tilde{y}})_{i,j+1/2} - (\phi_{\tilde{y}})_{i,j-1/2}}{\Delta \tilde{y}} = 0 \quad (2.18)$$

Substituting Eq. (2.17) into Eq. (2.18) and factoring yields

$$\left[K - (\gamma + 1)\left(\frac{\phi_{i+1,j} - \phi_{i-1,j}}{2\Delta x}\right)\right]\left[\frac{\phi_{i+1,j} - 2\phi_{i,j} + \phi_{i-1,j}}{(\Delta x)^2}\right]$$
$$+ \left[\frac{\phi_{i,j+1} - 2\phi_{i,j} + \phi_{i,j-1}}{(\Delta \tilde{y})^2}\right] = 0 \quad (2.19)$$

Eq. (2.19) is a second-order accurate difference operator for a Laplace-type equation in elliptic (subsonic) regions. The operator is stable by a linear stability analysis if the coefficient

$$(V_e)_{i,j} = K - (\gamma + 1)\left(\frac{\phi_{i+1,j} - \phi_{i-1,j}}{2\Delta x}\right) \qquad (2.20)$$

is positive.

Similarly, an implicit backward or upwind operator at $i,j$ may be written as

$$\frac{\{K\phi_x - [(\gamma + 1)/2]\phi_x^2\}_{i-1/2,j} - \{K\phi_x - [(\gamma + 1)/2]\phi_x^2\}_{i-3/2,j}}{\Delta x}$$

$$+ \frac{(\phi_{\tilde{y}})_{i,j+1/2} - (\phi_{\tilde{y}})_{i,j-1/2}}{\Delta \tilde{y}} = 0 \qquad (2.21)$$

or alternatively

$$\left[K - (\gamma + 1)\left(\frac{\phi_{i,j} - \phi_{i-2,j}}{2\Delta x}\right)\right]\left[\frac{\phi_{i,j} - 2\phi_{i-1,j} + \phi_{i-2,j}}{(\Delta x)^2}\right]$$

$$+ \left[\frac{\phi_{i,j+1} - 2\phi_{i,j} + \phi_{i,j-1}}{(\Delta \tilde{y})^2}\right] = 0 \qquad (2.22)$$

Eq. (2.22) is a first-order accurate difference operator for a wave-type equation in hyperbolic (supersonic) regions. The operator is stable by a linear stability analysis if the coefficient

$$(V_h)_{i,j} = K - (\gamma + 1)\left(\frac{\phi_{i,j} - \phi_{i-2,j}}{2\Delta x}\right) \qquad (2.23)$$

is negative.

During the iteration procedure, $(V_e)_{i,j}$ is computed at each grid point. If $(V_e)_{i,j} > 0$, the flow at that point is subsonic and the elliptic operator Eq. (2.19) is used. If $(V_e)_{i,j} < 0$ and $(V_h)_{i,j} < 0$, the flow is supersonic and the hyperbolic operator Eq. (2.22) is used. Closer examination is required, however, when the flow crosses the boundary from subsonic to supersonic regions at the sonic line and from supersonic to subsonic regions at a shock wave or sonic line.

As the flow accelerates through sonic velocity from subsonic to supersonic velocities, a point is reached where $(V_e)_{i,j} < 0$ and $(V_h)_{i,j} > 0$ [since $(V_h)_{i,j} = (V_e)_{i-1,j}$] and neither Eq. (2.19) nor Eq. (2.22) is stable. The difficulty is cir-

circumvented by introducing a parabolic point operator[27] for such points by setting $(V)_{i,j} = 0$ to yield

$$\frac{\phi_{i,j+1} - 2\phi_{i,j} + \phi_{i,j-1}}{(\Delta \tilde{y})^2} = 0 \qquad (2.24)$$

As the flow decelerates through sonic velocity from supersonic to subsonic flow, a point is reached where $(V_e)_{i,j} > 0$ and $(V_h)_{i,j} < 0$ and both Eq. (2.19) and Eq. (2.22) are locally stable. The original Murman and Cole scheme used the elliptic operator, Eq. (2.19), at this point.

## 2.3.3 Shock Point Operator

Results obtained using the above difference operators agree well with accepted exact solutions for continuous subcritical and supercritical shock-free flows. Furthermore, results for flows with embedded shock waves have agreed well with experimental data. However, the calculated shock pressure jump on the surface is consistently less than the theoretical value for a normal shock. This fact had been attributed[12] to a smoothing out of the previously discussed reexpansion singularity[24] at the foot of the shock by numerical truncation errors. However, several investigations using progressively finer grid spacing did not show an appreciable increase in the pressure jump with decreasing grid spacing as one would expect. Furthermore, Yoshihara[28] pointed out that no analysis had been presented to show that the calculated jump uniquely satisfies the jump contained in the governing equations. Murman[16] investigated this point further by comparing detached bow-wave solutions with time-dependent solutions[29]. This led to the introduction of the "shock-point operator"[16]

$$\frac{\{K\phi_x - [(\gamma + 1)/2]\phi_x^2\}_{i+1/2,j} - \{K\phi_x - [(\gamma + 1)/2]\phi_x^2\}_{i-1/2,j}}{\Delta x}$$

$$+ \frac{\{K\phi_x - [(\gamma + 1)/2]\phi_x^2\}_{i-1/2,j} - \{K\phi_x - [(\gamma + 1)/2]\phi_x^2\}_{i-3/2,j}}{\Delta x}$$

$$+ \frac{(\phi_{\tilde{y}})_{i,j+1/2} - (\phi_{\tilde{y}})_{i,j-1/2}}{\Delta \tilde{y}} = 0 \qquad (2.25)$$

which factors into

$$(V_e)_{i,j} \frac{(\phi_{i+1,j} - 2\phi_{i,j} + \phi_{i-1,j})}{(\Delta x)^2} + (V_h)_{i,j} \frac{(\phi_{i,j} - 2\phi_{i-1,j} + \phi_{i-2,j})}{(\Delta x)^2}$$

$$+ \frac{\phi_{i,j+1} - 2\phi_{i,j} + \phi_{i,j-1}}{(\Delta \tilde{y})^2} = 0 \quad (2.26)$$

This operator, whose x-differences are the sum of the x-differences of the elliptic and hyperbolic operators, is introduced at each grid point where $(V_e)_{i,j} > 0$ and $(V_h)_{i,j} < 0$.

Murman[16] has shown that this guarantees that the difference equations will give the correct weak solution to Eq. (2.3). For example, consider the normal shock solution for which $(dx)_s$ in Eq. (2.4) vanishes. Assume the shock lies somewhere between grid points $I - 1$ and $I$, with a uniform supersonic velocity $u_1$, upstream of the shock and a uniform subsonic velocity $u_2$ downstream. Sum the hyperbolic operator from $i = -\infty, \ldots, I - 1$, add the shock point operator at $i = I$ and sum the elliptic operator from $i = I + 1, \ldots, \infty$. Because of the cancellation of fluxes between neighboring grid points, the correct shock jump results:

$$\left(Ku - \frac{\gamma + 1}{2} u^2\right)_2 - \left(Ku - \frac{\gamma + 1}{2} u^2\right)_1 = 0 \quad (2.27)$$

Murman[16] has further generalized this example and shown that, in the limit of vanishing grid spacing, the correct shock jumps are obtained for oblique shocks when arbitrary grid spacing is used. For shock waves that jump from supersonic to subsonic velocities, the upstream velocity is $u_{I-3/2}$ and the downstream velocity is $u_{I+1/2}$ so that the jump is spread over three mesh points.

Now, if the shock point operator is replaced by the elliptic operator in the normal shock example given above, the result is

$$\left(Ku - \frac{\gamma + 1}{2} u^2\right)_2 - \left(Ku - \frac{\gamma + 1}{2} u^2\right)_1 = \left(Ku - \frac{\gamma + 1}{2} u^2\right)_{I-1/2,j}$$

$$- \left(Ku - \frac{\gamma + 1}{2} u^2\right)_{I-3/2,j} \quad (2.28)$$

The right-hand side can be viewed as a spurious source term that is caused by the noncancellation of fluxes at the shock point, $i = I$. Eq. (2.28) does not guarantee the correct shock jump, since, in general, the source is nonzero. In fact, the right-hand side vanishes only if the shock lies exactly at $i = I$, since then $u_{I-1/2,j} = u_{I-3/2,j} = u_1$.

A word should be said about calculating shocks when the flow downstream is supersonic. It has been demonstrated[27] that the first-order accurate hyperbolic operator Eq. (2.22) is dominated by dissipation errors, which lead to shocks smeared over 6 to 10 mesh points. Second-order accurate operators have a leading truncation error which is dispersive and often give poorer shock structure (e.g., overshoots and undershoots) and can suffer from instabilities. Hybrid combinations of first- and second-order operators[14,25] generally require so much dissipation for stability that the anticipated increase in sharpness is not realized.

### 2.3.4 Conservation Form and Consistency

The fact that the addition of the shock point operator gives the correct shock jump is a consequence of writing the difference operators in conservation form. That is, the integral properties of the governing equation are preserved by the difference operators. This is important at shock waves where spurious source terms resulting from the noncancellation of fluxes across mesh boundaries (if nonconservative differencing is used) may not vanish with vanishing mesh spacing. Thus, the calculated shock jump will be in error in proportion to the spurious source. It should be emphasized that, for smooth continuous regions, the choice of conservative or non-conservative differencing is irrelevant, but in regions of discontinuities, conservative form is imperative.

It is axiomatic that finite-difference operators be consistent with the differential equations being approximated, i.e., the difference equations reduce to the differential equations in the limit of vanishing grid spacing. At first glance, it appears that the parabolic operator, Eq. (2.24), and the shock point operator, Eq. (2.26), do not fulfill this requirement. It can be shown[16] that they both are, in fact, consistent with the differential equation, Eq. (2.3), in continuous regions where Eq. (2.3) is valid.

If one expands the coefficient $V = K - (\gamma + 1)\phi_x$ about the sonic value, $V = 0$, and substitutes in Eq. (2.3) the result to lowest order is

$$-\delta x (\gamma + 1)(\phi_{xx})^2 + \phi_{\tilde{y}\tilde{y}} + \ldots = 0 \qquad (2.29)$$

where $\delta x \equiv x - x_{sonic} \leq \Delta x$. As the mesh spacing vanishes, $\delta x \to 0$, showing that the parabolic operator, Eq. (2.24), is, indeed, consistent.

The Taylor series expansion of the shock point operator, Eq. (2.26), shows that its lowest-order approximation to Eq. (2.3) equals

$$2[K - (\gamma + 1)\phi_x]\phi_{xx} + \phi_{\tilde{y}\tilde{y}} + \Delta x \left\{ [K - (\gamma + 1)\phi_x]\phi_{xx} \right\}_x + \ldots = 0 \qquad (2.30)$$

If the flow decelerates through the shock points as a smooth recompression, the solution is continuous and, from the expansion Eq. (2.29), Eq. (2.30) is a consistent approximation with truncation error $O(\delta x)$. If the flow decelerates through the shock point as a shock with finite strength, the governing differential equation, Eq. (2.3), does not hold and the usual consistency condition is not violated. It should be noted, however, that in the limit $\Delta x, \Delta \tilde{y} \to 0$, the difference equations yield the correct integral properties of the governing equations.

## 2.3.5 Boundary Conditions

The flow tangency boundary condition on $\phi_{\tilde{y}}$, Eq. (2.14), is applied on the boundary $\tilde{y} = 0$ by writing either the approximation

$$(\phi_{\tilde{y}\tilde{y}})_{i,1} = \frac{2}{\Delta \tilde{y}} \left( \frac{\phi_{i,2} - \phi_{i,1}}{\Delta \tilde{y}} - \phi_{\tilde{y}} \Big|_{\tilde{y}=0} \right) \qquad (2.31)$$

with $j - 1$ placed on the boundary $\tilde{y} = 0$ or by

$$(\phi_{\tilde{y}\tilde{y}})_{i,1} = \frac{1}{\Delta \tilde{y}} \left( \frac{\phi_{i,2} - \phi_{i,1}}{\Delta \tilde{y}} - \phi_{\tilde{y}} \Big|_{\tilde{y}=0} \right) \qquad (2.32)$$

with $j = 1$ placed at $\tilde{y} = \tilde{y}/2$. In his treatment of lifting airfoils, Krupp[26] used a version of Eq. (2.32) for an unequally spaced $\tilde{y}$ mesh. The boundary condition $(\phi_{\tilde{y}})_{\tilde{y}=0}$ is incorporated into the expression for $\phi_{\tilde{y}\tilde{y}}$ at $\tilde{y} = h_1$ (see sketch E).

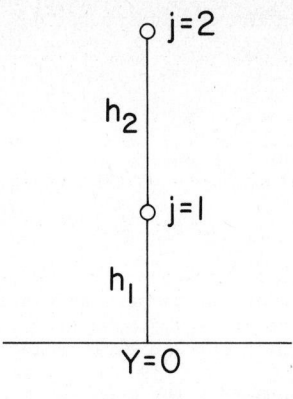

Sketch E

The difference operator, retaining the lowest-order truncation error, is given by

$$(\phi_{\tilde{y}\tilde{y}})_{i,1} = \frac{2}{h_2(h_2 + 2h_1)} (\phi_{i,2} - \phi_{i,1}) - \frac{2}{h_2 + h_1} \phi_{\tilde{y}}\bigg|_{\tilde{y}=0}$$

$$+ \frac{h_2^2 - 3h_1^2}{3(h_2 + 2h_1)} \phi_{\tilde{y}\tilde{y}\tilde{y}}\bigg|_{\tilde{y}=0} + O(h_2^2) \quad (2.33)$$

which shows that the truncation error is minimized for $h_2 = \sqrt{3}\, h_1$.

The outer boundary condition can be treated by either extending the computational domain to infinity through some transformation or by using a finite-domain and treating the infinity boundary condition in an approximate manner. The latter approach has been used in small disturbance computations reported. Approximate far field solutions have been derived[25,30] by writing Eq. (2.3) as an integral expression for $\phi$. The resulting approximations are separated into three terms representing the effect of thickness, lift, and the nonlinearity arising from the term $\phi_x^2$. This approximate treatment retains sufficient accuracy if the outer boundary is far enough from the origin, say $|x| \simeq 1.5$, $|\tilde{y}| \simeq 3$.

For lifting airfoils, the circulation $\Gamma$ which satisfies the Kutta condition must be obtained as part of the solution process for $\phi$. A cut is introduced at $\tilde{y} = 0$, $x \geq 1$ across which the potential jump must equal the circulation $\Gamma$. Modified difference operators for $\phi_{\tilde{y}\tilde{y}}$ are written that take into account the jump in $\phi$

across the cut while maintaining the continuity of $\phi_x$ and $\phi_{\tilde{y}}$. These difference operators are expressed as

$$(\phi_{\tilde{y}\tilde{y}})_{i,0^-} = \frac{1}{(\Delta\tilde{y})^2}[(\phi_{i,1} - \Gamma_i) - 2\phi_{i,0^-} + \phi_{i,-1}] \qquad (2.34a)$$

$$(\phi_{\tilde{y}\tilde{y}})_{i,1} = \frac{1}{(\Delta\tilde{y})^2}[\phi_{i,2} - 2\phi_{i,1} + (\phi_{i,0^-} + \Gamma_i)] \qquad (2.34b)$$

The iteration procedure for finding the proper circulation proceeds by choosing an initial circulation $\Gamma_0$ from which the far field solution is obtained. The circulation at the trailing edge is found from the jump in $\phi$, i.e.,

$$\Gamma_{te} = \phi_{i_{te},0^+} - \phi_{i_{te},0^-} \qquad (2.35)$$

On each iterative sweep of the grid, a new value of $\Gamma_{te}$ is found by linearly extrapolating the $\phi$'s from above and below. (It is recalled that, in the Krupp procedure, the grid points are at $\pm h_1$ above the airfoil boundary $\tilde{y} = 0$, $0 \leq x \leq 1$.) The new $\Gamma_{te}$ along with $\Gamma_0$ is used to determine the $\Gamma_i$, $1 < x < x_{max}$, by interpolation. As the iteration proceeds, new estimates for $\Gamma_0$ are made, depending on previous values of $\Gamma_0$ and $\Gamma_{te}$, until a converged solution for $\phi$ is obtained and $\Gamma_0 = \Gamma_{te}$. A simplified procedure for converging to the proper circulation has been developed,[31,32] which consists of simply setting $\Gamma = \Gamma_{te}$ along the entire cut during each iteration. This simple method gives both the same results and convergence rate as the method of Krupp.

The treatment of lift introduces an additional iteration into the basic relaxation procedure and can cause a significant increase in computation time. However, certain strategies exist to impove the efficiency of lifting calculations. For example, one can often begin calculations from a previous solution that is not far removed from the desired solution. Another strategy, suggested by Dr. Hall of the Royal Aircraft Establishment, is to update the potential in the entire field (not just the outer boundary) for the first few iterations according to the simple vortex solution. For the following iterations, the vortex solution is replaced by the lifting potential distribution found from the previous iteration.

## 2.3.6 Relaxation Procedure

Approximating the governing equation, Eq. (2.3), by the appropriate difference operators at each interior grid point and applying the boundary conditions results in a system of simultaneous equations for the value of potential at each interior grid point. The system is, in general, nonlinear in the grid variable $\phi_{i,j}$ because of the upwind difference operator used in supersonic regions. The solution is found by a successive line relaxation along a line of grid points at constant x. The equation system for each vertical line is written as

$$\underset{\sim}{A}\vec{\phi}_i = \vec{f}_i \qquad (2.36)$$

where $\vec{\phi}_i$ is the J dimensional column vector

$$\vec{\phi}_i = \begin{pmatrix} \phi_{i,1} \\ \cdot \\ \cdot \\ \cdot \\ \phi_{i,J} \end{pmatrix}$$

and the J×J dimensional tridiagonal matrix $\underset{\sim}{A}$ and J dimensional vector $\vec{f}_i$ are functions of $\vec{\phi}_{i+1}, \vec{\phi}_i, \vec{\phi}_{i-1}^+, \vec{\phi}_{i-2}^+$ where the superscript + refers to new values. After some initial guess on $\phi$, the iteration method consists of successively sweeping the grid from the upstream to downstream boundary, during which, new values of $\phi$ are obtained from Eq. (2.36) by direct elimination. Convergence is accelerated by the algorithm

$$\vec{\phi}_i^+ = \omega\vec{\tilde{\phi}}_i + (1 - \omega)\vec{\phi} \qquad (2.37)$$

where $\vec{\tilde{\phi}}_i$ is the solution to Eq. (2.36). Switching the difference operators, depending on the values of $V_e$ and $V_h$ with respect to zero, ensures that the matrix $\underset{\sim}{A}$ remains diagonally dominant and nonsingular. Note that in supersonic regions $\underset{\sim}{A}$ is a function of $\phi_{i,j}$ and the elimination algorithm may be successively iterated at columns that contain supersonic points until $\vec{\phi}_i$ satisfies a prescribed error bound before sweeping to the next column. Alternatively, one can consider $(V_h)_{i,j}$ as fixed coefficients and do the elimination only once. The later procedure gives a slightly better overall convergence rate.

The stability and rate of convergence of the relaxation algorithm depend on the choice of relaxation parameters $\omega$ in Eq. (2.37). The values of $\omega$ depend on the type of flow and acceptable values have been found to be $\omega \simeq 1.9$ in elliptic regions and $\omega \simeq 0.90$ in hyperbolic regions. Because the problem is nonlinear, these values of $\omega$ have been determined by numerical experimentation. A clue to the value in elliptic regions comes from standard references on relaxation methods, where it is shown that the line algorithm applied to linear elliptic equations is stable for $0 < \omega < 2$, with the optimum value approaching 2 with increasing grid refinement. For the linear wave equation, the well-known von Neuman stability test based on Fourier analysis (with successive iterations viewed as steps in pseudotime) shows that the supersonic relaxation algorithm is stable only if it is fully implicit, i.e., with $\omega = 1$. In actual transonic calculations, however, experience indicates that convergence difficulties are less likely to occur if $\omega$ is set to a value less than 1. It is noted that nonconservative relaxation schemes with both $V_e$ and $V_h$ computed by using central difference operators with data strictly from the previous sweep (thereby linearizing the equation from one sweep to the next) are reported to have no particular stability difficulties with $\omega = 1$. Such a modification is used in both the Garabedian-Korn and Jameson methods for the full potential equation (see section 3).

## 2.4 Results

Numerous calculated results obtained from the small disturbance relaxation method have been reported by Murman and Krupp, particularly in reference 25. Computation times are reported[26] to be from 3 to 15 minutes on an IBM 360/65 (or 1 to 5 minutes on a CDC 6600) although more recent improvements for converging the circulation have made the lower figure more typical. The bulk of the calculations were performed without incorporating the shock-point operator. Such results are termed "not fully conservative relaxation" (NCR) solutions. In Murman's[16] recent paper he compares some NCR solutions with those obtained using the shock-point operator, termed "fully conservative relaxation" (FCR) solutions. These results are highly significant and some of them are repeated here.

An example of the comparison between NCR and FCR solutions for an embedded shock is shown in Fig. 1. The NCR calculations show that its shock pressure jump does not approach the theoretical normal jump, even as the grid spacing is decreased. The FCR solution, however, shows that as the mesh is refined, the correct jump is obtained, followed by a well-defined reexpansion. The FCR computed shock is stronger and farther aft of the one obtained from the NCR method. This appears typical in comparisons of the two methods. In fact, as the strength of the shock increases, the disparity between the shock locations given by the two methods also increases. For example, the results in Fig. 1 for $M_\infty = 0.872$ show a difference in shock location of about 5 percent chord. The results shown in Fig. 2, on the other hand, indicate that at $M_\infty = 0.909$ the shock is stronger and the difference in location has increased to about 12 percent. Conversely, as the shock strength decreases, the difference in the predicted shock locations also decreases and, in regions of smooth shock-free recompressions, the two solutions are in essential agreement.

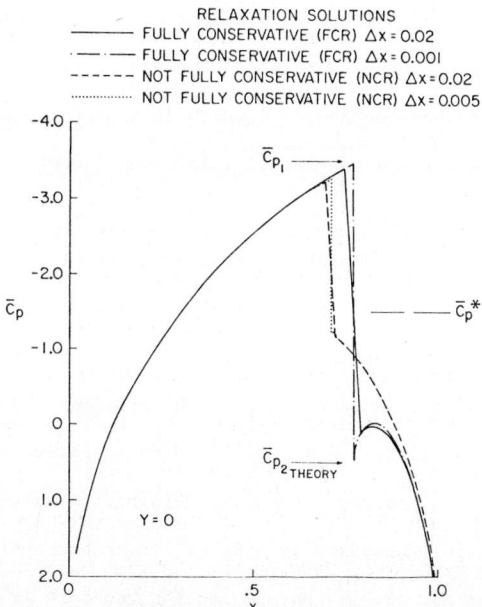

Fig. 1. Comparison of FCR and NCR solutions for 6 percent parabolic arc airfoil at $M_\infty = 0.872$[16] ($K = 1.8$).

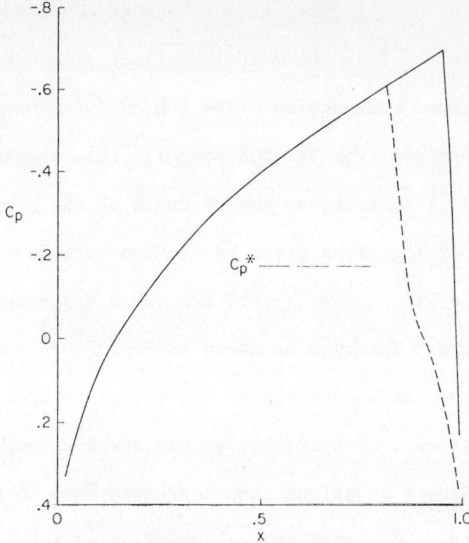

Fig. 2. Comparison of FCR and NCR solutions for 6 percent parabolic arc airfoil at $M_\infty = 0.909$[16] ($K = 1.25$).

Comparative results for flow with a supersonic free stream and a detached bow shock are shown in Fig. 3. The calculations were performed using the two relaxation methods and a time-dependent method,[29] which is also fully conservative. The FCR and time-dependent results are in essential agreement, whereas the NCR result shows too great a shock detachment distance. Fig. 4 gives the shock jumps for the three calculations in the form of hodograph plots and illustrates that the NCR method shock jumps are in considerable error for strong oblique shocks.

Further examples of NCR and FCR calculations for lifting airfoils are given in following sections. It should be noted that the existence of singular behaviors at the airfoil edges to Eq. (2.3) led Krupp[25] to do extensive experimentation with techniques for calculating surface pressure. His best results were obtained by finding $\phi$ on the airfoil boundary ($\tilde{y} = 0$) by linear extrapolation. (Recall from the boundary condition Eq. (2.33) that $\phi$ on the boundary is not computed directly.)

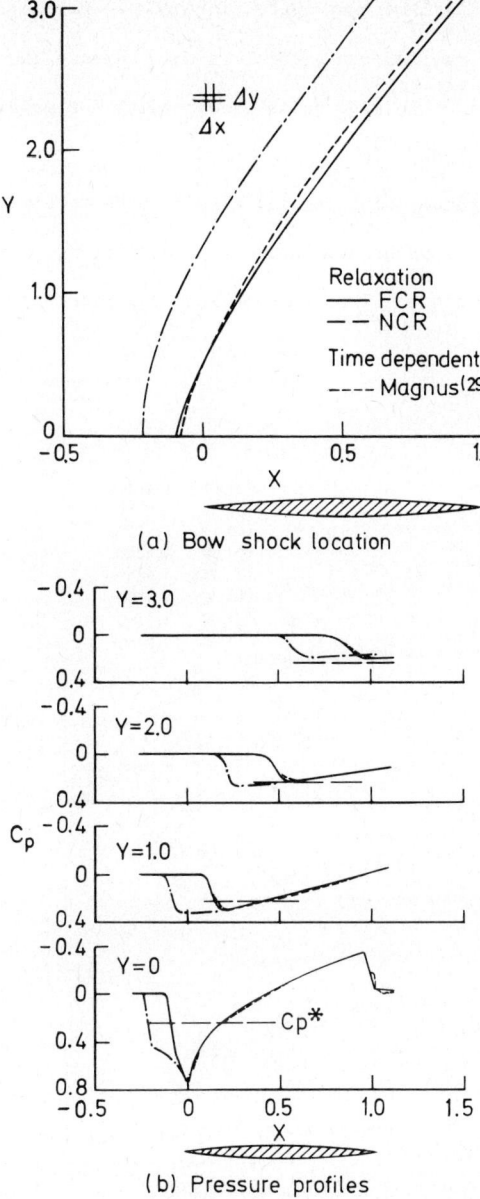

Fig. 3. Comparison of computational methods for 6 percent parabolic arc airfoil with detached bow wave at $M_\infty = 1.15$.[16]

While local irregularities may appear in the nose region for some solutions, the solution over the rest of the airfoil is unaffected. Thus, small disturbance solutions can be expected to give quite good results for moderately blunt airfoils at small angles of attack.

Small disturbance solutions can also be made to give better agreement with more exact solutions by appropriate choice of the transonic similarity forms which it is recalled are not unique. Through numerical experimentation, Krupp[25] found that the

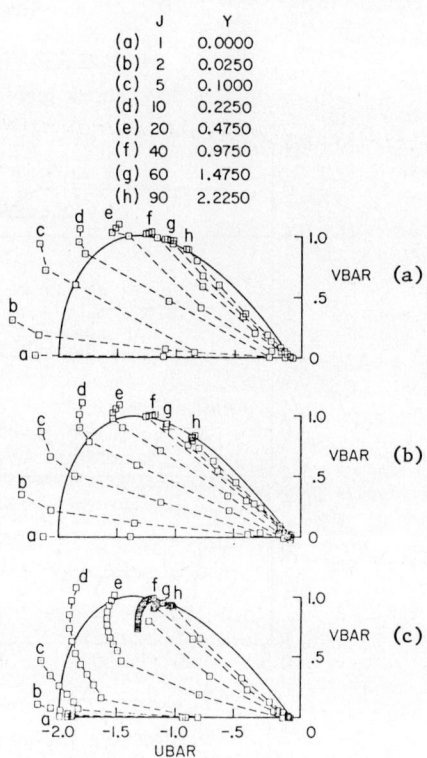

Fig. 4. Hodograph plots for detached bow wave.
    (a) Fully conservative relaxation.
    (b) Time-dependent.[29]
    (c) Not fully conservative relaxation.[16]

following scaling, when used by the above numerical method, gave improved agreement with full inviscid theory for symmetric shock-free airfoils. These forms are

$$K = \frac{1 - M_\infty^2}{\delta^{2/3} M_\infty}$$

$$\tilde{y} = \delta^{1/3} M_\infty^{2/3} y$$

$$C_p = \frac{-2\delta^{2/3}}{M_\infty^{3/4}} \phi_x$$

## 3. EXACT ISENTROPIC PROCEDURE IN TWO DIMENSIONS

### 3.1 Introduction

The equations for irrotational, inviscid, adiabatic flow of a perfect gas in two dimensions may be expressed as a second-order partial differential equation

$$(a^2 - u^2)\phi_{xx} - 2uv\phi_{xy} + (a^2 - v^2)\phi_{yy} = 0 \qquad (3.1)$$

for the velocity potential $\phi$. The velocity components are

$$u = \phi_x, \qquad v = \phi_y \qquad (3.2)$$

and the speed of sound is defined by Bernoulli's law

$$\frac{u^2 + v^2}{2} + \frac{a^2}{\gamma - 1} = \frac{1}{2} + \frac{1}{M_\infty^2 (\gamma - 1)} \qquad (3.3)$$

There are no assumptions of small disturbances and Eq. (3.1) is exact for subsonic inviscid flow. Furthermore, Eq. (3.1) is assumed valid for transonic flows under the assumption that any shock waves are sufficiently weak to introduce negligible rotation.

The flow equation can be written in the divergence form

$$(\rho\phi_x)_x + (\rho\phi_y)_y = 0 \qquad (3.4a)$$

$$\rho = \left[1 - \frac{\gamma - 1}{2}(u^2 + v^2)\right]^{1/\gamma - 1} \qquad (3.4b)$$

from which a weak solution can be derived that admits jumps analogous to the Rankine-Hugoniot relations. Steger and Baldwin[33] have shown that the component of momentum normal to the isentropic shock is not conserved through the shock. Since the total drag must vanish in a potential flow, the force that is due to the momentum jump at the shock is balanced by the drag on the body. Consequently, the solution to Eq. (3.1) may be used to give an approximation to the drag on an airfoil with shock waves.

Such estimates of inviscid wave drag are valid for relaxation solutions provided the isentropic shock wave is properly captured. However, results reported so far for the exact isentropic equation have failed to give the proper isentropic shock jump because the difference equation is an approximation to the nondivergence form of the differential equation, Eq. (3.1). As pointed out in section 2, conservative difference operators are required to calculate the weak solution correctly. Recall that in the small disturbance procedure, the conservative difference equation factored into coefficient V, multiplying second derivative operators in x. The change of sign of the coefficient V, depending on whether the flow is subsonic or supersonic, is necessary for stability in the Murman-Cole type-dependent scheme. Clearly, application of the appropriate difference operators to Eq. (3.1) will lead to the same stable properties. However, the finite-difference analog to the divergence form, Eq. (3.4) does not possess the straightforward factoring property of the difference analog to the small disturbance divergence form because of the complicated relationship between velocity and density. Further investigation is required to develop a method that gives the correct weak solution, either by conservative differencing or shock fitting. It is important to note, however, that, even though the present methods do not give the correct inviscid shock jumps, their solutions are often in remarkably good agreement with experimental results, as will be shown later.

The principal advantage of using the exact isentropic equation is that one can treat the airfoil surface boundary condition exactly, thereby obtaining more accurate solutions over blunt-nosed, thick airfoils at high angles of attack. Of course, the finite-difference grid must be introduced so that difference operators may be constructed accurately at the boundary and, in general, the airfoil itself must be a coordinate line, or nearly so.

Three relaxation procedures for obtaining solutions to Eq. (3.1) have been developed and are briefly described in the following sections.

## 3.2 Steger and Lomax Procedure

Steger and Lomax[13] chose to replace the actual airfoil by the blunt-nosed plate control surface shown in sketch F. The nose of the plate is taken to be the

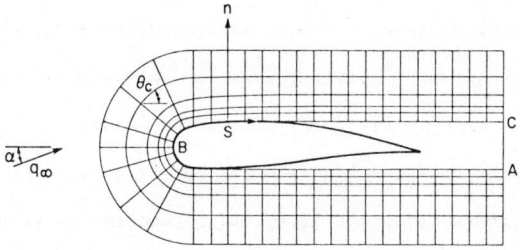

Sketch F

closest possible representation of the airfoil nose (in many cases exact). Over the aft portion of the airfoil, the flow tangency boundary condition is projected onto the control surface by second-order extrapolation. The coordinate system used in the calculation corresponds to the normals to the control surface and their orthogonal members. The far field boundary condition is taken to be a compressible vortex and is applied at some finite distance.

Eq. (3.1) is rewritten in terms of control surface coordinates from which the potential due to a uniform free-stream was substracted to yield

$$\left(\frac{a^2 - u^2}{H}\right)\left[\frac{1}{H}\phi_{ss} + \phi_s\left(\frac{1}{H}\right)_s\right] + (a^2 - v^2)\phi_{nn} - \frac{2uv}{H}\phi_{sn}$$

$$- \frac{1}{HR_c}\left[(a^2 - u^2)\phi_n + \frac{2uv}{H}\phi_s\right] = 0 \quad (3.5a)$$

where

$$a^2 = a_\infty^2 - \frac{\gamma - 1}{2}(u^2 + v^2 - q_\infty^2) \quad (3.5b)$$

$$u = q_\infty \cos(\theta_c - \alpha) + \frac{\phi_s}{H} \qquad (3.5c)$$

$$v = -q_\infty \sin(\theta_c - \alpha) + \phi_n \qquad (3.5d)$$

$$H = \frac{R_c(s) - n}{R_c(s)} \qquad (3.5e)$$

where $\theta_c$ is the angle the s-coordinate makes with a horizontal reference line and $R_c$ is the radius of curvature of the control surface. Type-dependent difference operators similar to that of Murman and Cole are written for Eq. (3.5), except that in hyperbolic regions fully second-order accurate operators are used.

The solution is obtained by a line relaxation scheme that sweeps about the airfoil, proceeding from A to C in sketch F. In lifting airfoils cases, the Kutta condition is enforced at the trailing edge and the appropriate value for the circulation is found by operator intervention via interactive computer graphics. Reported solutions were obtained in less than 20 minutes on an IBM 360/67 (6 minutes on a CDC 6600).

## 3.3 Garabedian and Korn Procedure

The Garabedian and Korn[14,34] approach is to map the exterior of the airfoil conformally onto the interior of the unit circle, with the point at infinity corresponding to the origin. This mapping procedure was introduced by Sells[35] and produces a polar coordinate system that greatly simplifies the fulfillment of the surface boundary condition. Furthermore, it produces a desirable distribution of grid points along the airfoil surface such that the density of grid points is greatest at the leading and trailing edges. The mapping is done numerically and requires the specification of the airfoil surface curvature. For details on the basic mapping procedure, the reader is referred to the paper by Sells[35] and the book by Thwaites.[36]

Assume that the mapping is known and given by

$$x + iy = F(re^{i\theta}) = \sum_{n=-1}^{\infty} a_n r^n e^{in\theta} \qquad (3.6)$$

with modulus

$$f = r^2 |F'(re^{i\theta})| \qquad (3.7)$$

In the new $(r,\theta)$ coordinate system ($\theta$ measured clockwise from the trailing edge back), Eq. (3.1) becomes

$$(a^2 - r^2 f^{-2} \phi_\theta^2)\phi_{\theta\theta} - 2r^4 f^{-2}\phi_\theta \phi_r \phi_{\theta r} + r^2(a^2 - r^4 f^{-2} \phi_r^2)\phi_{rr}$$

$$+ r(a^2 - r^2 f^{-2}\phi_\theta^2 - 2r^4 f^{-2}\phi_r^2)\phi_r$$

$$+ f^{-3}(r^2 \phi_\theta^2 + r^4 \phi_r^2)(f_\theta \phi_\theta + r^2 f_r \phi_r) = 0 \qquad (3.8)$$

This equation is used in the concentric region near the airfoil, $0 < r_o \le r \le 1$ and includes all supersonic points. For the inner concentric region, $0 \le r \le r_o < 1$, a disturbance potential is defined as

$$\Phi = \phi - f_o \frac{\cos(\theta + \alpha)}{r} \qquad (3.9)$$

where $f_o$ is a constant of the mapping. Use of the new dependent variable avoids the singularities at infinity, with $\Phi$ satisfying the equation

$$(a^2 - r^2 f^{-2}\phi_\theta)\Phi_{\theta\theta} - 2r^4 f^{-2}\phi_\theta \phi_r \Phi_{\theta r} + r^2(a^2 - r^4 f^{-2}\phi_r^2)\Phi_{rr} - 2r^3 f^{-2}\phi_\theta \phi_r \Phi_\theta$$

$$+ r(a^2 + r^2 f^{-2}\phi_\theta^2 - 2r^4 f^{-2}\phi_r^2)\Phi_r$$

$$+ f^{-3}(r^2 \phi_\theta^2 + r^4 \phi_r^2)(f_\theta \Phi_\theta + r^2 f_r \Phi_r)$$

$$= f_o f^{-3}(r^2 \phi_\theta^2 + r^4 \phi_r^2) \frac{f_\theta \sin(\theta + \alpha) + r f_r \cos(\theta + \alpha)}{r} \qquad (3.10)$$

and the vortex boundary values

$$\Phi = \frac{\Gamma}{2\pi} \tan^{-1}[\sqrt{1 - M_\infty^2} \tan(\theta + \alpha)] \qquad (3.11)$$

at $r = 0$. The Kutta condition requires that $\phi_\theta = 0$ at the trailing edge and that the potential jump across rays $\theta = 0$ and $2\pi$ be constant and equal to $\Gamma$.

The finite-difference scheme is similar to that of Murman and Cole. However, central difference operators are used to approximate all first derivatives in both subsonic and supersonic regions, and in supersonic regions a weighted average of first- and second-order accurate upwind operators is employed as follows for $\theta > \pi$ (similar expressions are derived for $\theta < \pi$):

$$\phi_{\theta\theta} = \frac{1}{(\Delta\theta)^2} [(\phi_{i,j} - 2\phi_{i-1,j} + \phi_{i-2,j}) + \varepsilon(\phi_{i,j} - 3\phi_{i-1,j} + 3\phi_{i-2,j} - \phi_{i-3,j})]$$

(3.12)

and

$$\phi_{\theta r} = \frac{1}{4\Delta\theta\Delta r} [2(\phi_{i,j+1} - \phi_{i-1,j+1} + \phi_{i-1,j-1} - \phi_{i,j-1})$$

$$+ \varepsilon(\phi_{i,j+1} - 2\phi_{i-1,j+1} + \phi_{i-2,j+1} - \phi_{i-2,j-1} + 2\phi_{i-1,j-1} - \phi_{i,j-1})] \quad (3.13)$$

By choosing $\varepsilon = 0$ the above operators are accurate to the first order in $\Delta\theta$; however, choosing

$$0 < \varepsilon = 1 - \lambda\Delta\theta < 1$$

leads to operators accurate to the second order which will be stable over a wide range of diffusive damping parameter, $\lambda$, because of the favorable damping given by the leading truncation error term.

The surface tangency condition at $r = 1$ is simply $\phi_r = 0$ and is handled by reflection.

In the relaxation procedure, the computational domain is swept in the direction of flow, i.e., from $\theta = \pi$ to $2\pi$ over the upper airfoil surface and then from $\theta = \pi$ to $0$ over the lower airfoil surface. During each cycle, the quantities $\phi_\theta$, $\phi_r$, and a are frozen at their values from the previous cycle. At each cycle, a new value of $\Gamma$ is obtained from the potential jump at the trailing edge and the increment in $\Gamma$ is used to update $\phi$ everywhere by use of Eq. (3.11). Solutions are reported to be obtained in 5 to 10 minutes on a CDC 6600.

## 3.4 Jameson Procedures

Jameson's method as described in reference 15 is essentially the same as that of Garabedian-Korn. However, Jameson avoids the use of two computational domains by writing a perturbation potential about a far field solution, represented by the sum of a doublet and pseudovortex. The resulting reduced potential

$$\Phi = \phi - \frac{\cos(\theta + \alpha)}{r} + \frac{\Gamma\theta}{2\pi} \qquad (3.14)$$

is everywhere finite and continuous. The governing equation becomes

$$(a^2 - u^2)\Phi_{\theta\theta} - 2uv\left(r\Phi_{\theta r} + \Phi_\theta - \frac{\Gamma}{2\pi}\right) + (a^2 - v^2)(r^2\Phi_{rr} + r\Phi_r)$$

$$+ (u^2 - v^2)r\Phi_r + (u^2 + v^2)(ur^{-1}f_\theta + vf_r) = 0 \qquad (3.15)$$

where

$$\left.\begin{array}{l} u = f^{-1}\left[r\left(\Phi_\theta - \dfrac{\Gamma}{2\pi}\right) - \sin(\theta + \alpha)\right] \\[6pt] v = f^{-1}[r^2\Phi_r - \cos(\theta + \alpha)] \end{array}\right\} \qquad (3.16)$$

At the airfoil surface, for $r = 1$, $\phi_r = 0$ so that the flow tangency condition becomes

$$\Phi_r = \cos(\theta + \alpha) \qquad (3.17)$$

At the airfoil trailing edge, for $r = 1$ and $\theta = 0$, the mapping is not conformal so that $f$ must vanish. Thus, the Kutta condition that the tangential velocity $u$ be finite at the trailing edge requires that

$$\Phi_\theta = \frac{\Gamma}{2\pi} - \sin\alpha \qquad (3.18)$$

at the trailing edge. At the far field boundary, for $r = 0$, the flow approaches the free-stream condition and $\Phi$ is given by

$$\Phi = \frac{\Gamma}{2\pi}\left\{\theta - \tan^{-1}\left[(1 - M_\infty^2)^{1/2}\tan(\theta + \alpha)\right]\right\} \qquad (3.19)$$

The relaxation procedure is the same as that of Garabedian and Korn except that operators accurate to the first order for $\Phi_{\theta\theta}$ and $\Phi_{\theta r}$ are used in hyperbolic regions. Jameson does not describe the procedure for obtaining the new value of $\Gamma$ at each cycle; however, it can easily be found from application of Eq. (3.18) at $\theta = 0$ and $\theta = 2\pi$ and $r = 1$. Jameson's procedure is very efficient, with solutions obtained in about 2 minutes on a CDC 6600.

It should be pointed out that Jameson differs from Murman in that all first derivatives are evaluated by using central operators with data from the previous iteration. In supersonic regions, the relaxation parameter, $\omega$, is set equal to 1.

Jameson[17] has recently extended his method to include supersonic free streams. The circle plane is not well suited for such cases because of the need to distinguish between the upstream infinity boundary, where Cauchy data are specified, and the downstream infinity boundary, where no condition is imposed. Jameson suggests that a more convenient coordinate system is obtained by mapping the circle plane to the upper half plane by the additional transformation

$$w = \sigma^{1/2} + \frac{1}{\sigma^{1/2}} \tag{3.20}$$

where $\sigma$ is the circle plane map function. Additional stretching of the coordinates is used to map the half plane into a rectangle. Thus, as shown in sketch G, the flow enters through the upper boundary, splits, and leaves through the two sides, with the airfoil being a segment of the lower boundary.

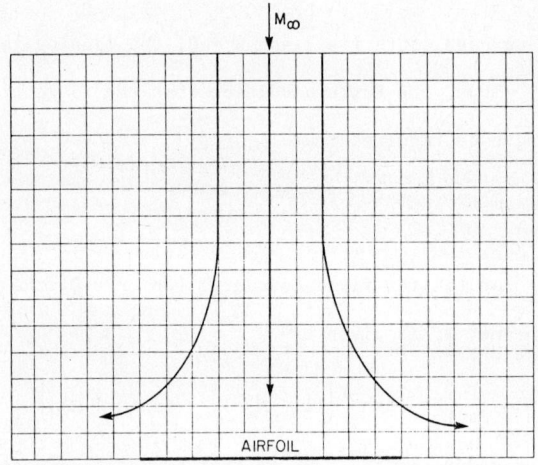

Sketch G

The remaining points on the lower boundary to the right and left of this segment correspond to points on either side of the slice across which the potential jump satisfying the Kutta condition is imposed. In the far field, the combined mappings approach a square-root transformation, and a reduced potential that is finite at infinity is obtained by setting

$$\Phi = \phi - (x^2 - y^2)\cos\alpha - 2xy \sin\alpha \qquad (3.21)$$

where x and y are coordinates in the transformed plane and $\alpha$ is the flow angle at infinity. The far field boundary conditions for subsonic flow at infinity are

$$\Phi = 0 \quad \text{on the top boundary}$$

and $\qquad\qquad\qquad\qquad\qquad\qquad\qquad\qquad\qquad\qquad\qquad\qquad\qquad$ (3.22)

$$\Phi = \pm\Gamma/2 \quad \text{on the side boundaries}$$

For supersonic flow at infinity, the conditions are

$$\Phi = 0, \ \Phi_y = 0 \quad \text{on the top boundary} \qquad (3.23)$$

with no condition imposed for supersonic outflow at the sides.

Jameson has considered a similar transformation, which applies the square-root transformation

$$z = w^2 \qquad (3.24)$$

about a point just inside the leading edge (at the center, say, of a circular nose) and generates parabolic coordinates in the physical plane. The airfoil becomes a bump on the lower boundary of the transformed plane. To facilitate a more accurate application of the tangency boundary condition, the coordinate parallel to the lower boundary is displaced to follow the contour of the transformed airfoil and leads to a slightly nonorthogonal coordinate system. The nonorthogonality introduces additional terms in the governing equation, as well as the expression for the surface boundary condition. In addition, care must be taken at the trailing edge to avoid corners in the coordinates and there is no automatic concentration of grid points near the trailing edge. Thus, this transformation does not appear as favorable as the previous one for two-dimensional computations, but, as is discussed later, it is used in Jameson's three-dimensional calculations.

## 3.5 Jameson's Rotated Difference Scheme for Supersonic Regions

The key to the Murman and Cole scheme is that x-derivatives in the transonic small disturbance equation are backward differenced in hyperbolic regions. In the small disturbance formulation, the x-direction is the local streamwise direction and thus disturbances in hyperbolic regions are prevented from propagating upstream. The principle that the domain of dependence of the difference equation include the domain of dependence of the differential equation it approximates is clearly met. The standard application of the Murman and Cole scheme to the difference equations approximating the full isentropic equation discussed in this section, however, is based on backward differencing in a coordinate direction, say x, which is not aligned with the local stream. Consequently, there will exist points for which $v^2 < u^2 < a^2 < u^2 + v^2$, that is, the x-component of velocity is subsonic in a supersonic region. Applying the central difference operator at such points allows upstream propagation of disturbances and may lead to instabilities. On the other hand, the y-coordinate line lies upstream of one of the characteristics (see sketch H), so that application of the backward difference operator leads to a scheme that uses the incorrect domain of dependence and may again lead to instability. Fortunately, this difficulty is of little consequence in many subsonic free-stream applications, since supersonic flow is confined to a region near the airfoil where the coordinate system is closely aligned to the stream.

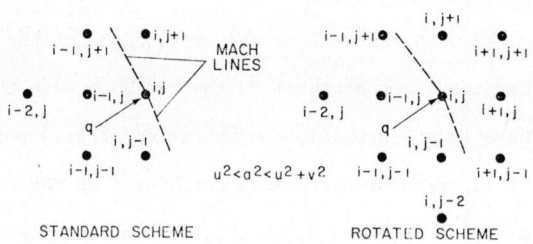

Sketch H

In cases where the flow at infinity is supersonic, the misalignment of the coordinates with the stream is of greater concern and led Jameson to developing the "rotated" difference scheme for supersonic flow regions. It was recognized that the Murman-Cole scheme should be applied to the governing equation written in terms of coordinates s in the local stream direction and n normal to the stream as follows

$$\left(1 - \frac{q^2}{a^2}\right)\phi_{ss} + \phi_{nn} = 0 \tag{3.25}$$

The derivatives $\phi_{ss}$ and $\phi_{nn}$ may be expressed in terms of the coordinate directions (x,y) locally by a rotation to give

$$\left.\begin{array}{l} \phi_{ss} = \dfrac{1}{q^2}(u^2\phi_{xx} + 2uv\phi_{xy} + v^2\phi_{yy}) \\[2mm] \phi_{nn} = \dfrac{1}{q^2}(v^2\phi_{xx} - 2uv\phi_{xy} + u^2\phi_{yy}) \end{array}\right\} \tag{3.26}$$

where $u/q$ and $v/q$ are the direction cosines. The Murman-Cole scheme is now properly applied by writing backward (or retarded) difference operators in x and y for the derivatives representing $\phi_{ss}$ and central difference operators for these representing $\phi_{nn}$.

Computation molecules for the standard and rotated schemes are shown in sketch H. A comparison of the schemes brings out two important features of the rotated scheme. First, because of the upwind y-difference operators used to approximate $\phi_{ss}$, the quantity $\phi_{i,j-2}$ appears. If the tridiagonal solution algorithm is to be used along the column, i, $\phi_{i,j-2}$ cannot be updated and its value from the previous iteration (old value) will appear in the right-hand side of Eq. (2.36). Second, due to the central x-difference operators used to approximate $\phi_{nn}$, old values appear along the column i + 1, preventing solution by a simple column-by-column marching procedure.

Extensive analysis of the stability and convergence of the rotated scheme is presented in reference 17 (also see references 37 and 38). The approach is similar to that of Garabedian's[39] theory for successive over-relaxation of Laplace's equation, in that iterations are viewed as steps in artificial time ($\tau$). The combination of new and old values in the difference operators is chosen so that the equivalent time-dependent equation (neglecting truncation terms) represents a properly posed problem whose solution approaches the solution of the time-invariant equation. In particular, the coefficient of $\phi_\tau$ is chosen to vanish and the coefficients of the remaining time derivatives chosen such that  s  is the time-like or marching direction in the hyperbolic time-dependent equation.

Jameson further shows that the von Neumann test of local stability for the difference equation

$$\sum_{p,q} (a_{pq} \phi_{i+p,j+q} - b_{pq} \phi^+_{i+p,j+q}) = 0 \qquad (3.27)$$

requires

$$\sum_{p,q} a_{pq} = \sum_{p,q} b_{p,q} = 0 \qquad (3.28)$$

The superscript + is used to denote new or updated values. Here, Eq. (3.27) is the linear equivalent of rotated scheme applied to Eq. (3.25) and the relaxation parameter is 1.

Upon combining the various conditions resulting from his analysis, Jameson writes the following difference operators.[37,38] The central difference operators contributing to $\phi_{nn}$ are

$$\left. \begin{aligned} \phi_{xx} &= \frac{\phi^+_{i-1,j} - \phi^+_{i,j} - \phi_{i,j} + \phi_{i+1,j}}{(\Delta x)^2} \\ \phi_{xy} &= \frac{-\phi^+_{i-1,j+1} + \phi^+_{i-1,j-1} + \phi_{i+1,j+1} - \phi_{i+1,j-1}}{4\Delta x \Delta y} \\ \phi_{yy} &= \frac{\phi^+_{i,j+1} - 2\phi^+_{i,j} + \phi^+_{i,j-1}}{(\Delta y)^2} \end{aligned} \right\} \qquad (3.29)$$

The upwind difference operators contributing to $\phi_{ss}$ when $u > 0$ and $v > 0$ (velocity coming from the upper left-hand quadrant) are

$$\left. \begin{aligned} \phi_{xx} &= \frac{2\phi^+_{i,j} - \phi_{i,j} - 2\phi^+_{i-1,j} + \phi_{i-2,j}}{(\Delta x)^2} \\ \phi_{xy} &= \frac{\phi^+_{i,j} - \phi^+_{i-1,j} - \phi^+_{i,j-1} + \phi^+_{i-1,j-1}}{\Delta x \, \Delta y} \\ \phi_{yy} &= \frac{2\phi^+_{i,j} - \phi_{i,j} - 2\phi^+_{i,j-1} + \phi_{i,j-2}}{(\Delta y)^2} \end{aligned} \right\} \qquad (3.30)$$

The central difference operators in Eq. (3.29) are constructed for the simultaneous solution of points along a y-coordinate line. The scheme may easily be modified for simultaneous solution of points along an x-coordinate by the obvious switching of $\phi_{xx}$ and $\phi_{yy}$ operator forms in Eq. (3.29). No modification to the upwind operators (3.30) is necessary.

Near the sonic line, a stabilizing term may be required to keep s the marching direction and is given by $\varepsilon(\Delta\tau/\Delta x)[(u/q)\phi_{x\tau} + (v/q)\phi_{y\tau}]$ where

$$\left. \begin{array}{l} \phi_{x\tau} = \dfrac{\phi^{+}_{i,j} - \phi_{i,j} + \phi^{+}_{i-1,j} + \phi_{i-1,j}}{\Delta\tau\,\Delta x} \\[2ex] \phi_{y\tau} = \dfrac{\phi^{+}_{i,j} - \phi_{i,j} + \phi^{+}_{i,j-1} + \phi_{i,j-1}}{\Delta\tau\,\Delta y} \end{array} \right\} \quad (3.31)$$

for $u > 0$ and $v > 0$. The quantity $\varepsilon$ is a small parameter which in practice may often be taken as 0.

### 3.6 Results

Numerous results obtained using the exact isentropic equations have appeared in the literature.[13,14,15,34,40] Comparisons between the numerical calculations and experimental results are particularly interesting but are complicated by the effects of viscosity and wind-tunnel walls. Such comparisons are given in section 5. Here, we show some theoretical comparisons of interest.

A comparison between the exact hodograph solution[41] and various relaxation solutions is shown in Fig. 5 for an NLR quasi-elliptical airfoil. The Jameson solution is not plotted since it is indistinguishable from the exact solution. Another comparison with the exact hodograph solution[14] for a Garabedian-Korn airfoil is shown in Fig. 6. Both the Garabedian-Korn relaxation solution and the Krupp-Murman solution* show a weak shock wave. In addition, the Krupp-Murman solution shows an under-expansion near the nose. Note that in the small disturbance case, the Mach number was increased by 0.01 to avoid formation of an additional shock wave farther forward.

---

*Calculation is the courtesy of Dr. Murman, NASA Ames Research Center, Moffett Field, Ca.

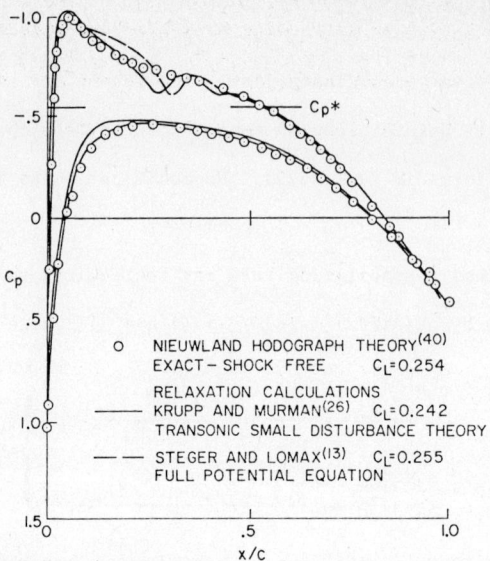

Fig. 5. Comparison of hodograph and relaxation solutions for NLR quasi-elliptical airfoil; $\delta$ = 12.12 percent, $\alpha$ = 1.32°, $M_\infty$ = 0.7557.

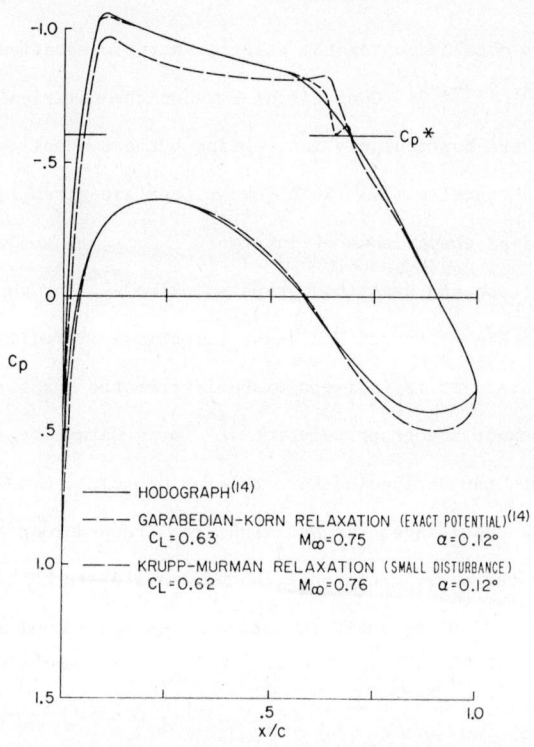

Fig. 6. Comparison of hodograph and relaxation solutions for Garabedian-Korn airfoil.

Superficial airfoils of the Garabedian-Korn type are extremely sensitive to small changes in Mach number, incidence, and inaccuracies in airfoil definition and thus are sensitive indicators of the accuracy of the calculations. It is of particular interest to note that at Mach numbers and angles of attack slightly below the design condition, the solution appears with multiple shock waves.

As mentioned previously, the relaxation methods for the exact equation do not use conservative difference operators and therefore do not fulfill the proper jump conditions. An indication of the error in fulfilling the shock jump is given in Fig. 7, which compares the solution obtained from Jameson's program with that obtained from the conservative time-dependent procedure for the isentropic equations described by Yoshihara.[17] As is expected from similar comparisons in the previous section, the conservative method gives a more nearly correct shock jump, with a shock location further aft.

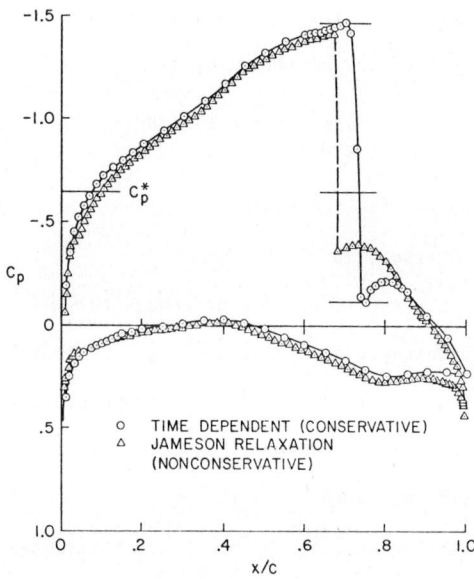

Fig. 7. Comparison of conservative time-dependent and nonconservative relaxation solutions of exact isentropic equation for the NACA 64A410 airfoil at $M_\infty = 0.735$ and $\alpha = 1°$.[7]

## 4. AXISYMMETRIC FLOW

We briefly turn our attention to axisymmetric flows. Such flows are two-dimensional and present no essential numerical difficulties. Because of spatial relief, axisymmetric flows have a smaller transonic Mach number range and have less pronounced transonic effects than corresponding two-dimensional planar flows. Considerable interest exists in developing numerical techniques for transonic flow about optimum bodies, which have longitudinal area distributions that exhibit high drag-rise Mach numbers. Upon application of the transonic equivalence principle (Mach-1 area-rule), such optimized configurations will presumably give a starting point from which to model the area distributions for transonic aircraft.

The transonic small disturbance theory may also be applied to axisymmetric flows over slender bodies and is the basis of axisymmetric relaxation methods reported by Krupp and Murman[26] and Bailey.[42] In the flow field, the only essential modification is the alteration of the governing equation so that the lateral term $\phi_{yy}$ is replaced by the radial term $(1/r)(r\phi_r)_r$. In addition, because of the logarithmic along the axis, the body boundary condition becomes

$$\lim_{r \to 0} (r\phi_r) = R(dR/dx)$$

where $R$ is the body shape. In the numerical method, the condition is applied on some small cylinder about the axis.

South and Jameson[37] have reported a procedure for calculating axisymmetric flows using the exact isentropic form of the governing equations. The method is a straightforward extension of Jameson's two-dimensional procedure including the rotated difference scheme. Fully conformal coordinates are used for closed spheres and ellipsoids. For blunt-nosed shapes with open tails and sharp corners, body-normal coordinates are used over the nose up to the horizontal tangent, followed by a nonorthogonal "sheared" cylindrical system, which consists of a family of vertical lines and a family of lines parallel to the body surface.

## 5. COMPARISONS WITH EXPERIMENT

### 5.1 Introduction

Checks on the accuracy and usefulness of inviscid transonic calculations depend heavily on comparisons with experimental results obtained by wind tunnel tests. However, flows with embedded shock waves are extremely sensitive to small changes in boundary parameters. Thus, significant differences can occur in comparisons of wind tunnel results and inviscid calculations because of viscous and wind tunnel interference effects. Although the precise isolation of these two effects is not possible, we shall consider separately their relationship to inviscid relaxation calculations.

### 5.2 Viscous Effects

We begin by considering, in Figs. 8 and 9, flow about nonlifting, symmetric airfoils with turbulent boundary layers in which the major viscous effect is the interaction between the shock wave and unseparated boundary layer. In Fig. 8, the solution from Jameson's program† shows excellent agreement with data[43] for flow about a symmetrical Boerstoel airfoil[44] at $M_\infty = 0.834$ and an interference corrected incidence of $-0.06°$. The data were obtained in the perforated NAE trisonic tunnel at a Reynolds number of $20 \times 10^6$ based on model chord. The free-stream Mach number correction is negligible. The symbols ● and ■ appearing directly beneath the calculated shock wave designate postshock values computed from the Rankine-Hugoniot and the isentropic jump conditions, respectively. The difference between these values is a measure of the error in pressure jump introduced by use of the exact isentropic flow equation. The difference between the isentropic value and the first computed subsonic point behind the shock wave is a measure of the failure of the nonconservative difference scheme to satisfy the isentropic jump conditions. Finally, the difference between the Rankine-Hugoniot value and the first experimental subsonic

---

†Calculations are the courtesy of Dr. Melnik, Grumman Aerospace Corp., Bethpage, N. Y.

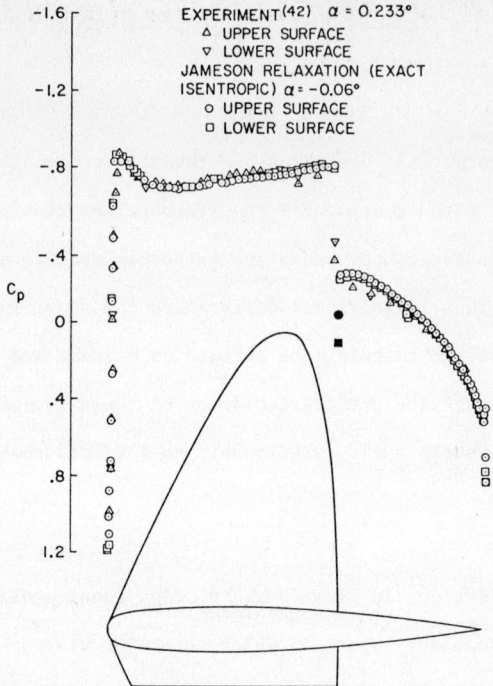

Fig. 8. Comparison Jameson relaxation solution with data for Boerstoel airfoil; $M_\infty = 0.834$

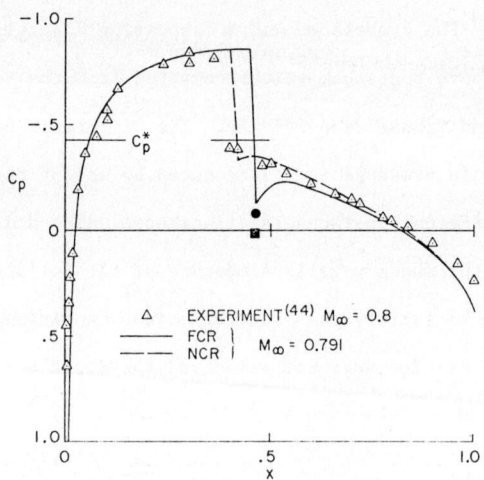

Fig. 9. Comparison of small disturbance solutions with data for NACA 0012 airfoil at $\alpha = 0°$.

point behind the shock is a measure of the weakening of the experimental shock due to its interaction with the boundary layer.

In Fig. 9, two small distrubance solutions are compared with data[45] for flow about an NACA 0012 airfoil at zero incidence and $M_\infty = 0.791$. The airfoil was tested at an uncorrected Mach number of 0.8 and at a moderate Reynolds number of $3.6 \times 10^6$ (boundary layer tripped at $x = 0.14$ to $0.16$) in a slotted wall tunnel for which the incidence correction was negligible and the experimentally determined Mach number correction was quite small at $-0.009 \pm 0.002$.[45] Calculations using both the nonconservative (NCR) and fully conservative (FCR) schemes are shown. The comparison between the data and NCR solution is very good, but the FCR solution predicts a stronger shock that is located farther aft. In this case, the symbol ■ represents the postshock value computed from the small disturbance jump condition.

It is suggested that the smaller shock jump predicted by the nonconservative schemes compensates, to a degree, for the weakening of the shock due to its interaction with the boundary layer. This appears to be quite typical as shown in Fig. 10. Here, a plot of shock pressure ratio versus the Mach number immediately upstream of the shock, $M_1$, is shown for a sample of nonconservative relaxation calculations and experimental results. Also shown for reference are the normal shock pressure ratios from the isentropic and Rankine-Hugonoit relations. Both calculated and experimental pressure ratios follow the same trend up to the point at which the shock separates the boundary layer ($M_1 \approx 1.3$). This is not a very comfortable state of affairs, however, because the nonconservative shock solution is not unique and does not account for viscosity in a rational manner.

We next consider flows over modern aft-cambered airfoils for which viscous effects are very significant. In Fig. 11, we repeat the results presented by Melnik and Ives[46] for an aft-cambered airfoil designed by Garabedian and Korn[14] at $M_\infty = 0.699$ and a corrected incidence of $3.6°$. The wind tunnel data were obtained in the NAE trisonic tunnel at a Reynolds number of $20 \times 10$.[47] The effect of tunnel interference on lift was corrected by a shift in angle of attack as determined by calibration tests. The calculations were obtained using Jameson's program in two versions: the standard one with the trailing edge Kutta-condition imposed and one

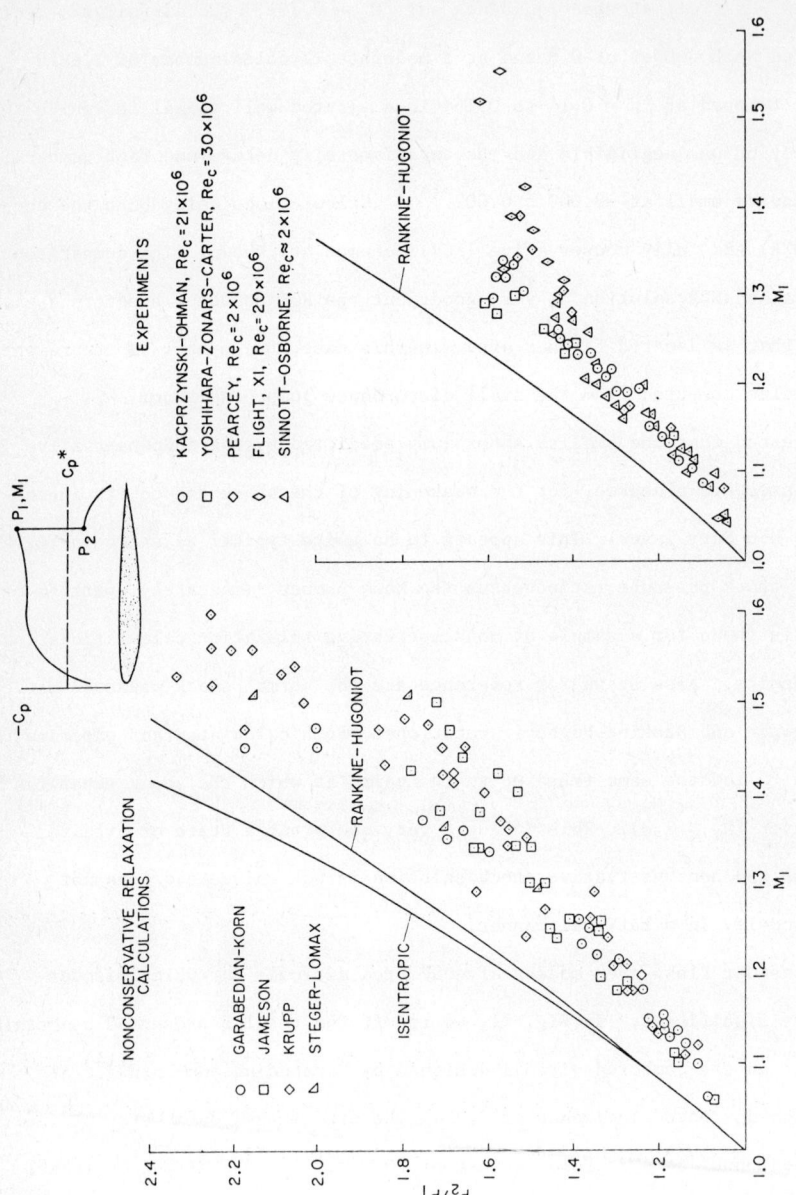

Fig. 10. Shock-wave pressure jump on airfoils in transonic flow. (a) Computed. (b) Experimental.

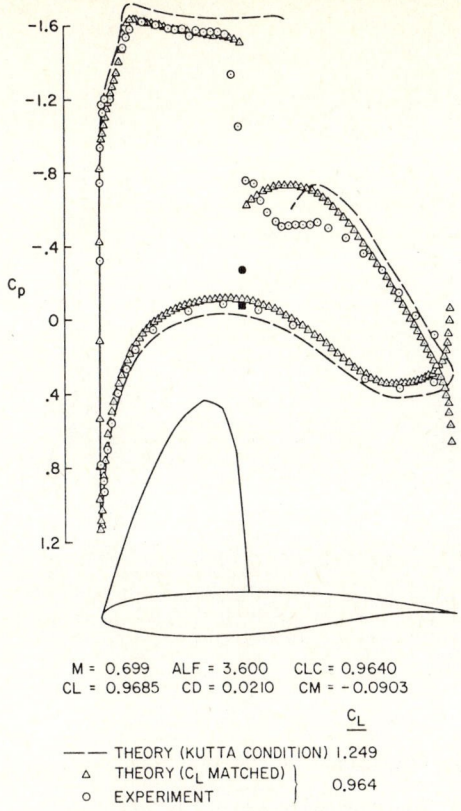

Fig. 11. Comparison of Jameson relaxation solution with data[46] for Garabedian-Korn airfoil.[45]

modified to accept a prescribed circulation constant determined by the experimental lift. The modified calculation shows better agreement with experiment except at the trailing edge.

A similar comparison with the FCR small disturbance solutions[16] is shown in Fig. 12 for the same airfoil at $M_\infty = 0.768$ and a geometric incidence of 1.38°. The data[40] were also obtained in the NAE tunnel but for a tunnel porosity of 6 percent instead of 20.5 percent.

In both Figs. 11 and 12 we see that the standard method gives a much larger lift coefficient than the measured value, as well as a large difference in pressure

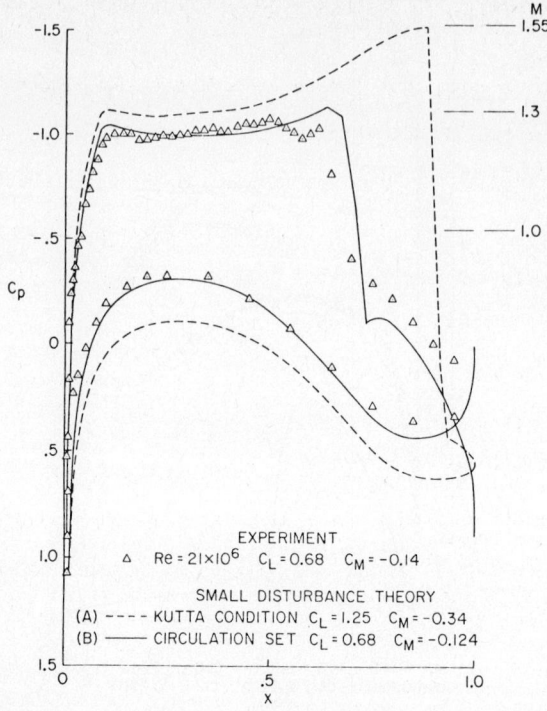

Fig. 12. Comparison of FCR solutions with data[47] for Garabedian-Korn airfoil; $\alpha = 1.38°$, $M_\infty = 0.768$.[16]

distribution and shock location. The modified results, on the other hand, show greatly improved agreement except, of course, at the trailing edge.

It appears that viscous effects are primarily responsible for the disagreement between the standard calculations and the experimental results. Thus, it is suggested that, when shock wave-boundary layer separation is absent, the principal viscous effect to account for is the reduction in circulation from the value given by the inviscid Kutta condition. While this strategy is useful, it does not yield a predictive procedure. Clearly, what is needed is a technique for solving the turbulent trailing-edge problem, thereby accounting for the reduction in lift and the displacement effects downstream of the shock wave.

## 5.3 Wind Tunnel Wall Effects

Although the use of ventilated transonic test sections reduces the magnitude of wall effects, uncertainties in the interference corrections still exist. The classical theory for predicting the corrections is based on linear subsonic theory with compressibility effects accounted for by the Prandtl-Glauert scaling laws.[48] Such an approach is generally inadequate in the transonic regime, particularly since it cannot account for the interference effect on the shock wave location. Thus, recource is often made to experimental calibration studies to predict the correct Mach number and angle-of-attack corrections.

With the availability of transonic finite-difference methods, however, it is now possible to study the nonlinear effects of various wall parameters by replacing the far field boundary with a tunnel wall boundary at the appropriate location. For solid or open jet tunnels, the usual boundary conditions of zero flow angle or constant pressure apply. For ventilated test sections — perforated or porous and slotted walls — simplified homogeneous wall boundary conditions proposed by Baldwin, Turner, and Knechtel[49] can be used.

The applicability of the transonic relaxation technique in simulating wall effects was demonstrated in reference 41, where calculations were made for flow about a parabolic arc of revolution with porous and open jet wall boundaries. Shown in Fig. 13 are results at $M_\infty = 0.99$ for various values of porosity parameter $P$ as compared with data[50] obtained in the Ames 14-foot perforated/slotted wind tunnel at a high Reynolds number of $27 \times 10^6$. Note that the shock wave moves forward with increasing porosity. The significance of wall interference near Mach 1 is illustrated in Fig. 14 by comparing experimental measurements with free-air and porous wall calculations of the transonic drag rise.

Murman[51] has extended the relaxation method to study the effect of perforated walls on lifting airfoils. He conducted an interesting numerical experiment in which calculations were made for a lifting airfoil in a simulated wind tunnel and in free air. The resulting wind tunnel lift and moment coefficients were then corrected to free-air conditions according to linear theory.[48] The results are given in Fig. 15

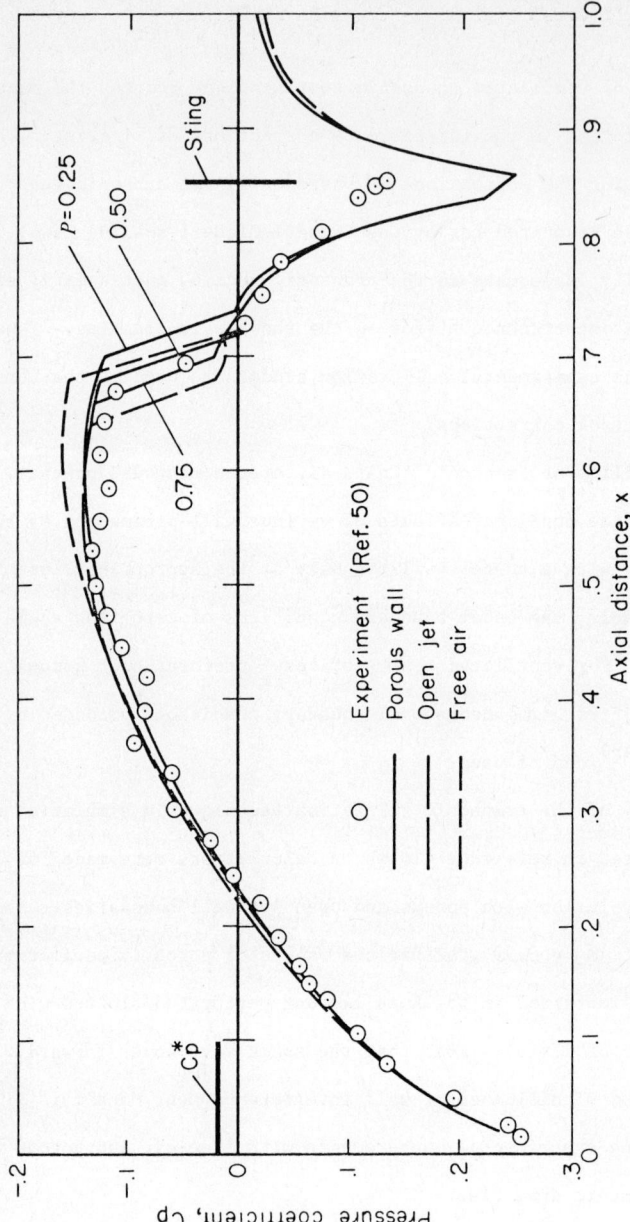

Fig. 13. Effect of wall conditions on body surface $C_p$ for parabolic arc of revolution with sting ($M_\infty = 0.99$ and $f = 10$).

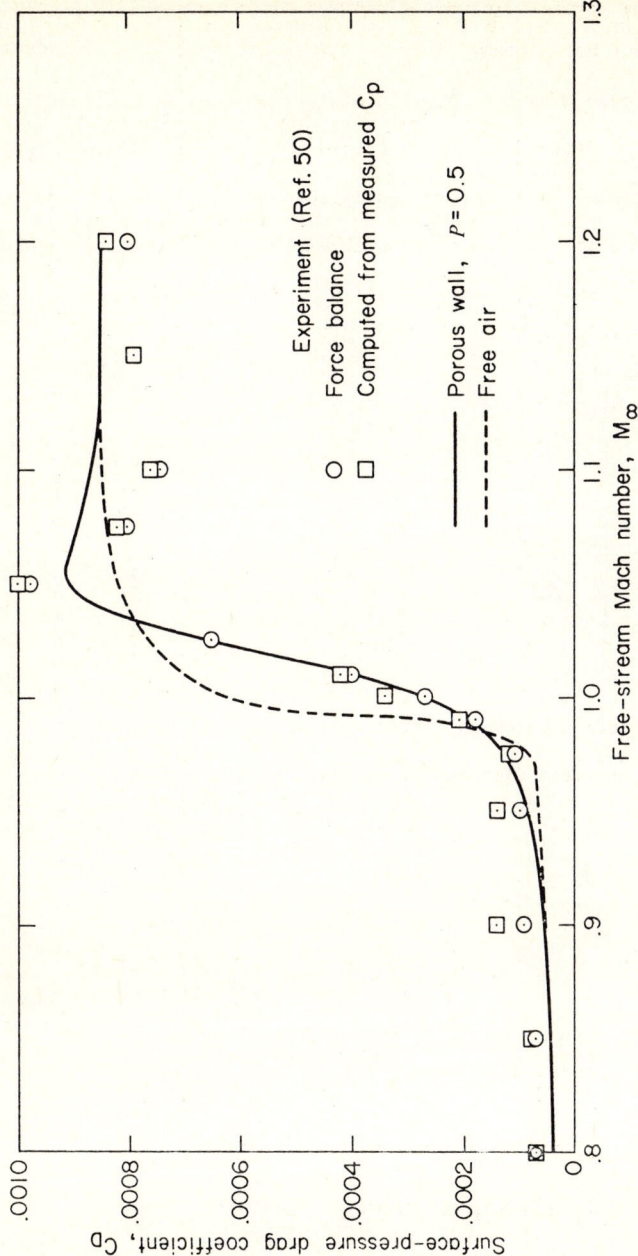

Fig. 14. Variation of surface pressure drag coefficient (based on body length) with Mach number for a parabolic arc of revolution with sting ($f = 10$).

and show that, in this case, the classical linear method adequately predicts the correction for lift but not moment. This is not entirely surprising because of the effect of wall interference on the location of the surface shock waves.

The interference effect of an ideal slotted wall on a nonlifting airfoil was also calculated by Murman[16] (using the fully conservative method). The comparison of free-air and slotted wall calculations with experimental results[45] obtained in a slotted tunnel for an NACA 0012 airfoil at $M_\infty = 0.80$ is shown in Fig. 16.

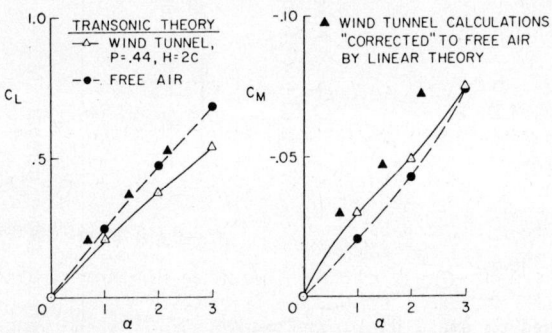

Fig. 15. Lift and pitching moment curves for NACA 0012 airfoil in perforated wind tunnel and free air, $M = 0.80$.[16]

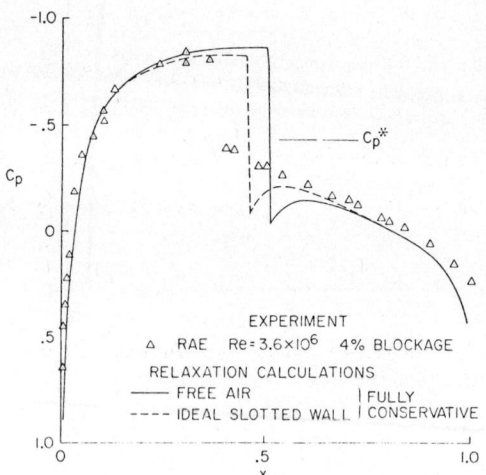

Fig. 16. Comparison of FCR solutions with data,[44] NACA 0012; $\alpha = 0°$, $M = 0.8$.[16]

## 6. SMALL DISTURBANCE PROCEDURE IN THREE DIMENSIONS

### 6.1 Introduction

The success of the Murman and Cole scheme in two dimensions has given rise to interest in applying the scheme to three-dimensional flows. The computational effort required to solve three-dimensional flows is not overly large for modern high-speed computers. For example, useful calculations for transonic flows about wings can be obtained using on the order of $10^5$ grid points with converged solutions obtained in about 15 minutes on a CDC 7600 or IBM 370/195.

Possibly the most difficult problem to be overcome in three-dimensional calculations is that of geometry. In particular, exact coordinate transformations, which have proven useful in two dimensions and which force the body to lie along the edge of a finite-difference grid, can be very difficult to apply to a complicated three-dimensional configuration. Thus, most of the three-dimensional calculations reported have been based on small disturbance theory applied to wings. (The exception is the yawed wing calculations of Jameson[38] which are discussed in the next section.) Small disturbance relaxation methods have been reported by Isom and Caradonna[52] and by Ballhaus and Caradonna[53] for transonic flow about a rectangular nonlifting helicopter rotor in hover and by Bailey and Steger[54] and Newman and Klunker[55] for rectangular lifting wings. Transonic flow about lifting swept wings and nonlifting wing-cylinder combinations have been treated by Ballhaus and Bailey.[31,32] The latter procedure is an extension of the Krupp-Murman NCR method discussed in section 2 and is discussed in some detail in this section.

### 6.2 Basic Formulation

The governing transonic small disturbance equation in three dimensions may be written (see sketch I) in similarity form as

$$[K_1 - (\gamma + 1)\phi_x]\phi_{xx} + K_2\phi_{yy} + \phi_{zz} = 0 \tag{6.1}$$

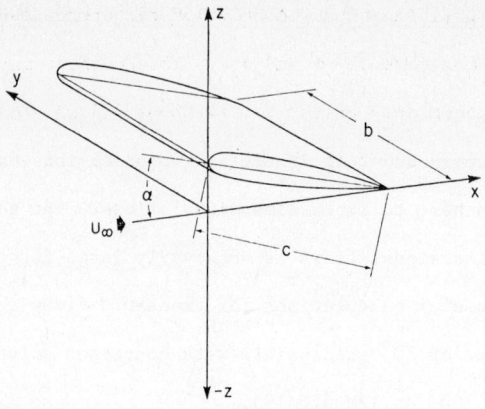

Sketch I

where

$$K_1 = \frac{1 - M_\infty^2}{\delta^{2/3} M_\infty^{4/3}}$$

$$K_2 = \frac{c^2}{b^2 \delta^{2/3} M_\infty^{4/3}}$$

The span coordinate, $y$, is scaled by the semispan, $b$, and the vertical coordinate, $z$, by $(\delta^{1/3} M_\infty^{2/3})^{-1}$. The pressure coefficient is given by

$$C_p = \frac{-2\delta^{2/3}}{M_\infty^{2/3}} \phi_x \qquad (6.2)$$

As in two dimensions, the flow tangency condition at the wing surface is linearized and applied on the mean wing plane $0 \leq x \leq 1$, $-1 \leq y \leq 1$, $z = 0$. In addition to satisfying the Kutta condition, provision must be made for a trailing vortex sheet downstream of the wing trailing edge. With the small disturbance assumption, the vortex sheet is flat and lies in the plane $z = 0$ with conditions that $\phi_x$ (pressure) and $\phi_z$ (flow angle) be continuous across it. The potential $\phi$ and its second derivative $\phi_{zz}$, however, experience a jump across the sheet. Because of the continuity of pressure across the vortex sheet, the jump in potential at any span station, $y = y_0$, is independent of $x$ and is equal to the circulation about the wing section

$$\Gamma(y_0) = -\oint d\phi(x, y_0, z) \qquad (6.3)$$

for any path enclosing the wing section. In the numerical procedure, the Kutta condition is satisfied by setting the potential jump across the vortex sheet equal to the value obtained at the trailing edge. A modified difference operator for $\phi_{zz}$ is written to account for the jump in $\phi$ and $\phi_{zz}$. The operator may be derived by noting that jumps in $\phi$ occur only at the vortex sheet and only odd functions may jump. Since the jump is independent of x, the solution at the vortex sheet decouples into even, $\phi^e$, and odd, $\phi^o$, solutions with $\phi^e$ satisfying Eq. (6.1) and $\phi^o$ satisfying

$$\phi^o_{zz} = -K_2 \phi^o_{yy} \tag{6.4}$$

At the sheet itself, the odd solution is given by

$$\phi^o(x,y,0^{\pm}) = \pm \frac{1}{2} \Gamma(y) \tag{6.5}$$

Therefore, $\phi_{zz}$ at the sheet can be written

$$\phi_{zz}\Big|_{0^{\pm}} = \phi^e_{zz}\Big|_{0^{\pm}} \mp \frac{K_2}{2} \Gamma_{yy}(y) \tag{6.6}$$

Approximating Eq. (6.6) at $z = 0^-$ by central difference operators and noting that $\phi^e$ can be related to $\phi$ by

$$\phi^e_{i,j,1} = \phi^e_{i,j,-1} = \frac{1}{2}(\phi_{i,j,1} + \phi_{i,j,-1})$$

$$\phi^e_{i,j,0^-} = \frac{1}{2}(\phi_{i,j,0^-} + \phi_{i,j,0^+}) = \frac{1}{2}(2\phi_{i,j,0^-} + \Gamma_j)$$

yields

$$(\phi_{zz})_{i,j,0^-} = \frac{1}{(\Delta z)^2}[(\phi_{i,j,1} - \Gamma_j) - 2\phi_{i,j,0^-} + \phi_{i,j,-1}]$$
$$+ \frac{K_2}{2(\Delta y)^2}(\Gamma_{j+1} - 2\Gamma_j + \Gamma_{j-1}) \tag{6.7}$$

The outer boundary conditions far from the wing and vortex sheet are given at some finite distance by an approximate analytical expression for the far field.[30] The dominant term in the expression is due to lift and is proportional to the circulation integrated over the span. The conditions at the downstream boundary, i.e., Trefftz plane, are found by iteratively solving Eq. (6.4) with condition Eq. (6.5), along with the rest of the flow field.

## 6.3 Relaxation Procedure

Consider first the extension of the Murman-Cole scheme to three-dimensional supersonic regions with the additional spanwise derivative approximated by the central operator

$$\phi_{yy} = \frac{\phi_{i,j+1,k} - 2\phi_{i,j,k} + \phi_{i,j-1,k}}{(\Delta y)^2} \tag{6.8}$$

and the remaining derivatives approximated by the appropriate operators given in section 2. A direct extension of the two-dimensional, fully implicit, marching procedure to three-dimensional supersonic regions requres a successive plane relaxation scheme (in contrast to the two-dimensional line scheme) in which new values of $\phi$ are obtained simultaneously in an x = constant plane before proceeding to the next downstream plane. Recall that in the two-dimensional method, new values of $\phi$ are obtained along an x = contant line by solving Eq. (2.36) by direct elimination. In three dimensions, the analogous procedure would require the direct solution of a similar equation with the elements of $\underset{\sim}{A}$ being themselves tridiagonal matrices. Efficient methods for the direct solution of this matrix equation have yet to be developed. However, this equation can be solved by relaxation. Thus, the fully implicit supersonic relaxation procedure is to pause at each x-constant plane and do a line relaxation within that plane, until all values of $\phi$ in the plane satisfy some error criterion, before moving to the next downstream plane. This fully implicit method ($\omega = 1$) is stable for the linear wave equation. It should be noted that if one does not pause, but rather sweeps immediately from one plane to the next, the scheme is no longer fully implicit. In addition, the von Neuman stability test shows that this procedure is unstable for small wave numbers when applied to the linear wave equation. However, such a scheme has been used successfully in three-dimensional calculations even though the linear stability criterion was violated. The reason for this is unclear, although contributing factors may be the influence of the boundaries, the grids are not sufficiently fine, the nonlinearity of the equation, and the use of a relaxation parameter less than 1.

Line relaxation schemes for supersonic regions that are not fully implicit, but that satisfy the stability test, can be derived by the method outlined by Jameson[17, 37, 38] (see section 3.5). For example, one can use operators in supersonic regions given by

$$\left.\begin{array}{l} \phi_{xx} = \dfrac{2\phi^+_{i,j,k} - \phi_{i,j,k} - 2\phi^+_{i-1,j,k} + \phi_{i-2,j,k}}{(\Delta x)^2} \\[1em] \phi_{yy} = \dfrac{\phi^+_{i,j-1,k} - \phi^+_{i,j,k} - \phi_{i,j,k} + \phi_{i,j+1,k}}{(\Delta y)^2} \\[1em] \phi_{zz} = \dfrac{\phi^+_{i,j,k-1} - 2\phi^+_{i,j,k} + \phi_{i,j,k+1}}{(\Delta z)^2} \end{array}\right\} \quad (6.9)$$

and sweep immediately from one plane to the next.

The supersonic procedures outlined above have been used successfully in actual three-dimensional calculations and they all converge to the same solution with nearly the same efficiency.

In subsonic regions the extension to three dimensions requires only the additional spanwise operator Eq. (6.8) and either plane or line relaxation may be used with $\omega \simeq 1.8$.

### 6.4 Nonrectangular Planforms

Consider next the application of the relaxation method to nonrectangular planforms (e.g., including sweep and taper). To facilitate the use of a high density of grid points at the leading edge and to retain the same number of chordwise grid points at each span station, it is convenient to use a coordinate transformation to map the planform into a rectangle. The transformation, valid for wings with finite tip chords, is given by

$$\left.\begin{array}{l} \xi(x,y) = \dfrac{x - x_{\ell.e.}(y)}{c(y)} \\[1em] \eta = y \\[0.5em] z = z \end{array}\right\} \quad (6.10)$$

where $x_{\ell.e.}(y)$ is the value of $x$ at the leading edge and $c(y)$ is the ratio of local chord to root chord. The governing small disturbance equation can then be written in terms of the new independent variables $\xi,\eta,z$ in the form

$$\left(K_1 - \frac{(\gamma+1)}{c}\phi_\xi\right)\frac{\phi_{\xi\xi}}{c^2} + K_2\xi_y^2\phi_{\xi\xi} + 2K_2\xi_y\phi_{\xi\eta} + K_2\xi_{yy}\phi_\xi + K_2\phi_{\eta\eta} + \phi_{zz} = 0 \quad (6.11)$$

In transformed coordinates, the pressure coefficient becomes

$$C_p = \frac{-2\delta^{2/3}\phi_\xi}{cM_\infty^{2/3}} \quad (6.12)$$

The transformation is not continued beyond the tip of tapered wings. In this case, $c(y)$ is held fixed beyond the tip and a smooth juncture is fit between the tapered and untapered regions.

At the wing root, the boundary condition is the required symmetry about the plane $y = 0$ and leads to

$$\phi_y = \phi_\eta + \xi_y\phi_\xi = 0 \quad (6.13)$$

Straightforward incorporation of the root boundary condition into the finite-difference analog of Eq. (6.11) has led to generally unsatisfactory results, both with respect to stability and accuracy. In reference 31, an interpolated or "skewed" scheme is discussed, which essentially leads to differencing the untransformed equation at the wing root and in general works well. It has been recently suggested by Dr. Hall of RAE that one modify the transformation such that the $\eta$ coordinate lines are normal to the symmetry plane. This is accomplished by turning the coordinate lines over a distance very small with respect to the wing semispan so that the deviation from the wing planform is not great. This approach is easily implemented and works quite well.

In writing the finite-difference operators for Eq. (6.1), it is recognized that in supersonic flow regions the domain of dependence of the finite-difference equation will contain the domain of dependence of the differential equation if upwind difference operators are used for x-derivatives and central difference operators are used for the y- and z-derivatives. This is taken into account in the difference analog to Eq. (6.8) by using central difference operators for $\phi_{zz}$ and the derivatives multiplied by $K_2$ (i.e., the term $\phi_{yy}$) and by using upwind operators for the remaining $\xi$-derivatives.

Because central operators are used in supersonic regions for $\xi$-derivatives contributing to $\phi_{yy}$ and these contain points downstream of a $\xi$ = constant plane, it is no longer possible to use a fully implicit supersonic marching scheme plane by plane. Stable calculations have been obtained, however, by the line relaxation procedure using essentially the operators given in section 2. A modified line relaxation scheme based on Jameson's method, which satisfies the linear stability test, has also been used. For this method, the $\xi$-derivative operator contributing to $\phi_{xx}$ is given by

$$\phi_{\xi\xi} = \frac{2\phi^{+}_{i,j,k} - \phi_{i,j,k} - 2\phi^{+}_{i-1,j,k} + \phi_{i-2,j,k}}{(\Delta\xi)^2} \tag{6.14}$$

the operators contributing to $\phi_{yy}$ are given by

$$\left.\begin{aligned}\phi_{\xi\xi} &= \frac{\phi^{+}_{i-1,j,k} - \phi^{+}_{i,j,k} - \phi_{i,j,k} + \phi_{i+1,j,k}}{(\Delta\xi)^2} \\ \phi_{\eta\eta} &= \frac{\phi^{+}_{i,j-1,k} - \phi^{+}_{i,j,k} - \phi_{i,j,k} + \phi_{i,j+1,k}}{(\Delta\eta)^2} \\ \phi_{\xi\eta} &= \frac{\phi_{i+1,j+1,k} - \phi^{+}_{i-1,j+1,k} - \phi_{i+1,j-1,k} + \phi^{+}_{i-1,j-1,k}}{4\Delta\xi\,\Delta\eta}\end{aligned}\right\} \tag{6.15}$$

and the z-derivative operator is given by

$$\phi_{zz} = \frac{\phi^{+}_{i,j,k-1} - 2\phi^{+}_{i,j,k} + \phi^{+}_{i,j,k+1}}{(\Delta z)^2} \tag{6.16}$$

It should be pointed out that, to avoid central differences of $\phi_{\xi\xi}$ across shock waves and thus computing sharper shock jumps, the earlier method given in reference 31 delayed upwind differencing until the flow normal to the local sweep was supersonic, and then the entire $\phi_{\xi\xi}$ term was upwind differenced. This procedure, however, can lead to erroneous results.

## 6.5 Results

Subcritical ($M_\infty = 0.752$) and supercritical ($M_\infty = 0.853$) results using the NCR method are shown in Figs. 17 and 18 for flow about a constant-chord, 23.75° sweptback wing with a Lockheed C-141 airfoil section (11.4 percent thick streamwise) at 2°

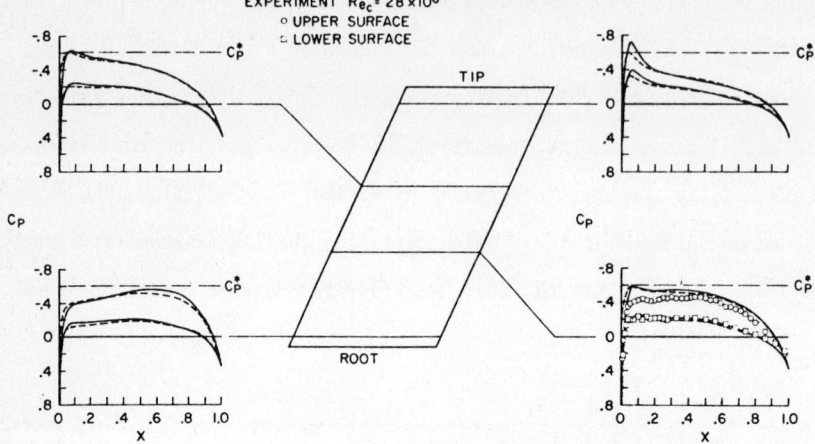

Fig. 17.  $C_p$ distribution on C-141 swept panel model, $M_\infty = 0.752$, $\alpha = 2°$.[31]

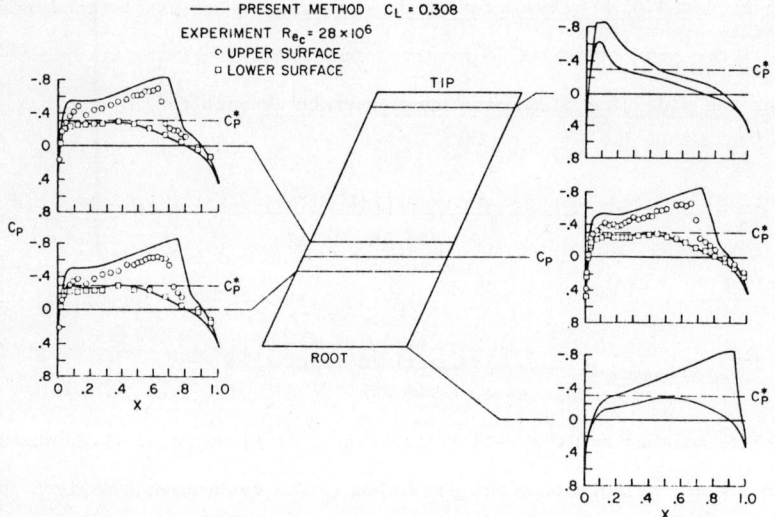

Fig. 18.  $C_p$ distribution on C-141 swept panel model, $M_\infty = 0.853$, $\alpha = 2°$.[31]

angle of attack. The calculation at $M_\infty = 0.752$ is compared in Fig. 17 with both experimental results[56] at $Re = 28\times10^6$ and results obtained by a subsonic panel method.[57] The relaxation results agree well with those obtained by the panel method but both calculations are in poor agreement with experiment on the upper surface. It is suggested that this disagreement is due primarily to the loss in lift caused by viscous effects at the trailing edge. Calculated results for the supercritical case shown in Fig. 18 are in even greater disagreement with experiment. Such a trend is to be expected, however, because of the shock-induced amplification of the trailing edge viscous effect. As in two dimensions, good agreement with experiment can be accomplished only through some consideration of viscous effects.

For the next example, consider the NCR calculation about a simulated C-141 wing given in reference 58. The wing had a leading-edge sweep of 25.6°, a taper ratio of 0.373, an aspect ratio of 8, a constant profile of 11.4 percent thick streamwise (the profile of the actual wing at 40 percent span) and a linear twist from 4° at the root to -1° at the tip. The calculated upper surface isobars for $M_\infty = 0.825$ is shown in Fig. 19. A shock wave swept at about 15° is indicated by the heavy band of coalesced isobars. In Fig. 20, the upper surface pressure distribution at the 40 percent span station is compared to wind tunnel and flight test results.[59] The wing angle of attack was adjusted to match the experimental leading-edge pressure gradient and peak pressure coefficient. The comparison between flight and wind tunnel data illustrates the importance of viscous scale effects on the surface pressure. Note that, in this case, a better prediction for the shock location is obtained from the calculation than from the wind tunnel experiment.

A final example is shown in Fig. 21 for flow at $M_\infty = 0.908$ about a 30° swept wing with a 6 percent biconvex section on a straight cylinder and on a symmetrically indented cylinder based on Mach-1 area-ruling. Note that the area-ruling eliminates the embedded shock waves on the wing. These NCR calculations were carried out on an equally spaced cylindrical coordinate system with the spacing adjusted such that $\Delta r = \Delta x/\tan \Lambda$, where $\Lambda$ is the sweep angle (see reference 32).

While the above results are encouraging, they are considered to be interim results and much needs to be done to improve the numerical procedure, particularly

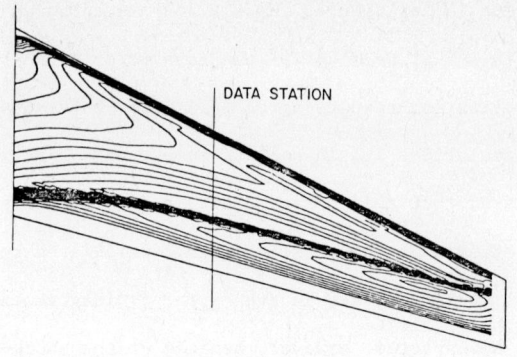

Fig. 19.  Calculated upper surface isobars for simulated C-141 wing at $M_\infty = 0.825$.[58]

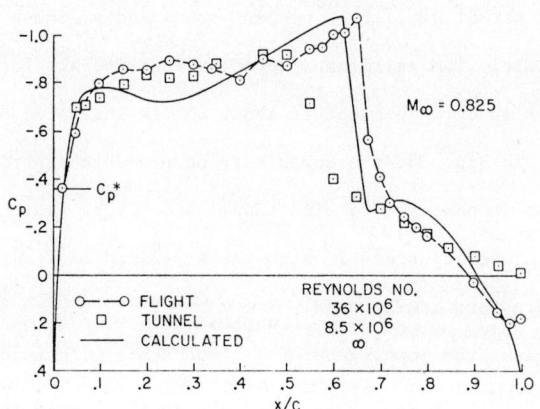

Fig. 20.  Wind tunnel, flight and computed upper surface $C_p$ distribution for C-141 wing at $y/b \approx 0.4$ and $M_\infty = 0.825$.[58]

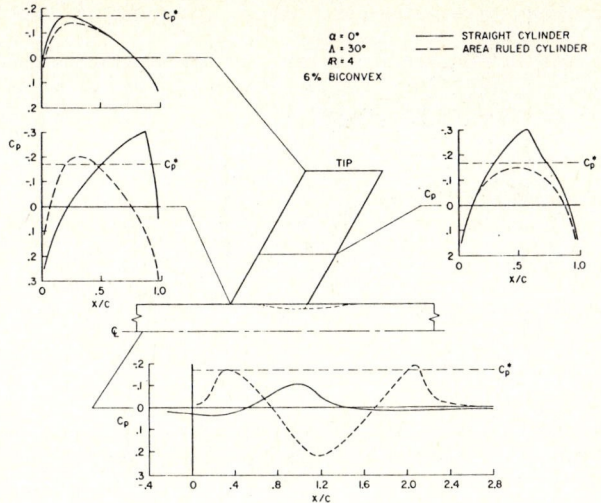

Fig. 21.  $C_p$ distribution on cylinder-wing combination at $M_\infty = 0.908$.[32]

with regard to developing a fully conservative method. This leads to the next topic — the capture of shock waves that are more oblique to the stream than the ones shown in these examples.

6.6  Swept Shock Waves

Transonic wings are nearly all swept; thus, it is of interest to investigate how well the transonic small disturbance equations approximate the jump across swept shocks that may be encountered on swept wings of large aspect ratio. The underlying basis for using wings with swept leading and trailing edges is generally derived by considering a sheared wing of infinite span and constant section. The principal assumption is that the velocity component parallel to an edge is constant or that the perturbation velocity parallel to an edge is zero. Under these conditions, a shock, if it occurs, would also have to be parallel to an edge, and its strength would depend only on the component of velocity normal to the edge. Thus, from the two-dimensional weak solution derived in section 2, the small disturbance normal shock solution written in terms of unscaled perturbation velocities normal to the leading edge is

$$u_{n_1} + u_{n_2} = \frac{2}{\gamma + 1}\left(\frac{1}{M_n^2} - 1\right) \qquad (6.17)$$

Now, the three-dimensional streamwise perturbation component of velocity (normalized by $u_\infty$) and free-stream Mach number are related to the two-dimensional normal perturbation components (normalized by $u_\infty \cos \theta$) by

$$\left. \begin{array}{l} u = u_n \cos^2 \theta \\[2mm] M_\infty = \dfrac{M_n}{\cos \theta} \end{array} \right\} \quad (6.18)$$

where $\theta$ is the angle of sweep with respect to the y-axis. Thus, Eq. (6.17) may be rewritten as

$$u_1 + u_2 = \frac{2\cos^2 \theta}{\gamma + 1} \left( \frac{1}{M_\infty^2 \cos^2 \theta} - 1 \right) \quad (6.19)$$

which represents the jump in streamwise velocity across a vertical shock swept parallel to the edge of an infinite sheared wing.

Consider next a nonsimilarity version of the three-dimensional transonic equation given by

$$\left[ (1 - M_\infty^2)u - M_\infty^2 \frac{\gamma + 1}{2} u^2 \right]_x + v_y + \omega_z = 0 \quad (6.20)$$

$$v_x - u_y = 0$$

$$w_y - v_z = 0$$

The weak solution to Eq. (6.20) is given by

$$\left\langle 1 - M_\infty^2 u - M_\infty^2 \frac{\gamma + 1}{2} u^2 \right\rangle \cos \alpha_1 + \langle v \rangle \cos \alpha_2 + \langle w \rangle \cos \alpha_3 = 0 \quad (6.21)$$

$$\langle v \rangle \cos \alpha_1 - \langle u \rangle \cos \alpha_2 = 0$$

$$\langle w \rangle \cos \alpha_2 - \langle v \rangle \cos \alpha_3 = 0$$

where $\cos \alpha_1$, $\cos \alpha_2$, and $\cos \alpha_3$ are the direction cosines of the shock with respect to the x, y, and z axes, respectively. If the shock is assumed vertical, i.e., $\cos \alpha_3 = 0$, and the wing is an infinite sheared wing, the condition that must be met across the shock is expressed by

$$u_1 + u_2 = \frac{2}{\gamma + 1} \left( \frac{1}{M_\infty^2 \cos^2 \theta} - 1 \right) \quad (6.22)$$

The disagreement between Eq. (6.19) and Eq. (6.22) shows the breakdown of traditional transonic small disturbance theory in its ability to calculate swept shocks. The difference is illustrated in Fig. 22 for $M_\infty = 0.85$, showing that the transonic small disturbance equation is a very poor model for flows with shocks that are more than 25° oblique to the free stream.

The question arises: is it possible to modify Eq. (6.20) such that a more accurate shock jump can be obtained in regions of swept shocks? Such a modified equation is considered in reference 58. Terms that appear in the perturbation form of the isentropic equations (see, e.g., reference 60) and are neglected in the transonic equation are added to Eq. (6.17) to give

$$\left[(1 - M_\infty^2)u - \underline{\left(\frac{3-\gamma}{2}\right)M_\infty^2 v^2} - M_\infty^2 \frac{\gamma+1}{2}u^2\right]_x + [v - \underline{M_\infty^2(\gamma - 1)uv}]_y + w_z = 0 \qquad (6.23)$$

The additional terms (underlined) are higher-order terms in the usual expansion process, so that they should not have a significant influence in continuous regions

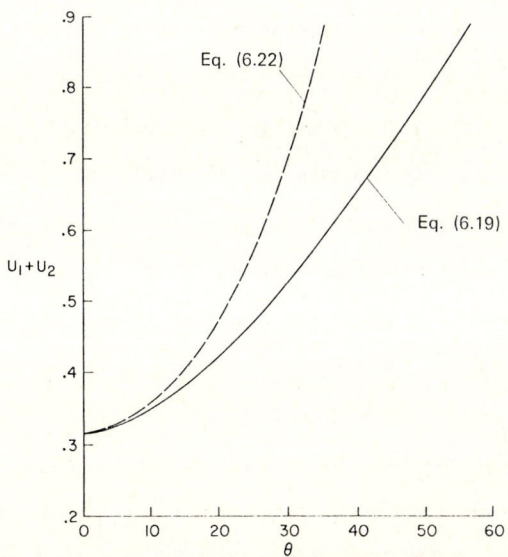

Fig. 22. Values of $(u_1 + u_2)$ from Eq. (6.22) and Eq. (6.19) for $M_\infty = 0.85$

of the flow. The weak solution to Eq. (6.23) with $w = 0$ is given by

$$\left. \begin{array}{c} u_1 + u_2 = \dfrac{2 \cos^2 \theta}{\gamma + 1} \left[ \left( \dfrac{1}{M_\infty^2 \cos^2 \theta} - 1 \right) + 2 \left( \dfrac{v_2}{\tan \theta} + u_2 \right) \tan^2 \theta \right] \\ \\ v_2 - v_1 = -(u_2 - u_1) \tan \theta \end{array} \right\} \quad (6.24)$$

If we consider the special case when $v_2 = -u_2 \tan \theta$, which exists when the component of the perturbation velocity parallel to the shock is zero (i.e., the special case when the condition of simple sweep theory applies), we see that Eq. (6.24) reduces to Eq. (6.13), the sweep theory result. It is concluded, therefore, that Eq. (6.23) provides a better model for approximating highly swept shocks as may occur on three-dimensional swept wings.

# 7. JAMESON'S EXACT ISENTROPIC PROCEDURE FOR YAWED WINGS

## 7.1 Introduction

In reference 38, Jameson presents a scheme for solving the exact isentropic equation in three dimensions for transonic flow about a yawed wing. The impetus for such calculations arises from the increasing interest in the yawed wing aircraft concept of R. T. Jones.[61] The method is restricted to straight leading edges but allows for a curved and tapered trailing edge. Many of the concepts used in Jameson's two-dimensional procedure are incorporated in the yawed wing scheme — notably the square-root plus shearing transformation in planes normal to the span and the rotated differencing scheme for supersonic flow regions.

The coordinate system is fixed to the wing leading edge and the yaw angle is introduced by rotating the free-stream velocity vector. The vortex sheet is assumed to lie flat in the wing mean plane and trail in the shadow of the wing. The need for asymptotic far field solutions is avoided by stretching the coordinates to infinity. At downstream infinity, the square-root transformation collapses the region influenced by the vortex sheet to the line of points containing the sheet.

## 7.2 Transformed Equation

The exact isentropic equation in three-dimensions is expressed as

$$(a^2 - u^2)\phi_{xx} + (a^2 - v^2)\phi_{yy} + (a^2 - w^2)\phi_{zz} - 2uv\phi_{xy} - 2vw\phi_{yz} - 2uw\phi_{xz} = 0 \quad (7.1)$$

where

$$u = \phi_x$$
$$v = \phi_y$$
$$w = \phi_z$$
$$a^2 = a_0^2 - \frac{\gamma - 1}{2} q^2$$
$$q^2 = u^2 + v^2 + w^2$$

Following the coordinate system shown in sketch I, the square-root transformation in the x-z planes is given by

$$\left. \begin{aligned} x + iz &= \frac{1}{2}(X_1 + iZ_1)^2 \\ y &= Y_1 \end{aligned} \right\} \quad (7.2)$$

If the wing surface is represented by

$$Z_1 = S(X_1, Y_1) \quad (7.3)$$

the shearing transformation, which displaces the vertical coordinates to be parallel to the wing surface, is expressed as

$$X = X_1, \quad Y = Y_1, \quad Z = Z_1 - S(X_1, Y_1) \quad (7.4)$$

A reduced potential $\Phi$, from which the singularity at infinity has been removed, is introduced as

$$\Phi = \phi + \left\{ \frac{1}{2}[X^2 - (Z+S)^2]\cos\alpha + X(Z+S)\sin\alpha \right\}\cos\theta + Y\sin\theta \quad (7.5)$$

where $\theta$ is the yaw angle and $\alpha$ the angle of attack in the cross plane normal to the leading edge.

Under the above transformations, the governing equation takes the form

$$A\Phi_{XX} + B\Phi_{YY} + C\Phi_{ZZ} + D\Phi_{XY} + E\Phi_{ZY} + F\Phi_{XZ} = H \quad (7.6)$$

Here, the terms A through H are expressed as functions of the local speed of sound, the orthogonal velocity components in $(X_1, Y_1, Z_1)$ space, the surface slopes and the mapping modulus given by

$$h^2 = X^2 + (Z + S)^2 \tag{7.7}$$

The condition that flow normal to the surface vanishes is expressed as

$$\phi_Z = -\frac{(S \cos \alpha - X \sin \alpha)\cos \theta + U_1 S_X + h^2 V_1 S_Y}{1 + S_X^2 + h^2 S_Y^2} \tag{7.8}$$

where

$$U_1 = \phi_X + (X \cos \alpha + S \sin \alpha)\cos \theta$$

$$V_1 = \phi_Y + \sin \theta$$

## 7.3 Numerical Method

As in Jameson's two-dimensional method, the proper domain of dependence in supersonic regions is taken into account by using a rotated differencing scheme. Let Eq. (7.1) be expressed in the nondivergence canonical form

$$(a^2 - q^2)\phi_{ss} + a^2(\Delta\phi - \phi_{ss}) = 0 \tag{7.9}$$

where $s$ denotes the stream direction and $\Delta\phi$ denotes the Laplacian

$$\Delta\phi = \phi_{xx} + \phi_{yy} + \phi_{zz} \tag{7.10}$$

The streamwise derivative can be expressed in terms of the x, y, and z derivatives as

$$\phi_{ss} = \frac{1}{q^2}(u^2\phi_{xx} + v^2\phi_{yy} + w^2\phi_{zz} + 2uv\phi_{xy} + 2vw\phi_{yz} + 2uw\phi_{xz}) \tag{7.11}$$

where $u/q$, $v/q$, and $w/q$ are the direction cosines. In the numerical procedure, the velocity components are computed using central difference operators evaluated from the previous cycle, and their values determine whether the flow is subsonic or supersonic at a given point. At subsonic points, all second derivatives are approximated by central difference operators. At supersonic points, all second derivatives contributing to $\phi_{ss}$ in the first term of Eq. (7.9) are approximated by upwind difference operators, while those contributing to $\Delta\phi - \phi_{ss}$ are approximated by central operators. Note that when the governing equation is written in curvilinear coordinates, such as Eq. (7.6), only the principal part need be rotated since the domain of dependence is determined by coefficients of second derivatives. Furthermore, the term H contains only first derivatives, which are always approximated by central operators.

An analysis of the three-dimensional scheme based on an equivalent time-dependent equation as discussed in section 3.4 is presented in reference 38. The analysis leads to central and upwind difference operators of the form given in Eqs. (3.27) and (3.28).

The body boundary condition is satisfied by incorporating an additional row of points behind the boundary at which $\Phi$ is assigned values that satisfy Eq. (7.8). Points on the surface are treated as field points. In addition, special treatment is required at the vortex sheet.

Jameson uses a line relaxation scheme in which the subsonic points are overrelaxed and the relaxation parameter is set equal to 1 at supersonic points. The line algorithm can be used in any coordinate direction as long as the iteration sweeps downstream. Jameson divides the x-z plane into three strips. The method then proceeds by marching towards the surface in the central strip, and outwards with the flow in the left-hand and right-hand strips.

## 7.4 Results

Fig. 23 shows results reported in reference 38 for flow about a wing with 30° yaw at $M_\infty$ = 0.866 and 3° incidence. The planform is shown in Fig. 23a and the upper surface pressure in Fig. 23b.

## 8. CONCLUDING REMARKS

The rapid advancement of relaxation methods over the past few years has led to a useful and efficient tool for the analysis of transonic flows. Two important advances have been made in the past year. One is the fully conservative differencing scheme that allows the correct calculation of the small disturbance shock jump. The other is the rotated differencing scheme that allows stable calculations regardless

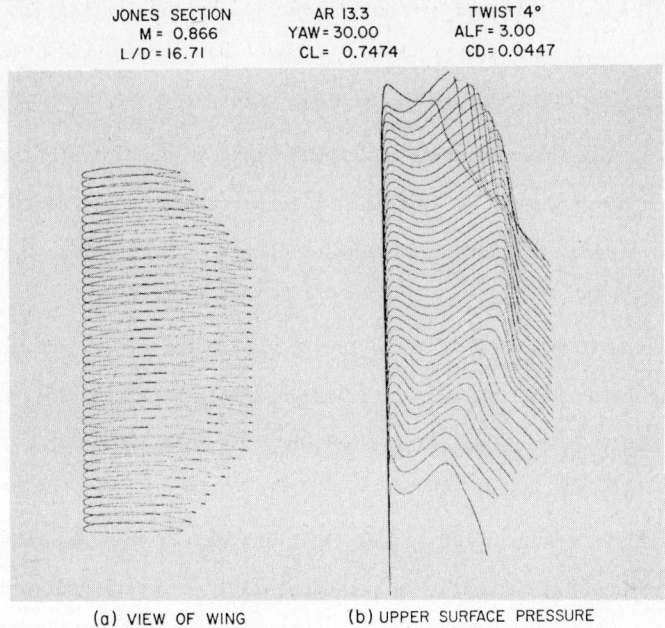

Fig. 23.  Yawed wing results for $M_\infty = 0.866$, $\alpha = 3°$, $\theta = 30°$.[38]

(a) View of wing.     (b) Upper surface pressure.

of the alignment between the flow and the finite-difference grid.  However, further improvements are clearly needed to obtain complete solutions of transonic flow problems.

While procedures for the exact isentropic formulation allow more accurate treatment of the boundary conditions, further improvement is required to calculate correct shock jumps, either by conservative difference operators or by explicitly fitting the shock waves as discontinuities and imposing the correct jump conditions. Because the exact isentropic jump and particularly the small disturbance jump become increasingly larger than the Rankine-Hugoniot jump with increasing shock Mach number, it is suggested that techniques be investigated for incorporating the Rankine-Hugoniot jump rather than the jump appropriate for the isentropic equation. Although such an approach is not rigorous, it may lead to a better approximation of the pressure distribution obtained from the exact inviscid equations of motion.  It is yet unclear how the correct computation of shock jumps (whether isentropic or not) will affect the apparent general good agreement between experimental jumps and those calculated by the nonconservative methods.

It is clear that viscosity plays a very important role in transonic flows and there remains the formidable task of incorporating turbulent viscous effects, particularly over the aft end of lifting airfoils. Although the development of a complete theory may take some time, more phenomenological methods based on modifications of the boundary layer approach with empirical adjustments may be developed for the short term. The urgent need is for predictive methods, however crude, that yield results for real flows.

Finally, we consider the additional complications of three-dimensional flows, which are centered about the increased difficulty of satisfying the boundary condition on complicated three-dimensional configurations. The small disturbance formulation considerably simplifies the boundary conditions and appears a reasonable near-term approach. In particular, it can be applied to wings on simulated fuselages to aid in the design of wing-fuselage junctures for minimum interference. However, efforts are needed to improve solutions near blunt leading edges and to improve the calculation of swept shocks, either through modifications to the equation or shock fittings.

## REFERENCES

1. Nieuwland, G. Y., "Transonic Potential Flow Around a Family of Quasi-Elliptical Aerofoil Sections," National Lucht-en-Ruimteraartlaboratorium (NLR) Technical Report T. 172 (Netherlands), 1967.

2. Korn, D. G., "Computation of Shock-Free Transonic Flows for Airfoil Design," Courant Institute of Math. Sci., NYO-1480-125, Oct. 1969.

3. Richtmyer, R. D., and Morton, K. W., Difference Methods for Initial-Value Problems, Interscience Publishers, Second ed., 1967.

4. Magnus, R., Gallaher, W., and Yoshihara, H., "Inviscid Supercritical Airfoil Theory," Transonic Aerodynamics, AGARD Conference Proceedings No. 35, Sept. 1968, pp. 3-1, 3-3.

5. Magnus, R., and Yoshihara, H., "Inviscid Transonic Flow Over Airfoils," AIAA Paper 70-47, Jan. 1970.

6. Murman, E. M., "Computational Methods for Inviscid Transonic Flows With Embedded Shock Waves," Numerical Methods in Fluid Dynamics, AGARD Lecture Series No. 48, 1972, pp. 13-1, 13-34.

7. Yoshihara, H., "A Survey of Computational Methods for 2D and 3D Transonic Flows With Shocks," Advances in Numerical Fluid Dynamics, AGARD Lecture Series No. 64, 1973, pp. 6-1, 6-35

8. Nieuwland, G. Y., and Spee, B. M., "Transonic Airfoils: Recent Developments in Theory, Experiment, and Design," Annual Review of Fluid Mechanics, Annual Reviews, Inc., Vol. 5, 1973, pp. 119-150.

9. Emmons, H. W., "The Numerical Solution of Compressible Fluid Flow Problems," NACA TN 932, 1944.

10. Emmons, H. W., "The Theoretical Flow of a Frictionless, Adiabatic, Perfect Gas Inside of a Two-Dimensional Hypersonic Nozzle," NACA TN 1003, 1946.

11. Emmons, H. W., "Flow of a Compressible Fluid Past a Symmetrical Airfoil in a Wind Tunnel and in Free Air," NACA TN 1746, 1948.

12. Murman, E. M., and Cole, J. D., "Calculation of Plane Steady Transonic Flows," AIAA Journal, Vol. 9, No. 1, 1971, pp. 114-121.

13. Steger, J. L., and Lomax, H., "Transonic Flow About Two-Dimensional Airfoils by Relaxation Procedures," AIAA Journal, Vol. 10, No. 1, 1972, pp. 49-54.

14. Garabedian, P. R., and Korn, D. G., "Analysis of Transonic Airfoils," Comm. Pure Appl. Math., Vol. XXIV, 1971, pp. 841-851.

15. Jameson, A., "Transonic Flow Calculations for Airfoils and Bodies of Revolution," Grumman Aerospace Corp. Report 390-71-1, 1971.

16. Murman, E. M., "Analysis of Embedded Shock Waves Calculated by Relaxation Methods," Proceedings of AIAA Computational Fluid Dynamics Conference, Palm Springs, Ca., July 1973, pp. 27-40.

17. Jameson, A., "Iterative Solution of Transonic Flows Over Airfoils and Wings, Including Flows at Mach 1," to appear in Comm. Pure Appl. Math.

18. Cole, J. D., and Messiter, A. F., "Expansion Procedures and Similarity Laws for Transonic Flow," <u>Zeit. ang. Math. u. Physik.</u>, Vol. 8, No. 1, 1957, pp. 1-25.

19. Cole, J. D., "Twenty Years of Transonic Flow," Boeing Scientific Research Laboratories Document D1-82-0878, July 1969.

20. Ashley, Holt, and Landahl, Martin, <u>Aerodynamics of Wings and Bodies</u>, Addison-Wesley Publishing Co., Inc., 1965.

21. Lax, Peter D., "Weak Solutions of Nonlinear Hyperbolic Equations and Their Numerical Computation," <u>Comm. Pure Appl. Math.</u>, Vol. VII, No. 1, 1954, pp. 159-193.

22. Oswatitsch, K., <u>Gas Dynamics</u>, Academic Press, 1956.

23. Nonweiler, T. R. F., "The Sonic Flow About Some Symmetric Half-Bodies," <u>J. Fluid Mech.</u>, Vol. 4, Pt. 2, 1958, pp. 140-148.

24. Oswatitsch, K., and Zierep, J., "Das Problem des senkrechten Stosses an einer gekrummten wand," <u>Zeit. ang. Math. u. Mech.</u>, Vol. 40, Supplement, T143-144, 1960.

25. Krupp, J. A., "The Numerical Calculation of Plane Steady Transonic Flows Past Thin Lifting Airfoils," Boeing Scientific Research Laboratories Report D180-12958-1, June 1971.

26. Krupp, J. A., and Murman, E. M., "The Numerical Calculation of Steady Transonic Flows Past Thin Lifting Airfoils and Slender Bodies," AIAA Paper 71-566, June 1971.

27. Murman, E. M., and Krupp, J. A., "Solution of the Transonic Potential Equation Using a Mixed Finite Difference System," <u>Lecture Notes in Physics</u>, Vol. 8, Springer-Verlag, 1971, pp. 199-206.

28. Yoshihara, Y., "A Survey of Computational Methods for 2D and 3D Transonic Flows With Shocks," GDCA-ERR-1726, Convair Aerospace Div., General Dynamics, Dec. 1972.

29. Magnus, R. M., "The Direct Comparison of the Relaxation Method and the Pseudo-Unsteady Finite Difference Method for Calculating Steady Planar Transonic Flow," TN-73-SP03, General Dynamics - Convair Aerospace Div., 1973.

30. Klunker, E. B., "Contributions to Methods for Calculating the Flow About Thin Lifting Wings at Transonic Speeds - Analytical Expression for the Far Field," NASA TN D-6530, 1971.

31. Ballhaus, W. F., and Bailey, F. R., "Numerical Calculation of Transonic Flow About Swept Wings," AIAA Paper 72-677, June 1972.

32. Bailey, F. R., and Ballhaus, W. F., "Relaxation Methods for Transonic Flow About Wing-Cylinder Combinations and Lifting Swept Wings," <u>Lecture Notes in Physics</u>, Vol. 19, Springer-Verlag, 1972, pp. 2-9.

33. Steger, J. L., and Baldwin, B. S., "Shock Waves and Drag in the Numerical Calculation of Isentropic Transonic Flow," NASA TN D-6997, 1972.

34. Bauer, E., Garabedian, P., and Korn, D., "Supercritical Wing Sections," <u>Lecture Notes in Economics and Mathematical Systems</u>, Vol. 66, Springer-Verlag, 1972.

35. Sells, C., "Plane Subcritical Flow Past a Lifting Airfoil," Proc. Roy. Soc. (London), Vol. 308A, 1968, pp. 377-401.

36. Thwaites, B., Incompressible Aerodynamics, Oxford Press, 1960.

37. South, J. C., and Jameson, A., "Relaxation Solutions for Inviscid Axisymmetric Transonic Flow Over Blunt or Pointed Bodies," Proceedings AIAA Computational Fluid Dynamics Conference, Palm Springs, Ca., 1973, pp. 8-17.

38. Jameson, A., "Numerical Calculation of the Three Dimensional Transonic Flow Over a Yawed Wing," Proceedings AIAA Computational Fluid Dynamics Conference, Palm Springs, Ca., 1973, pp. 18-26.

39. Garabedian, P. R., "Estimation of the Relaxations Factor for Small Mesh Size," Math. Tables Aids Comp., Vol. 10, 1956, pp. 183-185.

40. Kacpryzynski, J., Ohman, L., Garabedian, P., and Korn, D., "Analysis of Flow Past a Shockless Airfoil in Design and Off-Design Conditions," Paper presented at AIAA 4th Fluid and Plasma Dynamics Conference, June 21-23, 1971, Palo Alto, Ca. (see NRC Aeronautical Report LR-54 (Canada)), June 1972.

41. Lock, R. C., "Test Cases for Numerical Methods in Two-Dimensional Transonic Flows," AGARD Report No. 575, Nov. 1970.

42. Bailey, F. R., "Numerical Calculation of Transonic Flow About Slender Bodies of Revolution," NASA TN D-6582, 1971.

43. Kacpryzynski, J. J., "Wind Tunnel Tests of a Boerstoel Shockless Symmetrical Airfoil - 0.11-0.75-1.375," National Aircraft Establishment (NAE) Project Report 5x5/0061 (Canada), July 1972.

44. Boerstoel, J. W., "A Survey of Symmetrical Transonic Potential Flows About Quasi-Elliptical Airfoil Sections," National Lucht-en-Ruimtevaartlaboratorium (NLR) Technical Report T.136 (Netherlands), Jan. 1967.

45. Osborne, J., "A Selection of Measured Transonic Flow Pressure Distributions for the NACA 0012 Aerofoil: Provisional Data From an NPL Tunnel," Aerodynamics Dept., Royal Aircraft Establishment, June 1971.

46. Melnik, R. E., and Ives, D. C., "On Viscous and Wind-Tunnel Wall Effects in Transonic Flows Over Airfoils," AIAA Paper 73-660, July 1973.

47. Kacpryzynski, J., "A Second Series of Wind Tunnel Tests of the Shockless Lifting Airfoil No. 1," Report 5x5/0062 NRC (Canada), June 1972.

48. Garner, H. C. et al., "Subsonic Wind Tunnel Corrections," AGARDograph 109, Oct. 1966.

49. Baldwin, B., Turner, J., and Knechtel, E., "Wall Interference in Wind Tunnels With Slotted and Porous Boundaries at Subsonic Speeds," NACA TN 3176, 1954.

50. Taylor, R. A., and McDevitt, J. B., "Pressure Distributions at Transonic Speeds for Parabolic-Arc Bodies of Revolution Having Fineness Ratios of 10, 12, and 14," NACA TN 4234, 1958.

51. Murman, E. M., "Computation of Wall Effects in Ventilated Transonic Wind Tunnels," AIAA Paper 72-1007, Sept. 1972.

52. Isom, M. P., and Caradonna, F. X., "Subsonic and Transonic Potential Flow Over Helicopter Rotor Blades," AIAA Paper 72-39, Jan. 1972.

53. Ballhaus, W. F., and Caradonna, F. X., "The Effect of Planform Shape on the Transonic Flow Past Rotor Tips," <u>Aerodynamics of Rotary Wings</u>, AGARD Conference Proceedings No. 111, Paper 17, Sept. 1972.

54. Bailey, F. R., and Steger, J. L., "Relaxation Techniques for Three Dimensional Transonic Flow About Wings," AIAA Paper 72-189, Jan. 1972.

55. Newman, P. A., and Kunker, E. B., "Computation of Transonic Flow About Finite Lifting Wings," <u>AIAA Journal</u>, Vol. 10, No. 7, July 1972, pp. 971-973.

56. Cahill, J. F., and Stanewsky, E., "Wind Tunnel Tests of a Large-Chord, Swept-Panel Model to Investigate Shock-Induced Separation Phenomena," Air Force Flight Dynamics Lab. Report AFFDL-TR-69-78, Oct. 1969.

57. Saaris, G. R., and Rubbert, P. E., "Review and Evaluation of a Three Dimensional Lifting Potential Flow Computational Method for Arbitrary Configurations," AIAA Paper 72-188, Jan. 1972.

58. Lomax, H., Bailey, F. R., and Ballhaus, W. F., "On the Numerical Simulation of Three-Dimensional Transonic Flow With Application to the C-141 Wing," NASA TN D-6933, 1973.

59. Cahill, J. F., Teron, S. L., and Hofstetter, W. R., "Feasibility of Testing a Large-Chord, Swept-Panel Model to Determine Wing Shock Location at Flight Reynolds Number," AGARD Proc. 83, Paper 17, April 1971.

60. Liepmann, H. W., and Roshko, A., <u>Elements of Gas Dynamics</u>, John Wiley and Sons, New York, 1967.

61. Jones, R. T., "Reduction of Wave Drag by Antisymmetric Arrangement of Wings and Bodies," <u>AIAA Journal</u>, Vol. 9, 1971, pp. 114-121.

A CRITICAL REVIEW OF NUMERICAL SOLUTION OF NAVIER-STOKES EQUATIONS

by

Sin-I Cheng

PRINCETON UNIVERSITY

Department of Aerospace and Mechanical Sciences

(Separately distributed as Lecture Notes on Numerical
Solutions in Fluid Dynamics by v. Karman Institute
of Fluid Dynamics, AGARD, NATO, Belgium, February 1974
and as AMS Report #1158, Princeton University)

This research was conducted under the sponsorship
of the Office of Naval Research under Contract No.
N00014067-A-0151-0028.

Reproduction in whole or in part is permitted for
any purpose of the United States Government.

February 1974

A CRITICAL REVIEW OF NUMERICAL SOLUTION OF NAVIER-STOKES EQUATIONS

by

Sin-I Cheng
Princeton University
Department of Aerospace and Mechanical Sciences

## I. INTRODUCTION

This article is concerned primarily with the various practical problems encountered in using high speed electronic computers to obtain approximate solutions of various fluid flow problems, rather than with the general mathematical theory of difference approximations of partial differential equations. It is important to realize that, in the mathematical formulation of a given physical problem, the boundary conditions are as important as the partial differential equations which describe the phenomenon. There are complicated practical problems involved in discretizing the differential formulation (both the differential equations and the boundary conditions) into an appropriate difference formulation for numerical solution. Several aspects of the discretization procedure involve behavior quite different from those encountered in the more familiar differential analysis.

Fluid dynamicists usually ignore the question of convergence in asymptotic differential approximations obtained via perturbation arguments. They often consider the computational solution of the resulting system of ordinary differential equations as routine (albeit tedious), even though such systems are often ill-posed, especially for multi-eigenvalue problems. Under difficult circumstances, heuristic local treatments or various ad hoc methods are often introduced. Such hit-or-miss approaches have been carried over to the direct computational solution of the partial differential equations systems of fluid dynamics, resulting in much disappointment. While it may not be crucial to appreciate all of the details of the underlying mathematical theory, it is important to be aware of the implications of some fundamental mathematical results concerning the difference approximations of a partial differential equation. Accordingly, a brief review of these mathematical aspects will be outlined prior to the discussion of the practical art of numerically integrating the partial differential equations system of fluid dynamics.

Within the continuum description, the fluid will be considered to be homogeneous and to possess two independent thermodynamic (or state) variables, i.e., the density $\rho$ and the internal energy e per unit mass. There is an algebraic equation of state $p = p(\rho,e)$ relating the thermodynamic pressure p to the density $\rho$ and internal energy e. Let $u_i$ (i = 1,2,3) be the velocity vector of a fluid element in a three-dimensional space $x_i$. $u_i$, $\rho$ and e are the five dependent variables and will be considered as functions of $x_i$ and t. The Eulerian description of the time rate of change of these variables is represented by a set of five partial differential equations, expressing the conservation of mass, momentum, and energy (written here in divergence form) as:

$$\frac{\partial \rho}{\partial t} + \frac{\partial}{\partial x_j}\left[\rho u_j\right] = 0 \quad , \tag{1.1}$$

$$\frac{\partial (\rho u_i)}{\partial t} + \frac{\partial}{\partial x_j}\left[\rho u_i u_j + p\delta_{ij} - \tau_{ij}\right] = 0 \quad , \tag{1.2}$$

$$\frac{\partial (\rho e)}{\partial t} + \frac{\partial}{\partial x_j} \left[ \rho u_j (e + u_i u_i/2) + p u_j - q_j - u_i \tau_{ij} \right] = 0 \quad . \tag{1.3}$$

When the surface stress $\tau_{ij}$ is related linearly to the strain rate as

$$\tau_{ij} = \mu \left( \frac{\partial u_i}{\partial x_j} + \frac{\partial u_j}{\partial x_i} \right) + \left( \kappa - \frac{3}{2} \mu \right) \frac{\partial u_j}{\partial x_j} \quad , \tag{1.4}$$

and when the heat transfer vector $q_j$ is linearly related to the temperature gradient as

$$q_j = -k \frac{\partial \theta}{\partial x_j} = -\frac{\gamma}{Pr} \mu \frac{\partial e}{\partial x_j} \quad , \tag{1.5}$$

the system of equations (1.1-1.3) will be referred to as the Navier-Stokes equations for a compressible fluid. The Prandtl number Pr and the specific heat ratio $\gamma$ are properties of the fluid and are both of O(1). The shear viscosity coefficient $\mu$ is assumed to be a known algebraic function of temperature (or internal energy). The bulk viscosity coefficient $\kappa$ is often taken as zero, or is otherwise absorbed in $\mu$. In dimensionless form, a Reynolds number may be defined in terms of some characteristic length $L_o$ and velocity $U_o$ as $Re_o = \rho_o U_o L_o / \mu_o$, where subscript o indicates that the quantity is to be evaluated at some reference state. For most fluid dynamics applications, the Reynolds number is very large.

The divergence form of the Navier-Stokes equations (1.1)-(1.3) may be written as

$$\frac{\partial v}{\partial t} + \frac{\partial}{\partial x_j} F \left( v, \frac{1}{Re} \frac{\partial v}{\partial x_k} \right) = 0 \quad , \tag{1.6}$$

posed as an initial value problem for the vector unknown v having the five scalar components $\rho$, $\rho u_i$, and $\rho e$. F is the flux of v, given by the nonlinear quantities in the square brackets of Equations (1.1)-(1.3). When physically meaningful, initial and boundary data are prescribed, Equation (1.6) is expected to give a satisfactory description of the temporal development of the flow field at later times. This expectation is mathematically justifiable. The integration of this equation system is needed, for example, in weather forecasting, and in the determination of the temporal development of blast waves, hurricanes, and turbulent fluctuations (where the gravitational field and the coriolis forces are included where necessary). In most aeronautical applications, steady state (or quasi-steady state) problems, where the temporal dependence is neglected, are more often of primary interest. Thus Equation (1.6) becomes

$$\frac{\partial}{\partial x_j} F(v, \frac{1}{Re} \frac{\partial v}{\partial x_k}) = 0 \quad , \tag{1.7}$$

which is to be solved as a boundary value problem. The boundary conditions must, of course, be independent of time. But it is not clear how such boundary conditions should be specified to provide the required steady state solution or, indeed, any solution at all. Physical intuition often provides some meaningful guidance, but not all that is needed.

The stress and the heat conduction terms give rise to the second (and highest) order partial derivatives, with coefficients proportional to $Re^{-1}$. The steady state Navier-Stokes Equation (1.7) generally assumes elliptic behavior. When Re becomes large, the flow field may be divided into sub-regions. In the region sufficiently far away from any solid boundary, the inviscid approximation, obtained by dropping terms in (1.6) or (1.7) containing $Re^{-1}$, is a valid approximation, known as Euler's Equation:

$$\frac{\partial v}{\partial t} + \frac{\partial}{\partial x_j} F(v) = 0 \qquad (1.8a)$$

$$\frac{\partial}{\partial x_j} F(v) = 0 \qquad (1.8b)$$

The time-dependent inviscid Equation (1.8a) remains hyperbolic, and is posed as an initial value problem, as is Equation (1.6). The steady state Equation (1.8b), however, can be purely elliptic (subsonic), purely hyperbolic (supersonic), or mixed (i.e., with both elliptic and hyperbolic regions). The boundaries between different regions of a mixed problem will depend on the solution, and thus are not known before hand. This situation arises in the supercritical transonic inviscid flow problem, for example.

In the regions near a solid boundary, or near where there is large shear stress or heat conduction, some or all of the stress terms contained in $F(v, \frac{1}{Re} \frac{\partial v}{\partial x_k})$ have to be kept, despite the large Re. If this viscous region should extend along a coordinate surface $(x_1, x_2)$ such that the lateral extent (along $x_3$) of this viscous layer is small (compared with its physical extent along the $(x_1, x_2)$ surface), then Prandtl's boundary layer theory applies. Only the highest order partial derivative in this lateral direction $(\partial^2/\partial_3^2)$ will survive in the limit of very large Re. This asymptotic limit at large Re gives the boundary layer equations, which are parabolic. However, not all viscous layers are sheet-like, and, hence, not all are amenable to Prandtl's boundary layer approximation. For viscous layers like the near-wake and the interaction region between a shock wave and a boundary layer, the full Navier-Stokes Equation (1.7) will have to be used, and the problem becomes elliptic, at least in a significant portion of the flow field of interest.

The change of the mathematical character of the flow field in different regions when the Reynolds number is large is both a blessing and a cause for concern. It is a blessing in that, historically, it enabled the development of fluid dynamics in the forms of the inviscid (or perfect) fluid theory and the boundary layer theory. But it is also the fundamental difficulty in the analysis of the mixed flow regions which are characteristic of most interaction flow problems. Now there are significant differences in the numerical integration of the three types of partial differential equations. A method that has proved successful for one type need not be so for another. It is, therefore, important to recognize the type of partial differential equation at hand before formulating a difference approximation for its numerical integration. Clearly, then, there are difficulties in the numerical integration of mixed problems. Such difficulties are quite different from those encountered in the asymptotic analysis of mixed flow problems. In a few examples, these difficulties have been successfully resolved with appropriate cautionary measures. But there is no theorem to guarantee similar success in other problems.

If the elliptic steady state Navier-Stokes Equations (1.7) could be integrated for a given large but finite Re, why should the difficulties arising from the asymptotic limit of Re $\rightarrow \infty$ concern us? An obvious answer might be that the asymptotic form of the partial differential equations system is much simpler than the full system. However, a more fundamental reason is that, at large but finite Reynolds numbers, the asymptotic behavior of the flow in different regions bears strongly on the appropriateness of the difference formulation and on the numerical integration of the Navier-Stokes equations when the resolution (or the number of meshes per linear dimension of the field of computation) is severely limited.

For a flow problem in three space dimensions, an average of 30 meshes per linear dimension will give rise to $3 \times 10^4$ nodel points; and thus $1.5 \times 10^5$ words of storage space will be needed for the 5 unknowns at each point. This storage space should preferably be provided in the core of the computer unit for ready access. Such a requirement will stretch the core memory capacity of most of the currently available large computers, such as the CDC 6600 or the IBM 360-91. The solution of the full Navier-Stokes Equations (1.7) for a well-posed boundary value problem will need hours of computation in such machines. Parallel computers in advanced stages of development, like the ILLIAC IV and the STAR, cannot promise much improvement in this regard. To extend the core memory capacity of these parallel machines, a hierarchy of external storage devices will be provided. Frequent reference to such external storage, however, will greatly increase the time required for data management, due to the slowness of the input-output devices connected to the central processing unit. This input-output slowness is crucial in parallel computers, where the promised large gain in arithematic speed can be obtained only for specific modes of "parallel" or "vector" computations in which a huge amount of data must be properly processed and continuously fed into the arithematic unit(s).

The concept of parallel use of an array of mini-computers might appear to relieve the difficulty associated with any such specific mode of high speed arithematic operations. The benefit is likely to be illusory, however, at least for present applications. The use of such a system simply transfers to the users the tremendous problem of optimal coordination of the operations of the array of mini-computers, and the problem of data management among the diverse "internal" and "external" storage facilities. The users are generally not equipped with the expertise of the computer scientists who designed the possess "neighboring solutions." This means that when the initial-boundary data is slightly perturbed, the differential problem should still provide a solution which, hopefully, departs from the unperturbed solution of the problem only slightly. This is primarily a physical requirement, expounded by Hadamard, to insure that a mathematical formulation describes a physical situation reasonably. Mathematically speaking, the solution of the differential problem is said to vary continuously with the data; and the differential problem is said to be "well-posed." A given partial differential equation is well posed only when (among other things) the boundary conditions are properly specified. For example, the Laplace equation in two variables x and y,

$$\frac{\partial^2 u}{\partial x^2} + \frac{\partial^2 u}{\partial y^2} = 0 \quad , \quad (2.1)$$

is well-posed when the value of the function u(x,y) is specified on a boundary enclosing the domain of interest (Dirichlet Problem).

Now the function

$$u(x,y) = n^{-a} \sin nx \cosh ny \quad (2.2)$$

is an exact solution of the Laplace equation with the initial data

$$u(x,0) = n^{-a} \sin nx$$

$$\frac{\partial u}{\partial y}(x,0) = 0$$

This set of initial data is small everywhere on x with a > 0 and n sufficiently large. If the Laplace equation is to be solved when u(x,0) and $\frac{\partial u}{\partial y}(x,0)$ are specified, then a small perturbation of the initial data can introduce perturbations of the type (2.2) onto the solution of the problem.

possess "neighboring solutions." This means that when the initial-boundary data is slightly perturbed, the differential problem should still provide a solution which, hopefully, departs from the unperturbed solution of the problem only slightly. This is primarily a physical requirement, expounded by Hadamard, to insure that a mathematical formulation describes a physical situation reasonably. Mathematically speaking, the solution of the differential problem is said to vary continuously with the data; and the differential problem is said to be "well-posed." A given partial differential equation is well posed only when (among other things) the boundary conditions are properly specified. For example, the Laplace equation in two variables x and y,

$$\frac{\partial^2 u}{\partial x^2} + \frac{\partial^2 u}{\partial y^2} = 0 \quad , \tag{2.1}$$

is well-posed when the value of the function u(x,y) is specified on a boundary enclosing the domain of interest (Dirichlet Problem).
Now the function

$$u(x,y) = n^{-a} \sin nx \cosh ny \tag{2.2}$$

is an exact solution of the Laplace equation with the initial data

$$u(x,0) = n^{-a} \sin nx$$

$$\frac{\partial u}{\partial y}(x,0) = 0$$

This set of initial data is small everywhere on x with a > 0 and n sufficiently large. If the Laplace equation is to be solved when $u(x,0)$ and $\frac{\partial u}{\partial y}(x,0)$ are specified, then a small perturbation of the initial data **can** introduce perturbations of the type (2.2) onto the solution of the problem.

thought and modifications of existing methods." This statement is equally true today, particularly for the type of flow problems under consideration here.

## II. FUNDAMENTAL CONCEPTS

Consider now the problem of solving a partial differential equation, subject to a set of initial and boundary data, through numerical integration. A difference formulation, as an approximation to the differential problem, is obtained by replacing the differential coefficients by appropriate difference quotients. There will be some "errors" in the approximate formulation of the equation and of the initial and boundary data. When these "errors" vanish as the mesh sizes $\Delta t \to 0$ & $\Delta x \to 0$ in some manner, the difference approximation is said to be "consistent" with the differential problem. The solutions of this difference formulation provide a sequence of approximate solutions, which, in the limit of $\Delta t, \Delta x \to 0$, is supposed to "converge" to the solution of the differential problem in some sense; i.e., the "error" of the solution, as a measure of the departure of each member of the sequence of approximate solutions from the solution of the differential problem, tends to "zero." This convergence is, however, not guaranteed for a consistent approximate difference formulation. Various aspects of this situation will be considered in the following sections.

### 2.1 Well-Posed Differential Problem

Whether the problem is to be integrated analytically or numerically, the differential problem should not only possess a unique solution, but should also

This perturbation (2.2) is not small in the immediate neighborhood of y = 0, despite the small error in the initial data when n is large and a is positive. While the perturbation (2.2) does vanish at y = 0 for any value of n (including n → ∞), the value of u(x,y) given by (2.2) at some small but finite value of y becomes infinitely large as n → ∞. Thus the Laplace equation is not "well-posed" (or is "ill-posed") when u(x,0) and $\frac{\partial u}{\partial y}$ (x,0) are specified (Cauchy Problem). If we should proceed to integrate this "ill-posed" problem, the perturbed initial data would be expected to contain components like (2.2), and the numerical solution would not converge to the desired solution even if Δx → 0 (i.e., n → ∞).

If the gradient of u(x,y) is specified over a closed boundary (Neumann Problem), or if the gradiant is specified on part of a closed boundary and the value of u(x,y) is specified on the remainder, the problem of solving the Laplace equation is well-posed (provided that some integral conditions are met). Ill-posed problems will result otherwise, i.e., either when Dirichlet or Neumann conditions are specified only on an open boundary, or when Cauchy conditions are used anywhere. This statement is applicable to elliptic partial differential equations in general. Parabolic equations are well-posed under similar conditions, but only on an "open" boundary and when integrated in the "positive" direction. Hyperbolic problems are well-posed only when Cauchy conditions are specified on an appropriate "open" portion of the boundary. It becomes difficult, then, to specify the boundary conditions that will render a mixed differential problem well posed, even before attempting to formulate a difference approximation of the problem for numerical integration. From this point of view, the algebraic complexities of the full Navier-Stokes equations system, either for the time-dependent hyperbolic problem (1.6) or for the steady state elliptical problem (1.7), may well be tolerated to facilitate the formulation of a well-posed problem.

## 2.2 Well-Posed Difference Problem

To provide a convergent numerical solution, it is not only required that the differential problem be well-posed for a specific or selected class of initial data, but also that the difference problem be well-posed for a more general class of initial data. This is because the perturbations implicit in the numerical solution of the approximate difference formulation need not fall within the class of the initial data for which the differential problem is well-posed. The function

$$u(x,t) = \exp\left[i\alpha(x + t)\right] \tag{2.3}$$

satisfies the first-order hyperbolic equation

$$\frac{\partial}{\partial t} u - \frac{\partial}{\partial x} u = 0 \tag{2.4}$$

with the initial value

$$u(x,0) = \exp(i\alpha x).$$

The complex notation with $i = \sqrt{-1}$ is used here for simplicity, to mean that both the real and imaginary parts of the expressions should be valid simultaneously. A wide class of functions $u(x,0)$ can be formed by superposing various trigonometric initial data, corresponding to various choices of values of the constant $\alpha$. Each component can possess an arbitrarily assigned amplitude. By summing up the component solutions of different $\alpha$'s, the solution of the problem with generalized initial data is obtained. Any number of the component solutions can be perturbed, with a correspondingly small perturbation on the solution. The differential problem is thus well-posed.

Suppose now the forward-time, centered-space difference algorithm is used to provide a difference approximation to (2.4) as:

$$\frac{U_j^{n+1} - U_j^n}{\Delta t} = \frac{U_{j+1}^n - U_{j-1}^n}{2\Delta x} \tag{2.5}$$

$$U_j^0 = \exp(i\alpha x)$$

where $U_j^n = U(j\Delta x, n\Delta t)$.

An exact solution of the difference problem (2.5) is

$$U_j^n = U(j\Delta x, n\Delta t) = \left(1 + i\frac{\Delta t}{\Delta x}\sin \alpha\Delta x\right)^n \exp(i\alpha x), \tag{2.6}$$

where $n = t/\Delta t$. In the limit of $\Delta t \to 0$ & $\Delta x \to 0$, the difference solution $U_j^n$, (2.6), converges uniformly to the solution $u(x,t)$, (2.3) of the differential problem (2.4). The same holds true for all components, and for their sum, with generalized initial data. Now when the difference problem (2.5) is computed for any small $\Delta t$ and $\Delta x$, the computation is always unstable, as is well known. It is apparent that some components of the perturbations introduced by the computation of the difference form (2.5) cannot be represented by trigonometric data, and grow out-of-bounds during the calculation.

The Euler's equation (1.8a) for inviscid gas dynamics is easily cast into a Cauchy-Kowaleski type quasi-linear hyperbolic equation system

$$\frac{\partial u}{\partial t} + A(u)\frac{\partial u}{\partial x_j} = 0, \tag{2.7}$$

where $A(u) = \frac{\partial F}{\partial u}$. If the initial data $u(x, t=0) = f(x)$ and $A(u)$ are analytic, then the solution $u(x,t)$ for all $x$ and $t$ is analytic. The requirement of analyticity of the initial data might not appear to be very restrictive, in view of the fact that, according to the Weierstrass approximation theorem, any continuous function within a closed interval can be approximated arbitrarily closely by analytic functions (including polynomials and sinusoidal functions). But an arbitrarily close approximation of the initial data does not promise an arbitrarily close approximation of the solution. The examples (2.1) and (2.5) given above illustrate this point, both for the differential and the difference equations.

Equations (1.8a) and (2.7) for inviscid gas dynamics are well-posed for a fairly broad class of initial data. Even if it is presumed that a consistent difference approximation possesses a solution that converges uniformly to the solution of the differential problem, stable computation is not guaranteed. The instability of the computation is attributed to the fact that perturbations on the initial data, introduced by the computational procedure, are beyond the class of perturbations expressible in terms of piecewise analytic data. For a difference problem to be well-posed, its solution must vary continuously with a much wider class of perturbations on the initial data. This is the crux of the concept of computational stability.

Computational stability in general calls for the boundedness of all of the perturbations in the computed solution. Then, when the magnitudes of the perturbations in the initial data are made arbitrarily small (in the limit of vanishingly small mesh sizes), the resulting perturbations in the computed solution will likewise vanish. The computed neighboring solutions based on a consistent difference formulation will then converge to the solution of the differential problem; i.e., stability and consistency imply convergence. This is the essence of the equivalence theorem of Lax. Success in obtaining a convergent approximate solution through computation based on a given difference formulation therefore depends on:

(i) the consistency of the difference formulation with the well-posed differential problem, and

(ii) the stability of the difference formulation.

Here, the difference formulation means, collectively, all of the difference relations connecting the values of functions at different time levels and at all mesh points in the interior of, and on the boundary of, the field of computation.

## 2.3 Computational Stability

Computational stability is a characteristic of a set of difference equations, rather than of a particular difference algorithm indicating how a differential coefficient in the differential equation is to be replaced by a difference quotient. Thus it is incorrect to refer to an algorithm as stable or unstable. The same algorithm when applied to various differential equations can lead to different difference equations with entirely different stability characteristics. For example, the forward time and centered-space difference algorithm applied to the simple wave equation (2.4) leads to an always unstable difference equation (2.5). But, when the same algorithm is applied to the heat diffusion equation, the resulting difference equation is stable if $s = \frac{\Delta t}{\Delta x^2} \leq \frac{1}{2}$. More simple examples are given in Tables I and II.

Slightly different algorithms, applied to the same differential equation, may yield difference equations with quite different stability behavior. For the simple wave equation (2.4), the forward-time and backward-space difference algorithm will yield the always unstable difference equation

$$L(u) = \left(\frac{\partial}{\partial t} + c\frac{\partial}{\partial x}\right)u = 0$$

| | $L_\Delta(u)$ WITH $r = c\frac{\Delta t}{\Delta x} > 0$ | $e_t = L_\Delta(u) - L(u)$ | STABLE |
|---|---|---|---|
| 1) | $(u_j^{n+1} - u_j^n) + r(u_{j+1}^n - u_j^n)$ | $O(\Delta t, \Delta x)$ | UNSTABLE |
| 2) | $(u_j^{n+1} - u_j^n) + r(u_j^n - u_{j-1}^n)$ | $O(\Delta t, \Delta x)$ | IF $r \leq 1$ |
| 3) | $(u_j^{n+1} - u_j^n) + \frac{r}{2}(u_{j+1}^n - u_{j-1}^n)$ | $O(\Delta t, \Delta x^2)$ | UNSTABLE |
| 4) | $u^{n+1} - \frac{u_{j+1}^n + u_{j-1}^n}{2} + \frac{r}{2}(u_{j+1}^n - u_{j-1}^n)$ | $O(\Delta t, \Delta x^2)$ | IF $r \leq 1$ |
| 5) | $u_j^{n+1} - u_j^{n-1} + r(u_{j+1}^n - u_{j-1}^n)$ | $O(\Delta t^2, \Delta x^2)$ | ALL $r$ |
| | MOST IMPLICIT SCHEMES | | ALL $r$ |

TABLE I

$$L(u) = \left(\frac{\partial}{\partial t} - \nu \frac{\partial^2}{\partial x^2}\right) u = 0$$

| | $L_\Delta(u)$ WITH $s = \nu \Delta t/\Delta x^2$ | $e_t = L_\Delta(u) - L(u)$ | STABLE |
|---|---|---|---|
| 1) | $(u_j^{n+1} - u_j^n) - s(u_{j+1}^n - 2u_j^n + u_{j-1}^n)$ | $O(\Delta t, \Delta x^2)$ | IF $s \leq \frac{1}{2}$ |
| 2) | $\left(u_j^{n+1} - \frac{u_{j+1}^n + u_{j-1}^n}{2}\right) - s(u_{j+1}^n - 2u_j^n + u_{j-1}^n)$ | $O(\Delta t, \Delta x^2)$ | UNSTABLE |
| 3) | $(u_j^{n+1} - u_j^{n-1}) - 2s(u_{j+1}^n - 2u_j^n + u_{j-1}^n)$ | $O(\Delta t^2, \Delta x^2)$ | UNSTABLE |
| 4) | $(u_j^{n+1} - u_j^{n-1}) - 2s(u_{j+1}^n - u_j^{n+1} - u_j^{n-1} + u_{j-1}^n)$ | $O(\Delta t^2, \Delta x^2)$ | ALL $s$ |
| | MOST IMPLICIT SCHEMES | | ALL $s$ |

TABLE II

$$\frac{U_j^{n+1} - U_j^n}{\Delta t} - \frac{U_j^n - U_{j-1}^n}{\Delta x} = 0 \quad . \tag{2.8}$$

The forward-time and the forward-space difference algorithm will provide the difference equation

$$\frac{U_j^{n+1} - U_j^n}{\Delta t} - \frac{U_{j+1}^n - U_j^n}{\Delta x} = 0 \quad , \tag{2.9}$$

which is stable if $\Delta t/\Delta x \leq 1$. And, as mentioned previously, the forward-time and centered-space difference algorithm, Equation (2.5), is always unstable. The choice of a difference algorithm which yields a stable difference equation is not trivial.

A partial differential equation representing a physical principle may be written in different (but equivalent) forms in terms of different subsidiary variables. Moreover, a partial differential equation of higher order can sometimes be written as an equivalent system of lower order equations. When the same difference algorithm is applied to discretize these equivalent differential forms, the resulting difference equations are not equivalent, and may possess widely different stability behavior. Consider the simplest case of the second-order wave equation

$$\frac{\partial^2 \phi}{\partial t^2} = C^2 \frac{\partial^2 \phi}{\partial x^2} \tag{2.10}$$

which is differentially equivalent to a system of two first-order wave equations. We may write the system in terms of two different pairs of variables as:

$$\begin{cases} \frac{\partial \phi}{\partial t} = v \\ \frac{\partial v}{\partial t} = C^2 \frac{\partial^2 \phi}{\partial x^2} \end{cases} \tag{2.11a}$$

and
$$\begin{cases} \dfrac{\partial v}{\partial t} = C \dfrac{\partial u}{\partial x} \\ \dfrac{\partial u}{\partial t} = C \dfrac{\partial v}{\partial x} \end{cases} \qquad (2.11b)$$

When the forward-time and centered-space difference algorithm is used, the following difference equation systems result:

$$\begin{cases} \dfrac{\Phi_j^{n+1} - \Phi_j^n}{\Delta t} = V_j^n \\ \dfrac{V_j^{n+1} - V_j^n}{\Delta t} = C^2 \dfrac{\Phi_{j+1}^n - 2\Phi_j^n + \Phi_{j-1}^n}{\Delta x^2} \end{cases} \qquad (2.12)$$

and
$$\begin{cases} \dfrac{V_j^{n+1} - V_j^n}{\Delta t} = C \dfrac{U_{j+1}^n - U_{j-1}^n}{2\Delta x} \\ \dfrac{U_j^{n+1} - U_j^n}{\Delta t} = C \dfrac{V_{j+1}^n - V_{j-1}^n}{2\Delta x} \end{cases} \qquad (2.13)$$

System (2.12) is always unstable for any choice of $\Delta t$ and $\Delta x$ (as is easily verified by v. Neumann Analysis), while system (2.13) is stable if $C \Delta t/\Delta x \leq 1$. Note also that the similar difference equation (2.5) for the first-order wave equation (2.4) is always unstable. Thus, it is not a matter of trivial consequence to rewrite a partial differential equation into equivalent, but different, forms before discretization with a given difference algorithm.

The equations of fluid dynamics represent the three conservation laws of mass, momentum, and energy. They can be expressed in terms of a great number of dependent and independent variables, in terms of particular combinations of such variables, and in various coordinate systems. Second-order equations may be split into first-order systems. (For the moment, the question of non-linearity is put aside). When applied to these various physically and differentially equivalent systems of partial differential equations, a given difference algorithm will yield various difference forms with quite different stability and other computational behaviors.

The complete difference formulation of a fluid dynamics problem calls for the discretization not only of the differential equations, but also of the boundary conditions. The set of difference relations connecting the values of various functions at mesh points neighboring the boundary is generally different from the set of recursive relations for the interior points derived from the differential equations. This set of boundary difference relations may be unstable, while the recursive difference relations for the interior points are stable. Furthermore, apparently trivial modifications of the difference formulation of the boundary conditions often lead to substantial changes in the stability behavior.

In view of such a complicated situation and of the frequent experience of severe computational instability, it is highly desirable to be able to analyze the stability behavior of a given difference formulation; but there is no simple means available except the so-called "energy analysis." "Energy analysis" attempts to establish a finite bound on the solution (over the entire net or mesh space) in some suitably-chosen norm; if this is possible, then the formulation is, by definition, stable. When such a bound is established, the proof of convergence, existence, and uniqueness follows trivially. For a nontrivial boundary value problem, such a proof is very difficult and tedious, even for a simple equation. Such proofs are available for the Navier-Stokes equations for an incompressible fluid, but only for periodic boundary conditions - a case which is really not that much different from a pure initial value problem. With rather complicated boundary conditions, it is impractical, if not impossible, to ascertain the stability property of a difference formulation of a fluid dynamics problem via such an approach. At present, it is a practical art to draw both from experience with similar problems and from inferences of model analysis in formulating the recursive difference relations for the interior points. The formulation of the boundary conditions is approached on an individual (i.e., ad hoc) basis and modified where necessary. The entire algorithm is then tested in actual computation for its stability. Considerable work will be involved before stable computation is achieved; by then, quite a few modifications may have been introduced. It is opportune to check if the final difference formulation is consistent with the differential problem to be solved, with regard to both the differential equations and the boundary conditions.

It may well be that the difference boundary conditions which prove successful in computation are not consistent with the correct physical boundary conditions, or that some spurious terms are introduced into the differential equations that fail to vanish in the limit of $\Delta t, \Delta x \to 0$. The v. Neumann stability analysis for the local linearized model will most likely impose some restrictions on $\Delta t$ and $\Delta x$ for the computation to remain stable. This restriction should be observed by all approximate solutions, viewed as successive members in a Cauchy sequence converging toward the solution of the differential problem. The limit process in the t-x space is not to be taken in any arbi-

## III. STABILITY ANALYSIS

In the numerical integration of the Navier-Stokes Equations, an outstanding example of a complicated partial differential equations system, it is expected that quite serious practical difficulties will be encountered. Such difficulties can be grouped under the following three (not necessarily independent) considerations:

(i) Computational Stability - All disturbances should remain bounded in the computation. Otherwise, the value of some quantity would eventually become so large as to be beyond the capability of any computer, and no results would be obtained. Hence, stability is often referred to as "computability."

(ii) Convergence Rate - The solution, at some later time T or at the asymptotic steady state, should be obtained with a reasonable amount of computational work; i.e., the number of time or iterative steps in the solution must not be too large, and the computational work for each step not excessive, so that results can be obtained within a reasonable amount of time (and hence cost).

(iii) Accuracy - For it to be useful, the solution eventually obtained must be in some sense approximate the physical results in question. The criterion for an adequate approximation is, however, subject to judgment. The accuracy criterion imposes limitations on the fineness of the resolution (both temporally and spatially) which in turn determines the convergence rate.

Computational stability is clearly the most pressing problem, since it is the first one to be encountered in an attempt to get any solution. Much work has been devoted to this question. As explained in the previous chapter, trary manner; this restriction should be considered while investigating the consistency of the difference formulation.

Certain difference algorithms are often referred to as "unconditionally stable." This means that when such an algorithm is used to discretize a certain type of differential equation for the solution of pure initial value problems (or periodic boundary value problems), there will not be, according to the v. Neuman stability analysis of the linear equations, restrictive conditions on the choice of $\Delta t$ (or on the iterative steps) for a given set of $\Delta x$. When such an algorithm is used in the numerical solution of non-periodic boundary value problems, even for the same particular type of equations, computational instability will often result, especially for complicated boundary conditions and for non-linear equations. Even if no question of stability should arise, the apparent advantage of permitting the use of quite large time steps $\Delta t$ need not lessen the overall computing time, while inevitably decreasing the accuracy of the computed solution. Indeed, under such circumstances, it is advisable to verify the consistency conditions for both the equation and the boundary condition.

A case to illustrate this point is the following. The integration of the simple heat diffusion equation

$$\frac{\partial u}{\partial t} = \frac{\partial^2 u}{\partial x^2} \qquad (2.14)$$

with the formally second-order accurate, centered-time, centered-space algorithm of DuFort-Frankel:

$$\frac{U_j^{n+1} - U_j^{n-1}}{2\Delta t} = \frac{U_{j+1}^n - 2U_j^n + U_{j-1}^n}{\Delta x^2} + \frac{U_j^{n+1} - 2U_j^n + U_j^{n-1}}{\Delta t^2}\left(\frac{\Delta t}{\Delta x}\right)^2 \qquad (2.15)$$

is "unconditionally stable" for any positive values of $s = \frac{\Delta t}{\Delta x^2}$, so that $\Delta t$

tedious, even for a simple equation. Such proofs are available for the Navier-Stokes equations for an incompressible fluid, but only for periodic boundary conditions - a case which is really not that much different from a pure initial value problem. With rather complicated boundary conditions, it is impractical, if not impossible, to ascertain the stability property of a difference formulation of a fluid dynamics problem via such an approach. At present, it is a practical art to draw both from experience with similar problems and from inferences of model analysis in formulating the recursive difference relations for the interior points. The formulation of the boundary conditions is approached on an individual (i.e., ad hoc) basis and modified where necessary. The entire algorithm is then tested in actual computation for its stability. Considerable work will be involved before stable computation is achieved; by then, quite a few modifications may have been introduced. It is opportune to check if the final difference formulation is consistent with the differential problem to be solved, with regard to both the differential equations and the boundary conditions.

It may well be that the difference boundary conditions which prove successful in computation are not consistent with the correct physical boundary conditions, or that some spurious terms are introduced into the differential equations that fail to vanish in the limit of $\Delta t, \Delta x \rightarrow 0$. The v. Neumann stability analysis for the local linearized model will most likely impose some restrictions on $\Delta t$ and $\Delta x$ for the computation to remain stable. This restriction should be observed by all approximate solutions, viewed as successive members in a Cauchy sequence converging toward the solution of the differential problem. The limit process in the t-x space is not to be taken in any arbi-

## III. STABILITY ANALYSIS

In the numerical integration of the Navier-Stokes Equations, an outstanding example of a complicated partial differential equations system, it is expected that quite serious practical difficulties will be encountered. Such difficulties can be grouped under the following three (not necessarily independent) considerations:

(i) Computational Stability - All disturbances should remain bounded in the computation. Otherwise, the value of some quantity would eventually become so large as to be beyond the capability of any computer, and no results would be obtained. Hence, stability is often referred to as "computability."

(ii) Convergence Rate - The solution, at some later time T or at the asymptotic steady state, should be obtained with a reasonable amount of computational work; i.e., the number of time or iterative steps in the solution must not be too large, and the computational work for each step not excessive, so that results can be obtained within a reasonable amount of time (and hence cost).

(iii) Accuracy - For it to be useful, the solution eventually obtained must be in some sense approximate the physical results in question. The criterion for an adequate approximation is, however, subject to judgment. The accuracy criterion imposes limitations on the fineness of the resolution (both temporally and spatially) which in turn determines the convergence rate.

Computational stability is clearly the most pressing problem, since it is the first one to be encountered in an attempt to get any solution. Much work has been devoted to this question. As explained in the previous chapter, can be made as large as $\Delta x$ (or larger) without leading to computational instability. Most other explicit difference algorithms, when applied to the heat diffusion equation, will impose a stability limit like $s \leq 1/2$. This restriction on $\Delta t$ is particularly severe at small $\Delta x$. Now, in integrating Equation (2.15), it is tempting to use as large a $\Delta t$ as is practical, usually comparable to $\Delta x$, to save computing time. Indeed, this is often credited as the "merit" of the Dufort-Frankel scheme. Equation (2.15) is, however, consistent with the heat diffusion equation only when $\frac{\Delta t}{\Delta x} \to 0$ as $\Delta x \to 0$. Otherwise, it is consistent with the wave equation (2.15a), having the wave speed $\frac{\Delta x}{\Delta t}$.

$$\left(\frac{\Delta t}{\Delta x}\right)^2 \frac{\partial^2 u}{\partial t^2} + \frac{\partial u}{\partial t} = \frac{\partial^2 u}{\partial x^2} \tag{2.15a}$$

With $\frac{\Delta t}{\Delta x} = O(1)$, the computed solution is expected to display waves comparable in magnitude to the actual solution, and therefore, loses much of its value as an approximation to the solution of the diffusion problem (2.14). Even with $\Delta t/\Delta x^2 = s \leq 1/2$, for example, the computed solutions will still display oscillations, albeit of smaller amplitude. An averaged solution (taken over the waves) is not necessarily a meaningful approximation of the solution to the diffusion problem with Dirichlet boundary conditions - if a Neumann boundary condition is imposed, instability will often result. The qualitative statements mentioned here should not be generalized; the simple example is given above only to drive home the point that every individual problem should be carefully examined according to the fundamental principles. Our current understanding of the numerical integration of partial differential equations does not warrant any simple generalizations applicable to the complicated situations of fluid dynamics.

its fundamental nature is essentially understood, but there are quite a few subtle aspects in its implementation, even for simple examples. The practical difficulty encountered in achieving a stable computation for the complicated system of the Navier-Stokes Equations is expected to be formidable. The various heuristic approaches that promise to guide the formulation of a stable difference problem will be reviewed in the following chapter. Generally speaking, with some hard work a stable computation can usually be achieved, as may be verified in actual computation. It is important, however, to bear in mind that the convergence rate and the accuracy of the formulation should not be seriously compromised in an all-out effort to achieve stability of the computation. The objective of the computation is to obtain a valid approximation to a given physical problem. Therefore, the following review is intended to bring out primarily the mathematical assumptions and the physical implications of various approaches when they are applied to the solution of different types of practical problems.

## 3.1 v. Neumann Stability Analysis

A vector unknown $U(t,x_j)$ of dimension p is to be calculated over mesh spacings $\Delta x_1$, $\Delta x_2$, $\Delta x_3$ for successive increments of $\Delta t$ from the initial values of $U(t=0,x_j)$, based on a system of linear difference equations.

The general form of the linear difference relations may be that some linear combinations of the values of the function $U^{n+1}$ at a group of neighboring mesh points are given by some other linear combinations of $U^n$ at various neighboring points. If only the $U^{n+1}$ evaluated at a single mesh point is involved in the difference equations, the unknown values of $U^{n+1}$ at any given mesh point can be determined without reference to the advanced values of $U^{n+1}$ at other mesh points. Such difference equations are explicit. If the advanced values of $U^{n+1}$ at more than one mesh point are involved, a set of recursive difference relations written for all the mesh points have to be solved simultaneously, so that the advanced values of all the mesh points in the entire field of computation are obtained at the same time. Such difference equations are implicit. Sometimes it is preferable to solve simultaneously for the advanced values at special groups of mesh points in succession, such as by rows, columns, diagonals, blocks, or bands. Such difference equations are by nature partially implicit and partially explicit. The organization of the special group may change from one group to the next, and such different groups are often applied in alternating sequence, or in some special order. These techniques are then referred to as alternating direction methods. The difference algorithms that may be employed to represent a differential problem are indeed very numerous when these specific details are considered.

If all of the coefficients of the difference equations are constant, and if the system of equations is to be solved under periodic boundary conditions (or under the presumption that the boundary is so far away as to exert no influence on the solution, i.e., the pure initial value problem), the solution of the system of equations can be extended periodically beyond the field of computation, with both $U^n$ and $U^{n+1}$ represented by Fourier series. The linearity of the difference equation system permits the treatment of each Fourier component separately. Thus, by replacing U by $V(k_j) \exp\{ik_j x_j\}$ in the system of difference equations, and cancelling the common factor in each equation, an equation

$$H_1 V^{n+1}(k_j) = H_o V^n(k_j) \tag{3.1}$$

results. Here i is the complex number used to represent the sinusoidal functions with wave numbers $k_1$, $k_2$, $k_3$ in the $x_1, x_2, x_3$ directions respectively and $V(k_j)$ is the amplitude of the particular wave component under consideration. Each of the Fourier components may be considered either as a part of the proper solution U, or as a small perturbation (or error) superposed on the solution U. $H_1$ and $H_o$ are matrix operators depending on the constant coefficients of the difference equations and on $\Delta t$ and $\Delta x_j$. On the assumption that $H_1$ can be inverted, Equation (3.1) becomes

$$V^{n+1}(k_j) = G(\Delta t, \Delta x_j, k_j) V^n(k_j) \tag{3.2}$$

where

$$G(\Delta t, \Delta x_j, k_j) = (H_1)^{-1} H_o$$

Equation (3.2) gives the evolution of each Fourier component (interpreted either as a part of the solution or as a perturbing error). Accordingly, $G(\Delta t, \Delta x_j, k_j)$ is called the amplification matrix of the system of difference equations. The condition that the solution U be uniformly bounded requires each and every component to be so bounded. Since $\|V^n\| \leq \|G\|^n \cdot \|V^0\|$, it is necessary and sufficient that $\|G\|^n$ be so bounded for all wave components and for all $n = T/\Delta t$, where T is the time period for which U is to be calculated, with some choice of small but positive $\Delta t$. Now $\|G\|^n \geq R^n(\Delta t, \Delta x_j, k_j)$, where R is the spectral radius of G, i.e., the largest eigenvalue of G. Hence for such initial-periodic boundary value problems, the v. Neumann condition requires that all of the eigenvalues of the amplification matrix G be

$\leq 1+O(\Delta t)$. This is a necessary condition for computational stability. (The eigenvalues of the amplification matrix are often most conveniently obtained by the direct substitution of $u^{n+1} = \lambda u^n$ into the difference equation to obtain the determinant which vanishes when $\lambda$ takes up the eigenvalues.) The v. Neumann condition becomes sufficient for the stability of the stated problem when the matrix G is normal. Both this sufficiency aspect and the additional term $O(\Delta t)$ are without much practical significance for the present consideration, as will shortly become clear. The important points to recognize from the above are the physical implications of the various conditions under which the v. Neumann stability analysis is formulated.

## 3.2 Local Linearization

The application of the v. Neumann analysis for the stability of the numerical integration of a system of nonlinear partial differential equations such as (1.7) calls for quite a few important additional assumptions and approximations:

(i) The nonlinear **difference** (or differential) equation is linearized by considering the solution as the sum of a small perturbation (or variation) superposed on the local solution $u(x,n\Delta t)$ of the problem. By substituting the perturbed solution into the difference equation and keeping only the terms involving the first power of the perturbation, the result is the equation of the first variation. The coefficients in this equation of the first variation depend on the solution of the differential problem, and therefore, vary with x and t.

(ii) The coefficients are assumed to be slowly varying, so that these coefficients can be replaced by the constant local values at various mesh points. The system of equations of the first variation then becomes linear with constant coefficients, at each mesh point. The coefficients (and hence the difference relations) vary from mesh point to mesh point, however.

(iii) The stability behavior of the computation at each mesh point is assumed to be independent of its neighbors, so that the v. Neumann stability analysis may be applied locally at every mesh point to find the local stability limit on $\Delta t$ based on the local linear difference equation of the first variation with constant coefficients.

(iv) The local stability limit is evaluated at every mesh point in the interior with the local computed value $U^n(x)$ rather than the genuine solution $u(x, n\Delta t)$. The most restrictive of the local stability limits, computed over all the interior points, is then taken as the stability limit on $\Delta t$ for the integration of the difference problem.

The concept of local linear stability analysis applied to fluid dynamics problems is probably what led v. Neumann to develop the Fourier method for constant coefficient linear difference equations. This method is still the most valuable practical tool. It should be noted that a slight difference in the linearization procedure can lead to slightly different linearized equations of the first variation. They will then give slightly different local linearized stability criteria. Consider the following example, taken from Richtmeyer and Morton's book. P.P. 201-206:

$$\frac{\partial u}{\partial t} = \frac{\partial^2}{\partial x^2} (u^5) \tag{3.3a}$$

$$= \frac{\partial}{\partial x} (5u^4 \frac{\partial u}{\partial x}) \tag{3.3b}$$

with the initial condition

$$u_o = u(x,t=0) = \Psi[v(x_o-x)]$$

and the boundary conditions

$$u(0,t) = \Psi[v(vt+x_o)]$$

$$u(L,t) = \Psi[v(vt-L+x_o)]$$

The following is a solution representing a running wave with constant wave velocity v

$$u(x,t) = \Psi[v(vt-x+x_o)] \quad , \tag{3.4}$$

where the function $\Psi$ is given implicitly as the inverse of

$$\frac{5}{4}(u-u_o)^4 + \frac{20}{3}u_o(u-u_o)^3 + 15 u_o^2 (u-u_o)^2 + 20 u_o^3 (u-u_o)$$

$$+ 5 u_o^4 \ln(u-u_o) = v(vt-x+x_o) \quad . \tag{3.5}$$

The solution u is shown in Fig. 1 with a relatively sharp front and approximately a quartic curve far downstreams. It may be interesting to note that Equation (3.3) stands as a heat diffusion equation with variable diffusivity $5u^4$, rather than as an equation describing the steady propagation of a nondecaying wave.

Let Equation (3.3) be discretized with a forward-time difference, and with the spatial derivative evaluated as a weighted average of centered differences at the advanced and initial time steps, with weights $\theta$ and $(1-\theta)$ respectively:

$$U_j^{n+1} - U_j^n = \frac{\Delta t}{\Delta x^2} \{\theta[\delta^2(U^5)]_j^{n+1} + (1-\theta)[\delta^2(U^5)]_j^n\} \tag{3.6}$$

where the second order spatial difference operator is defined by

$$[\delta^2 (\ )]_j^n = (\ )_{j+1}^n - 2(\ )_j^n + (\ )_{j-1}^n \tag{3.7}$$

The parameter $\theta$ can be chosen at convenience. (3.6) is a nonlinear equation. The linearized approximation

$$(U^5)_j^{n+1} - (U^5)_j^n = 5(U^4)_j^n (U_j^{n+1} - U_j^n)$$

gives the equation of first variation of (3.6) as

$$(U_j^{n+1} - U_j^n) - \frac{5\theta \Delta t}{\Delta x^2} \left[ (U^4)_{j+1}^n (U_{j+1}^{n+1} - U_{j+1}^n) \right.$$

$$\left. - 2(U^4)_j^n (U_j^{n+1} - U_j^n) + (U^4)_{j-1}^n (U_{j-1}^{n+1} - U_{j-1}^n) \right]$$

$$= \frac{\Delta t}{\Delta x^2} \left[ (U^5)_{j+1}^n - 2(U^5)_j^n + (U^5)_{j-1}^n \right] . \tag{3.8}$$

Note that the equation is linear in the unknown $(U_j^{n+1} - U_j^n)$, if the values of the function U at all of the spatial mesh points at the time level n are known. Otherwise, the equation retains its nonlinear form. Alternatively, it is appropriate to linearize in many other ways. A particularly simple one is to take

$$\left[\delta^2(U^5)\right]_j^{n+1} - \left[\delta^2(U^5)\right]_j^n$$

$$= 5(U^4)_j^n \left[(\delta^2 U)_j^{n+1} - (\delta^2 U)_j^n\right]$$

and $\quad \left[\delta^2(U^5)\right]_j^n = 5(U^4)_j^n (\delta^2 U)_j^n$ .

Then the equation of the first variation of (3.6) becomes

$$(U_j^{n+1} - U_j^n) - 5\frac{\theta \Delta t}{\Delta x^2}(U^4)_j^n \left[(U_{j+1}^{n+1} - U_{j+1}^n) - 2(U_j^{n+1} - U_j^n) + (U_{j-1}^{n+1} - U_{j-1}^n)\right]$$

$$= 5\frac{\Delta t}{\Delta x^2}(U^4)_j^n \left[U_{j+1}^n - 2U_j^n + U_{j-1}^n\right] \quad (3.9)$$

This last equation is indeed the same as that which would result if the effective diffusivity $5u^4$ in Equation (3.3b) is treated as a constant before and during discretization.

With all $U_{j+1}^n$, $U_j^n$, and $U_{j-1}^n$ taken to be constant, the v. Neumann stability analysis for Equation (3.8) will require the following for all wave numbers k:

$$\left| \frac{1 - (1-\theta)s}{1 + \theta s} \right| \leq 1 \quad , \quad (3.10)$$

where s is the complex expression

$$s = 5(U^4)_j^n \frac{\Delta t}{\Delta x^2} \left[ 2 - (\alpha+\beta)\cos k\Delta x - i(\alpha-\beta)\sin k\Delta x \right]$$

$$\text{with} \quad \alpha = (U_{j+1}^n/U_j^n)^4$$

$$\text{and} \quad \beta = (U_{j-1}^n/U_j^n)^4 \quad .$$

The restriction on the value of $\frac{\Delta t}{\Delta x^2}$ can be computed for all k from (3.10) for the values of $\alpha$ and $\beta$ at every interior mesh point. This is a very tedious process. The v. Neumann stability analysis for Equation (3.9) leads to the same relation (3.10); but with $\alpha=\beta=1$. This provides an explicit limit on $\frac{\Delta t}{\Delta x^2}$, such that when $\theta < 1/2$,

$$5(U^4)_j^n \cdot \frac{\Delta t}{\Delta x^2} \leq \frac{1}{2(1-2\theta)} \quad , \quad (3.11)$$

with no limit on $\frac{\Delta t}{\Delta x^2}$ if $\theta \geq 1/2$. This is the well-known result for the simple heat equation.

To test the usefulness of the local linear stability criterion, computations were carried out with Equation (3.8), taking $\theta = 0.4$ and $\frac{\Delta t}{\Delta x^2} = 0.001$. The parameters $\nu$ and $U_o$ were chosen as $\nu \frac{\Delta t}{\Delta x} = 0.075$ and $5 U_o^4 \frac{\Delta t}{\Delta x^2} = 0.005$. The last value is much less than 2.50, as required by Equation (3.11) for local computational stability. As the computation proceeds, the values of U increase with t over the entire field of computation. According to the local stability criterion (3.11), we would expect instability to appear in the form of rapidly increasing amplitudes of oscillation when and where the values of $(U_j^n/U_o)$ exceed $(500)^{1/4} \sim 4.7$. This was what happened, as is illustrated in Figure (1). The computed points lie very close to the analytical solution except at the foot of each wave front, where the solution undergoes a rapid change; and in the region $U_j^n/U_o \stackrel{\sim}{>} 5$, where the computed solution oscillates, signalling the onset of computational instability.

It is remarkable that the simple local criterion deduced for the difference Equation (3.9) provides highly satisfactory guidance for the integration of Equation (3.8), even though $\alpha$ and $\beta$ generally differ from unity. When the stability boundary (in the complex plane) of Equation (3.8) with $\alpha$ & $\beta \neq 1$ lies within the stable region of Equation (3.9), the local linear stability limit deduced for (3.10) need not even be "necessary" at these interior mesh points represented by the region between the two stability boundaries. Such regions are likely to be small, however, if the model equation (3.9) in the above example is appropriately chosen. The local criterion is clearly not sufficient, since the v. Neumann stability condition itself is not sufficient and since the influence of the boundary conditions on computational stability has not yet been investigated. Nevertheless, the local linear stability analysis does appear to provide useful guidance in practical applications,

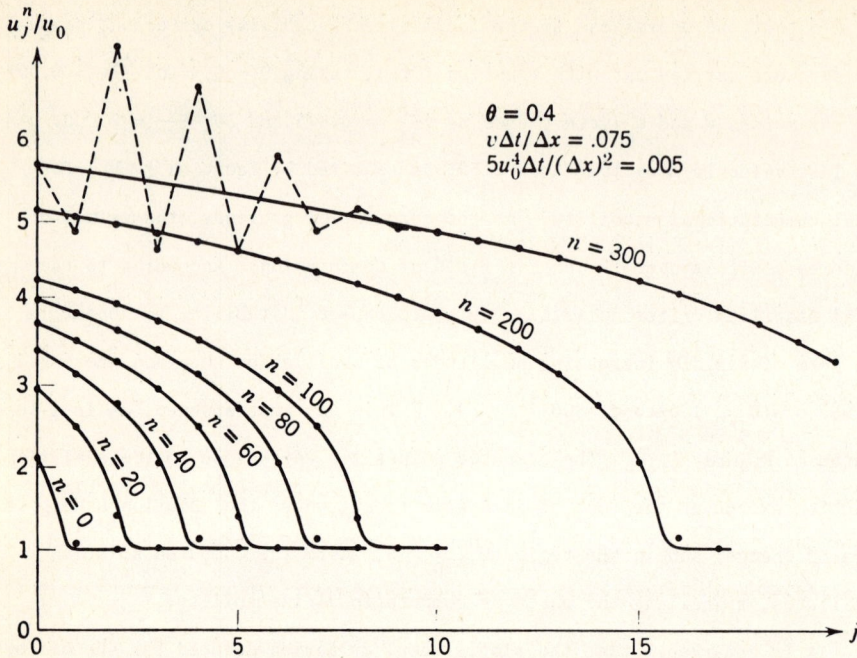

**Fig. 1.** Running-wave solutions of the non-linear equation $\partial u/\partial t = \partial^2(u^5)/\partial x^2$. The curves show the exact solution, given by equation (8.25) and the dots show the solution of the difference equation (8.27) with $\theta = 0.4$ and with $\Delta t$ and $\Delta x$ so chosen that $v\Delta t/\Delta x = 0.075$ and $5u_0^4 \Delta t/(\Delta x)^2 = 0.005$. The numbers on the curves are cycle numbers.

especially if the influence of the boundary conditions can be separately investigated, and if the linearized model for the difference relations at the interior points is properly selected. Such fortunate circumstances are, however, not to be presumed in complicated equations systems.

## 3.3 Application to Navier-Stokes Equations

The Navier-Stokes system is quasi-linear due to (i) the variable convective velocity, and (ii) the variable density and energy (and hence the variable diffusivity). The system is further complicated in the case of small diffusivity (or large Reynolds number), especially in multi-dimensional flow problems, where many viscous terms occur. If the standard procedure of local linearization is followed, the resulting linearized equations are very long. The v. Neumann stability analysis for such equations inevitably leads to unwieldy algebraic expressions, so that the explicit limit on $\Delta t$ at each mesh point can only be obtained at much more labor than that required for Equation (3.10). It is then impractical to consider checking the stability limit at many mesh points, even if infrequently. It appears imperative to look for simple but meaningful model equations, such as Equation (3.9) in the previous example. The search for such useful models is considerably complicated by the change of the asymptotic behavior of the Navier-Stokes equations system in different regions of the field of computation, as outlined in the previous chapter. Near solid boundaries, or where viscous effects are important, the region is locally parabolic or elliptic. Far away from solid boundaries, the direct viscous effect is negligible and the flow region is primarily hyperbolic. It is unfortunate that a difference algorithm, when applied to practical differential equations of different types, will lead to difference equations with quite different stability behavior.

Tables I and II illustrate the application of a few common difference algorithms to the simple wave equation and to the simple diffusion equation respectively. An algorithm often yields a stable difference equation for the diffusion equation (such as the forward time-centered space algorithm, Scheme 1 in Table II), while it provides an unstable difference equation for the simple wave equation (Scheme 3 in Table I). Friedrich's modification, which renders the wave problem stable (Scheme 4 in Table I), on the other hand, leads to an unstable diffusion problem (Scheme 2 in Table II). The centered-time and centered-space algorithm (given in the tables) is another example which illustrates the same point; there are many further examples like these. Such schemes are not useful for integrating the Navier-Stokes equations.

There exist many schemes which are stable for both types of equations, but where $\Delta t$ is subject to different restrictions in different regions. Usually $c \frac{\Delta t}{\Delta x} < 1$ is required for the wave equation, and $\frac{\Delta t}{\Delta x^2} \leq$ some fractional constant g for the diffusion equation; such is true for the forward-time, backward-space algorithm, Schemes 2 and 1 respectively in the two tables. The condition $c \frac{\Delta t}{\Delta x} \leq 1$ is known as the Courant-Friedrich-Levy (CFL) condition of zone of dependence, and is to be satisfied generally for difference forms of wave equations.[1] The CFL condition states that the zone of dependence of the difference formulation must include the zone of dependence of the differential equation. When such a scheme (stable for both types) is used in integrating the Navier-Stokes equations, computational stability might be expected if $\Delta t$ is locally chosen to be the more restrictive of the wave and diffusion limits:[2]

$$\Delta t < \text{Inf}_j \left[ \frac{\Delta x}{c}, \gamma \frac{\Delta x^2}{\nu} \right] \quad . \tag{3.12}$$

Here c is related to the local wave speed, $\nu$ is the local kinematic viscosity coefficient, and $\gamma$ is some constant less than unity. The precise values of c and $\gamma$ may be determined from the v. Neumann stability analysis of the linearized Navier-Stokes equations, after dropping the viscous terms or the dynamic terms respectively. The most restrictive of these local limits over all mesh points may then be taken as the $\Delta t$ for the next time increment. In actual computation, it is often necessary to reduce this most restrictive limit on $\Delta t$ further by introducing an empirical safety factor which may have to be rather small.

It might be thought that such a safety factor is needed because of the unknown effect of the boundary conditions. But actual computation often indicates that instability is initiated from the interior. Thus, this instability appears to be, at least in part, due to the fact that the pure diffusion and/or the pure wave equations are rather poor models for the interior points of the linearized Navier-Stokes equations. It is true that, in linearized form, the Navier-Stokes equations may be visualized as the superposition of a wave and a diffusion equation. The stability limit, however, is not generally the superposed diffusion and wave limits. This is because the determination of the eigenvalues of a linear equation, which requires finding the roots of a polynomial equation with constant coefficients, is not a linear problem. A small perturbation on a coefficient of the characteristic polynomial often leads to an inproportionately large change in the largest eigenvalue (or the spectral radius), depending on the specific difference algorithm.

To illustrate the situation, consider the one-dimensional Burgers' equation with constant c and $\nu$:

$$\frac{\partial u}{\partial t} + c \frac{\partial u}{\partial x} = \nu \frac{\partial^2 u}{\partial x^2} \quad . \tag{3.13}$$

When c and $\nu$ are taken as the local values at a mesh point, (3.13) serves as a linearized model of the Navier-Stokes equation in one space dimension, possessing the essential characteristic of changing type (of partial differential equation) in different regions. If Equation (3.13) is discretized with forward-time and backward-space differences for the convective term, and a centered-space difference for the diffusion term, the v. Neumann stability limit is

$$\Delta t \leq \left( c/\Delta x + 2\nu/\Delta x^2 \right)^{-1} \quad , \tag{3.14}$$

which is almost half of the hyperbolic limit $\Delta x/c$ or the diffusion limit $\Delta x^2/2\nu$, if they are approximately equal. Thus the safety factor to be applied to condition (3.12) should be about 1/2 (or less) for stable computation of the interior points alone.

The situation is even more critical for multidimensional flow problems. Consider the following two models for 2-D problems:

$$\frac{\partial u}{\partial t} + c \left( \frac{\partial u}{\partial x} + \frac{\partial u}{\partial y} \right) = \nu \left( \frac{\partial^2 u}{\partial x^2} + \frac{\partial^2 u}{\partial y^2} \right)$$

and

$$\frac{\partial u}{\partial t} + c \frac{\partial u}{\partial x} = \nu \left( \frac{\partial^2 u}{\partial x^2} + \frac{\partial^2 u}{\partial y^2} \right) \quad , \tag{3.15}$$

with the convective term $\nu \frac{\partial u}{\partial y}$ represented by $c \frac{\partial u}{\partial y}$ and zero respectively. The stability limits for the two cases, assuming $\Delta x = \Delta y$, are

$$\Delta t \leq \frac{1}{2} (c/\Delta x + 2\nu/\Delta x^2)^{-1}$$

and $\quad \Delta t \leq \quad (c/\Delta x + 4\nu/\Delta x^2)^{-1}$ \hfill (3.16)

respectively. This means that the safety factor to be applied to condition (3.12) should be ~1/4 or 1/3 for 2D flow problems, and should be even smaller for 3D flow problems. Thus, although it is simple and convenient, the stability condition (3.12) based on superposing the wave and the diffusion parts of the Navier-Stokes equations is not very useful.

The local stability condition based on the linearized Burgers' equation was found to be quite satisfactory for the integration of not only the nonlinear Burgers' equation without a safety factor, but also of the full Navier-Stokes equations with properly treated boundary conditions.[3] The one-dimensional Burgers' model should be applied locally to the flow along the streamline through a mesh point. This yields stability limits of the form of Equations (3.14) and (3.16), in which c should be interpreted as the local signal speed $|q| + |a|$, where q is the stream velocity. Both the local speed of sound a and the kinematic viscosity coefficient $\nu$ should be evaluated at the local temperature or energy. $\Delta x$ should be evaluated along the streamline in some manner, and may well be taken, for example, as the smaller of ($\Delta x$, $\Delta y$) for 2-D problems. For a given choice of the difference algorithm for discretization, the expression for the local stability limit on $\Delta t$ will depend on how the various local quantities are evaluated from the explicitly calculated variables. It is advisable to choose a simple (though perhaps less accurate) form of such an expression which is convenient for the explicit determination of the limit on $\Delta t$ at each point. This calculation is to be carried out at many points and at many time intervals for an estimate of the most restrictive limit on (the smallest value of) $\Delta t$ for the next time interval. It may also be convenient to check the local linearized stability limit once every few time steps rather than every time step, and to adjust the magnitude of $\Delta t$ adopted for the next few steps accordingly.

## 3.4 Treatment on the Boundary

When the appropriate local linearized stability limit is obeyed, computational instability at the interior points can usually be avoided, although oscillations of fairly large (but bounded) amplitudes are often present in the calculated results. These oscillations originate from the boundaries, both interior and exterior, and do not represent computational instability in the previously discussed sense of boundedness of the solution. Such bounded oscillations are often referred to as Nonlinear Instability, which is basically a different phenomenon more directly related to the question of accuracy, and which probably cannot be clarified by the heuristic local linear stability treatment[4] discussed in the previous section.

Genuine unstable computation can result when certain boundary treatments are applied to a given difference algorithm. For such cases, the local linearized analysis can often foretell the impending computational instability. Consider the integration of the inviscid gas dynamic equation (2.7) with the Leap-Frog scheme. (Scheme 5 in Table I):

$$U_j^{n+1} - U_j^{n-1} = -A_j \frac{\Delta t}{\Delta x} \left[ U_{j+1}^n - U_{j-1}^n \right] \quad , \tag{3.17}$$

which is second order accurate in both time and space and is always stable at all of the interior points for any value of $\Delta t/\Delta x$. To initiate the integration, both $U_j^0$ and $U_j^1$ should be available at all $j = 0,1,2,...J$, and boundary conditions must be provided at boundaries j = 0 and j = J. Note that both the initial value $U_j^1$ and the boundary data at j = J are not specified by the initial data of the differential problem for the propagation of a small wave in an unbounded flow field. These data are extraneous and are required by the use of a "higher-order accurate" difference algorithm in which a first order differential coefficient is replaced by a second order difference quotient.

The extraneous initial data $U_j^1$ are usually obtained from a Taylor series expansion about t = 0, where the necessary higher order temporal derivatives are evaluated from the initial data $U_j^0$ through use of the differential equation and its time derivatives. But, it is not obvious how the extraneous boundary data at j = J should be defined. One natural way is to extrapolate along x, assuming that $\frac{\partial}{\partial x} U$ is small:

$$U_J^n = U_{J-1}^n \tag{3.18}$$

This is not a bad physical approximation. Computationally it leads to the difference relation

$$U_{J-1}^{n+1} - U_{J-1}^{n-1} = -A_{J-1} \frac{\Delta t}{\Delta x} \left[ U_{J-1}^n - U_{J-2}^n \right] \tag{3.19}$$

for advancing the mesh value at the point J-1 immediately preceding the boundary point J. Being different from equation (3.17), equation (3.19) need not remain stable on the boundary although the computation in the interior is stable. In view of the presumption of the local linear analysis that the stability at a given mesh point is independent of its neighbors, we apply the v. Neumann stability analysis locally to this difference equation. With $A_{J-1}$ taken as a constant and U taken as a scalar unknown, the difference relation (3.19) is found to be locally always unstable with the amplification factor $|\lambda| = |U_{J-1}^{n+1}/U_{J-1}^n| > 1$. This is so because the v. Neumann analysis leads to the algebraic relation

$$\lambda - \frac{1}{\lambda} = -A_{J-1} \frac{\Delta t}{\Delta x} \left[(1-\cos k\Delta x) + i \sin k\Delta x\right] = -2(f_r + if_i) \quad , \quad (3.20)$$

where k is the wave number under consideration and $2f_r$ and $2f_i$ are the real and the imaginary parts of the right hand side. Thus

$$\lambda = -(f_r + if_i) \pm \left[1 + (f_r + if_i)^2\right]^{1/2} . \quad (3.21)$$

For some choice of k, $f_i$ will be zero and $|\lambda|$ will be greater than unity regardless of the magnitude of $A_{J-1} \frac{\Delta t}{\Delta x}$. Actual computation confirms the instability, i.e., that $|U_j^n|$ diverges as n. If $A_{J-1} \frac{\Delta t}{\Delta x}$ should be taken as unity, and if the initial data satisfies $U_j^n = (-1)^{j+n}$ for n=0 and 1 and all j = 0, 1...J-1, the solution of the difference equation can actually be shown to continue as

$$U_j^n = (-1)^{j+n} + (-1)^j F(j + n)$$

with $\quad F(j + n < J) = 0 \quad$ and

$$F(n + J) = (-1)^{n-1} 2n \quad . \quad (3.22)$$

Higher order accurate extrapolation formulas based on the assumption that higher order derivatives equal to zero (instead of Equation (3.18) will only change $f_r$ and $f_i$, and will still lead to computational instability in the same manner.

Careful examination of the local stability analysis suggests that stable computation will result if the extraneous boundary value $U_J^n$ is obtained as:

$$U_J^n = \frac{1}{2}(U_{J-1}^{n+1} + U_{J-1}^{n-1}) \tag{3.23}$$

i.e., $U_{J-1}^n$ in the first order extrapolation formula (3.18) is replaced by the average of its temporal neighbors. Then the difference relation on the boundary is

$$U_{J-1}^{n+1} = \frac{1-\alpha}{1+\alpha} U_{J-1}^{n-1} + \frac{2\alpha}{1+\alpha} U_{J-2}^n \tag{3.24}$$

where $\alpha = \frac{1}{2} A_{J-1} \frac{\Delta t}{\Delta x}$, with $\alpha > 0$. Thus

$$|U_{J-1}^{n+1}| \le \max. (|U_{J-1}^{n-1}|, |U_{J-2}^n|) \quad , \tag{3.25}$$

and the advanced values $U_{J-1}^{n+1}$ remain bounded. Alternatively, if the local v. Neumann analysis is followed, then

$$\lambda = \frac{1-\alpha}{1+\alpha} \frac{1}{\lambda} + \frac{2\alpha}{1+\alpha} e^{-ik\Delta x}$$

and $$|\lambda| \le |\frac{1-\alpha}{1+\alpha}| \frac{1}{|\lambda|} + \frac{2\alpha}{1+\alpha} \quad .$$

Thus $$-1 < -\frac{1-\alpha}{1+\alpha} < |\lambda| < 1 \quad \text{if } \alpha < 1 \quad ,$$

or $$-1 < |\lambda| < \frac{\alpha-1}{\alpha+1} < 1 \quad \text{if } \alpha > 1 \quad ,$$

and computational stability can be expected.

Thus the local linear stability analysis will help to avoid unfortunate choices of unstable boundary conditions and will sometimes suggest appropriate choices to secure stable computation. It must be cautioned that if a particular choice of the boundary condition fails to represent the physical situation, the computed stable solution need not be a good approximation to the genuine solution of the given physical problem. It is commonly found that oscillations of finite amplitudes appear to be generated at the various boundaries in a computed stable solution, and that such oscillations appear to propagate into the interior of the field of computation (or away from a shock wave or other interior boundary). These oscillations represent error components, superposed on the correct solution of the physical problem, and are likely introduced by the "errors" in the difference treatments of such boundaries. Indeed, there are also nonoscillatory errors caused by the difference treatments on the boundary; and such errors may actually be more serious because of their deceptively smooth appearance in the results of a stable computation. These errors tend to be overlooked, especially in view of the difficulty in securing a stable computation. An important aspect of studying the accuracy of computed results is to determine if the various boundary conditions are appropriate and to estimate the associated errors.

## IV. IMPLICIT COMPUTATION AND RATE OF CONVERGENCE

Implicit difference algorithms generally lead to stable difference equations when applied to simple wave and simple diffusion equations, as indicated in Tables I and II. The local linear stability analysis for equation (3.3) illustrates further that stability is "improved" when the fraction $\theta$ of the spatial derivative evaluated at the advanced time level (and hence implicitly) is increased from zero to 1/2. The system becomes unconditionally stable when $\theta \geq 1/2$. Implicit difference algorithms are traditionally used in the solution of Laplace or Poisson equations without any problem of computational stability. The implicit difference algorithm, then, appears to be the most desirable from the point of view of avoiding computational instability, especially for complicated problems with mixed behavior. It will be demonstrated that the merit of the implicit schemes is not without reservation, since there may indeed be other difficulties involved which are as serious as computational instability.

With implicit difference algorithms, the difference relation at a given mesh point contains the unknown advanced values of quantities at neighboring mesh points. Thus, it is necessary to treat the system of difference relations at all of the interior mesh points simultaneously; and hence, the solution of the difference formulation based on a totally implicit scheme will require the inversion of matrices of very large dimension. This imposes severe requirements on the memory capacity and on the arithmetic speed of the computer, and also calls for skill in rendering efficient inversion of sparse but large matrices, (inevitably through some iterative procedure). The rate of convergence, or the number of iterations required to solve the systems of equations to a prescribed accuracy, is of great concern. This is because the computational effort required to complete a "sweep" over the field of computation (i.e., to advance the values of the functions at all mesh points for one time step) is generally much larger for the implicit difference formulation than for the explicit difference formulation. It is hoped, however, that in the absence of a stability limit with an implicit difference formulation, the time steps may be taken so many times larger than that allowed by the stability limit of the explicit formulation, as to more than compensate for the much larger computational effort per time step for the implicit formulation. In the following sections, this question will be examined.

## 4.1. Simple Time Dependent Problem

The advantage of the implicit formulation is best illustrated in the solution of time-dependent heat transfer problems in multispace dimension,

(4.1a), or in the solution of Laplace equations for the steady state problem, (4.1b).

$$\frac{\partial u}{\partial t} = \nu \nabla^2 u \qquad (4.1a)$$

$$0 = \nabla^2 u \qquad (4.1b)$$

For such problems, the system of simultaneous difference equations to be solved can be conveniently arranged in the form

$$AU = f \quad , \qquad (4.2)$$

where U is the vector unknown representing the temperature at all the N interior mesh points, arranged in some appropriate order. Here f is a known vector of dimension N and A is an N x N tridiagonal matrix, often diagonally dominant. The solution of the system (4.2) for the unknown vector U is equivalent to the inversion of the matrix A, giving U as $U = A^{-1} f$. Computationally, a highly efficient method can be used to solve the system (4.2) with approximately 5N operation counts. This is to be compared with N counts for the solution of an explicit system. (Conventionally, each multiplication and division counts as one operation, while addition, subtraction and other data management operations are neglected. The evaluation of coefficients is ignored here on the presumption that the same amount of computational work is needed in both the implicit and the explicit cases). Thus, the computational effort to advance the solution for one time step with the implicit format is about 5 times as much as that with an explicit format. As illustrated in Table 2, most stable explicit schemes will possess a stability limit (easily verified by v. Neumann analysis) of the type $s = \frac{\nu \Delta t}{\Delta x^2} \stackrel{\sim}{<} (1/2, 1/4)$; here 1/4 is for two dimensional problems (see equation 3.16 with c = o.).

With good spatial resolution, i.e., a small $\Delta x$, the time step for the explicit scheme will be limited to $\Delta t \lesssim \frac{1}{2\nu}\Delta x^2$, which is indeed very small. Thus, if computation with the implicit formulation should be carried out with a time step larger than $\frac{5}{2\nu}\Delta x^2$ (or even say with $\Delta t = \Delta x$), considerable saving in the computational effort required for the determination of the temperature field U at a later time will result.

Such a benefit is illusory, however, if the determination of the solution at some specific later time is required to possess a specified accuracy. Assume that all variables are properly non-dimensionalized, and that it is required to achieve an accuracy of $10^{-2}$. This accuracy is presumed to be solely dependent on the truncation error (i.e., all other errors are suppressed in the formulation and computation). Suppose that the explicit scheme 1 in table II is used, which is first order accurate in time and second order accurate in space (i.e., $e_t = 0(\Delta t, \Delta x^2)$). Then the field of computation, defined by x = 0 to 1 and y = 0 to 1 for a two dimensional problem from time t = 0 to 1, should be divided into at least 10 equal parts in both the x and the y directions, i.e., $\Delta x = \Delta y = 1/10$ - preferably say with $\Delta x = \Delta y = 1/20$ to allow some margin of safety. The stability limit will require a $\Delta t$ (with time non-dimensionalized by the square of characteristic length divided by the diffusivity) as small as $\frac{1}{4}\Delta x^2 \approx 10^{-3}$ if $\Delta x = 1/20$, or $1/4 \times 10^{-2}$ if $\Delta x = 10^{-1}$. The relative magnitudes of $\Delta t$ and $\Delta x$ are such that the local truncation error $e_t = 0(\Delta t, \Delta x^2)$, and hopefully the computed results will remain consistent with the accuracy requirement. (In this case, the accumulation of the local truncation error will remain of the same order.)

Suppose that scheme (1) in Table II is now modified so that the spatial derivative is replaced by the implicit difference

$$s(\ U_{j+1}^{n+1} - 2U_j^{n+1} + U_{j-1}^{n+1} \ \ldots\ )$$

for both the x and y directions, with the same local truncation error $e_t = 0(\Delta t, \Delta x^2)$. This scheme (Laasonen) is unconditionally stable, i.e., $\Delta t$ can be taken arbitrarily large without suffering computational instability. However, with $\Delta t$ much larger than $\Delta x^2$, the local truncation error is of $0(\Delta t) \gg 0(\Delta x^2)$. Thus with $\Delta x = 1/20$, as in the explicit case, and with $\Delta t$ taken as $\Delta x/5$, which is 16 times larger than the stability limit of the explicit scheme, the computational effort will be only $\sim 1/3$ of that with the explicit scheme. However, the solution so obtained is less accurate, with $e_t = 0(\Delta t)$ and $\Delta t = \frac{\Delta x}{5} = 10^{-2}$. This is marginally acceptable to the required accuracy $10^{-2}$, allowing no room for the accumulation of the local truncation errors. Formally, the above solution from the implicit scheme should be compared with the solution from the explicit scheme taking $\Delta x = 10^{-1}$, with $e_t = 0(\Delta x^2)$ and $\Delta x^2 = 10^{-2}$. The computational effort of this explicit scheme is then actually 80% of the implicit scheme with the same local truncation error. Alternatively, if the implicit scheme is to produce a result with accuracy comparable to the explicit solution computed with $\Delta x = 1/20$ and $\Delta t = 1/4 \times (\frac{1}{20})^2$, then the time step $\Delta t$ for the implicit calculation should be taken at most as $\Delta x^2 = \frac{1}{400}$, so that $e_t = 0(\Delta t = \Delta x^2)$. Then the computational effort for the explicit format will again be 80% of that of the implicit scheme of comparable accuracy.

In the above example, the effectiveness of the implicit algorithm is largely nullified by the first order temporal accuracy of the difference scheme. It may be that implicit schemes with second order temporal accuracy will be more effective in reducing the overall computational effort, but such higher order schemes are cumbersome. From this point of view alone, the implicit schemes would certainly appear to be advantageous in the solution of steady state problems via asymptotic temporal approach, since the temporal accuracy is then of little concern. But, as will be discussed in the next section, it is not certain if such large temporal steps are conducive to rapid convergence to the steady state. It should be noted that, in the above example, the solution of the implicit formulation calls only for the inversion of a tridiagonal matrix, which can be implemented most efficiently in $\sim 5N$ operations. For fluid dynamics problems, the matrices resulting from an implicit formulation will be far more complex; and the solution of such matrix equations will be far more time consuming. It, therefore, appears prudent not to expect significant savings in computational effort by the use of implicit difference algorithms without some detailed investigation.

## 4.2 Iterative Solution of Steady State and Asymptotic Temporal Approach

Most of the fluid flow problems of practical interest are at a steady state or a quasi-steady state in which the temporal variations of the flow variables are negligible. Discretization of such steady state equations will generally lead to implicit difference relations in terms of the steady state values of various physical quantities at all the interior points and at the boundary points. Except for the solution of potential flow problems of incompressible fluids, the differential equations will be non-linear and considerably more complicated than the Laplace equation. The resulting implicit difference relations will give rise to a rather sparse matrix A, when written in the format of equation (4.2). This sparse matrix A will not, however, be tridiagonal or block-tridiagonal, or of any of the other special forms convenient for the solution of the system of equations. In fact, the nonlinear terms will first have to be quasi-linearized so that the coefficients in the matrix A can be evaluated with some assumed approximate values. The system of linear equations will then be solved iteratively until the solution from (4.2) agrees with the assumed solution, under certain convergence criteria.

Let superscript n indicate quantities evaluated with the $n^{th}$ iterate of U and use the system of difference relations (4.2) to calculate the $(n+1)^{th}$ iterate. Then equation (4.2) becomes

$$A^n U^{n+1} - f^n = 0 \quad , \tag{4.3a}$$

which is indeed the same as

$$A^n (U^{n+1} - U^n) = f^n - A^n U^n \quad . \tag{4.3b}$$

Equation (4.3b) can now be considered as obtained from a time-dependent equation in which the terms with spatial derivatives are the same as those in the steady state equation (4.2), but with an added temporal term

$$\lim_{\Delta t \to 0} \Delta t \, A^n \, \frac{U^{n+1} - U^n}{\Delta t} \stackrel{\sim}{=} \Delta t \, A(u) \, \frac{\partial u}{\partial t}$$

and with a forward temporal difference quotient replacing $\frac{\partial u}{\partial t}$ .

The iterative solution of a steady state problem based on an implicit algorithm is then not substantially different from the solution of a time-dependent problem, albeit the artificial temporal term may not correspond to the temporal terms in the time-dependent form of the Navier-Stokes equations. The physical meaning of the individual fictitious temporal terms can be easily identified when the matrix operator A is written in expanded form. The iterative index n can be identified with the temporal index n in the time-dependent formulation, although the equivalent time-dependent physical problem may contain artificial sources of mass, momentum and energy. These artificial sources are small, but are distributed over the entire field of computation - in the interior as well as on the boundary - and vanish in the steady state limit.

In the numerical solution of the Navier-Stokes equations in multi-space dimensions, there will be a few thousand mesh points and 4 or 5 unknown quantities at each mesh point. Thus, the dimension N of the vector U will commonly be $O(10^4)$ or larger. To solve equation (4.3a) for the successive approximations to the solution of the nonlinear equation (4.2) at each time (or iterative) step by the standard Gaussian elimination process, requiring $\sim \frac{1}{3} N^3$ operations per step, is out of the question. It is, therefore, imperative to develop highly efficient iterative methods. Thus in equations (4.3), the matrix operator $A^n$ is split into two parts, with $B^n$ operating on $U^{n+1}$ and $(A^n - B^n)$ operating on $U^n$. This gives

$$B^n U^{n+1} + (A^n - B^n) U^n = f^n \qquad (4.4a)$$

or

$$B^n (U^{n+1} - U^n) = f^n - A^n U^n \quad , \qquad (4.4b)$$

where $B^n$ should be some easily invertible matrix so that $U^{n+1}$ can be readily found. This $U^{n+1}$ will replace $U^n$ in the next iteration, until finally $U^{n+1} \tilde{=} U^n$ according to some steady state criterion. In this manner, the iterative solution of the quasi-linearized equation (4.3) has incorporated the iterations that were called for by the quasi-linearization of the nonlinear equation.

If B is chosen as the identity matrix I, equation (4.4b) is then identical to the explicit difference equation which would be obtained using a forward-time difference and the spatial difference algorithm of the implicit equation (4.3a). Thus, as in time-dependent explicit schemes, the iterative solution of equation (4.4b) with B = I corresponds to tracing the physical development in time of the flow field from an initial state toward the steady state. The local accumulations of mass, momentum and energy in the cell around each mesh point are precisely as they would be in the explicit scheme for time-dependent flows.

Alternatively, the matrix B may be chosen as diagonal, with its diagonal elements equal to the diagonal elements of A, i.e. $b_{ii} = a_{ii}$ and $b_{ij} = 0$ for $i \neq j$. Such an iterative process is then known as Jacobi iteration. Since $b_{ii} = a_{ii}$ are not identically unity, the temporal terms may be larger (or smaller) than the accumulation term in the physical, time-dependent flow. The excess (or deficiency) of a particular quantity U may be attributed to the presence of a source (or sink) of that quantity at the mesh point under consideration. These artificial sources (sinks) will tend to zero when the asymptotic steady state is approached.

If the matrix B is chosen to be the main tridiagonal elements of A, i.e. $b_{ij} = a_{ij}$ for $|i-j| \leq 1$ and $b_{ij} = 0$ for $|i-j| > 1$; then the artificial temporal terms will contain spatial derivatives. They then represent doublets and quadruplets around the mesh point. The situation is quite complicated algebraically and physically, but it is very natural physically how a steady state may be reached via such time-dependent states provided that all of these sources, and doublets, etc., properly vanish in the steady state limit. In practice, the choice of B is dictated by the desire to reduce the computational effort required to obtain the steady solution, irrespective of its physical correspondence to some temporal flow field. The purpose here is to show that the asymptotic temporal approach and the iterative solution of the implicit formulation to obtain steady state results are fundamentally similar. The iterative method does take much more computational effort per iteration or per time step. But it permits the use of a much wider variety of temporal artifices to produce a very rapid convergence to the steady state, possibly resulting in less overall computational effort. It is possible, of course, that for some choices of B, there may not be any steady state solutions; or that the steady state solutions reached through such computational artifices may be different from the physical solution which one wished to obtain.

## 4.3 Iterative Methods

One of the most popular choices for the matrix B is the lower-triangular part of A i.e. $b_{jk} = 0$ if $k > j$ and $b_{jk} = a_{jk}$ if $k \leq j$. This is the Gauss-Seidel iteration or successive relaxation procedure. The $(n+1)^{th}$ iterate is given by

$$U_j^{n+1} = \frac{1}{a_{jj}^n} \left( f_j^n - \sum_{k=1}^{j-1} a_{jk}^n U_k^{n+1} - \sum_{k=j+1}^{N} a_{jk}^n U_k^n \right) , \qquad (4.5a)$$

from which the successive scalar components of $U^{n+1}$ can be explicitly calculated in the order of increasing j, where the latest available mesh values are used throughout. This semi-explicit solution of $U^{n+1}$ can be given in matrix form as:

$$U^{n+1} = U^n + (B^n)^{-1} (f^n - A^n U^n) , \qquad (4.5b)$$

where $(f^n - A^n U^n)$ is the residue and $(B^n)^{-1}$ is the inverse of the matrix $B^n$.

If the vector calculated from equations (4.5) is taken as a provisional solution, and if the new iterate $U^{n+1}$ is evaluated as some weighted average of $U^n$ and this provisional value, with weights $(1-\beta)$ and $\beta$ respectively, then,

$$U^{n+1} = (1-\beta) U^n + \beta [U^n + (B^n)^{-1} (f^n - A^n U^n)] \qquad (4.6a)$$

which is the same as

$$U^{n+1} = U^n + \beta (B^n)^{-1} (f^n - A^n U^n) \qquad (4.6b)$$

or $\qquad U^{n+1} = U^n + (B^n/\beta)^{-1} (f^n - A^n U^n)$

$\beta$ is often called the acceleration (or relaxation) parameter. Equation (4.6b) suggests that $\beta$ may be interpreted alternatively as a multiplier of either the residue in equation (4.5), or of the operator $B^n$ operating on the artificial temporal sources in equation (4.4b). An appropriate choice of $\beta$ is expected to effect a faster convergence of the iterative sequence, with the process referred to as successive over (or under) relaxation when $\beta > 1$ (or $\beta < 1$). For the integration of the Laplace equations in a rectangular domain, the optimal relaxation parameter $\beta^*$ for the fastest convergence can be evaluated (as a function of the mesh spacing) and is usually around 1.8 - 1.5. For more complicated situations, the selection will have to be empirical and the optimal choice need not even be an over-relaxation. Unfortunate choices of $\beta$ can lead to diverging sequences, even for Laplace equations (i.e. beyond $2 \geq \beta \geq 0$).

Each Gauss-Seidel iterative step requires $N^2$ operations. This is to be compared with the count of $N^3/3$ for a Gauss elimination solution for the quasi-linear steady state. The iterative solution would, therefore, be advantageous if it converges within N/3 iterations, since the nonlinear iterations for the solution of equation (4.3) would then be avoided. Now with $N = O(10^3)$, it is hoped that by proper choice of the relaxation parameter $\beta$, much fewer iterations than N/3 may be needed to reach a steady state. In principle, if the steady state is defined by $||U^{n+1} - U^n||/||U^n|| < 10^{-m}$, the number of iterative steps required for convergence can be estimated by m/R, where R is the rate of convergence with $R \stackrel{\sim}{=} \log_{10}(\frac{1}{\rho})$, and $\rho$ is the geometric mean of the spectral radii of the matrices $(B^n)^{-1} A^n$ at successive iterative steps n. Such an estimate of R is not possible in practice because of the complexities of the matrix A and its dependence on the solution $U^n$.

For the integration of some form of the hydrodynamic equations, it is not uncommon that hundreds of such iterations are needed. This is partly due to the nonlinearity of the equations system and partly due to non-optimal choices of the relaxation parameter. It is also true that such iterations often fail to converge, despite a wide range of choices of the acceleration parameter. Now, if the physical state of the flow is steady or quasi-steady, the asymptotic temporal approach using the correct time-dependent equations (B=I) may be expected to converge on purely intuitive grounds, provided that the difference system is stable and consistent with the time-dependent Navier-Stokes equations. But when the implicit iterative method is used, its convergence to the steady state cannot be presumed on physical grounds, since artificial sources of mass, momentum and energy are introduced purely algebraically. The particular temporal variations of these sources need not provide any steady state, although in cases without such external artificial sources, nature has demonstrated that a steady state will eventually be reached. It might even be legitimate to question whether a steady state so reached would be the same as one reached under zero external sources, since the time integrals of the artificial sources may appreciably alter the integrals of motion of the system. It is regrettable that no useful answer can be derived physically.

Mathematically speaking, the matrix B in equation (4.4b) can be quite arbitrarily chosen, and can even be selected differently for different steps. Convergence to a steady state is assured provided that

$$\lim_{n \to \infty} (B^n)^{-1}(B^{n-1})^{-1}(B^{n-2})^{-1} \ldots (B^1)^{-1}(B^0)^{-1} = 0 \quad (4.7a)$$

and

$$\lim_{n \to \infty} [(B^n)^{-1}A^n][(B^{n-1})^{-1}A^{n-1}] \ldots [(B^0)^{-1}(A^0)] = 0 \quad . \quad (4.7b)$$

These relations can be secured if the spectral radii of all $(B^n)^{-1}$ and all $(B^n)^{-1}A^n$ are less than unity. If the form of B chosen should be the same for all iterations, (4.7b) is not really much different from the local linearized stability criterion of v. Neumann, with $B^{-1}A$ replacing the amplification matrix G. (See Chapter III, Section 3.1 and 3.2). The essential difference lies, then, in the freedom of choice of the form of the matrices $B^n$ at different iterative steps n. It is not clear whether condition (4.7a) implies the physical requirement of conservation of the integrals of motion. It is also not practical to find the spectral radii or bounds on the eigenvalues of these complicated matrices. There is no counterpart of the local linear stability analysis to provide some idea of the rate of convergence in a complicated problem. There is only the practical alternative of trying it out on the computer.

In practice, the possible choices of the form of B are severely limited to those which are easily invertible. It is difficult to find such a choice that shows significant improvement over the optimal overrelaxation process, if inferences from the study of the solution of Laplace equations are a reliable guide. A further substantial reduction of operational counts per iterative step can be derived, however, from cyclic processes built upon the Gauss-Seidel iterative procedure. If the field of computation constitutes p columns of q elements per row, with $p \cdot q \cong N$, the matrix B may be chosen as block-lower-triangular so that each of the q blocks consists only of the p (or q) elements in each column (row). Then $B^{n-q+1} B^{n-q+2} \ldots B^n$ can be taken as the lower triangular matrix in successive blocks, with zero elements everywhere else. This is the line Gauss-Seidel process operating on successive columns (or rows). Such a line process can be accelerated by employing some proper acceleration parameter.

The line processes along columns and rows (or diagonals or other convenient directions) may be employed in succession, such as the sequence of operators $(B^{n-q-p+1} \ldots B^{n-q})(B^{n-q+1} \ldots B^n)$ and its cyclic repetition. A set of acceleration parameters may be employed with the cyclic column-row sequence. This is known as the alternating direction method, or the method of Peaceman and Rachford[6] (who first demonstrated the power of such cyclic iterative methods for the solution of Laplace equations). Such line methods derive the benefit of reduced computational work from the basic fact that the operational count of the Gauss-Seidel process is proportional to the "square" of the vector length of the unknown. Thus the operational count of a complete cycle is, with $p = q = N^{1/2}$ for example,

$$p \cdot q^2 + q \cdot p^2 = (p+q)pq \sim 2N^{3/2} \quad , \tag{6.8}$$

compared to $N^2$ for the point Gauss-Seidel process. This means a decrease in the number of operations per sweep by the factor $2/N^{1/2}$, significant to an order of magnitude with $N = O(10^3)$. The extension of such a cyclic process to problems in three space dimensions with $p \sim q \sim r \sim N^{1/3}$ is obvious, in which case, the total operational count per cycle is $\sim 3N^{4/3}$, and the factor of operational count reduction will be $3/N^{2/3}$. The advantage enjoyed by the alternating direction iteration (ADI) or any such cyclic line iteration process over the point Gauss-Seidel relaxation process is clear. Success in reducing the overall computational effort in the solution of steady flow problems with such schemes requires, in addition, an appropriate choice of the acceleration parameters, suitable for the type of problems at hand and the class of prescribed boundary data. This is where the uncertainty resides.

For the solution of Laplace equations, the optimal acceleration parameters and the maximum rates of convergence of these processes can be explicitly determined. The ADI process is certainly the most efficient. This is likely to be true for the integration of purely elliptical equations, especially those with the Laplace operator as the leading term. For more complicated equations, including the equations of hydrodynamics, success depends on the ability to select appropriate acceleration parameters for the problem at hand and on a proper implementation of the boundary conditions. For hyperbolic problems with discontinuous solutions as interior boundaries, success with implicit methods is yet to be demonstrated.

## 4.4 Fractional Time and other Alternating Direction Methods

An alternating direction iterative method, known as the time splitting or fractional time step method, has been developed extensively in the Soviet Union by Yanenko, Marchuk, etc.[5] The key idea is to split the operator into a sum of implicit difference operators, each of which should lead to an easily invertible tridiagonal matrix. The successive split operations in a complete cycle serve as a "weak" approximation to the original operator. They prefer the unconditional computational stability and formal second-order accuracy of the Crank-Nicholson algorithm, as illustrated in Equation (3.6) when $\theta$ takes the value $\frac{1}{2}$. Second-order accuracy is needed, since a first order-accurate scheme can hardly meet the accuracy requirement of practical problems with the currently available computing machine. The development of this method and its relative merits when applied to gas dynamic applications is presented below.

Consider first the equation

$$\frac{\partial \phi}{\partial t} + L\phi = 0 \quad , \qquad (4.9)$$

where L is a linear spatial differential operator, explicitly independent of time t. Discretizing with the Crank-Nicholson algorithm (which is second-order accurate in both time and space) gives

$$\frac{\phi^{n+1} - \phi^n}{\Delta t} + L \left( \frac{\phi^{n+1} + \phi^n}{2} \right) = 0 \quad . \qquad (4.10)$$

Letting I be the identity operator, we have

$$(I + \frac{\Delta t}{2} L) \phi^{n+1} = (I - \frac{\Delta t}{2} L) \phi^n$$

or

$$\phi^{n+1} = (I + \frac{\Delta t}{2} L)^{-1} (I - \frac{\Delta t}{2} L) \phi^n = C \phi^n \quad .$$

For the simple heat diffusion equation $L_x \sim -\sigma \frac{\partial^2}{\partial x^2}$, the matrix $(I + \frac{\Delta t}{2} L_x)$ is tridiagonal, and the spectral radius of the matrix C can be obtained as

$$\rho(C) = \frac{1-S\psi}{1+S\psi} \quad \text{with} \quad \psi = 4 \sin^2(\frac{\pi}{2} \frac{j}{j+1})$$

where $0 \leq x = j\Delta x \leq (J+1)\Delta x$ .

Thus

$$||\phi^{n+1}|| \leq \frac{1-S\psi}{1+S\psi} ||\phi^n|| \leq \ldots \leq (\frac{1-S\psi}{1+S\psi})^n ||\phi^0|| ,$$

which establishes the boundedness and unconditional stability. Indeed, with $\Delta t/\Delta x$ taken as constant, the computational error is bounded as $||e|| \leq ||e_0|| + O(\Delta x^2)$. When the C.F.L. condition $\Delta t/\Delta x \leq 1$ for wave equations is satisfied, this scheme is expected to work for both the diffusion and the wave equations, and is hoped to work for Navier-Stokes type equations, at least in the 1-D case. (As shown in section 3.3, it does not necessarily follow that an algorithm successful for the wave and diffusion equations individually will automatically succeed for the Navier-Stokes.)

Consider now the heat diffusion problem in three space dimensions

$$\frac{\partial \phi}{\partial t} - \sigma(\frac{\partial^2}{\partial x^2} + \frac{\partial^2}{\partial y^2} + \frac{\partial^2}{\partial z^2}) \phi = 0,$$

and take $L = L_x + L_y + L_z$ or $L_1 + L_2 + L_3$. While the operators $(I + \frac{\Delta t}{2} L_x)$ can be easily inverted, the combined matrix $[I + \frac{\Delta t}{2} (L_x + L_y + L_z)]$ is no longer tridiagonal and, though highly sparse, cannot be simply inverted. So the equation is integrated in three successive steps for the time interval $t_n \leq t \leq t_{n+1}$, these fractional steps being formally designated as $t_{n+1/3}$, $t_{n+2/3}$ and $t_{n+3/3} = t_{n+1}$. For the step at $t_{n+\alpha/3}$, the Crank Nicholson algorithm

$$\phi^{n+\alpha/3} = (I + \frac{\Delta t}{6} L_\alpha)^{-1} (I - \frac{\Delta t}{6} L_\alpha) \phi^{n + \frac{\alpha-1}{3}}$$

is used, giving for the complete cycle

$$\phi^{n+1} = \prod_{\alpha=1}^{3} (I + \frac{\Delta t}{6} L_\alpha)^{-1} (I - \frac{\Delta t}{6} L_\alpha) \phi^n$$

$$= \left\{ I - \Delta t\, L + \frac{\Delta t^2}{2} [ L^2 + \sum_{\alpha=1}^{3} \sum_{\beta=\alpha+1}^{3} (L_\alpha L_\beta - L_\beta L_\alpha) + \ldots ] + O(\Delta t^3) \right\} \phi^n$$

and $\quad \phi^{n+1} = \left\{ (I + \frac{\Delta t}{2} L)^{-1} (I - \frac{\Delta t}{2} L) + O(\Delta t^3) \right\} \phi^n$

if $L_\alpha L_\beta$ is commutable.

Thus the split difference scheme will be second order accurate if the split operators are commutable; otherwise, it is only first order accurate. When such commutativity of the split operators for different dimensions (x, y, & z) does not hold, the split scheme of only first order accuracy can be arranged to yield second-order accurate results in two cycles if the second cycle is repeated in the opposite order. For the two consecutive cycles, i.e.

$$\phi^{n+1} = \prod_{\alpha=1}^{3} (I + \frac{\Delta t}{6} L_\alpha)^{-1} (I - \frac{\Delta t}{6} L_\alpha) \phi^n$$

and

$$\phi^{n+2} = \prod_{\alpha=3}^{1} (I + \frac{\Delta t}{6} L_\alpha)^{-1} (I - \frac{\Delta t}{6} L_\alpha) \phi^{n+1},$$

the two non-commutative terms cancel and the second order accuracy is resumed for non-commutative operators $L_\alpha$. This statement will be true even if the $L_\alpha$ involve differential operators with varying coefficients or if they depend on $\phi$ (as for gas dynamic quasi-linear equations), so long as such coefficients are smooth and are treated properly.

For unconditional stability, it is required that the operator L and the split operators $L_1, L_2$ & $L_3$ be semi-positive definite, that is, that the inner product $(L\phi, \phi)$ be $\geq 0$ for any arbitrary function and be defined over the entire field of computation. This condition is crucial in securing unconditional computational stability. Taking the norm of $\phi^{n+1}$, and defining the norm of an operator as the natural norm induced by any vector norm, gives

$$||\phi^{n+1}||^2 = \frac{[(I + \frac{\Delta t}{2} L)^{-1} (I - \frac{\Delta t}{2} L) \phi^n, (I + \frac{\Delta t}{2} L)^{-1} (I - \frac{\Delta t}{2} L) \phi^n]}{(\phi^n, \phi^n)} \cdot ||\phi^n||^2$$

Defining

$$(I + \frac{\Delta t}{2} L)^{-1} \phi^n = \xi^n,$$

then

$$||\phi^{n+1}||^2 = \frac{||(I - \frac{\Delta t}{2} L) \xi^n||^2}{||(I + \frac{\Delta t}{2} L) \xi^n||^2} \quad ||\phi^n||^2 = \Lambda^2 ||\phi^n||^2.$$

It follows that

$$||(I - \frac{\Delta t}{2} L) \xi^n||^2 = [(I - \frac{\Delta t}{2} L) \xi^n, (I - \frac{\Delta t}{2} L) \xi^n]$$

$$= ||\xi^n||^2 - \Delta t [L(\xi)^n, \xi^n] + \frac{\Delta t^2}{4} ||L(\xi^n)||^2$$

$$||(I + \frac{\Delta t}{2} L) \xi^n||^2 = [(I + \frac{\Delta t}{2} L) \xi^n, (I + \frac{\Delta t}{2} L) \xi^n]$$

$$= ||\xi^n||^2 + \Delta t [L(\xi^n), \xi^n] + \frac{\Delta t^2}{4} ||L(\xi^n)||^2.$$

Here $\Lambda^2$ corresponds to the square of the spectral radius $\rho(C)$ for the simple 1-D heat diffusion problem with the Crank-Nicholson algorithm. Since both

$||\xi||^2$ and $||L(\xi)||^2$ are positive, and since $\Delta t > 0$, the amplification factor $\Lambda^2$ will be $\geq$ or $<$ unity depending on whether $(L(\xi), \xi) \geq$ or $< 0$.

The successive application of split operators at each step leads to

$$||\phi^{n+1}||^2 = \Lambda_1^2 \Lambda_2^2 \Lambda_3^2 ||\phi^n||^2.$$

The conditions for $\Lambda_1^2$, $\Lambda_2^2$ & $\Lambda_3^2$ to be less than or equal to unity are the same as those required for the semi-positive definiteness of the split operators $L_1$, $L_2$ & $L_3$; i.e. $(L_\alpha \phi, \phi) \geq 0$ for $\alpha = 1, 2, 3$. This semi-positive definiteness is a sufficient (but not necessary) condition for unconditional stability of a complete computational cycle.

Now if this restriction of semi-positive definiteness is enforced, the applicability of the split scheme will be practically limited to the simple diffusion equation or the Laplace equation in a rectangular domain with Dirichelet boundary conditions. It seems intuitively logical that the method should be applicable to a wider class of circumstances than those for which proofs have been given. This situation is really no better off than that encountered in the question of stability for explicit schemes. Indeed, there is not even a necessary criterion for computational stability of this split method, comparable to the von Neumann stability criterion for explicit schemes.

In the theoretical treatment of gas dynamic flows by Marchuk and Yanenko[5] the semi-positive definiteness condition is satisfied by imposing special "periodic" boundary conditions on the problem; in which case it is clear that

$$(L\phi, \phi) = 0$$

so that $\Lambda^2 = \Lambda_1^2 = \Lambda_2^2 = \Lambda_3^2 = 1$, and the norm is preserved:

$$||\phi^{n+1}|| = ||\phi^n|| = \ldots = ||\phi^\circ||$$

This appears to be an excellent feature for initial value problems. But it also implies, for example, that any error in the initial data (if it is a guess) will not decrease (in the mean square norm) at later times. Therefore, the splitting scheme should not be used to obtain steady-state solutions with periodic boundary conditions, because the results will never be better (within the integral norm) than the initial guess.

For treating practical problems, the physical significance of this stability requirement $(L\phi,\phi) \geq 0$ needs to be more carefully examined. Post-multiplying the equation

$$\frac{\partial \phi}{\partial t} + L\phi = 0$$

by $\phi$, and summing (or integrating) over the entire field of computation gives

$$\frac{\partial}{\partial t} ||\phi||^2 + (L\phi,\phi) = 0,$$

i.e.

$$\frac{\partial}{\partial t} ||\phi||^2 = - (L\phi,\phi).$$

If L is semi-positive definite, i.e. $(L\phi,\phi) \geq 0$, then $\frac{\partial}{\partial t} ||\phi||^2 \leq 0$. This of course implies the boundedness of the solution at all times and guarantees a decreasing sequence of $||\phi||^2$. Now the gas dynamic equations (in primary physical variables) are conservation laws for mass, momentum, and energy. $L\phi$ is the net flux of these conserved quantities out of unit physical volume. If $\phi$, and hence $L\phi$, are periodic over a parallelopiped in physical space in order to secure $(L\phi,\phi) = 0$, then the outflux and the influx across the boundary of computation exactly balance. Thus, with $\phi$ identified as mass, momentum and energy, this condition excludes the loss of these quantities throughout the entire field of computation. This means that the computed results should not be expected to show body forces acting on some immersed body, or heat transfer to or from the body. Thus any lift, drag and heat transfer that may be presented in the computed results must originate from some computational artifices, and are physically meaningless.

If now the flow field is computed with periodic boundary conditions in the transverse plane, then $\Lambda_2^2 = \Lambda_3^2 = 1$. A deficit in the out-flux $L\phi$ (when there is a body drag or an energy sink to the body) and a positive $\phi$ will render $(L_1\phi,\phi) \leq 0$, and hence $\Lambda_1^2 > 1$. Thus $\Lambda^2 = \Lambda_1^2 > 1$, and the computation will be "unstable." To secure computational stability under such circumstances, it is necessary to modify the boundary conditions in the transverse plane, so that $\Lambda_2^2$ & $\Lambda_3^2$ are sufficiently smaller than unity to render $\Lambda_1^2 \Lambda_2^2 \Lambda_3^2 < 1$. Guidance is badly needed here for handling these boundary conditions properly to secure computational stability with the split schemes. And even if computational stability is achieved by some means, there is little idea how the calculated results of such important quantities as body drag, lift, and heat transfer will compare with the physical situation.

The fractional time step method outlined above was not meant to be applied to steady state problems, because each of the interative solutions ($\phi^{n+1/3}$, $\phi^{n+2/3}$ and $\phi^{n+1}$) satisfy different equations, none of which approximate the steady state equations. Even if the exact steady state solution of a given problem is used as the initial data, the fractional time step method will generate solutions that will not quite settle down to any sort of a steady state limit. This situation can be remedied by retaining the terms that were dropped in the fractional step method, and evaluating them with the previous (or otherwise known) iterate. One possible method is:

$\phi^{n+\alpha/3} = (I + \frac{\Delta t}{6} L_\alpha)^{-1} \{I + \frac{\Delta t}{6} L_\alpha - \frac{\Delta t}{3} \sum_\alpha L_\alpha\} \phi^{n+\frac{\alpha-1}{3}}$ , which would indeed be the same as the alternating direction iterative solution of the implicit formulation of the steady state problem with $B = (I + \frac{\Delta t}{6} L_\alpha)$ and $A = \frac{\Delta t}{3} \sum_\alpha L_\alpha$ given as equation (4.4a). This method is then similar to the Douglas and Gunn [7] extension of the Peaceman-Rachford Alternating Direction method for the solution of steady state problems. With these additional terms, it is not possible to conjecture what the stability behavior and the convergence rate of the difference formulation will be. Some experience of the research group at Langley Research Center, NASA (the author is grateful for this private communication) indicates that the overall computational effort in using such schemes (for the numerical integration of the Navier-Stokes Equations for some mixed supersonic-subsonic flow fields) is much larger than that experienced by the author on similar problems with explicit formulation.

While no generalization is implied, the fundamental reasons expounded in this and the previous sections, coupled with some practical experience, serve as an appropriate caution against being overly optimistic about the advantage of such implicit methods.

The split operator $L_x$ can be split further as $L_x = L_{xc} + L_{xv}$ (for example), where $L_{xc}$ is the convective part and $L_{xv}$ the viscous part of $L_x$. In this manner, each momentum equation is split into 6 parts, and each of the 6 parts give rise to either a wave operator or a diffusion operator. The question of rendering a stable computation for each step is somewhat simplified in the interior. There will be difficulties in formulating the boundary conditions and in achieving higher order accuracy, especially for time dependent problems. Future developments in such split schemes can be important, however, for computing flows in 3-space dimensions.

## V. ACCURACY AND CONSERVATIVE FORMULATION

The physical conservation laws of mass, momentum and energy are established for arbitrary macroscopic volumes of a homogeneous fluid. By reducing the volume to a macroscopically small "point," but a microscopically large domain (to justify the continuum model) the Navier-Stokes partial differential equations are derived. They are used as convenient mathematical relations governing smooth point functions in the flow field. Now, to facilitate the numerical integration of the partial differential equations system, the Navier-Stokes equations are discretized into a system of difference equations for finite elements of a spatial domain. Such difference equations may as well be obtained directly from consideration of the fundamental physical laws for such finite discrete spatial domains (with the help of interpolation formulas). It is, however, more common that discretization is effected by replacing a differential coefficient with a difference quotient according to a Taylor series truncated to some order of accuracy. The errors associated with the interpolation formula or the truncated Taylor series are called truncation errors, some of which are given as $e_t$ in Tables I and II. The mathematical requirement of consistency means simply that the truncation error will vanish as $\Delta t, \Delta x \to 0$.

The conservation laws for each finite spatial element are properly approximated to some formal order of accuracy (given by the truncation error) by the difference equations deduced in either manner mentioned above. However, when the difference forms of such conservation laws are summed over a large but arbitrary collection of such finite spatial elements, the conservation laws may be seriously violated. This is because the small higher-order errors will accumulate when summed over the very large number of the small discrete elements which make up the finite domain of computation. Now for an appropriate description of a physical problem to the accuracy of say $O(\Delta x^2)$, it is essential that such conservation laws should be accurate to $O(\Delta x^2)$ over not only the differential elements, but also over finite volumes. If the truncation errors of the conservation laws in finite space are to be of $O(\Delta x^2)$, the errors must not accumulate when neighboring mesh cells are summed up. If the truncation errors are allowed to so accumulate, the difference formulation used should be higher-order accurate, so that the accumulation of such small higher-order truncation errors over arbitrary mesh combinations throughout the field of computation will not exceed $O(\Delta x^2)$. But the difference form of Navier-Stokes equations, uniformly accurate to better than $O(\Delta x^2)$, is extremely cumbersome to construct and execute. Thus, with the limited spatial resolution currently available, it is imperative to pervent or limit the accumulation of truncation errors.

It is highly commendable to (a posteriori) verify the extent to which the computed results conserve mass, momentum and energy over the entire field of computation. This is not an alternative to requiring no accumulation of the truncation errors. The truncation errors are generally representative of dipoles or quadruples, rather than of simple sources or sinks. They distort the local flow field much more than they cause apparent deviations in the overall mass, momentum and energy balances. The consequence of such dipoles and the like is, indeed, familiar to aerodynamicists. A circular cylinder in a uniform incompressible flow can be represented by a doublet. A thin airfoil or a thin wing in a subsonic or supersonic flow can be represented by some distribution of sources and sinks or dipole pairs within the framework of the linearized theory known as the method of singularities. If a series of tiny little vanes or thin sheets is not to be tolerated in the test section of a windtunnel, then the distributed dipoles arising from the truncation errors of every computational cell must be correspondingly suppressed (if not completely eliminated) in numerical solutions. Such suppression can be achieved with some close attention to the formulation of the difference problem.

## 5.1 Conservative Difference Formulation

The conservation relations are written in divergence from as Equations (1.1) to (1.3) for the density $\rho$, the momentum $\rho u_i$, and the energy density e per unit volume. These five quantities are the scalar components of the vector function V in Equation (1.6), etc., and will be considered as the "Primary Dependent Variables" in terms of which the physical laws are stated and the practical results desired. The conservation laws provide the integrals of motion when proper initial and boundary data are specified over a specific but arbitrary volume. When neighboring volumes are summed, the contributions on their common boundary cancel identically, so that the integrated conservation laws retain the same form. This is the crucial property that enables the integral theorems of Stokes and Green to cast the conservation principles into field descriptions in terms of different variables (Dia. 1). An adequate approximation of the conservation laws in difference form should preferably retain this property, at least to the order of accuracy required. Such a summable property is implicit in the mathematical abstractions of continuity and differentiability of the functions in question. Thus, the differential formulations in terms of various dependent and independent variables are all equivalent, although the forms of the partial differential equations may be

CONSERVATION LAWS OF SOURCE-FREE FLUID FLOW FOR ARBITRARY VOLUMES
BOUNDED BY SURFACE S WITH FLUXES F CROSSING BOUNDARIES

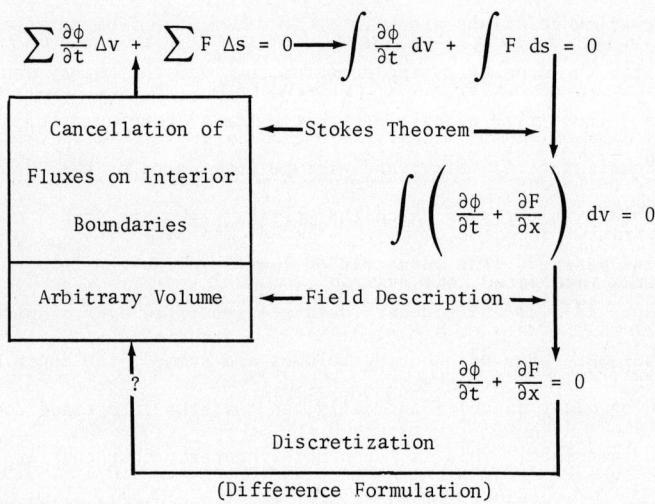

DIAGRAM 1

much different. This is not the case for the difference approximations of the conservation laws that may be formally "derived" from the varieties of forms of equivalent partial differential equations. This is because the difference functions are discrete or at least not differentiable beyond a certain order when the discrete values are joined by locally smooth functions. A summable difference formulation - in the sense that when cells in the field of computation are summed, the fluxes in the physical space $(x_j)$ of the primary dependent variables cancel identically along their common boundary - will be called a "Conservative Difference Formulation".[3,10] The computational space need not be the physical space, and the dependent variables computed need not be the primary ones. Nevertheless, the fluxes in physical space and of the primary variables are still those that are required to be summable for the conservative difference formulation.

For illustrative purposes, consider the discretization of the continuity relation from the integrated conservation law expressed in the primary variables $\rho$, $\rho u$, and $\rho v$, in the two dimensional physical space (x,y) divided into uniform rectangular cells $\Delta x \, \Delta y$. $\rho_{j,k}$ is the average density of the fluid in the cell $j\Delta x$, $k\Delta y$. The net increase of mass in the cell during $\Delta t$ is $(\rho_{j,k}^{n+1} - \rho_{j,k}^{n})\Delta x \cdot \Delta y$. The mass fluxes of $\rho U$ and $\rho V$ should be evaluated on the boundary, but $\rho U$ and $\rho V$ are known only as the average momenta of the fluid in the cells. Thus the boundary fluxes are evaluated through (second order accurate) linear interpolation, as the arithematic average of the mean momentum in neighboring cells. If increasing j and k are taken as the positive directions, the conservation of mass is stated as:

$$(\rho_{j,k}^{n+1} - \rho_{j,k}^{n})\Delta x \Delta y + \frac{\Delta t \Delta y}{2}\left\{\left[(\rho U)_{j+1,k}^{n} + (\rho U)_{j,k}^{n}\right] - \left[(\rho U)_{j,k}^{n} + (\rho U)_{j-1,k}^{n}\right]\right\}$$
$$+ \frac{\Delta t \Delta x}{2}\left\{\left[(\rho V)_{j,k+1}^{n} + (\rho V)_{j,k}^{n}\right] - \left[(\rho V)_{j,k}^{n} + (\rho V)_{j,k-1}^{n}\right]\right\} = 0$$

(5.1)

For the neighboring cell $(j-1)\Delta x \cdot k\Delta y$, the difference form of mass continuity relation can be obtained from (5.1) by replacing j by j-1. The two cells have a common boundary at $(j-\frac{1}{2})\Delta x \cdot k\Delta y$. The outflux from the cell (j-1,k) crossing this common boundary is $\frac{1}{2}[(\rho U)_{j,k}^n + (\rho U)_{j-1,k}^n]$, which is identically the same as in the influx to the cell (j,k). Thus, when the two mass continuity equations (5.1) for the cells (j,k) and (j-1,k) are added, the flux terms across the common boundary cancel out. The resulting difference equation is identical to the one obtained when the conservation law is applied directly to the combined cells, and is accurate to $O(\Delta x^2)$. The addition of other neighboring cells behaves in the same manner. Similar results will be obtained for the momentum and the energy relations; thus a conservative difference formulation accurate to $O(\Delta x^2)$ is formulated. It is easily verified that the same difference formulation will be obtained with the forward-time, centered-space difference algorithm applied to the differential equations system (1.1) to (1.3) written in divergence form. Indeed, the first order accurate algorithm of backward or forward spatial differences will also yield a conservative difference formulation, but of first order accuracy of $O(\Delta x)$, provided that the differential equation is discretized in divergence form and that the physical space is divided uniformly.

If the continuity equation should be written in expanded form for discretization, such as $u\frac{\partial \rho}{\partial x} + \rho \frac{\partial u}{\partial x}$ for the net mass flux in the x-direction, the centered-space difference algorithm can represent the net x-flux as

$$\frac{\Delta t \Delta y}{2}\left[U_j(\rho_{j+1} - \rho_{j-1}) + \rho_j(U_{j+1} - U_{j-1})\right] \qquad (5.2a)$$

or as $\frac{\Delta t \Delta y}{4}\left[(U_{j+1} + U_{j-1})(\rho_{j+1} - \rho_{j-1}) + (\rho_{j+1} + \rho_{j-1})(U_{j+1} - U_{j-1})\right]$ (5.2b)

The influx to the cell (j,k) from the cell (j-1,k), crossing the boundary at $(j - \frac{1}{2}) \Delta x$ is, (respectively):

$$\frac{\Delta t \Delta y}{2} \left[ U_j \rho_{j-1} + \rho_j U_{j-1} \right] \tag{5.3a}$$

or

$$\frac{\Delta t \Delta y}{4} \left[ (U_{j+1} + U_{j-1}) \rho_{j-1} + (\rho_{j+1} + \rho_{j-1}) U_{j-1} \right] \tag{5.3b}$$

The outflux from the cell (j-1,k) into the cell (j,k) crossing the same common boundary, as may be obtained from Equation (5.2a)(5.2b) by putting $j \to j-1$, is (respectively):

$$\frac{\Delta t \Delta y}{2} \left[ U_{j-1} \rho_j + \rho_{j-1} U_j \right] \tag{5.4a}$$

or

$$\frac{\Delta t \Delta y}{4} \left[ (U_j + U_{j-2}) \rho_j + (\rho_j + \rho_{j-2}) U_j \right] \tag{5.4b}$$

The outflux (5.4a) is identical to the influx (5.3a), and will cancel when the two cells are summed. Thus the difference algorithm (5.2a) will lead to a conservation difference formulation, without the differential equation being written in divergence form. But the outflux (5.4b) is different from the influx (5.3b). When the two cells are summed up, they do not cancel completely, but produce a net mass source of magnitude proportional to $\Delta x \cdot \Delta y \cdot \Delta t$ along the common boundary. This is formally negligible in a second-order accurate algorithm, but renders the difference formulation from algorithm (5.2b) not summable and not conservative. Even if such errors accumulate randomly over a field of computation with $1/\Delta x^2$ meshes, the accumulated truncation error will be $O(\Delta x)$ rather than $O(\Delta x^2)$. If the first order accurate backward or forward spatial difference algorithm is used for discretizing $u \frac{\partial \rho}{\partial x} + \rho \frac{\partial u}{\partial x}$ the net x-flux will be:

$$\frac{\Delta t \cdot \Delta y}{2} \left[ U_j(\rho_j - \rho_{j-1}) + \rho_j(U_j - U_{j-1}) \right] \qquad (5.5a)$$

or

$$\frac{\Delta t \cdot \Delta y}{2} \left[ U_j(\rho_{j+1} - \rho_j) + \rho_j(U_{j+1} - U_j) \right] \qquad (5.5b)$$

Neither of the two will lead to a conservative difference formulation, even to an accuracy of $O(\Delta x)$. The above examples demonstrate that both the centered difference algorithm and the divergence form of the differential equation are conducive to a conservative difference formulation with uniform mesh size in physical space. On the other hand, the difference formulation based on integrated conservation laws, even with only linear interpolation, leads straightforwardly to a conservative difference form of second order accuracy.

Consider now the effect of nonuniform mesh sizes in physical space, with

$$\frac{(\Delta x)_{j+1}}{(\Delta x)_j} = \eta_{j+1/2} \qquad \text{and} \qquad \frac{(\Delta x)_j}{(\Delta x)_{j-1}} = \eta_{j-1/2}$$

when the integrated conservation laws and linear interpolation are used to discretize the continuity relation. The net flux into the cell at $j\Delta x$, during the time interval $\Delta t$, is obtained in a straightforward manner (illustrated here only for x-fluxes):

$$+ \Delta t \cdot \Delta y \left[ \frac{\eta_{j+1/2}}{1+\eta_{j+1/2}} (\rho U)_j + \frac{1}{1+\eta_{j+1/2}} (\rho U)_{j+1} \right] \qquad (5.6)$$

$$- \Delta t \Delta y \left[ \frac{\eta_{j-1/2}}{1+\eta_{j-1/2}} (\rho U)_{j-1} + \frac{1}{1+\eta_{j-1/2}} (\rho U)_j \right].$$

The first bracket represents the outflux from cell j, and the second bracket represents the influx to cell j. If, in the first bracket, j is replaced by j-1, then the outflux from the cell at $(\Delta x)_{j-1}$ becomes identical to the influx into the cell at $(\Delta x)_j$, across their common boundary. They therefore cancel when the two cells are summed. Thus the algorithm (5.6) will, in physical space, lead to a conservative difference formulation despite the variable spacing. Algorithm (5.6) clearly indicates how the centered spatial difference algorithm should be modified to accommodate variable physical spacing, in order to achieve a conservative difference formulation and second-order accuracy. The choice of this particular weighted average of $(\rho U)_{j+1}$, $(\rho U)_j$, and $(\rho U)_{j-1}$ is, however, not obvious from the point of view of discretizing $\frac{\partial}{\partial x}(\rho u)$ with second-order accuracy through Taylor series expansions without the consideration of fluxes on the boundary.

Variable mesh sizes in physical space are commonly achieved through some transformation $x=x(\xi)$ of the independent variables, or inversely as $\xi = \xi(x)$. The difference formulation is then derived from the transformed differential equation by discretizing with a uniform mesh spacing $\Delta\xi$ in the transformed $\xi$-space, according to some difference algorithm. This transformation of the spatial coordinates is often suggested by the desire to bring the boundaries into coordinate lines-such as $\xi \sim x/1+x$, so that $x = \infty$ corresponds to $\xi = 1$-or the use of spherical, cylindrical **or other** convenient body coordinates is dictated by the contour of the solid body present in the flow field. The intuitive process of discretization in the $\xi$-space is not likely to produce a conservative difference formulation. Even with a uniform mesh spacing $\Delta\xi$, the cancellation of influx and outflux in the transformed space does not guarantee the same in physical space, due to the presence of the metric coefficients.

Consider the mass continuity relation in cylindrical polar coordinates $(r,\theta,z)$:

$$\frac{\partial \rho}{\partial t} + \frac{1}{r}\frac{\partial}{\partial r}(r\rho u) + \frac{1}{r}\frac{\partial}{\partial \theta}(\rho v) + \frac{\partial}{\partial z}(\rho w) = 0 \; , \tag{5.7}$$

where u, v, and w are the radial, azimuthal and axial velocity components. Even if the mesh spacings $\Delta r$, $\Delta \theta$, and $\Delta z$ are uniform, and the central space difference algorithm is adopted, there remains the question of how the metric coefficient r should be treated in discretizing Equation (5.7) to obtain a conservative difference form. Now the integrated conservation relations in the physical space with curviliner coordinates stand as:

$$\Delta r . \Delta z . (r_j \Delta \theta) \cdot \Delta_t(\rho)$$

$$= \Delta t . \Delta z \Delta_r(\rho u r . \Delta \theta) + \Delta t . \Delta z . \Delta r \Delta_\theta(\rho v)$$

$$+ \Delta t . \Delta r . (r_j \Delta \theta) \cdot \Delta_z(\rho w), \tag{5.8}$$

where $\Delta$ with subscript r, $\theta$, or z stands for the net flux of the quantity in the parenthesis in some difference form. The left hand side of Equation (5.8) represents the net increase of mass in the volume element. If the flux terms on the right hand side are expressed either in the form (5.1) for uniform mesh sizes, or in the form (5.6) for nonuniform mesh sizes, the difference form of the continuity equation will be conservative (or summable). Thus, the metric coefficient r arising in the volume element should be treated as $r_j$, while the metric coefficient r arising in the surface element should be treated differently for the influx and the outflux surfaces, depending upon the specific difference algorithm. It appears, therefore, that the conservative difference formulation can be more conveniently obtained by considering the integrated conservation relations in the physical space-despite the curvilinear coordinate system that may have to be adopted.

The treatment of the conservation relations of the momentum vector is considerably more complicated than that of the scalar mass, because of the stress and inertia terms due to curvature, and because of the need to consider the appropriate vector components. Complicated as this may be, the flux terms can be clearly identified, and conservative difference formulations can be obtained. Often it is desirable, for the purpose of achieving a simpler difference formulation, to relax the condition of identical cancellation of influx and outflux crossing the same common cell boundary. A more lenient requirement may be that the influx and outflux crossing the same boundary differ by a sufficiently small higher order quantity (allowing some error accumulation), possibly supplemented by identical cancellation of the fluxes over a group of say four neighboring cells. This may be permissible, since the ultimate objective of the conservative difference formulation is to prevent an undue accumulation of truncation errors over finite volumes which would cause serious deterioration of the accuracy of the computation.

With conservative difference formulation, the accumulated truncation error $E_T$ of a set of calculations can be estimated (to an order of magnitude) at any point within the field of computation. Moreover, the error of the computed results at a point can be separated into two parts (despite the fact that the difference problem is essentially nonlinear):
(i) the truncation error $E_T$, and (ii) the error at the point caused by the errors on the boundary of the field of computation.

## 5.2 Heuristic Error Estimate and Accuracy

The accuracy question has been little explored. This may be due partly to preoccupation with stability questions, and partly to the difficulty of constructing an upper bound on the error of a computation for the type of initial-boundary value problems found in fluid dynamics. It may be possible that those convergence proofs which naturally include an estimate of the error bounds can be extended from periodic boundary value problems to more realistic boundary conditions. Such a difficult, complicated, and rigorous a priori error estimate generally gives an error bound much too large to be practically meaningful. Heuristic, rough, a posteriori error estimates will often suffice. Indeed, it would be preferable to have an estimate that is simple and generally applicable, though not rigorous and precise. Inview of this, the nonlinear Burgers' equation is conveniently adopted for analysis as a one-dimensional model of the Navier-Stokes equations.[10] As shown in Section (3.2), it is a useful model for stability analysis, being quasi-linear and possessing both wave and diffusion characteristics. It is also convenient for the study of akcuracy because many exact solutions of this equation are known, so that computational errors can be quantitatively evaluated and compared with theoretical estimates.

The Burgers' equation (in dimensionless form) is:

$$\frac{\partial u}{\partial t} + u \frac{\partial u}{\partial x} = \frac{1}{R_e} \frac{\partial^2 u}{\partial x^2} \tag{5.9}$$

having the steady state solution:

$$u(x) = -\alpha \tanh(\alpha R_e x/2)$$

with $\quad u(x=0) = 0, \quad u(x=-1/2) = 1$

and $\quad |u(x=\pm\infty)| = \alpha = 1/\tanh(\alpha R_e/4)$. $\tag{5.10}$

This steady state solution for the range $-1/2 \leq x \leq 0$ has been calculated as the long-time limit of the temporal problem via several difference algorithms. The quasi-linear term $u \frac{\partial u}{\partial x}$ is always treated in the divergence form $\frac{\partial}{\partial x}(u^2/2)$, where

$$\left(\frac{U^2}{2}\right)_{j+1/2} = \left[\left(U_{j+1}^2 + U_j^2\right) + aU_{j+1} U_j\right] / 2(2+a) \qquad (5.11)$$

and

$$\Delta\left(\frac{U^2}{2}\right)_j = \frac{1}{\Delta x}\left[\left(\frac{U^2}{2}\right)_{j+1/2} - \left(\frac{U^2}{2}\right)_{j-1/2}\right]$$

Here "a" is a parameter. The simple centered spatial difference corresponds to $a = 0$. The centered-space difference in non-divergence form results when $a = \infty$, in which case,

$$\Delta\left(\frac{U^2}{2}\right)_j = \frac{U_j(U_{j+1} - U_{j-1})}{2\Delta x} \qquad (5.12)$$

If it is presumed that an approximate steady-state solution $U(t,x,\Delta t,\Delta x)$ will be reached, departing only slightly from the genuine solution (5.10), then a linearized differential equation for the error can be derived and solved. Linearization permits the separation of the errors, i.e., the truncation errors $E_T$ and the boundary errors $E_b$, although the difference equations derived from (5.11) are all nonlinear. The linearized differential error analysis implied (and hence the linearization procedure presumes) that the error created over the entire field of computation from a given source is proportional to the magnitude of the source, i.e., the cumulative error is of the same order of magnitude as the local error. Accordingly, for the results of the linearized error estimates to be applicable, it is imperative that the difference formulation of the nonlinear equation (5.9) to be conservative (or summable).

The linearized analysis shows that $E_T$ at any point in the field of computation is proportional to $(Re_{\Delta x})^2$ for the second order accurate conservative difference formulations derived from (5.11). Here $Re_{\Delta x}$ is the Reynolds number, based on the length $\Delta x$ and the velocity difference between the point $x = 0$ (with maximum velocity gradient) and the point $x = 1$ (with nearly the asymptotic velocity). A quantitative estimate of $E_T$[10] is:

$$\frac{E_T}{(Re_{\Delta x})^2} = M_o E_o + \frac{M_1 E_1 + (1+3a)M_2 E_2}{2 + a} + \frac{M_3}{2} E_3 , \qquad (5.13)$$

where $M_o$ is the constant defining the steady state criterion

$$\text{Sup} \left[ U_j^{n+1} - U_j^n \right] < M_o \Delta x^3 ,$$

$M_1 (Re_{\Delta x})^2$ and $M_2 (Re_{\Delta x})^2$ are the coefficients of the truncated quasilinear convective terms, and $M_3 (Re_{\Delta x})^2$ is the coefficient of the truncated viscous terms. $M_1$, $M_2$, and $M_3$ are expected to be of $O(1)$ for reasonable difference algorithms and for reasonably smooth solutions. $E_o$, $E_1$, $E_2$, and $E_3$ are universal functions of the genuine solution $u(x)$ that vanish on both aries and have their absolute magnitudes less than 0.1 (Fig. 2). For small values of $M_o$ and the parameter "a" in equation (5.11), the truncation errors $E_T$ are expected to be of the order of $(Re_{\Delta x})^2/10$ for second-order accurate schemes. Actual computations with $M_o = O(\Delta x)$ and $\Delta x = 1/20$

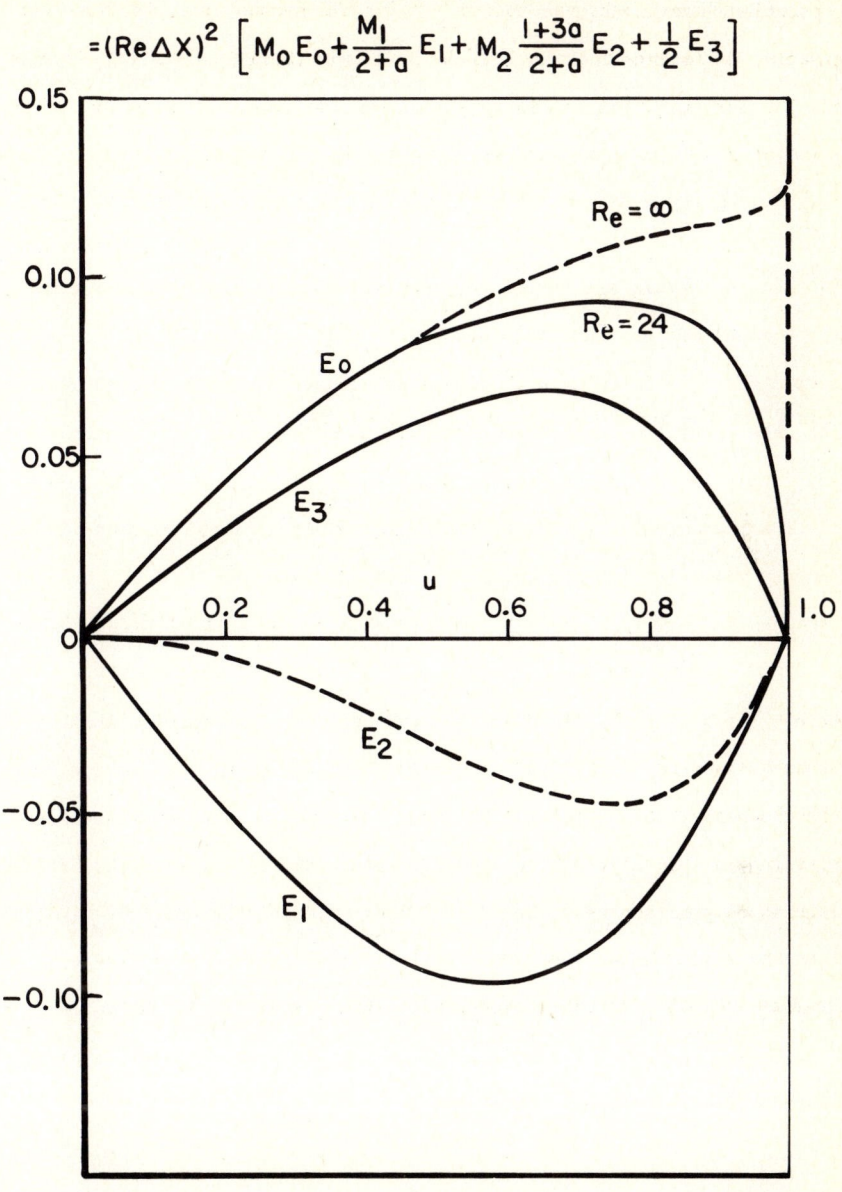

FIG. 2

for various schemes have verified the quantitative values of Equation (5.13) and the dependence of $\dot{E}_T$ on $(Re_{\Delta x})^2$.

For $Re_{\Delta x} = O(1)$ and for all of the finite values of $a = O(1)$ tested, the following estimate of the maximum absolute truncation error is valid:

$$E_T < 3 \times 10^{-2} (Re_{\Delta x})^2 \qquad (5.14)$$

This simple formula is, therefore, recommended as a preliminary estimate of the bound of the truncation errors of a second-order accurate conservative difference formulation. With a non-conservative difference formulation, the truncation errors can accumulate and can thus become considerably larger than the estimate given by Equation (5.14)

The boundary errors in the field due to a fractional error $\varepsilon_b$ in the boundary value is given by the linearized analysis as:

$$E_B = \varepsilon_b E_h, \qquad (5.15)$$

where $E_h$ is a universal function that is unity on the boundary where the erroneous boundary condition is applied, and decays very slowly toward the other boundary, where it vanishes. The decay is so slow that the error retains more than half its value until within the last few tenths of the field of computation near the other boundary, depending upon the magnitude of the Reynolds number. (Note that $E_h$ is plotted against $u(x)$ in Fig. 3. The decay into the field is even slower when $u(x)$ is replaced by $x$.)

For Neumann boundary conditions, the boundary error is still given by Equation (5.15) but $\varepsilon_b$ is evaluated as

# BOUNDARY ERROR $E_b(u) = \epsilon_b E_h$

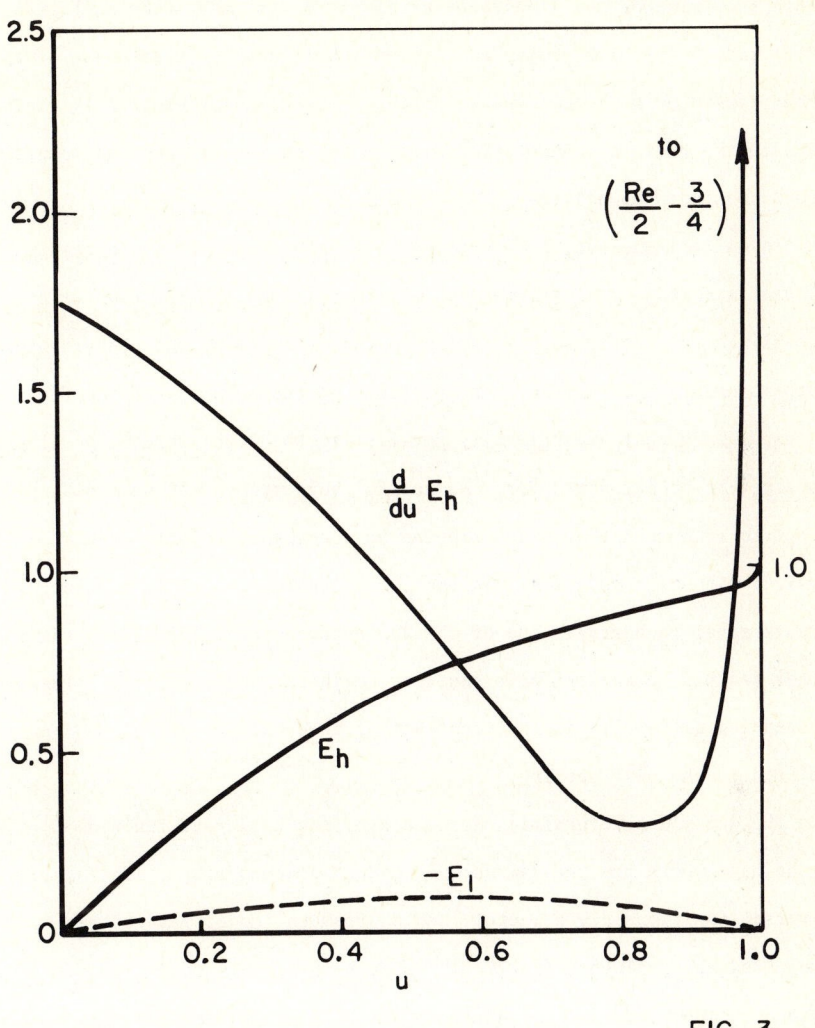

FIG. 3

$$\varepsilon_b \stackrel{\sim}{=} -2\varepsilon_b'/\alpha Re ,  \tag{5.16}$$

where $\varepsilon_b'$ is the fractional error in the spatial derivative on the boundary. Within the framework of linearized error estimates, the superposition of (5.15) and (5.16) with proper coefficients will enable an estimate of the errors caused by a Cauchy-type condition. The boundary error at a given point in the field of computation will be the sum of the decayed boundary errors from both boundaries.

In multidimensional flow problems, it is presumed that the results of the previous model analysis may apply primarily in the direction along streamlines, or nearly so. This leaves the estimate of the contributions of the boundary errors from those portions of the boundary of the field of computation that are primarily parallel to the local streamline directions yet to be accounted for. No helpful suggestions can be made here, except to recommend that a description be rendered as nearly correct as the physical situation suggests. In fact, the treatment of this portion of the computational boundary is one of the two outstanding difficulties that the author and his co-workers have experienced in various problems. (The other outstanding difficulty is the treatment of internal shockwaves, to be explored in the next section.)

The decay characteristics described by the universal function $E_h$ may be used where the one-dimensional model is appropriate. The various universal functions $E_o$, $E_1$, etc., and $E_h$ from the model results may be recognized as "influence functions" describing error propagation in the field of computation. They can be empirically established, a posteriori, by introducing a known error at a specific point (on the boundary for the specific boundary error and at chosen interior points for truncation errors) and then computing the solution under the modified condition. The difference between the two sets of solutions then gives the influence function E in question. Usually, during the developmental stage of a difference formulation for a given physical flow problem, such information can be derived from preliminary results and can be used for the purpose of a posteriori error estimation. Clearly, the a posteriori determination of such influence functions is desirable to provide additional checks on the behavior of the computational program.

Without referring to any specific computational problem, the following general observations can be inferred from the model study. They are applicable only for a conservative difference formulation in which the truncation errors do not accumulate, so that the truncation and the boundary errors can be treated separately and estimated by Equations (5.14) to (5.16).

(1) The steady state criterion $|U_j^{n+1} - U_j^n| < O(\Delta x)^4$ is sufficiently accurate for a second-order accurate scheme.

(2) The truncation error $E_T$ is expected to be $(Re_{\Delta x})^n$ for conservative difference formulations of nth order formal accuracy, and the influence functions $E_{1,2}$, etc. are not likely to possess maximum magnitudes much less than $10^{-1}$. With $Re_{\Delta x} > 1$ in practical cases, the maximum truncation error is not likely to be reduced appreciably from that of second-order accurate scheme, as may be estimated from (5.14)

(3) Boundary errors cannot be efficiently reduced by reducing the mesh sizes. They decay very slowly, and are generally considerably larger than the truncation errors in practical cases with $Re_{\Delta x} = O(1)$. The primary

effort required in achieving a reasonably accurate solution of complicated practical problems lies in the sophistication of the treatment of the various boundary conditions. The field of computation and the choice of coordinates should be properly defined to facilitate a more accurate implementation of the boundary conditions.

The general observations made above carry an important message for those interested in obtaining solutions for complicated fluid dynamics problems with reasonable accuracy to suit practical purposes. Much attention should be paid to the formulation of the problem. Attempts to improve the accuracy of the numerical solution of a poorly formulated problem by extending the computation to satisfy a more restrictive steady-state criterion or by refining the mesh (even with the help of much larger and faster computers) can prove to be not only expensive but frustrating.

A similar attempt at model analysis was made for time-dependent flow. It was found that for flows with slow and monotonic temporal variations, the behavior of error propagation in the second-order accurate conservative difference formulation is essentially similar to that described above for steady state problems. For oscillatory flows, conservation in the spatial domain apparently fails to help. Test calculations[3] for some simple damped oscillations as exact solutions of the Burgers' equation indicate the serious effect due to the phase errors of the different oscillatory components caused by the dispersive truncated terms; the computed results become highly inaccurate after one or two cycles. It has been illustrated [8, 9, 11] that fourth-order accurate difference algorithms will substantially improve the accuracy of the computed results beyond a few cycles of oscillations.

It is, however, a tremendous task to compute a complicated equation system like the Navier-Stokes with formal forth-order accuracy.

## 5.3 Shock Waves and Artificial Viscosity

In all of the previous discussions, the question of "non-smooth" or even "discontinuous" solutions is deferred. In problems of practical interest, shock waves and contact discontinuities are often the prominent features of the flow field. The presence of such discontinuities, (or in general, regions of very large gradient) causes difficulties in the computation.

Discontinuous initial and boundary data are often imposed on purely elliptic or parabolic problems. Such data may cause oscillations in the vicinity of the boundary, but they are never very serious. This is because of the inherent nature of these systems to smooth out any discontinuities in time and in space. The accuracy of the computed results may suffer somewhat (according to the modulus of continuity of the functions involved), but this can often be remedied by using a higher-order accurate difference algorithm. This inherent tendency to smooth out any discontinuity can also be troublesome as in treating flow problems involving an interfacial discontinuity formed by two different fluid media - especially when the interface is not stationary - since an initially sharp discontinuity diffuses in the course of the computation (if not artificially maintained).

For hyperbolic problems, a discontinuity in the initial-boundary data propagates into the field of computation and causes excessive computational disturbances downstream, particularly in its zone of influence. It also produces upstream influences. For quasi-linear gas dynamic problems, a shock discontinuity can physically arise from a perfectly smooth boundary due to the coalesence of smooth compression waves. Thus, when this flow field is computed with an algorithm that works well for smooth fields, quite severe oscillations can develop approximately at the location where the shock discontinuity would appear. Such oscillations are fairly large, but do not necessarily lead to the catastrophic divergence of linear instability. It may be that the amplitude of such shock-induced oscillations are limited by non-linear effects; thus the phenomenon may well be called nonlinear-instability. But this is certainly not instability in the sense of violating the requirement of boundedness discussed in Chapters II and III. Even if bounded, however, such oscillations are highly damaging to the accuracy of the results, not only in the vicinity of the shock, but over most of the flow field. Since practical interest is often centered in the vicinity of such a shock discontinuity, much has been done for computing a shock discontinuity.

It is natural to treat a shock front or an interfacial contact discontinuity as an internal boundary, and to compute the smooth solutions on both sides of the discontinuity separately. The jump conditions across the discontinuity will connect the two solutions together. This shock-matching or shock-fitting procedure is easily carried out in one space dimension for a known discontinuity, i.e., a discontinuous front propagating into a homogeneous medium at rest or in uniform motion. If the shock should be propagating into a non-uniform medium or a homogeneous medium in non-uniform motion, the shock strength and speed will vary, and the Hugoniot relations across the shock will have to be supplemented by some additional matching conditions to be derived form the difference results in the vicinity of the shock front. Oscillations often appear on one or both sides of the shock discontinuity, probably as a result of inaccuracies in the location of the shock and in the values of functions in its vicinity. The oscillations may be alleviated if the shock location is fixed at a mesh point and if the mesh dividions are rezoned at every time or iterative step. The computational procedure in terms of such shock coordinates rapidly becomes complicated.

In two space dimensions and with a curved shock of unknown shape and location, the computational details of such a shock matching procedure become more tedious and inaccurate. With fixed mesh points, the shock front is generally off the mesh points. Thus it becomes difficult to determine the direction normal to the front, resulting in a highly inaccurate matching process. The use of curvilinear shock coordinates is convenient, and may possess other desirable features for treating inviscid steady-state flow problems with uniform supersonic flow on the upstream side of the shock front.[12] They are not suitable, however, for a shock wave imbedded in a non-uniform inviscid flow field, or for viscous and inviscid flow fields involving more complicated shock configurations, such as shock intersections and Mach reflections, or transonic shocks that terminate in the flow field. The tedious shock matching can in principle, be implemented even for such complicated configurations, but the procedure is too complicated to be manageable, and the results so obtained are uniformly poor.

To avoid shock matching, v.Neumann and Richtmeyer[13] introduced the artificial viscosity method for computing shock propagation in an inviscid flow field. A quadratic viscous pressure term $\rho\alpha^2\Delta x^2 \left|\frac{\partial u}{\partial x}\right|\frac{\partial u}{\partial x}$, where $\alpha$ is a numerical constant chosen conveniently, is added to the differential equation before discretization. Quadratic dependence on the velocity gradient is to promote rapid decay of the artificial viscous term away from the shock front (which possesses a steep velocity gradient). With $\alpha < 1$, typical results of the calculation for one-dimensional shock propagation into a uniform field give a sharp shock front, spreading over $\sim 2$ meshes, and a calculated shock speed within 0.1% of the correct value. But sizable oscillations develop downstream over an extended range, without appreciable damping (spatially and temporally). By increasing $\alpha$ to $\gtrsim 2$, the magnitudes of the oscillations are reduced, but the shock front spreads wider, over 4 or more meshes. A reasonably smooth downstream solution is obtained only when $\alpha$ is so large as to be $O(\Delta x^{-1})$, and the shock front spreads over many meshes. By then the artificial viscous term is no longer small in the apparently smooth inviscid region, and the apparently smooth results of computation fail to be a satisfactory approximate solution near the shock front.

The artificial viscosity method is physically sound, simply implemented, and easily extended formally to multispace dimensions by including derivatives in the other spatial dimensions. The large spread of the shock front and the induced oscillations generally become more objectionable, however. Many artifices can and have been devised to improve the appearance of the computed results. The artificial viscous term may be dropped when the gradient of velocity becomes less than a pre-assigned value, or the downstream oscillations may be suppressed or eliminated by some smoothing process, or they may be limited to a permissible range about the mean through some filtering process. Excellent results can generally be obtained for simple test problems with known shocks. The merit of such procedures in computing shock propagation into non-uniform flow fields is yet to be demonstrated, particularly with respect to the accuracy of such smoothed results.

The Lax-Wendroff treatment [14] of a shock wave utilizes the fact that the Hugoniot relations are simply the conservation laws integrated over the discontinuity. Thus, with the inviscid equations written in divergence form for the physically conserved quantities, shock matching can be avoided because the difference equations for such conserved quantites are, indeed, the approximate form of the Hugoniot relations. (Note that the divergence form of the transformed dependent variables, rather than the physically conserved variables, may not result in such approximate Hugoniot relations). One-dimensional computations show that this method leads to a quite sharp shock front ($\sim 2\Delta x$) and accurate shock speed. But sizable oscillations are generated at the shock front, although they are rapidly damped and disappear within 8 to 10 meshes from the front. This damping is derived from the dissipative term $\Delta x^3 \cdot r(1-r^2)\frac{\partial^4 u}{\partial x^4}$, with $r = u\Delta t/\Delta x$, which may be visualized as an artificial viscosity that spreads out the shock front. The quadratic viscous terms adopted by v.Neumann and Richtmeyer does not appear to provide as much damping of the shock-induced oscillations as does this linear viscous term. But the peak amplitude of the shock-induced oscillation near the front is often larger for the linear than for the quadratic artificial viscous term. Additional artificial viscous terms are often introduced to reduce the amplitude of such oscillations.

The introduction of artificial viscous terms into the differential equation before discretization is fundamentally not much different from the process of dropping higher order terms in a truncated Taylor series during discretization. Since such viscous terms contribute to the stability of the difference formulation, artificial viscosity is very widely employed for problems without shocks. These artificially-introduced viscous terms are often substantially larger than the Navier-Stokes viscous stress terms evaluated with the physical viscosity coefficient of the fluid. This is justifiable in the solution of inviscid flow problems (i.e., flow problems visualized as the asymptotic limit where viscous stress terms are negligable), as long as the contributions due to the artificial viscous terms are "negligibly small" compared to those from the inviscid terms, and provided that the somewhat spread-out shock front is visualized as a "sharp" discontinuity. Such large artificial terms are clearly not tolerable for viscous flow problems, since the effect of the fluid viscosity will be overshadowed by the effect of the pseudo-viscosity.

There are many numerical solutions of the Navier-Stokes equations--some with first-order accurate algorithms, some with second-order accurate algorithms--using large artificial viscous terms, and at large Reynolds numbers (based upon fluid viscosity) of the order of $10^6$. These computed results are very insensitive to the large fluid Reynolds number[15]. This is understandable, since the pseudo-viscosity in such calculations is substantially larger than the real fluid viscosity, and therefore changes in the fluid Reynolds number will not significantly alter the effective Reynolds number (based on the total viscosity included in the difference formulation). If one wishes to quantitatively evaluate the viscous effects, both the artificial viscous terms introduced into the differential equations system and the pseudo-viscous terms implicit in the difference form should remain substantially less than the physical fluid viscous term. Thus for viscous flow problems, artificial viscosity terms of the type used by v. Neumann and Richtmeyer should satisfy

$$\alpha^2 \Delta x^2 \left(\frac{\partial u}{\partial x}\right)^2 \ll \nu \frac{\partial^2 u}{\partial x^2} \Delta x,$$

or dimensionally

$$\alpha^2 \frac{\Delta u \, \Delta x}{\nu} = \alpha^2 \, Re_{\Delta x} \ll 1. \tag{5.17}$$

With $Re_{\Delta x}$ generally larger than unity, the constant $\alpha$ must be chosen appreciably less than unity. This severely restricts the usefulness of an artificial viscous term, either for securing computational stability, or for suppressing shock-induced oscillations in viscous flow problems.

For a second-order accurate conservative difference formulation, the errors introduced by the pseudo-viscous terms are included in the truncation error $E_T$, the absolute upper bound of which may be estimated as $E_T < 3 \times 10^{-2} (Re_{\Delta x})^2$ according to the results based on the Burgers' model equation given in the previous section. Thus $Re_{\Delta x}$ may be as large as 1 or even 2 without having the cumulative truncation errors exceed a few percent. Note that this $Re_{\Delta x}$ is defined in terms of the local change in velocity per mesh when the Burgers' model is fitted to the "local flow field" of large velocity gradient. With a Reynolds number of $O(10^3-10^4)$ based on the viscous flow dimension and the reference velocity in the inviscid flow field, it is possible to provide sufficient number of mesh points over the linear dimension so that the local values of $Re_{\Delta x}$ will be considerably smaller than 10 and $E_T \lesssim$ a few percent except in the region of shock-induced oscillations. If the shock front is visualized as an interior boundary, and the shock-induced oscillation as a form of propagating boundary error, the errors in the results computed with the second-order accurate difference formulation will generally be dominated by boundary errors.

Shock-induced oscillations mar the appearance of the computed solution much more seriously than the less conspicuous sources from the exterior boundary, though they need not cause larger errors. The difficulty is compounded where a shock wave, either incident or emerging, intersects an exterior boundary. In the next section, the relation between boundary treatment and shock-induced oscillations will be explored.

## 5.4 Shock-Induced Oscillations

Shock-induced oscillations are often considered unavoidable when a shock wave is encountered in computation with a higher-order accurate difference algorithm. While a first-order accurate algorithm does not give rise to such oscillations, the smear of the shock front becomes excessive and the cumulative truncation errors become large. Thus, when a shock wave is encountered in a computation, it is often held to be necessary to choose between these two evils. The following is an attempt to clarify the origin of the spurious oscillations, and to show that a certain class of second-order accurate difference algorithms can, under favorable circumstances, avoid such spurious shock-induced oscillations.

Consider the solution of a linear steady state problem via the time-dependent approach. Let the spatial difference operator be split into two parts, $L_1(T)$ and $L_2(T)$, where $T$ is the shift operator for the spatial indices, i.e., $TU_j = U_{j+1}$, $T^{-1}U_j = U_{j-1}$, and $T^2 U_j = T \cdot TU_j = U_{j+2}$, etc. Construct the class of two-step difference algorithms for the time interval $n\Delta t$ to $(n+1)\Delta t$:

$$\hat{U}_j^n - U_j^n = L_1(T)U_j^n + L_2(T)U_j^n$$
$$U_j^{n+1} - U_j^n = L_1(T)\hat{U}_j^n + L_2(T)U_j^n \qquad (5.18)$$

where $\hat{U}_j^n$ is a provisional or predicated value of $U_j^{n+1}$. The second or final step is a corrector step. $L_1(T) + L_2(T)$ is second-order accurate and consistent with the differential operator in the steady state.

Let the boundary conditions applied in the first or provisional step be

$$B(T)\,\hat{U}_j^n = 0 , \qquad (5.19)$$

and let the boundary values of $\hat{U}_j^n$ derived from these boundary conditions used in the first step, be used in the second step for the computation of $U_j^{n+1}$ at the correspoinding boundary points. In this manner it is maintained that $U_j^{n+1} - \hat{U}_j^n \equiv 0$ at all of the boundary points for every time step. The boundary values at each boundary point may change from step to step and may contain errors implicit in the boundary conditions (5.19). By subtracting the two steps in the difference equations (5.18), the following difference relation is obtained:

$$U_j^{n+1} - \hat{U}_j^n = L_1(T)\left(\hat{U}_j^n - U_j^n\right) . \qquad (5.20)$$

In the event that a steady state is approached in the sense that $U_j^{n+1} = U_j^n$, then Equation (5.20) becomes (in the steady state limit):

$$\left[I + L_1(T)\right]\left(\hat{U}_j^n - U_j^n\right) = 0 . \qquad (5.21)$$

Thus $\hat{U}_j^n - U_j^n$ is governed by the linear system of difference equations (5.21), and is subject to zero boundary values over the entire boundary. If there are no eigen solutions to this system of equations, it follows that in the steady state limit $U_j^n = \hat{U}_j^n = U_j^{n+1}$. The solution in the steady state limit is thus the solution of the correct steady state equation

$$\left[ L_1(T) + L_2(T) \right] U_j^n = 0 \tag{5.22}$$

Now if the boundary values of $\hat{U}_j^n$ and $U_j^{n+1}$ are not kept the same in successive iterations, $\hat{U}_j^n$ must be eliminated from Equations (5.18). Then, in the limit of the steady state with $U_j^{n+1} = U_j^n$, the solution will be determined by the equation

$$\left[ I + L_1(T) \right] \left[ L_1(T) + L_2(T) \right] U_j^n = 0 \tag{5.23}$$

This solution will contain the "correct" steady state solution (5.22), to the extent that the boundary conditions $B(T)U_j^n = 0$ represent a correctly-posed situation. But it will also contain the nontrivial solutions of Equation (5.21) when $\hat{U}_j^n - U_j^n$ is not identically zero, as a result of the slight difference in the boundary values of $\hat{U}_j^n$ and $U_j^{n+1}$. Naturally, such extraneous solutions are possible sources of shock-induced oscillations, and can indeed be identified in the course of computation as being proportional to the difference between the provisional and the final solutions. From the practical point of view, it is simplest and most desirable to use the identical boundary values from (5.19) to suppress all of the spurious fundamental solutions arising from Equation (5.21).

There are many two-step difference algorithms, but most are not of the class (5.18), except for the Cheng-Allen scheme and Brailovskaya's scheme. For the linearized Burgers' Equation (3.13), the difference forms can be cast into: Cheng-Allen Algorithm[10,16]

$$\begin{cases} L_1(T) = \dfrac{1}{1+2s} \left[ \left( -\dfrac{r}{2} + s \right) T + \left( \dfrac{r}{2} + s \right) T^{-1} \right] \\ \\ L_2(T) = \dfrac{-2s}{1+2s} \end{cases} \tag{5.24}$$

Brailovskaya Algorithm[17]

$$\begin{cases} L_1(T) = r(T - T^{-1}) \\ L_2(T) = s(T - 2 + T^{-1}) \end{cases} \quad (5.25)$$

where $r = c\Delta t/\Delta x$ and $s = \nu\Delta t/\Delta x^2$. When (5.24) is substituted into Equation (5.23), the general solution $U_j$ is obtained as

$$U_j = \sum c_k \xi_k^j \quad k = 1, 2, 3, 4$$

where

$$\begin{cases} \xi_1 = 1 \\ \xi_2 = \dfrac{2s+r}{2s-r} = \dfrac{1+\frac{1}{2}\text{Re}_{\Delta x}}{1-\frac{1}{2}\text{Re}_{\Delta x}} \end{cases}$$

$$\xi_{3,4} = \left[ -(1+2s) \pm \left\{(1+2s)^2 + (r^2-s^2)\right\}^{1/2} \right] \Big/ (2s-r) . \quad (5.26)$$

$\xi_1^j$ and $\xi_2^j$ are the two proper fundamental solutions of the correct steady state equation $[L_1(T) + L_2(T)]U_j = 0$, because in the limit $\text{Re}_{\Delta x} \to 0$, they approach the two fundamental solutions 1 and $\exp(\text{Re} x)$ of the steady state differential equation, $c\dfrac{\partial u}{\partial x} = \dfrac{1}{\text{Re}}\dfrac{\partial^2 u}{\partial x^2}$. $\xi_3^j$ and $\xi_4^j$ are the two extraneous fundamental solutions of the two-step scheme that constitute the errors or "spurious solutions" arising from the solution of the equation

$$\left[ I + L_1(T) \right] U_j = 0$$

or of Equation (5.21).

With both $r$ and $s > 0$, and $\left|\dfrac{2s-r}{2s+1}\right| < 1$, it is found that

$$\xi_3 \sim -\dfrac{r+2s}{1+2s} < 0$$

$$\xi_4 \sim -\dfrac{(1+2s)}{2s-r} \gtreqless 0 \text{ as } r \gtreqless 2s.$$

Thus $\xi_3^j$ always represents a mesh-to-mesh oscillation, while $\xi_4^j$ can be either oscillatory or monotonic. The steady state limit of the difference $U^{n+1} - \tilde{U}^n$ can be given as:

$$\tilde{U}_j - U_j = c_3 \xi_3^j + c_4 \xi_4^j \qquad (5.27)$$

where $c_3$ and $c_4$ are determined by the difference in the values of $\tilde{U}^n$ and $U^{n+1}$ at $j = 0$ and $j = J$ on the boundary. When the boundary values of $\tilde{U}^n$ and $U^{n+1}$ are kept the same at every step, then $c_3 = c_4 = 0$ and no spurious solution will be present in the computed steady state result. Otherwise, oscillations can be expected.

If Brailovskaya's scheme (5.25) is substituted into Equation (5.23), the same proper fundamental solutions $\xi_1^j$ and $\xi_2^j$ are obtained, but the pair of extraneous solutions $\xi_3^j$ and $\xi_4^j$ are given somewhat differently as $\xi_{3,4} = [1 \pm (1 + 4r^2)^{1/2}]/2r$, with $\xi_4 < 0$ always. The overall situation is much the same, however.

It may be pertinent to repeat here that the spurious solutions will be suppressed so long as the same values of $\tilde{U}^n$ and $U^{n+1}$ are used on the boundary at every step. Such boundary values can be determined by the approximate boundary conditions $B(T)U_j^n = 0$, and may contain errors. In this event, they may cause errors in the constants $c_1$ and $c_2$ in the steady state solution

$$U_j = c_1 \xi_1^j + c_2 \xi_2^j . \qquad (5.28)$$

There will not be any catastrophe if the boundary values are not excessively in error and if the mesh size of the steady state solution is not too coarse, so that the inequality

$$Re_{\Delta x} < 2 . \qquad (5.29)$$

is maintained.

This last restriction $Re_{\Delta x} < 2$ has little to do with suppressing the spurious fundamental solutions, $\xi_3^j$ and $\xi_4^j$, but is rather to keep $\xi_2^j$ from becoming oscillatory and failing to be a valid approximation to the fundamental solution $\exp(Rej\Delta x)$ of the differential problem. It is clear from Equation (5.26) that when $Re_{\Delta x} > 2$, the appropriate form of $\xi_2^j$ is

$$\xi_2^j = (-1)^j \left[ \frac{1 + 2/Re_{\Delta x}}{1 - 2/re_{\Delta x}} \right]^j, \qquad (5.29)$$

which is oscillatory and rapidly amplifying with increasing j, and hence fails to serve as any meaningful approximation to $\exp(Rej\Delta x)$. Thus, to obtain a valid steady state solution without spurious oscillations based on algorithms (5.24) or (5.25), not only should identical boundary values be used at the provisional and the final steps, but also the mesh size must be sufficiently refined so that $Re_{\Delta x} < 2$. Sample calculations for steady state solutions of the linearized Burgers' equation (3.13) verified the abrupt change in the behavior from a smooth to a violently oscillatory limiting solution when $Re_{\Delta x}$ increases beyond the critical value of 2.

For linear problems with variable coefficients, the various fundamental solutions of the difference equations cannot be displayed. It is nevertheless expected that the spurious solutions will be suppressed if the same operators $L_1(T)$ and $L_2(T)$ and the same boundary values are used for the successive iterative steps in each time interval. Regarding the proper fundamental solutions of $[L_1(T) + L_2(T)]U_j = 0$, it is known that one of them must be unity to satisfy the consistency requirement. The other will become oscillatory for too large a $Re_{\Delta x}$. Whether the critical value of $Re_{\Delta x}$ will be 2, or how it may vary with x, is uncertain. For nonlinear problems with sufficiently smooth solutions, the complete suppression of spurious fundamental solutions in the first variation of the nonlinear difference operator at each time step may be expected. This is because the spurious fundamental solutions contained in the computed results of the nonlinear equations will have been reduced to higher order small quantities in $\Delta t$ by the stratagem described above. Such higher order small quantities in $\Delta t$ are of little significance in the steady state limit. Thus, the outstanding problem for eliminating shock-induced oscillations is to satisfy the requirement of sufficiently small mesh size $\Delta x$ corresponding to the restriction of $Re_{\Delta x} < 2$ for the linearized Burgers' equation. It is anticipated that, for nonlinear problems, there may not be such a sharp value for the critical $Re_{\Delta x}$. The transition from a smooth to an oscillatory steady state solution may take place gradually over some range of values of $Re_{\Delta x}$. This has been verified in actual computation. It is hoped that the following heuristic model will give a general idea of where this critical range of $Re_{\Delta x}$ may be.

When a second-order accurate conservative difference algorithm of the class (5.18) is used for the integration of the Navier-Stokes equations, and when the stratagem just described is followed in the treatment of the boundary conditions, the shock wave (if present in the computation) is not regarded as a discontinuity, but as a "smooth" region with large gradient, spread out by the pseudo-viscosity. This shock transition region usually spreads out over two or more mesh points to connect the smooth, asymptotically uniform flow fields both up and downstream of the shock region. The transition profile as calculated is not intended to be accurate. Its primary function is to accomplish a smooth connection, hopefully without inducing oscillations propagating into the smooth flow field in its neighborhood. Thus, the transition profile, joining a scalar function u with asymptotic values $u_\infty = \pm \alpha$ in the up and downstream regions respectively, might as well be computed approximately, based on the nonlinear Burgers' equation as a model for the local flow field. This means that the local profile might be approximated by the steady solution (5.10), with $x = 0$ and $u = 0$ located at the point of maximum slope in the transition profile actually computed with the full Navier-Stokes equations. Thus, the computed maximum value of $\frac{\partial u}{\partial x}$ (properly nondimensionalized in the transition region) will define the effective Reynolds number of the transition region.

$$\left(\frac{\partial u}{\partial x}\right)_{\text{max computed}} = Re/2 \tag{5.30}$$

In this manner, the poorly defined thickness of the transition region is avoided. The parameter $\alpha$ can be taken as unity when the reference velocity is taken as the change in the velocity (or the particular scalar quantity in dimensionless form) from the point of maximum gradient to the asymptotic value. If the computed transition profile is approximately symmetric with respect to the inflection point, this reference velocity will be half the jump across the shock.

Letting the asymptotic values of u across the shock transition region be $U_1$ and $U_2$, then assuming we have $U_1 > U_2$,

$$\left(\frac{\partial U}{\partial x}\right)_{\text{max}} = \frac{U_1 - U_2}{2} \left(\frac{\partial u}{\partial x}\right)_{\text{max}} = \frac{U_1 - U_2}{4} Re$$

$$\left(\Delta U\right)_{\text{max}} = \left(\frac{\partial U}{\partial x}\right)_{\text{max}} \Delta x = \frac{U_1 - U_2}{4} Re_{\Delta x} \tag{5.31}$$

Now it is pressumed that the critical value of this $Re_{\Delta x}$ is essentially the same as if the computation were done with the same algorithm, but based on the Burgers' equation so that oscillation-free computed results in the transition region can be effected with $Re_{\Delta x} < 2$. When expressed as an a posteriori criterion in terms of quantities directly available in the computation, according to (5.31) this condition becomes

$$\frac{(\Delta U)_{max}}{U_1-U_2} < \frac{1}{2} \quad ; \tag{5.32}$$

i.e, "the maximum change permissible in U per mesh, $(\Delta U)_{max}$, in order to avoid large shock-induced oscillations in the computed results, is one half of the jump $|U_1-U_2|$ across the discontinuity."

This statement implies that we cannot expect to obtain an oscillation-free shock front containing less than two meshes from a computational solution following the given strategem. Moreover, within the linearized framework, the criterion (5.32) might be equally applicable to any physical scalar variable sustaining a "jump" across some large gradient region, not necessarily a discontinuous front, even though $Re_{\Delta x}$ was defined in terms of flow velocity and viscosity provided that Burgers' model remains appropriate. Criterion (5.32) is explicitly independent of viscosity.

Condition (5.32) stands, however, only as an a posteriori criterion for achieving an oscillation-free shock solution. This is because $(\Delta U)_{max} = \left(\frac{\partial U}{\partial x}\right)_{max} \Delta x$ becomes known only after the completion of the computations; by then, there is no need of a criterion to find out if the computed solution is oscillation-free! Such an a posteriori criterion can, however, be of some help in practice, since $(\Delta U)_{max}$ can be estimated long before the computed solution reaches a satisfactory "steady state". Oscillations will be present in the "transient states" of the computation, whether or not the steady state limit will contain shock-induced oscillations. If the criterion should be satisfied at some transient stage, we may expect an oscillation-free steady state solution with further temporal steps. Otherwise, smaller mesh sizes may be needed.

It is more convenient if this criterion is put into some a priori form, even if it is then less precise (as it must be). Note that the magnitude

$|U_1-U_2|$ depends on the shock strength, the shock orientation relative to the coordinate axes (in a multidimensional problem), and the coordinate direction under consideration. If it is possible to estimate $|U_1-U_2|$, then

$$Re_{\Delta x} \stackrel{\sim}{=} |U_1-U_2|\Delta x/2\nu < 2$$

may be used directly as an a priori limit. This Reynolds number $Re_{\Delta x}$ must not be confused with $Re_{\Delta x,\infty}$, based on the uniform supersonic flow velocity $U_\infty$ far upstream of the flow field, i.e., $Re_{\Delta x,\infty} = U_\infty \Delta x/\nu$. In terms of this $Re_{\Delta x,\infty}$, the criterion becomes

$$Re_{\Delta x,\infty} = \frac{U_\infty \Delta x}{\nu} < \frac{U_\infty}{U_1} \frac{4}{1-U_2/U_1} \tag{5.33}$$

which can be useful a priori if there is some idea as to the shock strength $U_2/U_1$ and as to the ratio $U_\infty/U_1$ of the reference velocity $U_\infty$ far upstream to the velocity $U_1$ into which the shock wave is propagating. For complicated flow problems, however, such quantities are usually among the unknowns. Thus, the limit on $Re_{\Delta x,\infty}$ given by (5.33) will have to be based on some rough estimate, or on the "transient states" of the computed solution.

The previous heuristic development is equally applicable to any flow region containing a large gradient other than a shock front. In particular, oscillations originating from boundaries of the field of computation can be similarly alleviated. It is to be emphasized, however, that if the oscillatory extraneous fundamental solutions like $\xi_3^j$ and $\xi_4^j$ are not suppressed by the stratagem described above, these extraneous oscillatory solutions will propagate into the neighboring smooth flow fields, even if the mesh size is reduced much below that required by (5.33). At least one of these solutions will be amplifying away from the boundaries of the transition region, while propagating into the neighboring smooth regions on either side. On the other hand, if much too coarse a mesh size is used in the computation, large amplitude oscillations will result despite the fact that the strategem described above is followed, since one of the proper fundamental solutions of the difference equation fails to be a valid approximation to that of the differential problem. To produce an oscillation-free computational solution of a flow problem involving shock waves, it is recommended not only that some form of the two step algorithm (5.18) be used with identical boundary values applied to both iterative steps during a time interval, but also that the mesh size $\Delta x$ be kept sufficiently small according to the condition (5.33). This recommendation is based on the results of analysis of a simple linear model for the numerical solution of the much more complicated and nonlinear gas dynamic equations. It is recommended in the same spirit that the local linear stability analysis of von Neumann be used to help in achieving computational stability. The practical merit of this recommendation is yet to be examined in greater detail by the computational community.

The previous development has guided the author quite successfully in his early attempts at integration of the Navier-Stokes equations for some complicated flow problems, such as the near wake flow behind a flat base with a sharp corner in the supersonic flow[16], and the hypersonic flow over the sharp leading edge of a highly-cooled flat plate.[18] The flow situations encountered in these examples are just too complicated to provide any meaningful quantitative tests of the validity of the above-mentioned criterion and the accuracy of the computed results. In the following, a simple case will be described which may serve to support and to illustrate that, despite the heuristic arguments for their application to the integration of the Navier-Stokes equations, the strategem and the criterion outlined above are indeed useful in practice.

The Cheng-Allen two-step algorithm, as a member of the class (5.18), is used to integrate the complete Navier-Stokes equations for the propagation of a planar shock wave into a uniform supersonic flow at Mach No. 2, with the shock front inclined at an angle $\beta = 41.84°$ to the uniform inflow.[19] The gas density $\rho_1$, velocity $u_1$, energy $e_1$, and pressure $p_1$ are taken to be unity in dimensionless form. The theoretical values of these variables downstream of the shock, given by the Hugoniot relations, agree with the values computed at $Re_{\Delta x,\infty} = 10$ to better than 0.1%. The critical Reynolds number per mesh is $(Re_{\Delta x,\infty})_c = 4/(1-0.837) = 24.5$. No oscillations are found, and the shock front is sharp and straight. It is verified that the a posteriori criteria (5.32) are satisfied for the density $\rho$, the x-velocity component u, the y-velocity component v, the energy e, and the pressure p across the shock. (Figure 4 and Table 3)

When the computation is repeated at $Re_{\Delta x,\infty} = 50$, exceeding the critical value $(Re_{\Delta x,\infty})_c = 24.5$ for the same flow configuration, substantial oscillations are present immediately downstream of the shock. The a posteriori criteria (5.32) for all of the physical variables are found violated. The peak amplitude of the oscillation is about 10%, but such oscillations are essentially damped out a few meshes downstream of the shock. The downstream asymptotic values are reached well within the field of computation; the results obtained from the computation at $Re_{\Delta x,\infty} = 50$ are correct to within 0.3% of the Hugoniot values. (Figure 5)

The smooth incident shock computed at $Re_{\Delta x,\infty} = 10$ was then allowed to be reflected from an inviscid wall. For the reflected shock, the critical Reynolds number is $(Re_{\Delta x,\infty})_c = 4/(0.837 - 0.646) = 21$, which exceeds the $Re_{\Delta x,\infty} = 10$ used in the computation. A smooth, straight reflected shock is obtained. All of the computed downstream asymptotic values agree with the theoretical values to better than 0.1%, and there are no oscillations.

|   | FLOW REGION | | | |
|---|---|---|---|---|
|   | 2 | | 3 | |
|   | NUMERICAL | THEORETICAL | NUMERICAL | THEORETICAL |
| $\rho$ | 1.573 | 1.575 | 2.460 | 2.457 |
| u | 0.837 | 0.837 | 0.646 | 0.648 |
| v | -0.181 | -0.181 | 0.000 | 0.000 |
| e | 1.214 | 1.213 | 1.466 | 1.463 |
| p | 1.910 | 1.910 | 3.600 | 3.597 |
| $\theta$ | -12.23° | -12.23° | 12.23° | 12.23° |
| $\beta$ | 41.84° | 41.84° | 46.23° | 46.14° |

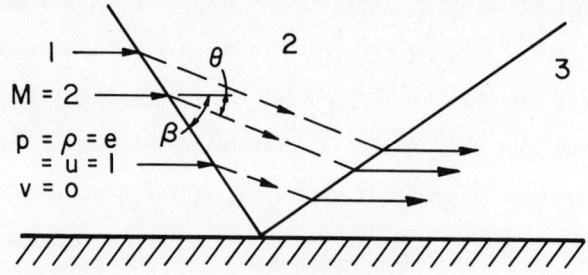

TABLE III
INVISCID SHOCK-REFLECTION CALCULATION

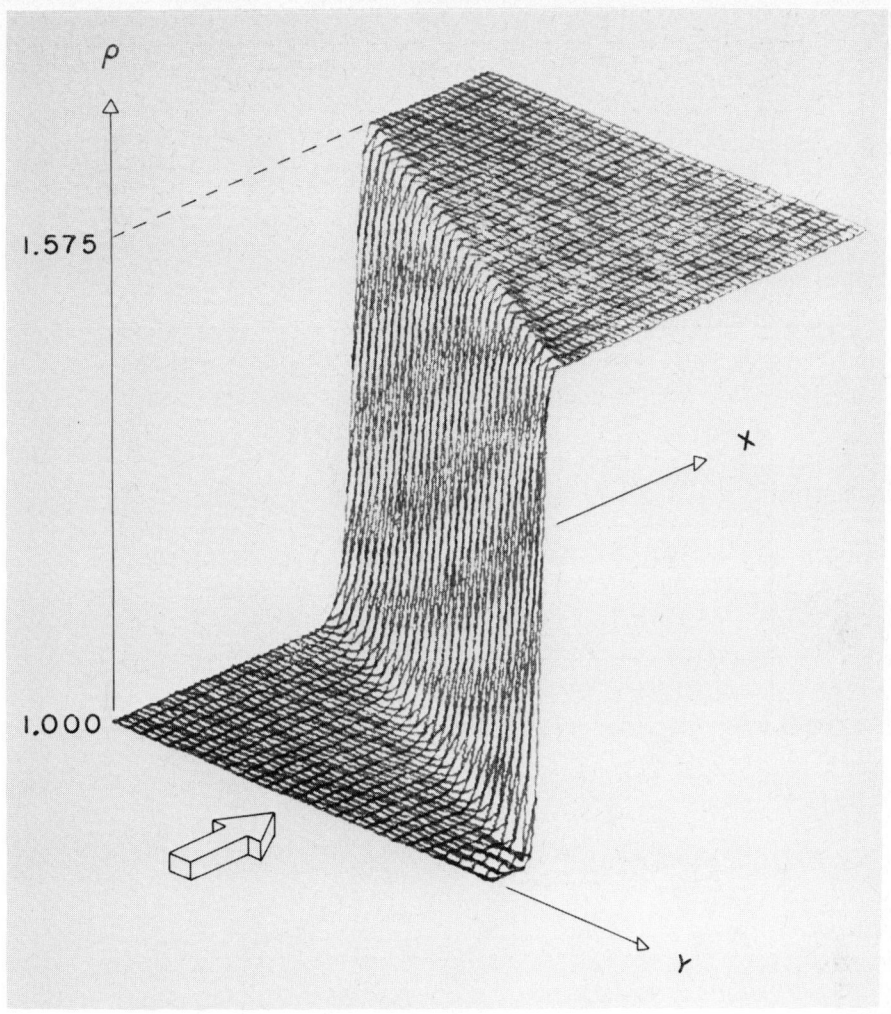

**STEADY STATE DENSITY PROFILES**

COMPUTED AT $Re_{\Delta x, \infty} = 10$

FIG. 4

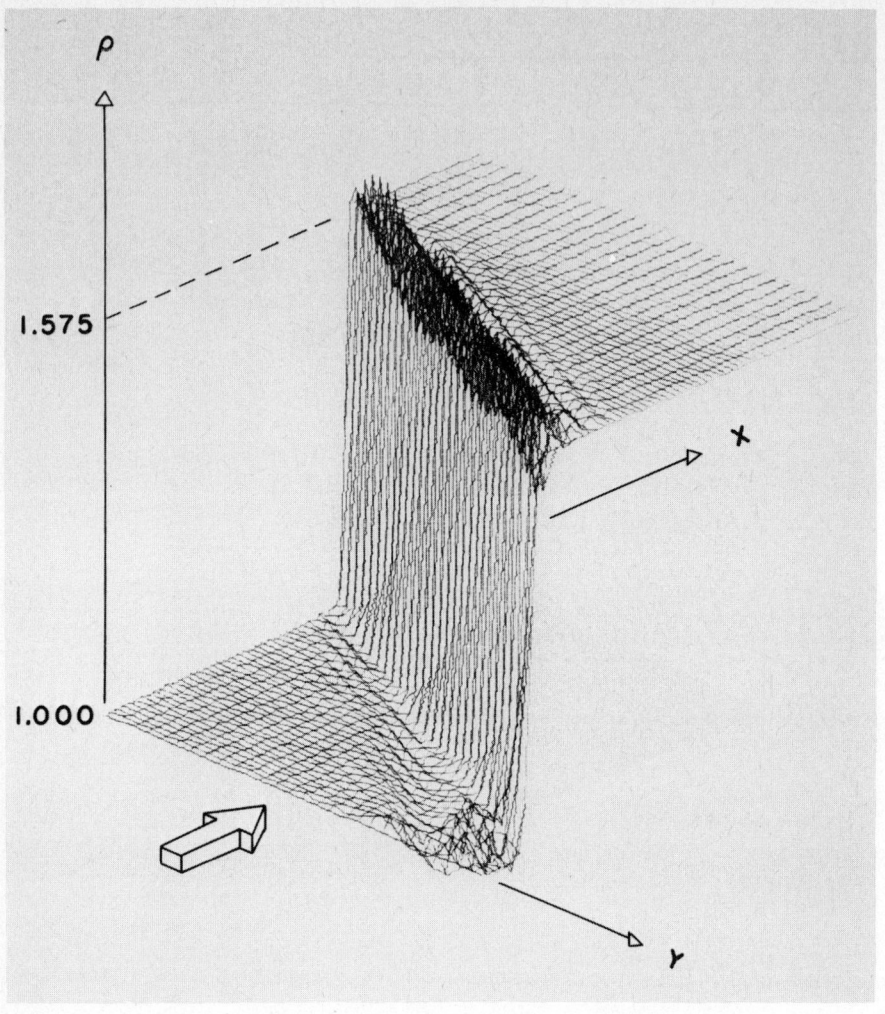

**STEADY STATE DENSITY PROFILES**

COMPUTED AT $Re_{\Delta x, \infty} = 50$

FIG. 5

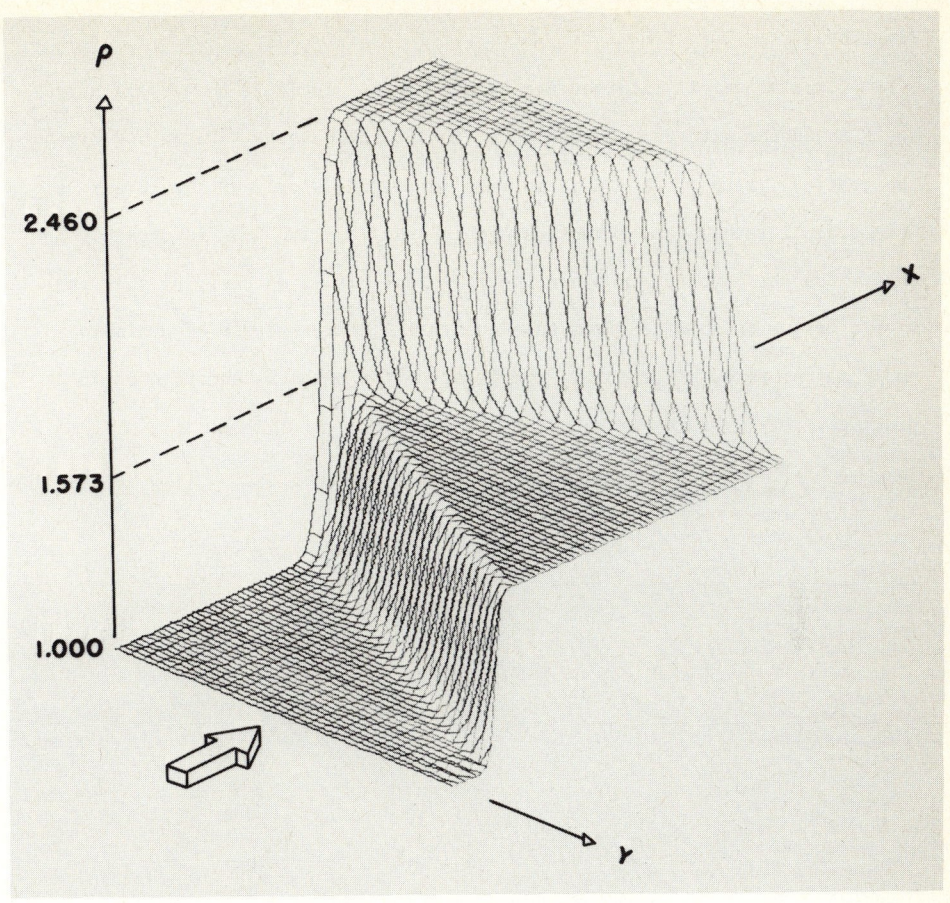

**STEADY STATE DENSITY PROFILES**

COMPUTED AT $Re_{\Delta x, \infty} = 10$

FIG. 6

(Figure 6)

Computations at intermediate values of $Re_{\Delta x}$ indicate that oscillations begin to appear with $Re_{\Delta x}$ exceeding 10 to 15, increase fairly rapidly around the critical value of 20 - 30, and keep increasing slowly with a larger $Re_{\Delta x}$. This gradual rather than abrupt change in behavior with $Re_{\Delta x}$ is probably what should be expected in a nonlinear system. It is encouraging that the simple criterion obtained from an elementary linear analysis of a simple model may prove to be useful in complicated flow problems encountered in practice.

## VI. CURRENT STATUS AND FUTURE PROSPECT

The various problems associated with the numerical integration of the Navier-Stokes equations have been reviewed in the previous chapters, as to the mathematical origin of the problems and the basis of various current techniques for dealing with them. This approach was chosen in preference to a review (in the form of a glossary) of various solutions from the literature to facilitate the presentation of an overall view of the problem.

In the days of mechanical desk calculators or card programmed calculators (CPC), the numerical integration of the hydrodynamic equations was attempted. The primary concern at that time was the limitation on the computational speed offered by these machines. While the question of computational stability was known to mathematicians[1], it was not of much concern to the practitioners. The dawn of high-speed electronic computers in the mid-1940's changed all that, demonstrating how often an apparently straightforward computation will lead to unbounded meaningless results. This problem of stability deserves to be the first and the most pressing one presented by high speed computation, because unless the stability question is successfully resolved, no results of any kind can be obtained. Since the mid-1940's, this stability question has been studied very extensively, both mathematically and empirically. As described in Chapter III, much has been learned and understood since then. But when complicated sets of partial differential equations such as those of gas dynamics are to be integrated, computational stability remains a formidable problem. As in the older days, so much work is still needed to achieve a stable computation that one often hesitates to ask any further questions about any reasonably looking computed solution. For those interested in the use of computational methods for practical purposes, computational stability is not the single major problem in obtaining a numerical solution of a partial differential equation system, but is only a first step in achieving a solution of value.

With the help of suitable model studies and appropriate choices of difference algorithms, computational stability can generally be obtained after some hard work as may be tested in actual machine computation. Now it is the time to be concerned with obtaining not only some qualitatively correct solutions, but also quantitatively accurate answers and some estimate of the error bounds on the computed solution. In applications, the primary purpose of a computed solution is to seek some reasonably accurate quantitative estimate of some physical quantities in the flow field. Of course, the accuracy requirements for different applications may vary greatly. Whether or not a solution is sufficiently accurate for a specific application can only be judged under criteria dictated by considerations external to the mathematical analysis. But such a judgment can be made only when the computed solution is accompanied by some error bound, if not by a strict error estimate. The error bounds on a computed solution are no less important than the error bars of a set of experimental data, if such computed solutions are to be practically useful. With this in mind, the preliminary developments on computational accuracy given in Chapters IV and V are quite important in practice, although may not be widely appreciated. Most of the solutions available in the published literature were probably obtained primarily to demonstrate qualitatively what can be done, rather than to solve specific problems in application. Little attention has been paid to the accuracy of those computed results. In the few examples described below, we hope to illustrate that, with proper attention to certain details, quantitatively accurate and useful results can be obtained for some complicated fluid flow problems.

## 6.1 Hydrodynamics

The flow of an incompressible viscous fluid in two space dimensions probably represents a simple, non-trivial form of the Navier-Stokes equations. It is most often treated in the stream function-vorticity formulation. The mass continuity equation in two space dimensions (x,y)

$$\frac{\partial u}{\partial x} + \frac{\partial v}{\partial y} = 0 \qquad (6.1)$$

can be satisfied by a scalar stream function $\Psi$ defined by

$$u = \frac{\partial \Psi}{\partial y} \quad \text{and} \quad v = -\frac{\partial \Psi}{\partial x} , \qquad (6.2)$$

while the vorticity component $\omega$ normal to the x-y surface is

$$\nabla^2 \Psi = \frac{\partial^2 \Psi}{\partial x^2} + \frac{\partial^2 \Psi}{\partial y^2} = -\omega(x,y) . \qquad (6.3)$$

The curl of the momentum equation reduces to the vorticity transport equation

$$\frac{\partial \omega}{\partial t} + \frac{\partial \Psi}{\partial y} \cdot \frac{\partial \omega}{\partial x} - \frac{\partial \Psi}{\partial x} \cdot \frac{\partial \omega}{\partial y} = \nu \nabla^2 \omega \qquad (6.4)$$

The divergence of the momentum equation gives the $\nabla^2 p$ in terms of $\Psi$ and $\omega$. Thus the static pressure p can presumably be found independently after the stream function $\Psi$ and vorticity $\omega$ have been determined. The solution of a hydrodynamic problem is therefore posed as the simultaneous solution of two elliptic problems for $\Psi$ and $\omega$ (represented by Equations 6.3 and 6.4) subject to Dirichlet and/or Neumann boundary conditions on a closed boundary. The physical boundary conditions depend on the particular problem.

A simple case is the decay of a vortex in a closed rectangular box, in which case u = v = 0 on the boundary (taken as x = 0, y = 0, x = 1, y = 1). This set of physical boundary conditions has to be translated into boundary conditions of $\Psi$ and $\omega$. By definition, $\Psi = 0$ may be assigned on the boundary. Equation (6.3) then serves to determine $\Psi(x,y)$ completely, when $\omega(x,y)$ is given over the field. The remaining physical boundary conditions are

$$\frac{\partial \Psi}{\partial y} = u = 0 \quad \text{on} \quad x = 0 \quad , \quad x = 1$$

$$-\frac{\partial \Psi}{\partial x} = v = 0 \quad y = 0 \quad , \quad y = 1 \tag{6.5}$$

A practical question arises concerning how (6.5) may be expressed as boundary conditions on $\omega$ in the solution of Equation (6.4). In practice, this question is by-passed by first solving Equation (6.3) for the advanced values of $\Psi(x,y)$, and then estimating the boundary values of $\omega$ from the most recently available advanced values of $\Psi$ near the boundary. This can be done with or without the conditions (6.5) taken into consideration. In principle, the boundary conditions (6.5) should at least be checked a posteriori. There is clearly an error $\tau_B$ in the boundary values of $\omega$ of the order of $\Delta t$, $\Delta x$, and/or $\Delta y$ depending on the formal order of accuracy of the algorithm how the boundary values of $\omega$ are calculated from the values of $\Psi$ near the boundary.

Now if Equation (6.4) is intergrated over the volume (x = 0 to 1 and y = 0 to 1) and over the time period (t = 0 to t) of the integration, the total decay of the vorticity is

$$\int_V [\omega_0(t = 0) - \omega(t)] dV$$

$$= \nu \int_0^t dt \int_V \nabla^2 \omega \, dV$$

$$= \nu \int_0^t dt \int_S (\vec{\nabla} \cdot \omega) \cdot \vec{dn} \tag{6.6}$$

i.e., it is proportional to the total outflux of the gradient of vorticity $\vec{\nabla} \cdot \omega$ on the boundary. (The three dimensional analog is obvious.) Thus the non-random cumulative error on the total decay of the vorticity in the box will be of the order $NJ\tau_B$, where N is the number of time steps intergrated and J is the number of spatial meshes in a linear dimension. $\vec{\nabla} \cdot \omega$ on the boundary is assumed to be of the same order of the error in the boundary vorticity $\tau_B$ itself (although it is likely much larger). The use of the integral formula has implied that the accumulation of truncation errors over all interior points in the difference calculation has been neglected. Even so, the total decay of the vorticity at later times depend very importantly on how accurately the boundary vorticity is formulated in the computation, and on whether and how the errors associated with such a formulation will accumulate in space (along the boundary) and in time. The question involves more than the local truncation error of the difference formulation of the vorticity boundary condition, since the correct physical boundary condition Equation 6.5 - which represents some integrated condition on the vorticity field rather than the local values of the vorticity - was ignored.

The use of the stream function and the vorticity as the dependent variables is the fundamental reason for the difficulty in implementing the boundary conditions. It also causes considerable complications in rendering a conservative formulation in order to prevent the accumulation of the truncation errors over the interior points. If the physical variables u and v are used as the dependent variables in the difference formulation, the difficulty with the boundary condition is eliminated for the above example, and the conservation of the difference formulation can be readily implemented. The advantage of the vorticity-stream function formulation in reducing the number of partial differential equations may be outweighed by this difficulty alone. The determination of pressure field often brings more serious problems.

For hydrodynamic problems with inflow and outflow boundaries in the field of computation, the boundary treatment in the difference formulation poses a difficulty of a different nature. This is because the physical boundary conditions are prescribed very far up and downstream of the field of computation. The vorticity-stream function formulation does not aggravate this situation much further, and therefore may be preferred for the numerical integration of the hydrodynamic equations. Poisson-type equations can be efficiently solved in different ways. There are many such solutions in the literature. Most of such results cannot be analyzed for an error estimate, primarily because of the non-conservative form of the difference formulation which permits the accumulation of the local truncation errors. Experimental data is generally not available to provide a quantitative estimate of the error in the computed results. Most of such computations serve to demonstrate over and again the feasibility of computing some "reasonable" approximate solutions for different flow fields, but fail to demonstrate their quantitative value. A numerical study of the steady flow of a uniform stream over a sphere will be presented below to illustrate the point.[10] (A sphere was preferred to a circular cylinder since the sphere data are not subjected to the experimental uncertainties as to the two dimensionality of the test configuration).

The flow field of a uniform stream over a sphere is conveniently described by using the spherical polar coordinates. To extend the outer boundary of the field of computation as far downstream as possible (to facilitate the implementation of the boundary conditions), $z = \ln r$ is used in place of the physical radius r. Three different sets of numerical integration have been made by different authors at common Reynolds numbers of 40 and 100.[20,21,22] There is also a set of experimental data by Taneda[23] of some characteristic quantities of the recirculatory wake flow field at these and other Reynolds numbers. Such measured values of wake length and locations of the separation point and the vorticity centers provide for comparisons of the detailed flow field in the most sensitive region, in addition to the overall drag coefficient acting on the sphere.

Jenson,[20] and Hamielec, et al[21] used similar difference relaxation procedures and the same downstream boundary conditions approximating uniform out flow, (Table 4). Both cases were carefully executed and examined very carefully

TABLE IV

Outflow boundary conditions. Sphere wake calculations based on Navier-Stokes equations.

| $Re_D$ | Authors | Location radii | Vorticity $\omega$ | $\Delta\omega_{Oseen}$ | Stream function | Velocity $q-q_{Oseen}$ | Mesh size $\Delta\theta, \Delta z$ |
|---|---|---|---|---|---|---|---|
| 40 | Jensen | 3 | Extrap. | $5 \times 10^{-1}$ | $\psi = \psi_\infty$ | $5 \times 10^{-1}$ | $6°, \frac{1}{20}$ |
| | Hamielec, Hoffman, and Ross | 7<br>14 | 0<br>0 | $2 \times 10^{-1}$<br>$1/3 \times 10^{-2}$ | $\psi = \psi_\infty$<br>$\psi = \psi_\infty$ | $2 \times 10^{-1}$<br>$10^{-1}$ | $6°, \frac{1}{20}$ |
| | Rimon and Cheng | 20 | 0 | $10^{-3}$ | $\frac{\partial\psi}{\partial x} = 0$ | $10^{-2}$ | |
| 100 | Hamielec, Hoffman, and Ross | 7 | 0 | $5 \times 10^{-2}$ | $\psi = \psi_\infty$ | $2 \times 10^{-1}$ | $3°, \frac{1}{40}$ |
| | Rimon and Cheng | 20 | 0 | $10^{-3}$ | $\frac{\partial\psi}{\partial x} = 0$ | $10^{-2}$ | $6°, \frac{1}{20}$ |

numerically, making sure that the steady state results obtained are essentially independent of further reduction in the mesh spacing from $\Delta\theta = 6°$ and $z = 1/20$. They obtained a drag coefficient $C_D$ in agreement with that expected from the experimentally well-established "standard drag curve". However, the details of the two solutions were much different. For example, the two results for the vorticity on the wake side of the sphere surface differ by a factor of 2 to 3 for the case with $Re_D = 40$, (Fig. 7a). The streamline patterns in the recirculatory wake are visibly different, although qualitatively similar. Such differences in the detailed results clearly demonstrate the importance of the cumulative effects of the truncation errors due to the non-conservative nature of the difference algorithms which are equivalent to their relaxation procedures, despite the good agreement in such overall results like the drag coefficient $C_D$. Jenson's results depart considerably further from Taneda's wake data than do the results of Hamielec, et al at $Re_D = 40$, (Fig. 8). Hamielec, et al also calculated the case $Re_D = 100$. They found it necessary to refine the mesh to $\Delta\theta = 3°$ and $\Delta z = 1/40$ to secure a reasonable steady state, and also had to introduce some fine adjustments in order to reproduce the experimental value of the drag coefficient $C_D$ at $Re_D = 100$.

Rimon and Cheng[22] employed the Gauss-Seidel, over-relaxation procedure, and succeeded in developing a conservative difference form that is still reasonably simple despite the contracted curvilinear coordinates and stream function-vorticity formulation. The same mesh size $\Delta\theta = 6°$ and $\Delta z = 1/20$, as used by the previous authors, was employed. The conservative nature of the difference formulation permits an estimate of the upper bound of the cumulated truncation error via Equation (5.14), in which the $Re_{\Delta x}$ should be replaced by $Re_{\Delta z}$ for this calculation in terms of $\Delta\theta$ and $\Delta z$. The magnitudes of $Re_{\Delta z}$ for the two cases with $Re_D = 40$ and $100$ can be estimated from the computed solution, based upon the velocity gradient in the region near the isolated rear stagnation point in the

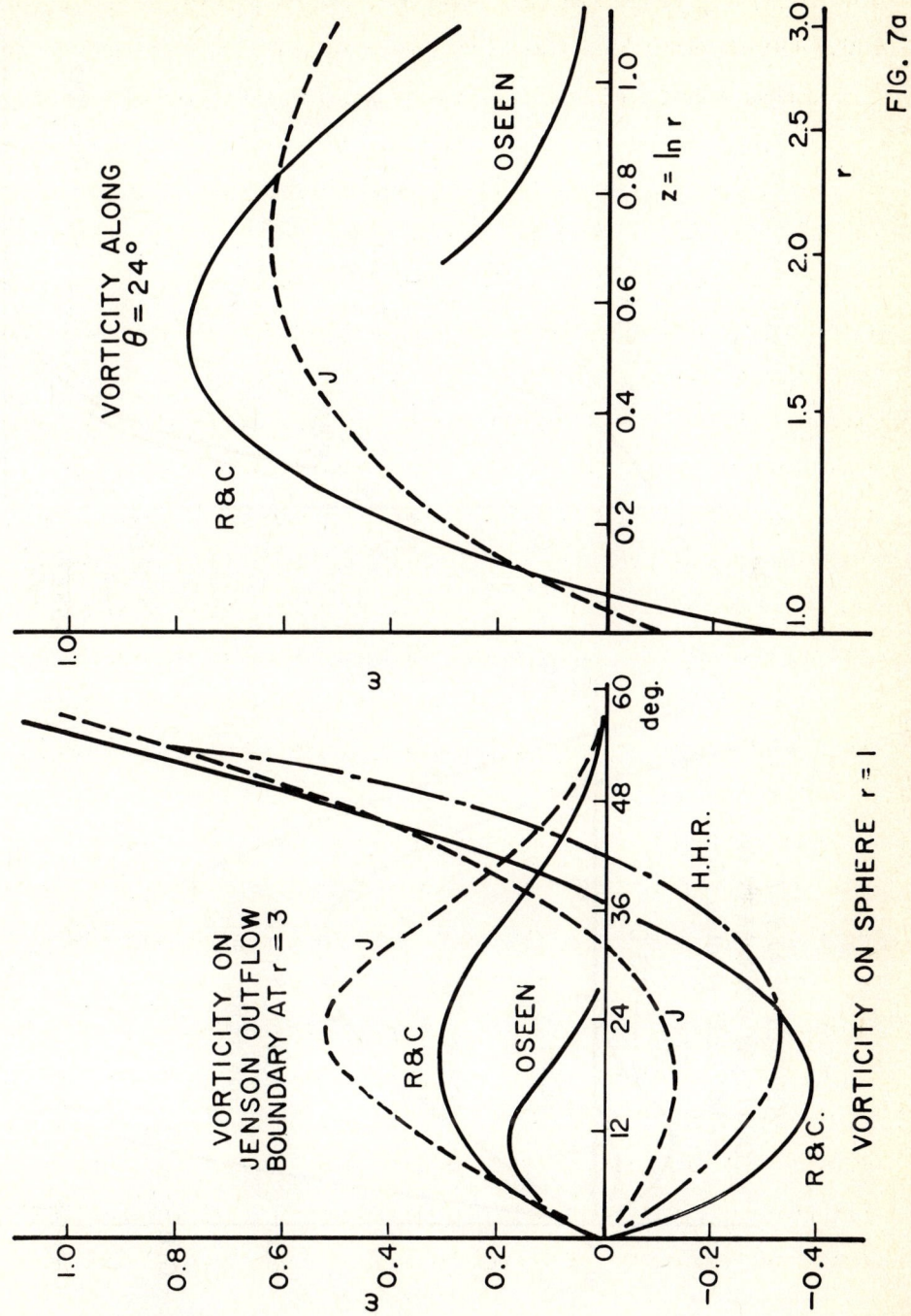

FIG. 7a

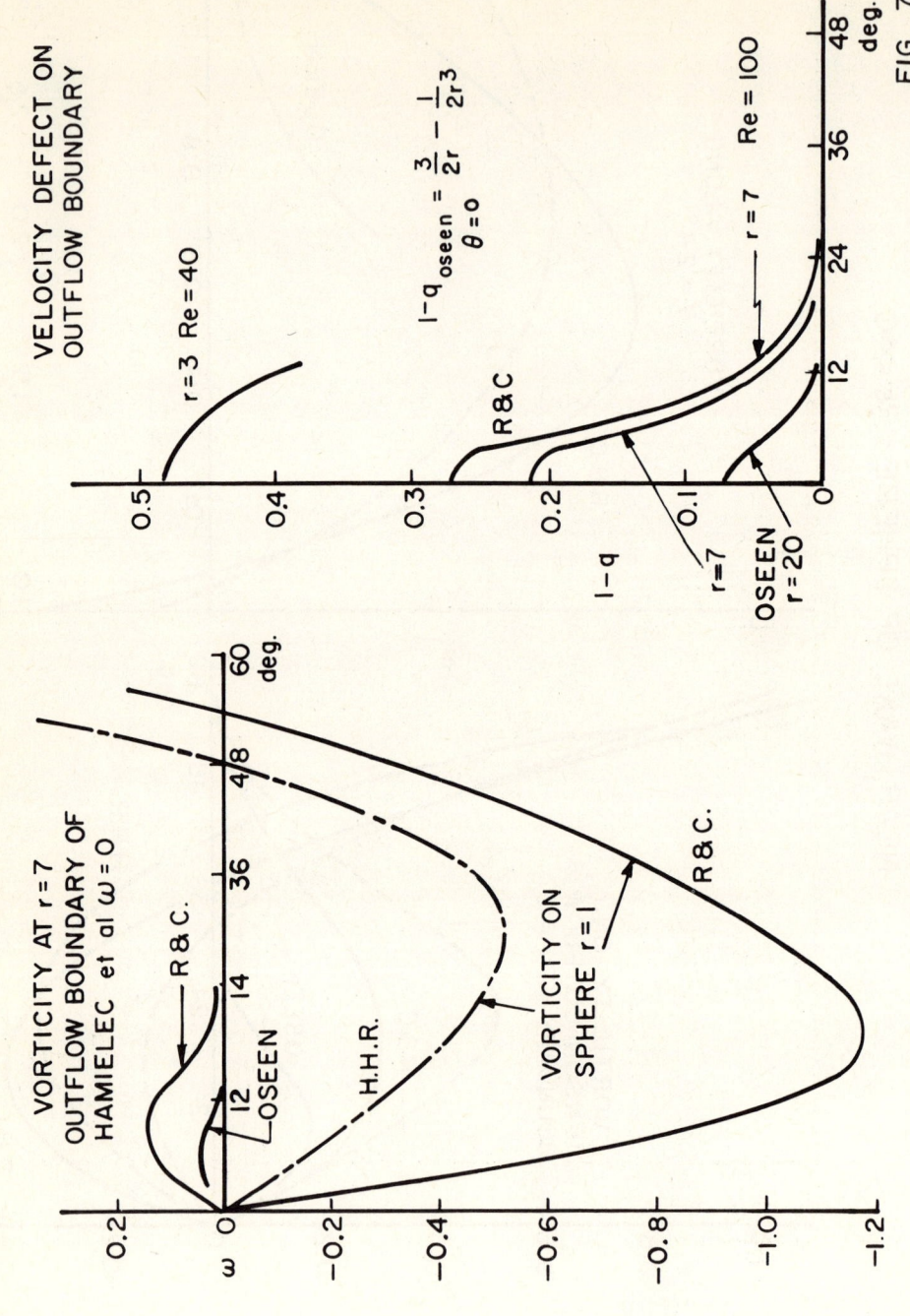

FIG. 7b

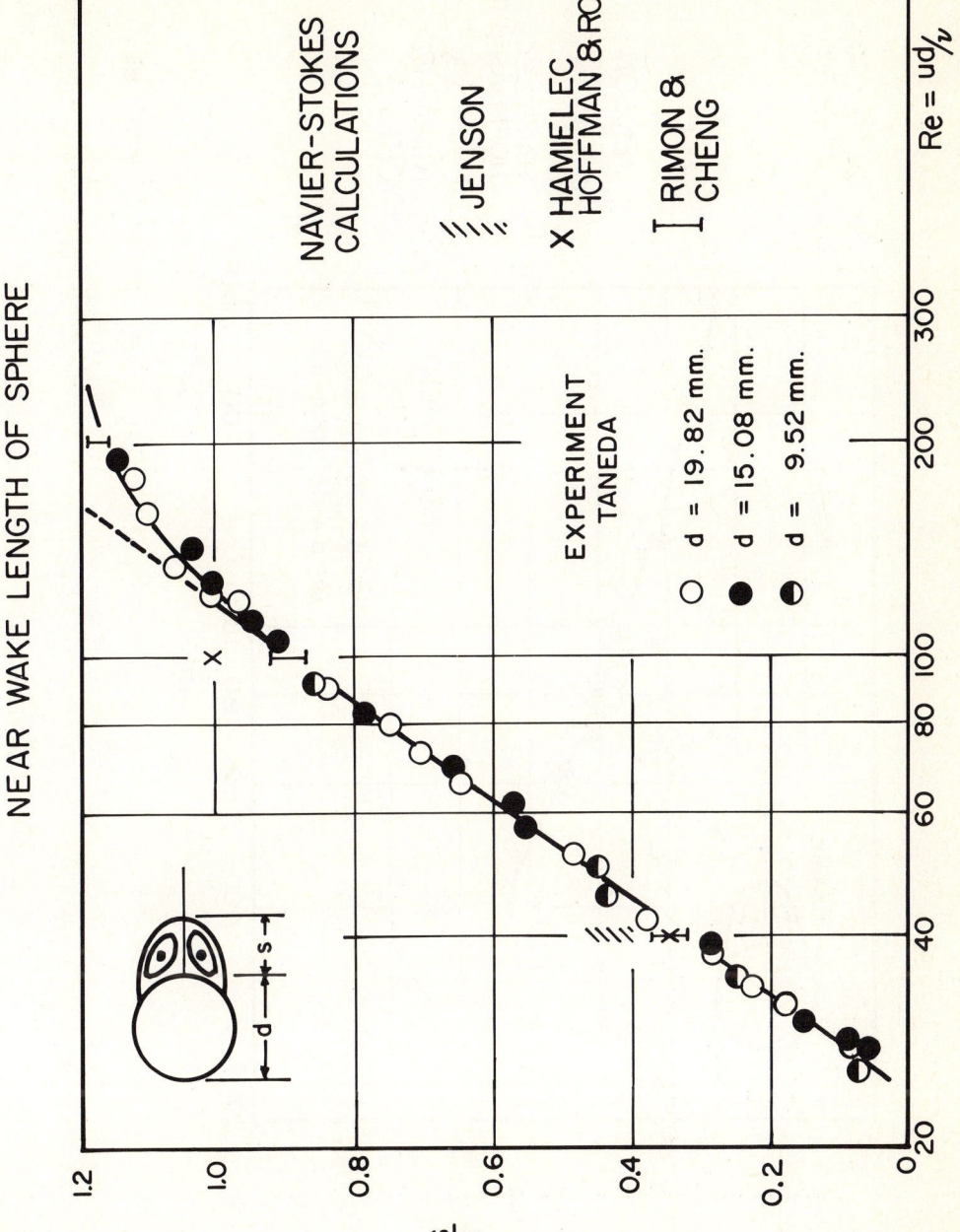

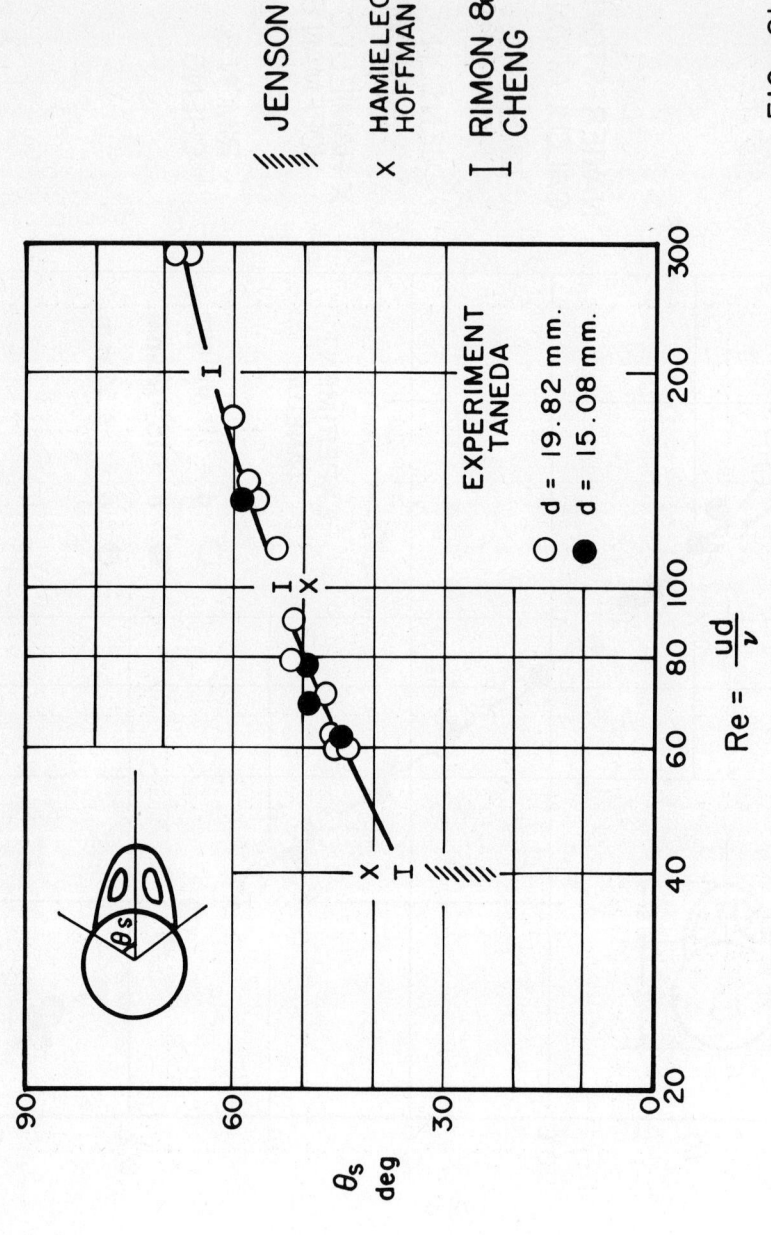

FIG. 8b

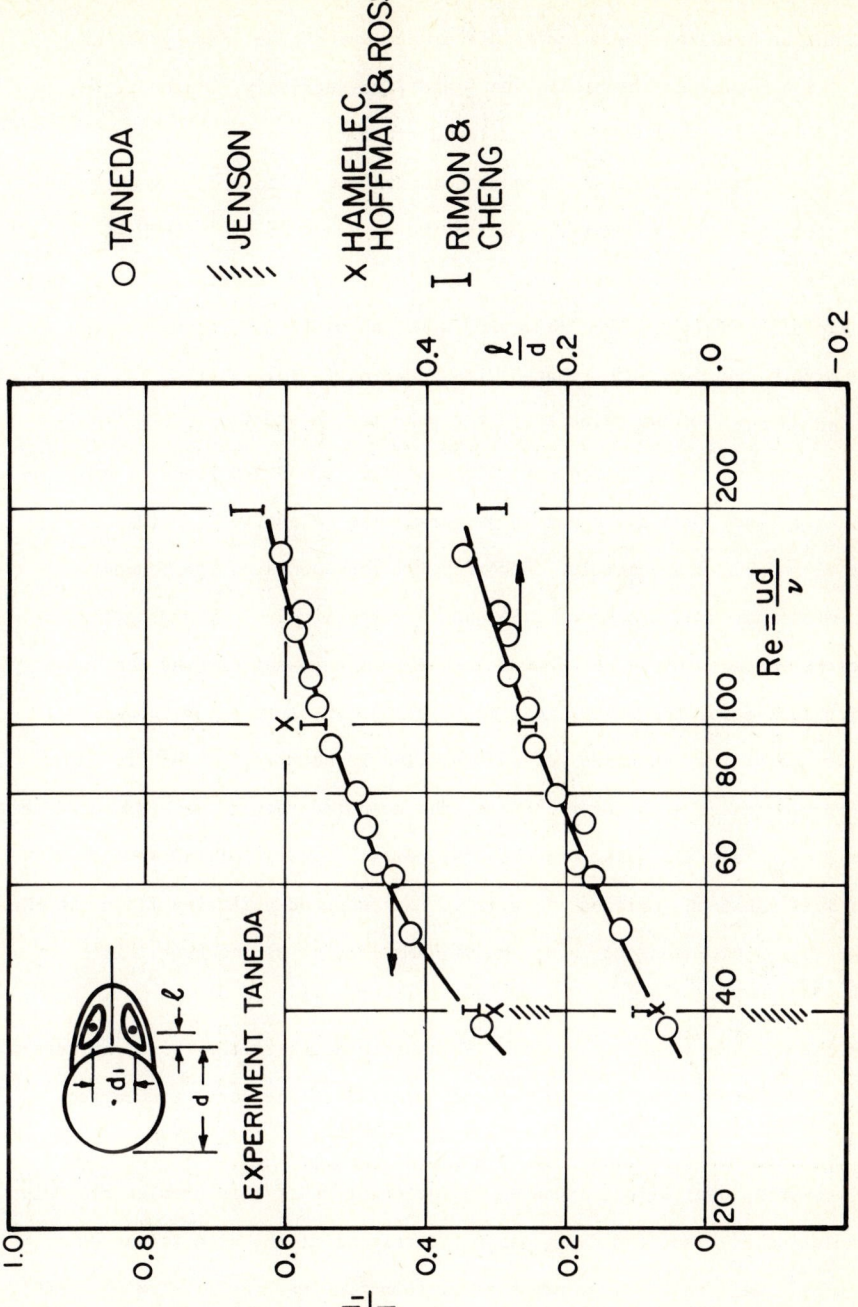

FIG. 8c

wake according to Equation (5.31) with the reference velocity of this mesh Reynolds number based on the velocity difference across the large gradient region. These magnitudes are less than $\frac{1}{2}$ and 1 respectively. Accordingly, the absolute upper bounds of the accumulated truncation errors are $3 \times 10^{-2} \times Re_{\Delta z}^2 \sim 1$ and 3% respectively. The extrapolation condition at the downstream boundary gives the largest contribution to the boundary error. (Both $\frac{\partial \psi}{\partial x} = 0$ and $\omega = 0$ on the out flow boundary commit a fractional error as much as 100%. They are not expected to err in sign, however). The absolute upper bound of the boundary errors may then be estimated with Equation (5.16), where $\varepsilon_b' = 1$, and Re is based on the maximum velocity in the wake region and the length from the rear stagnation point to the out flow boundary in the z-θ plane of computation. This is more than two sphere diameters. The effective Reynolds numbers are then 80 and 200 respectively. Accordingly, the bounds on the boundary errors are estimated as $2\varepsilon_b'/Re$ of 2.5% and 1% respectively. By adding the estimates of the absolute upper bounds of the truncation errors and the boundary errors for each case, the overall estimates of the absolute error bounds are about 3.5% and 4% for the cases $Re_D = 40$ and 100 respectively. This is quite satisfactory engineering accuracy. Thus, the computed results were expected to agree well with Taneda's wake data even for certain details of the wake flow fields. This has been verified, (Fig. 8). The computed vorticity fields in the near wake region of Rimon and Cheng and of Hamielec, et al, however, differ by a factor of 2 or more in the case with $Re_D = 100$, while they differ by much less for the case $Re_D = 40$, (Fig. 7b). This again demonstrates the significance of larger mesh Reynolds numbers on the accumulation of the local truncation errors.

The computational effort expanded in the solution of this problem following the formulation of Rimon and Cheng was not excessive at the time it was done, and is rather small in terms of present-day computing machines. $61 \times 31 = 1891$

mesh points were used. A steady state solution was obtained in about an hour computation on the IBM 7094, with the potential flow field taken as the initial data. In terms of CDC 6600 machine time, the solution would take less than 10 minutes. Fortran language was used without paying much attention to programming efficiency. The computational time can be appreciably reduced if an approximation more accurate than the inviscid flow field should be used as the initial data, and if more attention should be paid to programming efficiency. It is therefore believed that with conscientious effort in constructing the difference formulation, useful quantitative results may be obtained from numerical solution of the Navier-Stokes equations for hydrodynamic flow problems, somewhat more complicated than the sphere problem dealt with here.

The extension of such calculations to steady flows in three dimensional space and to higher flow Reynolds numbers will, however, be more complicated. It will need not only substantially more computer time, but also some analysis in order to gain understanding of certain intricacies in the truly 3-D problems such as the computations in the vicinity of the "separation lines". With greatly increased capability of high speed computers in the foreseeable future to provide the much needed speed and resolution, it is hopeful that good quantitative results even for these practical steady flow problems in three spatial dimensions may be obtained.

Time-dependent hydrodynamic problems in three space dimensions are considerably more difficult and demanding. This is especially true if hydrodynamic turbulence is the subject of investigation. The high frequency components of the turbulent fluctuations can doubtfully be treated with a reasonable accuracy, despite the giant stride in the capability of computing machines foreseen in the future. It appears that some phenomenological theory for the high frequency turbulent components will be needed, while the low frequency components can perhaps be satisfactorily handled by computational methods. This statement is meant to apply whether the integration takes place in the physical space for the physical variables or in the Fourier space for the Fourier components of the physical variables. Much work is needed in any case.[24,25,26]

## 6.2 Supersonic Gas Dynamics

The gas dynamic equations are basically the same as the hydrodynamic equations, except for the variations in the gas density and in the diffusivities, and for the addition of the equation of energy balance (1.3). The outstanding feature of supersonic flow fields is the presence of shock waves, either generated from within the field, or incident on the flow field from without. Most of the practical problems that call for a numerical treatment of the Navier-Stokes equations involve the generation of shock waves due to the interaction of the inviscid and viscous streams. The computation of a shock wave of unknown strength and location presents considerable difficulty, as was discussed in the previous chapter. The shock-induced oscillations in its neighboring flow field are detrimental to the appearance of the computational solution. Such solutions are often presented after some artificial averaging or filtering procedure, and can therefore be of qualitative value only. Indeed, those solutions relatively free from this criticism owe their success to avoiding the serious consequences of a shock standing in an important part of the flow field. By carefully selecting the field of computation for the problems to be investigated, the consequences of shock-induced oscillations are minimized.

Allen and Cheng[16] treated the near wake flow imbedded in a supersonic stream turning over a sharp shoulder of a flat base with a "recompression shock" generated from the turning of the supersonic stream caused by the closing of the recirculatory wake. In the steady state solution of this problem, the small oscillations caused by the recompression shock appreciably distort the computed results only in the far downstream portion of the rejoined wake flow field near the downstream boundary. Although the oscillations of the flow properties in the flow field are equivalent to those induced by an oscillation of the shock front of only $1/4\Delta x$, they remain as one of the two largest sources of computational errors. It is conjectured that the likely source of the small oscillation is the inaccurate extraneous difference treatment where the shock emerges from the downstream boundary of the field of computation. The conservative difference form of the class (5.18) was used, and the criterion (5.35) was satisfied (although without a substantial margin). Unfortunately, comparable experimental data are not available, and the extension of this calculation to the range of practical Reynolds numbers of $10^3 - 10^4$, and for a somewhat more complicated geometrical configuration, was beyond available means then (computation time and storage capacity).

Ross and Cheng[27] studied the question of the permissible ranges of Reynolds numbers and Mach numbers such that the computational solutions with the previous formulation will possess an absolute upper bound on the error of no more than 10%. They limited the number of mesh points to 2100, used an "optimal" ratio of $\Delta x/\Delta y$, and modified their boundary treatment in a non-essential (but simplifying) way. The computational effort was limited to 10-15 minutes of computing time on the IBM 360-91 (equivalent roughly to 20-30 minutes on the CDC 6600, or 4 to 10 hours on the IBM 7044, originally used by Allen). When other restrictions of purely a fluid mechanical nature are superposed, it was established that the range of validity of the computational formulation can be extended to $M \overset{\sim}{=} 4$ and Reynolds numbers of $\sim 1\text{-}2 \times 10^3$ (based on half width of the base.) To extend this computation to the practical range of interest would require substantial refinement in the mesh size, with a corresponding increase in the computational effort. The storage limitation of the computer did not seem restrictive, but rather the computer time and cost that was prohibitive. It may be that an absolute upper bound of 10% is too restrictive, since the maximum fractional error in the solution is likely to be substantially less than the absolute upper bound. A substantial decrease in the estimate of the computational effort will follow a modest reduction of the accuracy requirement - if the method of error estimate described in Chapter V should be granted in the absence of any direct comparison with reliable, appropriate experimental data.

Carter[28] chooses to integrate the Navier-Stokes equation for a steady supersonic viscous flow over a compression ramp or corner with an imbedded separated region. The compression waves will eventually coalesce into a shock wave. Carter kept the upper boundary of the field of computation sufficiently close to the viscous region so that the waves generated from the viscous layer may be treated (without serious error) as isentropic waves, and utilized the simple wave extrapolation condition on the upper boundary. This stratagem, as was used in the treatment of the near wake problem,[16,27] serves to eliminate the major part of the undesirable wave reflections from the upper boundary. By restricting the field of computation to such a narrow strip, and by using a highly refined mesh with Brailovskaya's difference algorithm (a member of the class (5.18) ), results which compare favorably with experimental data can be obtained in the comparable Reynolds and Mach number ranges. This difference formulation is probably not quite conservative, due to the use of the "curved" body coordinates. But the curvature is sufficiently small (or otherwise localized) so that the accumulation of truncation errors may not be excessive. While an estimate of the error bounds has not yet been made, the evidence seems to indicate that this calculation may have come very close to directly generating some useful practical results. Admittedly, the computational effort in this calculation seemed to be excessive from the academic point of view (two or more hours of CDC 6600 per case), but it does not appear prohibitive from the view of engineering development. Moreover, there is substantial room for improvement if an error estimate can be made. The 4th generation computers that will be operational shortly promise a further substantial increase in speed of computation and in storage capability.  When successfully implemented, this may render the computational effort of less concern in solving such practical problems.

An academic program has been devoted to developing techniques for handling the difficulty of computing shock waves in a complicated flow field.  The results reported in Section 5.4 demonstrate some progress in this direction.  There are still tremendous difficulties ahead in cases where a shock wave interacts with other incident waves or when the criterion of (5.33) becomes much too restrictive.  Nevertheless, even in their present unsatisfactory state, computational results can be useful in fluid dynamics research to supplement experimental and other efforts.  The following treatment of the hypersonic leading edge problem may illustrate the situation.

Over the leading edge of an infinitely thin flat plate, placed in a hypersonic or supersonic stream at zero incidence, a shock wave will develop due to viscous effects in the vicinity of the plate.  In this region, the hypersonic strong interaction theory, based on boundary layer type arguments of various forms, fails to provide even a qualitatively adequate description of the flow field.  It is not clear to what extent the flow situation will have to be described by the kinetic theory of gases.  We feel that the continuum theory, when appropriately modified for the slip effects, should provide a good approximate description of the flow field very near the leading edge and fair smoothly into the results of the hypersonic strong interaction theory further downstream.  Thus, asymptotic approximations were introduced only in the formulation of the surface slip conditions, and the full Navier-Stokes equations system was integrated numerically.

Physically, a rather strong oblique shock wave develops rapidly from the leading edge, and produces, in the downstream gas, a high pressure and temperature, both proportional to $M^2 \sin^2 \theta$, where $\theta$ is the local inclination of the shock front to the incoming uniform stream.  It is very clear then that any small oscillations in the shock front will produce, in the downstream, correspoinding oscillations of significant magnitudes when the upstream flow Mach number is $\sim$ 20. It is therefore critical to eliminate or suppress shock oscillations from the computation.

The conservative two-step algorithm of Cheng and Allen was used with a 40 × 30 mesh in the physical space x-y and with y = 0 describing the plate surface.[18] The leading-edge shock emerges from the downstream outflow boundary. The downstream outflow boundary is treated by second-order accurate extrapolation along the shock direction where the shock emerges, along the plate on the plate surface, and along directions linearly interpolated in between. Slip conditions are derived from two stream molecular distribution function with the molecules emitted from the plate diffusedly and accommodated fully to the plate conditions. The various computed profiles at constant $y = (i-1)\Delta y$ from the plate are given in Fig. 9. Around the plate leading edge point a fairly large oscillation is generated by the discontinuous boundary, but dies out rapidly away from the plate leading edge. A minor localized oscillation developed farther downstream at about 2-4 $\Delta y$ possibly due to some inappropriate difference treatment of the boundary conditions on the plate. This localized oscillation (in the thermodynamic variables) imposes no significant error on the solution.

The absolute upper bound of the errors in the smooth part of the computed solution due to the downstream extrapolation boundary condition is evaluated according to Equation (5.16) to be < 7%. The absolute upper bound of the truncation error is estimated from Equation (5.14) to be also less that 7%. With both the round-off error and the error due to the steady state criterion both less than 1%, the absolute upper bound of the error in the computed solution, away from the immediate vicinity of the leading edge and the out flow boundary is about 16%.[29]

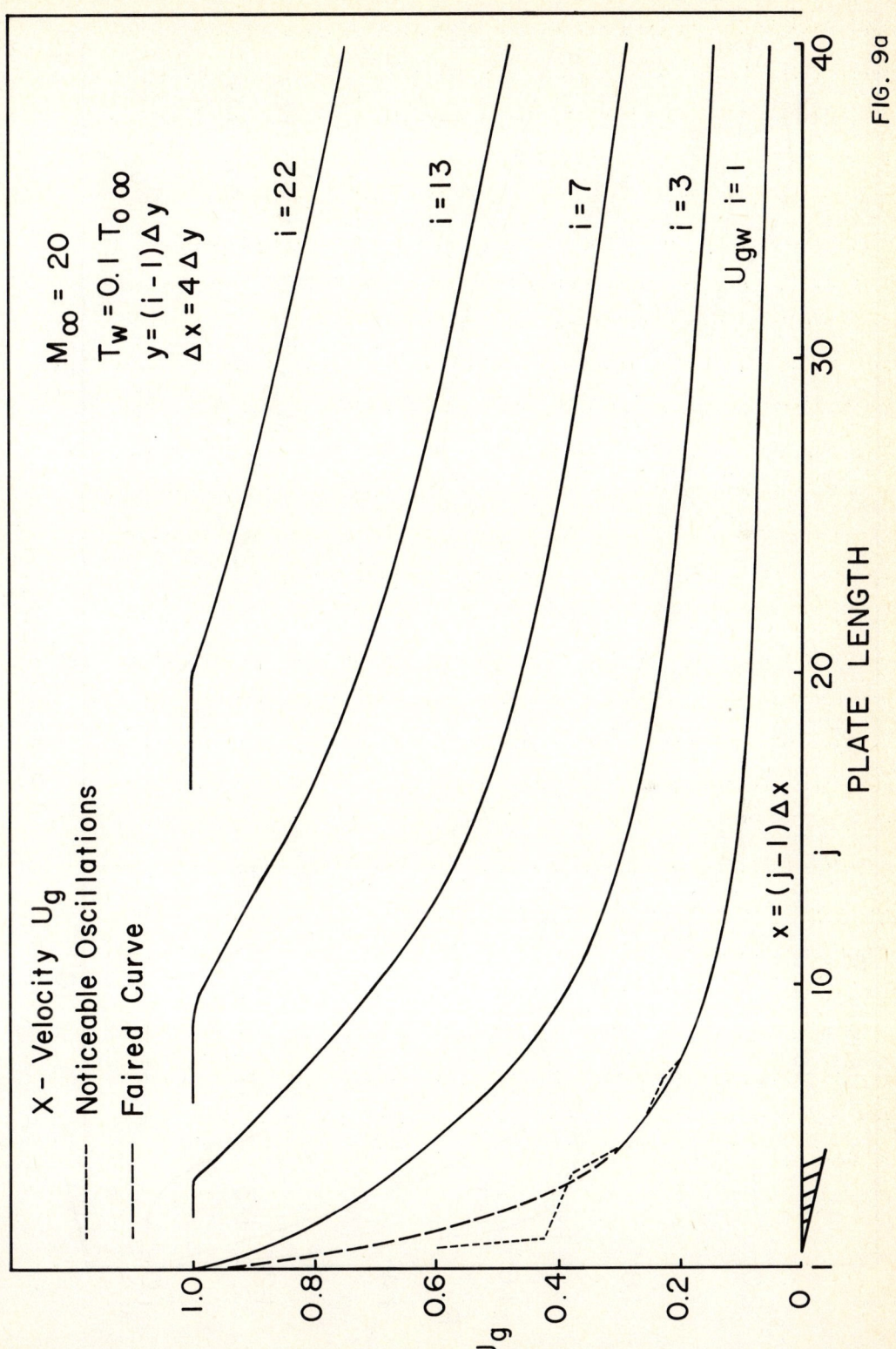

FIG. 9a

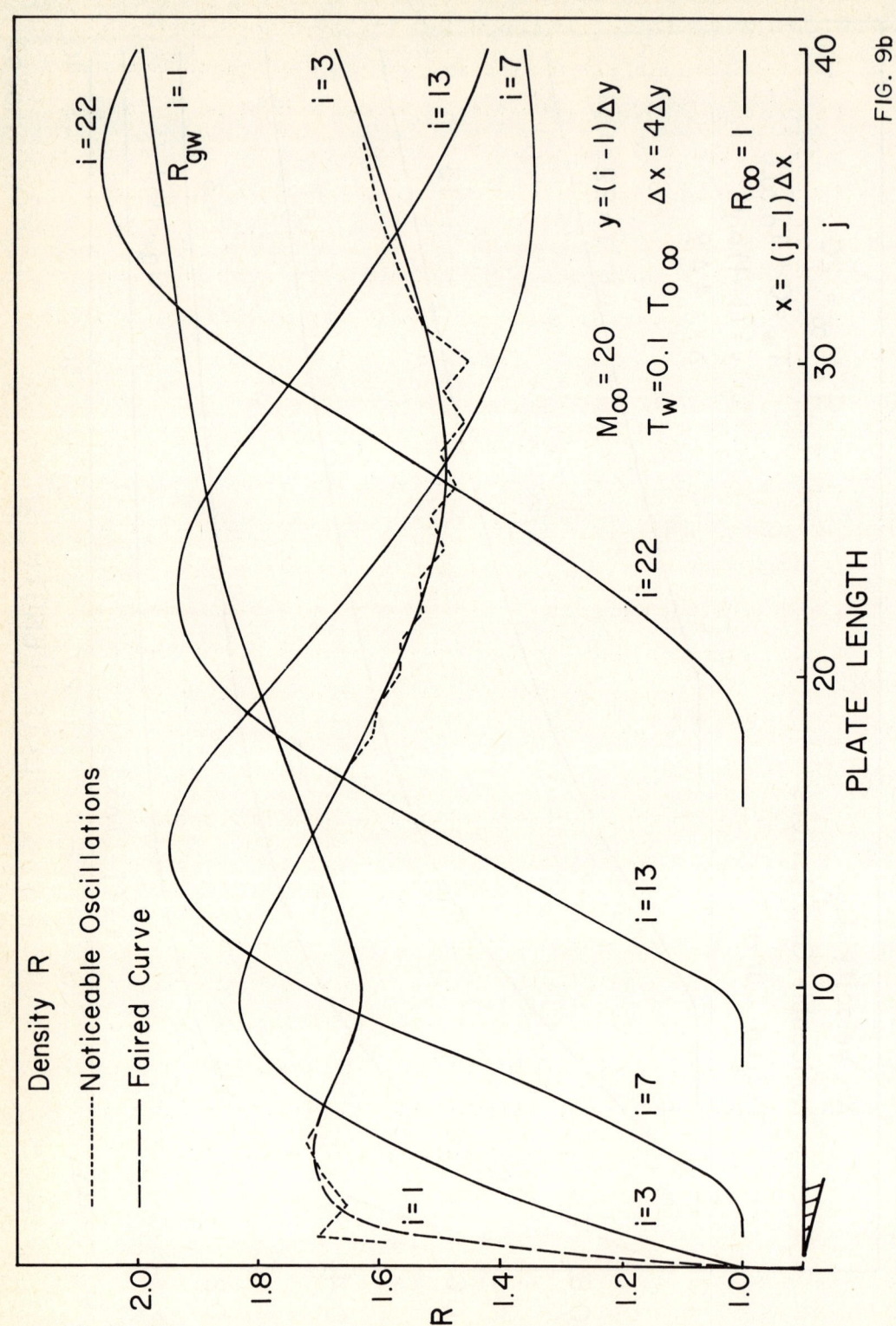

FIG. 9b

There is a collection of measured data from two different hypersonic wind tunnels at Cornell Aeronautical Laboratories and at Princeton University. The test conditions do not correspond precisely but encompassing the case computed and shown above, the hypersonic tunnels and the instrumentations were developed through many years. The model testing was tedious and difficult. The surface pressure data, reduced to dimensionless parameters, agree in general trend; but quantitatively the data from the two sources differ by a factor of two or more. Figure 10 shows how the computed results compromise the two sets of data. Examination of the details help to identify the region of validity of each set of data and the cause of divergence between the two. Figures 11a,b show how the computed results of slip velocity and slip temperature of the gas along the plate surface compare with available experimental data. Figures 12a,b show the computed and measured dimensionless parameters of surface friction and heat transfer rate. The agreement is good and is without any adjustable parameters. Thus computational methods with reasonable accuracy can provide results directly useful in engineering development.

The above computational solution also contributes to the fundamentals of continuum fluid dynamics. It provided a positive indication that the continuum description of fluid flow by Navier-Stokes equations system with appropriate slip conditions is valid for the transition regime, and that the proper surface slip conditions should be consistent with diffused emission of fully accommodated molecules from the gas-solid interface.

In the above review, there are important omissions of many interesting and significant results in the development of computational methods relevant to aerospace applications. They are omitted here to facilitate the presentation of the major themes, hopefully with as little digression as possible. While computational stability remains a problem, difficulties can generally be overcome with some hard work. Stability problems should not be permitted

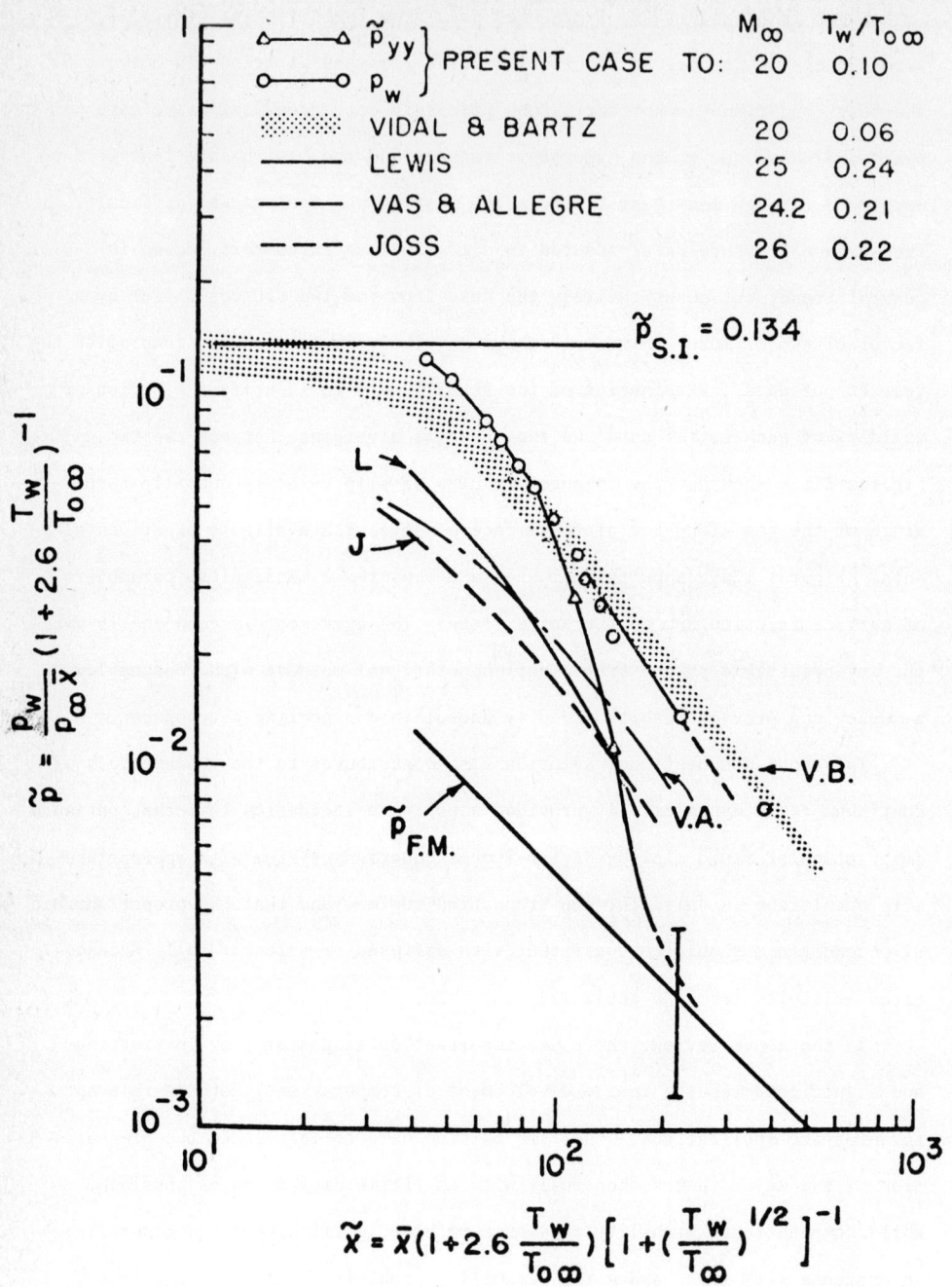

FIG. 10

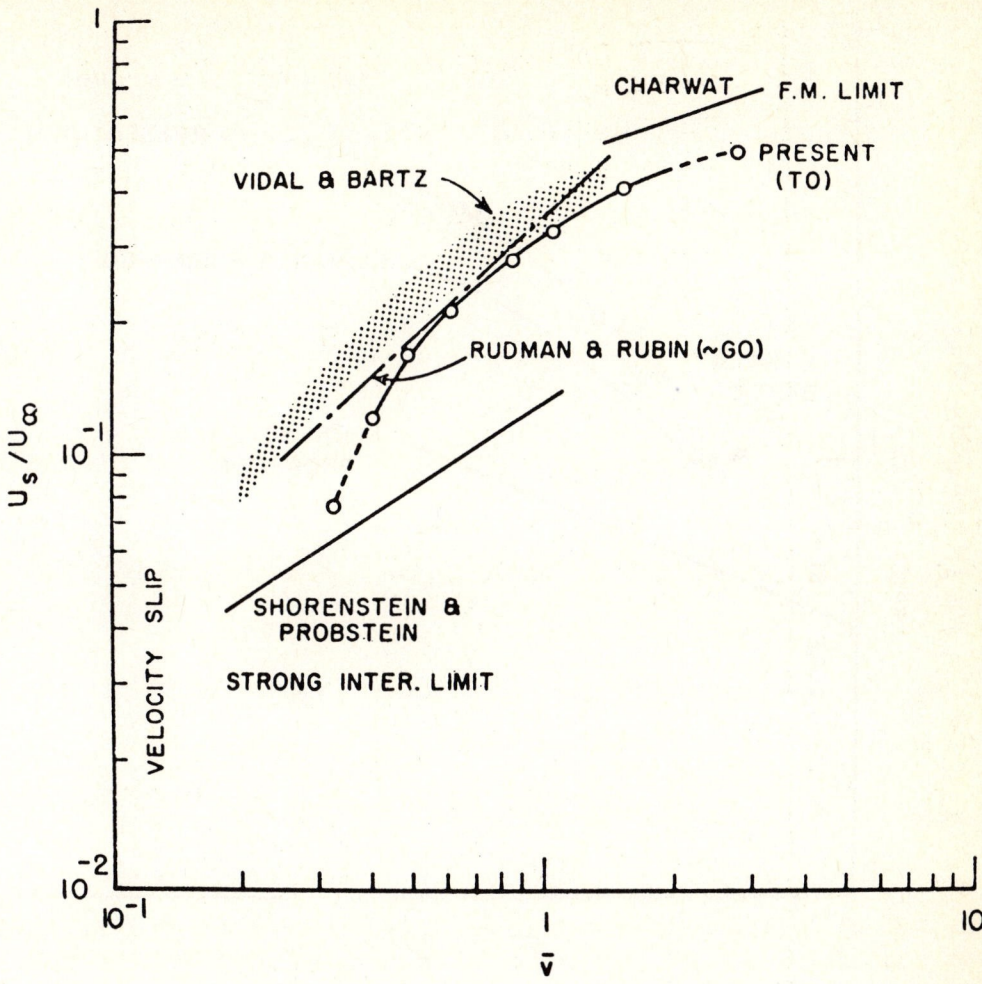

FIG. 11a

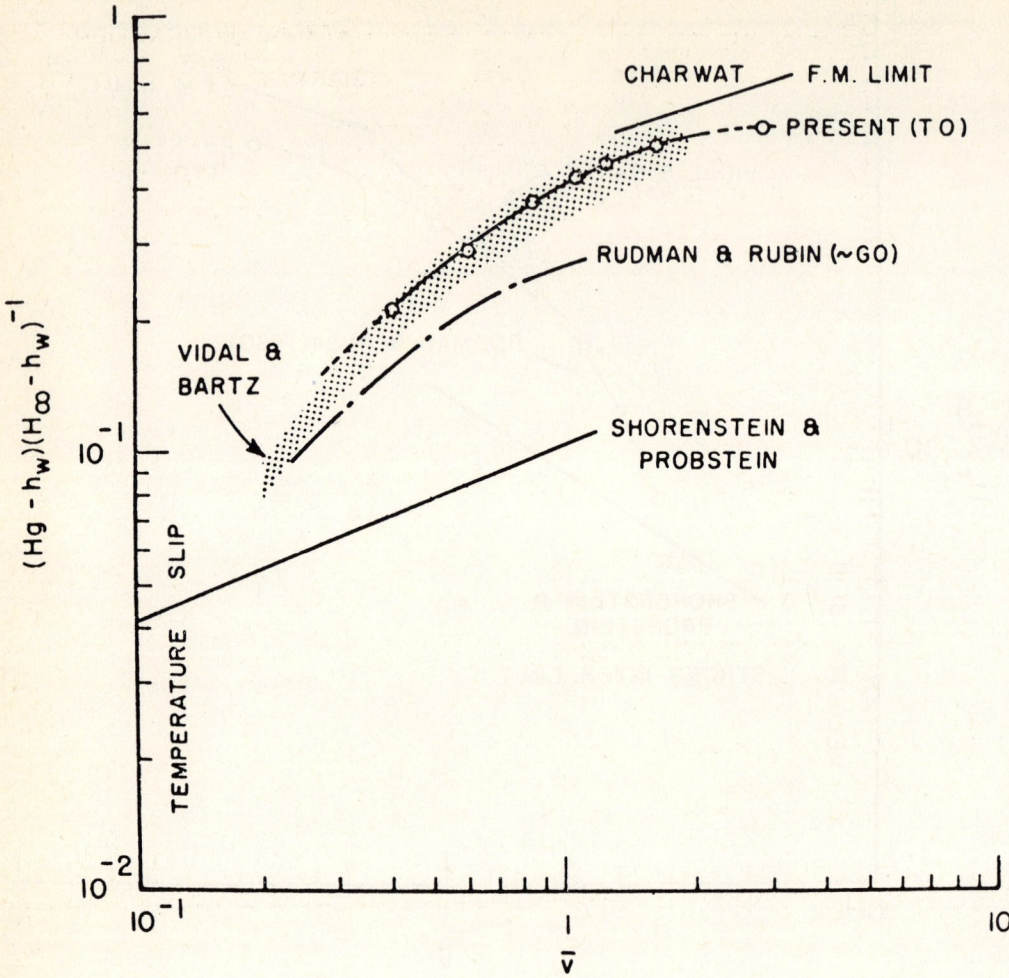

FIG. IIb

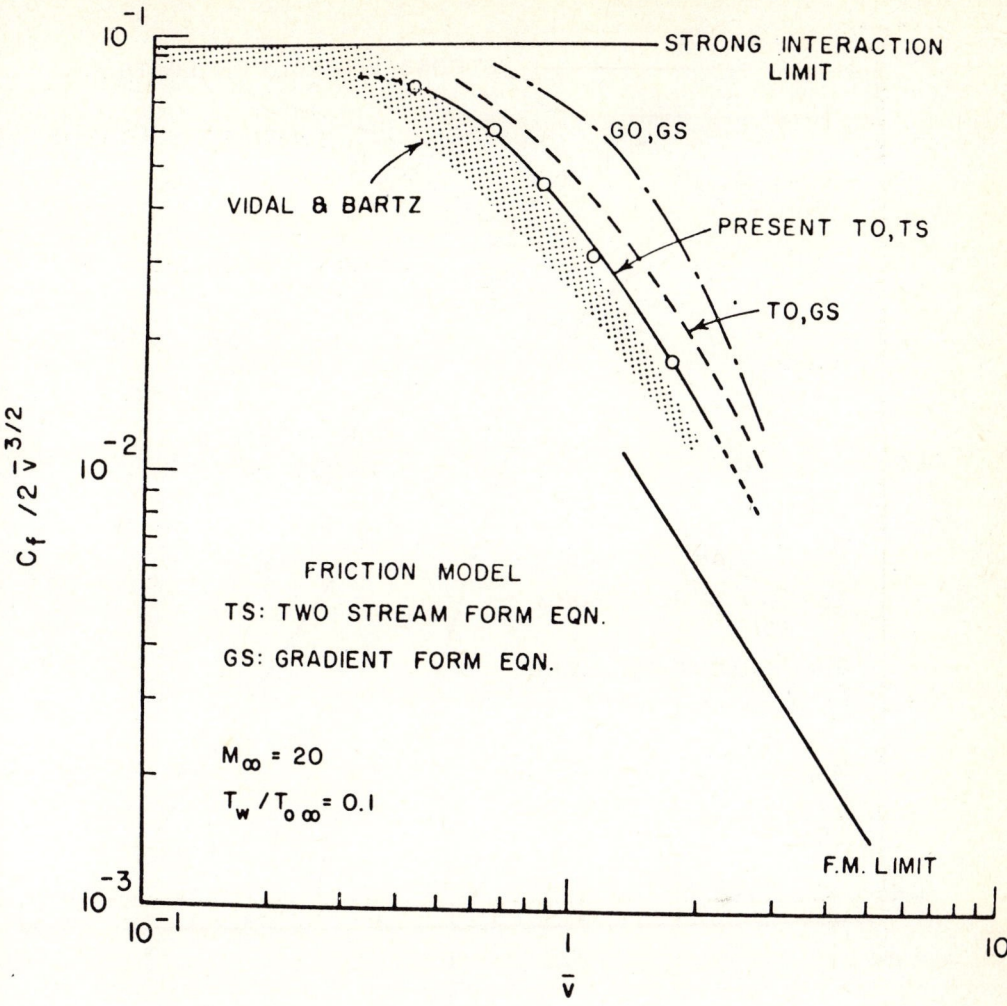

FIG. 12a

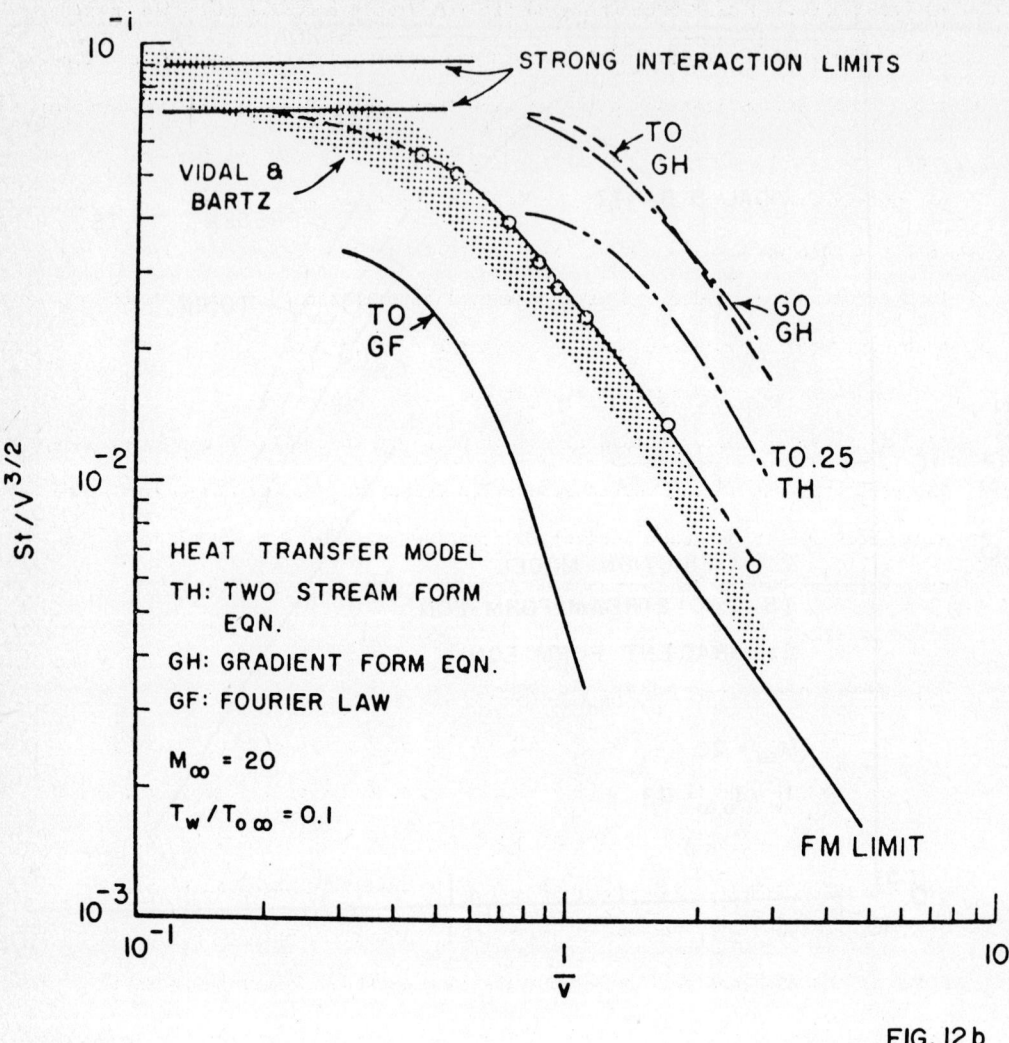

FIG. 12b

to draw attention away from the need for reasonably accurate computed results.
Stable and smooth computational results are encouraging, but can be very deceiving.  From the applications point of view, the question of accuracy is crucial.
Accordingly, the approach described above to secure "accurate" formulation is
of fundamental importance (crude as it is).  How such crude criteria may be
used and incorporated is demonstrated in this chapter.  Much development in
this direction is needed.  Some fundamental aspects should be understood, and
practical methods developed to deal with the various situations.  Such
problems will not fade away because of the dramatic advances in computer
capabilities.  Indeed, there are serious problems that will be encountered in
the efficient use of the fourth generation computers, if any meaningful speed
advantages are to be reaped.  Therefore, a few words on the prospects of the
coming fourth generation computer will serve to bring to conclusion the
present review.

## 6.3  Future Prospects with the Fourth Generation Computers

It has been a constant allusion that faster and bigger computers will
provide the solution to many difficulties associated with the numerical
integration of partial differential equations.  Such larger and faster
computers are needed, but they do not provide the brute force to resolve
all computational difficulties without conscientious efforts.  Certain aspects of the problems must be fundamentally understood before being satisfactorily dealt with, such as the questions of stability and accuracy.  Moreover, the development of computer hardware has reached the point that order of
magnitude improvement in the speed of information processing through
miniaturization cannot be expected, as in the past.  Fourth generation
computers promise to bring about a large improvement in speed through
"Parallelism" which is very much dependent on the sophistication of software

and on the nature of specific problems to be solved. These computers will bring complicated problems to the users, as well as to the manufacturer of the machines.

"Parallelism" is effected primarily in two different ways. Burrough Company's ILLIAC IV speeds up the arithematic process by using 64 arithematic units, receiving the same instruction from a common command module to simultaneously process 64 sets of raw data. Thus arithematic results can be "effectively" obtained 64 times faster. This is often referred to as a "single Instruction Multiple Processor" machine (SIMP). Control Data Corporation's STAR (the STring ARay processor) employs the assembly line (or "pipe line") technique in which a string of data is "continuously" fed into the "pipe line" to be processed by a standing instruction. In this manner, the arithematic unit does not become idle when the instructions are being fetched, decoded, and installed in place to direct the computation, or when the newly computed data is being sent out of the arithematic unit, or the raw data is being brought into the arithematic unit. This is often referred to as the pipe-line machine. Both the ILLIAC IV and the STAR machines possess virtual memory capacity, i.e., the machines will manage automatically the data stored in the external memory units used to extend the storage capacity of the machine. Texas Instrument Corporation's ASC machine (Advanced Science Computer) incorporates both the multi-processor and the pipe-line concept, but possesses no virtual memory capability. All of these machines are about to be (or have already been) delivered by the various manufactuers and are to become operational shortly.

ILLIAC IV is most efficient when the 64 arithmetic processors can be fully utilized. Any vacant processors are simply idling (doing no useful work) when an operation is performed on less than 64 sets of data. Thus the demonstration of the speed of ILLIAC IV vs currently available computers is often in terms of the inversion of a 64 x 64 matrix. STAR is most efficient when a large amount of raw data (a long string of data) is to be processed through the same operation (i.e. single instruction), so that the "filling time" of the pipe becomes negligible. The machine will provide a 64-fold increase in the effective speed since each word in the STAR contains 64 bits of binary information. The ASC machine possesses intermediate behavior. Each manufacturer has developed powerful and intricate software to implement and enhance the advantages of the hardware. But they are all subject to the inherent limitations of a SIMP or a pipe-line machine.

For any one of these machines, a huge amount of data must be stored, arranged, and retrieved from storage facilities. This must be done efficiently, commensurate with the processing speed of the machine. Such can be done for the data in core memory, directly accessible to the central processing unit (CPU), but it cannot be done for the data stored in external memories. The speed of a search operation or of a data transmission through the interface to the CPU is orders of magnitude slower than the arithematic speed of the machine. If the CPU asks for data in the external storage too frequently, the CPU would be doing little useful computation, instead, it would be spending time transmitting the data in and out of the external memory units under its virtual memory operation. If the user should prefer to deprive the machine of its virtual memory capability, then the user-programmer must assume the responsibility of managing the data across the interface. An alternative solution to this problem is to expand the core memory of the CPU of the computer to match its processing speed. This is unfortunately a very expensive proposition. There are also other problems of data management in the CPU (though probably not so serious as the ones just mentioned) more intimately related to the specific characteristics (hardware and software) of each computer. These are problems which the user cannot do much about. On the other hand, these machines present problems to the users which the manufacturer of the machines cannot alleviate.

Currently available computers are serial machines that process and advance the data at one point after another. Simultaneous solution of unknowns at many points, as is required by implicit algorithms, is handled through special procedures such as matrix inversion. If a program designed for the serial machine should be run on parallel computers, no speed advantage will result. (Indeed there will be some loss.) The 64 parallel processors of ILLIAC IV will only have one processor doing useful work. The STring-ARray processor of STAR will operate in its scalar mode (versus the "vector mode" for string array processing). There is not, and will not be, software that will translate an existing serial program into a reasonably efficient "parallel program" for a specific parallel machine. Such a translation is not a matter of translating one language into another; it is a matter of changing the logic in solving a problem. It asks essentially for a new formulation of a specific problem, if one wishes to exploit the speed advantage offered by a specific machine. The user is asked to start anew, for each problem and for each specific parallel computer. The user must pay considerable attention not only to the formulation of a problem for solution, but also to the storage of the data in the external memory in order to match the demand of the data, according to the formulation of the problem.

In writing such a program for use with a specific parallel computer, it is not a simple matter to take advantage of a successful serial program used with the current serial machines. It may indeed be doubtful that the existence of a successful serial program offers any advantage in constructing a good parallel program. Without further elaboration, it may be noted, even for simple problems, that:

    1. An efficient serial algorithm need not lead to an efficient

parallel algorithm, while an inefficient serial algorithm may lead to an efficient parallel algorithm.

2. An algorithm that is apparently serial and was constructed for use with a serial computer may possess a great deal of hidden parallelism which can be exploited to suit the particular mode of operation of a specific parallel computer.

3. A parallel program may behave quite differently in the difference solution of a partial differential equation than the corresponding serial program. Here "behavior" refers to the stability of the computation, the rate of convergence to the desired solution, and the accuracy of the solution.

The last note is particularly important. It asks the user to gain as much understanding as possible of the various fundamental problems of difference methods, such as stability and accuracy. With a better understanding, it is hoped that the years of tedious and painful trial-and-error learning that occurred in the development of difference techniques for the serial machines will not be repeated, or at least may be greatly reduced.

For many important practical problems the solution of the Navier-Stokes equations in three spatial dimensions will be required. Even for the steady state solution of such problems, computation for a reasonably accurate solution will require the speed and storage capacity promised by these parallel computers. Complicated boundary conditions do not lend themselves to efficient parallel treatments, and interfere with efficient organization for the parallel computations of fluid flow problems. These problems are in addition to the fundamental difficulties noted above. It is hoped that what has been learned from the serial machines may benefit the development of computational programs which can reap the promised speed advantage of the parallel computer. For this purpose, it is especially important to gain some fundamental understanding of the complicated computational difficulties particular to fluid dynamics. Such understanding cannot be expected from computer scientists, who have a full share of difficulties associated with the operation of the parallel computers in general. Those wishing to solve complicated flow problems with the Navier-Stokes equations must learn how to resolve such difficulties for themselves. The task ahead is formidable. The potential reward is also immense.

## ACKNOWLEDGEMENT

A portion of the material included in this manuscript is part of the, as yet, unpublished results of research supported by the Office of Naval Research, U. S. Navy, under Contract Number N00014-67-A-0151-0028.

The author is grateful for the support and also for the permission to report such information.

## GENERAL TEXTS FOR BACKGROUND MATERIALS

1. Forsythe, G. E. and Wasow, W. R., <u>Finite Difference Methods for Partial Differential Equations</u>, John Wiley and Sons, Inc. (1960).

2. Isaacson, E. and Keller, H. B., <u>Analysis of Numerical Methods</u>, John Wiley and Sons, Inc. (1966).

3. Richtmeyer, R. D. and Morton, K. W., <u>Difference Methods for Initial Value Problems, second edition</u>, Interscience Publishers, John Wiley and Sons, Inc. (1967).

4. Morse, P. M. and Feshback, H., <u>Methods of Theoretical Physics</u>, McGraw-Hill Book Co. (1953).

5. Goldstein, S. (Editor), <u>Modern Development in Fluid Dynamics</u>, Oxford Clarendon Press (1938).

6. Howarth, L. (Editor), <u>Modern Development in Fluid Dynamics High Speed Flow</u>, Oxford Clarendon Press (1953).

Background materials in Mathematics and Physics in Chapters 1 - 4 are contained in the above general texts and others; and they are not referenced specifically. The physical interpretations of the various results in the present review represent the opinion of the present reviewer whose view may or may not be in full agreement with opinions of the authors of these references. The present review is to put forth and to illustrate, with simple examples, some physical perspective of these mathematical results to help in the numerical integration of the complicated system of equations of fluid flows. It is inevitable that, at places, such inferences may appear far-fetched. The following are the specific references relevant to these physical discussions in the order they appear in the manuscript.

## SPECIFIC REFERENCES

1. Courant, R., Friedricks, K. O., and Levy, H., <u>Uber die Partiellen Differenzen gleichungen der Mathemetischen physik</u>, Mathematics Annual, Vol. 100 (1928).

2. Fromm, J. E., "The Time Dependent Flow of An Incompressible Fluid" <u>Methods in Computational Physics</u>, Vol. 3, Academic Press, N. Y. (1964).

3. Cheng, S. I., "The Numerical Integration of Navier-Stokes Equations," J. of American Institute of Aeronautical and Astronautics, Vol. 8, No. 12, (1970).

4. Hirt, C. W., "Heutristic Stability Theory for Finite Difference Equations," J. of Computational Physics, Vol. 2, (1968).

5. Yanenko, N. N., The Method of Fractional Steps, English translation by M. Holt, Springer Verlag (1971).

6. Peaceman, D. W. and Rachford, H. H., Jr., "The Numerical Solution of Parabolic and Elliptic Differential Equations," Journ, Soc. Industrial and Applied Mathematics, Vol. 3, (1955).

7. Douglas, J. and Gunn, J., "A General Formulation of Alternating Direction Methods," Numerical Mathematics, Vol. 6, (1964).

8. Kreiss, H. O. and Oliger, J., "Comparison of Accurate Methods for the Integration of Hyperbolic Equations," Tellus XXIV 3 (1972).

9. Fromm, J. E., "A Numerical Study of Buoyancy Driven Flows in Room Enclosures," Proceedings of the 2nd International Conference on Numerical Methods in Fluid Dynamics, Berkeley, California, Sept. (1970), Springer Verlag.

10. Cheng, S. I., "Accuracy of Difference Formulation of Navier-Stokes Equations" The Physics of Fluids, Supplement II, Dec. 1969.

11. Fromm, J. E., "Practical Importance of Convective Difference Approximations of Reduced Dispersion," The Physics of Fluids, Supplement II, Dec. 1969.

12. Moretti, G. and Bleich, G., "Three Dimensional Flow around Blunt Bodies," Jour. of American Institute of Aeronautics and Astronautics, Vol. 5, No. 9, (1967).

13. v. Neumann, J. and Richtmeyer, R. D., "A Method for the Numerical Calculations of Hydrodynamic Shocks," Jour. of Applied Physics, Vol. 21, (1950).

14. Lax, P. and Wendroff, B., "Systems of Conservations Laws," Communications on Pure and Applied Mathematics, Vol. 13, (1960).

15. Thoman, D. C. and Szewczyk, A. A., "Time Dependent Viscous Flow over a Circular Cylinder," The Physics of Fluids, Vol. 12, (1969).

16. Allen, J. and Cheng, S. I., "Numerical Solutions of the Compressible Navier-Stokes Equation for the Laminar Near Wake," The Physics of Fluids, Vol. 13, No. 1, (1970).

17. Brailovskaya, I. Y., "A Difference Scheme for the Numerical Solution of the Two-Dimensional Unsteady Navier-Stokes Equations for a Compressible Gas," Soviet Physics Doklady, Vol. 10, No. 2, Aug., (1965).

18. Cheng, S. I. and Chen, J. H., "Finite Difference Treatment of Strong Shock over a Sharp Leading Edge with Navier-Stokes Equations," Proc. of 3rd International Conference on Numberical Methods in Fluid Mechanics,

Vol. II, held in Paris, France, July 1972, Springer-Verlag, Berlin.

19. Messina, N. A. and Cheng, S. I., "A Study of the Computation of Regular Shock Reflection with Navier-Stokes Equations," presented at the Symposium on Application of Computers to Fluid Dynamics Analysis and Design, PolyTech. Institute of Brooklyn, Jan. 1973.

20. Jenson, V. G., "Viscous Flow Round a Sphere at Low Reynolds Number," Proc. of Roy. Soc. London, A249, (1959).

21. Hamielec, A. E., Hoffman, T. W., and Ross, L. L., "Numerical Solution of the Navier-Stokes Equations for Flow Past Non-Solid Spheres," Journal of American Institute of Chemical Engineers, Vol. 13, No. 2, March, 1967.

22. Rimon, Y. and Cheng, S. I., "Numerical Solution of a Uniform Flow over a Sphere at Intermediate Reynolds Numbers," The Physics of Fluids, Vol. 12, No. 5, (1969).

23. Taneda, S., "Studies on Wake Vortices, Experimental Investigation of the Wake Behind a Sphere at Low Reynolds Numbers," Journal of the Physical Society of Japan, Vol. 1, (1956).

24. Chorin, A. J., "Computational Aspects of the Turbulence Problem," Proc. of the Second International Conference on Numerical Methods in Fluid Dynamics, held at Berkeley, California, U.S.A., Sept. 1970.

25. Daly, B. J. and Harlow, F. H., "Inclusion of Turbulence Effects in Numerical Fluid Dynamics," Proc. of the Second International Conference on Numerical Methods in Fluid Dynamics, held at Berkeley, California, U.S.A. Sept. 1970.

26. Orzag, S., "Numerical Simulation of Turbulence," (Fourier or Spectral Method), Proc. of Symposium on Statistical Models and Turbulence, held at San Diego, California, U.S.A., July 1971.

27. Ross, B. B. and Cheng, S. I., A Numerical Solution of the Planar Supersonic Near Wake with its Error Analysis," Proc. of the Second International Conference on Numerical Methods in Fluid Dynamics, held at Berkeley, California, Sept. 1970.

28. Carter, J. E., "The Navier-Stokes Equations for the Supersonic Laminar Flow over a Two-Dimensional Compression Corner," NASA TR R385, July 1972.

29. Cheng, S. I. and Chen, J. H., "Slips, Friction, and Heat Transfer Laws in Merged Regimes," to appear in The Physics of Fluids.

# VARIATIONAL PRINCIPLES IN FLUID MECHANICS and FINITE ELEMENT APPLICATIONS

B. FRAEIJS de VEUBEKE

Aeronautics Laboratory - University of Liège - Belgium

## TABLE OF CONTENTS

1. Eulerian and Lagrangian coordinates
2. Lagrangian and Eulerian variations
3. The Hamilton principle for an inviscid fluid
4. Derivation of an Eulerian principle
5. A self-supporting Eulerian variational principle
6. Elimination of the Lagrangian variation of position
7. The pressure integral
8. The particular case of incompressible flow
9. The vector potential
10. Orthogonality aspects of isochoric and irrotational flow
11. Bounding of the kinetic energy
12. Finite element implementation of the Rayleigh-Ritz processes
13. Variational principles for viscous flow
14. References

## 1. EULERIAN AND LAGRANGIAN COORDINATES

The fundamental theorems of classical mechanics deal with closed systems, that is fixed sets of material particles which are followed in their motion. In most problems of fluid mechanics, one is rather interested in the phenomena that occur in a fixed region of space traversed by the particles. This modification of point of view requires some essential transformations to the classical variational formulations of Hamiltonian dynamics.

By $a = (a_1, a_2, a_3)$ we denote generalized lagrangian or "material" coordinates identifying a particle. They may, but need not necessarily, represent the space coordinates $(x_1, x_2, x_3)$ occupied by the particle at a conventional epoch, usually denoted by $t = 0$. Their general définition is that of an independent set of integration constants of the differential equations of trajectories

$$\frac{dx_1}{u_1(x,t)} = \frac{dx_2}{u_2(x,t)} = \frac{dx_3}{u_3(x,t)} = dt \tag{1}$$

In this differential system, $u_i(x,t)$ is the velocity field of the particles expressed as a function of space location and time. Any set of three independent first integrals of (1)

$$a_i = a_i(x,t) \tag{2}$$

provides an implicit description at a regular point of the parametric equations of the trajectories of particles

$$x_j = X_j(a,t) \tag{3}$$

At a regular point in the field, the Jacobian determinant

$$J = \frac{D(x_1, x_2, x_3)}{D(a_1, a_2, a_3)}$$

is different from zero and the volume element containing the particles with material coordinates $\hat{a}_i$ in the set $a_i \leq \hat{a}_i \leq a_i + da_i$ is given by

$$d\Omega = J \, da_1 da_2 da_3 \tag{4}$$

The symbol $D_t$ is used to denote the material time derivative ; $D_i$ to denote the partial derivative with respect to the material coordinate $a_i$ under fixed time. Both are partial derivatives of any intensive variable of the field when expressed in the form of $f(a,t)$ and we have the commutative property

$$D_t D_i f = D_i D_t f.$$

Similarly $\partial_t$ will be the symbol of local time derivative; $\partial_j$ that of partial derivative with respect to $x_j$. Both are partial derivatives of intensive variable f when it is expressed in Eulerian form $f(x,t)$ and we have the commutative property

$$\partial_t \partial_j f = \partial_j \partial_t f.$$

In general, all transformations will be performed on the Eulerian description of variables and, for intensive variables, there follows from the definitions

$$D_t f = \partial_t f + \partial_j f \, D_t X_j$$

$$D_t X_j = \frac{\partial}{\partial t} X_j(a,t) = U_j(a,t) = u_j(x,t) \tag{5}$$

so that

$$D_t f = \partial_t f + u_j \partial_j f \tag{6}$$

In particular, since a material coordinate is attached to a particle throughout its motion

$$D_t a_i = \partial_t a_i + u_j \partial_j a_i = 0 \tag{7}$$

and (2) may also be considered to be a solution of the partial differential equation (7).

To compute the material time derivative of the volume element, consider the Laplace expansion of the Jacobian determinant

$$J = e_{mnp} D_m X_1 D_n X_2 D_p X_3$$

where use is made of the permutation symbol $e_{mnp}$.

$$D_t J = e_{mnp} (D_t D_m X_1 \, D_n X_2 \, D_p X_3 + D_m X_1 \, D_t D_n X_2 \, D_p X_3 + D_m X_1 \, D_n X_2 \, D_t D_p X_3)$$

However,

$$D_t D_m X_1 = D_m D_t X_1 = D_m U_1 = \partial_i u_1 D_m X_i$$

hence

$$e_{mnp} D_t D_m X_1 \, D_n X_2 \, D_p X_3 = \partial_i u_1 e_{mnp} D_m X_i \, D_n X_2 \, D_p X_3$$

$$= \partial_i u_1 \, e_{i23} J = (\partial_1 u_1) \, J$$

With a similar treatment of the other terms, ther finally comes

$$D_t J = (\partial_j u_j) \, J$$

or, in view of (4)

$$D_t \, d\Omega = (\partial_j u_j) \, d\Omega \qquad (8)$$

Formulas (6) and (8) funish a justification of the general statement about the material time derivative of any extensive quantity

$$D_t \int_\Omega f \, d\Omega = \int_\Omega D_t (f d\Omega) = \int_\Omega \{\partial_t f + u_j \partial_j f + f \, \partial_j u_j\} \, d\Omega$$

$$= \int_\Omega \{ \partial_t f + \partial_j(u_j f) \} \, d\Omega$$

or, after application of the divergence theorem

$$D_t \int_\Omega f \, d\Omega = \int_\Omega \partial_t f \, d\Omega + \int_{\partial\Omega} f(n_j u_j) \, dS \qquad (9)$$

where $n_j$ denote the direction cosines of the outward normal to the surface $\partial\Omega$ bounding the set of particles.

## 2. LAGRANGIAN AND EULERIAN VARIATIONS

The preceding reminder of well known results is useful in order to establish a complete analogy with similar conclusions relating material and local variations. In Hamiltonian mechanics the real motion of each particle is compared to perturbed or "varied" motions. We may, for instance, consider a family of virtual motions

$$x_j = X_j(a,t;\varepsilon) \qquad (10)$$

of which the real motion (3) would correspond to the value zero for the parameter . The material or Lagrangian variation of position of a particle can then be defined as

$$\Delta X_j = \frac{\partial}{\partial \varepsilon} X_j \bigg|_{\varepsilon=0} d\varepsilon \qquad (11)$$

Inversion of (10)

$$a_i = a_i(x,t;\varepsilon) \qquad (12)$$

leads naturally, for the material coordinates, to a concept of local or eulerian variation, in which the space coordinates are kept fixed

$$\delta a_i = \frac{\partial}{\partial \varepsilon} a_i \bigg|_{\varepsilon=0} d\varepsilon \qquad (13)$$

Since by definition $\delta x_j = 0$, we obtain from (10), considering a back-substitution of the material coordinates through (12),

$$\Delta X_j + \delta a_i \, D_i X_j = 0 \qquad (14)$$

Conversely, becouse $\Delta a_i = 0$ by definition,

$$\delta a_i + \Delta X_j \partial_j a_i = 0 \qquad (15)$$

which is the analogue to (7). Thus there is an equivalence by one to one correspondence between $\Delta X_j$ and $\delta a_i$; (14) and (15) are indeed the inverse relationships to one another, since for $\varepsilon = 0$

$$D_i X_j \partial_j a_m = \delta_{im} \qquad \partial_j a_i D_i X_m = \delta_{jm} \qquad (16)$$

More generally, the variations of an intensive variable $f(x,t;\varepsilon)$ are related by

$$\Delta f = \delta f + \Delta X_j \, \partial_j f \qquad (17)$$

which is the analogue of (6), or by

$$\delta f = \Delta f + \delta a_m \, D_m f$$

that follows immediately from its alternative representation as a function of $(a,t;\varepsilon)$.

Obviously, $\Delta$ commutes with $D_i$ and $D_t$, while $\delta$ commutes with $\partial_j$ and $\partial_t$. From a computation similar to that of $D_t J$, we obtain the analogue to (8)

$$\Delta J = (\partial_j \Delta X_j) \, J \qquad \text{or} \qquad \Delta d\Omega = (\partial_j \Delta X_j) \, d\Omega \qquad (18)$$

and finally, the analogue to (9)

$$\Delta \int_\Omega f d\Omega = \int_\Omega \delta f d\Omega + \int_{\partial\Omega} f(n_j \, \Delta x_j) \, dS \qquad (19)$$

The operators $\partial_t$ and $\delta$ keeping the space coordinates fixed, we have also

$$\partial_t d\Omega = 0 \qquad \qquad \delta d\Omega = 0 \tag{20}$$

## 3. THE HAMILTON PRINCIPLE FOR AN INVISCID FLUID

In Hamilton's principle the set of particles is kept fixed and must be followed throughout its motions, a fact that will be stressed in the formulas by writing $\Omega(t)$ and $\partial\Omega(t)$ for its volume and bounding surface. The Lagrangian per unit mass will be

$$L = \frac{1}{2} D_t X_i\, D_t X_i - U - G \tag{21}$$

where G is a gravitational potential, assumed to be a function of the space coordinates only $G(x)$, so that

$$g_j = -\partial_j G \tag{22}$$

is the local gravitational acceleration acting on a particle, and

$$\Delta G = -\partial_j G \Delta X_j \qquad \qquad \delta G = 0 \tag{23}$$

The specific internal energy U is in general a function of $\rho$, the mass per unit volume, and of the specific entropy S. To obtain a true variational principle, it will be necessary to make the assumption that there are no heat exchanges between the particles, nor momentum exchanges. Thus, neglecting conductivity and viscosity the entropy of each particle remains the same at any time. In addition we assume, for simplicity, that the entropy of each particle is the same (homentropic flow).
It is then possible to ignore entirely the dependence of U on S; the thermodynamical pressure becomes defined by

$$p(\rho) = \rho^2 \frac{dU}{d\rho} \tag{24}$$

and the fluid is barotropic.

after, again, a separate

$D_t(\rho d\Omega) = 0$

If due account is taken
yields the natural bound

$p = \bar{p}$      on    ∂

4. DERIVATION OF AN EULE

A step towards the de
consists in an applicati
Thus we must have

$$\int_{t_1}^{t_2} \int_{\Omega(t)} \delta(\rho L) d\Omega dt =$$

and in view of (25)

$$\int_{t_1}^{t_2} \int_{\Omega(t)} \delta(\rho L) d\Omega dt +$$

$$- \int$$

The correctness of this
exactly Eulerian in the
the motion of the volume
accounted for.

The difference betwee

$$\delta \int_{t_1}^{t_2} \int_\Omega \rho L d\Omega dt$$

Hamilton's principle asserts that

$$\Delta \int_{t_1}^{t_2} \int_{\Omega(t)} \rho L d\Omega dt - \int_{t_1}^{t_2} \int_{\partial_2 \Omega(t)} \bar{p}\, n_j\, \Delta X_j\, dS\, dt = 0 \tag{25}$$

provided $\Delta X_j = 0$ at $t = t_1$ and $t = t_2$. The second term represents the virtual work of a prescribed $\bar{p}$ in part $\partial_2 \Omega$ of the boungary.
On the complementary part $\partial_1 \Omega$ the fluid may be assumed to glide along a fixed or moving wall so that the constraint

$$n_j \Delta x_j = 0 \qquad \text{on} \qquad \partial_1 \Omega \tag{26}$$

must be applied independently.

As it is stated the principle does not take care of conservation of mass that is also to be entered as a side constraint

$$\Delta(\rho d\Omega) = 0 \qquad \text{or} \qquad \Delta\rho + (\partial_j \Delta x_j)\rho = 0 \tag{27}$$

This gives

$$\int_{t_1}^{t_2} \int_{\Omega(t)} \rho\, \Delta L\, d\Omega\, dt - \int_{t_1}^{t_2} \int_{\partial_2 \Omega(t)} \bar{p}\, n_j \Delta x_j\, dS\, dt = 0$$

Now, in view of (23) and (24)

$$\Delta L = D_t X_j\, D_t \Delta X_j - \frac{p}{\rho^2} \Delta\rho - \partial_j G\, \Delta X_j$$

is in the time integrations by parts which require the $\partial_t$ operator in the first case, the $D_t$ operator in the second. The terms requiring integration by parts in time in $\delta(\rho L)$ are

$$\rho u_i \delta (D_t X_i) \, d\Omega$$

We have from (17)

$$\delta D_t X_i = \Delta D_t X_i - \Delta X_j \partial_j u_i = D_t \Delta X_i - \Delta X_j \partial_j u_i$$

whence

$$\rho u_i \delta (D_t X_i) \, d\Omega = D_t (f \, d\Omega) - E_j \Delta X_j \, d\Omega \qquad (31)$$

where $\quad f = \rho u_i \Delta X_i$

and

$$E_j = \rho D_t u_j + \rho u_i \partial_j u_i \qquad (32)$$

Equation (31) is in the form required by the second case. It will generate two terms that vanish at the time limits and a contribution $-E_j$ to the Euler equation. If we now transform in (31)

$$D_t (f \, d\Omega) = (\partial_t f) \, d\Omega + \partial_j (u_j f) \, d\Omega$$

it follows that for the first case we generate again terms that vanish at the time limits, a surface term

$$\int_{t_1}^{t_2} \int_{\partial \Omega} (n_j u_j) \rho u_i \Delta X_i \, dS dt$$

and the same contribution to the Euler equation. As a consequence we do not alter the Euler equation by switching from the quasi-Eulerian functional to the really Eulerian one, that involves a fixed region $\Omega$ of space; but in so doing, we introduce a complicated combination of Lagrangian and Eulerian surface integrals. This is not surprising as the boundary conditions represented by free surfaces or moving walls are essentially Lagrangian by nature. In the sequel we must be satisfied with taking Eulerian variations of the Eulerian functional

$$\int_{t_1}^{t_2} \int_{\Omega} \rho L d\Omega dt \qquad \text{and fit whatever boundary conditions that are}$$

"natural" to the situation.

## 5. A SELF-SUPPORTING EULERIAN VARIATIONAL PRINCIPLE

To avoid the necessity of dealing separately with conservation of mass, the functional can be augmented by means of a Lagrangian multiplier to include the satisfaction of eq. (27) . This step was taken originally by Herivel (Ref. 4) but is known to be insufficient when the variations on particle displacement are transferred to material variations of the velocity field; it restricts the flow to the irrotational case.
A logical step to remove this restriction was taken by the author (Ref. 7) in 1965, it consists in augmenting the functional further by incorporating the constraints :

$$D_t X_i - u_i = 0 \qquad (33)$$

by means of a vector Lagrangian multiplier $\psi_i$. We thus examine the Eulerian variations of the new functional

$$\int_{t_1}^{t_2} \int_{\Omega} [\rho L + \theta(\partial_t \rho + \partial_i(\rho u_i)) + \rho \psi_i (D_t X_i - u_i)] \, d\Omega dt \qquad (34)$$

where L may now be written as

$$L = \frac{1}{2} u_i u_i - U(\rho) - G(x) \qquad (35)$$

and $\delta\rho$, $\delta\theta$, $\delta\psi_i$, $\delta u_i$, $\Delta X_i$ are independent variations.

The variations on the Lagrangian multipliers raise (27) and (33) to the status of Euler equations. If we collect the terms due to the variation of

$$(\frac{1}{2} u_i u_i - \frac{d}{d\rho}(\rho U) - G) \delta\rho + \theta \partial_t \delta\rho + \theta \partial_i (u_i \delta\rho) + \delta\rho \psi_i (D_t X_i - u_i),$$

take into consideration that (33) is satisfied and prepare the required integrations by parts

$$\partial_t (\theta \delta\rho) + \partial_i (\theta u_i \delta\rho) - \delta\rho (\frac{d}{d\rho}(\rho U) + \partial_t \theta + u_i \partial_i \theta + G - \frac{1}{2} u_i u_i)$$

we obtain as Euler equation

$$\delta\rho \rightarrow \qquad D_t \theta = \frac{1}{2} u_i u_i - G - \frac{d}{d\rho}(\rho U) \qquad (36)$$

The variation on $u_i$ alone generate the terms

$$\rho u_i \delta u_i + \theta \partial_i (\rho \delta u_i) - \rho \psi_i \delta u_i = \partial_i (\theta \rho \delta u_i) + \rho (u_i - \partial_i \theta - \psi_i) \delta u_i$$

and the corresponding Euler equations

$$\delta u_i \rightarrow \qquad u_i = \partial_i \theta + \psi_i \qquad (37)$$

For $\Delta X_i$ we must manipulate

$$\delta D_t X_i = \Delta D_t X_i - (\partial_j u_i) \Delta X_j = \partial_t \Delta X_i + u_j \partial_j \Delta X_i - (\partial_j u_i) \Delta X_j$$

generating the terms

$$\rho \psi_i \delta D_t X_i = \partial_t (\rho \psi_i \Delta X_i) - \partial_t (\rho \psi_i) \Delta X_i + \partial_j (\rho \psi_i u_j \Delta X_i) - \partial_j (\rho \psi_i u_j) \Delta X_i$$

$$- \rho \psi_j \partial_i u_j \Delta X_i$$

and obtain the Euler equation

$$\Delta X_i \rightarrow \qquad \partial_t (\rho \psi_i) + \partial_j (\rho \psi_i u_j) + \rho \psi_j \partial_i u_j = 0$$

In view of (29) this simplifies to

$$\Delta X_i \rightarrow \quad D_t \psi_i + \psi_j \partial_i u_j = 0 \qquad (38)$$

From the various contributions we can also derive the following integral at the time limits

$$\int_\Omega (\theta \delta \rho + \rho \psi_i \Delta X_i) d\Omega \Bigg|_{t_1}^{t_2}$$

and the surface terms related to possible boundary conditions

$$\int_{t_1}^{t_2} \int_{\partial \Omega} (\theta(u_i n_i)\delta\rho + \rho\theta(n_i \delta u_i) + \rho(n_j u_j)\psi_i \Delta X_i) \, dS \, dt$$

They will be discussed later, after elimination of the only remaining Lagrangian variation $\Delta X_i$.

It should be observed that none of the Euler equations correspond directly to the Newtonian equations of motion. They are, however, contained as combinations. First of all, we find from (24)

$$\frac{d}{d\rho}(\rho U) = U + \rho \frac{dU}{d\rho} = U + \frac{p}{\rho} = I(\rho) \qquad (39)$$

the specific enthalpy considered as a function of $\rho$. If we then take the material derivative of (37) and eliminate $\psi_i$ by using (38), there comes

$$D_t(u_i - \partial_i \theta) + (u_j - \partial_j \theta)\partial_i u_j = D_t u_i - (\partial_t + u_j \partial_j)\partial_i \theta - \partial_j \theta \partial_i u_j$$

$$+ \partial_i \frac{u_j u_j}{2} = D_t u_i - \partial_i D_t \theta + \partial_i \frac{u_j u_j}{2} = 0$$

or, finally, using (36)

$$D_t u_i + \partial_i (I+G) = 0 \qquad (40)$$

which is a classical form of the equations of motion.

## 6. ELIMINATION OF THE LAGRANGIAN VARIATION OF POSITION

To eliminate the use of $\Delta X_i$ we must solve the corresponding Euler equations (38) and substitute solution into the functional. Equation (38) states that the $\psi_i$ field is a constant circulation one; on any small segment $dx_i$ carried by the particles the circulation of $\psi_i$ does depend on time :

$$D_t (\psi_i dx_i) = 0 \qquad (41)$$

Indead, this is equivalent to

$$D_t\psi_i dx_i + \psi_j D_t dx_j = D_t\psi_i dx_i + \psi_j dD_t X_j = D_t\psi_i dx_i + \psi_j du_j$$

$$= dx_i (D_t\psi_i + \psi_j \partial_i u_j) = 0$$

Equation (41) indicates that the Pfaffian form $\psi_i dx_i$ depends only on material coordinates. In any of its canonical representations

$$\psi_i dx_i = d\gamma + \alpha d\beta \qquad (42)$$

the variables $\alpha, \beta, \gamma$ are material variables :

$$D_t \gamma = 0 \qquad D_t \alpha = 0 \qquad D_t \beta = 0 \qquad (43)$$

From (42) follows then the general solution of (38)

$$\psi_i = \partial_i \gamma + \alpha \partial_i \beta \qquad (44)$$

and this, substitued into (37) yields the general Clebsch representation (Ref. 1) of the rotational flow of an inviscid fluid :

$$u_i = \partial_i \phi + \alpha \partial_i \beta \qquad (45)$$

where $\phi = \theta+\gamma$ is a velocity potential and $\alpha$ and $\beta$ are material variables. If the potential $\phi$ is single-valued the velocity field retains the constant circulation property for closed contours carried by the flow. Moreover

$$\text{rot } \vec{u} = \text{grad}\alpha \times \text{grad}\beta \tag{46}$$

and we have the statement that the vortex lines which are the intersections of the surface families $\alpha = $ constant and $\beta = $ constant, are carried by the flow. The constant circulation property indicates the existence of an acceleration potential, indeed,

$$D_t u_i = \partial_t(\partial_i\phi + \alpha\partial_i\beta) + u_j\partial_j(\partial_i\phi + \alpha\partial_i\beta)$$

$$= \partial_i(\partial_t\phi + \alpha\partial_t\beta) + \partial_t\alpha\partial_i\beta - \partial_i\alpha\partial_t\beta + u_j\partial_i(\partial_j\phi + \alpha\partial_j\beta)$$

$$+ u_j\partial_j\alpha\partial_i\beta - u_j\partial_i\alpha\partial_j\beta$$

$$= \partial_i(\partial_t\phi + \alpha\partial_t\beta + \frac{u_j u_j}{2}) + \partial_i\beta D_t\alpha - \partial_i\alpha D_t\beta$$

and the two last terms vanish by (43). With this result and (40), we obtain the generalized Bernoulli integral of the equations of motion

$$\partial_t\phi + \alpha\partial_t\beta + \frac{u_j u_j}{2} + I + G = h(t) \tag{47}$$

Since the potential $\phi$ contains an arbitrary additive function of time only, there is no restriction in making $h(t) = 0$.

To eliminate $\Delta X_i$ replace in (34)

$$\psi_i D_t X_i = (\partial_i\gamma + \alpha\partial_i\beta)D_t X_i = D_t\gamma - \partial_t\gamma + \alpha(D_t\beta - \partial_t\beta) = -(\partial_t\gamma + \alpha\partial_t\beta)$$

Then

$$\rho\psi_i(D_t X_i - u_i) = -\rho(\partial_t\gamma + \alpha\partial_t\beta) - \rho u_i(\partial_i\gamma + \alpha\partial_i\beta)$$

If in addition we transform

$$\theta\{\partial_t \rho + \partial_i(\rho u_i)\} = \partial_t(\rho\theta) + \partial_i(\theta\rho u_i) - \rho\partial_t\theta - \rho u_i \partial_i \theta$$

the two contributions combine into

$$\theta\{\partial_t \rho + \partial_i(\rho u_i)\} + \rho\psi_i(D_t X_i - u_i) = \partial_t(\rho\theta) + \partial_i(\theta\rho u_i) - \rho D_t \phi - \rho\alpha D_t \beta$$

Thus discarding the term that goes to time limits and the divergence term, we obtain a functional

$$\int_{t_1}^{t_2} \int_\Omega \rho K d\Omega dt$$

$$K = \frac{1}{2} u_i u_i - U - G - D_t \phi - \alpha D_t \beta \qquad (D_t = \partial_t + u_i \partial_i) \qquad (48)$$

The Eulerian variation of this functional yields the following Euler equations :

$$\delta\rho \rightarrow \frac{u_i u_i}{2} - I - G - D_t \phi - \alpha D_t \beta = 0 \qquad (49)$$

$$\delta u_i \rightarrow \rho(u_i - \partial_i \phi - \alpha \partial_i \beta) = 0 \qquad (50)$$

$$\delta\phi \rightarrow \partial_t \rho + \partial_i(\rho u_i) = 0 \qquad (51)$$

$$\delta\alpha \rightarrow D_t \beta = 0 \qquad (52)$$

$$\delta\beta \rightarrow \partial_t(\rho\alpha) + \partial_i(\rho\alpha u_i) = 0 \qquad (53)$$

The last being equivalent to $D_t \alpha = 0$ in view of (51).
The time limits term is

$$-\int_\Omega \rho(\delta\phi + \alpha\delta\beta) d\Omega \, \Big|_{t_1}^{t_2}$$

and can be deleted under the vonvention that the variations on $\alpha$ and $\beta$

vanish for $t = t_1$ and $t = t_2$.

The surface terms are

$$-\int_{t_1}^{t_2}\int_{\partial\Omega} \rho(\delta\phi + \alpha\delta\beta)(n_i u_i)\, dS\, dt$$

The simpler boundary condition is that of a fixed wall. Freedom in the variations of either $\phi$ or $\beta$ at such a boundary wall will give the corresponding requirement $n_i u_i = 0$ as a natural boundary condition. If a normal velocity $(n_i \overline{u_i})$ is imposed at a part $\partial_1\Omega$ of the boundary we add to the functional the term

$$\int_{t_1}^{t_2}\int_{\partial_1\Omega} \rho\phi(n_i u_i)\, dS\, dt$$

and the free variation of $\phi$ will impose $n_i u_i = n_i \overline{u_i}$ on $\partial_1\Omega$. The free variation on $\rho$ in this additional term will cause $\phi = 0$ on the same boundary.

## 7. THE PRESSURE INTEGRAL

Consider the energy per unit volume

$$f(\rho) = \rho U(\rho)$$

The variable conjugate to $\rho$ is by definition

$$\frac{df}{d\rho} = U + \frac{p}{\rho} = I$$

A co-energy is then defined as in elasticity theory by the Legendre transformation

$$\rho I - f = \rho(I-U) = p(I) \tag{54}$$

and turns out to be the pressure to be considered as a function of the enthalpy. Differentiation of (54) produces then the involutory of conjugate variables

$$\rho dI = dp \tag{55}$$

Precisely, when (49) is used to eliminate the consideration of  as a variable, the Kernel of the functional reduces to

$$\rho K = \rho(I-U) = p$$

We obtain one of Bateman's Eulerian variational principles (Ref. 3), the so-called pressure integral

$$\int_{t_1}^{t_2} \int_\Omega p(I) d\Omega\, dt \tag{56}$$

in which the enthalpy must be considered to be expressed through (49) as

$$I = -\frac{u_i u_i}{2} - G - D_t \phi - \alpha D_t \beta \tag{57}$$

From (55) and (57) there comes

$$\delta p = \frac{dp}{dI} \delta I = \rho(u_i \delta u_i - \delta D_t \phi - \delta \alpha D_t \beta - \alpha \delta D_t \beta)$$

and the Eulerian equations are still given by (50), (51), (52) and (53); nothing is changed concerning the time limit and surface terms.

The pressure integral can be further simplified by accepting a priori the Euler equation (50). Hence substituting the Clebsch representation

$$u_i = \partial_i \phi + \alpha \partial_i \beta$$

we obtain the pressure integral (56) with the enthalpy given this time by

$$I = -(\frac{1}{2}(\partial_i \phi + \alpha \partial_i \beta)(\partial_i \phi + \alpha \partial_i \beta) + G + \partial_t \phi + \alpha \partial_t \beta) \tag{58}$$

as would result from the generalized Bernouilli integral (47).

This principle depends only on the potential $\phi$ and the Lagrangian variables of the Clebsch representation. Their variations produce the Euler equations (51), (52) and (53); again the time limits and surface terms are unaltered.

The principle has received a good deal of attention in the problem of the perturbation of a uniform flow of a compressible fluid by aerodynamic bodies. Using a pressure coefficient

$$P = \frac{p - p_\infty}{\frac{1}{2}\rho_\infty U^2}$$

in place of the pressure itself; introducing the Mach number

$$M = \frac{U}{a_\infty} \qquad \text{with } a_\infty^2 = \gamma \frac{p_\infty}{\rho_\infty}$$

and the variable

$$Z = \frac{I_\infty - I}{U^2}$$

instead of the enthalpy itself, the relationships

$$I - I_\infty = c_p(T - T_\infty) \qquad \text{and} \qquad \frac{p}{p_\infty} = \left(\frac{T}{T_\infty}\right)^{\frac{\gamma}{\gamma-1}}$$

of gas dynamics yield the explicit law

$$P = \frac{2}{\gamma M^2}\left[(1-(\gamma-1)M^2 Z)^{\frac{\gamma}{\gamma-1}} - 1\right] \tag{59}$$

While, if the flow depends only on the potential $\phi$, and a perturbation potential $\eta$ of the uniform flow along $x_1$ be introduced by

$$\phi = U(x_1 + \eta)$$

$$Z = \partial_1 \eta + \frac{1}{U}\partial_t \eta + \frac{1}{2}\partial_i \eta \partial_i \eta \tag{60}$$

An approximate determination of the perturbation potential is possible by application of the Rayleigh-Ritz method via the variational principle

$$\delta \int_{t_1}^{t_2} \int_{\Omega} \left[ (1-(\gamma-1)M^2 Z)^{\frac{\gamma}{\gamma-1}} - 1 \right] d\Omega \, dt = 0$$

with Z given by (60). The principle is also useful as a theoretical tool for delivering coherent approximations to the field equation governing the perturbation potential and its boundary conditions, by assuming small pressure and velocity perturbations and expanding the Kernel by the binomial theorem.

## 8. THE PARTICULAR CASE OF INCOMPRESSIBLE FLOW

Incompressible flow is an idealized case where the pressure is no more of thermodynamical origin but constitutes a purely mechanical reaction against changes of volume. One can, however, consider it as a limiting case of the enthalpy formula through (55) since then

$$I = \int \frac{dp}{\rho} = \frac{p}{\rho}$$

and $\frac{p}{\rho}$ is sometimes called the specific pressure energy.

Thus the general pressure formulation applies here in the form (56) with

$$p = \rho \left( \frac{u_i u_i}{2} - G - D_t \phi - \alpha D_t \beta \right) \tag{61}$$

There is no loss in generality in dropping the constant factor $\rho$ in the Kernel of the principle. It will also be observed that G plays no role in the variational equations and may be dropped in the Kernel that becomes:

$$\delta \int_{t_1}^{t_2} \int_{\Omega} \left( \frac{u_i u_i}{2} - D_t \phi - \alpha D_t \beta \right) d\Omega \, dt = 0 \tag{62}$$

However, G retains its role as additional hydrostatic pressure when the pressure is computed from (61) after the potential and Lagrangian functions have been determined.

Consider now the very special case of stationary potential flow of an incompressible inviscid fluid. The assumptions can be summarized in

$$\partial_t \vec{u} = 0 \qquad \text{rot } \vec{u} = 0 \qquad \text{div } \vec{u} = 0$$

and the problem is almost purely grometrical in nature.
Because of the stationarity assumption, the time integral may be dropped in the variational principle. The second assumption allows to retain only $\phi$, and (62) degenerates into

$$\int_\Omega (u_i \partial_i \phi - \frac{u_i u_i}{2}) d\Omega - \int_{\partial_2 \Omega} \phi \overline{u_\nu} \, dS - \int_{\partial_1 \Omega} (n_i u_i)(\phi - \overline{\phi}) dS$$

$$\begin{array}{c|c} \min & \max \\ \phi & u_i \end{array} \qquad (63)$$

The sign of the functional has been changed and surface terms added to provide for natural boundary conditions throughout.
Those and the Euler equations are in fact

$$\delta u_i \quad \text{in } \Omega \quad \rightarrow \quad u_i = \partial_i \phi$$

$$\delta u_i \quad \text{on } \partial_1 \Omega \quad \rightarrow \quad \phi = \overline{\phi}$$

which is equivalent to the imposition of the velocity components tangent to this boundary,

$$\delta \phi \quad \text{in } \Omega \quad \rightarrow \quad \partial_i u_i = 0$$

$$\delta \phi \quad \text{on } \partial_2 \Omega \quad \rightarrow \quad n_i u_i = \overline{u}_\nu$$

the imposition of the velocity component normal to this boundary.

Principle (63) is in the so-called canonical (in the sense of Hamilton) or involutory form advocated by Friedrchs and whose analogue in elasticity theory is better known under the name of Reissner. It is a saddle point principle in which, after looking for a maximizing choice of the velocity field under a given potential, one looks after the minimum of all those maxima for the choice of the potential.

From it, two simpler single-field principles may be derived, whose dual character enables the kinetic energy estimates of the flow, obtained from Rayleigh-Ritz approximations, to be bounded from below and from above respectively.

The first is obtained by accepting a priori the potential character of the flow. If we add to this the a priori satisfaction of $\phi = \bar{\phi}$ on $\partial_1\Omega$, we obtain

$$\int_\Omega \frac{1}{2} \partial_i\phi \partial_i\phi \, d\Omega - \int_{\partial_2\Omega} \phi \, \bar{u}_\nu \, dS \qquad \min_\phi \qquad (64)$$

and the principle accounts simply for the incompressibility condition

$$\partial_i u_i = \partial_i \partial_i \phi = 0$$

and for the boundary conditions on $\partial_2\Omega$.

If, on the contraty, we want to simplify (63) by a priori satisfaction of the incompressibility condition plus the boundary condition in $\partial_2\Omega$, it becomes necessary to transform the functional by an integration by parts :

$$-\int_\Omega (\phi \partial_i u_i + \frac{u_i u_i}{2}) \, d\Omega + \int_{\partial_2\Omega} \phi(n_i u_i - \bar{u}_\nu) \, dS + \int_{\partial_1\Omega} n_i u_i \phi \, dS$$

Accepting now a priori the constraints

$$\partial_i u_i = 0 \quad \text{and} \quad n_i u_i = \bar{u}_\nu \quad \text{on} \quad \partial_2\Omega$$

we obtain the dual single-field principle (the sign has again be changed)

$$\int_\Omega \frac{1}{2} u_i u_i \, d\Omega - \int_{\partial_1\Omega} n_i u_i \bar{\phi} \, dS \qquad \begin{array}{c} \min \\ u_i \text{ constrained} \end{array} \qquad (65)$$

## 9. THE VECTOR POTENTIAL

The implementation of the incompressibility constraint on the $u_i$ field calls naturally for the use of a vector potential $\vec{A}$ :

$$\vec{u} = \text{rot } \vec{A} \rightarrow \text{div } \vec{u} = 0 \tag{66}$$

but introduces interpretation difficulties for the boundary terms. For this reason we carry out the required transformations on (63) instead of (65). Since the use of a vector potential

$$u_i = e_{ipq} \partial_p A_q$$

automatically entails $\partial_i u_i = 0$, the functional in (63) may already be transformed to

$$-\int_\Omega \frac{u_i u_i}{2} d\Omega + \int_{\partial_2 \Omega} \phi(n_i u_i - \bar{u}_\nu) dS + \int_{\partial_1 \Omega} \bar{\phi} n_i u_i dS$$

Or, with the understanding that $\phi = \bar{\phi}$ on $\partial_1 \Omega$,

$$-\int_\Omega \frac{u_i u_i}{2} d\Omega + \int_{\partial\Omega} \phi n_i u_i dS - \int_{\partial_2 \Omega} \phi \bar{u}_\nu dS$$

The free variation $\delta\phi$ on $\partial_2 \Omega$ produces the natural boundary condition

$$\vec{n} \cdot \vec{u} = \bar{u}_\nu \qquad \text{on } \partial_2 \Omega,$$

The variation $\delta u_i = e_{ipq} \partial_p \delta A_q$ gives

$$-\int_\Omega \delta\vec{A} \cdot \text{rot } \vec{u} \, d\Omega - \int_{\partial\Omega} n u_i e_{ipq} \delta A_q dS + \int_{\partial\Omega} \phi n_i e_{ipq} \partial_p \delta A_q dS = 0$$

The Euler equation is obviously rot $\vec{u} = 0$, as was to be expected. The last term, that contains derivatives of the variations of the vector potential, is transformed as follows :

$$\int_{\partial\Omega} \phi \vec{n} \cdot \text{rot } \delta\vec{A} \, dS = \int_{\partial\Omega} \vec{n} \cdot \text{rot}(\phi \delta \vec{A}) \, dS - \int_{\partial\Omega} \vec{n} \cdot (\text{grad}\phi \times \delta A) \, dS$$

where, on account of

$$\vec{n} \cdot (\text{grad}\phi \times \delta\vec{A}) = \delta\vec{A} \cdot (\vec{n} \times \text{grad}\phi)$$

the scalar potential has only to be defined on the surface.

As $\int_{\partial\Omega} \vec{n} \cdot \text{rot}\,(\phi\delta\vec{A})\,dS = 0$, we finally obtain for the surface terms

$$\int_{\partial\Omega} \delta\vec{A} \cdot [\vec{n} \times (\vec{u} - \text{grad}\phi)]\,dS = 0 \qquad \text{with } \phi = \bar{\phi} \text{ on } \partial_1\Omega$$

The boundary conditions are thus finally obtained in the form

$$\vec{n} \times \vec{u} = \vec{n} \times \text{grad}\bar{\phi} \qquad \text{on} \qquad \partial_1\Omega$$

$$\vec{n} \cdot \vec{u} = \bar{u}_\nu \qquad \text{on} \qquad \partial_2\Omega$$

## 10. ORTHOGONALITY ASPECTS OF ISOCHORIC AND IRROTATIONAL FLOW

Consider on the one hand an irrotational flow described by a scalar potential :

$$u_i = \partial_i \phi \quad \rightarrow \quad \text{rot}\,\vec{u} = 0$$

on the other hand, and isochoric flow, described by a vector potential :

$$v_i = e_{ipq} \partial_p A_q \quad \rightarrow \quad \text{div}\,\vec{v} = \partial_i v_i = 0$$

and define a scalar product between the two as

$$(u,v) = \int_\Omega u_i v_i\,d\Omega$$

From a first type of integration by parts

$$(u,v) = \int_\Omega v_i \partial_i \phi\,d\Omega = \int_{\partial\Omega} \phi n_i v_i\,dS - \int_\Omega \phi \partial_i v_i\,d\Omega = \int_{\partial\Omega} \phi n_i v_i\,dS \qquad (67)$$

It is apparent that this scalar product vanishes if the bounding surface is subdivised in parts :

$$\partial_1\Omega \qquad \text{over which} \qquad \phi = 0$$

$\partial_2 \Omega$     over which     $n_i v_i = \vec{n}.\text{rot } \vec{A} = 0$

The second type of integration by parts

$$(u,v) = \int_\Omega u_i e_{ipq} \partial_p A_q d\Omega = \int_{\partial\Omega} n_p u_i e_{ipq} A_q dS + \int_\Omega \vec{A}.\text{rot } \vec{u} \, d\Omega \text{ , or}$$

$$(u,v) = -\int_{\partial\Omega} \vec{A} \, (\vec{n}\times\vec{u}) \, dS = +\int_{\partial\Omega} \vec{u}.(\vec{n}\times\vec{A}) \, dS \tag{68}$$

leads to the same conclusions. On $\partial_1\Omega$ the imposition of $\phi = 0$ is equivalent to the requirement $\vec{n}\times\vec{u} = 0$. On $\partial_2\Omega$ the requirement $\vec{n}.\text{rot } \vec{A} \neq 0$ is satisfied by the somewhat stronger one $\vec{n}\times\vec{A} = 0$.

The equivalence between the two surface integrals to which the scalar product reduces follows also from the general statement

$$\int_\Omega \text{div rot } \vec{B} \, d\Omega = \int_{\partial\Omega} \vec{n}.\text{rot } \vec{B} \, dS = 0$$

with $\vec{B} = \phi A$

This gives indeed, from

$$\text{rot}(\phi\vec{A}) = \phi \text{ rot } \vec{A} + \text{grad}\phi \times \vec{A}$$

the result

$$\int_\Omega \phi \vec{n}.\text{rot } \vec{A} \, dS = \int_{\partial\Omega} \text{grad } \phi.(\vec{n}\times\vec{A}) \, dS \tag{69}$$

The orthogonality property is thus found to hold between an irrotational flow, whose tangential velocity component vanishes on $\partial_1\Omega$ and isochoric flow whose normal velocity component vanishes on the complementary part $\partial_2\Omega$.

## 11. BOUNDING OF THE KINETIC ENERGY

Consider a flow that is both irrotational and isochoric and satisfies non homogeneous boundary conditions on $\partial_1\Omega$, where the tangential velocity component is specified, and $\partial_2\Omega$ where the normal component is specified.

In keeping with the preceding section, denote by u an irrotational flow that satisfies the homogeneous condition on $\partial_1\Omega$ (no tangential velocity) but is left unspecified on $\partial_2\Omega$, while $u_o$ denotes any particular irrotational flow complying with the non homogeneous data on $\partial_1\Omega$.

Similarly, v will denote any isochoric flow satisfying the homogeneous condition on $\partial_2\Omega$ (no normal velocity component) and without specification on $\partial_1\Omega$, while $v_o$ will denote any particular isochoric flow satisfying the non homogeneous data on $\partial_2\Omega$. We then find

$$(u_o,v) = \int_{\partial_1\Omega} \overline{\phi\,(\vec{n}.\text{rot}\,\vec{A})}\,dS = +\int_{\partial_1\Omega} \overline{\vec{A}.(\vec{n}\times\text{grad}\phi)}\,dS \qquad (70)$$

$$(u,v) = \int_{\partial_2\Omega} \overline{\phi\,\vec{u}\cdot\vec{v}}\,dS = -\int_{\partial_2\Omega} \overline{\text{grad}\phi.(\vec{n}\times\vec{A})}\,dS \qquad (71)$$

In approximating the flow by a numerical analysis of Rayleigh-Ritz type, we may either consider the irrotational flow to contain adjustable parameters in u to satisfy in some best sense the incompressibility condition and the boundary data on $\partial_2\Omega$, or the isochoric flow to contain adjustable parameters in v to satisfy in some best sense the irrotationality condition and the boundary data on $\partial_1\Omega$.

Both viewpoints are combined in the requirement that the squared "distance" between the two adjustable fields by minimized:

$$(u+u_o-v-v_o,\ u+u_o-v-v_o) = (u+u_o,u+u_o)+(v+v_o,v+v_o)-2(u+u_o,v+v_o)$$
$$\text{minimum}$$

Because of the orthogonality property $(u,v) = 0$, this condition naturally splits into the two independant requirements

$$(u+u_o,u+u_o) - 2(u,v_o) \qquad \underset{u}{\text{minimum}} \qquad (72)$$

$$(v+v_o,v+v_o) - 2(v,u_o) \qquad \underset{v}{\text{minimum}} \qquad (73)$$

The term $-2(u_o,v_o)$ has been dropped as constant.

Now $u + u_o$ is the potential flow $u_i = \partial_i \phi$ where $\phi = \bar{\phi}$ as specified on $\partial_1 \Omega$, and the first requirement is identical to our previous variational principle (64) :

$$\frac{1}{2} \int_\Omega \partial_i \phi \partial_i \phi d\Omega - \int_{\partial_2 \Omega} \phi \, \overline{u_\nu} \, dS \qquad \text{minimum}$$

Similarly, $v + v_o$ is the isochoric flow $\vec{v} = \text{rot } \vec{A}$ where $\vec{n}.\text{rot } \vec{A} = \overline{u_\nu}$ is specified on $\partial_2 \Omega$, and the second requirement is identical to the irrotational principle (65) implemented by a vector potential

$$\frac{1}{2} \int_\Omega \text{rot } \vec{A} \text{ rot } \vec{A} \, d\Omega - \int_{\partial_1 \Omega} \bar{\phi} \, (\vec{n}.\text{rot } \vec{A}) \, dS \qquad \text{minimum}$$

We obtain a bounding of the kinetic energy of the flow by considering the separate problems :

Problem 1 : The data specified on $\partial_1 \Omega$ are non homogeneous ($u_o \neq 0$) but homogeneous on $\partial_2 \Omega$ ($v_o = 0$)

Problem 2 : The complementary problem : $u_o = 0$, $v_o \neq 0$.

We may note that the general problem can always be handled by linear superposition of problems 1 and 2.

In problem 1 we must find the best approximations to

$$(u + u_o, u + u_o) \qquad \text{minimum} \tag{74}$$

$$(v,v) - 2(v,u_o) \qquad \text{minimum} \tag{75}$$

Set $u = \sum_1^n \alpha_j u_j$

where each $u_j$ field is generated by an assumed potential that is zero on $\partial_1 \Omega$. The best coefficients $\hat{\alpha}_j$ are given by equating to zero the partial derivatives of the quadratic form

$$(u,u) + 2(u,u_o) = \Sigma\Sigma \alpha_j \alpha_k (u_j, u_k) + 2\Sigma \, \alpha_j (u_j, u_o)$$

Thus

$$\sum \hat{\alpha}_k (u_j, u_k) + (u_j, u_o) = 0 \qquad j = 1, 2, \ldots n$$

Denoting by

$$\hat{u} = u_o + \sum \hat{\alpha}_k u_k$$

The best approximation, those equations are equivalent to

$$(\hat{u}_j, \hat{u}) = 0 \qquad j = 1, 2, \ldots, n$$

Multiplying each by its coefficient $\hat{\alpha}_j$ and summing

$$(\hat{u} - u_o, \hat{u}) = 0 \qquad \text{or} \quad (\hat{u}, \hat{u}) = (\hat{u}, u_o) \tag{76}$$

The exact solution s, which is both irrotational and isochoric satisfies the similar equation

$$(s, s) = (s, u_o) \tag{77}$$

Indeed, s is both a v-type field ($v_o = 0$) and simultaneously $s - u_o$ is a u-type field, so that $(s-u_o, s) = 0$ by orthogonality.
Furthermore, since the minimum in (74) is not necessarily reached,

$$(\hat{u}, \hat{u}) \geq (s, s) \tag{78}$$

We can give a similar treatment to

$$v = \sum_{1}^{n} \beta_j v_j$$

each $v_j$ field being generated by a vector potential such that $\vec{n} \cdot \text{rot} \vec{A} = 0$ on $\partial_2 \Omega$.

$$(v, v) - 2(v, u_o) = \sum\sum \beta_j \beta_k (v_j, v_k) - 2\sum \beta_j (v_j, u_o) \quad \text{minimum}$$

furnishes the linear system

$$\Sigma \hat{\beta}_k (v_j, v_k) - (v_j, u_o) = 0$$

or with $\hat{v} = \Sigma \hat{\beta}_k v_k$, the best approximation,

$$(v_j, \hat{v}) - (v_j, u_o) = 0 \qquad\qquad j = 1, 2, \ldots, n$$

Multiplying by each $\hat{\beta}_j$ and adding

$$(\hat{v}, \hat{u}) - (\hat{v}, u_o) = 0 \tag{79}$$

Since the minimum of (75) is not necessarily reached

$$(\hat{v}, \hat{v}) - 2(\hat{v}, u_o) \geq (s,s) - 2(s, u_o)$$

This inequality is transformed by (79) and (77) into

$$- (\hat{v}, \hat{v}) \geq - (s,s)$$

and this result combined with (78) gives the kinetic energy bounding

$$(\hat{v}, \hat{v}) \leq (s,s) \leq (\hat{u}, \hat{u}) \tag{80}$$

A similar treatment of Problem 2 yields the reverse bounding

$$(\hat{u}, \hat{u}) \leq (s,s) \leq (\hat{v}, \hat{v}) \tag{81}$$

where $\hat{u} = \Sigma \hat{\alpha}_j u_j$ and $\hat{v} = v_o + \Sigma \hat{\beta}_j v_j$

## 12. FINITE ELEMENT IMPLEMENTATION OF THE RAYLEIGH-RITZ PROCESSES

The simply connected region $\Omega$ is divided into adjacent subdomains $\Omega_\alpha$, the so-called finite elements. Any integral extended over the whole region is understood to be the sum of integrals over the $\Omega_\alpha$. Whenever an integration by parts is applied, the boundary terms involve the whole set of boundaries $\partial\Omega_\alpha$ of each subdomain and can be regrouped as a sum of integrals covering the external boundary $\partial\Omega$ of $\Omega$ and a sum of integrals involving the two faces of interfaces $I_\beta$ of the subdomains

$$\sum_\alpha \int_{\partial\Omega_\alpha} n_i f_i dS = \int_{\partial\Omega} n_i f_i dS + \sum_\beta \int_{I_\beta} n_i (f_i^+ - f_i^-) dS$$

In the last terms the convention is adopted that the normal $n_i$ to the interface is that of one of its faces, denoted by the superscript +. Since for outward normals

$$n_i^- = -n_i^+ = -n_i$$

the minus sign of the contribution of the other face is understood.

Consider a first subdivision into finite elements, in each of which a scaler potential $\phi_\alpha$ is defined, usually in the form of a complete polynomial of chosen degree with unknown coefficients. The transition conditions to be satisfied at the interfaces can be found by examination of the orthogonality condition, generalizing (67)

$$(u,v) = \sum \int_{\Omega_\alpha} v_i \partial_i \phi_\alpha \, d\Omega = -\sum \int_{\Omega_\alpha} \phi_\alpha \partial_i v_i d\Omega + \int_{\partial\Omega} \phi_\alpha n_i v_i dS +$$

$$+ \sum \int_{I_\beta} n_i (\phi_\alpha^+ v_i^+ - \phi_\alpha^- v_i^-) dS$$

To obtain orthogonality with an isochoric flow ($\partial_i v_i = 0$) satisfying $n_i v_i = 0$ on the part $\partial_2 \Omega$ of the outer boundary, while $\phi_\alpha = 0$ on $\partial_1 \Omega$, we must still ensure that at the interfaces

$$\sum \int_{I_\beta} n_i (\phi_\alpha^+ v_i^+ - \phi_\alpha^- v_i^-) dS = 0$$

This must hold in particular for a continuous isochoric flow, hence $v_i^+ = v_i^-$ at the interfaces and

$$\sum \int_{I_\beta} n_i v_i (\phi_\alpha^+ - \phi_\alpha^-) dS = 0$$

It is thus sufficient, although admittedly not necessary, that there be continuity of the scalar potentials at the interfaces. It turns out that in the case of complete polynomials, it is extremely easy to enforce the interface continuity conditions, both in 2 and 3 dimensions. For the two-dimensional case, taking triangular finite elements, the coefficients of the polynomial defining the scalar potential inside can be determined in terms of local values of the potential at the vertices and along the sides, plus, as turns out ot be the case for degrees higher or equal to 3, at some interior points. If, at an interface, the local values of the potentials $\phi^+$ and $\phi^-$ coincide, the potentials coincide along the whole interface.

Similarly, for the same or another subdivision into finite elements, for each of which a vector potential is assigned containing unknown coefficients, the transition conditions follow from (68)

$$(u,v) = \Sigma \int_{\Omega_\alpha} \vec{u}.\text{rot } \vec{A}_\alpha \, d\Omega = \Sigma \int_{\Omega_\alpha} \vec{A}_\alpha.\text{rot } \vec{u} \, d\Omega - \int_{\partial\Omega} \vec{A}.(\vec{n}\times\vec{u}) \, dS + \Sigma \int_{I_\beta} (\vec{A}.(\vec{n}\times\vec{u})^+ + \vec{A}.(\vec{n}\times\vec{u})^-) dS$$

To obtain orthogonality with an irrotational flow (rot $\vec{u}$ = 0) satisfying $\vec{n}\times\vec{u}$ = 0 on part $\partial_1\Omega$ of the outer boundary, while $\vec{A}_\alpha$ = 0 on part $\partial_2\Omega$, it is sufficient to have continuity of the vector potential at the interfaces.

Again, this is quite easily implemented for polynomial approximations of the vector potential. Here in the two-dimensional cases of plane flow or axisymetric flow, a scalar stream function replaces the vector potential.

## 13. VARIATIONAL PRINCIPLES FOR VISCOUS FLOW

There are no true variational principles yielding as Euler equations the Navier-Stokes general equations. There is, however, a principle that governs the dissipation in steady state flow for cases of such low Reynolds numbers that the acceleration terms are negligible. Limiting ourselves to incompressible fluids, the dissipation

$$F = \mu \theta_{ij} \theta_{ij}$$

$$\theta_{ij} = \frac{1}{2}(\partial_i u_j + \partial_j u_i)$$

and the functional yielding the equations of motion with negligible inertia force terms can be taken as

$$J = \int_\Omega (\rho g_i u_i + p(\partial_i u_i) - F)\, d\Omega + \int_{\partial_2 \Omega} \bar{t}_i u_i\, dS$$

with $u_i = \bar{u}_i$ on $\partial_1 \Omega$.

The pressure p appears here as a Lagrangian multiplier, whose variations enforce the incompressibility condition. With the viscous stresses

$$\sigma_{ij} = \frac{\partial F}{\partial \theta_{ij}}$$

the Euler equations stemming from variations on the velocity field are

$$\rho g_i - \partial_i p + \partial_j \sigma_{ij} = 0$$

and the natural boundary conditions on $\partial_2 \Omega$ are

$$n_j(\sigma_{ij} - p\delta_{ij}) = \bar{t}_i$$

As shown by Debongnie (Ref. 9), this principle can be extended by the Friedrichs technique to a canonical form involving simultanéously variations on the viscous stresses themselves.

Applications have been made in several directions. To biomechanics by P. Tong and Y.C. Fung (Ref. 8). To oil bearing problems and flow over deep wells by Debongnie (Ref. 9).
In applying the finite element methods to the two-dimensional cases, advantage may be gained from the remarkable analogy with Kirchhoff plate bending problems. The analogy comprises that between the stream function of the flow and the transverse plate flexure, the viscosity stresses and the bending moments tensor.

## 14. REFERENCES

1. CLEBSCH, A. : J. Reine und Angew.Math. 54, 293, 1857.
   56, 1, 1959.

2. LICHTENSTEIN, L. : Grundlagen der Hydrodynamik. Chap. 9.
   Berlin, Springer, 1929.

3. BATEMAN, H. : Proc. Royal Soc. London, Ser. A, 125, 598, 1929.

4. HERIVEL, J.W. : Proc. Cambridge Phil. Soc., 51, 344, 1955.

5. SERRIN, J. : Handbuch der Physik, Band VIII/1, 125.
   Berlin, Springer, 1959.

6. ECKART, C. : The Physics of Fluids, 3, 421, 1960.

7. FRAEIJS de VEUBEKE, B. : Variational principles in fluid mechanics. in Fluid Dynamics Transactions, vol. 3, (Sumposium-Jurata, 1965), p 111, Polish Academy of Sciences.

8. TONG, P. and FUNG, Y.C. : Slow particulate viscous flow in channels and tubes. Applications to biomechanics.
   J. of Applied Mechanics, 1971, p. 721.

9. DEBONGNIE, J.F. : Application de la méthode des éléments finis en mécanique des fluides.
   Université de Liège, Faculté des Sciences Appliquées, 1973.

RECENT DEVELOPMENTS OF FINITE-DIFFERENCE APPROXIMATIONS FOR BOUNDARY-LAYER EQUATIONS

E. KRAUSE

AERODYNAMISCHES INSTITUT
RHEINISCH-WESTFÄLISCH TECHNISCHE HOCHSCHULE AACHEN, GERMANY

ABSTRACT

Finite-difference solutions for Prandtl's boundary-layer equations are described for steady, two- and three-dimensional laminar and turbulent flows. For three-dimensional flows only boundary sheets are considered and curvature effects in the direction normal to the wall are being neglected. The governing equations are presented in form of a matrix-vector equation. Its numerical stability is discussed for elementary finite-difference molecules. Non-orthogonal coordinates are shown to affect the stability limits for the convective terms. If the momentum equations and/or the energy equation are decoupled by splitting the main part of the differential equations additional conditions must be observed for stable solutions. Finite-difference approximations with truncation error of fourth order are introduced to enable either increased accuracy or shortened calculation times, in particular, for three-dimensional problems. Studies of the behaviour of the overall error of the solution and several applications to real flow situations supplement the general considerations. Finally, a brief discussion is given for second-order closure problems.

1. INTRODUCTION

Although considerable effort has been spent on the analysis of turbulent boundary layers, our knowledge about such flows and our ability to predict them is rather limited. The major - so far unsurmountable - difficulties nest in the closure problem. Solutions cannot be obtained unless some empiricism is introduced at some point in the development of the solution. Aside from the physical problems there are computa-

---

This lecture is based on a paper [1] presented the AIAA-Computational Fluid Dynamics Conference, Palm Springs, Cal., July 19 - 20, 1973 and extensions thereof.

tional problems, if a solution is sought by means of finite-difference techniques. The computational problems are caused by the very nature of turbulent flow: A steep increase of the time averaged tangential velocity components in the immediate vicinity of the wall and the presence of large Reynolds stresses almost throughout the entire boundary layer. Their maximum value is much larger than that of the Newtonian stresses and numerical solutions which do not account for this peculiar behaviour of the dependent variables and of the coefficients of the differential equations are bound to be ineffective, in particular for three-dimensional flow problems.

This paper deals mainly with problems concerning the numerical integration of the boundary-layer equations for turbulent flows. Closure assumptions are only briefly discussed as the analysis presented herein is centered on an attempt to improve the numerical tools and techniques in order to make existing solution procedures more efficient. A survey of finite-difference methods was recently given in Ref. [2]. The finite-difference solutions presently being used can be divided into two groups: The first group is characterized by the common assumption of hyperbolic differential equations for the description of the time averaged velocity components and of the Reynolds stresses. These methods are described in [3],[4]and [5]. The change of the type of the differential equations is introduced by a particular approximation of the equation for the turbulent kinetic energy. As the slope of the characteristics at the wall is infinite the numerical solution fails there and a law of the wall must be matched to the numerical integration procedure. The method can only be applied to fully turbulent flows as the Newtonian part of the stress tensor has been completely neglected. An attempt to improve the law of the wall for three-dimensional flows was recently made in [6].

The second group of solutions uses parabolic equations in conjunction with a gradient-type representation for the cross-correlations. The approximations are, in general, extensions of first-order closures used in the analysis of two-dimensional flows. The validity of these concepts must be considered very critically when they are applied to three-dimensional flows. There is experimental evidence [7] that first-order closure can only be employed in mildy three-dimensional flows. Description of these solutions may be found in [2], [8], [9] and [10]. Numerical improvements of the accuracy of the solutions for parabolic equations were presented in [11] and [12]. For laminar flows [13] considerable savings of computation time were obtained for constant accuracy. In this lecture two fourth-order discretization procedures will be derived for parabolic equations which are written in matrix-vector form for non-orthogonal curvilinear coordinates. Both developments can be casted into a form identical with that of the difference equations for the second-order solution. Only the coefficients have to be redefined. If the differential equations are locally linearized, the coefficient matrix is tridiagonal for implicit formulation and the commonly used recursion relations can be employed in the solution.

## 2. GOVERNING EQUATIONS FOR BOUNDARY SHEETS

We begin the development by listing the momentum equations for those threedimensional boundary-layers which are categorized as boundary sheets. Curvature effects in the direction normal to the wall will not be included. Let $V_1$, $V_2$, $V_3$ be the three time averaged velocity components, $V_3$ being the normal component and $V_1$ and $V_2$ the two tangential components, and $q_1$, $q_2$, $q_3$ corresponding non-orthogonal curvilinear coordinates. With the boundary-layer assumption of constant pressure normal to the wall, the two momentum equations for the directions of $q_1$ and $q_2$ may be written as a matrix-vector equation of the following form (the flow is assumed to be steady and incompressible):

$$A_0 F + A_1 \frac{\partial F}{\partial q_1} + A_2 \frac{\partial F}{\partial q_2} + A_3 \frac{\partial F}{\partial q_3} + A_4 \frac{\partial^2 F}{\partial q_3^2} + B = 0 \tag{2.1}$$

All quantities are properly normalized and F is a column vector with components $V_1$ and $V_2$; $A_0$, $A_1$, $A_2$, $A_3$ and $A_4$ are matrices and B a vector defined below:

$$A_0 = \begin{pmatrix} k_1 v_1 + k_2 v_2 & k_3 v_2 \\ l_1 v_1 + l_2 v_2 & l_3 v_2 \end{pmatrix} \tag{2.2}$$

$$A_1 = \frac{V_1}{h_1} I \quad ; \quad A_2 = \frac{V_2}{h_2} I \tag{2.3}$$

where I is the identity matrix of order two. The matrices $A_3$ and $A_4$ are of the following form

$$A_3 = \left(V_3 - \frac{\partial \varepsilon_1}{\partial q_3}\right) \begin{pmatrix} 1 & 0 \\ 0 & 1+e_1 \end{pmatrix} \tag{2.4}$$

$$A_4 = -(1+\varepsilon_1) \begin{pmatrix} 1 & 0 \\ 0 & 1+e_2 \end{pmatrix} \tag{2.5}$$

In the last equation, $\varepsilon_1$ is the component of the eddy viscosity in the direction of $q_1$. The excentricities $e_1$ and $e_2$, being defined by

$$e_1 = \left[\frac{\partial}{\partial q_3}(\varepsilon_1 - \varepsilon_2)\right] / \left(v_3 - \frac{\partial \varepsilon_1}{\partial q_3}\right) \tag{2.6}$$

$$e_2 = (\varepsilon_1 - \varepsilon_2)/(1+\varepsilon_1) \tag{2.7}$$

vanish, if the eddy viscosity is assumed to be a scalar (i.e. $\varepsilon_1 = \varepsilon_2 = \varepsilon$). Then the matrices $A_3$ and $A_4$ can again be defined in terms of the identity matrix. Because of the introduction of non-orthogonal curvilinear coordinates both components of the vector B contain the pressure gradients for the directions $q_1$ and $q_2$:

$$B = -\frac{h_1 h_2}{gm} \begin{vmatrix} \frac{h_2}{h_1} & -\frac{g}{h_2} \\ -\frac{g_1}{h_1} & \frac{h_1}{h_2} \end{vmatrix} \begin{bmatrix} \frac{\partial p}{\partial q_1} \\ \frac{\partial p}{\partial q_2} \end{bmatrix} \tag{2.8}$$

The metric coefficients $k_1$-$k_3$, $l_1$-$l_3$, $h_1$, $h_2$, g and m are defined in [1]. They will not be repeated here. Eq. (2.1) can easily be adapted for twodimensional flows by identifying F with V, and setting $A_2$ equal to zero. If compressible flows are considered, the energy equation can also be written in a form identical to that of Eq.(2.1), and the components of F are $V_1$ and either h, $h_s$ or T depending on what variable is used. For threedimensional compressible flows, F contains the three components $V_1$, $V_2$ and T, or $h_s$, the stagnation enthalpy.

The normal velocity component is determined from the continuity equation which for three-dimensional flows reads

$$\frac{\partial}{\partial q_1}\left(\frac{m}{h_1}v_1\right) + \frac{\partial}{\partial q_2}\left(\frac{m}{h_2}v_2\right) + m\frac{\partial v_3}{\partial q_3} = 0 \tag{2.9}$$

The boundary conditions to be imposed on Eqs.(2.1) and (2.9) are

$$F(q_1, q_2, 0) = 0 \quad ; \quad \lim_{q_3 \to \infty} F = Fe \tag{2.10}$$

$$v_3(q_1, q_2, 0) = f_1(q_1, q_2) \tag{2.11}$$

where $f_1(q_1, q_2)$ must be prescribed in terms of the surface coordinates $q_1$ and $q_2$; $f_1(q_1, q_2)$ vanishes identically for an impermeable wall, is negative for the case of suction and positive for normal injection. As Eqs. (2.1) and (2.9) are given in a nondimensionless form in which the normal coordinate and the normal velocity component are stretched by the square root of the characteristic Reynolds number, the function $f_1$ must be of order unity so that the boundary-layer assumptions are satisfied. Initial conditions are to be prescribed for F along some initial surface such that

$$F(q_{1i}, q_{2i}, q_3) = F_i(q_{1i}, q_{2i}, q_3) \qquad (2.12)$$

where $F_i$ is a known vector function specifying its components on a surface normal to the body erected over the line specified by $q_{1i}$ and $q_{2i}$. For twodimensional problems the surface on which the initial conditions are specified collapses into the surface normal of the body.

For closure of the problem, the eddy viscosity introduced earlier may be approximated to first order by a scalar function of the form

$$\varepsilon = l^2 \left[ \left(\frac{\partial v_1}{\partial q_3}\right)^2 + \left(\frac{\partial v_2}{\partial q_3}\right)^2 \right]^{1/2} \qquad (2.13)$$

where $l$ is the mixing length, which may be taken proportional to $q_3$ in the inner part of the boundary layer and equal to a constant in the outer. Several models are compared in [2]. The validity of Eq. (2.13) must be considered very critically as there is experimental evidence that this assumption does not hold true in general [7]. As the closure assumption is not relevant for the following discussion, no justification for the adoption of the mixing length hypothesis and the eddy viscosity concept is given; it is only mentioned that most finite-difference solutions derived for parabolic equations rest on the validity of Eq. (2.13). If compressible flows are considered, an equation of state and laws specifiying the laminar viscosity and the thermal conductivity in terms of the temperature must be given. First-order closure for turbulent flows would require a turbulent Prandtl number.

The use of non-orthogonal coordinates for the numerical solution is advocated mainly for two reasons: If an algorithm is derived from implicit linearized difference equations the coordinates used affect only the coefficients but do not change the form of the recursion relations. The more complicated expression for the pressure gradient term is of little importance as it can be calculated before the integration is initiated and need not be determined repeatedly. The second reason is that it can only be decided, which coordinates are suitable

when the particular problem to be investigated is specified.
Eqs. (2.3) - (2.9) can always be reduced to an appropriate form and
for example, orthogonal - either external flow or surface orientated-
coordinates are obtained by setting g in Eqs. (2.8) - (2.9) equal to
zero. Although non-orthogonal curvilinear coordinates offer the possibility of applying the solution to a wide range of problems, they also
influence the stability conditions, which will be briefly discussed
in the next section.

## 3. REMARKS ON THE NUMERICAL STABILITY

The stability of the finite-difference approximations for Eq.(2.1) has
been discussed repeatedly, e.g. in [2] and earlier in [14] and [15].
Therein it was shown that the implicit finite-difference approximations
of Eq. (2.1) are only stable if the Courant-Friedrichs-Lewy condition
is satisfied for the convective terms; that is to say that on the surfaces parallel to the surface of the body the numerical domain of dependence must include the domain of dependence of the differential
equation. The latter is defined by the "Raetz-influence-principle" [5],
which will be repeated here to clarify matters: If initial conditions
for $V_1$ and $V_2$ are specified on a surface normal to the surface of the
body and if the line of intersection is of finite length and does not
coincide with the projection of a streamline, then the solution of
Eqs. (2.1) and (2.9) is completely defined in terms of the initial
conditions only over a region of influence of finite extent. The
region of influence is bounded by the surface on which the initial
conditons are specified and two other surfaces which are normal to the
surface of the body and intersect the initial surface in its end points.
The bounding surfaces are erected over a limiting and/or the projection
of an external streamline such that the enclosed area on the surface
of the body attains a minimum. The flow outside of the domain of dependence cannot be computed as it is advected from points for which
no initial data are available.

Within the domain of dependence the implicit solution is stable only
if the convective terms in Eq. (2.1) are substituted for by advective
finite-difference approximations [16], i.e. the integration must always follow the main direction of the flow. In [14] and [15] the von-
Neumann analysis was shown to predict the stability limits accurately
for cartesian coordinates. The solution became immediately unstable

as soon as the stability limits were exceeded. In the following we outline the von-Neumann test for curvilinear coordinates. By freezing the coefficients in Eq. (2.1) one can derive locally valid stability limits which are defined in terms of the stability parameter

$$\Gamma = \frac{v_2 h_1 \Delta q_1}{v_1 h_2 \Delta q_2} \tag{3.1}$$

In comparison to cartesian coordinates $\Gamma$ in Eq. (3.1) may be more restricted in stable regions. This is caused by the appearance of the length parameter $h_1$ and $h_2$ in the expression for $\Gamma$. In addition for curvilinear non-orthogonal coordinates lower-order instabilities may arise from the curvature terms: Consider a simple difference molecule depicted in Fig. 1. In this case the derivatives in the direction of $q_3$ are approximated with second-order accuracy and those in the directions of $q_1$ and $q_2$ with first order.

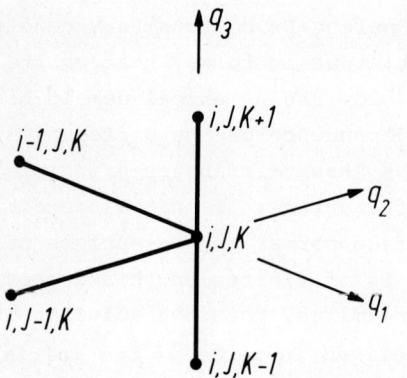

If the pressure gradient term in Eq. (2.1) is neglected and the matrices $A_1 - A_4$ are assumed to be constant with $e_1 = e_2 = 0$ the amplification matrix for the direction of $q_1$ is

Fig. 1 Simple finite difference molecule for implicit integration

$$G(\underline{K}, \Delta q_1) = \frac{h_1 \Delta q_1}{D} \begin{vmatrix} E + l_3 \frac{v_2}{v_1} & -K_3 \frac{v_2}{v_1} \\ -\left(l_1 + l_2 \frac{v_2}{v_1}\right) & E + K_1 + K_2 \frac{v_2}{v_1} \end{vmatrix} \tag{3.2}$$

where E is an abbreviation of the complex expression

$$E = \frac{1}{h_1 \Delta q_1} \left[ 1 + \Gamma Z_1 - \frac{2(1+\epsilon)}{(\Delta q_3)^2} \frac{h_1 \Delta q_1}{v_1} Z_2 + \left(v_3 - \frac{\partial \epsilon}{\partial q_3}\right) \frac{h_1 \Delta q_1}{v_1 \Delta q_3} Z_3 \right] \tag{3.3}$$

with

$$Z_1 = 1 - \cos(K_2 \Delta q_2) + i \sin(K_2 \Delta q_2) \tag{3.4}$$

$$Z_2 = 1 - \cos(K_3 \Delta q_3) \tag{3.5}$$

$$Z_3 = i \sin(K_3 \Delta q_3) \qquad (3.6)$$

The vector $\underline{K}$ in Eq. (3.2) is defined by the two integer components $K_2$ and $K_3$. The quantity D is the determinant of the matrix in Eq.(3.2). From Eq. (3.2) and Eq. (3.3) it is clear that the absolute values of the complex eigenvalues satisfy the von-Neumann condition as long as $\Gamma$ is properly restricted (as shown in [14] ) and the curvature terms are of order unity. However, small step sizes $\Delta q_1$ may be necessary when the curvature terms are large. This can easily be verified by setting $Z_1$, $Z_2$ and $Z_3$ equal to zero. Then Eq.(2.1) reduces to an ordinary differential equation [17], which for large curvature terms requires small step sizes $\Delta q_1$, if the direction of $q_1$ is assumed to be the marching direction. These results imply that the length elements $h_1$ and $h_2$ should not be too different from each other; in addition, the curvature terms should be of order one so that the step size in the direction of the tangential coordinates does not have to be restricted unnecessarily.

Another difficulty may be encountered, if the main part of the differential equation (2.1) is split in order to decouple the equations. Then the second-order derivatives of all components of the solution vector may appear in each of the equations (2.1). It is, in general, possible to solve the resulting difference equations simultaneously without decoupling. Since this method of solution would require matrix inversion the equations are often decoupled -for the sake of convenience- so that they can be solved one after the other. The component of the solution vector in question is then written in implicit formulation and the rest of the main part of the differential equation is discretized explicitly. These terms are evaluated from the last station computed, and act as a forcing function, comparable to pressure-gradient terms in the momentum equations. Such a decoupling may be necessary when the eddy viscosity is not assumed to be a scalar. To demonstrate the point we consider a simplified form of Eq. (2.1)

$$\frac{\partial F}{\partial q_1} + A_4 \frac{\partial^2 F}{\partial q_3^2} = 0, \qquad (3.7)$$

the matrix $A_4$ is assumed to have four positive elements $a_{ij}$ instead of two as in Eq. (2.5). If the terms with coefficients $a_{11}$ and $a_{22}$ are written in implicit formulation and those with $a_{12}$ and $a_{21}$ explicitly, the amplification matrix of (3.7) becomes

$$G(\underline{K}, \Delta q_1) = \begin{vmatrix} \dfrac{1}{1+g_{11}} & \dfrac{-g_{12}}{1+g_{11}} \\ \dfrac{-g_{21}}{1+g_{22}} & \dfrac{1}{1+g_{22}} \end{vmatrix} \qquad (3.8)$$

The abbreviations $g_{ij}$ are defined as

$$g_{ij} = \frac{2 a_{ij} \Delta q_1}{(\Delta q_3)^2} (1 - \cos K_3 \Delta q_3) \qquad (3.9)$$

The two eigenvalues of Eq. (3.8) are of the form

$$\lambda_{1,2} = \frac{1}{2}\left(\frac{1}{1+g_{11}} + \frac{1}{1+g_{22}}\right) \pm \sqrt{\frac{1}{4}\left(\frac{1}{1+g_{11}} - \frac{1}{1+g_{22}}\right)^2 + \frac{g_{12}\, g_{21}}{(1+g_{11})(1+g_{22})}} \qquad (3.10)$$

In order to satisfy the von-Neumann condition the absolute values of the eigenvalues must be less than unity. This is always true when the matrix elements $a_{12}$ and $a_{21}$ are equal to zero. Since $g_{11}$ and $g_{22}$ are non-negativ for all values of $k_3 \Delta q_3$, the eigenvalues are positive and less than unity. This is the expected result and the finite-difference solution in implicit formulation is stable. On the other hand, the terms along the Spur may vanish, i.e. $a_{11} = a_{22} = 0$. This condition is encountered if the eddy viscosity does not depend on the component of the solution vector considered but only on the forcing function. The eigenvalues become for $a_{11} = a_{22} = 0$

$$\lambda_{1,2} = 1 \pm \sqrt{g_{12}\, g_{21}} \qquad (3.11)$$

The second eigenvalue yields the stability condition

$$\Delta q_1 \leq \frac{1}{2} \frac{(\Delta q_2)^2}{\sqrt{a_{12}\, a_{21}}} \qquad (3.12)$$

for explicit integration [+], but the first eigenvalue is always larger than unity so that the solution of the difference equations is unstable, if the elements along the Spur vanish. If neither one of the $a_{ij}$ is zero, the first eigenvalue yields the condition that the product $a_{12}\, a_{21}$ must be less than $a_{11}\, a_{22}$ otherwise $\lambda_1$ (which is positive) would exceed unity. The second eigenvalue $\lambda_2$ leeds to a condition

$$\left[(a_{12}\, a_{21} - a_{11}\, a_{22}) \frac{\Delta t}{(\Delta q_3)^2} - \frac{1}{2}(a_{11} + a_{22})\right] \frac{\Delta t}{(\Delta q_3)^2} < \frac{1}{4} \qquad (3.13)$$

---

[+] It was pointed out by J.J. Smolderen that with $a_{11} = a_{22} = 0$ the solution should always be unstable. This is clearly confirmed by the first eigenvalue of Eq. (3.11).

Since $a_{11}$ and $a_{22}$ are positive the bracketed term in Eq.(3.13) is negative if

$$a_{11} a_{22} \geq a_{12} a_{21} \qquad (3.14)$$

so that stability can be guaranteed if Eq.(3.14) is satisfied. From physical considerations there is no need to impose the restriction given by Eq. (3.14) on the elements of the matrix $A_4$, as they are independent of each other and can be chosen arbitrarily i.e. $a_{ij} > 0$. Although numerical tests have not been carried out the above derivations show that decoupling by explicit-implicit formulation may not always leed to stable difference equations. These considerations also apply to multidiffusion problems, if the diffusional flux of each one of the chemical species is expressed though the sum of the others and the decoupling of the equations is carried out as described above. The terms which are incorporated in the finite-difference approximation as explicit terms may therefore have a destabilizing effect as they act as forcing functions. We next turn now to a description of higher-order schemes.

## 4. FOURTH ORDER DIFFERENCE APPROXIMATIONS

In numerical solutions of the boundary layer equations (2.1) and (2.9) second-order finite-difference approximations have been used predominantly. Higher-order solutions are applied in order to achieve an increased accuracy or to reduce the computation time when only moderate accuracy is desired. Although both problems seem to be identical, experience has shown that this is only true when all flow variables and their derivatives are of order one. In turbulent boundary layers, not only the derivatives of the tangential velocity components are large (in the vicinity of the wall) but also the dimensionless turbu-

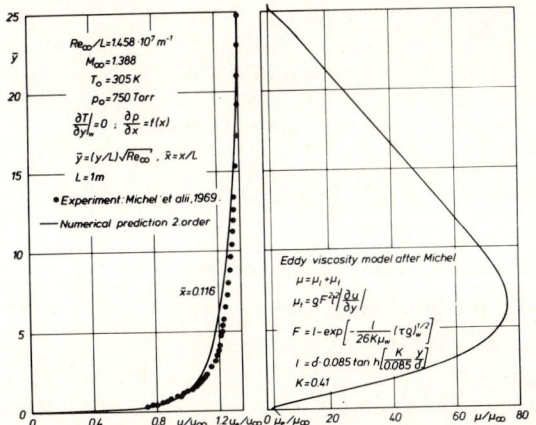

Fig. 2 Typical profile of tangential velocity component and turbulent viscosity

lent viscosity is large compared to unity and exhibits steep gradients on both sides of its maximum value. Even in the outer portion of the boundary layer where the velocity gradients are small do the gradients of the turbulent viscosity remain large. This behaviour is common to all viscosity models and can be seen in Fig. 2 where a sample calculation of [18] is shown for a twodimensional compressible boundary layer and compared to experimental data. Depicted is a profile of the tangential velocity component and of the effective turbulent viscosity, which was calculated from Michel's equation for the mixing length

$$\frac{l}{\delta} = 0.085 \, th\left(\frac{K}{0.085} \frac{q_3}{\delta}\right) \tag{4.1}$$

and Eq. (2.13) reduced to two-dimensional flows. The behaviour near the wall is determined by the van Driest damping factor

$$F = 1 - exp\left[-\frac{l}{26K\mu}(\tau \varrho)^{1/2}\right] \tag{4.2}$$

Other approximations [2] for the eddy viscosity yield comparable data. This is shown in Fig. 3 where for a typical case, Equs. (2.13), (4.1) and (4.2) are compared with Pletcher's polynomial curve fit of experimental data:

$$\left(\frac{l}{\delta}\right)_i = K\left[1 - exp\left(-q_3^*/\delta\right)\right](q_3/\delta) \tag{4.3}$$

$$0 \leq q_3/\delta \leq 0.1$$

$$\left(\frac{l}{\delta}\right) = \left(\frac{l}{\delta}\right)_i + \sum_{n=2}^{n=4} a_n \left(q_3/\delta - 0.1\right)^n \tag{4.4}$$

$$0.1 < q_3/\delta \leq 0.6$$

$$a_2 = -1.53506; \quad a_3 = 2.75625; \quad a_4 = -1.88425$$

$$\frac{l}{\delta} = 0.089 \qquad 0.6 < q_3/\delta \tag{4.5}$$

Often Klebanov's intermittency factor is used to describe the eddy viscosity in the outer portion of the boundary layer:

$$\varepsilon_0 = k_1 V_e \, \delta^*/\left[1 + 5.5 \left(q_3/\delta\right)^6\right] \tag{4.6}$$

In the above relations k is von Kármán's constant, $k_1 = 0.0168$; $q_3^*$ is defined in terms of the shear velocity. It is this characteristic dependence of the effective turbulent viscosity and the form of the tangential velocity profile, that complicates the integration of the

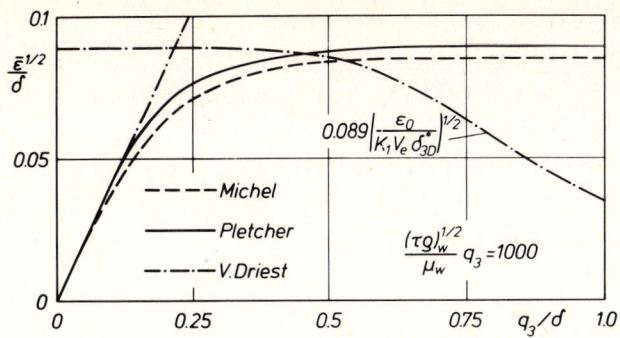

Fig.3 Comparison of several approximations for the eddy viscosity.

boundary-layer equations for turbulent flows. For this reason it is necessary to construct accurate finite-difference approximations as otherwise numerical errors can be attributed to the failure of the closure relations chosen and may leed to wrong conclusions.

There are several ways to improve the accuracy of numerical solutions. Richardson extrapolation has been used successfully, for example, in Refs. [19] and [20]. Here an alternative approach will be discussed. The basic idea is that the first higher-order derivatives which are neglected in the second-order solution are eliminated through auxiliary relations obtained either by Taylor series development or from the differential equations. In order to show the major steps of the development we will start with the Taylor series and define the two difference expressions.

$$(\delta F)_k = F_{k+1} - F_{k-1} \tag{4.7}$$

$$(\delta^2 F)_k = F_{k+1} - 2F_k + F_{k-1} \tag{4.8}$$

where the subscript K designates a net point and K + 1 and K - 1 neighbouring points being a constant $\Delta q$ away from K. The expressions $\delta F$ and $\delta^2 F$ possess a Taylor series representation of the form

$$(\delta F)_k = 2\left[\left(\frac{\partial F}{\partial q}\right)_k \Delta q + \frac{1}{3}\left(\frac{\partial^3 F}{\partial q^3}\right)_k (\Delta q)^3 + \cdots\right] \tag{4.9}$$

$$(\delta^2 F)_k = 2\left[\frac{1}{2!}\left(\frac{\partial^2 F}{\partial q^2}\right)_k (\Delta q)^2 + \frac{1}{4!}\left(\frac{\partial^4 F}{\partial q^4}\right)_k (\Delta q)^4 + \cdots\right] \tag{4.10}$$

In the second-order solution only the first term on the right of the last two equations is retained, while all other terms are neglected. The finite-difference representation may now be improved, if the third- and fourth-order derivatives are eliminated. First the series (4.9) and (4.10) are repeated for the first- and second-order derivatives: There result the four expressions [11]

$$\left[\delta\left(\frac{\partial F}{\partial q}\right)\right]_k \Delta q = 2\left[\left(\frac{\partial^2 F}{\partial q^2}\right)_k (\Delta q)^2 + \frac{1}{3!}\left(\frac{\partial^4 F}{\partial q^4}\right)_k (\Delta q)^4 + \cdots\right] \quad (4.11)$$

$$\left[\delta^2\left(\frac{\partial F}{\partial q}\right)\right]_k \Delta q = 2\left[\frac{1}{2!}\left(\frac{\partial^3 F}{\partial q^3}\right)_k (\Delta q)^3 + \frac{1}{4!}\left(\frac{\partial^5 F}{\partial q^5}\right)_k (\Delta q)^5 + \cdots\right] \quad (4.12)$$

$$\left[\delta\left(\frac{\partial^2 F}{\partial q^2}\right)\right]_k (\Delta q)^2 = 2\left[\left(\frac{\partial^3 F}{\partial q^3}\right)_k (\Delta q)^3 + \frac{1}{3!}\left(\frac{\partial^5 F}{\partial q^5}\right)_k (\Delta q)^5 + \cdots\right] \quad (4.13)$$

$$\left[\delta^2\left(\frac{\partial^2 F}{\partial q^2}\right)\right](\Delta q)^2 = 2\left[\frac{1}{2!}\left(\frac{\partial^4 F}{\partial q^4}\right)_k (\Delta q)^4 + \frac{1}{4!}\left(\frac{\partial^6 F}{\partial q^6}\right)_k (\Delta q)^6 + \cdots\right] \quad (4.14)$$

Eqs. (4.9) - (4.14) can now be combined to yield the following four linearly independent expressions:

$$(\delta F)_k = 2\left(\frac{\partial F}{\partial q}\right)_{k+1}\Delta q - \frac{2}{3}\left[\left(\frac{\partial^2 F}{\partial q^2}\right)_{k+1} + 2\left(\frac{\partial^2 F}{\partial q^2}\right)_k\right](\Delta q)^2 + \frac{2}{45}\left(\frac{\partial^5 F}{\partial q^5}\right)_k (\Delta q)^5 + \cdots \quad (4.15)$$

$$(\delta F)_k = 2\left(\frac{\partial F}{\partial q}\right)_{k-1}\Delta q + \frac{2}{3}\left[\left(\frac{\partial^2 F}{\partial q^2}\right)_{k-1} + 2\left(\frac{\partial^2 F}{\partial q^2}\right)_k\right](\Delta q)^2 + \frac{2}{45}\left(\frac{\partial^5 F}{\partial q^5}\right)_k (\Delta q)^5 + \cdots \quad (4.16)$$

$$(\delta F)_k = 2\left(\frac{\partial F}{\partial q}\right)_k \Delta q + \frac{1}{6}\left[\delta\left(\frac{\partial^2 F}{\partial q^2}\right)\right]_k (\Delta q)^2 + \frac{1}{180}\left(\frac{\partial^5 F}{\partial q^5}\right)_k (\Delta q)^5 + \cdots \quad (4.17)$$

$$(\delta^2 F)_k = \frac{1}{12}\left[\left(\frac{\partial^2 F}{\partial q^2}\right)_{k+1} + 10\left(\frac{\partial^2 F}{\partial q^2}\right)_k + \left(\frac{\partial^2 F}{\partial q^2}\right)_{k-1}\right](\Delta q)^2 - \frac{1}{240}\left(\frac{\partial^6 F}{\partial q^6}\right)_k (\Delta q)^6 + \cdots \quad (4.18)$$

If now all terms of fifth and higher order are neglected the last four equations contain three unknown first and three unknown second-order derivatives. The truncation error has been reduced to fourth order. The finite-difference representation just given will now be used to replace the derivatives in the direction normal to the wall.

For the elimination of the six unknown derivatives in Eqs.(4.15)-(4.18) three additional relations are necessary. They are obtained from the momentum equation (2.1). If it is assumed that appropriate difference approximations have been introduced for the derivatives in the direction of $q_1$ and $q_2$, the momentum equations can be written in the following form for the points K + 1, K, and K - 1 :

$$G_0 + A_{3l}\left(\frac{\partial F}{\partial q_3}\right)_l + A_{4l}\left(\frac{\partial^2 F}{\partial q_3^2}\right)_l = 0 \qquad l = K-1, K, K+1 \qquad (4.19)$$

where G is the finite-difference approximation of the first three terms and of B in Eq. (2.1)

$$G = A_0 F + A_1 \frac{\partial F}{\partial q_1} + A_2 \frac{\partial F}{\partial q_2} + B \qquad (4.20)$$

Eqs. (4.15) - (4.2o) yield now a set of difference equations which have the same form as those of the second-order implicit solution

$$M_{1K} F_{K+1} + M_{2K} F_K + M_{3K} F_{K-1} + M_{4K} = 0 \qquad (4.21)$$

and can be solved with the algorithm

$$F_K = P_j F_{K+1} + Q_j \qquad (4.22)$$

The definitions of $P_j$ and $Q_j$ follow from Eq. (4.21). The major difference is, however, that F is determined with an error

$$\varepsilon = O[(\Delta q_3)^4] + O[(\Delta q_1)^2] + O[(\Delta q_2)^2],$$

if the matrices $A_1$ - $A_4$ are calculated to the same degree of accuracy. In order to do so five net points will be necessary.

This method derives its name ("Mehrstellen"-method) from the fact that collocation is enforced at three net points instead of one for the second-order solution. Approximations similar to the one just outlined were described earlier in [21] and [22], and the method has been applied to boundary layers in [11], [13], and [23].

In [17] it is shown how a fourth-order solution can be obtained for the heat conduction equation in a manner different from the one just outlined. That approach can also be extended to the boundary-layer equations and a brief derivation will be given here: While in the development of the "Mehrstellen"-method auxiliary relations for the elimination of the third- and fourth-order derivatives are obtained from Taylor series expansions, they may also be obtained from the differential equation (2.1). If G is redefined as

$$G = -A_4^{-1}\left[A_0 F + A_1 \frac{\partial F}{\partial q_1} + A_2 \frac{\partial F}{\partial q_2} + B\right] \qquad (4.23)$$

and

$$H = A_4^{-1} A_3 \qquad (4.24)$$

Eq. (4.19) can be written as

$$G = H\frac{\partial F}{\partial q_3} + \frac{\partial^2 F}{\partial q_3^2} \qquad (4.25)$$

This expression can be differentiated with respect to $q_3$; after elimination of the second-order derivatives there results

$$\frac{\partial^3 F}{\partial q_3^3} = -HG + \frac{\partial G}{\partial q_3} + \left(H^2 - \frac{\partial H}{\partial q_3}\right)\frac{\partial F}{\partial q_3} \qquad (4.26)$$

and a second differentiation gives

$$\frac{\partial^4 F}{\partial q_3^4} = \frac{\partial^2 G}{\partial q_3^2} - \frac{\partial}{\partial q_3}(HG) - \left[\frac{\partial}{\partial q_3}\left(\frac{\partial H}{\partial q_3} - H^2\right)\right]H^{-1}G \\ - \left\{\frac{\partial H}{\partial q_3} - H^2 - \left[\frac{\partial}{\partial q_3}\left(\frac{\partial H}{\partial q_3} - H^2\right)\right]H^{-1}\right\}\frac{\partial^2 F}{\partial q_3^2} \qquad (4.27)$$

With the following abbreviations introduced

$$B_0 = -HG + \frac{\partial G}{\partial q_3} \qquad (4.28)$$

$$B_1 = H^2 - \frac{\partial H}{\partial q_3} \qquad (4.29)$$

$$C_0 = \frac{\partial^2 G}{\partial q_3^2} - \frac{\partial}{\partial q_3}(HG) - \left[\frac{\partial}{\partial q_3}\left(\frac{\partial H}{\partial q_3} - H^2\right)\right]H^{-1}G \qquad (4.30)$$

$$C_1 = -\frac{\partial H}{\partial q_3} + H^2 + \left[\frac{\partial}{\partial q_3}\left(\frac{\partial H}{\partial q_3} - H^2\right)\right]H^{-1} \qquad (4.31)$$

in Eqs. (4.9) and (4.10) one obtains for the derivatives of first and second order

$$\left(\frac{\partial F}{\partial q_3}\right)_k = \left[I + \frac{(\Delta q_3)^2}{6}B_{1K}\right]^{-1}\left[\frac{(\delta F)_k}{2\Delta q_3} - \frac{(\Delta q_3)^2}{6}B_{0K}\right] + O\left[(\Delta q_3)^4\right] \qquad (4.32)$$

$$\left(\frac{\partial^2 F}{\partial q_3^2}\right)_k = \left[I + \frac{(\Delta q_3)^2}{12}C_{1K}\right]^{-1}\left[\frac{(\delta^2 F)_k}{(\Delta q_3)^2} - \frac{(\Delta q_3)^2}{12}C_{0K}\right] + O\left[(\Delta q_3)^4\right] \qquad (4.33)$$

After substitution of the last two expressions into Eq. (4.25) there results again a finite-difference approximation with a truncation error

$$\varepsilon = O\left[(\Delta q_3)^4\right] + O\left[(\Delta q_1)^2\right] + O\left[(\Delta q_2)^2\right] \;.$$

Just as before, only three net points are necessary, if the quantities

$B_0$, $B_1$, $C_0$, $C_1$ contain no higher than second-order derivatives. By comparing Eq. (2.4) with Eq. (4.3o) it is seen that third- and fourth-order derivatives appear in Eqs. (4.29) - (4.31). In Ref. [17] a transformation is suggested to overcome this difficulty for the case that the excentricities in Eqs. (2.4) and (2.5) are zero, i.e. $\varepsilon_1 = \varepsilon_2 = \varepsilon$

$$\eta = \int \frac{1}{(1+\varepsilon)} \, dq_3 \qquad (4.34)$$

Then Eq. (2.1) can be written as

$$(1+\varepsilon)\left(A_0 F + A_1 \frac{\partial F}{\partial q_1} + A_2 \frac{\partial F}{\partial q_2}\right) + A_3 \frac{\partial F}{\partial \eta} - \frac{\partial^2 F}{\partial \eta^2} + (1+\varepsilon) B = 0 \qquad (4.35)$$

$$A_3 = (1+\varepsilon)\left(\frac{\partial \eta}{\partial q_1} A_1 + \frac{\partial \eta}{\partial q_2} A_2\right) + v_3 I \qquad (4.36)$$

For flow fields for which (4.34) is applicable, the quantities $B_0$, $B_1$, $C_0$, and $C_1$ need only be evaluated with second-order accuracy as they are multiplied by $(\Delta q_3)^2$. Recently, W. Kordulla investigated the transformation (4.34) in his doctoral dissertation 24 . He showed that the transformation can only be employed when $\varepsilon$ is of order unity. This result was obtained from the following test case: A known tangential velocity profile was used to evaluate the turbulent effective viscosity from Michel's approximation. Eq. (4.34) was then integrated numerically yielding $\eta$ as a function of y. In Fig. 4 the inverse transformation is shown as a function of $\eta$. Because of the steep increase of the effective turbulent viscosity there is a very large contraction in $\eta$; while y increases from zero to six, $\eta$ varies only from zero to 0.5. For larger values of y the contraction is zero and y

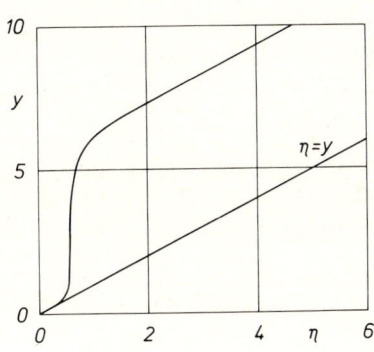

Fig. 4 The inverse transformation Eq. (4.34)

increases linearly with $\eta$. The effect of the contraction on the velocity profile is demonstrated in Fig. 5, where in customary representation the profile of the dimensionless tangential velocity component is shown as a function of the normal coordinate y and the transformed coordinate $\eta$. The contraction changes the velocity profile in two ways: first, the external flow is reached for $\eta = 0,7$ while for the same value of y, the value of the velocity in untransformed coordinates is only about 0,25. Secondly the contraction distortes the velocity profile completely, causing an unusual S-shaped form.

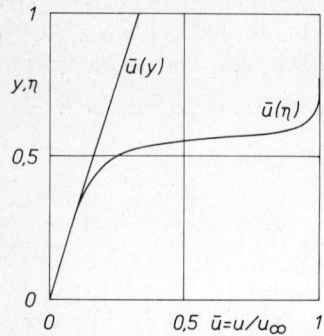

Fig. 5 Tangential velocity profile for the transformed coordinate $\eta$

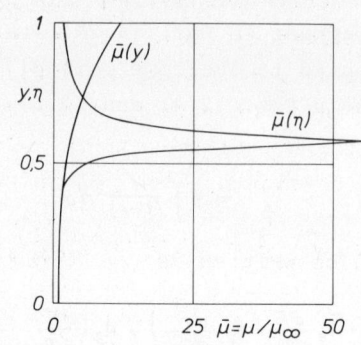

Fig. 6 Shape of the profile of the effective turbulent viscosity for the transformed coordinate $\eta$.

The integration of the momentum equation in the form of Eq. (4.35) could not be facilitated. The failure is due to the shape of the viscosity profile, which is depicted in Fig. 6.

It is seen that $\mu(\eta)$ shows a sharp peak near $\eta$ =0,6 with very large gradients on both sides of the maximum. It is clear that this function is not suitable for numerical integration, unless particularly fine resultion is used. Thus the transformation suggested by Richtmyer and Morton is not applicable to turbulent flows, but may be in solutions for laminar flows as long as the dimensionless viscosity is of order unity. This result does by no means invaliditate the use of Eq. (4.25) together with the fourth-order approximations for the first-and second-order derivatives normal to the wall, Eqs. (4.32) and (4.33). It is only necessary to evaluate the third-and fourth-order derivates in the coefficients Eq. (4.28) - (4.31) with second-order accuracy, which requires five net-points. In the field the usual difference approximations are

$$\left(\frac{\partial^3 F}{\partial q^3}\right)_K = \frac{1}{2}\left[F_{K+2} - 2(F_{K+1} - F_{K-1}) - F_{K-2}\right]/(\Delta q)^3 + O\left[(\Delta q)^2\right] \quad (4.37)$$

$$\left(\frac{\partial^4 F}{\partial q^4}\right)_K = \left[F_{K+2} - 4F_{K+1} + 6F_K - F_{K-1} + F_{K-2}\right]/(\Delta q)^4 + O\left[(\Delta q)^2\right] \quad (4.38)$$

Eqs. (4.37) and (4.38) cannot be used for the first net point close to the wall, because of the appearance of $F_{K-2}$. Here the coefficients are determined from the law of the wall. This assumption is, as far as the order of the truncation error is concerned, at the first glance inconsistent with the above derivations, but can be made compatible with the fourth-order accuracy scheme: The law of the wall results from the exact momentum equations Eq. (4.25) by setting the first three terms in Eq. (4.23) equal to zero. This simplification is justified as all velocity components and the effective turbulent viscosity vanish for $q_3 \rightarrow 0$. Thus in the frame of the finite-difference approximation the law of the wall is consistant with the fourth-order scheme as long as

$$\left| H \frac{\partial F}{\partial q_3} - A_4^{-1} \left[ A_0 F + A_1 \frac{\partial F}{\partial q_1} + A_2 \frac{\partial F}{\partial q_2} \right] \right| \leq c_1 (\Delta q_3)^4 \qquad (4.39)$$

The left-hand side of Eq. (4.39) can always be evaluated from the initial profile. Then the location of the point nearest to the wall must be chosen so that the above condition is satisfied. This approximation should not be confused with the use of the law of the wall in [3]. It was pointed out earlier that in the solution of Ref. [3] the slope of the characteristics at the wall is infinite and the numerical solution fails there. For that reason the law of the wall must be employed over a distance of finite extent in the direction normal to the wall until the order of magnitude of the slopes of the characteristics approaches unity, so that the truncation errors become of order $O[(\Delta q_3)^2]$. In the present approximation the distance between the first net point and the wall can be made arbitary small, i.e., the smaller it is the better the approximation.

The integration of the continuity equation (2.9) can be carried out with fourth-order accuracy with the iteration method developed in [25] for two-dimensional flows. For second- and fourth order accuracy the integration procedure has been tested successfully. According to this method, the integration starts with an initial guess for the profile of the normal velocity component, say $v_3=0$, and all velocity components are then calculated iteratively from the continuity equation and momentum equations until the solution converges within prescribed error bounds. They must again be of order $O[(\Delta q_3)^4]$.

The difference form of Eq. (2.9) is

$$a_{K+1} v_{3K+1} + a_K v_{3K} + a_{K-1} v_{3K-1} = b_{K+1} c_{K+1} + b_K c_K + b_{K-1} c_{K-1} \qquad (4.40)$$

$$c_K = -\frac{1}{m} \left[ \frac{\partial}{\partial q_1} \left( \frac{m}{h_1} v_1 \right) + \frac{\partial}{\partial q_2} \left( \frac{m}{h_2} v_2 \right) \right]_K \Delta q_3 \qquad (4.41)$$

In Eq. (4.40) the normal velocity component at the point next to the wall must also be prescribed together with the boundary condition for

$q_3 = 0$. Here again, an approximation similar to the one chosen for the momentum equations must be used. By adjusting the stepsize in the vicinity of the wall the integration of the continuity equation can be initiated. The coefficients $a_k$ and $b_n$ are determined from Eqs.(4.15)-(4.18). They result from eliminating all second-order derivatives in these equations; since the coefficients change, depending on where they are evaluated they will not be given here. They are obtained without difficulty.

## 5. DISCUSSION OF NUMERICAL RESULTS

The accuracy of the numerical results obtained with the method described in the foregoing sections depends on several parameters. The most important ones are 1) the order of the truncation error, 2) the stepsize $\Delta q$, 3) the error of the iteration process for the normal velocity component $\varepsilon_{v3}$, 4) the error with which the edge conditions are approximated $\varepsilon_e$, 5) the accuracy of the finite-difference approximation of first- and second-order derivatives at the wall, and 6) indirectly the Reynolds number.

Fig. 7 shows a comparison of the shearing stress at the wall as calculated with the second-order solution and the Mehrstellen-method. The initial conditions were again taken from laminar flow and transition to turbulent flow was enforced by using an eddy-viscosity model in the solution. Several step-sizes were employed in the calculation and the influence of the step-size is clearly reflected in the results. The wave-like oscillations, which appear for large step sizes are caused by the error $\varepsilon_\delta$; such a behaviour is typical for turbulent flows.

The outer-edge conditions must be satisfied to an appropriate degree of accuracy or else the effect of the error $\varepsilon_\delta$, is transmitted throughout the entire boundary layer.

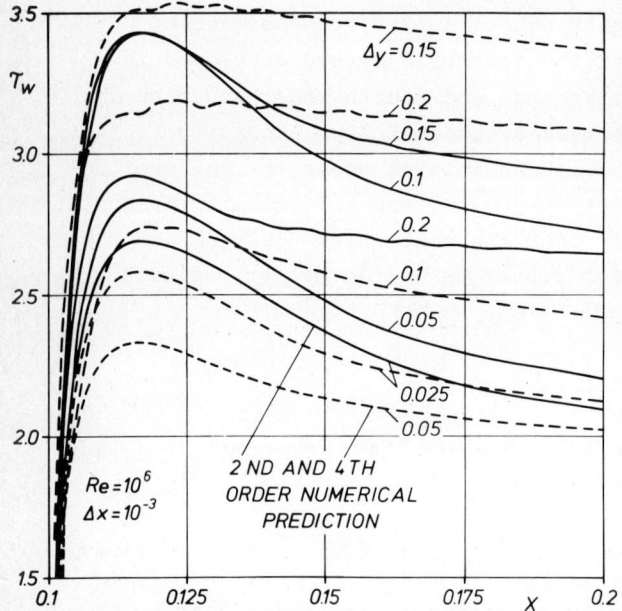

Fig.7 Effect of step size on shearing stress distribution at the wall

Fig. 8 shows the effect

of the error $\varepsilon_\delta$ on the effective turbulent viscosity. It is seen that a small change of from $10^{-5}$ to $5 \cdot 10^{-4}$ change the maximum value from 125 to 85. Unless a convention is introduced, through which the edge is properly defined, this error may result in noticeable changes in the velocity profiles. This result, again, shows that the prediction of turbulent flows can greatly be influenced by the numerical accuracy.

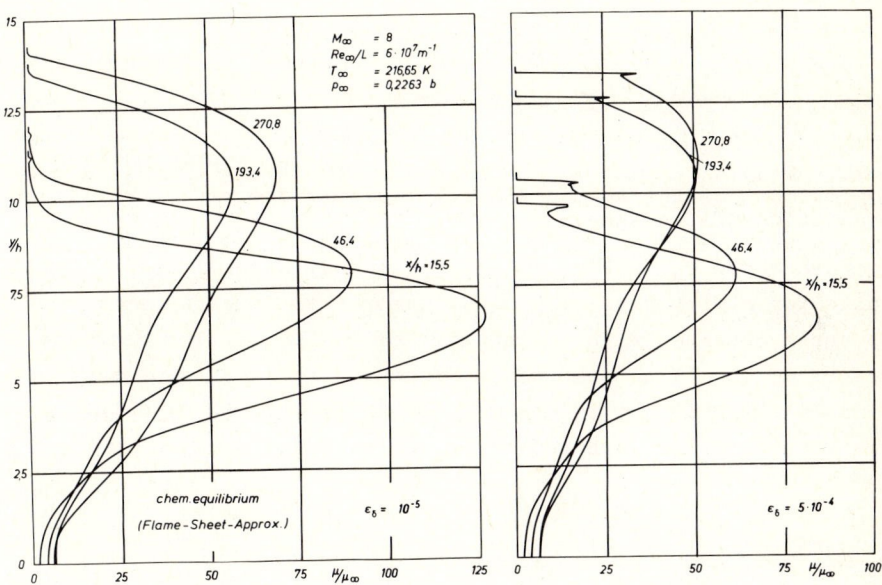

Fig.8 Effect of the accuracy with which the boundary layer is calculated on the profiles for the turbulent viscosity.

It was shown in Fig. 2 that the effective turbulent viscosity is large and exhibits steep gradients on both sides of its maximun value. The accuracy of the second- and fourth-order solution (Mehrstellen-method) can be improved substantially if Eq. (2.1) is divided by $\mu = 1 + \varepsilon$ and $\partial(\ln \mu)/\partial q_3$ is approximated by a finite-difference formula. The improvement of the accuracy can be seen in Fig.9, where the error of $\tau_w$ is plotted versus the step size h for the direction normal to the wall. The curve $C_1$ gives the results for matrix $A_3$ written in the form of Eq. (2.4), while the curve $C_3$ gives the same results, when the derivative is taken of $\ln \mu$.

The value of the shearing stress depends also on the form of the finite-difference approximation used for the point on the wall. If the end-point formula (either second- or fourth-order) is replaced by the

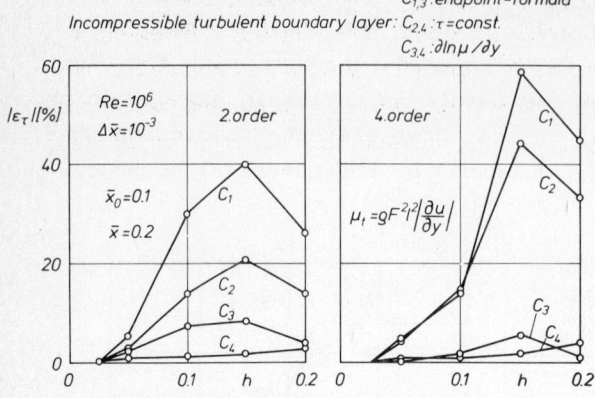

Fig.9 Improvement of the accuracy for the prediction of the shearing stress

assumption that $\tau$ remains constant for the first step of integration for the direction normal to the wall -as outlined in the preceding section- and if $\tau_w$ is calculated from the resulting expansion, $\tau_w$ is less sensitive to an increase of the step size (curve $C_2$).

The two approximations just described provide a marked increase in accuracy (compare curve $C_4$ in Fig. 5). There is only a small deviation of the results for a step size of h = 0,2 (less than five percent) compared to those obtained with a step size of h = 0,025. The decrease of the curve $C_1$ for large step sizes is caused by a cross-over of the over-all error to negative values. It should be kept in mind that all errors mentioned earlier are reflected in the results given in Fig.9.

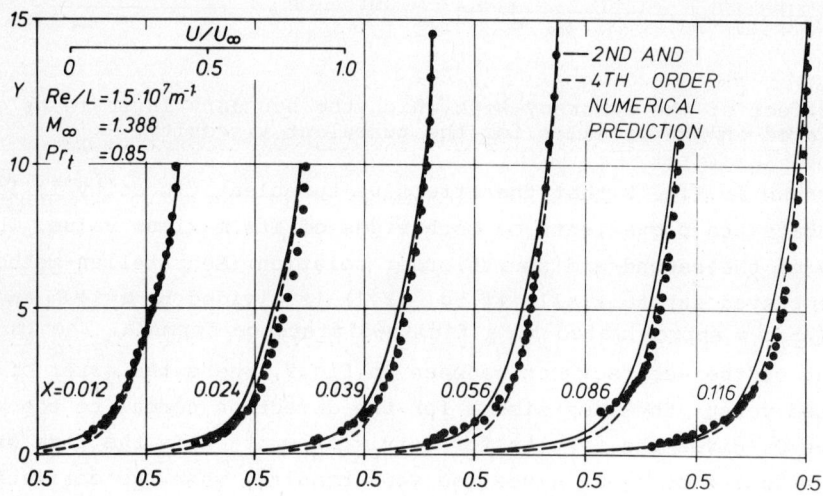

Fig. 1o Comparison of the Merstellen-method and 2nd order solution with experimental data. (Velocity Profiles.)

Finally, in Fig 1o and 11 the Mehrstellen-method is compared with the second-order solution and axperimental data. The better agreement of the Mehrstellen-method with the measurement clearly demonstrates the necessity of accurate numerical solutions, which, no doubt, will be indispensible for future analysis of turbulent flows. This is briefly pointed out in the next section.

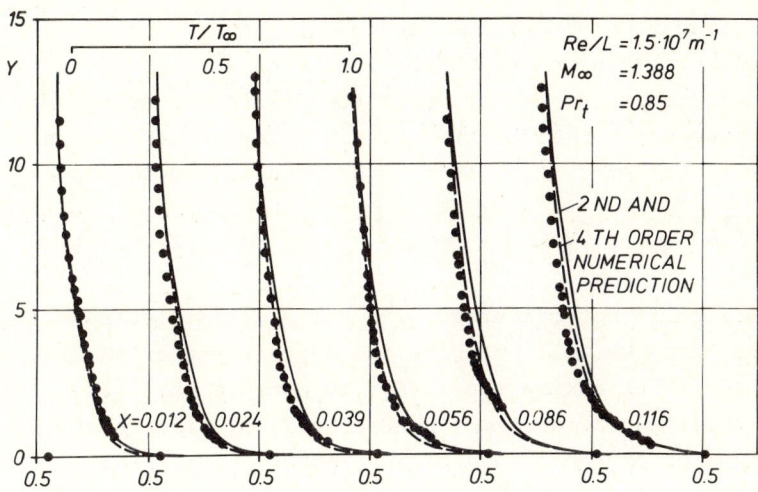

Fig. 11 Comparison of the Mehrstellen-method and 2nd order solution with experimental data. (Temperature Profiles)

## 6. REMARKS ON HIGHER-ORDER CLOSURE OF THE TRANSPORT EQUATIONS

As pointed out in section 2, the momentum equations (2.1) may be made determinate by a first-order model as, for example, by Eq.(2.13). For simple flows, such an approximation is sufficient and reasonable agreement with experimental data can be obtained. For more complex flows the system of equations (2.1) must be supplemented by differential equations for the Reynolds stresses and the kinetic fluctuation energy. These additional equations require naturally more assumptions than the first-order closure. Expressions for the turbulent dissipation, the pressure-shear velocity correlation term, the kinetic energy diffusion and the shear diffusion must be introduced. Several approximations presently being used are discussed in [26] for two-dimensional incompressible high Reynolds number flows. With the one exception described in [27], the differential equation for the Reynolds stresses and the kinetic energy are parabolic in nature and numerical solutions described in the preceeding sections can be employed. If the turbulent length scale L, which is the characteristic length of the eddies carrying the energy, and appears in the expression for the rate of dissipation, is held constant, only relatively simple flows can be predicted, as is shown in [26]. These short-comings due to over-simplifying the turbulence model may be remedied, if a transport equation for the length scale is introduced. Such an equation is given in [26]; although its structure is very complicated, it is again parabolic in nature. The closure assumptions which have to be introduced for the production term require an expansion of the derivative of the mean flow in the direction normal to the wall in a Taylor series. In the notation of [26] the production term is written in the following way:

$$\frac{3}{16}\left[\left(\frac{\partial U}{\partial y}\right)_y \int_{-\infty}^{\infty} R_{21}\, dr_y + \int_{-\infty}^{\infty}\left(\frac{\partial U}{\partial y}\right)_{y+r_y} R_{12}\, dr_y\right] = \overline{uv}\left[L_{12}\frac{\partial U}{\partial y} + \sum_{n=2}^{\infty} L_{12,n}^n \frac{\partial^n U}{\partial y^n}\right] \quad (6.1)$$

As this discussion is not concerned with the physical interpretation of the various terms we will not give the definitions of the integrals of Eq. (6.1) but advise the reader to consult Ref. [26]. Therein attempts are reported to carry out a numerical solution in which a two-term expression of the length scale production term was included in the transport equation. The solution proved to be unstable and according to Ref. [26] the instability had to be attributed to the third-order derivative. This may be due to various reasons as, for example, explicit formulation, the way of decoupling of the equations or the difference approcimations, which would require more than three net points. If, however, the instability is caused by this term alone, a convenient procedure can be devised in order to restrict the number of necessary net points to three and eliminate the third-order derivate from the truncated series in Eq. (6.1). Let the corresponding two-term expansion be designated by $P_2$ such that

$$P_2 = \overline{uv}\left[L_{12}\frac{\partial U}{\partial y} + L_{12,2}^2 \frac{\partial^2 U}{\partial y^2} + L_{12,3}^3 \frac{\partial^3 U}{\partial y^3}\right] \quad (6.2)$$

and write Eq. (4.17) for two-dimensional flows (in cartesian coordinates), i.e.

$$U\frac{\partial U}{\partial x} + V\frac{\partial U}{\partial y} + \frac{\partial p}{\partial x} - \frac{\partial^2 U}{\partial y^2} = -\frac{\partial \overline{uv}}{\partial y} \quad (6.3)$$

then, by inserting the continuity equation there results

$$-U\frac{\partial V}{\partial y} + V\frac{\partial U}{\partial y} + \frac{\partial p}{\partial x} - \frac{\partial^2 U}{\partial y^2} = -\frac{\partial \overline{uv}}{\partial y} \quad (6.4)$$

The third-order derivative can be expressed in terms of second-order derivatives

$$\frac{\partial^3 U}{\partial y^3} = -U\frac{\partial^2 V}{\partial y^2} + V\frac{\partial^2 U}{\partial y^2} + \frac{\partial^2 \overline{uv}}{\partial y^2} \qquad (6.5)$$

and finally the two-term expansion $P_2$ becomes

$$P_2 = \overline{uv}\left[L_{12}\frac{\partial U}{\partial y} + \left(L^2_{12,2} + L^3_{12,3,V}\right)\frac{\partial^2 U}{\partial y^2} - L^3_{12,3} U\frac{\partial^2 V}{\partial y^2} + L^3_{12,3}\frac{\partial^2 \overline{uv}}{\partial y^2}\right] \qquad (6.7)$$

The right hand side of the last equation can then be discretized in the usual manner if the equations are written in implicit formulation or explicitly with a three-level scheme in the x-direction.

## 6. CONCLUSIONS

Prandtl's boundary-layer equations were discussed for the analysis of two-and three-dimensional incompressible laminar and turbulent flows. Only boundary sheets were considered and curvature effects normal to the wall were neglected. The governing equations, written for non-orthogonal curvilinear coordinates, were put into a form suitable for implicit finite-difference integration. The numerical stability of the difference equations was investigated by freezing the coefficients and applying the von-Neumann analysis. The solution was found to be stable if the finite-difference representation of the convective terms is advective. Lower-order instabilities may arise when the curvature terms are large.

It was then shown how the order of the truncation error can be reduced by applying the Mehrstellen-method. The resulting-fourth order solution needs only three net-points for the direction normal to the wall if the coefficient matrices do not contain derivatives for the same direction. It was shown that for special cases this difficulty can be avoided by a suitable transformation. For the general case, however, five point formulae must be used to approximate the coefficients with proper accuracy. The difference equations are still tridiagonal in form and rest on three net-points only. Compared to the second order solution the Mehrstellen-method enforces collocation at these three points and thereby provides a better accuracy.

The method was applied to several flow fields. The additional alge -

braic relations require about ten percent more program statements than the second-order solution does. Results obtained so far indicate that the new method is superior to second-order integration as it gives either better accuracy or smaller calculation times if the coeffi‑ cient matrices are properly normalized. Further improvements are possible. Finally it is shown how third-order terms arising in the transport equation for the length scale can be eliminated by introducing a recursion of the momentum equation.

## REFERENCES

[1] Krause, E., Hirschel, E.H., and Kordulla, W., Fourth Order "Mehrstellen"-Integration for Three-Dimensional Turbulent Boundary Layers. AIA-Computational Fluid Dynamics Conference, Palm Springs, Cal., 19-2o July, 1973, Conference Proceedings.

[2] Krause, E., Numerical Treatment of Boundary-Layer Problems. AGARD LS 64, 1973, Brussels.

[3] Bradshaw, P., Calculation of Three-Dimensional Turbulent Boundary Layers. J. Fluid Mech. (1971), Vol. 46, Part3, pp.417-445.

[4] Wesseling, P., Lindhout, J.P.F., Three-dimensional incompressible turbulent boundary layers: comparison between calculations and experiments. Paper presented at the EUROMECH Colloquium 33 "Three-dimensional turbulent boundary layers", 25 to 27 September 1972, Berlin.

[5] Nash, J.F., Patel, V.C., Three-Dimensional Turbulent Boundary Layers, SBC Technical Books, 1972.

[6] Van den Berg, B., The Law of the Wall in Two-and Three-Dimensional Turbulent Boundary Layers. NLR TR 72111U, 1973.

[7] East, L.F., Measurements of the turbulent boundary layer on a slender wing. Paper presented at the EUROMECH Colloquium 33,1972, Berlin.

[8] Fannelop, T.K., A simple finite difference procedure for solving the three-dimensional laminar and turbulent boundary-layer equations. Paper presented at the EUROMECH Colloquium 33,1972,Berlin.

[9] East, Jr., J.L., Pierce, F.J., Explicit Numerical Solution of the Three-Dimensional Incompressible Turbulent Boundary-Layer

Equations. AIAA Journal, Vol. 1o, No. 9, (1972), pp.1216-1223.

[1o] Klinksiek, W.F., and Pierce, F.J., A Finite-Difference Solution of the Two- and Three-Dimensional Incompressible Turbulent Boundary Layer Equations. Transactions of the ASME. Journal of Fluid Engineering Vol. 95, Series 1, No. 3, September 1973.

[11] Krause, E., Mehrstellenverfahren zur Integration der Grenzschichtgleichungen, DLR Mitt. 71-13 (1971),S. 1o9-138.

[12] Krause, E., Hirschel, E.H., Kordulla, W., Finite difference solutions for three-dimensional turbulent boundary layers. Paper presented at the EUROMECH Colloquium 33, 1972, Berlin.

[13] Hocks, W., Korschelt, D., Küster, H., Peters,N., Arbeitsbericht der Projektgruppe "Turbulente dreidimensionale Grenzschichten", Teil I: Das numerische Verfahren.Inst. f. Thermo- und Fluiddynamik, Technische Universität Berlin (1972).

[14] Krause, E., Hirschel, E.H., Bothmann, Th., Numerische Stabilität dreidimensionaler Grenzschichten, ZAMM Sonderheft 48 (1968),T 2o5.

[15] Krause, E., Hirschel, E.H., Bothmann, Th., Die numerische Integration der Bewegungsgleichungen dreidimensionaler laminarer kompressibler Grenzschichten. Fachtagung Aerodynamik, Berlin 1968, DGLR-Fachbuchreihe Bd. 3, Braunschweig (1969).

[16] Krause, E., Comment on Solution of a Three-Dimensional Boundary-Layer Flow with Separation, AIAA Journal, Vol.7, p. 575.

[17] Richtmyer, R.D., Morton, K.W., Difference Methods for Initial Value Problems, Interscience Publishers Inc., New York (1967), Second Edition.

[18] Kordulla, W., An Improved Calculation Method for Compressible Turbulent Boundary Layers. Paper presented at the EUROMECH 43 Colloquium " Heat transfer in turbulent boundary layer with variable fluid properties", 14 to 16 May 1973, Göttingen.

[19] Sells, C.C.L., Two-dimensional Laminar Compressible Boundary Layer Programme for a Perfect Gas. RAE TR 66243, Aug. 1966.

[2o] Keller, H.B., Cebeci, T., Accurate Numerical Methods for Boundary Layer Flows, I. Two-dimensional Laminar Flows. Proceedings of the Second International Conference on Numerical

Methods in Fluid Dynamics, 1970, Berkeley, Lecture Notes in Physics No. 8, Springer, 1971.

[21] Collatz, L., The numerical treatment of differential equations. Springer, 1960, Vol. 60, 2nd printing of 3rd edition 1966.

[22] Falk, S., Eine Variante zum Differenzenverfahren. ZAMM Vol. 45, 1965, Sonderheft T 32.

[23] Wirz, H.J., Eine Erweiterung des Verfahrens der Zwischenschritte auf allgemeinere parabolische und elliptische Differentialgleichungen. ZAMM 52, 1972, S. 329-336.

[24] Kordulla, W., Helium -und Wasserstoff-Wandstrahlen in atmosphärischen Überschallgrenzschichten. Doctoral Dissertation. Aerodynamisches Institut, Aachen, 1974

[25] Krause, E., Numerical Solution of the Boundary Layer Equations, AIAA Journal. Vol. 5 No.7 (1967) pp. 1231-1237.

[26] Rotta, J.C., Recent Attempts to Develop a Generally Applicable Calculation Method for Turbulent Shear Layers. AGARD Conference Proceedings No. 93 on Turbulent Shear Flows North Atlantic Treaty Organisation. September 1971.

[27] Bradshaw, P., Calculation of Three-Dimensional Turbulent Boundary Layers. J. Fluid Mech. (1971), Vol. 46, Part 3 pp. 417-445.

COMPUTATION OF THREE-DIMENSIONAL,

INVISCID SUPERSONIC FLOWS


Paul Kutler

Ames Research Center, NASA

## Table of Contents

Title Page . . . . . . . . . . . . . . . . . . . . . . . . . . . . . 287

Table of Contents . . . . . . . . . . . . . . . . . . . . . . . . . 288

1. Introduction . . . . . . . . . . . . . . . . . . . . . . . . . . 293
2. Gas-Dynamic Equations . . . . . . . . . . . . . . . . . . . . . 295
    2.1 Euler Equations . . . . . . . . . . . . . . . . . . . . . 295
    2.2 Decoding Conservative Variables . . . . . . . . . . . . . 297
    2.3 Eigenvalues of Governing Equations . . . . . . . . . . . 299
    2.4 Conservative Versus Non Conservative Variables . . . . . 300
3. Coordinate Systems . . . . . . . . . . . . . . . . . . . . . . 304
    3.1 Basic Orthogonal Systems . . . . . . . . . . . . . . . . 304
    3.2 Surface Alignment Transformations . . . . . . . . . . . 306
    3.3 Self-Similar Transformations . . . . . . . . . . . . . . 308
    3.4 Point Concentration Transformations . . . . . . . . . . 311
4. Finite-Difference Schemes . . . . . . . . . . . . . . . . . . 312
    4.1 First-Order Scheme . . . . . . . . . . . . . . . . . . . 314
    4.2 Second-Order Scheme . . . . . . . . . . . . . . . . . . 315
    4.3 Third-Order Scheme . . . . . . . . . . . . . . . . . . . 317
    4.4 Solution of $u_t + (u^2/2)_x = 0$ . . . . . . . . . . . . 318
5. Boundary Conditions . . . . . . . . . . . . . . . . . . . . . 322
    5.1 Impermeable Boundaries . . . . . . . . . . . . . . . . . 323
    5.2 Permeable Boundaries . . . . . . . . . . . . . . . . . . 329
6. Initial Conditions, Step Size, and Convergence . . . . . . . . 335
7. Numerical Results . . . . . . . . . . . . . . . . . . . . . . 338
    7.1 Two-Dimensional Wedge and Axisymmetric Cone Flow . . . . 338
    7.2 Planar Delta Wing . . . . . . . . . . . . . . . . . . . 340
    7.3 Conical Wing-Body Combination . . . . . . . . . . . . . 346
    7.4 Internal Corner Flow . . . . . . . . . . . . . . . . . . 348
    7.5 Two-Dimensional Blunt Body . . . . . . . . . . . . . . . 352

Table of Contents (Continued)

7.6 Interfering Shock Problem . . . . . . . . . . . . . . . . . . . . 355

7.7 Three-Dimensional Supersonic Flow . . . . . . . . . . . . . . . . 357

References . . . . . . . . . . . . . . . . . . . . . . . . . . . . . . . 371

## List of Figures

| Figure | Title | Page |
|---|---|---|
| 1. | Three-dimensional interfering shock problem; to determine unsteady flow field interactions . . . . . . . . . . . . . . . . . . . . | 294 |
| 2. | Typical shock wave and contact surface structure for interfering shock problem . . . . . . . . . . . . . . . . . . . . . . . . . . . | 294 |
| 3. | Spherical coordinate system $(r, \theta, \phi)$ . . . . . . . . . . . | 296 |
| 4. | Approximation square wave using first several harmonics . . . . . | 301 |
| 5. | Conservative variable distribution through shock generated by a wedge (a and b) or cone (c and d) . . . . . . . . . . . . . . . . | 302 |
| 6. | Supersonic flow over a pointed ogive. . . . . . . . . . . . . . . | 303 |
| 7. | Supersonic blunt-body flow. . . . . . . . . . . . . . . . . . . . | 303 |
| 8. | Planform shock pattern for space shuttle orbiter. . . . . . . . . | 304 |
| 9. | Surface-oriented coordinate system. . . . . . . . . . . . . . . . | 305 |
| 10. | Result of transformation to align body with a coordinate direction. | 306 |
| 11. | Configurations and coordinate systems for coordinate alignment with body. . . . . . . . . . . . . . . . . . . . . . . . . . . . . . . | 307 |
| 12. | Body and shock coordinate alignment . . . . . . . . . . . . . . . | 307 |
| 13. | Three-dimensional coordinate alignment; (a) normalization between body and outer boundary, and (b) normalization between body and peripheral shock. . . . . . . . . . . . . . . . . . . . . . . . . | 308 |
| 14. | Coordinate system and mesh description for planar delta wing. . . | 309 |
| 15. | Two-dimensional interfering shock problem with self-similar planes. | 310 |
| 16. | Rectangular and shock-aligned computation boundaries for interfering shock problem . . . . . . . . . . . . . . . . . . . . | 311 |
| 17. | First-order solution of Eq. (4.2b) using Lax's scheme for Courant numbers of 1.0 and 0.5. . . . . . . . . . . . . . . . . . . . . . | 319 |
| 18. | Second-order solution of Eq. (4.2b) using MacCormack's scheme for Courant numbers of 1.0 and 0.5; (a) version I, and (b) version II . | 320 |
| 19. | Comparison of second- (versions I and II permuted) and third-order solutions of Eq. (4.2b) for Courant numbers of 0.9 and 0.1. . . . . | 320 |
| 20. | Calculation of a weak shock in the presence of a strong shock; (a) third-order method with a constant $\omega$, (b) third-order method with a variable $\omega$, and (c) second-order method (versions I and II permuted) . . . . . . . . . . . . . . . . . . . . . . . . . . . . | 321 |
| 21. | Reflection technique for flat surface in x-z plane; (I) image point approach and (II) nonimage point approach . . . . . . . . . | 323 |
| 22. | Comparison sketch of method of characteristics and reflection or one-sided, finite-difference techniques . . . . . . . . . . . . . | 325 |

List of Figures (Continued)

| Figure | | Page |
|---|---|---|
| 23. | Unsteady shock for two-dimensional supersonic flow in polar coordinates (t, r, $\theta$)................................. | 330 |
| 24. | Steady shock for three-dimensional supersonic flow in cylindrical coordinates (z, r, $\phi$)................................. | 332 |
| 25. | Supersonic outflow and inflow computational boundaries; (a) blunt body, and (b) planar delta wing-compression side.......... | 334 |
| 26. | Computation of simple supersonic wedge flow using first- and second-order methods................................. | 339 |
| 27. | Computation of axisymmetric supersonic cone flow using first- and second-order methods................................. | 340 |
| 28. | Spanwise pressure distribution on compression side of planar delta wing; $M = 4$, $\Lambda = 50°$, $\alpha = 5°$, $10°$, and $15°$.......... | 343 |
| 29. | Compression side-shock shapes; $M = 4$, $\Lambda = 50°$, $\alpha = 5°$, $10°$, and $15°$ | 343 |
| 30. | Spanwise pressure distribution on expansion side of planar delta wing; $M = 3$, $\Lambda = 45°$, $\alpha = 4°$, $8°$, and $12°$............ | 344 |
| 31. | Spanwise pitot pressure distribution on planar delta wing; $M = 2.94$, $\Lambda = 44.7°$, $\alpha = 12°$................... | 345 |
| 32. | Comparison with experiment of shock wave and conical sonic line for planar delta wing; $M = 2.94$, $\Lambda = 44.7°$, $\alpha = 12°$.......... | 345 |
| 33. | Windward centerline pressure distributions beneath planar delta wing; $M = 2.7$, $\Lambda = 55°$, $\alpha = 1.8°$................ | 346 |
| 34. | Coordinate system for conical wing-body combination....... | 347 |
| 35. | Computed location of shock and expansion waves around wing-body combination; $M = 4$, $\Lambda = 50°$, $\alpha = 5°$................ | 347 |
| 36. | Surface-pressure distribution on wing-body combination; $M = 4$, $\Lambda = 50°$, $\alpha = 5°$................................. | 348 |
| 37. | Coordinate system and typical wave structure............. | 349 |
| 38. | Computational plane for internal corner flow.............. | 350 |
| 39. | Comparison of numerical and experimental shock patterns; $M = 2.98$, $\delta_1 = \delta_2 = 9.49°$................................. | 351 |
| 40. | Comparison of numerical and experimental surface-pressure distributions; $M = 2.98$, $\delta_1 = \delta_2 = 9.49°$.............. | 352 |
| 41. | Comparison of numerical and experimental shock patterns for unequal wedge angles; $M = 3.17$, $\delta_1 = 3.5°$, $\delta_2 = 12.2°$.......... | 353 |
| 42. | Shock shape for two-dimensional blunt body; $M = 4$ and $10$...... | 354 |
| 43. | Surface-pressure distribution for two-dimensional blunt body; $M = 10$................................. | 354 |

## List of Figures (Continued)

| Figure | | Page |
|---|---|---|
| 44. | Stagnation streamline pressure distribution for two-dimensional blunt body; M = 10. | 354 |
| 45. | Density contours for two-dimensional interfering shock problem; $M_w$ = 3.15, $\delta$ = 30°, $M_i$ = 2, $\lambda$ = 60° | 357 |
| 46. | Pressure contours for two-dimensional interfering shock problem; $M_w$ = 3.15, $\delta$ = 30°, $M_i$ = 2, $\lambda$ = 60° | 357 |
| 47. | Schlieren photograph of two-dimensional interfering shock problem; $M_w$ = 3, $\delta$ = 30°, $M_i$ = 2, $\lambda$ = 60°. | 358 |
| 48. | Coordinate system for three-dimensional configurations. | 359 |
| 49. | Mesh description for three-dimensional problem | 360 |
| 50. | Typical body cross section. | 361 |
| 51. | Surface-pressure distribution for cone at angle of attack; M = 3, $\alpha$ = 15°, $\sigma$ = 7.5° | 362 |
| 52. | Crossflow Mach number contour plot for cone at angle of attack; M = 3, $\alpha$ = 15°, $\sigma$ = 7.5°. | 363 |
| 53. | Cross-sectional shock shape for cone at angle of attack; M = 7, $\alpha$ = 15° and 30°, $\sigma$ = 20°. | 364 |
| 54. | Density distribution behind shock wave for cone at an le of attack; M = 7, $\alpha$ = 15° and 30°, $\sigma$ = 20° | 364 |
| 55. | Crossflow Mach number contour plot for cone at incidence; M = 7, $\alpha$ = 30°, $\sigma$ = 20°. | 365 |
| 56. | Shock location for pointed-nose configuration; M = 7.4, $\alpha$ = 0°. | 367 |
| 57. | Shock location for lung-nose configuration; M = 7.4, $\alpha$ = 15.3°. | 368 |
| 58. | Propagation of canopy and recompression shocks through shock layer in leeward plane of symmetry; M = 7.4, $\alpha$ = 15.3°. | 369 |
| 59. | Radial pressure and density distribution through entropy layer and wing leading-edge shock; M = 7.4, $\alpha$ = 15.3° | 369 |
| 60. | Longitudinal surface-pressure distribution for the 0°, 90°, and 180° meridians; M = 7.4, $\alpha$ = 15.3°. | 370 |
| 61. | Comparison of shock location for blunt-nose configurations; M = 26.26, $\alpha$ = 15.3°, altitude = 76 km. | 371 |

COMPUTATION OF THREE-DIMENSIONAL, INVISCID SUPERSONIC FLOWS

by

Paul Kutler

Computational Fluid Dynamics Branch
Ames Research Center, NASA
Moffett Field, California 94035

## 1. INTRODUCTION

The numerical computation of three-dimensional, inviscid flow fields for either perfect or real gases about supersonic or hypersonic airplanes and reentry spacecraft can be of considerable importance to the vehicle designer. The continual increase in complexity of such prototype aerospace vehicles (e.g., the space shuttle) requires thousands of hours of costly wind-tunnel time (approximately $1000 per hour) to provide the aerodynamic flow simulations necessary for their development and design. Even with this investment of time, it is necessary to accurately scale the wind-tunnel results to real flight conditions, which is not always possible. Consequently, computer simulations offer an inexpensive supplement to the experimental data and, in certain instances, can completely eliminate the need for experimental testing. This paper describes some numerical procedures capable of determining the complicated supersonic flow fields about wings, bodies, and wing-body combinations.

The flow field about such configurations can contain multiple shocks, expansion waves, and slip surfaces. Basically, two philosophically different approaches can be used to compute such a flow field. The "shock-capturing technique" is inherently capable of predicting the location and strength of all flow discontinuities and their interaction without knowledge of their presence. The "sharp-shock technique" attempts to treat all known shock waves as sharp discontinuities by predicting their motion and applying the Rankine-Hugoniot equations across them. The shock-capturing technique has the single big advantage of being easy to apply while at the same time yielding an accurate solution. The flow discontinuities, rather than appearing as discrete jumps, are spread over several mesh intervals; however, can be precisely located within that region.

Probably all supersonic-flow problems involving multiple shock waves and their intersections could be solved using a sharp-shock procedure. To allow for all possible types of interactions and reflections, however, would be a formidable task. Consider, for example, the flow field generated by a planar oblique shock passing over a cone at angle of attack in supersonic flight (Fig. 1). The resulting flow field is shown in Fig. 2. This time-dependent problem can lead to a variety of possible shock patterns depending on the incident shock-wave inclination angle and strength. This particular problem, however, is well suited for solution by the shock-capturing

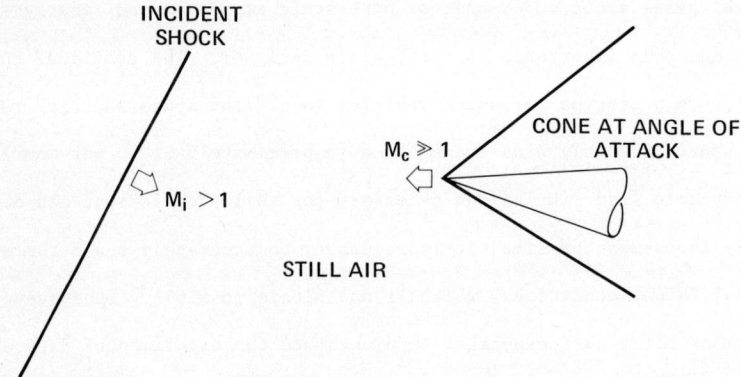

Fig. 1. Three-dimensional interfering shock problem; to determine unsteady flow field interactions.

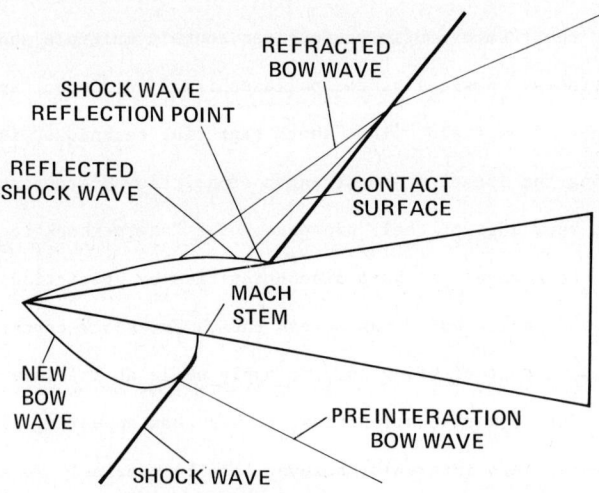

Fig. 2. Typical shock wave and contact surface structure for interfering shock problem.

approach because of its ability to accurately predict the location and intensity of all shock waves without any special treatment. Examples of the equivalent two-dimensional problem are presented later.

In applying the shock-capturing technique, the appropriate hyperbolic equations that govern inviscid flows are written in conservation law form; that is, the dependent conservative variables ($\rho u$, $\rho u v$, $p + \rho u^2$, etc.) are composed of the product and sum of the individual state (nonconservative) variables ($p$, $\rho$, $u$, $v$, etc.) and yield a set of partial differential equations (pde's) whose coefficients are unity. They are then integrated using a finite-difference scheme of the desired accuracy with the appropriate boundary conditions being applied at the extremities of the computational domain.

In the following sections, the pde's for both unsteady and steady flows are presented. First-, second-, and third-order finite-difference schemes are discussed briefly. Boundary condition procedures used in the numerical computations are also reviewed and discussed. The computational solutions discussed here, which have all been presented or published elsewhere, include supersonic flow about cones, delta wings, conical wing-body combinations, internal corners, blunt bodies, and three-dimensional wing-body configurations.

## 2. GAS-DYNAMIC EQUATIONS

### 2.1 Euler Equations

The basic equations of gasdynamics include those for the conservation of mass, conservation of species, conservation of momentum, and conservation of energy as well as an equation of state. These nonlinear partial differential equations are written in terms of four independent variables; time, plus three space dimensions. Under the assumptions of an inviscid, non-heat-conducting gas in local thermochemical equilibrium, these equations are written in the following conservation law form for a generalized orthogonal coordinate system:

$$\frac{\partial U}{\partial t} + \frac{\partial E}{\partial x_1} + \frac{\partial F}{\partial x_2} + \frac{\partial G}{\partial x_3} + H = 0 \qquad (2.1)$$

where

$$U = h_1 h_2 h_3 \begin{pmatrix} \rho \\ \rho u \\ \rho v \\ \rho w \\ e \end{pmatrix}, \quad E = h_2 h_3 \begin{pmatrix} \rho u \\ p+\rho u^2 \\ \rho uv \\ \rho uw \\ (e+p)u \end{pmatrix}, \quad F = h_1 h_3 \begin{pmatrix} \rho v \\ \rho uv \\ p+\rho v^2 \\ \rho vw \\ (e+p)v \end{pmatrix}, \quad G = h_1 h_2 \begin{pmatrix} \rho w \\ \rho uw \\ \rho vw \\ p+\rho w^2 \\ (e+p)w \end{pmatrix}$$

$$H = \begin{pmatrix} 0 \\ \rho uvh_3 \frac{\partial h_1}{\partial x_2} + \rho uwh_2 \frac{\partial h_1}{\partial x_3} - (p+\rho v^2)h_3 \frac{\partial h_2}{\partial x_1} - (p+\rho w^2)h_2 \frac{\partial h_3}{\partial x_1} \\ \rho vwh_1 \frac{\partial h_2}{\partial x_3} + \rho uvh_3 \frac{\partial h_2}{\partial x_1} - (p+\rho w^2)h_1 \frac{\partial h_3}{\partial x_2} - (p+\rho u^2)h_3 \frac{\partial h_1}{\partial x_2} \\ \rho uwh_2 \frac{\partial h_3}{\partial x_1} + \rho vwh_1 \frac{\partial h_3}{\partial x_2} - (p+\rho u^2)h_2 \frac{\partial h_1}{\partial x_3} - (p+\rho v^2)h_1 \frac{\partial h_2}{\partial x_3} \\ 0 \end{pmatrix}$$

where $t$ and $x_i$ are the independent variables and $h_i$ are the metric coefficients (or arcual derivatives - $h_i = \partial S_i / \partial x_i$, where $S_i$ is the arc length measured in the $x_i$ direction with the remaining two independent variables fixed). For example, the metric coefficients for a spherical coordinate ($x_1$, $x_2$, $x_3 = r$, $\theta$, $\phi$) system (Fig. 3) are

$$h_1 = \partial S_1 / \partial r = 1$$
$$h_2 = \partial S_2 / \partial \theta = r \sin \phi$$
$$h_3 = \partial S_3 / \partial \phi = r$$

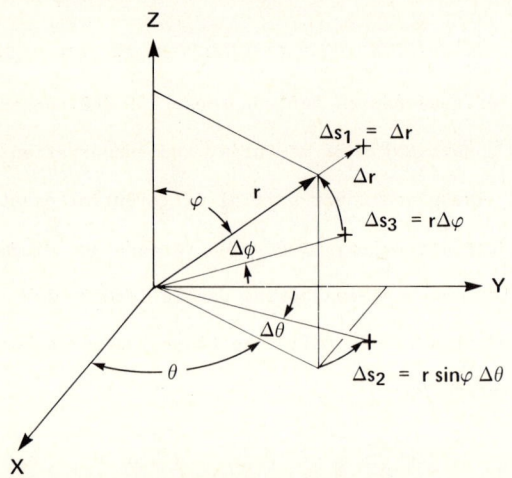

Fig. 3. Spherical coordinate system ($r$, $\theta$, $\phi$).

In Eq. (2.1), p represents the pressure; $\rho$, the density; u, v, and w, the velocity components in the $x_i$ directions, respectively; and e, the total energy per unit volume. The energy e is related to p, $\rho$, u, v, and w by

$$e = \rho \left[ h(p,\rho) + \frac{u^2+v^2+w^2}{2} \right] - p \qquad (2.2)$$

where $h(p,\rho)$ is the state equation for static enthalpy. The specific formulation for h depends, in particular, on whether the gas is assumed to be perfect or everywhere in local thermodynamic equilibrium. For a perfect gas, $h(p,\rho)$ is simply related to pressure and density ($h = (p/\rho)[\gamma/(\gamma-1)]$), and total energy is thus given by

$$e = \frac{p}{\gamma-1} + \rho \frac{u^2+v^2+w^2}{2} \qquad (2.3)$$

For a real gas, no such simple explicit functional relationship exists. The conventional procedure[1,2] for evaluating real gas state relations is to use a combination table lookup and curve-fitting procedure.

For steady flow, the differential form of energy equation (2.1) can be replaced by the integrated form, yielding the equation for total enthalpy:

$$H_t = h(p,\rho) + \frac{u^2+v^2+w^2}{2} = \text{constant : real gas} \qquad (2.4a)$$

$$H_t = \frac{p}{\rho} \frac{\gamma}{\gamma-1} + \frac{u^2+v^2+w^2}{2} = \text{constant : perfect gas} \qquad (2.4b)$$

## 2.2 Decoding Conservative Variables

It is well known that Eq. (2.1) is hyperbolic for all flow regimes. It is also known that, for steady flow, Eq. (2.1) is hyperbolic with respect to the $x_1$, $x_2$, or $x_3$ coordinate if the velocity component in that direction is greater than the local speed of sound. When one solves such hyperbolic equations by finite-difference procedures, prior to each integration step, the physical flow variables p, $\rho$, u, v, w, and e must be obtained from the components $u_i$ of U for unsteady problems (p, $\rho$, u, v, and w from $e_i$ of E for steady problems ($x_1$-hyperbolic)) to form the other conservative variables (E, F, and G, unsteady; F and G, steady).

For the unsteady case,

$$\left.\begin{aligned} \rho &= u_1 \\ u &= u_2/u_1 \\ v &= u_3/u_1 \\ w &= u_4/u_1 \\ e &= u_5 \end{aligned}\right\} \text{real or ideal gas} \qquad (2.5)$$

The pressure can be obtained directly from Eq. (2.3) for an ideal gas and iteratively or possibly directly in conjunction with gas property tables from Eq. (2.2) for a real gas.

For the steady case, the decoding procedure necessitates the solution of five simultaneous, nonlinear equations consisting of Eq. (2.4) together with the four elements $e_i$. The velocity components $v$ and $w$ are given by

$$v = e_3/e_1, \quad w = e_4/e_1 \qquad (2.6a)$$

If the $e_i$ along with the above relations are used to eliminate the explicit dependence of $p$, $\rho$, $v$, and $w$ from Eq. (2.4a), the following implicit expression for the velocity $u$ is obtained:

$$D(u) = u^2/2 + h[p(u), \rho(u)] - \Gamma/2 = 0 \qquad (2.7a)$$

where

$$\left.\begin{aligned} p(u) &= (e_2 - e_1 u)/h_2 h_3 \\ \rho(u) &= e_1/h_2 h_3 u \\ \Gamma &= 2H_t - (e_3^2 + e_4^2)/e_1^2 \end{aligned}\right\} \qquad (2.7b)$$

The decoding procedure is now reduced to a problem of root finding—that is, the $x_1$—velocity component $u$ that satisfies Eq. (2.7a). Two roots exist, one corresponding to subsonic flow, the other to supersonic flow. We seek the supersonic root because the flow in the $x_1$ direction is assumed to be supersonic, which resulted in the $x_1$ hyperbolicity of our equations. The procedure for solving Eq. (2.7a) depends on whether a perfect or real gas is being considered and, consequently, on the function $h(p,\rho)$.

For an ideal gas,

$$h(p,\rho) = \frac{\gamma}{\gamma-1} \frac{p}{\rho}$$

and, when combined with Eq. (2.7a), yields a quadratic equation that can be solved, resulting in an algebraic expression for the supersonic velocity u:

$$u = [-B + (B^2 - 4AC)^{1/2}]/2A \qquad (2.6b)$$

where

$$A = \frac{\gamma+1}{2\gamma}$$

$$B = -e_2/e_1$$

$$C = \frac{\gamma-1}{2\gamma}(2H_t - v^2 - w^2)$$

To find the roots of Eq. (2.7a) for a real gas, a root-finding algorithm is used in conjunction with gas property tables. According to Kutler et al.,[3] the successive linear interpolation scheme described by Dekker[4] was found to be very efficient and required, on the average, about seven iterations to find the desired supersonic root.

## 2.3 Eigenvalues of Governing Equations

The solution of initial value problems using finite difference procedures requires an integration step size. The value of this step size (discussed in a later section) is a function of the eigenvalues of the coefficient matrices of the governing pde's when written in the form:

$$\frac{\partial U}{\partial t} + P \frac{\partial U}{\partial x_1} + Q \frac{\partial U}{\partial x_2} + R \frac{\partial U}{\partial x_3} + S = 0 \; ; \quad \text{unsteady} \qquad (2.8a)$$

$$\frac{\partial E}{\partial x_1} + J \frac{\partial E}{\partial x_2} + K \frac{\partial E}{\partial x_3} + L = 0 \; ; \quad \text{steady } (x_1\text{-hyperbolic}) \qquad (2.8b)$$

where P, Q, R, J, and K are the Jacobian matrices $\partial E/\partial U$, $\partial G/\partial U$, $\partial F/\partial E$, and $\partial G/\partial E$, respectively.

Equations (2.8) are difficult to derive algebraically, and once the derivation is complete, it is even more difficult to determine their eigenvalues. An easier way to obtain the same result is to rewrite Eq. (2.8) as

$$\frac{\partial U}{\partial t} + A \frac{\partial U}{\partial x_1} + B \frac{\partial U}{\partial x_2} + C \frac{\partial U}{\partial x_3} + D = 0 \; ; \quad \text{unsteady} \qquad (2.9a)$$

$$\frac{\partial U}{\partial x_1} + M \frac{\partial U}{\partial x_2} + N \frac{\partial U}{\partial x_3} + A^{-1}D = 0 \; ; \quad \text{steady} \qquad (2.9b)$$

where $U = [u,v,w,p,\rho]^t$, $M = A^{-1}B$, and $N = A^{-1}C$.

The eigenvalues of the coefficient matrices A, B, C, M, and N are

$$\left.\begin{array}{ll}\sigma^A_{1,2} = (u\pm c)/h_1 \;, & \sigma^A_{3,4,5} = u/h_1 \\ \sigma^B_{1,2} = (v\pm c)/h_2 \;, & \sigma^B_{3,4,5} = v/h_1 \\ \sigma^C_{1,2} = (w\pm c)/h_3 \;, & \sigma^C_{3,4,5} = w/h_1 \end{array}\right\} \text{unsteady} \quad (2.10a)$$

$$\left.\begin{array}{ll}\sigma^M_{1,2} = \dfrac{h_1}{h_2}\left[\dfrac{uv\pm c\sqrt{u^2+v^2-c^2}}{u^2-c^2}\right] \;, & \sigma^M_{3,4,5} = \dfrac{v}{u}\dfrac{h_1}{h_3} \\ \sigma^N_{1,2} = \dfrac{h_1}{h_3}\left[\dfrac{uw\pm c\sqrt{u^2+w^2-c^2}}{u^2-c^2}\right] \;, & \sigma^N_{3,4,5} = \dfrac{w}{u}\dfrac{h_1}{h_2} \end{array}\right\} \text{steady} \quad (2.10b)$$

The $\sigma$ terms in Eq. (2.10a) can be recognized as the slopes of the characteristics and streamlines in the $t-x_1$, $t-x_2$, and $t-x_3$ planes, while the $\sigma$ terms in Eq. (2.10b) are the slopes in the $x_1-x_2$ and $x_1-x_3$ planes. Note that any secondary transformation of the independent variables of Eq. (2.1) will logically change the eigenvalues of the governing equations (as shown in a later example).

## 2.4 Conservative Versus Nonconservative Variables

As mentioned in the Introduction, shock-capturing techniques are used to determine the supersonic flow fields presented here. As Lax[5] points out, it is necessary to formulate the governing equations, therefore, in conservation law form and integrate them using a conservative finite-difference procedure to guarantee that any discontinuities in the flow will be processed correctly, for example, shock waves will be of the correct intensity and in the correct position. It was demonstrated by Lax,[5] Gary,[6] and Abbett[7] that use of the nonconservative form of the equations can produce significant errors in the speed of the shock wave, while Longley[8] showed that the conservation form yielded the correct shock speed for a variety of finite-difference schemes.

The shock waves captured using such a procedure, although correctly positioned and of the proper strength, generally will not appear as sharp discontinuities, but will be spread over several mesh intervals. For second- and higher-order, finite-difference schemes,[9] the solution will display post- and precursor oscillations of the dependent variables in the vicinity of the shock. The simple reason that these discrepancies occur is that the dependent variables being differenced, although conservative, can be discontinuous across the shock, and the finite-difference scheme approximates the solution by passing a polynomial of some degree through the discontinuity. (The degree equals the order of the finite-difference scheme.) This is analogous to approximating a discontinuity by the first few terms of a Fourier series (Fig. 4).

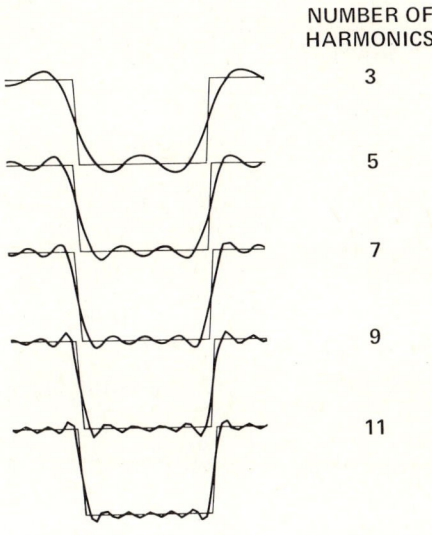

Fig. 4. Approximation square wave using first several harmonics.

Spreading of the shock and oscillations near the shock wave will not always occur with a shock-capturing approach. Consider, for example, the steady supersonic flow over a wedge (Figs. 5(a) and (b)). The flow properties (nonconservative variables) on either side of the wedge shock are constant. For polar coordinates $[(x_1, x_2 = r, \theta);$ $h_1 = 1, h_2 = r]$, the conservative variables $F$ of Eq. (2.1) are continuous across the shock (Fig. 5(b)) since $F_{\text{free stream}} = F_{\text{wedge}}$, which are simply the Rankine-Hugoniot equations for a normal shock. Therefore, any conservative finite-difference approximation of $\partial F/\partial \theta$ in the free stream, across the shock, or in the shock layer will be zero, and will not produce oscillations of the dependent variables. Because of this, the shock will span only one mesh interval.

Consider the steady supersonic flow over a cone, again in polar coordinates (Figs. 5(c) and (d)). The flow properties in the shock layer are continuous but not constant, while the conservative variable $F$ is continuous everywhere, but with a discontinuous first derivative ($\partial F/\partial \theta$) at the shock ($F_{\text{free stream}} = F_{\text{cone}}$ at shock).

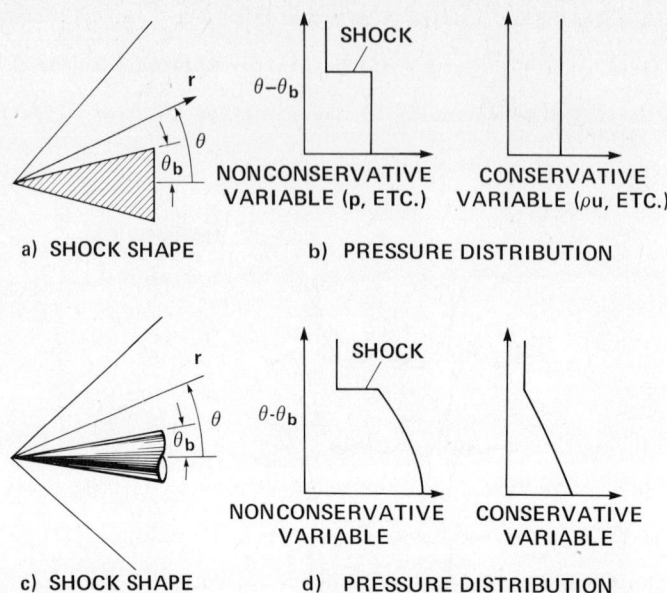

Fig. 5. Conservative variable distribution through shock generated by a wedge (a and b) or cone (c and d).

Therefore, differencing across the shock in this case will generate oscillations in the vicinity of the shock.

In both examples mentioned above, one of the coordinate lines ($\theta$ = const) was aligned with the shock wave, which resulted in the continuously varying F conservative variables across the shock. If the coordinate system is chosen so that the shock is not parallel to one of the coordinate lines, then none of the conservative variables will be continuous across the shock, which will induce added oscillations at the shock. Therefore, the more skewed the shock is with respect to the coordinate lines, and the more the flow variables change near the shock, the greater the oscillations will be in the vicinity of the shock. Examples presented later show that although captured shocks exhibit oscillations, the remaining flow field is still accurately predicted.

As noted, the time-dependent Euler equations (Eq. (2.1)) are hyperbolic and generally can be used to solve any unsteady or steady three-dimensional problem using finite-difference procedures. However, it would be inappropriate to solve for the steady supersonic flow over a pointed ogive, for example, using the unsteady equations

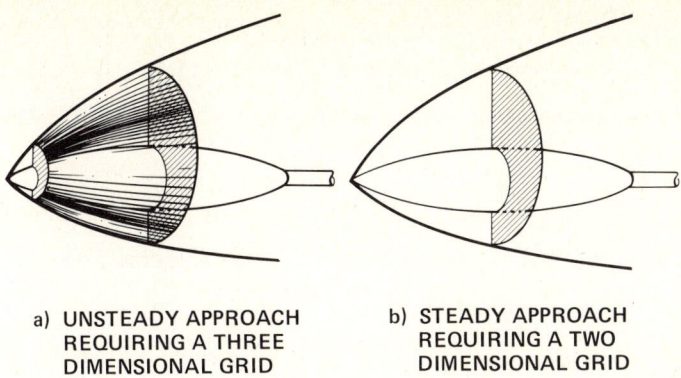

a) UNSTEADY APPROACH REQUIRING A THREE DIMENSIONAL GRID

b) STEADY APPROACH REQUIRING A TWO DIMENSIONAL GRID

Fig. 6. Supersonic flow over a pointed ogive.

that require a three-dimensional grid (Fig. 6(a)) when the steady equations are hyperbolic in the longitudinal direction and can be solved with a marching procedure requiring only a two-dimensional grid (Fig. 6(b)).

As another example, consider the flow over a three-dimensional, blunt-nosed configuration in which the last plane of data must be normal to the body axis and in the supersonic flow region. Again, the unsteady equations could be used to solve the entire problem (Fig. 7(a)). However, a more efficient procedure is to discretize only the embedded three-dimensional subsonic region for solution by the unsteady approach as did Rizzi and Inouye[10] (Fig. 7(b)) and then use a steady marching approach from the warped unsteady boundary to the required axis normal plane (Rizzi et al.[11]).

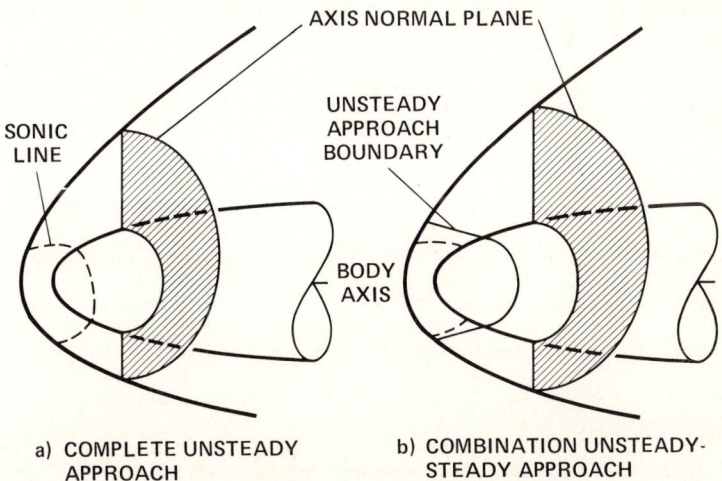

a) COMPLETE UNSTEADY APPROACH

b) COMBINATION UNSTEADY-STEADY APPROACH

Fig. 7. Supersonic blunt-body flow.

When one solves supersonic flow problems involving three-dimensional geometries, it is quite possible that embedded regions of subsonic flow may exist at other places in the field than near the blunt nose. In Fig. 8, for example, the supersonic flow over a space shuttle orbiter generates both a bow shock and wing shock which, when they intersect, can result in a small region of locally subsonic flow. Determination of the flow in a region such as this requires a local solution of the unsteady equations, which may not be a trivial matter.

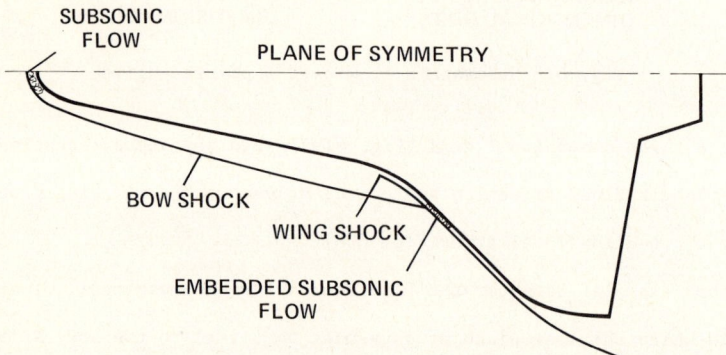

Fig. 8. Planform shock pattern for space shuttle orbiter.

Note that although the inclusion of the time derivative in the governing pde's affords us the ability to calculate transient flows, some workers[10,12] are interested only in the steady-state solution. In such instances, one should strive to obtain the solution without the rigors required to maintain a truly time-accurate procedure if this speeds convergence.

## 3. COORDINATE SYSTEMS

As briefly pointed out in the previous section, a judicious choice of the independent variable can have pronounced effects on the resulting numerical solution. Thus some forethought should go into the choice of coordinate system and subsequent independent variable transformations that are to be used.

### 3.1 Basic Orthogonal Systems

Table 1 lists three of the most commonly and one not so commonly used orthogonal coordinate systems along with their metric coefficients. Some explanation should be given to better understand the surface-oriented coordinate system (Fig. 9). The coordinates $\mu$ and $\xi$ lie on the surface, with $\mu$ being the distance measured along the surface from an origin $\xi$ the distance along the surface from the $\xi = 0$ line, normal to $\mu$ = const lines. The third coordinate $\eta$ is the distance measured normal to the surface. The metric coefficients for this system involve the radii of curvature $R^\mu$ and $R^\xi$ of the surface in the $\mu$ and $\xi$ directions. Note that this system is somewhat difficult to work with, but slight variations of it are particularly useful.

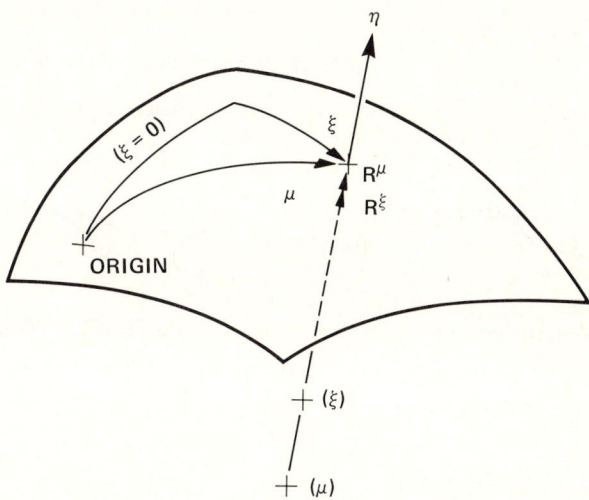

Fig. 9. Surface-oriented coordinate system.

The last three coordinate systems listed in Table 1 contain singularities due to the transformation from a Cartesian system that has no singularities in a finite region; for example, spherical coordinates (Fig. 3) are singular when $\phi = 0$ or $r = 0$. In most instances when these various coordinate systems are used, computation near the singularities is not required. However, when it is, a simple application of

Table 1.

Metric Coefficients for Some Orthogonal Coordinate Systems

| Coordinates | $x_i$ | $h_i$ |
|---|---|---|
| Cartesian | x, y, z | 1, 1, 1 |
| Cylindrical | z, r, $\phi$ | 1, 1, r |
| Spherical | r, $\theta$, $\phi$ | 1, r sin $\phi$, r |
| Surface oriented (Fig. 9) | $\mu$, $\eta$, $\xi$ | $1+\eta/R^\mu$, 1, $1+\eta/R^\xi$ |

l'Hospital's rule yields a new set of governing equations to be used at the singular points (see, for example, Bohachevsky and Mates[13]).

## 3.2 Surface Alignment Transformations

Once the basic orthogonal coordinate system is selected, subsequent independent variable transformations can be made to align various surfaces with a particular coordinate and/or concentrate grid points at a given location or in a particular area of the discretized flow region. One of the goals underlying the choice of the coordinate system or transformation should be to align the surface of the body with a coordinate surface (Fig. 10). This eliminates the necessity of unequally spaced grid points at

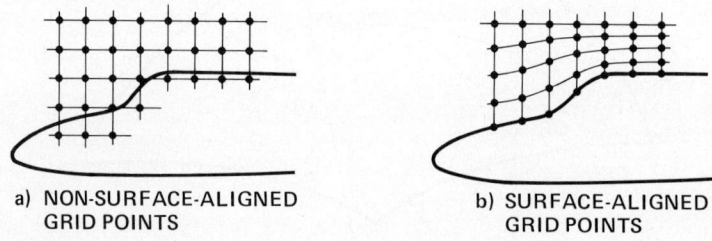

a) NON-SURFACE-ALIGNED GRID POINTS

b) SURFACE-ALIGNED GRID POINTS

Fig. 10. Result of transformation to align body with a coordinate direction.

the body (Fig. 10(a)) and the subsequent formation of instabilities in the numerical calculation (see, for example, Burstein[14]). For some problems, the choice of coordinate system is such that one of the coordinates is already coincident with the surface of the body and need not be transformed. Consider, for example, the following problems and their coordinate systems as shown in Fig. 11:

1. Wedge flow (Cartesian)

2. Conical wing-body combination (spherical)

3. Two-dimensional or axisymmetric pointed ogive (surface oriented)

    ($h_1 = 1 + y/R^x$, $h_2 = 1$, $h_3 = y \cos \theta_b + r_b$, where $\theta_b$ is the local body angle and $r_b$ is the cylindrical body radius).

4. Two-dimensional blunt body (polar)

In most simple, supersonic flow problems, a single shock separates the free stream from the disturbed flow region surrounding the body. In obtaining a solution to the blunt-body problem, Morretti and Abbett[12] introduced a nonorthogonal coordi-

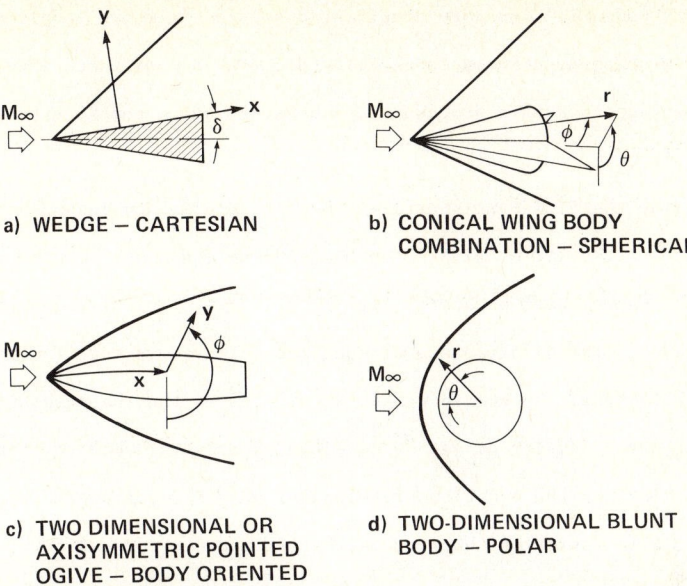

Fig. 11. Configurations and coordinate systems for coordinate alignment with body.

nate transformation that normalized the distance between the body and such a shock (which was treated as a sharp discontinuity). Both surfaces become coordinate surfaces as shown in Fig. 12. A similar procedure was developed by Morretti et al.[15]

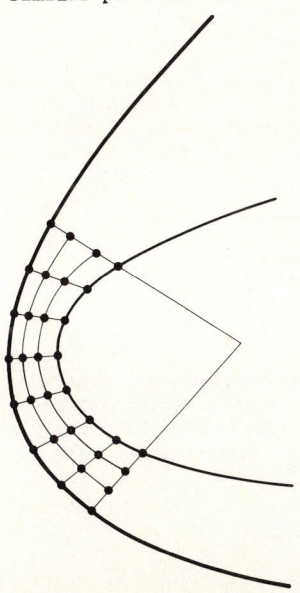

Fig. 12. Body and shock coordinate alignment.

and Marconi and Salas[16] for more complicated supersonic flows involving multiple shock waves, in which each known shock coincided with a coordinate line. The logic involved in developing such a procedure is, however, quite complicated and rather cumbersome for automatic computation.

To determine the flow over shuttle-like configurations using a complete shock-capturing approach, Kutler et al.[17] normalized the equations between the body and an analytically known outer boundary (Fig. 13(a)) that completely encompassed the outermost shock wave. The disadvantage of such a procedure was that the peripheral shock location was not known. By combining the attributes of the sharp shock and shock-capturing procedures, Kutler et al.[3] developed a computer code for three-dimensional bodies that normalized the equations between the body and peripheral or outermost shock (Fig. 13(b)). Interior shock waves that formed due to such things as canopy, wing, or recompression waves were captured, while the peripheral shock was treated as a discontinuity. Since only special treatment of the finite-difference procedure is required at the body and shock, this particular formulation is rather well suited for automatic computation, especially on the new computers being developed that make use of parallel processing (such as the ILLIAC IV designed by Burroughs Corp.).

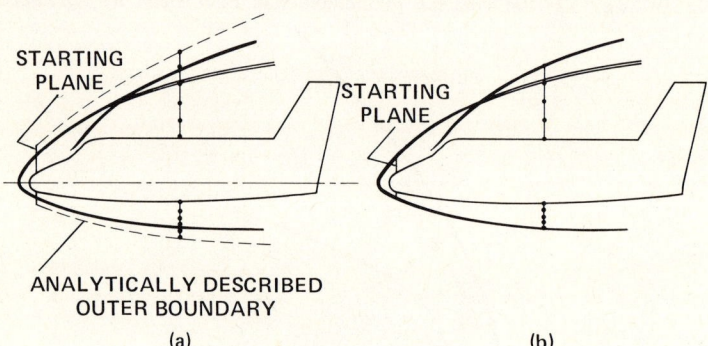

Fig. 13. Three-dimensional coordinate alignment; (a) normalization between body and outer boundary, and (b) normalization between body and peripheral shock.

3.3 Self-Similar Transformations

Some problems encountered in supersonic inviscid flow are self-similar; that is, the flow field is invariant with respect to a particular independent variable. One of the prime examples is the wide range of conical flow problems. This self-similar feature of certain problems can be used as the basis for solution and can be instituted easily using a nonorthogonal coordinate transformation. Take, for example, the flow about a supersonic edge delta wing (Fig. 14). The basic coordinate system is selected as Cartesian with the origin at the vertex of the wing. The governing equations are then transformed according to the conical transformation:

$$\zeta = x, \quad \eta = y/x, \quad \xi = z/x \qquad (3.1)$$

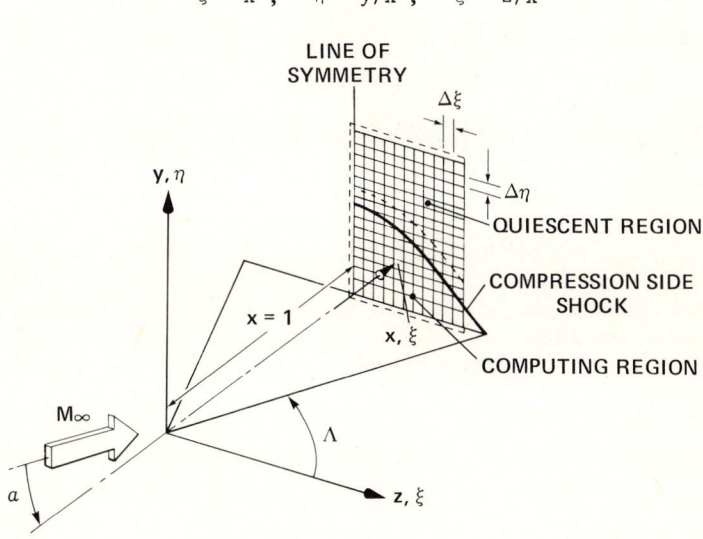

Fig. 14. Coordinate system and mesh description for planar delta wing.

In the $\eta,\xi$ plane ($\zeta$-derivatives zero), the governing equations are mixed elliptic-hyperbolic, but if the $\zeta$-derivative terms are included, the resulting set of equations is hyperbolic with respect to $\zeta$. These equations can thus be solved iteratively using finite-difference procedures until the $\zeta$-derivative terms become zero, which implies the establishment of a conical flow field.

Another interesting self-similar problem is posed by the flow field generated by passing a planar oblique shock over a wedge or cone in supersonic flight. The nonexistence of a characteristic length associated with the body and the fact that the incident wave is planar are the basis for the self-similarity with respect to time. Consider the two-dimensional problem shown in Fig. 15 where a wedge traveling at Mach number $M_w$ is struck by an oblique shock wave moving in the opposite direction at

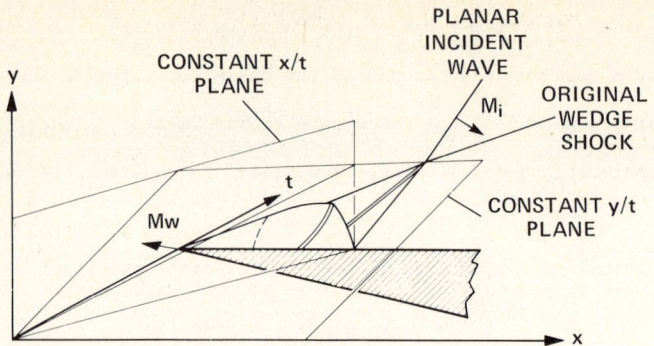

Fig. 15. Two-dimensional interfering shock problem with self-similar planes.

Mach number $M_i$. By transforming the Euler equations in Cartesian coordinates according to the following nonorthogonal transformation,

$$\tau = t, \quad \xi = x/t, \quad \eta = y/t \qquad (3.2)$$

the time-dependent problem can be made self-similar. In effect, the unsteady problem has now been reduced to a steady-flow problem.

As mentioned previously, it is desirable when using the shock-capturing approach to align the shock with one of the coordinate directions. For the previous example, it is possible through another coordinate transformation to align the incident planar shock, the original wedge shock, and the new wedge shock with certain coordinates by use of the following transformation:

$$\tau = t, \quad \xi = \frac{x-b(t,y)}{t}, \quad \eta = y/x \qquad (3.3)$$

where $b(t,y) = y/\tan \lambda + b_o t$. This transformation yields the network shown in Fig. 16. As opposed to discretizing the desired flow region with a rectangular grid using Eq. (3.2) (Fig. 16), this transformation results in a more efficient use of the points, that is, more points appear in the unknown flow regions than in the known, in addition to its shock alignment properties.

It was mentioned earlier that the basic coordinate system can contain singular points. It is also possible to create other singularities by the subsequent nonorthogonal transformation. For example, in the transformation given by Eq. (3.3), singularities occur at $t = 0$ and $x = 0$. If computation is required in regions near these

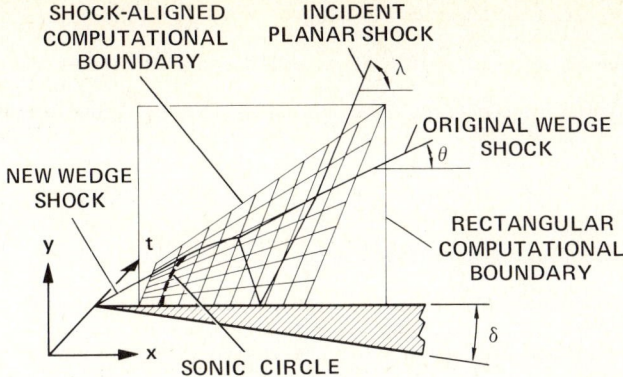

Fig. 16. Rectangular and shock-aligned computation boundaries for interfering shock problem.

singularities, it will generally result in a reduced overall step size, an increase in the number of iterations required for convergence, and thus a greater amount of computer time. However, in most instances, it is believed that the resulting enhanced accuracy of the numerical solution under the transformation will warrant the additional increase in computer time.

### 3.4 Point Concentration Transformations

As mentioned earlier, the other purpose of a coordinate transformation is to cluster or concentrate points in a particular region where the dependent variables are changing rapidly. Basically, there are two procedures by which clustering can be instituted: (1) by physically inserting points where desired, and (2) by an analytic transformation of the independent variables. Both Blottner and Roache[18] and Kalnay de Rivas[19] agree that the latter approach is best and can result in a significant improvement in accuracy over the former.

The physical insertion of points approach has been successfully applied by Chu and Powers,[20] however, in their method-of-characteristics technique for three-dimensional flows. On the other hand, using a finite-difference procedure, Kutler et al.,[3] in determining the flow over three-dimensional winged bodies, used the simple transformation:

$$\eta(\phi) = \tan^{-1}(\kappa \tan \phi) \qquad (3.4)$$

(where $\kappa$ controls the degree of clustering) to group points in the circumferential direction near the leading edge of the wing ($\phi = 90°$); good results were obtained. In determining the flow field over a blunt delta body, Thomas et al.[21] used a clustering transformation in the circumferential direction to group points near the leading edge and in the radial direction to capture the thinning entropy layer generated by the blunt nose.

The mechanics of using a transformation as opposed to a manual change of the mesh is somewhat simpler. For example, with an analytic transformation, the same finite-difference scheme can be used for the entire grid, whereas for the mesh change the finite-difference scheme must change when transitioning from one mesh to the next.

The coordinate systems mentioned and the nonorthogonal transformations discussed in this section are by no means an exhaustive discussion of the existing possibilities. Rather, a few have been mentioned to describe the importance of the proper choice in formulating and simplifying a given problem, and, more basic, how this choice facilitates and improves the solution obtained.

## 4. FINITE-DIFFERENCE SCHEMES

Our main interest in computing three-dimensional supersonic flow fields in an Eulerian mesh is to accurately predict the location and intensity of all shock waves along with the continuous portions of the disturbed region. At most, only one shock wave will be treated as a sharp discontinuity. All others therefore must be captured by the finite-difference solution. Thus we rely heavily on the ability of the finite-difference algorithm in conjunction with the boundary conditions to correctly describe multiple shocked flows.

It is not the purpose of this section to survey all existing finite-difference schemes or even a small number of them. Only three explicit schemes containing no explicit "artificial viscosity" terms are considered: the first-order scheme of Lax,[5] the second-order scheme of MacCormack[22] (a Lax-Wendroff variant), and the third-order scheme of Warming et al.[23] (a Rusanov[24] or Burstein and Mirin[25] variant). In discussing the properties of finite-difference schemes, we use the following terms, which are based on simple linear partial differential equations (see Richtmyer and Morton[26]):

1. <u>Properly posed initial value problem</u>. The solution of the governing pde exists, it is unique, and it depends continuously on the initial data.

2. <u>Truncation error</u>. A measure of how well a solution of the pde satisfies the finite-difference equation.

3. <u>Consistency</u>. The difference equation is said to be a consistent approximation of the pde if the truncation error approaches zero as the step size ($\Delta t$) approaches zero.

4. <u>Accuracy</u>. The order of the truncation error is the formal accuracy of the finite-difference scheme.

5. <u>Convergence of iterations</u>. In solving a problem iteratively, as the number of iterations approaches infinity, the difference between the solution at the nth iterate and the solution at infinity approaches zero for a fixed step size.

6. <u>Convergence</u>. The solution of the difference equation approaches the solution of the pde as the step size approaches zero. (Lax's Equivalence Theorem:[26] for a properly posed intial value problem, the consistency of approximation plus the stability of the scheme is a necessary and sufficient condition for convergence.)

7. <u>Stability</u>. Depends solely on the difference scheme and not the pde being solved, requires that the solution be bounded as the step size approaches zero.

8. <u>Modified equation</u>.[27] The pde that is actually solved numerically. It is derived by expanding each term of the finite-difference equation into a Taylor series and then eliminating time derivatives higher than first order (including mixed time and space derivatives) by repeated use of the expanded equation.

9. <u>Dissipation</u>. The ability of the finite-difference scheme to damp high-frequency terms. The effect of dissipation is indicated by the even-order spatial derivatives of the modified equation.

10. <u>Dispersion</u>. The ability of the finite-difference scheme to propagate waves of different wavelengths at the same speed. The effect of dispersion is indicated by the odd-order spatial derivative of the modified equation.

11. <u>Diffusion</u>. A property of the finite-difference scheme that results in a spreading or smearing out of a discontinuity, generally due to both dissipative and dispersive effects.

The analysis of finite-difference schemes is generally constrained to simple linear pde's of the form:

$$\frac{\partial u}{\partial t} + c \frac{\partial u}{\partial x} = 0 \qquad (4.1a)$$

or for a system of equations,

$$\frac{\partial U}{\partial t} + A \frac{\partial U}{\partial x} \qquad (4.1b)$$

where A is a constant matrix with eigenvalues $\sigma_i$. But this convective equation is of interest since it carries the main features of the inviscid fluid-flow equations. Application of the conclusions drawn for the linear equations can be generalized to the nonlinear modified form of Burgers'[28] equation:

$$\frac{\partial u}{\partial t} + u \frac{\partial u}{\partial x} = 0 \quad \text{nonconservative} \qquad (4.2a)$$

or

$$\frac{\partial u}{\partial t} + \frac{\partial (u^2/2)}{\partial x} = 0 \quad \text{conservative} \qquad (4.2b)$$

which is a more accurate model of the inviscid equations.

In describing the three finite-difference schemes, we use the modified equation approach developed by Warming and Hyett[27] for the analysis of such schemes. The finite-difference schemes themselves are presented in a form applicable for use in Eq. (2.1).

## 4.1 First-Order Scheme

Lax[5] proposed a finite-difference scheme for calculating time-dependent, one-dimensional, compressible fluid flows containing strong shocks. His single-step scheme, which uses central differences for the spatial derivatives and a forward difference for the time derivative, when applied to Eq. (2.1), becomes

$$\begin{aligned} U_{i,j,k}^{n+1} = \frac{1}{6}\Big(&U_{i+1,j,k}^{n} + U_{i-1,j,k}^{n} + U_{i,j+1,k}^{n} + U_{i,j-1,k}^{n} + U_{i,j,k+1}^{n} + U_{i,j,k-1}^{n}\Big) \\ &- \frac{\Delta t}{2\Delta x_1}\Big(E_{i+1,j,k}^{n} - E_{i-1,j,k}^{n}\Big) - \frac{\Delta t}{2\Delta x_2}\Big(F_{i,j+1,k}^{n} - F_{i,j-1,k}^{n}\Big) \\ &- \frac{\Delta t}{2\Delta x_3}\Big(F_{i,j,k+1}^{n} - F_{i,j,k-1}^{n}\Big) \end{aligned} \qquad (4.3)$$

where

$$U^n_{i,j,k} = U(n\Delta t, i\Delta x_1, j\Delta x_2, k\Delta x_3)$$

$$E^n_{i,j,k} = E\left(U^n_{i,j,k}, n\Delta t, i\Delta x_1, j\Delta x_2, k\Delta x_3\right), \text{ etc.}$$

The modified equation for Lax's scheme applied to Eq. (4.1a) is

$$\frac{\partial u}{\partial t} + c\frac{\partial u}{\partial x} + \left(\frac{c^2\Delta t}{2} - \frac{\Delta x^2}{2\Delta t}\right)\frac{\partial^2 u}{\partial x^2} + \left(-\frac{1}{3}c\Delta x^2 + \frac{c^3\Delta t^2}{3}\right)\frac{\partial^3 u}{\partial x^3}$$
$$+ \left(\frac{1}{12}\frac{\Delta x^4}{\Delta t} - \frac{1}{3}c^2\Delta x^2\Delta t + \frac{c^4\Delta t^3}{4}\right)\frac{\partial^4 u}{\partial x^4} + \cdots = 0 \quad (4.4)$$

The coefficient of the lowest-order error term is

$$\frac{c^2\Delta t}{2} - \frac{\Delta x^2}{2\Delta t}$$

so the scheme is first-order accurate in $\Delta x$ and $\Delta t$. The scheme can be inconsistent since, as $\Delta t$ and $\Delta x$ approach zero (e.g., in the ratio $\Delta x^2/\Delta t$), this error term does not go to zero. The stability bound is shown to be

$$\nu = \frac{c\Delta t}{\Delta x} < 1 \quad (4.5)$$

where, for Eq. (4.1b), $c$ is replaced by $|\sigma_{max}|$, where $\sigma_{max} = \max(\sigma_i)$. The parameter $\nu$ is referred to as the "Courant number." The dissipation of the scheme (lowest-order even derivative of error terms) is of order 2, while the dispersion (lowest-order odd derivative) is of order 3. Phase errors generated using Lax's scheme lead to the exact solution.

## 4.2 Second-Order Scheme

MacCormack,[22] in studying hypervelocity impact cratering, developed a noncentered, two-step, finite-difference scheme. Basically, the scheme uses one-sided differences (forward or backward, hence the term "noncentered") to replace the spatial derivatives as opposed to the centered differences of Lax's[5] or Richtmyer's[26] scheme.

For the two-dimensional plus time version of Eq. (2.1), MacCormack's scheme is written

$$U_{i,j}^{(1)} = U_{i,j}^n - \alpha_1 \left\{ \frac{\Delta t}{\Delta x_1} \left[ (1-\varepsilon_1) E_{i+1,j}^n - (1-2\varepsilon_1) E_{i,j}^n - \varepsilon_1 E_{i-1,j}^n \right] \right.$$

$$\left. + \frac{\Delta t}{\Delta x_2} \left[ (1-\varepsilon_2) F_{i,j+1}^n - (1-2\varepsilon_2) F_{i,j}^n - \varepsilon_2 F_{i,j-1}^n \right] + \Delta t H_{i,j}^n \right\} \quad (4.6a)$$

$$U_{i,j}^{n+1} = \frac{1}{2}\left(U_{i,j}^n + U_{i,j}^{(1)}\right) - w_1 \left\{ \frac{\Delta t}{\Delta x_1} \left[ \varepsilon_1 E_{i+1,j}^{(1)} + (1-2\varepsilon_1) E_{i,j}^{(1)} + (\varepsilon_1 - 1) E_{i-1,j}^{(1)} \right] \right.$$

$$\left. + \frac{\Delta t}{\Delta x_2} \left[ \varepsilon_2 F_{i,j+1}^{(1)} + (1-2\varepsilon_2) F_{i,j}^{(1)} + (\varepsilon_2 - 1) F_{i,j-1}^{(1)} \right] + \Delta t H_{i,j}^n \right\} \quad (4.6b)$$

where $\alpha_1 = 1$, $w_1 = 1/2$, $U_{i,j}^n$ and $E_{i,j}^n$ are as defined before, and

$$E_{i,j}^{(1)} = E^{(1)}\left[ U_{i,j}^{(1)}, (n+\alpha_1)\Delta t, i\Delta x_1, j\Delta x_2 \right]$$

This scheme allows four possible variations for replacing the space derivatives in the predictor and corrector steps:

$$\left. \begin{array}{ll} \text{I:} & \varepsilon_1 = 0, \quad \varepsilon_2 = 0 \\ \text{II:} & \varepsilon_1 = 1, \quad \varepsilon_2 = 1 \\ \text{III:} & \varepsilon_1 = 0, \quad \varepsilon_2 = 1 \\ \text{IV:} & \varepsilon_1 = 1, \quad \varepsilon_2 = 0 \end{array} \right\} \quad (4.7)$$

MacCormack[22] suggests that in applying this scheme to general flow problems the four variations (I-IV) be cyclically permuted to obtain the most unbiased results. The generalization to three dimensions plus time is straightforward.

The modified equation corresponding to MacCormack's scheme (which reduces to the Lax-Wendroff[29] scheme for linear equations) is

$$\frac{\partial u}{\partial t} + c \frac{\partial u}{\partial x} + \frac{c}{6} (\Delta x^2 - c^2 \Delta t^2) \frac{\partial^3 u}{\partial x^3} + \frac{c^2 \Delta t}{8} (\Delta x^2 - c^2 \Delta t^2) \frac{\partial^4 u}{\partial x^4} + \cdots = 0 \quad (4.8)$$

Therefore, the scheme is uniformly second-order accurate in both time and space. The scheme is consistent, and the stability bound is the same as for Lax's scheme, namely,

$$\nu = c \frac{\Delta t}{\Delta x} < 1$$

According to Lax's equivalence theorem, the scheme is convergent.

The dissipation of the scheme is of order 4 while the dispersion is of order 3. Phase errors generated using MacCormack's scheme will be predominantly lagging.

## 4.3 Third-Order Scheme

Warming et al.[23] derived a third-order scheme that is a variant of Rusanov's[24] and Burstein and Mirin's[25] scheme. It is a three-step method that uses the first two steps of MacCormack's method. The algorithm can be written as

$$U^{(1)}_{i,j} = \text{same as right side of (4.6a) with } \alpha_1 = 2/3 \tag{4.9a}$$

$$U^{(2)}_{i,j} = \text{same as right side of (4.6b) with } \alpha_1 = 2/3 \text{ and } w_1 = 1/3 \tag{4.9b}$$

$$\begin{aligned}
U^{n+1}_{i,j} = U^n_{i,j} &- \left[(\omega_1)^n_{i+1/2,j}/24\right]\left[U^n_{i+2,j} - 3U^n_{i+1,j} + 3U^n_{i,j} - U^n_{i-1,j}\right] \\
&+ \left[(\omega_1)^n_{i-1/2,j}/24\right]\left[U^n_{i+1,j} - 3U^n_{i,j} + 3U^n_{i-1,j} - U^n_{i-2,j}\right] \\
&- \left[(\omega_2)^n_{i,j+1/2}/24\right]\left[U^n_{i,j+2} - 3U^n_{i,j+1} + 3U^n_{i,j} - U^n_{i,j-1}\right] \\
&+ \left[(\omega_2)^n_{i,j-1/2}/24\right]\left[U^n_{i,j+1} - 3U^n_{i,j} + 3U^n_{i,j-1} - U^n_{i,j-2}\right] \\
&- \frac{1}{24}\left[(\Delta t/\Delta x_1)\left(-2E^n_{i+2,j} + 7E^n_{i+1,j} - 7E^n_{i-1,j} + 2E^n_{i-2,j}\right)\right. \\
&\left. + (\Delta t/\Delta x_2)\left(-2F^n_{i,j+2} + 7F^n_{i,j+1} - 7F^n_{i,j-1} + 2F^n_{i,j-2}\right) + 6\Delta t H^n_{i,j}\right] \\
&- \frac{3}{8}\left[(\Delta t/\Delta x_1)\left(E^{(2)}_{i+1,j} - E^{(2)}_{i-1,j}\right) + (\Delta t/\Delta x_2)\left(F^{(2)}_{i,j+1} - F^{(2)}_{i,j-1}\right) + 2\Delta t H^{(2)}_{i,j}\right]
\end{aligned} \tag{4.9c}$$

It should be emphasized here that $U^{(1)}_t$, $U^{(2)}$, $F^{(1)}$, etc., are evaluated at the t coordinate $[n+(2/3)]\Delta t$. The free-parameter terms of Eq. (4.9c), that is, the brackets with multiplicative coefficients $\omega_1$ and $\omega_2$ have been differenced conservatively in both the $x_1$ and $x_2$ directions, and formulas for them are given later. Since these terms represent a fourth-order difference operator,[23] they do not affect the third-order accuracy of the algorithm. Any of the four possible variations of MacCormack's method are applicable for the first two steps (Eqs. (4.9a) and (4.9b)), and each is consistent with the third-order accuracy of the final step.

The modified equation corresponding to this difference algorithm is

$$\frac{\partial u}{\partial t} + c\frac{\partial u}{\partial x} + \frac{\Delta x^4}{24\Delta t}(\omega - 4\nu^2 + \nu^4)\frac{\partial^4 u}{\partial x^4} + \frac{c\Delta x^4}{120}[-5\omega + (4\nu^2+1)(4-\nu^2)]\frac{\partial^5 u}{\partial x^5} + \cdots = 0 \tag{4.10}$$

where $\nu = c\Delta t/\Delta x$. Therefore, the scheme is uniformly third-order accurate in both time and space. It is consistent and stable if[24]

$$4\nu^2 - \nu^4 < \omega \leq 3 \text{ and } |\nu| < 1 \tag{4.11}$$

The third-order method can have either a leading or lagging phase error, depending on the choice of the free parameter $\omega$.[23] The difficulty is in choosing the correct value for the free parameter. The modified equation for this scheme, however, affords some insight into the proper choice. If one wishes to minimize the dissipation, then $\omega$ is chosen so that the lowest-order, even derivative coefficient of the modified equation (Eq. (4.10)) is zero or

$$\omega = 4\nu^2 - \nu^4 \tag{4.12}$$

To minimize the dispersion, the coefficients of the lowest-order odd derivative is set to zero; that is,

$$\omega = (4\nu^2 + 1)(4 - \nu^2)/5 \tag{4.13}$$

Warming et al.[23] and Kutler et al.[17] were successful in using the free parameter $\omega$ to enhance the shock-capturing ability of the third-order scheme by allowing it to vary from grid point to grid point. Examples presented later demonstrate the variable free-parameter effects.

Again, note that the analysis of finite-difference schemes is based on the use of a linear pde; however, Hirt[30] has argued that certain stability criteria are applicable to nonlinear equations with variable coefficients. In addition, since no complete rigorous nonlinear analysis exists, we must rely on the theory developed for the linear case and account for the nonlinear effects by conservative estimates of the integration step size.

## 4.4 Solution of $u_t + (u^2/2)_x = 0$

To determine the relative merits or deficiencies of a particular finite-difference algorithm for solving the gasdynamic equations, the scheme can be applied to the modified Burger's equation, Eq. (4.2b), which is representative of the inviscid Euler equations. Because of its simplicity, the computer coding is easier and the core requirements and computer time are minimal. Kutler[31] and Warming et al.[23] performed such studies, and some of their results are presented here for the three schemes discussed in this section.

Of prime interest is how well the finite-difference scheme can predict and follow discontinuities in the flow. Therefore, the initial condition for Eq. (4.2b) is chosen as a step discontinuity that is supposed to simulate a shock moving from left to right. Solutions are obtained for different step sizes or Courant numbers (Eq. (4.5)) to study the effects of dispersion, dissipation, and diffusion.

The results obtained using Lax's first-order method, Eq. (4.3), for Courant numbers of 1.0 and 0.5 are shown in Fig. 17. There is no overshoot or undershoot for either case; for $\nu = 1.0$, the discontinuity is spread over three mesh intervals, while for $\nu = 0.5$ it is spread over approximately six. This diffusion of the discontinuity indicates that Lax's method is highly dissipative. However, the location of the discontinuity is predicted quite well by this scheme.

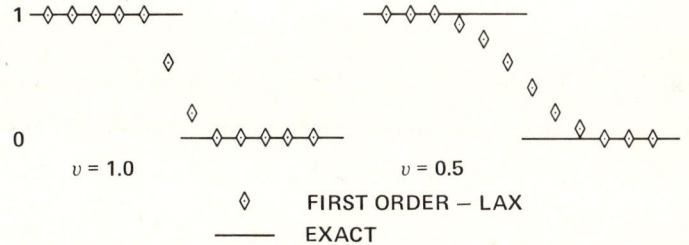

Fig. 17. First-order solution of Eq. (4.2b) using Lax's scheme for Courant numbers of 1.0 and 0.5.

MacCormack's second-order scheme has been termed "preferential" by Kutler,[31] which means that the solution obtained will be more favorable, depending on the version (Eq. (4.7)) of MacCormack's scheme used. In particular, for discontinuities that propagate in the direction of increasing i (in the present case, to the right), the preferred version of MacCormack's scheme is I, in which forward space differences are used in the predictor and backward space differences are used in the corrector. This preferential behavior is shown in Fig. 18 by the results for Version I (Fig. 18(a)) and version II (Fig. 18(b)) for the right-moving discontinuity. For $\nu = 1.0$, with version I (the preferred scheme), there is no overshoot or undershoot and the discontinuity is only spread over two mesh intervals, whereas for version II (the nonpreferred scheme) there is a slight overshoot. For a Courant number of 0.5, both versions exhibit oscillations following the discontinuity (a result of dispersion errors), with version II having the larger amplitudes. The discontinuities are still

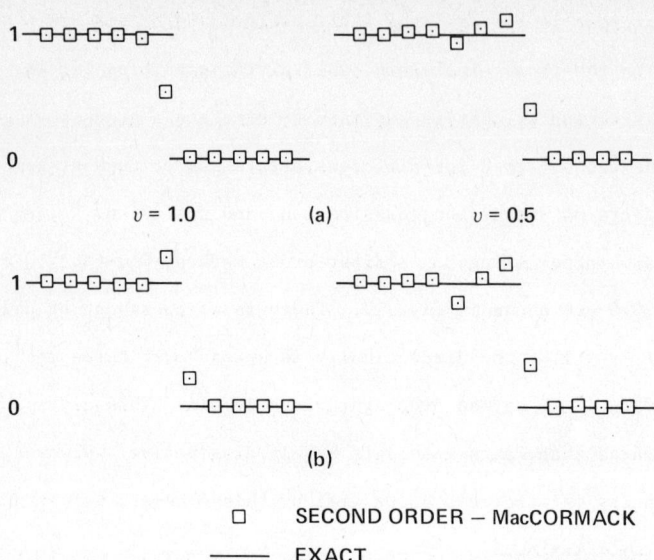

Fig. 18. Second-order solution of Eq. (4.2b) using MacCormack's scheme for Courant numbers of 1.0 and 0.5; (a) version I, and (b) version II.

only spread over two mesh intervals, indicating the improvement in the diffusion properties over Lax's scheme.

If versions I and II are permuted as suggested by MacCormack,[22] this results in the solutions in Figs. 19(a) and 19(d) for Courant numbers of 0.9 and 0.1. The dis-

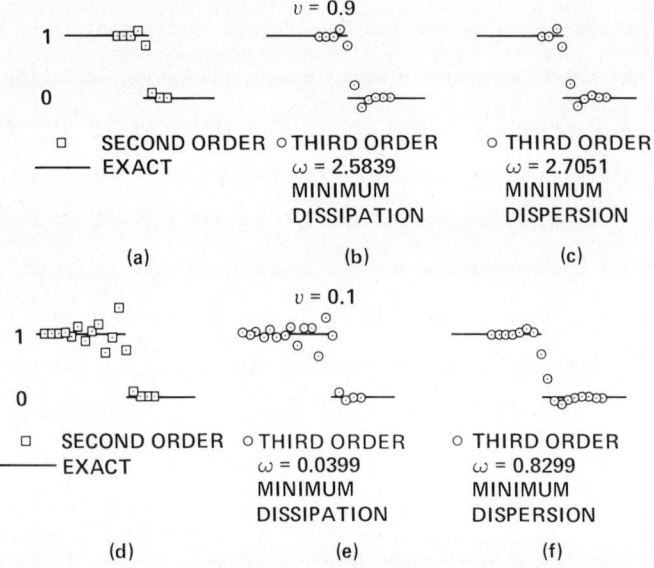

Fig. 19. Comparison of second- (versions I and II permuted) and third-order solutions of Eq. (4.2b) for Courant numbers of 0.9 and 0.1.

continuity is captured as well as that using either version I or II, but the overshoot is greater than version I and less than version II. For $\nu = 0.1$, the dispersion errors are predominant and result in oscillations behind the discontinuity.

The analysis governing the properties of finite-difference schemes, including the free parameter of the third-order scheme, was based on a linear equation and, strictly speaking, is invalid for nonlinear problems. However it provides a guide of what to expect, and for the third-order method, what value of the free parameter to use in the nonlinear case. Figure 19 shows the results obtained for Eq. (4.2b) using the third-order method with values of $\omega$ for minimum dissipation and dispersion and four Courant numbers of 0.9 and 0.1. These results are compared with the second-order permuted MacCormack scheme. For the large Courant number, there is not much difference between the second- and third-order solutions. However, for a Courant number of 0.1, the third-order method using $\omega$ for minimum dispersion results in the best solution for the captured discontinuity.

The previous examples have shown that the resolution of discontinuities computed by the third-order method is rather sensitive to the choice of the parameter $\omega$. In complicated flow patterns with multiple shocks, an optimum choice of $\omega$ at some spatial point will probably result in poor shock-capturing ability in other regions of the flow field if $\omega$ is constant throughout the flow. Figure 20(a) depicts a weak shock computed in the presence of a strong shock for the nonlinear Eq. (4.2b). The

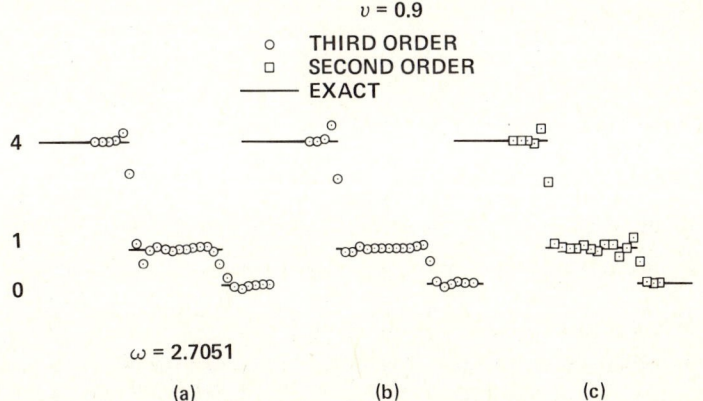

Fig. 20. Calculation of a weak shock in the presence of a strong shock;
(a) third-order method with a constant $\omega$,
(b) third-order method with a variable $\omega$, and
(c) second-order method (versions I and II permuted).

numerical solution was computed for a Courant number $\nu = |\sigma|_{max} \Delta t/\Delta x = 0.9 \Delta t/\Delta x = 0.225$, and with $\omega = \omega(0.9) = 2.7051$ calculated from Eq. (4.13). The local value of the Courant number for the weak shock is $\nu = 0.225$ and, consequently, the value of $\omega$ used is too high for this lower Courant number, resulting in a rather smeared shock.

It is possible to make $\omega$ a local function of the Courant number $\nu$ rather than keep it constant throughout the computational mesh.[22] Figure 20(b) shows the same double-shock system as in Fig. 20(a), except $\omega$ was assumed to be a variable calculated locally for minimum dispersion from Eq. (4.13). The result, while not showing dramatic improvement, indicates that the weak shock is less smeared since the jump that takes essentially three mesh intervals in Fig. 20(a) has been reduced to two mesh intervals in Fig. 20(b). For comparison, Fig. 20(c) illustrates the double-shock solution using the second-order method.

With regard to programming logic and basic core storage requirements, Lax's method is the easiest to program and requires minimum storage, while the third-order method is the most difficult and requires the most core storage. The choice of the finite-difference scheme to be used, therefore, will depend strongly on the problem to be solved and the computer used to solve it.

## 5. BOUNDARY CONDITIONS

Probably the single most important aspect in the successful application of any numerical technique to the solution of fluid-flow problems is the proper treatment of the impermeable and permeable boundaries that encompass the computational plane. An impermeable boundary is one across which no mass can flow, such as the solid surface of a body, a plane of symmetry, or a contact discontinuity, and along which therefore the tangency condition must be satisfied. A permeable boundary, such as a shock wave or inflow or outflow boundary, allows mass to flow through its surface. Of all these boundaries, the impermeable surface of a solid body has probably received the most attention by the numerical modelist, and rightfully so. It is this boundary, in conjunction with the free-stream conditions, that generates the behavior of the surrounding flow field.

## 5.1 Impermeable Boundaries

A wide variety of body boundary condition schemes exists, some of which are discussed by Abbett,[32,33] Moretti,[34] and Roache.[35] Three of these procedures (used in the examples presented later) are discussed, namely, (1) the reflection technique, (2) the explicit one-sided derivative technique, and (3) the simple wave corrector technique of Abbett.[33] All these schemes are easy to apply in that they attempt to treat the boundary points as regular points of the interior, and when used properly, they yield quite accurate results.

The "reflection principle" or "reflection technique" is only truly applicable for simulating the slip condition on a plane or flat wall in which one of the coordinates lies along the wall. It forces all nonconservative flow variables other than the normal velocity component to behave as even functions with respect to the wall. And it forces the normal velocity to behave as an odd function, thus yielding a zero normal velocity at the wall. If the conservative variables are used, all but the normal momentum component behave as odd functions since they are multiplied by the normal velocity component.

Two approaches can be used in applying the reflection technique (Fig. 21, areas I and II): (1) image point approach (area I), which requires a sequence of grid points one $\Delta y$ below or inside the body and thus allows the wall points to be treated as regular interior points of the flow or (2) nonimage point approach (area II), which

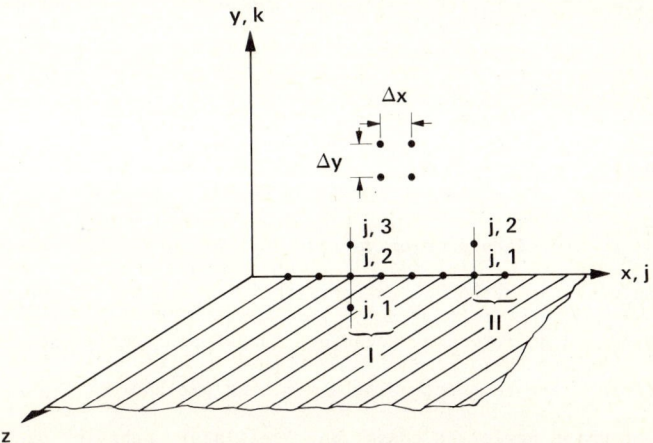

Fig. 21. Reflection technique for flat surface in x-z plane; (I) image point approach and (II) nonimage point approach.

requires no subwall points but requires a simple change in the finite-difference scheme at the body.

Thus, in applying the reflection technique using the image point approach with conservative variables (see F in Eq. (2.1)), the values of $F_{(1)}$, $F_{(2)}$, $F_{(4)}$, and $F_{(5)}$ at points (j,1) are set equal to the negative of the values at points (j,3), while $F_{(3)}$ at (j,1) is set equal to the value at (j,3). In using the nonimage point approach, as with MacCormack's scheme, when a backward difference is required at the wall, it is computed using the conservative variables at points (j,1) and (j,2) only (see area II); that is, $\partial F/\partial y|_{back} = F_{(1,2,4,5)_{j,1}} + F_{(1,2,4,5)_{j,2}}$ and $\partial F/\partial y|_{back} = F_{(3)_{j,1}} - F_{(3)_{j,2}}$.

The reflection technique, although exact only for planar bodies, has been used for nonplanar bodies with moderate success by a number of investigators, including Bohachevsky and Mates,[13] Bohachevsky and Rubin,[36] Kutler,[31] and Kutler and Lomax.[37] The accuracy is directly proportional to the curvature of the body, the number of grid points used in the direction normal to the body, and how well behaved the flow variables are near the body.

A rather simple and easily implemented procedure for modeling the tangency condition is to use the normal interior point finite-difference scheme with one-sided differences at the body, along with the fact that the normal velocity component is zero. For example, in using version I of MacCormack's scheme, Eq. (3.10), the predictor step at the body is the same as for the interior. The subsequent corrector step, however, is modified so that the required backward difference in the body normal direction is replaced by a forward difference. Following the corrector, the normal velocity component, which will normally not be zero, is set to zero. Again, the success of this scheme depends on the body geometry, number of points, and flow variable behavior.

Abbett,[32] in his discussion of various surface boundary condition procedures, made comparisons with the method of characteristics for both the reflection technique and explicit one-sided differencing technique for simple compression and expansion flows—both of which were computed using a marching procedure. Figure 22 is a sketch of the comparison which depicts a convergent oscillatory behavior of the two approximate procedures. The noteworthy characteristic of this curve is that as x increases

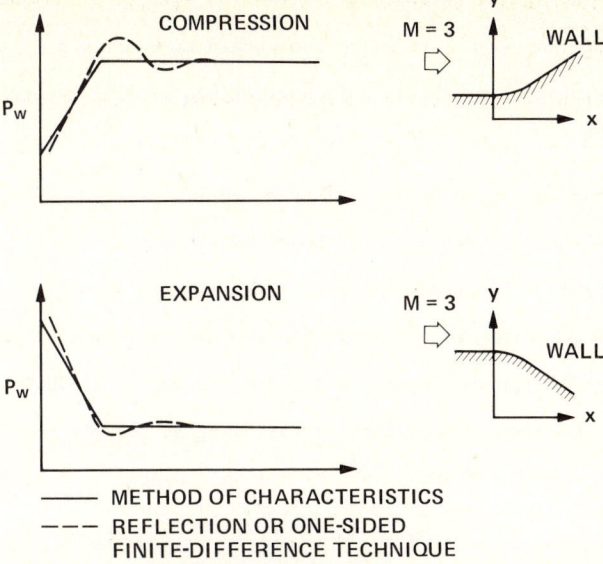

Fig. 22. Comparison sketch of method of characteristics and reflection or one-sided, finite-difference techniques.

both techniques approach the method of characteristics solution, which implies that if an iterative procedure is used as opposed to a marching procedure, these boundary condition techniques will yield acceptable results. Examples of self-similar flow problems involving multiple shock waves using only an iterative approach are presented later; these demonstrate solutions obtained using the two boundary condition procedures, which incidentally are capable of properly treating shocks impinging on the body.

It should be concluded from the above discussion that reflection and one-sided, finite-difference boundary condition techniques are best used for iterative solutions and that, in using a marching procedure for three-dimensional supersonic flows, a more accurate boundary condition technique is required. Again, many procedures are available; some are quite accurate but difficult to apply, while others are inaccurate but easy to apply.

Abbett's[32] concept of the simple-wave corrector technique is selected because it possesses the attributes of being both accurate and easy to apply. The details of the scheme are presented by Kutler et al.,[3,17] but are repeated here for completeness. The three-dimensional supersonic flow-field program is based on a cylindrical coordinate system (see Table 1) marching in the $z$ direction and uses version I of MacCormack's scheme (Eq. (4.6)) to solve the governing equations.

This boundary condition procedure is basically a predictor-corrector technique in that the flow variables at the surface are first predicted using finite-difference algorithms and then corrected using a simple compression or expansion wave to satisfy the tangency condition. The first step of MacCormack's scheme, Eq. (4.6a), is applied at the body to yield the first predicted conservative variable $U^{(1)}$. It is followed by Eq. (4.6b) with the backward difference in the radial direction replaced by a forward difference and yields the "second predicted" conservative variable $U^{(2)}$. These variables are then decoded (see discussion following Eq. (2.4)) to obtain $p^{(2)}$, $\rho^{(2)}$, $u^{(2)}$, $v^{(2)}$, and $w^{(2)}$ at the station $z^{n+1} = z + \Delta z$. Generally, the resulting velocity vector $\vec{q}^{(2)} = u^{(2)}\hat{i}_z + v^{(2)}\hat{i}_r + w^{(2)}\hat{i}_\phi$ will not satisfy the surface tangency condition $\vec{q} \cdot \vec{n}_b = 0$, where $\vec{n}_b$ is the outward unit normal vector to the body and, in fact, will be rotated out of the surface tangent plane by a small angle $\Delta\theta$. This angle can be determined from

$$\Delta\theta = \sin^{-1}\left[\vec{q}^{(2)} \cdot \vec{n}_b / q^{(2)}\right] \quad (5.1)$$

where $q^{(2)}$ is the magnitude of $\vec{q}^{(2)}$ and the unit normal $\vec{n}_b$ can be calculated from

$$\vec{n}_b = \frac{\nabla f_b}{|\nabla f_b|} = \frac{-r_{b_z}\hat{i}_z - \hat{i}_r - (r_{b_\phi}/r_b)\hat{i}_\phi}{\left[r_{b_z}^2 + 1 + (r_{b_\phi}/r_b)^2\right]^{1/2}} \quad (5.2)$$

where $f_b = r_b - r_b(z,\phi) = 0$ describes the body surface. If $\Delta\theta$ is positive, then an expansion wave is necessary for the rotation of $\vec{q}^{(2)}$ and if $\Delta\theta$ is negative, a compression wave is required. The corrected value of the static pressure is found from the integral relation[38] for the Prandtl-Meyer turning angle $\nu(p; H_t, s)$, which depends on pressure and has the total enthalpy and entropy as parameters. The corrected value of pressure is found by solving

$$\nu(p^{n+1}; H_t, s) = \nu(p^{(2)}; H_t, s) + \Delta\theta \quad (5.3)$$

for the pressure $p^{n+1}$. In this equation, $\Delta\theta$ is given by Eq. (5.1). If $\Delta\theta$ is sufficiently small, Eq. (5.3) can be inverted and solved analytically for $p^{n+1}$ only for a perfect gas to yield

$$\frac{p^{n+1}}{p^{(2)}} = 1 - \frac{\gamma(M^{(2)})^2}{[(M^{(2)})^2 - 1]^{1/2}} \Delta\theta + \gamma(M^{(2)})$$

$$\times \left\{ \frac{(\gamma+1)(M^{(2)})^4 - 4[(M^{(2)})^2 - 1]}{4[(M^{(2)})^2 - 1]^2} (\Delta\theta)^2 \right\} + O[(\Delta\theta)^3] \qquad (5.4)$$

where

$$M^{(2)} = \frac{q^{(2)}}{c^{(2)}} \quad \text{and} \quad c^{(2)} = \left[ \frac{\gamma p^{(2)}}{\rho^{(2)}} \right]^{1/2}$$

For a real gas, Eq. (5.3) can be inverted by the use of a table lookup method. The isentropic flow assumption requires that the table be generated only once at the very beginning of a flow-field calculation when the entropy on the body stream surface is known. The table elements are pressure and Prandtl-Meyer turning angle $\nu$. The procedure for generating the table is described by Hayes and Probstein.[38]

The pressure $p^{n+1}$ in Eq. (5.3) is determined by first finding $\nu(p^{(2)}; H_t, s)$ from the table with the predicted pressure $p^{(2)}$ as the argument. The angle $\Delta\theta$ given by Eq. (5.1) is then added to the result and the desired value for the corrected pressure $p^{n+1}$ is then found from the same table with $\nu(p^{(2)}; H_t, s) + \Delta\theta$ as the argument. The remaining flow variables $\rho^{n+1}$, $u^{n+1}$, $v^{n+1}$, and $w^{n+1}$ are then determined as follows.

From the starting solution, all surface flow variables are known along with the value of entropy at the body, and since entropy is assumed to be constant over the entire body, that constant can be determined from

$$\left. \frac{p^n}{(\rho^n)^\gamma} \right|_{\text{starting plane}} = \text{const} \quad \text{(nonconical flow)} \qquad (5.5a)$$

When a cone solution is generated, the surface entropy during the iteration procedure is calculated from

$$\left. \frac{p^n}{(\rho^n)^\gamma} \right|_{\text{windward shock}} = \text{const} \quad \text{(conical flow)} \qquad (5.5b)$$

since the entropy throughout the shock layer in the windward plane of symmetry is known to be constant.

If constant entropy is assumed along the body, the density $\rho^{n+1}$ can therefore be calculated from

$$\rho^{n+1} = (p^{n+1}/\text{const})^{1/\gamma} \tag{5.6}$$

The velocity magnitude $q^{n+1}$ can then be determined from the energy equation (2.4) as

$$q^{n+1} = \left[2\left(H_t - \frac{p^{n+1}}{\rho^{n+1}}\frac{\gamma}{\gamma-1}\right)\right]^{1/2}$$

Finally, it is necessary to determine the individual components of $\vec{q}^{n+1}$. Since $\vec{q}^{(2)}$ was rotated through an angle $\Delta\theta$ in the plane of $\vec{n}_b$ and $\vec{q}^{(2)}$, it follows that the direction of the final velocity $\vec{q}^{n+1}$ must be in the direction of the vector $\vec{q}^{(2)} - \left(\vec{q}^{(2)} \cdot \vec{n}_b\right)\vec{n}_b$. Thus,

$$\vec{q}^{n+1} = q^{n+1}\vec{n}_t \tag{5.7}$$

where

$$\vec{n}_t = \frac{\vec{q}^{(2)} - \left(\vec{q}^{(2)} \cdot \vec{n}_b\right)\vec{n}_b}{\left|\vec{q}^{(2)} - \left(\vec{q}^{(2)} \cdot \vec{n}_b\right)\vec{n}_b\right|} \tag{5.8}$$

The velocity components obtained from Eq. (5.7) are

$$u^{n+1} = q^{n+1}(u^{(2)} + r_{b_z} M/N)/L \tag{5.9a}$$

$$v^{n+1} = q^{n+1}(v^{(2)} - M/N)/L \tag{5.9b}$$

$$w^{n+1} = q^{n+1}[w^{(2)} + (r_{b_\phi}/r_b)(M/N)]/L \tag{5.9c}$$

where

$$M = (-u^{(2)} r_{b_z} + v^{(2)} - w^{(2)} r_{b_\phi}/r_b)/N$$

$$N = [r_{b_z}^2 + 1 + (r_{b_\phi}/r_b)^2]^{1/2}$$

$$L = \left[u^{(2)} + r_{b_z} M/N + (v^{(2)} - M/N)^2 + \left(w^{(2)} + \frac{r_{b_\phi}}{r_b}\frac{M}{N}\right)^2\right]^{1/2}$$

and $r_{b_z} = \partial r_b/\partial z$, etc.

A comparison of this boundary condition scheme for the simple two-dimensional compression and expansion flows mentioned earlier showed virtually no differences with the method of characteristics. The three-dimensional version just described relies on the two predictor steps to yield an accurate flow description in the $\phi$ direction.

Results presented later establish the accuracy of this procedure.

The impermeable boundary created by a plane of symmetry is simply simulated numerically by applying the refelection technique along it. This is an exact boundary condition treatment and therefore does not contribute to the numerical error of a solution.

## 5.2 Permeable Boundaries

As with the surface boundary condition, there is a variety of schemes to treat the permeable boundary created by a shock wave. Abbett[39] discusses and compares the most widely used techniques. Based on personal investigations and the conclusions of Abbett, a modified version of Thomas' scheme[40] (pressure approach) is adopted here for the supersonic flow-field calculations presented that used a sharp-shock approach. The procedure is presented for both the two-dimensional unsteady (which can easily be generalized to three dimensions) and the three-dimensional steady cases. In both cases, one of the constant coordinate lines is assumed to lie along the shock wave.

The pressure approach method of Thomas, originally derived for the steady flow nonconservative equations, is relatively simple to implement and yields quite accurate results. The Rankine-Hugoniot relations can be written as a function of the pressure downstream of the shock wave. This pressure is predicted by the first step of MacCormack's method (version I), Eq. (4.6a), from the decoded conservative variables, and through the Rankine-Hugoniot relations, the other predicted variables can be found. The pressure is then recomputed by the corrector step, Eq. (4.6b), and the rest of the procedure is repeated. The details for the unsteady case assuming a perfect gas follow.

Figure 23 depicts a two-dimensional unsteady shock with a shock velocity $q_s$ in a polar coordinate system whose surface is described by

$$r_s = r_s(t,\theta) \tag{5.10}$$

where $r_{s_t} = \partial r_s/\partial t = q_{s_r}$ and $r_{s_\theta} = \partial r_s/\partial \theta$. From geometrical considerations, the shock angle $\beta$ is

$$\beta = \frac{\pi}{2} - \theta + \tan^{-1}(r_{s_\theta}/r_s) \tag{5.11}$$

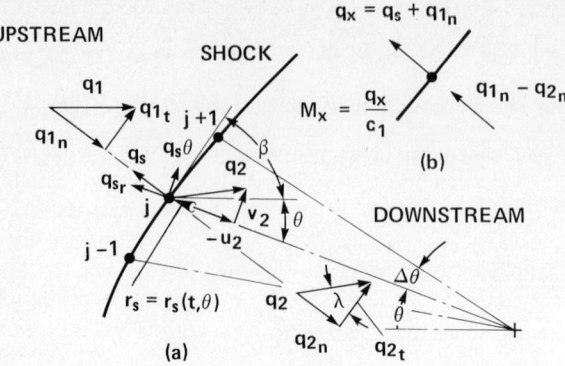

Fig. 23. Unsteady shock for two-dimensional supersonic flow in polar coordinates $(t, r, \theta)$.

The pressure behind the shock wave is known from the finite-difference scheme; therefore, the shock Mach number $M_x$ (Fig. 23(b)) is given by

$$M_x = \{[(\gamma+1)p_2/p_1 + (\gamma-1)]2\gamma\}^{1/2} \tag{5.12}$$

The density behind the shock is given by

$$\rho_2 = \rho_1(\gamma+1)M_x^2/[(\gamma-1)M_x^2 + 2] \tag{5.13}$$

The upstream velocity components normal and tangential to the shock are

$$\left. \begin{array}{l} q_{1_n} = q_1 \sin \beta \\ q_{1_t} = q_1 \cos \beta \end{array} \right\} \tag{5.14}$$

From kinematical relations, the shock velocity is given by

$$q_s = M_x c_1 - q_{1_n} \tag{5.15}$$

where $c_1 = (\gamma p_1/\rho_1)^{1/2}$ and thus

$$q_{s_r} = r_{s_t} = q_s \sin(\beta+\theta) \tag{5.16}$$

The normal velocity behind the shock is given by

$$q_{2_n} = c_2 \left[ \frac{(\gamma-1)M_x^2 + 2}{2\gamma M_x^2 - (\gamma-1)} \right]^{1/2} - q_s \tag{5.17}$$

where $c_2 = (\gamma p_2/\rho_2)^{1/2}$.

The velocity components in the $r$ and $\theta$ directions are therefore

$$\left. \begin{array}{l} u_2 = -q_2 \cos \mu \\ v_2 = q_2 \sin \mu \end{array} \right\} \quad (5.18)$$

where $q_2 = (q_{2_n}^2 + q_{1_t}^2)^{1/2}$ and $\mu = \beta + \theta - \lambda$, where $\lambda = \tan^{-1}(q_{2_n}/q_{1_t})$.

The shock wave is propagated using the following Euler predictor/modified Euler corrector in conjunction with the predictor-corrector philosophy of computing interior points:

$$r_s^{(1)} = r_s^n + q_{s_r}^n \Delta t \quad \text{(predictor)} \quad (5.19a)$$

$$r_s^{n+1} = r_s^n + \frac{1}{2}\left[q_{s_r}^n + q_{s_r}^{(1)}\right]\Delta t \quad \text{(corrector)} \quad (5.19b)$$

where $\Delta t$ is the time step. The partial derivative $r_{s_\theta}$ required in the Rankine-Hugoniot equations is found numerically (Fig. 23(a)) using the second-order, central-difference formula:

$$r_{s_\theta} = (r_{s_{j+1}} - r_{s_{j-1}})/2\Delta\theta \quad (5.20)$$

The above equations are used as follows. Initially, $p_2$, $\rho_2$, $u_2$, $v_2$, $r_s$, $r_{s_\theta}$, and $r_{s_t}$ are known along the shock at time step $n$. The pressure at the shock $p_2^{(1)}$ is predicted using Eq. (4.6a) with a backward difference in the radial direction. The shock wave is then moved using Eq. (5.19a), and $r_{s_\theta}^{(1)}$ is calculated from Eq. (5.20). From Eq. (5.11), $\beta^{(1)}$ can then be found, followed by the upstream velocity components given by Eq. (5.14). The density, shock velocity, and velocity components behind the shock can be found from Eqs. (5.13), (5.16), and (5.18), respectively. The same procedure is used in the corrector step except that Eq. (4.6b) is used to correct the pressure and Eq. (5.19b) is used to correct the shock position. Results obtained using this procedure at the shock for the supersonic flow over a two-dimensional blunt body are presented later.

To apply a sharp-shock procedure in steady three-dimensional supersonic flow of either an ideal or real gas for cylindrical coordinates $(z, r, \phi)$, the pressure approach can again be used. Consider the three-dimensional shock shown in Fig. 24 for which the governing equations are integrated in the longitudinal direction $z$. The free-stream velocity vector $\vec{q}_1$ at an angle of attack $\alpha$ is given by

$$\vec{q}_1 = (u_1, v_1, w_1) = q_1 \cos \alpha \hat{i}_z - q_1 \sin \alpha \cos \phi \hat{i}_r + q_1 \sin \alpha \sin \phi \hat{i}_\phi \quad (5.21)$$

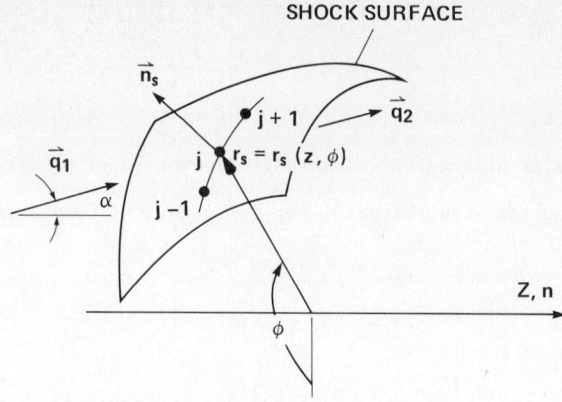

Fig. 24. Steady shock for three-dimensional supersonic flow in cylindrical coordinates $(z, r, \phi)$.

Two quantities that appear in the following equations are inherently dependent on equations of state, the upstream component of velocity normal to the shock surface $\tilde{u}_1$ and the downstream density $\rho_2$:

$$\tilde{u}_1 = \tilde{u}_1(p_2; p_1, \rho_1) \tag{5.22}$$

$$\rho_2 = \rho_2(p_2; p_1, \rho_1) \tag{5.23}$$

Here the quantities upstream and downstream of the shock-wave discontinuity are denoted by subscripts 1 and 2, respectively. The procedure used to evaluate Eqs. (5.22) and (5.23), which depends on whether a real or perfect gas is considered, is covered later. For the present it is assumed that such relations exist.

The vector components of velocity normal and tangential to the shock wave are given by

$$\vec{\tilde{u}}_1 = -(\vec{q} \cdot \vec{n}_s)\vec{n}_s \tag{5.24}$$

$$\vec{\tilde{v}}_1 = \vec{q}_1 - \vec{\tilde{u}}_1 \tag{5.25}$$

where $\vec{n}_s$ denotes the outward unit normal to the shock surface. The formula for the shock surface normal is identical with that for the body surface normal, Eq. (5.2), except that subscript b is replaced by subscript s.

The magnitude of the normal velocity component $\tilde{u}_1$ is found as a function of shock surface derivatives by use of Eq. (5.24). The resulting expression is then inverted to yield the following representation for the derivative $r_{s_z}$:

$$r_{s_z} = u_1\Omega + \tilde{u}_1\sqrt{\Omega^2 + [1 + (r_{s_\phi}/r_s)^2]/(u_1^2 - \tilde{u}_1^2)} \qquad (5.26)$$

where

$$\Omega = \frac{v_1 - w_1(r_{s_\phi}/r_s)}{(u_1^2 - \tilde{u}_1^2)}$$

The downstream velocity $\vec{q}_2$ is given by either

$$\vec{q}_2 = u_2\hat{i}_z + v_2\hat{i}_r + w_2\hat{i}_\phi \qquad (5.27a)$$

or

$$\vec{q}_2 = \vec{\tilde{u}}_2 + \vec{\tilde{v}}_2 \qquad (5.28a)$$

The tangential component $\vec{\tilde{v}}_2$ is conserved across the shock wave and hence its value is the same as $\vec{\tilde{v}}_1$. This variable is eliminated from Eq. (5.28b) by use of Eq. (5.25) and, in addition, mass conservation across the shock wave is introduced in the form $\tilde{u}_2 = \tilde{u}_1\rho_1/\rho_2$ to eliminate $\tilde{u}_2$. The result is

$$\vec{q}_2 = \vec{q}_1 - r_{s_z}a\hat{i}_z + a\hat{i}_r - \frac{r_{s_\phi}}{r_s}a\hat{i}_\phi \qquad (5.29)$$

where

$$a = \frac{|\tilde{u}_1|(1 - \rho_1/\rho_2)}{\sqrt{r_{s_z}^2 + 1 + (r_{s_\phi}/r_s)^2}}$$

As in the unsteady case, the shock wave is moved using the following Euler predictor/modified Euler corrector:

$$r_s^{(1)} = r_s^n + r_{s_z}^n \Delta z \quad \text{(predictor)} \qquad (5.30a)$$

$$r_s^{n+1} = r_s^n + \frac{1}{2}(r_{s_z}^n + r_{s_z}^{(1)})\Delta z \quad \text{(corrector)} \qquad (5.30b)$$

where $\Delta z$ is the integration step size. The quantity $r_{s_\phi}$ is evaluated according to the formula (Fig. 23):

$$r_{s_\phi} = (r_{s_{j+1}} - r_{s_{j-1}})/2\Delta\phi \qquad (5.31)$$

Equations (5.19) and (5.20) for an ideal gas can be written explicitly as

$$\tilde{u}_1(p_2, p_1, \rho_1) = \frac{p_1}{2\rho_1}\left[(\gamma+1)\frac{p_2}{p_1} + (\gamma-1)\right] \qquad (5.32)$$

$$\rho_2(p_2, p_1, \rho_1) = \rho_1 \frac{\frac{p_2}{p_1} + \frac{\gamma-1}{\gamma+1}}{1 + \frac{\gamma-1}{\gamma+1}\frac{p_2}{p_1}} \tag{5.33}$$

Equivalent analytic representations for a real gas are not available. However, a table-lookup scheme can also be adapted here as in the body boundary condition scheme. At the beginning of the flow-field calculation after $p_1$ and $\rho_1$ are specified, a pair of tables is generated that contains the upstream normal velocity $\tilde{u}_1$ and the downstream density $\rho_2$ as elements with the pressure $p_2$ as the argument. The table lookup procedure can then simultaneously return values $\tilde{u}_1$ and $\rho_2$ for a given pressure $p_2$. The procedure used to generate the table is similar to that described by Vincenti and Kruger[41] (p. 179) in their discussion on steady shock waves.

The procedure used to apply the above equations for a steady three-dimensional shock is basically the same as that used in the unsteady example presented earlier and therefore is not repeated here. Again, results presented later use this procedure and demonstrate the obtainable accuracy.

In the computation of supersonic flow problems, two other types of permeable boundaries are encountered: the outflow or downstream boundary and the inflow or upstream boundary. Figure 25 presents examples of both types.

The computational region for determining the supersonic flow about a blunt body (see Fig. 25(a)) is bounded by the body, bow shock, plane of symmetry, and the line $\theta = \theta_{max}$. This line is a supersonic outflow boundary and must be chosen downstream of the sonic line, that is, $q_\theta$ along $\theta_{max}$ must be greater than the local speed of sound

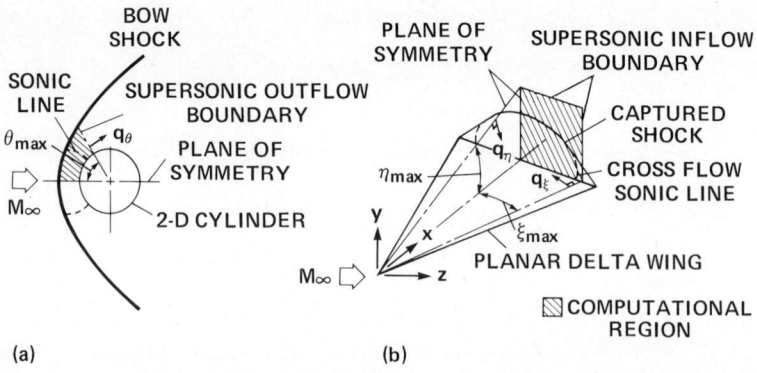

Fig. 25. Supersonic outflow and inflow computational boundaries; (a) blunt body, and (b) planar delta wing-compression side.

in order that the time-dependent problem be well posed. A variety of techniques exists for determining the dependent variables along such a boundary, but the simple linear extrapolation, or equivalently one-sided differencing, has been found to work well and is usually used. Roache[35] discusses other procedures for accomplishing the same thing.

Supersonic inflow boundaries are quite common in the examples presented later. Two such boundaries occur in the determination of the conical supersonic flow over the compression side of a planar delta wing (Fig. 25(b)). The computational boundary for conical coordinates in this case consists of the body, a plane of symmetry, and the two supersonic inflow boundaries along the lines $\eta_{max} = (y/x)_{max}$ and $\xi_{max} = (z/x)_{max}$. For this problem to be well posed, the fluid velocity $q_\xi$ and $q_\eta$ normal to these boundaries and at every point along them must be greater than the local speed of sound. The exact flow conditions along this type of boundary must be known at each step during the integration procedure; in general, they are usually constant. In Fig. 25(b), the dependent variables along the line $\eta_{max}$ assume the values of the free stream, while along the line $\xi_{max}$ they assume values of both the free stream and "sliding wedge" flow.

The boundary condition procedures discussed in this section are not meant to be the best possible for solving supersonic flow problems. But when used properly, however, they yield solutions of more than acceptable quality.

## 6. INITIAL CONDITIONS, STEP SIZE, AND CONVERGENCE

To initiate a given calculation, the values of the dependent variables at each grid point in the computational plane must be specified. This initialization procedure depends on whether a marching technique or an iterative approach is being used to obtain the solution.

For an iterative approach in which one is interested only in the converged solution, the initial data, in most instances, can be a rather rough approximation of what the actual solution is believed to be. In using a complete shock-capturing approach, for example, it is a common practice to set the flow variables at the interior points equal to the free-stream variables. In doing this, imposition of the tangency condition at the body creates either a compression or expansion wave that propagates into the field and eventually settles down to its correct location as the solution converges.

Initialization for the blunt-body problem in which the bow shock is treated as a discontinuity is somewhat more complicated. In addition to initializing the dependent variables at the interior points, one must estimate the shock position and slope. Usually, this simply requires that the shock be specified analytically, thus yielding its slope and the flow variables behind it. In conjunction with a simple approximation for the body variables for example, modified Newtonian flow followed by a linear interpolation for the flow variables between the body and shock, the initialization procedure is complete.

The initial data required when using a marching procedure in which the solution at each step is of interest are usually determined from some other source and supplied to the marching code. For example, when solving for the supersonic flow over a three-dimensional, blunt-nose configuration (Fig. 13(b)), a blunt-body computer program supplies the data in the starting plane. This includes all flow variables between the body and the shock, the shock position, and shock slopes.

Once the initialization procedure is complete, a step size must be selected that is small enough to be commensurate with the stability bound, but large enough to finish the computation with a minimum of computer time. Use of the largest possible step size for hyperbolic equations ensures that the finite-difference scheme is as nearly compatible with the method of characteristics or the "perfect shift condition" (see Kutler and Lomax[37] or Warming et al.[23]) as possible. To determine the range of values the step size should have, many authors rely on amplification matrix theory because of its ability to predict a stability condition conservatively and quickly. The method is based on a locally linear analysis of the governing partial differential equations coupled with a discrete harmonic analysis of the linear-difference scheme. In Section 4, the modified equation approach was used to get a stability bound. Both theories yield the same result.

The partial differential equation system for the linear analysis is given by Eq. (2.9a) for the unsteady case and by Eq. (2.9b) for the steady case. The stability theories, at least for $(t, x_1)$ space in unsteady flow and $(x_1, x_2)$ space in steady flow, require that

or
$$\frac{\Delta t}{\Delta x} \leq \frac{1}{|(\sigma_\ell^A)_{max}|} \quad ; \quad \text{unsteady} \tag{6.1a}$$

$$\frac{\Delta x_1}{\Delta x_2} \leq \frac{1}{|(\sigma_\ell^M)_{max}|} \quad ; \quad \text{steady} \tag{6.1b}$$

$\ell = 1, 3$

where $(\sigma_\ell^A)_{max}$ and $(\sigma_\ell^M)_{max}$ are the maximums of the local maximum eigenvalues (Eq. (2.10a) and (2.10b)) of all the points at a particular constant $t$ or $x_1$ plane, respectively. Similar relations can be obtained for the $(t, x_2)$, $(t, x_3)$, and $(x_1, x_3)$ spaces:

$$\frac{\Delta t}{\Delta x_2} \leq \frac{1}{|(\sigma_\ell^B)_{max}|}$$

$$\frac{\Delta t}{\Delta x_3} \leq \frac{1}{|(\sigma_\ell^C)_{max}|}$$

unsteady, $\ell = 1, 3$ \quad (6.2a)

$$\frac{\Delta x_1}{\Delta x_3} \leq \frac{1}{|(\sigma_\ell^N)_{max}|} \quad \text{steady} \tag{6.2b}$$

This planar analysis has been shown[3,17,31,42] to give a good bound on the step size in multidimensional problems if the right-hand size of Eqs. (6.1) and (6.2) are multiplied by a constant $C \leq 1$, which can be varied during the computation and is usually assigned a value of approximately 0.9.

For multidimensional problems in unsteady flow, for example, $\Delta x_1$, $\Delta x_2$, and $\Delta x_3$ are known. It is therefore necessary to determine the step size from the minimum $\Delta t$ predicted by Eqs. (6.1a) and (6.2a). This ensures that all inequalities are satisfied. This same procedure is followed for multidimensional steady flows. In flow fields where the dependent variables are changing rapidly, the step size should be recalculated after each complete integration step to eliminate the possibility of an instability.

Independent variable transformations change the structure of the eigenvalues and hence the step size. Consider, for example, the following transformation applied to the steady flow equations (Eq. (2.9b)):

$$\zeta = x_1$$
$$\eta = \eta(x_1, x_2, x_3) \qquad (6.3)$$
$$\xi = \xi(x_1, x_2, x_3)$$

Applied to Eq. (2.9b), this yields

$$U_\zeta + PU_\eta + QU_\xi + A^{-1}D = 0 \qquad (6.4)$$

where

$$P = (\eta_{x_1} + M\eta_{x_2} + N\eta_{x_3})$$
$$Q = \xi_{x_1} + M\xi_{x_2} + N\xi_{x_3}$$

The eigenvalues of the matrices P and Q can be determined and then used in Eqs. (6.1b) and (6.2b) to calculate the integration step size. An example of this effect is presented later.

The convergence of an iterative solution is recognized when the flow variables, to the accuracy of the method being used, are not changing. All calculations presented in the following section were obtained using a cathode ray display tube (CRT) linked with the computer. This allowed the solution to be displayed after each integration step so that convergence could be judged.

## 7. NUMERICAL RESULTS

This section presents the numerical results for a number of different problems ranging from simple wedge flow to multiple-shocked three-dimensional flows. The majority of these computations were performed on an IBM 360/67 computer system linked with an IBM 2250 cathode ray display tube, which allowed on-line interaction with the computer while simultaneously displaying the results.

### 7.1 Two-Dimensional Wedge and Axisymmetric Cone Flow

The pedagogical problems of supersonic flow over a wedge and a cone at zero angle of attack are by no means difficult to solve. They are used here to demonstrate the effects of the shock-capturing, finite-difference approach on solutions of the inviscid Euler equations in comparison with solution of the modified Burger's equation discussed earlier. Results are presented using the first-order method of Lax and the second-order method of MacCormack.

To solve the wedge problem, a Cartesian coordinate system is used in which the x coordinate lies along the surface of the wedge and the y coordinate is normal to the surface (Fig. 26(a)). The reflection principle is applied at the body, and the flow variables are initially set equal to the free-stream variables. The governing equations are integrated from $x = 1$ to $x = 2$ and then stepped back to $x = 1$. This procedure is repeated until the transients have been damped. The shock wave during the integration from 1.0 to 2.0 propagates upward (or forward) in the computational line as did the simulated shocks when solving the modified Burger equation, thus allowing for an easy comparison of the two solutions.

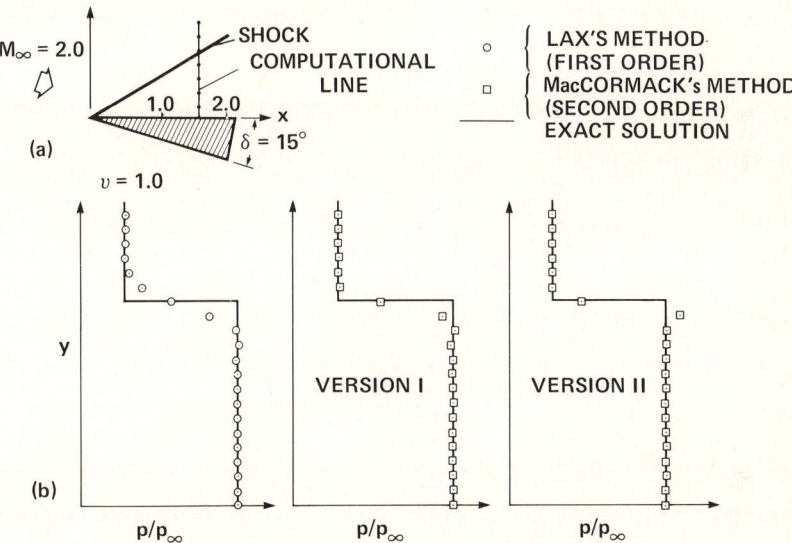

Fig. 26. Computation of simple supersonic wedge flow using first- and second-order methods.

The wedge solutions are shown in Fig. 26(b). Using Lax's method, the captured shock is spread over approximately four mesh intervals, and its location agrees quite well with the exact shock location. This same behavior was observed in Fig. 17 for Burger's equation. Using version I of MacCormack's scheme (the preferred version for this problem), the shock is spread over two intervals and has no noticeable overshoots or undershoots as does the solution obtained using version II (the nonpreferred version.

A spherical coordinate system is used in solving the cone at zero angle of attack

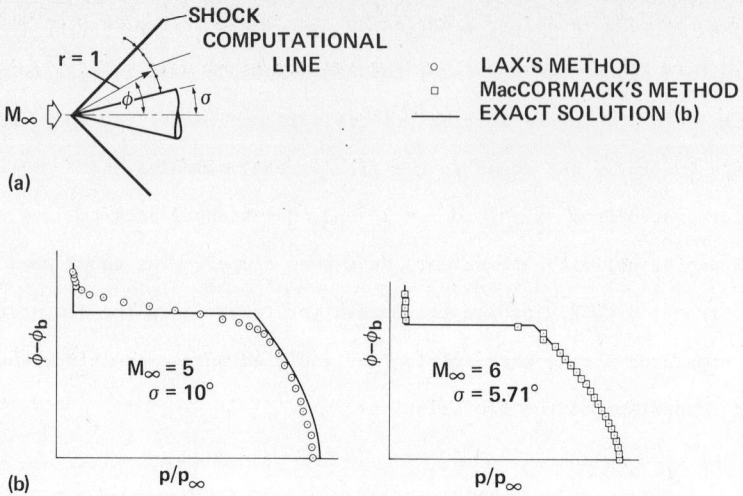

Fig. 27. Computation of axisymmetric supersonic cone flow using first- and second-order methods.

problem (Fig. 27(a)). Again, the reflection principle is used at the body, and the flow variables are set equal to the free stream initially. The governing equations are integrated iteratively with respect to r until converged. Solutions obtained using Lax's method and MacCormack's method are shown in Fig. 27(b). The first-order scheme smears the shock badly while the second-order scheme yields a rather sharp shock. The shock wave in the computational line for the near-converged solution does not move. The conservative variables in the $\phi$ direction therefore are continuous through the shock (as shown in Fig. 5(d)), but their first derivative is discontinuous. When differencing across the shock in this case, it is this discontinuous behavior that results in the minor oscillations of the second-order solution.

The conclusions to be drawn from this simple study are that (1) the modified form of Burger's equation can be used to represent the inviscid Euler equations for numerical studies, (2) the numerical solutions obtained using MacCormack's second-order scheme are far superior in their shock-capturing ability than the solutions obtained using Lax's scheme, and (3) shock alignment with one of the coordinate directions yields captured shock waves that are better defined.

## 7.2 Planar Delta Wing

The supersonic flow field surrounding a lifting delta wing with supersonic leading edges has been the object of many numerical, theoretical, and experimental studies in the past. The purpose here is first to determine the flow fields on both the compression and expansion sides of a planar delta wing and, second, to combine these two solutions at the trailing edge to form an initial data plane that can be integrated downstream to yield the inviscid flow in the wake of the delta wing.

Compression side numerical calculations have been obtained by such investigators as Fowell,[43] South and Klunker,[44] Babaev,[45] Beeman and Powers,[46] and Voskresenskii.[47] The flow field on this side of the delta wing poses no great problem for the sharp-shock techniques used by these investigators, and their results are comparable.

Expansion side calculations have been attempted by Fowell,[43] Babaev,[48] and Beeman and Powers.[45] This flow field is somewhat more complicated than the compression side since, at some distance inboard of the leading edge, an embedded shock wave is produced because of the deceleration of the supersonic crossflow velocities.

In the past, no attempt has been made to determine the complete inviscid flow field in the wake of a lifting delta wing. Oswatitsch and Sun[49] used the method of characteristics in conjunction with a limiting procedure to handle the trailing-edge expansion to determine the influence of the near-field flow in the far-field wave formation beneath the delta wing. Their main conclusion was that the bow shock, due to attenuation by the trailing-edge expansion wave, terminates a finite distance from the wing. Roe,[50] in a subsequent experiment, found that the bow shock did not disappear, but the wave pattern beneath the planar delta wing developed into the classical "N" wave.

The near-field flow behind the delta wing is complicated not only by the existing compression and expansion side-flow fields, which contain various combinations of shock and expansion waves, but also by the shock and expansion waves generated at the trailing edge. This class of problems, which would be difficult to solve using a complete sharp-shock approach, is a good test for the usefulness of the shock-capturing technique.

To solve this problem, a Cartesian coordinate system is used, and the wing with respect to this system is oriented as shown in Fig. 14. An independent variable transformation to conical coordinates, normalized with respect to the tangent of the wing angle $\beta$ ($\zeta = x$, $\eta = y/x \tan \beta$, $\xi = z/x \tan \beta$) is performed on Eq. (2.1). The resulting equation is rearranged in conservation law form, and since it is hyperbolic with respect to $\zeta$, it is integrated cyclically from $\zeta = 1$ to $\zeta = 1 + \Delta\zeta$ until conical flow is established. Plane-of-symmetry boundary conditions are applied at the left-hand boundary (Fig. 14) of the mesh since the flow field is symmetrical to it. The uppermost part of the mesh is chosen so that it remains entirely in the free stream, and the boundary conditions there are fixed accordingly. Exact boundary conditions are applied at the right-hand side since these can be computed from the oblique-shock or Prandtl-Meyer relations which apply along supersonic leading edges. At the body, the reflection principle, which is exact in this case, is used. For both the compression and expansion side calculations, initial conditions are supplied by using the values of the flow variables in the free stream.

After the complete flow field is determined on both sides of the delta wing, the two solutions are combined at the trailing edge to form an initial data plane that can then be numerically integrated downstream through the wake. In this case, the only boundary condition imposed is that the free stream exist along all edges of the mesh where symmetry does not apply.

Computations were performed (see Kutler and Lomax[42]) to determine the flow field over the compression side of a 50° swept, planar delta wing. Figure 28 shows the results of those computations for angles of attack of 5°, 10°, and 15° at Mach 4. The semispan pressure distributions are compared with the results of South and Klunker,[44] who used a method of lines technique. South, in turn, made comparisons with Voskresenskii[47] and found good agreement, and with Babaev[45] and found poor agreement. The present results substantiate the results of South and Voskresenskii. Figure 29 compares the shock shapes for the above flow conditions. There is very little disagreement with South's results. The shock shape obtained using the shock-capturing technique was located using a weighted gradient technique coded into the program.

The surface-pressure coefficient on the expansion side of a 45° swept delta wing in Mach 3 flow for 4°, 8°, and 12° angle of attack is shown in Fig. 30. The results are compared with a method-of-characteristics technique devised by Beeman and Pow-

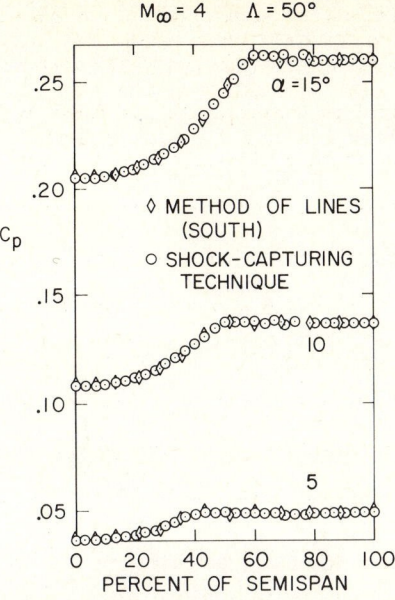

Fig. 28. Spanwise pressure distribution on compression side of planar delta wing; M = 4, Λ = 50°, = 5°, 10°, and 15°.

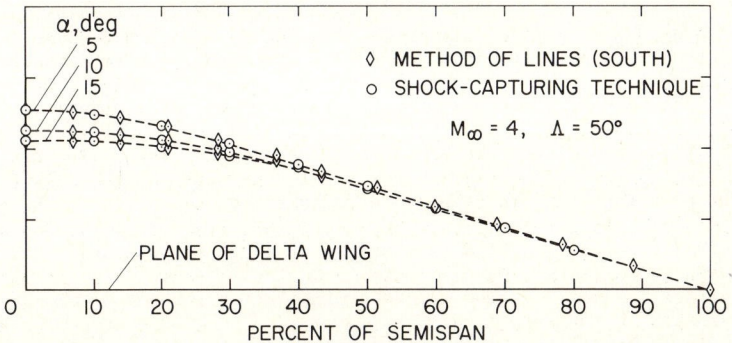

Fig. 29. Compression side-shock shapes; M = 4, Λ = 50°, α = 5°, 10°, and 15°.

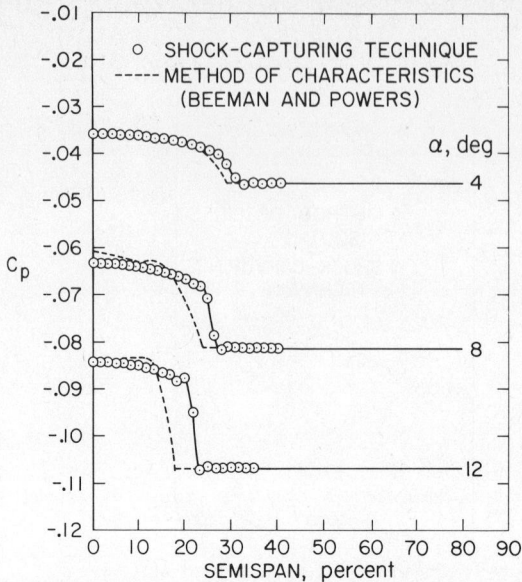

Fig. 30. Spanwise pressure distribution on expansion side of planar delta wing; $M = 3$, $\Lambda = 45°$, $\alpha = 4°$, $8°$, and $12°$.

ers,[46] who chose to neglect the weak crossflow shock, assuming instead an isentropic compression. The disagreement in the location of the embedded shock is believed to be the result of their assumption. However, the pressure distributions on either side of the shock are in good agreement. The grid size used for these problems consisted of 34 points normal to the body and 26 points parallel to the body, and computation times were on the order of 10 min on the IBM 360/67.

Bannink and Nebbeling[51] obtained very good experimental results on the expansion side of a 44.7° swept delta wing at 12° angle of attack in Mach 2.94 flow. The identical case was solved numerically and plots of the spanwise pitot-pressure distribution at various heights above the wing are compared with the experimental results in Fig. 31. The locations of the crossflow shock and conical sonic line are compared in Fig. 32. The agreement in both figures is remarkable.

The complete inviscid flow field in the wake of a 55° swept, planar delta wing at 1.8° angle of attack in Mach 2.7 flow was determined after the compression and expansion side flow fields were determined. The results of this calculation clearly show the formation of the trailing-edge shock wave on the leeward side and expansion wave on the windward side. The formation of the secondary recompression shock on the wind-

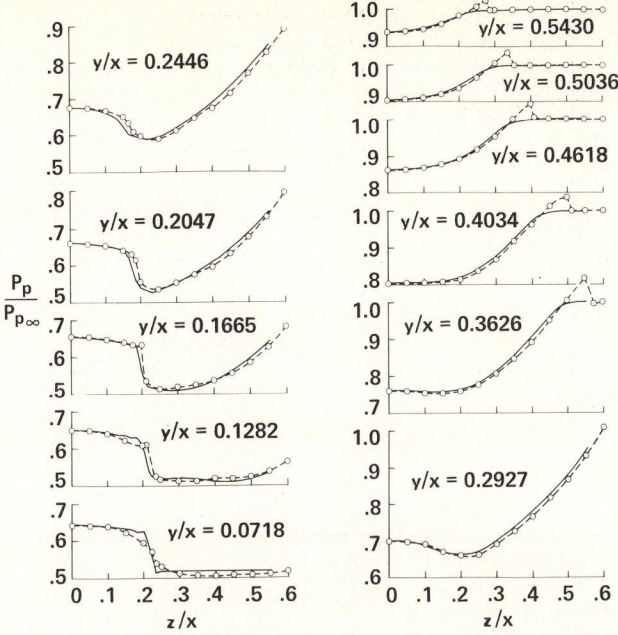

Fig. 31. Spanwise pitot pressure distribution on planar delta wing; $M = 2.94$, $\Lambda = 44.7°$, $\alpha = 12°$.

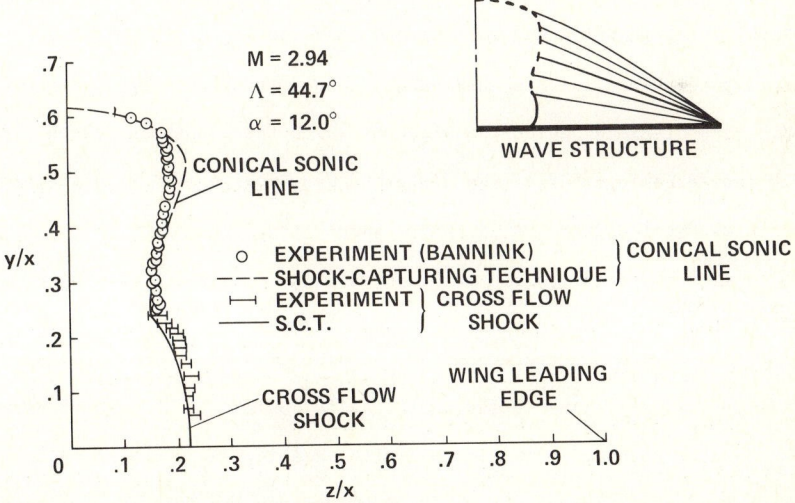

Fig. 32. Comparison with experiment of shock wave and conical sonic line for planar delta wing; $M = 2.94$, $\Lambda = 44.7°$, $\alpha = 12°$.

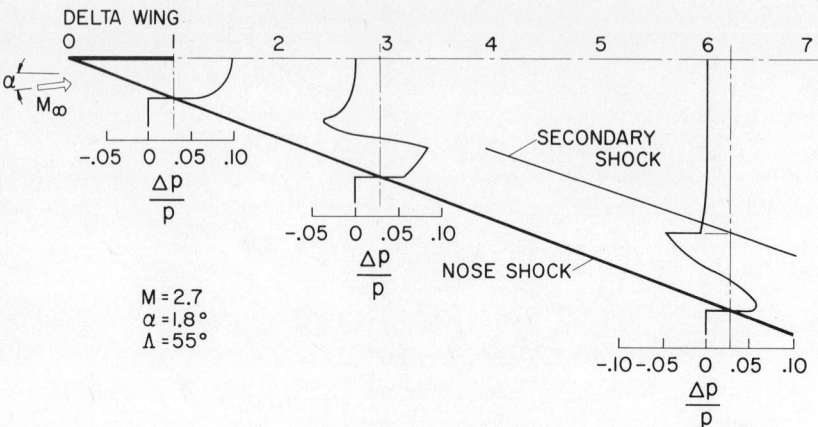

Fig. 33. Windward centerline pressure distributions beneath planar delta wing; M = 2.7, Λ = 55°, α = 1.8°.

ward side is also clearly recognizable. Figure 33 shows the plane-of-symmetry, compression side-shock locations, and normal pressure distributions between the plane of the wing and the free stream at various stations downstream. The pressure curves shown were faired through the numerical data, and the actual shock waves did not appear as sharp discontinuities but were spread over two mesh intervals.

The results obtained in this wake study did not reveal the disappearance of the bow shock for the distance behind the wing for which the equations were solved. The results did show a rapid decay of the disturbed flow region away from the plane of symmetry, but always indicated an N wave beneath the wing in the plane of symmetry.

## 7.3 Conical Wing-Body Combination

The supersonic flow about the compression side of a circular cone/planar delta wing combination was solved by Kutler and Lomax[42] using the shock-capturing technique. The results obtained compared well with existing experimental data. Results are now presented for a similar wing-body configuration for both the compression and expansion side-flow regions.

Consider the quarter-body in Fig. 34. The basic coordinate system is again Cartesian, and the governing equations are transformed to conical coordinates. They are

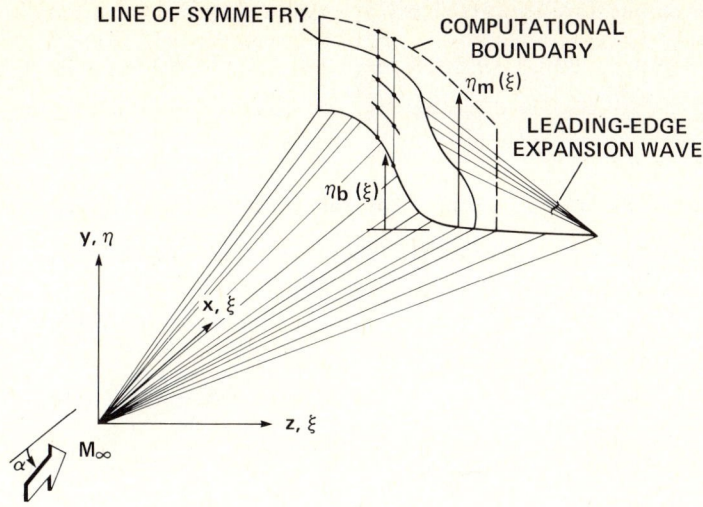

Fig. 34. Coordinate system for conical wing-body combination.

transformed again to normalize the distance between the body given by $\eta_b = \eta_b(\xi)$ and the upper computational boundary given by $\eta_m = \eta_m(\xi)$ as follows:

$$\left. \begin{aligned} \zeta &= \zeta \\ \eta' &= \frac{\eta - \eta_b(\xi)}{\eta_m(\xi) - \eta_b(\xi)} \\ \xi &= \xi \end{aligned} \right\} \qquad (7.1)$$

The resulting equation is then rearranged in conservation law form and integrated with respect to $\zeta$ to establish conical flow.

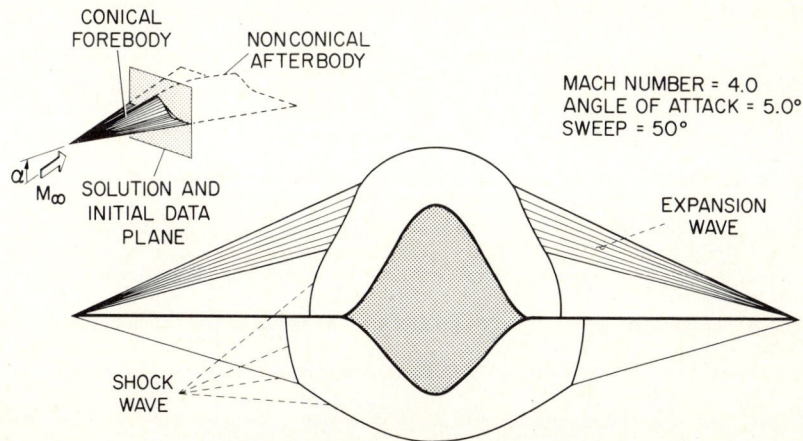

Fig. 35. Computed location of shock and expansion waves around wing-body combination; $M = 4$, $\Lambda = 50°$, $\alpha = 5°$.

The results of such a computation for a cosine shaped body and planar delta wing at 5° angle of attack in Mach 4 flow are shown in Figs. 35 and 36. The computed shock and expansion wave patterns are shown in Fig. 35. On the compression side, there exists a slip surface (not shown) emanating from the triple point and extending to the crossflow stagnation point on the body. The surface-pressure distribution for both sides of the vehicle is shown in Fig. 36. The discontinuous behavior in the curves results from the embedded shocks striking the body.

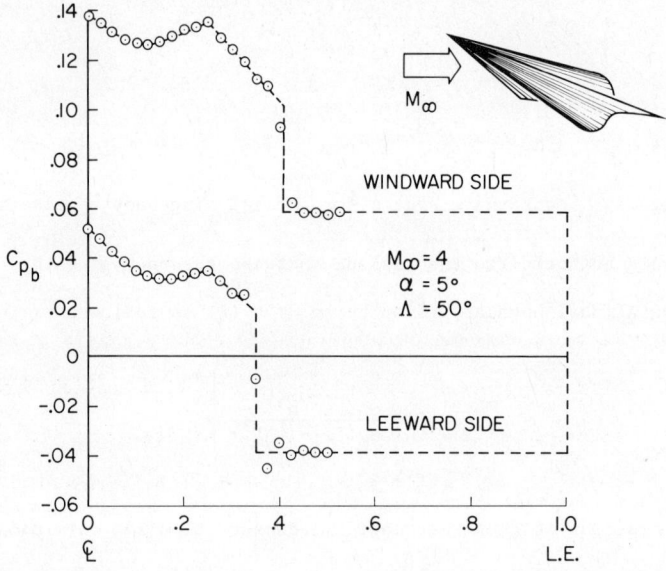

Fig. 36. Surface-pressure distribution on wing-body combination; M = 4, $\Lambda = 50°$, $\alpha = 5°$.

## 7.4 Internal Corner Flow

The supersonic flow field generated by an internal corner contains multiple shocks and slip surfaces, but it is easily determined using the shock-capturing approach.[52,53] The structure of the conical flow generated by two intersecting wedges immersed in a supersonic stream is shown in Fig. 37. The shock structure consists of the planar shocks emanating from the leading edge of each wedge (with angles $\delta_1$ and $\delta_2$), a corner shock that joins the two wedge shocks, and two embedded shocks that stretch from the body to their respective triple points. Stretching between each of triple points and the axial corner is a slip surface or inviscid shear layer. A vor-

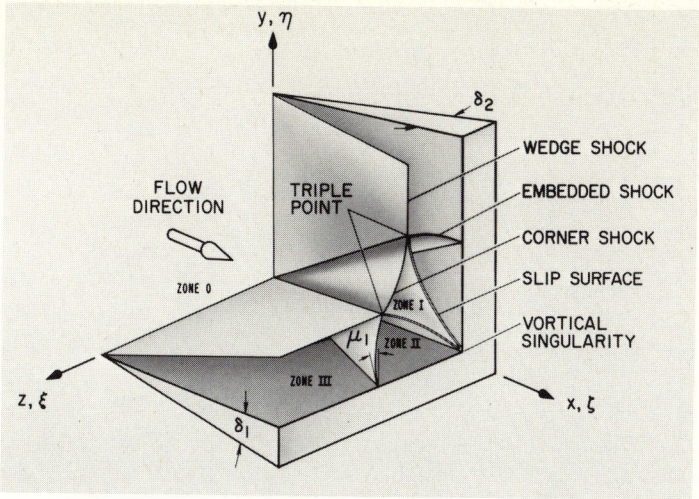

Fig. 37. Coordinate system and typical wave structure.

tical singularity (a point with multiple values of entropy) exists at the axial corner of the two wedges. It is generated as a result of the flow passing through different points of the curved embedded and corner shocks and converging at the axial corner.

The regions bounded by the shocks and slip surfaces are denoted as zones 0, I, II, and III (as illustrated in Fig. 37). Zone 0 corresponds to the free stream, and zone III contains simple wedge flow; both have constant flow properties. The flow in zones I and II is rotational because of the convex corner shock and concave embedded shock (viewed from corner). The conical crossflow velocity (the component that results when the total velocity is projected on a sphere whose center is at the origin of the coordinate system) is supersonic in zone III and subsonic in zones I and II. Therefore, the conical problem is mixed elliptic-hyperbolic. If the three-dimensional steady-flow equations (Eq. (2.1)) in Cartesian coordinates are transformed into non-orthogonal, conical coordinates ($\zeta = x$, $\eta = y/x$, and $\xi = z/x$), they are made hyperbolic with respect to $\zeta$.

A rectangular region that completely encompasses the shock structure in the corner is discretized and results in the computational plane shown in Fig. 38. In the

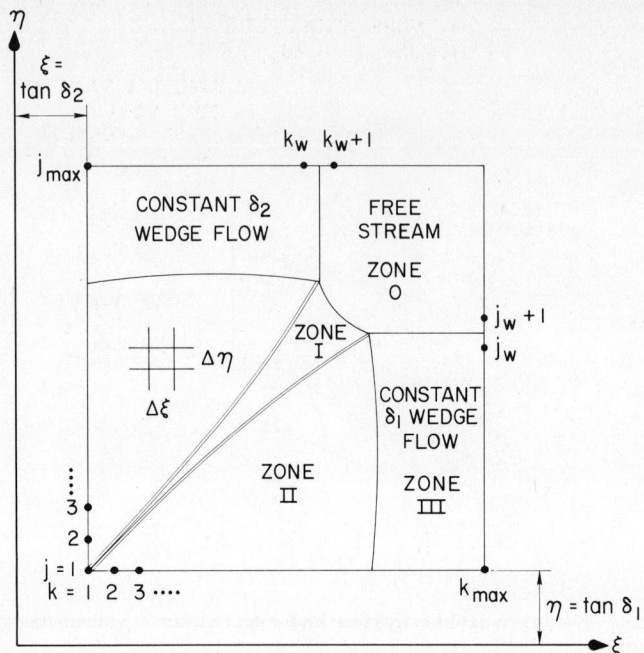

Fig. 38. Computational plane for internal corner flow.

$\eta$ direction, the lower boundary is the wedge surface, $\eta = \tan \delta_1$ where $j = 1$ (along with the tangency condition is satisfied using one-sided finite differences), while the upper boundary, $j = j_{max}$, is chosen to fall in a region of known flow properties (well outside the wedge-flow Mach cone from the corner). An analogous procedure is used in the $\xi$ direction. All interior points are assigned values of the free-stream variables initially.

The second-order-accurate, predictor-corrector scheme of MacCormack is used to integrate the governing equations iteratively until the term $E_\zeta$ is zero, which implies the establishment of a conical flow field. Shock waves and slip surfaces that should exist form automatically and are correctly positioned within the computational network of points.

The most recent published experimental data obtained for the corner flow problem are by West and Korkegi.[54] They tested an equal wedge angle ($\delta_1 = \delta_2 = 9.49°$) configuration in Mach 2.98 flow over a Reynolds number range from $0.4 \times 10^6$ to $60 \times 10^6$, which included laminar, transitional, and turbulent boundary layers. A numerical so-

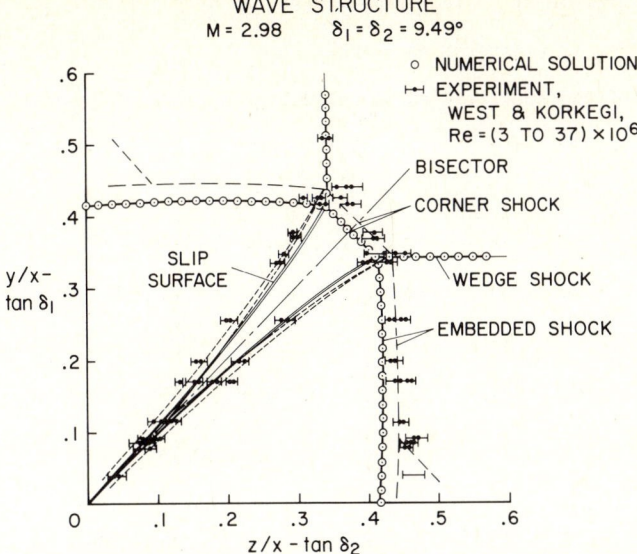

Fig. 39. Comparison of numerical and experimental shock patterns; $M = 2.98$, $\delta_1 = \delta_2 = 9.49°$.

lution* for the corresponding inviscid case was obtained, and the shock wave and slip surface structure are compared with the high Reynolds number experiment in Fig. 39.

The inviscid embedded shock is slightly concave when viewed from the origin and falls inside the location of the corresponding experimental shock. The corner shock, which is slightly convex when viewed from the origin, also falls inside the experimental shock. The position of the experimental and numerical wedge shocks agrees exactly. It appears, therefore, that the displacement effects of the boundary layer in the region bounded by the corner and embedded shocks result in an effective thickening of the body, and this forces the shock structure outward.

The slip surface locations for this case can be found from plots of density and are shown as the thin double line that stretches from the triple point to the origin in Fig. 39. The slip surface is slightly curved and asymptotically approaches the bisector near the origin. The experimental shear layer is also curved, but it appears to merge before the origin is reached. Since the positions of the numerical and experimental triple points are different, the comparison between the inviscid slip sur-

---

*For the numerical results presented, a 30×30 rectangular grid was used. Each computation, consisting of 400 iterations, required approximately 20 min of CPU time on an IBM 360/67.

face and viscous shear layer, which originate at the triple points, is unfair. Qualitatively, however their basic shapes are the same.

A comparison of the numerical and experimental (turbulent boundary layer) surface pressures is shown in Fig. 40. The first pressure rise in the experimental data (decreasing $z/x$) indicates the onset of separation. This is followed by a reduced gradient region that indicates separation and again a rapid pressure rise that indicates reattachment. The pressure between the reattachment point and the origin is greater than that of the inviscid result. This higher pressure indicates an apparent thickening of the body in this region due to boundary-layer displacement effects.

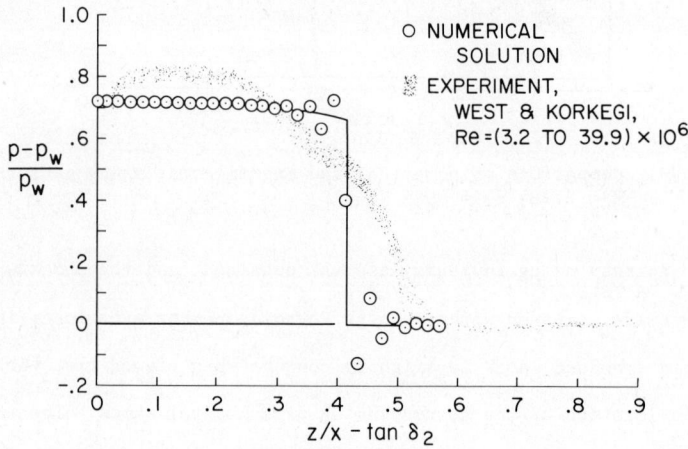

Fig. 40. Comparison of numerical and experimental surface-pressure distributions; $M = 2.98$, $\delta_1 = \delta_2 = 9.49°$.

Figure 41 shows the distortion in the numerical and experimental wave structure that results from an asymmetrical configuration with $\delta_1 = 3.5°$ and $\delta_2 = 12.2°$ in $M = 3.17$ flow. The experiment was performed by Charwat and Redekeopp.[55] Both the computed and experimental vertical embedded shocks are practically straight, while both horizontal embedded shocks curve rapidly into the triple point. Again, the position of the experimental wave pattern is displaced outward when compared with the numerical result, but both exhibit the same asymmetrical behavior.

## 7.5 Two-Dimensional Blunt Body

The blunt-body problem has been solved by various investigators in various ways. Our goal is not to devise a new approach but to determine the flow field that results

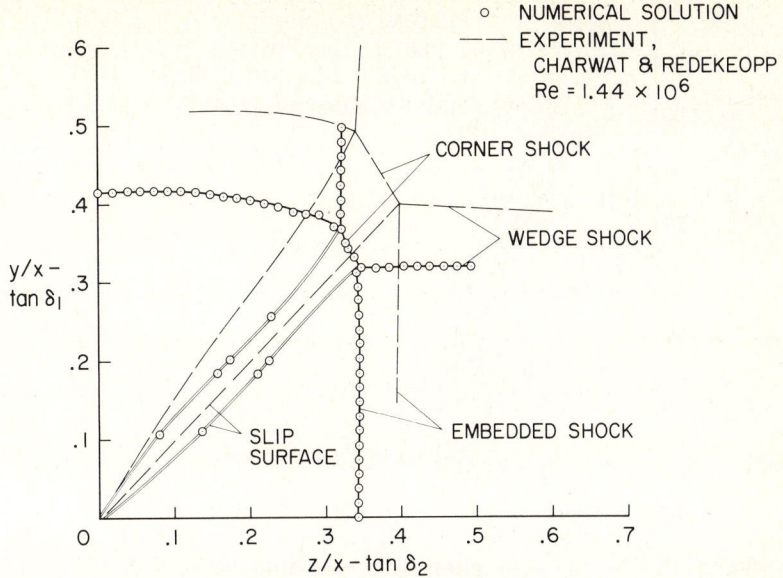

Fig. 41. Comparison of numerical and experimental shock patterns for unequal wedge angles; M = 3.17, $\delta_1 = 3.5°$, $\delta_2 = 12.2°$.

when a planar shock wave intersects the bow shock generated by a blunt body. The analysis and results presented here, however, are only for the two-dimensional, blunt-body solution and do not include the effects of the impinging shock.

The basic orthogonal coordinate system chosen is polar (t, r, θ) (Fig. 11(d)). The unsteady equations are then transformed to normalize the distance between the body and shock, which is treated as a sharp discontinuity in this case. The resulting computational plane is shown in Fig. 25(a). The unsteady shock relations discussed earlier are applied at the shock boundary, and data at the supersonic outflow boundary (θ = $θ_{max}$) are obtained using a second-order extrapolation technique. Plane-of-symmetry conditions are applied along the line θ = 0, while the surface tangency condition is satisfied at the body using the "normal momentum equation approach" discussed by MacCormack and Warming.[56]

The grid points are initialized according to a procedure discussed earlier, and the time-dependent equations are integrated using MacCormack's scheme until a steady

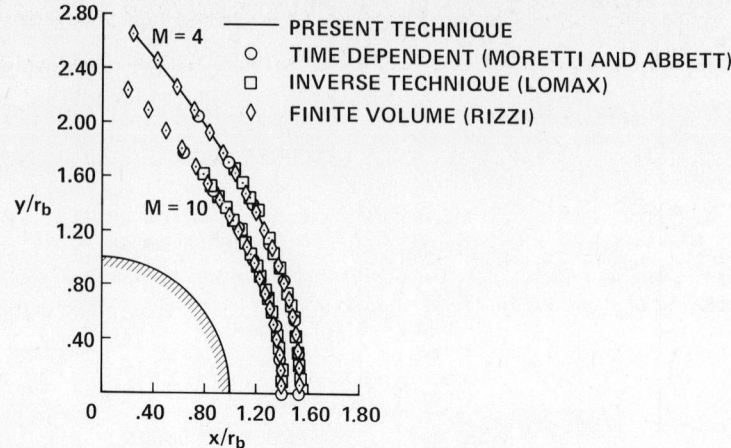

Fig. 42. Shock shape for two-dimensional blunt body; M = 4 and 10.

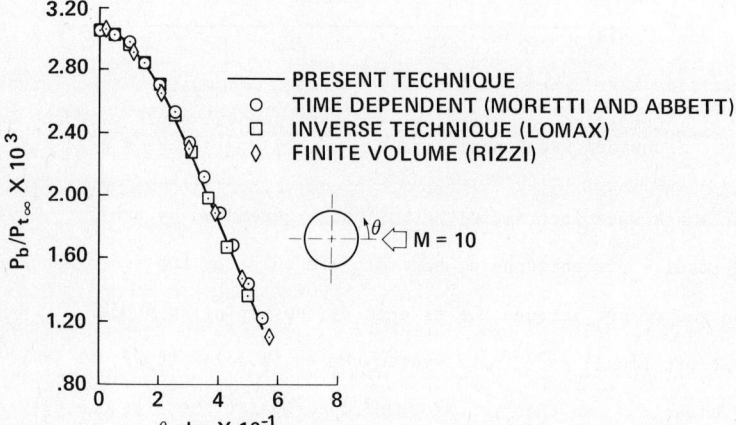

Fig. 43. Surface-pressure distribution for two-dimensional blunt body; M = 10.

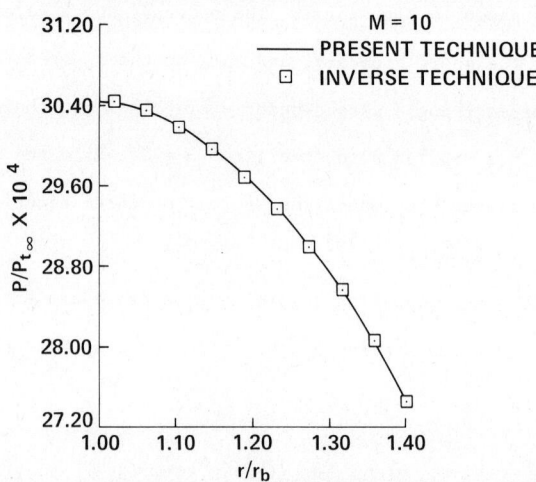

Fig. 44. Stagnation streamline pressure distribution for two-dimensional blunt body; M = 10.

state is reached. Results* of typical calculations are shown in Figs. 42-44. The shock shapes for Mach numbers 4 and 10 are shown in Fig. 42 and compared with the existing solutions of Morretti and Abbett,[12] Lomax and Inouye,[2] and Rizzi and Inouye.[10] The surface-pressure distribution for Mach 10 is shown in Fig. 43 along with the other numerical solutions. Figure 44 is a plot of the pressure distribution along the stagnation streamline, which is compared with the results from the inverse solution only. All comparisons are excellent and no numerical difficulties were encountered during the converging process.

## 7.6 Interfering Shock Problem

A rather interesting unsteady problem and a good test for the shock-capturing approach is the flow field that results when a moving planar shock wave interferes with the supersonic flow over a pointed cone (Fig. 1). The resulting shock wave and contact surface structure for a typical encounter is shown in Fig. 2. To develop the numerical procedure required to determine this three-dimensional flow field, the two-dimensional counterpart of this problem was first solved.[57] This analysis and the resulting solutions are now presented.

The basis for solving this unsteady problem is that it is self-similar—that is, as time increases, the wave structure expands linearly (assuming that at $t = 0$ the incident shock is at the wedge tip) and thus in constant $x/t$ and $y/t$ planes (Fig. 15), the flow field is invariant with time. This self-similarity is generated because there is no characteristic length associated with the body, that the incident shock wave is planar. Thus, if one applies a nonorthogonal coordinate transformation based on self-similarity to the unsteady gasdynamic equations, the unsteady problem is reduced to a steady problem.

From discussions in previous sections, it has been shown that shock waves, if they are aligned with one of the coordinate directions, will be captured with a minimum of post- and precursor oscillations. Because of the complicated shock structure in this problem, it is not possible to align all the shock waves. By an appropriate transformation of the independent variables, however, the incident planar shock can be

---

*This work was performed in conjunction with Mr. James Daywitt, Graduate Assistant at Iowa State University and Reese Sorenson of Ames Research Center.

aligned with one of the coordinate directions, and the original and new wedge shocks, since they are rays from the wedge vertex, can be aligned with the other coordinate direction. It was also mentioned previously that one should also strive to align the body with one of the coordinate directions. The independent variable transformation to satisfy these criteria, which is applied to the two-dimensional unsteady version of Eq. (2.1), is

$$\tau = t$$
$$\xi = [x - b(t, y)]/t \qquad (7.2)$$
$$\eta = y/a(x)$$

where

$$a(x) = x \tan \theta$$
$$b(t,y) = y/\tan \lambda + x_b t$$

where $x_b = x_{min}$ at $t = t_{initial}$.

The above transformation results in the shock-aligned computational plane shown in Fig. 16, where the left-hand boundary is chosen to be upstream of the sonic circle, the right-hand boundary is chosen to be downstream of the intersection point of the incident shock and original wedge shock, and the top boundary is chosen to be at an angle greater than the new wedge-shock angle. Along all these supersonic inflow boundaries, the flow conditions are known and held fixed during the entire computation. Along the lower boundary, which corresponds to the wedge surface, the tangency condition is satisfied by use of a one-sided, finite-difference procedure. MacCormack's scheme is used to advance the interior points in the $\tau = 1.0$ plane, which are initially set equal to free-stream values.

Merritt and Aronson[58] performed an experiment in which they obtained Schlieren photographs of the two-dimensional, shock-wave interactions generated by a 30° wedge at Mach 3 and a head-on ($\lambda = 60°$), $M_i = 2$, planar incident shock. This same case was calculated numerically and the results are shown in Figs. 45 and 46. Figure 45 is a density contour plot of the computational plane, which clearly shows all the shock waves and slip surfaces. The discontinuities in the flow that are not aligned with a coordinate direction are spread over approximately two mesh intervals, but their precise location can be pinpointed as denoted by the broad white dashed lines (shock waves) and the thin dotted lines (slip surface) superimposed on the contour plot. The

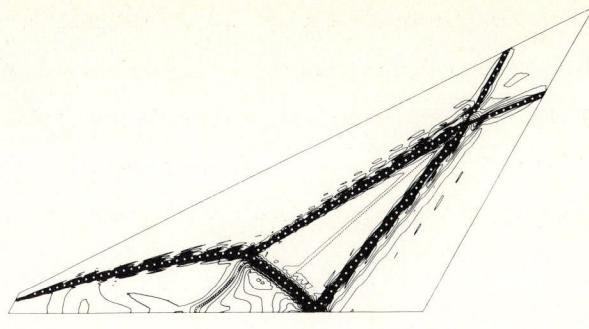

Fig. 45. Density contours for two-dimensional interfering shock problem; $M_w = 3.15$, $\delta = 30°$, $M_i = 2$, $\lambda = 60°$.

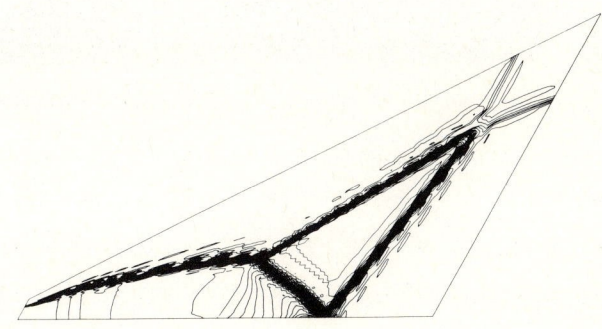

Fig. 46. Pressure contours for two-dimensional interfering shock problem; $M_w = 3.15$, $\delta = 30°$, $M_i = 2$, $\lambda = 60°$.

existence of a slip surface can be seen by comparing the pressure contour (Fig. 46) with the density contour. Since pressure is continuous across the slip surface, the constant-pressure lines do not build up where the slip surface exists.

The experimental wave structure for this case is shown in Fig. 47, and compares well with the numerical results of Fig. 45. Note, however, that in the experiment the original wedge shock, if extrapolated toward the wedge vertex, does not intersect it. This indicates that there were some nonuniformities in the tunnel flow conditions.

## 7.7 Three-Dimensional Supersonic Flow

In this section, a numerical procedure (see Kutler et al.[3]) is discussed that

Fig. 47. Schlieren photograph of two-dimensional interfering shock problem; $M_w = 3$, $\delta = 30°$, $M_i = 2$, $\lambda = 60°$.

is capable of determining the inviscid supersonic flow field for either pefrect or real gases about three-dimensional wing-body configurations, in particular, vehicles similar to the space shuttle orbiter. The complicated geometry of such a configuration traveling at supersonic velocities results in an intricate pattern of intersecting shocks, expansion waves, and slip surfaces—a natural problem for the shock-capturing approach.

In this procedure, the outermost shock—that is, the shock that separates the free stream from the disturbed region generated by the body—is treated as a sharp discontinuity. For example, before the canopy or wing is reached, the outermost shock is that generated by the nose of the vehicle. If the shock generated by the canopy intersects the bow shock, the resulting coalesced shock then becomes the outermost shock. When the shock generated off the wing leading edge intersects the bow shock, it becomes the outermost shock and is then treated as a sharp discontinuity. Hence, there are segments of the outermost shock that could consist of the original nose shock, the canopy shock, and the wing leading-edge shock. The resulting flow field beneath the body and outermost shock is treated in a shock-capturing fashion and therefore allows for the correct formation of secondary internal shocks.

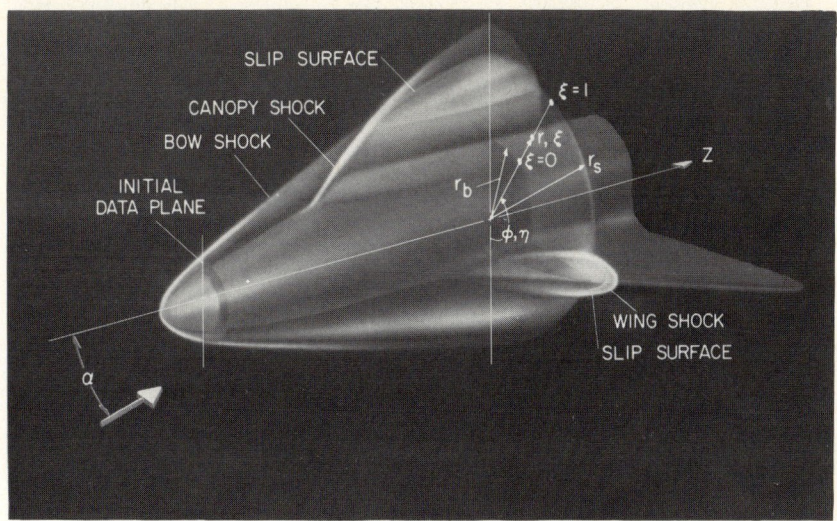

Fig. 48. Coordinate system for three-dimensional configurations.

The basic coordinate system used for this problem is cylindrical; its orientation with respect to the body is shown in Fig. 48. The vehicle body geometry and the location of the outer or peripheral shock surface are represented by functions of the form

$$r_b = r_b(z,\phi)$$
$$r_s = r_s(z,\phi)$$
(7.3)

The function $r_b$ is known, and $r_s$ is determined during the numerical computation. As is common practice in problems of this type, the distance between the body and peripheral shock is normalized (Fig. 49(a)) by a transformation of the radial variable r. This yields a rectangular computational plane whose boundaries consist of the plane of symmetry and the body and shock surfaces as shown in Fig. 49(b).

In regions where the body curvature is large, the flow variables change rapidly in the meridional direction and to avoid degrading the rest of the solution, it is necessary to cluster points in such a region. As was pointed out earlier, this is best accomplished by an independent variable transformation such as that given by Eq. (3.4), which allows for clustering only at the $\phi = 90°$ meridian. Thomas et al.[21] used a transformation that clusters points about any meridian, given by

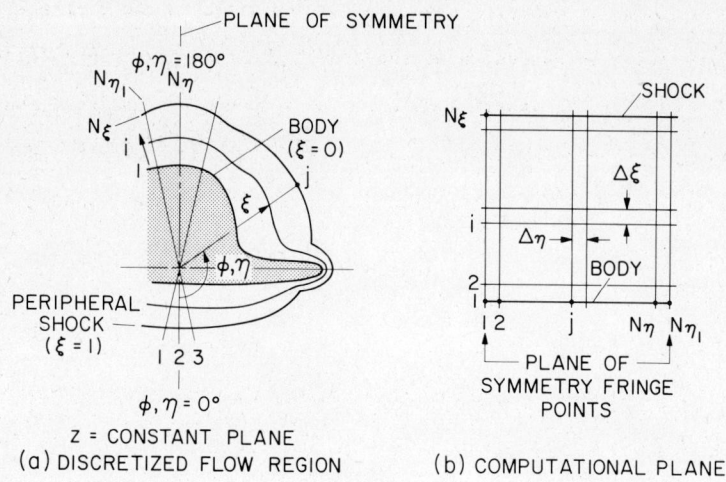

Fig. 49. Mesh description for three-dimensional problem.

where
$$\left.\begin{array}{l} \eta(\phi) = \pi \left\{ C + \dfrac{1}{\beta} \sinh^{-1}\left[\left(\dfrac{\phi}{\phi_o} - 1\right)\sinh(\beta C)\right]\right\} \quad \beta > 0 \\[1em] C = \dfrac{1}{2\beta} \ln\left[\dfrac{1 + (e^{\beta}-1)\phi_o/\pi}{1 - (1-e^{-\beta})\phi_o/\pi}\right] \\[1em] \eta(\phi) = \phi \quad \beta = 0 \end{array}\right\} \quad (7.4)$$

The angle $\phi_o$ is the point about which clustering occurs while $\beta$ is the parameter that controls the degree of clustering. Either the above transformation or the one given by Eq. (3.4) is used in the results presented later.

Thus, the equations of the independent variable transformations are

$$\left.\begin{array}{l} \zeta = z \\ \xi(z,r,\phi) = [r - r_b(z,\phi)]/[r_s(z,\phi) - r_b(z,\phi)] \\ \eta = \eta(\phi) \end{array}\right\} \quad (7.5)$$

This transformation is applied to the three-dimensional steady version of Eq. (2.1), and the resulting equation is then rearranged in conservation law form. The steady-flow energy equation for either a real or perfect gas is used.

The pressure approach discussed earlier is used to treat the peripheral shock wave as a sharp discontinuity while the simple-wave corrector scheme is used at the body to satisfy the surface tangency condition. Symmetry conditions are applied at the $\phi = 0°$ and $180°$ planes.

MacCormack's scheme is used to integrate the equations in the z direction from a given initial data plane downstream over the body. The computer code relies on an external program to provide the starting data if the body has a blunt nose, but it is capable of generating a solution for a pointed cone at angle of attack; results are presented later which describe the flow field surrounding circular cones at large angles of attack.

The function $r_b(z,\phi)$ that describes the body is a known analytic function. A typical body cross section is composed of various segments (Fig. 50) (such as straight lines, ellipses, etc.) governed by certain parameters that vary longitudinally as cubic polynomials.

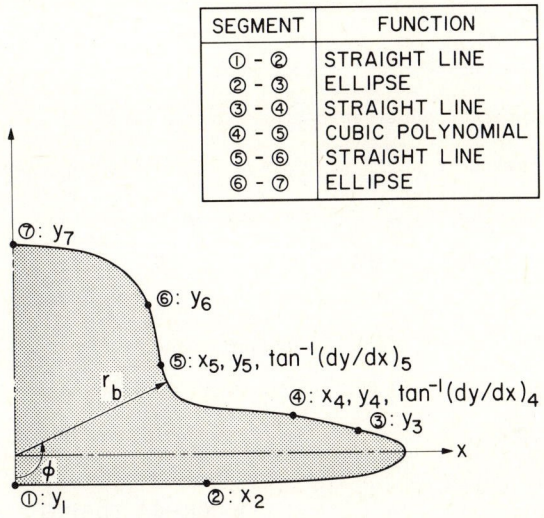

| SEGMENT | FUNCTION |
|---|---|
| ① - ② | STRAIGHT LINE |
| ② - ③ | ELLIPSE |
| ③ - ④ | STRAIGHT LINE |
| ④ - ⑤ | CUBIC POLYNOMIAL |
| ⑤ - ⑥ | STRAIGHT LINE |
| ⑥ - ⑦ | ELLIPSE |

Fig. 50. Typical body cross section.

As mentioned earlier, to determine the integration step size, the eigenvalues of the matrices of Eq. (6.4) for this problem under the above transformation are

$$\left.\begin{aligned}\sigma^P_{1,2} &= \frac{1}{\tilde{c}}\left[\tilde{a} + \frac{u(v+\tilde{b}w/r) \pm c[(v+\tilde{b}w/r)^2 + (u^2-c^2)(1+\tilde{b}^2/r^2)]^{1/2}}{u^2-c^2}\right] \\ \sigma^P_{3,4,5} &= \frac{1}{\tilde{c}}[\tilde{a} + (v+\tilde{b}w/r)/u]\end{aligned}\right\} \quad (7.6)$$

where

$$\tilde{a} = -r_{b_z} - \xi(r_{s_z}-r_{b_z}) \; , \quad \tilde{b} = -r_{b_\phi} - \xi(r_{s_\phi}-r_{b_\phi})$$

$$\tilde{c} = r_s - r_b$$

and

$$\left.\begin{array}{l}\sigma^Q_{1,2} = \frac{1}{r}\left[\frac{uw \pm c(u^2+w^2-c^2)^{1/2}}{u^2-c^2}\right]\eta_\phi \\ \sigma^Q_{3,4,5} = (w/ur)\eta_\phi\end{array}\right\} \qquad (7.7)$$

The three-dimensional program can be used to determine the flow field about cones at large incidence ($\sigma$ is the cone half-angle and $\alpha$ is the angle of attack) by a distance asymptotic approach. The conical flow problem, when solved in the crossflow plane, is elliptic for small angles of attack and mixed elliptic/hyperbolic for large angles of attack. The problem is made totally hyperbolic (with respect to the marching coordinate $z$) by treating it three dimensionally. The governing equations are thus integrated downstream over the cone until a conical flow field has been established.

Two large angle-of-attack cone flow solutions are presented. In the first case ($M = 3$, $\alpha/\sigma = 2$), the embedded supersonic crossflow is confined to a small region near the body. In the second case ($M = 7$, $\alpha/\sigma = 1.5$), this supersonic crossflow encompasses a large region stretching from the body to the shock.

The results of the first case are shown in Figs. 51 and 52. To obtain this so-

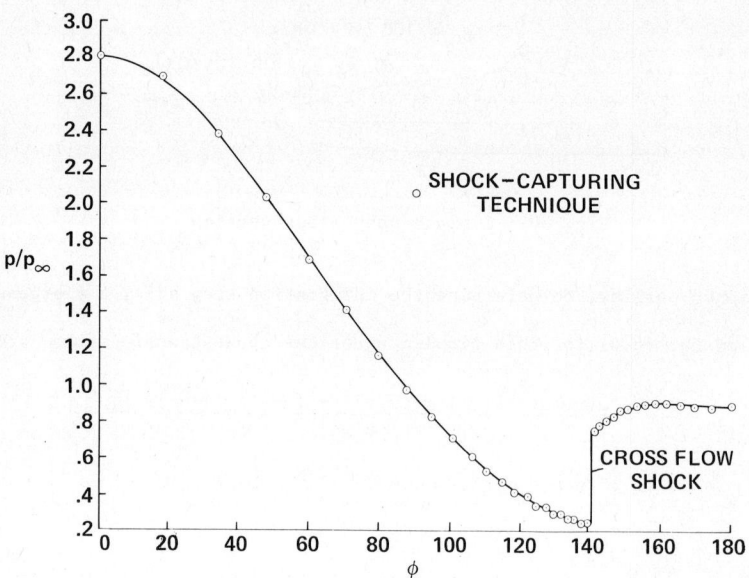

Fig. 51. Surface-pressure distribution for cone at angle of attack; $M = 3$, $\alpha = 15°$, $\sigma = 7.5°$.

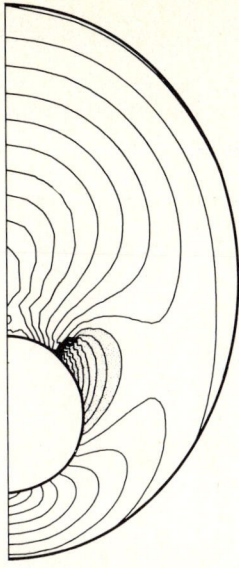

Fig. 52. Crossflow Mach number contour plot for cone at angle of attack; $M = 3$, $\alpha = 15°$, $\sigma = 7.5°$.

lution, a 22×37 point $(r,\phi)$ grid was used with clustering ($\beta = 5$ in Eq. (7.4)) at the 140° meridian. The surface pressure distribution for this case is shown in Fig. 51. Near the $\phi = 140°$ plane, a crossflow shock exists that results from the deceleration of the supersonic crossflow velocity. This shock was captured by the numerical scheme. If the crossflow Mach number in front of this shock is known, the Rankine-Hugoniot relations yield the conditions just downstream of it. The pressure from such a calculation is plotted in Fig. 51, and it agrees well with the computed result.

Figure 52 is a crossflow Mach number contour plot of the conical flow field. The shaded portion is the embedded supersonic crossflow region, and the coalescence of contours is the crossflow shock. For this case, the vortical singularity in the leeward plane of symmetry lifted from the body. The program encountered no numerical difficulties as a result of the vortical singularity since it is a "weak solution"[5] of the governing partial differential equations (the radial and circumferential conservative variables are continuous through it).

Under certain conditions, the embedded supersonic region can encompass a large portion of the flow field in the crossflow plane. Results for such conditions are shown in Figs. 53-55. The cone half-angle for this case is 20° and the free-stream

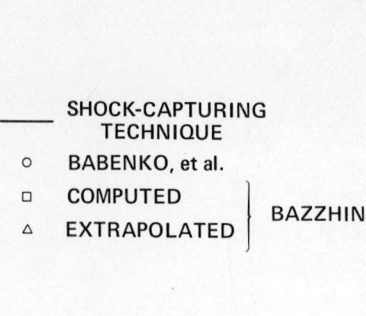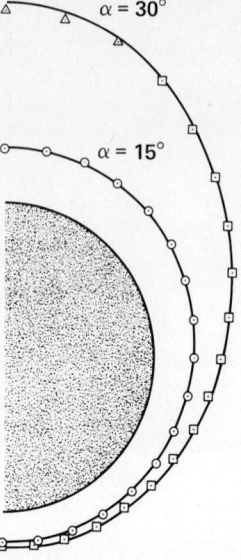

Fig. 53. Cross-sectional shock shape for cone at angle of attack; $M = 7$, $\alpha = 15°$ and $30°$, $\sigma = 20°$.

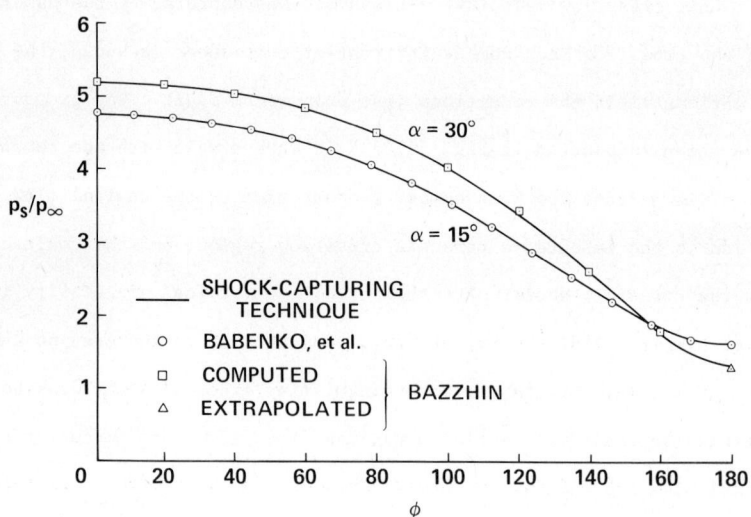

Fig. 54. Density distribution behind shock wave for cone at angle of attack; $M = 7$, $\alpha = 15°$ and $30°$, $\sigma = 20°$.

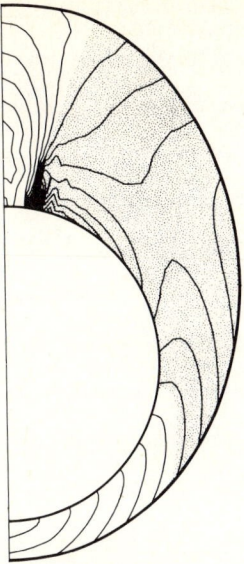

Fig. 55. Crossflow Mach number contour plot for cone at incidence;
$M = 7$, $\alpha = 30°$, $\sigma = 20°$.

Mach number is 7. Solutions were obtained for an angle of attack of 15° and are compared with the results of Babenko et al.[59] and for 30°, which were compared with the incomplete results of Bazzhin.[60] Figure 53 is a plot of the shock shapes for both angles of attack, and both are in excellent agreement with the results of Babenko and Bazzhin. The density distribution behind the shock wave for the two cases is shown in Fig. 54, and it also compares well with the other numerical solutions. A crossflow Mach number contour plot is shown in Fig. 55, and the large shaded portion indicates the supersonic crossflow region. There is a crossflow shock near the 165° meridian, and its strength dissipates rapidly with distance from the body.

Cone solutions such as these are easily generated and can be used to supply starting data for determining the supersonic flow over three-dimensional bodies. When blunt-nose starting solutions are required, the inverse blunt-body computer code of Lomax and Inouye[2] is used.

To test the ability of the numerical procedure to describe the multi-shocked flow field surrounding a shuttle-like configuration, a body was designed that used segments 2-3 (bottom ellipse) and 6-7 (top ellipse) of Fig. 50. The longitudinal variation of the required geometrical parameters was obtained from drawings of a delta-wing shuttle orbiter that is now obsolete. The resulting analytical configuration modeled the exact shape in both the planform and profile views but crudely approximated the body cross section in the wing region. The actual models tested in the wind tunnels also varied somewhat from the blueprint designs because of replication problems such as mold shrinkage. Such effects cause additional discrepancy between the analytical and experimental body shapes. The flow conditions for this test were Mach 7.4 and 0° angle of attack. These particular conditions are of interest computationally because available experimental shadowgraphs[61] show two shock-shock intersection regions: one when the canopy shock intersects the bow shock and the other when the wing leading-edge shock intersects the bow shock.

To eliminate any difficulties associated with the thinning entropy layer due to a blunt nose, a 23.07° pointed cone was used to simulate the nose of the vehicle for this test case. The grid size in the radial direction consisted of 18 points initially and was increased to 31 points just before the canopy was encountered. The number of meridional planes was held fixed at 19 for the entire calculation; however, the clustering parameter $\kappa$ of Eq. (3.4) was varied discretely from 1.0 initially to 0.13 for the last few steps. Its variation was based on the surface-pressure distribution in the region of the wing leading edge as observed on the CRT. This calculation, which consisted of approximately 700 streamwise integration steps and covered more than 90 percent of the body, required about 36 min on an IBM 360/67.

The shock locations in both the planform and profile views are compared in Fig. 56 with the experimental shadowgraphs made by Cleary.[61] When the results obtained by the numerical solution coincide with those of the experiment, only the numerical solution is shown. The agreement is excellent even though the actual nose was approximated by a pointed cone. The canopy shock location disagrees somewhat from that of the experiment. This can be attributed to the fact that the simulated canopy was a little steeper than the actual canopy. When the canopy shock intersected the bow shock, the shock-fitting procedure automatically began to treat the canopy (outermost) shock as a discontinuity and no difficulty was encountered in making the transition. The slip surface or inviscid shear layer that results when two shocks of the same family intersect was observed as a rapid change in a small region of the radial den-

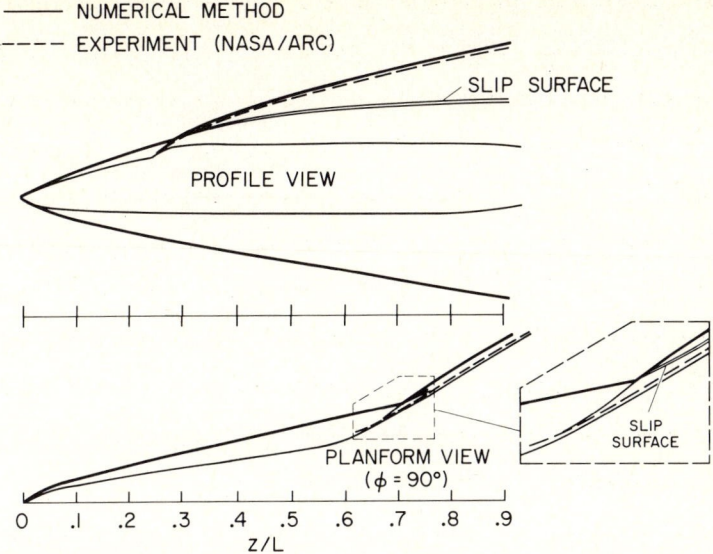

Fig. 56. Shock location for pointed-nose configuration; $M = 7.4$, $\alpha = 0°$.

sity distribution (Fig. 56). It agrees identically with that seen in the shadowgraph. In the planform view, the intersection of the nose and wing leading-edge shocks is shown along with coalesced shock and slip surface. Also shown is the experimental wing shock. There is disagreement between the locations of the numerical and experimental shocks since, in the numerical calculation, the actual wing is crudely approximated on the upper surface by a much thicker wing, which results in a larger standoff distance.

Some interesting results are obtained when a similar configuration is tested—this time with a blunt nose and at angle of attack. The flow conditions are a Mach number of 7.4 and angle of attack of 15.3°. The radial distribution of points was varied from 21 initially to 31 finally. The number of meridional planes was kept constant at 19, while the clustering parameter $\kappa$ was changed when necessary.

The planform and profile shock shapes are shown in Fig. 57 and compared with the experimental shadowgraphs and with the method of characteristics.[62] The windward portion of the shock agrees quite well with experiment, and the slight variance at its latter stations can be attributed to the disagreement between the numerical and experimental body shapes on the forward portion of the lower surface. On the leeward size,

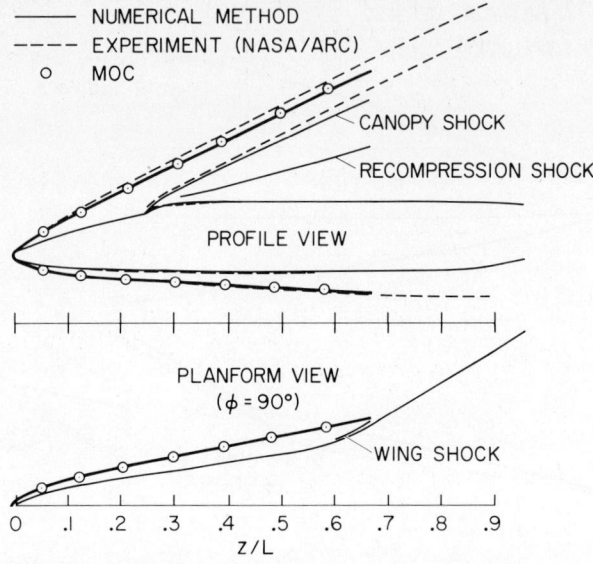

Fig. 57. Shock location for lung-nose configuration; $M = 7.4$, $\alpha = 15.3°$.

the canopy shock was captured, but its location disagreed somewhat from that of the experiment, again due to the differences in bodies. Because of the overexpansion of the flow around the canopy, a recompression shock is formed (Fig. 57) that is weaker than the canopy shock (not observed in this shadowgraph). However, this shock has been observed in other experiments.[63] The shock generated by the wing leading edge is shown in the planform view ($\phi = 90°$) of Fig. 57. Its location in this view agrees well with the experiment since the bottom ellipse closely approximates the lower surface of the shuttle and also controls the shock standoff distance at the leading edge.

Figure 58 shows the pressure distribution in the radial direction for the leeward plane of symmetry at two longitudinal stations, in which both canopy and recompression shocks are recognizable. Both shocks are captured within two or three mesh intervals.

Radial pressure and density plots through the merged entropy layers as well as the wing leading-edge shocks are shown in Fig. 59. The wing leading-edge shock in this plane is spread over four mesh intervals. Although good definition of the entropy layers is lost, their presence posed no difficulties until their thickness became less than one mesh interval, at which time oscillations began to occur.

The longitudinal surface-pressure distribution for three meridians is shown in

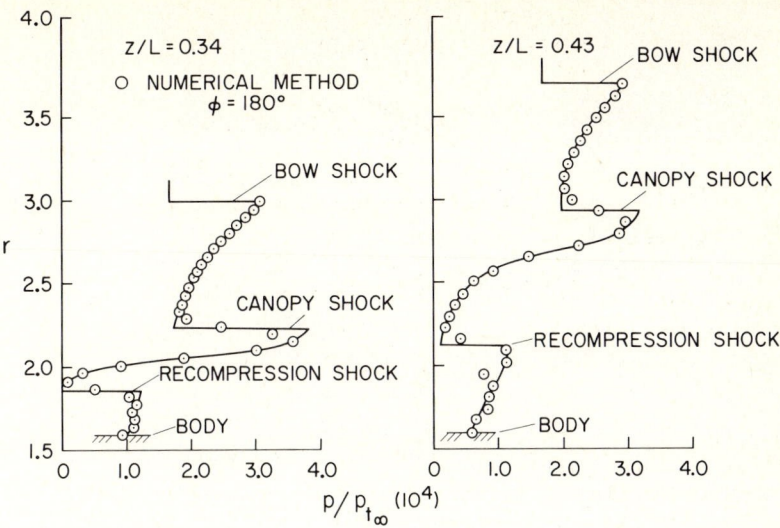

Fig. 58. Propagation of canopy and recompression shocks through shock layer in leeward plane of symmetry; $M = 7.4$, $\alpha = 15.3°$.

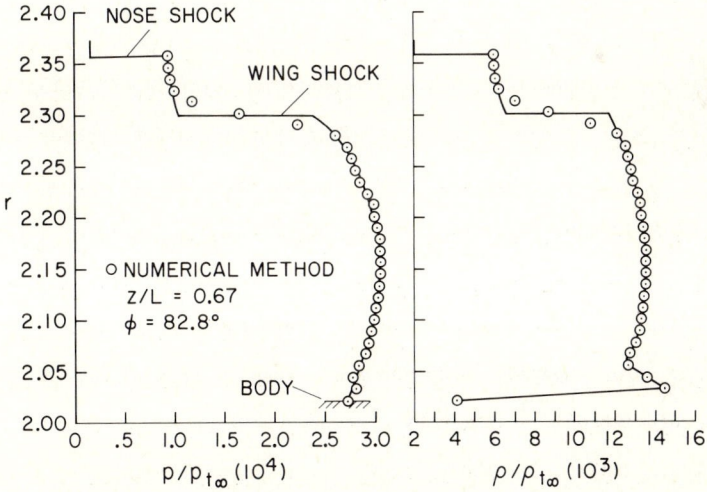

Fig. 59. Radial pressure and density distribution through entropy layer and wing leading-edge shock; $M = 7.4$, $\alpha = 15.3°$.

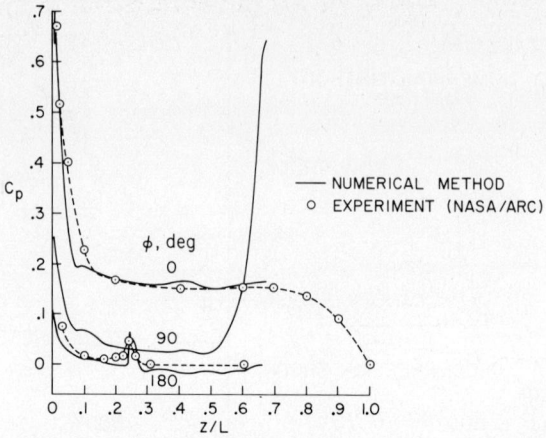

Fig. 60. Longitudinal surface-pressure distribution for the 0°, 90°, and 180° meridians; M = 7.4, α = 15.3°.

Fig. 60 and compared with experimental data obtained from the NASA/ARC 3-1/2-foot hypersonic wind tunnel. As the integration proceeds downstream, the pressure in the 85° plane continually rises, causing a corresponding decrease in the u component of velocity, to the extent that u approaches its local sonic value. This eventually causes the calculations to be terminated since the equations are then no longer hyperbolic. These near-sonic velocities occur only within the entropy layer, and the velocities are well above sonic outside this layer.

To demonstrate the capability of the method to calculate equilibrium air flow, starting conditions were chosen representative of a point on the orbiter's trajectory, i.e., an altitude of 76 km, a velocity of 7.3 km/sec (M = 26.26), and an angle of attack of 15.3°. Such free-stream conditions are difficult to simulate in existing wind-tunnel facilities. The results of calculations for the forward fuselage of a shuttle-like configuration are shown in Fig. 61 where the shock shapes for both perfect and real gases are compared. Also shown are results from a real-gas, method-of-characteristics calculation[64] (given by circles). The agreement between both numerical methods is excellent. Also shown in Fig. 61 is a small segment of the secondary shock originating from the front of the canopy. Here, no differences between the perfect- and real-gas solutions are observed.

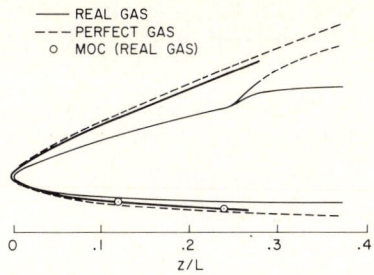

Fig. 61. Comparison of shock location for blunt-nose configurations; M = 26.26, α = 15.3°, altitude = 76 km.

## REFERENCES

1. Rakich, J. V., "Calculation of Hypersonic Flow over Bodies of Revolution at Small Angles of Attack," AIAA J., Vol. 3, pp. 458-464, March 1965.

2. Lomax, H., and Inouye, M., "Numerical Analysis of Flow Properties About Blunt Bodies Moving at Supersonic Speeds in an Equilibrium Gas," NASA TR R-204, 1964.

3. Kutler, P., Reinhardt, W. A., and Warming, R. F., "Multishocked, Three-Dimensional Supersonic Flowfields with Real Gas Effects," AIAA J., Vol. 11, No. 5, pp. 657-664, May 1973.

4. Dekker, T. J., "Constructive Aspects of the Fundamental Theorem of Algebra," B. Dejon and P. Henrici, eds., John Wiley & Sons, Inc., p. 37, 1969.

5. Lax, P. D., "Weak Solutions of Nonlinear Hyperbolic Equations and Their Numerical Computation," Commun. Pure Appl. Math., Vol. 7, pp. 159-193, 1954.

6. Gary, J., "On Certain Finite Difference Schemes for Hyperbolic Systems," Math. Computation, pp. 1-18, 1964.

7. Abbett, M. J., "Boundary Condition Computational Procedures for Inviscid Supersonic Steady Flow Field Calculations," Aerotherm Corp., Mt. View, Calif., Final Rept. 71-41, 1971.

8. Longley, H. J., "Methods of Differencing in Eulerian Hydrodynamics," Los Alamos Scientific Lab., Los Alamos, New Mexico, LASL Rept. LAMS-2379, 1960.

9. Godunov, S. K., "Finite Difference Method for Numerical Computation of Discontinuous Solutions of the Equations of Fluid Dynamics," Math. Skornik, Vol. 47(89), No. 3, p. 271, 1959.

10. Rizzi, A. W., and Inouye, M., "A Time Split Finite Volume Technique for Three-Dimensional Blunt Body Flow," AIAA J., Vol. 11, Nov. 1972.

11. Rizzi, A. W., Klavins, A., and MacCormack, R. W., "A Generalized Numerical Method for Three-Dimensional Supersonic Flow," to be published.

12. Moretti, G., and Abbett, M., "A Time-Dependent Computational Method for Blunt Body Flows," AIAA J., Vol. 4, pp. 2136-2141, 1966.

13. Bohachevsky, I. O., and Mates, R. E., "A Direct Method for Calculation of the Flow about an Axisymmetric Blunt Body at Angle of Attack," AIAA J., Vol. 4, pp. 776-782, 1966.

14. Burstein, S. Z., "Numerical Methods in Multidimensional Shocked Flows," AIAA J., Vol. 2, pp. 2111-2117, 1964.

15. Morretti, G., Grossman, B., and Marconi, F., Jr., "A Complete Numerical Technique for the Calculation of Three-Dimensional Inviscid Supersonic Flows," AIAA Paper 72-192, 1972.

16. Marconi, F., and Salas, M., "Computation of Three-Dimensional Flows about Aircraft Configurations," Computers & Fluids, Vol. 1, No. 2, June 1973.

17. Kutler, P., Lomax, H., and Warming, R. F., "Computation of Space Shuttle Flow Fields Using Noncentered Finite-Difference Schemes," AIAA J., Vol. 11, No. 2, pp. 196-204, Feb. 1973.

18. Blottner, F. G., and Roache, P. J., "Nonuniform Mesh Systems," J. Computational Phys., Vol. 8, pp. 498-499, 1971.

19. Kalnay de Rivas, E., "On the Use of Nonuniform Grids in Finite-Difference Equations," J. Computational Phys., Vol. 10, pp. 202-210, 1972.

20. Chu, C. W., and Powers, S. A., "Determination of Space Shuttle Flow Field by the Three-Dimensional Method of Characteristics," NASA TM X-2508, 1972.

21. Thomas, P. D., Vinokur, M., Bastianon, R., and Conti, R. J., "Numerical Solution for the Three-Dimensional Hypersonic Flow Field of a Blunt Delta Body," AIAA J., Vol. 10, No. 7, July 1972.

22. MacCormack, R. W., "The Effect of Viscosity in Hypervelocity Impact Cratering," AIAA Paper 69-354, pp. 1-7, 1969.

23. Warming, R. F., Kutler, P., and Lomax, H., "Second- and Third-Order Noncentered Difference Schemes for Nonlinear Hyperbolic Equations," AIAA J., Vol. 11, No. 2, pp. 189-196, Feb. 1973.

24. Rusanov, V. V., "On Difference Schemes of Third Order Accuracy for Nonlinear Hyperbolic Systems," J. Computational Phys., Vol. 5, pp. 507-516, 1970.

25. Burstein, S. Z., and Mirin, A. A., "Third Order Difference Methods for Hyperbolic Equations," J. Computational Phys., Vol. 5, pp. 547-571, 1970.

26. Richtmyer, R. D., and Morton, K. W., Difference Methods for Initial-Value Problems, John Wiley & Sons, Inc., New York, 1967.

27. Warming, R. F., and Hyett, B. J., "The Modified Equation Approach to the Stability and Accuracy Analysis of Finite-Difference Methods," J. of Comp. Phys., Vol. 14, No. 2, Feb. 1974.

28. Hopf, E., "The Partial Differential Equation $u_t + uu_x = \mu u_{xx}$," Commun. Pure Appl. Math., Vol. 3, pp. 201-230, 1950.

29. Lax, P. D., and Wendroff, B., "Difference Schemes for Hyperbolic Equations with High Order Accuracy," Commun. Pure Appl. Math., Vol. 17, pp. 381-398, 1964.

30. Hirt, C. W., "Heuristic Stability Theory for Finite-Difference Equations," J. Computational Phys., Vol. 2, No. 4, pp. 339-355, June 1968.

31. Kutler, P., "Application of Selected Finite Difference Techniques to the Solution of Conical Flow Problems," Ph.D. Thesis, Dept. of Aerospace Engineering, Iowa State Univ., 1969.

32. Abbett, M. J., "Boundary Condition Computational Procedures for Inviscid Supersonic Steady Flow Field Calculations," Aerotherm Corp., Mt. View, Calif., Final Rept. 71-41, 1971.

33. Abbett, M. J., "Boundary Condition Computational Procedures for Inviscid Supersonic Flow Fields," Proceedings, AIAA Computational Fluid Dynamics Conference, 1973.

34. Moretti, G., "Importance of Boundary Conditions in the Numerical Treatment of Hyperbolic Equations," High-Speed Computing in Fluid Dynamics, The Physics of Fluids Supplement II, 1969.

35. Roache, P. J., Computational Fluid Dynamics, Hermosa Publishers, Albuquerque, New Mexico, 1972.

36. Bohachevsky, I. O., and Rubin, E. L., "A Direct Method for Computation of Nonequilibrium Flows with Detached Shock Waves," AIAA J., Vol. 4, pp. 600-607, 1966.

37. Kutler, P., and Lomax, H., "The Computation of Supersonic Flow Fields about Wing-Body Combinations by 'Shock-Capturing' Finite Difference Techniques," Second International Conference on Numerical Methods in Fluid Dynamics, Sept. 1970; also Lecture Notes in Physics, Vol. 8, pp. 24-29, 1971.

38. Hayes, W. D., and Probstein, R. F., Hypersonic Flow Theory, 2nd ed., Academic Press, New York, p. 485, 1966.

39. Abbett, M. J., "Sharp Shock Computational Procedures for Inviscid, Supersonic, Steady Flow Field Calculations," Aerotherm Corp., Mt. View, Calif., Final Rept. 72-50, 1972.

40. Thomas, P. D., "On the Computation of Boundary Conditions in Finite Difference Solutions for Multi-Dimensional Inviscid Flow Fields," Lockheed Palo Alto Research Lab., Palo Alto, Calif., LMSC 6-82-71-3, March 1971.

41. Vincenti, W. G., and Kruger, C. H., Jr., Introduction to Physical Gas Dynamics, John Wiley & Sons, Inc., 1965.

42. Kutler, P., and Lomax, H., "Shock-Capturing, Finite-Difference Approach to Supersonic Flows," J. Spacecraft Rockets, Vol. 8, No. 12, pp. 1175-1182, Dec. 1971.

43. Fowell, L. R., "Exact and Approximate Solutions for the Supersonic Delta Wing," J. Aeronaut. Sci., Vol. 23, 1956.

44. South, J. C., and Klunker, E. B., "Methods for Calculating Nonlinear Conical Flows," NASA SP-228, pp. 131-158, 1969.

45. Babaev, D. A., "Numerical Solution of the Problem of Supersonic Flow Past the Lower Surface of a Delta Wing," AIAA J., Vol. 1, No. 9, pp. 2224-2231, Sept. 1963.

46. Beeman, E. R., and Powers, S. A., "A Method for Determining the Complete Flow Field Around Conical Wings at Supersonic/Hypersonic Speeds," AIAA Paper 69-646, 1969.

47. Voskresenskii, G. P., "Numerical Solution of the Problem of a Supersonic Gas Flow Past an Arbitrary Surface of a Delta Wing in the Compression Region," Izv. Akad. Nauk SSSR, Mekh, Zhidk. Gaza, No. 4, pp. 134-142, 1968.

48. Babaev, D. A., "Numerical Solution of the Problem of Flow Round the Upper Surface of a Triangular Wing by a Supersonic Stream," Zh. vychislitel'noi matematiki i matelmaticheskoi fizika, Vol. 2, pp. 278-289, 1962.

49. Oswatitsch, K., and Sun, Y. C., "The Wave Formation and Sonic Boom Due to a Delta Wing," Aeronaut. Quart., Vol. XXIII, May 1972.

50. Roe, P. L., "Wind Tunnel Measurements of Sonic Boom Due to a Plane Lifting Delta Wing," Preliminary results presented to the Euromech 31 Meeting, Aachen, West Germany, May 1972.

51. Bannink, W. J., and Nebbeling, C., "Investigation of the Expansion Side of a Delta Wing at Supersonic Speed," AIAA J., Vol. 11, No. 8, Aug. 1973.

52. Kutler, P., "Numerical Solution for the Inviscid Supersonic Flow in the Corner Formed by Two Intersecting Wedges," AIAA Paper 73-675, 1973.

53. Kutler, P., "Supersonic Flow in the Corner Formed by Two Intersecting Wedges," AIAA J., Vol. 12, No. 5, pp 577-578, May 1974.

54. West, Major J. E., and Korkegi, R. H., "Interaction in the Corner of Intersecting Wedges at a Mach Number of 3 and High Reynolds Numbers," ARL 71-0241, 1971.

55. Charwat, A. F., and Redekeopp, L. G., "Supersonic Interference Flow Along the Corner of Intersecting Wedges," AIAA J., Vol. 5, No. 3, pp. 480-488, March 1967.

56. MacCormack, R. W., and Warming, R. F., "Survey of Computational Methods for Three-Dimensional Supersonic Inviscid Flow with Shocks," AGARD Lecture Series No. 64 on Advances in Numerical Fluid Dynamics, AGARD-LS-64, 1973.

57. Kutler, P., Sakell, L., and Aiello, G., "On the Shock-on Shock Interaction Problem," AIAA Paper No. 74-524, 1974.

58. Merritt, D. L., and Aronson, P. M., "Wind Tunnel Simulation of Head-On Bow Wave-Blast Wave Interactions," NOLTR 67-123, Aug. 1967.

59. Babenko, K. I., Voskrensenskiy, G. P., Lyubimov, A. N., and Rusanov, V. V., "Three-Dimensional Flow of Ideal Gas Past Smooth Bodies," NASA TT F-380, 1966.

60. Bazzhin, A. P., "Some Results of Calculations of Flows Around Conical Bodies at Large Incidence Angles," Lecture Notes in Physics, Vol. 8, 1971.

61. Cleary, J. W., "Hypersonic Shock-Wave Phenomena of a Delta-Wing Space-Shuttle Orbiter," NASA TM X-62,076, 1971.

62. Rakich, J. V., and Kutler, P., "Comparison of Characteristics and Shock Capturing Methods with Application to the Space Shuttle Vehicle," AIAA Paper 72-191, 1972.

63. Cleary, J. W., "Subsonic, Transonic, and Supersonic Stability and Control Characteristics of a Delta Wing Orbiter," NASA TM X-62,066, 1970.

64. Kutler, P., Rakich, J. V., and Mateer, G. G., "Application of Shock Capturing and Characteristics Methods to Shuttle Flow Fields," NASA TM X-2506, Vol. 1, p. 65, 1972.

NUMERICAL AND PHYSICAL EXPERIMENTS
IN VISCOUS SEPARATED FLOWS

Thomas J. Mueller
Department of Aerospace and Mechanical Engineering
University of Notre Dame, Notre Dame, Indiana 46556


1. INTRODUCTION

1.1 General Remarks

Efficient design and/or accurate prediction of performance of fluid dynamic systems requires that the entire flow field be calculable. This requires a simultaneous calculation of the inviscid flow field, the viscous boundary layer along solid surfaces as well as viscous separated or wake flow regions. Numerical calculation of inviscid and attached boundary layer flows using large high speed computers has recently been quite successful because of the simplified mathematical form of the governing equations. Since viscous separated flow regions do not fall within the limitations of the simplified boundary layer equations, one must look to the most complete mathematical model in Newtonian fluid dynamics - the full Navier-Stokes equations. No general solutions of the Navier-Stokes equations are known and it is very unlikely that such a solution will ever be obtained. As a result of the non-linear nature of these equations, in general, and the complex behaviour of separated flows in particular, only approximate methods would appear to be feasible. One approximate method, finite difference numerical analysis, is being used more and more frequently to solve the Navier-Stokes equations for separated flow problems. An excellent description of the formidable difficulties arising in the numerical solution of these equations is given in reference 1. With the advent of faster and larger electronic computers, as well as more efficient numerical techniques, these approximate solutions have and will become more practical and more nearly exact.

It now appears that recent advances in computer technology have steadily reduced the cost of numerical flow field simulation (Ref. 2). In fact, on the basis of cost, numerical experiments are now competitive with physical experiments for many complex fluid dynamics problems. Figure 1 obtained from Ref. 2 illustrates this trend of relative computational cost. It should be remembered that unless the physical experiment is performed full scale and under actual operating conditions, it is often as much of a flow field simulator as is the computer. There is of course no substitute for the real thing.

A recent example of the practical value of finite difference solutions of the Navier-Stokes equations is provided by the complex problem of heat pipe design. For steady operation within the working range of many heat pipes, the Reynolds numbers are quite low so that the flow may be considered laminar. Furthermore, the vapor velocity in the evaporator is low enough so that the density is approximately constant (Ref. 3). Although operable heat pipes and experimental data have been available for several years, the recent work of Bankston and Smith (Ref. 3) presents the quantitative means for laminar heat pipe design. In the introduction to their work, these authors state that "Because of the limitations of previous studies as to Reynolds number or geometry, the rational design of real heat pipes has awaited a solution of the full Navier-Stokes equations for a pipe of finite length and with both evaporation and condensation." Of course, only time will determine the extent to which this statement is true.

Before committees, of either national or international scope, are formed to do away with wind tunnels [1] - existing or planned - an attempt should be made to present a rational perspective. The computer should be viewed as a partner to, not a replacement of, the wind tunnel. In a particular engineering problem one or the other of these simulators may be more advantageous. More advantageous from the point of view of obtaining the desired result either cheaper or faster in real time. Or in some cases one approach may be more flexible and lead to a better understanding of the more general physical phenomena involved. For some extremely complex problems, both physical and numerical experiments may be necessary in order to gain sufficient understanding of important small scale details of the flow.

The basic fluid dynamic problems which have been solved up to the present must be considered to be only a foundation for the future. As always, the foundation must be free from flaws if the future structure is to withstand the test of time or be worth building upon at all. In the spirit of building a foundation, therefore, the great majority of finite difference solutions to the Navier-Stokes equations have been for incompressible, two-dimensional flow with relatively simple geometric boundaries. For an engineer, the decision of whether or not the numerical foundation is adequate must lie in its favorable comparison with the appropriate experimental data. Once this is established for these basic flows, three-dimensional steady and unsteady flows may be approached with confidence. Thus a need exists for careful correlations between finite difference numerical and experimental investigations.

The happy marriage of wind tunnel and computer will undoubtedly result in a greater understanding of the physical processes occurring as well as provide fast, accurate, and therefore practical solutions to the important engineering problems of the present and future. It is to this happy and lasting marriage that the present lecture is directed. May they flourish in each others company and be proud of their offspring.

## 1.2 Occurrence of Separated Flows

Separated flows have long been known to be detrimental to the performance of hydrodynamic and aerodynamic systems. This type of flow is characterized by relatively slow reverse flows which are distinct from the main flow. They result in an increase in the drag force and usually present complex heat and mass transfer problems. Internal flow separation is common in propulsive nozzles, inlet and wind tunnel diffusers, turbomachinery passageways, and heating and ventilating distribution duct networks to name just a few. External separation often occurs from airfoils or hydrofoils at angle of attack, from surface protuberances such as vortex generators, from struts and rapid changes in external geometry as well as at the termination of the body in the form of a wake. Most of these examples occur at moderate to very high Reynolds numbers (usually turbulent) whether the flow is compressible or incompressible.

---

[1] The term wind tunnel is intended to represent all physical facilities and techniques in this context.

Recently an interest has also developed in moderate to low Reynolds number separated flows occurring in a broad class of environmental and physiological applications. The environmental problems frequently concern the wind or sea loading of stationary structures or the entrainment of pollutants on the lee side of these structures. For problems of this type encountered in water, the flow may be considered to be laminar in many cases. Although the Reynolds number may be only moderate, flows of this type in air are almost always turbulent. Physiological flow separation usually results from aberrations of the circulatory system caused by atherosclerosis (especially near bifurcations), atheroma, heart valve stenosis and aneurysms (particularly common in the aorta). Unnatural separated flows are also introduced into the human circulatory system with such prosthetic cardiovascular devices as occluder heart valves or assist pumps. In these flows where blood is the working fluid serious long term mass transfer problems arise (i.e., thrombi formation) in addition to the immediate performance loss due to increased resistance to the flow. It is indeed difficult to find viscous flows of practical importance where flow separation does not occur.

## 1.3 Scope of the Present Work

The purpose of this lecture is to compare the results of finite difference solutions to the Navier-Stokes equations with the results of appropriately designed physical experiments. The separated flows reviewed include those incompressible planar flows produced by the blunt base and front step (see Fig. 2a). Other similar separated flows which have received considerable attention in the literature, such as the flow over rectangular cavities and the circular cylinder, will not be presented due to limitations of time and space. A comparison of various finite difference techniques and a comparison of numerical results with experiments for the rectangular cavity may be found in the recent paper by Bozeman and Dalton (Ref. 4). Although there are still more published finite difference works of this type (e.g., the incompressible flow over a backstep, ramp, protuberance, rotating plate as well as compressible backstep, ramp, frontstep, and cavity flows) little or no physical data are reported for these cases. At low to moderate values of Reynolds number, with steady upstream flow, these planar separated flows though laminar may be either steady or unsteady.

The slightly more complicated axisymmetric flow through a fully open disc type prosthetic heart valve shown in Fig. 2b will also be presented. The only other axisymmetric separated flows that have received considerable attention in the literature are the flow past a paraboloid of revolution and a sphere. No physical data appear to be available for the paraboloid of revolution, however, a comparison of physical and numerical experiments for the axisymmetric flow about a sphere may be found in the recent paper of Liu and Lee (Ref. 5). It should be mentioned that for a steady upstream flow, the confining nature of the numerical axisymmetric assumption allows only steady separated flows to be produced.

The finite difference investigations to be presented have used standard, explicit, time-dependent computational methods. The time-dependent approach seems particularly suited to separated flows which often exhibit a time-dependent behaviour, e.g., oscillating wake problems. Although implicit techniques are currently very popular for steady flow solutions, the new parallel process computers (e.g. Illiac IV) appear to favor explicit methods. The important differences in the numerical investigations include the treatment of some boundary conditions, mesh geometry and estimated accuracy of results. These methods have been found, mostly by numerical experimentation, to be consistent, stable and thus convergent to within the desired tolerance over a wide range of Reynolds numbers. Although comments will be made when possible, detailed information concerning these questions of consistency, stability, convergence, and behavioral errors of numerical schemes may be obtained from the recent text of Roache (Ref. 6) and the current literature.

The physical experiments at low Reynolds numbers are actually more difficult than their numerical counterparts. Producing a truly planar or axisymmetric separated flow in the laboratory is always difficult. In addition, one must face the equally difficult problem of measuring velocity and/or pressure in such low Reynolds number flows. Thus it will become evident that the question of accuracy of the physical experiment is often as difficult to answer and/or improve as that of numerical accuracy.

## 2. THE NAVIER-STOKES EQUATIONS

That a solution to a particular incompressible problem exists is usually either assumed from physical intuition or known from observation. The difficult and yet incomplete mathematical question of the uniqueness of such a solution for the prescribed initial and boundary conditions has apparently been resolved only for two-dimensional incompressible flows (Ref. 7).

The numerical treatment of the Navier-Stokes equations involves deriving the desired form of the equation, choosing a suitable mesh system, developing the finite difference form of the equations and solution procedure, determining the stability of the resultant scheme, and examining the question of accuracy of the solution in view of computational costs as well as the use to be made of the results. The following section presents a brief review of this procedure for the incompressible separated flow problems to be studied later.

### 2.1 Incompressible Planar Flow

For two-dimensional incompressible flow, the Navier-Stokes equations and continuity equation in a rectangular Eulerian coordinate system may be expressed as

$$\frac{\partial v_x}{\partial t} + v_x \frac{\partial v_x}{\partial x} + v_y \frac{\partial v_x}{\partial y} = -\frac{1}{\rho} \frac{\partial P}{\partial x} + \alpha \left[ \frac{\partial^2 v_x}{\partial x^2} + \frac{\partial^2 v_x}{\partial y^2} \right] \tag{1}$$

$$\frac{\partial v_y}{\partial t} + v_x \frac{\partial v_y}{\partial x} + v_y \frac{\partial v_y}{\partial y} = -\frac{1}{\rho} \frac{\partial P}{\partial y} + \alpha \left[ \frac{\partial^2 v_y}{\partial x^2} + \frac{\partial^2 v_y}{\partial y^2} \right] \tag{2}$$

$$\frac{\partial v_x}{\partial x} + \frac{\partial v_y}{\partial y} = 0 \tag{3}$$

The vorticity in such a two-dimensional flow can be written

$$\xi = \left( \frac{\partial v_y}{\partial x} - \frac{\partial v_x}{\partial y} \right) \tag{4}$$

Eliminating the pressure terms in equations (1) and (2) by cross-differentiation, applying equation (3) to this result and then using the vorticity relation of equation

(4), the following equation with the vorticity as dependent variable is obtained,

$$\frac{\partial \xi}{\partial t} + v_x \frac{\partial \xi}{\partial x} + v_y \frac{\partial \xi}{\partial y} = \alpha \left[ \frac{\partial^2 \xi}{\partial x^2} + \frac{\partial^2 \xi}{\partial y^2} \right] \quad (5)$$

local      advection      viscous diffusion
term       terms          terms

This form of the Navier-Stokes equations is referred to as the Vorticity Transport equation.

By adding the definition of vorticity (4) to both sides of the continuity equation (3) and introducing the incompressible stream function defined by

$$\frac{\partial \psi}{\partial y} = v_x, \qquad \frac{\partial \psi}{\partial x} = - v_y \quad (6)$$

the following Poisson equation results

$$\frac{\partial^2 \psi}{\partial x^2} + \frac{\partial^2 \psi}{\partial y^2} = - \xi \quad (7)$$

Thus, the Navier-Stokes equations and the continuity equation are reduced to a parabolic Vorticity Transport equation (5) and an elliptic Poisson equation (7) for the stream function. If the slightly modified version of continuity

$$\xi \left( \frac{\partial v_x}{\partial x} + \frac{\partial v_y}{\partial y} \right) = \xi \frac{\partial v_x}{\partial x} + \xi \frac{\partial v_y}{\partial y} = 0 \quad (8)$$

is added to both sides of equation (5), then an alternate and often used form of equation (5) is obtained namely,

$$\frac{\partial \xi}{\partial t} + \frac{\partial (v_x \xi)}{\partial x} + \frac{\partial (v_y \xi)}{\partial y} = \alpha \left[ \frac{\partial^2 \xi}{\partial x^2} + \frac{\partial^2 \xi}{\partial y^2} \right] \quad (9)$$

Equation (9) is referred to as the "conservation form" of the Vorticity Transport equation since it may be shown that the transport property $\xi$ is conserved (Ref. 6). Although conservation does not necessarily imply accuracy (Ref. 6), experience indicates that conservation systems generally produce more accurate results (Refs. 8,9).

By rendering the terms of equations (7) and (9) dimensionless, it is possible to extend their range of applicability by using Reynolds principle of similarity. Therefore, if L and $v_\infty$ are the characteristic length and velocity respectively, then

$$x = x^* L \qquad\qquad y = y^* L$$
$$v_x = v_x^* v_\infty \qquad\qquad v_y = v_y^* v_\infty$$
$$\psi = \psi^* v_\infty L \quad (10)$$
$$t = \frac{t^* L}{V_\infty} \qquad\qquad \xi = \frac{\xi^* v_\infty}{L}$$

and the dimensionless conservation Vorticity Transport equation can be written as

$$\frac{\partial \xi^*}{\partial t^*} + \frac{\partial (v_x^* \xi^*)}{\partial x^*} + \frac{\partial (v_y^* \xi^*)}{\partial y^*} = \frac{1}{Re_L} \left[ \frac{\partial^2 \xi^*}{\partial x^{*2}} + \frac{\partial^2 \xi^*}{\partial y^{*2}} \right] \tag{11}$$

where the dimensionless vorticity and stream functions are related by the following Poisson equation

$$-\xi^* = \frac{\partial^2 \psi^*}{\partial x^{*2}} + \frac{\partial^2 \psi^*}{\partial y^{*2}} \tag{12}$$

Although it is possible to obtain numerical solutions of the Navier-Stokes equations in the primitive form (i.e., equations 1, 2 and 3), most successful numerical solutions for incompressible flows have used the vorticity-stream function form of equations 11 and 12. The parabolic equation (11) is solved by explicit marching in time from some initial conditions. The steady-state solution (if it exists) is attained asymptotically in time. At each time step, the elliptic equation (12) is solved iteratively by overrelaxation. The velocity components are easily obtained from the $\xi - \psi$ solution by using the definition for the stream function. However, the determination of the pressure requires some care and a reasonable amount of effort (Refs. 6 and 10).

The next logical step in the solution procedure would be to construct the finite difference mesh to fit the particular problem of interest. This will be deferred until the discussion of each of the specific separated flow problems in later sections. Since all of the separated flow problems to be discussed later make use of the same differencing techniques and calculational procedure, a discussion of these common methods and techniques is appropriate.

The basic method used for equation (11) at interior field points is as follows: the velocity components are obtained from the stream function distribution by centered differencing:

$$v_{x_{ij}} = \frac{\psi_{i,j+1} - \psi_{i,j-1}}{2\Delta y} ; \qquad v_{y_{ij}} = -\frac{\psi_{i+1,j} - \psi_{i-1,j}}{2\Delta x} \tag{13}$$

The vorticity is then advanced in time

$$\xi_{ij}^{n+1} = \xi_{ij}^n + \Delta t \left[ -\frac{\delta (v_x \xi)^n}{\delta x_{ij}} - \frac{\delta (v_y \xi)^n}{\delta y_{ij}} + \frac{1}{Re_L} \frac{\delta^2 \xi^n}{\delta x_{ij}^2} + \frac{1}{Re_L} \frac{\delta^2 \xi^n}{\delta y_{ij}^2} \right] \tag{14}$$

and the diffusion terms are represented by the centered difference form, as in

$$\frac{\delta^2 \xi}{\delta x_{ij}^2} = \frac{\xi_{i+1,j}^n + \xi_{i-1,j}^n - 2\xi_{ij}^n}{\Delta x^2} \tag{15}$$

The advection or convection terms are represented by the method of upwind differencing. This one-step, explicit, two-time-level method which achieves stability of advection terms involves one-sided, rather than space-centered, differencing. Meteorologists have long known of the stabilizing effects of "upwind" or "weather" differencing. The upwind difference form of the advection terms of equation (11) is

$$\frac{\delta(v_x\xi)^n}{\delta x_{ij}} = \begin{cases} \dfrac{(v_x\xi)^n_{i+1,j} - (v_x\xi)^n_i}{\Delta x} & \text{for } v_x < 0 \\[2ex] \dfrac{(v_x\xi)^n_{i,j} - (v_x\xi)^n_{i-1,j}}{\Delta x} & \text{for } v_x > 0 \end{cases} \quad (16)$$

Similar forms are used for $\dfrac{\delta(v_y\xi)^n}{\delta y_{ij}}$. In this first order method, information is advected into a cell only from those cells that are upwind of it[+] (Refs. 10, 11, 12). Therefore, information is advected from a cell only into those cells which are downstream of it. This, of course, is physically correct and leads to the following definition of the Transportive Property. A finite difference formulation of a flow equation possesses the Transportive Property if the direction of a perturbation in a transport property is advected only in the direction of the velocity. Upwind differencing methods inspired by this physical reasoning possess this property. In any method using space centered differences for the advective terms, the effect of a perturbation in a transport property is advected upstream against the velocity. A finite difference method which possesses the Transportive Property maintains the integral kinematic property of the continuum solution in the same way that one which possesses the Conservation Property maintains the integral Gauss divergence property of the continuum solution. Of course, space-centered differences are more accurate than unidirectional upwind differences based upon the formal Taylor series expansion. However, the transportive property appears to be as fundamentally important and physically significant as the conservative property (Ref. 6). Furthermore, it should be remembered that the accuracy of the result compared to the appropriate physical experiment is the final test of the numerical procedure and not simply the order of accuracy. Although the upwind differencing method introduces an artificial viscosity effect which must be carefully examined when assessing the accuracy of results, it has the further advantage that it is not stability limited by a cell Reynolds number as are forward-time space-centered methods. The physical relevance of upwind differencing which seems particularly appropriate for separated flows with their large backflow regions, has been discussed by many authors (see Ref. 6 for a list of references).

Numerical stability requires that the time dependent solution cannot proceed at time increments greater than some critical value. The following expression for dynamic stability was obtained from a discrete perturbation analysis of a linear model equation (Refs. 11 and 12).

$$\Delta t_{crit} \leq \frac{1}{\dfrac{|v_{x_{ij}}|}{\Delta x} + \dfrac{|v_{y_{ij}}|}{\Delta y} + 2\alpha\left[\dfrac{1}{\Delta x^2} + \dfrac{1}{\Delta y^2}\right]} \quad (17)$$

---

[+]When $v_x$ reverses sign near a mesh point, a modification to the basic upwind difference scheme is required in order for strict conservation to hold.

The $\Delta t$ used for a particular problem is usually some fraction of $\Delta t_{crit}$. The stability of this method has been demonstrated over a wide range of Reynolds numbers for various separated flows (Refs. 11, 12).

Once the new $\xi$ distribution at time (n+1) is obtained from equation (14), the new $\psi$ distribution is found from equation (12) by iteration using successive over-relaxation. Convergence criteria will be discussed later for each separated flow problem studied.

The accuracy of the upwind differencing method in resolving viscous effects usually deteriorates at high $Re_L$ because it implicitly introduces an effect which resembles an artificial viscosity effect. This numerical or artificial viscosity effect simply reduces the effective Reynolds number $\frac{v}{\alpha}$ to $\frac{v}{\alpha + \alpha_{es}}$. Although this numerical viscosity $\alpha_{es}$ is not unique to upwind differencing it appears to be the predominant source of error in the numerical scheme described above. Recently, Roache (Refs. 13 and 6) has considered the artificial viscosity errors for multi-dimensional viscous flow problems. By considering the application of upwind differencing in a two-dimensional flow and using the appropriate form of equation (14) for constant $v_{x_i}$, $v_{y_i} > 0$, the following equation was obtained:

$$\frac{\partial \xi}{\partial t} = \frac{\partial (v_x \xi)}{\partial x} - \frac{\partial (v_y \xi)}{\partial y} + (\alpha + \alpha_{ex}) \frac{\partial^2 \xi}{\partial x^2} + (\alpha + \alpha_{ey}) \frac{\partial^2 \xi}{\partial y^2}$$

$$+ \text{ higher terms and differentials} \qquad (18)$$

In the transient analysis

$$\alpha_{ex} = \frac{1}{2} v_x \Delta x (1-C_x) \qquad \alpha_{ey} = \frac{1}{2} v_y \Delta y (1-C_y) \qquad (19)$$

where $C_x$ and $C_y$ are the Courant numbers defined by

$$C_x = \frac{v_x \Delta t}{\Delta t} \qquad C_y = \frac{v_y \Delta t}{\Delta y} \qquad (20)$$

In the steady-state analysis

$$\alpha_{ex} = \frac{1}{2} v_x \Delta x \qquad \alpha_{ey} = \frac{1}{2} v_y \Delta y \qquad (21)$$

Although these relations for the artificial viscosity only apply in the limit as $\Delta x$ and $\Delta y$ approach zero (Ref. 6), they are useful for purposes of discussion. For transient solutions, according to equation (19), the numerical or artificial viscosity effect will be at a minimum for $C_x$ and $C_y$ as close to unity as possible. The question of the values of $C_x$ and $C_y$ is further complicated by the inviscid stability restriction obtained from linear theory that $C_x + C_y \leq 1$ (Ref. 6). In practical problems therefore, it would be impossible, to simultaneously have both $C_x$ and $C_y$ near unity. Consequently some artificial viscous effects will always be present. Equation (21) indicates that for steady-state the directional cell Reynolds numbers must be much less than 2. While this condition is the requirement for formal accuracy, in some physical situations it is not quite this discouraging (Refs. 6 and 11). For example in regions where the boundary layer approximations are valid $\partial^2 \xi / \partial x^2$ is small and the term $(\alpha + \alpha_{ex}) \partial^2 \xi / \partial x^2$ in equation (18) will be small.

Furthermore, $v_y$ is also small so that $\alpha_{ey}$ will be smaller than $\alpha$. It may also be possible to control this effect to some degree by using a variable mesh where a large number of mesh points are concentrated in regions of steepest gradients. An example of this approach will be presented and discussed later.

In view of equations (19) and (21) it is clear that for Eulerian mesh systems in multidimensional problems, the artificial viscosity varies spatially, e.g., in x- and y-directions for two-dimensional situations. This may occur with a uniform mesh (i.e., $\Delta x = \Delta y$) because $v_x$ and $v_y$ vary throughout the flow field or with a variable mesh because $\Delta x$ and $\Delta y$ as well as $v_x$ and $v_y$ vary in the region of interest. For this reason an exact determination of the artificial viscosity error is usually not possible. However, an order of magnitude estimate of this type of error may usually be obtained.

Upwind differencing has often been found to provide the best compromise between accuracy and computer time for separated flow problems (Refs. 11, 12, 4). The choice of this method must be closely related to the desired accuracy and/or the relative difficulty and cost of obtaining similar or more accurate results from other methods. Since directional differencing is not stability limited by a cell Reynolds number, as is the forward-time, space-centered method, it is particularly useful in the study of complex separated flows, where only qualitative accuracy may be required at high Reynolds numbers.

## 2.2 Incompressible Axisymmetric Flow

The Navier-Stokes equations and the continuity equation in a cylindrical $(r, \theta, z)$ Eulerian coordinate system for two dimensional axisymmetric (i.e., $v_\theta \equiv 0$ and $\frac{\partial}{\partial \theta} \equiv 0$) incompressible flow may be expressed as

$$\frac{\partial \xi^*}{\partial t^*} + \frac{\partial (v_r^* \xi^*)}{\partial r^*} + \frac{\partial (v_z^* \xi^*)}{\partial z^*} = \frac{1}{Re_R} \left[ \frac{\partial^2 \xi^*}{\partial r^{*2}} + \frac{\partial^2 \xi^*}{\partial z^{*2}} + \frac{1}{r^*} \frac{\partial \xi^*}{\partial r^*} - \frac{\xi^*}{r^{*2}} \right] \quad (22)$$

This is the conservative Vorticity Transport equation in dimensionless form where the vorticity and stream function are related by the Poisson equation

$$-\xi^* = \frac{1}{r^*} \left[ \frac{\partial^2 \psi^*}{\partial z^{*2}} + \frac{\partial^2 \psi^*}{\partial r^{*2}} - \frac{1}{r^*} \frac{\partial \psi^*}{\partial r^*} \right] \quad (23)$$

The comments made in the previous section concerning the solution procedure also apply to the axisymmetric case.

## 3. PLANAR SEPARATED FLOWS

Although a truly two-dimensional flow is achieved numerically, it is usually very difficult - if not actually impossible in a strict sense - to achieve in physical experiments. Furthermore, duplicating the exact inflow and outflow boundary conditions for a finite computational region is very difficult - if not actually impossible in a strict sense. Thus a large amount of determination and at least some poetic license are necessary if one is to proceed.

For each case studied, a brief description of the physical experiment and an estimate of the accuracy of the measured results will be presented. The procedure for numerical experimentation will then be presented along with the question of accuracy of results. Finally, a comparison of the results of both methods will be discussed.

### 3.1 Blunt Base

The flow over a blunt-based body represents one of the most convenient and fundamental examples of unsteady separated flow. This oscillating wake is one of the most widely studied problems in fluid dynamics. Particular interest has been generated in the wake of blunt-based airfoils which could provide significant advantages at high speeds, if the drag penalty of the oscillating wake at low speeds could be overcome. A recent numerical and experimental study of this problem is reported in reference 14. The primary goal of this study was to provide numerical solutions which would enhance the understanding of the mechanism by which an oscillating wake was formed. A complete description of the three types of wake oscillations found may be obtained from references 14, 15, 16. Only the highest Reynolds number case (i.e., the third type of oscillation) will be discussed here since accurate quantitative experimental data are available for comparison with the numerical solution.

3.1.1 <u>Physical Experiments</u>. The experimentation in the Reynolds number range $Re_h \approx 1.6 \times 10^4$ was designed to yield: a velocity profile at the same location as the inflow boundary of the finite difference grid; the wake Strouhal number; and the free stream Reynolds number based on the base height $\frac{v_{x\infty} h}{\alpha}$. These experiments were conducted in one of the University of Notre Dame's low-speed, low-turbulence wind tunnels. The model, a 12 in. (30.48 cm) long, 6 in. (15.24 cm) wide and 2 in. (5.08 cm) thick flat plate with an elliptical nose and lucite side plates, was mounted in a two square foot (0.1858 m$^2$) test section fitted with a DISA hot wire probe and probe traversing mechanism. The hot wire probe was calibrated with a pitot tube connected to a micromanometer (Ref. 16). The experimental procedure included: traversing the flow field along the inflow station, thereby obtaining the free stream velocity and the velocity profile at the inflow station; and traversing the wake to determine the frequency of oscillation of the wake. The traversals were performed along four lines in the flow field as shown in Fig. 3. The first traverse produced the velocity profile one base height upstream of the base from which the free stream velocity and boundary layer thickness were obtained. The other three traversals were all parallel to the first, but located one-eighth, one, and two base heights, respectively, downstream of the base.

The velocity profile obtained one base height upstream of the base is plotted in Fig. 4 in terms of the ratio of local velocity to free stream velocity versus base heights above the surface. The calibration of the hot-wire probe before and after data were taken indicated that the free stream velocity was measured to within about 2% of the pitot value. The accuracy of this type of velocity measurement is known to decrease as the probe approaches the surface of the model as a result of interference effects as well as the lower velocities encountered. The boundary layer thickness was defined as the distance from the surface at which the local velocity was 99 percent of the free stream value. A fourth order polynomial was then fitted to the data points lying below this height. The resultant curve was considered to be the velocity profile in the boundary layer. The computed velocity profile curve and the data points to which it was fit are shown in Fig. 5. The boundary layer thickness was calculated to be 0.1210 base heights. The Reynolds number was 16,295.

The second section of the experiment was the determination of wake Strouhal numbers. The frequency of oscillation was determined during the hot wire traversals. The frequency was taken to be the average frequency recorded over a ten second measuring period. Hot wire voltages were displayed on the oscilloscope. Photographs of the oscilloscope trace were taken at the locations marked on Fig. 3. The letter designation of these locations corresponds to the letter designations of Fig. 6 which shows the trace photographs.

Figure 6a shows two traces of the hot wire voltage in the boundary layer at the position where the velocity profile was determined. The small amplitude oscillatory character of the velocity in this region is immediately apparent. The oscillations appear to be fed back upstream from the large amplitude oscillations of the wake. The laminar character of the boundary layer is also confirmed by this figure. Figure 6b, taken outside the boundary layer, also shows the oscillations to be present in the free stream. Figure 6c shows the oscilloscope trace at the location of optimum signal clarity. As in the experimental work of Bearman (Refs. 17 and 18), this position was found to be one base height downstream of the base and one base height above the centerline. The frequency in this region was determined to be 23.80 c.p.s. at a free stream velocity of 15.29 f.p.s. (4.66 m. p.s.), giving a Strouhal number of 0.2594 at a Reynolds number of 16,295. Frequency measurements in this range are known to be accurate to within 1%.

Moving towards the centerline, Fig. 6d shows that fluctuations in the local velocity are superimposed on the fluctuations due to the wake oscillation. The wake oscillation pattern is thus partially obscured. At the centerline, these local fluctuations are large enough to completely obscure the periodic character of the wake (Fig. 6e). Displacing the probe an additional base height downstream gives a single trace similar to Fig. 6e, only having a large amplitude. However, a multiple trace photograph reveals that the wake oscillation frequency is well defined in this region despite the large local fluctuations, Fig. 6f. Figure 6g shows the hot wire trace with the probe positioned one-eighth base height behind the base and on the centerline. The local velocity fluctuations are of small amplitude, and the wake oscillation is not apparent at this position, probably being of equally small amplitude.

3.1.2 <u>Numerical Experiments</u>. In the finite difference approximation, to the solution of the governing equations, approximations to the actual values of the variables are obtained at a finite number of points within the flow field. When the grid lines are equally spaced in all areas of the flow field, the spacing is governed by that necessary to obtain the desired accuracy in the area of largest gradients, leading to a high density of grid points in areas where there are low gradients. Fortunately, it is possible, in some cases, to tailor the grid spacing to the particular problem decreasing the grid point density in the areas of low gradients and increasing this density in the areas of high gradients. This may be accomplished without losing the advantages of a rectangular grid.

In the present problem, the largest gradients occur in the boundary layers on the body and in the region one and one-half base heights either side of the centerline, downstream of the base. A grid tailored to concentrate points in the proper locations for the blunt base problem is shown in Fig. 7. The grid used during computation was finer than that of Fig. 7, consisting of 56 grid spaces in the stream-wise direction and 112 grid spaces in the cross stream direction. The grid or mesh aspect ratio, $\frac{\Delta x}{\Delta y}$, varied from 20 to 2. In terms of the base height, the flow field computed was seven base heights square. The nomenclature for the finite difference mesh is demonstrated in Fig. 8. The nonuniform nature of the mesh or grid structure requires a special formulation of the finite difference approximations to the partial derivatives.

Finite Difference Derivatives

In order to formulate the governing equations in finite difference form, it is necessary to obtain finite difference expressions for the first and second derivatives. Standard Taylor series expansions yield for the first derivative in the x-direction

$$\frac{\partial f_{i,j}}{\partial x} = \frac{\Delta x_{i-1} \, f_{i+j,j}}{\Delta x_i (\Delta x_{i-1} + \Delta x_i)} - \frac{\Delta x_i \, f_{i-1,j}}{\Delta x_{i-1} (\Delta x_{i-1} + \Delta x_i)}$$

$$- \frac{(\Delta x_{i-1} - \Delta x_i) f_{i,j}}{\Delta x_i \Delta x_{i-1}} \qquad (24)$$

and for the second derivative in the x-direction

$$\frac{\partial^2 f}{\partial x^2} = \frac{2 f_{i+1,j}}{\Delta x_i (\Delta x_{i-1} + \Delta x_i)} + \frac{2 f_{i-1,j}}{\Delta x_{i-1} (\Delta x_{i-1} + \Delta x_i)} - \frac{2 f_{i,j}}{\Delta x_i \Delta x_{i-1}}$$

$$- \frac{(\Delta x_{i-1} - \Delta x_i)}{3} \frac{\partial^3 f}{\partial x^3} - \frac{\Delta x_i \Delta x_{i-1}}{24} \frac{\partial^4 f}{\partial x^4} \qquad (25)$$

If this last expression is truncated before the term containing $\frac{\partial^3 f}{\partial x^3}$, the approximation is not necessarily accurate to the order of magnitude of $(\Delta x^2)$. However, if the grid is constricted in such a fashion that the order of magnitude of $(\Delta x_{i-1} - \Delta x_i)$ is the same as the order of magnitude of $(\Delta x_{i-1} \Delta x_i)$ truncation prior to this term is permissible, while limiting truncation errors to the order $(\Delta x^2)$. In this specific case, the expression for $\frac{\partial^2 f}{\partial x^2}$ is given as

$$\frac{\partial^2 f}{\partial x^2} = \frac{2 f_{i+1,j}}{\Delta x_i (\Delta x_{i+1} + \Delta x_i)} + \frac{2 f_{i-1,j}}{\Delta x_{i-1} (\Delta x_{i-1} + \Delta x_i)} - \frac{2 f_{i,j}}{\Delta x_i \Delta x_{i-1}} \qquad (26)$$

The derivations of $\frac{\partial f}{\partial y}$ and $\frac{\partial^2 f}{\partial y^2}$ are completely analogous to the above derivations with $\Delta x$ replaced by $\Delta y$, and the index j varying. As mentioned earlier, it is the absolute accuracy and not simply the order of accuracy which is important. Therefore the grid may be expanded somewhat faster than just described if it is sufficiently fine.

Boundary and Initial Conditions

As in the solution of any time dependent partial differential equation, it is necessary to specify the conditions on the boundaries of the system and the initial state of the system.

Upstream Mesh Boundary

At the inflow or upstream boundary layer, surfaces 1, Fig. 8, the experimentally determined velocity profile, $v_x$, was integrated to provide the necessary stream function values and $v_y$ was allowed the freedom to adjust with time. The vorticity on this boundary was computed directly from Poisson's equation, using a centered difference in the y-direction and a forward difference in the x-direction.

Upper and Lower Mesh Boundaries

The upper and lower mesh boundaries, surfaces 2, Fig. 8, were assumed to be undisturbed stream lines. The actual condition at an infinite distance from the body was thus brought to within a finite distance of the body. Following the approach of Roache and Mueller (Ref. 10) and Mueller and O'Leary (Ref. 19), the vorticity was specified as equal to the vorticity one grid space within the mesh.

Downstream Mesh Boundary

Three boundary conditions were tried on the outflow boundary, surface 3, Fig. 8. The first was simply setting the vorticity on the boundary equal to the vorticity one grid point upstream. While both Roache and Mueller (Ref. 10) and Mueller and O'Leary (Ref. 19) imply that this condition may be interpreted physically as no production of vorticity between these grid points, it would appear that this is correct only under steady state, converged conditions. If a variation of the vorticity value at the point one grid space upstream of the boundary exists, the interpretation would be quite different. Under such conditions the boundary condition implies the production or dissipation of vorticity in the requisite amount to bring both grid points to the same state at the same time. The condition was abandoned as too restrictive. The second condition tried was a mixed time and space derivative. This boundary condition, first used by Roache and Mueller (Ref. 10), was abandoned as it resulted in the production of large amount of vorticity at the boundary with the subsequent effect of producing a catastrophic instability in the solution. The last approach tried was based on the assumption that vorticity was a linear function of the "x" spatial coordinate over the last three grid points. This resulted in a linear extrapolation of vorticity to the boundary. While still rather restrictive, this condition was felt to allow the flow more freedom at this boundary. The downstream boundary condition on stream function was also handled by a linear extrapolation.

Solid Surfaces

As the stream function on the body surface was chosen to be identically zero there was never any need to re-compute this value. Following the work of Roache and Mueller (Ref. 10), the vorticity on surface 4, Fig. 8, was computed using a one sided difference. The stream function and vorticity on the base of the body, surface 5, Fig. 8, were computed in a similar manner to those on the upper surface of the body.

Corners

The value of the stream function at the corners, like all other places on the body, was set to zero. Again using the approach of Roache and Mueller (Ref. 10), the corner points were assigned two values of vorticity. If, while computing a point above or below the corner, the value of vorticity at the corner was required, this value was computed as if the corner point lay on the upper or lower surface, respectively. If, however, the value at the corner was required while computing a point behind the base, the corner vorticity was computed as if it lay on the base of the body.

Initial Conditions

Three types of initial conditions were used successfully. The first defined the stream lines as straight lines, parallel to the surface upstream of the base, which were turned through an angle at the plane of the base and projected to the downstream boundary. The second defined the stream line to be parallel to the centerline both upstream and downstream of the base except within one grid space downstream of the plane of the base. In this region the stream lines underwent a sharp vertical deflection. This condition was felt to best approximate the impulsive starting condition. In both of these initial conditions a slight asymmetry was introduced by deflecting the zero stream line one grid point vertically from the centerline. The third condition was the use of a previously attained solution as the starting point for a new case.

3.1.3 <u>Method of Solution</u>. The upwind differencing technique described earlier was applied to the solution of the planar Vorticity Transport equation (11). The effect of upwind differencing was to bias the solution so that vorticity could be advected only in the direction of flow. The technique, however, presented no such bias to the diffusion of vorticity. It was felt that the use of this technique approximated more closely the physical situation.

Once new values of vorticity were obtained at all interior grid points, it was necessary to compute the new values of the stream function, which satisfied Poisson's equation and were compatible with the vorticity field values. Poisson's equation was solved (Ref. 16) by an iteration technique called successive overrelaxation by Young and extrapolated Liebmann by Frankel (Ref. 20). The iteration was continued until the net change between two successive iterates, at each point, was less than $5 \times 10^{-6}$.

Once the solution to Poisson's equation was obtained, the boundary conditions on vorticity were applied. A new time step was then computed, the appropriate data recorded and the sequence restarted at the calculation of vorticity at the new time level. The repetition of this sequence continued until the flow pattern repeated itself at a definite frequency. The oscillatory solution was then considered to have been reached. This took from 50 to 70 hours of UNIVAC 1107 time for three cycles.

Interpretation of Plotted Fields

Nearly all results from the numerical phase of this work are presented in the form of plots of constant stream function value, stream lines. This method of presenting the results was chosen as it enhanced the investigators' understanding of the flow field. Only the portion of the grid, which was required to observe the region of interest, was plotted. The plots therefore, do not necessarily represent the entire calculated field.

A linear interpolation between grid points was used to locate the intersections of stream lines with grid lines. Therefore, it should be noted that the locations and contours of the plotted stream lines are only as accurate as a linear interpolation along grid lines. However, the high grid point density, particularly in the region of high gradients, resulted in a reasonably smooth and accurate plot. The increments in stream function between adjacent plotted stream lines were not uniform throughout the plotted field. Rather, they were chosen to best demonstrate the character of the flow and minimize plotting time.

A bifurcation of the zero stream line, where it separates from the body, is evident in nearly all plots. This bifurcation is not indicative of two separation points. Rather, it is a characteristic of the plotting routine and the limits of the solution. The finite difference solution cannot locate the position of separation, it can only specify the two grid points on the body between which separation occurs. In a manner consistent with this limit of the solution, the plotting routine draws a line to both grid points. The point of separation, then lies between the two intersections of the legs of the bifurcation with the body.

3.1.4 <u>Discussion of Results</u>. Using the results of the experiment, the inflow velocity profile with boundary layer thickness of 0.121 h and Reynolds number of $Re_h = 16,295$ were inserted into the numerical procedure and the impulsive initial conditions were used. A circulation region formed behind the upper portion of the base and subsequently entrained stream lines which had passed as far as a half base height below the lower surface of the body. This circulation region fed back upstream on the upper surface of the body. Eventually, two circulation regions were formed by the division of the single original region at the corner. As the circulation in both regions was in the same sense, an interface between them was unsupportable, leading to the production of a third circulation region between the two original ones. This region entrained the stream lines from above the base carrying them entirely across the base to the lower corner. The region originally behind the base moved downstream and the circulation region on the upper surface decreased in intensity. Eventually, the region on the upper surface had completely dissipated, the loop of the stream lines from above the body to below and back to above had moved away from the base and a small region of circulation had formed on the upper portion of the base. This recirculation region grew and entrained stream lines that had passed below the base. This sequence is shown in Fig. 9. The oscillatory solution for this case is shown in Fig. 10.

The experimental criterion for transitioning of the shear layer presented by Roshko and Lau (Ref. 21) indicates that the shear layers should transition prior to the formation of the detached circulation regions. The obscuring of the periodic oscillation on the oscilloscope trace is most likely due to the onset of turbulence. It appears, however, that the finite difference solution continues to closely approximate the gross flow patterns of the wake, even though it does not take this transitioning into account. For this type of oscillation, at $Re_h = 16,295$, the numerically determined Strouhal number for the full period was 0.222 compared to the experimental value of 0.259. These two values differ by about 14%. Physically, one could attribute some of this difference to the facts that the experiment shows signs of turbulence and that the flow produced was not strictly two-dimensional due to the finite size of the model. The predominant source of error in the numerical scheme is the numerical or artificial viscosity effect. In addition, for oscillatory flows phase errors caused by dispersion could also become serious (Ref. 8). Both of these types of errors will be discussed.

Although an exact determination of the artificial viscosity effect cannot be given for this multidimensional viscous flow, arguments - mostly from computational experience - will be given. The simplest argument is based upon the estimate that the artificial viscosity error in the boundary layer is about $\mu \frac{\Delta y}{\delta}$

or simply proportional to $\frac{\Delta y}{\delta}$ (Ref. 11). In the present case, $\Delta y$ varied considerably because of the variable mesh. The region of largest gradients in the boundary layer was approximately contained between the minimum value, $(\Delta y)_{min}$ = 0.00625 h, and the value $\Delta y = 0.0214$ h. Since the experimentally determined boundary layer thickness was 0.121 h, one could estimate that the local artificial viscosity error would be between

$\frac{(\Delta y)_{min}}{\delta}$ x 100 = 5.17%     and     $\frac{\Delta y}{\delta}$ x 100 = 21.4%. The region of largest gradients in the wake was about three fourths of a base height either side of the centerline. However, there is no convenient parameter (i.e., like $\delta$) available with which to estimate the error in the wake. Because the boundary layer assumptions are not valid in the wake, one would expect a larger artificial viscosity effect in this free shear layer. In view of Equation (19), although $\Delta x > \Delta y$, $v_x$ in the shear layer where viscous effects are important is usually only a fraction of the free stream value. This is the reason given by Roache (Ref. 6) for the fact that viscous finite difference solutions with non zero $(\alpha_e)_{steady\ flow}$ are often more accurate than might be expected from evaluating $(\alpha_e)_{steady\ flow}$ based on free stream conditions. Based on the work of Runchal, Spalding and Wolfshtein (Ref. 22), it appears that artificial viscosity may be examined from the point of view of stream line angle. They found that the artificial viscosity could be approximated by $\alpha_e = 0.36\ v_x\ \Delta x \sin(2\theta)$, where $\theta$ was the stream line angle. In reference 22, Runchal, Spalding and Wolfshtein used an upwind difference method for the driven cavity problem. At Reynolds number of 100 with their non-uniform mesh of 13 x 13 they found that their results compared favorably with computations made with a uniform mesh of 51 x 51. Their reasons for this surprising result is that their mesh not only concentrated more points in regions of steepest gradients, but that the mesh was generally aligned with the stream line pattern. In regions where this was not true (i.e., in the corners $\theta$ is large and approaches 45°) the velocity was small so that $\alpha_e$ was probably small. These same arguments also appear to apply to the oscillating wake solution presented above.

By studying a damped oscillation, Cheng (Ref. 8) arrived at the following conclusion concerning phase errors caused by dispersion. A spatial resolution of 30 meshes per wave length and 300 time steps per cycle can provide engineering accuracy for the first wave length for a second order accurate scheme. In the blunt base oscillating wake solution, there were more than 30 meshes per wave length and between 6000 and 7000 time steps per cycle. It therefore seems reasonable, in accordance with Cheng's result, to conclude that phase errors were not serious in this case.

Finally, the recent work of Bozeman and Dalton (Ref. 4) for the cavity problem shows clearly that directional differencing with the conservation form of the equation produced better solutions than using the non-conservative equation at Reynolds number of 1000. Furthermore, with centered differencing at this Reynolds number, neither the conservative nor the non-conservative equations converged to the steady state solution.

3.1.5 <u>Concluding Remarks</u>. If you are interested in Strouhal numbers, velocity profiles or lift and drag values, with accuracy of 1 or 2%, physical experiments will probably be the fastest and cheapest approach, especially if the necessary wind tunnel and instrumentation are available. If, however, you are interested in studying the detailed mechanism of formation of the oscillating wake and/or the oscillatory pressure and shear stress components throughout the entire flow field, numerical experiments can be obtained if a large amount of computer time is available.

3.2 **Symmetric Channel Contraction - Frontstep**

The complexity of internal flows is a result of the simultaneous presence and interaction of different fluid phenomena. One such example is that of the flow in an abruptly converging duct as shown in Fig.2a. Here there is superposition of two opposing factors, the pressure drop associated with the acceleration of the main flow in the duct and the locally increasing pressure near the duct walls due to blockage. The latter effect results in separation of the flow from the walls. To date there has been little numerical or experimental research directed toward the low Reynolds number frontstep problem (Ref.23). A more complete description of this problem may be obtained from reference 23. Only the zero bleed case of reference 23 will be discussed here. Since accurate experimental data have been difficult to find in the literature for this low Re case, a qualitative experiment was performed in support of this discussion.

3.2.1 <u>Physical Experiments</u>. A two-dimensional symmetrical channel with an approximate contraction of 2 to 1 was set on the water table. The channel extended 50 cm from the rounded entrance to the contraction and 30 cm from the contraction to the downstream end. The two sections of the channel were approximately 5 cm and 2.5 cm apart with 1.25 cm frontsteps. The centerline velocity was determined by measuring the time necessary for a very small particle of wood to move 15 cm on the water surface in the upstream channel section. The average of three runs was used, the approximate separation point was found visually by alternately injecting a small amount of blue dye far upstream at the wall, and in the separation region. A summary of these qualitative data is given below in the order taken.

| Upstream Water Depth (cm) | $v_{x_{\mathbb{C}}}$ (cm/sec) | $Re_D$ | $Re_h$ | $\frac{x_s}{h}$ | Comments |
|---|---|---|---|---|---|
| 2.5 | 5.00 | 1400 | 700 | 0.71 | 3-D effects |
| 2.5 | 2.73 | 770 | 385 | 0.50 | "         " |
| 2.5 | 6.53 | 1830 | 915 | 0.86 | "         " |
| 4.5 | 3.62 | 1162 | 581 | 0.71 | "         " |
| 5.0 | 2.34 | 656 | 328 | 0.57 | Plexiglas lid i.e. no free surface. |

Note that all but the last case were true water table experiments containing a free surface. The probable error in these experiments is at least $\pm 10\%$. These data are plotted in Fig.11. No noticeable upstream influence of the contraction was observed about two step heights upstream.

3.2.2. <u>Numerical Experiments</u>. The location of the mesh points was found by overlaying the geometry of the upper-half channel, as shown in Fig.12, with a rectangular mesh which was uniform throughout the flow field. The aspect ratio, $\frac{\Delta x}{\Delta y}$, of the mesh was two. The number of grid lines, corner locations and mesh nomenclature are shown in Fig.12. The upstream boundary was located four step heights from the contraction and the downstream boundary three step heights from the contraction.

Boundary and Initial Conditions

Somewhat different boundary conditions were used for this problem than for the blunt base problem. The initial conditions, however, were almost identical.

Upstream Boundary

The inflow or upstream boundary is surface (2) in Fig. 12. Initially, Poiseuille flow was specified at the inflow boundary (i.e., $v_x = v_{x_\mathbb{C}}(1-(\frac{y^2}{D^2}))$ and $v_y = 0$).

During the numerical solution, however, these conditions were allowed to vary from time step to time step permitting the inflow $v_x$ and $v_y$ to be sensitive to the solution as it developed downstream. This represents an extension of the concept proposed by Roache (Ref. 12) for the treatment of the upstream boundary. Roache allowed only $v_y$ the freedom to adjust with time. This proved insuitable for the internal flow studied here because the blockage effect of the front step produced a larger upstream influence than that produced by the back step studied by Roache. In the present study, at the conclusion of a time step, new values of $\psi$ at the inflow boundary points were obtained by a 2nd order extrapolation of $\psi$ from the next three points downstream. A compatible value of vorticity was then generated by applying the Poisson equation at the inflow boundary under the assumption that $\psi_{xx}$ remains constant over the first $\Delta x$.

Plane of Symmetry

Because the flow field studied was specified to be symmetric, the center surface (1) of Fig. 12, represents the plane of symmetry. The stream function along surface (1) was constant and was arbitrarily set equal to zero and the vorticity was set equal to zero.

Solid Wall Boundaries

The solid walls, surfaces (3), (4), (5) and (6) in Fig. 12 were no-slip boundaries. The stream function was constant along each of these boundaries and all equal to $\psi$ along surfaces (3) if there was no bleed flow. Vorticity was computed using a one-sided difference (Ref. 12).

Downstream Boundary

The stream function on this boundary surface (7) of Fig. 12, was obtained by a linear extrapolation from adjacent interior points. The vorticity at surface (7) was set equal to the vorticity at the adjacent interior points. No computational instabilities were encountered using these downstream boundary conditions.

Step Corner

The stream function at the step corner, since it is part of the solid walls, was a constant. Using the approach of Roache and Mueller (Ref. 10), the corner point was assigned two values of vorticity. When computing the velocity of a point upstream of the corner, this value was computed as if the corner lay on the step surface. However, if the value at the corner was required while computing a point below the corner, this value was computed as if the corner lay on the downstream wall, i.e., surface (6). Another investigation supporting the use of this double-valued treatment of the vorticity in flows with sharp corners was provided recently by Stevenson (Ref. 24).

Initial Conditions

It has been shown that the initial condition need not have physical significance (e.g., Ref. 19). In the present study, the transient solution serves only as a numerical technique in approaching the asymptotic case and need not represent a physical development of the flow field. Naturally, it is advantageous to pick the initial condition as close to the steady state solution as is conveniently possible to reduce the ensuing computation time. In the present study, two types of initial conditions were used. One, termed the "cold start" initial condition similar to the first type discussed in the blunt base problem, was used for the initial solution of a series of solutions, all having the same mesh structure and inflow condition. The second was used for succeeding cases, in which only the Reynolds number or the value of $u_B$ varied from a previous case. The converged solution of that previous case was used as an initial condition for the new case.

3.2.3 <u>Method of Solution</u>. The method of solution including the upwind differencing technique was described earlier. In evaluating the relative convergence of the numerical solutions, several criteria were employed. At the conclusion of each step, the following four quantities were computed:

$$\sum_{i,j} \left| \xi_{i,j}^{n+1} \right| \tag{27}$$

$$\sum_{i,j} \left| \psi_{i,j}^{n+1} \right| \tag{28}$$

$$\sum_{i,j} \left| \xi_{i,j}^{n+1} \right| - \sum_{i,j} \left| \xi_{i,j}^{n} \right| \tag{29}$$

$$\sum_{i,j} \left| \psi_{i,j}^{n+1} \right| - \sum_{i,j} \left| \psi_{i,j}^{n} \right| \tag{30}$$

The first two expressions simply represent the total magnitude of vorticity and stream function throughout the finite difference field. They indicate the production or dissipation of vorticity and the corresponding development of the separated flow pattern with increasing time steps. Expressions (29) and (30) represent the total production or dissipation rates of $\xi$ and $\psi$ in the field.

In judging the relative convergence of the numerical scheme, the solution was continued until expressions (27) and (28) remained constant to five significant figures over at least 50 time steps. Usually expression (29) had reached a value less than $5.0 \times 10^{-4}$ and expression (30) less than $3.0 \times 10^{-4}$ by that time. In the solution of Poisson's equation by successive over-relaxation, a relative convergence criteria was used to terminate the iterative solution of the stream function. The iterative solution was continued until the change between two successive iterates, at each point, was less than some fixed fraction of the maximum value, usually $10^{-6}$. Criteria such as this represent a subjective judgment based on an examination of the computer output and the total computer time available.

3.2.4 Discussion of Results. Numerical solutions were obtained over a range of Reynolds numbers based on the channel half-width of from 500 to 1500. The corresponding Reynolds number range based on the frontstep height was 250 to 750. Only the no bleed results will be discussed here (see Ref. 23 for the bleed results). Contour plots of stream function and vorticity for six Reynolds numbers from 500 to 1500 are presented in Fig. 13. Stream function is reflected about the channel centerline and plotted in the lower half of the figure with the vorticity directly above. There are several physical characteristics apparent in these contour plots. Although the stream lines present a general view of the flow pattern that occurs, more information can often be found in the vorticity plots. The most obvious feature is the large wall vorticity gradient near the sharp corner as well as the downstream wall. This is of course due to the high shearing stress in these regions. Note the volume flow beneath the lower two stream lines in the stream function plot. All of this fluid squeezes past the sharp corner and is confined to a very thin viscous region near the downstream wall. Also, note the dotted curved line, representing $\xi = 0$, which extends between the upstream wall and the step face in the stagnant corner region. Where the wall vorticity goes through zero, the wall shear stress is also identically zero. Thus, this vorticity contour line locates both the separation and reattachment points of the dividing stream line. With increasing Reynolds number, the corner eddy increases in size and intensity and the vorticity gradients become more severe near the walls.

Figure 14 depicts typical velocity profiles for two different Reynolds numbers, $Re_D$ of 500 and 1500. Profiles at six different stations are plotted for each Reynolds number, at x equal to 4, 1, and 1/2 step heights upstream and 1/2, 1, and 3 step heights downstream of the corner. The profiles show the anticipated development from the Poiseuille profile at $\frac{x}{h} = -4$ to an inflected profile, characteristic of a point near separation, at $\frac{x}{h} = -\frac{1}{2}$. Downstream, the flow rapidly approaches the Poiseuille profile again. At $Re_D = 500$, the actual separation point occurs at approximately $\frac{x}{h} = -0.540$; at $Re_D = 1500$, it occurs at approximately $\frac{x}{h} = -0.791$.

Figure 11 summarizes results for the no bleed cases. This figure is a plot of the location of the separation point, in non-dimensional step heights upstream of the step, versus Reynolds number. The distance $x_s$ was determined by locating $\xi_w = 0$ along the upstream wall in the vorticity solution. Figure 11 indicates that the effect of Reynolds number is to produce an upstream movement of $x_s$ for an increase in R. This observation is in agreement with existing experimental results for laminar flow separation in general and with the qualitative experiments in particular. Wall shear stress distribution were also obtained from the numerical solution and are presented and discussed in reference 23.

The present numerical study was conducted on a CDC 6600 computer. A typical solution, consisting of 1514 lattice points, required approximately 15 min. of central processor time. Stability analysis of the upwind differencing method (Ref. 12) results in a $\Delta t$ restriction that depends upon the maximum $v_x$ and $v_y$ components in the field. During the transient phase of the solution, the critical time step was re-evaluated after each time step, utilizing the current maximum velocities, so as to always use the largest $\Delta t$ permissible. Typically $\Delta t$ was on the order of 0.016 and about 800 time steps were required to satisfy the convergence criteria. Successive over-relaxation of Poisson's equation for $\psi$ required only a single iteration to satisfy the relative convergence criteria after the initial 50 or so time steps.

In any computer simulation of a time dependent flow field, a choice is made on the fineness of the lattice grid, size of the computational time step, and convergence criteria. The choices are not arbitrary but influenced by computer core limitations and the excessive costs of lengthy computation. The question of artificial or effective viscosity inherent with the approximate numerical methods used here will be discussed in view of the results obtained. As in all approximate techniques this represents an error, the severity of which must be evaluated in light of the cost and effort one would expend to reduce or eliminate it.

Roache has shown in reference 6 that a multi-dimensional analysis of the upwind differencing method leads to the conclusion that a steady state solution is subject to an artificial viscosity which is dependent upon the size of $\Delta t$ as well as $\Delta x$. This dependence of artificial viscosity on $\Delta t$ was not observed in the present study so that one must resort to numerical experimentation in this matter.

An examination of artificial viscosity was performed on the converged solution of $Re_D = 500$, $u_B = 0$. Figure 11 implies that this case would be most sensitive to changes in viscosity (i.e., Reynolds number) if a change in $x_s/h$ was used as a judging criteria. The converged solution represented a non-dimensional time, $t = 13.26$. To that point $\Delta t$ had been set at 90% of the critical time step for stability ($\Delta t_c$). At this point $\Delta t$ was reduced to 20% of $\Delta t_c$ and the solution continued until $t = 25.46$. Consistent with previous experience with this numerical methods, no detectable change was observed in the location of separation or reattachment points of the corner eddy. No significant changes occurred in the other flow parameters. Hence, one concludes that the steady solution is not subject to an artificial viscosity that depends on $\Delta t$. A second test was conducted to investigate the artificial viscosity dependence on $\Delta x$. A case of $Re_D = 500, u_B = 0$ was computed with $\Delta x$ and $\Delta y$ set at $\frac{1}{2}$ their previous values, resulting in a lattice consisting of 5,842 points. This solution was computed to $t = 12.75$ $x_s/h$ and $y_R/h$ changed by 4.2% and 2.3% respectively. From a practical engineering point of view, these changes would usually be considered insignificant. The increase in accuracy could not justify the expenditure of approximately 1.75 hours of CDC 6600 central processor time required to compute this solution.

In this case it is not surprising that the artificial viscosity effect introduced by the directional differencing is small since, except for the small region near the step, the boundary layer approximations are valid. Therefore, $\frac{\partial^2 \xi}{\partial x^2}$ is small and the term $(\alpha + \alpha_{ex}) \frac{\partial^2 \xi}{\partial x^2}$ in equation (18) will be small. Also, $v_y$ is small so that $\alpha_{ey}$ will be small and not appreciably affect the $(\alpha + \alpha_{ey}) \frac{\partial^2 \xi}{\partial y^2}$ term. Another way of arriving at the same conclusion is to consider the argument presented by Runchal, Spalding and Wolfshtein (Ref. 22) based on the stream lines angle measured with respect to the grid. The stream line angles are very small except near the step (see Fig. 13). In the separated portion of this region the velocities are low so that even when $\theta$ is large, the overall effect on $\alpha_{ex} = 0.36\, v_x \Delta x \sin(2\theta)$ is probably small. This overall situation is aided, of course, by the low values of Reynolds number used.

3.2.5 <u>Concluding Remarks</u>. Low Reynolds number separated flow of this type may be studied quickly and relatively cheaply by numerical methods. Numerical experiments offer greater flexibility than do physical experiments since the effects of upstream velocity profile shape, positive and negative base bleed, etc., may be easily obtained. Furthermore, values of shear stress and pressure may be readily determined throughout the flow field. To obtain accurate data of this type from physical experiments as these low Reynolds numbers would be much more difficult and costly.

## 4. AXISYMMETRIC SEPARATED FLOW

### 4.1 Disc-Type Artificial Heart Valve

Artificial heart valves produce serious short and long term problems associated with the separated flows they produce. Separated flows, characterized by relatively slow reverse flows which are distinct from the main flow, may occur upstream and downstream of the sewing ring and behind the occluder as shown in Fig. 2b. The slow reverse flow traps lipids, platelets, and other debris making this type of region thrombogenic. Furthermore, it is thought that all artificial valves are sufficiently hemolytic to enhance thrombus formation through the accumulation of the resulting ghosts, fragments and other debris. Although artificial heart valves have been available for well over ten years, there is relatively little quantitative data concerning the extent of thrombogenic separated flow regions produced by these valves since most experiments have been of the qualitative flow visualization type. Because flows of this type occur at relatively low values of Reynolds number, they appear to be very interesting from the computational viewpoint. The numerical and experimental investigation described in this section is for the flow through an axisymmetric fully open disc-type heart valve (Refs. 25, 26, 27).

4.1.1 <u>Physical Experiments</u>. The experiments were performed in a closed loop steady flow apparatus consisting of reservoir tank, a bellmouth entrance section to 1.00 inch (2.54 cm) inside diameter transparent acrylic tube. Five anti-turbulence screens were attached to the inlet of the bellmouth and a disc type heart valve in the fully open position was located 18 tube diameters from the tube entrance. The acrylic tube continued downstream of the heart valve for about 16 tube diameters where an elbow directed the liquid to the pump. The flow rate and therefore the Reynolds number ($Re_D$) was varied by means of the pump bypass system.

These experimental studies were directed toward studying the largest separated region produced, i.e., the region behind the disc as shown in the sketch inset in Fig. 15. Data were obtained for Reynolds numbers based on the tube diameter and average velocity upstream of the sewing ring ($Re_D$) of from 50 to almost 10,000. The Reynolds number in vivo in the aortic region varies from zero to a maximum of about $Re_D = 6300$. The length and shape of this separated region was determined using two methods of flow visualization.

An electrochemical technique referred to as the Thymol Blue (thymolsulphonephthalein) method was found to be useful only at very low Reynolds numbers, i.e., from 50 to 100. This method takes advantage of a proton transfer reaction near a current carrying wire in a Thymol Blue solution which turns the

the solution dark blue. This dark blue fluid is neutrally buoyant and is carried downstream by the flowing yellow fluid. Photographs of the flow patterns for values of $Re_D$ were obtained and the length of the separated region behind the disc was taken from the photographs.

For the dye injection experiments, a special sliding tube injector was constructed. This dye injector, attached to the center of the disc, consisted of a slotted guide hypotube, 0.050 inch (0.0197 cm) outside diameter, internally fitted with a movable dye injection hypotube. The injection hypotube contained an orifice which could therefore be translated along the geometric center of the test section. A very small amount of neutrally buoyant dye was injected at a constant rate using an infusion-withdrawal pump. The reattachment location or downstream end of the separated region behind the disc was determined by moving the dye injection orifice until a change in flow direction was observed.

These experiments and additional experiments using the hydrogen bubble method indicated that the separated region behind the disc was steady, axisymmetric and laminar up to $Re_D \approx 200$. From $Re_D \approx 200$ a small swirl component appears in the flow while for $400 < Re_D \leq 2000$ the separated region becomes unstable though laminar. This instability is the precursor of a complete breakdown into turbulent flow. At Reynolds numbers greater than 2000, the flow was very difficult to observe because of the rapid diffusion of dye caused by the high mean flow velocities and random small scale motion. For the largest Reynolds numbers the fluid motion appeared to be turbulent.

4.1.2 <u>Numerical Experiments</u>. The location of the grid or mesh points was determined by overlaying the geometry to be studied (shown in Fig. 16) with a square mesh (i.e. $\Delta r = \Delta z$) which was uniform throughout the flow field. Figure 16 along with Table 1 describes the mesh nomenclature and the various mesh sizes used.

Boundary and Initial Conditions

Since the boundary and initial conditions are almost identical to those used in the previously described cases, they will be presented as briefly as possible.

Upstream Boundary

The inflow or upstream boundary, surface 1 of Figure 16, was specified as a parabolic $v_z$- velocity profile for all the cases to be discussed in this article. Although $v_z$ was specified in this manner, $v_r$ was allowed the freedom to adjust with time.

Centerline

The centerline is labeled surface 2 in Fig. 16. Assuming axial symmetry, the vorticity and stream function at the centerline were set equal to zero and the velocity in the r-direction was also set equal to zero.

Solid Boundaries

The solid boundaries are labeled (3) in Fig. 16. The value for stream function along the top boundary, including the sewing ring, were given a constant value determined from the integration of the inflow velocity profile. The value of stream function for the disc was the same as for the centerline, zero. The velocity in both r and z directions were zero. Vorticity on the solid boundaries was computed using the definition of vorticity.

### Corners

The values of vorticity for the corners of the solid boundaries were computed using one sided differences as described in the frontstep and blunt base cases.

### Downstream Boundary

The outflow or downstream boundary is labeled 4 in Fig. 16. The boundary condition for stream function and vorticity used by Fanning and Mueller (Ref. 15) and described in the blunt base problem was used for the outflow. Thus a linear extrapolation in the z direction over the last three points was made for the values of stream function and vorticity. This allows the flow to continue in the general direction dictated by the two interior points adjacent to the outflow boundary.

### Initial Conditions

Initial conditions similar to those described in the frontstep and blunt base cases were used.

4.1.3 <u>Method of Solution</u>. The method of solution including upwind differencing for advection terms and convergence criteria, was essentially the same as for the frontstep problem described earlier, except of course equations (22) and (23) were used.

4.1.4 <u>Discussion of Results</u>. Figure 16 along with Table 1 describe the geometries and mesh sizes used. The first mesh used was the coarse mesh. A converged solution at $Re_D = 100$ was reached rapidly, however, the nature of this solution was questionable since no wake was apparent behind the disc. Experiments were performed using mesh sizes two and three times smaller than the coarse mesh. Unfortunately, the Univac 1107 did not have sufficient storage for the finest mesh. In order to accommodate the finest mesh it was necessary to shorten the geometry by one disc length on both upstream and downstream ends. The results for the three runs at $Re_D = 100$ on the length of the separated region downstream of the disc were very instructive. The Reynolds number $Re_D$ is based upon the average inflow velocity and the tube diameter. The medium mesh gave results which appear reasonable, i.e., wake behind the disc. The length of this wake or separated region behind the disc was even larger for the fine mesh. The flow also separated closer to the corner of the disc for the fine mesh than for the medium mesh. While still finer meshes might give more accurate results, these calculations indicated that the improvement would be quite small and probably not compensate for the increased computer time required. Further numerical experiments were performed to study the effects of inflow velocity profile shape and inflow location and are reported in reference 26. Recently, the components of the shear stress have been extracted from these solutions in order to locate regions with very high or very low values. Results of this type have considerable significance from the medical point of view (Ref. 28). Numerical calculations using the fine mesh produced the same trend as the physical experiments up to $Re_D \approx 500$ as shown in Fig. 15. The corrected numerical results shown in Fig. 15 are significantly different from those presented earlier in references 25, 26 and 27. The latest results were obtained after finding and correcting a local conservation error in the computer program. This agreement might be further improved if the actual velocity profile approaching the heart valve could be used in the numerical calculations.

Although much more time and effort was involved in obtaining the experimental data shown in Fig. 15, than in the frontstep case, it was only possible to improve the measurement of the Reynolds number (i.e., probable error of the order of 3%). The accuracy of determining the length of the wake behind the disc was never better than $\pm$ 10%. In the high Reynolds number region, where the wake was unstable this value was often exceeded as the interpretation of the wake length became more difficult and thus more subjective.

It appears that in this case the artificial viscosity effect will be rather large as either the Reynolds number increases or as the mesh size increases from the fine mesh used. One would not expect the boundary layer assumptions to be valid except in small regions near the upstream and downstream ends of the geometry, i.e., from the sewing ring until downstream of the wake $\frac{\partial^2 \xi}{\partial z^2}$ and $v_r$ are both large. From the streamline angle point of view (Ref. 22), significant areas of this flow have large values of $\theta$ with respect to the grid together with large values of velocity so that $\alpha_{er}$ and $\alpha_{ez}$ are probably large. In particular, the regions between the sewing ring and the disc and near the downstream end of the wake have streamline angles around $45^\circ$.

4.2.5 <u>Concluding Remarks</u>. While it appears that for this simple geometry, the numerical experiments offer some advantages over the physical experiments at low Reynolds numbers, great care must be exercised in the choice of the method and mesh configuration used. This seems to be the type of problem where both physical and numerical experiments should be performed simultaneously as a check on each other.

## 5. SUMMARY

From this study of three quite different viscous separated flow problems using the same numerical techniques, it is apparent that experimentation is as important in the numerical sense as it is in the physical sense. The time-dependent conservative equations with upwind differencing for advection terms produced stable solutions over a wide range of Reynolds numbers. The actual accuracy of the numerical solutions varied with the flow problem and mesh geometry. A variable mesh, concentrating mesh points in regions of steepest gradients, appears to be a convenient method of reducing the, ever present, artificial viscosity effect. Numerical solutions with engineering accuracy can be obtained if great care is taken to control this artificial viscosity effect. Furthermore, they allow the study of basic flow phenomena which would be more difficult to produce and study in physical experiments. These methods, however, are still in the developmental stages and are not available in foolproof form for use by design engineers.

There should be no doubt that, at present and for the foreseeable future, the computer and wind tunnel are and will be dependent upon each other for the practical solution of complex separated flow problems.

# REFERENCES

1. WIRZ, H.J. and SMOLDEREN, J.J.: Numerical integration of Navier-Stokes equations.
   AGARD Lecture Series 64: Advances in numerical fluid dynamics, 5-9 March 1973, pp 3-1 - 3-13.

2. RAKICH, J.V.: Introduction to the Proceedings of the Symposium on Computational Fluid Dynamics.
   Proceedings of the AIAA Computational Fluid Dynamics Conference, Palm Springs, Cal. July 19-20, 1973.

3. BANKSTON, C.A. and SMITH, H.J.: Vapor flow in cylindrical heat pipes.
   ASME Transact. Series C, J. of Heat Transfer, Vol.95, No.3, August 1973, pp 371-376.

4. BOZEMAN, J.D. and DALTON, C.: Numerical study of viscous flow in a cavity.
   J. of Computational Physics, Vol.12, No.3, July 1973, pp 348-363.

5. LIU, C.L. and LEE, S.C.: Transient state analysis of separated flow around a sphere.
   Computers and Fluids, Vol.1, No.3, Sept. 1973; pp 235-250.

6. ROACHE, P.J.: Computational fluid dynamics.
   Hermosa Publishers, P.O. Box 8172, Albuquerque, New Mexico 87108, 1972.

7. LIONS, J.L. et PRODI, G.: Un theoreme d'existence et unicite dans les equations de Navier-Stokes en dimension 2.
   C.R. Academie Sci. Paris, 248, 1959, pp 3519-3521.

8. CHENG, S.I.: Accuracy of difference formulation of Navier-Stokes equations.
   The Physics of Fluids, Supplement II, High speed computing in fluid dynamics; Vol.12, No.12, Part II, December 1969, pp II-34 - II-41.

9. ALLEN, J.D.: Numerical solution of the compressible Navier-Stokes equations for the laminar near wake in supersonic flows.
   Princeton University, Ph.D. Dissertation, Princeton, New Jersey, 1968.

10. ROACHE, P.J. and MUELLER, T.J.: Numerical solutions of laminar separated flows.
    AIAA J. Vol.8, No.3, March 1970, pp 530-538.

11. THOMAN, D.C. and SZEWCZYK, A.A.: Time dependent viscous flow over a circular cylinder.
    The Physics of Fluids, Supplement II, High speed computing in fluid dynamics; Vol.12, No.12, Part II, December 1969, pp II-76-II-86.

12. ROACHE, P.J.: Numerical solutions of compressible and incompressible laminar separated flows.
    Ph.D. Dissertation, Dept. of Aero-Space Engineering, University of Notre Dame, Notre Dame, Indiana, Nov. 1967.

13. ROACHE, P.J.: On artificial viscosity.
    J. Computational Physics, Vol.10, October 1972, pp 169-184.

14. FANNING, A.E. and MUELLER, T.J.: Numerical and experimental investigation of the oscillating wake of a blunt based body.
    AIAA J., Vol.11, No.11, Nóv.1973, pp 1486-1491.

15. FANNING, A.E. and MUELLER, T.J.: A numerical and experimental investigation of the oscillating flow in the wake of a blunt based body.
    AIAA Paper 71-603, Palo Alto, Cal., 1971.

16. FANNING, A.E.: A numerical and experimental investigation of the oscillating flow in the wake of a blunt based body.
    M.S.Thesis, U. of Notre Dame, Notre Dame, Indiana, August 1970.

17. BEARMAN, P.W.: Investigation of the flow behind a two-dimensional model with a blunt trailing edge and fitted with splitter plates.
    J.Fluid Mechanics, Vol.21, Part 2, 1965, pp.241-255.

18. BEARMAN, P.W.: The effect of base bleed on the flow behind a two dimensional model with a blunt trailing edge.
    The Aeron.Qua., Vol. XVIII, August 1967, pp 207-224.

19. MUELLER, T.J. and O'LEARY, R.A.: Physical and numerical experiments in laminar incompressible separating and reattaching flows.
    AIAA Paper 70-763, presented at the AIAA 3rd Fluid and Plasma Dynamics Conference, Los Angeles, Cal. June 29-July 1,1970.

20. SMITH, G.D.: Numerical solution of partial differential equations.
    Oxford University Press, 1965.

21. ROSHKO, A. and LAU, J.C.: Some observations on transition and reattachment of a free shear layer in incompressible flow.
    Proc.1965 Heat Transfer and Fluid Mechanics Institute, Los Angeles, Cal., June 21-23, 1965.

22. RUNCHAL, A.K., SPALDING, D.B., WOLFSHTEIN, M.: Numerical solution of the elliptic equations for transport of vorticity, heat and matter in two-dimensional flow.
    The Physics of Fluids, Supplement II, High speed computing in fluid dynamics, Vol.12, No.12, Part II, December 1969, pp II-21 - II-28.

23. CAMPBELL, D.R. and MUELLER, T.J.: Effects of mass bleed on an internal separated flow.
    Proc. Symp. on Application of Computers to Fluid Dynamics Analysis and Design at Polytechnic Institute of Brooklyn, New York, Jan.3-4, 1973. (Submitted to Computers and Fluids for publication).

24. STEVENSON, J.F.: Flow in a tube with a circumferential wall cavity.
    ASME Transact., Series E, J. of Applied Mechanics, Vol.40, No.2, June 1973, pp 355-361.

25. UNDERWOOD, F.N. and MUELLER, T.J.: Numerical studies of the steady, axisymmetric flow through a disc-type prosthetic heart valve.
Proc. 25th ACEMB, Bal Harbour, Florida, October 1972, p. 273.

26. UNDERWOOD, F.N.: Numerical and experimental studies of the steady, axisymmetric flow through a disc-type prosthetic heart valve.
M.S. Thesis, U. of Notre Dame, Notre Dame, Indiana, August 1972.

27. MUELLER, T.J., et al.: On the separated flow produced by a fully open disc-type prosthetic heart valve.
ASME 1973, Biomechanics Symposium Proceedings, AMD-Vol.2, Atlanta, Georgia, June 1973, pp 97-98.

28. MUELLER, T.J., LLOYD, J.R. and UNDERWOOD, F.N.: Unpublished data.
University of Notre Dame, Notre Dame, Indiana, 1973.

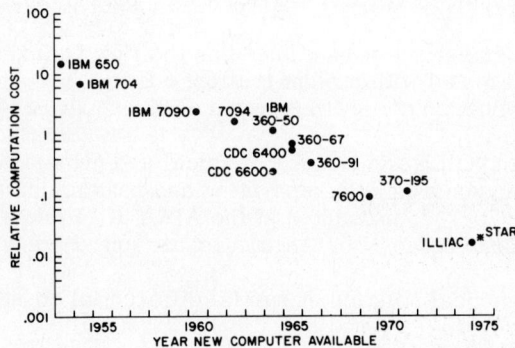

Fig. 1 - Trend of computational cost for computer simulation of a given flow (from Ref.2)

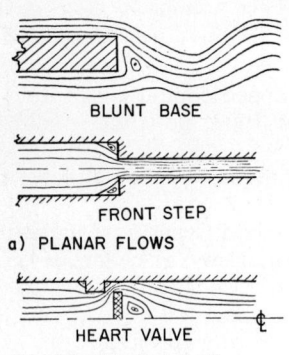
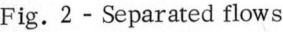

Fig. 2 - Separated flows

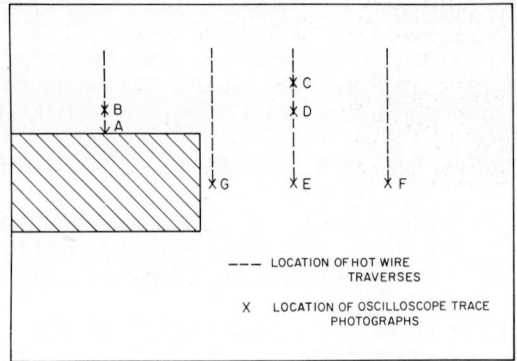

Fig. 3 - Locations of anemometer traverses and oscillograph photographs

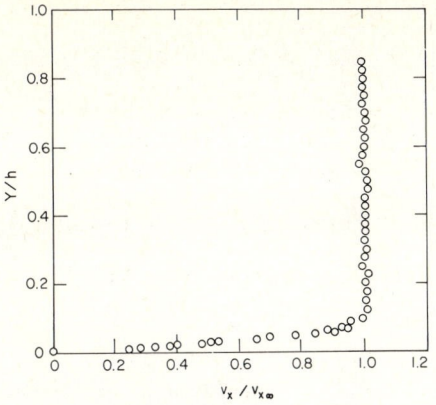

Fig. 4 - Inflow velocity profile, $Re_h = 16,295$

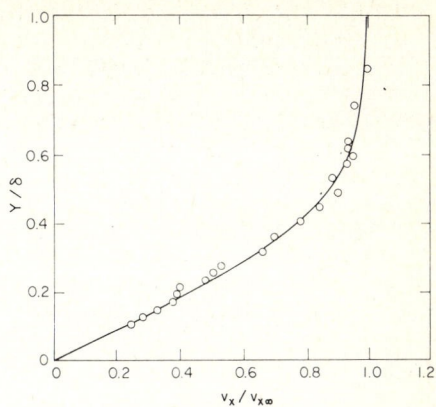

Fig. 5 - Boundary layer velocity profile, $Re_h = 16,295$, $\delta = 0.121\,h$

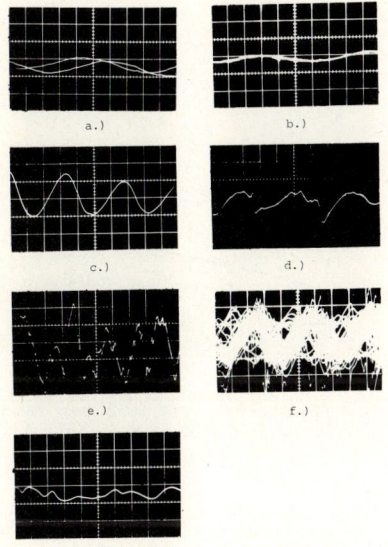

Fig. 6 - Hot wire voltage-oscilloscope photographs

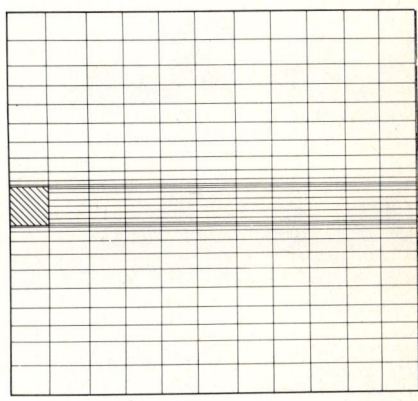

Fig. 7 - Variable rectangular grid

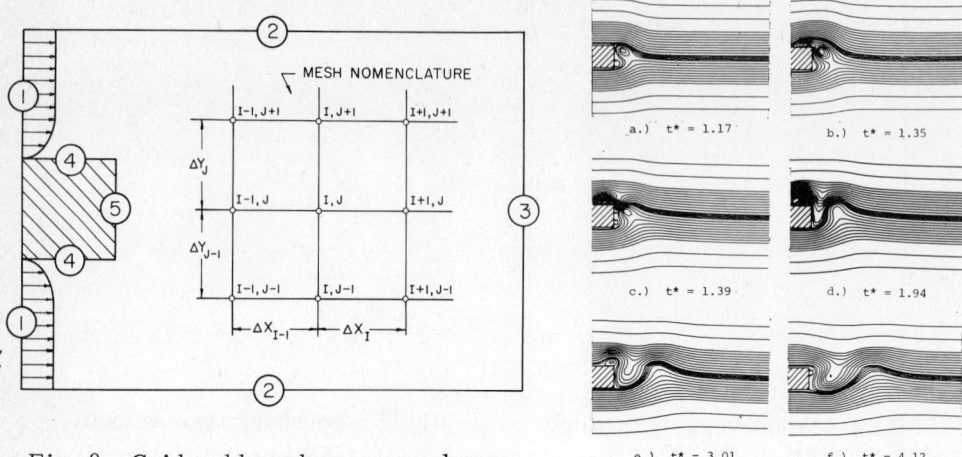

Fig. 8 - Grid and boundary nomenclature

Fig. 9 - Numerical development
$Re_h = 16,295$,
$\delta = 0.121\,h$

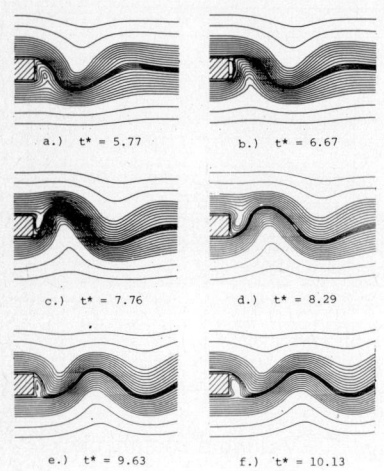

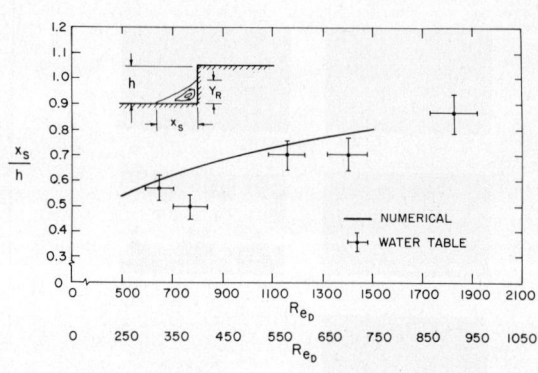

Fig. 11 - Separation point versus Reynolds number for zero bleed (i.e., $u_B = 0$)

Fig. 10 - Numerical solution,
$Re_h = 16,295$,
$\delta = 0.121\,h$

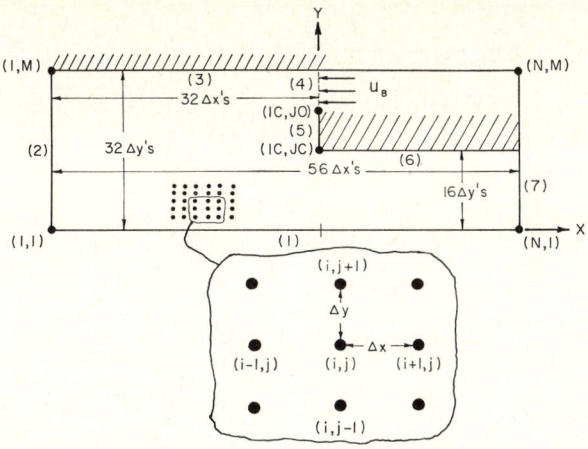

Fig. 12 - Front step geometry, boundary labeling convention, mesh nomenclature

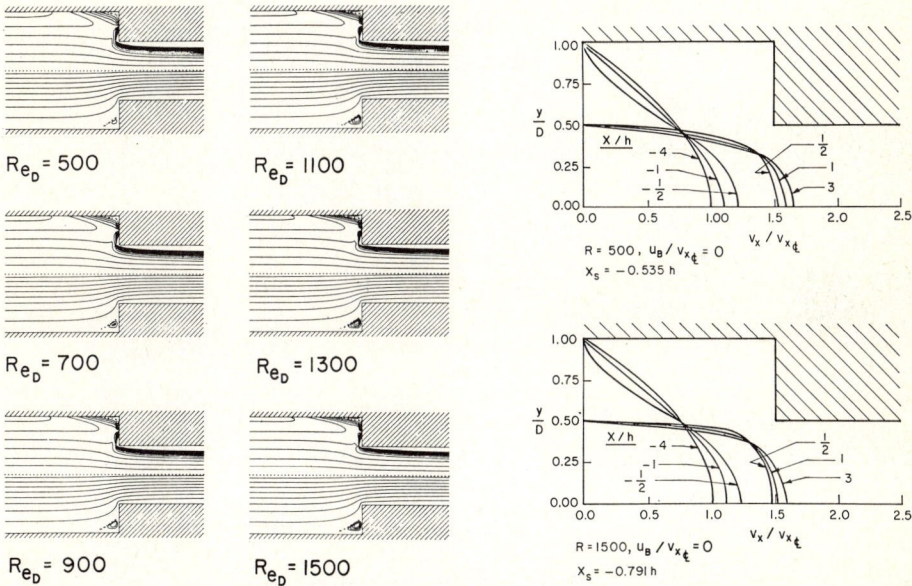

Fig. 13 - Contour vorticity-stream function plots for zero bleed

Fig. 14 - Velocity profiles up and downstream of the step at $Re_D$ = 500 and 1500, zero bleed

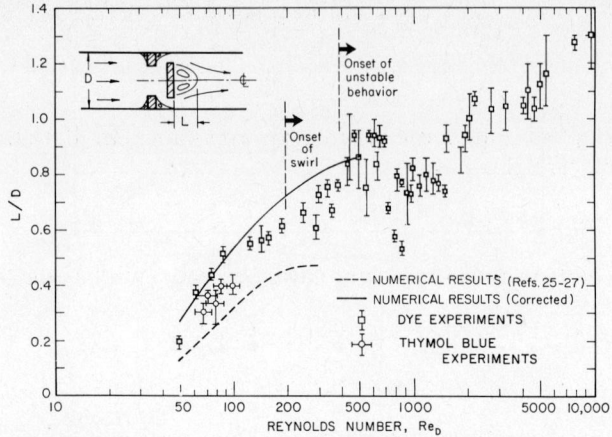

Fig. 15 - Length of separated region behind disc versus Reynolds number

Table 1

Mesh Coordinates

| Mesh | B | | C | | D | | E | | F | |
|---|---|---|---|---|---|---|---|---|---|---|
| | I | J | I | J | I | J | I | J | I | J |
| Coarse | 21 | 9 | 26 | 9 | 30 | 11 | 32 | 11 | 62 | 15 |
| Medium Test | 41 | 17 | 51 | 17 | 59 | 21 | 63 | 21 | 123 | 29 |
| Medium Reg. | 61 | 17 | 71 | 17 | 79 | 21 | 83 | 21 | 165 | 29 |
| Fine | 61 | 17 | 76 | 25 | 88 | 31 | 94 | 31 | 184 | 43 |

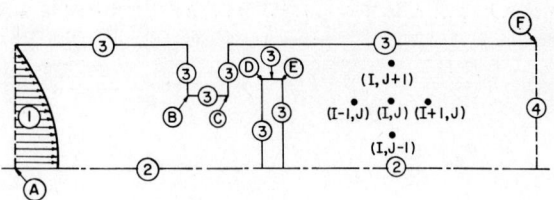

Fig. 16 - Geometry, mesh nomenclature, and boundary labeling convention

## LIST OF FIGURES

Figure No.

1     Trend of computational cost for computer simulation of a given flow (from Ref. 2)

2     Separated flows

3     Location of anemometer traverses and oscillograph photographs

4     Inflow velocity profile, $Re_h = 16,295$

5     Boundary layer velocity profile, $Re_h = 16,295$, $\delta = 0.121\,h$

6     Hot wire voltage-oscilloscope photographs

7     Variable rectangular grid

8     Grid and boundary nomenclature

9     Numerical development, $Re_h = 16,295$, $\delta = 0.121\,h$

10     Numerical solution, $Re_h = 16,295$, $\delta = 0.121\,h$

11     Separation point versus Reynolds number for zero bleed (i.e. $u_B = 0$)

12     Front step geometry, boundary labeling convention, mesh nomenclature

13     Contour vorticity-stream function plots for zero bleed

14     Velocity profiles up and downstream of the step at $Re_D = 500$ and 1500, zero bleed

15     Length of separated region behind disc versus Reynolds number

16     Geometry, mesh nomenclature, and boundary labeling convention

## NOMENCLATURE

| | |
|---|---|
| C | Courant number |
| D | diameter or channel half width |
| f | arbitrary function |
| h | base height or step height |
| L | length of separated region behind disc or characteristic length |
| P | pressure |
| $Re_D$ | Reynolds number based upon D |
| $Re_h$ | Reynolds number based upon h |
| $Re_L$ | Reynolds number based upon L |
| r | radial direction |
| t | time |
| v | velocity |
| x,y | cartesian coordinates |
| z | axial direction |
| $\alpha$ | kinematic viscosity |
| $\alpha_e$ | effective or artificial viscosity |
| $\Delta$ | increment |
| $\delta$ | increment or boundary layer thickness |
| $\theta$ | streamline angle or cylindrical coordinate |
| $\mu$ | absolute viscosity |
| $\xi$ | vorticity |
| $\rho$ | density |
| $\tau$ | shear stress |
| $\psi$ | stream function |

## NOMENCLATURE (continued)

### Subscripts

| | |
|---|---|
| B | base bleed |
| $\mathcal{CL}$ | centerline |
| r | radial |
| ij | condition at ij mesh point |
| crit | critical value |
| max | maximum value |
| s | steady state value or separation |
| x | Cartesian coordinate |
| y | Cartesian coordinate |
| z | axial |
| $\infty$ | free stream |

### Superscripts

| | |
|---|---|
| n | time level |
| * | dimensionless |

# STABILITY OF EXPLICIT TIME DEPENDENT TREATMENT

## OF HYPERBOLIC BOUNDARY PROBLEMS

J. SMOLDEREN

von Karman Institute for Fluid Dynamics
Rhode St Genèse, Belgium

## 1. INTRODUCTION

It is well known that the explicit time-marching finite difference reatment of hyperbolic equations may lead to severe stability problems. von Neumann (Ref. 1) has given a necessary and often sufficient condition for stability in the case of linear equations with constant coefficients and uniform mesh. The criterion has been widely and successfully used in more general cases, including linearized versions of non linear problems, the only limitation in its use being the complexity of the algebraic manipulations required to work out the criterion for partial differential systems of high order or involving more than two independent variables.

Unfortunately, the von Neumann analysis does not generally apply to problems involving boundary conditions. Many examples show that instability may occur even if the von Neumann criterion is satisfied. The condition is still necessary but far from sufficient.

A general theory, due to Godunov and Ryabenkii (Ref. 2) leads to a more restrictive criterion which is usually found to be sufficient to ensure stability in the presence of boundary conditions.

A simplified presentation of this theory and the resulting criterion will be outlined and illustrated by a simple example.

A more thorough mathematical treatment will be found in a recent paper by Kreiss (Ref. 3).

## 2. EXPONENTIAL SOLUTIONS OF FINITE DIFFERENCE EQUATIONS

Finite difference discretization of a partial differential equation or system with constant coefficients leads to a linear difference equation or system, the coefficients being also constant, if a uniform mesh is used. Exponential solutions exhibiting separation of variables therefore also exist for the difference equation.

Consider, for instance, the simplest case of two independent variables t and x, t being the time-like marching variable (in a steady state supersonic problem, the time-like variable will be the streamwise coordinate). Let the regular mesh system be defined by

$$t_k = t_0 + k\Delta t \qquad (k = 0,1,2,\ldots)$$

$$x_j = x_0 + j\Delta x \qquad (j = 0,1,2,\ldots)$$

and let $u_j^k$ be the approximate values of the unknown function(s) at the mesh point $(t_k, x_j)$, resulting from the difference equations. These equations being linear with constant coefficients, it is easy to construct particular solutions with separated variables of the form

$$u_j^k = \text{const.} \; \rho^k \lambda^j \qquad (1)$$

which are analogous to the exponential and Fourier modes for the corresponding differential equations.

Substituting the above expression(s) in the difference equation(s) one obtains after cancelling the common factor, a relation connecting $\rho$, the temporal amplification factor and $\lambda$, the spatial amplification factor :

$$F(\rho,\lambda) = 0 \qquad (2)$$

This represents the characteristic relation for the difference scheme. In the case of a system of equations, this relation is obtained by expressing that the determinant of the linear algebraic system for the constant coefficients introduced by (1) is zero.

The von Neumann criterion expresses that the temporal amplification factor $\rho$ (generally a complex number) must have a modulus bounded by $1 + O(\Delta t)$ for all values of $\lambda$ which represent spatial Fourier modes, i.e., for

$$\lambda = \exp\,(i\pi n/N) \qquad (n = 1,2,\ldots,N) \qquad (3)$$

(N being the number of spatial meshes used).

If boundary conditions are imposed at either one or both boundaries, $x_0$ and $x_0 + N\Delta x$, of the spatial domain considered, then these Fourier modes will generally not be acceptable solutions of the problem because of incompatibility with the boundary conditions.

However, during an initial part of the progression in time, the influence of the boundary conditions will not be felt inside the numerical region of dependence of the initial data. The solution in this region will blow up if the von Neumann criterion is not satisfied so that the criterion still represents a necessary condition for stability.

Let us assume that the boundary conditions are also linear with constant coefficients. Considering the perturbations to a given solution, one may reduce the study to the case of homogeneous boundary conditions of the form

$$\sum_{j,\ell} a_{j,\ell} u_j^{k-\ell} = 0 \qquad (4)$$

where the summation involved a fixed number of indices, defining a few neighbouring points to the boundary and a few earlier time steps.

It is obviously possible to combine solutions of the form (1) corresponding to the same value of $\rho$ to satisfy a suitable set of boundary conditions of the type (4). Indeed, for $\rho$ given, the characteristic relation (2) represents an algebraic equation for $\lambda$ say of the $r^{th}$ degree with r roots : $\lambda_1, \ldots \lambda_r$. (In the case of equal roots there will exist polynomial-exponential solutions of the form

$$u_j^k = \text{const } P(j) \rho^k \lambda^j$$

where P is a polynomial in j).

A linear combination of the form

$$u_j^k = \rho^k \sum_{\nu=1\ldots r} A_\nu \lambda_\nu^j \qquad (5)$$

will be solution of the boundary problem if the boundary conditions (4) allow unique determination of the coefficients $A_\nu$. It can easily be shown that the number of boundary conditions to be specified in order to define the time marching procedure is indeed equal to r, the number of $\lambda$ roots of the characteristic equation (2). This number may actually be higher than the order in x of the partial differential equation or system to be treated, if one uses a discretization of order of accuracy higher than the first. In such case, additional boundary conditions, which are not at all specified by the physical situation to be treated, must be invented, with suitable regard for accuracy requirements. This need for a choice involving a degree of arbitrariness, represents a serious difficulty as it may strongly influence the stability of the calculations.

## 3. STABILITY OF MODES COMPATIBLE WITH THE BOUNDARY CONDITIONS

Substitution of the expression (5) of the combined mode in the r boundary conditions of type (4) will yield a linear algebraic system of r equations for the r unknown coefficients $A_1, \ldots, A_r$. A non trivial solution will exit only if the determinant of the system is zero. This yields a new algebraic condition connecting $\rho, \lambda_1, \ldots, \lambda_r$.

Expressing that $\lambda_1, \ldots, \lambda_r$ are the r roots of the characteristic equation (2) will lead, after considerable algebraic manipulations, to a new algebraic equation for the temporal amplification $\rho$, the roots of which may be considered to be eigenvalues for our linear homogeneous boundary problem.

A new necessary condition for stability may then be established, by requiring that the roots of the final equation in $\rho$ are all of modulus smaller than $1 + O(\Delta t)$.

The inextricable complexity of this approach will be understood if it is realized that conditions may be prescribed at both boundaries of the spatial region, so that factors of the type $\lambda^N$ will occur in the equations defining the coefficients A and in the corresponding determinant, N being the number of spatial meshes. We must therefore expect that the final equation for $\rho$ will be of a degree which increases indefinitely with N, and the same will be true for the number of its roots.

This apparently hopeless situation can fortunately be resolved by showing that the number of unstable modes is necessarily bounded for all values of N.

## 4. UNSTABLE BOUNDARY MODES

The number of exponential modes compatible with suitable boundary conditions have been shown to be increasing with the number of spatial meshes, as is the case for the Fourier modes (eq. 3). However, the new family of modes has very different properties, in general, and the coefficients of an expansion in terms of these modes may not be bounded for increasing N.

However, we are interested only in stability conditions here, and may therefore limit ourselves to the study of the eventual unstable modes corresponding to $|\rho| > 1 + \varepsilon$ ($\varepsilon$ positive, fixed).

It may be shown that if the finite difference scheme satisfies the von Neumann criterion, then there occurs, for $N \to \infty$, a decoupling of the influence of the boundary conditions applied at different boundaries of the spatial domain, for the unstable modes. Each boundary may therefore be considered separately and this introduces powers of $\lambda$ with low exponents independent of N. The resulting equation in $\rho$ for the unstable modes will therefore also be of a relatively low degree and independent of N.

Of course, the number of stable modes will always be unbounded, for increasing N, because the total number of modes is unbounded.

It may actually be shown that if s boundary conditions are imposed at the lower boundary (j = 0) and r - s at the upper boundary (j = N), then the characteristic relation (2) will have exactly s roots $\lambda$ with modulus smaller than unity and (r-s) roots with modulus larger than unity, for all $\rho$ such that $|\rho| > 1$ (unstable modes).

This important lemma leads to the following property. At the limit $N \to \infty$, the determinant of the algebraic system for the coefficients A defining the mode (5) may be factored and the condition on the $\lambda$ reads

$$P_s(\lambda;\rho) \, P_{r-s}(\lambda;\rho) = 0$$

where $P_s$, $P_{r-s}$ are polynomials of degree s and r-s respectively. The coefficients of $P_s$ depend only in the lower boundary conditions and those of $P_{r-s}$ on the upper boundary conditions. This is the decoupling property which may be expressed as follows. Possible unstable modes will be of the form

$$u_j^k = \rho^k \Sigma A_\nu \lambda_\nu^j \qquad \text{with } |\lambda_\nu| < 1 \text{ for } 1 \leq \nu \leq s \qquad (6)$$

$$u_j^k = \rho^k \Sigma A_\nu \lambda_\nu^j \qquad \text{with } |\lambda_\nu| > 1 \text{ for } s+1 \leq \nu \leq r \qquad (7)$$

The modes (6) are called lower boundary modes and must satisfy the s boundary conditions imposed at the lower boundary. The upper boundary modes (7) must satisfy the upper boundary conditions. Such a decoupling will not occur for stable modes.

These considerations, which dramatically reduce the algebraic manipulations, may also be generalized to multi-dimensional spaces and even curved boundaries may then be treated, using a local approach.

It should be mentioned that the establishment of a stability criterion, expressing that the moduli of $\rho$ for all boundary modes are smaller than $1 + O(\Delta t)$, is still very tedious in non trivial cases and considerably more difficult to work out than the von Neumann criterion.

Kreiss has shown that the conditions so obtained are not always sufficient (Ref. 3) but the example he used to show the existence of non exponential, polynomial modes, must be considered as rather marginal (Leap-fog scheme).

## 5. EXAMPLE : SUFFICIENT STABILITY CRITERION FOR AN ADDITIONAL BOUNDARY CONDITION

Using the concept of boundary modes, it is sometimes possible to obtain a sufficient condition for the absence of unstable exponential boundary modes, without even specifying the scheme and its characteristic relation (eq. 2). We illustrate this using the example of a single hyperbolic equation of the first order for the unknown function $u(x,t)$. Assume that a higher order scheme is used so that an additional condition must be introduced at say $j = 0$. This assumes that the characteristics are running downward in the $(t,x)$ plane.

The new value $u_0^{k+1}$ must then be defined to proceed with the marching scheme. Let us select a linear condition expressing $u_0^{k+1}$ in terms of the earlier values at the neighbouring points $j = 0$ and $j = 1$ :

$$u_0^{k+1} = a\, u_0^k + b\, u_1^k$$

First order accuracy at the boundary (which is compatible with second order accuracy of the scheme) will require

$$a + b = 1$$

According to the theory described in section 4, there will be only one possible unstable boundary mode of the form

$$u_j^k = A\rho^k \lambda^j \qquad\qquad |\rho| > 1; \; |\lambda| < 1$$

This leads to the following homogeneous equation for A :

$$\rho A = aA + (1-a) A\lambda$$

Therefore, the mode will exist only if

$$\rho = a + (1-a)\lambda \qquad\qquad\qquad\qquad\qquad\qquad (8)$$

This mode will represent an unstable lower boundary mode only if $|\rho| > 1$, $|\lambda| < 1$. If these inequalities cannot be simultaneously satisfied, taking account of (8), then no unstable exponential mode will exist (note that this will represent a sufficient but not always necessary condition, because $\lambda$ and $\rho$ must also satisfy the characteristic relation of the scheme, which may not be possible for $|\rho| > 1$).

Obviously, the image in the complex $\rho$ plane of the unit circle of the $\lambda$ plane, under the linear transformation (8), is a circle with radius $|1-a|$ centered at $\rho = a$. No unstable exponential mode will exist if this circle is entirely inside the unit circle $|\rho| = 1$. This will be the case if

$$-1 < 2a-1 < 1, \qquad -1 < a < 1$$

hence, if

$$0 < a < 1 \qquad\qquad\qquad\qquad\qquad\qquad\qquad\qquad (9)$$

(9) therefore represents a sufficient condition for stability as far as exponential modes are concerned.

The following interpretation of condition (9) is interesting: $u^{k+1}$ is taken equal to the value of u corresponding to the preceding time step k, at some point located between j = 0 and j = 1 (weighted average). But we have assumed that the characteristics of the hyperbolic equation run towards decreasing values of x for increasing t (otherwise an essential boundary should have been imposed at j = 0 to define the solution). Therefore, the additional condition (8), taking account of the criterion (9), turns out to be in qualitative agreement with the "characteristic rule" advocated by Moretti (Ref. 4), on the basis of physical arguments. One should, however, be careful about the use of physical arguments in the discussion of a purely numerical problem.


REFERENCES

1. O'BRIEN, G.G., HYMAN, M.A. and KAPLAN, S.: A study of the numerical solution of partial differential equations.
   J. Math.and Phys., Vol. 29, 1950, pp 223-251.

2. GODUNOV, S.K. and RYABENKII, V.S.: Special stability criteria for boundary condition problems for non self-adjoint finite difference equations.
   Uspekhi Mat.Mauk. Vol. 18, 1969, p. 3.

3. KREISS, H.O.: Boundary conditions for difference approximations of hyperbolic differential equations.
   in Advances in numerical fluid dynamics, AGARD Lecture Series No 64, 1973.

4. MORETTI, G.: The importance of boundary conditions in the numerical treatment of hyperbolic equations.
   Brooklyn Polytechnic Institute, PIBAL Report No 68-34, 1968.

# IMPROVING OF THE NUMERICAL SOLUTIONS
# BY USING ANALOGUE SUBROUTINES

## Listing of the graphs

TABLE I : analog versus digital computer

Fig. 1. : Computation spectrum

Fig. 2. : Unilateral hybrid analog/digital systems

Fig. 3. : Bilateral hybrid system

Fig. 4. : Error vs. frequency diagram comparison of analog and digital implementation (from W. Giloi)

Fig. 5. : Discrete – space   continuous – time method

Fig. 6. : Continuous – space   discrete – time method

Fig. 7. : DSDT Hybrid System


## Table of contents

- Introduction to a hybrid solution approach
- Analog computer oriented approach : two ways of solving partial differential equations
- Digital computer oriented approach : the advantage of using analog subroutines
- Application to a DSDT problem
- Conclusion.

# IMPROVING OF THE NUMERICAL SOLUTIONS
# BY USING ANALOGUE SUBROUTINES

*G.C. VANSTEENKISTE*
*Professor of Engineering*
*University of Ghent*
*Coupure Links 533*
*B-9000 Ghent*
*Belgium*

INTRODUCTION

There exist many approaches to the reduction of the time required to obtain numerical solutions using general-purpose digital computers. A number of these involve the utilization of special-purpose peripheral devices which function as subroutines, to be called by the digital computer program as required. Most frequently these peripheral devices are digital in nature, containing the memory, arithmetic, and control required to perform computations which would be much more time-consuming if performed by the central processor unit (CPU). A less widely used technique involves the use of analog devices in the peripheral unit. In this case, the digital computer is coupled to an analog unit by means of interface hardware.

Such a system is effective in increasing the rate at which the digital computer can solve certain classes of problems because the analog device is essentially a fully parallel computer, the solution time being independent of the problem complexity (number of arithmetic operations). The use of such a peripheral, therefore, involves essentially a trade-off between the time required for the data to pass through the interface in the two directions and the time that would be required to perform the calculations in the CPU.

The present text is directed to a specific application : the treatment of fluid flow problems. A variety of basic techniques are available for the numerical solution of transient fluid flow problems, such as Monte Carlo methods, Methods of Characteristics, Finite Element Methods and Finite Difference Methods. The last ones however are used almost exclusively for the treatment of complex systems (fig. 1).

## HYBRID SYSTEMS

The possibility of operating many analog computing elements in parallel permits real-time simulation of large dynamical systems. As a matter of fact, computing-element bandwidths make it possible to simulate many systems on a speed-up ("fast") time scale. Unlike the situation in digital machines, this computing speed is difficult to trade off for increased accuracy.

The term true hybrid is applied to those combined computing systems containing analog as well as digital hardware in appreciable amounts. The ways in which analog and digital computer installations can be used together can be classified into two broad categories : *Unilateral operation*, in which information flows across the interface between the analog and the digital sections in only one direction ; and *bilateral operation*, in which the flow across this interface is in both directions. Both methods require conversion equipment at the interface. Figures 2a and 2b illustrate two types of unilateral systems. Note that only one type of converter, either analog-digital or digital-analog is required at each interface. In such systems the analog or the digital computer can be regarded as playing the part of a complex and elegant input or output device. Fig. 3 illustrates a bilateral hybrid system. Such systems are characterized by a closed loop formed by the digital computer, the digital-analog conversion devices, the analog computer, and the analog-digital converters. In addition to those major units bilateral hybrid computer systems also include a number of other important devices. *Multiplexers* and *demultiplexers* are employed to permit the converters, which translate continuous DC voltages into digital code and vice versa, to be time-shared. *Hold devices* are required to maintain the continuously varying analog signals at constant values for a time sufficiently long to permit conversion, and to maintain the output voltage of digital-analog converters at constant levels while conversion is taking place. *Buffers* are required to adjust voltage levels and pulse shapes in a manner compatible with the digital and analog computers in use. Finally, *timing and control circuitry* is required to synchronize the processes in the various units comprising the hybrid loop. Each of these units and subunits manifests input-output relationships which deviate from the ideal or specified behavior. In designing hybrid computer systems and in evaluating their performance it is therefore necessary to determine the effect of the non-ideal behavior of each sub-unit upon the overall system dynamics. An important major application of hybrid computer systems involves the interconnection of the analog-digital loop with major items of hardware. Because of their wide-spread application in telemeter and communications systems, unilateral hybrids no doubt outnumber bilateral systems by a wide margin.

It is possible to identify certain general computational requirements which suggest the hybrid computer approach. In this connection, it should be noted that hybrid techniques are frequently employed to overcome certain shortcomings in present-day analog or digital computers. As these limitations are reduced or eliminated, it is possible that some of the applications for hybrid computing systems will disappear (table I).

The increasing speed and decreasing cost of general-purpose digital computers as well as the advent of time-shared on-line digital systems may well narrow the range of applications for hybrid equipment. On the other hand, the introduction of integrated circuitry makes possible the realization of linkage equipment in increasingly simple, reliable and economical form thus making hybrid techniques increasingly attractive in areas in which pure analog or pure digital computers may be adequate. The following are, the chief motivations for interconnecting digital and analog computers :

- *To combine the speed of an analog computer with the accuracy of a digital computer.*
- *To permit the use of system hardware in a digital simulation.*
- *To increase the flexibility of an analog simulation by using digital memory and control.*
- *To increase the speed of a digital computation by utilizing analog subroutines.*
- *To permit the processing of incoming data which are partially discrete and partially continuous.*

Not only analog hardware but also human operators make necessary the development of an analog-digital interface in such sophisticated computer systems. Once the necessity for an interface has been established, it becomes possible to examine each computational task to determine whether it can better be performed on the analog or the digital side of the hybrid computer system.

Combined simulation is motivated by the hope of combining analog-computer speed in some parts of the simulation with digital accuracy and function-generating power in other parts of a simulation. Digital storage and analog output of several complicated functions of two to four variables is a frequent application of combined-simulation techniques.

Applications of this type combine not only the *best* features of analog and digital computation, but also their *worst*, viz., analog-computer inaccuracy and the sampled-data bandwidth limitations of the digital computer. Digital operations imply *sampled-data operations, digital processing delays,* and *quantization,* all of which produce essential errors in the representation of continuous dynamical-system variables. These errors must be evaluated and mitigated through careful choice of the portion of the simulation carried out on the digital computer. While quantization errors rarely cause trouble, digital sampled-data operations and processing delays limit the digital part of a combined simulation to slowly varying variables.

Even so, subtle loop-instability effects are encountered ; it is best to check each problem on a reduced time scale to see whether sampling rates are fast enough for stability.

The most effective utilization of hybrid computers has to be expected for those problems which allow the full use of the pass-band of new analog elements ; in these cases, the competitivity of hybrid computers vs. purely digital ones may be higher than for analog computers in the past.
Often this point is not sufficiently taken into account, and the evaluation of hybrid computers is done for applications concerning the solution of sets of slow ordinary differential equations, leading to poor comparison with full digital simulation.

Let us assume that today's typical digital computer used for simulation purposes has a word length of 24 bit, at least. Hence, the local round-off error, which is equivalent to the 'static' error in analog computers, is less than $10^{-7}$. The dynamic error in a digital simulation program is caused by the truncation error of numerical integration and depends on the actual integration formula, used in the program, and on the step size. Because a digital simulation program has to be executed in a quasi-parallel way, the step size of any integration is equal to what is called the "frame-time", i.e. the total execution time of all operations within one step of integration.

As given in reference [1] fig. 4 shows a comparison of the error vs. frequency for the above digital computer and a modern analog computer (with 0,01 % static accuracy and a 300 KHz, 3dB pass-band for amplifiers). The comparison is made for a typical dynamic model, of a size corresponding to a 100 amplifiers analog computer (with a typical implementation of integrators, summers, multipliers and function generators) ; the execution on the digital computer of one time step for this model, with leasttime programming (in machine language), requires about 4000-5000 memory cycles, depending on the integration formula used (frame-time of 8-10ms, for a memory cycle of 2 µs.). Fig. 4 shows the result of an error analysis for three different integration formulas (Euler-, trapezoidal- and Adams-Bash-forth-integration) assuming a frame time of 10 ms. As the diagram shows, the "bandwidth-to-accuracy ratio" even of the Adams-Bashforth-formula (which is of relatively high order, resulting in small dynamic errors) is 1 - 2 decades smaller than that of the analog computer. The situation is much worse in the case of one-step formulas such as the trapezoidal rule or even the Euler integration. Additionally, one has to consider, that for large-scale problems a frame time of 10 ms can be considered as being the lower boundary, even if the computer is very fast.

The difficulties of pure digital simulation are not entirely characterized by yet unsatisfying computation speed of appropriate computers.

Even more serious problems arise by the potential instability of numerical integration. If truncation errors would be the only problem, this could easily be overcome by using multistep methods of adequate high order (disregarding for the moment the starting problems). What makes the point crucial is that the risk of causing instabilities in the solution of differential equations by discrete variable methods increases with the order of a multistep formula.

For a detailed analysis of hybrid systems, the reader is referred to reference [1].

## ANALOG COMPUTER ORIENTED APPROACH

In analog computer oriented hybrid systems, relatively elegant and expensive analog computers perform the bulk of the computations, usually involving the integration of systems of ordinary differential equations, while the digital partner is employed in a subsidiary capacity for control, function generation, memory, etc.

In the continuous-time-discrete-space (CTDS) hybrid method, continuous integration with respect to time is performed by analog integrators. The space domain to be simulated is broken up into two or more sections, and analog elements are provided only for a single section. The analog system is then used repeatedly to provide solutions for each of the sections of the space domain. If now an analog system is used to represent only a portion of the overall field, the "boundary" conditions at the two ends of this system are generally not known but are rather a part of the solution being sought. It is therefore necessary to employ iterative techniques to "match" all the time-shared sections.

Fig. 5 shows a simple three-integrator system. A digital computer together with the necessary linkage equipment is employed to simulate adjacent sections in the positive and negative x-directions by applying to the analog network the transient potentials which would, as indicated in fig. 5, be generated by integrators immediately to the left and to the right of the section shown, and to record the potentials generated by the analog system. The latter transients become the "boundary" potentials to be applied to the analog system when it is used subsequently to simulate adjacent sections in the space domain. The analog system is used successively to represent the sections of the space domain starting with the left-most section and ending with the right-most section. Initially, the "boundary values" for the interior sections are arbitrarily assumed. After the first iterative pass through the system, the digital computer will have stored in its memory the first "solution values" generated by the analog system in each section. These, then, serve as the boundary excitations for the succeeding iterative cycle in which the analog system again sequentially simulates each of the sections in the space domain. These iterative cycles are repeated until convergence to the correct solution has been obtained.

The need for this high number of iterations as well as the errors introduced in the hybrid loop ; greatly limit the applicability of this approach. It has merit when large numbers of nonlinear one-dimensional diffusion equations must be treated.

In the continuous-space-discrete-time (CSDT) hybrid method, the problem time variable is discretized ; so that solutions are generated at successive time levels. In approximating the time derivative, two possibilities exist : forward difference and backward difference approximations. Equations employing forward differences, are solved explicitly, a process which is relatively simple computationally but which has the inherent possibility of computational instability. If the ratio of the time increment to the space increment is too large, round-off errors made in the course of the solution will gradually build up until they overshadow the solution, thus making it worthless. In order to obtain satisfactory solutions by this method, it is necessary to make the time increment relatively small, that is to take many time-consuming steps. Using backward differences, the one-dimensional diffusion equation results in :

$$\frac{d^2 u_i}{dx^2} - \frac{1}{\Delta t} u_i = u_{i-1}(x) - S_i(x)$$

with boundary conditions

$$u_i(0) = u_0(i\Delta t) , \quad \frac{du_i}{dx}(1) = 0$$

and with

$$S_i(x) = S(x, i\Delta t)$$

A digital computer offers an obvious means to provide the functions $S_i(x)$ and $u_{i-1}(x)$. The $S_i(x)$ functions are stored originally as part of the problem statement whereas $u_{i-1}(x)$ has been stored as a result of the previous solution at the i-1 interval (fig. 6).

Unfortunately, there are a number of severe problems which limit drastically the usefulness of this scheme. First of all, at each time interval we must solve a boundary condition problem. Starting at x = 0 and integrating towards x = 1 we must guess initially
$\frac{du_i}{dx}(0)$ in order to have the derivative vanish at x = 1.
This implies an iterative process in itself to converge on the initial condition which generates the correct solution satisfying the final condition. The real problem however, is that the above equation is unstable, and the smaller we make $\Delta t$, the more severe is the instability.

This will make it difficult to repeat solutions and will put a definite lower limit on Δt.

On the other hand the backward difference representation for ∂u/∂t is rather inaccurate, having a large residual error given by

$$\frac{\Delta t}{2} \left. \frac{\partial^2 u}{\partial t^2} \right|_i$$

This implies that Δt should be made quite small for reasonable accuracy, which is quite incompatible with the stability problem described in the previous paragraph. Thus the continuous-space, discrete-time method for hybrid solution of partial differential equations would appear to be inferior to the conventional discrete-space continuous-time method.

## DIGITAL COMPUTER ORIENTED APPROACH

Since the accuracy of analog operations is limited by the quality of the electrical components, the use of analog subroutines may entail a degradation of solution accuracy. However, as is the case in the method described below, the use of the analog subroutine in an error-correction mode entirely obviates this disadvantage. The approach is applicable to elliptical, parabolic, hyperbolic as well as biharmonic partial differential equations. Problems are programmed for convention digital computation, and the digital computer flow chart is analyzed to determine if some particularly time-consuming blocks could be better handled by analog rather than digital techniques, that is, by an analog subroutine. An analog unit is then especially constructed for this computational task. Because of its special-purpose nature, such a unit is far less expensive than a general-purpose analog computer and entails few of the usual programming or maintenance problems. A computer system, embodying this concept has been developed and has been operating successfully at the University of California, Los Angeles, for over five years. The system was designed specifically to assist in the solution of a class of nonlinear partial differential equations, and a wide variety of engineering problems have been successfully treated (reference [2]. A similar hybrid system is now under development at the University of Ghent and will be used for partial differential equation studies in collaboration with the Von Karman Institute.

When transient field problems are treated on a digital computer, all partial derivatives must be approximated by finite difference expressions. As seen above, in approximating the time derivative, for parabolic partial differential equations, backward differences are employed. The computational procedure is implicit with no danger of computational instability but requires now the solution of a large number of simultaneous algebraic equations at each time level which involves time-consuming matrix inversion of large sparse matrices. A variety of techniques for solving these simultaneous difference equations have been introduced over the years ; the so-called successive over-relaxation method and the alternating direction implicit method are by far the most widely used. It is here that the hybrid computer makes its principal contribution. The analog subroutine approach, as utilized in the so-called discrete-space-discrete-time (DSDT) computer constitutes indeed an alternative, designed to save computer time at the expense of additional hardware. A principal advantage of the DSDT hybrid method, is furthermore its interactive capability permitting the user to combine his heuristic insight into the physics of the problem with formal mathematical and algorithmic methods. The difficulty of studying systems whose dynamics are characterized by partial differential equations in more than one space dimension lies not only in the complexity of the problem but also in the fact that it is virtually impossible to express all the constraints in an algorithmic form. This bottleneck has severely limited the utility of the conventional computer approach to complex inverse problems. The DSDT hybrid computer method can make an important contribution by permitting powerful and useful computational algorithms to be programmed on the digital computer, while allowing the specialist to introduce his judgments and insights as they are required in the computational process, without first translating them into an abstract programming language. Another advantage of the approach, when compared to competing digital and analog methods, is its efficiency in handling nonlinear problems. A disadvantage lies in the fact that the number of finite difference grid points which can be treated efficiently with a given system is limited by the available hardware.

Consider the general mathematical problem (see ref. [2])

$$L(\phi) = d \qquad (1)$$

where $\phi$ and d are either vectors, functions, or matrices, and $L$ is an operator. Such a problem is frequently treated by iterative techniques. For the rth iterative cycle,

$$M(\delta^{(r)}) = d - L(\phi^{(r)}) \qquad (2a)$$
$$\phi^{(r+1)} = \phi^{(r)} + \theta\delta^{(r)} \qquad (2b)$$

where $M$ is an invertable linear operator, $\theta$ is a scalar relaxation factor, and $\delta$ is a correction term. Provided that the convergence criteria are satisfied, $\phi^{(r)}$ will converge to $\phi$, the solution of (1). The rate of convergence is influenced by the choice of $M$ and $\theta$. If $L$ is a linear operator, the solution $\phi$ is obtained after a single iteration by choosing, $M$ equal to $L$ and $\theta = 1$. Using analog subroutines, the computations represented by (2) are carried out as follows :

- An error vector $\Delta^{(r)} = d - L(\phi^{(r)})$ is computed digitally.
- $\Delta^{(r)}$ is scaled and converted into a set of analog signals.
- The equation $M(\delta^{(r)}) = \Delta^{(r)}$ is solved for $\delta^{(r)}$ by an analog technique.
- The analog signals $\delta^{(r)}$ are converted into digital form and unscaled.
- $\phi^{(r+1)}$ is computed digitally using (2b).

This sequence is repeated until

$$||\Delta^{(r)}|| < \varepsilon \qquad (3)$$

where $||\ ||$ is a suitably chosen norm, and $\varepsilon$ is a scalar parameter controlling solution accuracy.

The basic reason for calculating $\delta^{(r)}$ by analog means is to reduce the time required to solve (2). The analog subroutine presents a computing speed advantage relative to digital methods for two reasons. The parallel- computing nature of analog circuitry permits the term $\delta^{(r)}$ to be calculated more rapidly ; more important, however, as demonstrated below is that the number of iterations (r) required to attain convergence of (2) is usually far smaller.

It is important to recognize that errors or inaccuracies in the analog circuitry do not directly affect the solution accuracy provided only that convergence is achieved. This is the case because the analog circuitry is employed only to determine the error term $\delta^{(r)}$. By suitably scaling the analog signals so as to utilize the maximum analog dynamic range during each iteration, the analog errors are made to constitute only a small percentage of $\delta^{(r)}$, regardless how small this correction term becomes as convergence is approached. It is this feature of the method that makes it possible to employ relatively simple and inexpensive analog components.

The structure of the analog unit is determined by the choice of the linear operator $M$. This operator should be selected so as to produce as rapid a rate of convergence as possible. For optimum speed advantage, each problem to be solved would require a different analog unit. As is shown below, however, it is possible to design analog subroutines which can accommodate large classes of problems without change of structure, and at the same time effect impressive increases in computing efficiency.

## APPLICATION TO THE DSDT APPROACH

An important class of problems of the form of (1) is the linear algebraic system

$$L\phi = d \qquad (4)$$

where $\phi$ and $d$ are N-vectors, and L is a N x N matrix. If all the eigenvalues of L have positive real parts, (4) can be solved by the iterative scheme

$$\Delta^{(r)} = d - L\phi^{(r)} \qquad (5a)$$

$$\delta^{(r)} = M^{-1}\Delta^{(r)} \qquad (5b)$$

$$\phi^{(r+1)} = \phi^{(r)} + \theta\delta^{(r)} \qquad (5c)$$

where M is a N x N matrix while $\Delta^{(r)}$ and $\delta^{(r)}$ are N-vectors.

Fig. 7 is a block diagram of the hybrid computer implementation of (5), where the analog network constitutes a realization of the matrix M. Since all mathematical operations, which must be performed by the analog network in order to generate the solution vector, are algebraic in nature, no integrators, capacitors, or other memory or delay elements are required in the analog network. If, moreover, M is a Stieltjes matrix (a symmetric positive-definite matrix all of whose off-diagonal elements are zero or negative), no electrical components other than passive resistors are required to realize M. The analog subroutine functions in the following manner :
- During each iterative cycle (r) the vector $\Delta^{(r)}$ is read out of the digital computer in a serial fashion. Each component of this vector is transformed into analog form (i.e., a scaled analog voltage proportional to its magnitude) by means of the digital/analog converter (DAC).
- The analog voltages generated sequentially by the DAC are distributed to an array of sample-hold units. Each of these units accepts an analog voltage (present for a brief period of time at the output of the demultiplexer) and maintains this constant voltage, until its input voltage is updated during the following iterative cycle. Each sample-hold unit, therefore, acts as a memory of one element of the vector $\Delta^{(r)}$. At the end of the digital computer readout, all these elements exist simultaneously at the outputs of the array of sample-hold units.
- The output of each sample-hold unit forms a separate input to the analog network. This network is essentially a parallel-operating algebraic equation solver. As soon as the entire vector $\Delta^{(r)}$ is available at the outputs of the sample-hold units, this network "relaxes" to the correct solution of (5b). Since the analog network contains no reactances, the setting time required for the "relaxation" is less than 1µs. The vector $\delta^{(r)}$, therefore, is immediately available at the output node points of the analog network.
- By means of the multiplexer, the output node points of the network are sampled sequentially.
- Each component of the vector $\delta^{(r)}$ is translated in turn into digital form by means of the analog/digital converter (ADC).
- The elements of the vector $\delta^{(r)}$ are read into the digital computer.
- Equation (5c) is solved on the digital computer to complete the rth iterative cycle.

Any errors introduced by imperfections in the hybrid loop affect only the error vector $\delta^{(r)}$, and are, therefore, second-order effects. If, for practical reasons, M cannot be made closely equal to L, then it is important that an optimal or near-optimal value be chosen for $\theta$. If both L and M are symmetric and positive definite, it can be shown that the eigenvalues of $M^{-1}L$ are all real and positive. Let $\lambda_{max}$ and $\lambda_{min}$ denote the largest and smallest of these eigenvalues, respectively. The value of $\theta$ which maximizes the rate of convergence is then given by

$$\theta_{opt} = \frac{2}{\lambda_{min} + \lambda_{max}}$$

Although the exact calculation of $\lambda_{max}$ and $\lambda_{min}$ can be time-consuming, simple formulas for estimating them are often available.

This method is applicable to all systems of the type of (4) in which L is a stability matrix. Of particular interest, however, are classes of problems in which L is a sparse matrix of a special type. In the solution of partial differential equations by finite-difference techniques, the system of difference equations leads to a matrix L having only 3, 5, or 7 nonzero elements in each row, depending upon whether the problem is formulated in one, two, or three space dimensions. N is then equal to the number of finite-difference grid-points in the space domain. The development of efficient techniques for the solution of such a system of algebraic equations is important because N is often very large and because the system of equations must usually (in the case of nonlinear problems) be solved several times at each of a large number of time levels.

To illustrate the efficacy of the analog subroutine approach to such a problem consider the equation

$$\frac{\partial^2 \phi}{\partial x^2} + \frac{\partial^2 \phi}{\partial y^2} = \frac{\partial \phi}{\partial t} \tag{7}$$

with the boundary conditions : $\phi = 1$ everywhere on the boundary for all t ; and the initial conditions : $\phi(x, y, 0) = 1 - \sin \pi x \sin \pi y$. Using a backward-difference approximation, the finite-difference approximation for (7) is

$$\frac{-\phi_{i-1,j,k} - \phi_{i+1,j,k} + 4\phi_{i,j,k} - \phi_{i,j+1,k} - \phi_{i,j-1,k}}{h^2} = -\frac{\phi_{i,j,k} - \phi_{i,j,k-1}}{\Delta t} \tag{8}$$

where

$$\phi_{i,j,k} \equiv \phi(i\Delta x, j\Delta y, k\Delta t)$$

Letting $\Delta x = \Delta y = h = 0.10$, and $\Delta t = 0.01$, (8) becomes

$$-\phi_{i-1,j,k} - \phi_{i+1,j,k} + 5\phi_{i,j,k} - \phi_{i,j-1,k} - \phi_{i,j+1,k} = \phi_{i,j,k-1}$$

This set of finite-difference equations may be expressed in vector-matrix form as

$$L\phi_k = d_k = \hat{d}_k + b$$

where

$$L = \begin{vmatrix} L^\alpha & -I & 0 & 0 & 0 & 0 & 0 & 0 & 0 \\ -I & L^\alpha & -I & 0 & 0 & 0 & 0 & 0 & 0 \\ 0 & -I & L^\alpha & -I & 0 & 0 & 0 & 0 & 0 \\ 0 & 0 & -I & L^\alpha & -I & 0 & 0 & 0 & 0 \\ 0 & 0 & 0 & -I & L^\alpha & -I & 0 & 0 & 0 \\ 0 & 0 & 0 & 0 & -I & L^\alpha & -I & 0 & 0 \\ 0 & 0 & 0 & 0 & 0 & -I & L^\alpha & -I & 0 \\ 0 & 0 & 0 & 0 & 0 & 0 & -I & L^\alpha & -I \\ 0 & 0 & 0 & 0 & 0 & 0 & 0 & -I & L^\alpha \end{vmatrix} ; b = \begin{vmatrix} b^{\alpha 1} \\ b^{\alpha 2} \\ b^{\alpha 2} \\ b^{\alpha 2} \\ b^{\alpha 2} \\ b^{\alpha 2} \\ b^{\alpha 2} \\ b^{\alpha 2} \\ b^{\alpha 1} \end{vmatrix}$$

$$\hat{d}_k = \phi_{k-1}$$

and where

$$L^\alpha = \begin{vmatrix} 5 & -1 & 0 & 0 & 0 & 0 & 0 & 0 & 0 \\ -1 & 5 & -1 & 0 & 0 & 0 & 0 & 0 & 0 \\ 0 & -1 & 5 & -1 & 0 & 0 & 0 & 0 & 0 \\ 0 & 0 & -1 & 5 & -1 & 0 & 0 & 0 & 0 \\ 0 & 0 & 0 & -1 & 5 & -1 & 0 & 0 & 0 \\ 0 & 0 & 0 & 0 & -1 & 5 & -1 & 0 & 0 \\ 0 & 0 & 0 & 0 & 0 & -1 & 5 & -1 & 0 \\ 0 & 0 & 0 & 0 & 0 & 0 & -1 & 5 & -1 \\ 0 & 0 & 0 & 0 & 0 & 0 & 0 & -1 & 5 \end{vmatrix}$$

$$b^{\alpha 1} = \begin{vmatrix} 2 \\ 1 \\ 1 \\ 1 \\ 1 \\ 1 \\ 1 \\ 1 \\ 2 \end{vmatrix} \qquad b^{\alpha 2} = \begin{vmatrix} 1 \\ 0 \\ 0 \\ 0 \\ 0 \\ 0 \\ 0 \\ 0 \\ 1 \end{vmatrix}$$

and I is the 9 by 9 identity matrix.

The analog network has nine internal node points in the x and the y directions. The solution was carried out for 50 time levels with 6 decimal-place precision for each solution point. A total of 110 iterative cycles were required to traverse the entire time domain. The same problem was then solved by the successive overrelaxation method using the optimum overrelaxation factor. In this case, 334 iterative cycles were needed. The solutions by the two methods agreed at all points to better than five decimal places, demonstrating that the analog subroutine method, although using analog components limited by the quality of the electrical components, does not introduce any appreciable degradation in solution accuracy while providing an appreciable reduction in the number of computer runs. The analog subroutine is used in an error-correction mode which entirely obviates the disadvantage of component quality.

In the solution of problems of the type of (7), the so-called alternating direction implicit (ADI) method is sometimes used. In this technique, the iterations at each time level are usually minimized through the utilization of the tridiagonal algorithm. Where applicable, this method has been found to be somewhat faster than the analog subroutine approach. On the other hand the ADI method is often found to be impractical where the field geometry is irregular, where the problem is formulated in three space-dimensions, or where irregular finite-difference grids are employed. The analog subroutine approach is not subject to any of these limitations.

## CONCLUSION

Experience with a wide variety of engineering field problems (references [3] and [4]) has demonstrated that the approach described in this text is highly effective in reducing the digital computer time required for the solution of partial differential equations. This gain in speed results primarily from the reduction in the number of iterations. The analog subroutine approach is especially well adapted to the treatment of systems of algebraic equations since in that case the analog network has a particularly simple configuration. There exist, however, many other problem areas for which the general approach described here may prove to be beneficial.

## REFERENCES

[1] VANSTEENKISTE G.C., *Analog and Hybrid Computation*, course notes Von Karman Institute for Fluid Dynamics, Brussels (1970)

[2] KARPLUS W.J. and DRACUP J.A., *Technical Completion Report*, UCLA - ENG - 7142

[3] SHIH CHAU and DRACUP J.A., *Simulation of Evaporation from Constant Source with Finite Areas*, Water Resources Research, vol.5, n°1, Feb. 1969, pp.281-290

[4] STOIKE D. and KARPLUS W.J., *Heat transfer in pyrolytic graphite in a re-entry environment*, Journal Spacecraft Rockets, vol.5, Dec. 1968, pp. 1491-1493.

TABLE I

| ANALOG COMPUTER | DIGITAL COMPUTER |
|---|---|
| - DEPENDENT VARIABLES TREATED IN CONTINUOUS FORM | - HANDLING OF ALL DATA IN QUANTIZED OR DISCRETIZED FORM |
| - ACCURACY LIMITED BY THE QUALITY OF THE COMPUTER COMPONENTS | - ACCURACY DETERMINED BY THE NUMBER OF BITS CONTAINED IN MEMORY REGISTERS AND UPON THE SPECIFIC NUMERICAL TECHNIQUE SELECTED FOR A SPECIFIC PROBLEM |
| - PARALLEL OPERATION, ALL ELEMENTS OPERATING SIMULTANEOUSLY | - SERIAL OPERATION, TIME-SHARING OF ALL OPERATIONAL AND MEMORY UNITS |
| - HIGH SPEED OR REAL-TIME OPERATION, COMPUTING SPEEDS LIMITED BY BANDWIDTH OF THE ELEMENTS AND NOT BY COMPLEXITY OF THE PROBLEM | - SOLUTION TIMES RELATIVELY LONG, DETERMINED BY THE COMPLEXITY OF A PROBLEM; ABILITY TO REDUCE ERRORS BY INCREASING LENGTH OF TIME REQUIRED TO OBTAIN THE SOLUTION ON THE COMPUTER |
| - ABILITY TO PERFORM EFFICIENTLY MULTIPLICATION, INTEGRATION, ADDITION, NONLINEAR FUNCTION GENERATIONS, LIMITED ABILITY TO MAKE LOGICAL DECISIONS, STORE NUMERICAL DATA, PROVIDE TIME-DELAYS | - ABILITY TO PERFORM A LIMITED NUMBER OF ARITHMETIC OPERATIONS : ADDITION AND MULTIPLICATION; INTEGRATION AND DIFFERENTIATION REQUIRE APPROXIMATE TECHNIQUES; FACILITY FOR MEMORIZING DATA INDEFINITELY AND TO PERFORM LOGICAL OPERATIONS AND DECISIONS |
| - PROGRAMMING TECHNIQUES BASED ON SUBSTITUTION OF ANALOG COMPUTING ELEMENTS FOR PHYSICAL SYSTEM ELEMENTS | - PROGRAMMING TECHNIQUES BEAR LITTLE DIRECT RELATIONSHIP TO THE PROBLEM UNDER STUDY, BUT ARE FACILITATED BY COMPILERS AND ROUTINES |
| - FACILITY FOR INCLUDING ANALOG HARDWARE FROM A SYSTEM UNDER STUDY IN THE COMPUTER SIMULATION | - FLOATING-POINT OPERATIONS ELIMINATE SCALE FACTOR PROBLEMS |
| - PROVISIONS TO PERMIT THE ENGINEER TO EXPERIMENT BY ADJUSTING POTENTIOMETER SETTINGS ON THE COMPUTER; THEREBY GAINING DIRECT INSIGHT INTO SYSTEM OPERATION | - FACILITY FOR ALTERING AND CONTROLLING THE TOPOLOGY OF THE DATA FLOW WITHIN THE MACHINE ON THE BASIS OF CALCULATIONS |
| - SUITED FOR : PHYSICAL SIMULATION REAL TIME SIMULATION ENGINEERING EXPERIMENTATION INTEGRATION OF DIFFERENTIAL EQUATIONS | - SUITED FOR : STORAGE OF DATA LOGICAL FUNCTIONS AND DECISIONS HIGH SPEED ARITHMETIC SOLUTION OF ALGEBRAIC EQUATIONS |

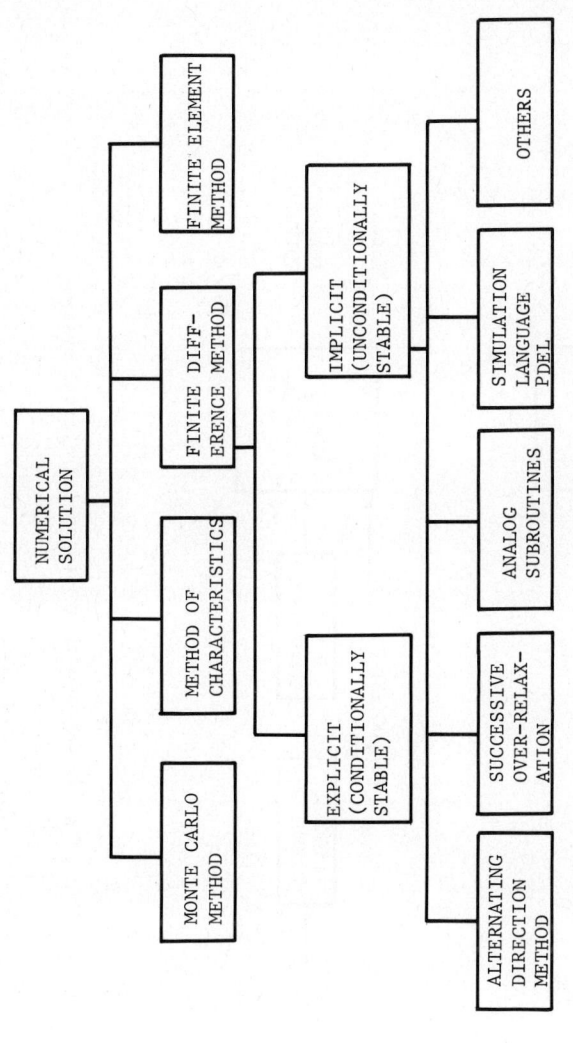

Fig. 1. Computation spectrum

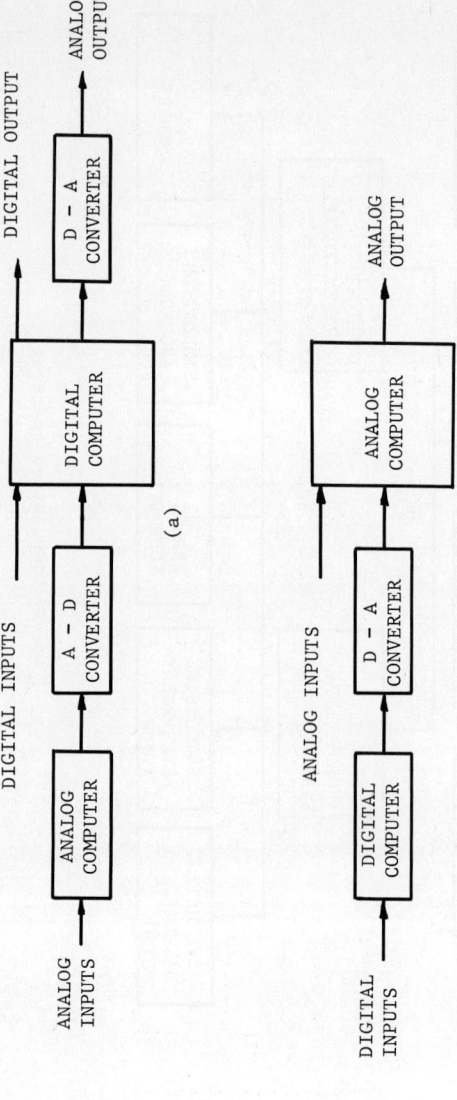

Fig. 2. Unilateral hybrid analog/digital systems

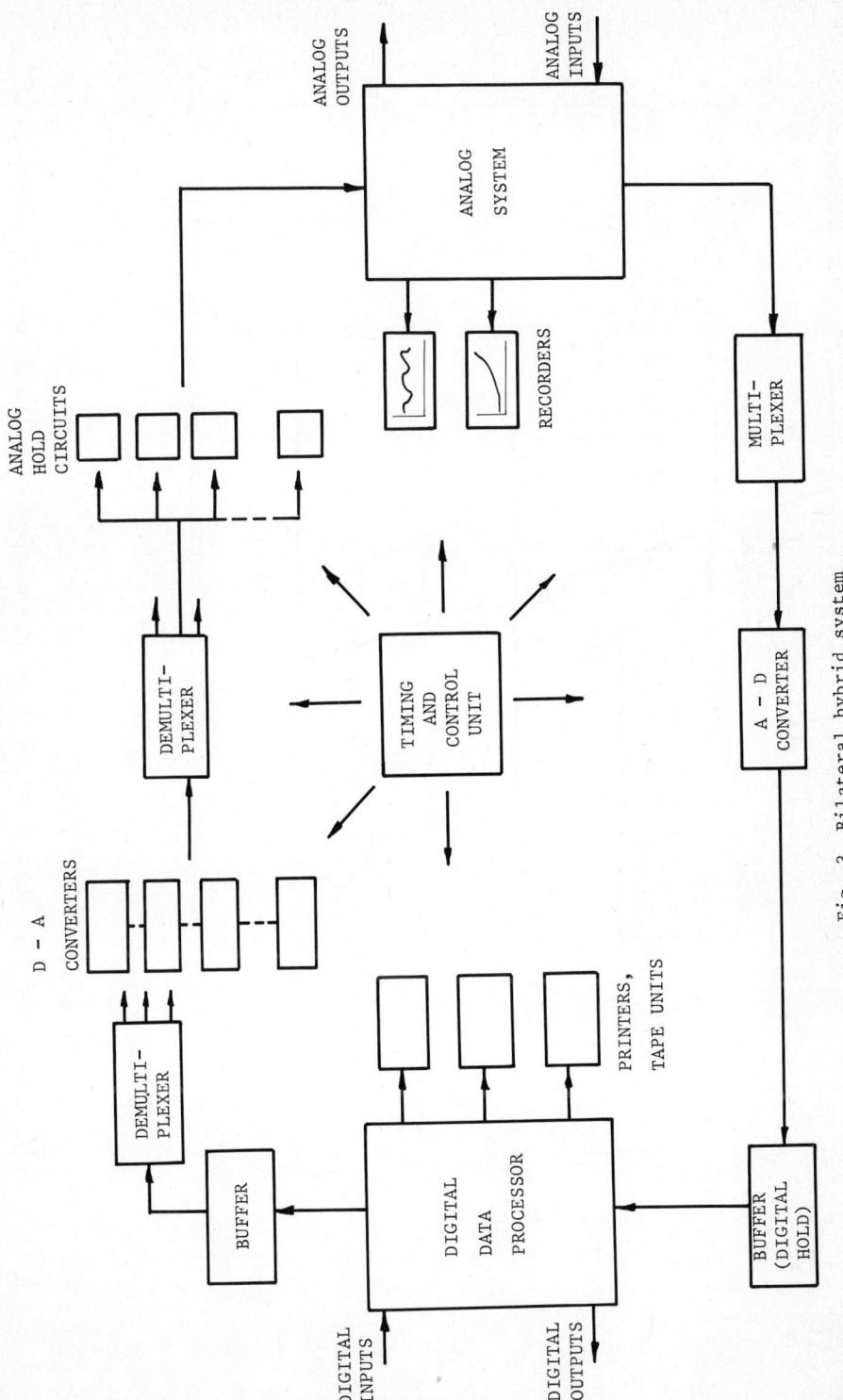

Fig. 3. Bilateral hybrid system

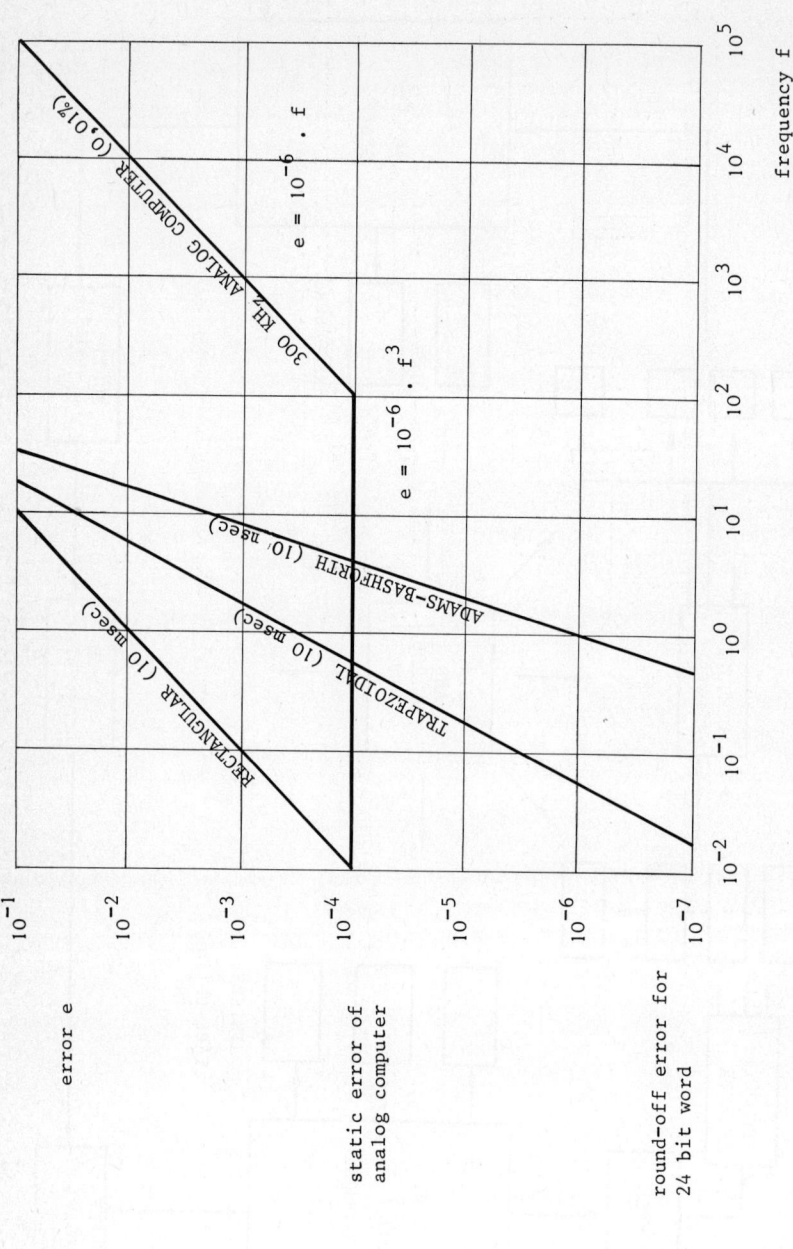

Fig. 4. Error vs. frequency diagram comparison of analog and digital implementation (from W. Giloi)

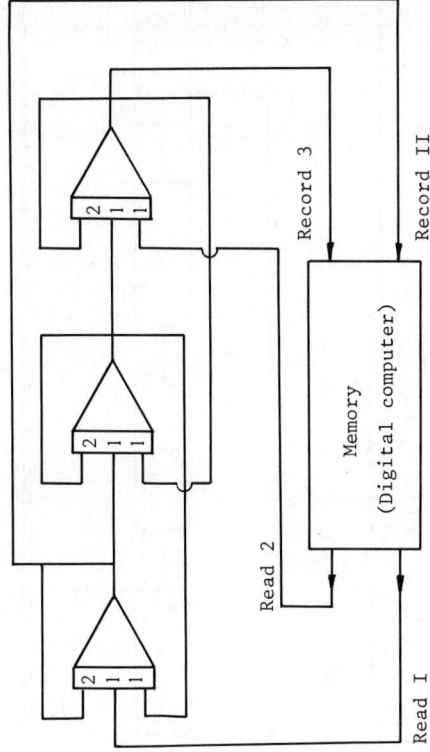

Fig. 5. Discrete - space continuous - time method

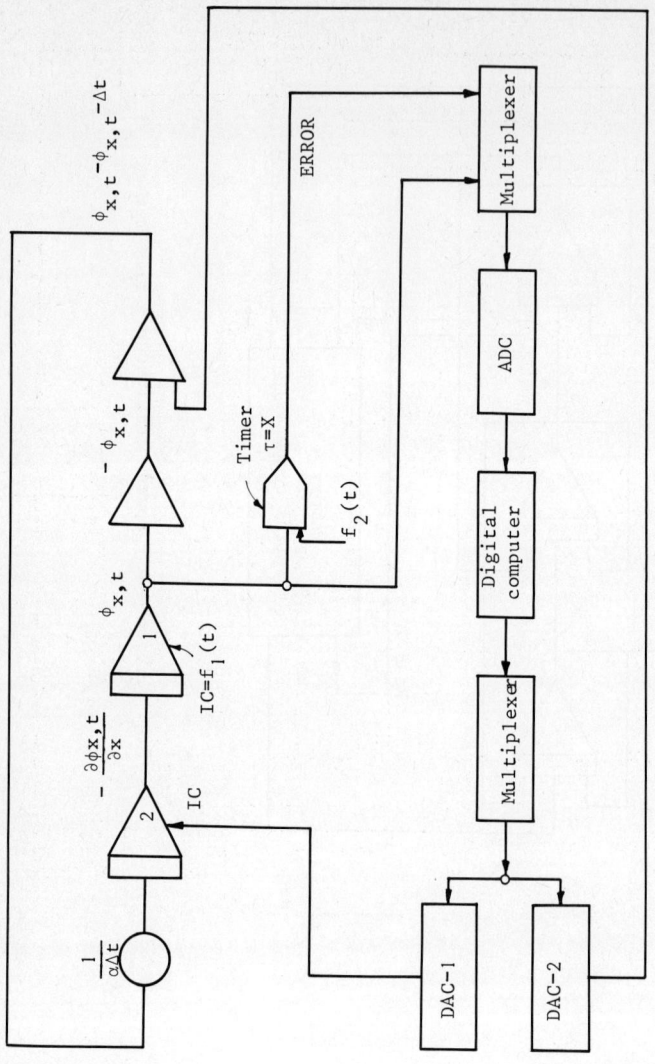

Fig. 6. Continuous - space discrete - time method

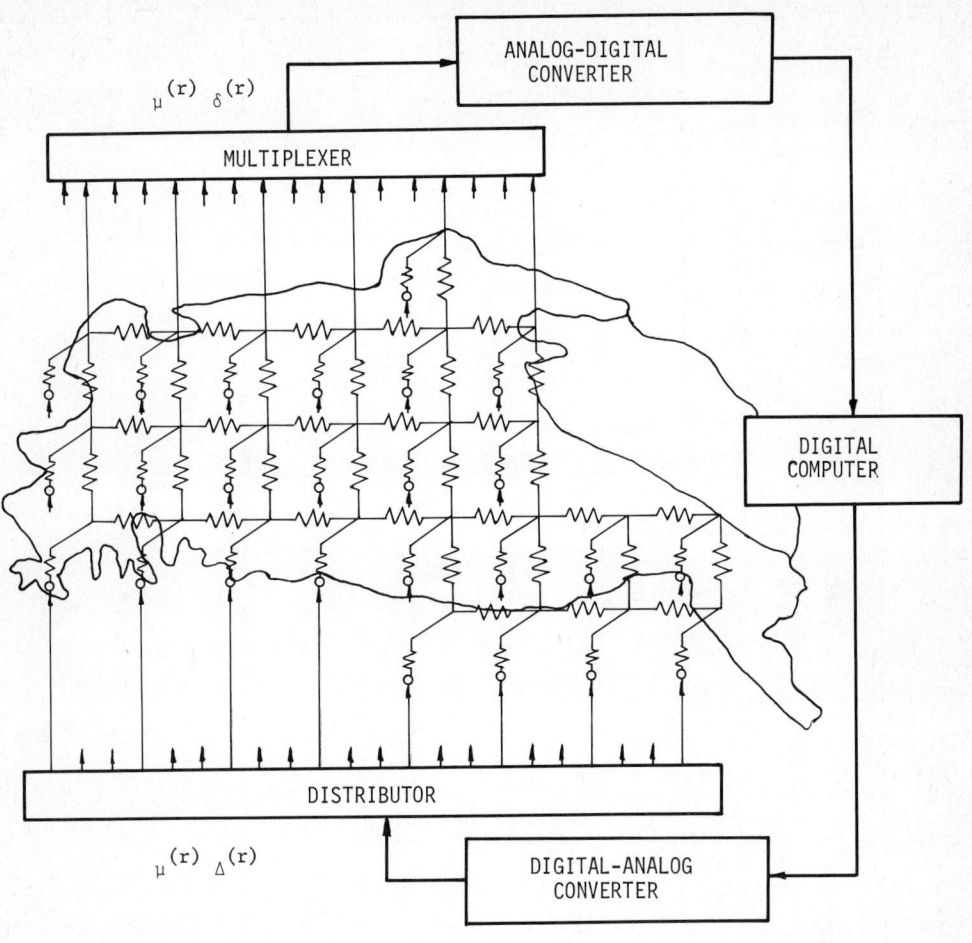

Fig. 7. DSDT Hybrid System

# COMPUTATION OF UNSTEADY BOUNDARY LAYERS

H.J. WIRZ

von Karman Institute for Fluid Dynamics
Rhode St Genese, Belguim

and

DFVLR, Germany

ABSTRACT

Starting with a brief discussion of some basic unsteady boundary layers (Rayleigh, Stokes), the fundamental equations describing three dimensional unsteady, laminar and turbulent compressible boundary layers are presented.

In order to facilitate the computation of unsteady boundary layers, various boundary layer transformations have been employed; their applicability is investigated.

Two different approaches to solve approximately (integral and finite difference method) the governing equations are discussed in some detail. Special attention is given to finite difference methods.

Finally, some available results are reported, indicating that the increasing capabilities of digital computers have made it possible to obtain solutions of some of these complex flow patterns.

1. INTRODUCTION

The subject of unsteady boundary layers, that is the addition of unsteadiness to viscous flows near boundaries, has again attracted considerable attention in recent years. The proceedings of the IUTAM symposium on Unsteady Boundary Layers (Ref. 1), 1971 trace out an impressive and vivid picture of the various activities in this particular field.

Unsteady boundary layers play an important role for the understanding of particular flow problems in many technical applications such as turbomachines, helicopter rotors, shock tubes, propellers, unsteady flight problems, duct and nozzle flows, combustion chambers, charging and discharging motions, etc.

The increasing capabilities of digital computers have made it possible to obtain solutions of some of these complex flow patterns in a reasonable amount of time. These results, however, are still only of limited usefulness to design engineers due to the many difficulties which remain to be solved.

Although several comprehensive summaries of the state of the theory of unsteady boundary layers have been prepared by Schlichting and Gersten (Ref. 2),, Rott (Ref. 3), Stuart (Ref. 4) and Stewartson (Ref. 5), the present state and the development of computational methods to solve approximately the basic equations is usually treated rather briefly.

At this point it is worthwhile to take note of some basic unsteady boundary layers which may serve as instructive examples for more general boundary layers.

Although the concept of boundary layer theory was introduced first by Prandtl 1904, as well known, the very first and simplest unsteady boundary layers, the Stokes and the Rayleigh layer, being linear, stem for an earlier period, the mid 19th century (Stokes 1851).

Consider a two-dimensional semi-infinite region of incompressible fluid in the domain $y > 0$, bounded by a rigid impermeable wall $y = 0$. If the flow is assumed to be independent of the coordinate x along the wall, then the Navier-Stokes and the continuity equations reduce to

$$\frac{\partial u}{\partial t} = -\frac{1}{\rho}\frac{\partial p}{\partial x} + \frac{\partial^2 u}{\partial y^2} \ ; \qquad \frac{\partial p}{\partial y} = 0 \qquad (1)$$

where $u(y,t)$ is the velocity in the x-direction, to is the time, p is the pressure (required to be linear in x), $\rho$ is the density and $\nu$ is the kinematic viscosity. These equations represent essentially an analogue to the heat conduction equation with heat addition. In the case of zero pressure gradient, equation 1 reduces to the simpler diffusion equation

$$\frac{\partial u}{\partial t} = \frac{\partial^2 u}{\partial y^2} \qquad (2)$$

The first basic layer, the Stokes layer, is periodic in t and satisfies the boundary conditions (zero pressure gradient)

$$\begin{array}{lll} y = 0 & u = u_w \cos\omega t & \\ y \to \infty & u = 0 & \end{array} \qquad (3)$$

and the solution is

$$u = u_w e^{-\eta} \cos(\omega t - \eta) \qquad (4)$$

where

$$\eta = y\left(\frac{\omega}{2\nu}\right)^{1/2} \qquad (5)$$

$\omega$ being the frequency. Another form of the Stokes layer arises from the boundary conditions:

$$\begin{aligned} y = 0 &: u = 0 \\ y \to \infty &: u = U_\infty \cos\omega t \end{aligned} \qquad (6)$$

with

$$-\frac{1}{\rho}\frac{\partial p}{\partial x} = -\omega U_\infty \sin\omega t$$

and the solution is

$$u = U_\infty \cos\omega t - U_\infty e^{-\eta} \cos(\omega t - \eta). \qquad (7)$$

As can be seen from these solutions there is no outflow from the boundary layers. Secondly, the thickness of the Stokes layer is proportional to $\left(\frac{\nu}{\omega}\right)^{1/2}$, and thirdly, the solutions (4) and (7) exhibit an important phase shift. The skin friction leads the velocity at the edge of the layer by $\frac{\pi}{4}$.

The Rayleigh layer, which represents the flow generated by a sudden movement of the plane $y = 0$, arises from the boundary conditions

$$\begin{aligned} t = 0 &\quad u(y,0) = 0; \quad y > 0 \\ y = 0 &\quad u = U_0 \\ y \to \infty &\quad u = 0 \end{aligned} \bigg\} \; t > 0 \qquad (8)$$

and the solution is

$$u = U_0 \, \mathrm{erfc}\left(\frac{y}{2(\nu t)^{1/2}}\right) \qquad (9)$$

The analogue form of (9) satisfies the following boundary conditions

$$t = 0 \quad u(y,t) = U \ ; \quad y > 0$$

$$y = 0 \quad u = 0$$
$$\qquad\qquad\qquad\qquad\qquad t > 0 \qquad\qquad\qquad\qquad (10)$$
$$y \to \infty \quad u = U_0$$

and the solution is

$$u = U_0 \ \text{erf} \ \frac{y}{2(\nu t)^{1/2}} \qquad\qquad\qquad\qquad (11)$$

Again, these solutions do not exhibit an outflow since the velocity at infinity is not allowed to depend on x, whilst the thickness of this layer is proportional to $(\nu t)^{1/2}$.

A third basic unsteady viscous layer is the critical layer (Stuart, Ref. 6) which occurs when a vorticity wave propagates in a shear flow $u(y)$. This flow is governed by the Heisenberg-Tollmien equation and its characteristic feature is the promotion of phase differences between the velocity components, yielding concomitant Reynolds stresses.

As long as stability problems are not considered, the Stokes and the Rayleigh layer serve as the simplest examples for many unsteady boundary layers.

Although it is convenient (Stuart, Ref. 7) to subdivide the subject into the following sections :
(i) the response of steady boundary layers to imposed fluctuations;
(ii) the generation of steady streaming by a purely oscillatory motion;
(iii) impulsive and other non-oscillatory boundary layers;
(iv) effects of rotation;
(v) stability of unsteady flows,
we here prefer to discuss a number of problems arising from the development of computational methods which numerically solve the basic parttial differential equations. Thus we may classify this work as follows
(i) governing fluid flow equations;
(ii) boundary layer transformations;
(iii) computational methods;
(iv) discussion of results.

## 2. GOVERNING FLUID FLOW EQUATIONS

For three-dimensional unsteady compressible laminar boundary layer flow, these equations may be written in terms of a cartesian coordinate system (inertia system) as

Continuity :

$$\frac{\partial \rho}{\partial t} + \frac{\partial}{\partial x}(\rho u) + \frac{\partial}{\partial y}(\rho v) + \frac{\partial}{\partial z}(\rho w) = 0 \tag{12}$$

Momentum :

$$\rho \frac{Du}{Dt} = -\frac{\partial p}{\partial x} + \frac{\partial}{\partial y}\left(\mu \frac{\partial u}{\partial y}\right) ; \tag{13}$$

$$\rho \frac{Dw}{Dt} = -\frac{\partial p}{\partial z} + \frac{\partial}{\partial y}\left(\mu \frac{\partial w}{\partial y}\right) ; \quad \frac{\partial p}{\partial y} = 0 \tag{14}$$

Energy :

$$c_p \rho \frac{DT}{Dt} - \frac{D_e p_e}{Dt} = \frac{\partial}{\partial y}\left(\lambda \frac{\partial T}{\partial y}\right) + \mu\left(\left(\frac{\partial u}{\partial y}\right)^2 + \left(\frac{\partial w}{\partial y}\right)^2\right) \tag{15}$$

where u, v, w are the boundary layer velocities in the x, y, z directions respectively; t is the time coordinate, $\rho$ is the density, $\nu$ is the viscosity, T is the temperature, p is the pressure, $\lambda$ is the heat conduction coefficient, $c_p$ is the specific heat at constant pressure. Finally, we have the operators

$$\frac{D}{Dt} = \frac{\partial}{\partial t} + u\frac{\partial}{\partial x} + v\frac{\partial}{\partial y} + w\frac{\partial}{\partial z} \tag{16}$$

and

$$\frac{D_e}{Dt} = \lim_{\substack{u \to u_e \\ w \to w_e \\ v \to 0}} \frac{D}{Dt} \tag{17}$$

where the subscript e denotes the flow at the edge of the boundary layer. The outer flow velocities and the temperature are connected with the pressure through

$$\rho_e \frac{D_e u_e}{Dt} = -\frac{\partial p}{\partial x} ; \quad \rho_e \frac{D_e w_e}{Dt} = -\frac{\partial p}{\partial z} \tag{18}$$

$$\frac{\partial p}{\partial t} = \rho_e \frac{D_e}{Dt}\left(c_p T_e + \frac{(u_e^2 + w_e^2)}{2}\right) \tag{19}$$

In order to complete these equations a thermal and caloric equation of state together with a specification of the fluid properties ($\mu, \lambda$) must be given. Usually the following laws are applied (perfect gas)

$$p = \rho RT, \quad c_p = \text{const.} \tag{20}$$

and $\mu = \mu(T)$ together with $\lambda = \dfrac{\mu c_p}{Pr}$ (21)

where R is the gas constant and Pr is the Prandtl number, which is assumed to be constant.

The incompressible case of these equations is derived by setting $\rho$ constant. Additionally, in the energy equations (15), the second term on the left side does not appear, and the dissipation term in (15) is usually neglected.

The very simplest case for two-dimensional and incompressible flows has been treated to some extent, so that it is worthwhile to write down these equations explicitly.

Continuity :

$$\frac{\partial u}{\partial x} + \frac{\partial v}{\partial y} = 0 \tag{22}$$

Momentum :

$$\frac{\partial u}{\partial t} + u \frac{\partial u}{\partial x} + v \frac{\partial u}{\partial y} = -\frac{1}{\rho} \frac{\partial p}{\partial x} + \nu \frac{\partial^2 u}{\partial y^2} \tag{23}$$

where $\nu$ is the kinematic viscosity. The pressure gradient is given by

$$-\frac{1}{\rho} \frac{\partial p}{\partial x} = \frac{\partial u_e}{\partial t} + u_e \frac{\partial u_e}{\partial x} \tag{24}$$

The set of partial differential equations given so far has to be completed by appropriate boundary and initial conditions. The formulation of boundary conditions (zero velocity difference between fluid and wall at the wall together with either a prescribed temperature or heat flux at the wall, and at the edge of the layers, the free stream conditions for velocities and temperature) usually do not involve any problems. However, it must be realized that in most of the practical problems the outer flow field is not known, especially for three dimensional unsteady problems.

Additionally, initial conditions for the t, x, z coordinates must be prescribed. Their explicit formulation is usually a difficult and complicated problem.

We will discuss some aspects of this problem in more detail in connection with the presentation of solved problems.

So far we have mentioned only laminar flows. In most of the practical problems, however, turbulent flows are of even greater importance than laminar flows.

In the simplest case of an incompressible two-dimensional flow the usual derivation of such equations leads to the following system

$$\frac{\partial u}{\partial x} + \frac{\partial v}{\partial y} = 0 \tag{25}$$

$$\frac{\partial u}{\partial t} + u \frac{\partial u}{\partial x} + v \frac{\partial u}{\partial y} = - \frac{1}{\rho} \frac{\partial p}{\partial x} + \frac{1}{\rho} \frac{\partial \tau}{\partial y} \tag{26}$$

where the shear stress is given by

$$\tau = \mu \frac{\partial u}{\partial y} - \rho \overline{u'v'} \tag{27}$$

the latter term being the Reynolds shear stress.

Cebeci and Keller (Ref. 8) use the eddy viscosity concept (composite layers) to relate the Reynolds shear stress to the mean flow velocity, and discuss differences and similarities between an spatially one dimensional unsteady flow and a steady two dimensional flow.

Another concept to close the above system of equations is achieved by making use of the turbulent kinetic energy equation. This approach has been used by Patel and Nash (Ref. 9) in the manner suggested by Townsend (Ref. 10) and Bradshaw, Ferris and Altwell (Ref. 11).

Based on three essential assumptions, the following equation for the Reynolds shear stress $\tau$ (the shear stress involving the molecular viscosity is regarded as negligible) has been treated by Patel and Nash to compute some unsteady turbulent boundary layers:

$$\frac{\partial \tau}{\partial t} + u \frac{\partial \tau}{\partial x} + v \frac{\partial \tau}{\partial y} - 2a_1 \tau \frac{\partial u}{\partial y} + 2a_1 \frac{\tau_{max}}{\rho U_e} \frac{\partial}{\partial y} (a_2 \tau)$$
$$+ \frac{a_1}{L} \tau^{3/2} \rho^{1/2} = 0 \tag{28}$$

For the present purpose, here it is sufficient to note that the coefficient $a_1$ is assumed to be a universal constant (equal to 0.15), while $a_2$ and L are universal empirical functions of $\frac{y}{\delta}$, $\delta$ being the boundary layer thickness. A sketch of these functions is shown in figure 1.

Two different cases have been treated numerically. The first is a flat plate turbulent boundary layer subjected to periodic oscillations in the free stream. Only two sets of measurements, those due to Karlson (Ref. 12) and Miller (Ref. 13), seem to be available for the purpose of comparison. Additionally, only time averaged (over a complete cycle) mean velocity profiles are reported, so that a detailed comparison is not possible.

The second case is a boundary layer subjected to an adverse free stream velocity gradient which remains constant in the x-direction and is periodic in time. No experimental results are available.

The essential difficulty in predicting such flows arises from the so-called 'closure problem' and not primarily from computational aspects. This problem has not been resolved satisfactorily up to now, even for steady turbulent boundary layer flows.

## 3. BOUNDARY LAYER TRANSFORMATIONS

The set of equations describing compressible three dimensional unsteady laminar boundary layer flows (12-21) have been written in physical cartesian coordinates, which are of course usually the simplest ones. In most practical problems, however, further transformations are often needed. The necessity for such transformation arises mainly from three sources.

The boundary layer flow over a real body requires, in general, the formulation of the boundary layer equations in curvilinear coordinates (see for example reference 14). The choice of these coordinates (usually orthogonal ones) may depend on special physical conditions, on the availability of the free stream data, but also on the (numerical) determination of the metric coefficients. Streamlines of the outer flow at a fixed time and their orthogonal trajectories together with the outer normal of the body may form a suitable system of curvilinear coordinates. Such a system is reported by Piquet and Zeytounian (Ref. 15).

Many unsteady flow phenomena may be better described in moving or rotating coordinates, which are then no longer inertia systems. Additional 'forces' as for example Coriolis and centrifugal ones, will appear in a rotating coordinate system. The system of equations for unsteady, incompressible boundary layer flow about a rotating airfoil has been recently studied by McCroskey and Yaggy (Ref. 16) in order to numerically investigate a few problems of helicopter rotor boundary layers.

Many of the difficulties associated with the computation of unsteady boundary layers may be removed by special coordinate transformations. We shall discuss these aspects in some detail.

In order to avoid the explicit calculation of the density in the basic set of equations, the following transformation may be employed. Additionally, the continuity equation (12) is integrated identically in defining two functions ,

$$\xi = x; \quad \eta = \int_0^y \frac{\rho}{\rho_\infty} dy \ ; \quad \zeta = z \ ; \quad \tau = t \tag{29}$$

$$u = \frac{\rho_\infty}{\rho} \frac{\partial \psi}{\partial y} \ ; \quad w = \frac{\rho_\infty}{\rho} \frac{\partial \chi}{\partial y} \ ; \quad v = - \frac{\rho_\infty}{\rho} (\frac{\partial \psi}{\partial x} + \frac{\partial \chi}{\partial z} + \frac{\partial \eta}{\partial t}) \tag{30}$$

where $\rho_\infty$ is a constant reference density. Introducing a velocity $v^+$ through

$$v^+ = -(\psi_\xi + \chi_\zeta) \tag{31}$$

the operator $\frac{D}{Dt}$ remains nearly unchanged

$$\frac{D}{Dt} = \frac{D}{D\tau} \equiv \frac{\partial}{\partial \tau} + u \frac{\partial}{\partial \xi} + v^+ \frac{\partial}{\partial \eta} + w \frac{\partial}{\partial \zeta} \tag{32}$$

The resulting set of equations thus may be written as
Continuity :

$$u_\xi + v^+_\eta + w_\zeta = 0 \tag{33}$$

Momentum :

$$\frac{Du}{D\tau} = -\frac{1}{\rho_e} \frac{\partial p}{\partial \xi} \frac{T}{T_e} + \frac{\partial}{\partial \eta} (\frac{\rho \mu}{\rho_\infty \rho_\infty} \frac{\partial u}{\partial \eta}) \tag{34}$$

$$\frac{Dw}{D\tau} = -\frac{1}{\rho_e} \frac{\partial p}{\partial \zeta} \frac{T}{T_e} + \frac{\partial}{\partial \eta} (\frac{\rho \mu}{\rho_\infty \rho_\infty} \frac{\partial u}{\partial \eta}) \tag{35}$$

Energy :

$$c_p \frac{DT}{D\tau} - \frac{1}{\rho_e} \frac{D_e p_e}{D\tau} \frac{T}{T_e} = \frac{\partial}{\partial \eta}\left(\frac{\lambda \rho}{\rho_\infty \rho_\infty} \frac{\partial T}{\partial \eta}\right) + \frac{\mu \rho}{\rho_\infty \rho_\infty}\left(\left(\frac{\partial u}{\partial \eta}\right)^2 + \left(\frac{\partial w}{\partial \eta}\right)^2\right) \tag{36}$$

This transformation is originally due to Dorodnitzyn (Ref. 17), and may be further extended.

In order to remove some of the difficulties associated with the leading edge singularities, the following transformation is often employed. Consider a two dimensional unsteady boundary layer, written in a non dimensional form :

$$u_x + v_y = 0 \tag{37}$$

$$u_t + uu_x + vu_y = \frac{\partial U_e}{\partial t} + u_e \frac{\partial U_e}{\partial x} + u_{yy}$$

subjected to the following transformations :

$$\xi = x \; ; \quad \eta = \left(\frac{U_e}{2x}\right)^{1/2} y \; ; \quad \tau = t \tag{38}$$

$$f' \equiv \frac{\partial f}{\partial \eta} = \frac{u}{U_e} \; ; \quad \bar{v} = v + \frac{1}{2}(\beta_\xi - 1)f' + \frac{1}{2}\beta_\tau \eta \tag{39}$$

The momentum equation then takes the form

$$\frac{\xi}{U_e}\frac{\partial f'}{\partial \tau} + f'\frac{\partial f'}{\partial \xi} + \bar{v}\frac{\partial f'}{\partial \eta} = \beta_\xi(1 - f'^2) + \beta_\tau(1 - f') + \frac{1}{2}\frac{\partial^2 f'}{\partial \eta^2} \tag{40}$$

where $\beta_\xi$ and $\beta_\tau$ are

$$\beta_\xi = \frac{\xi}{U_e}\frac{\partial U_e}{\partial \xi} \; ; \quad \beta_\tau = \frac{\xi}{U_e^2}\frac{\partial U_e}{\partial \tau} \tag{41}$$

The advantages of such a trandformation, which may be applied also to the three dimensional case, (see Dwyer, Ref. 18), are :
(i) possible leading edge singularities are removed;
(ii) an equation(s) to determine the initial conditions along $\xi = 0$ may be obtained by taking the limit $\xi \to 0$;
(iii) the boundary layer thickness is very nearly constant in terms of the transformed coordinate ($\eta \simeq 6$);
(iv) the derivatives of the independent variables are stretched so that high accuracy may be obtained with relatively large step sizes.

Another transformation (Crocco, Ref. 19) which removes the usual difficulty with the location of the outer edge of the boundary layer (the coordinate y has to be taken finite), is defined through

$$\xi = x \ ; \quad \eta = \frac{u}{U_e} \ ; \quad \tau = t \tag{42}$$

$$\phi = \frac{1}{U_e} \frac{\partial u}{\partial y} \tag{43}$$

The boundary layer equation (37) in the new form is :

$$\phi^2 \frac{\partial^2 \phi}{\partial \eta^2} + A \frac{\partial \phi}{\partial \eta} - B\phi - \frac{\partial \phi}{\partial \tau} - \eta U_e \frac{\partial \phi}{\partial \xi} = 0 \tag{44}$$

while the usual boundary conditions, now transformed, yield

$$\eta = 0 \qquad \phi \frac{\partial \phi}{\partial \eta} + C = 0$$

$$\eta = 1 \qquad \phi = 0.$$

The coefficients A, B, C are given functions of the independent variables

$$A = (\eta^2 - 1) \frac{\partial U_e}{\partial x} + (\eta - 1) \frac{1}{U_e} \frac{\partial U_e}{\partial \tau}$$

$$B = \eta \frac{\partial U_e}{\partial x} + \frac{1}{U_e} \frac{\partial U_e}{\partial \tau} \tag{46}$$

$$C = \frac{\partial U_e}{\partial x} + \frac{1}{U_e} \frac{\partial U_e}{\partial \tau}$$

This type of transformation has been extensively used in the work of Piquet (Ref. 20). The advantages are obvious : (i) the integration domain in the $\eta$ direction is bounded ($0 \leq \eta \leq 1$), (ii) the main equation (44) is linear except for the first term, (iii) the extension of this transformation to systems of two dimensional unsteady boundary layers is possible.

On the other hand, this transformation has also disadvantages, of which the problem of uniqueness of the solutions in cases where the velocity profile exhibits an overshoot, is the severest one. The necessary and sufficient condition is $\phi \neq 0$ in $0 < \eta < 1$. Since it is well known that unsteady boundary layers are especially liable to exhibit the effect of an overshoot, care has to be taken.

Finally, a group of transformations needs to be considered which reduces the partial differential equations for unsteady boundary layers to differential equations with fewer independent variables than the original ones. The solutions of these equations (usually called similarity solutions) are extremely helpful for many reasons.

In cases where one succeeds in reducing the partial differential equations to nonlinear ordinary ones, their solutions are normally easy to obtain. Besides their physical relevance, they may be used to check computational procedures designed to solve the complete partial differential equations. Sometimes these solutions may be used in the construction of approximate methods of the von Karman-Pohlhausen type.

For incompressible two dimensional unsteady boundary layers, similarity solutions with one independent varaible have been reported by Schuh (Ref. 20) and Geis (Ref. 21). The free stream is of the form $U_e = \frac{mx}{t}$ or $U_e = ct^n$, while Yang (Ref. 22) treated the case $u_e = x/(a+bt)$, where a, b are constants. A class of similarity solutions for unsteady spatially one dimensional compressible boundary layers is considered by Yang and Huag (Ref. 23), the free stream velocity being again of the form $u_e = ct^n$. Gabbert (Ref. 24) and Wirz (Ref. 25) finally derived a set of similarity solutions for spatially two dimensional compressible flows with free stream velocities of the form $u_e = \frac{mx}{t}$; $u_e = mx$; $u_e = \frac{m}{t}$.

Another important aspect of these similarity (only one independent variable) and semi-similarity (more than one independent variable) solutions is associated with the problem of obtaining initial conditions to start a general computational method designed to solve the complete partial differential equations. It is often possible to derive approximate initial conditions in making use of special similarity or semi-similarity solutions. Semi-similarity solutions have been reported by Tani (Ref. 26), who considered the case $u_e = U_0 - \frac{x}{T-t}$, $U_0$, T being constants. A more general class of this type of solution is discussed by Hassan (Ref. 27) (see also Hayasi, Ref. 28).

## 4. COMPUTATIONAL METHODS

The problem of theoretically predicting unsteady boundary layer flows with sufficiently general boundary and initial conditions usually requires, in the simplest case, the calculation of approximate solutions of at least one partial differential equation with three independent variables. The situation is even more complicated if three dimensional unsteady boundary layers are considered, leading to systems of differential equations with four independent variables.

Two basic approaches have been successfully developed, which we will discussed here in some detail.

The first one, usually referred to as the integral method, is a natural extension of the well known von Karman-Pohlhausen procedure to unsteady boundary layers. Mathematically speaking, these methods belong to a wider class of approximate methods based upon weighted residuals.

Schuh (Ref. 29) presented in 1953 the first integral method of this type to calculate unsteady two dimensional incompressible boundary layers on bodies with arbitrary shape and arbitrary varying free stream velocities.

Although this type of approximate methods is still employed, more recently, the finite difference approach has attracted more attention because of its wider and easier applicability to complicated problems.

The basic idea of the integral method applied to unsteady boundary layers may best be explained by considering the following set of equations describing the development of momentum and thermal laminar boundary layers in an incompressible laminar fluid.

Continuity

$$\frac{\partial u}{\partial x} + \frac{\partial v}{\partial y} = 0 \tag{47}$$

Momentum

$$\frac{\partial u}{\partial t} + u \frac{\partial u}{\partial x} + v \frac{\partial u}{\partial y} = \frac{\partial U_e}{\partial t} + U_e \frac{\partial U_e}{\partial x} + \frac{\partial^2 u}{\partial y^2} \tag{48}$$

Energy

$$\frac{\partial T}{\partial t} + u \frac{\partial T}{\partial x} + v \frac{\partial T}{\partial y} = \frac{1}{\sigma} \frac{\partial^2 T}{\partial y^2} \tag{49}$$

together with the boundary conditions :

$$y = 0, \quad u = v = 0, \quad T = T_w$$
$$y \to \infty, \quad u = U_e(x,t), \quad T = T_e, \tag{50}$$

$T_w$ and $T_e$ being constants.

These equations, written here in a nondimensional form, where u,v are the velocities and T is the temperature and $\sigma$ is the Prandtl number, have been treated to some extend by Yang (Ref. 30) and Miller (Ref. 31). The work of Schuh (Ref. 29) is based on the momentum equation only, plus an additional equation for the balance of mechanical energy.

If the velocity component v is eliminated from the momentum and energy equation by using the continuity equation and each term in equation 48 and 49 is integrated with respect to y from 0 to $\infty$, the so called integral momentum and energy equations are obtained :

$$\frac{\partial}{\partial t}(U_e \delta_1) + U_e^2 \frac{\partial \delta_2}{\partial x} + U_e \frac{\partial U_e}{\partial x}(\delta_1 + 2\delta_2) = \left(\frac{\partial u}{\partial y}\right)_0 \tag{51}$$

$$\frac{\partial}{\partial t}(\theta_1) + U_e \frac{\partial \theta_2}{\partial x} + \frac{\partial U_e}{\partial x} \theta_2 = -\frac{1}{\sigma}\left(\frac{\partial \theta}{\partial y}\right)_0, \tag{52}$$

where

$$\delta_1 = \int_0^\infty \left(1 - \frac{u}{U_e}\right) dy, \qquad \delta_2 = \int_0^\infty \frac{u}{U_e}\left(1 - \frac{u}{U_e}\right) dy \tag{53}$$

are the displacement and the momentum thickness, and $\theta_1$ and $\theta_2$ are defined with $\theta = (T-T_e)/(T_w-T_e)$ by

$$\theta_1 = \int_0^\infty \theta \, dy \qquad \theta_2 = \int_0^\infty \frac{u}{U_e} \theta \, dy \tag{54}$$

If each term in the original momentum equation is multiplied by u before integrating as before, the so called integral (mechanical) energy equation is obtained

$$\frac{U_e}{2} \frac{\partial \delta_1}{\partial t} + \frac{1}{2} \frac{\partial}{\partial t} (U_e^2 \delta_2) + \frac{1}{2} \frac{\partial}{\partial x} (U_e^3 \delta_3) = \int_0^\infty \left(\frac{\partial u}{\partial y}\right)^2 dy \qquad (55)$$

where

$$\delta_3 = \int_0^\infty \frac{u}{U_e} \left(1 - \left(\frac{u}{U_e}\right)^2\right) dy \qquad (56)$$

is the "energy-" thickness of the boundary layer.

The generalization of obtaining additional integral equations is obvious. Such an approach has been explored in the work of Koob and Abott (Ref. 32).

The system of integral equations (51) and (52) contains, in principle, six unknowns, whereas only two equations are given so that a closure of the problem is only achieved if additional equations (algebraic or differential equations) for the remaining quantities can be formulated. This is the key problem of all approximate methods based on integral equations.

The integral methods have been frequently used and are still in common use to calculate steady boundary layers, where the basic equations reduce to ordinary differential equations. However, this advantage of the method is lost, if unsteady problems or steady three dimensional boundary layers are considered. In all these cases still partial differential equations must be solved numerically by finite difference methods, although one might say that the reduction of one independent variable is always a clear advantage with respect to the computer storage to be needed.

In order to close the basic integral equations, the following ideas have been employed :
Assuming that all unsteady velocity and temperature profiles for a specific problem, satisfying the boundary conditions, belong to a single parameter family of curves, the quantitites $\delta_1$, $\delta_2$, $\theta_1$, $\theta_2$ and $\left(\frac{\partial u}{\partial y}\right)_0$ and $\frac{1}{\sigma} \left(\frac{\partial \theta}{\partial y}\right)_0$ are functions of this parameter only, so that all unknowns may be expressed in terms of the thicknessess $\delta_2$ and $\theta_2$, for instance. These relations, often termed as "universal functions" are usually rather complcated but may be calculated in advance. The essential parameter is

usually derived from a so called compatibility condition, which may be the partial differential equation evaluated at the wall. Schuh (Ref. 29), Yang (Ref. 30) and others use the following parameter

$$\lambda \equiv - \frac{\delta_2^2}{U_e} \left(\frac{\partial^2 u}{\partial y^2}\right)_0 = \delta_2^2 \left(\frac{\partial U_e}{\partial x} + \frac{1}{U_e} \frac{\partial U_e}{\partial t}\right) \tag{57}$$

which is the natural extension of the parameter frequently used in steady two dimensional boundary layers.

The accuracy of the results depends strongly on the choice of the single parameter family of profiles for velocity and temperature. Fourth order polynomials, Hartree-profiles and similarity solutions of the unsteady equations have been applied, yielding slightly different results, if the region of separation where remarkable differences occur, is excluded.

In order to improve the accuracy, profiles with more than one parameter need to be considered. Although these profiles may be found rather easily, a greater number of integral equations (partial differential equations in x and t) must be solved numerically. In addition, all the "universal functions" are now two parametric functions, which need to be calculated and stored. Thus, we see that the involved numerical work is strongly increasing being comparable with the pure finite difference methods. Because of the lack of any convergence proof, even with higher order methods, the accuracy of the solutions cannot be estimated.

A clear advantage, however, needs finally to be mentioned. The formulation of the initial conditions for unsteady boundary layers does not involved the dependency on the y-coordinate any more and is therefore often much more easy to obtain.

In trying to assess the relative merits of the integral methods, which have been successfully applied to a number of unsteady problems, the limitations (lack of generality and accuracy) indicate that only special unsteady boundary layers may be treated with easy success.

The second method is entirely characterized by the use of finite differences to transform the partial differential equations into a set of algebraic equations, which then are solved simultaneously on a computer. The exploration of this approach is still developing, although quite a number of papers have already been published.

In order to study the method and the associated difficulties (approximation of the differential equation, stability and convergency, initial conditions, computational procedures), consider the following simple model problem, which represents, to some extend, the basic features of unsteady boundary layers

$$\frac{\partial u}{\partial t} + U(y) \frac{\partial u}{\partial x} = \sigma \frac{\partial^2 u}{\partial y^2} \tag{58}$$

where $u(x,y,t)$, say the velocity, is the single unknown, $t,x,y$ are the independent variables, $U(y)$ is a prescribed function and $\sigma$ is a positive constant. The domain of integration may be given as

$$B = \{x,y,t \mid x \geq 0, \quad t \geq 0, \quad 0 \leq y < 1\} \tag{59}$$

together with boundary and initial conditions, which we do not specify at this point.

Although general solutions of the linear differential equation are not known, we easily derive a special solution for u, if U is assumed to be constant, say $U_0$. This solution writes

$$u(x,y,t) = \sum_\rho A_\rho(\xi) e^{-\sigma k_\rho^2 t} e^{\sqrt{-1} k_\rho y} \tag{60}$$

where the lines $\xi = x - U_0 t$, $\xi = $ const, form the characteristics along which the solution is convected and where the $A_\rho(\xi)$ are functions defined by the initial conditions, the $k_\rho$ being constants. The important physical aspects of this simple solution are that the flow quantity u is convected along the characteristic line $\xi = x - U_0 t$ and attenuated with increasing time, due to the (double) parabolic nature of the equation. In the more general case, the characteristics are given by

$$\frac{dx}{dt} = U(y) \tag{61}$$

so that in each plane $y = $ const. the slope of the characteristic is different. The maximum turning angle between these characteristic direction is given by the formula

$$\phi = \arctan \frac{U_{max} - U_{min}}{1 + U_{max} U_{min}} \; .$$

The limiting characteristic directions at a point P of the x-t plane form the domain of dependence and the domain of influence, which must be taken into consideration in order to specify correctly the initial conditions. In the simpler case of $U = U_0$, the turning angle is zero, or physically speaking, the dispersion is zero.

Another important feature of our simple equation with $U = U_0$ may be seen as follows. If each term of the equation 59 is multiplied by u and integrated with respect to y between the boundaries $y = 0$ and $y = 1$, the following equation is obtained:

$$\frac{\partial}{\partial t} \int_0^1 u^2 dy + U_0 \frac{\partial}{\partial x} \int_0^1 u^2 dy = 2\sigma u \frac{\partial u}{\partial y}\bigg|_0^1 - 2\sigma \int_0^1 \left(\frac{\partial u}{\partial y}\right)^2 dy \qquad (63)$$

where no boundary conditions have been inserted. This equation represents in a sense the balance of the "energy" of the system. The first term on the right hand side represents the work of the "shear stress" at the boundaries and the latter one the "dissipation". In order to have a bounded solution of our problem, the boundary conditions cannot be chosen arbitrarily; the right hand side of equation 62 must always be less than zero. Fortunately, in boundary layer problems, this condition seems to be always fullfilled.

Many of the features mentioned so far are quite similar to those associated with the problem of integrating three dimensional steady boundary layers. For a discussion of these problems, the reader may refer to Krause (Ref. 33).

In the following chapter we will discuss a few finite difference schemes, which solve our basic equation 58 numerically. A grid system of equal mesh size in the domain B is introduced in writing

$$\begin{aligned} x_i &= i\Delta x, & i &= 0, 1, 2, \ldots \\ y_j &= j\Delta y, & j &= 0, 1, 2, \ldots, N \\ t_k &= k\Delta t, & k &= 0, 1, 2, \ldots \end{aligned} \qquad (64)$$

where $\Delta x$, $\Delta y$, $\Delta t$ are the space and time increments, respectively. The approximate solution is denoted by

$$u_{i,k}^j \approx u(x_i, t_k, y_j)$$

and in addition we introduce two step parameters:

$$\lambda_j = \frac{\Delta t}{\Delta x} U(y_j), \qquad s = \sigma \frac{\Delta t}{(\Delta y)^2}, \qquad \text{s being always positive.} \qquad (65)$$

Although the methods to be presented now solve only our model problem, the extension to the more complicated unsteady boundary layers is straightforward.

In figure 2 we have depicted five different schemes, two explicit and three implicit ones, which we will further investigate.

By taking first order differences for the x and t derivatives and second order centered differences for the diffusion term, the explicit schemes may be written as

$$u_{i+1,k+1}^j = E_j\, u_{i,k+1}^j + F_j\, u_{i+1;k}^j + G_j\, u_{i,k}^j \qquad (66)$$

where the operators $E_j$, $F_j$ and $G_j$, which depend on the y-coordinate, are given through

Scheme a)  $\quad E_j = 0$

$\qquad\qquad F_j = \left((1-\lambda_j)\delta + s\delta_y^2\right)$  $\qquad\qquad (67)$

$\qquad\qquad G_j = \lambda_j$

Scheme b)  $\quad E_j = \dfrac{1}{\lambda_j}\left((\lambda_j-1)\delta + s\delta_y^2\right)$

$\qquad\qquad F_j = 0$  $\qquad\qquad (68)$

$\qquad\qquad G_j = \dfrac{1}{\lambda_j}.$

In these equations, the unity operator $\delta$ and the usual central difference operator with respect to the y-coordinate, $\delta_y^2$, have been employed.

The truncation error of these consistent schemes can be shown to be of the order $O(\Delta x + \Delta t + \Delta y^2)$. In order to guarantee the convergence of these step by step procedures, the stability must be investigated. If we omit from the analysis the influence of the boundary conditions, a rather simple way of obtaining sufficient stability limits of the above schemes is the requirement that all operators $E_j$, $F_j$, $G_j$ must be positive. This condition leads to the following equations

Scheme a) $\quad \lambda_j > 0$, $\quad s \leq \frac{1}{2}(1-\lambda_{max})$,

and additionally (69)

$\lambda \leq 1$

Scheme b) $\quad \lambda_j > 0$; $\quad s \leq \frac{1}{2}(\lambda_{min}-1)$

and (70)

$\lambda > 1$.

The second condition concerning $\lambda$ expresses the fact that the domain of dependence of the numerical scheme must include the domain of dependence of the partial differential equations, i.e., the fullfillment of the Courant-Friedrichs-Lewy (CFL) condition.

Because of the above limitations, explicit schemes are very seldom employed. In order to avoid these difficulties, only implicit schemes are practically used for the integration of the unsteady boundary layers.

The implicit consistent schemes for our model problem may generally be written as (see Fig. 2, schemes c),d),e)) :

$$T_j^j \, u_{i+1,k+1} = E_j^j \, u_{i;k+1} + F_j^j \, u_{i+1,k} + G_j^j \, u_{i,k} . \quad (71)$$

The various operators are collected in Table 1. The first one (scheme c) is a Laassonnen type scheme with a truncation error of the order $O(\Delta x + \Delta t + \Delta y^2)$. The second one is a Crank-Nicholson type scheme (d) with a truncation error of the order $O(\Delta x^2 + \Delta t^2 + \Delta y^2)$, while the third one is a Mehrstellen-scheme (e) with the highest order of truncation error, being of order $O(\Delta x^2 + \Delta t^2 + \Delta y^4)$. In contrast to the explicit schemes, the finite difference equation 71, written down for all values of $1 \leq j \leq N-1$, forms a system of linear equations for the unknown values $u_{i+1,k+1}^j$ with a tridiagonal matrix, which must be inverted at each point in the x-t plane.

The investigation of the stability of these schemes is now carried out with the von Neumann analysis, which is strictly valid only, inside the domain B, for difference equations with constant coefficients. Thus any influence of the boundary conditions on the stability is excluded from this analysis. The amplification factors, multiplied with their complex conjugate, are the following ones :

Laasonnen - scheme :

$$\rho\bar{\rho} = \frac{1}{(1+4s \sin^2 \frac{k_2}{2} \Delta y)^2 + 4\lambda(1+\lambda+4s \sin^2 \frac{k_2}{2} \Delta y^2)\sin^2 \frac{k_1}{2}\Delta x} \qquad (72)$$

Crank-Nicholson - scheme :

$$\rho\bar{\rho} = \frac{\cos^2 \frac{k_1}{2} \Delta x (1-2s \sin^2 \frac{k_2}{2} \Delta y) + \lambda^2 \sin^2 \frac{k_1}{2} \Delta x}{\cos^2 \frac{k_1}{2} \Delta x (1+2s \sin^2 \frac{k_2}{2} \Delta y) + \lambda^2 \sin^2 \frac{k_1}{2} \Delta x} \qquad (73)$$

Mehrstellen - scheme :

$$\rho\bar{\rho} = \frac{\cos^2 \frac{k_1}{2} \Delta x (1-2s \sin^2 \frac{k_2}{2} \Delta y)^2 + \lambda^2 \sin^2 \frac{k_1}{2} \Delta x (1-\frac{1}{3} \sin^2 \frac{k_2}{2} \Delta x)^2}{\cos^2 \frac{k_1}{2} \Delta x (1+2s \sin^2 \frac{k_2}{2} \Delta y)^2 + \lambda^2 \sin^2 \frac{k_1}{2} \Delta x (1-\frac{1}{3} \sin^2 \frac{k_2}{2} \Delta y)^2} \qquad (74)$$

where $k_1$, $k_2$ are arbitrary wave numbers. By inspecting these amplification factors, we see that all schemes are unconditionally stable, $\lambda$ being constant. Note that the stability analysis of the explicit schemes does not require the assumption of constant values of $\lambda$.

If we consider now again the equations at the beginning of this chapter (eqs. 47 to 50) subjected to any of the transformations mentioned in chapter three, the following type of partial differential equation (or equations) is obtained

$$A_1 F_{\eta\eta} + A_2 F_\eta + A_3 F + A_4 + A_5 F_\xi + A_6 F_\tau = 0 \qquad (75)$$

where the coefficients $A_1$ to $A_6$ may depend on the independent variables $\xi$, $\eta$, $\tau$, various given parameters and the solution F which introduces a nonlinearity. In compressible flows, a deak dependency of the coefficients $A_1$ to $A_6$ on the temperature is introduced if F represents the normalized velocity for example.

This equation (or equations) may now be discretized with finite difference methods following the ideas outlined before. The resulting system of (linear) equations with a tridiagonal matrix is readily solved by the well known Thomas algorithm. Because of the nonlinearities in equation 75, iterations at each point in the $\xi$-$\tau$ plane are usually required.

## 5. DISCUSSION OF RESULTS

In order to demonstrate the applicability of the computational methods to predict the development of unsteady boundary layers, we will discuss in this last chapter a selected number of solved problems.

As a first example consider the problem of a boundary layer flow over an impulsive started flat plate. The motion of the plate is parallel to itself, impulsively started from rest with uniform velocity. Because of the breakdown of the boundary layer assumptions near the leading edge, attention is confined to a region sufficiently far downstream from the leading edge.

The development of the flow in time has two simple features. Initially, the convective terms are negligible, so that the flow is described by the Rayleigh solution (eq. 11). At large times the flow settles down to a steady state, described by the Blasius solution. The problem is to explore the development of the flow from the initial to the steady state.

This problem has been studied by Stewartson (Ref. 34), Schuh (Ref. 29), Oudart (Ref. 35), Cheng (Ref. 36), Cheng and Elliot (Ref. 37), Lam and Crocco (Ref. 38), Hall (Ref. 39), Tani and Neng-Jong Yu (Ref. 40) and Piquet (Ref. 52).

The governing equations, written in a dimensionless form, are

$$\frac{\partial u}{\partial x} + \frac{\partial v}{\partial y} = 0 \tag{76}$$

$$\frac{\partial u}{\partial t} + u \frac{\partial u}{\partial x} + v \frac{\partial u}{\partial y} = \frac{\partial^2 u}{\partial y^2} \tag{77}$$

subjected to the boundary conditions

$$\begin{aligned} y = 0 \quad & u = v = 0 \\ y \to \infty \quad & u = 1 \end{aligned} \tag{78}$$

Schuh, Oudart and Tani obtained their results with an integral method, assuming a one parameter family of curves, while Hall developed a Crank-Nicholson type difference scheme applied to the above equations. Finally, Piquet solved the equations, subjected first to the Crocco transformation, employing also a Crank-Nicholson type difference scheme.

The initial data in Hall's procedure is obtained by making use of the known similarity solutions, i.e., the Rayleigh and the Blasius solutions, in an iterative manner.

In figure 3 the local wall shear stress is plotted as a function of the dimensionless time. The collected results differ only slightly from each other, so that an assessment of the various methods with respect to this problem seems to be useless.

Next, we consider the problem of a flat plate in a free stream with small harmonic velocity oscillations about a steady mean in an incompressible fluid. This problem has attracted also many investigators, see for instance Schlichting and Gersten (Ref. 2). It has been treated sufficiently general, most with integral methods, by Lighthill (Ref. 41), Teipel (Ref. 42) and Miller (Ref. 31), while Farn and Arpaci (Ref. 43) developed an explicit finite difference scheme.

The free stream velocity U varies with time in the following complex form

$$U_\infty = U_0 (1+\varepsilon e^{i\omega t})$$

where $\varepsilon$ is some small quantity, $\omega$ being the frequency. In order to facilitate the solution of the problem, the following expressions for the dimensionless velocity components u and v are usually assumed

$$u = u_0(x,y) + \varepsilon u_1(x,y)e^{i\omega t} + O(\varepsilon^2)$$
$$v = v_0(x,y) + \varepsilon v_1(x,y)e^{i\omega t} + O(\varepsilon^2)$$
(79)

Inserting these equations into the integral equations, a system of ordinary differential equations in the streamwise direction x is obtained, which is integrated with the Runge-Kutta method (Miller, Ref. 31).

In figures 4 and 5 the results of this calculation are depicted together with experimental data, obtained by Hill and Stenning (Ref. 44). The accordance between computed results and experimental data is remarkable. The dimensionless coordinates $\eta$, $\zeta$, and y are given through

$$\eta = \frac{y}{\zeta} \quad \text{with} \quad \zeta = \sqrt{\frac{\omega X}{U_0}}, \quad \text{and} \quad y = \sqrt{\frac{\omega}{\nu}} Y,$$

where X,Y are the streamwise and normal coordinates, $\nu$ being the kinmatic viscosity.

In two dimensional laminar boundary layers, the vanishing of the skin friction is usually the criterion for separation. However, in unsteady boundary layers, this criterion is not any longer meaningful, as Moore (Ref. 45), Rotta (Ref. 46) and Sears (Ref. 47) seem to have pointed out first. In order to study this rather striking feature of unsteady boundary layers, Phillips and Ackerberg (Ref. 48) and Telionis et al. (Ref. 49) carried out some numerical investigations with finite difference schemes of the Crank-Nicholson type, solving the differential equations for two dimensional, incompressible unsteady boundary layers, where regions of back flow occur. The flow situation near the region of back flow is illustrated schematically in Fig. 6, while in Fig. 7 the skin friction versus the streamwise coordinate s for a steady flow with a moving wall is plotted. It is clearly observed that the skin friction goes through a point of zero without any sign of singularity. This feature has been observed also elsewhere. The criterion of separation being proposed by Moore, Rott and Sears is defined by the two conditions $\frac{\partial u}{\partial N} = 0$ at a point inside the flow, where u is, in addition, zero.

In order to continue the calculation in reversed flow regions physically meaningfull, an "upwind difference" scheme for the streamwise coordinate has been established by Telionis et al., trying to take into account the appropriate data in the region of the field where the velocity profile is reversed. This concept, however, needs to be explored further.

A heat transfer problem in connection with unsteady boundary layers has recently been investigated in order to study some unsteady effects in combined forced and free convection. A finite difference scheme of the Laasonnen type to solve numerically the following dimensionless set of equations, describing the unsteady boundary layer flow along vertical walls has been developed by Wirz and Elsholz (Ref. 50):

$$\frac{\partial u}{\partial x} + \frac{\partial v}{\partial y} = 0$$

$$\frac{\partial u}{\partial t} + u\frac{\partial u}{\partial x} + v\frac{\partial u}{\partial y} = -\frac{\partial p}{\partial y} + \frac{\partial^2 u}{\partial y^2} + \varepsilon T \tag{80}$$

$$\frac{\partial T}{\partial t} + u\frac{\partial T}{\partial x} + v\frac{\partial T}{\partial y} = \frac{1}{Pr}\frac{\partial^2 T}{\partial y^2} \quad ,$$

subjected to the following boundary conditions

$y = 0 \qquad u = v = 0 \qquad T = T_w(x,t)$

$y \to \infty \qquad u = u(x,t) \qquad T = 0 \ .$ \hfill (81)

In these equations, u,v are the velocities, T is the temperature, $\varepsilon$ is a parameter, either +1 or -1 according to the flow situation (aiding or opposing flows) and Pr is the Prandtl number.

Based on a set of similarity solutions of the above set of equations, obtained by Wirz (Ref. 51), a check of the finite difference scheme employed was easy to perform, giving sufficient agreement between the exact similarity solution and the first numerical results, plotted as points in Fig. 8.

To close this chapter, an approach to solve a rather complicated three dimensional and time dependent problem will be considered. A finite difference method of the Laasonnen type has been developed by Dwyer (Ref. 18) and successfully applied to a rotating flat plate in forward flight, which is of direct interest to helicopter rotors. A sketch of the flow geometry is given in Fig. 9. The appropriate laminar, incompressible boundary layer equations for this problem in terms of the x, y, z coordinates are :

Continuity :

$$\frac{\partial u}{\partial x} + \frac{\partial v}{\partial y} + \frac{\partial w}{\partial y} = 0$$

x-Momentum :

$$\frac{\partial u}{\partial t} + u\frac{\partial u}{\partial x} + v\frac{\partial u}{\partial y} + w\frac{\partial u}{\partial z} - 2\Omega w = -\frac{1}{\rho}\frac{\partial p}{\partial x} + \nu\frac{\partial^2 u}{\partial y^2} + \Omega^2 X \qquad (82)$$

z-Momentum :

$$\frac{\partial w}{\partial t} + u\frac{\partial w}{\partial x} + v\frac{\partial w}{\partial y} + w\frac{\partial w}{\partial z} + 2\Omega u = -\frac{1}{\rho}\frac{\partial p}{\partial z} + \nu\frac{\partial^2 w}{\partial y^2} + \Omega^2 Z$$

where u, v, and w are the boundary velocities in the x, y, z directions respectively, t is the time and $\nu$ the kinematic viscosity. These equations are subjected to the following transformations :

$$\xi = x \; ; \qquad \eta = y \sqrt{\frac{U_e}{2x}} \; ; \qquad \zeta = z \; ; \qquad T = t \; ; \qquad f' = \frac{u}{U_e} \qquad (83)$$

yielding a system of equations where the formulation of initial conditions is facilitated, although it is still a formidable problem. Some of the results obtained by Dwyer are collected in Fig. 9. Significant changes of the flow quantities appear, near the retreating blade portion of the cycle, where retreating blade stall has been a recurring problem. These results promise a detailed understanding of the complicated flow structure, although their validity has not been proven yet.

## REFERENCES

1. EICHELBRENNER, E. (Ed.): Recent research on unsteady boundary layers.
    Proc. IUTAM Symposium 1971, Quebec 1972.
2. SCHLICHTING, H.: Grenzschichttheorie, 5. Aufl., 1965.
    G. Braun, Germany.
3. ROTT, N.: Theory of time dependent flows, in
    Theory of laminar flows, F.K. Moore ed., Princeton U.Press, 1964.
4. STUART, J.T.: Unsteady boundary layers, in
    Laminar boundary lauers, L. Rosenhead, ed., Oxford U.Press, 1963.
5. STEWARTSON, K.: The theory of unsteady laminar boundary layers, in
    Advanced in Applied Mechanics, Vol. VI, H.L Dryden and Th. von Karman, eds., Academic Press, N.Y., 1960.
6. STUART, J.T.: Inaugural lectures.
    Imperial College, 109, 1967.
7. STUART, J.T.: Unsteady boundary layers, in
    Recent Research on Unsteady Boundary Layers, E. Eichelbrenner, ed., Quebec, 1972.
8. CEBECI, T. and KELLER, H.B.: On the computation of unsteady turbulent boundary layers, in
    Recent Research on Unsteady Boundary layers, E. Eichelbrenner, ed., Quebec, 1972.
9. PATEL, V.C. and NASH, J.F.: Some solutions of the unsteady two dimensional turbulent boundary layer equations, in
    Recent Research on Unsteady Boundary Layers, E. Eichelbrenner, ed., Quebec, 1972
10. TOWNSEND, A.A.: Equilibrium layers and wall turbulence.
    J. Fluid Mechanics, Vol. 11, 1961.
11. BRADSHAW, P., FERRIS, D.H., ATWELL, N.P.: Calculation of boundary layer development using the turbulent energy equation.
    J. Fluid Mechanics, Vol. 28, 1967.
12. KARLSSON, S.K.F.: An unsteady turbulent boundary layer.
    J. Fluid Mechanics, Vol. 5, 1959.
13. MILLER, J.A.: Heat transfer in the oscillating turbulent boundary layer.
    ASME Paper 69-GT-34
14. ROSENHEAD, L., ed.: Laminar boundary layers.
    Oxford U. Press, 1963.
15. PIQUET, J., ZEYTOUNIAN, R.Kh.: Recherches récentes dans le domaine des couches limites instationnaires, in
    Recent Research on Unsteady Boundary Layers, e. Eichelbrenner, ed., Quebec, 1972.
16. McCROSKEY, W.J., YAGGY, P.F.: Laminar boundary layers on helicopter rotors in forward flight.
    AIAA J., Vol. 6, No 10, 1968.

17. DORODNITZYN, A.A.: Prikl. Math. Meh. 6, 1942.
18. DWYER, H.A.: Calculations of unsteady and three dimensional boundary layer flows.
    AIAA.P. 72-109, 1972.
19. CROCCO, L.: A characteristic transformation of the equations of the boundary layer in gases.
    ARC, London, 4582, 1939.
20. SCHUH, H.: Uber die ähnlichen Lösungen der instationären laminaren Grenzschichtgleichungen in inkompressibler Strömung, in 50-Jahre Grenzschichtforschung, H. Görtler und W. Tollmien, eds., Vieweg, Braunschweig, Germany, 1955.
21. GEIS, T.: Bemerkungen zu den ähnlichen instationären laminaren Grenzschichtströmungen.
    ZAMM, Bd 36, Nr 9/10, 1956.
22. YANG, K.T.: Unsteady laminar boundary layers in an incompressible stagnation flow.
    J. Appl. Mechanics, Vol. 25, 1958.
23. YANG, W.J. and HUAG, H.S.: Unsteady compressible laminar boundary layer flow over a flat plate.
    AIAA J., Vol. 7, 1969.
24. GABBERT, C.H.: Similarity of unsteady compressible boundary layers.
    AIAA J., Vol. 5, 1967.
25. WIRZ, H.J.: Similarity solutions of unsteady, compressible plane and axisymmetrical laminar boundary layers, in Recent Research on Unsteady Boundary Layers, E. Eichelbrenner, ed., Quebec, 1972.
26. TANI, I.: An example of unsteady laminar boundary layer flow.
    Grenzschichtforschung - IUTAM Symposium, Freiburg, 1957.
27. HASSAN, H.A.: On unsteady laminar boundary layers.
    J. Fluid Mechanics, Vol. 9, 1960.
28. HAYASI, N.: On semi-similar solutions of the unsteady quasi-two-dimensional incompressible laminar boundary layer equations.
    J. Phys. Soc. Japan, Vol. 16, 1961.
29. SCHUH, H.: Calculation of unsteady boundary layers in two dimensional laminar flow.
    ZFW, Vol. 5, 1953.
30. YANG, K.T.: Unsteady laminar boundary layers over an arbitrary cylinder with heat transfer in an incompressible flow.
    J. Appl. Mech., June, 1959.
31. MILLER, R.W.: Analysis of unsteady thermal boundary layers.
    NASA TN D-7054, 1972.
32. KOOB, S.J. and ABOTT, D.E.: Investigation of a method for the general analysis of time dependent two dimensional laminar boundary layers.
    ASME Transact., Series D, J. Basic Engrg, Vol. 90, 1968.
33. KRAUSE, E.: Numerical treatment of boundary layer problems.
    AGARD, LS 64, 1973.
34. STEWARTSON, K.: On the impulsive motion of a flat plate in a viscous fluid.
    Qua. J. Mech. & Appl. Math., Vol. 4, 1951.
35. OUDART, A.: Mise en régime de la couche limite de la plaque plane dans l'impulsion brusque à partir du repos.
    Recherche Aérospatiale, No 31, 1953.
36. CHENG, S.I.: Some aspects of unsteady laminar boundary layer flows.
    Quart. Appl. Math., Vol. 16, 1957.
37. CHENG, S.I. and ELLIOT, D.: The unsteady laminar boundary layer on a flat plate.
    ASME Transact., Vol. 79, 1957.
38. LAM, S.H. and CROCCO, L.: Shock-induced unsteady laminar compressible boundary layers on a semi-infinite flat plate.
    Princeton U., Report 428, 1958.

39. HALL, M.G.: The boundary layer over an impulsively started flat plate.
    Proc. Roy. Soc., Vol. A 310, 1969.
40. TANI, I. and YU, Neng-Jong: Unsteady boundary layers over a flat plate started from rest, in
    Recent Research on Unsteady Boundary Layers, E. Eichelbrenner, ed., Quebec, 1972.
41. LIGHTHILL, M.J.: The response of laminar skin friction and heat transfer to fluctuations in the stream velocity.
    Proc. Roy. Soc., Vol. A 224, 1954.
42. TEIPEL, I.: Ein Integralverfahren zur Berechnung von inkompressiblen oszillierenden Grenzschichtströmungen.
    DLR FB 69-09, Germany, 1969.
43. FARN, C.L.E. and ARPACI, V.S.: On the numerical solution of unsteady laminar boundary layers.
    AIAA J., Vol. 4, 1966.
44. HILL, P.G. and STENNING, A.H.: Laminar boundary layers in oscillatory flows.
    ASME Transact., Series D., J. Basic Engrg, Vol. 82, 1963.
45. MOORE, F.K.: Research on rotating stall in axial flow compressors.
    WADC TR 59-75, Part II, 1959.
46. ROTT, N., see Ref. 3.
47. SEARS, W.R., unpublished notes.
48. PHILLIPS, J.H. and ACKERBERG, R.C.: A numerical method for interpreting the unsteady boundary layer equations when there are regions of back flow.
    J. Fluid Mechanics, Vol. 58, No 3, 1973.
49. TELIONIS, D.P., TSAHALIS, D.Th., WERLE, M.J.: Numerical investigation of unsteady boundary layer separation.
    Physics of Fluids, Vol. 16, No 7, 1973.
50. WIRZ, H.J. and ELSHOLZ, E.: The numerical solution of unsteady boundary layers with combined forced and free convection.
    Unpublished report.
51. WIRZ, H.J.: Unsteady combined forced and free convection in boundary layers.
    Proceedings of the 5th International Heat Transfer Conference, September 1974, Tokyo.
52. PIQUET, J.: Calcul numérique de couches limites laminaires compressibles en régime instationnaire.
    J. de Mécanique, Vol. 11, No 1, 1972.

TABLE 1 - IMPLICIT FINITE DIFFERENCE SCHEMES FOR UNSTEADY BOUNDARY LAYERS

$$T_j^j u_{i+1,k+1} = E_j^j u_{i,k+1} + F_j^j u_{i+1,k} + G_j^j u_{i,k}$$

| Scheme | $T_j$ | $E_j$ | $F_j$ | $G_j$ |
|---|---|---|---|---|
| c) Laasonnen | $(1+\lambda_j)\delta - s\delta_y^2$ | $\lambda_j$ | 1 | 0 |
| d) Crank-Nicholson | $(1+\lambda_j)\delta - \frac{s}{2}\delta_y^2$ | $(\lambda_j-1)\delta + \frac{s}{2}\delta_y^2$ | $(1-\lambda_j)\delta + \frac{s}{2}\delta_y^2$ | $(1+\lambda_j)\delta + \frac{s}{2}\delta_y^2$ |
| e) Mehrstellen | $S_y + S_y^* - \frac{s}{2}\delta_y^2$ | $S_y^* - S_y + \frac{s}{2}\delta_y^2$ | $S_y - S_y^* + \frac{s}{2}\delta_y^2$ | $S_y + S_y^* + \frac{s}{2}\delta_y^2$ |

Operators :

$\delta\phi_j = \phi_j$

$\delta_y^2\phi_j = \phi_{j-1} - 2\phi_j + \phi_{j+1}$

$S_y\phi_j = \frac{1}{12}(\phi_{j-1} + 10\phi_j + \phi_{j+1})$

$S_y^*\phi_j = \frac{1}{12}(\lambda_{j-1}\phi_{j-1} + 10\lambda_j\phi_j + \lambda_{j+1}\phi_{j+1})$

$s = \sigma \frac{\Delta t}{\Delta y^2}$

$\lambda_j = \frac{\Delta t}{\Delta x} U(y_j)$

Addendum
Lecture Notes in Physics, Vol. 41
By mistake the following 9 figures have not been bound at the end of the contribution:
H.J.Wirz,Computation of Unsteady Boundary Layers.    Pages 442 - 471.
We therefore attach the remaining sheets 473 - 476 with the figures 1 - 9.

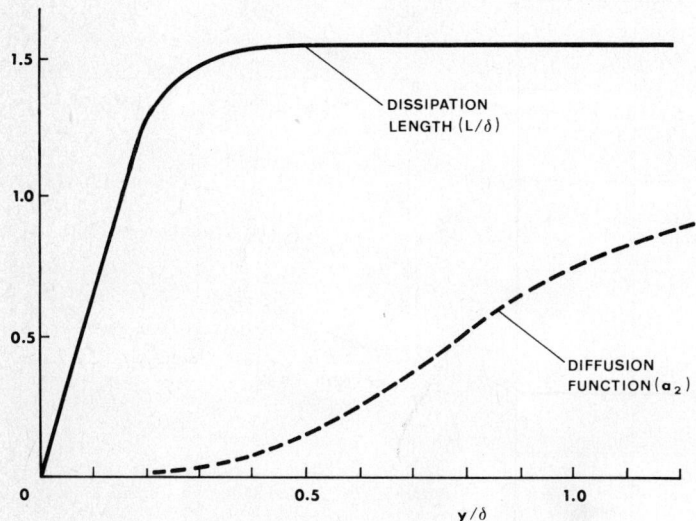

FIGURE I EMPIRICAL FUNCTIONS

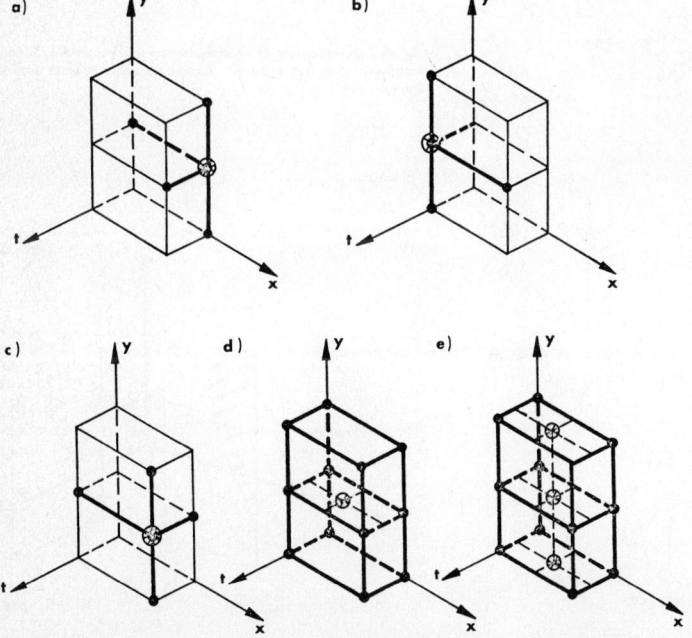

FIG.II FINITE DIFFERENCE SCHEMES FOR UNSTEADY BOUNDARY LAYERS

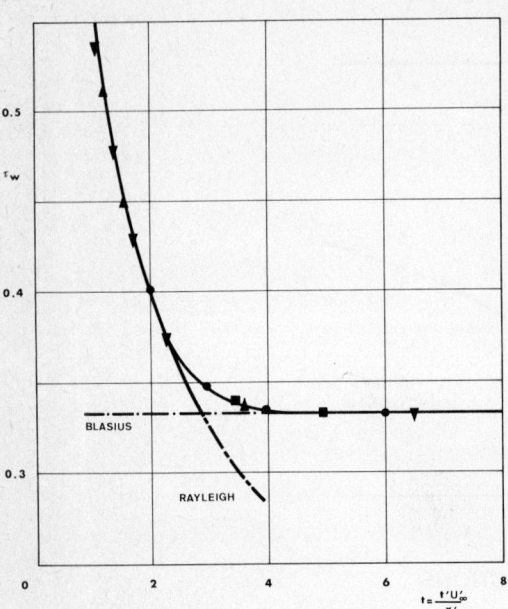

**FIG. III WALL SHEAR STRESS**

- ● HALL ▲ TANI
- ■ LAM and CROCCO
- ▼ PIQUET

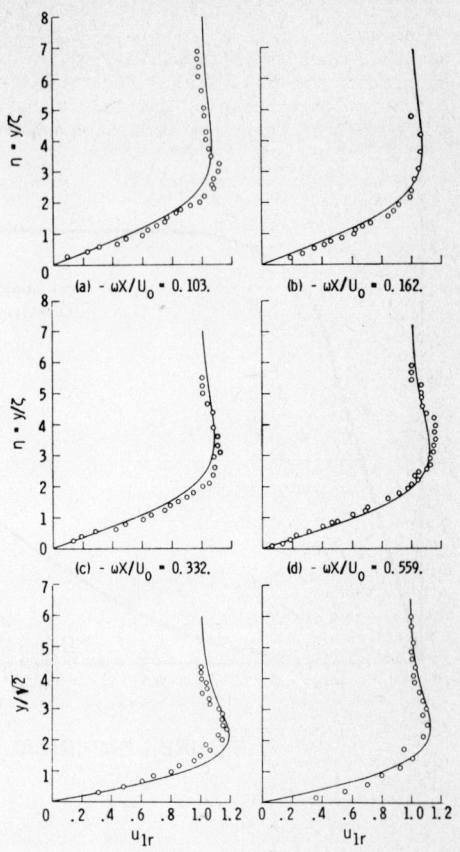

**Fig. 4** Development of velocity component magnitude along flat plate with oscillating free stream. Circles are experimental data of Hill and Stenning [44].

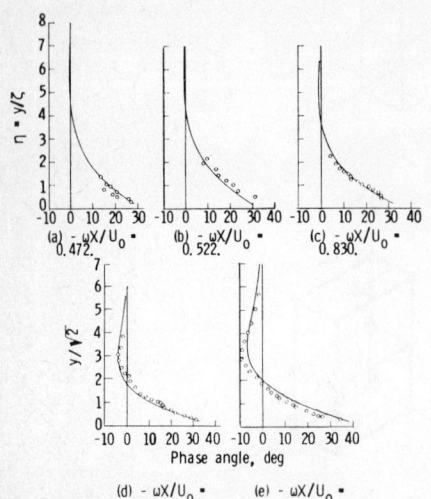

**Fig. 5** Development of phase angle between in-plane and out-of-phase velocity components along flat plate with oscillating free stream. Circles are experimental data of Hill and Stenning [44].

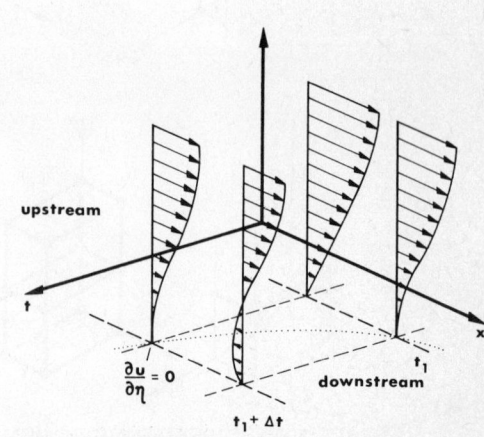

**Fig.: 6** Schematic flow field

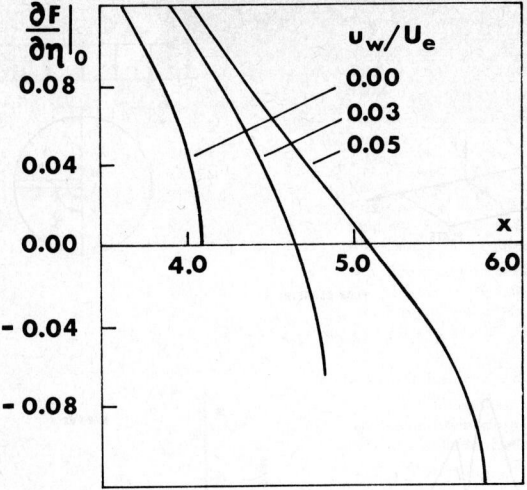

**Fig.: 7** Skin friction function versus the distance x for steady flow over fixed or moving walls.

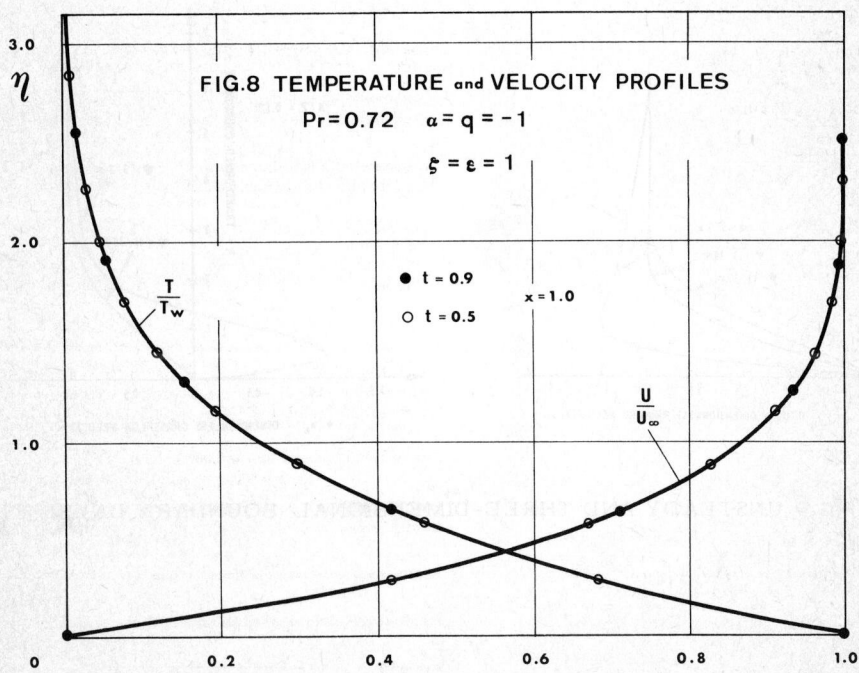

# SPRINGER TRACTS IN MODERN PHYSICS

Ergebnisse der exakten Naturwissenschaften

Editor: G. Höhler

Associate Editor: E. A. Niekisch

Editorial Board:
S. Flügge, J. Hamilton,
F. Hund, H. Lehmann,
G. Leibfried, W. Paul

## Volume 66
30 figures. IIi, 173 pages. 1973
ISBN 3-540-06189-4

### Quantum Statistics
in Optics and Solid-State Physics

R. Graham: Statistical Theory of Instabilities in Stationary Nonequilibrium Systems with Applications to Lasers and Nonlinear Optics.
F. Haake: Statistical Treatment of Open Systems by Generalized Master Equations.

## Volume 67
III, 69 pages. 1973
ISBN 3-540-06216-5

S. Ferrara, R. Gatto, A. F. Grillo:

### Conformal Algebra in Space-Time
and Operator Product Expansion

Introduction to the Conformal Group in Space-Time. Broken Conformal Symmetry. Restrictions from Conformal Covariance on Equal-Time Commutators. Manifestly Conformal Covariant Structure of Space-Time. Conformal Invariant Vacuum Expectation Values. Operator Products and Conformal Invariance on the Light-Cone. Consequences of Exact Conformal Symmetry on Operator Product Expansions. Conclusions and Outlook.

## Volume 68
77 figures. 48 tables. III, 205 pages. 1973
ISBN 3-540-06341-2

### Solid-State Physics

D. Schmid: Nuclear Magnetic Double Resonance — Principles and Applications in Solid-State Physics.
D. Bäuerle: Vibrational Spectra of Electron and Hydrogen Centers in Ionic Crystals.
J. Behringer: Factor Group Analysis Revisited and Unified.

## Volume 69
13 figures. III, 121 pages. 1973
ISBN 3-540-06376-5

### Astrophysics

G. Börner: On the Properties of Matter in Neutron Stars.
J. Stewart, M. Walker: Black Holes: the Outside Story.

## Volume 70
II, 135 pages. 1974
ISBN 3-540-06630-6

### Quantum Optics

G. S. Agarwal: Quantum Statistical Theories of Spontaneous Emission and their Relation to Other Approaches.

## Volume 71
116 figures. III, 245 pages. 1974
ISBN 3-540-06641-1

### Nuclear Physics

H. Überall: Study of Nuclear Structure by Muon Capture.
P. Singer: Emission of Particles Following Muon Capture in Intermediate and Heavy Nuclei.
J. S. Levinger: The Two and Three Body Problem.

## Volume 72
32 figures. II, 145 pages. 1974
ISBN 3-540-06742-6

D. Langbein:

### Theory of Van der Waals Attraction

Introduction. Pair Interactions. Multiplet Interactions. Macroscopic Particles. Retardation. Retarded Dispersion Energy. Schrödinger Formalism. Electrons and Photons.

## Volume 73
110 figures. VI, 303 pages. 1975
ISBN 3-540-06943-7

### Excitons at High Density

Editors: H. Haken, S. Nikitine
Biexcitons. Electron-Hole Droplets. Biexcitons and Droplets. Special Optical Properties of Excitons at High Density. Laser Action of Excitons. Excitonic Polaritons at Higher Densities.

## Volume 74
75 figures. III, 153 pages. 1974
ISBN 3-540-06946-1

### Solid-State Physics

G. Bauer: Determination of Electron Temperatures and of Hot Electron Distribution Functions in Semiconductors.
G. Borstel, H. J. Falge, A. Otto: Surface and Bulk Phonon-Polaritons Observed by Attenuated Total Reflection.

Springer-Verlag
Berlin
Heidelberg
New York

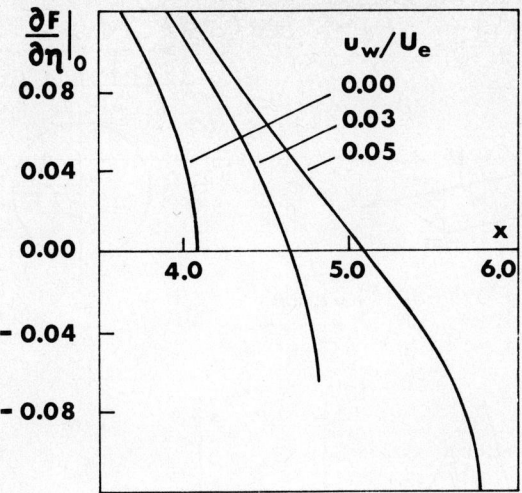

**Fig.:7** Skin friction function versus the distance x for steady flow over fixed or moving walls.

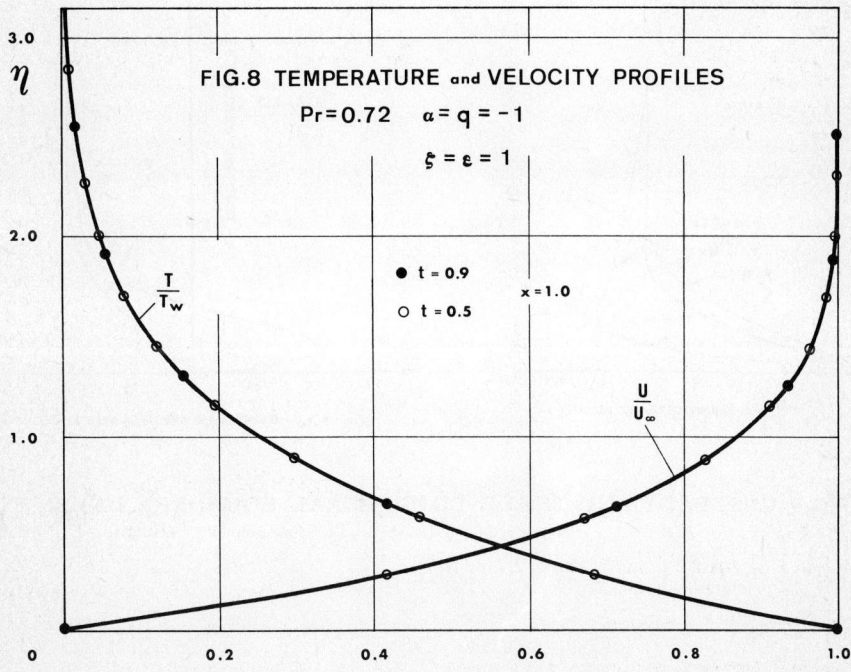

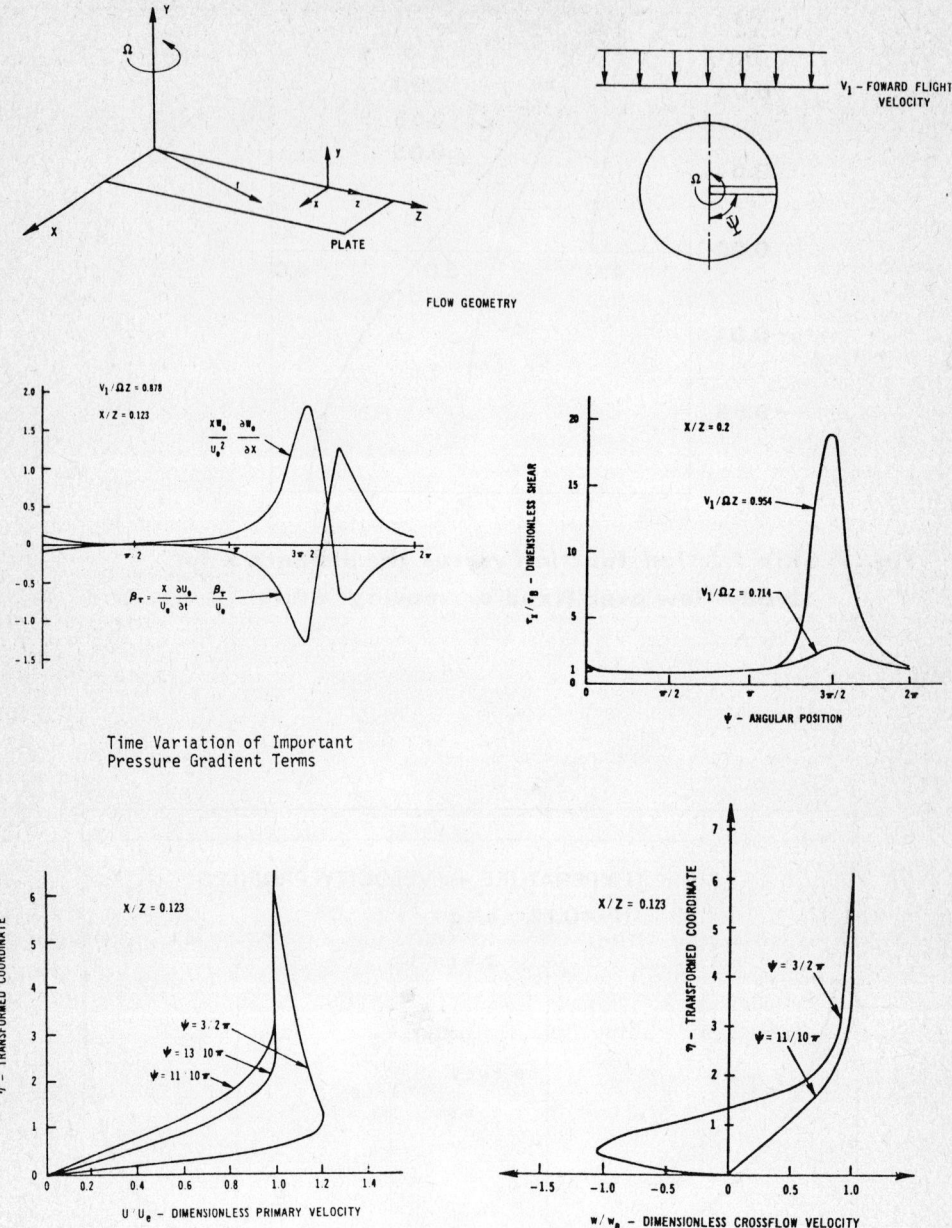

FIG.9 UNSTEADY AND THREE-DIMENSIONAL BOUNDARY LAYER FLOWS

# Lecture Notes in Physics

**Bisher erschienen/Already published**

Vol. 1: J. C. Erdmann, Wärmeleitung in Kristallen, theoretische Grundlagen und fortgeschrittenene experimentelle Methoden. 1969.

Vol. 2: K. Hepp, Théorie de la renormalisation. 1969.

Vol. 3: A. Martin, Scattering Theory: Unitarity, Analyticity and Crossing. 1969.

Vol. 4: G. Ludwig, Deutung des Begriffs physikalische Theorie und axiomatische Grundlegung der Hilbertraumstruktur der Quantenmechanik durch Hauptsätze des Messens. 1970. Vergriffen.

Vol. 5: M. Schaaf, The Reduction of the Product of Two Irreducible Unitary Representations of the Proper Orthochronous Quantummechanical Poincaré Group. 1970.

Vol. 6: Group Representations in Mathematics and Physics. Edited by V. Bargmann. 1970.

Vol. 7: R. Balescu, J. L. Lebowitz, I. Prigogine, P. Résibois, Z. W. Salsburg, Lectures in Statistical Physics. 1971.

Vol. 8: Proceedings of the Second International Conference on Numerical Methods in Fluid Dynamics. Edited by M. Holt. 1971. Out of print.

Vol. 9: D. W. Robinson, The Thermodynamic Pressure in Quantum Statistical Mechanics. 1971.

Vol. 10: J. M. Stewart, Non-Equilibrium Relativistic Kinetic Theory. 1971.

Vol. 11: O. Steinmann, Perturbation Expansions in Axiomatic Field Theory. 1971.

Vol. 12: Statistical Models and Turbulence. Edited by C. Van Atta and M. Rosenblatt. Reprint of the First Edition 1975.

Vol. 13: M. Ryan, Hamiltonian Cosmology. 1972.

Vol. 14: Methods of Local and Global Differential Geometry in General Relativity. Edited by D. Farnsworth, J. Fink, J. Porter and A. Thompson. 1972.

Vol. 15: M. Fierz, Vorlesungen zur Entwicklungsgeschichte der Mechanik. 1972.

Vol. 16: H.-O. Georgii, Phasenübergang 1. Art bei Gittergasmodellen. 1972.

Vol. 17: Strong Interaction Physics. Edited by W. Rühl and A. Vancura. 1973.

Vol. 18: Proceedings of the Third International Conference on Numerical Methods in Fluid Mechanics, Vol. I. Edited by H. Cabannes and R. Temam. 1973.

Vol. 19: Proceedings of the Third International Conference on Numerical Methods in Fluid Mechanics, Vol. II. Edited by H. Cabannes and R. Temam. 1973.

Vol. 20: Statistical Mechanics and Mathematical Problems. Edited by A. Lenard. 1973.

Vol. 21: Optimization and Stability Problems in Continuum Mechanics. Edited by P. K. C. Wang. 1973.

Vol. 22: Proceedings of the Europhysics Study Conference on Intermediate Processes in Nuclear Reactions. Edited by N. Cindro, P. Kulišić and Th. Mayer-Kuckuk. 1973.

Vol. 23: Nuclear Structure Physics. Proceedings of the Minerva Symposium on Physics. Edited by U. Smilansky, I. Talmi, and H. A. Weidenmüller. 1973.

Vol. 24: R. F. Snipes, Statistical Mechanical Theory of the Electrolytic Transport of Non-electrolytes. 1973.

Vol. 25: Constructive Quantum Field Theory. The 1973 "Ettore Majorana" International School of Mathematical Physics. Edited by G. Velo and A. Wightman. 1973.

Vol. 26: A. Hubert, Theorie der Domänenwände in geordneten Medien. 1974.

Vol. 27: R. Kh. Zeytounian, Notes sur les Ecoulements Rotationnels de Fluides Parfaits. 1974.

Vol. 28: Lectures in Statistical Physics. Edited by W. C. Schieve and J. S. Turner. 1974.

Vol. 29: Foundations of Quantum Mechanics and Ordered Linear Spaces. Advanced Study Institute Held in Marburg 1973. Edited by A. Hartkämper and H. Neumann. 1974.

Vol. 30: Polarization Nuclear Physics. Proceedings of a Meeting held at Ebermannstadt October 1–5, 1973. Edited by D. Fick. 1974.

Vol. 31: Transport Phenomena. Sitges International School of Statistical Mechanics, June 1974. Edited by G. Kirczenow and J. Marro.

Vol. 32: Particles, Quantum Fields and Statistical Mechanics. Proceedings of the 1973 Summer Institute in Theoretical Physics held at the Centro de Investigacion y de Estudios Avanzados del IPN – Mexico City. Edited by M. Alexanian and A. Zepeda. 1975.

Vol. 33: Classical and Quantum Mechanical Aspects of Heavy Ion Collisions. Symposium held at the Max-Planck-Institut für Kernphysik, Heidelberg, Germany, October 2–5, 1974. Edited by H. L. Harney, P. Braun-Munzinger and C. K. Gelbke. 1975.

Vol. 34: One-Dimensional Conductors, GPS Summer School Proceedings, 1974. Edited by H. G. Schuster. 1975.

Vol. 35: Proceedings of the Fourth International Conference on Numerical Methods in Fluid Dynamics. June 24–28, 1974, University of Colorado. Edited by R. D. Richtmyer. 1975.

Vol. 36: R. Gatignol, Théorie Cinétique des Gaz à Répartition Discrète de Vitesses. 1975.

Vol. 37: Trends in Elementary Particle Theory. Proceedings 1974. Edited by H. Rollnik and K. Dietz. 1975.

Vol. 38: Dynamical Systems, Theory and Applications. Proceedings 1974. Edited by J. Moser. 1975.

Vol. 39: International Symposium on Mathematical Problems in Theoretical Physics. Proceedings 1975. Edited by H. Araki. 1975.

Vol. 40: Effective Interactions and Operators in Nuclei. Proceedings 1975. Edited by B. R. Barrett. 1975.

Vol. 41: Progress in Numerical Fluid Dynamics. Proceedings 1974. Edited by H. J. Wirz. 1975.

# SPRINGER TRACTS IN MODERN PHYSICS

Ergebnisse der exakten Naturwissenschaften

Editor: G. Höhler

Associate Editor: E. A. Niekisch

Editorial Board:
S. Flügge, J. Hamilton,
F. Hund, H. Lehmann,
G. Leibfried, W. Paul

Springer-Verlag
Berlin
Heidelberg
New York

## Volume 66
30 figures. IIi, 173 pages. 1973
ISBN 3-540-06189-4

### Quantum Statistics
in Optics and Solid-State Physics

**R. Graham:** Statistical Theory of Instabilities in Stationary Nonequilibrium Systems with Applications to Lasers and Nonlinear Optics.
**F. Haake:** Statistical Treatment of Open Systems by Generalized Master Equations.

## Volume 67
III, 69 pages. 1973
ISBN 3-540-06216-5

**S. Ferrara, R. Gatto, A. F. Grillo:**

### Conformal Algebra in Space-Time
and Operator Product Expansion

Introduction to the Conformal Group in Space-Time. Broken Conformal Symmetry. Restrictions from Conformal Covariance on Equal-Time Commutators. Manifestly Conformal Covariant Structure of Space-Time. Conformal Invariant Vacuum Expectation Values. Operator Products and Conformal Invariance on the Light-Cone. Consequences of Exact Conformal Symmetry on Operator Product Expansions. Conclusions and Outlook.

## Volume 68
77 figures. 48 tables. III, 205 pages. 1973
ISBN 3-540-06341-2

### Solid-State Physics

**D. Schmid:** Nuclear Magnetic Double Resonance — Principles and Applications in Solid-State Physics.
**D. Bäuerle:** Vibrational Spectra of Electron and Hydrogen Centers in Ionic Crystals.
**J. Behringer:** Factor Group Analysis Revisited and Unified.

## Volume 69
13 figures. III, 121 pages. 1973
ISBN 3-540-06376-5

### Astrophysics

**G. Börner:** On the Properties of Matter in Neutron Stars.
**J. Stewart, M. Walker:** Black Holes: the Outside Story.

## Volume 70
II, 135 pages. 1974
ISBN 3-540-06630-6

### Quantum Optics

**G. S. Agarwal:** Quantum Statistical Theories of Spontaneous Emission and their Relation to Other Approaches.

## Volume 71
116 figures. III, 245 pages. 1974
ISBN 3-540-06641-1

### Nuclear Physics

**H. Überall:** Study of Nuclear Structure by Muon Capture.
**P. Singer:** Emission of Particles Following Muon Capture in Intermediate and Heavy Nuclei.
**J. S. Levinger:** The Two and Three Body Problem.

## Volume 72
32 figures. II, 145 pages. 1974
ISBN 3-540-06742-6

**D. Langbein:**

### Theory of Van der Waals Attraction

Introduction. Pair Interactions. Multiplet Interactions. Macroscopic Particles. Retardation. Retarded Dispersion Energy. Schrödinger Formalism. Electrons and Photons.

## Volume 73
110 figures. VI, 303 pages. 1975
ISBN 3-540-06943-7

### Excitons at High Density

Editors: **H. Haken, S. Nikitine**
Biexcitons. Electron-Hole Droplets. Biexcitons and Droplets. Special Optical Properties of Excitons at High Density. Laser Action of Excitons. Excitonic Polaritons at Higher Densities.

## Volume 74
75 figures. III, 153 pages. 1974
ISBN 3-540-06946-1

### Solid-State Physics

**G. Bauer:** Determination of Electron Temperatures and of Hot Electron Distribution Functions in Semiconductors.
**G. Borstel, H. J. Falge, A. Otto:** Surface and Bulk Phonon-Polaritons Observed by Attenuated Total Reflection.